About the Author

Oxford-educated Louise Bagshawe was the youngest ever contributor to *The Tablet* at the age of fourteen. Young Poet of the Year in 1989 and former President of the Oxford University Rock Society, she worked in the record business before leaving at twenty-three to write full time. A bestselling novelist and screen writer, Louise Bagshawe has had her work published in nine languages. She lives with her husband in New York.

Also by Louise Bagshawe

Venus Envy
A Kept Woman
When She Was Bad...

Louise Bagshawe

Three Great Novels

Career Girls
The Movie
Tall Poppies

ORION

Career Girls © 1995 Louise Bagshawe
The Movie © 1996 Louise Bagshawe
Tall Poppies © 1997 Louise Bagshawe

All rights reserved

The right of Louise Bagshawe to be identified as the
author of this work, has been asserted by her in accordance
with the Copyright, Designs and Patents Act 1988.

This omnibus edition first published in Great Britain in 2002 by
Orion
An imprint of Orion Books Ltd
Orion House, 5 Upper St Martin's Lane, London WC2H 9EA

ISBN: 0 75285 268 X

A CIP catalogue record for this book is
available from the British Library

Typeset in Minion by Deltatype Ltd, Birkenhead, Merseyside

Printed and bound in Great Britain by
Clays Ltd, St Ives plc

Contents

Career Girls

This book is dedicated to
Barbara Kennedy-Brown, my partner-in-crime

Thanks to

Jacob Rees-Mogg, Nicky Griffiths, Ed, Damian, Tiz, Margaret, Rod, James Robertson, James Ross, Nick Edgar, Alexia, Jeremy, Arabella, Stephanie, Melanie, Katherine, Harvey, Nick Little, Edna, Brenda, Marion, Tristam, Pete, Adrian, Alex, Jeremy Green, Sebastien and all my friends at Christ Church and the Union – you know who you are; Gary Williams, Andy Stevens, Luc Vergier, Rachel Robinson and everybody at Sony International; Brian McWheat and Frank Hannon; the infinitely cool Brian Celler; Tom and Claire Zutaut; John and Gina Florescu, Tom Silverman of Tommy Boy; Suicidal Tendencies, Tom Abraham and the crew (ahem); Nigel Kennedy; John Watson and Colin Bell of London Records, James Harman, Rod MacSween, Dave Bates, the C.R.A.B.S., Sean McAuley, Lizzie Radford, Roger Holdom, Vanessa Warwick, Brent Hansen, Brian Diamond, Max Loubière, Lucy, Kate, Sandy, Paul, Paula and Barry at EMI and especially Keith Staton; Pippa, Belinda, Isabella and everyone at Biss Lancaster; Dawn Harris, Angelica Passantino and family, and Claire Bryant.

Special thanks to: Mum, Dad, Tilly, James, Alice, Seffi and all the family; my genius of an agent, Michael Sissons, and the wonderful, brilliant and very kind Fiona Batty; my awesome editor, Rosie Cheetham, for her guidance, patience and encouragement, and the whole team at Orion, especially Katie Pope for everything and Caroleen Conquest, my copy-editor; Lisa Anderson, the first woman in Britain to run a major label, and Sharon Osbourne, one of the best managers in the world, my all-time heroines – words cannot express my gratitude; Conrad Miles; Jane 'Heaven is . . .' Edwards; Fred 'Court Jester' Metcalf; Nigel Huddlestone and Chris Hall; Richard Hamer; Ged (pronounced 'God') Doherty, Lynn Seager; Andrew Snelling, the world's only rock 'n' roll bank manager; Cliff Burnstein, for three hours of life philosophy at the Don Valley stadium; and to Def Leppard, Joe Elliott, Phil Collen, Vivian Campbell, Rick Savage, Rick Allen and the late, great Steve Clark for the music and the inspiration.

And finally, my thanks to the most appropriately named man in the music industry, Peter Mensch, for taking me along for the ride.

Part 1
OXFORD

1

Topaz burst through the door of the President's Office.

'Oh – my – God!' she yelled. '*Oh my God*! I got it! I got it! I can't believe it! Rowena, you're a genius. How can I ever repay you? I don't know what to say!'

She flung herself on one of the faded velvet armchairs, pushing a handful of red curls back from her face.

Rowena turned away from the computer with a sigh. Her delicately pitched letter of invitation to Gary Lineker to come down to Oxford and speak had reached a crucial paragraph. She smiled at her friend. 'What are you talking about?'

'*The Times, The Times*! They read the draft, they like it, they want eight hundred words on student benefits! I'm going to be published in a national! Oh babe, I can't thank you enough,' said Topaz.

'Topaz, that's great. That's really great. I'm so pleased,' said Rowena. 'You're the best, and they're lucky to have you.'

'It's all down to you. I wouldn't have got it without you.'

'That's rubbish and you know it. All Dad did was make sure the right person got to read it. Stevens wouldn't have commissioned it if it wasn't any good,' said Rowena firmly.

The two girls glowed at each other.

'Talent is the only thing that counts,' said Rowena.

'In which case, you'll never have any problems,' said Topaz.

They made a great team. Everyone said so. They were so unlikely to get along, it was almost inevitable that they should become best friends: Topaz Rossi, the brashest, loudest, and by far the most attractive American in Oxford, and Rowena Gordon, willowy, blonde, coldly determined, every inch a gentleman's daughter.

Topaz had interviewed Rowena for *Cherwell*, the university newspaper, in their second term at college, when her sophistication and poise had taken the Union by storm, winning an election to the Secretary's committee by a record margin. The American girl had turned up with a paper and pen cordially prepared to hate her guts: Rowena Gordon, another stuck-up British aristo dabbling in student politics before settling down to a suitable marriage. She despised girls like that. They were the enemy, a living reproach to every woman who'd struggled for the right to work for a living.

When she actually saw Rowena, her second impression was worse than the first; she was dressed in an Armani suit that would have cost Topaz her year's budget, with long, blonde, precision-cut hair, expensive scent, immaculate make-up and delicate gold jewellery.

'Why do you think you won this election?' Topaz asked in a bored monotone.

Rowena had looked at her equally coolly. *Bloody Americans!* Look at this girl, those thrusting breasts in a low-cut top, those long legs stretching up for miles into a suede mini at least three inches too short, and a riot of ruby curls tumbling halfway down her back. Swaggering in here like she owns the place. It was obvious how she managed to be a staffer on the student paper in less than a term.

'Because I worked hard all term, made speeches I believed about, and raised more sponsorship money than anybody else,' she answered shortly. 'Why do you think you're doing this feature?'

'Because I'm the best writer on the paper,' Topaz shot back.

For a second they glared at each other. Then, slowly, Topaz smiled and held out her hand.

By the end of the day, both women had made their first ally.

Over the next two weeks, they became firm friends. At first, this amazed other students who knew them; after all, Rowena was cold, reserved and richer than hell, whereas Topaz was a red-blooded Italian-American, sensual, pushy and scraping by on a scholarship.

But their backgrounds were more similar than most people realized. Both of them had already made one major mistake in the eyes of their parents: they'd been born female.

The Gordons of Ayrshire had been an unbroken line of Scottish farmers for more than a thousand years. Give or take a few acres, the Gordon estate and coat of arms had passed smoothly from father to son down the generations, until Rowena's father, Charles Gordon, had failed to provide a son of his own. There had been three miscarriages, and Rowena was conceived despite doctor's orders. When Mary Gordon, after all the heartache, was finally delivered in Guy's Hospital in London, her proud husband waited all night in the room closest to the ward, turning over names in his mind – Richard, Henry, Douglas, William, Jacob. At 3 a.m. the nurse came in beaming.

'Is he all right?' Charles asked anxiously.

'She's fine, sir,' the nurse smiled. 'You have a beautiful baby daughter.'

Gino Rossi would have sympathized with Charles Gordon. He might also have felt a touch of condescension: after all, he already had three fine sons. He was the envy of his neighbours. But he wanted another, and his wife was getting tired. Gino had already decided this would be the last time for her. When the baby turned out to be a girl, he felt cheated. What should Gino Rossi do with a daughter? He hadn't even had any sisters. No, he patted the little infant on the head and left her to her mother to raise. Anna Rossi called her daughter Topaz, after her favourite gemstone, and because she had a little tuft of red-gold baby hair.

Rowena Gordon wanted for nothing. From the moment she was wrapped in her heirloom christening gown of antique lace, everything was provided for her. When she was six, a pony. When she was seventeen, a car. In between, the finest clothes, the smartest skiing holidays, ballet lessons, a Harley Street orthodontist and anything else her father could think of. Anything that would allow him to ignore his real feelings for her, the acute disappointment, the sense of betrayal. Until Rowena was six, he merely avoided her. After that, he would either lose his temper over the smallest childish offence, or treat her with cold courtesy. Mary Gordon was no better. She resented her daughter as the reason for her husband's coldness towards her. When Rowena was sent away at seven to boarding school, she felt only relief.

When Rowena was ten, a minor miracle occurred. Mary Gordon, at the age of forty-one, got pregnant again and carried the baby to term. This time Charles's prayers were answered: at forty-seven he had fathered a son, James Gordon, sole heir to the estate and the family name. Both parents were overjoyed; the new baby was the apple of their eye, and Charles Gordon never snapped at his daughter again. From that day forth, he simply ignored her.

Rowena accepted her parents' attitude. Things were the way they were, and no amount of wishing would change it. Her reaction was simple: from now on, she would be in control. She would shape her own world. She would rely on herself.

The grades she was earning at school ceased to be an effort to win their love. Now they became a passport to college. University meant independence, and independence meant freedom. And Rowena discovered something else: she was good at work. She was, in fact, the brightest girl of her year. It was a new revelation. Rowena worked coldly and with complete dedication until she topped the class in everything except art. She had her rivals, Mary-Jane and Rebecca, happy, pretty girls who were much more outgoing and popular than her. They provided a benchmark. They were the ones to beat. If Rowena got only 74 per cent in an exam, she didn't mind, providing Becky and Mary-Jane got only 73 per cent. She discovered she would rather come top than get an A. In most cases she did both.

Across the Atlantic, little Topaz Rossi was also disappointing her family. Where Rowena became arrogant, cold and withdrawn, Topaz threw tantrums, burst into tears and demanded attention. Like the unruly mop of red curls she was sprouting – nobody knew where *that* came from, as Gino remarked – the girl was proving rebellious. She flirted with boys, her poppa hit her. She started to wear make-up, her mom made her go to Mass every day for a month. Her mom tried to love her, but she was worn out. And Topaz was so different! She refused to learn to cook! She wanted a career, like she couldn't find a nice boy, looking like she did! What was wrong with the child, didn't she know she was a *girl*?

Topaz burnt with the injustice of it. In truth, she was more like her father than any of his sons; smart, feisty, passionate when angry. She was so desperate for them to love her. Or at least understand! She was making the best grades in grade school! She was making the best grades in high school!

When Topaz was sixteen, her parents ordered her to quit school and come help in the shop. She refused. She wanted more. Her teachers thought she could get a scholarship to Oxford University, no less. She wanted to make something of herself.

Sullenly, Gino refused his permission. All Topaz's tears were to no avail. Deep down inside, he knew he was wrong, that if Emiliano had been offered such a chance he would have burst with pride, but he was angry. Why did the Lord give him three ordinary sons, no better than the next man's, and suddenly this wild little daughter, who made straight As in courses her brothers couldn't even *spell*? What business did she have, being brighter than her family?

Gino was jealous for his sons. He was jealous for himself. No, he refused permission. She should not take this exam. At eighteen, she would help her mother.

Topaz felt her tears and rage crystallize into a hard diamond of fury. So be it, she thought. If her father turned his back on her, she would turn from him. She took the exam in secret and, as she had known they would, they awarded her the bursary.

Two days later she packed up her few decent clothes, kissed her brothers and mother goodbye and got in a cab for JFK. Her father refused her his blessing.

Though her heart was breaking, Topaz hardened her face. Very well. From now on, she was on her own.

For both girls, Oxford was the way out. In that glorious summer, the beautiful old city nestling in the heart of the soft Cotswold hills represented an opportunity to make a name for yourself. If you were doing it properly, Oxford was a dress rehearsal for real life.

Topaz and Rowena were doing it properly.

Topaz wanted to be a journalist more than anything else in the world. She wanted to talk to everyone and see everything and serve it back up to the public in graceful phrases and snappy paragraphs, underneath a photo of herself and a byline. She would make them laugh, and shock them, and make and break people, and change perceptions. She wanted to give people spectacles, so that when they looked through them they would see life the way she did. She would expose, observe, amuse and enlighten. And make a ton of money doing it.

When Topaz arrived in Oxford, she staggered up the staircase to her room, unpacked her clothes and made a cup of coffee. Then she went down to the porters' lodge at the college entrance, signed her name in the register of new undergraduates, and examined the sixty-odd leaflets stuffed into her pigeonhole from university societies desperate to get freshers – as the new batch of students were traditionally termed – to sign up. One of them was from *Cherwell*, the student newspaper, advertising for volunteers. Topaz folded the little sheet of paper and tucked it neatly in her purse. She threw everything else away without looking at it.

Rowena Gordon was just as sure about what she wanted to do, but she knew Oxford wouldn't give her much help with it. She wanted to go into the record business. Over her last two years at school, Rowena, the icy blonde who was famous for never even *looking* at a boy, discovered rock and roll. It was the first thing she'd felt moved by. The wild, dark rhythms of the music, the blatantly sexual lyrics, the dangerous looks of the musicians – it scandalized all her friends, but it excited Rowena. Hard rock was a world of its own, a totally different world to the one she was used to. It made her feel strange.

Her parents heard about her passion from the housemistress, but could hardly believe it. How could their troublefree girl possibly be involved in that kind of trash? So the teacher kept her counsel, disapprovingly. It didn't do to upset Mr Gordon. But having known Rowena for some years, she sensed in the girl what her parents did not; a disturbing sexuality buried in that virgin flesh, in the new sashay of her long, slim legs, and the promise of her soft, plump lips.

Rowena was intelligent, and she kept her ambitions to herself. Music would have to wait until she'd graduated, and meanwhile, there was Oxford to attend to.

Her first term, Rowena, newly up at Christ Church, joined the Oxford Union. It was the most important society in Oxford, and so Rowena Gordon intended to be President.

Three-quarters of all undergraduates were members of the Union. It owned its own buildings in the centre of the city, and possessed a cheap bar and cocktail cellar that were always packed out. It was regarded as a nursery for Britain's political elite – prime ministers and cabinet members from Gladstone to Michael Heseltine had been officers and presidents. The programme of speakers and events for Topaz and Rowena's first terms had included Henry Kissinger, Jerry Hall, Warren Beatty and the Princess Royal within the space of eight weeks.

Rowena fell in love. She couldn't write, like Topaz, but she could certainly talk. She learnt how to debate and found she adored the almost sexual charge of passionately exhorting a crowd, joking, rebuffing, challenging, holding them locked into her eyes and voice. She started running in the Union elections and found she loved that too; the bitter feuds, the pacts made and broken, the secret meetings in the officers' offices. She loved the rhetoric and the protocol – 'Madam Librarian', 'Mr Chairman', 'the honourable lady from St Hilda's'.

'What's the motion next week again?' Topaz asked, trying not to seem too absorbed in her own triumph. *Published in a national! Published in a national! Editor of Cherwell was one thing, but* this! . . .

'This House Believes that Women Are Getting Their Just Deserts,' recited Rowena.

Topaz laughed. 'I can't believe they're letting you off the leash on that one in a Presidential, Madam Librarian.'

Rowena allowed herself a quick smile. 'Nor can I, to be honest,' she admitted. 'Gilbert is such a prat about feminism.'

The Presidential Debate took place once a term and was the final showdown between officers and other candidates for the top job. Rowena's only real competition was the Secretary, Gilbert Docker; one hundred per cent public schoolboy, blood so blue it was obscene. Gilbert found it appalling that women should even be allowed to join the Union, let alone run for office. In the good old days, they had had to watch silently from the visitors' gallery, with all the other peasants.

'You'll have *Cherwell* right behind you,' Topaz assured her.

Rowena smiled. 'Yeah, well. At least you and I can count on each other. Let's go and have a beer.'

They wandered down Broad Street towards the King's Arms, a perennial favourite for students from the university and polytechnic. Most of the tourists that crowded Oxford's lovely streets had climbed back on their buses by six o'clock, and the early evening air was warm and soft. The scent of mown grass drifted towards them from the gardens of Trinity College.

'Have you seen Peter this week?' Rowena asked.

Peter Kennedy was one of the better-known students at Oxford, and Topaz Rossi's boyfriend. They'd been seeing each other for a couple of months, and Rowena was intrigued by the romance. She gathered that Peter was – well – more from her own kind of background, to be honest. He wasn't the type she'd expect to be interested in Topaz Rossi, nor he in her. Still, by all accounts he was drop-dead gorgeous.

'Yes,' said Topaz. She blushed. 'I really like the guy. He's pretty ... pretty interesting.'

'Pretty spectacular, you mean,' said Rowena. 'Let's not kid ourselves.'

They turned into the pub, grinning at each other with perfect understanding.

'Nice job, Topaz!' called Rupert Walton from the bar. 'I heard about *The Times*.'

'Cheers, Rupert.' Topaz waved to her deputy editor.

'Hey, Rupe,' Rowena called.

'Madam President,' he said.

'Bloody hell, don't say that,' Rowena protested, fighting her way through the crowd. 'Gin and tonic, Labatt's, and whatever Rupert's drinking, please. You'll jinx it.'

'Nothing can jinx it after the piece on him I'm running next week,' he said smugly. 'It's not even editorial condemnation. It's just a long list of his own quotes, starting with "Working mothers are responsible for the crime rate," and ending with "Oxford was designed for the sons of gentlemen, and it ought to be kept that way." I'll have a Guinness, please. Thanks.'

They threaded their way back to the table, nodding at friends. Chris Johnson and Nick Flower, two of Rowena's candidates, were sitting next to Topaz.

'Look out, Rupe, hacks in the area,' she teased. 'You go out for an innocent drink with Miss Gordon, you end up in the middle of a slate meeting.'

'Right,' said Rupert. 'You'll wind up civil servants, the lot of you, and serve you right. No fate is too bad.'

'How's it looking, guys?' asked Rowena. 'Ignore the budding Fleet Street scum over here.'

'Christ Church is solid,' said Nick, 'as ever. Oriel's not.'

'Surprise.'

'Hertford'll give you a hundred and fifty line votes.'

'God bless Hertford,' said Topaz.

'Amen,' Rowena concurred.

'We've got Queen's, Lincoln, Jesus and St Peter's wrapped up. Balliol's a problem. So is John's.'

'Why?' asked Chris.

Nick shrugged. 'Because Peter Kennedy's decided he wants to support Gilbert, and he's mobilizing the old school ties.'

A slight chill fell over the table and Rowena felt her heart sink. Gilbert, really, had never been that much of a threat. Peter was another matter.

Topaz touched her sleeve. 'Don't worry. I'll go see him, talk some sense into him. He'll be cool.'

'Thanks, sweetheart,' Rowena said, wondering what she'd do without her. She didn't want Topaz dragged into a political row between her best friend and her boyfriend. 'But I'll do it. This one's really my problem. I'll sort it out.'

Peter Kennedy versus Rowena Gordon, Rupert thought, looking at the two beautiful girls. Now, that *will* be interesting.

2

'Can you tell me where Mr Kennedy lives, please?' asked Rowena politely.

The porter touched his bowler hat gravely, whether in deference to herself or Peter Kennedy she wasn't sure.

'Certainly, madam. Mr Kennedy has rooms in Old Library, number five on the first floor.'

'Thank you,' said Rowena.

She took a quick glance at the spacious lodge, littered like most of Oxford's college entrances with leaflets advertising lectures, plays, jobs and pizza discounts. It was Friday, which meant that a large pile of that week's *Cherwell* had just been delivered, dumped underneath the window next to the noticeboard. She grabbed a copy before they all disappeared.

He *would* be at Christ Church, she thought.

It was the largest, most prestigious and most arrogant college in the university. Only St John's was richer, and only Oriel more despised by everyone else. Not that either of these things bothered the House, as it was traditionally nicknamed; John's was full of 'grey men', hard-working, brilliant undergraduates destined for fellowships and research posts – boring idiots in other words – and Oriel was a poor relation. Christ Church had produced something like twelve prime ministers and nineteen viceroys of India. Its hall was one of the architectural wonders of England. It had a private picture gallery, boasting drawings by Michelangelo and Van Dyck.

Peter Kennedy could not possibly have gone anywhere else, Rowena thought. She smiled. *And neither could I.*

She walked through magnificent Tom Quad, admiring the grey Elizabethan stone, lit gently by the setting sun. Tom Tower, rearing up behind her, began to strike the hour five minutes early, because the college was exactly one degree west of Greenwich. She felt very nervous, as if even the ancient walk ways and carved gargoyles were ranking up behind Gilbert, now that Kennedy was on his side. She'd have to talk him out of it. That was all there was to it.

Under the soaring archways of the walk into hall, someone had pinned up the standard-issue poster announcing the Union elections, listing the candidates and somewhat improbably requesting that any breach of the rules be reported to J. Sanders, Exeter, Returning Officer. Since the rules stated that no candidate should solicit votes, much less form an electoral pact – a slate, in other words – they were universally ignored, except on polling day, when the deputy returning officers had fun making life even more miserable for the hacks than it was already. Every hack, once they stopped running, had a go at being a DRO and enjoyed it immensely.

Rowena examined the poster for graffiti and was pleased to find that someone had scrawled 'Prat' after Gilbert's name. She also noticed, laughing, that someone had carefully written 'TOPAZ ROSSI, ST HILDA's' at the top of the list of standing-committee nominees. My friend the sex symbol. She'd tried to get Topaz to run a million times, but unless she could interview it, report on it or give it an impossible deadline, Topaz wasn't interested. 'Tina Brown didn't have time for the Union,' she'd said dismissively.

Rowena strolled through the glorious cathedral cloisters to Old Library. The door to the staircase was heavy, solid wood, studded with metal bolts like a dungeon entrance. Maybe, thought Rowena fancifully, they locked Protestants in here when Bloody Mary was queen.

She bounded up the narrow stairs to Kennedy's room, her heart hammering, and knocked loudly. I *am* Librarian of the Union, she told herself firmly, and he's a threat, that's all, to be dealt with like any other threat.

Peter, tall and tanned from rowing, opened the door. 'Miss Gordon, delighted to meet you', he said. 'I've been expecting you. Won't you come in?'

Rowena stepped into the most luxurious undergraduate rooms she'd seen anywhere. 'Thank you,' she said. 'Please call me Rowena, Mr Kennedy.'

'Only if you'll agree to call me Peter,' he said, smiling, waving her to an armchair. 'I am seeing your best friend, after all. I'm amazed that we haven't managed to meet up before now.'

'Then that's settled,' said Rowena, ashamed to find herself momentarily jealous.

Christ, the guy was attractive. He was wearing a dark blue Boat Club tracksuit, with HOUSE emblazoned on the back in large white letters, the colour emphasizing his blue eyes and luxuriant blond hair. To Rowena, his size and strength made him seem even older than twenty-three, perhaps nearer to twenty-five. There was discreet evidence of immense wealth displayed all over the room; an antique gold carriage clock, a couple of leather-bound first editions on his table without library stickers on them. The bed was made up with a feather duvet and crisp Irish linen, and she doubted even Christ Church would run to that. Peter Kennedy was studying Anglo-Saxon under the legendary tutelage of Richard Hamer, one of the most learned and pleasant dons at Oxford, but there were textbooks on advanced economics stacked in rows on his bookshelves. Two pairs of oars were mounted across the bed; blades, traditionally awarded to the finest rowers. And God only knew he was that, Rowena thought.

'Coffee?' he enquired.

'Yes, please,' said Rowena. It might be a little easier when those handsome eyes weren't staring her down.

'You presumably know why I'm here,' she said. 'Word has it that you'll be supporting Gilbert Docker this term. You must realize that without your intervention I'm cruising home.'

'So how can one outsider's influence make any difference to you, more or less?' asked Peter calmly, stirring the coffee.

'I'm not sure,' said Rowena, deciding that honesty might charm him, 'but I'd prefer not to chance it. Believe me, I know how popular you are, how widely you can pull out the Old Etonian vote, the sports vote' – she hesitated, but added, 'the female vote . . .'

Peter handed her her coffee.

'I don't feel that anything could make Gilbert look good,' she said, 'but if there were something, it would be your support.'

He sat opposite her, sizing her up. Nice. Long blonde hair, green eyes, slim body, long legs, a lady evidently. A virgin for sure.

'Why should I support you?' he asked. 'Gilbert's the son of a friend of my father's. You'll have to give me some very good reasons to withdraw my backing from him.'

My God, Rowena thought. He's considering it. Is he seriously interested in my qualifications for the job? Most people couldn't give a monkey's about that.

'I'm the best candidate by miles,' she said, 'and you're rumoured to be a meritocrat, Peter.'

He smiled, amused. That was a clever slant.

'As Secretary, I doubled the number of social events and made a profit on entertainments for the first time in four years. As Librarian, I managed to get speakers from David Puttnam to Mick Jagger. I've served time on every Union committee. I've debated for Oxford in the world championships.'

'Did we win?' asked Kennedy, interested.

'We came second to Edinburgh,' Rowena grinned. 'The Cambridge judges were copping an attitude.'

'Classic inferiority complex,' agreed Kennedy.

'Gilbert ran straight for Secretary, just scraped in on the OE vote because there was no serious opposition, can't be bothered to turn up for standing-committee meetings, and has put on exactly two parties, using hangover sponsors from my term. He only wants to put "President of the Union" on his application to the merchant banks. He probably wouldn't bother with his own debates, if he got it.'

Kennedy nodded, accepting this. 'I need some more time to think about it,' he said. 'I won't give you a glib answer.'

Rowena got up and offered him her hand to shake, pleasantly surprised.

He turned it over, raised it slowly to his lips and kissed it. A shiver ran with little electric feet all over her body.

'Really, Topaz is terrible,' he said. 'Keeping you away from me like this. If I'd had the pleasure of knowing you beforehand, I wouldn't have committed myself to Gilbert in the first place.'

For a second Rowena wondered how on earth Topaz had managed to hook up with this devastating guy. She was amazed that he would choose an American. Still . . .

'Well, thank you for seeing me,' she said. 'I'll be in touch.'

Topaz and Rowena sat in Topaz's cramped room in Hall Building in St

Hilda's, companionably drinking huge mugs of tea and stuffing their faces with chocolate biscuits, leafing through back copies of *Cherwell* to select the best pieces for Topaz's portfolio. What there was of Topaz's room was very nice, as it had once belonged to a don, but in order to create two separate rooms for lowly undergraduates someone had partitioned it straight down the middle. Topaz thus had half a window, which looked out on to the river, past the gorgeous Hilda's gardens which were ablaze with roses and thick honeysuckle. Both girls loved it here.

'God, I'm so tired,' Topaz complained. 'The fucking computers crashed at three o'clock this morning and we all had to stay up and retype everything. Ever tried drinking out of a Coke can someone just used as an ashtray? No? Well, don't bother.'

Rowena smothered a laugh, her mouth full of Hob-nob.

'I've got a tutorial first thing tomorrow on Molière, and I can't skip it because I went sick on the last one, so that means essay crisis tonight . . . and I gotta pick something out here to show the big boys when I'm job-hunting, and I'll just screw it up because I'm pissed-off.'

'You're always pissed-off, Topaz,' said Rowena.

'I brought you a present,' Topaz said, throwing her the latest issue of *Vanity Fair*. 'It's got a massive piece on David Geffen in it.'

'Oh, great!' said Rowena, grabbing it. 'David Geffen –'

'– is God, I know, I know,' said Topaz.

Rowena worshipped David Geffen, the legendary American music mogul who had started two record companies from scratch and made a huge success out of both of them. He was a self-made billionaire who had started out without a cent to his name. She kept a *New York Times* profile on him tacked above her bed.

'So?' said Rowena defensively. 'You'd walk a mile over broken glass for five minutes with Tina Brown.'

'I'd walk ten miles,' sighed Topaz, imagining it. Tina Brown was young, beautiful, happily married and the greatest magazine powerhouse the world had ever seen, or at least that's what Topaz Rossi thought. She had left Oxford, gone into editing and seemed to double the circulation of any magazine in whose direction she glanced. Now she ran *Vanity Fair*, and had produced a cocktail of glitz and gravitas that made it the hottest title on the shelves, hotter even than *Cosmopolitan*, if that were possible.

'I want what she's got, damn it!' Topaz said.

'You've got *Cherwell*.'

'It's hardly *Vanity Fair*, now is it?' asked Topaz sarcastically.

'It's a start,' Rowena insisted. 'It got you *The Times*.'

'That's true,' admitted Topaz, her bad mood evaporating. 'How's the debate coming along?'

'I've got no problems,' said Rowena, supremely confident. 'Gilbert Docker? I'll slaughter him.'

'What did Peter say?' Topaz asked, with an uncharacteristic blush. Somehow, talking about Peter in front of Rowena always made her feel a bit dirty. Rowena was still a virgin, amazingly enough.

'He said he'd think about it,' Rowena told her. 'Are you seeing him tonight?'

'Yeah,' Topaz said. She was glad Rowena had dealt with it herself. She'd hate to have to discuss slate politics with Peter.

There was a slight pause.

'Let's get on with it, then,' Rowena said, picking up a feature on the Magdalen May Ball.

Topaz arched her back from the pleasure of it, feeling the night dew of the meadow wet beneath her. Over her head she could see the spires of the ancient city, black against the night. They were a few feet away from the riverbank and somewhere under the urgent heat of her pleasure she could hear the gentle murmuring of the water. God, it was so beautiful. In New York the neon lights of the city obliterated all the stars; here, under Peter's exquisite touch, she could see them scattered across the whole sky, like sherbet.

Peter's tongue was flicking up and down her spine, his fingertips lightly tracing her ribcage, half tickling, half caressing. Her whole body felt sensitized, alive. Topaz parted her legs, ready for him, enjoying the weight of him, the feeling of his large, thick erection pushing into her. She liked his strength. Sometimes she might even have liked it a little rougher, but that wasn't Peter's style; sex was an art for him.

She felt his fingers slide around and underneath her, reaching for her belly, for the delicate little skin patches just under her hips, wanting to stroke them, to feel them flutter under his touch. It sent a new spasm of wetness through her, and she moaned. He had taken his time discovering her body. He knew where he could turn her on. Topaz pressed against him, squirming into his hands. He liked that. His cock leapt against her.

Topaz moved with him, getting hotter. She was close, she could feel it. She wriggled about, so she could push up against his cock with the cheeks of her ass. Peter gasped when she did that, surprised by a new surge of desire. He pulled back, positioned himself to enter her. Topaz opened herself wider, waves of heat spreading through her.

'Now, baby,' she urged, and Peter began to thrust, in and out, pulling so far back he was almost withdrawn, and then plunging back inside her, slick with her juice. He was getting harder inside her, he was nearly there. He put his hands on her shoulders, gripping her hard, pushing into her faster, pleasuring her. Topaz sobbed. Maybe someone would walk across the meadows. Maybe someone would see them. She moaned, she was going to come. The block of pressure in her stomach dissolved and shattered, rippling through her, a long shiver of orgasm. Peter went rigid with pleasure, came, and relaxed on top of her.

Topaz kissed his shoulder. 'You were amazing,' she said.

'Me? Oh, baby,' he said. 'You're fantastic.'

He rolled off her, and they lay on the riverbank together, exhausted.

'This is so romantic,' Topaz said. 'I just can't believe it.'

She was incredibly happy. Peter was so gentle, so imaginative, so tender with her. The fumbling boys back in Brooklyn had never been like this. And her father had wanted one of them for her husband! If Gino could see this stunning, rich English gentleman, he'd throw a fit. Topaz had a brief, vengeful fantasy about taking Peter back for dinner and watching her poppa fall over himself to kiss his ass. Not that she'd ever darken *that* asshole's door again.

'I'm glad you think so,' Peter said. He grabbed his jacket, took out a packet of cigarettes and lit up. The smoke curled up in the darkness, white and fragrant. 'Your friend Rowena came to see me today,' he added. 'About the Union. She wants me to drop out of supporting Gilbert.'

'She mentioned it,' Topaz said, warily. One thing she had learnt was that Union politics got deadly serious. She suppressed the memory of her friend's mute appeal for help this afternoon; she didn't want Peter to think she was interfering.

'Trouble is, I'm committed to him,' Peter said easily. 'Are you cold, darling? No? I might get out of it, but it'd be tricky.'

Topaz curled against the warmth of his side. She still tingled from his caress. 'You guys can sort it out,' she said.

Peter allowed his arm to drop round her, enjoying the feeling of her firm, full breasts. It was pleasant, being with Topaz Rossi. She was eager, enthusiastic and fun. He was slightly surprised that Rowena Gordon was her friend. They were so different.

Idly he pictured Rowena as she had come to deal with him that morning. The shimmering blonde hair. The graceful poise. The confident manner. If being with Topaz was exploring the exotic, talking to slim, elegant Rowena Gordon was like looking in a mirror. And that was something else Peter Kennedy enjoyed.

'Leave it to us, sweetheart,' he said. We'll find some solution. Tell your friend to come and see me again.'

3

'Topaz, please,' Rowena said, twisting her fingers around under her cuffs.

The two girls were walking down the wide gravel path that bisected Christ Church meadows, strolling down to the river. It was the middle of Eights Week, the traditional summer rowing contest. Every college fielded male and female teams – except St Hilda's, which didn't admit men – and the students took it very seriously indeed. Topaz had two whole teams of *Cherwell* reporters asigned to it, and every hack in the Union took up position outside their college boathouse first thing in the morning. Ambition aside, where else could you be? The sun was beating down, the water was glittering and the alcohol was flowing. Thousands of kids were packing the riverbank, this year like every year. Rowena and Topaz were threading through a crowd on their way down there, and it was only ten in the morning. The crack of dawn. Normally they wouldn't even be awake.

'No. Jesus, how many times? I said no, and I meant it,' Topaz answered, with something of an edge to her tone. 'I'm not gonna discuss it with Peter for you. I don't want to get involved. *Capisci?*'

'I get that, but I need your help,' Rowena said, hammering away. 'I *have* to get Peter, if not to go with me, at least to hold back from supporting Gilbert.'

'What part of "no" don't you understand?' Topaz asked, sarcastically. 'The guy's my boyfriend. This stuff is as important to him as it is to you. If I start interfering, he's gonna be turned off like a light switch. I'm devoting every damn issue of the paper to what an asshole Gilbert Docker is. Isn't that enough?'

'Yeah, and you know I'm really grateful, but –'

'No. No buts,' Topaz interrupted her impatiently, pushing a handful of scarlet curls away from her forehead, and yet again Rowena was struck by how terrific, how brazen, her friend looked. Today she was wearing cut-off denim shorts that fitted snugly round her taut, curvy ass, the tiny threads on the fringes just kissing the tops of firm, tanned thighs, and a yellow-checked shirt tied above her flat midriff, the fabric pulled hard against those overripe breasts. She felt another quick burst of frustrated envy, immediately followed by a stab of guilt.

'You'll have to talk him into it yourself, Rowena. That's your specialty, anyway.'

'I'm seeing more of him than you are, these days,' Rowena said softly.

For a second Topaz glanced across at her. 'You can't hate his company as much as you're making out,' she said. 'Peter's not so bad. Hey, you're gonna have to get to like him. You'll have to dance with him at our wedding. That's in the chief bridesmaid's job description, says so in all the books.' She grinned.

'Wedding! Don't you think you might be rushing this just a little bit?' Rowena exploded.

'Maybe. Let's not talk about it any more,' Topaz begged. 'I don't want to have a row with you. But I'm not getting involved. OK?'

'OK,' Rowena said, looking away. She swallowed her fury. 'I'll see you later, Tope, all right? I want to see how we're getting on.'

'Sure,' her friend said, giving her a cheerful wink as she headed towards a hot-dog stand.

Rowena fought her anger all the way down the riverfront as she strolled towards the Christ Church boathouse. Not that anyone watching her would have known it; she walked slowly, waving at anyone who looked even vaguely familiar and flashing a dazzling smile at everyone else.

She looked good, she knew that. Beautiful and happy, confident and stylish. The brilliant sunshine made her blonde hair look almost platinum, and the long cotton dress she'd picked out that morning flowed closely round her slim body. She'd picked out just a kiss of make-up – clover lips, beige eyeshadow – and in her own way she looked just as sexy as Topaz Rossi.

But it was Topaz Rossi who was dating Peter Kennedy, not her.

Yes, and he'd really dump her for bringing up politics, Rowena thought, blowing a playful kiss to Emily Chan, a friend of hers from Lady Margaret Hall. Why can't she just do this for me? Why do I have to be closeted with her fucking boyfriend? If I was dating some guy at a national paper I'd talk to him about *her* . . .

The path exploded with cheers as Merton's women's crew tore past, oars slicing up the water with powerful strokes, and Oriel only seconds behind.

'Go *on*, Merton!' she shouted, jumping up and down. Ancient college rivalry between Christ Church and Oriel. Anybody was preferable to those guys winning . . .

'Yeah, move it!' a voice agreed behind her. The sun was blacked out by a Christ Church scarf being looped around her head from behind, knotted and pulled tightly together. 'Guess who?' the voice whispered in her ear. A low male voice, laughing at her.

'Cut it out, Kennedy,' Rowena snapped.

He loosened the scarf, letting her see again. 'You're too easy, Rowena. Don't look where you're going. You could get into all kinds of trouble that way.'

She reached up to her neck and ripped it off. 'What are you doing here?'

He raised an eyebrow. 'Same thing you are. Supporting Sam and the guys.' He nodded towards the Christ Church boat, moored just ahead of them, where Sam Wilson, Captain of Boats, and the main men's crew were waiting to race. 'That *is* what you're doing, right?'

'Of course,' Rowena replied icily.

Damn, why did he have to look at her like that? Look her up and down like that? What was she supposed to do about it? Say, 'Hey, you belong to Topaz'?

'Sure you're not here to hack?' he teased her. 'All these votes, within such easy reach . . .'

'Sure you're not here to relive past glories?' she countered.

Last year Peter Kennedy had been Captain of Boats and had led Christ Church to a record victory. There had been talk of Olympic trials, but Kennedy had chosen to give up sport to concentrate on his finals. Now Sam Wilson looked as though he might be leading them to Head of the River again, and the Olympic coaches were sniffing round new stars, like Johnny Searle.

'You know how to hit where it hurts,' Peter said, not taking his eyes off her. He made it sound vaguely obscene. 'Rowing meant a lot to me. Still does.'

'I can see that,' Rowena answered, struck by the closeness of his body, the broad, tanned chest in a white T-shirt inches from her face. Peter Kennedy would have graced any beach in California.

'Are you flirting with me?' Peter asked, catching her green eyes on his body.

Ridiculously, Rowena felt her breath catch in her throat. Where the fuck's Topaz? she thought.

'Don't be absurd,' she said coldly.

'Maybe you *should* flirt with me. Kiss up to me a little,' Peter suggested, smiling at her with a lazy grin. 'You do want my help, right?'

'Not that badly.'

'Don't be so uptight. I'm just kidding,' he said, putting one hand on her waist and steering her towards their boathouse. 'Topaz wouldn't want us to quarrel.'

Despite herself, Rowena stiffened beneath his touch.

Peter Kennedy smiled.

'Rowena! Peter! Hurry up!' said James Gunn, a friend of theirs, pulling the two of them into the Christ Church crowd. 'You nearly missed it, we're about to start.'

Rowena felt herself surrounded by bodies in college colours, hundreds of them, all seething forward towards the bank, shouting and clapping. Somebody flung an arm round her. She flung an arm round somebody. The college was going berserk.

'*House! House!*'

They were about to cut the boat loose. Rowena was lost in a press of navy blue, thrown forward towards the mooring boards. 'I can't see anything!' she complained to no one in particular.

Suddenly she felt herself being lifted up from behind, as lightly as a doll, and hoisted backwards over the heads of the crowd. Amazed, she looked down, to see Peter ducking between her legs, supporting her on his shoulders. She had a perfect view of the boat, the river, everything.

The back of Peter Kennedy's strong neck pressed against her white cotton panties.

It felt good.

'Put me down!' she insisted, weakly.

He grinned up at her. 'Later.'

With a roar from the crowd, the Christ Church boat sprang away from its moorings, finding the stroke at once. The eight rowers moved in perfect harmony into the water, their oars churning it up at terrific speed, chasing the Oriel first boat. The supporters on the bank immediately broke up and started to run alongside it, screaming encouragement at the tops of their voices and cursing the rival crew amicably. Peter ran with them, carrying Rowena above him, his hands holding her thighs in an iron grip, ignoring her protests. Her weight was evidently nothing to him.

Rowena, startled, cheered and shouted with the rest. It was too much fun. Besides which, she couldn't help but think, every single person here could see her getting into it, supporting her college – she'd be kind of hard to miss, with her fair hair streaming out behind her like a banner, piggybacking on top of Peter Kennedy.

There was a cry of triumph as Christ Church inexorably rammed into the tail of the Oriel boat.

'Bumped!' Peter yelled. He reached up and swung Rowena gracefully down from his back with one hand.

She touched her feet to the ground, smoothing down her dress, suddenly embarrassed, wondering what to say.

'We win again,' he said.

'Thanks, Peter,' she muttered.

He raised her hand to his lips and kissed it, casually. 'That was fun. Let's do it again some time,' he suggested.

Rowena Gordon blushed bright red, nodded as coldly as she could, and walked off down the path.

Cherwell was buzzing.

It was two weeks to the Union elections, and it looked like they were going to be close. Every college was being hacked full-throttle by eager candidates from the opposing slates. Each new day brought a fresh crop of rumour, treachery and malicious gossip; Tori had defected, Joss wasn't pulling his weight, rival candidates were still sleeping with each other . . . Topaz loved it. It was an editor's dream.

Of course, the biggest rumour of all was that Peter Kennedy and Rowena Gordon were on the verge of doing a deal. If *that* happened, all bets were off. Rowena would be home free, the first woman President of the Union for five years. Gilbert Docker needed Peter to survive.

Whenever Rowena or Gilbert went round to Peter, the news trickled back to *Cherwell*. Mostly Topaz didn't report it. She wanted to throw as much weight as she could behind her best friend, and she concentrated on articles about Gilbert's sexism or the bully-boy tactics of his followers. God only knew they made the best reading; one of her writers at St Anne's had come in just that morning with a story of how Gilbert's Secretary candidate, a popular Scottish guy reading law, had stuck a ten-inch carving knife into the door of his female opponent on Rowena's slate. Topaz had been ecstatic; the story was dynamite. She'd lead this Friday's edition on it.

The only thing she would *not* do was interfere personally. Rowena had asked her to take over with Peter three times this week, but Topaz always turned her down flat. She knew what the Presidency meant to Rowena, but even so, she couldn't risk her boyfriend over it.

'Have you seen my layout for the jobs pages?' Rupert asked, weaving in between their rickety photocopiers with a full cup of coffee. 'I'm sure I left it on top of my desk . . .'

Topaz shook her head, preoccupied with the carving knife. College authorities had pulled it out of Lisa's door, and she was wondering if she could get away with sticking a similar knife in the door and taking a photo of that.

'You're bloody useless, Rupe,' Gareth Kelly said. 'We had two thousand quids' worth of advertising from McKinsey in that.'

'I'll find it, OK?' promised her deputy editor, sounding harassed. Rupert was scatty and untidy, but a great journalist. Topaz could see that clearly. Even on a college paper he had a knack for ferreting out the real stories: single-parent students, harassing tutors. Rupe had been the first to congratulate her on her *Times* commission. He was the only person on the staff who realized it meant more than a £150 cheque.

'Here it is,' shouted Jane Edwards, the features editor. Rupert leaned gratefully across and grabbed it, answering the phone at the same time and slopping coffee all over his desk.

'*Cherwell*. Yeah. Who should I say is calling?'

He handed the receiver to Topaz with a wink. 'It's for you. Geoffrey Stevens at *The Times*.'

Topaz grabbed the phone, swinging her long legs over the desk to reach it. Every guy in the place sighed mentally.

'Miss Rossi?' asked a cool voice.

'That's me,' Topaz replied, trying to sound flip and unconcerned. She'd posted off her article two days ago. What if the guy hated it?

'This is Geoffrey Stevens,' he said. 'We received your article on student benefits yesterday. We were wondering if you might like to consider a new use for it?'

Topaz's heart sank. It wasn't good enough for the *Educational Supplement*. 'What did you have in mind?' she asked.

'I think this is a bit too good to tuck away in a supplement,' Stevens said. 'I've shown it to the features editor and he agrees with me – we want to use it in the main paper.'

Topaz put out a hand to steady herself against the desk. She was too stunned to speak.

'I know what you're thinking,' Stevens went on, 'you're wondering where we're going to put it. And you're right, of course, that's a problem just at the minute. We're full up, but if you can bear to wait a fortnight we'll run it two weeks on Monday. Would that be OK?'

'That'd be fine,' Topaz said, trying not to sound too overjoyed.

'Terrific! I hoped I could count on you. And send me some more, if you've got it. We're always looking for new talent.'

'Thanks, I will,' said Topaz. She hung up, and looked at the six faces gazing at her expectantly.

'Oh my God!' she exclaimed. 'I'm *in*!'

Rowena planned her campaign with military care. Every speech was dramatic. Every outfit was sexy. Every hack on her slate had his or her orders, and everyone followed them. Rowena had found out who the weak links were early on, kept them out of slate meetings and assigned them to the smallest colleges. She just wasn't taking risks.

She wanted to be President of the Union.

She wanted it *badly*.

She would do almost anything to win.

And that was the problem. Because in this case, 'anything' involved Peter Edward Kennedy, her best friend's boyfriend, the power behind Gilbert's throne. The one man who could hand her what she wanted on a golden plate.

Since that first meeting, Kennedy had swung back and forth like a pendulum. Yes, he would support her. No, he'd given his word. OK, Gilbert was a sexist and an elitist. He would back her slate. Well, maybe he wasn't sure . . .

Rowena knew she could not let this go. However annoyed, however exasperated she got, she never let it show. If Peter Kennedy could be won over, it was worth any effort. It was worth going to see him four times a week.

And that was the *real* problem.

Rowena Gordon, the proverbial ice maiden, was having to deal with something more than annoyance. Something so new she didn't even recognize it at first, but which slowly took a hold of her, until it was all she could do to control herself. She was falling for Peter.

Every day she had to deal with it. He forced her to sit in his rooms and discuss politics with him, a subject which normally fascinated her. But with Peter Kennedy she found she was tuning out. She wasn't listening to him, she was watching his lips move. The square, bold set of his jaw. The thick flaxen hair. The well-developed muscles sliding under the brown, healthy skin.

Peter entranced her. He was so intelligent, so masculine, so assured. Normally Rowena despised men of her own class: wimpy chinless wonders, the lot of them. Gilbert Docker was a typical specimen. But Peter Kennedy wasn't like that. He was a thorough gentleman, but he was sexual too. He was graceful, but he obviously knew how to fight. He was accomplished, but he was also a fiercely competitive athlete. He interested her. He *excited* her.

'What do you *want* out of life?' he asked her. 'When is it enough?'

'I want everything!' Rowena replied. 'It's never enough!'

'When you die, they'll put "Dreamer" on your gravestone,' Peter said, looking at her admiringly. 'You remind me of something Henry Ford once said – "Whether you think you can, or whether you think you can't, you are right."'

She'd glowed with pleasure at his approval.
She knew it was dangerous. She knew it was wrong.

Topaz was in love with him, for God's sake! But what could she do? Without Peter's backing she might fail. And failure was something Rowena Gordon wouldn't stand for.

She began to get angry with Topaz. Why couldn't *she* do this? Peter was her boyfriend. He'd listen to her. If Topaz would talk to him, she wouldn't have to torment herself, but no, her friend just refused to help. It was the first breach that had come between them. Topaz wouldn't even discuss it. She's too absorbed with her goddamn paper, Rowena thought angrily. Student Journalist of the Year. Young Editor of the Year. Future *Times* columnist.

So Rowena walked in and out of Christ Church's magnificent Tudor stone four times a week, because Kennedy refused to let her off the hook. He wanted to be persuaded, talked into it. He told Rowena he enjoyed her company, that she was beautiful, brilliant and enthralling, and that since he had all the cards, she'd have to humour him.

Rowena tried to convince herself that this annoyed her.

Silk. Satin. Swirling chiffon. The lawns of St Hilda's were covered in ballgowns. Thin, sparkling sheaths clung tightly to their owners' bodies, short, bias-cut numbers displayed miles of pretty calves, and old-fashioned crinoline gowns swept regally to the ground, their delicate hems brushing the close-mown grass. The only women's college left at Oxford was preparing for the Union Ball.

'What do you think?' Topaz demanded. She struck a pose against an oak tree wreathed in white dog-roses.

'Very sexy,' Rowena said. Topaz was wearing a tiny, barely-there outfit of navy velvet which contrasted beautifully with her auburn hair, bright blue eyes and healthy tanned skin. The dress was boned at the ribs to emphasize her magnificent breasts, and cut off six inches above the knee, displaying acres of firm, rounded thighs. It was a knockout; even the old porters couldn't stop staring at her.

Rowena tried to hide her disapproval. What *did* Topaz think she was wearing? She looked like a tramp. That little scrap of fabric hardly hid her underwear. How could – she tried to smother her snobbery, but failed – a gentleman like Peter Kennedy want to date her? She was so brazen!

'Do you think it's possibly a little short?' she added coldly.

'What's the matter, am I embarrassing you? Huh?' Topaz grinned. 'Wondering what Peter's going to do with me when he checks this out?'

Rowena blushed scarlet.

'Hey, hey, I'm only teasing,' Topaz said hastily. 'You're getting a little uptight these days, that's all.'

'Election pressure,' offered Rowena, ashamed of herself. She was letting jealousy sour her friendship.

'You look wonderful,' Topaz said warmly. 'Fantastic. It's a little conservative for me, but I'm sure it'll win you hundreds of votes. Who could see you tonight and *not* vote for you?'

Rowena had chosen a family heirloom, an antique Regency gown in light pink silk. It was embroidered with a subtle design of heather sprigs, picked out on the bodice in cloth-of-gold. She was wearing her long hair straight, letting it tumble in a blonde curtain over her shoulders. Her shoes were satin heels from Chanel, and she was carrying a small fan and an elegant clutch bag. Long washed-silk gloves reached up to her elbows. Cinderella would have been proud.

'Thanks,' Rowena smiled. 'That's the idea.'

Topaz glanced at her again, more slowly. 'You devious bitch,' she said affectionately. 'They could stick a picture of you in the dictionary next to "ladylike". It's all part of the masterplan, am I right? Look feminine, talk feminist? You'll hook the women with their ears and the men with their eyes.'

Rowena laughed. 'For a foreigner, you're a quick learner.'

A porter shuffled across the manicured lawns towards them. 'Taxi, Miss Rossi,' he said.

'So when are they printing it?'

'Two weeks from yesterday,' Topaz said. The taxi crawled across Magdalen Bridge, the Gothic splendour of the college rearing up to her right. Undergraduates in full evening dress were picking their way along the High Street, but Rowena didn't want to walk. Not that the locals paid any attention. Every year, ball dresses, dinner jackets and drunken students were a standard fixture in the summer term. 'And he asked me to give him some more stuff, said they were always looking for talent . . .'

Excitement and happiness bubbled in her voice.

'They'll print it right after the election,' remarked Rowena. It was so close now. Anxiety balled in her stomach like a fist. She *must* win, she must! The Presidency of the Union would be her crowning achievement so far. After she graduated, she was going to give everything up, sink herself into rock music, carve out a new life. Mavericks like David Geffen were her heroes. But all that had to wait. Rowena Gordon was totally single-minded, it was part of her control. If she was going to drop out later, fine. But she had to drop out as a winner, and the Presidency was the ultimate prize.

'Yeah,' Topaz agreed. 'And it means I'm on my way. I can't get over what you did for me, getting your dad to make Geoffrey Stevens look at my work. I could wind up working for *The Times* now.'

'For *The Times*?' asked Rowena, confused. 'Won't you go back to New York?'

'I was planning to, but not any more,' Topaz said. She stretched luxuriously. 'Not now I've met Peter.'

The car took a right down Cornmarket towards the Union. The early evening air was mild and warm, perfect weather for a ball. The event was sold out, and student politicians from both slates would be there, hacking the crowd for all they were worth. Rowena dragged her mind away from Peter Kennedy. There were more important things at stake.

'James!' Rowena said. She fought her way through the glittering crowd of bright young things crowding the lobby, dragging Topaz with her. 'Topaz, you must meet my escort, James Williams. He's running for Treasurer with us.'

'As if I didn't know,' Topaz smiled, shaking hands with a gorgeous young second year in army dress uniform. James Williams was a rising star, honest, popular and very good-looking. He was also up at Oxford on a military bursary, and even in the left-wing student atmosphere that commanded grudging respect.

'Delighted,' James said, gripping her hand firmly. '*Cherwell* gets better every week. I see you've won a fistful of awards.'

'You certainly know how to charm a reporter,' Topaz said. 'And everybody else, I hear.'

'What's this, Williams?' demanded Peter Kennedy, coming up behind them. 'Chatting up my girlfriend? We can't allow that, can we?'

James grinned. Peter had been in the year above him at Eton. 'When are you going to do the decent thing and back us, Kennedy?' he demanded.

'Subtle as an H-bomb,' Rowena apologized.

Peter just smiled at her, and turned to kiss Topaz's hand. 'What a sensational dress.'

You're nearly wearing, finished Rowena silently. Watching Peter Kennedy eat Topaz alive with his eyes was just too much. She burned with envy and total inadequacy. God, Topaz had curves on her curves, while she was a mere stick insect. And Topaz was probably his fantasy in bed, as well. She was just a frustrated, ignorant little virgin. How could she ever have imagined she could compete with a sassy, gorgeous American? It was politics that interested Peter. Not her.

'And Rowena,' he said. 'Stand back and let me look at you.'

Rowena took a pace back, aware of a crowd of onlookers watching her, including some of Gilbert's supporters, dismayed to see Peter Kennedy getting so friendly with her. She managed a radiant smile.

'Breathtaking,' Peter said, after what seemed like an eternity. 'James, you are a lucky bastard.'

A shiver of delight rippled through her. He almost sounded like he meant it.

'Come on, babe, they've got business to attend to,' Topaz grinned. *And so have we*, she thought. *Somewhere dark and private.*

'Absolutely,' said Peter, gently squeezing her hand. He nodded at Rowena. 'You and I will have to hook up again later, Miss Gordon. I've come to a decision.'

'Come on, Rowena. Let's get some champagne,' James said, not wanting to push him.

Topaz was having a good time. The crowd was partying hard, the music was great, the food was plentiful and Peter was with her. How could she not enjoy herself? They'd been to the masseur, the video room, the manicurist, the fortuneteller and the handwriting expert, who proclaimed that Peter was trustworthy and confident and that Topaz had a good sense of humour.

'I wonder why they never see anything bad in there,' Topaz commented afterwards.

'With you, there's nothing bad to see,' Peter said.

They'd found a wildly drunk bunch of her compatriots who tried and failed to teach Peter 'The Star-Spangled Banner', danced cheek-to-cheek to a chamber music quartet, and roasted marshmallows together in a bonfire lit in the gardens.

'At least I found one American custom you like,' Topaz teased him.

'Oh, I like a lot of American things,' Kennedy replied, letting his right hand slip to the back of her dress.

When he took her in his arms and kissed her by the firelight, she felt pure happiness flood through her. All the time she'd struggled in New Jersey, for attention from her family, for popularity at school, to make *something* of the only life she had, she'd never dreamed college could be like this. More friends than she could count, English and American. A student paper she ran by herself. A best friend whom she relied on completely. And a boyfriend whom she could easily fall in love with.

'You mean the world to me,' she said breathlessly when they stopped kissing.

Peter smoothed her hair, gently. 'You're incredible,' he said.

She's far more innocent than she makes out, he thought. He lifted her to her feet. 'We ought to get back inside,' he suggested. 'I have to abandon you for a few minutes. I need to find Rowena. Anyway, I don't want you catching cold.'

'All right,' Topaz agreed, looking lovingly at him.

Peter didn't like it. Why did she have to get that devoted shine in her eyes? He wasn't her father, for Christ's sake.

Laughing. Smiling. Applauding loudly. Flirting. Joking. Rowena was on automatic pilot. Three hours of this rubbish and she could hardly bear to tell one more overweight postgraduate how stunning she looked in cherry velveteen, but she did it anyway. You had to lead from the front, right? All her female politicos were going through the same thing. Rowena didn't worry about the men. *They* didn't have to cope with heels.

'Brought you a margarita,' Chris Johnson said, shoving through a crowd of freshers to get to her. Chris was her Librarian candidate, a clever, nice, scatty guy with a shock of brown hair that made him look like a young Albert Einstein.

'You lifesaver,' she said gratefully, taking a refreshing sip. 'How's it going downstairs?'

'Oh, pretty well,' he nodded. 'All our lot are pouring double measures into every drink they serve.'

Rowena grinned. Handing out ridiculously generous measures of drink was a time-honoured way of making yourself popular with the voters.

'Not my money,' she and Chris said in unison, and laughed.

'You should go up to the masseur,' she suggested. 'A bunch of helpless voters trapped in a queue.'

'You got it,' he said.

Rowena finished her drink slowly, glad of the break, and smoothed down the fragile silk of her dress. Amazingly enough she'd managed to prevent it from getting torn in the crush, God knew how. She was fond of this gown, it had been in the family for generations and she'd like to see her daughter wear it to a ball some day. Better than turning up semi-naked like Topaz.

'Rowena,' Peter Kennedy said.

She spun round to find him standing at the foot of a pillar draped in gold streamers and ivy leaves, watching her. He was leaning against the wall, casually, his black dinner jacket slightly crumpled from holding Topaz outside.

'Hello, Peter,' she said, flushing red. 'Are you enjoying yourself?'

He nodded absently. 'I wonder if you could spare me five minutes?' he asked.

God, how beautiful she is, he thought. Attractive in exactly the opposite way to Topaz. Rowena was so obviously embarrassed, blushing whenever he turned up, trying to get out of coming to see him. He felt the familiar twitch in his thighs. Rowena Gordon was a challenge, much more of a challenge than her best friend. A virgin. And very loyal to Topaz, or so people said.

She was struggling with herself.

She *wanted* him.

'Of course,' Rowena said. She glanced around her at the ballgoers cramming every available inch of space in the main building. Only one thing for it.

'We can go into the Officers' Offices,' she suggested, beckoning him to follow her. She turned into what looked like an under-stair cupboard and punched a code into a security lock. The Officers' Offices, for the Librarian, Treasurer and Secretary, were a little back annexe closed off to the public. It was about the only place that would be private.

Peter shut the door behind him and whistled softly. 'Ali Baba's cave,' he said.

Rowena shook her head. 'Hardly. They don't even heat it. A few computers, some files and leftover cans of low-alcohol beer don't add up to limitless riches.'

She couldn't look him in the face. Suddenly, they were out of all the noise and the crush and she was alone with him. Her best friend's man.

How *can* you be with Topaz! Rowena thought angrily. You're so different from her!

'You said you'd come to a decision,' she said, as coolly as she could.

'That's right,' Peter agreed. He moved closer to her, and she could smell the faint scent of his cologne. 'You've talked me into it. I can't actively campaign for you, but I'll withdraw my support from Gilbert. I'm going to break it to him tomorrow.'

Rowena felt overwhelmed with relief. He'd just handed her the election. Gilbert Docker had a snowball's chance in hell without Peter Kennedy's help. He was talentless, elitist and completely disorganized. At the debate on feminism next week she intended to prove that.

'I don't know how to thank you,' she said, beaming with delight.

Peter took a step towards her. 'I do,' he said. He bent forward and kissed her lightly on the lips.

A second later, Rowena pulled back. But it was a second too long. Kennedy had already felt her soft mouth welcoming his embrace, her nipples stiffen against his shirt – he could feel them through her dress – the telltale brightness in the eyes and the shortness of breath. Desire surged through him. Topaz Rossi was a skilled, passionate lover, but Rowena's timidness and uncertainty was something else. He wanted to have her. To teach her about sex. He'd never taken a girl's virginity. The thought of it aroused him almost unbearably.

'What are you *doing*?' Rowena hissed. 'What about Topaz?'

He nearly said, 'What about her?' but stopped himself in time.

'I know, I feel so guilty,' Peter admitted, undressing her with his eyes. Oh, look. She was blushing from head to toe. How sweet. 'Topaz is a great girl, and I'm fond of her too, but . . . I can't help the way I feel about you.'

'Topaz is my friend,' Rowena insisted. 'That's all there is to it.'

God, she wanted him.

'We'd never have lasted together,' Kennedy said smoothly. 'You know that. She's American, she wants different things out of life to me. I only realized it once I started seeing you and talking to you. We're the same, Rowena. We might have a chance together. Let me talk to Topaz and explain things to her.'

'No, no,' said Rowena. She felt as though she could hardly breathe. To hear Peter say what she'd been thinking for so long . . . it was killing her. 'Just leave me alone. I can't talk to you again,' and she wrenched open the door and ran out, her eyes brimming with tears.

Peter Kennedy watched her go.

Not long now, he thought.

4

The air in the chamber was thick with tension.

Rowena sat on the opposition benches, her beautiful face frozen in stone. She appeared to be listening gravely to Gilbert Docker's bumbling, inept attempt at proposing the motion.

At the moment, he was making jokes about male executives having their innocent, appreciative comments towards female juniors totally misconstrued by dykey feminists. It wasn't going down too badly, on the face of it; a crowd of drunk, upper-class rugby players and Oriel boaties had turned up and were cheering every sexist innuendo to the rafters. Gilbert's normally squeaky voice was climbing higher and higher with pleasure, and his face had gone red and sweaty from the heat; he was annoying everyone else, Rowena noticed.

She put a delicate hand to her temple, trying to make the sick, dizzy feeling go away. Why me? she thought. Why now?

Chris Johnson, who as top of standing committee was sitting in the Secretary's chair while Gilbert spoke, glanced across at his slate boss. He was very worried. The chamber was packed solid with students, cramming the benches, squeezed up on the floor, thronging the gallery upstairs. It was Wednesday; the election would be on Friday week. Presidential Debates and officer hustings were usually held on the night before the election, but Crown Princess Victoria of Sweden was due to speak that day, so tonight's showdown had been brought forward. The unusual timing made the debate even more crucial for their slate; Oxford would have more than a week to reflect on this evening's performances.

And Rowena Gordon was a star. A brilliant speaker. She could wipe the floor with Gilbert Docker, ninety-nine times out of a hundred. Indeed, a large chunk of the crowd had turned up specifically to see a bloodbath.

Oh, there'll be a bloodbath, OK, Chris thought grimly. But it might not be Gilbert's blood.

Rowena *looked* stunning. No problems there. She was wearing a strapless ballgown of crushed red velvet, a Balenciaga original of her mother's which emphasized her perfect small breasts and tiny waist, and then cascaded to the floor in sumptuous raspberry folds. The richness of the colour picked out her shimmering hair, and her ice-mint eyes were sharp and glittering.

Glittering far too brightly, Chris thought. The girls who were looking at her enviously and the guys who were sizing her up hadn't seen her like he had this morning, her hair slick with perspiration, her skin pale and shining with sweat. They'd called the doctor: Rowena Gordon, on the morning of her Presidential Debate, had a temperature of 103 and was immediately confined to bed. Chris, as her friend, had tried to talk her out of it, but as soon as the doctor had left, she got up, staggered over to her sink and swallowed ten Nurofen.

'It's not worth it, for Christ's sake,' Chris had said, aghast. 'You'll kill yourself.'

Rowena, shivering with fever, looked at him.

'No I won't,' she said levelly. 'I'll kill Gilbert.'

In the gallery, Peter Kennedy was watching Rowena intently.

Something's wrong, he mused. I know it is.

He thought about how amusing it would be to console her for the loss of the Presidency. Ladies simply had to learn not to bite off more than they could chew. He looked at her again, unsure exactly what it was, but confident that Gilbert would be fine now.

He had a killer's instinct for weakness.

Topaz Rossi was really trying hard to concentrate on the debate, but couldn't. Rowena looked great and she'd cruise it. And if, by some disaster, she did say anything stupid now, or miss some chance to shred Gilbert, Friday's *Cherwell* would wrap it up for her.

Rowena tried to think her way through the lightness and fuzz in her brain. She tugged at the red silk wrap around her shoulders. *Get it together, girl, get it together.* She knew the drugs had sent her ten miles high.

She smiled at her friend, Richard Black, the Treasurer-elect, who was sitting directly opposite her. He grinned tentatively back, but was making frantic gestures at his chest.

Rowena raised an eyebrow. What are you trying to say?

Richard just kept on gesticulating. In the end, unable to work out his signals, she shrugged amiably and turned a contemptuous gaze on Docker.

Gilbert sat down to polite applause, punctuated by whoops from the Oriel contingent.

Jack Harcourt, the President, got up to introduce Rowena. 'And I'd like to thank the Secretary very much indeed for that speech, and it now gives me great pleasure –'

'Oh, Jesus, no,' Chris said.

'– to call upon Rowena Gordon, Christ Church –'

Other people were noticing it now. Murmurs and laughter started to bubble through the chamber.

'– Librarian, to come and oppose the motion.'

Rowena mustered a brilliant smile and got to her feet, making her way to the dispatch box.

For a moment there was a stunned silence. Then the chamber erupted into the loudest roar of cheers and applause Rowena had ever heard. She smiled, bewildered. Not even Gary Lineker had had this enthusiastic a reaction.

People were yelling, smiling, drumming their feet on the floor. She smiled again. They were going insane.

Then she saw Gilbert's smug grin and Chris's stricken expression. *Oh my God*, she thought.

She glanced down at herself, and time seemed to freeze, and then pool like treacle.

Her strapless dress had slipped; the bodice was hanging down, useless, at the waist. She was standing semi-naked at the podium, displaying her breasts to the entire chamber.

Afraid she might faint, Rowena grabbed at her wrap and pulled it across her chest, clutching on to it for dear life. The cheers had by now turned into roars of laughter; a thousand students all clapping and whistling. Everybody on the Gordon slate just wanted to die. Of all the ways to lose an election . . .

In the gallery, Topaz, jolted out of her daydreams, had started to cry from shock and compassion.

Peter Kennedy was quietly beside himself. Those perfect little exposed breasts had given him a rock-solid erection.

Rowena stood frozen at the centre of the storm, paralysed like a rabbit in the glare of headlights. She felt hot tears prickling at the back of her eyes, nausea welling in her throat. She would never live this down as long as she stayed at Oxford.

The cheering went on and on.

Why don't they shut up? Rowena screamed silently. *What are they waiting for?* Then she realized. They were waiting for her to burst into the inevitable tears and run from the chamber. She looked at Gilbert Docker, who shot her a triumphant smile of pure malice. Something inside her snapped back into place. Still clutching at her wrap with her left hand, she raised her right hand for quiet, and, surprised, the audience shut up.

Rowena waited until she had total silence, and then she smiled. 'Well, Mr President,' she said in a loud, clear voice, 'there's only one lesson to be learnt from what just happened – and that is that the Proposition should watch themselves.'

She took a step forward. All eyes were now fixed on her. 'Be warned,' she went on, turning dramatically to Gilbert, still grinning. 'Because for those of us on this side of the House, no sacrifice is too dramatic, no humiliation is too great, *to win this bloody motion!*' and she laughed.

The chamber erupted again, but there was a different quality to this applause. As the bravery of what she had just done sank in, people started to rise from their seats, and all of a sudden she had a standing ovation. Rowena wasn't finished yet, though. Still covered by her wrap, she pulled up her bodice with her free hand and held it against her. Then she let the wrap fall.

'Mr President,' she said loudly, 'if – given the appalling speech the honourable Secretary just made – it isn't against his principles to assist a woman, I wonder if Mr Docker would give me some help with my zip? I seem to be having a little trouble with it.'

And she immediately turned round, presenting her back to a helpless Gilbert, who got up and fastened his rival's dress, boot-faced with anger.

Chris, Topaz and Nick led a fresh round of cheering.

By the time the debate was over it was the middle of the night and rain was thundering down in the Union gardens. Students spilled out into the street, rushing back to their colleges or sordid digs, or attempting to shove themselves into the sardine-like Union bar for last orders. Baby hacks from the Secretary's committee stood outside in the downpour, arguing furiously over whether Rowena had done it on purpose. She had gone on to deliver a moving, passionate speech, and had won the motion by a huge margin.

'We'll still win the fucking election,' Gilbert Docker snapped at Chris Johnson on the way out.

Chris just laughed in his face. He'd already had the pleasure of turning down Gilbert's Treasurer candidate, who'd rather pathetically tried to switch sides.

Topaz cannoned out of the chamber, whooping, kissed Rowena, and ran in the other direction.

'Hey, where are you going?' she yelled.

'*Cherwell*,' Topaz shouted back at her. 'I've been dying to get on that computer since the second you sat down! What a story, girl! I'll have you on the front page!'

'OK, if you say so,' Rowena shouted at her friend's departing back.

It was true, it *was* a great story, and Topaz had been so wrapped up in it she didn't notice the way Peter had stiffened beside her when she hugged him in elation.

Rowena, utterly euphoric, accepted congratulations and pumped hands like a dutiful hack for an hour and a half before slipping back to her tiny digs in Merton Sreet, hardly noticing the soaking rain.

In the *Cherwell* offices, Topaz flicked on the lights and turned on her Apple, trying out a few headlines. Everything came up *Sun*-speak: 'MAY THE BREAST WOMAN WIN,' 'GORDON BENNETT!' 'TREASURE CHEST!' Topaz laughed out loud. Maybe it *was* time for a break from the quality tradition, after all! She tapped in a huge headline: BREAST FOOT FORWARD, and lit a cigarette.

'You thought you'd seen it all before,' Topaz typed away, 'until last Thursday's sensational speech by Rowena Gordon, 34–22–32 (obviously).'

Around her, the empty *Cherwell* offices were quiet and deserted, the silence broken only by the soft hum of the computer and her own breathing. She enjoyed a brief fantasy about how different it would be in a year's time, working on a real paper in London.

Topaz felt contentment seep through her. Rowena would be President of the Union. She would get to be a journalist – *The Times*, no less, and maybe, just maybe, Mrs Peter Kennedy, too.

Peter bawled Gilbert out.

'It's not my fault,' he whimpered for the hundredth time.

'Look,' Kennedy snapped, losing his temper, 'just go home, OK, Docker. I'm going to sort it out now.'

'There's nothing you can do,' Gilbert whined, and then, seeing Peter's face, thought better of it.

Peter started to walk towards Merton Street. Christ Almighty, why did he always have to do everything himself?

Rowena sat in her study sipping a cup of weak tea and watching the fire crackle in the grate. She was comfortable and warm in her thick soft towelling bathrobe, her half-dry blonde hair hanging fresh and glowing around her shoulders. The summer rain drummed against the dark skylight; through the streaming glass she could see the slippery, melting lights of the stars.

She was far too excited to sleep.

She glanced at the faded article on David Geffen, pinned over the bed. When she was President, she'd be able to invite him over to speak . . . She was still fantasizing about what she'd say when they were introduced when the doorbell rang.

'Let yourself in, sweetheart,' she called to Topaz.

'That was a warmer welcome than I expected,' Peter Kennedy said, ducking his head as he stepped into the room.

Rowena shot out of her chair, belting her robe even tighter around her. 'What are you doing here?'

'You asked me in, I believe,' said Peter calmly, shutting the door behind him and offering her a cigarette. She declined; he shrugged and lit up. 'It was a good speech, if I may say so. Very gutsy of you to carry on.'

'Thank you,' said Rowena, relaxing slightly. She couldn't help it, she was glad to see him. Peter hadn't come round since that kiss at the Union Ball a week ago. Who don't I trust? Rowena asked herself. Him, or me?

'It was that or give up on the whole thing, and nothing would persuade me to do that. I've got a duty to the other guys on the slate, anyway.'

He took a long drag on his cigarette. 'Nothing could persuade you to drop out?'

'Nothing,' said Rowena, wary again. There were only two reasons, in this university, for someone like Kennedy to be in her rooms at this hour: sex or politics. And he was still dating her best friend, so it couldn't be the former. 'Tell me what I can do for you, Peter.'

'I want you to withdraw from the election.'

Rowena leant back, and took another sip of her tea. She was surprised, but not shocked; she'd seen too much of this stuff, treachery, indecision, switching sides, on her way up the ladder, to be taken aback now. Plenty of it had been last-minute, too. She wondered for a second if Topaz had known, and then dismissed that idea: Topaz was her closest friend. This was a blow, when it looked as if she had everything wrapped up, but it wasn't all that serious. She doubted even Peter Kennedy could save Gilbert now, not after this evening's triumph.

'I have no intention of doing any such thing, I'm afraid,' she said coolly. 'I rather thought you were supporting me, Peter.'

'Then you thought wrong,' Kennedy said with equal coldness.

'Does Topaz know you're here?' Rowena asked. Her heart was hammering now. Why had Peter come? Why had he switched sides again? Because she'd turned him down?

She looked at the handsome face, the muscular body, the golden hair soaked from the rain. She didn't want him to be angry with her. She wanted him to like her.

'I can't go back on my word to Gilbert,' Peter said, furiously. 'Why can't you see that? Why are you making me feel like this?'

'You gave your word to me, too,' Rowena answered. He looked so angry and guilty and mixed-up. She knew he was battling with himself to sort out his motives, do the right thing. She was stupidly pleased by it, that the way he felt about her had confused him. A small ache of lust began to gather inside her.

'I know,' Kennedy said. The sapphire eyes stared directly at her. 'I should never have said it. I couldn't help myself.'

For the second time that evening Rowena felt time slow down around her. For a few seconds she didn't reply, and they listened to the fire crackling in the grate and the gathering storm outside, the wind moaning across the Elizabethan gables of the house.

Finally she asked, 'What do you mean?'

Her heart was hammering in her chest, her mouth was dry, waiting for his answer.

Peter reached out tenderly and stroked her cheek. 'You know exactly what I mean,' he said. 'Tell me I was wrong. Tell me you have no feelings for me. That you don't think about me. That I can never be more to you than your friend's boyfriend.'

Overcome with desire, Rowena was silent. His touch on her skin sent a small, burning ribbon of heat down between her legs.

'Tell me any of those things,' he said, 'and I'll leave.'

For a split second Rowena remembered Topaz telling her how much Peter meant to her. How she'd stay in England because of him.

Then she looked again at the handsome, aristocratic face, the hard, masculine body, and the way he was watching her, and put the thought out of her mind.

'No,' she said. 'You weren't wrong.'

5

Life seemed to carry on as normal.

In the run-up to the election, Rowena was as ordered and focused as she'd always been: drawing up college lists, organizing secret car runs to carry friendly voters in from around the city, planning speeches and working parties and making sure everybody on the slate did the same. Peter was definitely sticking with Gilbert and they had to work twice as hard. This would be close.

The tourists who crowded into Oxford this summer like every other would have been amazed if they could have seen what was going on behind the bicycles, the billowing academic gowns, and the spires and turrets and champagne picnics – a dirty, bitter struggle for power that would have done credit to a Congressional race. The public schoolboys were going to fight for their turf, and Rowena's assortment of non-privileged candidates couldn't afford to underestimate them.

They had allies, of course. *Cherwell* for one, which had supported them all term. Colleges of their own. Kids that turned up to debates regularly. Anyone who had heard about Rowena's performance in the debate.

But to the other side, merit didn't matter. A socialist idea. Gilbert *wanted* to be President, so he should be. Support the old school. His father's regiment. His mother's receptions. All the old, solid things that had been certain fifty years ago and in the late eighties meant absolutely nothing – except to the disinherited youth which liked to pretend that they did.

Words were had in the appropriate places. The Gridiron Club. Vincent's, where Oxford sporting Blues with matching blue blood liked to get very drunk on fine port. The Disraeli Society. And all the older, established colleges, which despite their PR to the outside world liked things exactly the way they had always been – Oriel, Lincoln, Jesus, Balliol, Queen's, and especially Trinity. Only Christ Church held back. Rowena was one of their own.

And that was what really got the boys going. Because Rowena was being defiant. Charles Gordon's daughter, educated at St Mary's, Ascot, she should have known better. Gilbert and Peter could have arranged the Presidency for her next term. But she still insisted on fighting them. And on picking her own team.

It was obvious that Gordon was walking away from the whole deal. She had hung around with that brash American practically since she came up. She talked loudly about going into the music industry, of all things.

She was a feminist.

She was a traitor.

They would teach her a lesson.

If Gilbert Docker could have seen underneath the cool mask Rowena was presenting to Oxford, he might have relaxed a little. At the moment, with all the organizing and whispering and trading of favours he could pull off, the relentless work of the other slate still put them ahead, and most people saw Rowena herself as their greatest strength.

They didn't know what Peter Kennedy did.

Rowena Gordon was out of control.

She gasped. Peter's hands had moved from her thighs to her nipples, brushing her skin with the featherlight touch he knew fired her up most. She was slippery wet between the legs, loving how he felt inside her, his cock pushing deeper and deeper into the quick heart of her pleasure, his gentle rhythm never faltering, never letting up, sending a light, sweet orgasm rippling across her stomach, and then another a few minutes later, just enough pressure for one or two contractions, keeping her hot, never letting her reach the final climax.

'It's not so bad, is it?' Peter teased. 'Sleeping with the enemy?'

'I'm Mata Hari,' Rowena managed. 'Using you.'

He gave a low, confident chuckle and answered her with an exquisite little twist of the hips, stroking her inside her body, letting her response speak for itself.

Rowena moaned with pleasure. This close to orgasm, she forgot all the other emotions that crowded into her mind whenever Peter came round. The guilt. The jealousy, because he was still seeing Topaz. The shame, at not being able to dismiss him. And the bittersweet joy at seeing him again.

Every time, Rowena said it was the last.

It never was.

She was simply no match for him. Closed away in a convent school, a virgin, faintly contemptuous of boys, Rowena had never come across anyone who called to her body like Peter did. She had been a cold girl, determined, closed-off, proud; Topaz Rossi had been the first really close friend she'd had. For the sake of that friendship, she'd tried to hide her feelings. She'd even turned Peter down at the ball.

It wasn't enough. Her desire was too strong.

She drew back from Topaz, refusing to admit to herself what she was doing. After all, there were a thousand excuses. Topaz was all wrong for Peter. Too brazen. Too foreign. Too poor. And she was perfect: from the same country, the same background, the same class. Kennedy was a gentleman, she was a lady. Prejudices which Rowena had fought against all her life, which she'd always despised, she started using to convince herself of what she needed to believe. She became cold and distant when Topaz tried to talk to her. Told herself the friendship was a mismatch from the start.

'Do it again,' Rowena said, intently. Her nipples were throbbing with pleasure. 'Again. Now.'

'You're good,' Peter whispered, excited. It was true. She was a natural at sex. She loved it. The way she leapt under his touch aroused him. She responded to every tiny caress, every hot glance, every touch of his fingers.

Even that first time, she had come.

Cold, haughty Rowena Gordon.

Kennedy grinned to himself, thrusting deeper into her. Life was full of surprises.

Topaz Rossi walked along Broad Street, heading towards Christ Church. She was in a good mood. Unlike all the English kids who took it for granted, the beauty of Oxford always enchanted her. Compared with small-town New Jersey, this is another planet, she thought, looking across at the wrought-iron gates protecting Trinity's immaculate gardens, the spectacular busts of the Roman emperors ringed round the entrance to the Sheldonian Theatre.

Some scholars cycled past her, long black robes billowing out behind them, on their way to Blackwell's, the university's bookstore of choice. She smiled, wondering whether they were picking up obscure textbooks or a sex-packed trashy novel. One of the things Topaz liked best about studying here was that it could just as easily be either.

She turned down towards the main Hertford entrance, glancing into the courtyard of the Bodleian, Oxford's main library and one of the finest in the world. Topaz walked around there sometimes just for the sheer beauty of it, but you couldn't take out books there, so she didn't use it often. She was a modern girl. She preferred to study in her rooms, where she could make a cup of coffee and listen to Aretha Franklin.

A couple of young *Cherwell* wannabes waved hi to her. They were assigned to the arts pages, covering some new student production at the Playhouse.

'How's the report going?' she asked.

'Well,' the younger girl replied. 'Looks like a couple of West End scouts were in the audience last night. I want to interview Mary Jackson, since she's directing.'

'What she means is, she wants a part in the next one,' her friend said, grinning. The other girl hit her.

'As long as we get our story,' Topaz told them, feeling extremely grown-up. She wasn't in the mood to rain on anybody's parade just now. She was on her way to surprise Peter, she couldn't wait to see him. Life was good.

The two girls waved and walked away.

Topaz pushed back her mass of red curls from her face, enjoying the easy camaraderie of the moment. Some American kids had a tough time here; not understanding the dry English teasing, they left Oxford convinced that the natives hated all foreigners with a passion and Americans in particular. Topaz knew better.

Or maybe Rowena's just blinded me to their faults, she thought.

Or maybe Peter has.

Her skin still felt warm where he'd caressed it that morning. Where he'd licked off the champagne. 'A congratulations present,' he'd said, 'for finishing your second article for a national paper.'

It was a good article, too. She'd submit it as soon as the first one had been published, after the elections. Rowena would be thrilled, once she was a bit less nervous and stressed-out. She'd been acting weird lately.

Topaz paused for a second at the top of Oriel Square, the back entrance into Peter's college, thinking about her article, her lover and her friend, letting it all shimmer round her head. The soft warmth of the sunshine beat down on the nape of her neck. She felt like she was taking a bath in pure happiness.

Rowena felt the fist in her chest again. Like she couldn't breathe, certainly couldn't cry. A gut reaction, probably, to help her keep control.

'We have to stop,' she said bleakly. 'I shouldn't have done this.'

Peter offered her a cigarette, but she shook her head.

'But you did do it,' he said.

A sense of power came to him. That every time he could overcome her scruples, her conscience, whatever. It appealed strongly to his vanity to know that he could fuck both Topaz Rossi and Rowena Gordon in the same day.

Not that Rowena knew that, of course. But she knew he was still seeing her best friend. And that counted.

'I've told you before, I have to let Topaz down gently,' he continued. 'I thought we'd agreed on that.'

Rowena was silent, staring at the wall. Shame and heartache and restless desire were all mixed up inside her.

'What is it? The election?' Peter demanded. 'You know how I feel. I have to keep my word. What we have together is nothing to do with politics.'

She shook her head, no. They both knew that the sex was better because they were opponents. It added another edge.

'What about your word to Topaz?'

'You said it was the last time yesterday,' he reminded her cruelly.

Rowena flushed. It was true. Yet again she'd given in; partly as a result of her deep craving for him, partly because he'd refused to let up. He'd climbed up the drainpipe outside her window, sent her two dozen red roses and a bottle of vintage champagne. He'd sat next to her at every meal in Hall. Waited for her in the porters' lodge when she came to get her morning post. He had been as insistent as a Sherman tank and as romantic as Lord Byron. It was almost a relief to give in to him, to let him do what she longed for him to do.

We're at the same college, Rowena thought. I can't get away from him.

Out loud, she said, 'I mean it. This isn't about not hurting Topaz. It's about you refusing to give either of us up.' She wanted to cry.

'You're the one I want,' Peter said carefully, hearing a new note in her voice. He took her in his arms.

Despite herself, Rowena felt too weak to resist. She wanted him to comfort her. To tell her he loved her, that it would all be OK.

'Topaz is my best friend,' she said. A fresh wave of shame beat up in her. How could she say that? She'd sneered at her, despised her, pulled rank on her, the works. All because Topaz had done the unforgivable thing. She'd been betrayed. And Rowena had let a guilty person's dislike for their victim take over.

Peter looked down at the sexy, lithe body, stiff in his arms. At those full lips set dead against him, strong with rejection.

Neither of them noticed the door swing open. Neither of them saw they were being watched.

'What are you talking about?' he said. 'You were the person who told me the whole thing was crazy. A hick from New Jersey and a girl like you. She wouldn't even help you with *me*, remember? I seem to recall you told me last night you'd break if off after the election. She does edit *Cherwell*, after all.'

He touched her cheek, softly. 'Don't blame Topaz Rossi for what you feel about me. She doesn't matter to you. Don't try and hide behind that. You owe me better.'

'Hide what?' Rowena murmured. The smell of him, the nearness of him. She wanted to cling to him. She didn't want to let him go.

'The fact that you don't love me,' Peter said.

'That's not true.'

There was a pause, while he sensed her sexual heat blossom again.

'Show me,' he said, and Rowena, with a little sob of capitulation, lifted her lips to his.

At the door, Topaz found her eyes had brimmed over with tears, so she could hardly see. She blinked, and felt the salt water roll away down her cheeks. In total silence, she backed into the corridor.

Neither of them noticed her go.

The *Cherwell* offices were crammed. It was Wednesday, the final review meeting day for copy. Everything had to be filed by Thursday afternoon and they went to print that night. The atmosphere was fun, a cocktail of apprehension, excitement, moaning about the work. Seventh week of Trinity Term was going to be a thick edition, too. There was sports news from the rowing, gossip from the various college balls, a bundle of recruitment ads, advice on the final examinations for unfortunate third and fourth years, and, of course, the Union elections. And that didn't even touch on the features: benefits, computing and the city homeless. Students were jamming the place. It was a good paper to write for, a good thing to put on the résumé. And, since Topaz Rossi had taken over, everybody read it. Shock and amaze your friends! They were future media barons. They were ready to go.

People stopped chattering when Topaz and Sebastien walked in together. The editors had that kind of presence: good for a laugh, motivational, fun to work with, but you shut up when they told you to. Topaz never settled for second-rate writing, photography or design.

You got it right, or you were out.

'OK', Topaz said. She was wearing a sexy outfit, a cutoff black tank top that emphasized her magnificent breasts and bared her flat midriff, teamed with low-slung black 501's which hugged her ass. Her red hair was wound into a coil and piled loosely on the top of her head, letting a few rebellious strands swing round her temples. Uncharacteristically, she was also wearing make-up: a dash of colour on her high cheekbones, soft brown eyeshadow, an inviting pink lipstick. Long chain earrings swung from her lobes, following every movement of her head. Her eggshell-blue eyes were sparkling with fierce determination.

Half the male journos in the room found they didn't know where to look.

'We've got one major change this week,' Topaz said. Her Italian-American accent seemed more pronounced than ususal. 'Roger Walpole, I'm afraid it affects you.'

Roger, sitting in one of the comfortable black chairs, looked across at her. 'What's up?' he asked. 'You didn't like the piece?'

He'd been writing the lead story on a Student Union plot to increase the price of alcohol, a matter of concern to every undergraduate in the city, if not a personal tragedy. It would have been a terrific headline.

'No, it's superb, as usual,' Topaz smiled. 'It's going on the front page. But we're running a new lead. I've written it.'

A murmur of surprise ran round the room. 'About what?' somebody asked.

Topaz paused for effect, feeling the white-hot rage, the burning satisfaction of a tiny measure of revenge.

'About Rowena Gordon's candidacy for President of the Union.'

The place erupted, with everybody shouting questions at once.

'I thought you were friends,' Phil Green said.

Topaz shrugged. 'A story's a story.'

'What are you going to say?'

'That I've discovered that Rowena plans to cheat on her own slate; she's not going to pull any votes for anyone but herself. That the whole thing with her dress in the debate was a deliberate publicity stunt. That she made up the story about the knife in Joanne's door just to slander Gilbert.'

'Is it *true*?' Roger asked, shocked.

Topaz looked him straight in the eye. 'Every word.'

'What a bitch,' said Jane. 'But we come out on Friday morning. The morning of the election.'

There was another burst of noise as the room realized what that meant. 'She'll be destroyed!' someone yelled.

Topaz waited for them to quieten down, then looked at them calmly. Every eye was fixed on her.

'That's the idea,' she said.

Rowena Gordon felt good about herself for the first time in weeks. She'd actually done it, she'd told Peter Kennedy to go screw himself and she'd meant every word. He'd sent flowers at lunch, she refused delivery. She put the phone down on him three times. When he turned up at her door, she threatened to call the porters if he didn't leave.

It was madness, she told herself, but it passed.

Of course, it nearly hadn't done. After that kiss this morning, she must have been seconds away from falling back into bed with him. She had no idea what gave her the strength to pull back. To push him away. To insist that he leave, and actually make him do it.

Rowena brushed her long fair hair, standing in front of the wall mirror in her chilly bedroom. The silky fall of the fine strands against her back was a sensual feeling. She moved and pirouetted, admiring her own slender, leggy reflection, the pale pink nipples on her small, tight breasts. She'd always envied Topaz her magnificent figure, but tonight she decided she was happy with her body. It would look graceful, sitting in the President's chair.

There was a hard knock on the door.

'Who is it?' Rowena demanded, reaching for a silk bathrobe. If her rooms weren't quite the picture of luxury that Peter's were, Charles Gordon, with his customary disregard for money, had seen to it that they were handsomely equipped.

'It's Topaz,' came the reply.

Rowena felt little spiders of fear crawl up and down her spine. She'd nearly said, 'Get lost, Peter.'

'Just coming,' she shouted, tying back her hair. She found herself blushing. Should she confess to Topaz? she wondered, and in a split second decided against it. That would only salve her own conscience at the expense of her friend's happiness.

She took a deep breath, and opened the door.

Topaz walked into the familiar room quite calmly. She'd rehearsed this meeting over and over in her mind, so she'd get to take it slow, say everything she needed to. She didn't want to lose anything in the heat of passion.

Rowena, that cold, betraying English bitch, was looking her normal immaculate self. Topaz checked out the robe, noticing the expensive designer-green silk. A lot of things in this room were expensive, she guessed. The feather duvet. The bottle of port on the sideboard. Rowena's brushed-leather overcoat, hanging on the back of the door.

Things that were way too good for a hick from New Jersey, right?

Topaz sauntered past Rowena, looking at her with the deepest contempt.

Rowena felt her heart leap into the roof of her mouth. She had seen Topaz act like this only a couple of times before. When one of the *Cherwell* old guard had called her a Yank wop and tried to kill some of her early stories. It had been one of the reasons she'd liked Topaz so much in the first place.

'You should know something about Italian-Americans,' Topaz had told him, right in front of Rowena. 'We always avenge an insult.'

Two months later, the guy had resigned from the paper. Topaz never offered to tell her what had happened and Rowena never asked. It was just there for all to see.

I am who I am. Don't fuck with me.

She had that same look on her face now.

'You know,' Rowena said.

'Yeah, I know,' Topaz said. 'And please don't insult me with an excuse.'

Rowena couldn't look at her. Shame overcame her. 'I left him, today,' she said, eventually.

'Did you?' Topaz asked. She suddenly wanted to cry. The double rejection came back at her again, with the force of a kick in the stomach. Her friend. Her lover. Had they laughed about her together? she wondered. 'It didn't look like that when I saw you in his arms this morning.'

Rowena sat down heavily on the bed. 'I can explain –' she said.

Topaz shook her head. 'It's over, Rowena,' she said. Her eyes were hard. 'I brought you a copy of *Cherwell*'s front cover story for tomorrow. I thought you might like a preview.'

Her hands trembling, Charles Gordon's daughter picked up the story that would wipe out three years of dedicated work. That would deny her the last prize she wanted before she dropped out of society. That would brand her as a traitor and a liar in front of her whole university.

She finished the story in silence. When she turned to Topaz, her face was drained of blood.

'If you print this,' she said, 'I'll call my father and I'll have him speak to Geoffrey Stevens. Your article will never see the light of day.' She drew herself up, rigid and haughty. 'I promise you.'

'I thought of that,' replied Gino Rossi's daughter. Her face was murderously angry. 'It's worth it, to see you crash and burn.'

She paused, looking for the right words. 'You see, Peter doesn't matter,' she said. 'He was nothing. He was good in bed, he was charming, I'd have found out what he really was soon enough. It's *you* that matter, Rowena. Because I was your friend. Because we trusted each other.'

Topaz leant closer. 'I promise *you* something,' she said. 'I promise you this is just the beginning. When you find what you really want to do – records or whatever – I'll be waiting for you. Wherever you go. And I'll have my revenge. I swear it.'

'A nice speech,' Rowena answered coldly.

Topaz turned at the door, the two beautiful girls staring at each other with candid hatred.

'You never had to fight for a thing, did you? Life's just a fucking tennis match for you, right?'

Topaz nodded at the *Cherwell* article spread out over the bed. The headline, in black type three inches high, read FOR SHAME, ROWENA.

'Fifteen-all,' she said, and slammed the door.

Part 2
RIVALS

6

Sophistication was the first thing to go.

'*You* wanna rent this place? You must be joking,' the third landlord said when Rowena turned up to view his bedsit. He examined her camel-coloured wool coat, her Armani pantsuit, her delicate shoes. His eyes narrowed. 'You're mucking me about. What do *you* wanna live in Soho for?'

'It's the only thing I can afford,' Rowena answered. She wished the guy would step back; his breath recked of garlic and curry. She tried to smile, to make him want to rent to her. The first two places she'd seen, the landlords had taken one look at her and slammed the door in her face.

Rowena was getting desperate. The money she had from her own account was running very low, she couldn't find a job in the record business anywhere, and her parents had cut her off without a penny until she agreed to come home and give up any idea about working in music. Rowena had refused point-blank. When she graduated, she'd decided to conquer the world. There was no way she was crawling back to Scotland to apologize and behave, like a beaten puppy.

'Sure,' the landlord said. He leered at her. 'On the game, are we, darlin?'

'I beg your pardon?' asked Rowena, stunned.

He winked. 'Oh, don't look like that. I won't tell if you won't. It's fifty-five down and cash at the start of each month, in advance.'

For a second she didn't understand. 'You're renting it to me?'

'I ain't giving it to you,' he said, extending a sweaty hand.

Rowena hurriedly opened her purse and gave him the notes. She'd already learnt not to offer a cheque.

'Any problems, please don't bother me with them,' the guy said, leering at her again and waddling out of the room.

Rowena took a long, hard look at herself in the grimy mirror. A high-class prostitute? *Her*?

Then she took another look. The figure-hugging clothes. The impeccable make-up. The precision-cut hair shimmering down her back.

He was right. It wasn't Soho.

The next day, Rowena took all her designer clothes down to an exchange store and sold every one of them. She hawked her brooches, her Patek Phillipe steel watch and her gold pendant, and forced herself to haggle over

51

the price. The woman upped her offer by 30 per cent. Rowena knew she was probably still being ripped off, but it felt like a victory. She was learning.

She invested in a good pair of Levi's, some ankleboots, sneakers and a black leather jacket. T-shirts were cheap and she picked up Indian-print scarves at the markets. By day she traipsed round London, looking for a job. By night, she practised her cooking – not being able to afford Marks & Spencers was a revelation – and went to every cheap rock gig she could scam her way into.

Looking back on that first month, Rowena wondered how she'd ever got through it. All her romantic notions about rebelling against her parents and living in poverty until she found the job of her dreams! How come she'd never stopped to wonder what 'poverty' actually meant? To be cold, hungry, watching every penny all the time – Rowena Gordon, who'd never so much as compared the price of two lipsticks the whole time she was at college! How come the image of bravely tramping the pavement, banging on every door in sight, had never included the sick feeling of failure that consumed her whenever she lost out on another entry-level position?

Two or three times she nearly gave up. She didn't have to do this, after all. She had a good degree and a useful set of A-levels. She could have become a lawyer, joined a management consultancy – all sorts of high-pay, high-respect jobs where doing well at Oxford would count for something. She was only getting rejection after rejection because she wanted to go into the record business, where a degree was a negative, not a positive, and nobody gave a monkey's if your hobbies were riding and skiing.

But in the sweaty little clubs, packed out with bikers and rock fans, filled with acrid smoke from the dry ice and Guns 'n' Roses pumping loudly on the stereo, Rowena Gordon had her first taste of freedom. She became accepted on the scene. She got to know the bartenders, some of the regular kids, and they accepted her for what she was. Without questions. Without judgments. Another 21-year-old kid that liked music.

And there *was* the music.

Rowena got to know all the coming bands. Most of them were tired, derivative rubbish – pale imitations of the LA glitter boys, or the New York metalheads. But sometimes, just *sometimes*, she'd hear a band that excited her. And that made it all worth it.

Arrogant, cool Rowena Gordon was surprising herself.

She couldn't bear to give up on the dream.

One night she walked into the Arcadia, in Camden Town, to find the place almost deserted.

'What's up?' Rowena asked, walking up to Richard, the barman and a friend of hers, who was chatting to an old man in a trenchcoat. 'Did Blue Planet cancel?'

He nodded.

'That's OK, they're overrated anyway,' she shrugged, perching on a barstool. 'Can I get a Jack Daniels and Diet Pepsi, please?'

Richard pushed across her drink, glancing slyly at the guy he'd been talking to. 'I hear Musica Records just signed them for two hundred grand.'

Rowena chuckled. 'They would. Musica can't tell a rock band from a rubber band.'

The old man coughed. 'Why do you say that, missy?' he demanded, in a brittle American accent.

Rowena blushed. 'Are you their manager? I'm sorry.'

'No, I'm not their manager,' he said. 'But I'll buy you that drink if you tell me what you think's wrong with them.'

'You should listen to Rowena,' Richard told him. 'She goes to every gig in town. Every club, too.'

'Rich girl?' the old man asked.

Rowena laughed. 'Hardly. I don't *pay* for any of it. Friends let me in. You know how it is.'

'Yeah, I know how it is,' he said wryly, trying to remember what it was like hanging out at New York Jazz dives in the thirties.

Rowena took a swallow of her drink. Her friends from Oxford wouldn't have recognized her; sitting without make-up, comfortable and relaxed in a scruffy pair of jeans, she looked even younger than she actually was. She'd lost weight, developed muscle tone, and pulled her long hair back in a casual pigtail. She looked terrific.

'You want to know why it was a bad deal for Musica Records?' she asked cockily. 'Fine. I'll tell you.'

Ten minutes later, her eyes sparkling with enthusiasm, she was still talking about dime-a-dozen unsigned bands.

'Enough, enough,' Richard laughed, putting a hand on her arm. 'He gets the message.'

'No, that's OK,' the old guy said. 'What do you do when you're not fighting for a place in the front row, missy?'

She shrugged. 'Nothing. I want to work in a record company, but I can't get a job. I'm still trying, though. Who's asking?'

As Richard grinned, the American pulled out a gold-edged business card from his battered wallet. 'My name's Joshua Oberman,' he said shortly. 'You know who I am?'

Rowena felt herself spread crimson from head to toe. Josh Oberman was an industry legend. He was also President of Musica Records UK.

'Yes, sir,' she said.

'I said my name was *Joshua*. Don't act cute. Just report in to my Personnel division at ten tomorrow morning. You're hired,' he added as an afterthought, and got up to leave.

'What as?' asked Rowena, stupefied.

'A talent scout, of course,' Oberman snapped. 'What do you think?'

The first day Rowena walked through the doors of Musica Records as an employee was one of the happiest of her life. She took one look at the futuristic lobby, its black leather and polished chrome, the young, hip secretaries strolling in and out of reception with their T-shirts and attitude, and the wall-mounted TVs pumping out music videos, and knew she'd found her vocation.

Nothing could dent her mood. Not the surly, prim woman in Personnel who filled out her details and insisted on calling the president's office to get confirmation that Rowena wasn't making it up; not the way the other A&R scouts refused even a pretence of friendliness to the new competition when she was being shown round; not even her tiny cubbyhole of an office, or the minute amount of money she'd be getting paid, which meant she'd still have to keep her seedy apartment.

Rowena was prepared to sweat blood for Musica Records. They had given her a chance.

'Hi, welcome to the team,' said Matthew Stevenson, with a total lack of enthusiasm. 'Have a seat.'

He waved Rowena to a cavernous armchair in soft buttery leather at one corner of his huge office. Sun came streaming through the windows overlooking the Thames, illuminating the state-of-the-art stereo system and the framed gold and platinum discs that covered the walls.

'I'm the head of A&R, or Artists and Repertoire,' Stevenson said, sighing. He was a fat, bald, hook-nosed industry veteran and he liked to pick his own scouts. But Oberman got what Oberman wanted, and he'd taken a shine to this girl.

Stevenson had seen it happen before: some kid would impress Josh at a concert or write him a good pitch letter and Oberman, always hungry to discover a new David Geffen, would stick them in Marketing or International and there was nothing anyone could do about it. They usually lasted a few months, maybe even a year, and then lost interest and quit or got fired after a decent interval. He was sure this girl would go the same way. But what could he do about it? The old man was capricious.

'That means we try and sign talented bands to the label, and then we help them develop repertoire, i.e. songs. That used to mean we'd choose songs for them to cover, but these days it mostly involves helping a band choose the right producer. Is that clear?'

Rowena nodded eagerly. She knew all this stuff backwards, of course, but she didn't want to look cocky.

'Your job,' her boss continued, 'is to listen to tapes the hopefuls send in, mail them back with a rejection letter, and go out at night looking for bands.'

'But what if someone sends in a good tape?'

'If they're good, they play live. Someone has heard of them. They have a manager. Understand?'

Rowena crossed her legs. She didn't want to annoy her new boss, but she couldn't help herself. 'Then why do we bother listening to them at all?'

'Just in case I'm wrong,' Stevenson answered with an unpleasant grin, and held out a clammy hand. 'Welcome to the music business.'

He wasn't wrong. After three days, Rowena was quite clear on that point. Every morning, the secretary she shared with four other scouts dragged a huge sackful of tapes into her cubbyhole and left Rowena staring at them in dismay. At first, wanting to be fair on everybody, she listened to half of each tape. When she discovered that one sack was replaced by two, and two by three, as she made no inroads at all on the mountain of work, she cut it back to one song. Eventually, Jack Reich, the scout who worked next to her, took pity on her hopeless amateurism.

'Look, Rowena,' he said, yanking her headphones off her ears. 'Thirty seconds, OK? *Thirty seconds*. You've got hundreds of these suckers to go through, *and* all the paperwork, *and* all the bands that are serious enough to actually play gigs. Ninety per cent of these acts you're making notes about have split up by now.'

He grabbed the tape she was listening to and held it up. 'See the date of that? September. Five months ago. That's how long it takes to get round to unsolicited tapes.'

'Thirty seconds?' Rowena repeated.

'Thirty seconds,' Jack insisted 'is *generous*.'

He wasn't kidding. Rowena was getting disillusioned about musicians. She'd had no idea how much bad music it was possible to make until she started looking for a band good enough to invest in. Her days were filled with tape after tape of utter rubbish – people would submit tapes of themselves singing along to Karaoke machines. Her nights were filled with long, backbreaking drives around the country, watching a succession of lacklustre singers and laughably dreadful rock bands. She got to know every mildewed, dank little club from Oxford to Truro, and as the lowest scout on the totem pole she was never allowed within ten feet of more juicy chances.

It was difficult to make friends at work. Jack Reich treated her kindly, but he was an A&R manager with three signed acts, and always busy. The other scouts, all male and all younger than herself, refused to give her the time of day. The secretaries made it clear that they preferred flirting with the boys to typing up her paperwork, and Matthew Stevenson called by her office every week like a circling vulture, Rowena thought, itching to sack her.

'Found anything yet?' he'd smirk, and she'd have to say, 'No, not yet.'

God, she really wanted to! It was heartbreaking! Here she was, a rock fan, a music junkie, and now a talent scout for a major label, pleading, begging to be impressed. And she saw or heard hundreds of bands a month, all of whom were begging her to be impressed by them.

But she couldn't. She couldn't do it. There was no answer to Matthew, because everything she checked out was so awful, every song was so dire.

She ploughed on, feeling more and more isolated and depressed. Maybe she should forget the whole thing, become a lawyer. Maybe there was a talent drought in Britain. Maybe there was nothing *to* find.

And then she stumbled across Atomic Mass.

7

Topaz was miserable. It was not supposed to turn out like this, she told herself for the millionth time as she huddled over the street brazier, frozen to the marrow of her bones. There is nothing on God's earth so cold as a New York winter, and Topaz Rossi was catching the full brunt of it.

She stared across the river of grimy traffic, crawling though the slush, at the marbled Fifth Avenue skyscraper from which David Levine obstinately refused to appear. Persistence, Topaz told herself, persistence is 99 per cent of what makes a good reporter. True, she could duck into Rockefeller Plaza and grab a cup of hot chocolate – with whisky – and a slice of warm sachertorte. But if she did, and God knows she was longing to, it was a hundred to one on that Levine would choose that exact moment to appear and she'd lose her shot at an interview with the hottest film star on the planet. Not to mention her job.

Topaz stuck her hands into the pockets of her snug black jeans, cut to show off every curve of her magnificently pert ass. She may have felt like shit, but she looked like a million dollars, even if the tips of her ears were so cold they matched her lipstick. The guy selling chestnuts on the brazier raked over the coals some more, in the hope that it'd be warm enough to keep this incredible babe standing there for just a bit longer. Maybe if he got *really* lucky, she'd stamp her feet again to warm up, because when she did that she jiggled slightly under the clinging cashmere jacket, showing him a little bit of paradise right here on earth. He wondered, not for the first time, who she was waiting for. If it was a guy, he was one hell of a lucky sonofabitch.

Topaz let her mind drift back as to why she was there, answering her own questions as usual. This might be a cold fucking assignment but it was a lot better than none at all. She had a vision of herself just three months ago, clutching a smart little leather folder full of neatly mounted examples of her work on *Cherwell* and letters of recommendation from her tutors, hawking herself around the New York magazine houses until her feet bled. It was the same story everywhere.

'I'm sorry, we have nothing for you.'

'You do need *some* experience to write for the *New Yorker*, kid. Sorry to have to break it to ya.'

'We have no vacancies at this time.'

'He's in a meeting.'

'She's in a meeting.'

'He's still in a meeting.'

'What is this stuff? You're bringing me stuff from *school*? We're a national publications group, Ms Rossi. If you don't realize that this isn't good enough without me telling you, you aren't cut out to be a journalist,' said Nathan Rosen, not unkindly.

Topaz felt as though two or three big rocks were sitting leaden in her stomach. It was her sixth interview of the day.

'I was commissioned to write a piece on student benefits for the London *Times* once,' she murmured miserably.

Rosen brightened. 'Well, that's different. I'd like to see the piece, you got it with you?'

She shook her head. 'It didn't come off.'

Rosen looked at her sceptically.

Rowena Gordon, I hope you rot in the hottest corner of hell, Topaz thought, suddenly pierced with a white-hot anger. She pushed back her chair.

'Mr Rosen, I'm obviously not suited for *Westside*. Thank you for seeing me. I won't waste any more of your time.'

Hey, hey, wait up,' Rosen said softly. 'I didn't say you could go. One of the juniors in entertainment is off sick this month. You'd be pasting, setting, making coffee, typing . . . it's pretty menial stuff, but it's a way in. You want the job?'

No I don't want the job, Topaz screamed silently. *I'm the most intelligent goddamned woman that ever set foot in your stinking rathole office, and I'm nobody's fucking gofer!*

It was the only thing she'd been offered in more than a hundred interviews.

'What's the pay like?'

'It's shit,' said Nathan Rosen.

'I'll take it,' said Topaz.

For the next two weeks she seemed to run on adrenalin, substituting the electric atmosphere of the office for more normal human fuels like food and sleep. She lost weight and learnt how to gulp down a cup of coffee whilst running from the art department to the newsdesk with six different layouts in her hand. She typed up articles, corrected spellings, pasted photographs on to mockups, checked up on facts for investigative pieces. She made coffee, typed letters, photocopied headlines and hated herself. She suggested captions and ideas to the journalists and felt she was making a mark. She pushed herself in everyone's face.

The first Saturday Topaz had off, she slept all day.

She learnt quickly because she had a fast eye and instincts about people. Jason Richman was writing a piece on the weirdest food in New York? Topaz had seen a guy selling chocolate pizza off West 4th Street. Josie Simons complained at the top of her voice that there was no one in the whole world with a fresh take on rock 'n' roll, and Topaz suggested she interview the doorman at CBGB's. Josh Stein, the art director, couldn't fit a long headline on to a page? Splice it across the diagonal, maybe, said Topaz. Write the article around it.

'I need a title for this piece!' bellowed Nathan Rosen across the features desk, drowning out the incessant whirr of telephones, voices and computer typewriters.

'What's it on?' asked Elise DeLuca, the deputy features editor.

'Modern art at the Met ... Henry Kravis is thinking of endowing a national collection of American avant-garde stuff – its the lead story next week,' Rosen yelled. 'Biggest thing since J. P. Getty got the painting bug.'

'Modern Masters,' said Elise.

'The Tate comes to NYC.'

'New York, New Pictures.'

'Cutting-Edge Kravis.'

'All of those suck. *They suck!*' bellowed Rosen. 'All I'm asking for is one good goddamned line!'

'How about "State of the Art, Art of the State"?' murmured Topaz, passing his desk with two armfuls of photocopies.

Rosen looked at her. 'That's good. I'll use that,' he said quietly.

Later in the afternoon Rosen stopped by her desk, where she was typing up some hack's drastically edited play review for setting. 'See if you can do something with this one, Rossi,' he said, trying not to stare at the beautiful firm young cleavage positioned directly under his nose. 'I got two pages in the business section on Häagen-Dazs ice cream and how good it's doing in Europe – four hundred per cent growth a year, stuff like that.'

'I'm not surprised,' said Topaz, remembering the Häagen-Dazs café in Cornmarket and how it was full of undergraduates even in December.

'Yeah, well. This is a real smart piece of business reporting but it's just that – business. I'd like to get some feel of ice cream in there, remind people what Häagen-Dazs tastes like. Association makes the figures a lot more interesting. So.'

He held up a sheet with the article, entitled 'Häagen-Dazs Spearheads Growth of Upmarket Snacks'. It was one and three-quarter pages of close text, with a tub of rum-raisin filling the upper left-hand corner of the second sheet.

'I need a killer caption for the packshot,' said Rosen.

'OK. Gimme just a second,' said Topaz. She had the line already, she'd thought of it the moment he explained the article, but she wanted to bask in Nathan Rosen's presence for a few more seconds. Hey, any junior would be flattered to have the editor by their deskk. The fact that he was so good-looking had nothing to do with it.

'No hurry,' said Rosen impatiently.

'Well,' said Topaz slowly, 'how about if you put "Häagen-Dazs: not so much of an ice cream, more of a religious experience."'

'Could you say that again?' asked Nathan Rosen, wondering if he could have heard her right.

'Not so much of an ice cream, more of a religious experience,' Topaz repeated.

Nathan pulled himself together. The sentence was perfect. 'OK. Let me get a few other suggestions. You make sure you stop by my office when you get off work today.'

'Whatever you say, boss,' Topaz smiled. *I'm getting there*, she thought.

'You won't get a better caption than that one!' she shouted after his retreating back.

The editorial rooms of *Westside* were quieter by 8 p.m.; there were still a few journalists hunched over their consoles, faces lit by the flickering screens, who might well be slaving over their pieces till one or two in the morning. Topaz heard a telephone ring in the art department, a fax machine whirr on the newsdesk. But basically the place was emptying out. She felt slightly sick with excitement as she looked at the editor's office, still flooded with golden light. She was exhausted after another gruelling day; the job left her feeling like a human punchbag.

Better check myself out first, Topaz told herself, slipping into the ladies. Hardly the most luxurious restrooms in the universe, at least they had adequate supplies of what she needed most right now: lights and mirrors.

She glanced at her reflection, dabbing a little cover-up over the shadows under her eyes. Pretty good. Her black Donna Karan tunic emphasized her large bust and tiny waist, the latest stack mules made her calves look thinner, there were a few long curly red strands which had escaped from her swept-back look, but that was cool; they looked sexy, and they looked like she'd been working.

'Yes. I am a working girl. I am going to get a promotion,' Topaz told herself, then she took a deep breath, left the ladies, and strode across the floor to Nathan Rosen's office.

Rosen watched her coming. She excited him every way he looked at it. Day-to-day, she was a free-range magazine-improver and staff-energizer. Mentally, he felt a rush of joy as one print man discovering another; looking at her, he saw a female version of his younger self: all journalistic brilliance and brass balls wrapped up in an intense love of the story and how to tell it. She would make it in spades, and he would be her guru. But physically – damn it! – he had distinctly unpaternal feelings which refused to go away. He watched the tight muscles of her ass rolling under her clothes as she came across the room, her breasts rising and falling, her legs clicking and pumping . . . he felt that treacherous tickle in his groin . . . God, look at the way she moved when she walked! It was poetry, it was a symphony to the beauty of the human female.

Stop it! Right now! Rosen lectured himself. She's twenty-one years old, I'm thirty-nine. I could be her father.

Topaz knocked and came in, smiling.

My God, she's attractive, thought Rosen. 'Sit down,' he said coldly.

Topaz sat.

'You're coming up with some good stuff, Topaz,' he said, leaning forward. 'Really good. And I know you realize this. I also know you realize that you're outperforming your job description, and that you deserve a pay rise and a promotion.'

Topaz nodded intently. *This is it. I did it. He's gonna make me a reporter.*

'Well, you can have the pay rise,' Rosen said. 'But I'm not gonna make you a reporter. That, you can forget. You've only been here a month. You got five months to go before I'll even consider it. And I don't want you making any waves around the office – all the assistants are jealous enough of you as it is and I can tell you right now, some of the junior reporters feel threatened.'

'What?' said Topaz, bewildered.

'You gotta pay your dues and that's just the way it is. I'm sorry if you don't like it. That's all. Congratulations on your pay rise,' said Nathan bluntly, and turned to a file on his desk in dismissal.

For a second there was silence, as Topaz was suffocated with fury. But only for a second.

'Fuck that! And *fuck you*,' she spat. 'So that's it, huh? Six months of typing from seven a.m. to eight p.m. so the other secretaries can feel comfortable! How can you sit there and tell me talent means nothing, pay your dues? You're scared of your junior reporters? I'll tell you why they're threatened – because I prove every day out there that I can do what they do *better*. You practically said so yourself. Who's the editor here? You or them?'

'*I* am!' roared Rosen, out of his chair now and incensed. '*Me*, not *you*! And don't you *ever* forget it!'

He sat down again heavily, enraged. 'You listen to me, Rossi,' he said. 'You're lucky I don't fire you on the spot' – Topaz went white – 'for the way you just spoke to me. I've been running this ship for ten years and you've been here five minutes. I've seen hotshots like you before, you come in the door, put in long hours, come up with a couple of snappy lines and you think you're Ralph J. Gleason. Well, coming up with a title or a caption does not make a reporter. You know what it makes? *An advertising copywriter!*' he bellowed again. 'You wanna sell ice cream? Take a cab to Madison Avenue!'

Topaz trembled. It was like standing directly in the path of a ballistic missile.

'I'm sorry,' she mumbled, and was appalled to hear her voice quiver. Oh God, she panicked, I think I'm going to cry.

Rosen looked at his protégée, staring at her lap and obviously terrified. He had been violently angry, but that had passed and now he kind of admired her spirit. And she looked so vulnerable. Part of him wanted to soothe her, kiss her, stroke her hair. Part of him wanted to throw her over the desk and fuck her right here in the office. *Don't think about that! Be fair. But be just.*

'OK, look,' he said. 'I can't go on with you like this, it's disruptive. But you think I'm holding you back, you're as good as the junior reporters . . . so. I'm giving you a chance to prove it. David Levine has a meeting at the GE building at three o'clock tomorrow, I got a tip-off, nobody else knows. You know nobody's been able to get a comment from him on this story that he hit a teacher at his kid's school. Get a comment. You know where he'll be, follow him, get a comment. You do, you get a promotion and a secretary. Screw up, and you're out on your ass. Understood?'

'Understood,' said Topaz, and now she was glowing.

David Levine emerged out of the General Electric building, and across the street Topaz felt time, her heartbeat and the revolution of the planets ground to a resounding halt. She sucked in her breath. He was unmistakable even at this distance; the golden hair that had introduced a generation of American pubescent girls to their own sexuality glinted in the thin winter light, and she could see his broad, tall frame and arrogant jawline from here. David Levine combined an intense, Jewish, Richard Gere-type sensuality with the looks and physique of a Viking. Topaz had seen ten of his movies herself. He was one of a handful of stars who could 'open' a movie nationwide; and now ugly rumours were surfacing which could wreck his career if they were true. Certain sussed journalists had heard that America's Mr Romantic was a woman-beater, and had broken the nose of his mistress, a young teacher at his son's primary school. Not a word had appeared in print. The woman was too scared to talk. Levine was too powerful to libel.

Topaz felt for her Dictaphone recorder, securely in her pocket, and dashed through the traffic. 'Mr Levine!' she gasped, running up to him. 'Excuse me, sir?'

Levine turned round, noticed a girl with a great-looking body in shades and a baseball cap, blushing furiously. He gave her a lazy smile. 'Hey, sweetheart,' he said. 'Not too loud. I don't want to get mobbed. Who shall I sign it to?'

He thinks I'm an autograph-hunter!

'Oh no, I'm not a fan,' she blurted. 'Well, I am a fan. It's just – I mean, I'm a reporter . . . you know, there's a story going round that you hit a teacher. I was wondering if you had any comment, you know, to clear your name?'

David Levine's green eyes had crystallized into chips of ice.

'Get lost, you cheap whore,' he slurred. 'And you can tell that tramp from me, if she's been talking . . .'

'What?' demanded Topaz. 'You'll finish the job?'

All of her nervousness had evaporated. She was right in the middle of a breaking story, and this bastard was high.

Levine glared at her. 'Print a word of this, slut, and I'll sue you to kingdom come. I don't see a tape recorder.'

And he stepped into a swooping cab.

Topaz barely had time to register that he was right, she hadn't had the Dictaphone switched on. She hailed the next taxi in line. 'Can you follow that car? And don't let the guy know.'

'No problem, lady,' said the driver, pleased to have his boring day livened up.

The cars tore through glittering Manhattan, weaving through the traffic like it was water. Topaz stared out of the window, at the mirrored skyscrapers jabbing into the sky like accusing fingers, and raced through her information. Number one, he was guilty as hell. Number two, he was on some kind of drugs, and not totally together – maybe she could get something past him. Number three, the way he spoke, she'd bet her last dime the teacher was not the only woman he'd hit . . .

Topaz thought for a second. Then she took off her cap and shades and stuffed them in her bag, unbuttoned her jacket and unpinned her hair so that it fell round her shoulders like a blazing waterfall. She loosened the top three buttons on her shirt, took out her lipstick . . .

David Levine relaxed some more. It was good cognac, good coke and a nice club, the kind where people were too cool to bother him. He'd screwed three more points on the gross from them in the meeting today, and told a dyke reporter where she could get off. And now he was here, talking to Jo-Ann, some Texan chick with wide baby eyes, soft lips and awesome tits. She had a good attitude, too. She appreciated her luck in getting to sit with him. She was the type that liked a strong man. He could hardly wait to stick it to her.

'... though you prob'ly don't approve, being a New Yorker,' she murmured, eyes downcast. 'Y'all are prob'ly one of those feminists.'

She pronounced the word with a delicate distaste.

Levine roared with laughter. 'No, ma'am. No way.'

'Well, that's good to hear,' she said. 'I know I'm real old-fashioned, but I swear that's the way the good Lord intended it to be. It tells us so in the Bible. I admire a man who keeps discipline in his own house, although you don't meet too many of those in this day and age.'

Levine wondered if she'd get off on being spanked before he took her. Well, no matter, he was going to do it anyway. The thought of her delicious Southern ass exposed across his knees started to give him a hard-on.

'Well, you got one here, Jo-Ann,' he said. 'Last time my ex-girlfriend decided to get out of line ... let's just say she never did it again.'

Topaz leant forward, pressing her breasts together, the rolling Dictaphone whirring under her dress.

'My!' she purred. 'Why don't you tell me *all* about it?'

8

The subway car was crammed, absolutely full to the brim. Smart business-men in crisp linen suits stood shoulder-to-shoulder with maintenance men in their overalls and joggers in tight Lycra on their way home. Topaz didn't mind; not even the fat Italian housewives clutching shopping bags bothered her any more.

For the first couple of weeks, she'd felt uncomfortable, wondering if all these big-city slickers could see through her no-nonsense jeans and trainers, her tight little skirts and black briefcase. She'd felt transparent, like everybody could tell by looking at her she shouldn't be here: Topaz Rossi, a pushy kid from New Jersey, playing at being a journalist on a big magazine. She imagined that everybody could tell she was earning slave wages, living in a scuzzy walk-up on the Lower East Side. Who was she kidding? Nobody'd be fooled because she'd learnt to *dress* right. She was bound to look gauche and awkward. To make a fool of herself.

Three weeks after that, she'd become neutral, tuning out like everybody else.

Today, she was loving every minute of it.

The David Levine article, typed, neatly laid out and over eight thousand words long, was safely folded in her briefcase, together with a copy of the tape of her interview. She felt as though it must be burning a hole right through the leather, this thing was so hot. It had taken her all night to write it up, and it was worth every second. She didn't feel tired. She felt young, and terrific, and bursting with energy. She was on her way.

Topaz smoothed her skirt down on her hips, oblivious to the admiring glances of the men around her. Her mind was racing with plans, with exactly how she should present this to her editor, with what she could get out of him in return.

Because this was it.

This was her big break.

Nathan Rosen had given her Mission Impossible, and against all the odds she'd come through. Yeah, she mused, he won't be expecting *this*. He wanted to punish me, show me I'd been getting too big for my boots, that I couldn't handle the stuff I was asking for. He probably expected me to come see him a couple of days later, in tears, begging him not to sack me. Topaz shook her beautiful head, sending her earrings jangling about her throat. The scene wasn't gonna play that way.

The train pulled up at 53rd Street and 7th, and Topaz pushed out of the doors, looking forward to the walk to the office. Several bored commuters admired her ass as she strode purposefully up the escalator, enjoying the rare sight of a girl with curves. Topaz had an hourglass figure, and she refused to starve it into waiflike submission. If Kate Moss wanted to look like a boy, fine. She doubted men like Nathan Rosen would look twice at Kate Moss.

Broadway glittered in the early morning sun as Topaz stepped out of the station. The air was faintly humid and warm, promising a baking hot day later on. She shivered with pleasure, feeling enthusiasm and energy beat up out of the streets towards her. Her sneakers seemed to bounce off the pavement. Midtown Manhattan! Why *shouldn't* she love it?

All the way to the American Magazines tower, Topaz Rossi was bubbling with excitement. When you were young and on your way, New York was the only place to be, paying no attention to where you were from, just where you were going.

And I, Topaz thought, pushing through the revolving doors into the marble lobby, am going straight to the top. No more Gino putting me down. No more Rowena Gordon, stamping on me with her blue-blooded feet. No more sons-of-bitches like Peter Kennedy tricking their way into my pants. And no more assholes like Geoffrey Stevens refusing to take my calls –

'Topaz? Anybody home?' Jason Richman asked. 'God, where are you *at* this morning? I called out to you three times on the street, but you just walked right past with your head in the clouds.'

She smiled at him apologetically as they both walked into the elevator. 'Jase, I'm sorry. I had my mind on a story.'

'Yeah? Whose? Did Rosen ask you to copy-edit that Josie Simons thing on ticket scalpers?'

Topaz shook her head, grinning. 'Not exactly. This is one of my own.'

'Of yours?' asked Jason, surprised. Topaz was obviously very good, but Nate Rosen would surely never promote her so quickly. She'd only been at *Westside* a month. Even Elise had had to wait six months before she got a reporting gig.

She nodded. 'It's kind of a . . . a test. He wanted to see what I could do.'

The heavy metal doors hissed smoothly open, and they stepped out together onto *Westside's* floor. The offices were deserted at this time in the morning. Only Jason liked to get into work early; he left early too, to hit the cool, crowded little restaurants he reviewed before the rush started. Today, Topaz wanted time to think, to go over what she could get out of this hot little bombshell. If only she could keep a lid on her excitement long enough to think straight.

'I'm intrigued,' Jason said. 'Spill it, Topaz. What did he say? You want some coffee?'

'Yes please,' she said, already a shameless caffeine addict. 'Black, no sugar. Can you keep a secret?'

'Sure,' said Jason, curiously.

'He asked me to get an interview with David Levine. Said that if I did, he would make me a reporter, and if I screwed it up, I was fired.'

'No!' said Jason, perching on the edge of his desk. He handed her the coffee. 'That's not like Nathan, to be hard on a junior like that. He's normally so laid-back. You must really have pissed him off, Topaz. Would you like me to talk to him? See if I can calm him down?'

Topaz grinned. 'I got the story, Jason.'

'Get out of here.'

'I did, I did!' she burst out, unable to control the huge grin spreading across her face. 'I trailed him! In disguise! And I taped him! And it's dynamite!'

Jason laughed at her affectionately. 'Come on, babe, you're not Lois Lane, and this isn't the *Daily Planet*. What did you do, make something up? I'm not gonna report you. Nathan'll probably let you off for being inventive.'

Without another word, Topaz bent down and unclipped her briefcase. Gingerly she extracted the double-spaced typescript of her story and handed it to her friend.

Jason read it in silence, occasionally raising an eyebrow or letting his lips move in surprise. It was extremely well written. And it was indeed dynamite.

At the end, he said simply, 'Topaz, can you prove this?'

She nodded, eyes sparkling, and threw him the tape of their conversation. Richman slotted it into the cassette player by Elise DeLuca's desk.

'. . . tell me *all* about it,' said Topaz in a soft Southern drawl.

'Well, Susie should have known better,' David Levine's unmistakable voice asserted loudly.

Jason sat bolt upright, staring down at the pages in his hand. He realized what he was hearing, but he still couldn't quite believe it.

'She was a teacher. Seemed like *I* had to teach *her* a lesson,' Levine went on, his voice clipped and tight.

'Coke?' Jason asked, reaching for the off-switch. He didn't want to hear any more. The stuff Levine admitted in this article made his stomach turn.

'Yeah. And he was on something different when I first stopped him in the street,' Topaz answered. She was swelling with pride. Jason's reaction was exactly what she'd hoped for. 'He told me he'd sue if I printed anything, because he didn't see a tape recorder. So I switched my Dictaphone on and . . . and I hid it inside my bra,' she explained.

Jason glanced involuntarily at her firm, full bust. Damn, the girl had no business looking like that. It was distracting when he was trying to concentrate on the scoop of the goddamn year.

He sighed. 'Topaz, do you know what you've got here?'

'A story that'll make me a reporter,' she said confidently.

Richman marvelled. For a smart, independent kid, Rossi could sometimes be incredibly dumb.

'What you've got here,' he explained patiently, 'is a front-page lead item on the six-o'clock-news-type story. An exclusive that could sell millions of papers. That will ruin a major film star's career, embarrass his studio, and make you personally into a celebrity, at least for a few days. Now you *could* hand in a story like that to your boss and get made into a reporter, on twenty-five thousand dollars a year. That's a big step up from where you are now, of course.'

He gathered up his stuff, wanting to get over to the Gotham Café in SoHo for breakfast. 'Or you could figure out what a story like that is worth. To Nathan Rosen or anyone else. Don't be a *putz*, Topaz. You're not in Kansas any more.'

And with that he winked at her and strolled out the door.

Nathan Rosen stepped into his kitchen, wondering what to fix for breakfast. French vanilla coffee and a toasted bagel with lox, perhaps. Nothing too heavy. It was too warm a morning to want to eat heavy food.

A few years ago he'd have just grabbed some ice cream from the fridge, or made himself a chicken sandwich. Or more likely skipped breakfast altogether and picked up a doughnut at the office. Things were simpler then. After the divorce, eating what he liked where he liked had taken on a delicious sense of luxury.

But Rosen was a born New Yorker, and a high achiever at that. He liked to be the best at everything, and he liked the attentions of women. And somewhere in the mid-eighties, how you looked became as important as what you were.

As usual, Nathan refused to be left behind. He joined a gym and worked off his soft belly and spreading thighs, and cut excess fat from his diet. He still ate like a horse, but he ate high-protein, high-carbohydrate foods. The one thing he couldn't give up was ice cream, but then again, he was only human.

It had been a struggle. But it was worth it, Rosen thought with a touch of vanity, checking himself out in the wall mirror. His large frame was now solid muscle. He had a clean, strong jawline with no hint of fat around the chin. There was nothing he could do about his thinning hair and the flecks of grey at the side of his skull, but basically Rosen looked good. And he knew it. Hell, how could he fail to notice? He was getting laid so much more. Women came on to him at the gym. After the workout class. While he was out jogging. At parties. At baseball games. Yeah, Nate Rosen was a big fan of the exercise revolution.

He'd dated a few of the women he met socially, but not for long; no relationship since his marriage had lasted more than five months. But that didn't bother him. He was in no rush to get another thin gold band. After years of fidelity to a sexually selfish woman, Rosen was enjoying his freedom too much to give it up. If the right person came along, fair enough. But it was a case of proceed with caution. He'd been wrong the first time.

Rosen switched on the percolator, waiting for the pleasantly bitter coffee smell to fill the airy kitchen. He loved this time in the morning that he had for himself, swinging into his stride, psyching himself up for another day in the office. *Westside* was a fun magazine to edit; not only cutting-edge, but, since he'd taken over the editor's job, highly profitable.

In fact, the rumour was that he was about to be promoted. Henry Birnbaum, the director of American's East Coast operations, was due to step down in the fall. Nathan had been told by the President, Matthew Gowers, that he was first in line for the job.

Director. It would be a good way to turn forty, Nathan thought, grinning.

He looked out of his window towards Central Park, enjoying the clear blue skies, the sunlight, his own feelings of success.

Maybe he'd been a little hard on Topaz Rossi.

Now where the hell did that come from? Rosen wondered, angry with himself. What *was* this thing he had about some new kid? Some talented, pushy new kid who'd only been in the office a month? He could not stop thinking about her. Getting enchanted by her enthusiasm, fascinated by her intelligence, enraged by her arrogance. He'd never had so much chutzpah at her age. At least, he thought not. And she had been way out of line the other night, no question. But would he have reacted in that way if she'd been a guy? Wouldn't he just have laughed at her, told her to calm down? What was with this stupid do-or-die mission he'd sent her on? David Levine? Right. Like some kid could manage to swing an interview with *him*. She was probably over there this morning, cleaning out her desk. And she had talent, Topaz Rossi; Nathan reckoned she'd make a good writer some day. It wasn't his job as her boss to be taking out his feelings on her.

Because, Rosen admitted to himself, spreading lox on his bagel, I *do* have feelings for that girl. I like her. And I want her.

But that was natural. She was beautiful, with those delicate blue eyes and that mass of curly red hair. It was impossible not to think about the hair elsewhere on her smooth, young body. And she was stacked, with a waist he could encircle with his two hands swelling out to an invitingly curvy ass. Rossi would grace the cover of *Sports Illustrated*'s swimsuit issue, so it was only to be expected that he imagined her the way he did. On a beach, in a tiny bikini. Naked on top of him. Being made love to, slowly, in his jacuzzi upstairs.

Rosen, feeling the first stirrings in his groin, dragged his thoughts away from those images. Topaz was way too young. He despised middle-aged men who chased students. And he had enough girls without screwing around on his doorstep. In the nineties, the office romance was totally taboo. It had always been bad news, but these days you didn't even think about things like that. The office *compliment* was taboo, for Christ's sake. If Topaz was a little older, she'd understand these things. She wouldn't come on to him so damn obviously, with those smiles and little breathless glances and tight T-shirts. She was a nice kid. He had to be a responsible adult.

This morning, Rosen decided, I'll call the kid in and let her off with a warning. A *stern* warning.

David Levine and Topaz Rossi? he thought, grinning. It would be Christians and Lions all over again.

'What's up with Topaz?' Elise asked Josie. 'She's been locked on the phone all day.'

'And circling property ads in the *Village Voice*,' the music writer agreed. 'I don't know. I guess she's moving house.'

'On what we're paying?' Elise shrugged.

Topaz felt her heartbeat speeding up. Adrenalin coursed through her. Thank

God for Jason Richman! Thank God she'd even got to talk to him! How *could* she have been so blind?

She was holding for Geoffrey Stevens. Amazing how good this felt. It had come to her like a blinding flash of inspiration, after Jason left this morning. So the article was worth $50,000 and she hadn't spotted it? Fine. Well, now she was going to make it $100,000. And get herself a little revenge into the bargain.

She had to move secretly. And she had to move fast.

'Miss Rossi.'

There it was, at last. That clipped English accent she thought she'd never hear again, not once Charles Gordon had killed her student articles with one phone call. Oh, she remembered all that. 'Mr Stevens is unavailable.' 'Mr Stevens is not in the office.' 'Mr Stevens has asked me to tell you we can't use your material, Miss Rossi. Sorry if there was any misunderstanding.'

Topaz felt her Italian blood pump through her, thrilled at the prospect of revenge.

'I got your fax,' Stevens said. 'A very interesting snippet.'

Yeah, you're interested in this *material, right, you limey prick?*

'There's more where that came from, Mr Stevens. A lot more. And a tape to go with it.'

There was a pause. Topaz could almost see the greedy asshole licking his lips.

'We would be very interested in publishing this story, Miss Rossi. You would have a byline, of course. And a picture.'

She almost laughed out loud. He must think she was still at college. 'Of course,' she agreed. 'That's standard. Now we must discuss the small matter of my fee.'

'My budget is limited, Miss Rossi,' Stevens said coldly, as if to imply his contempt for such a mercenary attitude.

Topaz grinned. 'My options aren't,' she observed.

Silence. He could feel it slipping away. 'What do you want?'

'Seventy thousand pounds,' said Topaz coolly. The office fax wasn't numbered, and she wanted him to think she was still in England. That was an important part of the plan. 'Today. Paid directly into my bank account. You get a European exclusive, and it has to run in the *Sunday Times* next week. I'll fax you the first half of the story today, with a tape to match, Fed ex'd to the office. If I get my money, you'll get the second half of the story tomorrow.'

'How do I know it isn't a complete fabrication?'

Topaz held her Dictaphone up to the receiver and pressed play, letting the tape run for twenty seconds.

'That should be enough, Mr Stevens. If you can't trust me, just say so, I'll sell it to the *Mail on Sunday*. Do we have a deal?'

'Yes, damn it!' the man spat.

Topaz heard the line click dead.

Smiling, she called her bank.

Nathan arrived at *Westside* about eleven fifteen and went straight into his office, refusing all calls and his mail, and worked solidly through the proposed budget for a new colour supplement the board wanted to see installed. Nobody disturbed him; it had been Rosen's habit for years to concentrate completely on the most immediate problem they had, and sort other things out later. If Elise wanted a new features layout or Josie wanted to run a rock concert promotion, they got to see Nathan Rosen – but only after lunch. If you got summoned to the office before 2 p.m., everybody knew something was up.

At noon the internal phone buzzed on Topaz Rossi's desk.

'Yeah,' she said absently, hunched over mortgage calculations.

'Topaz? This is Oriole,' said Nathan's assistant, sympathetically. 'Could you come over to the editor's office right away, please? He wants to talk to you.'

'Sure,' Topaz said, feeling her palms begin to sweat. God, she hoped she'd done the right thing. Not that she should worry. She'd made herself rich. Or at least richer. Seventy thousand pounds is $100,000, Topaz told herself firmly, trying to calm her nerves, to control the ball of anxiety in her stomach. She got up, tugging her skirt round her hips, futilely trying to make it a little longer, pulling back her snaking red curls into a neat ponytail. It was no use. Her reflection stared back at her from Elise's glass door, the long, well-turned legs stretching up for miles, the smart black leather hugging her ass provocatively, the tiny waist emphasized by a leather belt, and the full breasts, tilting youthfully upwards from her ribcage, blossoming under the tight pull of her crisp white shirt. In fact, the ponytail somehow *added* sex appeal – it made her look like an overripe schoolgirl.

Blushing, she unfastened the blue velvet scrunch that held it in place, grabbed her story and her tape and marched across the corridor to Nathan Rosen's office.

Why should I care if he fires me? Topaz thought rebelliously. I can get another job in a second. I don't need *Westside*.

But she knew that she did care. Very much. Because Nate Rosen worked at *Westside*.

'Hi, Topaz,' Oriole said. 'You can just go right in.'

She sauntered into Rosen's office, looking over the spectacular city view. Nathan, jabbering furiously into the phone in Yiddish, motioned to her to take a seat. Topaz sat gratefully down in a black leather chair opposite his desk, trying to look like someone who knew how to bargain. Someone who sold a major story to two papers every day of the week. And not someone who was terrified she'd just blown her career.

Nathan growled into the phone and hung up, then sat down heavily, glaring at her. 'So you remember our last conversation,' he said.

Topaz summoned up her courage. 'Yes I do,' she said. 'And I got you the interview.'

Her editor raised an eyebrow.

'I taped it,' Topaz blurted. 'I mean, I disguised myself and I taped it secretly. I hid the Dictaphone . . . on me, and he admitted everything, so I transcribed it in a story and I have copies of the tape and . . . and it's all there,' she finished breathlessly, shoving her typescript and the tape towards him.

Nathan looked at his protégée for a long moment, then glanced at the top page of the interview, not bothering to flick through it. Then he looked slowly at Topaz again.

'OK, kid,' he said coldly. 'What have you done?'

'Wh – what do you mean?' she stammered.

Rosen sighed. 'Ms Rossi,' he said, 'I've been editing this magazine for two years. I've been a journalist for eighteen years. I think I can read a case of guilty nerves pretty well. I'm sure you *did* get this story, like you say. Now that ought to be a coup, am I right? But you walk in here like you've been summoned to the principal's office, not like you wanna tell me you're up for the Pulitzer. So please don't insult my intelligence. Just save us both some time and tell me what you've done.'

Topaz swallowed, hard. 'OK,' she said. 'I – I've sold the European rights on the story to the *Sunday Times* and they're running it next week. But they think I'm still in England. They don't know I'm here, so they didn't ask for world rights. Which means that we can lead Wednesday's edition with it and still be first with the story.'

'Let me get this straight,' Nathan said slowly. 'You have sold this story to another publication, a major international paper, and you are proposing to doublecross them by having us print the story in America first. Where it will, of course, make the news around the world, thus making it almost useless to them.'

'Yes,' Topaz admitted weakly.

Rosen's voice was calm. 'How much did you get for it?'

'A hundred thousand dollars,' she mumbled.

'One hundred thousand dollars,' he repeated. 'I see. And what did you want from me? A chunk of the stock, perhaps?'

'No, no,' Topaz protested. 'I swear. I just wanted you to make me a reporter ...' Her voice trailed off miserably and she stared at her skirt.

'Sit there,' Nathan ordered. 'While I read this *lucrative* piece of investigative journalism.'

Topaz waited for five minutes that seemed like five hours, squirming on her seat in embarrassment as Rosen worked through the article, his face impassive. She was obviously about to get fired. Nathan seemed to think she'd torn up the rule book of news ethics. *Santa Maria*, and she only wanted to please the guy! He was so gorgeous! And yet he never seemed to notice she was alive, unless it was to yell at her or reprimand her for some little thing. The shorter her skirts, the more figure-hugging her blouse, the less interest Nathan showed. She couldn't understand it. She'd never come across a man that didn't at least *look* at her appreciatively. And Nathan Rosen was definitely not gay – according to the other girls in the office, outside of *Westside* he was a goddamn womanizer. So what the hell, Topaz thought angrily, is *wrong* with me?

Finally, Rosen looked up, and to her astonishment she saw he was smiling.

'What kind of a reporter did you want to be?'

'Excuse me?' she said, bewildered.

'Come on, Rossi,' Nathan said. 'Pitch me. Tell me what you want to do. Tell me how you can sell more magazines for me.'

'I could write a column,' Topaz said. It was the first thing that came into her head. 'About New York. As an out-of-towner who's new here. Things most people wouldn't notice – it'd make them look at Manhattan with a fresh eye. I'd call it "NY Scene".'

'What about your salary?' asked Rosen, still smiling.

'Thirty-five thousand dollars,' Topaz said boldly.

Nathan shrugged. 'That's ten thousand more than new reporters get.'

'But I'd be a *columnist*. And like I told you before, I'm better than they are.'

'Don't push it,' Nathan said. He extended one hand across his desk and Topaz grabbed it eagerly, feeling a little electric shock of sexuality as his flesh touched hers.

'Congratulations, kid,' he said. 'You scored.'

'You're not mad at me for selling it to an English paper?'

Nathan chuckled. 'Rossi, that was the first piece of real initiative you've shown since you got here.'

'And thirty-five thousand a year!' she breathed.

Nathan smiled at her again. 'With a story like this, you could have asked for fifty thousand. But you wouldn't welsh on a handshake, right?'

'You sonofabitch,' Topaz said, angrily.

Nathan laughed. 'Relax. Consider it valuable vocational training. You're not the only one who can pull a fast trick, kid. Just remember – I'm still better at this than you are.'

For a second she glared at him, and then broke down under the warmth of his teasing and smiled. Damn, damn, *damn*, he was attractive.

'Want to grab a beer with me to celebrate?' she asked, tentatively.

Nathan Rosen looked her over, the thrusting breasts, the handspan waist, the round ass and long, beautiful legs, and felt himself sorely tempted. Her desire was written in a bright glow on her face, on those delicious half-stiffened nipples.

'No, I have to work,' he said. 'Unlike some people I could mention.'

She turned away, trying not to show her disappointment.

'Topaz,' Nathan said. 'You can take the day off. Go find a new apartment. You did good.'

'Thanks, boss,' she said lightly, and walked out of his office, closing the door behind her.

After she'd gone, Nathan Rosen stared at the typescript on his desk for a long moment. He'd have to watch this girl carefully. Because unless all his instincts were mistaken, the pushy little Italian was a force to be reckoned with.

9

It wasn't a promising start. Of all the places Rowena least liked having to trek to see bands, working men's clubs in the north of England rated amongst the worst. Usually she had to argue for forty minutes with some surly bloke who blew smoke in her face before he'd even let her in, and then stand at the back and do her best to blend into the chipped paint or peeling wallpaper. Not easy, when drunk fifty-year-olds were wandering up to you and making breathtakingly obscene comments every five minutes. The only women welcome in those dives were strippers, and the punters made sure Rowena knew it.

So some bunch of talentless Northerners called Atomic Mass are playing Crookes Working Men's Club in Sheffield, Rowena thought as she parked her battered mini down the road. Terrific. Great. And Musica Records, right on the cutting edge as usual, is here to check them out.

Once she got inside, she bought two triple Jack Daniels and Diet Cokes, and finished one off before the band even hit the stage. She was obviously going to need them. The place was mercifully half-empty, but the barman had taken great pleasure in informing her that Atomic Mass were a bunch of young kids who'd got together at college, with an American from the university on lead guitar. Bound to be strictly amateur-hour stuff. By the time they wandered onstage, Rowena was seething with resentment at Matthew Stevenson for making her waste an evening like this.

And then they started to play.

Barbara Lincoln, elegantly dressed in an Armani pantsuit in cream linen that set off her slim figure and soft chocolate skin, was trying to figure something out. Her secretary had brought in her mail that morning – the usual stuff every Business Affairs executive had to deal with in a record company – and one memo. Not that she didn't normally get memos. But this one was different: hand-delivered early in the morning, and from a talent scout in A&R, Rowena Gordon, some new girl whom Barbara had never met.

It was so weird.

She glanced at it again. *Dear Ms Lincoln, I would be grateful if you could allow me ten minutes for a meeting with you today. My extension is 435. Regards, Rowena Gordon, Artists and Repertoire.*

Why on earth did one of Stevenson's *scouts* want to meet with her? Why not Matthew himself? He was the one who handled contract negotiations.

Barbara was twenty-five and the number two in Musica's Legal and Business Affairs Department, and she'd never met a scout in her career. There was just no reason for it.

Intrigued, she dialled Rowena's extension.

'I wanted some advice,' Rowena said nervously, shutting the door behind her. Maybe this hadn't been such a good idea. Barbara Lincoln's secretary had shot her a strange look when she'd turned up for her appointment, dressed in her normal office clothes of jeans and trainers. Over in Business Affairs, the look was obviously more formal. Christ, Lincoln dressed the way she had at Oxford, in the old days when money was no object. That seemed several lifetimes ago now.

Barbara eyed her up. She looked intelligent, a well-spoken young girl for a talent scout. There was something about this one she couldn't pin down.

'I don't mind at all,' she said. 'I'm just curious as to why you wouldn't tell me what this was about.'

Rowena nodded. 'I understand,' she said, 'but I couldn't say in front of Matthew Stevenson. You see, I've found a band I think the company should sign, and I don't think Matthew will listen to them with an open mind if I play them for him.'

'Why not?' Barbara enquired calmly.

'Because Josh Oberman hired me himself,' Rowena said.

Barbara smiled. 'Did you know that's how I got hired?' she asked.

'That's why I'm here,' Rowena said simply. 'You've obviously survived. I hoped you might be able to help me to.'

Barbara laughed. 'Very inventive. Did you bring a tape with you? I'll put the headphones on.'

The older girl listened in silence for several minutes, then slid the headpiece off and looked at Rowena with something approaching respect. 'Well, I'm into business, not music,' she said, 'but it seems to me like you have something here. If I were you I'd go to see Oberman direct.'

'How would I get an appointment?'

Barbara picked up her phone and tapped in some numbers. 'Josh?' she asked. 'Hi, it's Barbara Lincoln. Fine, thanks. Look, Josh, I was just wondering if you could see Rowena Gordon some time today.'

Rowena, her face flaming red, made a lunge for the phone, but Barbara stood up, grinning, and held it out of reach. 'She's found a good act and she wants you to hear it. Doesn't think Matthew will give a rock band a chance, and she's too shy to tell you herself. Yeah, OK. OK. I understand. Thanks, boss.'

She hung up and turned to a mortified Rowena. 'He wants to see you in his office in five minutes,' Barbara told her. 'And don't look like that. He's not gonna fire you. I've been working with Josh for a couple of years, and I tell you, that guy knows the score. He's been doing this since before either of us were born. He'll understand Matthew's problem. He'll only think well of you for coming to me.'

'Are you sure?' Rowena asked, anxiously.

Barbara gave a self-assured nod. 'I am. And come and see me when you're through. We should go out for a drink.'

Rowena smiled. 'I'd like that,' she said.

Joshua Oberman sat hunched in his chair, listening to the tape. The sound quality was dreadful, the production non-existent, and Gordon didn't have so much as a picture to show him.

They were *awesome*.

Excitement rippled through his withered veins. Seventy years old, and good music could still turn him on. He couldn't get an erection any more but he still felt like a teenager when he heard stuff like this. It was the old Guns 'n' Roses syndrome. The thrill of hearing an act nobody else had heard of, and knowing, just *knowing* that in a couple of years they'd be packing stadiums and making thousands of teenage chicks cream their pants. Fat bass. Fresh guitar. Great vocals. Cool songs.

The kind of stuff that got arena seats ripped up.

Music that caused riots.

'So where did you see this act?' he asked impassively, staring sternly at little Rowena Gordon, sitting fidgeting in her chair like she was up before God at the Day of Judgment.

'At a working men's club in Sheffield,' Rowena admitted. 'They're really young, Josh. And they look really good.'

'Music sells music, kid,' Oberman growled. 'Remember that.'

She nodded hastily, but couldn't help adding. 'And they moved really well live ... hardly anyone was there but they still played their guts out ... '

'Where are they playing next?' Oberman asked casually.

'At the Retford Porterhouse,' Rowena told him. She leant forward on her seat. 'Josh, you've got to come and see them. Please.'

She groped for something he would understand. 'Look, they'll sell records in America,' she tried. 'I'm just sure of it.'

Josh Oberman raised an eyebrow. He'd grown up on the Brooklyn Heights, his career had spanned three continents, and for the past fifteen years he'd ruled the British record industry with a rod of beat-up platinum discs. In all that time he'd found exactly three European bands who'd had substantial success in America. Now there was a pretty little English rosebud sitting in his office, telling him she was *sure* this unknown act of hers would break in America.

The trouble was, he agreed with her.

'Listen to me, kid,' he growled. 'It's seven years since I've been to a fleapit rock concert. So you'd better be right about this, because I've got six companies to run here.'

Rowena took a deep breath. So she was gambling her career. So what? If she couldn't get *these* boys signed, she was in the wrong industry.

'I'm right, Josh,' she insisted. 'If you don't agree, I'll quit.'

Oberman pretended to think about it. 'OK, Gordon. You have yourself a deal. I will neglect all the needs of the Musica group of companies in the UK and go see –'

'Atomic Mass.'

'Atomic Mass, right. And you should pray that they're good. Come pick me up tomorrow night, and don't bother to bring your car. We'll take a limo.'

What an incredible-looking girl, Oberman thought as he watched Rowena leave his office. All legs and hair and pouty lips.

He wished he was young enough to wish he could fuck her.

Rowena could hardly make it through Wednesday, she was so excited. And nervous. And hopeful. And scared.

If Josh didn't like them, that was the end of it. Forget about music. Forget about dropping out. It would be back to the drawing board, and a nice safe life as a lawyer or something.

But if he *did* like them –

She hardly dared think about it.

As soon as the time on her computer flashed 6.30, Rowena logged out, stood up and almost ran out of A&R to the president's office. She'd taken great care with her appearance this morning; black jeans, a tight black body to emphasize her minute waist, fashionable workmen's boots and a black leather jacket. A sexy look. A tough-girl look. She hoped she seemed like someone who knew a talented rock band when she heard one.

'Goddamn, what the hell are you wearing?' Oberman demanded, thinking how hot she looked. The long blonde hair shimmering down her back was almost obscenely golden against the black leather.

'What's wrong with it?' Rowena asked, practically dragging her boss out to the lifts.

'You look like you're gonna mug me,' the old man grumbled, leading her towards his car.

Rowena took a step back. Of course, she was hardly unused to luxury. And she realized that the presidents of record companies don't drive Renault 5s. But this was something else. A liveried chauffeur holding open the back-seat door on a long, gleaming black monster that looked like it had driven straight out of a Jackie Collins novel.

'Well, what are you gaping at?' Oberman demanded, secretly amused. The kid was half brilliant and half totally naive. 'Get in and quit wasting time. They're only the support act. You want me to miss them, or what?'

'No, no, sir,' Rowena said hastily, slipping into the back seat with a refined movement. Josh noticed that, too. So she was used to chauffeurs. Although she'd been dirt poor when he found her, and she was earning a pittance right now. Curiouser and curiouser, as Alice said in Wonderland.

He clambered in next to her and told his driver where to go, and the limo pulled smoothly out of the car park and melted into the early evening traffic.

Rowena glanced at her watch.

'Don't worry, kid, we'll get there,' Oberman said. 'Lewis is a good driver. Knows all the short cuts. Right, Roger?'

'Right, Mr Oberman,' the chauffeur answered briskly in a soft Welsh accent.

Rowena paid no attention. She was trying not to stare at the incredible array of equipment in Oberman's car. Two phones. A fax machine. A television. A CD-player on a stack system. Discreet Surround Sound speakers built into the camel leather. An IBM computer and a drinks cabinet.

'The swimming pool's out back,' Oberman added dryly, and chuckled when she spun round. 'I do a lot of work in the car,' he explained. 'Works out cheaper than a second office.'

She nodded, trying not to feel that she was way, way out of her depth. What was she thinking of, dragging her boss out to a tiny, sweaty club in the provinces? That was her job, not his!

'OK,' Oberman said briskly. 'Tell me everything you remember about the first time you saw these guys play.'

The limo pulled up in a grimy street a couple of hours later. The summer evening sky was black with rain, and by the time she'd shown him across the road to the club they were both soaked to the skin. She stumbled into the entrance, drenched, and gave their names to the doorman, who insisted on making Oberman wait outside in the downpour while he laboriously searched the guest list. Rowena's heart sank. She could see that this gig was packed out with kids, no place for an old man to have to stand listening to a new act. And he was bound to be in a filthy mood at the weather and the delay.

'Yeah, all right,' the doorman yelled. 'Oberman, Joshua. 'E can go in.'

'Thank you,' Rowena yelled back, pulling her president inside.

'No readmittance,' the doorman added sourly.

Oberman's face was murderous.

Rowena swallowed hard and pushed through the open doors, grabbing her boss's hand and forcing a way through the slamming crowd, so they had somewhere to stand. It was tough going. She was used to metal crowds, but she was still a girl. And acting as a bodyguard for an old man was a tough gig. At least he's tall, Rowena thought gratefully, craning to see Atomic kicking up a storm on the tiny stage.

Josh Oberman watched the band in silence, a huge grin on his weatherbeaten face. He was pleased that Gordon couldn't see him. He didn't want to let her know how delighted he was with her.

In front of him, a bunch of five kids looking as though they were barely out of school were tearing up the little hothouse of a club as though the world would end tomorrow. Jesus, Oberman thought, the drummer looks like he's never fucking *shaved*. The songs were original and new and had an insistent beat, clever harmonies and a crashing bass. The front rows were a mass of flailing bodies, teenage boys slamming into one another, slick with sweat and rebellion.

They had passion.

They had music.

They had youth.

And, Joshua Zachary Oberman told himself when the house lights came up, they had a record deal.

'Come with me,' he said to Rowena. 'We're going backstage.'

Knowing better than to ask him to wait a few minutes, Rowena followed her boss round to the side, picking her way across puddles of beer and crushed styrofoam cups and flyers. The security guards spoke briefly to Josh, then ushered the two of them into a minute dressing room, where Atomic Mass, drenched in sweat and towelling off, looked at them questioningly.

'Hi, I'm Joshua Oberman, president of Musica Records,' Josh said.

Two cans of beer halted simultaneously in mid-air.

Oberman shoved Rowena forward, noting the appreciative glances the lads shot her. 'And this is Rowena Gordon, an A&R girl who works for me. She thinks we should give you a record deal. And so do I.'

10

In the sweltering heat of the *Westside* offices on Seventh Avenue, the phone rang on Topaz's desk.

'Rossi,' she said briskly.

'Topaz?' crackled the voice at the other end.

'*Rupert?*' shrieked Topaz, delighted. 'Rupe! How *are* you? Give me your number, I'll call you right back.'

'It's OK, I'm at the Union,' said Rupert, with the airy disregard of someone not paying the phone bill.

'How's it going down there?' she asked. The comparative peace and quiet of college seemed very attractive right now.

'I made editor,' said Rupert. 'James Robertson's President for Michaelmas Term; and Rod Clayton made another great speech.'

'Rod's great, I wish I'd been there,' sighed Topaz. Rod Clayton's speeches made her laugh till her stomach hurt. She glanced down at her piece on the demise of the Mets; no matter how hard she reworked it, it wouldn't come right. Much like the Mets, in fact. Topaz was a big Mets fan and she wasn't having history's best day.

'Anyway, I didn't call you about that,' Rupert went on. 'I called about Rowena.'

Topaz froze. 'What about Rowena?' she asked casually.

'Didn't you hear? You *must*'ve heard,' said Rupert incredulously. 'First she just disappeared from sight for months. Then it turns out she's got a job at Musica Records, right, and she barges into the president's office or something and told him he was a prat. Apparently things like that get you big brownie points in the music business. Anyway, he goes to see this brilliant band she'd found and offers them a deal on the spot! So now he thinks Rowena's a genius, and he's making her AR or something – that means she gets to sign acts...'

Topaz Rossi had suddenly become oblivious to the flashing phone lights and deadlines and spewing fax machines and all the office chaos. She sat still as a statue. Rowena's success was a white-hot knife in her heart.

'Everyone at Oxford's taking bets on which of you guys is going to make it first,' Rupert went on. 'Someone faxed your *Westside* exposé of that bastard David Levine to *Cherwell* – we led on it! It was *unbelievable*, Topaz, even for you.'

'Thanks, Rupe,' said Topaz mechanically. 'It's going OK here.'

Then it dawned on her that this would get back to Rowena. 'In fact, I'm probably going to get a syndication deal,' she added quickly. 'I got creative control, I report direct to Nathan – he's the editor – and *Westside* just gave me my own column.'

'Bloody *hell*, Topaz!' said Rupert, astonished.

'I've even bought a little apartment,' said Topaz, 'so if you're ever in New York ... it's on Clarkson Street in the Village ...'

'In the *Village*?' spluttered Rupert. 'Are you rich, too?'

'I'm getting by,' said Topaz.

Choke on it, Rowena.

Nathan Rosen passed her office, flashing her a 'rescue me' look. A tall, thin, blonde woman in a fur coat was propelling him towards his own, one hand on his shoulder ostentatiously flashing a gold Rolex.

'Who is that?' hissed Elise to Topaz.

'No idea,' she whispered, shaking her head. 'Ask Jason.'

Elise buzzed Jason Richman.

'Don't you guys recognize her?' Jason asked. 'That's Marissa Matthews.'

'The gossip columnist?' demanded Elise in a strangled screech. Marissa Matthews' bitchy chronicles of New York high society made her the highest-read journalist in America.

'His ex-wife,' Jason added.

'His *what*?' gasped both women.

'Nathan was married?' asked Elise, who'd been at *Westside* two years.

'For seven years,' Jason said. 'He doesn't talk about his private life.'

'Jesus! You can say that again!' muttered Elise, twisting her own wedding ring.

Topaz was shocked at the wave of jealousy surging through her. Nathan Rosen was going to be hers. He'd resisted all her advances so far, but he'd see reason. They were having dinner this evening to talk about the column, and she had high hopes even for tonight.

'I'm getting him out of this,' she said to Elise, jumping out of her chair and striding across the floor to the editor's office.

'Topaz Rossi's on the warpath,' said one of the features subs to a secretary, catching sight of her face.

'So what else is new?'

'Baby!' Topaz purred, throwing open the editor's door. 'What time are we meeting up tonight? Oh, hi,' she added warmly to Marissa. 'I'm Topaz Rossi. I see you've met my boyfriend, but I don't think we've been introduced! Nathan, you're such a forgetful boy.'

She gave Marissa a dazzling smile.

Rosen suppressed a wild desire to laugh.

'Sweetheart, I don't think you've met my ex-wife, Marissa Matthews. Marissa, this is my girlfriend Topaz Rossi, a rising star at *Westside*,' he said pleasantly.

Marissa stared at her with a look that would have lowered the temperature at the North Pole as Topaz sauntered over to Nathan and ran her hand affectionately over the seat of his pants.

'Nathan and I were together for a very long time,' she informed Topaz acidly.

'Oh well! Shit happens, huh?' said Topaz, with a cheerful smile. 'Still, every cloud has a silver lining,' she added maliciously, standing on tiptoe to kiss Nathan's cheek, which she did slowly and luxuriantly, touching his rough skin with the hidden tip of her tongue.

Rosen felt flames of lust lick up and down his body.

Marissa's thin lips pursed in disapproval. *What a foulmouthed little Italian tramp!* 'I must be going, Nathan,' she snapped.

'Let's do lunch!' called Topaz after her retreating back, letting go of Nathan's hand reluctantly.

Rosen smiled at her, wondering how long he could hold out. She was just a child, damn it, and she worked for him. He absolutely must *not* take advantage of a young girl's crush.

'Thanks, Rossi,' he said. 'I owe you one. How's "NY Scene" coming along?'

'Great,' shrugged Topaz. 'I just spent a day in Central Park, interviewing everyone who used the carousel.'

'Sounds good,' Rosen nodded curtly, pleased because it did. 'We'll talk more at dinner.'

'Sure,' Topaz said, turning to go.

Work, work, work, she thought sadly. You never look at anything else, do you?

Rosen drove down Baxter Street into Little Italy.

'Where are we going?' demanded Topaz, pissed-off because he hadn't noticed her low-cut dress.

'Silver Palace,' said Nathan, keeping his eyes locked on the road, as if that would help him forget about those incredible breasts staring him in the face. *Dear God, please don't let me get hard right in front of her.* 'I hear they have incredible dim sum.'

'I want Italian,' said Topaz mutinously.

'Well, I want Chinese,' replied Nathan amiably, 'and I'm paying.'

'You're the boss,' Topaz snapped.

He turned into Hester Street, heading for the Bowery, and ignored her. Topaz watched the high tenement houses with their beautiful iron fire escapes slip past her. She felt more relaxed out of the office, in crowded Little Italy with its cafés and Chinese shops and almost European sense of clutter. Anyway, watching the scenery might take her mind off the close-shaven grey and black hair at the side of Nathan's head.

Miraculously, they got to the restaurant without another row.

'What do you want?' Nathan asked, as one of the dim sum carts wheeled its way across the packed floor towards them.

'Spring rolls, prawn dumplings, steamed pork dumplings,' said Topaz, somewhat reconciled to Chinese from the mouthwatering scent of the food all around them.

Nathan heaped his plate. He worked out three times a week, drank no alcohol, and considered good ice cream the ultimate human pleasure this side of sex, so he'd pig out if he damn well felt like it.

Talking of sex, he was getting hard for Rossi. Her skirt had blown up just a little as she'd climbed the stairs in front of him. He couldn't help himself.

'. . . and I think it'd be a great twist, you ask six celebrities what they read at school . . .'

'. . . that would be a winner, Nate, for the men's titles – "My Favourite One-Night Stand" by sportsmen . . .'

Rosen, making notes, choked on a spring roll. 'Rossi!' he protested, shocked.

'Why not? Sex sells, especially men's titles. And I think you should suggest a cover-mount CD for *White Light*. Some books tried it in England last year when I was at school, circulation quadrupled.'

Nathan jotted it down. It was fantastic, a never-ending torrent of ideas. Where did she get it all from? He'd talk to Harry Birnbaum about her, he'd have to. There was a vacancy for a features editor over at *US Woman*, and Topaz Rossi was obviously perfect for it. Whoever heard of a features editor with only one year's experience? Well, they were about to.

He watched her, leaning towards him, blue eyes sparkling with passionate enthusiasm.

'I thought we were gonna talk about "NY Scene", not what you'd do if you ran American Magazines,' he said weakly.

Topaz shrugged. 'You got a problem with "NY Scene"?'

'No.'

'We getting a good reader response?'

'Pretty good,' Nathan conceded. In fact, *Westside* had never seen so many letters.

'So what's to discuss?' demanded Topaz.

He looked at her. 'Young lady, I should take you across my knee and spank you.'

Topaz felt herself getting slick between the legs. 'Promises, promises,' she said, touching him with her shoe.

Nathan battled with himself. He was as hard as a rock. 'Quit that,' he said through gritted teeth.

'Quit what?' asked Topaz innocently.

They stared at each other for a long moment.

'I'll get the check,' murmured Topaz, jumping up and turning to the counter to pay. She almost ran down the stairs and out of the door, waiting for him. She needed to get him out of the crowded restaurant.

Rosen emerged on to the sidewalk two seconds later, grabbed her by the shoulders and backed her up against the wall.

Then he kissed her, his body stretched along hers, the hard weight of him pushing against her right there on the street, so her soft breasts were crushed into his chest and she could feel his erection.

Nathan softly prised her mouth open and ran the tip of his tongue along the underside of her top lip.

Topaz moaned.

He pulled away from her and stared into her eyes, wild and surprised and aroused and scared. 'Topaz Rossi,' he whispered in her ear, 'I'm going to fuck your brains out.'

Topaz sat rigid in the cab in the darkness, trying not to betray herself in front of the driver. Nathan had his left hand, hidden by her coat, in her panties, and was stroking her very gently with two fingers, relentlessly, back and forwards.

'We'll go to the American Magazines tower on Seventh, please,' he said casually. 'I got a little unfinished business at the office.'

The two of them walked into the marble lobby, Nathan supporting Topaz while he collected his keys. Once the elevator door had shut he ran his hands all over her, barely able to restrain himself. Topaz was faint with desire. She was burning for him over her whole skin, her entire body sensitized to his touch. He put both his palms on the insides of her thighs, caressing her, tantalizingly close to her ass and her pussy but never quite touching them.

'Please, Nathan,' she gasped, '*please . . .*'

For answer he led her out of the elevator and across the deserted *Westside* office. Barely able to walk, Topaz stumbled after him.

Nathan opened his office but didn't bother flicking on the lights; the dull neon glow of New York at night was more than enough to see by. He looked round the room at his Eames chair and his files and his silent computer. Then he looked at Rossi, leaning against the door for support, squirming with longing for him. Rosen stared at her for a second, mesmerized by her; the flawless young skin, her lips wet and parted, the blue eyes liquid with desire.

Jesus Christ, she's every man's fantasy, Nathan thought, overwhelmed with lust. His cock was so hard he was starting to ache. He felt half frightened to touch her, unsure what she could do to him, where this would take him.

He'd sworn he wouldn't do this.

She'd shown him what she wanted.

He wondered who was seducing who.

'That's a nice dress,' he said hoarsely, 'but it'd look a lot better in a crumpled heap on the floor. Take your clothes off.'

Topaz stripped, her fingers fumbling from her heat. She saw Nathan Rosen gazing at her, transfixed. A new flush of sex rippled through her – look what she could do to him, look at the way he was staring. She unhooked her bra deliberately, delicately, letting him see the wisps of chocolate-coloured lace brush against her erect nipples, shrugging the tiny silk panties slowly off her thighs.

'Well?' Topaz asked insolently. She pirouetted for him, displaying herself, taunting him.

Rosen could hardly believe her body. His cock reared in his pants. 'Come here,' he breathed.

Topaz crossed the room and reached for him, sliding her hand across his fly, feeling the hardness of him through the denim. Nathan's rough hands gripped her shoulders, moving over the sleek skin, the pressure betraying his impatience. She reached for the buttons of his Levi's and undid them, slipping her hand over him, hard as flint, hot against her palm, and opened and closed her fingers around him in a smooth, fluttering movement, feeling him pulse under her touch, his breath catching in his throat.

Rosen moaned, harshly, utterly unable to control himself a second longer. He caressed her, squeezing her ass and stroking her firm full breasts with their exquisite swollen nipples, before turning her gently round and pushing her down over the desk.

A second later she felt him slide into her, in and out, in and out, and all her pent-up desire crystallized into a huge block and she looked round and saw Nathan behind her and above her, smiling, fucking her slowly, and she felt the sweet pressure spread out across her body and she started to come, feeling it in her fingers and toes, and her whole skin, convulsing in orgasm . . .

11

Rowena Gordon leant back against the soft fabric of her seat as the plane dipped sharply in the sky, veering in to the landing approach. She craned her neck, trying to catch a glimpse of the Manhattan skyline spread out below her, full of threats and promises. At this very moment, a cab assigned to her would be pulling up at JFK. Waiting to take her to Mirror, Mirror, the famous, luxurious and totally exclusive New York studios. Nicknamed the 'Dream Factory'. Where good bands went to become great ones. Where stars went to become multi-platinum supernovas. Where a kind of weird magic descended on the recording of just a handful of albums each year, turning them into volcanic eruptions of sound that could blow you away even on a tinny home stereo. Magic that transformed your bedroom into Madison Square Gardens. That gave drums a wild kick, guitars a glittering distortion, vocals a savage precision, and shot your record to the top of the charts and the cover of *Rolling Stone*.

Because Mirror, Mirror was the studio where Michael Krebs recorded.

And Michael Krebs was the best producer in the world.

And Rowena had to have him.

At first she'd just been dreaming out loud. Things were going so well, after all: Josh had signed Atomic Mass, she'd got a big promotion and pay rise – and a nice new flat in Earl's Court, thank God – and the band were media darlings of the week. Their small shows became bigger shows. The bigger shows sold out. No less than five major acts offered them the support slot on their tours. And in the middle of all the excitement, the boys were keeping their heads screwed on and writing some incredible songs . . .

So Rowena had joked to Josh Oberman that they should get Michael Krebs to produce. Yeah, right. The *legendary* Michael Krebs. Who only ever worked with superstar bands, who was probably booked for a decade upfront, and who'd expect a couple of million dollars for his services alone.

Of course, a multi-platinum record can make six or seven million. So for a huge act, it wasn't unreasonable.

But Atomic Mass were a tiny new band, freshly signed, with not even a single to their name. And Rowena's budget was £100,000.

So it *was* a joke.

Christ Almighty, what am I doing here? she thought, smoothing her long blonde hair into a ponytail and trying to look cool, as though she flew Business Class to New York all the time. What am I going to say to him? A hundred and fifty thousand dollars? He'll laugh in my face. I'll probably crack a rib when his security goons throw me out on the pavement.

But that was Joshua Oberman for you! When the old guy liked an idea, he really liked an idea.

'You think Krebs should produce Atomic Mass?' he'd asked his protégée.

'Oh, sure,' Rowena grinned. She patted her demo tapes like a proud mother. 'They're the best band around, they should have the best producer. And just as soon as I've saved up a spare million, we'll hire him for them.'

Oberman got up and padded around the soft carpet of his office, like a twitchy leopard.

'I know Michael from way back when,' he said suddenly. 'Gave him his first job when I was working for Elektra. In seventy-four. He'll see you if I ask him to.'

'Josh, you can't be serious,' Rowena protested. 'He'd cost more than ten times our budget for the whole thing!'

'We could go to a hundred and fifty thousand dollars,' Oberman replied with an air of reckless generosity.

'You must be –'

'No buts,' Oberman insisted. 'You fly to New York and meet with him. Take a demo. If he likes the stuff, he might do it for that money. Starting a band from scratch could appeal to Michael. He's a risk-taker. I'll have him send a cab to bring you to the studio, and I'll let you take it from there.'

'Boss, you are out of your mind. This will never work in a million years.'

Oberman looked across at her, with a strange expression. 'Atomic Mass are your band, Rowena,' he'd said. 'Make it work.'

'Can I take your champagne glass, ma'am?' asked a handsome steward in a gentle American accent. 'We'll be coming in to land in just a few moments.'

'Thank you,' Rowena said, startled out of her thoughts. God, she was really doing this! Coming to New York for the first time. Trying to pull off a deal with a superproducer. In person. By herself.

There it was, look! The Statue of Liberty!

'Oh God,' said Rowena out loud.

She had never felt so nervous in her life.

'What kind of business?' the customs officer asked pleasantly. Not that he gave a damn. The girl was obviously not a drugs smuggler, criminal or illegal immigrant, but as long as he could ask her questions he could enjoy the sight of her long, slender legs in those tight pants, the gentle swell of her breasts under the clinging Lycra body, her tumbling blonde hair, her almost obscenely sexy lips, soft, plump, with a slight natural pout that belied the businesslike jacket and smart briefcase.

'I have a meeting,' she replied, in crisp English tones. The officer brightened even more. What a babe. She sounded like Princess Diana, all haughty and impatient. Made him want to warm her up.

'With who?'

'With a producer.'

'Oh,' he said, glancing at her slyly. 'An actress, huh?'

Rowena shook her head, smiling. 'Not that kind of producer.'

'Well, welcome to the United States,' the guy said, sighing. Back to the grind. Fat tourists and screaming kids. Terrific . . .

Rowena, glad to have it over with, pushed her trolley through into the arrivals hall, praying that the Mirror cab hadn't given up on her and driven back. This was impossible enough without her annoying Michael Krebs. She peered through the throng of relatives, company reps and minicab drivers, jostling against the barrier with their little cardboard signs. Nothing. She checked again. Definitely no 'Gordon', Damn! She'd have to call and explain . . .

'Ms Gordon?' asked a respectful voice.

She spun round, and was confronted with a tall chauffeur, decked out in full uniform – peaked cap, grey suit, the works.

'Yes, I am,' she answered, trying not to stare.

'Mr Oberman gave us a description, ma'am,' he explained, taking her trolley. 'If you'd like to follow me, I've got your limousine parked round the front. Mr Krebs wanted to know if you'd like to come and see him straight away, or if you'd prefer to go to the hotel first?'

'We should just go straight to the studios,' said Rowena. *A limo! Jesus Christ!* 'If it's convenient for Mr Krebs to see me now.'

The chauffeur touched his cap respectfully and led her to the exit, Rowena walking three paces behind him in the vague hope that everyone might stop staring at her. She couldn't believe this. It was a message to Musica from Krebs. When Oberman suggests he might send a cab, he responds . . . with . . .

Rowena, emerging into the bright sunlight, felt her mouth open in astonishment.

Parked in front of the regular car queue was the biggest, longest, most ecologically unsound car she'd ever laid eyes on. It stretched out in front of her, gleaming, polished and totally ostentatious. It had *three* back doors. The chauffeur was loading her suitcases into a vast trunk with infinite care, as if they were Louis Vuitton filled with the crown jewels instead of her scruffy T-shirts and Marks & Sparks pyjamas. As he walked round and held open the third of the back doors, she forced herself to stop gawping and try to behave naturally. What would Josh do? Probably wouldn't bat an eyelid.

A small knot of people had gathered outside the airport doors, watching the scene curiously. Rowena felt centuries of gentlemanly Scottish restraint screaming in protest at such vulgarity. She blushed scarlet and hastily clambered into the car, shutting the doors, thankful that this monster came with one-way mirrored glass. At least nobody could see who it was in here. They'd probably assume it was Madonna . . .

Forty minutes later, she'd relaxed a little. The car was so smooth it felt like they were floating. She'd called London from the in-car phone, switched on the TV and turned it to MTV – wherever you go in the world, some things stay the same – and pulled out her Walkman. *Remind yourself why you're here.*

Atomic Mass's newest, best demo flooded into her head as they spun through midtown Manhattan. Dazzled by the beauty of the city – soaring skyscrapers, vast neon billboards – she settled into her leather seat and just let herself enjoy it. Oh, she could get used to this, Rowena thought, as they turned off Times Square, heading for the studios. So what if Krebs wanted to send a limo? He might still agree to $150,000 for a new band. After all, they *were* very good. And like Josh said, he was a risk-taker.

A little voice inside her head said she had to be kidding.

There was no way this was gonna work.

And Oberman had told her to *make* it work.

Jesus.

The limo purred to a halt. Rowena switched off her music and looked outside; they'd stopped in front of a square, low-slung, black granite building.

'We're here, ma'am,' the chauffeur announced. 'If you care to go inside. I'll take your cases on to the hotel for you.'

'Thank you,' said Rowena, nervously overtipping him $20 and stepping outside.

Her reflection gazed back at her from the car: hair long and tousled, eyes tired from the flight. She should have freshened up at the hotel first. Oh well. Too late now!

Rowena took a deep breath and walked into the reception area, automatic doors hissing open in front of her. The studio lobby was decorated in sumptuous apricot tones, a Persian rug spread on the carpet, dark mahogany furniture everywhere, soft lighting arrangements on the ceiling and walls giving an instantly soothing effect, and a kidney-shaped reception desk bearing a huge crystal vase crammed full of white roses.

'Can I help you?' asked the immaculately dressed receptionist, giving Rowena a disapproving once-over. She felt hopelessly awkward, standing in this bloody palace in her crumpled clothes, with her two-bit little demo tape and pocket-change offer for Michael Krebs. Lord, even his receptionists wore Chanel.

'I'm here to see Mr Krebs,' she said, as confidently as she could. 'He's expecting me. My name is Rowena Gordon, from Musica Records in London.'

The girl tapped the name into her computer and gave Rowena a more friendly look. 'Yes, ma'am. I'll just let him know you're here.'

She spoke quietly into an internal phone, then turned back to her. 'That's fine. If you want to walk right through those doors, someone will meet you and escort you up to his office,' she added, giving Rowena the benefit of several thousand dollars' worth of cosmetic dentistry. Rowena nodded briskly and went though into the main recording complex, feeling her heartbeat speeding up.

Come on. You can do this.

'Ms Gordon?' asked another polite minion. 'If you'll just step this way –' and Rowena followed the guy through three studios to the main office, where he held open the door for her with a beaming smile.

Rowena tucked her hair back behind her ears and stepped into the producer's office. It was a large room – all gleaming chrome, black leather and hi-tech luxury. Michael Krebs was working on something at a desk made entirely of cut glass, heaped with phones, faxes, an expensive-looking IBM and a range of sound equipment.

Her heart sank. Offering this guy $150,000 would be an insult. But that was her goddamn budget! As far as her boss would go . . .

'Michael Krebs?' she asked.

He stood up, punched a few keys on his computer and turned round to her, smiling.

'Rowena, good to see you,' Krebs said, walking over to her and shaking her hand warmly. She noticed the way his eyes ran quickly over her body, checking her out. 'Josh Oberman's a big fan of yours. Told me everything about you, except why you're here.'

'I'm grateful you could find time to fit me in,' Rowena replied. 'And thank you for the car.'

She was dismayed to find herself blushing. Oh, God! Why hadn't she gone to the hotel and changed first? He was absolutely, totally drop-dead gorgeous.

Michael Krebs was in his early forties, about twenty years older than her. He was tall, muscular and lean, with intelligent black eyes and grey hair round his temples. He carried himself with a natural air of total confidence and power; Rowena noticed he was wearing a sweatshirt, jeans and sneakers, no Rolex or jewellery or any kind of status symbol. Even these magnificent offices had no gold or platinum discs anywhere in sight, and she knew he could have wallpapered the entire complex with them if he'd wanted to. Everything about him said *I don't need to boast.*

But it was the eyes that she couldn't get over; mesmeric, gripping eyes, fringed with the most incredible thick dark lashes, lush as a woman's. She could not break his gaze. She felt transparent, as if he could see right through her.

A small point of sexual heat started to burn between Rowena's legs.

'The car? That was nothing. We keep some on-site for the acts that record here,' Michael said. He waved to the black leather couch. 'Won't you have a seat? I hate to keep you standing up. You must be exhausted.'

'Thanks,' she said, sitting down and reaching for her demo. She felt sick with nerves. Michael Krebs was a world-class producer, and she'd flown across the Atlantic to ask him to work with a totally unknown act with a Mickey Mouse budget. She didn't know where to start.

Krebs pulled a chair up opposite her and sat down, completely relaxed. What a great-looking girl. Fantastic hair. Very sensual lips. He had a brief vision of her giving head with those lips. And *endless* legs, Jesus, a guy could get lost in there. Almost made him wish he was single. It was too cute, the way she was obviously completely terrified and doing such a lousy job of hiding it. Poor kid, Oberman had probably got some crazy idea into his head and sent a stunning babe over here to do his dirty work for him.

What had the old buzzard said? That this kid was bright, ballsy and a great talent scout? 'A natural feel for rock music,' wasn't that it?

Looking like that? *Sure.*

'To what do I owe the pleasure?' he asked gently.

Rowena started, and fished in her bag for the demo tape. She held it out to him. 'We'd like you to produce this band we've signed,' she said. 'We think you'd be perfect for them. They're called Atomic Mass.'

Michael Krebs shook his head, perplexed. 'Atomic Mass? Doesn't ring any bells,' he said. 'I must've blanked out. Remind me what their last album was called.'

Rowena swallowed hard. 'They've never made a record,' she replied. 'This would be the first.'

He stared at her. 'Oberman wants *me* to work on a *baby act*? Now I've heard everything,' he said. 'He's gonna spend that kind of money on a new band?'

Oh, God, thought Rowena. 'We could offer you' – *Josh will* kill *me* – 'two hundred thousand dollars.'

Krebs, amazed, broke into a huge grin. 'Did I hear you right? Two hundred thousand?'

Rowena nodded. She was still clutching her little demo like an idiot. He hadn't bothered to take it from her.

'Ms Gordon, you've been misinformed,' Krebs told her. 'I do have a space in my schedule for the next two months, but the price is a million. At *least*. And I never work with unestablished bands.'

'But wouldn't you like to break a new act? From scratch? I thought you were a risk-taker, Mr Krebs,' Rowena said, rather coldly. To her surprise she was getting angry. How could he just dismiss Atomic like that when he hadn't even heard them?

Michael heard the challenge in her voice. Interesting. Maybe the girl did have some balls after all.

'I used to do that. But times have changed,' he answered, equally coldly. 'And the price is one million dollars, minimum.'

'We don't *have* a million.'

'I wouldn't get out of bed for two hundred thousand.'

Rowena stood up, furious.

Too bad Oberman hadn't bothered to explain the rules of the game to the girl, Michael thought. She seemed smart and passionate. He'd give a good report of her back to Josh when he rang him up to yell at him for wasting his time. But that was Oberman for you; the guy was completely fucking insane, he played by his own rules.

'I'm sorry you've had a wasted trip,' he said, smiling at her.

Rowena lost her temper. 'Times *have* changed, haven't they? You used to be a hero, Mr Krebs. A real visionary. Christ, I had articles about you on my walls at college. It's incredible what a few platinum records will do, isn't it?'

She threw the demo at him. 'Take it, it's a present. Might remind you what a bunch of teenagers who give a damn are capable of. But I guess you don't care about music any more. Just the chinging of cash tills, right?'

She sprang to her feet. 'Don't bother to get up. I'll show myself out.'

Astonished, Michael Krebs watched her go.

Rowena turned round in the shower, letting the hard jets of water pummel her neck and shoulders, massaging away the strains in her muscles. She pushed her long wet hair down her back, squeezing the conditioner out of it, rinsing it clean.

There's nothing like washing your hair to refresh you, she thought, switching the water off and pulling on one of the hotel's soft white bathrobes. The shower had made her whole body feel alive again, her nipples hard from the cool air of the room, her skin warm and vital. She would definitely go out tonight. She'd slept, and she felt good. Maybe she'd buy a copy of the *Village Voice* in the lobby and check out what bands were playing.

Rowena had one night in New York. She wasn't going to waste it sitting in her room. Outside her window, Manhattan stretched in front of her, sparkling in the night, traffic moving through the gridlike roads in melting rivers of light. It was exciting and alive. She wanted to move into the slipstream, to be part of it.

There was a loud knock on the door.

'Come in,' Rowena yelled, belting her robe. Great. She was starving. She'd ordered a huge pastrami sandwich on rye and a chilled beer – when in Rome, after all . . .

'Hello again,' Michael Krebs said, walking in.

Rowena jumped out of her skin, automatically clutching the bathrobe tighter around her. 'What are you doing here?' she gasped.

'We had the hotel address, remember? We sent your luggage ahead of you,' he reminded her. 'I thought I better come and see you before you flew back.'

She didn't reply.

'You know, it's been a long time since somebody told me to go to hell,' Krebs remarked, glancing at the slim lines of her body under the robe. *Stop that!* he ordered himself. 'Oberman said you were pushy. He wasn't wrong.'

Rowena, embarrassed, started to apologize, but the producer cut her off. 'So I listened to your band. I was curious,' he said. 'They're pretty good.'

'Yes they are,' she agreed, holding her breath. Was he about to say what she hoped he was?

'OK, I'll do it,' Michael Krebs told her, black eyes glittering. 'But not for two hundred thousand. If I'm gonna chance working with these boys, I want a stake in their future. Musica doesn't pay me at all, but I get a five per cent royalty. Of the gross.'

'Five per cent gross? That could be a lot of money,' Rowena countered, trying to contain her excitement.

Krebs looked at her. 'Don't push it, kid. Do we have a deal, or what?'

'Yes, sir,' Rowena said, feeling triumph flood through her. 'Thank you, Mr Krebs. I'm sure you won't regret it.'

Michael Krebs! Michael *Krebs* was going to produce Atomic Mass! It was the coup of the fucking century!

'I'd better not. And you can call me Michael,' Krebs said, enjoying her reaction. He checked her out again. His wife was visiting her parents this week, and he didn't have to get home. And this girl was intriguing him;

talented, brave, smart, a little reckless . . . Well, he rationalized, I'm working with her now.

'Why don't you get dressed, Rowena?' he said. 'I'll show you New York.'

12

'So it's between those two, then,' the chairman concluded, toying with one of the files on his desk.

'I would have said so.'

Nathan Rosen stared out of the glass walls of the penthouse office, somewhat uneasily. He didn't normally suffer from vertigo, but this was the sixtieth floor, the summit of the American Magazines tower. It was a famous quirk of Matt Gowers, the CEO, that the walls of the top floor should be three feet of clear glass, so he could survey the whole of New York, right out to the ocean. 'Because journalism is observation,' Gowers had reportedly said.

Nathan Rosen was new to the American Magazines board, and he wasn't used to the effect. Anyway, he preferred to convince himself it was the view that made him nervous, not the fact that he was secretly dating one of the candidates he was recommending to his boss.

'Kind of young, aren't they?' Gowers commented.

Joe Goldstein was thirty; Topaz Rossi, twenty-three.

'Yes, sir. Child prodigies,' Nathan smiled, only forty-one himself. 'But they've both proved they can run magazines. Circulation and revenue are up and costs are down on all the books they cover.'

Gowers nodded, acknowledging this. 'I have a lot of money riding on this project.'

'Yes sir, I know.'

'Joe Goldstein's got an MBA, from Wharton,' said the chairman. 'Does Rossi?'

'She's completing her first year. She's taking a course in the evenings and at weekends, doesn't want to take time out from the job.'

'Is the programme Ivy League accredited?'

'Yes it is.'

Gowers considered this. 'That's a good attitude,' he said. 'That's good. Have these two kids met each other yet?'

'No. Goldstein's only just moved to New York. He used to work out of the Los Angeles office.'

'Get them together, Nathan,' the chairman ordered. 'They've got a right to check out the competition.'

Joe Goldstein was in a bad mood.

I just don't want this shit, he thought angrily. I don't need any of this bullshit. It's not like we have time to waste here.

He fiddled aimlessly with an already perfect bow tie. God, he hated wearing a tux. It made him feel stiff and awkward, and he thought he looked like a waiter. But you don't turn down an invitation to dinner with Nathan Rosen, director of American Magazines, East Coast. And if it says 'Black Tie,' you wear black tie.

A handsome and annoyed young man glared back at him from the mirror. Joe regarded his reflection coolly, his impassive gaze sweeping across the jet-black hair trimmed ruthlessly short, the dark, intense eyes flecked with silver, the broad, clean-shaven jaw. Goldstein was darkly attractive, his smooth skin tanned to a deep brown from the California sun, and he had a muscled chest and long sturdy legs, uncomfortably encased in stiff black linen. He frowned.

At thirty Joe Goldstein was resolutely single, and doing a pretty good impression of the Man Who Had Everything. He had been born the eldest of four sons to a moderately wealthy Massachusetts retailer, and the power and responsibility of being a big brother had lent him the air of someone who naturally expects to be put in charge. Joe had been ambitious all his life. He'd excelled in high school, firstly to show his brothers, Cliff, Martin and Sam, how to do it, and later because excelling had become second nature. Joe Goldstein made straight As, was a quarterback in the football team, and was voted 'Most Likely to Succeed' three years running. His parents, who believed in hard work, God and family values, set standards for their eldest son which he followed almost absolutely.

Joe helped old people across the road, gave part of his allowance to charity every week, and stood when a lady entered the room. Only two things prevented Goldstein from being a caricature of the perfect Republican All-American boy: first he was Jewish; second, he was an inveterate womanizer.

The Goldstein boys had been sent to a private school that stretched the limits of what their parents could afford. It was an old, prestigious establishment, and although they were not the only non-Christian pupils attending, they were part of a tiny minority, swamped in a sea of rich Boston kids with trust funds and establishment backgrounds. Joe never felt completely secure there. One day he went to check on his youngest brother, Sam, then aged six, and saw him sobbing in a corner of the playground. Some older boys were kicking and punching him and shouting abuse. The eldest was repeatedly giving the Nazi salute, and appeared to be trying to force little Sam to do the same. Joe tore across the concrete.

He was seventeen, twice as big as any of them, and when he crashed into the group they instantly laid off his baby brother and looked terrified.

Two of them burst into tears. The ringleader, a fourteen-year-old, spat at him. 'Kike,' he said.

He gave the Nazi salute, right in Goldstein's face. He wasn't about to worry over a punch or two. Everyone knew what the Yid quarterback was like; he wouldn't really hurt a kid half his size.

Joe glanced at his brother. 'You OK?' he asked.

Sam snuffled yes.

Joe grabbed hold of the ringleader's right wrist and held it in a vicelike grip. He turned to the other bullies, who were watching horrified.

'This is what kikes do to fascists,' he said.

Then he broke his arm.

None of them were bothered again, but Joe never forgot that incident. He ceased making any attempt to fit in socially with people he despised. From then on, he became highly selective of his friends, choosing to spend time only with the boys whose morals and dedication matched his own. Academic achievement became a matter of pride, too. Joe worked harder and won bigger, as if proving his worth to himself. His only distractions were sport, and later, women.

Girls came easily to Goldstein from puberty onwards, and he took full advantage of the situation. He used to tell himself it was because he was a football player, but once he reached Harvard and turned to the *Lampoon* instead of the sportsfield, the flow of women did not dry up. Nor did it dry up once he graduated *cum laude* and lunged straight into Wharton Business School.

And Joe indulged. Why not? He was good-looking, muscular and well-endowed. He was also, more importantly, a skilful, sensitive lover who took care that his partners were pleased. He practised safe sex and was upfront about what he wanted. Joe had a strictly defined set of rules: he didn't get involved with girls who got involved. He liked female company, he liked sleeping with women, but that was it, and he made that clear. And even under those conditions they flocked to him, Jewish girls and shiksas, white girls and black girls, Asian girls and Hispanics. Joe didn't discriminate. He just liked women, all kinds of women.

There was only one type of girl Goldstein didn't get on with, and certainly didn't want in his bed, and that was the driven, aggressive career woman. He thought feminism was OK, to a degree – that is, he thought ladies should be *respected*. But he didn't like women who pretended to be men. Joe admired compassion and nurturing in women; protecting and providing he reserved for himself. His old-fashioned values ran all the way down the line. He thought Naomi Wolf's *The Beauty Myth* was a bunch of hysterical nonsense. He knew a lot of men privately agreed with him.

Joe Goldstein had turned out a nice guy, but a sexist.

Joe did *not* like women like Topaz Rossi. He didn't like having to eat dinner with them. And he particularly didn't like having to pretend to compete with them for the managing director's job on a new, upmarket economic title. A man's title. A title clearly earmarked for him, but one he'd have to pretend to compete for, so American Magazines could look politically correct.

He hated to waste time.

Topaz sighed. 'God,' she remarked to a pigeon, 'I envy that guy.'

She'd never met Joe Goldstein and didn't know much about him. One thing she was certain of, however, he was a man. Therefore he was to be envied at times like these. For Nate and Mr Goldstein, 'Black Tie' were two simple words, not a command to strike fear into the soul.

She twisted round in her sixth outfit, wondering if this would do. She was wearing a short skirt of supple brushed leather from Norma Kamali, a chocolate-brown silk shirt from DKNY, and slingback mules from St Laurent. A mixed heap of gold bangles jingled on her right arm, and her slender legs shimmered in light-reflecting hose from Wolford's. It was an aggressive, expensive look, the sexy-but-businesslike style that was the height of fashion at the moment. And after all, fashion was what she did for a living, so looking good and looking professional were synonymous for her these days.

Outside her window, Central Park shone green and gold, bathed in the evening sun. Topaz permitted herself a smile. Even by New York standards, her rise had been meteoric. She'd only been features editor of *US Woman* for a few months before the managing editor's job at *Girlfriend* magazine fell vacant when the boss left to get married. At first, Topaz hadn't even considered applying. She'd only just got a major promotion, and anyway, nobody gets to run a flagship teen title at twenty-three. But then the board had announced internally that they were opening the vacancy to group tender; any executive or senior enough editor could pitch for it, anonymously, by submitting a blind portfolio of ideas, covering everything from layout to advertising strategies to subscriptions. The portfolios would be anonymous, so, like an exam, the judges would not know whom they'd liked or disliked until the results were out.

The initiative had come direct from the chief executive, Mr Gowers. It was an attempt to bolster internal competition, and Topaz realized that as a features editor, she was eligible to apply – and nobody would know if she failed.

She changed her mind. For two months she immersed herself in teen fiction, teen music, teen television and hundreds of teenage magazines. She researched statistics on box-office young audience figures and called account executives at fifteen major advertising agencies. She worked nights and weekends and told nobody she was pitching, not even Nathan.

The dummy issue she came up with was dynamite, a mixture of baby feminism, cheap makeover ideas, New Kids on the Block and Sega games. The accompanying dossier of financial projections and consumer profiles was eighteen pages of taut research.

Topaz's submission was outstanding, so much the best it wasn't even funny. She became the youngest managing editor in the history of the group, and within six months the new-look *Girlfriend* had increased its market share by 16 per cent.

She was beautiful, successful, and just twenty-three years old.

She became a media property herself, although Nathan, on his way to the board and once again her immediate superior, forbade her to agree to a *Vanity Fair* profile. 'Sell magazines for American, not Condé Nast,' he said.

Oh yeah? thought Topaz to herself, adjusting a cuff. Somehow she suspected the new director had a more personal reason for wanting the spotlight away from her vicinity. And that attitude presented her with a big problem, one she would soon have to turn her attention to.

But forget about that, for now. Tonight was not about her personal life. When it was announced that American would be looking for an editor for *Economic Monthly* from inside the company, Topaz had spent two whole weeks on her application. She had no experience of finance, or men's magazines, but she put her ideas across with such passion and clarity that Nathan *had* to put her forward to Cowers. Although he'd made it clear that the other contender was by far the favourite.

So tonight was about this Goldstein guy, and the formidable opposition he represented to her next step up the ladder. Because Topaz was determined to prove that a woman was good for more than one woman's title. She wanted to demonstrate that she was an all-rounder.

She wanted to be a *player*.

She wanted *Economic Monthly*.

Nathan Rosen, the newest director of American Magazines, prayed Topaz would behave herself. She was the only element in his life he couldn't control.

He paced round his apartment, checking for the millionth time the immaculate table setting of Irish linen and Italian glassware. He forced himself to take a deep breath, and looked round the drawing room, finding some comfort in the emblems of his success all around him – the marble fireplace, the small Cézanne hanging above the Chippendale cabinet. The place was a model of discreet bachelor luxury, from the soft, buttery leather armchairs to the wafer-thin stereo system, currently playing 'Eine Kleine Nachtmusik'. This was one of the most exclusive co-ops on the Upper East Side.

Not bad for forty-one, Nathan reminded himself. I can handle Rossi.

He stopped pacing and smiled. Maybe that last thought could have been better phrased. It was his inability to *stop* handling Topaz that was causing him problems.

Rosen had been seeing Topaz ever since that wild night when he fucked her over the desk in the *Westside* editor's office. He couldn't help himself. To this day, he could remember her teasing over that meal, taunting him with her body and her beauty, challenging him to come and take her. Well, he had, and it'd been fantastic. It had been the best sex he'd ever known. Nathan had no doubt at all that half the pleasure of that night had derived from the fact that he'd been fighting his desire for Topaz from the moment she'd walked into his office.

The million reasons why he shouldn't have fucked her then remained just as true now – she was so young, he was her boss. And if anything, they seemed to have been amplified by time. There was a larger downside too, given that those two years had seen her make editor of one magazine, and him become a director, with responsibility for New York and the rest of the East Coast.

Which led to situations like this. Where he, Nathan, was going to sit on a panel choosing between two candidates. And he was dating one of them.

Topaz told him the simple answer was to just admit it. To see her publicly. To tell Matt Gowers that they were lovers, and see what the CEO said about it, which she insisted would be nothing at all.

Nathan wasn't so sure.

And the fact was, he was totally embarrassed about becoming a living cliché – 41-year-old man with his 23-year-old girlfriend. What did they call them? Jennifers, yeah, that was it. It was the modern equivalent of wearing a T-shirt saying MIDLIFE CRISIS IN PROGRESS! And he was *not* having a goddamn midlife crisis! He was doing very well and he knew exactly where he was going – two doors down the hall, to Matt Gowers' office. By the time he was fifty-four, he thought his life's ambition would be within his reach.

On the other hand, he couldn't give Topaz up. She was no Jennifer, no dumb ditzy blonde. She was one hell of a strong, confident girl, and a natural print woman. Her intelligence and enthusiasm charmed the pants off him. So to speak. Oh God, the sex . . . he couldn't help being pleased that she wanted him, when he knew for a fact that half the guys in the company would give a month's wages to touch her breasts *once*. She had evolved sexually too: she would throw him down on a bed, mount him and walk out when she'd finished, just as often as she wanted him to dominate. Topaz needed variety and experimentation. Which was partly why he stayed so hot for her.

He was going to have to make a decision; she'd said to him last week that she either moved in or moved on. God Almighty! Rosen thought. To have Topaz around all the time . . . that red hair, those creamy breasts, everything about her that drove him nuts, wandering around this place all the time. And she'd need satisfying, *all the time* . . .

The idea was breathtaking!

The idea was terrifying!

He'd asked for grace, to be allowed to think about it after this selection process, but she refused flat out. 'What you and I do out of hours has nothing to do with business,' she said. He could see her clearly right now, moving closer to him, her hand on his thigh, pushing that tricky, sexy, maddening tongue into his ear.

'I can't be patient. I want you. I *love* you,' she whispered, and Nathan Rosen had felt the familiar silver tendrils of desire trawl across his body, sending little hooks and claws digging into his groin, and he'd had to get her out of the office.

He passed a hand through his greying hair, unsure whether to be furious or elated. Man, he never thought he'd be going through this again. Checking into hotels at lunchtime because his need for a woman was so urgent he couldn't wait.

The selection procedure, Rosen, Nate reminded himself, dragging his thoughts back to this dinner. Maybe that would enable him to prove to the board that there was no undue favouritism going on here, because, he was certain, he'd be voting for Joe Goldstein. A new title like *Economic Monthly* was *designed* to be run by somebody like Joe. Rosen didn't think that Topaz, smart though she was, talented as she had proved herself to be, was yet ready for a serious, big-budget, male-orientated title like this one, and Nathan planned to vote impartially for the best candidate for the job.

And unless Joe really screwed his application up, that would not be Topaz Rossi.

She wouldn't hold it against him. She was fair where business matters were concerned. His only worry was that she'd tease him in front of Joe, let something slip. If that happened, his relationship with Goldstein, which he valued, would be jeopardized.

The doorbell rang. *Oh God*, Nathan Rosen thought.

He let his guests in, Joe just before Topaz. They had arrived within seconds of each other.

'Nate Rosen,' Joe greeted his old friend.

'Hey, Joe, how are you finding Manhattan?' Nathan welcomed his first discovery, grasping him in a bear hug.

Rosen had first noticed Goldstein at the *Lampoon* and hired him while he was still at Wharton, to work in the finance division of two titles. Goldstein had been another sensational success. Nathan smiled at his friend; what a great talent-spotter I am, he thought complacently. He had no doubt that Joe would be as brilliant a manager of the new title as he already was of *American Scientist, Executive Officer* and *Week in Review*.

'Hi, Topaz,' he added.

He wished she'd gone for something a little more formal; the best he could hope for was that she'd make a useful friend and ally in Joe. She could learn a good deal from him, he had a grasp of formal business strategies that were outside Topaz's experience. He doubted Goldstein would approve of this look for a businesswoman; it was too feminine, too distracting.

Well, it was distracting *him*, goddamnit.

'Joe Goldstein, meet Topaz Rossi, our managing editor at *Girlfriend*,' Rosen introduced them. 'I know you've seen Joe's résumé, Topaz.'

'Nice to meet you,' said Topaz, offering Joe her hand to shake. Why hadn't he been sent *her* résumé? She sized him up. Handsome, muscular, pleased with himself. She disliked him on sight.

Goldstein shook hands with her briskly, suppressing his annoyance. He was being asked to compete with *this*? The girl was barely out of diapers, and just look at that skirt. No need to ask how she'd got this far this young. He'd never seen so much T&A in all his life.

'How do you do,' he said.

Nathan handed them both a glass of champagne. 'Let's eat,' he suggested.

They sat down to a starter of Jerusalem artichokes with asparagus butter.

'So, Ms Rossi,' Joe said. 'Do you know much about economics?'

Rosen shrank in his chair. *Oh no. Oh no. Please, no . . .*

'Why wouldn't I know about economics, Mr Goldstein?' asked Topaz, angered by his tone. 'Because I'm a woman?'

Not only a bimbo, thought Joe, a militant feminist bimbo. Wonderful! OK, you want the gloves off, cutie? Fine.

'It was an innocent question, Ms Rossi. Perhaps you'd prefer it if I were more specific. What nation do you see as having the greatest potential for growth in the next five years?' he enquired, waiting indifferently for the inevitable reply: 'Japan'.

Topaz considered for a few seconds. 'Korea,' she replied. 'Although the question's way too general. How can anyone accurately predict where we'll be in two years, let alone five?'

Joe was surprised, but caught himself. So she'd read a few back issues of *The Economist.* So what?

He decided to play hardball. 'Korea is yesterday's news,' he said. 'You should be looking to China. Growth rates indicate –'

'Yesterday's news!' Topaz interrupted. 'I'll tell you what's yesterday's news: looking at the provinces which border Hong Kong and assuming that the rest of China can get just as rich just as quick, without the whole economy totally overheating –'

'There's nothing to stop it from doing so,' Joe snapped. 'But doubtless fashion shoots in Beijing have made you an expert.'

Topaz flushed. She knew all Goldstein's existing titles were aimed at the exact same market as *Economic Monthly,* totally unlike her own. 'I'm an expert at selling magazines,' she retorted.

Unnoticed to either of them, Nathan had sunk his head in his hands.

He'd *known* this damn dinner was a stupid idea.

'Well, Rosen, how did they get along?' Gowers asked.

'I – I think it's safe to say that there will be a healthy spirit of competition for this title, sir,' said his director.

The chairman chuckled. 'Fireworks, were there?'

'It was the Fourth of July, sir,' said Nathan.

Over the next two months, the battle for *Economic Monthly* became the American Magazines spectator sport of choice. Joe and Topaz were scrupulously polite to each other at management meetings, but that was the extent of their co-operation. People were fascinated by the open rivalry, and betting on the board's decision became a minor cottage industry, although after the first week nobody would accept a bet on Goldstein, even at 15 to 1 on. Only the staff of *Girlfriend, US Woman* and a few *Westside* reporters, who'd watched their former colleague pull off wildly improbable promotions twice already, would risk putting money on Topaz. Joe Goldstein, after all, was five years older, had his MBA, and ran three books to Topaz's one – all of them pitched at the educated, affluent male.

The more Joe saw of Topaz Rossi, the less he liked her. At the second editors' meeting they attended together, she chewed him out for opening the door for her. Goldstein hardened his resolve. So be it. As far as he was concerned, she had now renounced all special consideration to which a lady was entitled.

Topaz took her seat, laughing inwardly at Goldstein's face when she'd flown at him. She did it on purpose to annoy him. Goldstein was the worst type of jerk; he put women on pedestals and gave them no real respect at all. And on top of her dislike for his attitude problem, she was well aware that the whole building thought that *Economic Monthly* was as good as assigned to Joe already. They dismissed her chances, and she blamed him for that.

Early in the meeting, Jason Richman, who'd replaced Rosen as *Westside*'s editor, discussed his forthcoming series on leading women clergy.

Joe laughed. 'As Dr Johnson remarked,' he said, ' "a woman's preaching is like a dog's walking on his hinder legs. It is not done well; but you are surprised to find it done at all." '

There was a hush around the table as the execs waited to see if Topaz Rossi would come back. She didn't disappoint them.

'As Topaz Rossi remarked,' she mimicked him. 'Dr Johnson was a stupid asshole who probably couldn't get it up.'

There was laughter.

'Why don't you just back off, and save us both some time?' Joe murmured to Topaz when they left the room.

'Go fuck yourself,' she hissed. 'I could do the job just as well as you.'

'Oh, don't worry, honey,' said Joe. 'There's a place for you at *Economic Monthly* – I've always got room for an assistant with a cute tush.'

He patted her on the backside and walked out, leaving Topaz speechless with fury.

The next morning, *Executive Officer* began running the first in a series of in-depth profiles of leading economic figures; Joe Goldstein, the managing editor, was personally interviewing Alan Greenspan of the Federal Reserve. The article received wide acclaim, and was discussed on WHRT's *Good Morning Manhattan*.

Topaz Rossi and Joe Goldstein would present to the board in six weeks' time.

13

'Let's look at the situation,' Joshua Oberman said.

He pointed to the bright graphics on the presentation stand, showing the board of Musica Records what they wanted to see. Profits were up. Costs were down. And for the first time in years, Musica had some promising new acts.

'We can be happy with the results we have now,' he told them. 'Sam Neil and Rowena Gordon have each signed three good acts. Sam prefers to concentrate on mainstream pop, and Rowena has managed to find us talent from various' – he groped for the formal marketing term – 'niche sectors. Her soul singer, Roxana Perdita, had a debut album that went silver, and a rave act, Bitter Spice, has the number eight single this week.'

Blank faces greeted this summary around the table. Oberman sighed inwardly. Why did he bother? The bottom line was the only music to their ears.

'And Sam's bands have done equally well,' he concluded. 'But I feel that we are losing market share by limiting our search for talent to England and Europe.'

'But we have no base in America,' objected Maurice LeBec, President of Musica France.

'Which is what I propose to set up,' Joshua replied. 'It's true that we've always been a European company. But being the only major label in the world *not* to have a base in the States is becoming a liability.'

Hans Bauer, President of Musica Holland, sniffed sceptically.

Josh took his meaning at once. *You would say that. You're an American.* Bauer was his main rival for the job of chairman of Musica Worldwide, when John Watson retired next year.

'Gentlemen,' the old man went on, 'I need hardly remind you that only the English company has successfully found any new acts that sold albums last year. Now I have an executive with a particular gift for developing offbeat talent. Just the sort of talent that's crowding New York. And for her to operate properly she needs a company base there. I don't want to lease her out to Warners or PolyGram and have them poach her.'

'How much will this cost?' the chairman asked.

Oberman named a figure.

'That's a lot of money,' Hans said disapprovingly.

'We could make it back off three big records.'

'Just how talented is this girl, Joshua?' the chairman asked.

Oberman smiled at his boss. 'John,' he said, 'Michael Krebs is producing her act for *free*.'

'Do it again, Joe,' Krebs insisted.

Rowena sat on a spare chair behind the production console, watching them work. Joe Hunter, the singer, was laying down vocals for 'Karla', the album's big ballad.

'Rowena, make him stop,' Joe said into the mike, so she could hear. 'This has to be against the bloody Geneva Convention!'

'Michael's in charge,' she shrugged helplessly, grinning at him. 'Far be it from Musica to interfere in the creative process.'

'This is the fourteenth time we've done this take, Michael,' the singer complained. 'And it's one bloody line of the song . . . '

'Come on, Joe, you'll get it,' Krebs ordered him implacably. 'We don't settle for second best, right? Not for Atomic Mass. Go again.'

'Slavedriving bastard,' said the singer, but he did it again.

Rowena hugged herself for pure pleasure. It was so good to be involved like this, exactly what she'd wanted. Joe and the rest of the boys were all friends of hers now, and Barbara Lincoln had quit her job at the record company to manage them. So Rowena had got to be involved at every stage of their career – finding a live agent, getting them a good accountant and planning the tour, as well as the normal A&R stuff like supervising marketing. She cared like hell about all her acts, but Atomic were the only band that kept her up at night.

'That's good,' Krebs agreed. 'You can go from "it's good to see you again" now.'

'Wow, the second line,'Joe growled sarcastically, but he looked pleased.

Michael glanced at Rowena and winked.

He was wearing a black sweater and black jeans and he looked amazing. Rowena thought Michael should live in black. It picked out his eyes. It made him even more attractive than usual.

She loved to be with him.

It had started in New York four months ago, when he'd come to the hotel and said he'd show her the city.

That wasn't fair. He'd had her at a disadvantage – first he blew her out, then he offered her the break of the fucking century, then he put her in another of those monster black limos and showed her some of the sights. A man whom Rowena had hero-worshipped for years, whom she'd literally fantasized about talking to, was driving her to the Russian Tea Rooms for dinner, and ordering her strawberries and champagne. Then he took her to an Aerosmith concert at Madison Square Gardens, where they had access-all-areas passes and got to stand at the side of the stage.

Everyone they met treated Michael like a king. Rowena felt dizzy from the glory of it.

Krebs was intense. That was the main thing about him. She'd met guys as good-looking as he was, or at least she thought so – but never, never, had she found someone so completely in control of every situation. He'd decided that

Rowena Gordon was of interest to him, and that was it. At the Aerosmith show, he'd introduced her to so many record moguls they dissolved into a smiling blur. She was 'Musica's great white hope'. 'A rising star'. 'Incredibly talented'. And Krebs had told absolutely everyone that Rowena had personally convinced him to produce her band for nothing.

She'd had record company *presidents* lining up to shake her hand. Several of them offered to double her salary on the spot.

But Rowena shook her head, smiling and overwhelmed.

'Why didn't you take them up on it?' Krebs asked.

'I owe Josh,' Rowena said simply, smiling at him, and Michael Krebs looked at her, her long, freshly washed hair gleaming in the bright lights, and thought how glad he was she'd walked into his offices.

'Yeah, you do,' he said severely. 'And don't forget it.'

In the car on the way home, he'd demanded Rowena tell him her entire life story. 'I want to know *everything*. And you have to tell me. You owe me, because I took you to Aerosmith.'

'Took me to a show? Michael, you're producing my band.'

Krebs shook his head, giving her a smile that melted her bones. 'You don't owe me for that, honey. I have five per cent of the album. I'll get mine,' and she believed him.

When the limo pulled up outside her hotel, and Michael kissed her hand gallantly as she got out – man, it was weird to have an American heavy-metal producer do that – Rowena suspected she was in big trouble.

And when she got to JFK the next morning and found that Krebs had arranged for her to be upgraded to first class, she *knew*.

Her return home had been fairytale stuff. Although he had wanted this, Oberman could hardly believe Rowena had actually pulled it off. He gave her a senior manager title and another pay rise. Atomic Mass, meanwhile, were dumbfounded by the idea of working with Michael Krebs, and their extreme gratitude turned into friendship, as Rowena found them places to live in London and took charge of their affairs. When Barbara quit to manage them, they got even closer.

The two women had a lot in common. Barbara wasn't the music freak Rowena had turned into, but she was cool, logical and very ambitious. She had no interest at all in the secretaries' gossip, or who was fucking whom, nor did she give a damn if Manchester United won the league. The result was that she was branded a cold bitch, stuck-up and the rest of it. Nobody understood what Joshua Oberman could possibly see in Ms Lincoln. Behind her back, and sometimes even to her face, they called her 'the token black woman', a piece of positive-discrimination window-dressing.

Rowena knew better. In fact, Barbara made her feel small; she'd only had to fight sexism, the disapproval of a privileged circle and prejudice on account of her looks. Barbara had clawed her way up by herself: law at London University, an MBA at nightclasses, and heavy specialization in entertainment law. Her tutors wrote her glittering reports, her papers were published in eminent legal journals. And then she had suffered the utter humiliation of being turned down again and again at record companies, always getting to the final interview, never getting hired.

'Overqualified', 'underexperienced'. What they never said was 'Black'.

At first Barbara had thought she was being paranoid. Maybe she was just presenting herself wrongly. But when she asked for a list of senior black personnel at the seven major labels from industry associations, the reply confirmed all her worst suspicions.

There were none.

Not 'one or two', not 'a bare handful', *none.*

She refused to give up. She went on trying, banging on the Human Resources doors and doing everything else she could think of. Finally, she had written a long letter to Joshua Oberman, President of Musica UK, and marked it 'Private and Personal'.

Oberman had seen her. And he'd hired her on the spot.

Rowena learnt all this from Josh himself on the drive back from the Retford Porterhouse, and she'd bought Barbara lunch the next day – partly as a thank-you for getting Oberman to hear her tape, and partly to satisfy her curiosity.

Now they were best friends – the first woman Rowena had been close to since Topaz Rossi.

Whom she never thought about.

Whom she buried deep in her mind.

She was, she told herself firmly, a different person now. One who'd totally outgrown social snobbery. One who would never betray a friend.

Barbara enjoyed watching Rowena adjust to having money of her own, money she'd *earned*, for the first time in her life, helping her buy a flat in Holland Park, start shopping for her food in Marks & Spencer's and, most importantly, dress designer. Since she'd been disowned by her father, Rowena had almost forgotten how.

'I can't believe how much this *costs!*' she gasped, holding up a sexy little Krizia dress.

'If you want to be a player, you better dress that way,' Barbara laughed, folding the dress over her arm.

Rowena abandoned the elegant, refined clothes she used to wear in favour of younger, brighter, more confident stuff. Where Barbara preferred Armani, she liked to slink around in Donna Karan. When Barbara wore Chanel to industry parties, Rowena turned up in shimmering Valentino. They complemented each other perfectly.

They were inseparable.

And then, on 15 March, Michael Krebs arrived.

'Can you come up to Oberman's office?' Barbara asked, sticking her head round Rowena's door. 'We've got a visitor.'

She'd gone upstairs without thinking, totally preoccupied with how Bitter Spice were playing in the clubs. Too preoccupied to notice the sidelong glances that Barbara was giving her, and the jealous looks from the secretaries on the executive floor. When her friend opened the door of the president's office for her, Rowena jumped out of her skin.

There he was. A week before she'd expected him. Michael Krebs, dressed in beat-up jeans and sneakers and a Mets baseball cap, chatting to Josh Oberman as though he did this every day of the week.

He looked so fucking gorgeous, Rowena's heart stood still.

'Miss Gordon, we meet again,' Krebs said, giving her a beaming smile and standing to greet her. 'Oberman, I tell you, you are so lucky to have this young lady working for you it isn't even funny.'

Josh snorted.

'You're early, Michael,' Rowena managed.

He shrugged. 'I had a free week. I thought we might do a little pre-production. Think you can get the band together for me?'

'Oh, I expect we can manage that,' she replied, glad to be on safe professional grounds.

'Good,' Krebs said, looking her over slowly. Rowena felt a wave of desire flood through her, and she coloured, hoping Barbara wouldn't notice.

'And you'll have to show me London, too. If I'm going to be here for a few months, I'll need some help getting around.'

'I'm not sure how good I'd be as a tour guide,' Rowena said, but Krebs shook his head.

'You'll be fine,' he said implacably.

'You can't steal my A&R manager, Krebs,' Oberman objected. 'She's got three bands to look after.'

'Relax,' Michael said, not taking his eyes off Rowena. 'She'll have plenty of time. I just want to show her how I record an album.'

'You never let a record company within ten miles of your studio,' Oberman scoffed.

Krebs turned back to his friend with a shrug. 'Rowena's different,' he said.

For two weeks, Rowena held out. She never saw him alone. She tried not to think about him. She kept herself busy, going scouting for bands, attending parties, seeing stupid amounts of films. Because Michael Krebs spelt danger. Heady, reckless danger, the kind any intelligent girl should avoid.

He was an extremely powerful man.

He was twenty years older than her.

He was married.

Rowena knew all that. So she did her best to resist her feelings for him. Because whenever she did have to see Michael – with Barbara, or with the band – she only became more fascinated by him. More attracted to him.

Not only was the guy a legendary producer, he was also highly intelligent and well educated, to Rowena's surprise. He had two degrees, from the Universities of Chicago and Boston. He was an exercise fanatic and went to the Harbour gym in Chelsea every morning. He loved dogs. He loved history, and made Rowena take him round the National Gallery and the British Museum.

And he loved the record business. With a passion.

'I'm gonna teach you everything you need to know,' he told her.

'You can spot talent. And that means the sky's the limit,' he said.

'You're going to surpass me by miles,' he said. 'You can conquer the world. Believe it.'

Rowena was half embarrassed, half thrilled by his interest in her. It overjoyed her to see how well Atomic were getting on with him – Zach Freeman, the lead guitarist, and Alex Sexton, the bassist, especially – and what incredible depth he was bringing to the album. Even the quality of the songs the boys were writing had improved dramatically. It was as though everybody was outdoing each other to impress Krebs. He had that effect on people, Rowena thought. Like any born leader, he made you want desperately to please him.

It felt like he was producing her life.

Of course, she couldn't be sure she was right about how he felt. Maybe he *was* just a friend. Maybe he only wanted to mentor her. He did flirt with her outrageously, and she responded in kind, but there was nothing wrong with that. He never made a pass, he never avoided questions about his family, and he bugged Rowena about getting herself a boyfriend. So she was confused. She told herself she was being ridiculous.

But sometimes, when she caught him watching her in the evenings, she thought differently.

As the days went by, Rowena's attitude changed. Without even admitting it to herself, she started to try to make Michael Krebs notice her – as a woman, not a record executive. She began to wash and condition her hair every day. She wore Red by Giorgio Beverly Hills whenever she went down to the studio. She selected her sexiest outfits, the clinging grey cashmere dress by Georges Rech, the black Donna Karan suit, the Ann Klein miniskirt. And she put on make-up.

Michael reacted by ceasing to even flirt with her.

'He doesn't know I'm alive!' Rowena complained to Barbara.

'Don't be pathetic. I feel like holding up a match between you two, to see if it'll catch fire,' her best friend replied. 'The sexual energy you guys are giving off could power the National Grid.'

'He's married,' Rowena said, with an air of finality.

'I *know* he's married. That's what makes me nervous,' Barbara replied. 'Rich, powerful men like Michael Krebs eat girls like you for breakfast.'

'So you think all the stuff he says about me being talented is rubbish, then?' Rowena asked, winding a strand of blonde hair round her fist.

Barbara shook her head. 'Actually, no,' she said. 'He believes all that. And he really likes you as a friend. The trouble is, he's having trouble suppressing his sexual feelings.'

'No he isn't,' Rowena said. 'He's stopped flirting with me now. He doesn't ask me to dinner. He's even stopped introducing me to people.'

'You want to know why? Because you're a threat now. When it was harmless to flirt with you, he enjoyed it. But now you've turned up the heat, and he wants you.'

'I think you're wrong.'

'You'll see,' said Barbara calmly.

So now, at the end of the session, Rowena watched Michael wrap it up with Joe with her normal mixture of interest, admiration and confused longing.

'OK, my man. You're out,' Krebs told the singer dryly, flicking a couple of switches on the production console.

Joe raised a hand to the two of them and walked straight off the studio floor, without further pleasantries.

'Nice manners. Maybe I'm working them a little too hard,' Krebs remarked unrepentantly.

'The song sounds good, though,' Rowena said. She curled on her chair, a sinewy, catlike movement.

'What would you know?' he asked gruffly. 'You can't tell take one from take fifteen. You've got ears like Beethoven.'

'Oh, I just look for the big picture. I let guys like you sweat the details,' Rowena said, smiling at him.

There was a pause. Both of them were acutely aware that they were now alone together.

'Are you free for dinner tonight?' Rowena asked suddenly.

Krebs spun round slowly on the big leather producer's chair, looking at her. He'd been preparing for a moment like this for weeks. What he would say. How he'd let her down. How he could preserve a great friendship without risking anything further.

Except that if she'd waited a second longer, he'd have asked Rowena the exact same question.

Dinner's just dinner.

'Why do you want to have dinner with me?' he asked, almost savagely. 'On our own?'

'Just for the pleasure of your company,' Rowena answered quickly, blushing bright red.

'For the pleasure of my company? That's sweet, but you've been in my company all day,' Krebs said, hearing his own cruelty but unable to stop himself. He couldn't tear his eyes off Rowena, her long, slender legs tumbling out of a light blue Krizia dress, her firm thighs shimmering in reflective hose, her small breasts clearly visible through the white Bill Blass shirt she'd chosen that morning. Her long hair fell loose and sleek around her shoulders, and her eyes were wide, her lips parted.

For weeks now she'd been like a trembling reed in his presence, so brimming with desire that he could practically smell it.

For weeks now a general appreciation of an attractive, intelligent girl had become a raging lust which he could scarcely control.

And Michael Krebs was always in control.

He ached to fuck this woman. To really have her. To put her through her paces in ways she'd never dreamed of.

'Hey, it's no big deal,' Rowena said, her green eyes flashing.

'You've got a crush on me, Rowena,' Krebs insisted, his expression unreadable. 'And I'm married. I have three sons.'

'Nonsense, Michael,' Rowena said coldly. 'I'm not remotely attracted to you.'

They glared at each other.

The phone rang, shattering the tension.

'Krebs,' Michael said shortly, picking it up. 'Oh, hi, Oberman. No, it went fine. Yes, she is.' He held out the receiver to Rowena.

'Can you come over to the office and see me?' the old man asked. 'I need to talk to you about something urgently. Right now, Rowena.'

'Of course,' Rowena said, dragging her mind back to business with an effort. 'Is something wrong?'

'Nothing's wrong. Just be here,' Oberman said testily, and hung up.

She looked at Michael. 'I have to go.'

'Rowena –' he said suddenly, but she moved away from him, not wanting the quarrel to get any deeper.

'I really have to go. I'll see you tomorrow.'

'Call me tonight,' Krebs said, and although Rowena wanted to tell him to go to hell, she knew he wouldn't take no for an answer.

'I will.'

'You'd better,' Michael said, grinning at her in that way of his that weakened her knees. She felt a great rush of wanting sweep through her, and turned away from him as fast as she could, almost running out of the studio.

'Tell me something, Rowena. What do you think of New York?' Oberman asked her forty minutes later, as she sat across from his desk.

God, she looks stunning, he thought. I don't know what's happened to this girl lately. She was always special-looking, but now she's something else. Check out that pale blue dress with those light green eyes! Goddamn, no wonder Stevenson had resented her! How could a babe this beautiful be so good at her job?

'What do I think of New York?' Rowena repeated, bewildered. 'I've only been there once, Josh. It's a great city. What can I tell you?'

'What do you think of the bands there?' Oberman pressed her.

Rowena shrugged, a cascade of blonde hair falling about her shoulders. 'Right now, it's got the best bands in the world.'

The old man gave a satisfied grunt. 'OK. Now let's play a different game. What if I made you Managing Director – and don't get too excited, the title's only protocol – of a small subsidiary? A *tiny* subsidiary, just a name really, an outpost company. Your only job at first would be to look for talent, but over time I'd expect you to build it up. Do you think you could handle it, working on your own for a couple of years? With just an accountant and a secretary?'

'Of course,' she replied, wondering what the hell he was talking about.

'You mean that? You think you could be totally self-sufficient?'

Rowena shifted in her chair. It dawned on her that Oberman wasn't just playing 'Let's Pretend'. 'What about Atomic Mass? I wouldn't want to be too far from them right now.'

He made an expansive, dismissive gesture. 'Thought of that. We'd transfer them to record at Mirror, Mirror.'

He paced around behind his desk, looking at his protégée as though he was trying to see past her actual flesh and bones to her character, her self-reliance.

'I got the impression that you'd made a conscious decision to change your life when you got into this stuff, Rowena,' he said. 'Well, I hope that *was* what you wanted. Because I've just come back from an extended board meeting and I think I can guarantee that your life is about to change completely. Congratulations, Miss Gordon. You're gonna run a new label for us.'

He leant forward towards her, his craggy old face broken by a mischievous grin.

'In New York.'

Rowena didn't get back to her flat until 11 p.m., she'd spent so long talking about this with Josh, and Barbara, and even a little with Alex and Mark, the bassist and drummer for Atomic, who were in Barbara's management offices when she drove over there. She felt nervous and excited at the same time.

She flicked on the dimmer switch, letting a soft light flood the drawing room of her flat, illuminating the oyster-white carpet, the elegant chintz sofa and Georgian writing desk. As she slipped off her shoes and padded across to the kitchen, wanting to make herself a gin and tonic and a light supper before she crashed out, the phone rang.

With a sigh of annoyance, Rowena picked it up.

'I thought you were gonna call me,' Michael Krebs said.

It was like an electric shock. Small prickles of desire crawled all over her skin at the sound of his voice, teasing, friendly, definitely turned on.

'I meant to. I've been so busy, I only got home a second ago.'

'Rowena, you can always make time for your friends,' Krebs said softly.

Rowena took a deep breath. 'I thought I was making too much time for you,' she answered.

'I didn't mean to bite your head off,' he said. 'But I was right, though, wasn't I?'

She felt her palm holding the receiver go moist with sweat.

'You *have* been thinking about it, haven't you? For a while, now, I guess.'

'And you haven't,' she managed.

'We're not talking about me, we're talking about you,' he said relentlessly.

'Christ! Michael, you're so arrogant,' Rowena replied. 'I haven't got the faintest interest in you.'

There was a pause. She could almost feel his desire reaching down the telephone line. It was late at night, there was no one to see them, no one to stop them. She knew that they were trembling right on the cusp, on the brink of something from which there was no going back.

'Rowena,' Michael said.

It was just one word. A light rebuke. A tease, as if to say *Come on.* But his knowing, mocking tone pushed her over the edge.

To Rowena's astonishment, she heard herself moan with lust. A soft, wild sound she couldn't control.

Michael heard it, and his erection pressed so hard against his zipper it hurt.

'I'm at the Halcyon Hotel, in room 206,' he said. 'Get in a fucking cab. *Now.*'

It took twelve minutes for Rowena to get to the hotel, and during that time Krebs paced the room, thinking about her, imagining her in different positions, lightly touching himself from time to time. His erection remained rock-solid. When he heard her timid knock, he had to restrain himself from running across the room to wrench the door open.

'Hi, Rowena,' he said. 'Come in.'

She stepped into his suite, hearing the heavy door lock itself behind her. She was squirming and wet between the legs. Her heart was crashing and thudding so loudly against her ribcage she was sure he must hear it. She stood awkwardly in the middle of the room, not sure where to put herself.

Krebs regarded her impassively, his arms folded, for a few moments, looking her over at his leisure. She blushed deeper. She wanted him so desperately now she thought she might collapse.

Michael calmly picked up the phone and spoke to the operator, not taking his eyes off Rowena. 'This is Mr Krebs in 206,' he said. 'Hold all my calls, and have room service send up some champagne and leave it outside the door. I'm taking a shower.'

He replaced the receiver and beckoned to her. 'Come here.'

She walked unsteadily towards him.

'Closer,' Michael ordered, and she moved nearer, until her lips, wet and slightly parted, were inches from his face.

Staring deep into Rowena's eyes, Krebs shoved his hand up her dress and roughly yanked down her panties, pressing his hand against the damp hair between her legs, and slid a finger inside her, finding the hot, melting centre of her.

Rowena sobbed with pleasure, her legs shaking.

'What happened to "I'm not remotely attracted to you", "I haven't got the faintest interest in you"?' he enquired, caressing the urgent knot of heat in her belly.

She couldn't speak. She couldn't take her eyes off him. The mesmeric quality Krebs had always had, the dominating influence he'd had over her, in sex became a control so complete it sent spasms of ecstasy convulsing through her. Rowena couldn't believe what she was feeling. Not with Peter, nor with the other men she'd dated since, had she ever experienced anything like this. She was almost hypnotized. The force of his will was like a ten-ton truck.

And she was amazed at the depth of her response. She'd felt desire before. She'd felt pleasure. But never, *never*, had she felt anything like the heat that was flooding her body now.

'Say it,' he insisted. 'I want to hear you say it.'

'Michael, I – I think you're the most attractive man I've ever seen in my life, and I always wanted you,' Rowena said, half choking on the admission. She pressed herself against him, feeling his thick erection, letting him understand how great her need was. She pressed her lips to his throat, covering it with kisses. 'Please,' she said.

Michael took her head in his hands and twisted it about, looking at her like he wanted to drink in her face. Then he kissed her, fiercely, crushing her lips, running his hands over her body, under her dress, unsnapping her bra and playing with her erect nipples, stroking her in between the legs until she was weak with pleasure.

'I have dreamed about this,' he said. 'You're so beautiful. You're so different, you could drive a man mad.'

Then he pulled back, forcibly holding her away from him. 'I fantasized about you that first time,' he said. 'I looked at your mouth. I want to see your lips round my cock. I want to see it disappear into your mouth.'

He pushed her down on her knees before him. 'And tie your hair back,' he added. 'So I can see what you're doing.'

Rowena fumbled with her hair, barely able to get her fingers to work properly. She was already approaching orgasm, her feelings were so strong. She had trouble unbuttoning his fly because the denim was pushed out tight from his cock hard against it. Krebs did not help her.

When she finally freed him, Rowena drew breath.

He was big. No doubt about it. Long and thick. The thought of that inside her was almost frightening. She longed to taste him.

Rowena had always flatly refused to give head, no matter how much her partners had begged her. The thought of it disgusted her. But there was no question, now, of refusing Michael Krebs anything he wanted. She was being completely controlled and she loved it.

She wanted him inside her mouth. She wanted to please him. To submit to him.

Delicately, gingerly at first, and then bolder, harder, more confidently, she began to suck him.

Krebs felt the sweet relief of her tongue and pleasure surged through him, violent, intense sexual pleasure. He knew it was her first time, and that somehow made it better. He watched her, her eyes shut in rapture, her soft, plump lips caressing him eagerly.

When he finally forced himself to pull out of her mouth, he dropped down beside her without a word, spread her legs and entered her immediately, holding her head steady in his hands so he could watch her come.

Rowena felt the orgasm seconds before it started, the waves of sex running through her gathering and deepening, rushing towards her groin from her fingertips, her toes, her neck. The ecstasy was so intense she felt dizzy, and all she could see was Michael's face, and those brilliant dark eyes watching her, and she was coming, a huge, crashing climax ripping through her, and she thrashed about in Michael's arms, and she felt him erupt inside her with a groan of bliss, and she was still coming, and then finally it subsided, and she was staring into his eyes again, and she knew, with absolute, helpless certainty, that she had just found the one great passion of her life.

14

From 7 p.m. onwards, fleets of limos streamed down the Avenue of the Americas, towards the Victrix, the smartest hotel in Manhattan.

It was the party of the year.

It was the party of the decade.

Invitations had been harder to come by than tickets to the best Clinton Inaugural Ball, more sought-after than A-list places at the late Swifty Lazar's annual post-Oscars bash. An invitation to this party marked you out as the cream of the New York crop; fail to get one, and you failed to make the grade. Social death. Effective immediately.

Because there was something different about this party, quite aside from the eleven million dollars it had reputedly cost. This was no ordinary hymn to American excess, with a safe guest list drawn up from the usual social old guard: Mr and Mrs Billionaire Financier, Mr and Mrs Millionaire Publisher, and their summer neighbours from the Hamptons. Elizabeth Martin couldn't care less about those sort of people. She wasn't interested in the richest. She was only interested in the best.

Elizabeth was twenty-eight years old and married to the wealthiest man in the Western world, which meant that money no longer concerned her. Achievement was all she gave a damn about, and she threw parties for the people at the top of each individual tree, their bank balance being incidental. Your ancestors came over on the *Mayflower*? So what? If you couldn't compete on a worldwide scale, Elizabeth didn't have time for you.

Her parties were strictly for the great. The good could take care of themselves.

Young, cool, competitive Manhattan was hosting the Meritocrats' Ball.

Topaz Rossi and Rowena Gordon had both been invited.

Oberman arrived at Rowena's new apartment on West 67th street at 8 p.m. There had never been any question that he wouldn't fly over for this one, and in any case Rowena needed an escort, since she didn't know any of the American players yet, and invites were for one person only; no wives, no husbands, no lovers.

'Just come in, Josh, it's open,' called Rowena from the bathroom. He took a look round, pleased with himself; with no time to hunt for a place, Gordon had taken the first thing he recommended, and he obviously hadn't failed her. The co-op had a façade of elegant white stone, with Gothic carvings of gargoyles entwined around the porch, which led into a lobby of polished black granite with efficient, discreet 24-hour security. Rowena had four huge, high-ceilinged rooms with breathtaking views over Central Park, and she'd decorated them with a few small English watercolours and exquisite Georgian furniture. He nodded to himself, satisfied. No disgrace for Musica's youngest-ever MD to live somewhere like this.

'Holy shit,' he said as Rowena walked into the drawing room.

She was wearing a white chiffon gown by Ungaro, high-waisted in the Regency style and bias-cut in the skirt, so that it flowed around her, following every slight swing of her hips. The chiffon was studded with tiny fabric roses, complementing her classic peaches-and-cream complexion. Her blonde hair was swept up into a regal pile, secured by tiny ebony combs. Rubies glittered at her ears, throat and wrists, the dangling earrings in particular giving a sexy emphasis to the movement of her head and setting off her sparkling green eyes. Delicate pink satin heels peeped out from under her hem.

'Do you like it?' asked Rowena anxiously.

'You look unbelievable, toots,' said Oberman, with fatherly pride. 'Have a drink. You'll need it.'

'If you say so.' She smiled at him. What a sweetheart he was. She hoped she'd get the same reaction from the two people she was really dressing for: Michael Krebs and Topaz Rossi.

Topaz received her gold-embossed invitation at the office, just as she was winding up a particularly tough advertising deal for *Girlfriend*. She was one of only four people invited from American Magazines.

Mrs Alexander Martin requests the pleasure of Miss Rossi's company on Wednesday, 28 June, for a party in four acts.
The Victrix Hotel, 8.30 p.m.
Dress as you please.

She spent a fortnight agonizing over what to wear, and then decided that less was more and went for a Chanel sheath in light green silk with matching shoes. She wore her hair loose, and no make-up or jewellery of any kind. The dress let her figure speak for itself, hugging her curves like a second skin, and the sea-green colour lit up the deep cobalt of her eyes. It was a look to stop traffic.

Nathan Rosen, Marissa Matthews and Joe Goldstein were coming too, and since they were all ridiculously busy people, they met up in the limo.

Nathan was wearing a tux.

Joe was wearing a tux.

Marissa was wearing a golden creation in six layers of organza, laced with silver thread and covered head to foot in solid gold sequins. She had added a three-row pearl choker and sapphire and diamond bracelets.

'What's the matter, honey? Couldn't you at least have *hired* something to go in?' she asked as Topaz settled into the leather seat, furious because neither Nathan or Joe would stop stripping her with their eyes.

'I didn't realize it was a fancy-dress party, darling!' Topaz countered. 'How original of you to come as a Christmas tree!'

Nathan hastily turned a snort of laughter into a cough, and the limo eased smoothly away.

Rowena clutched on to her boss's arm, trying to catch her breath.

What was normally the ballroom of the Victrix Hotel, occupying the entire twenty-fourth floor, had been turned into a landscaped garden, with mossy turf laid down wall to wall and ancient-looking stone paving. To the right and left were orchards of orange trees in full blossom, delicately scenting the air. Footmen in full court livery paraded around with mahogany trays of caviar and truffles, and maids appeared and disappeared silently, ensuring that no glass was ever less than half full of vintage champagne. Tiny bells had been garlanded into the branches of the trees, filling the room with soft, delicious chimes. White peacocks wandered among the crowd.

And what a crowd! Rowena had passed Madonna on her way in, and then found that she and Josh were sharing an elevator with Arnold Schwarzenegger and Si Newhouse, mogul head of Condé Nast magazines. Oberman had had to edge past Henry Kissinger, deep in conversation with Henry Kravis, just to get Rowena some champagne.

'Come on, kid,' he said, seventy-two and unshakeable. 'I'll introduce you to a few people.'

For the next ten minutes Rowena Gordon, who lived and died for the record business, was catapulted straight to heaven.

'Ahmet Ertegun, Rowena Gordon.'

'Rowena, you haven't met Sylvia Rhone, have you?'

'Tommy Mottola. Clive Davis. Michelle Anthony. Joe Smith. Alain Levy.'

Rowena shook hands, suppressing the urge to curtsy.

'This is Rick Rubin,' said Josh, steering a huge man who looked like a bear towards her.

Dear God, thought Rowena, as she shook hands with the ultimate Heavy Metal prince, you can almost smell the testosterone. The guy's masculinity must walk into a room three paces in front of him.

'I like the rushes of that Atomic Mass record Krebs is working on,' growled Rubin. 'Word of mouth on that band is huge.'

'Yeah, they're great,' agreed Rowena, glowing with pride. 'I thought you did an awesome job on "Licensed to Ill".'

'Thanks,' said Rubin.

'Stop flirting with everybody, Rowena,' said Josh loudly, making her blush even worse.

'Get out of my face, Oberman,' said Rubin amiably.

'Oh my God, Batman and Robin,' said Oberman, grabbing a pair of guys who were walking their way. 'Hello, gentlemen, come say hi to Musica's new woman in New York. Rowena, say hello to Q-Prime, and then go sign me an act they can handle.'

Rowena was afraid she might drop her glass. If it was good and it used a guitar, Q-Prime represented it. *Sweet Jesus! The two most legendary managers in the world . . .*

'Hi, nice to meet you,' said Cliff Burnstein and Peter Mensch.

'How are you finding New York?' asked Burnstein, who basically didn't give a shit about anything and had turned up in a Metallica shirt and jeans.

'Er, it's very big,' muttered Rowena, her powers of conversation deserting her. They kindly agreed that it was indeed very big, and then launched into an animated discussion of the prospects for the Mets that season, finishing off each other's sentences.

'Do me a favour,' Oberman murmured to her after they'd moved away. 'Never, ever fuck with those guys.'

'I wasn't planning to, Josh.'

At the other end of the garden Topaz had also taken up residence on cloud nine, because Nathan had finally introduced her to Tina Brown, and the editor of *Glamour* had complimented her on *Girlfriend*.

'Excuse me, Marcelle,' simpered Marissa, dragging a highly reluctant Topaz away from the exquisitely dressed editor of British *Cosmopolitan*. 'Topaz, didn't you know Rowena Gordon when you were at school?'

'What about it?' snapped Topaz.

'Because she's right over there,' Marissa purred.

At that moment, Rowena happened to glance to her left, and froze, paralysed to the spot.

They had not laid eyes on each other for three years.

'Ladies and gentlemen,' announced a waiter. 'Dinner is served.'

Elizabeth Martin had outdone herself this time, everybody agreed. The menus announced 'Act II: A fairytale meal', and she had certainly delivered.

The dining hall looked like a missing chapter of *Charlie and the Chocolate Factory*. It seemed as if Alexander Martin must have bought the entirety of F. A. O. Schwarz to decorate it. The centrepiece of the room was a table for 200 people crafted out of hard-baked, solid gingerbread. Miniature trains ran round the table, laden with quails' eggs and celery salt in one carriage, Godiva chocolates in the next, and still more caviar in the third. Humanoid robots stumbled about, bearing various trays of drinks: champagne cocktails, fine wines, fresh pressed raspberry juice, even ready-mixed Long Island Ice Teas and Cokes in glass bottles. With a fine disregard for the seasons, various trophies of childhood festivals stood around; pumpkins complete with flickering candles and jagged smiles, fireworks for the Fourth of July, Easter eggs and chocolate bunnies, and Christmas trees everywhere, strung with tinsel and baubles and laden with gifts to which guests were expected to help themselves: Rolex watches, silver cufflinks, Hermès scarves, bottles of Joy and Chanel No. 5. You just didn't know where to look first.

'Fucking fantastic!' laughed Joe Goldstein, seated on one side of Topaz.

'Awesome!' agreed Nathan, and indeed all around them the movers and shakers of New York had started to laugh in wonder, smile and relax. Nobody had ever seen anything like it. You almost saw the pressures of the city lifting and the years evaporating. Normality was suspended.

As waiters dressed in penguin suits served them with starters of smoked salmon mousse or honey-glazed roast vegetables, guests started unwrapping the presents laid beside each individual place setting, parcels of various different shapes and sizes. A chorus of gasps arose amongst the delighted hubbub. Someone had spent a long time on the known preferences of each guest; Elizabeth had apparently cast herself as everyone's fairy godmother. Beside each plate was an object of desire longed for by the recipient, but never acquired.

'Oh my God,' said Topaz, delicately lifting the gauze off a letter to an academic written, and signed, by J. R. R. Tolkien.

'I don't believe it,' said Josh Oberman, pulling out a small Fabergé egg. 'It can't be what I think it is.'

'Look at *this*,' said Rowena in astonishment, holding up a first-pressing copy of the Def Leppard EP and a bootleg tape of the MC5.

'Look, Joe,' said Nathan Rosen, showing him his battered football with the autographs of the entire Giants team.

Silence descended on the room as people started to enjoy the food.

Topaz couldn't eat anything. She toyed with her meal, trying not to stare at Rowena. The force of her loathing gripped her inside her stomach, twisting her guts. God, she was just the same: English, cold, haughty. So stunningly beautiful, so perfectly tasteful. Rowena could wear as many rubies as she liked and carry it off, whereas Marissa just seemed vulgar. Look at her. She didn't give a damn about anybody or anything.

I worshipped you, you hateful bitch, Topaz thought, choked. I shared everything with you. And it obviously meant nothing to you.

She felt weak, she thought she might cry. The bitter pain of Rowena's treachery came flooding back, and the terrible hurt of betrayal by the only friend to whom she'd ever fully revealed herself; the hurt of Rowena, whom she'd totally trusted, teaching her that sisterhood was a sham, and that the only person in this life that Topaz Rossi would ever be able to believe in was herself.

Rowena sliced up her duckling breast, precisely and automatically. She was determined not to show how badly she felt, knowing Topaz Rossi's cruel blue eyes were boring into the back of her neck.

She had betrayed a friend. Cheated on her. Stolen her lover. And used her class and breeding to excuse herself – as her father had done to justify his own rejection of her. It was a system she had previously denounced as an archaic, imperialist British hangover, best forgotten.

But you used it against an Italian Yank when it suited you, accused a nagging little voice in her head.

Rowena shook her head, as though she could dispel the past. She hadn't given Topaz a second thought! Why should she be looking at her like this now? Water under the bridge, right? Christ, they were only kids at college.

Trust Topaz Rossi to get worked up about it.

Anger mingled with her guilt. That terrible *Cherwell* headline flashed in front of her.

Deliberately, Rowena pushed back her chair, and stood up, smoothing down her dress. The room was seriously overstocked with men, and at least thirty pairs of eyes followed the flow of the material over her breasts.

There was a tension in the air. The main course wasn't even finished. What was she doing?

'Sit down,' hissed Josh Oberman.

Rowena, apparently, could not hear her boss. She walked carefully over to where Topaz was sitting, and the other woman shot out of her chair to meet her.

Two places down, Marissa Matthews was ecstatic. Something was very wrong indeed, and very right for Friday's column. She strained to listen.

'It must be hell for you, Rowena,' said Topaz, in bitter, measured tones, 'having to break bread with all these ghastly colonials.'

'I see that you're doing well in American Magazines, Topaz,' said Rowena evenly, 'although I'm not surprised, since journalism is a profession where the scum usually rises to the top. Do you find a better class of interviewee to sleep with these days?'

'No wonder you're succeeding in the record business, Rowena,' answered Topaz, barely restraining her fury. 'So few women to get in your way, and you can contribute to the feminist agenda by promoting male heavy-metal bands. But then this sister was only ever doing it for herself, wasn't she?'

They stared at each other, constrained by the presence of the glittering crowd.

'This is my patch,' hissed Topaz.

'This *was* your patch,' spat Rowena.

There was a moment's hung silence. Then, slowly, both girls turned aside and returned to their seats.

Michael Krebs moved casually towards Rowena across the dance floor. He didn't enjoy dancing, but he did enjoy watching his beautiful woman whirl gracefully from the arms of one mogul to the next. Her intelligence and her poise were captivating the whole of New York. All of these men thought she was the ice queen. He knew better.

'Do you mind if I cut in?' he said to the deeply famous movie director, who was pissed-off because he wanted to get Rowena to consult on his project for the life and times of Led Zeppelin.

Rowena, who'd been searching for him all night, tried to stop herself melting into his arms with relief. Michael hated emotion. He demanded complete detachment. Maybe it took his mind off the wedding ring glinting on his left hand, she thought with renewed agony.

Krebs took her easily into the sedate rhythm of the waltz, one hand on the curve of her waist. He felt her body respond to his touch as if he'd given her an electric shock, and immediately his cock started to swell for her. The intensity of her lust was almost frightening. He knew he could get her wet just by looking into her eyes. It sent a flood of powerful joy through him, to do this to her. Her own sexuality had her in chains.

'You look lovely,' he told her quietly.

'Thank you, Michael,' said Rowena, determined to keep her cool. 'It's quite a party.'

'Yeah,' said Krebs, adding matter-of-factly, 'you'll meet me in the lobby downstairs in ten minutes. Don't excuse yourself to Joshua, just come downstairs.' Rowena felt the familiar convulsions of longing.

'I can't,' she murmured.

'You can and you will,' said Michael Krebs, and she looked at his determined brown eyes, and his wiry salt-and-pepper hair, and his beautiful, callous face, and knew she would do whatever he wanted.

'But the party –' she protested weakly.

'I know what happens now,' said Michael in her ear, 'so you won't have to stay to see. For Act Three, everyone goes downstairs to the fourteenth floor, which they've turned into a giant ice rink. Then for Act Four, everyone goes up to the roof garden and gets into a fleet of helicopters which ferry them to Alex Martin's private airstrip, and then two Gulfstream 4 jets take everybody out and back for six hours' dancing in the Florida Keys.'

'You're kidding,' breathed Rowena.

Krebs made an impatient movement with his hand. 'No, I'm not kidding. But I want to fuck you, so you're not going.'

He took another look at her in that cream-and-roses dress, the rubies sparkling round her long neck as she moved. She reverted to type, they all did, these aristocratic little rich girls playing around in business. She was a class piece, a European lady, the kind that he dreamt about in college but would have stammered in front of if he'd actually had to speak to her. Now he was everything she hoped to be; now, in this new universe where class counted for nothing, he was a lord and she was still a peasant.

Michael Krebs, twice Rowena Gordon's age, her mentor in business, her tutor in sex.

He splayed his fingers over her ribcage, feeling her slight involuntary squirm. He would have her like this, exactly like this. He wouldn't let her change a thing. He wanted to see this English lady in her fine clothes down on her knees with her mouth round his cock, with her warm soft lips and eager tongue working him so he could come in her mouth. That would be first. Then a little later, before he was even hard again, he'd make her take his limp prick in between her lips and hands and work him back up to erection, so he could put her on her hands and knees on a hotel bed, shove up that elegant chiffon and screw her from behind, just fuck all that British reserve right out of her. She'd have to please him like that. She'd have to earn her sex.

Topaz fastened her seatbelt as the Gulfstream soared into the skies above New Jersey. She'd got a second burst of energy now, even without the aid of the poppers and speed pills which most of the guests were on. Stewardesses in the navy uniform of Martin Oil moved up and down the spacious aisles of the private jet, presenting passengers with orchids, cigars and miniatures of cognac.

Marissa, orgasmic at the confrontation she was announcing to the world, had already phoned in her copy to 'Friday's People'.

Topaz knew it and she welcomed it. There would only be one winner in this war. New York was her turf, born and bred, and the stuck-up bitch would never survive. Everybody knew she hadn't even lasted this party, whereas, she, Topaz, had tied up two joint ventures and optioned a bestseller.

She tapped Joe Goldstein on the shoulder. He was an arrogant, sexist bastard, but she had a use for him.

'Yeah, Rossi,' he said, engrossed in his *Wall Street Journal.*

'Joe,' she asked, 'what do you hear about a rock band called Atomic Mass?'

Rowena gripped on to the edge of the mixing desk with one hand, her feet splayed against a Marshall stack, her other hand in her mouth, muffling herself.

Michael stood in between her legs, rocking his cock into her with perfect control, in and out, making her look at it as he fucked her. He felt her pussy rippling round him, young and tight and hot with pleasure. She was trembling on the brink of orgasm, mutely imploring him to push her over it.

'Absolutely,' he said into the phone. 'No, the second Atomic album, Josh, I'll make the time. Yeah, well, what can I tell you. Two per cent of nothing is nothing! Sure! You know I love doing business with you, Oberman, and with Rowena Gordon as well. She's a very good friend of mine. Yes, very talented.'

He could feel the insistent clutching of her belly, unable to resist him much longer.

'Well, I'll catch you later,' he said casually, and put the phone down.

He moved deeper into her. 'You like that, don't you?' he asked her conversationally. 'You like having me fuck you while I'm doing business.'

Rowena had her head back, and her eyes were wild. She couldn't speak. She made little choking noises, which he loved, as she gasped in ecstasy.

'God these rivers of passion,' he said. 'You're a slave to it, aren't you? Is this everything you dreamed it would be? Is it as good as you remember it?'

'Michael! Michael!' Rowena sobbed, abandoned utterly to pure desire. Krebs grinned to himself, as the pleasure in his own loins began to build. She was in New York for good. Now she belonged to him.

15

Topaz stood in front of her new bedroom window, looking across the Village.

The blue expanse above the warm red brick of the elegant townhouses shimmered, holding out the promise of another scorching day. She stared at the view below her, drawing strength from it. After all, she was a New Yorker now.

Like the city itself could help her stay on top of things.

She turned away from the window and padded towards her dressing room, across the lush blue carpeting of the bedroom, noting with satisfaction the Art Deco table, the Lalique lamps, the huge Moston bed with its silk sheets still rumpled from the way Nathan and she had christened it last night.

Nathan Rosen. Her lover. Her partner.

He'd been superb last night, probing, stroking, kissing her everywhere. Almost as good as the first few weeks they'd been lovers. And she was glad of that. She couldn't understand why Nathan wanted to take it slow. 'Let's pace ourselves.' 'Later.' 'Sweetheart, I'm beat right now.' He'd been like that for weeks.

Not that they hadn't made love. *Sometimes.*

Topaz adjusted the belt of her Yves St-Laurent silk gown, feeling it flow round her magnificent body like water. Her full breasts still thrust upwards despite their weight, tilting towards the sky with the confidence of youth.

She caught sight of her reflection in their full-length wall mirror, and pirouetted, pleased with that at least. No way she needed an uplift, Topaz thought. Although the second she did she was gonna get one. Why should she have sagging breasts, when she had plenty of money to ensure otherwise? Of course, Rowena Gordon would probably think plastic surgery was low-rent. Well, she could go fuck herself. This was America. Where pasty complexions and sexual repressions weren't something to be proud of.

Topaz shook her head, as if to dispel thoughts of Rowena. Time enough for that when she got into the office. Christ, she'd kept that anger bottled up for years. It could wait a few more hours.

Her Italian blood was raging for revenge. She still couldn't believe Rowena Gordon had had the chutzpah to actually get up in the middle of dinner and confront her. Of course she'd known Rowena would be there. Just like she knew she'd been posted to New York, and that her act Atomic Mass were being talked about all over knowing circles in the city.

British live sensation.

Michael Krebs producing. No fee. Just a piece of the action.

Five young boys with looks MTV would eat alive.

Debut single out this week.

If the rumours were true, Atomic Mass were about to burst on an unsuspecting world as the biggest new band since Nirvana.

Topaz made it her business to know these things. Somebody else might have sneered at the hype, dismissed it as gossip flavour-of-the-month stuff. But she remembered Rowena's passion for music – yeah, she remembered *everything* about Rowena. In those days, in the cloisters of Oxford, it had been the one rebellious trait in her personality. She'd had the elegant clothes, the social grace, the ever-present volume of medieval poetry or some other scrupulously academic book tucked under her arm. Rowena Gordon wouldn't have dreamt of relaxing with a Jackie Collins or a John Grisham. But her rock 'n' roll Rowena loved too much to hide, even for the sake of her precious image.

And Topaz wasn't about to underestimate her opponent. That was a mistake for amateurs. That was what Rowena Gordon did to Topaz Rossi, and was she ever going to pay for it.

I said I wasn't going to think about her now! Topaz lectured herself, and strolled into the kitchen. Light was streaming in from the windows and skylights, flooding the polished wood floor, the expensive oak table and the European Aga cooker, which Topaz had insisted on. In fact she'd insisted on the whole thing. Moving in together. Nathan selling his co-op. Her selling her chic single-girl's apartment. If they were going to be partners, she'd persuaded Nate, they ought to be *partners*. In love. Money. Everything.

And who could deny that it was a good move? she asked herself, setting up the coffee machine so Nate could get his fix when he came back from his early morning jog. Pooling their resources, they'd been able to buy a *house*, an actual house, in the middle of Manhattan! West 10th Street, prime Village property and very suitable for a media couple. And their place even had a garden. OK, so it was a tiny scrap of a garden, but in New York that was saying something.

Specifically, that was saying, *we are very rich.*

So? Topaz thought. They *were* rich. Who could deny it? Nathan was a director for American Magazines, and she was editor of *Girlfriend* and about to become editor of *Economic Monthly*.

Whatever Joe Goldstein thought.

Joe thrust again, twisting his hips a little, pushing himself deep into the pulsing heart of her, feeling for the hot, wet core that would send her crashing over the edge. The excitement in his cock seemed to feed through into his whole body, making his bloodstream sing as though it were liquid fire. He gently caressed her fine, pointed breasts, taking the swollen nipples into his mouth and circling each of them with his tongue, then sucking them, while she moaned and gasped with delight, making those small guttural sounds in the back of her throat that turned him on even more. They rolled over and she was on top, her dyed blonde hair tumbling round her face, eyes still closed in bliss. He hadn't missed a beat.

Joe pushed up her breasts in his hands, more urgently now, feeling the first tremors of orgasm start to build. The ecstatic expression on Lisa's face had triggered it; he took pleasure in the woman's pleasure, always making sure they came several times, always leaving them hungry for more.

On automatic pilot he gathered himself for the final seconds and plunged deep, deep inside her, hitting the g-spot, the little tender melting spot on the wall of the vagina, the place some sexologists and most women swore didn't exist. But not the ones who'd slept with Joe Goldstein.

Well, it had taken men a while to discover the clitoris, Joe reckoned. They'd get round to the g-spot eventually.

Of course, it helped to be a connoisseur of women.

Of course, it helped to have a twelve-inch cock.

'*Joe!*' Lisa screamed, her entire, perfectly flat belly visibly rippling with the force of her convulsions. 'Joe! Joe! Oh, my God!'

'Lisa,' he breathed, feeling his orgasm tear through him and explode inside her.

They were immobile for a few seconds, gasping for breath, recovering.

'Jesus Christ, you are the best,' she said, rolling off him and pushing the damp hair out of her eyes.

'You're something special yourself,' replied Joe automatically. 'You always were.'

She got up and sauntered towards the shower, displaying a firm, full body, with nice breasts and legs, maybe a little chunky around the hips, and sassy, uneven blonde hair with the roots showing. Joe and Lisa had screwed on and off for years. She was married in name only to a Wall Street financier who could rarely get it up, and she was as careful in choosing her lovers as Joe was in choosing his: no involvement, no commitment, and plenty to offer in the sack. Lisa Foster was a sensualist, but she was also a materialist. She didn't want to take any risks. And neither did Joe.

'Baby, you could fuck for World Champion,' was her parting comment to him as she left, wrapped in a garish pink Ungaro suit.

Joe smiled and kissed her hand. He liked Lisa. Girls like her were worth missing sleep for. They were easy to please and fun to screw, and they didn't insist on beating you up with a big feminist stick. She didn't want to debate the difference between men and women for five hours, she just wanted to enjoy it. He supposed Topaz Rossi would despise a girl like Lisa. Living off her husband's money, or whatever it was she'd say.

Goldstein lit a cigarette, annoyed. Even thinking about that woman ruined his good mood. He wandered into the kitchen, spread a couple of bagels thickly with cream cheese and put on a fresh pot of coffee, switching on his IBM. The notes for his presentation to the board flashed up on the screen, the speech amusing, well paced and lucid.

That made him feel better. The speech was a killer. It should nail *Economic Monthly*, if it hadn't been nailed before. The title had his name on it anyway – a serious new monthly: glossy, upmarket, aimed at men. He ran three magazines just like it for American Magazines already, and he ran them very successfully. And it wasn't just the circulation of his own titles that he had to offer the group. Since the time he'd been at Wharton and discovered by Nate Rosen, he'd been using his *cum laude* MBA to American's advantage, submitting cost-cutting proposals, helping to review supplier contracts, helping out on acquisition titles.

Goldstein was more than a hotshot editor. He was a businessman. And he saw *Economic Monthly* as a direct leap to the board.

Topaz Rossi! What made her a goddamn candidate? OK, so after a couple of weeks at American's New York offices he realized he'd been wrong about her, at least at first. She was a very talented journalist, dynamite columnist, had been a good features editor at *US Woman* and had done wonders for the circulation of *Girlfriend*. Fair enough, she had more going for her than her physical charms. But still, the girl was in charge of only one magazine. Aimed at teenage girls. And she had no corporate or business experience at all – well, a little MBA work at night school, big deal. God, she'd never been within a mile of running a high-profile men's magazine.

So why am I letting her get to me? thought Joe angrily. I'm gonna *cream* her over *Economic Monthly*. And that's all. End of story.

But it wasn't.

Topaz Rossi was under Joe Goldstein's skin, and he didn't like it. She annoyed him and she bothered him and she made him mad. Usually, when he met a woman he couldn't stand, he put her out of his mind. He had better things to do. Annoyance was a futile, pointless emotion, and Joe Goldstein didn't indulge in time-wasting.

But Rossi refused to get out of his mind.

Maybe it was the harsh feminism, but he met a lot of feminists. Maybe it was her personality. That brash, bold, in-your-face way Topaz had about her. She seemed to be everywhere he went, shouting encouragement to the *Girlfriend* staffers, carrying great stacks of layouts past his office to her own, greeting everybody in the goddamn building like they were her bosom buddies. And it seemed most of them were, which made it worse. In meetings, she was polite and courteous to him, but that was as far as it went. She was curt. Blunt. Almost dismissive of him. In the LA bureau where Goldstein had been operating, people compromised from time to time to let something get done. Not Ms Rossi, though. 'Compromise' was not in her dictionary. That girl would argue for two hours rather than concede *anything*.

She was fucking *relentless*.

Maybe it was her dress sense, Joe thought, moving back into the kitchen to finish off his bagel. He glanced at his Rolex. Eight forty. He'd have to get a move on; lucky the Brooks Brothers suit was already pressed and ready to go, the white shirt hanging on the back of his closet. Yeah, her dress sense. Totally inappropriate for the working environment, he thought severely. Always showing off her figure. Bright colours. Designer names. Rich fabrics. By rights, she should come over as vulgar, but her innate self-confidence and sense of style enabled her to carry it off. He'd never met another redhead who could wear a shocking-pink suit by Vivienne Westwood and get away with it. It was just so – so – off-putting, this bold, brassy, ballsy Italian girl storming round the place like an ongoing nuclear explosion.

Joe dressed quickly, without fuss or undue worries about his reflection. He never thought about that stuff.

Of course, he'd fantasized about Topaz. Or tried to. Hell, she was awesomely beautiful and she had the best body he'd seen outside the covers of *Playboy*.

But something was wrong with that picture. Every time he tried to imagine her naked on a rug, he found himself remembering something annoying about her, like the last time she'd shaken his hand at an editors' meeting with all the warmth of your average iceberg.

He ran off a new copy of his speech notes and put them in his custom-made briefcase. No time to think about that now. There was only one day to go before the board got to pick the first editor of *Economic Monthly*.

Joe Goldstein had worked hard on the construction of his speech for this presentation, harder than he'd worked on anything for some time. Possibly he was being underconfident. After all, he was meant to be a dead cert for this job.

But he wanted to polish this speech till it gleamed.

There was no way he was gonna lose out to Topaz Rossi.

'I wanted to break it to you myself,' Josh Oberman said, spearing a stuffed mushroom with vigour.

He was meeting Rowena Gordon for breakfast at the Pierre. When back in New York on business, Oberman always stayed at the Pierre and he always had the same suite. He knew what he liked. Elegant décor, impeccable service and a nice view of Central Park. The Royalton or the Paramount were the music-industry hotels of choice right now, with their futuristically equipped rooms and ultra-hip atmosphere, but Joshua Oberman sneered at that. Hotels were somewhere you slept when you were doing business. Period. He couldn't give a damn about how good-looking the bellboys were.

'Break what to me, boss?' Rowena asked, picking at her fruit salad. The New York body fascism was already starting to get to her, but she didn't mind. How could she? Her slim, naturally blonde figure seemed to be the American ideal. And she wanted to be perfect for Michael, absolutely perfect. Her desire for him was fast becoming obsession.

'The reaction Warners had to the first Atomic Mass single,' Josh said gravely.

Rowena stiffened, little prickles of fear rising on the nape of her neck. Warners were going to distribute the first Atomic record in the States, just like they packaged, shipped and sold all the Musica records out here. Rowena's little talent-scout outpost of a label notwithstanding, the company had no real presence in America. So they did a deal with a major, like every other semi-independent, and took a royalty payment on each of their CDs sold out here.

So if Warners hated the single, forget it. Her band were sunk.

'What reaction?' she demanded. ' "Karla" is brilliant! It's *brilliant*! How could they not love it?'

Josh let her hang for a second, savouring the moment. He admired her outfit again, a shaped black suit by Anna Sui, legs tapering down in sheerest black nylon to stack-heeled mules from Chanel. Her long hair, shaped with a soft new fringe at the front and precision cut at the back, swung behind her like a shining golden curtain.

'Relax,' he said. 'They did love it. More than that, even.'

Rowena leant back in her chair, feeling relief flood through her. She smiled at her boss. Capricious old bastard! She shouldn't have risen to it like that, but any teasing about Atomic Mass hit straight home. The first single was about to be released, the record was nearly done, and everyone connected with the band was wound up as tight as a bedspring.

The boys themselves, naturally, were completely at their ease, just glad to be wrapping up *Heat Street* and going back on the road. And they were still getting to know New York. The bars. The clubs. And the women. *Especially* the women. Christ, they weren't even known here yet, and they were getting snowed under with girls. She'd never seen anything like it. No, the band weren't uptight, the band were in seventh bloody heaven.

'I wish I could draw you a picture of Bob Morgado's face when he heard it,' Oberman said, smiling broadly at the memory. 'Oh, they thought Christmas came early this year. If the rest of the album matches up to "Karla", we're looking at the top of the priority list.'

He attacked his cheese omelette, cackling. 'Know how I really know they loved it?' he asked. 'They wanted to renew the Atomic contract. Separate from the general Musica deal. I guess they must realize we plan to get our own distribution going sooner rather than later, and they still want a piece of Atomic Mass.'

'What did you tell them?' Rowena demanded.

'I said we'd think about it. Depending on how good a job they do with *Heat Street*,' Oberman grinned, thoroughly pleased with himself. 'And how are you settling in, kid?'

'Oh, fine,' said Rowena vaguely. She wasn't about to belabour her boss with her business problems. The office. The overwork. The commercial fucking Siberia she found herself in as a lone gun.

Fix it first, talk about it later.

'Good. Haven't seen you since you ducked out of Elizabeth Martin's party – without saying goodbye,' Oberman added severely. 'No, don't give me whatever excuse you're desperately trying to cook up. You don't want to jet to Florida, it's your problem. Who was that woman you were catting with at the dinner, Rowena? The stunning redhead? Is it something I should be concerned about?'

'She's nobody. A magazine executive I didn't get on too well with at Oxford, that's all,' answered Rowena, her tone going cold. She resented Topaz shoving herself into a conversation she was having with Joshua Oberman. Josh was her mentor. Josh was sacred.

Oberman lifted his fork, warning her. 'Babe,' he said, 'nobody at that party was nobody.'

The sixtieth floor of the American Magazines tower on Seventh Avenue was pleasantly cool, despite the blazing sun that streamed into it through the glass walls in every director's office. Lower floors in the building were at their normal, mind-melting level, but not this one. The board had the benefit of the latest Japanese air-conditioning systems, silent and effective, so that they could run America's second-largest magazine empire with total concentration, the freezing winters and baking summers of New York being totally immaterial.

Indeed, to the unwary visitor used only to the rest of the building – editors barking orders, reporters yelling into phones, computers and printers clattering, photocopiers whirring and the rest – the sixtieth floor could seem like another planet. Chaos and bleeping phones and mundane things like deadlines seemed miles away from the calm, almost churchlike tranquillity of the executive floor.

Nathan Rosen, the company's young director, East Coast – a mere forty-one years old – sometimes missed the constant hustle of actual magazine offices. But not often. He'd been working up to his current position all his life. He was ready for the big picture work now – acquisitions, sales, disposals. It *was* busy up here. It was just that you'd never know it.

At least, Topaz Rossi didn't seem to know it.

'I can't talk,' Nathan protested. 'Not today.' He gave a small shrug, the tightness of his movement betraying his annoyance. 'You and Joe are presenting *tomorrow*, Topaz, for Christ's sake.'

'Why does that matter? I know you'll be objective,' Topaz said, moving towards him.

She knew she shouldn't be here. But she couldn't help it. Some innate desire to tease her lover had proved too strong to resist. She loved seeing his face like that, taut with anger and impatience, as though he despaired of her. Topaz knew it reminded him of the difference in their ages, and she played on that mercilessly. Making him do things he'd sworn not to do. Forcing him to consider all the taboos he was breaking with her. Forcing him to remember *why* he was breaking them.

Anything to provoke.

Anything to arouse.

Anything to help his passion, his vitality, match up to hers.

Nathan leant across his desk and took her head in his hands, gazing at the soft, tanned skin, the sparkling blue eyes, the wild red hair. She'd picked out a short Mark Eisen suit in bright yellow, set with pretty enamel buttons shaped like large daisies. She was wearing some fresh, summery perfume – Chanel No. 19, he thought. She was sensational.

Rosen pressed his lips down on hers, her riot of colour muted by the sober navy of his Savile Row suit. 'Think Jewish, dress British.' One of the only pieces of advice his father had bothered to give him, and pretty good advice too, Rosen had always thought.

He pushed his tongue into her mouth, enjoying her instant response, enjoying her surprise.

The young are so arrogant, Rosen mused.

'Now get out of here,' he said firmly as he pulled off her. 'You've got work to do, Ms Rossi. Didn't you tell me this morning that you were planning a piece on that new girl over at Musica Records? The one who's just set up here? I thought you were hot on doing some kind of exposé for *US Woman*. She's got quite a reputation already, this girl. What's her name again?'

'Rowena Gordon,' said Topaz, drawing back from him. Her face had taken on a new hardness. 'But she's not important. It's the band I'm interested in. There has to be a story there.'

Nathan looked up. Interesting. Now she was fidgeting, couldn't wait to get back downstairs. He sighed. The girl was a mystery to him.

'OK, good,' he said curtly. 'Atomic Mass, isn't that their name? Joe told me you were digging around them, now I come to think of it. Should make a good story. The rumours about them are wild. Apparently they're the next –'

'I know,' she said shortly.

He smiled at her. She was crazy and mixed up, but he adored her.

'I'll see you tonight,' Nathan said, as she turned to go. 'I love you. And by the way, Rowena Gordon *is* important, Topaz. If she makes something of this new company, she'll be in a very powerful position.'

Thursday, 6 July dawned muggy and overcast. Grey skies loomed over the city, hardly dissipating the heat that seemed to steam up from the crowded sidewalks and logjammed roads.

The two candidates for editor of American Magazines' new upmarket glossy, *Economic Monthly*, rode the elevator to the boardroom on the fifty-ninth floor, one floor down from Gowers' glass cradle of power. Both were wearing suits and immaculately groomed, but Joe Goldstein looked by far the more confident and relaxed.

He was carrying a large canvas folder containing charts and statistics for his presentation. It was an understandable, witty and highly expert summary of macroeconomic conditions, designed to demonstrate once and for all how suitable he was to edit this title – if his existing magazines hadn't already established that beyond doubt.

He glanced at Topaz, who'd come armed with nothing at all. She was nervously tapping one hand against her thigh.

Joe hardened his heart. Little girls that bite off more than they can chew get hurt; if Topaz Rossi insisted on playing out of her league, she was just going to have to learn her lesson the hard way.

He looked her over again, surreptitiously.

He'd been right about that cute ass, though.

The senior committee watched Joe Goldstein giving the most polished, urbane performance of his life. They were fascinated, laughing and nodding from time to time. Nate Rosen glanced at the papers of the man seated next to him; he'd made a note to call his broker.

Actually, Nate thought Goldstein was being pretty gracious about this. He was paying Topaz the compliment of giving it his best shot, not just showing up to have management rubber-stamp a decision which was basically already made.

He glanced at Topaz, sitting in a chair against the far wall, watching Joe with polite attentiveness. She was dressed soberly – navy Dior, rebellious red curls swept back in a severe bun – and she seemed anxious. Rosen felt a pang. He wanted to comfort her, to tell her it didn't matter, that she was only twenty-three, there'd be plenty more titles for her later. He noticed the way her full breasts rose and fell as she breathed, pushing against the stiff linen of her jacket. He wanted her.

Nathan turned resolutely back to Joe, embarrassed. He was supposed to be concentrating. Damn it, this whole situation was his fault. His judgment wasn't sober or impartial, not these days. He veered too far one way, then too far the other. This so-called contest for *Economic Monthly*, for example. It was one instance where he thought she was totally off-track competing for it and Matt Gowers was just trying to look liberated by fielding a woman candidate. But it was his fault too. He had endorsed her for it, when she'd insisted on trying out. He'd sat there in the chairman's office and told his boss it was between Joe and Topaz.

Who was he trying to kid? Joe was always going to destroy her, and now here he was, destroying her right on cue. He, Rosen, both as Topaz's lover and her boss, should have been cruel to be kind and refused to put her name forward. Now his own judgment would be called into question.

But that was his mistake, his error. And he'd been making Topaz pay for it. Coming down on her like a ton of bricks in the editors' meetings. Cutting her dead in front of their colleagues.

' . . . if it's dinars or dollars,' Goldstein concluded to warm laughter and applause, and walked over to the chair next to Topaz, offering his hand to her as he sat down. She shook it briskly, avoiding eye contact with him, murmuring congratulations. The board at the table in front of them had their heads down scribbling brief comments on their sheets of paper. But it was obvious from the genial smiles on their faces what they thought.

He did look terrific up there, Topaz admitted to herself. Absolutely terrific. It's a shame he's such a jerk, because that is one handsome, self-possessed sonofabitch.

'And now,' said the presiding secretary, 'the board will hear Ms Topaz Rossi, editor of *Girlfriend* magazine and still a journalistic contributor to many of our other titles. Ms Rossi, if you please.'

Topaz got to her feet and regarded the seven pairs of eyes looking at her with little more than polite interest.

'Mr Goldstein's presentation was the best, and the funniest, piece of economic analysis I think I've ever heard,' she began in a clear voice. 'And if he were applying for the job of chief correspondent or senior features writer, I would give it to him without hesitation.'

She paused.

'But it isn't the editor's job to write the magazine. I had dinner with Mr Goldstein last month, and I admitted to him then that I was no expert in economics. I said that I *was* an expert in selling magazines. And that's still true.'

The seven pairs of eyes now looked considerably more interested.

'The job of editor – the *editor*, mind you – at *Economic Monthly* will not be to explain the General Agreement on Tariffs and Trade. It will be to take advertising and circulation away from *The Economist, Forbes, Fortune* and *Business Week.* And this is how I would do that.'

'*Holy Shit!* thought Nathan Rosen.

The board watched her, riveted.

16

The public rivalry started with Marissa Matthews' column, 'Friday's People', published two weeks after the party.

Seeing Topaz with Nathan as a couple in public, and hearing what had happened at the *Economic Monthly* pitch, Marissa didn't pull any punches. On either of them.

Catfight at the most important party of the year . . . Musica Records executive embarrassing her boss . . . Fiery redhead Topaz Rossi . . . innuendo about 'sleeping with interviewees' . . . do we remember the mysterious David Levine exclusive? . . . Watch out, Manhattan, here come the Career Girls!

'Ridiculous!' said Topaz, annoyed. She flung the paper on to the kitchen table and dialled Marissa Matthews at home. 'What do you mean by this?' she demanded.

'Who is it, please?' purred Matthews, as if she didn't know.

'It's Topaz Rossi,' replied Topaz, furious.

'Darling!' Marissa crooned. 'Are you a little bit upset about the column?'

'Marissa, I –'

'Journalistic integrity, sweetie. You, of all people, should understand that. I mean, just look what you did to that ravishing film star.'

'He was a woman-beater!' Topaz snapped, incensed at the comparison.

'Well, darling, I haven't ruined your career, now have I? It's simply the truth that you and your friend did make a scene at dear Elizabeth's party, and it was so very dramatic! All that wonderful stuff about territory, and sleeping with people to get interviews! Not that I *personally* believe it, of course, but one always wondered how you got that story . . . it did kick-start your career in the most fabulous way, and I *do* have a duty to my readers.'

She paused, then repeated with relish, 'To my many *millions* of readers, especially in New York – I mean, sweetie, anyone who is anyone in this town reads . . .'

Topaz slammed the phone down on her in disgust.

'I think it's funny,' Michael Krebs told her. 'It's a hell of a way to announce your arrival, though. You have some kind of history with this girl?'

'I don't want to talk about it,' Rowena answered wearily. Her phone had been going all day from reporters wanting to run a 'Rivals' story in various magazines.

Krebs nodded. A story like this was bad news.

'Did Oberman have anything to say?'

'Yes he did,' she said shortly. Her chairman had the 'Friday's People' column faxed to him every week, and was none too pleased to see his newly appointed MD starring in what was described as a bitch-fight during the most important social event of the year. He'd given her a lecture on businesslike conduct, ending up with 'You know what, Rowena? A lot of people in this industry don't like me putting a woman in charge. Don't make it harder for me by giving them ammunition.'

She had burned with shame at the rebuke, more so because he was right.

'Forget about it,' Krebs told her. 'You've got enough to do setting up this label. I know it's been tough.'

'It has. It is,' she said, under pressure and anxious.

'I could help,' Michael offered, brushing her hair out of her eyes. She felt the cool metal of his wedding ring against her temple.

'It's my problem. I'll handle it,' Rowena said, but already part of her was wondering if she could.

BOOM! Atomic Mass were everywhere. And that meant *everywhere.*

Displays in the store windows. Ads in the music magazines. Billboards across the city, cleverly designed to show a picture of the boys, slouching together against a wall and looking meanly at the cameras, like five long-haired versions of James Dean. The one-word strapline at the base of the posters said simply: COMING.

MTV had an exclusive right to show the video, and it was making good use of it. God, sometimes heavy rotation means *heavy rotation,* Rowena thought, delighted, as she switched on yet again and found it pumping away.

Zach Freeman, holding his guitar like an offensive weapon.

Alex Sexton, strumming hard at the bass and checking out the girls in the front, cute pieces of jailbait with the darkly kohled eyes that were in fashion amongst the alternative music crowd right now. Despite the perfect street-cred calling cards, the camera showed all the women in a very old-fashioned state of high sexual excitement.

Mark Thomas attacking his drumkit like it just insulted his mother. Pan to shots of guys in the audience, screaming approval and hurling themselves into a raging mosh-pit.

Jake Williams, rhythm guitarist, grinding out a swing that you wouldn't believe.

And Joe Hunter, lead singer, six foot three of Lancashire muscle, with his tumbling brown hair and handsome, slightly slanted eyes, taking total control of the stage, prowling like a wild panther, all his youth and inexperience counting for nothing. He didn't need experience.

He was a natural.

He was a star.

'But is it on the radio? We need airplay,' Josh fretted, ringing her the first day Warners had released the track to radio.

'Oberman,' his new managing director soothed him, 'it's on the radio. It's on the playlist for every Top Forty station in New York. The song is a fucking phenomenon.'

'Is it getting out to the other markets? Dallas, LA, Chicago, Minnesota?' Josh asked the next day. 'Warners swear it is. But they would. You tell me.'

'It's breaking out like a rash. Like it was contagious,' Rowena assured him.

'You know what? This business is going to rot your brain,' he told her. 'Forget that Oxford education, your vocabulary is about to contract into two sentences – "It's a hit." "It's not a hit."'

'This,' said Rowena firmly, 'is a hit.'

Oberman laughed, his grating roar reaching across the Atlantic, rich with satisfaction. 'I think you might be right,' he said. 'That bastard Krebs! I thought he was doing us a favour, but he was just spotting talent. Now he gets five per cent off the top. Sonofabitch! I've known the guy for long enough, I should have guessed.'

Rowena couldn't resist it. 'If you'd come up with a million five in the first place,' she pointed out, 'we wouldn't be getting royally screwed now. Anyway, why *did* you tell me to go and get Michael Krebs for a hundred and fifty thousand dollars? You must have known that was never gonna happen.'

'I did,' Oberman admitted. 'I dunno, kid, it was an impulse. I wanted to send you in to get him with your back against the wall. See what you'd come up with. I had a sense that you two would be good together, and I wanted him to get interested in you. With the right amount of money, you'd have been just another client to him. And Atomic Mass would have been just another band.'

Rowena put the phone down, feeling yet again that Josh Oberman was one of the most cunning, knowing men alive. How well he'd understood Michael Krebs. How well he'd understood *her*.

And the rise of Atomic Mass continued at full force.

Barbara Lincoln had flown over and checked into the Paramount and Rowena was to meet her there every morning to begin the promotional round. Officially, it was none of her business. Rowena worked for Musica, and until they built up a distribution network Atomic Mass's label in the States was Elektra. But Barbara and the band insisted, so that was that. Rowena, and usually Michael Krebs, too, piled into the limo with the guys as they headed off to the Warners building to start the day's round of interviews, photoshoots and radio phone-ins.

She had no time to attend to the new label. Forget that, Rowena thought. It'll wait.

'Hey, Rowena! How's it going?' Barbara asked her, kissing her on the cheek. She admired the burgundy Donna Karan tunic, the Charles David pumps, the silk hose from Wolford's. 'You look terrific.'

'So do you,' her friend said, returning the kiss and the admiring glance. Barbara was dressed in a silk slip Armani dress, complete with beaded straps, Italian heels and a Hermès scarf. Every day she turned up in something impossibly glamorous and totally impractical. Barbara made no concessions to minor matters like the dirt of Manhattan or the fact that all the Warners people wore jeans.

Let's face it, Rowena thought, smiling. Barbara makes no concessions to anything.

'It's the only reason we're working with you,' Mark teased them. 'Can't be surrounded by anything except beautiful women now. Bad for our image.'

'Our image! You fucking prat,' Joe snarled, pushing his drummer in the shoulder.

'Hangover?' asked Krebs, who was sitting directly across from Rowena in the limo. He'd nodded curtly at her as she got in the car, and that was about it. Michael was super-cautious these days. The old gushing about her talents had gone completely, and since she'd arrived in New York he had scarcely complimented her publicly. Rowena had been forced to point out to him that unless he acknowledged that they were at least friends, everyone would assume they were having an affair. You don't go from red-hot to ice-cold without a good reason. God, men were so stupid. Especially the smart ones.

Joe nodded, grimacing. 'Went down to Continental Divide. I was on shorts all night.'

'You'll pay,' said Michael, like a stern father.

The singer shrugged as their limo pulled smoothly away into the traffic. 'What he doesn't say is that he was up all night with these three girls who –'

'Zach!' Krebs warned sharply, glancing at their manager, but the guitarist grinned.

'Barbara don't give a fuck about that,' he said, quite accurately.

She nodded, smiling at the producer with elegant indifference. Rowena marvelled at how changed she was. Just a few months looking after a rock band, and Barbara already understood the first instinctive rules. Like, you don't mess with your act's sex life.

'They can do what they like. They're not old married men like you, Michael,' Barbara said. *And even so I wouldn't give a fuck*, her tone implied.

Krebs grunted.

When the band and Barbara had got deep into a discussion of promotion for the album launch, he finally looked over at Rowena. Cute dress. She looked like a schoolgirl in that dress. Michael felt himself getting aroused. He was disturbed, he'd planned on giving her up by now. Any longer and something must surely slip, she'd tell Barbara, she'd mention something to Josh, the band would pick up on it. There was no way he could risk Debbie finding out.

He loved his wife, and he lived for his sons. The family. It was the most important thing in life, Michael always said. His own parents had provided for him, but little more; to this day he resented them for it. Ten thousand dollars' worth of therapy swore his control-freak tendencies came directly from that. And Michael thought it was true. He could remember deciding that if that was the way it was gonna be, then he was going to be in full control. Permanently.

Maybe that was the lure of Rowena Gordon, Krebs thought, letting his dark gaze travel slowly up those slender calves, to the shadow under the fall of her skirt, and then further up, as if he could see through the darkness through sheer force of will, please himself by gazing at those pale, supple thighs and the delights that lay between them. There had been many women, some more beautiful, more skilled in bed than Rowena. But few so intelligent as she was. Michael Krebs, like many Jewish men, prized intelligence in everyone, including women. It didn't scare him off, it attracted him. Amongst other things it meant that Rowena came to him with her eyes open, having understood the hopelessness of her position, but coming to his bed anyway. And maybe that was the lure. His complete control over her.

I love my wife. I've been a good father to my sons, better than my father was to me, Krebs thought, and then Rowena shifted in her seat and caught him staring at her. He watched her instant reaction, the lips parting, the blood rushing to the face, her green eyes glancing at him, then away again, pretending to watch midtown Manhattan through the limo's tinted windows. His cock hardened in his pants. Bang, just like that. He had her again.

The band and Barbara were still jabbering away at each other.

'Rowena,' Michael said softly. Her name, a command.

She looked at him, her thighs flaming from the feeling that he'd been looking at her, thinking about her, reminding himself of the last things they'd done together. Lust started to lick at her. It had been four days ago, just before the release of the record. Michael had taken her to her apartment on West 67th and made her undress for him in her bedroom, removing her clothes exactly as he instructed. He had been excruciatingly slow, making her wait, turn and move as he directed, so that by the time she was naked Rowena was so aroused she could hardly stand up. Krebs had sat there, fully clothed, his erection clearly visible under his jeans, and made her just stand before him, naked, while he talked to her about what he was going to do with her and how, getting Rowena hotter and hotter, until she was weeping with sheer desire, but he'd still made her stand there. She remembered how the combination of being so exposed in front of a clothed man, and what he was saying, and her submission to him, had brought her so close to the brink that when Krebs stood up and came across to her, still not touching her, and had very deliberately walked round her, staring at the whole of her body, her ass, her breasts, her legs, and finally let his gaze trail obviously and slowly between her legs, Rowena's haunches had shuddered in an uncontrollable movement and she'd climaxed, coming for Michael Krebs when he hadn't even laid a finger on her.

'Yes, Michael?' she replied now, the coolness of her tone belying the wild heat in her belly.

What's wrong with me? Rowena thought. I can't even be near the guy without melting all over the seat.

Krebs smiled, his liquid brown eyes refusing to accept her outward calm. 'Wanna have lunch?' he asked casually. 'I can play you the final mixes for the b-sides.'

'Sure,' Rowena said, anticipation oozing from every pore.

Oh, love was a drug. It made you higher than acid or ecstasy or anything. Michael, Michael, the universe itself was less important than his smile, he was the first thing she thought of when she woke in the mornings and the last image in her mind at night. There was the trial of setting up the label. The triumph of watching Atomic Mass break. The danger of Topaz Rossi, something Rowena sensed, feared, and knew she'd have to deal with.

But over that and above it was Michael Krebs, and the heady, maddening passion Rowena felt for him. Love. Like a fine, golden mist, settling over everything. Informing everything she did. The backdrop to life. *What will Krebs think? When can I tell him? What would Michael do? Where is he now?*

Yes, she knew he was married.

Yes, she knew he had children.

Yes, she knew it was wrong.

But Rowena Gordon didn't care. She was in love, in that rare, complete thraldom that true first love demands. Anyone who has ever experienced it knows exactly what it's like. Rowena, as she sat in that car, looking at her married lover, was prepared to sacrifice anything and everything in order to keep him around. Her pride. Her heart. Her principles. Her honour.

'It's your turn, I think,' Michael said, holding her in their private conversation, locking her gaze in his.

'To buy lunch? Yeah, I think so too,' Rowena agreed, inflecting her tone with just that subtle shade of extra meaning Michael had used.

They both knew what he meant. That Michael had pleasured Rowena the last time they met, and it was her turn now. She would do what he loved, sweeping her long, fine hair across his body so it teased him with millions of featherlight strokes, then moving down with her lips and her tongue until she reached his groin, then teasing the wiry grey hairs around the flat of his stomach, circling the base of his cock until he couldn't stand it any more, and grabbed her head by the hair, insistently pushing her down on him. Sometimes Rowena licked him first, the tip of her tongue running round the tip of his cock, flicking at the sensitive little triangle just under the crown, and then when the pleasure got too much for him to bear without coming, moving down to the base again, then holding him hard and wet in her hands, using her fingers and tongue to bring him to a crashing orgasm. Other times, she simply responded by taking him deep, deep into her mouth, carefully angling his thickness so it got to the very back of her throat. Michael could only take a little of that before he came, erupting into her with a groan of satisfaction, staggered at how incredible it felt to see this girl swallow him whole. She was so good at sucking cock, he thought he'd died and gone to heaven. And she loved it. That was what truly aroused Michael so much that sometimes he woke up in the night, next to his wife, with a raging hard-on for Rowena that refused to go away. Other women would either refuse or grudgingly agree to it, as a special favour to their men. You could order a groupie to do what you liked, of course. But that was quid pro quo. Rowena was so into Michael, so wild with lust for him, that she *fantasized* about doing it to him. She begged for it. And he'd never known *anything* – not on tour, not with girlfriends, not with his wife – like the rapture he felt when Rowena Gordon was kneeling in front of him, her long blonde hair halfway down her back, her little bud nipples erect, giving him head, her eyes closed in sexual frenzy, making those tiny choking sounds at the back of her throat that drove him fucking crazy, as he rammed himself into her, roughly, forcing her to take it all in, asking her how he tasted, if she wanted more, if she loved it. Once she'd even reached up blindly, groping for his hands, and he hadn't known what she wanted until with a fresh rush of sex he understood she was putting them on the back of her head, asking for it harder, deeper, more.

Michael felt his hard-on swelling.

Rowena saw it.

A conspiratorial look passed between them, shared desire, shared annoyance at being in company, shared helplessness to do anything about it. And then Rowena grinned, and Krebs winked at her, and they felt a huge surge of affection and friendship, on top of the desire.

Christ, I like *him so much*, Rowena marvelled.

That girl is terrific, Michael thought.

The limo purred to a halt outside the Warners offices, and as it did so, a small crew of photographers ran forward, poised to snap pictures of the band.

'Get used to it, guys,' Barbara said, glancing at her producer and A&R girl with evident satisfaction. 'You'll need to.'

HEAT STREET – OUT NEXT WEEK, screamed the banner ads.

New British Invasion? asked *RIP* magazine, giving a picture of Joe space on the cover.

Oh, You Pretty Things, cooed the *Village Voice*.

'What's heavy metal got that rap and country don't?' asked *Rolling Stone*. 'Precious little, if recent sales are anything to go by. Except, of course, metal can lay claim to Atomic Mass, a new band from England who are causing a sensation on MTV with "Karla", the first single on their Krebs-produced debut *Heat Street*, out on Warners next week. Playing music brutal enough to appeal to fans of early Metallica, and good-looking enough to steal young girls from the teenybop bands, the act are tipped as the next Led Zeppelin. Can you say *crossover*?'

Overhyped. Overrated. Over here. ran the headline in *Westside*'s influential music section atop a devastating attack, sneering at alternative fans for falling at the feet of a band 'snug in the arms of the machine, protected by Warners' marketing might and Michael Krebs's Midas touch'. The Wednesday that article ran, the band's low-key gig at CBGBs was half empty.

'Fuck 'em, if they want to stay away because some paper tells them to,' Jake snarled, but he wasn't used to playing to an audience with gaps in it and it pissed him off.

'Is Topaz Rossi behind this?' Josh Oberman demanded from London, spitting with rage. 'I've got the fucking *NME* and *Melody Maker* all ready to run articles on Atomic Mass being a heavy metal Suede. And MTV Europe reported the CBGB show on the news.'

'Yes, she is,' Rowena said, her anger returning.

'That bitch!' her boss swore. 'Is this her idea of revenge?'

Rowena smiled grimly. 'Oh, this isn't Topaz's revenge,' she told him. 'This is just a calling card.'

Topaz needn't worry herself, Rowena thought. She was having enough trouble here without needing any help.

Everyone took Atomic Mass seriously.

No one took Musica Records seriously.

As the scout who'd signed the flavour of the month, Rowena Gordon was respected, regularly showered with job offers, and had her ass kissed by promoters and agents and anyone who thought she might have some clout with Barbara Lincoln.

As the 'Managing Director' – *yeah, right!* – of Luther Records, the name she'd given to Musica's new subsidiary in New York, she couldn't persuade an act to sign with her. No big-time managers would commit their new acts to a European company that was just tinkering around in the United States. No, they were all happy to deal with Musica in Europe, but let a US major sign the act first and then rent it out to Musica for Europe.

The trouble with that was that the US label took a royalty. Just like Musica did when Elektra sold an Atomic Mass single.

And they'd go on missing American repertoire.

And she, Rowena, would have failed.

Rowena looked out at the lights of Manhattan from Luther's tiny, cramped offices at the top of a narrow building on Leonard Street, and knew there was no way she was giving up. Michael Krebs lived here, Atomic Mass were tasting their first big success here, and fifty per cent of all the records in the world were sold here. Anyway, she loved New York. She'd made friends in her building, friends in the clubs, friends down at the Marquee, the Bottom Line, and all the other venues where her face was getting known. Josh Oberman had been right about her wanting to change her life.

Here people were interested in what she did, not who her parents were.

Hadn't Rick Rubin managed it? Rowena reminded herself sternly, after another door slammed in her face. Surely she could do it. All she had to do was find a really talented, really good new band who'd be happy to sign with her despite the risks. A band so new they didn't *have* a fucking manager.

She stared out at the city. It was the place to be, she could feel that in her bones. Lady Liberty, wasn't she the patron saint of career girls?

Fuck you, Topaz Rossi, Rowena thought. *I'm here to stay.*

All she had to do was sign a good band. Fast.

17

The rivalry escalated with Joe Hunter on *Oprah*.

'But why do you guys get such adulation from some of the press, and yet other magazines are . . .'

She held up a copy of *White Light*, the cover plastered with a shot of Mark Thomas taken during some gig, in motion. His mouth was open and his eyes were shut in a pose that made him look like a moron. The strapline was WORST BAND IN THE WORLD?

The audience laughed. Oprah held the magazine between thumb and forefinger, as if it were a piece of trash, the wry expression on her face making her distaste clear.

'Oh, it don't bother us,' Joe answered firmly, the northern accent making some women on the audience visibly squirm on their seats in delight. 'We don't care about the press, we only care about the fans. We've just hit number one in America with our first single and we're on tour with bloody Guns n' Roses. *White Light* can go . . . stuff themselves,' he finished carefully, remembering just in time that they were on coast-to-coast TV.

The host smiled, charmed by the singer's forthright speaking. In an age where most rock stars' *hairdressers* had publicity agents, and said exactly what they were told, Atomic Mass obviously couldn't care less. The smoked, they drank, they ate red meat, they screwed a lot of girls and they said things like '*White Light* can go stuff themselves' on primetime shows.

They were likeable.

They were dangerous.

They meant *ratings*.

'Fair enough,' she said. 'And you have no idea why opinion on you is so split?'

Joe gestured to the magazine she was holding. 'With that one there I do,' he said. 'That article was written by Josie Simons. She writes in-house on music for American Magazines, and her boss is a girl called Topaz Rossi, who's an old rival of our A&R girl, Rowena Gordon – the woman who gave us a record deal. Rowena's working in New York now, and Topaz Rossi is determined to give her a really hard time. So she gets at us. There's hardly been one article published by magazines in that company that don't slag us off. So we ignore it.'

'Are you sure?' Oprah asked, scenting something interesting. Like a high-profile libel case, for a start.

Joe shrugged. 'Barbara Lincoln, our manager, went through all the American Magazines articles with us. They're all the same. Maybe it's coincidence, but I don't think so.'

'And how do you feel about that?'

Hunter leant forward and looked straight into the camera, his brown eyes angry. He knew this girl Rossi would be watching.

'It's what you expect, right?' he replied. 'Rowena Gordon's a doer. Rowena participates, and Topaz commentates. It don't mean nothing to Atomic Mass.'

With her perfect sense of timing, Oprah let the tension hang in the air for just long enough. Then she waded in to break it up.

'A female talent scout, a female manager – we don't think of Atomic Mass as exactly leading the feminist charge,' she remarked to loud laughter. The first album wasn't even out yet, and already the stories of what they got up to on the road were being printed in the *National Enquirer*. 'Do you like working with women?'

Joe gave the camera a wink.

'We like doing *everything* with women,' he replied.

'It reflects badly on the company,' Matt Gowers said. 'I take on board what you're saying, Topaz – and we all know your work on *Girlfriend* is terrific and your journalistic contributions to *US Woman* are invaluable.'

Joe Goldstein kept his face impassive as he watched Rossi burning up with humiliation. She was obviously itching to defend herself, but he'd noticed Nathan Rosen kick her under the table, and she was now biting her lips in order to force herself to keep quiet.

'And we couldn't be happier with the way *Economic Monthly* is selling,' Gowers added.

For once, the reference to his recent defeat didn't hit Joe in the solar plexus. No, it was Rossi's turn to try to hold her head up in front of her colleagues. *Don't smile, don't smile, don't smile*, thought Joe. Topaz had gloated when she surprised everybody by beating him out of the new glossy. She'd lost a lot of friends that way.

He glanced round the editors' meeting. A number of them were looking down and smirking. This was the first real setback Topaz had had since she joined the company, and many of them weren't sorry. The girl had started to act like she was the Queen of Sheba. Like she was invincible.

Well, that long-haired English boy had had other ideas.

Not that this was a threat to Topaz's career, as the chairman was making clear. But it was her first fuck-up. Rap-on-the-knuckles time.

Joe Goldstein was enjoying himself.

'But even if, as you say, you didn't bring pressure to bear on Josie or Tiz or Jason, Topaz, it looks bad. Our lawyers have told us we'd have a tough time bringing a case. So unless there's a real story, lay off this band, OK?'

'Yes, sir,' said Topaz, ashamed and enraged. The fact that Gowers was obviously right only made it worse. She could feel the eyes of her co-workers crawling over her skin.

Topaz glanced at Joe Goldstein, who wasn't looking at her. Apparently he was fascinated by the meeting agenda. She knew that it was an act, he was faking it to be polite.

Self-righteous jerk! she thought.

Rowena Gordon watched the sun sinking over Central Park from her luxurious apartment window, and felt her heart sinking with it. Another night of futile talent-hunting. Another night when she didn't want the acts that were prepared to sign with Luther Records, and the ones she did want wouldn't sign.

She pulled on her clothes. Tailored black slacks by Ralph Lauren. Long-sleeved Soundgarden shirt. Ankleboots by Manolo Blahnik.

That day at work, the Luther offices had been almost silent. Lucy, her secretary, had taken exactly four calls; three of them from Josh Oberman about work on the new Roxana Perdita record back home – Jack Reich was supervising her career now, but Rowena liked to keep in touch with her other two acts – and one from Matthew Stevenson, sneeringly asking when they might see a New York band in exchange for their investment. He'd pretended it was a joke, but Rowena knew better.

It wasn't like she was in danger of getting fired. As long as Roxana, Bitter Spice and of course Atomic Mass kept selling records, she was safe. Even without the protection of Joshua Oberman and Michael Krebs.

But there was a timebomb under her, and she knew it. Oberman had been given leave to develop an American operation over the objections of other board members, and there was a time limit on her bringing home some bacon. Three months. After that, they'd close the American company and bring her back to run Atomic's career in Europe.

She was one month down.

Rowena walked into the bedroom to grab her bag, and was greeted with the sight of her rumpled bed, the Irish linen sheets tumbled from her sex with Michael Krebs that afternoon. A mixed-up pang of lust and longing ran through her, and she buried her face in the bedclothes, drinking in the scent of him. She felt like crying. Michael had been so detached this afternoon, so cold. When he was dressed, he'd turned to her and said, 'I'm just gonna call my wife and then I'm gonna get back to the studio,' and when he'd seen her stricken expression, Krebs had added, annoyed, 'Come on, Rowena. I'm not rubbing it in your face. We're friends and that's it.'

She could still feel the inexpressible chill that had run through her. *My wife. My sons. My family, which is a tight little club from which you are excluded.*

And even worse, the subtext. *I love my wife. I don't love you. I'll never love you.*

Why was he so bloody honest about it? Rowena thought bitterly. At least if he lied, she could hate him. She could blame him. She could say she was tricked, deceived like all the other mistresses from time immemorial with promises that he loved her, he'd leave his wife for her. But Michael Krebs was a stand-up guy. He followed his own rules and he wouldn't lie to her. In fact, he preferred almost anything to discussing their relationship.

'Let's talk about us,' Rowena would say. If she was feeling brave.

'Us? There is no *us*,' Michael would answer with displeasure. 'We're *friends*. I've said it before.'

'I try to measure what I do by whether you would do it,' Rowena said to him, as they stood together in a private box at Madison Square Gardens, waiting for Atomic Mass to come on and play their support set.

Michael gave her an affectionate smile. 'Except that you should try to be the most moral and ethical person you can be.'

She felt a great sense of distress. 'But Michael, you are, totally moral and ethical,' she said.

'Except in one respect.'

'That's my fault,' Rowena said.

'No, it's my fault,' he replied, sadly.

She hated to hear him say he felt guilty, when guilt was eating her alive. She hated to think of herself as a mistress, but was furious when he refused even to call her that. She could see, quite clearly, as though she were watching someone else, how hopeless and destructive this affair was for both of them, but especially her. After all, Michael wasn't in love.

Rowena Gordon had decided – a cold, academic, intelligent decision – that she was not going to end up like all those other women. Abandoned by a lover who ran back to his wife, frozen out of the society of mutual friends, begging the guy to call her again. She'd seen it happen to girlfriends of the band. All of a sudden you were out of the charmed circle, doors shut, access revoked. Well, *she* was a career girl, even if her progress was a little slow right now. She was young, beautiful, well-bred and self-reliant. She wasn't about to immolate herself on the altar of a married man twice her age – even if he was a musical genius, frighteningly, ferociously intelligent, devastatingly handsome, one of her all-time heroes, spectacular in bed . . . *oh, Christ Almighty. Oh, dear God*, Rowena thought, forcing herself to pull her face out of the sheets. She'd have to tell him to get lost. At least as far as sex went.

But in her heart she knew they were empty words. Rowena was so in love with Michael Krebs she couldn't see straight.

'Come on,' she said aloud. 'Let's go to work.'

The *Girlfriend* offices were busy as hell. Phones were ringing off the hook, the staff writers were yelling at each other, teen models in Gap outfits traipsed round the desks, waiting for Sasha Stone or Alex Waters to call them into the photo room for that week's fashion layout. In one corner, the sales and advertising team were busiest of all, sitting in almost permanent crouches over their desks, either dealing with desperate make-up companies, fighting over the last square inches of ad space, or logging yet more orders from new retailers, mom-and-pop stores outside the national loop.

Success, success, success. It was only the editor's insistence that stopped them from doubling the thickness of each issue with glossy ads, or raising the cover price by ten cents. Topaz let nothing interfere with the magazine itself. *Girlfriend* was a sensation, and she planned on keeping it that way.

'Where's the editor? I need to speak to the editor,' a stylist begged Tiz Correy, the talented twenty-year-old features editor.

Topaz had hired her own crew, and she'd hired carefully: young, gifted kids barely older than their target readers. The strategy had proved brilliant, and Rossi had repeated it over at *Economic Monthly*, where the most media-friendly Harvard experts had columns next to guest industrialists, powerful figures who wrote every month on their personal rules for profitability – Ross Perot, Rupert Murdoch, Michael Eisner. With both her titles, Topaz followed her gut instincts. With both of them, she followed what she thought was a fundamental trait in the American psyche – the need to hero-worship. For teenage girls, that meant Madonna. For businessmen, that meant Bill Gates. But the rule was the same.

'American Magazines' new flagship comes across as *Vanity Fair* meets *The Economist*,' sneered the *Wall Street Journal*, but as far as Topaz was concerned, the only good title was one that sold.

Economic Monthly was selling.

'The boss is busy,' Tiz shrugged, gesturing to the editor's office, the door of which was firmly shut. Even over the din of the offices, the sound of raised voices – a man's and a woman's – could be heard.

'But Sasha won't let me dress Jolene in her Jean-Paul Gaultier jacket. And it would look *divine*,' the little man pouted. 'Who's she talking to, anyway?'

'Mr Rosen. He's a director of the board,' Tiz answered firmly, hoping to shut him up. 'And Jolene will wear the Gap like everyone else. *Girlfriend* readers can't afford Jean-Paul Gaultier.'

'How could you not let me know? I am so goddamn embarrassed!' Nathan shouted. '*White Light. Westside.* Fucking *Girlfriend* magazine. Article after article on this goddamn band! We look so stupid, Topaz! And I get it shoved in my face on fucking *Oprah!*'

'I didn't write them all,' Topaz said sullenly. Couldn't he give it a break? She'd had the lecture this morning.

'Yeah, but you let your feelings be known to the people whose pay cheques you sign. In no uncertain terms. Am I right?' demanded Nathan, stalking round her office. The blue vein at the side of his grey temple was pulsing, and he looked awkward in the tailored suit.

'Can't we talk about it later?' Topaz asked.

Rosen felt anger rise up in his throat, half choking him. He felt so stressed-out, his blood pressure must be off the scale. First that damn *Oprah* show airs yesterday, and no one has the guts to mention it to him because the girl he's living with is the one being criticized. Then Topaz and he had a fight last night because she wanted to make love again, and he didn't. Who did she think he was? Superman? And to cap it all, Matt Gowers had called him into his office this morning and fucking carpeted him.

As director of the East Coast, he was responsible for editorial policy. As Topaz Rossi's line manager, he was responsible for her actions. And as a board member living with one of the staff, he'd better be damn sure he didn't get any wires crossed.

'I value you and I value Topaz,' Gowers had said dryly. 'And what you do in your spare time is nobody's business but yours. *Except* when it interferes in our affairs. You should have seen this and stopped it, Rosen. Don't let it happen again.'

'No, sir,' Nathan said, nodding.

It was his textbook nightmare, come to life.

'No we *cannot* talk about it later!' he roared, suddenly *Westside*'s editor again, faced with an impertinent junior. 'Later is *personal*. This is *business*!'

He wrenched open the door. 'I hope to hell you can separate the two of them, Topaz,' he said. 'Because we don't have a future if you can't.'

Rowena threaded her way through the crowd to Joe, precariously balancing two large vodkas on the rocks. CBGBs was only half full, the narrow corridor of the club still giving her space to breathe. Not like a week ago, when Atomic had played a warm-up gig to start the tour. Tonight she could actually see Velocity, the new band, onstage, as well as hear the dark, brittle frenzy of their movement. It pounded through the club, hard as diamonds, heavy as lead.

Joe was slouching against one of the far walls, which was papered with flyers. She could see the intent expression on his face as he watched the band, carefully, the way one musician watches another. Rowena felt happiness wash through her. This was what made it all worthwhile. A dark club, a great band, optimism, music. To the kids in the crowd she was just another girl, a pretty student type from NYU. They accepted her as one of them, without comment, and she loved that.

'What do you reckon?' she asked Joe, handing him his drink.

'I think you should go for it,' he replied, not taking his eyes off the stage.

'That's what I think, too,' Rowena said happily.

They were both too engrossed with Velocity to notice the short, unassuming brunette a few paces behind them, watching them both and making notes.

On his way home – he and Topaz never left the office together – Nate Rosen was struck by a pang of remorse. Topaz's stricken face when he threatened to break up with her had been on his mind all day. He saw something that had been absent from her personality almost as long as he'd known her.

Fear.

The Topaz Rossi he knew was not about fear. She was about stupid risks, naked aggression and brilliant journalism. She was about imagination and a refusal to give up. The Topaz who'd shot down David Levine. Who'd surprised the whole board by creaming Joe Goldstein for *Economic Monthly*.

That vote, he remembered guiltily, had been unanimous, not just cast by him. And the sales figures on the title showed what a great job she was doing. True, maybe Joe could have done better, but it would be close.

Topaz had changed from the pushy kid he'd first hired. No doubt about it. Ever since 'NY Scene' had been syndicated, she'd grabbed her success and hung on to it with both hands. It was like the eighties had never finished: Chanel, St-Laurent, Dior. Bright colours, high heels and lots of jewellery. Interior-designed apartment. Joy perfume. A black Porsche 911 Turbo. Rolex. Patek Philippe, and dinners for two at 21 and the Four Seasons.

She was different in the office, too. At first she'd settled in slowly to her role as editor of *Girlfriend*, testing the waters, being cautious and polite to the staff. But as it became clear that Topaz's ideas in the dummy she'd produced were good ones, ones that worked in practice, she started to change. Overriding the old features editor. Personally designing new layouts. Sometimes even yelling at the staff writers.

The approach had caused outrage. Who was this Italian kid in her early twenties who thought she could show them how to run *their* magazine? With her colourful clothes and her board director boyfriend, the girl had had one scoop and thought she was Si Newhouse. Resentment was high, but so was the new circulation. Topaz, finding herself in charge for the first time in her life, had apparently turned into Attila the Hun in couture. She stuck rigidly to her guns and if her authority was challenged she fired the challenger. After the third month, she started firing people anyway and replacing them with younger, hipper, more talented journalists and photographers. Topaz Rossi was intent on making *Girlfriend* the best and when staff called her a loudmouthed Italian bitch she just shrugged.

'Whatever it takes,' was her attitude.

Nobody interfered. Topaz was selling magazines and she was selling ads and she was keeping down costs. It had been her idea to use teenage models for the cover, and from the second she'd sat down in the editor's office, *Girlfriend* had never employed another supermodel.

'They cost too much. They're too thin, too famous and a bad role model for the American teenager,' she told the editors' meeting. '*Girlfriend* readers like Janet Reno, Nancy Kerrigan and Winona Ryder.'

Nathan remembered it now, the sensation of pride and lust he'd had watching her give it to them, standing there in a dark green tunic by Gianfranco Ferre, the simplicity of the dress countered by an armful of glittering glass bracelets from Butler & Wilson. Amongst the army of sombre dark suits and the occasional neutral dress, Topaz had stood out like a sore thumb encrusted with rubies. Joe Goldstein had remarked to Nathan later – apparently forgetting their relationship – that Topaz used her beauty like an offensive weapon.

'And we will never run another advert featuring Kate Moss,' Topaz went on, daring anybody to contradict. 'Anorexia isn't glamorous.'

At which point every man in the room had involuntarily looked up and down her own incredible curves until Nathan had hastily thanked her for her presentation, and called on Richard Gibson at *White Light* to give his report.

Rosen shifted in his seat, feeling his anger dissolve and the first stirrings of desire take its place. Every guy at American would give a month's wages to trade places with him for five minutes, and he knew it. But Topaz was his. She wanted him. Not only that, but she'd pursued him relentlessly. It was flattering.

And he'd been in therapy long enough to see some of what was causing this heady materialism, this need for display and aggression. Topaz was nervous and scared. It was a classic reaction; the girl was hiding her insecurity behind fitted Versace, and her terror behind naked aggression. She was worst of all with Joe Goldstein; Jesus, those two were such competitors now it was almost a joke. The unstoppable force and the immovable object.

The gaudy clothes? That was simpler still. Not that she didn't look great in them – a girl like Topaz Rossi could carry that look with ease. But she used to dress in a far simpler, less attention-grabbing style and he could date the change exactly from the night of Elizabeth Martin's party: when Topaz had worn a Chanel sheath and that Rowena Gordon girl, the record executive, had turned up in a huge sweeping ballgown, with spectacular ruby earrings.

Which also explained her fury over the way Atomic Mass had shot to stardom. And her pain this morning when he'd threatened to break it off with her.

Topaz Rossi had been rejected by her father and betrayed by her best friend. No wonder the poor kid was bruised. It was insensitive of him not to remember that.

Rosen picked up the car phone and dialled Mellenick's, the exclusive Fifth Avenue florist. Fuck business. Fuck Matt Gowers. Topaz was his girl, and he was happy about that. Still.

'If you want them, go get them.'

'I can't, Josh. I don't have a budget authorized yet,' Rowena said, shivering. The heating in Luther's offices had given up the ghost, and she was beginning to feel like her American career was, too. How could I have been this disorganized? Rowena thought. First I can't find a band. Then I get sick with worry over finding a band and now, because I neglected to hire a good accountant, I can't *sign* the fucking band.

She felt totally incompetent. Jesus, maybe she was just a talent scout. Obviously there was more to running even a small company than that and she wasn't sure she had what it took.

'The money I've been allocated so far was for leasing space, hiring an assistant, basic overheads ... I don't get any more until there's a solid financial plan with sales projections.'

'You should have completed that by now, Rowena.'

She was silent.

'I might have known it wouldn't be a social call. OK, Gordon, I'll see what I can do.'

Her boss sighed; she could hear the faint scratching of his pen, making notes.

'Hans Bauer hated giving you this job in the first place, you know. He'll really love me for insisting on an emergency A&R budget for you.'

'If we want Velocity, we've got to move,' she said. 'They won't stay secret for ever.'

'Goddamnit, I'll go as fast as I can!' Oberman growled. 'Just make sure you don't lose the act. I don't want you making a fool of me.'

'I'll get them,' Rowena promised him. 'You just get me a budget.'

He grunted. 'By the way, I saw a tape of the *Oprah* show. Pretty funny. Did you put him up to that?'

'No, it was a surprise,' Rowena answered, smiling a little. She'd enjoyed Joe doing that for her. Topaz could see where her pathetic attempts at revenge would get her. From what little she knew about journalism, that would have caused her some embarrassment. Good. Pushy bitch, the English girl thought, glad to have someone she could openly dislike.

'Has that girl been causing you problems?' Oberman asked.

Rowena drew herself up a little in the shabby room. Embattled, ignored and struggling in Manhattan, her sense of class superiority came right back to her.

'She's nothing. Topaz Rossi is the least of my problems,' she said with contempt.

Nathan Rosen thrust again, savouring Topaz's low moans. His hands moved gently over her swollen nipples, and he lapped at them softly with his tongue, tugging them and pulling them into full erection. Her hands were all over him, stroking, clutching, sometimes reaching under him to trail her fingers gently over his balls, in that way that drove him crazy. He refused to be hurried, and for once she wasn't rushing him. They both enjoyed slow, bridge-building sex like this that lasted for hours and ended in long-drawn-out orgasms as relaxing as a scented bath. This was Nathan's pace, not Topaz's. But she was happy to give in to him tonight.

Topaz moved under her partner, her supple body keeping pace with his rhythm. She smiled into his eyes, feeling tenderness, mild arousal and the relaxation of tension. She hadn't wanted to lose Nate. He was her family, and family was important. He was the first person truly to care for her and not just lust after her. That was worth a little sexual incompatibility. She kissed his shoulder, remembering yesterday, when flowers from Mellenick's, chocolates from Godiva and vintage champagne had all been delivered to the house and they'd made love on the kitchen floor to celebrate.

'I love you, Topaz,' Nathan gasped, feeling his whole body bathed in a pre-orgasm sweat. He glanced down at her superb breasts, pressed hard against him. 'Oh, God, I love you. I love you,' and she murmured, 'I love you too,' knowing that he was coming, nowhere near climax herself, but wanting him to come, wanting him to be pleased, wanting him to love her.

'Ohhhh,' Rosen groaned, erupting inside her with a surge of white-hot bliss. Topaz put her arms round him, holding him to her, kissing the handsome line of his jaw, until he eventually, reluctantly, pulled out of her. He rolled off her and lay in the bed next to her, feeling like a young lion.

She was so giving, so generous in bed. Compared with Marissa's tight-assed sufferance of his pleasure, Topaz was Mother Earth and Venus rolled into one.

Her only fault is to want too much of me, Rosen told himself, with a flash of vanity. The idea pleased him. Put like that, her overdemanding attitude to sex − as he saw it − wasn't so bad after all.

'Will you marry me?' Rosen asked suddenly.

'Do you want to?' Topaz asked, surprised, propping herself up on one elbow to look at him. Her red hair tumbled down her back and her breasts thrust themselves towards his face. Incredibly, Nathan sensed the renewed stirrings of desire.

He suppressed his misgivings. 'Yes I do,' he said. 'Absolutely.'

Topaz felt her eyes fill with tears. She'd never expected him to ask her so soon; to have a successful career, be a wife with a loving husband, maybe even a mother – it was exactly what she'd dreamt of.

Now all she had to do was to find some way of dealing with the two things that still bothered her. Joe Goldstein, her newest rival, still with one more magazine than she had and still determined to block her career at American Magazines. And Rowena Gordon.

Maybe her recent humiliation *had* been her own fault, but then she'd been careless. And unsubtle. Flinging insults at a band that were already on their way was futile, as well as obvious. No, she wanted to really do Rowena some harm. Topaz had done a fair amount of research on her situation at Musica and she knew that it wasn't as secure as it looked. She also knew that Rowena was having trouble signing a band. And that Atomic Mass were getting pretty wild on tour. There had to be some possibilities there. Topaz didn't want Rowena to just fail to make it and go home – she had to *help* her to fail. Yeah, sure, she knew nice girls didn't pursue revenge. They forgave and forgot.

Fuck that. She betrayed me.

Topaz smiled at Nathan, putting Rowena from her mind.

'The answer is yes,' she whispered, and kissed him.

18

'Married?' demanded Joe Goldstein. He pushed back his chair and stood up, black eyes luminous with anger. 'Married? To Topaz Rossi?'

'Who else?' Nathan replied coolly. He hadn't expected this reaction from Joe. *American Scientist, Week in Review* and *Executive Officer* were all flourishing now that Goldstein had moved to New York, and he had taken good care to see that Topaz was never unduly favoured over Joe. Goldstein was still favourite to succeed Nathan to the board. He thought he'd made that clear.

'Is that what she wants?' Joe asked. He was struggling to contain himself, so great was the rage sweeping through him. Topaz Rossi *marrying* Nathan Rosen? It was all wrong, totally wrong. His old mentor was thinking with his dick and Rossi was just a stupid child. Either that or climbing the ladder horizontally.

'I guess so,' Rosen answered.

'Well, I hope you'll be happy,' Goldstein said shortly.

'Thank you,' Nathan Rosen said, looking at his protégé with a new wariness.

'Married! *Now* you tell me!' Gino Rossi said, his disapproval echoing down the phone. 'Is he Catholic?'

Amazing, thought Topaz, how much this still hurt. She called her father for the first time in years, to tell him she was getting married, and all he could say was 'Is he Catholic?' No 'How are you, where have you been?' Even fury would have been preferable to this total lack of interest in her life – anger would have meant he gave a damn.

'No, Poppa, he's Jewish,' she replied.

'A Jew! My daughter is marrying a fucking Jew? How did we bring you up, for you to be –'

Topaz slammed the phone down, feeling the shame and rejection all over again.

Thank God I got away from them, she told herself fiercely, determined to ignore the dull ache in her heart. Nate Rosen was marrying her and *he* hadn't seen anything to despise. She glanced at her reflection in the door of her office: a pretty blue dress, elegant shoes, ethnic bangles. Good enough for Nathan, good enough for anybody.

Her assistant buzzed her. 'It's John Aitken.'

'Show him in,' Topaz ordered, her mind switching gears. If John had come through the way she hoped, the scores would be settled and there'd be one less thing on her mind.

'Well?' she asked, as the journalist walked into her office. His Rage Against the Machine T-shirt was crumpled and his eyes were bloodshot, as though he'd been up all night.

'I've got something,' Aitken said, handing her a sheaf of dirty notes.

Topaz tore through them, her mind racing. When she'd finished, she looked up at him with an expression of pure triumph. 'Can we run with this now?' she asked.

'There's a launch party for the album in a fortnight, at Madison Square Gardens,' John told her. 'If I were you I'd wait. This is a real killer.'

Topaz thought about it. Maybe she *could* wait. This would be the second punch in a one-two jab at Rowena that would put an end to her unfinished business with that woman.

She'd had the first real break yesterday night.

'Can you see what I'm getting at?' Tiz Correy had yelled in her ear.

Tiz was setting up the October issue, and wanted her boss to come with her and check out a scene – the new industrial music in New York, epitomized by bands like Cop Shoot Cop, which was attracting a new wave of young, pissed-off female punks, art students and assorted misfits. Topaz had vetoed the idea at once. She didn't think that was what *Girlfriend* readers were looking for – more like lipstick, fashion and *Beverly Hills 90210*.

'It will made a great feature,' her staffer repeated angrily. 'You should trust me, Topaz. I haven't been wrong before. All you think about these days is impressing the guys over at *Economic*.'

Topaz flinched. 'That's not fair.'

'It is. OK, look: you come check out one of the bands, they're playing CBGB's tonight, have a look at what I'm talking about for yourself. If you want to kill the story after that, fair enough. Is it a deal?'

Topaz, trapped, nodded. 'What's the band?'

'Hot new group, no record deal. They're called Velocity.'

'Never heard of them.'

'You will.'

'Can you see what I'm getting at?' Tiz yelled in her ear. 'These girls are wild! We run something like, "She's a Rebel" and a few shots of this mayhem crowd stuff, a list of the bands, a picture of Axl Rose . . .'

'I like pictures of Axl Rose,' Topaz yelled back, knowing what was indisputably good for circulation. 'OK, Tiz, it's your call. Run whatever you want.'

She gestured at the stage, where Velocity's female bassist was hammering out a blitzkrieg run. 'Is this stuff popular?'

'What, are you kidding me? This band is the edge of the cutting-edge.'

'You were always the rock fan,' Topaz shrugged.

To her, it sounded like meaningless white noise designed to make the ears bleed. But that was why she'd given Tiz her head on the article. Tiz Correy was only twenty; she could remember what it was like to be fifteen. Topaz, on the other hand, was twenty-four and starting to forget; and anyway, even at fifteen, she would never have gone for this.

'The rumours about them are hot,' Tiz enthused.

'Really?' Topaz enquired politely, not giving a damn. She'd paid her dues, now she wanted to go home. Yes, the girls in the audience would take some interesting pictures. Yes, it might make a good feature. Enough! Do I have to endure the whole show? she wondered.

'Oh yeah. The guy behind the bar told me your Rowena Gordon was here last week. She's been to see them a few times now, and he noticed her talking to the manager last time she was here.'

Topaz turned to face her, slowly.

'Are you telling me Rowena Gordon wants to offer this band a record deal?'

'Does it matter?' Tiz asked, surprised at her boss's sudden intensity. 'Sure, I think she does. Like I told you, they're cutting-edge, real new and hot. I expect she wants to get them for Musica before that situation changes.'

'Can she do that?'

'I don't know, I'm not a record company executive. I guess so. Wasn't that how she got Atomic Mass, signing them up before word got out?'

'Tiz, you're a genius!' Topaz exclaimed.

'What? Are we doing a profile on Rowena Gordon?' Tiz asked, thoroughly confused. 'I thought you didn't like her. The female anarchy thing will make a better piece.'

Her boss ignored her. 'Will the manager be here tonight?'

'Probably. Do you want an introduction?'

'Yeah,' Topaz said, grinning. 'We can't have a cutting-edge band like Velocity snapped up for next to nothing, can we?'

She smiled at Tiz. 'You like the band, right? If I arrange for you to write a large guest feature in *White Light*, do you want to introduce them to Manhattan?'

'Of *course!*' said her features editor, excited. 'If I do it tonight, we could make their Thursday edition.'

She looked back at the stage. 'I could start a bidding war for these guys!'

'Exactly,' said Topaz.

'So did you get the tape?' Rowena asked Michael.

'Yeah,' he said. 'I got it this morning. I didn't get a chance to listen to it yet.'

'Well, hurry up,' she said. 'I want to know what you think.'

'What if I hate them?'

'I'm signing them anyway,' Rowena said firmly, 'because *I* think they kill. A bloke called Andrew Snelling manages them; he's a sharp guy, very good with money. We're exchanging contracts on Friday.'

'How did you come up with a budget?'

'I got Josh to wring some emergency funds out of the board.'

Krebs laughed. 'You must be everyone's favourite little girl.'

'Hey,' she said defiantly, 'I'll sign the act, they'll be a flagship band for this subsidiary, and Holland will stop concerning themselves with my ability.'

'Babe, you have nothing to prove to me . . . I'm sure you'll sign them, if you want them.'

'Of course I'll sign them,' she said. 'No one else has even heard of them.'

Joe Goldstein sat in his office at *American Scientist*, seemingly staring into space.

From time to time his secretary looked through the blinds, but knew better than to disturb him; when Mr Goldstein closed his door and stared at the air like that, it would take Wall Street crashing or a new cure for cancer to rouse him.

Joe was deep in thought. His office was situated high up in the building, and the gleaming skyscrapers of Seventh Avenue towered everywhere outside the three glass walls of the room, but he was impervious to urban beauty today. Today he was wondering about his future. He had made a grave error of judgment – underestimating a rival – and had, he felt, been humiliated in front of the entire company by failing to add *Economic Monthly* to his portfolio of business titles. Possibly for the first time in his life he was discovering what it felt like to fail. It was not an experience he wanted to repeat.

The worst thing, though, was that Nathan Rosen had voted for Topaz. That was something he just could not understand. It was Nate, after all, who'd brought him into the company in the first place, become his close friend, and eventually acted as his mentor. It was also Nathan who had engineered his transfer to New York, and considering that Rosen had become the director for the East Coast, he'd kind of counted on his vote.

In fact, forget 'kind of'.

And yet, and yet, and yet, Goldstein mused. Topaz had performed quite brilliantly. He remembered as if it had been yesterday the way his heart had sunk as he'd listened to her pitch, and if he was honest, he might have voted for her too.

But now Topaz was going to marry Nathan.

He couldn't work out why this annoyed him so much, but he'd found it hard even to be civil to Nathan this morning. In fact, since he'd found out when he first got here that the two of them were dating, Joe had seen his longstanding friendship with Nathan go down the tubes. And when they'd moved in together, a week before the *Economic Monthly* pitch, it had disappeared completely. He started turning down all Nathan's invitations to drinks or baseball games. He went with buddies from his own titles or he picked up women for company.

And he worked. He worked his balls off. For all Topaz Rossi's flamboyance, Joe Goldstein still edited one more magazine than she did and he still submitted business memos to the board. She wasn't the only one who could push up circulation. *American Scientist* and *Week in Review* had both posted record figures this month.

Joe knew he'd made a fundamental error with his pitch. It was readers and revenue that counted, not content – content of a magazine was the means, not the end. It was the bait. Topaz had demonstrated that and it was a lesson Joe was determined not to need twice.

The next time they set a title up, Goldstein thought darkly, there won't even be an open pitch.

His mind strayed back to Topaz Rossi. No male rival had ever got him going like this, but then no male rival had ever looked like that girl. Maybe that was it. It just didn't sit well with him to see an attractive woman so goddamn obsessed with the nine-to-five. Or the eight-to-ten, in her case. He'd heard that outside the office Nathan and she didn't have much of a life.

Not for one second did it occur to Joe that the same thing was said about him.

He flicked through yesterday's *Westside*, noting the article on some odious-looking band called Velocity – distinctly *not* Goldstein's speed. When he wanted to hear music he generally headed for the Lincoln Center. There was a pull-out quote by the writer, Tiz Correy, pointing out that Rowena Gordon, the girl behind Atomic Mass, was looking to sign them up.

Joe recognized a clarion call to every other player when he saw one. He wondered if Gordon had them inked on the dotted line yet, because if not, she didn't stand a prayer now. Assuming it was true, and she was interested in the first place. But he was inclined to believe it.

He scanned the article again. There was no mention of Topaz Rossi anywhere in it.

Joe smiled grimly. As if that mattered.

Nathan Rosen walked up the steps to his house at half-six, carrying a small package from Cartier. It was a cool evening, a light breeze rustling the tops of the trees in his street. You could almost call it quiet.

Topaz was waiting for him in the kitchen. There was a silver candlestick on the table, and the soft light from its flame was the only illumination in the room. Dinner for two was set with their best porcelain, a bottle of his favourite Perrier-Jouet champagne chilling in an ice bucket and small heaps of caviar glinting on their plates as a starter. She'd served it just the way he liked it: neat, no messing around with chopped egg or blinis. Perlman was playing Beethoven's Violin Concerto gently on the stereo.

Rosen stopped at the door, struck with the perfection of the moment.

His fiancée was wearing a muted, floating full-length gown in dusty blue chiffon, which flowed round her curves like cream. Her hair was pinned up in a formal style, swept back and secured with a tortoiseshell comb. She had no jewellery, nothing to spoil the line.

She took his breath away.

'I brought you something,' Rosen said, walking up to her and handing her the box.

She opened it, smiling at him. Inside was an engagement ring, a cluster of sapphires exquisitely set on a band of white gold.

'I love you,' Topaz told him, kissing his cheek, then his mouth. There were tears in her eyes as he slid the ring on to her finger.

'Are you sure you want to do this?' Rosen asked her. 'Be with me, I mean?

Even though I'm so sedate, so laid-back? Are you sure I'm not too slow for you?'

She shook her head and kissed him again. 'Things are going to be different now,' she told him. 'I'm going to relax. Be less uptight.'

'You?' he repeated, smiling. 'Why?'

Topaz pictured the look on Rowena's face when she found out. The first blow would be bad. The second would finish her off.

They were quits.

She could forget about Rowena, and get on with her life.

'Just because,' she said.

'No, it's OK, Andrew,' Rowena said, 'I understand. Business is business.'

Her knuckles were white with fury, gripping the phone.

'I'm afraid not,' she replied. 'I called my chairman already. We can't match that kind of money. No, I have no hard feelings. 550 Music is a great label, you'll do fine, and I wish you well.'

It was true. She didn't blame the manager, not for a second. It was his job to get the best deal for the act and she knew she'd have done exactly the same thing.

'I should have moved faster,' she said.

Rowena replaced the receiver and stared towards Seventh Avenue. Topaz Rossi was in one of those buildings.

The phone went again. 'Gordon,' she said.

'Would you care to explain to me what the fucking hell is going on?' snapped Josh Oberman.

19

'I guess that's everything,' John Aitken said.

'Thanks,' his editor told him. 'Richard Gibson's real pleased with the story, John. There'll be a rise for you in this.'

'I hope so,' he replied with feeling.

'Fax me the final draft at home, could you?' she asked. 'I want to see it as soon as it's done.' Her long fingers were absentmindedly rolling a tennis ball round on her desk.

'OK,' he said, ringing off.

Topaz surveyed her empty office.

'Bullseye!' she said.

It was autumn in Manhattan, and Rowena was still surviving. Just. After the Velocity fiasco, only one thing had saved her from recall to London; Barbara Lincoln and Michael Krebs had both insisted she stay and be put in charge of the album launch for *Heat Street*. It might be a Warners record for North America, but it belonged to Musica for the rest of the world, as Krebs pointed out to Oberman.

'She needs to find a band, Michael,' Josh told him.

'I know,' Krebs said. 'She will.'

A week later, Rowena found Obsession, a talented rap act from Brooklyn, and signed them, very quietly.

After the deal was done, she sent a tennis ball over to American Magazines, for the attention of Ms Topaz Rossi, with a note attached: 'Thirty-fifteen.'

'I'm impressed!' Barbara said.

'So you should be,' said Rowena.

Josh Oberman didn't say anything, as he was calculating the exchange rate of dollars to pounds and wondering if this would get him promoted. One more album like this, and they'd make him President for Life.

'Hi, this is Alex Isseult on MTV News,' said the stunning brunette on the limousine TV, smiling at them engagingly. 'Britain's newest supergroup Atomic Mass are rumoured to be planning a huge launch party for their debut album, *Heat Street*, at Madison Square Gardens in New York. A spokeswoman for Musica Records admitted that they were waiting for a go-ahead from city authorities. Atomic Mass, currently enjoying their second number one single with "Trapped", will be issuing free invitations at dates on their sold-out US tour, which follows earlier supports to the mighty Guns n' Roses.'

She paused to give them another dazzling smile.

'*Heat Street* will receive its first-ever playback at the stadium, and fans attending will also be issued with vouchers entitling them to a discount when they buy the album . . .'

'Can I believe my ears?' asked Oberman in theatrical disgust as the car glided past a huge billboard proclaiming THE ATOMIC AGE BEGINS 2 NOVEMBER. 'You can't do that.'

'Why can't I?' asked his Managing Director defensively.

'Because it's a carbon copy of what Burnstein and Mensch did to launch Metallica's last record.'

'So?' said Barbara impudently. 'I've always believed in learning from the masters.'

'Look, Lincoln,' began Oberman, who'd gone pale, 'you –'

'Calm down, Josh, I asked for permission,' Rowena said soothingly.

The old man visibly relaxed.

'Mensch said, if I wanted to be totally fucking unoriginal it was fine by him.'

'*Metallica* didn't sell twenty trillion copies because they threw a launch party at Madison Square Gardens,' Barbara pointed out. 'It sold twenty trillion because it was a phenomenal album.'

'Absolutely,' said Josh and Rowena in unison.

'We've done two million in firm pre-sales, Josh,' said Rowena. 'Firm, not shipped. I have point-of-sale in stores across the country and two independent promoters on the album. I have radio promos and competitions in four key markets for November. We're taking print ads, radio ads, MTV ads . . . marketing spend is huge . . . the whole thing is huge. It has to launch in style, and that was still the best idea anyone ever had . . .'

'OK, OK,' said Josh, throwing his hands in the air. 'Do what you like.'

'This album will sell itself,' Barbara insisted.

'Fine. We'll cancel the marketing budget,' grinned Rowena as Barbara glared at her.

Rowena had Press type up a list of the international TV and radio stations and magazines that were being flown in for the *Heat Street* launch and faxed it to the Musica affiliates around the world. It was four pages long, excluding American media. She copied Michael on it; he called her back almost immediately.

'I want you to know that I'm proud of you,' he said. 'You really did good here, Rowena.'

'Thank you,' she replied, suffused with pleasure.

'I really mean it,' Krebs insisted. 'You're one of the best I've ever seen.'

'They wouldn't have happened without you.'

'Sure they would. Maybe not so big,' he conceded.

There was silence for a moment.

'I want to be with you,' Krebs said gently. 'Can I come round tomorrow?'

'I would love that,' said Rowena.

She stared at the phone for a few seconds, luxuriating in happiness. For these infinitely rare moments of tenderness and affection she lived and died. She loved him so hard, so fiercely, perfectly aware he didn't love her back. He had never pretended to. She ought to leave him. God only knew she'd tried.

The first time had been a big deal, maybe because Rowena assumed Krebs would respect her wishes. They'd been together in Dublin, checking out a new band, and after some of the hottest sex she could remember he'd started talking about his wife. Feeling his insensitivity like a kick to the stomach, Rowena stood there and told him it was over.

'We'll talk about it in the morning.'

'No we won't,' Rowena said, her voice thick with the pain gathering at the back of her throat. 'I never want to see you again.'

'Never?' Krebs asked, propping himself up in bed on one elbow.

Rowena felt as if some sadist was performing open-heart surgery on her without an anaesthetic.

'Never!' she managed, tears trickling down her cheeks.

'Come back here,' Krebs said, but she ran away from him, barely reaching her own room before collapsing on to the bed. It was anguish, it was torture. For all he was a sonofabitch, the thought of never being with Michael again was sheer agony. She had to sit on her hands to stop herself calling his room and telling him she'd changed her mind. She sobbed for three hours, and cried herself to sleep.

In the morning, she got up early and checked out. The stewardess on board the Aer Lingus flight asked her if she was feeling ill. Rowena said no and refused all food and drink. She thought about Michael Krebs every second of the five-hour flight home.

She'd lasted a week and lost half a stone, hardly eating, hardly sleeping. Getting through each day was like running a marathon. Krebs was her first thought in the morning, her last thought at night. After three days, relentless sexual longing started to mix with the misery.

And then he'd called.

'This has gone on long enough. You can't still be mad at me,' Michael said.

Rowena was dumbstruck. 'You think this is *funny*?'

'Absolutely,' Krebs said firmly. 'I'm just gonna laugh at you, Rowena. All this angst . . .'

'*Angst*?' she spluttered. 'I *hate* you!'

'You hate me now?'

'Yeah,' she said sullenly, trying to ignore the flood of limitless joy that had surged through her at the sound of his voice.

'And you're never gonna sleep with me again?'

'No I'm not.'

'That's a shame,' Krebs said softly.

Lust swept a long, lazy, feathery caress right across her body.

'Is it OK if I reminisce, then? Because I have to tell you, I've been thinking about it . . .'

'No . . .'

'About Sweden. Remember that? I enjoyed that, Rowena.'

Sweden. Christ. He'd grabbed her by the nape of the neck and shoved her, belly down, across the desk in the hotel room. The lamp and all his papers had gone crashing to the floor. She'd come so many times that night she'd lost count.

'Shut up, Michael . . .'

'How did my cock feel, Rowena? Do you remember that? Sliding into you? You were so hot it wasn't even funny.'

She stifled a gasp. 'Fucking shut *up*, Michael . . .'

'You're gonna have to hang up on me.'

'I can't hang up on you. You know that . . .'

'If I was there now, we wouldn't be talking. I don't know, I might start with your breasts this time. I keep thinking about your nipples. They're so sharp when you're turned on . . . You know what I'd like to do? I'd like to lick them for a couple of minutes and then put a hand in between your legs. Then you could tell me how much you hate me.'

No.'

'Yes. Yes. You know, baby. You could tell me how you couldn't stand me while I was stroking you. I'd be real gentle, you wouldn't even know I was there. Probably wouldn't notice me lifting you up and pulling you down on my cock. I'd fuck you very, very slowly. Deep thrusts. Give you time to say whatever you've got on your mind. How about that? I mean, you hate me, right? Having me fuck you right in front of a mirror so you could watch it going in, that wouldn't make any difference . . .'

'Michael!'

'Don't tell me you *like* that idea.'

'Stop this.' Her stomach was contracted. Her whole body was shaking with desire.

'No. I won't. Because I know what's happening to you.'

She couldn't speak.

'I'll be there in five minutes,' Krebs said firmly, hanging up.

Rowena had never forgotten it. By the time he arrived, she was so racked with lust she couldn't stand up. When Krebs walked through the door and saw what he'd done to her, he pushed her up against the wall and took her where she stood, just unsnapping her jeans and shoving into her.

She'd tried to walk five or six times after that. But Michael wouldn't hear of it, and his sexual hold over her was absolute.

The American Magazines tower was buzzing. Gowers and the rest of the board had called an emergency editorial meeting.

'Are you sure we can run with this?' Jason Richman demanded.

'I'm sure. Our lawyers have gone through it with two fine-tooth combs,' Topaz assured him.

'How are you spreading it?' Joe Goldstein. Cold and businesslike.

'Over three issues initially. Maybe more to come, we're still digging.'

'Why don't you wait for the whole thing?'

She glared at him. Every damn meeting the guy tries to crucify me, she thought.

'Because I don't feel we can sit on this for even a day. It'll be leaked.'

'I agree completely,' Nathan snapped. Goldstein must be out of his mind. The story was so hot you could fry eggs on it.

'They're right,' Matt Gowers said, with an air of finality. Goldstein flushed slightly. Gowers added, 'We'll need a bigger print-run for the third and second issue.'

He turned to the meeting. 'It only remains for me to congratulate Topaz Rossi. You all know that most of the time American Magazines is in the business of great features, not breaking news, so it's good to see that we can handle that properly too, when the need arises. You also know that *White Light* has been lagging in the music press market. I think this could be the solution. So Topaz, well done indeed.'

The meeting broke into applause, although she noticed angrily that Joe Goldstein just shuffled his notes instead. As everyone left to get back to their offices, she grabbed him by the arm.

'What?' he snapped, shaking her off with an expression of distaste.

'Look, Joe,' she said patiently, 'I know we've had our differences but –'

He cut her off. 'Oh, spare me the "can't we be friends" spiel,' he said coldly. 'We work for the same company. That's about the extent of it. Now if you'll excuse me –'

'What's your problem?' shouted Topaz, losing her temper.

He seemed to consider whether or not to reply. Then, regarding her, he said, 'The fact is, I don't have any respect for people who fuck their way to the top.'

As she stiffened in shock, he turned and walked out.

Nathan was cooking supper when she got home.

Topaz relaxed against the doorway and enjoyed the sight of him, carefully and methodically fiddling with the pan. He'd even put an apron on. How sweet, just like him. She could see it now: *no applesauce is going to get the better of Nathan Rosen!*

He was barechested, apart from the apron, just cooking in jeans. That did something to her, the sight of his broad back, the muscles shifting under the skin as he moved. Topaz looked appreciatively over his tight, lean ass. Lust began to tug at her, mingling with the overwhelming sensations of triumph she'd been feeling all day. She padded up behind him and slid her hands round his waist, kissing his shoulderblades, and then started to brush his crotch through the denim.

'Hey, cut it out,' he said. 'This has reached a delicate stage.'

Topaz ignored him and silently slipped out of her shirt and bra. She began to brush across his spine with her nipples.

He groaned, immediately becoming erect beneath her hands.

Topaz started to unbutton his fly and rubbed him gently through the silk of his boxers. He moved with her, trying to press himself against her hands. She tickled and stroked him lightly for a minute or so, and when she felt him thickening and distending under her touch smartly withdrew and backed towards the kitchen table. Then she unhooked her skirt and slowly wriggled out of her panties, starting to touch herself.

'Topaz,' Rosen breathed, his hard-on chafing against his pants. He wanted to be where her fingers were. To come where her fingers were. But he sensed she wanted something else first and he came towards her, ripping off his jeans to free his swollen cock, and dropped to his knees, burying his face in the tiny, wiry red hairs of her pussy, hearing her groan.

Nathan started to kiss her softly, marvelling at how wet she was, and when he felt her thighs relax slightly, he began to lick her, slow, sure strokes, aiming to please.

Oh God, thought Topaz.

She reached down and moved his head, arrogantly guiding him for her pleasure. When she thought she could sense orgasm, she grabbed his wrists and pinioned his arms behind his head, kissing him.

Nathan shivered with desire, watching this beautiful young girl astride him, her magnificent breasts swaying just out of reach, her soft mouth suddenly determined and lustful, crashing down on his.

Christ, what was she doing now . . .

Topaz had loosened her ponytail and was brushing his cock with her hair, in long, sweeping caresses, stroking him with a million feathery touches. He felt desire and surprise rip through him. Then she grabbed him with her right hand and positioned herself, slick and open, above him.

'Do you want it? Tell me how much you want it,' she whispered.

He stared up at her, aroused and amused.

'Or I guess I could just leave you here,' she teased.

'No! I want it, OK. Just fuck me, damn it,' Rosen gasped, and Topaz smiled and lowered herself on to his straining cock and flung her head back, her body arching, and he exploded inside her a second later.

She collapsed against him, panting.

'What was that all about?' Nathan murmured, stroking her hair.

Topaz smiled and kissed him.

'I think you burnt the applesauce,' she said.

Rowena stretched comfortably in bed and flicked on MTV. The morning sun streamed through the windows.

'This is Alex Isseult with MTV News,' said the TV excitedly. Rowena waved at her lazily, registering her constant little thrill of pleasure at seeing the Atomic Mass logo on MTV.

'British supergroup Atomic Mass look certain to run into trouble this morning, as the current issue of *White Light* magazine, which hit the stands last night, reveals that two of the band members have previously undisclosed criminal records, including possession of drugs.'

'*What?*' Rowena screamed, sitting bolt upright.

'MTV News can exclusively confirm that New York authorities have already issued a statement banning the group from holding its planned launch party at Madison Square Gardens. The move is sure to cost Musica Records hundreds of thousands of dollars in wasted air fares and promotional costs. However, that may be the least of their problems: spokesmen for the DEA and the Justice Department have already said that they are actively considering deporting the band if the allegations are proven, meaning the cancellation of a sell-out tour and huge costs . . .'

'*What?*' she screamed again.

Downstairs, insistently, the phone began to ring.

20

'How could you do this to me? I must have been insane to give you this label! Didn't you anticipate the press would dig around an act of this size?'

'Josh, I –'

'No!' he screamed. 'Don't give me excuses! I have Holland on the phone every five minutes! Our goddamned fax is jamming because the worldwide MDs are having a mass panic!'

Rowena passed her hand across her forehead, cursing technology. Oberman might be three thousand miles away but he sounded like he was in the next room.

'Gordon, this is not a game!'

'I know that, Josh, I –'

'You report to me, I look like a fool. And I can tell you right now that Hans Bauer wants you recalled.'

She went pale.

'I can't cover your ass for ever. If it ever happens again, you're through. This is a fucking fiasco.'

'Understood,' said Rowena faintly.

Oberman slammed the phone down.

It was the last call in a long, long day, most of which had been spent in trying, fruitlessly, to get hold of the band and repeating 'The allegations are being investigated. We have no further comment at this time,' over and over again.

She was totally shattered.

When Michael rang the apartment doorbell at nine, she was in floods of tears.

'I'm sorry,' she said, mortified. 'I forgot you were coming over – let me wash my face . . .'

'Ssh,' Krebs said, kissing her gently. 'It's OK, you go ahead and cry. I think it's kind of cute, actually, the great Rowena Gordon showing weakness.'

She fled to the bathroom and doused herself in cold water, blew her nose and slapped on some foundation. Amazing, pathetic really, how even in this state she couldn't bear him to see her looking less than beautiful.

'Get out here, Rowena,' Michael called.

She went back out to him, embarrassed by her appearance, her spectacular failure, forgetting he was coming over, everything. Also, the familiar sensation of desire was starting to crawl over her. Merely to be in the same room as him was usually enough.

He came towards her, sensing the shift in her mood immediately. His kiss this time was less consoling, harder, sexual. 'What shall I do with you this evening?' he said. 'I was going to take you out to dinner somewhere discreet, to celebrate, but I guess that's inappropriate now.'

She nodded mutely.

'Take off your shirt,' he said. 'I want to play with your breasts while I'm thinking about it.'

He started to lightly caress her, discussing various different positions he might take her in in a calm, detached tone of voice, as if talking to himself.

After two minutes she broke down, gasping.

'Can't hold it?' Michael asked, smiling. 'God, you're really out of control today, Rowena, aren't you? I didn't even touch you between your legs yet.'

She started to unbutton his jeans, freeing his erection. He was red and swollen, and she wondered again how he managed to master his arousal so completely when she couldn't hide hers for a second. Krebs could often go from erection to ejaculation without making a single sound.

He spun her round so she was facing the wall, tugged down her skirt and panties and entered her, moving in aggressive, rhythmic strokes. As she shut her eyes in ecstasy he ran one hand across her groin, the other tracing a firm line up and down her spine possessively. She choked out his name as she came.

Michael tightened his grip on her shoulders and climaxed.

He held her firmly for a few seconds, just to make a point, and then kissed her affectionately. 'Always the best cure for stress,' he said.

She smiled ruefully. 'My problems are still there, though.'

'Come shower with me,' Krebs said. 'You have no problems. Let me explain something to you, Rowena: you're a friend of mine, and so are the band. When some little writer fucks with you, and fucks with Atomic Mass, they fuck with me.'

She glanced at him.

'Nothing has been proved, and nothing will be. There *are* other stadiums in America, and you should also bear in mind,' he added with heavy sarcasm, 'that I have produced for a few other companies besides Musica Records. I have a lot of favours coming to me.'

He paused. 'Do you know who's responsible for this?'

'I think so,' said Rowena.

'Good. Because you and I are going to talk to the press in a language which they'll understand, believe me.'

'Michael!' said Rowena.

She was excited now. She believed he was going to get her out of this. Gratitude and relief and the giddy prospect of revenge surged through her; and then admiration; and then a slow, deep wave of almost violent desire.

He watched her redden. 'You can consider this a continuation of your education,' he said. God, how hot he could get her. She was the most passionate girl he'd ever seen in his life. He felt his erection returning.

'Come here and pay me for it,' he said.

The next day she was her old self. There was something great about dealing with a crisis of this size; Rowena kicked into action, pouncing on phones, yelling at reporters and faxing 'please await further information' messages to her affiliates around the world. Krebs, meanwhile, called Freddy deMann, Doug Goldstein and Warren Entner, and Madonna, Guns n' Roses and Faith No More all cancelled exclusive interviews with *White Light*. Historically, artists are not fond of people or publications that smear other artists.

Michael was enjoying himself. 'It's just something for them to think about,' he said. 'Wait till I find Paul McGuinness. Then they can forget their U2 Christmas issue, as well.'

Rowena's secretary stuck her head round the door. 'Sorry to interrupt,' she said, 'but I've got Barbara Lincoln on line one.'

'Put her through!' said Rowena. 'On the speakerphone!'

'Why the fuck haven't you called?' Krebs demanded.

'We had the phones disconnected while I talked to the band,' Barbara explained. 'Sorry, you guys.'

'Sorry!' Rowena exploded, furious. 'Do you have *any idea* what it's been like in New York? Christ, Barbara –'

'Look, most of it's not true –'

'Why don't you just tell me what's true and what isn't,' Krebs said calmly.

'I want to speak to the band,' Rowena demanded, still furious.

'Hey, this is me, Rowena!' Barbara protested. 'Me, your best friend, remember? Now take a deep breath, and listen to this.'

'I don't understand it.'

Richard Gibson, *White Light*'s editor, was presenting to the editors' meeting.

'I mean I really do not get this. The Atomic Mass issue quadrupled our circulation, I have extra print-runs for the next three issues. I mean these magazines are just flying out of the stores and everybody knows it.'

'So what's the problem?' Nathan asked.

'I can't sell advertising space. I mean not at all. Musica Records pulled their ads, OK, this I understand. But now Geffen is pulling, Mercury is pulling, Epic pulled a whole page ad for Screaming Trees this morning. Said they decided to run it in *Spin* magazine instead.'

'Anything else?' asked Topaz.

'Yeah. All our cover stories are cancelling interviews.'

'Like who?' Joe Goldstein asked, making notes.

'Ever heard of U2?' Richard replied, with the withering sarcasm music journalists reserve for money men. 'Suddenly they can no longer fit us into their press schedule. Bang goes my Christmas double issue.'

'Madonna?' Topaz probed gently.

'Gone. Out of here,' Gibson snapped. 'I mean, this is *insane*. I have a music magazine which, right now, has triple the circulation of *Rolling Stone*, and I can't get an interview or sell an ad.'

Joe Goldstein shot a baleful look at Topaz. 'Richard, my friend,' he said, 'they're going to shut you down.'

Gibson considered it. 'No,' he said. 'It did cross my mind, OK. But the record business is highly competitive. Why would Geffen care if Musica screws up?'

'It's Rowena Gordon!' Topaz burst out.

Joe rounded on her. 'Gordon doesn't have that kind of reach, Rossi,' he said. 'If you could keep your little private vendetta out of this, you'd realize that. No; there's somebody else involved now, and whoever it is, they're going to shut you down.'

There was a silence.

'Joe's right,' Nathan said, eventually. 'There's no other explanation.'

Topaz and Nathan walked home at sunset, holding hands.

'Don't worry about Goldstein,' he said. 'He's just jealous of you. He'll come round.'

'He blames me for what's happening to *White Light*,' Topaz said, and then added, 'I guess they all do.'

'Hey,' Nathan told her, kissing her. 'It is absolutely not your fault. OK? There isn't one of them wouldn't have run that story, and there isn't one of them that wouldn't have used our only music magazine to run it in. So relax.'

She was quiet all the way home. Nathan led her to the sofa and they sat down, and he clasped both her hands in his.

'Tell me what's bothering you,' he murmured. 'I can't bear to see you like this.'

She looked at him, her eyes brimming. 'I don't know,' she said. A large tear rolled down her cheek, and then another.

'What is this?' asked Nathan, kissing her. 'This is not like my girl.'

'Do you think' – she faltered – 'do you think I fucked my way to the top?'

'What? No!' he said, almost laughing, but she looked so upset he stopped himself. 'Is that what this is about? Come on, Topaz! I didn't make you MD of *Girlfriend*, did I? And I voted for you for *Economic Monthly* because you gave the best presentation. You stupid woman, it was a unanimous decision by eight people.'

She was really crying now. 'Don't leave me, Nathan,' she sobbed.

'Who said anything about leaving you?' he said, bewildered. 'I *live* with you! I *love* you, for God's sake.'

She cried herself out for a couple of minutes, then wiped her eyes.

'Are we finished yet?' Rosen asked.

'Yeah,' Topaz snuffled. 'Sorry.'

'I'm not going to leave you, or reject you, like your dumb-ass parents or your college friend. You got that?'

'Yes,' said Topaz meekly, kissing him.

'Come to bed,' he said.

They lay entwined in each other's arms. 'What are you thinking about now?' Nathan asked her.

'Ice cream,' said Topaz, honestly. She smiled lazily at her lover, and added, 'Coffee ice cream.'

'If I go get you some coffee ice cream, what will you do for me then?' asked

Nathan, looking down at her, wondering how he'd ever got this damn lucky. God, she was so beautiful.

'I'll marry you twice.'

'OK,' he said. 'I'll be right back.'

Topaz lay in bed and thought how gorgeous he was, and how smart, and played naming their kids again: Nate and Louise and Nick and Rosie, she thought. After he'd been gone a quarter of an hour she started to worry, so when the bell buzzed she was relieved.

She opened the door.

There was a cop in the porch.

'Do you live here, ma'am?'

'Yes I do,' she said, clutching her robe around her. 'What's the problem?'

'Are you any relation to Nate Rosen?'

Topaz went cold. 'I'm his fiancée,' she whispered.

'I'm very sorry, ma'am,' the cop said.

Musica Records issued a press statement. The whole thing was an exaggeration. Mark Thomas, drummer for Atomic Mass, had been convicted of possession of two joints of marijuana at the age of sixteen and let off with a fine. Alex Sexton, the bassist, had borrowed his dad's car without permission, but that had been a mistake and no charges had ever been brought. Yes, it was true that the head of security hired for the tour had a criminal record for grievous bodily harm, but the band and their representatives had not been aware of it until now. The man had been dismissed and deported.

Rowena had rarely enjoyed a press conference so much.

'But dope is still a drug...' protested one journalist, desperate to keep some controversy alive.

'What can I tell you?' shrugged Rowena. 'He didn't inhale.'

There was laughter and applause.

The *Heat Street* launch was back on.

'I'm not risking more delay in New York,' Oberman insisted. 'You saved your ass this time, but who knows what that goddamn magazine will come up with next?'

'Nothing at all,' she assured him. 'We're closing them down.'

'Yeah, well. I heard you and Krebs were stirring things up for them.'

'I still think we should have it here or in LA.'

'I said *London*, and I was still your boss last time I looked,' snarled Oberman. 'The subject is closed. Oh, and kid –'

'Yes, commander?'

'Wear something nice.'

Two days later, a thick, stiff, expensive-looking cream envelope arrived for Richard Gibson at the *White Light* offices on Seventh Avenue, sent registered delivery and marked 'Personal'. Inside, to Gibson's blinding fury, were two invitations to the launch of the Atomic Mass album *Heat Street* at the Earl's

Court Exhibition Centre in London, and a short handwritten note from the Managing Director of Luther Records.

Dear Mr Gibson,

I have great pleasure in enclosing an invitation to our launch party, and hope that your doubtless enormous advertising revenue will enable you to afford the air fare. You will be most welcome, although regrettably, due to the sheer volume of interview requests from TV, radio and major magazines –

Fuck you, thought Gibson furiously

– we will not be able to give interview time to White Light *on this occasion. I also enclose an invitation for Ms Topaz Rossi, who I gather has been advising you on your editorial policy. I'm sure her advice has greatly benefited your magazine. I am quite sure that you, as editor, are aware how useful she has been to you and will therefore want to pass on our invitation to her yourself.*

With best wishes.

Rowena Gordon.

Yeah. She's been real useful, Gibson thought bitterly.

He tore the envelope up.

'I love it! I think it's fantastic,' Michael said. 'You're really coming on. I never knew you had this kind of a vindictive streak in you.'

'Normally I don't,' Rowena said, 'but Topaz Rossi and I have a long history. This was the closest she's come to screwing up my career. I want the guy we're putting out of business to know exactly who's responsible for this. I want her management to see she's unreliable, short-termist, lets personal stuff affect her business decisions.'

Krebs was not used to the edge in her voice.

'You look good,' he said, changing the subject.

'Thank you,' she smiled, instinctively tossing back her long blonde hair. It was an adolescent gesture, totally appealing. She's a hot little thing, he thought, pleased.

'I wanted to look good for the band,' she said. 'You should too. It's a moment of triumph for you. It's such a great record.'

'Thanks, babe,' Krebs said.

He wasn't listening; his eyes were still fixed on her dress. It was a long, sleeveless figure-hugging Dior creation in moss-green velvet, a classic, but cut to emphasize the small, inviting swell of her breasts, the soft, delicate line of her bare shoulders and her long, slim legs. Her hair, normally tied back in a ponytail for convenience, spilled down her shoulders and the bare skin of her back. Long diamond drop earrings dangled and glittered against it. She looked aristocratic, unattainable.

'How are you getting there?'

'I'm going on Concorde, tomorrow morning.'

'I'm flying out this evening, so I'll see you there,' he said. 'Make sure you wear this outfit. And don't wear panties.'

'Why? Are you going to fuck me?' she asked, getting excited.

'Yes, I think so,' he said, getting up and coming behind her. He put one hand on the small of her back, just above the fabric of the skirt, and laid the other open on her stomach. 'I always want to fuck you when you look like this. Just to remind you that you belong to me.'

He could feel the heat begin to stir under her skin. She moved slightly under his hands.

'You can be as much of a hard-nosed bitch as you want with everyone else,' he said, speaking low and close to her ear, 'as long as you remember your place with me. On your knees, at my feet. Or bent over a flight case. Or spreadeagled on my bed . . .'

She gasped with desire.

'It's true, isn't it?' Krebs pressed her. 'Yes or no?'

'Yes!' she whispered. His hands were still on her. 'Now. Please, Michael. Now.'

He turned her head to face him, her pupils dilated with wanting.

'No,' he said. 'You'll wait my pleasure. Tomorrow.'

'OK,' she murmured, fighting to control herself.

He smiled and kissed her, a luxurious, possessive kiss, letting her press herself against his erection.

'I'm sorry, miss,' said the policeman. 'All the roads to Earl's Court are blocked. It's pandemonium down here.'

She leant out of the driving seat window. He was right. A mob of fans and photographers was blocking the way.

'I'm with Musica Records,' she said, showing him her company ID. 'Can you get me through to the reserved parking?'

'Certainly, madam,' said the policeman, with a friendly smile.

That's *one* thing I don't miss about New York, Rowena thought, grinning.

A police escort guided her through a crowd comprised mostly of screaming, hysterical girls to the backstage door.

'The pop group is going to play live, miss,' one of them explained, 'and Capital Radio gave tickets away on the air, so those as didn't manage to get in are going mad.'

'Sorry,' she sympathized. This was great; she'd had no idea the boys were so popular back home. She'd get a number one album on both sides of the Atlantic.

'Oh, I seen it before,' the policeman said with a worldly air. 'I done security at a U2 concert.'

This guy is equating my band with *U2*? she thought, delighted. Oh my God!

'This is worse, though,' he added.

'Rowena! Come over here,' Josh Oberman said as she stepped backstage, threading her way through a jungle undergrowth of camera leads, lighting cables and microphones. 'Come meet my head of Press, Rachel Robinson,' he added, without drawing pause for breath. 'She's desperate for someone to say something about Atomic Mass to a bunch of important press people who're having to wait their turn with the band – everyone's working flat out, we still can't meet demand. And make sure you *shout*,' he bellowed unnecessarily, waving a wrinkled hand at the auditorium behind them, which was packed out with yelling, whistling, clapping kids waiting for the band to come on.

'Did you have to have them play? I thought we were just going to put the CD on,' said Rowena.

'They wanted to play,' Oberman shrugged.

'Artists!' she said, using the same tone of voice women normally reserve for 'Men!'

Her boss laughed.

'Is Michael Krebs here?' Rowena asked casually.

'Yeah. He arrived four hours ago; Rachel's been setting him up for interviews with *Guitar World, Bassist Magazine, Drums Unlimited*, et cetera, et cetera.'

She looked to her right and saw Krebs standing against the stage scaffolding, surrounded by reporters, greatly enjoying himself.

'. . . so by the time we got to the drum fills stage, we had about seventy-five fills on this one song, and Mark also wanted a different sound on the hi-hat, so we . . .'

'Rowena? I'm Rachel,' said an incredibly slim woman who looked about nineteen.

She reluctantly dragged her gaze away from her lover.

'Could you come and talk to *Kerrang!*? They want the story of how you discovered Atomic. And when you're done, so do sixteen others . . .'

'Of course, I'll talk to *Kerrang!*. It's an honour to talk to *Kerrang!*!' she exclaimed, laughing. 'But why do people want to interview backroom boys?'

'Are you kidding?' Rachel exclaimed. 'The band is so hot right now their dustman could sell an exclusive to the *News of the World* on what they ate for breakfast this morning!' The scandal in the States was pretty good for them, too.' She looked slyly at Rowena. 'Did you plant it?'

An hour later, she was finally allowed out of the press tent, if only because Atomic would be hitting the stage in fifteen minutes. They would play a four-song mini-concert, and then the *Heat Street* playback would start. Some teenage girls in the front row had become hysterical with anticipation and were being given first aid by medics. She wanted to go and say hi to Barbara and the boys, but was warned away from the dressing rooms by a burly security guard, and felt too exhausted from the flight and the interviews to argue.

'Where am I supposed to go now?' she asked him.

He examined her perfectly valid all-access laminate sourly.

'Well,' he conceded, 'it says here that you can go up on the stage.'

'Good,' she snapped, and stalked up the ramps to the wings of the stage, finding an amp she could hide behind to watch the show. Out in front of her, the exhibition centre stretched out, brilliant with lights and banners of *Heat Street* and the blue and gold Atomic Mass logo. Oh, Jesus, this was exciting. This was *her* little band that she'd found a few years ago in a Yorkshire club. All those people, just banks of people, kids all crushed and sweating and unbearably excited, fields of them right in front of her, jamming every inch of space in the arena until it had to shut the gates because of the fire risk – all these kids here for Atomic.

She was Mistress of the Universe tonight.

'Like the view?' Michael Krebs murmured in her ear, standing directly behind her.

He ran his hands over her ass, and smiled, satisfied. 'Good,' he said. 'I won't have to waste time taking your panties off.'

She blushed. He was feeling her naked under the dress, enjoying her obedience.

'We can't really do anything,' she objected softly. 'The whole record business is here.'

'I keep telling you, Rowena,' he said, 'that I will have you wherever I want, whenever I want. If I tell you to march out there and do it for the cameras, you will.'

He had pushed her legs apart, and was stroking her gently at the top of her thighs. She pressed slightly backwards, into his hands, staring straight ahead of her, trying to look as though she were having a normal conversation.

'Please don't do this,' she said.

'Don't do what? Don't get you hot? Don't turn you on?' he teased.

The arena lights dimmed. There was a huge roar of anticipation from the crowd, waves of sound sweeping over the stage.

'We did this, you and me,' he said in her ear, leaning in towards her to counteract the noise. 'This gig. This record. This launch. Your enemy, what's her name – Rossi? – we had total victory over her.'

As the boys hit the stage running, to screams of joy from the arena, Rowena Gordon felt a light, sweet, spontaneous orgasm rush across her groin. Krebs felt it, and thrust up the velvet of her dress in the darkness, brushing his thumb firmly against the slick nub of her clitoris.

She cried out, the noise drowned in howling guitars, and came again instantly, against his hand.

He spun her round to face him, tugging her dress back down. 'Come with me,' he said, hardly able to control himself. 'I told you you'd wait my pleasure. It's my pleasure right now.'

He led her to centre backstage, behind the drum riser, above a little stairway going downwards.

'There's a room under the riser,' he said. 'It's got a trapdoor which locks.'

'Right here?' she whispered.

'Right here,' he said. She put her hand on his cock, rock-solid through his jeans, and he grabbed it and held it there.

'Do you think I can wait?' he asked.

'No.'

'Can you wait?'

'No!' she gasped. 'Oh, Michael! Oh!'

He practically threw her down the stairs before they were interrupted by a stagehand, slamming the trapdoor under the base of the drumkit and bolting it. The little room was crammed with clean towels for the band, two guitars and a bass, flight cases, bottles of Gatorade and other musician clutter. They were swamped by music and the audience out front going crazy. The dull boom-boom-boom of the drums pulsed loudly above them.

Alone with him, Rowena couldn't look him in the face.

'Don't groupies usually end up down here?'

'Yes they do,' he said.

'Why don't you show me what happens to them?'

He came over towards her, twisting a piece of flex in his hands. 'Do managing directors and groupies fuck in the same way?' he said, teasing her again. 'Put your hands up by the crossbeam.'

He lashed her wrists to the ceiling, so she was perched on a case, helpless and aroused before him.

'That's tight,' she protested, tugging futilely at the cable.

Krebs looked her over, all velvet and pearls, her breasts unprotected beneath the fabric, her arms over her head.

'You can't touch me,' he said. 'You can't free yourself. You can't caress me, you can't brush my hand away. Do you understand? I can do whatever I like to you. You're at my mercy.'

'I know,' she whispered.

'Do you like it?'

'Yes,' she said. 'You know I do.'

For a moment he didn't move, just stood there looking at her.

She twisted impatiently. 'Do you want me to beg?'

Krebs reached forward and eased her dress away from her shoulders, kissing and licking the collarbone. She moaned, quietly. He unsnapped her bra in a practised movement, freeing her breasts, swollen with lust, the nipples red and erect with longing. As she gasped with pleasure, he started to lick slowly round the left areole, flicking his tongue back and forwards across the peak, which was getting bigger and harder in his mouth.

'That's OK,' he said. 'Your body is begging for you.'

Then he moved to her right breast, and when she was practically incoherent, he took the whole thing in his mouth and sucked.

She screamed, little rivers of sensation coursing through her to her crotch, which was beating, throbbing with need. She tried to press herself against him but he held her back, smiling.

'What do you want?' he whispered. 'Tell me. Tell me exactly what you want me to do.'

'I want you to put your cock inside me!' she gasped. The sound of the band and the screaming fans was all around them; her triumph heightened his every touch. She had never in her wildest dreams thought her body capable of such feelings.

About to burst, he shoved up her dress and pulled her legs open, freeing himself and thrusting into her, hard, as far as he could go, grinding into her. Krebs had his hands on velvet and warm skin, feeling his woman clench around him like she wanted to milk him dry. Christ, she felt so good. He fucked her even harder. Oh, she was great. She was the best. Look at her bucking and writhing against him, pleading with him not to stop . . .

'I'm gonna come, Rowena,' he said thickly. She was already there; he looked down and saw her stomach literally convulse beneath him, one, two, three times . . .

He called out her name over and over as he came.

'It was *amazing*! I've never seen a reaction like that,' gushed the *Music Week* reporter to her an hour later, at the glittering post-launch party at the Dorchester. 'I've never felt like that during a concert.'

'I felt good during that concert too,' Michael Krebs said, joining them with a glass of champagne for Rowena. She bit her lip to stop herself from laughing; Krebs winked at her.

The reporter looked from one to the other, bewildered. 'There's obviously a great friendship between you two,' he said.

'Not really,' Rowena grinned. 'Michael produces great records, so I just pretend to like him so he'll keep working with me.'

'Ha, ha, ha!' laughed the reporter sycophantically. 'But would you go on the record as saying you make a great team?'

'Yes, indeed,' said Michael.

'I'll go on the record too,' Rowena added, dropping her voice conspiratorially, 'as saying –'

The reporter hastily took out a biro and a scrap of paper.

'– Atomic Mass are a really, really great band.'

Krebs made a strangled coughing noise.

'– really great band,' the reporter wrote earnestly.

'Excuse us,' Krebs said, pulling her away to dance.

The hotel ballroom was full of media types, celebrities, musicians and executives from Musica and other record companies. Both Rowena and Michael had networked the place for hours, and finally wanted to relax. The playback had been another huge success; Michael's laborious, fat production had brought out the best in the band, who were fantastic to start off with, and it looked tonight as if *Heat Street* might become the bestselling album of his career. Rowena watched, burning with pride, as suit after suit came up to pay homage. She accepted her own tributes with one eye on him, absentmindedly spooned beluga caviar into her mouth while staring at him smiling and shaking hands across the room. Half the other women there were doing the same thing.

'I'm jealous,' she said lightly. She could feel the pressure of his hands, pulling her closer towards him. She loved the way the black dinner jacket picked out his eyes. 'All these other girls are looking at you.'

'Don't you think I see the guys stripping you with their eyes?' he smiled. 'But I know who you want. And I only want you.'

What about Debbie? she thought, but didn't say it.

'Come over tonight,' he said, '47 Park Street. We'll take up where we left off.'

'I'll check my diary,' she said, laughing.

God, I like this woman so much, Krebs thought affectionately, smiling at his friend.

As she was about to leave – ten minutes after Michael – a rough hand grabbed her shoulder.

'Rowena,' said Joe.

She looked at her singer, who was hoarse, sweating and exhausted.

He held out his hand for her to shake. 'Thank you,' he said. 'For everything.'

'Oh, Joe,' she said, clasping it, and her eyes filled with tears.

That night, Michael was tender and gentle with her.

'I love you,' said Rowena afterwards, and regretted it instantly.

'Come on, Rowena, don't spoil it,' he said, pulling his jeans back on. 'You're not my girlfriend.'

'What am I, then?' she asked, astonished.

'You're my friend,' Michael said breezily. 'You're my good friend, who I happen to enjoy having sex with. Debbie and I are absolutely secure in our relationship.'

He said this without a trace of irony.

Topaz organized the funeral. It was merciful that she had something to do, it took her mind off the loneliness and the loss.

Nathan had died instantly, hit by a drunk-driver, crossing the road. He'd been carrying coffee ice cream. When she saw it spattered over his shirt, mixed with dirt and blood, Topaz had felt grief so violent she'd fainted.

They held the service at Mt Hebron Synagogue, his favourite. She drove upfront in a long black limousine and stared out numbly at Fifth Avenue, at the cold sidewalks and crawling traffic. She thought about Nathan the whole time. The synagogue and the roads were jammed with his friends, the ones she knew and dozens she'd never met; a sister, a cousin; all weeping for him and praying for his soul.

Topaz felt her pain as if it were a great stone, physically blocking her breath and the tears that might clean her. She had loved Nathan and felt safe and comforted in his presence; her initial hot sexual crush had mellowed into friendship and alliance over the months. Up until now, she hadn't realized just how dependent on him she had been. Nathan had made all these friends; real friends, crying because he was dead. Topaz had companions, her buddies from the office, who'd all come round and been honestly sorry for her. But amongst them all, there was not one real friend. She had not one soul whom she could call on in the night, when she lay awake staring into space.

Nathan Rosen was the only person she'd allowed to truly befriend her since Rowena's betrayal.

His sister, Miriam, began the eulogy. Topaz crossed herself, and beseeched the Blessed Virgin to intercede for his soul.

'Thank you again, Miss Rossi,' Miriam Rosen said, kissing her on the cheek. 'I'll be thinking of you. You make sure and call me if there's anything you need.'

'I will, Miriam,' said Topaz. 'Goodbye now. Thank you.'

She shut the door on her and breathed out. That was the last guest gone; now she could clear up the wake and just sit and think. Maybe cry some.

Joe Goldstein cleared his throat.

She jumped and spun round.

'I'm sorry,' he said. He was standing in the kitchen doorway. 'I didn't mean to startle you.'

'It's OK,' she said.

'I – I wanted to wait until everyone else had gone,' he said. 'I have to say something to you.'

She gestured wearily at the sideboard and tables, covered with plates and glasses. 'Can it wait until Monday, Joe? I'm really busy.'

'It's not that, it's not work.' He shifted slightly, uncomfortable. 'I wanted to apologize to you. For the record, not just because Nathan . . . ' He petered out.

'I know.'

'What I said about the two of you was unforgivable. And it wasn't true. I was just jealous, I guess I felt humiliated when you got *Economic*. You know Nathan was my mentor; I could see you meant more to him than I did.'

Topaz looked levelly at him. Man, it was really costing him something to come out with this stuff.

'OK, I accept your apology,' she said. 'It's decent of you to admit it.'

He nodded curtly, obviously debating with himself whether to say something more, decided against it and walked to the door.

'You make sure and –'

'– call you if I have any problems, OK, Joe,' finished Topaz, a shade sarcastically.

He smiled ruefully at her. 'You know, I do realize you're very talented,' he said, and let himself out.

The phone rang, shatteringly loud in the darkness.

Goldstein glanced wearily at his bedside clock. It was 3.30 a.m. 'Goldstein,' he said.

'Joe?'

'Topaz, is that you?' he asked, wide-awake. She was crying so hard he could barely make the words out, but it was her, definitely.

'Could you come over, please? I can't be alone . . .'

'I'm on my way, OK? Don't do anything,' said Joe, illogically, reaching for his slacks.

She opened the door for him, red-eyed and haggard.

'I'm sorry,' she said. 'I don't know what came over me.'

'It's OK,' said Joe. 'Honestly.'

'I know it's pathetic,' said Topaz, 'but I don't have anyone I can call,' and she started to cry again.

He shut the door and guided her into the kitchen, putting on the kettle.

'So I'm nobody, right? You never stop,' he said, and she made a weak attempt at a smile.

'Grief comes at bad hours for the people who really care,' he said. 'You need to mourn him, and not just by yourself. You know what sitting shiva is?'

'I *am* a New Yorker,' said Topaz indignantly, through her tears.

'Oh, OK. Sorry.'
'Stop saying sorry.'
'OK.'
There was silence for a minute or so.
'I brought some cheese popcorn over,' said Joe.
'I love cheese popcorn.'
'Wanna talk about him?'
'Yes I do,' she sobbed.

Joe stayed with her till dawn.

21

Nathan Rosen's death changed a lot of things.

In practical terms, it meant that Topaz Rossi, the main beneficiary of his will, became a very rich woman overnight, with a net worth of more than four million dollars. She was also that rarest of creatures in New York, a house owner.

It left a vacant seat on the American Magazines board. Joe Goldstein, in confident possession of his MBA – Topaz had given up on hers due to pressure of work – was determined to occupy it. He mourned his friend and bitterly regretted his behaviour towards him over the Rossi business. But he knew that Rosen was dead, no amount of sorrow could change it. And life – and business – went on.

Joe planned on being on the board by forty and president by fifty. Gowers wouldn't stay in the game for ever. He hoped Topaz Rossi would be content to consolidate and build on her three magazines – because he'd annihilate her if she went for this one, and he was beginning to enjoy her company.

Topaz grew up. She took a step back from her work, made time for her friends. She was appalled to discover how little she knew about the people she'd been working with for years. She had dinner with Elise and her husband, and baby-sat for her secretary. Josh Stein, who'd moved from *Westside* to be art director for *US Womam*, introduced her to his boyfriend. Socially, she was awkward and stilted, but people made allowances. She began to feel less alone.

She got herself an accountant and a lawyer and a realtor, who sold the house for a huge amount of money. Topaz didn't want to mess up her head any worse, thinking about Nathan promising to be right back. The realtor plunged all the money straight into a new apartment – a fashionable triplex on 5th Avenue, with lots of bare space and natural light.

Topaz spent the better part of half a million dollars redecorating it. It gave her something to do, and it seemed appropriate. After all, she was going to be the youngest board member of a major magazine group in history. She hoped Joe wouldn't fight on this one; she'd beaten him before and would do it again if she had to, but she was really getting fond of the guy.

Heat Street sold a million records in six months.

Michael Krebs made a fortune off the deal.

Joshua Oberman succeeded John Watson as the new chairman of Musica.

Rowena set up Luther as a full company. She found a building with a knockdown rent across the park and called it Musica Towers – not exactly Black Rock, but it'd do. She bought five pairs of jeans and twenty T-shirts and stopped caring what she looked like. She was in the office by eight every morning, fine-tuning Oberman's distribution deals, supervising computer systems and decorators and huge wall-mounted TVs that could blast out MTV and VH1 twenty-four hours a day. She stomped about in a cloud of dust and woodshavings, losing her temper. She started hiring, and that was the fun part; there was so much talent going begging it wasn't true. She hired people like herself, young, clever hustlers who were also music junkies. Nobody older was going to work for a fledgling company anyway. She did try to recruit a few established names, and failed miserably. It didn't bother her superiors much, though; young hungry staff were more motivated – and they came cheaper.

There were plenty of role models in New York: André Harrell, ruling at Uptown; Richard Griffiths at Epic, another expat Brit and one whose roster made her sick with envy – Spin Doctors, Brad, Screaming Trees, Rage Against the Machine, Eve's Plum, etc, etc; Monica Lynch of Tommy Boy and countless others.

Obsession had a little success; the second act Rowena signed, Steamer, a thrash band, had more.

People started to fill offices, and Luther mixed the whine of chainsaws with whirring computer printouts and stereos pumping out Ice Cube and Sugar. Rowena filled one floor with phones and faxes and started the promotion department right away; Roxana was being worked at urban radio and Atomic Mass at Metal and CHR within a week.

In all her life, she'd never felt so alive.

She'd learnt her lesson and made sure they had good accountants and administrators as well as talented staff. By the end of the year Luther was a growing concern, and Josh Oberman finally thought that if they could just arrange to market more product, they could set up their own distribution.

Rowena was still obsessed with Michael, but slowly, painfully, from a lack of oxygen, hope was starting to die. Still, she just could not give him up, and Michael had no intention of letting her go. He liked her. He desired her. And though he would never admit it, Rowena was more to him than either a friend or a piece of ass.

Michael needed her admiration, he enjoyed her intelligence, and there was a part of him – the part whose parents had neglected him, whose first real girlfriend had cheated on him, whose wife was more interested in their children – that revelled in being the object of such blind, heedless, reckless love.

He wasn't an intentionally cruel man. He told Rowena, and he believed it when he said it, that he wanted her to have other lovers. To be happy. To find an available guy. But he knew her intimately, and he knew that there was never any real competition for him from the occasional dates that Rowena forced herself to go on for a week or so, something she hated doing, something she forced herself to do to prove to herself that she wasn't helpless.

Rowena met plenty of men, but so far she had been blind to them all. Krebs filled her dreams, her fantasies, her life.

It was true love.

It was terrible.

'I got some news for you,' Mary Cash, her assistant, smiled at Topaz as she handed her her coffee. 'Strictly gossip, though.'

'That's usually the most reliable source,' Topaz said. She meant it; not only was Mary a brilliant office manager, she was plugged into the nerve centre of the secretarial mafia.

'Well, word is that the boys upstairs are scouting to buy a sports property.'

'Really?' her boss asked. It made sense.

'Yeah, and when they've found one, they'll be picking some people to work on the buyout, monitoring the team . . .'

'And promoting the best person to the board?'

'You got it.'

Topaz felt a rush of pure adrenalin flood through her. She hadn't been this excited since Nathan died.

'And for what it's worth,' added Mary, pleased to see her interested again, 'the same person who told me was talking privately with Linda this morning.'

Linda was Joe Goldstein's secretary.

'Aha,' said Topaz, thoughtfully.

'Aren't you guys going to another Mets game tonight?' asked Mary archly. 'Will this get in the way?'

'Yes we are, and maybe,' said Topaz. 'But you know what? If it does – tough!'

They laughed.

'Are you sure?' Joe pressed Linda.

'Mary Cash. I swear.'

'OK, thanks.'

He took his finger off the buzzer and stared out of the window. It was a spectacular view from the forty-third floor, the tops of the skyscrapers and the Hudson and the long, straight roads with their glittering little cars. That was the prize: New York. Nothing less, as far as he was concerned. New York was media city, and only two types of men really ruled here: media bigshots and the Wall Street crowd. It would have been television, if he had had his choice.

But even someone as driven as Joe couldn't complain about the speed of this rise.

The American Magazines board, before he was thirty-five!

It was a bright autumn day in Manhattan, the sun streaming weakly into the chill air, nothing but dry, crisp brilliance outside his warm office.

He truly hoped Topaz would not take it personally, but he wouldn't give this up. For anyone.

'Seeing much of David?' Rowena asked Barbara, cradling her phone with her shoulder as she studied the Bitter Spice sales figures.

'Not really,' Barbara said. David Hammond, head of A&R at Funhouse Records in the UK, had been dating her for years. 'He took up with some Central European girl and carried on with me at the same time.'

Rowena winced. 'That must've hurt.'

'Yeah it hurt. And you know I slept with someone else once, two years ago, when David and I had just broken up?'

'But he wasn't seeing you.'

'I know. But he keeps referring to it, every time. As if my seeing this guy once is the same thing as him taking Elvira to every bloody industry event . . .'

'And he's still sleeping with you?'

'I know.' Barbara sighed. 'It's pitiful. But I'm sexually addicted, and I love him, however much of a bastard he is. What women will do, how low women will sink when they're in love.'

'I know,' said Rowena, thinking about Michael.

'Your head can be fully aware that the guy's no good. It's all very well, magazines saying that if you can see what a jerk he is you'll be cured. That's bullshit.'

'Your heart rules.'

'Every time.'

'It's an occupational hazard of being female,' Rowena said.

'How's business? Apart from us.'

'Apart from you, pretty good; including you, sensational. I've been consolidating, building, nothing flashy. Oberman's looking to set up a soundtrack deal, a label/studio-type deal – an exclusive arrangement.'

'You'd do all the soundtracks for one movie studio?'

'Exactly. And they'd own a piece of the label.'

'Sounds interesting. It could kick you up the corporate ladder, too.'

'No one ever said you were dumb, honey.'

'Nice change-up,' said Topaz appreciatively. 'Maybe we have a chance in this one.'

'I wouldn't bet on it,' said Joe, demolishing the first third of his hotdog. He swallowed and added, 'Pitching's OK, just. Hitting sucks. Us and the Padres have the lowest hitting average in the league, remember.'

'Thanks for the recap,' said Topaz, glaring at him. She hated defeatists. 'I love sports,' she added.

Joe stared fixedly at the field.

'And I love magazines,' she added.

Joe turned to her, dragging his gaze away from the game. 'Look, Rossi,' he said, 'if this is your attempt at subtlety, it's not working. I take it you heard about the sports title.'

'Right.'

'And . . . will you be requesting an assignment to the takeover team?'

'You mean am I pitching for the board?'

'That's what I mean,' said Goldstein.

'Are you?'

They looked at each other for a long moment, regretfully.

'Let's make it a clean fight.'

'OK.'

'No resentment,' Topaz insisted. 'Either side.'

'Fine by me.'

'Let's make it a rule never to talk about business after hours.'

'Let's watch the damn game, Topaz.'

Gary Sheffield strode on to the field, pinch hitting for Pat Rapp.

'Oh no,' said Joe.

'That's never in the pitch zone! Oh, no!' said Topaz, jumping up in her seat. 'No!'

Sheffield swung and hit a low outside fastball in a soaring curve towards the leftfield stands.

'It's history,' moaned Goldstein, a man in pain. 'Oh God. I can't bear it.' Topaz covered her eyes with her hands to avoid the gruesome sight of another enemy home run.

'I want you to know that I'm not gonna back off or ease up in any way on this,' Joe said.

'No business.'

'OK.'

Topaz drove them to René Pujol's on West 51st Street for dinner. 'They have a melting chocolate cake that's the closest thing to heaven this side of a cemetery,' she said.

'French food. Makes a change,' Joe remarked.

'What do you normally eat?'

'Italian.'

She smiled at him.

They talked a lot at dinner, about politics, religion, music. Topaz discovered that Goldstein had been pretty lonely since transferring to the East Coast; he hadn't done as badly as her, but he still missed his friends.

'I gotta get back,' said Joe eventually, checking his watch. 'I got a girl waiting.'

'Oh, I'm sorry,' Topaz said. 'I didn't know you had a girlfriend.'

Joe laughed. 'She's not my girlfriend, she's just some girl. I told the porter to let her in at ten so I'd better not be much longer.'

'Some girl?' repeated Topaz.

'Yeah. Joanna or Joanie or something. I met her at a bar, arranged to see her tonight.'

'Just to get laid?'

'Right,' said Joe pleasantly.

'Does this woman realize you call her "some girl" and don't even know her name?'

'Don't preach at me, Topaz,' said Joe less pleasantly. 'She's going to get what she wants out of it. Girls who hang around that kind of pick-up joint aren't looking for a "meaningful relationship".' He put quotes around the phrase.

Topaz found herself getting angry. 'You were hanging around that kind of pick-up joint too, Joe. What does that make you? A gigolo?'

Goldstein flushed. 'It's different for men, and you know it.'

'Damn right it's different for men. Men don't get labelled as whores for having sexual desires.'

Joe flinched. 'I don't like hearing a lady talk dirty.'

Topaz paused, then reached for her wallet and threw two hundred-dollar bills on the table.

'Fuck you, Joe Goldstein. And fuck the double standard,' she said calmly, and walked out.

The team working on the buyout of *Athletic World* was announced internally. Only two people of the requisite seniority had applied: Joe Goldstein and Topaz Rossi. Employees graffitied notices with 'Round Two' and 'The Rematch'.

Topaz sent Joe a copy of *Backlash: The Undeclared War Against American Women* by Susan Faludi.

In return, he sent her a copy of *The Way Things Ought to Be* by Rush Limbaugh.

Athletic World proved a complicated deal. The magazine was still family-run, one of the only major sports magazines not part of a publishing conglomerate – 'yet,' as Matthew Gowers said. The trouble was that it didn't stand alone. *Athletic World* was part of a small group of sports companies – the middle-aged man who'd founded it had also acquired a gym and a company that made personalized shoelaces for trainers, in addition to a medium-sized operation selling *Athletic World* merchandise.

Joe suggested the board look for an easier target.

They turned him down, unanimously. American Magazines was tired of risky start-up ventures. American Magazines was shopping for a little goodwill, for a brandname.

Topaz played to her strengths and requested that she be assigned to profile the magazine, circulation and advertising, how it could be improved. Joe set to work with due diligence, finding an investment bank, finding buyers for the other parts of the group.

Both of them were in their element, completely. The chairman and the board kept close tabs, and were extremely impressed.

'Let me get this straight,' Kirk said. Kirk was Joe's closest friend; they jogged together before work. He swallowed a mouthful of doughnut.

'She's smart, she's funny, she has a great body –'

'Knockout. Absolutely knockout.'

'And she *likes baseball*?'

'Yup.'

'And you let her go? You really screwed up,' commented Kirk.

'Yeah, well,' said Joe. He pummelled the punchbag. 'That's the problem. She's too masculine.'

'Tomboys are usually great in bed,' said Kirk.

'I didn't fuck her, OK. I'm talking about losing a friend here.'

'But you guys were inseparable for the past six months! You couldn't pull her in all that time?' Kirk teased.

'Jesus, Kirk. I said it wasn't like that. We just talked, about politics, art, you know.'

'Uh-huh.'

'Oh, please,' snapped Joe, exasperated. 'The goddamn bitch is fighting me for the board. For the *board*. She refuses to budge an inch. I mean I've had it with her. She's too young and totally inexperienced and I am going to *cream* her. *Fuck* her. I'm out.'

He savagely laid into the punchbag.

Kirk chuckled. 'Joe, my friend,' he said, 'you've got it bad.'

It was 7 p.m. and the *Girlfriend* offices were emptying out. Topaz wrapped up her discussion with Sue Chynow, the editor-in-chief, and went to fix herself a fresh pot of coffee.

It was going to be a long night.

'I got takeout,' Joe said as she appeared in his office five minutes later. 'Chinese, is that good for you?'

'It's fine,' Topaz said coldly, drawing up a chair and briskly opening a file. 'Coffee?'

'Yes, thank you. Black,' said Joe, equally briskly.

They both began to study cashflow charts in aggressive silence.

An hour later, they were having what politicians term 'a free and frank discussion'.

'But women working out are *totally different* to women sports fans!' roared Topaz. 'Just like men, you stupid asshole! Working out is not a sport! It's exercise!'

'No. You're wrong,' Joe said, through clenched teeth. 'They're into Flo-Jo because she wears make-up, not because of her speed.'

'No. *Men* are into Flo-Jo because she wears make-up.'

'Take women *out* of the goddamn reader profile!' yelled Joe.

'I will not. It alters the finance –'

'Don't tell me about financing, Rossi! What do you think I've been doing for the last month –?'

'Looking in the mirror and jerking off, probably,' said Topaz rudely.

Joe went white with anger. 'What did you say?'

'You heard.'

'If you were a man, I'd knock you out.'

'Oh! Big guy,' sneered Topaz contemptuously. Why was he so gorgeous and such an asshole? 'I want you to remember that I kicked your ass over *Economic Monthly*. Think about that, Joe. Consider it a dress rehearsal.'

Goldstein got up and came towards her. 'You just don't get it, do you, cutie? This job's mine already. You couldn't buy out a loaf of bread, and they know it. You'll be reporting to me, and I'm truly going to enjoy it.'

Topaz was an inch away from him. 'Who are you calling cutie?' she hissed.

'Who do you think, babe? What are you gonna do? Sue me for sexual harassment?'

She looked at him, black-haired, handsome, taunting her furiously. He was wearing jeans and an expensive-looking Oxford shirt.

'Oh, that's not sexual harassment, pretty boy,' Topaz said. '*This* is sexual harassment.'

And she grabbed the collar of his shirt and ripped it down the front, sending the little ivory buttons clattering on to the boardroom table.

His chest was strong, lean and covered in tiny wiry black curls. Topaz steadied herself. An incredible, overwhelming rush of desire surged through her.

'What the fuck?' said Joe softly. Oh God, he shouldn't have brought up this sex-tension thing. The touch of her hand against his neck – even that sharp, angry touch – had set him off. He wondered if he dared kiss her. Damn, he was hard. He didn't dare look down in case he drew her attention to it.

'I'm sorry . . . I got carried away . . .' murmured Topaz. 'Maybe I can get a pin and fix it for this evening – I'll replace it, of course . . .'

She tried to pull his shirt together, her hands on his chest, his ribcage.

'Quit touching me, damn it,' growled Joe.

'Fine,' Topaz snapped back. 'I –'

She gasped. Goldstein grabbed her shoulders and pushed her back on the hard table.

'What are you doing?' whispered Topaz.

'Take an educated guess,' said Joe, and took her face in his two hands and kissed her impatiently, sucking on her top lip, thrusting his tongue into her mouth.

I *shouldn't do this*, thought Topaz.

Heat flooded her belly.

She kissed him back, hard.

'No! Go on,' said Marissa, utterly fascinated.

'Well, apparently,' said Lisa, 'the janitor heard screams at one in the morning, like woman's screams, upstairs in the boardroom, so he runs upstairs and Joe goes, "Everything's OK," but he insists on going in to check, and Topaz Rossi was sitting there all red-faced with her buttons done up wrong and her breath's coming short –'

'No!' said Marissa, trying to suppress a jealous rage. Joe Goldstein was the best-looking man in the company.

'– and Joe was tucking his shirt back into his pants,' finished Lisa triumphantly.

'What a tramp!' Marissa trilled. 'She let him do . . . *that* with her in the *boardroom*? First Nathan, now this. Well, he'll want nothing more to do with her now, of course.'

Lisa wasn't so sure about that, but kept her counsel. Marissa Matthews was a powerful columnist.

'Topaz Rossi just preys on older, rich men. I shall tell everybody.'

'Everybody knows,' said Lisa, 'and he's not that much older.'

Joe called Topaz.

'Wanna go to the game on Saturday?'

'Sure,' she said, delighted.

Fernandez pitched some brilliant high-heat balls and struck out six enemy batsmen.

22

The flight from JFK to LAX takes five hours, and Rowena spent most of it working. Generally speaking, she loved to fly. She liked to have a few hours away from the phones to read a novel or daydream. She enjoyed the lift in her stomach at takeoff and landing, and even now she felt a small thrill of adventure at jetting from one city to another. But this time it was different.

She pencilled another note next to the paragraph on royalty breaks, wishing for the millionth time that she had a better grasp of maths. It was one hell of an important deal for her. Every per cent in every clause had to be exactly right.

'Champagne, Ms Gordon?' enquired the stewardess, hovering solicitously. So far this elegant businesswoman had refused the chocolates, cashew nuts, cocktails, and main meal of fillet of Dover sole, lobster or roast pheasant which was the envy of every other first-class service in America. She injected a pleading note into her voice.

Rowena relented. 'That would be lovely. Thank you.'

The attendant tilted her crystal glass slightly and filled it with the light golden nectar, which delicately spat and bubbled as it poured. Rowena smiled her thanks.

'Busy trip, ma'am?' She glanced at the pile of contracts on the empty seat.

'Just slightly,' Rowena said.

Interesting that she's English, the stewardess thought as she moved on. The Brits don't usually dress that well.

Rowena leant back to sip her champagne, glad of the break. She was wearing a soft Liz Claiborne pantsuit, flowing and loose, in a gentle fawn. She'd teamed it with chestnut shoes from Pied à Terre, and a crisp white shirt. Her make-up was equally subtle: buttery eyeshadow, matt bronze lips, the faintest hint of blusher. Her long blonde hair was gathered at the nape of the neck in a tortoiseshell clip. She looked every inch a nineties player: beautiful, casual, absolutely businesslike.

She allowed the drink to refresh her and ran over her schedule for the trip. She was staying in a house in the Hollywood hills, permanantly rented for visiting Musica executives. Lunch with John Metcalf was all set for noon tomorrow, and that, she reflected wryly, would be an all-mineral-water meal. That would be one conversation where she could *never* afford to drop her guard. Then the Coliseum, where Atomic Mass were headlining their first stadium gig. She felt proud and anxious all at once; no matter how many copies *Heat Street* had sold, this was the first date of the tour, and they'd never filled a venue of that size before.

Even Atomic Mass could run into problems.

The ticket printout she'd seen two days ago showed only a 75 per cent gate sale, and the world's journos were poised with sharpened pencils and unforgiving cameras, ready to label them an overblown hype.

She shuddered. In the music business, 'has been' is a dangerous insult – it often became a self-fulfilling prophecy, and nobody, but nobody, was immune from media backlash – look what it did to Michael Jackson's last record!

Everyone's a critic, she thought furiously, and that bitch Topaz Rossi is the Queen Bee. Ever since Atomic Mass had launched the album in London, Topaz had done what she could to hurt the band, hurt Rowena, and hurt Luther.

She won't stop until she's brought me down, Rowena reflected. Venomous tramp. She wants her revenge.

She knew Rossi had primed at least three people in MTV and one at *Rolling Stone* to trash this gig, probably more. And anyone who worked for American Magazines knew what they thought of the show without turning up to see it, at least they did if they valued their jobs.

I won't dwell on it, Rowena told herself. The boys will be OK. They're the best band in the world. I have a deal to do here.

She wondered if Michael would find time to call her.

She was still working on release obligations when the plane banked into its descent. The ocean shone in the moonlight, and Los Angeles was spread out in the darkness like a sparkling, jewelled grid. Mercifully, for once VIP arrival service was fast and effortless, and her Gucci cases were amongst the first off the carousel.

In the limo she relaxed. She was pretty sure of what she wanted from Metcalf now.

And I'll get it, too, she thought. They say he's pretty tough. But I'm tougher. And I'm hungrier than he is for this thing.

The car took a left at the Hyatt on Sunset and snaked up the steep, winding hills. A little while later it stopped at the house, and Rowena let the chauffeur unlock the gates and carry her luggage into the porch. She tipped him twenty bucks. Why not? She was rich.

She flicked on the lights and took a look around, interested in what the company provided for its top people – but you're not top people yet, she reminded herself. Maybe tomorrow you'll be top people.

There was a note for her from the maid on the kitchen table, propped against a huge vase full of orchids. Towels, cosmetics, toiletries, bathrobes and pyjamas had been provided for her convenience. There was food and drink in the refrigerator and cinnamon coffee on the stove. The office next to the bedroom was equipped with a computer and fax machine, and had a range of exercise equipment set up for her use. There was a selection of books and videos in the drawing room. The chauffeur and herself were on call twenty-four hours. She hoped everything was to Ms Gordon's satisfaction and that Ms Gordon would have a nice day.

Cinnamon coffee? Rowena wondered.

The phone rang.

'Rowena Gordon.'

'Miss Gordon?' asked a warm male voice.

'Yup, that's what I said,' said Rowena, slightly irritated.

'This is John Metcalf.'

'Oh,' said Rowena. 'Hi,' she added lamely.

'Did you have a good flight?' Metcalf asked, sounding amused at her discomfiture.

'Yes thanks,' said Rowena. 'Good of you to call.' She didn't ask how he got her number. I'll let him make the running, she thought.

'I got your number from Musica in New York,' he said. 'Thought I'd call and check you were OK in LA by yourself.'

'Hey, that's nice of you,' she said. 'But I'm a big girl, and I carry a gun at all times.'

Why am I snapping his head off: I'm supposed to be pitching this guy.

Metcalf chuckled. 'Point taken. Will the Ivy be good for you tomorrow?'

'It'll be fine. I hear they have amazing soft-shell crabs.'

'Rowena! You mean you've never tried them? You haven't lived until you've tasted those things,' he said.

Well, we've moved on from 'Miss Gordon' pretty quickly, Rowena thought. But she didn't really mind. He sounded so friendly and warm, not kissy and LA-insincere like she'd expected.

'I'll look forward to it, and I'll look forward to meeting you,' she said pleasantly.

'It goes double here – the legendary Rowena Gordon!' he said.

The legendary Rowena Gordon? OK, so it was just a line, but she liked the way it sounded. She liked it a *lot*.

'See you tomorrow, Mr Metcalf.'

'Please call me John. I hope you look as good as you sound,' he said, and rang off.

Cheeky bastard, Rowena thought. But she was grinning.

She flicked a switch on the stove to heat the coffee. When in LA, after all ... the fridge was lavishly stocked with ham, chicken, ice cream, smoked salmon, olives; food enough for a starving army of gourmets. In the drinks door there was a pitcher of margaritas, a chilled magnum of champagne, and a bottle of Gordons next to three cans of Schweppes tonic water. *Nice touch!*

She fixed a weak G&T, clinking oversized ice cubes into a large frosted glass, and padded round the apartment. Everything was state-of-the-art, everything was the height of luxury. The drawing room projected on to the side of the hill and was three walls glass, so you could look out over Hollywood and the glittering city set at its feet, quiet from this height, moving calmly in rivers of light. In stark contrast to New York's concrete forest, there were only two clusters of skyscrapers visible on the horizon.

Rowena looked out over Los Angeles, towards Century City. John Metcalf might still be in his office there, making deals, rubbishing scripts, green-lighting pictures. He held sway over the destinies of hundreds of directors, actors, producers, agents. And right now, one record company executive.

Michael rang the next morning.

'I was thinking about you last night,' he said. 'I was having sex with someone else, and I was thinking about you going down on me.'

Rowena couldn't help herself. She felt her nipples stiffen in response to his lust.

'I put my cock inside her,' he said, 'and I fucked her, and I thought about you sucking me. You want to do that right now, don't you?'

'Yes,' whispered Rowena, wet for him already.

'Are you playing with yourself?'

'Yes.' She was.

'I can hear it in your voice,' Michael said, satisfied. 'You can't come unless I say so. If you were here I'd come in your mouth, and I wouldn't let you touch yourself.'

Rowena moaned.

'If you're sucking my cock, I expect it done properly,' he said. 'You have to lick my balls, and swirl your tongue over my cock, and suck me real, real slow, and make me come. I haven't got time for you to touch yourself. It's not my problem.'

She shuddered, uncontrollably aroused.

'I'm gonna make you beg for it,' he said. 'I'm going to take my cock out and rub it over your cheeks and lips until you beg me to put it back in your mouth.'

'Please,' Rowena sobbed. 'Please.'

'Have some control,' Michael teased her. 'You can't come yet. Then I'm going to shove it back in your mouth, right down the back of your throat. I'm going to grab the back of your head with my hands and push you down on my cock. I'm going to fuck your mouth ... maybe I'll have you stop in the middle and tell me how much you love it, what I taste like ... '

Her breathing was ragged and strained.

'You'll give me head whenever I ask for it,' he said harshly.

'Yes,' she managed.

'I can have you at my whim.'

'Yes.'

'Now come for me,' Michael ordered.

She gasped as she climaxed, her body arching, her splayed fingers soaked in her own juices.

Michael's voice came smiling down the phone. 'Good girl,' he said. 'I have to go now.'

'Goodbye,' she whispered. She put the phone down and wondered if she had ever felt cheaper. But she still longed for him. God, how she longed for him.

I'm a junkie, thought Rowena. *I'm addicted to Michael Krebs.*

She stepped out on to the patio, wet and silken from her shower, swathed in a huge white towelling bathrobe, a mug of very delicious cinnamon coffee steaming in her hand. The warm scent of hundreds of flowers hit her straight away. She settled into a green wicker chair, breathing in the gentle humid morning air, birds singing all around her.

'Bloody hell,' she remarked to a starling. 'I could get used to this.'

Work, work, work, her New York brain screamed at her. *What do you think you're doing? You're supposed to be setting up a soundtrack deal with the third-biggest studio in the world! Whole record companies have been established on less. This is a deal that could push Musica one, maybe two places up the world rankings, and as for your own position . . . bottom line, you want to wind up president, or not? You think Ahmet Ertegun would be out here drinking coffee? Haul ass, woman!*

Rowena sighed.

Now! it added.

Reluctantly, she drained the mug and went off to study the diagrams of unit sales in relation to box-office takings.

By lunchtime she was sick with nerves. She changed her outfit four times, eventually settling on loafers, black Calvin Klein jeans, a Def American T-shirt, and a very, very expensive pair of sunglasses. She wanted to look Californian and give the impression that she was too important to bother with dress codes. Damn it! I am important! she told herself. I'm Rowena Gordon, MD of Luther Records and the hottest music business executive in New York!

He was just a studio head. That was all. Right?

The limo glided through LA. Rowena stared out of the windows, mirrored from the outside, watching the landmarks of Sunset Boulevard slip past her . . . the Rainbow, the Roxy, Geffen Records . . . it was a city designed only for drivers. She stepped out at the Ivy looking sleek and confident, trying to feel the same way.

Relax! It's a breeze. It's a done deal.

'Rowena Gordon for John Metcalf,' she announced to the maître d'.

'Of course, ma'am. This way,' he said cheerfully, leading her through the packed restaurant to the best and most secluded table in the place. 15–0 to Metcalf, Rowena thought, using her metaphor for the war with Topaz Rossi. He was studying a wine list as she approached, immaculately dressed in a dark suit by Hugo Boss with discreet gold cufflinks. She pulled at her T-shirt and felt like an idiot. 30–0.

'Mr Metcalf,' she said, extending her hand. 'I'm Rowena Gordon.'

She was shocked, and tried not to show it. She was so used to being the youngest player in any deal. But he couldn't be more than a few years older than her; he was smooth-skinned, he had a large, taut, muscular body, and thick hazel hair with just the faintest grey flecking the sides. Christ, he was gorgeous, and what astonishing eyes. Thirty-five, tops.

'Good to see you, Rowena. Have a seat, please. And the name's John.'

She wanted to reply that he could call her Rowena, but forced herself to swallow the rebuke. It was his show.

'Please, indulge me, don't insist on sticking to the mineral water,' he said.

'The kir royales here are exquisite. I'll order for us both, so you won't be at any negotiating disadvantage. Please. I beg you.'

She looked at the handsome man smiling opposite her, who then batted his eyelids in a theatrical gesture of persuasion.

What a character, she thought with complete approval. The kind of guy you'd call a record man. Except that he's in movies.

She decided to throw away the script.

'OK, you win,' she said. 'I hate to see a grown man cry.'

The two-hour lunch turned into a three-hour lunch, and a three-hour lunch turned into tea, complete with china cups and a fake Georgian silver teapot.

'Cucumber sandwiches! Bring me cucumber sandwiches,' Metcalf demanded. 'I have an English lady here.'

'You're a jerk, John,' said Rowena, grinning. 'No one in England eats cucumber sandwiches. And no one eats muffins either. And we don't all know Princess Diana.'

'Next thing you'll be telling me there's no Victoria's Secret in England,' Metcalf protested.

'There isn't.'

'No Victoria's Secret, English lingerie, in England?' he asked.

'None,' said Rowena mercilessly.

Metcalf considered this disconsolately. 'What about the tooth fairy?'

'Oh, she's real,' she reassured him, and they both started to laugh.

'Twelve per cent rising one per cent, point five, point five, point five in the four years.'

'Get out of my face,' she said.

'That's the deal, take it or leave it,' John insisted. 'I can take it to PolyGram tomorrow.'

'They'll leave it too,' she said. 'I won't make this deal unless the numbers are right. And you can forget about reversion of rights. Musica does not surrender its masters. We're only in the market to buy, we're not interested in renting.'

'You're a tough bitch, Ms Gordon, anyone ever tell you that?'

'Frequently, Mr Metcalf. Frequently.'

'So I hope I can tempt you along to the gig tomorrow,' Rowena said.

'What, go see the hottest band in the world with the best-looking woman in the universe? I'll have to check my diary,' Metcalf teased her, shaking her hand.

Rowena opened the door of the limo and gave him what she hoped was a businesslike smile. 'I feel like I just went nine rounds with Mike Tyson,' she said.

He gave her a quick, intelligent glance. 'You did,' he said.

'But I'm still standing.'

'For now,' said John Metcalf. 'For now.'

23

'. . . And this is Gloria Roberts, *live* from 105.5, KNAC, always there at all the really *big* concerts, and we are *backstage* at the Coliseum and Joe Hunter of British rock sensations Atomic Mass is here with me! Welcome back, Joe.'

'This lady I am talking to,' said Hunter, in his rich Lancashire burr, 'was one of the first people *ever* in America to play Atomic Mass on the radio! Can you remember?'

'I *do* remember!' said the DJ, immensely flattered.

John Metcalf spun the steering wheel lightly with one hand, cruising down the Santa Monica freeway towards the Coliseum, listening to the band on KNAC, where Joe, the singer, was playing the interviewer like a guitar. He flicked a few buttons on the multi-play sound system, trying to find a Top 40 station that wasn't wall-to-wall Atomic Mass. He failed.

'And this is "Big Cat" from *Animal Instinct . . .*'

'. . . That was "Frozen Gold", a little Atomic Mass for ya there . . .'

'. . . from a record which just sold and sold and *sold.*'

'. . . making the British rock combo only the third act ever to sell out the Coliseum . . .'

'. . . *live* from Venice Beach, where our "what would *you* do for a pair of tickets for Atomic Mass" contest is reaching its climax.'

'And that was "Sea Diver" by Mott the Hoople . . .'

John rolled his eyes in mock relief.

'. . . who, by the way, are cited as one of the biggest influences on *the* band of the moment, Atomic Mass, headlining the Coliseum tonight on the *very first* show of the *Animal Instinct* world tour 1995 . . .'

He groaned in delighted defeat. He couldn't get away from them, which meant he couldn't get away from her. At least his baby label was in good hands. What a woman! What an executive! What a . . . what a *babe*!

She had sat in his office, commandeered a spare telephone and fixed the problem.

'OK. This is how it is,' she had said briskly, slapping a sheet of ticket sales in front of him. 'Gate is eighty-five per cent. And that's not good enough. I need a hundred per cent.'

'But why do you care?' he'd asked, amused. 'You're fine at eighty-five. They'll make money!'

'That's not the point. It's how the band are perceived. We open at the

Coliseum, we sell out the Coliseum. That's it. No argument. I want people clamouring for tickets they can't buy.'

'Otherwise what? They look bad?'

'Congratulations, you win a cigar,' said Rowena, as if to a particularly stupid child. 'The boys are hot property today and I want them to be hot property tomorrow and the day after that.'

'But the gig is tomorrow,' he pointed out, admiring the silver-blonde cascade of hair tumbling to her slender waist. Her iced-mint eyes were sparkling with the challenge.

'That gives me three hours,' said Rowena.

'You can't do anything in three hours!' laughed John.

'Oh yeah?' she said. 'Watch me.'

And he'd watched her. He'd watched the elegant turn of her calf in her tight jeans, the tight sweet swell of her small breasts under her bodystocking, the way she sat with her legs apart like a man, tapping her knee with one beautiful, unpainted hand. He'd tried not to stare too hard at her crotch, gently outlined under the protecting denim. He wanted to undo the buttons of her fly and slide his hand in there, and guide her slowly, slowly, to spasm, till she was whimpering and begging, and maybe he'd take a couple of handfuls of that fountain of blonde hair and twist her head roughly about while she squirmed against his palm . . . God, he'd be patient with her, and when he put his cock in that soft silver wetness he'd take her with a slow intensity, deep, long strokes, ignoring her pleas to fuck her brains out. He'd teach her what sex was really about, and she'd come like it was the end of the world, and then . . . and then . . . and then he'd marry her, the gorgeous fucking creature.

And occasionally he'd watched how goddamn great she was at her job.

'So can I speak to the PD? Hey, Ken? Rowena Gordon! Uh-huh? You too, up book *again* I see . . . Look, I got a trade for you . . . stick on the Catch-22 single. No, listen, you play it, I got five hundred tickets for Atomic Mass at the Coliseum tomorrow . . . that's right, completely sold out . . . great.'

'Sam Goody in Sacramento please – Richard Brown? Rowena Gordon – you got a nice Mass display up there, babe? Cause I'm thinking maybe the boys might drop in on their way out to the plane . . . shit, you know I can't guarantee it . . . No, the show's totally sold out, but you wanna run a promotion I can cut you a deal – a hundred, two hundred? two fifty? I don't know, it's tough – call Simon at TicketMaster and tell him it's on Musica corporate rate. Anything for my favourite store manager.'

'Joseph Moretti. This is Rowena Gordon. Of course top brass work the promo phones! This is Musica, not MCA! Here it is. Show is totally sold out. I want tomorrow to be Atomic Mass day on KXDA – you get one thousand tickets and ten pairs of all-access passes, I get three tracks an hour every hour minimum – I can fix interviews – no, that's fine! I don't know, what are the three most beautiful words in the English language? A done deal? Ha ha ha! You got it . . .'

She put the phone down on Tower on Sunset two and a half hours later, and Atomic Mass had an exclusive franchise on every major radio station and record store in southern California.

'You're just a show-off,' said John, shaking his head.

Rowena lit a cigarette and took a deep pull, satisfied. He noticed she neither asked for permission to smoke nor apologized for it.

'What now?'

'Now I fax Musica's head of PR in New York with a press release.'

'Which says what?' he asked, completely fascinated.

'Which says,' she grinned, 'that the show is sold out, the only way to get tickets is through radio and in-store competitions, and that police have been warned of possible riots by crowds of disappointed fans unable to get in.'

He laughed. 'Woman, you are incredible. I can't believe it. I gave you a phone, and you delivered Los Angeles.'

'With red ribbons and a cherry on top,' Rowena agreed.

'So modest.'

'Fuck modest!' she said, feeling powerfully happy. 'I'm the best.'

He drove her to Morton's for dinner, and the night air was charged with jasmine and sex. She was wearing a grey dress, a little silken thing that poured over her slim body like water. Her long legs were naked down to the designer sandals. He wanted her so badly it ached.

John Metcalf was a studio president, and attractive in his own right. He was rich, he was powerful, and he was straight, in one of the most hedonistic cities in the world. There had been a lot of women, not all of them stupid.

But he knew within days of meeting her that Rowena Gordon was quite different from all of them. It wasn't a blinding revelation, the flash of light and cosmic neon arrows and everything else an Angeleno expects.

It was just a quiet certainty that this girl was the one.

He wanted to own her and possess her. He wanted to put his ring glittering on her finger and scream to the world that she was his alone. The contradictions of her entranced him – that cool, ladylike English voice wheeling and dealing with the appetite of a Brooklyn hustler; that delicate rosy beauty throwing itself into brutal male music like heavy metal and hardcore rap; her classically educated brain focusing its laser intelligence with total absorption on music he didn't understand and names he didn't recognize – techno, glam, swingbeat. She seemed interested in making money, even greedy, and yet completely uninterested in making it anywhere other than the record business. The day after the soundtrack deal was finalized, he'd offered her a vice-presidency at the studio, with stock options, at triple what she was making at Musica. She'd smiled and asked him to explain to her why she should trade down.

He wondered about her sexuality as his dark eyes swept over her lithe athletic body. He wondered if she realized how obvious she was about what she wanted. She flung her success down like a sexual gauntlet. She couldn't have made it clearer if she'd gone out in a T-shirt saying DOMINATE ME in big black letters. And she evidently had some lover, some man who was giving her what she thought she wanted.

John Metcalf pressed his foot on the accelerator, thinking murderous, aroused thoughts. The cool night air rushed past them, lifting Rowena's blonde hair like a golden banner streaming in the darkness. That made it worse. *Whoever he is, he's history,* Metcalf thought grimly. *I wonder what he made her do for him. I wonder if he made her swallow. I wonder if he put her on her hands and knees and screwed her from behind. Jesus! If he touches her again, he's a dead man.*

Rowena stretched in the seat, lifting her arms above her head. Her body bent into a slight bow, and he could see her delicate little nipples, hardened by the cold, push slightly against her dress.

I'm going to have you, Rowena Gordon, he said to himself. *I'm going to make you come so hard you weep. I'm not just going to shove it into you the way you think you like it. I'm going to make love to you an inch at a time, until you're so sensitive to my touch you get wet when my fingers brush your elbow. If you think about me when you're walking down the street, the friction of your legs will make you come . . .*

Rowena sipped her champagne, frustrated. Was it possible he didn't find her attractive? Maybe he was gay.

'Well, it's fifty million dollars' worth of business,' she said. 'That's worth getting excited about in my book.'

John Metcalf smiled, indulgent and infuriating. 'Maybe so, for music,' he said. 'If I could bring a movie in so cheap, I'd be a happy guy.'

'Oh, these numbers are chickenfeed to you,' she snapped sarcastically.

'Yes they are,' he said. 'Absolutely.'

She felt a rush of lust. Damn, he was good-looking. Well-muscled, confident, masculine. His jaw was hard-set and his lips fairly unremarkable. But there was something about him, she wasn't sure . . . she didn't know . . .

Rowena felt a disturbing confusion. She'd only spent a few days with John Metcalf. She didn't even know him. He wasn't *Michael,* was he? Michael was who she loved. Always and for ever and no matter what.

John Metcalf knew nothing about music, nothing about her, nothing about all the ties that bound her to Krebs. And he was an arrogant sonofabitch, sitting here telling her the most important deal of her life was chopped liver!

'I bet you're really selfish in bed,' she said, furious.

There was a pause. Metcalf looked at her over the table, slowly swallowing his steak.

'Selfish?' he asked.

Silence.

'I have a boyfriend,' Rowena whispered, suddenly frightened.

'Oh?' Metcalf enquired politely. 'That's nice.'

'I love him,' she insisted.

He tilted his glass towards her, courteously. 'Congratulations.'

'I must go,' said Rowena, flustered. 'I have to see to the arrangements for soundcheck. I'll get a cab.'

'Sorry you have to go,' he said, completely at his ease. 'I'll walk you to the car.'

He opened the cab door for her and stood aside so she could get in. Rowena turned round to thank him, intensely disturbed by how close together they were standing.

'It was good of you to take me to dinner, John,' she said.

'Thank you for coming,' he replied. With a barely perceptible movement, he took hold of her waist, thumbs in the hollows of her hipbones, his fingers resting on the top of her ass.

His touch changed everything.

The electricity was instantaneous.

Rowena stared at him, her groin dissolving with pleasure and panic.

'I'm not going to do anything to you that you don't want,' he said. 'And when we go to bed, you'll be mine. And there won't be any going back.'

24

All Rowena's worlds exploded at once.

Everything, suddenly, was falling into place, and everything was being decided tonight.

She looked out over the ocean of people before her and below her, stretching out into the night as far as she could see, small points of light filling the stadium as the fans clicked their lighters and held them above their heads. The gig wasn't due to start for twenty minutes yet, but the band, eager to amplify the already intense atmosphere, had dimmed the stadium floodlights, pumped up the huge house PA system to blare music into the darkened arena, and turned one brilliant light on the vast curtains sealing off the stage.

The Atomic Mass logo – a spinning molecule in gold on blue – shone like a massive raised beacon above the audience, demanding homage. Rowena could make out waves in the crowd, as people started to slam to Guns 'n' Roses' 'Paradise City'. She paced, alone in the executive box. Michael Krebs was locked in Mirror, Mirror, recording with another huge band. Rowena had asked him to come, but he was adamant – nothing took Krebs away from a record. She'd resented it; for Atomic Mass, he might have made an exception. If she'd played mother to their careers, Michael Krebs had played father.

Can't we be together in anything?

The Musica board should have been here an hour ago.

Atomic Mass, her band, her boys. They were poised on a knife-edge between 'major act' and 'legend'. It had taken everything she had to sell out this gig, and Musica would have to grin and bear an unprecedented promotional cost. The world was watching this evening. I can't help you now, she thought. Do or die, lads. Do or die.

Then, Musica. Everything she'd struggled for all her adult life. Luther was profitable; Atomic were the biggest band on the planet, at least for the next five minutes; and Picture This was a movie/music deal even Peter Paterno might have been proud to sign.

One thing's for certain, Rowena admitted to herself. That's it. That's the best I can do.

If they didn't give her North America now, they never would. It was that simple. And when – if? – Joshua Oberman finally made it to the gig, he'd tell her in person. She didn't know if that was good or bad.

The tension mounted in the Coliseum. The slow, heavy chords of Metallica's 'Enter Sandman' filled the night air, and Rowena shivered with joy as tens of thousands of voices took up the anthem:

Exit light
Enter night

What an awesome lyric, she thought. She swayed to the grind of the bass, her long legs taking up the beat, her golden hair sweeping from side to side. The excitement in the air was so strong you could taste it. Where was Oberman? And where, she wondered with a strange ache of longing, was John?

The final song blasted out of the PA. It was AC/DC. She couldn't help laughing at the irony.

It's a long way
Such a long way
It's a long way
To the top
If you wanna rock 'n' roll . . .

Topaz leant back in her chair and tried not to cry. *Damn it, take it like a man. I mean take it like a woman! Do some work or go for a walk. I mean do* something, *just don't sit here moping . . . just don't . . .*

It was no use. A large tear trickled down her cheek, and then another, and another . . .

She put a hand over her mouth to stifle a great wrenching sob. Embarrassed by her own reaction, and frightened one of the assistants stationed outside her office might see her, she rose from her desk and went to stand by the window, and then, with her back to the door, she leant wearily against the sill and wept.

Ten minutes later she wiped her face clumsily, pulled on a pair of shades and rang for a cab.

So I'll take the rest of the day off, she thought grimly, and I'll cry or whatever and I will deal with this. I'll congratulate Joe like a professional. OK, it hurts like hell. Big fucking deal. Mama always said I had eyes bigger than my belly . . . Bottom line, if I don't have what it takes, it's better to find that out now than when I'm fifty.

The phoned buzzed. *Oh Jesus Christ, get lost.*

'Hey, Topaz.' Marissa's jealous, smarmy voice greased its way down the line. 'I heard. You must be devastated.'

Topaz glanced out of the window at the tiny yellow ladybug cabs, crawling along Seventh Avenue in the impersonal sunshine. She felt a little welcome steel creep back into her soul.

'What can I tell you, Marissa? Shit happens. I'll get another chance.'

'Well, I wouldn't count on that, honey. American Magazines moves on real fast . . . Joe Goldstein calls the shots now.'

'And he's a great man to do it,' Topaz said firmly. 'I'm looking forward to being a part of his team.'

Marissa sighed theatrically. 'Oh, Topaz. I don't think you should rely on ... how shall I put it? A *close* working relationship that you had in the past ...'

Topaz's knuckles were white as she gripped the phone.

'Past, present and future, sugar,' she said sweetly. 'In fact, as the second most senior MD, Joe's asked me to look at redefining the roles for our star reporters. We both think that your talents are just wasted on the society circuit, babe ... Joe thought you'd be ideal for a major series in *Economic Monthly*, something serious you could get your teeth into.'

'Like what?' asked Marissa warily.

'Like six months covering the Midwest farming depression,' spat Topaz. 'That way you could report on things closer to your own level. Such as pig sewage.'

She slammed the receiver down, feeling a little better.

The phone rang again.

'Look, whoever you are, just fuck off, OK?' she shouted. 'I'm not in the goddamned mood!'

'That's a nice way to greet an old friend,' said Joe mildly.

'Oh, shit,' said Topaz, blushing. 'I'm sorry, Joe. I didn't know it was you.'

'Evidently,' he said.

Topaz bit the bullet. 'Congratulations, Joe. Really. I mean it. The best man won, and all that stuff ... you'll do a great job ... obviously you'll have my resignation by the end of the week, and no hard feelings.'

Joe chuckled. Topaz flushed a deeper red, this time from resentment. *There's no need to laugh at me on top of everything else. Winner's privilege, I guess.*

'Of course you're not going to resign, Rossi,' he said.

'Oh yes, I am,' said Topaz stubbornly. It'll be a cold day in hell before I report to you, Joe Goldstein, she thought.

'Topaz Rossi,' Joe insisted, 'I do not accept, and American Magazines will not accept, the resignation of the best print woman in the country.'

'If I was the best, I'd have got the job,' snarled Topaz, ashamed of herself but unable to be gracious.

'However,' Joe continued, ignoring her completely, 'we do need to talk about your future role. Why don't you come over to my place tonight? I'll cook something and we can discuss it over dinner.'

With a herculean effort, she swallowed a hundred smart-ass replies.

'Good idea. I'll be there at eight thirty,' she said.

'Look forward to it,' Joe said, and rang off.

Oh Joe, Topaz thought miserably. My best friend and worst enemy. I wish you were here. Then I could cry on your shoulder and kick you in the balls at the same time.

The phone rang again.

'What? *What?*' she shrieked.

'Uh, cab, Ms Rossi,' whispered a terrified receptionist.

'Oh. Cool,' said Topaz, a little gruffly. 'I'll be right down.'

The private jet was halfway from Stockholm to Los Angeles, and the four men were still arguing.

'But that was your point six months ago, Hans,' said Joshua Oberman. 'And Luther's already turning a profit. Not only that, but she's got three or four baby acts that are selling albums, not singles. I wanted a presence in domestic repertoire, and she is delivering.'

The president of Musica Holland and new group director of Finance glowered at him with all the anger fifty-three years and a red moustache could muster.

'It's insanity, putting an A&R man in a senior corporate job, Joshua. Name me one example where it's worked out.'

'Roger Ames at PolyGram.'

'Apart from Roger Ames.'

'Clive Davis at Arista.'

'Those are two freak instances,' said Hans Bauer.

'David Geffen,' said Josh Oberman. 'Rick Rubin. Russell Simmons. Charles Koppleman . . .'

'You can't put a *woman* in charge of North America!' Maurice LeBec objected.

The old man glared at his executive committee.

'Well, by my watch, you have three hours to persuade me not to, gentlemen,' he said.

It was early evening in Manhattan, and the summer air was balmy and cool, rustling the branches of the trees in Central Park. As far as the city ever feels relaxed, it was relaxed in New York that May. Topaz watched little children sucking noisily at their ice creams, and the horses trotting alongside the park, uncomplainingly hauling their carriages full of tourists.

She felt *weird*.

She sat on her apartment balcony, sipping Cristal. She was wearing a dark green dress by Ann Klein, which fell invitingly in folds of soft cotton round her magnificently curvy body, and then cut sharply off at the knees to reveal a pair of heart-stopping calves. She'd done her hair Renaissance-style, half of it piled on top of her head in a luxuriant coil, half tumbling down the sides of her face in long ruby curls. There was a thick gold bracelet on her left wrist, and jet-black mules from Chanel framed the sexy turn of her ankle.

She felt rich, and stunningly beautiful.

She felt like a wretched failure.

She hated Joe Goldstein. He'd beaten her hands down.

She wanted to fuck his brains out.

Mind you, I always wanted to do that, from the first moment I laid eyes on him, she reminded herself. But now, now I should hate him! He cost me my seat on the board, the bastard . . . Marissa was right about that one . . . American Magazines, like the rest of this town, doesn't cut losers a lot of slack.

Rowena Gordon, of course, had the world at her aristocratic feet.

Topaz felt little prickles of hatred crawl across her skin at the thought of it. The bitch had done everything right. She'd been born to the right parents, for a start. She'd gone to a prestigious school. And she'd betrayed her best friend, who loved her like a sister, at the first opportunity ... At least you can't write 'President of the Union' in that sparkling biography, she thought with satisfaction.

Across the park, Musica Towers glinted in the sun.

The satisfaction evaporated.

She'd come home, flicked on her wide-screen TV and been confronted by some inane MTV VJ getting orgasmic over Atomic Mass. What had the bitch done to sell out the Coliseum? She was damn sure it had been a quarter empty on Monday. Just wait for the reviews, Rowena. Your band will be about as hip as Whitesnake.

It was a small measure of comfort, and Topaz took a slow sip of champagne, trying to banish the vision of her enemy's triumph. I don't need this, she thought. I won't give her that final victory. I won't let her sour my life.

She got up and strolled to the fridge, checking her reflection in the wall mirror. She was a knockout. 'Better than Joe Goldstein deserves,' she said, smiling. Well, she'd do it in style, at least. She'd bought two sensational bottles of wine to congratulate him: vintage Moët et Chandon champagne and a Château Lafite 1953. Maybe she'd take off the bracelet and wear her diamond necklace instead. After all, she still ran two of the most profitable magazines in the United States.

When the chauffeur buzzed up to the apartment, Topaz was ready for him.

She blew a kiss at her exquisite reflection, clutching a bottle in each hand. Wow! The original playgirl of the Western World. Joe would be blown away.

Oh, face one more thing while you're at it, Rossi. You're head over heels in love with your boss. Again.

The curtain was ripped away from the front of the stage and hundreds of lasers spun into the sky, crossing and recrossing in spectacular webs. The ecstatic screams of about 80,000 girls rent the California skyline. They stayed screaming.

Rowena Gordon, twenty-seven years old, label boss, businesswoman, A&R goddess, rammed her knuckles into her mouth to stop herself doing the same thing.

It was absolute, total, mass hysteria.

And then the band came on.

I'm telling you, the men won't work with her,' Maurice said, purple with rage and struggling to control himself. Unbelievable. A woman had never sat on the board of a major label, never in the whole history of the record business. It was farcical. The old idiot would make fools of them all.

'She's not even thirty years old,' moaned Hans, reading his thoughts.

'She's got no experience in classical,' said Jakob van Rees, clutching at straws.

Josh Oberman looked at them all, whining, whingeing, carping. Pathetic. He remembered Rowena storming into his office five years ago, hurling an armful of CDs on to his desk, passionate and furious. What were these snivelling Eurotrash? Glorified fucking accountants.

'If people won't work with her, we'll just have to replace them, won't we?' he said with deadly calm.

Maurice and Hans swallowed nervously.

'You'll be able to work with her though, won't you?' he wondered aloud.

'Oh yes,' said all three men, hastily.

'What do you see in her, Joshua?' asked Jakob miserably.

He fixed the three group presidents with a contemptuous glance.

'She's the son I never had,' he said.

Joe Hunter stood centre stage, Zach's guitar howling beauty into the blackness. Alex was running over to the left-hand monitors, his bass swinging against his body, greeting the sea of crazed fans on that side of the stadium. He felt the glory of it course through his veins. It was better than power. Better than riches. Better than sex.

He started to sing.

> Why don't we start at the end
> It's great to see you again
> Have you heard anything new . . .

The answering roar shook the foundations of the building.

'Hi Rowena,' John Metcalf said.

Just when she'd thought it couldn't get any better.

'John!' she exclaimed, shocked at how pleased she was to see him. 'Oh, it's so good to see you, it's so good that you're here!'

This might possibly be the best moment of her life, and she found she was delighted to have him there to share it with her. He was wearing jeans and a white T-shirt, which threw his large, tanned body into sharp relief. An all-access crew laminate hung on his muscled chest.

Rowena smiled at the thought of a movie mogul humping flight cases around; although, if circumstances were different, he'd be big enough and strong enough for the job . . .

'Quite a show, young lady,' John congratulated her. 'Makes me tempted to try music for a couple of years.'

'Maybe I can find a place for you somewhere,' said Rowena.

John shook his head. 'Are you kidding? I couldn't take the cut in salary.'

'God, you *asshole*,' said Rowena, livid. 'You fucking . . .'

'Oh, shut up,' said John Metcalf gently, and gathered her into his arms and kissed her.

She didn't even bother with a token protesting squirm.

Atomic Mass were blasting through 'Karla' when the Musica board finally made it to the executive box, panting from the effort of climbing so many stairs, even though hordes of respectful security guards had shown them every short cut in the book. The group presidents were all wincing from the violent music and the delirious screams of the fans; Jakob was trying to hide an unimpressive hard-on which he'd got on passing two teenage girls, who, mad with worship, had torn at their shirts so much that they'd exposed their breasts, bouncing around in time to the beat. Josh Oberman noticed them too, and wished he was forty years younger. He was ecstatic with the job his protégée had done; the scene reminded him of the Beatles at Shea Stadium.

'*It's getting closer, It's getting clearer, I don't believe you, I'm getting out of here,*' soared Joe's spectacular voice.

The board stopped dead in their tracks. Maurice, Hans and Jakob were overjoyed. Surely now he would see reason.

Rowena Gordon, managing director of Luther Records, lay flat on her back, stretched underneath John Peter Metcalf III, chairman of Metropolis Studios, kissing him wildly, pressing herself into his caressing hands. Metcalf had thrust her skirt up almost to her panties, exposing her magnificent right thigh.

Joshua roared with laughter. 'How's it going, John?' he bellowed. 'I see you've met the president of our North American operations!'

Joe Goldstein liked to think he had the best apartment in TriBeCa. It was basically one huge room, with a separate bathroom. He had stripped the pine floorboards himself and painstakingly coated them with a dark varnish. The gentle light from his soft red lamps gleamed on the wood. He sat on the couch, underneath his poster of Sid Fernandez, pitcher for the Mets and all-time Goldstein hero. Northwards outside his window the spires of the Empire State Building stared back at him.

Good, he thought. I'm going to enjoy this.

The bell rang, and he went to open the door. He was wearing a flannel shirt, beat-up jeans and sneakers.

Topaz stood there in full evening dress, defiant and nervous and utterly beautiful. Diamonds glittered on her throat and ears, sending little points of light dancing over her blue eyes and red hair. Her deep green gown hugged her bosom and ass provocatively, taunting him. She was without question the most attractive woman he'd ever seen.

'Jesus Christ,' he said, staggered.

'Don't say that! You're not a Christian,' snapped Topaz, weak with longing for him. *Oh my God, you beautiful bastard.*

She pushed her way past him into the apartment, trying to catch her breath from the sudden rush of desire.

'I brought you a congratulations present,' she said, roughly thrusting the two bottles at him. 'Well done.'

She sounded nearly as awkward as she felt. But what could she say? *It should've been me! Damn you to all hell for ruining my life! Let's go to bed?*

'Come on, Topaz. You're hardly the good Catholic girl, now are you?' demanded Joe, opening the Moët and wondering how long he should let her stew before he told her.

'Don't you insult my fucking religion,' said Topaz, perhaps not as piously as she might have done.

Joe courteously pulled out a chair for her, and they sat down.

The mahogany table was covered with silver candlesticks and pink and white roses, and Joe had set out fresh mango slices as a starter. He poured champagne into two Lalique crystal glasses.

'To the director of American Magazines, East Coast,' said Joe, raising his glass.

Topaz swallowed her anger. Once, just once, she'd allow him to gloat over her. 'To Joe Goldstein,' she said, saluting him.

Joe regarded her across the table. Unless he was very much mistaken, her nipples were erect. All this battling must be getting to her, he thought. He remembered how much he'd hated the pushy, masculine bitch that night, and how furious he'd been when his cock seemed to have other ideas . . . and how she'd hated him right back . . . until that one touch had set everything off . . . and he remembered screwing her so hard on that desk, their mutual need so urgent and demanding that it blocked out all reason . . .

Topaz licked a drop of mango juice off her lips.

That's it, Joe thought. Forget about teasing her. If I get any more turned on, this table is going to lift an inch from the ground.

'I wasn't toasting myself,' he said shortly. 'That's your title now. I'm not taking the job.'

'What?' gasped Topaz.

'Don't you understand English? I've been offered a programming position at NBC. I'll have to drop a rung to do it, but that gets me into television, which is where I've always wanted to go.'

Topaz took an unladylike slug of her drink. The room was spinning.

'So! You just reckoned you'd let me stew for a day, did you, you asshole?' she demanded, trying to hide her joy. *Poor Marissa*, she thought bitchily.

'Why don't you shut up,' said Joe thickly, 'and ask me nicely if I'll fuck you, like you want me to.'

'I do not,' denied Topaz, unconvincingly.

'Yes you do, Rossi,' said Joe, rising from his chair and walking round the table towards her. 'Yes you do. You've been hot for me all day. You're wet for me now. Did you fantasize about it? Huh? Did you wonder if I'd sit in that big black chair in the director's office and make you kneel under my desk and suck me off?'

Topaz was so aroused she could hardly breathe. She sat transfixed in her chair, watching Joe come slowly towards her, a colossal erection straining under his jeans.

'Why should I bother fucking you?' she asked dismissively. 'You're not even a print man any more.'

Joe towered over her, his crotch right next to her face. 'I'll enjoy making you pay for that,' he said.

Topaz stared at the outline of his cock, and was seized with a paralysing longing to have it inside her.

'Beg me to fuck you,' said Joe.

'Please fuck me, Joe,' whispered Topaz, dying of lust.

'Louder,' Joe demanded, trying to control the urge to jump her bones immediately.

'Please fuck me,' she said, shaking with need.

'I'll fuck you when I'm good and ready,' Joe said, and then he knelt down and seized her left ankle in a vicelike grip, and slowly licked the tender hollow under the anklebone.

Topaz moaned.

Joe worked his way up her legs inch by inch, refusing to hurry his pace, holding her down if she tried to shove herself against him. Eventually he reached the top of her thighs, and roughly pulled down her panties.

Topaz tensed. 'Joe ... I've never ...'

But he could smell the beautiful thick musk of her desire.

'I'm going to give you what you want, Topaz Rossi,' he growled. Then, as she was shuddering with longing, he languidly trailed the tip of his tongue back and forward over her clitoris.

'Oh, Jesus!' Topaz screamed. 'Oh, my God!'

'Don't blaspheme,' Joe teased her. Then he licked her some more.

'Oh, Joe! I love you! I love you! Oh, Jesus! Please fuck me! Fuck me!' Topaz begged, insane with pleasure.

Joe's erection was swollen almost to the point of pain. Continuing to lick Topaz out, he kicked off his shoes and pants. 'You do want it, don't you,' he said. 'Catholic girl. You want my Jewish cock in your pussy. Isn't that right?'

Topaz writhed against his tongue, completely incapable of speech.

Joe pulled her roughly off the chair, and, unable to wait a second longer, shoved himself inside her, losing himself in the pleasure of her tight wet heat around him.

They moved together.

'I love you,' said Joe.

'I love you too,' said Topaz.

'You're going to get me pregnant,' said Topaz.

'I know that,' said Joe.

'Will you marry me?' asked Topaz.

'Oh yeah,' said Joe Goldstein, entering her for the fourth time. 'Yeah.'

25

Once again, Elizabeth Martin was throwing a party.

Once again, both Topaz Rossi and Rowena Gordon were invited.

And this time, *everyone* was watching them.

'You can't get an invite. Nobody can,' Rowena told John.

'If you lived in New York she'd have chosen you like a shot, but you're from LA. Elizabeth isn't David Geffen or Mike Ovitz. Running a movie studio won't give you any clout with her.'

'I'll get an invite,' Metcalf told her with supreme confidence, and he had.

'How did you manage that?' Rowena asked, surprised, when he rang her a week before the bash. 'That's impossible.'

'Nothing's impossible,' John teased, refusing to say. 'I'll pick you up at eight.'

'What are you going to wear?' Joe asked Topaz. Since they'd been living together, Goldstein had developed an intense interest in women's fashion, as far as it related to Topaz. The style and boldness with which she wore clothes used to infuriate him, but now he adored it. So what if the look disturbed her co-workers? Topaz was answerable to nobody. Topaz was a free spirit. That was exactly why he hadn't been able to forget her.

'You can wait and see,' she replied.

'You'll be the most beautiful woman in the place,' Joe said, coming up to her and taking her in his arms.

'I haven't told you what I'm wearing yet,' she pointed out.

'You'll be the most beautiful woman there if you turn up in a sack,' he said, kissing her.

'You can't avoid me for ever,' Michael Krebs said. 'We'll both be at Elizabeth's party.'

His tone was taut with what Rowena knew to be controlled anger. For a month now she'd been communicating with him by fax, talking to Barbara or letting a deputy negotiate for her. When he called her at home, she had the answering service take a message. She wanted to let her relationship with John develop, and that meant not talking to Michael.

Eventually she'd called him back, in his office, at 11.45 a.m. A nice, safe time when others of his staff might be there.

She took a deep breath. 'And so will John Metcalf,' she said. 'Who I'm going out with.'

There was a pause at the other end.

'Good!' said Michael, brightly. 'Congratulations, Rowena, that's great. But what does that have to do with us?'

'I can't do anything with you any more, Krebs,' said Rowena, with a slight smile. Some things never changed.

'Of course you can,' he said simply. 'You always did before.'

'John's different.'

Krebs gripped the phone, his knuckles white around the handset. He couldn't believe how angry he felt. Insulted. Cheated. Rejected. Of course John Metcalf was different – a young, attractive man, single, president of a movie studio, rich. A guy who made the 'America's Most Eligible Bachelors' list every summer.

A man richer and more powerful than him.

A *younger* man.

'Well, it's your choice,' he told her, as casually as he could manage. 'But I think you're being dumb. We had a lot of fun.'

Unexpectedly, Rowena found her eyes had filled with tears. 'Yes, we did,' she admitted.

Both of them had an instantaneous vision of the last time they'd had sex – in a hotel in Munich on the European leg of the *Heat Street* tour, when they'd barely been able to make it inside before ripping their clothes off and grabbing at each other. Krebs had fucked Rowena standing up, her back to the wall, while she was still half-dressed.

'Rowena –' Michael began.

'I have to go,' she said hurriedly, and replaced the receiver.

It had to end some time, Krebs told himself. I don't give a damn. It was fun while it lasted, that was all.

Rowena was the one who'd stressed out about it all the time. He, Michael, had been totally consistent in his attitude. Debbie was his wife and he loved her. Rowena – well – he shouldn't have done it, but she was so *good*. And he enjoyed her company, when she wasn't moaning and complaining and getting weepy on him.

John Metcalf, eh? Well, he was pleased for her.

'Eli, goddamnit!' Krebs roared. 'Where the fuck are my notes?'

Sometimes you work through a day and don't realize how tired you are until you sit down. And sometimes you can work through several years and not realize how lonely you are until you meet a guy. It had happened to Rowena Gordon in Los Angeles; first, the nervousness she'd felt around John Metcalf that none of her other lovers had provoked; then the simple happiness at finding her body responding to a man who didn't dominate her; and finally, the surprise at seeing him at her door every evening, the flowers that arrived every morning, the endless compliments and proclamations of love. She'd found herself extending her time in LA indefinitely, and then, one morning, Rowena Gordon had woken up in a beautiful bedroom in Beverly Hills, in her lover's arms, and decided that John made her happy.

Being with him made her happy. Being paraded in public made her happy. Getting complimented made her happy and making love to him made her happy. He couldn't drive her to the sexual nirvana that Michael could, but then again, John wasn't married and he was offering her love.

And she wasn't twenty-two any more. She was kissing thirty, and she hadn't had a serious relationship since the day she met Michael Krebs.

Yeah, she was a high achiever. She'd struggled in London, struggled in New York, and come through both times. She was the president of Musica North America and a powerful figure in her chosen industry. Of course, there was still a long way to go, but she was well on target. Rich in her own right. Famous amongst her peers. Music business magazines referred to her by her first name alone – now *there* was a sign of making it.

But she was unmarried and childless. Another New York career girl, alone and unhappily attached to a man who didn't love her back and didn't even pretend to.

No! I have choices! Rowena told herself that morning, looking at Metcalf's handsome face on the pillow beside her. There was nothing great about being a victim, a role-reversed Lancelot sighing for an unattainable Guinevere.

She would choose happiness. She chose John.

Topaz selected her outfit with great attention. She'd always cared about her looks, but this time it was important. She had to dress appropriately to her new position as director of American Magazines, East Coast – the youngest in the company's history and only the third woman to rank so highly. Last month *People* had called her 'the new Tina Brown' and Topaz had been completely thrilled. Shamelessly thrilled. If she got another chance to meet Tina Brown, she wanted to look dynamite for the photo. Rowena would call that shallow. *She* called it honest.

Also, she had to be a knockout for Joe. It was the first time they'd have been out socially since they got engaged.

Give Marissa something to write about.

And then she had to look better than Rowena Gordon.

Topaz still burned with resentment whenever she thought about that woman. The pain of her first betrayal had faded with time, but the cold arrogance of her attitude hadn't. She *had* taken a band from under Rowena's nose, but after that all the scoring was on the other woman's side. Musica's success, Atomic Mass, surviving that drugs story – *Jesus, how I hate writers that don't check their sources* – and selling out the Coliseum.

She'd wanted to get even, that was all. She was an Italian. Nobody spurned her and got away with it.

Yet Topaz might have let it go, all the same. She hadn't been *in* love with Nate Rosen – though only since she'd known Joe had she realized that – but she had loved him, and his death had changed her frantic attitude to life. And with Joe Goldstein, she was a woman blissfully in love, with a great career.

But Rowena Gordon had pushed her over the edge again.

It was the day after Joe had proposed to her. The day after Atomic Mass had played the Coliseum to wild reviews. Topaz had just got into the office, ready for a very pleasant meeting with Matt Gowers. After all, Joe had just resigned and would formally appoint Topaz to the board that morning. What with Joe, and the job, she was so happy that day that not even the sight of a triumphant Joe Hunter on *Good Morning America* had been able to dent her mood.

But then her assistant had come in with a large parcel. 'This came from Luther Records, this morning,' she said. 'I had to sign for it. Do you want me to send it right back?'

'No. I'll open it,' Topaz answered, curious.

She'd torn off the brown paper and felt a shock of rage.

It was a Dunlop tennis racket, with a small typed note attached. The note read: 'Advantage Miss Gordon.'

She picked it up, almost disbelievingly. Three years in the United States, and Rowena's fucking blue limey blood hadn't warmed up one degree. She'd never apologized, never explained, and she treated the whole thing like a game. She was fucking *laughing* at her.

That day she decided it was war. She was going to destroy Rowena Gordon, however long it took her.

You want to play this out? You got it.

Topaz twisted round, checking herself out in the full-length wall mirror. The dress was her first piece of fitted haute couture, a one-off original, with a price tag to match – but right now, she thought it had been worth every cent.

It was a sweeping ballgown in oyster-pink satin, the fitted bodice dusted over with hand-embroidered tiny gold beads, the skirt ruched over folds of stiff gold brocade. Watching her reflection carefully in the huge mirror, Topaz took out her favourite ebony combs and caught her hair up in a silken pile on the crown of her head, pinning it securely in place and then fixing it with a burst of Elnett hairspray, a regal style which exposed her long, elegant neck. She added dangling coral earrings and a ruby necklace, a magnificent piece from Cartier which Joe had bought her two weeks after they got engaged.

'What's this for?' Topaz had asked in delight, when he'd presented her with the box over dinner at Elaine's. A woman at the next table had given an involuntary gasp when Topaz, stunned, held up the perfect string of rubies to the light.

'Just for being alive,' Joe answered, feeling his heart almost burst with love at the sight of the tears in her eyes.

Being apart was torture. Every day, when they kissed each other goodbye, they took too long about it, not wanting to let go. They met each other for lunch, and one was always waiting to pick the other up after work. They walked everywhere holding hands like teenagers. Topaz sometimes called Joe on his direct line at NBC and told him in detail what she wished she were doing to him, so that he couldn't get up for fifteen minutes because of the erection surging in his pants. Nate would never have allowed it; Joe revelled in it. When he got home those evenings, if Topaz wanted to make love three times, Joe wanted to do it five. Where Nathan would have pushed her away, Joe asked for more. And where Nathan had made her feel good, Joe made her scream.

'I want to have your children,' she'd whispered to him in the restaurant, and Goldstein, feeling choked up himself, replied, 'I think that can be arranged.'

They hadn't even made it through the starter before Topaz called for the check.

'Can I come in now?' Joe yelled from the kitchen.

'Yeah,' she yelled back, spraying on a burst of Joy. She turned round as he appeared in the doorway, holding up her skirt with one hand as she slipped into her shoes, a pair of gold heels from Kurt Geiger.

'Do you like it?' she asked nervously.

Joe Goldstein looked his fiancée up and down, slowly, taking in the delicate pink and gold satin, the sexy earrings, and the way his rubies sparkled against the creamy backdrop of her full breasts, pushed up even further by the clever corsetry of the bodice. Her blue eyes looked anxiously at him, fringed with those delicate red lashes, and her hair gleamed softly in the light.

'It's beautiful,' he said neutrally, 'but there's something missing.'

'What? You think I should take a purse? A purse would be all wrong with this gown . . .'

'No. Not a purse.' He handed her a small jeweller's box with 'Asprey & Co' written on the top. 'I've been waiting for the right moment to actually give you this.'

Her heart hammering, Topaz opened the box, and was confronted with an exquisite engagement ring, a dark emerald set in diamonds. When she could drag her eyes away, she saw that Joe had sunk to one knee before her.

'I know you asked me,' he said, 'but I'm a traditionalist . . . Topaz Rossi, will you marry me?'

'Yes,' Topaz said, 'oh yes, oh, Joe, I love you.'

'You look good,' John said, when Rowena showed him in. He glanced round her apartment. 'Very New York.'

Rowena had chosen a long slip dress, a narrow silhouette in silver silk by Isaac Mizrahi. She had matched it with silver leather sandals from Jimmy Choo, a white Hermès scarf and a silver cross on a simple thong. Her hair was loose, hanging down her back in a curtain of pale gold. It was a look she preferred these days, slim and minimalist. A year ago she'd had her apartment redesigned to match – the Georgian furniture and English watercolours had given way to spare Japanese tables, a low couch and rice matting – all the hi-tech paraphernalia of a busy executive taking up the least space possible.

John noticed the fax machine and phone by the bed, the slimline stereo speakers on the walls.

'Never stop working, right?'

She took a slim clutch bag from the dresser and slipped her arm through his.

'What else is there?' she asked, and he thought for a second he heard a touch of regret.

Flashbulbs popped around them like out-of-control firecrackers.

Rowena, conscious of the press, nodded at Topaz Rossi with an icy smile. John was already off, working the room like a pro, but Joe Goldstein was at his girlfriend's side. Rowena recognized his picture from the LA trades – the new VP programming over at NBC, right?

Well, yet again, I outranked you, she thought triumphantly.

She looked at Goldstein with frank curiosity. He was very attractive, not Topaz's type, she thought. Rossi was looking sensational; Rowena was childishly jealous of the stunning gown, the womanly figure and the breathtaking necklace. Next to Topaz, her stylish simplicity was just outgunned.

'Good evening, Rowena,' Topaz said pleasantly.

That accent's got thicker since she's been in New York, Rowena decided, not bothering to answer.

'Have you met my fiancé, Joe Goldstein?' Topaz continued. 'Joe left American Magazines to work in television. I guess you've heard that I'm the new director for New York.'

'Yes,' Rowena replied, her tone contemptuous.

Topaz felt her anger bubbling up like oil. Same old Rowena Gordon, for whom friendship was a matter of convenience, and low-rent girls stayed low-rent girls, however far up the greasy pole they climbed.

'You're not concerned,' she said.

Rowena looked at Topaz, standing in front of her with Joe's hand circling protectively round her waist, her engagement ring glinting on her hand, looking beautiful and triumphant. She was radiant with happiness, but at the same time, bristling with defiance. And the older, colder side of Rowena, the one she thought she had buried, the one that refused to face up to her first betrayal, the one that had been prepared to win at all costs, the one that still knew exactly how to hurt, surfaced, longing to wound.

'Why should I be concerned with *you*, Ms Rossi?' she replied, emphasizing the American prefix. 'You mean less than nothing to me. You're just a journalist, and your efforts to stop me so far have come to precisely nothing. It's just like the girl I remember at Oxford to get obsessed by some insignificant quarrel.'

She opened her clutch bag and took out a small spray of Chanel No. 5, casually scenting her wrists in an aristocratic gesture.

'Sticks and stones may break my bones, but words will never hurt me,' she said with a smile, and then turned away from them, walking across to John Metcalf and kissing him on the cheek.

Topaz stared after her for a long moment.

'What a bitch,' Goldstein said.

'Is Josh here?' Barbara Lincoln asked, sweeping up to them in a barebacked white organza dress which looked stunning against her black skin. She embraced Rowena on the cheeks and added, 'You look like you've seen a ghost.'

'I'm fine,' Rowena told her. 'He couldn't make it, he's getting a little old to be shuttling across the Atlantic.'

'Is it true that they're restructuring the board? Hi, John, baby, how are you?' she added, leaning forward and kissing him on the cheek. 'Still looking after my best friend?' She gave Rowena an approving wink over Metcalf's shoulder. Barbara was still the only girl she knew who sized men up as if they were livestock.

'I'm still getting looked after,' John answered. 'Rowena and I are trying to figure out how to make as much money as you.'

'That's a tough one,' Barbara said, her every movement sending little showers of light out from the diamonds that sparkled at her throat, wrists and ears. 'I have twenty per cent of the biggest band in the world and the second record is out in a month. I'm shopping for my own country right now. Something modest, like Malta or St Kitts . . . but the board, Rowena. You didn't answer my question.'

Her friend jumped, taking her gaze off the man who had just entered the ballroom and was standing talking to Rudolph Giuliani.

'What? Oh, yeah,' she confirmed. 'It's true. Oberman could be outvoted now, not that the new members are likely to want to . . . it's some lawyer from France and an English management consultant.'

'Should we be worried?' Barbara asked, watching the new guest detach himself from the ex-mayor and wander towards them. She knew there had been objections to Rowena's promotion.

'Not since you signed Atomic Mass direct to Luther for the second album,' John pointed out. 'Rowena would have to be a mass murderer to get fired now.'

'Hello, Michael,' Barbara said, greeting her friend as he walked up to them. Krebs kissed her on the cheek.

Rowena stiffened.

'Hey, honey, how's it going?' he asked pleasantly, adding, 'Hi, Rowena.'

'Oh, the usual,' Barbara smiled. 'Sold-out stadiums, promoters on their knees begging for multiple dates.'

Michael chuckled. 'Who's tour managing this time? Still Will Macleod?'

'The one and only,' Barbara agreed. 'Who else? Are we sitting together at dinner, Rowena?'

'No, she's next to Jake Williams,' John said, checking the seating plan.

Rowena was looking at Michael Krebs, feeling her heart thudding against her chest. It was the first time she'd seen him since before she left for LA. He was wearing a dark suit by Gieves and Hawkes; again, the ebony cloth picked out those awesome black eyes. The grey hair was a little thinner at his temples, but it made no difference to Rowena. Michael Krebs was like Sean Connery, she thought, one of those men who got more attractive as they got older.

Krebs had barely acknowledged her, and hadn't looked at her blond escort at all.

I hope he's not going to make a scene, she thought.

'You'll have to excuse him if he gets up to powder his nose,' Barbara said, grimly.

'Is there a problem?' Rowena asked, worried about her rhythm guitarist. She knew what *that* meant.

'Yeah, I'd say so,' the manager replied, giving Rowena a tiny glance that said, *Not here.*

'You're the producer, Michael, right?' Metcalf asked. 'You must be working very closely with Rowena on this.'

Krebs turned to face the younger man, his movement deliberate. 'That's right,' he said, neutrally. 'We've known each for a while. John Metcalf, isn't it? She told me about you.'

Rowena looked from one man to the other, her smiled fixed on her face. Out of the corner of one eye she could see the gossip columnist, Marissa Matthews, hovering ominously.

'Anyway, it was nice to meet you,' Michael said politely. 'I should go and talk to the band. Barbara, Rowena,' and to her amazement he shook John's hand and walked away, without so much as a backward glance.

Rowena couldn't believe it. No anger, no hostility, nothing.

'My lords, ladies and gentlemen,' announced a footman loudly. 'Dinner is served.'

'You can't let her get away with that,' Joe muttered to Topaz as they sat down.

'Don't worry,' she said, settling into her mahogany chair in a rustle of satin and gold brocade. 'This thing will be finished tonight.'

'Tonight? How are you going to manage that?'

'Just something she said about how I hadn't changed,' she replied. 'It gave me an idea. Back to basics.'

'What? Tell me,' Joe asked, intrigued.

Topaz shook her head. 'That would spoil the surprise.' She smiled at him, and added, 'Lovely flowers, don't you think?'

Goldstein, mystified, glanced at the arrangements of orchids and tiger lilies placed on every table. 'What the hell have flowers got to do with it?' he asked.

'You'll find out,' she said.

This year's surprise wasn't in the form of gifts; tonight it was the food. Liz Martin's chefs had prepared dishes of such shameless opulence that every fresh course brought gasps of appreciation and amazement from the guests. The starter was a large mound of beluga caviar, served neat to each guest with a wedge of lemon in individual ice sculptures, six hundred fantastic mini-masterpieces, each different, little gleaming fragments of art destined for just a few minutes of display. Rowena's was a transparent ballerina, supporting the delicious black pearls over her head in an intricate basket. Joe Goldstein's was a crouching baseball player, cupping caviar in his catcher's mitt. It was followed by hen lobsters in a sorrel sauce, served with piles of real truffles; a warm salad of pheasant and grouse; impeccable grapefruit sorbet, to clear the palate; and finally a luscious dish of vanilla ice cream, served with a bitter chocolate sauce and tiny, perfect martins, the birds that were the corporate logo for Martin Oil, created out of glazed spun sugar.

Jake Williams, apparently, had lost his appetite.

'Try it,' Rowena prompted him, spearing some pheasant salad and proffering it to her rhythm guitarist.

He shook his head. 'Not hungry.'

Rowena was concerned. In the space of a couple of months, Jake had lost over a stone. He was frowning and tense, he'd snapped at her all evening, and he'd turned up to the most exclusive party of the year in one of Atomic's own T-shirts. Totally out of character.

'I suppose you're gonna tell me that I shouldn't do drugs,' he added nastily, rounding on her.

She shrugged, sending ripples of silver silk across her dress. 'Do drugs if you want to, man. I mean, I've had a few tabs of E in my time. It's a perk of the job, everybody does it. The trick is not to let drugs do you.'

Michael found Rowena at the end of the party, while John was deep in conversation with George Stephanopolous.

'If you come over next week I'll play you the roughs of the new record,' he said. '*Zenith* they're calling it.'

'*Zenith*. OK, I will,' she replied, waiting for him to say something else, to tell her he couldn't leave his wife, to tell her John Metcalf was a *putz*, to order her back to his bed. She would turn him down flat.

'Great,' Michael said, his dark eyes expressionless. 'I'll see you then. You have a good night,' and he walked off to the cloakroom.

She watched him go, cursing herself for being so hurt.

'Are we done?' asked John, coming up behind her and scooping her into his arms. Rowena pressed back against his chest, grateful for his familiar warmth, for the comfort, for the fact that someone she cared about would make love to her tonight.

I wonder if Debbie Krebs sees it like that.

Topaz Rossi and Joe Goldstein were among the last to leave. Joe couldn't remember when he'd had so much fun outside of a huge Mets victory; he'd spent a golden night being congratulated by New York's best and brightest on the NBC job, and then recongratulated as word of his engagement spread through the room. Topaz had her fair share of corporate homage, too, and the dress was a genuine sensation; in a party crammed full of designer labels, she'd been photographed for *Vanity Fair, GQ, Vogue* and *Women's Wear Daily*, and Liz Smith had asked her for details of her couturier. Goldstein had fairly burst with pride.

'You'll make a pretty good trophy wife,' he said.

'You'll make an adequate trophy husband,' she shot back, and they'd stared into each other's eyes for a second, wanting to kiss, not able to in such a crowd, luxuriating in the sexual tension.

'Later,' Joe whispered in her ear.

She had been fairly sizzling all night, her smile effortlessly charming, her laughter genuine and relaxed, enjoying every introduction, savouring the food, joking with all their friends.

'What got into you?' Goldstein demanded as they came to leave, taking his fiancée in his arms and kissing her lightly on the bridge of the nose.

'You did. About four hours ago,' Topaz teased.

'Nothing else?'

'Well, maybe there was *one* other consideration,' she admitted, beckoning to him to follow her over to a table in the centre of the room.

'That's where Rowena Gordon was sitting,' Joe exclaimed. 'Topaz, what the hell have you done?'

Grinning at him, Topaz reached down into her cleavage, fiddled about a little, and pulled out a small tape recorder.

'Remember that David Levine interview?'

'Of course,' he answered.

'Well, this hasn't been clasped to my bosom all night, but –'

'The *flowers*! You're telling me you hid a tape recorder in the vase?'

'That's what I'm telling you,' said Topaz, and she smiled.

26

Will Macleod, Atomic Mass's tour manager, strode around backstage, looking ferocious as usual, and people didn't mess with him. He was constantly in motion, searching for something that might go wrong before it happened, checking the band were OK, sorting out a billion problems a night ranging from water in the PA to trucking permits to landing schedules for the private jet, and always, incessantly, checking and rechecking the guest list. His all-access tour personnel laminate bounced against his chest as he ran, but guards across Europe, America and the Far East rarely demanded to see it. Basically, you took one look at Will and you did not get in his way. Not if you valued your mobility.

It's something of a rule, especially in hard rock, that the crew's tough exterior conceals warm-hearted family men who are constantly dreaming of their wives and baby daughters back home in Alabama. In Will Macleod's case, the tough exterior concealed a tough interior. He was single, Glaswegian, and hard as all hell. He cared about running a good show, he cared about getting paid, getting laid and getting drunk. He also cared about his mates. Macleod had no family and didn't want one, he was completely addicted to life on the road, but when he did make a friend, he stayed loyal to them for life.

Over the course of three world tours, Atomic Mass, and to an extent their wives and girlfriends, had become his friends. And so had their manager, Barbara Lincoln.

Macleod was slightly surprised to find himself in this position. Barbara was about as likely to wind up a friend of his as a gay rights activist. She was, to say the least, not his style. For a start, she was a woman, which under most circumstances would have knocked her right out of the running. Second, she was a woman who was also his boss. That stretched the bounds of credibility, as far as Will was concerned. Third, she was about a million miles away from being 'one of the boys'. On the (very) rare occasions when he had the misfortune to encounter a woman on the road – no, scrap that, to encounter a woman *working* on the road – a catering girl, a wardrobe assistant, the rarer-than-hens'-teeth instance of a female truck driver or rigger or something – at the very least, he expected the lass to bend over backwards to fit in with the lads, to laugh the loudest at all the dirty jokes, turn a blind eye if one of the roadies wanted to 'entertain' a groupie behind the generator trucks, swear like a squaddie and generally do her best to blend into the wallpaper.

Barbara, inexplicably, had refused to do any such thing.

She showed up on the road dressed in Chanel or Armani, full make-up and often wearing jewellery. She didn't joke around with the crew, and if the boys were reading porn magazines when Ms Lincoln showed up, they had to stuff them under sofa cushions. Not that she wasted much time socializing. Normally, she'd go and see that the band were happy, then find the promoter and the local record company rep, introduce herself and get straight down to business. She would be in total command of the production office from five minutes after she hit a venue. Watching her, Macleod was surprised that the phone wasn't surgically attached to her ear.

He asked the band about it once.

'What you gotta understand about Barbara,' Joe told him, 'is that she's clever. I mean she is *really* smart. And she can make sure that we're not getting screwed financially, with the promoters and the agents and stuff, and on the record side – she used to work for the company. So she understands exactly what's going on, and she also knows them all. We got a perfect relationship with them, y'know? She takes care of everything, and she lets you take care of the road.'

Will took a lot of convincing. He finally became a fan on the one hundred and third show of the *Heat Street* tour, in Rio. He'd come into the production office to find Barbara, dressed in delicate black silk, arguing with the promoter.

'Not very practical,' Will said, looking disapprovingly at her outfit. It was in the nineties out there, it was total chaos setting up the stage and supervising the dodgy electrical systems, and most of Macleod's boys had sweat pouring down their backs. Barbara, barely pausing in her yelling at Vasquelez, the promoter, turned round to Will, screamed, 'You can keep your fucking mouth shut, I wear what I fucking like,' and went back on the attack. Somewhat taken aback, Macleod started to listen to what she was saying.

'I can no afford it,' the guy was whining. 'It is inflation.'

'It is theft,' Barbara snarled, 'and you will refund what you overcharged, my friend, or we are not going on.'

'You cannot do that, you have contract –'

'Yeah, so do you. And the contract says ten bucks a head. Not seventeen.'

'You, also, you get more money,' wheedled Vasquelez, spreading his hands in a gesture of powerlessness. 'I have more, band has more, everybody is happy, I am an honest man, I will pay you also –'

'Our *fans* are not happy, you little fuck,' screamed Barbara. 'I don't give a damn about more money for the band! We came out here to play for everybody, not for the fucking rich kids with swimming pools! You go out there and you announce that anyone with a seventeen-dollar ticket can show the stub at the back gate for a cash refund, right now, and every new ticket sells for the equivalent of ten dollars or we are not going on. And don't try anything on, because I checked the exchange rate before I left the hotel this morning.'

'Is impossible,' shrugged the guy. 'I cannot do this.'

Barbara turned round to Macleod. 'Will,' she said, 'how long will it take the boys to get everything packed away?'

'Two hours, tops,' he said, smiling broadly.

'Great,' she said. 'Have them make a start, will you?'

'No problem, boss,' Macleod said, nodding.

The promoter stared at him wildly. 'No! You cannot do this thing! There is hundred thousand people waiting! There will be a riot!'

Macleod looked at the manager, questioningly.

'Will,' she said, 'you saw the ticket price agreement, right?'

'Yeah,' he said.

'Tell me something,' Barbara said. 'It seems to have slipped my mind. We'd agreed a special ticket price for the poorer territories, right?'

'That's right,' Macleod said, glaring down at the promoter.

'Uh-huh. I thought so. Could you remind me what it was?'

'Ten dollars in local money,' growled Macleod, enjoying himself.

'*Ten* dollars. Not seventeen.'

'Definitely not seventeen.'

'Absolutely, definitely not seventeen.'

'Ten dollars.'

'Well, you know what?' Barbara said. 'Amazingly, some kids in Brazil are being charged seventeen dollars to see Atomic Mass.'

'By ticket touts?'

'By the promoter. What do you think we should do about that, Will?'

Vasquelez glanced nervously at Macleod. The Scotsman towered over him.

'I think we should go on home,' said Will, airily. 'And make sure to let other bands know about the promoter.'

'Pack up our gear, Will.'

'No! No!' pleaded the little man. 'They will riot! They will kill me!'

'Really?' asked Barbara, not sounding remotely interested.

Vasquelez gave a wail of despair. 'OK, OK. I give the seven dollars back . . .'

Barbara shoved her face into his. 'You do that,' she hissed. 'Exactly the way I said. You give that money back now, not tomorrow, not next week, right now. And I'll tell you what else. My tour manager here is going to supervise it, in case you have any more last-minute problems with your arithmetic. If you make any mistakes,' she said, with icy calm, 'he's gonna rip your balls off and shove them down your throat. Do I make myself clear?'

Vasquelez gulped. 'Yes, señora,' he said.

Macleod was beside himself. 'She's fantastic,' he said to Mark Thomas, when they were packing away the kit that night.

'Oh, she's the business,' the drummer agreed. 'Best female manager since Sharon Osbourne.'

Will Macleod became a good friend to his boss and a trusted ally. They didn't have deep conversations all that often, mainly because he knew nothing about designer clothes, million-dollar deals or two-timing lovers, and she knew nothing about football. On the other hand, when they did talk, they usually agreed about the important stuff – the band, the show, the venue and the travel arrangements. Barbara Lincoln left him to get on with his job. Right up until this summer, it had been a solid partnership.

This summer, Jake Williams started taking cocaine.

At first, Will didn't comment. If Jake had been on the crew Will would have bawled him out the first time and sacked him the second time. But he wasn't on the crew, he was the rhythm guitarist.

'Is Jake out of control?' Barbara asked Macleod.

Will hesitated. He knew that as the album was exploding worldwide, Barbara was less and less able to get out on the road. Will had become her eyes and ears. She trusted him. She believed him.

He thought about every beer he'd ever had with Jake Williams, every football game they'd played, and the fundamental, basic code of the road. Which includes the commandment, *Thou shalt not get thy mates fired*.

'No, he's fine,' Macleod answered, and started avoiding her calls.

Of course, he faxed in gate reports regularly and called the office, picking times when she'd be busiest and one of her associates would deal with him. It was a betrayal of trust.

But what the fuck can I do? Macleod thought.

And the band weren't stupid, either. They recognized the signs, and Macleod knew they didn't like it. At first, it looked under control: Jake never indulged in front of Atomic, he rarely indulged at a show, and he didn't talk about it at all. You could almost ignore it. Almost, but not quite.

The *Heat Street* tour wound on and on, moving from the big arenas to headlining the Monsters of Rock that summer, to filling stadiums to capacity. As the album sold and sold around the world, Barbara's office multiplied dates, booking four nights in cities that had originally asked for one, and added further legs to the tour as new territories got in on the game; now they were heading for New Zealand and Australia, then he had to make room for Japan, Hong Kong, Taiwan and Thailand, and finally the hot areas newly added to the international touring map – Jakarta, Indonesia and Singapore, as well as the Indian subcontinent.

One year turned into eighteen months, eighteen months became two years, and still there was no sign of stopping. The crew were now working in shifts, staggering the three-week vacation periods, except Will who couldn't and didn't want to go home. The adrenalin rush kept him hooked. He was chief of the Mongol hordes, in complete control of this vast juggernaut crisscrossing the world.

Apart from the band and a handful of others, the tour manager rules over *everybody* on a tour. His authority is absolute. His word is law.

And Will Macleod was good at his job. He was a fair guy to work for, and the crew respected him. He made sure that everyone got paid in full and on time, but if he caught somebody slacking or committing an unforgivable breach of etiquette, he docked their wages or sacked them. (Selling your allocation of tickets was unforgivable; getting a groupie to give you head in exchange for some fifth-rate, no-access pass was not. Feminism had pretty much passed Will by.) Macleod ran a smooth ship, and he got off on the adventure and the atmosphere and the camaraderie of the band and crew.

He also got off on the money. Atomic Mass were generous, and as the stadiums sold out and the CDs flew off the shelves, there was suddenly a lot of serious cash flying around. Merchandizing broke sales records across America, and Brockum, their T-shirt manufacturers, could hardly keep up with the demand. Will noticed it everywhere, in bars, in airports, in newsagents. Wherever he went there was somebody wearing an Atomic shirt. The gold molecule on the blue background was becoming as popular as Metallica's grinning skulls or the Guns n' Roses logo.

Everybody was getting rich. Even on the road, away from the obvious symbols like houses and cars, you could see that. One tour accountant turned into three. The singer's wife was dripping in diamonds. Alex, the bassist, started wearing a gold Rolex. Zach, the lead guitarist, routinely ordered bottles of champagne for the whole crew when one leg was finished, and that ran into hundreds of people. The band stopped leasing a private jet and bought one of their own.

And Jake Williams took more cocaine.

Will knew now he'd made a mistake. He shouldn't have deferred to him, he shouldn't have been too embarrassed to interfere. The lad was getting sick. He wasn't careful any more, he kept coming out of the loos with an ugly white smudge on his pallid skin. If Macleod pointed it out, he'd curse at him and wipe it away. He was getting painfully thin; he'd always been slender but nowadays he just looked anorexic. His clothes hung off him. He would become mean, nasty and petty when he was high, traits which Will knew weren't part of his personality. And furthermore, he had no reason to stop.

Jake Williams had no boss and he was making hundreds of thousands of dollars a month. He could run a full-on addiction to every drug known to man and service his habit to his heart's content without even noticing the cost.

For another two months, he still played OK.

Then he started to miss rehearsals.

Then he started to fuck up onstage.

Yesterday, for the first time since Macleod began working with him, Jake missed a flight. Will sent the band on ahead and booked two first-class seats on the next plane to Rome. Then he tore back to the hotel and only managed to get into Jake's room by a succession of lavish bribes and heavyhanded threats. He found his guitarist passed out on the bed, his gaunt body half dressed, a syringe jutting out of his arm. Macleod pulled it out as gingerly as he could.

Smack. Jesus, it was heroin now . . .

The local doctor, called and even more lavishly bribed to keep his mouth shut, roused him and gave him an emetic to make him throw up.

'You can thank whichever god it is you worship that he's alive,' he told Will, who'd seen this story before and had never known a happy ending.

At least it wasn't an overdose. Macleod dressed Jake himself and dragged him half-conscious to the plane, got him strapped in and told the stewardess he was sick.

He had to *do* something. Fast.

His heart in his mouth, Macleod called Barbara Lincoln at home.

'Can I speak to Joshua Oberman, please?' Topaz Rossi said, politely. In front of her, the huge glass windows of the sixtieth floor revealed the island of Manhattan, spread out below her. If she turned to her right, she could see Musica Towers, the tall building by Central Park glinting in the light of the sun.

It looks so tranquil.

Not for long.

'Yeah?'

Topaz smiled at the gruff voice, intrigued to hear what Rowena's boss sounded like. Old, crabby, intelligent.

'Mr Oberman, this is Topaz Rossi at American Magazines.'

'I know exactly who you are,' Oberman said coldly. 'And I presume you have a good reason for making this call.'

She smiled. 'Yes sir, I think I do. We've had a reporter out on the first leg of Atomic Mass's *Zenith* tour for a month, and we plan to run a big story in next week's *Westside* magazine on Jake Williams' addiction to heroin and cocaine.'

There was a pause.

'No comment.'

'I understand that, Mr Oberman. I'm just calling for the record as to Musica Entertainment's official policy on the use of illegal narcotic drugs.'

'Policy? We don't permit it or condone it. Obviously,' Oberman snapped.

'So if an employee of your company was encouraging a musician to take illegal narcotics, that would be grounds for instant dismissal?'

'Yes, but none of my employees would ever do any such thing,' Oberman barked. 'Is that all, Ms Rossi? I'm a busy man.'

'Thank you, Mr Oberman; you've been most helpful,' said Topaz sweetly.

She hung up, grinning.

Barbara walked the last hundred yards or so along the Paseo Virgin del Puerto, where the cab had been forced to drop her because of police barriers, towards the Vicente Calderon Stadium, looming huge in the deepening twilight, floodlit from all sides. Music was blasting into the street from the PA, the earth-shaking rap/rock of House of Pain at the moment. Fans were out in their thousands, clogging the streets, crowding the various entrances to different sides of the stadium, sitting on the concrete with beer and hotdogs and joints, swarming round the bootleg merchandizing stalls, yelling in Spanish and various other languages. She had her laminate, hanging round her neck on an inconspicuous black cord, tucked safely inside her shirt. In fact, she'd tugged the little plastic square down between her breasts and was using her bra to clip the cord against her chest, so it wouldn't flap. If one of these kids saw she was wearing a laminate, they might very well rip it off her and that would be it. She'd never get backstage without a pass. She spoke no Spanish and security at an Atomic Mass gig these days would be adequate for the average head of state.

Barbara threaded her way through the fans around the side of the stadium; backstage had to be over there because she could see all the generator trucks parked in a monolithic cluster, thick powercords and rubber-insulated pipes running from them into the back entrance of the arena. She loosened her laminate as she got further away from the crowd, pulling it out of her shirt when she got to the first row of security guards.

They glanced at it and hundreds of pounds of forbidding muscle just melted away. Fans crowding round the security cordon gazed at her in awe and shouted pleadingly at her in Spanish. Barbara strode into the tunnel leading to the backstage area, looking for someone she recognized, perhaps a sign to the dressing rooms or production office. Crew members scurried about with guitar stands and extra drumsticks, making little finishing touches to the Atomic stage set and taking support band gear away. She wondered how the Knuckleheads, a newish act on as support, had gone over with the crowd. She'd have liked to see them, too, but had decided it was best to keep away from the venue until showtime; any earlier and somebody would have noticed her and told Macleod, or told Jake, and she didn't want to give them time to hide him. Nobody knew she was here. She wanted it to stay that way.

She rounded a corner and emerged into catering. Long trestle tables were set at the back of the amphitheatre, with a buffet of hot and cold food, huge steaming urns of tea and coffee, and an icebox with Cokes and beer and mineral water. Roadies were serving themselves and bantering with the catering girls as Barbara walked in.

She strode up to the main table and addressed the biggest guy she could see. 'Will Macleod in here?'

'Not in catering, sweetheart,' he replied, not recognizing her. 'You can try the production office, about a hundred yards ahead and to your left, right under the stairs. If he ain't there, the dressing rooms are on the first landing just up those same stairs. You can find that OK?'

'Sure,' Barbara said. Score one, she thought. 'I guess . . . Jake Williams isn't around, is he?'

'Don't waste your time,' the big guy grunted, not unkindly. 'He's here. But he's not available for business. He's seen his connection already this evening, you know what I mean? Will Macleod takes care of his shit.'

'Do you guys mind?' Barbara asked, controlling her voice.

General shrugs. 'Will keeps him out of our faces mostly,' the big guy said. 'Yeah, he can be a grade-A bitch, but that's the drugs talking.'

'Well, that ain't *my* fucking problem,' said his neighbour.

'He used to be a real sweet guy,' the big man said angrily. 'And he's dying, so make some fucking allowances, would you?'

'Thanks, I appreciate it,' said Barbara, walking away.

The sky was darkening out front, she could see it behind the stage scaffolding. She'd never been to this venue before, but most backs of stadiums are the same: expanses of concrete, the constant smell of petrol, people rushing about, groups of roadies manhandling huge flight cases so heavy they need wheels.

A roadcrew in operation is an impressive sight, like a colony of strong worker ants with beer-guts. They can raise a vast stage set in an afternoon and tear it down in two hours. You don't get in their way when they're moving gear. Barbara scattered out of the path of several guys and thus got slightly lost, but eventually found the production office without too much hassle. To her left, the way out to front of house was being illuminated by coloured spotlights, racing round the stadium. They'd stopped piping music to the PA.

Her watch showed thirty minutes to showtime.

Barbara took a deep breath. Then she flung the door open.

Macleod was bent over a prostrate figure, sprawled on the couch. Barbara had to look twice to see that it was Jake. He was wearing his normal T-shirt and jeans, but they hung off him obscenely, in loose, flapping folds, his ribs poking through his skin. His emaciated chest heaved spasmodically as though it was an effort for him to breathe.

One skeletal hand was clasped round a small vial which Macleod was trying to prise loose; she could see grains of white powder dusting his hands.

Barbara's hand flew to her mouth in horror.

'Jake's sick,' Macleod growled without turning round. 'Whoever you are, get lost.'

Barbara, shocked rigid, burst into tears.

27

For the first time since she'd started working, Rowena Gordon was an unmitigated success.

It hadn't been easy. Finding her first band had been tough, getting Michael Krebs involved had been tough, signing an American act had been tough, doing the Picture This deal had been tough.

But finally she'd come through. She was the first woman to run the North American division of a major label, many of her discoveries had reached stardom, and one had reached the true superstardom that founds empires, something that happens to one band in a million. She had power, money and a good-looking boyfriend even more successful than herself.

But like thousands of men before her, Rowena was finding that achievement brought its own set of problems.

'I'm so tired, I can't think straight,' she complained to John.

'You should move down to LA,' he suggested. 'It's just as good as New York for the record business and at least you could cut out the shuttle flights every other weekend.'

'I can't do that. All the good bands are up here.'

'You're not a talent scout any more, babe. Since when did you last have time to go to a club?'

'That's true,' she admitted, feeling old. Luther Records had a bunch of teenagers finding bands for it now.

'Think of the sunshine. Think of the jacuzzis,' John tempted her. 'You know what we'd be doing if you were here this evening? We'd be out at my house in the hills, naked, in a warm hot tub in the open air, looking at the stars and sipping champagne.'

Rowena tried to imagine it. Her first three months as division head had been more physically and emotionally taxing than she could possibly have imagined. Running Luther as a one-man outpost, and even heading up a small team that shovelled product into somebody else's pipeline, was a whole different ballgame to this.

She was supervising the birth of a seventh major American label. That meant having to make decisions every minute of every day, about things she'd never have dreamt of dealing with before. At Luther her only concern had been music. At Musica North America, her job involved marketing, promotion, budgeting, tax structures and distribution.

Rowena found herself picking between haulage systems, flying to Detroit and Minnesota to meet with truck companies. She had to set whole days aside to talk to investment bankers and accountants. She had to become competent to judge advertising agencies and indie promotion. Her days seemed to melt one into the other, in a sense of urgency and unremitting rush. If John hadn't insisted they spend time together at weeknds, she wouldn't have had any free time at all.

And now, Atomic Mass's second album, *Zenith*, was nearly finished.

'Feeling warmed up, kid?' Josh Oberman cackled, in town on a flying visit. 'Because the fun's just about to start.'

Initially he'd wondered whether to mention Topaz Rossi's call to Rowena, but decided against it. No point in bothering her with that venomous little journo now, when they were under such pressure. She was only trying to stir things up, and Joshua Oberman never went for hype.

Rowena groaned. 'Don't you think Frank Willis should handle it? He's in charge of Marketing.'

Oberman shook his head. 'No way. After what you did with that Coliseum gig? Nobody handles this record but you.'

'Christ,' she muttered, pushing a hand through her hair.

'You haven't been talking to Michael Krebs much these days,' her chairman added shrewdly. 'That has to stop. I've heard the final mixes, and they're terrific – they make *Heat Street* sound like it was recorded in Joe's bedroom in a couple of weeks. I want Michael involved in strategy for radio promotion and tour support.'

'But that's not a producer's job.'

'Krebs isn't just a producer.'

She didn't want to do this.

She didn't want to see him.

It was unavoidable.

What could she say? 'Boss, I'm uncomfortable with Michael because I used to sleep with him'? 'I think Krebs would prefer working with someone who hasn't dumped him'? 'I never want to see him again'?

But she *did* want to see him.

And that was the problem.

America the beautiful. America the free, Rowena thought as she dressed for her meeting. America, where the national pastime is reinventing yourself and taking control of your own life.

Hadn't she done that? Hadn't she walked away from one way of life and carved herself a place in another? She had all the accoutrements of the modern American woman. An apartment of her own, with furniture pared down to the bare essentials. A regular gym class, where she worked out in Lycra and Nike. A smart wardrobe of classic basics. A refrigerator stocked with lots of mineral water, fruit and vegetables. Everything designed for the Manhattan way of life; maximum style, maximum efficiency.

Yet Rowena failed the test in one respect. In the most important respect. Her love life had been screwed up from the word go. Until she was twenty-two, she'd had a few boyfriends, a handful of lovers, nice unthreatening boys whose names she could hardly even recall now. The boyfriends had often complained that she was driven, she never made time for herself, she'd never love anyone. Rowena had laughed and kissed them, but her heart was an impregnable fortress. Not one of them could get through.

But when I fell, I fell hard.

Michael Krebs. Everything a first love should not be. Twice her age. A different religion. A different background. A different country. The father of three sons. The husband of his high-school sweetheart.

And the other strikes against him? He was a close colleague. He was in a position of power over her. He was insensitive. He was domineering. But they had been good friends. He had been her mentor. All of which, of course, had evaporated into thin air when Rowena met somebody else, because the only way to eliminate Michael Krebs was to cut him off, cut him out.

Rowena wondered what the hell to wear. Something plain, but flattering, she decided; if she dressed deliberately frumpy, Krebs would think she was sending him a signal. She had to look like this was no big deal. He was married, she had a terrific partner, and they worked together.

What was in the past will stay there.

She picked a loose Armani sweater dress in buttery cashmere and teamed it with sandals and a thick wooden bangle, brushing her hair to one side and choosing a bare foundation with a muted berry lipstick; a natural, stylish look, nothing too provocative. She finished it off with a spritz of scent: 360°, by Perry Ellis, a clean, fresh fragrance.

Yeah. That's perfect, Rowena told herself, heading out of the door.

She looked put-together and in control.

She could handle this.

'Hey, it's good to see you again,' beamed Amy Tritten, the Mirror, Mirror receptionist, with complete insincerity when Rowena's white Lotus Esprit pulled into the parking lot. She was walking across to the main studio with a sheaf of papers, immaculate in a navy Adrienne Vittadini suit. None of the women who worked with Krebs had ever been glad to see Rowena Gordon.

'Did you want Ms Lincoln? Because she called to say she needed to see Michael right away, but she can't get here for a couple of hours.'

'No,' Rowena answered, wondering why Barbara needed to see Krebs so urgently. 'I have an appointment with Michael to discuss the new record.'

Amy smiled slightly. 'He's in the office. I'll take you.'

Rowena followed the younger woman through the studio complex, trying to calm her nerves, smiling brightly at all the engineers and technicians who waved hello. This was going to be OK. Actually, it was a good thing that they have this discussion. She could use some help with the *Zenith* launch right now, and Michael was an expert on radio. He seemed to be able to tell what programmers would go for merely by *looking* at a CD.

She was shown into the office. Krebs was drinking a cup of coffee, talking animatedly to a pretty woman in her late thirties, her sleek brown hair cut in a neat bob. As Rowena walked in, she gave her a friendly smile.

'Rowena, I'm glad you could make it,' Michael said. 'Have you met my wife?'

How she got through that day, Rowena could never figure out.

Deborah Krebs was just the start. Not a bimbo, not a frump, not a bitch; an attractive, intelligent, pleasant woman, who took an interest in Rowena's career, and who obviously loved her husband. She had one hand in his throughout their conversation; less a signal of ownership than the relaxed, natural posture of a woman completely at ease with her partner.

Rowena had felt a fist of jealousy clutch at her stomach with almost physical force. She felt her legs tremble. For a second, she couldn't breathe.

'Debbie, right? It's nice to meet you,' she said.

And at that moment she blessed every unhappy moment she'd spent at an English boarding school. The old reflexes snapped into focus: *composure, composure, composure.* She told his wife how much she'd heard about her. She asked meaningless questions about the health of her boys. She rhapsodized about John Metcalf.

And she avoided Michael's eyes.

When they moved on to *Zenith,* Rowena took notes, knowing that Oberman would ask her about the meeting and she wasn't registering a single word Michael said. She didn't hurry, she didn't rush, and when she got up to leave she shook both their hands and told them that they must all have dinner when John was next in New York. All the way across the complex to her car, she had a happy, contented expression on her face, like someone who's just finished a production meeting with an old friend. And when she finally, blessedly, pulled out of the parking lot, she still didn't cry. The pain was far too deep for that.

But there was worse to come.

She knew something was wrong the moment she walked through the doors.

At 11 a.m. on a Wednesday morning, Musica Towers should be buzzing – job candidates waiting anxiously in the foyer, bikers dropping off DATs and artwork, visitors being shown up to offices and her motley crew of staffers running everywhere. But today there was nothing. The lobby was completely empty, the black polished marble of the walls and floor ominously silent. Not even the duty receptionist was at the front desk.

Has there been a fire or something? What the hell's going on? Rowena thought.

At that moment, a security guard in the Musica Entertainment uniform, accompanied by a short man in a dark suit, marched into the lobby from the ground-floor corridors. She didn't recognize either one of them.

'Ms Gordon?' asked the man.

'Yes,' she replied, suddenly scared.

'My name is Johnson. I'm with Harman, Kennedy and Co.'

Her heart contracted. What in God's name did that mean? Harman, Kennedy & Co represented the parent company's legal affairs.

'I am here to inform you that your employment with Musica Entertainment has been terminated with immediate effect.' He walked forward and handed her a small sealed envelope. 'Furthermore, this letter notifies you of a breach-of-contract suit being brought against you by the company. The guard and I are to supervise your removal of any personal effects you may wish to take from your office.'

'What?' Rowena gasped.

'I am furthermore required to inform you that you are to cease and desist from claiming to represent the company in any way whatsoever. Your security classification and system password have been revoked. Any papers pertaining to company business which may be at your home or elsewhere in your possession must be returned to Musica Entertainment forthwith, or the company will take legal action to recover them.'

'I want to speak to Joshua Oberman,' Rowena said.

She was standing paralysed. This could not be happening, it just *couldn't*. What the hell was the reason for it? She'd spoken to Josh two days ago and he'd been fine. God in heaven, her boss was one of her closest friends!

'I am acting under direct instructions from Mr Oberman,' the lawyer replied. 'If you care to open that letter, Ms Gordon, you can check his signature yourself.'

With trembling fingers, Rowena ripped it open. She couldn't take in the official-looking type, but Oberman's spidery hand was unmistakable at the bottom of the page.

'I see,' she managed. Then she lifted her head. 'I do have some things I want to remove from my office,' she told them in a clear voice. 'If you could take me up there, please.'

Thank God for the executive elevator, she told herself as they stepped out on to the twenty-fourth floor. She knew instinctively that she had to behave with dignity right now; whatever the fuck had happened, she, Rowena Gordon, was not about to run sobbing from her own company like a postroom boy caught stealing stamps. Nevertheless, only shock was keeping her upright. The humiliation of being frogmarched upstairs in front of the rest of the staff would have overwhelmed her.

As it was, when she reached her own office and saw her secretary, Tamara, standing weeping outside, she barely retained control.

'It's OK, Tammy. Nobody died,' Rowena told her.

She wanted to ask the girl if she knew what was happening, but there was no way she'd do it in front of these men. While they watched, Rowena took a plastic crate and packed up all her personal stuff: the printed note that came with Michael's flowers the day she'd arrived in New York; her personal platinum records, presented to her by Musica for Roxana, Bitter Spice, Steamer and Atomic Mass; a photo of herself and Joe Hunter at the launch of *Heat Street*, a cartoon Barbara had clipped for her. Nothing much.

Christ Almighty.

She felt Tammy thrust something into her hand. A sheet of newsprint. Without looking at it, Rowena folded it up and put it inside her desk diary.

'You have my home number, honey, right?' she asked her loudly.

Weeping, Tammy nodded. Rowena put a hand on her shoulder. 'It'll work out,' she said gently, and turned to the two men.

'Right, gentlemen,' she said. 'I'm ready if you are.'

The sense of unreality stayed with Rowena all the way home as she threaded her way through the midday traffic on Broadway up to West 67th Street. The doorman touched his cap to her as she entered her apartment building and handed her a small parcel, neatly wrapped in brown paper. When she unlocked her door and shut it behind her, she was still half dazed from shock.

Automatically she put down the orange plastic crate, thinking how strange it was to be in her apartment in the middle of a weekday. She reached for her diary and took out the piece of paper Tammy had slipped her. It was the cover of the new issue of *Westside*. Rowena unfolded it, and started to read.

As she did so, she felt herself swaying. The whole room seemed to go dark.

DETONATION: HOW ATOMIC MASS BLEW UP JAKE WILLIAMS, read the headline. Underneath was a picture of the guitarist, obviously taken illicitly, slumped on the side of a flight-case, his eyes wild, his body skeletally thin. Next to that, she saw with dawning horror, was a picture of herself, looking poised and relaxed in the silver dress she'd worn to the Martins' party. There were several pull-out quotes in the middle of the text, but the one that screamed up at her said, *Do drugs if you want to . . . it's a perk of the job.*

Unsteadily, Rowena took the small parcel the doorman had given her and opened it.

Inside was a small silver cup, a replica of a sports trophy, and a note.

It read: 'Game, set, match and championship.'

PART 3
WAR

In the Wall Street offices of Maughan Macaskill, the prestigious investment bankers, Gerald Quin stared at his Quotron screen. It was flashing up a takeover: Mansion Industries had bought out Pitt Group, a small magazine company based in Minneapolis. The deal was a tiny one, scarcely worthy of the market's notice. But it interested Gerry.

Everything Mansion did interested Gerry.

Quin was twenty-six, happily married, a *cum laude* graduate of Wharton Business School and a skilled analyst. He was a rising star at Maughan Macaskill, and his specialization was tracking the movements of big conglomerates, predicting what they might do next. Months of harrowing research hell in the company library, grunt work on structuring deals and an instinctive feel for what makes a great entrepreneur tick had paid off, and Gerald was very, very good at his job.

He watched Lords Hanson and White. He watched Sir James Goldsmith. He watched Barry Diller. He watched Rupert Murdoch. And he watched Connor Miles of Mansion House.

Gerald took a sip of coffee from the plastic beaker on his desk. The takeover had been hostile, but Pitt hadn't put up much of a fight. Who could blame them? David and Goliath wasn't in it. Pitt Group was an old family company, running two local papers and a sports magazine. Three years ago they'd gone public, and recently a stock flotation meant that the family had – just – lost control. And Mansion's all-encompassing, predatory eye saw that as an open invitation.

Mansion Industries. A monolith so vast it crisscrossed the entire globe, and yet most people had never heard of it. Of course they knew about the individual companies it owned: Pemberton Diamonds in South Africa; Freyja Timber in Sweden; Natural Foods in France. Connor Miles was a bottom-fisher, like Larry Tisch, which was to say he bought undervalued companies cheap, then broke them down and sold them off or merged them into each other for economies of scale. Tradition, staff policy, product quality – all these meant nothing to Miles. Money was the only bottom line. On every company he took over he imposed his own supervisors, and in ninety per cent of cases fired the incumbent management. Who cared if they'd been there for generations? If they couldn't give Mansion the profits they demanded, they were *out*. End of story.

In the business community, Connor Miles was feared.

In the banking community, he was admired. And Gerald Quin was his number one fan. To watch Connor Miles at work, he thought, was to watch the shift in world profit centres: after the war, Mansion had been heavily into construction; in the sixties, pharmaceuticals; in the seventies, computing; in the eighties, any upmarket quality product – God, the eighties was a great decade, you made money just breathing – and in the nineties, entertainment and leisure.

He knew their big shopping spree wouldn't start for a few months. But Pitt Group was one of the first symptoms, although it was too small for most analysts to notice.

But Maughan Macaskill noticed, Quin thought, and he smiled.

28

As far as Topaz was concerned, it was over. She put Rowena Gordon out of her mind. There were a million other things to think about.

'Temple wedding,' Joe said. 'We're getting married under a wedding canopy and that's it.'

'But you haven't been to a synagogue for years. You're not religious,' Topaz retorted, outraged. 'We're getting married in St Patrick's Cathedral.'

'No way.'

'*Yes* way.'

They settled on a justice of the peace, with a rabbi and a priest blessing them afterwards.

'Have you got any plans for restructuring the division?' Matt Gowers asked his new director.

'How long have you got?' she replied, crossing a terrific pair of ankles in Ann Klein heels.

Gowers mentally cursed the fashion for long skirts, but part of him was relieved to see Rossi bang up-to-date as usual. Her flair for fashion had pushed American's women's titles to the front of the newsracks; refusing to use editorial space on see-through bras, designer grunge or thigh-high minis designed with an anorexic teenager in mind had won them a lot of friends amongst American women, who'd had it with being told to aspire to a body shape biologically impossible for most of them.

'Try me,' he offered.

'OK,' Topaz said. 'I want to rehaul *US Woman*, close down *White Light* altogether, take *Westside* national and start an entertainment glossy to rival *Vanity Fair*, except we won't bother with stories about businessmen – ours will be wall-to-wall stars.'

'Nate Rosen never tried anything so radical,' her boss commented.

Topaz shrugged. 'I'll need your support, Matt.'

'You have it,' said Gowers, mildly amused at her boldness. 'Aren't you getting married soon? You're going to be pretty busy.'

'Ain't that the truth,' his director answered with feeling.

'I've moved house so many times I can't do it again,' Topaz complained. 'What's wrong with your place?'

'It's not big enough. Neither is yours.'

'They were big enough for us before.'

Joe pulled her to him, running a large tanned hand across her stomach. 'They're not big enough for children,' he said.

'Children?' she repeated.

'Yeah,' Joe said, grinning at her. 'You know, sons, daughters. The indispensable accessory for the modern married couple.'

She picked up a beanbag and threw it at him, and Goldstein reached forward with a lightning thrust, grabbed her wrist and twisted her underneath him. Topaz felt him hardening on top of her as they stared breathlessly at each other, smiling, eyes alight with desire.

'Let's practise,' Joe murmured, hands reaching down to unbutton her silk cardigan.

She remembered that summer as one of the hottest, stickiest, busiest, most terrifying, aggravating, exhilarating, passionate times she'd ever spent in her life.

Work exploded. Financial projections, design reworks, marketing changes – it was a miracle she ever got out of the building. But the restructuring was screaming to be done and Topaz had decided to do it. She was the boss now, with no one but Matt able to countermand her, and at twenty-eight she'd learnt to trust her own instincts.

Some things were painful, like making the staff on *White Light* redundant. But the magazine had never recovered from the Atomic Mass fiasco, and it was better to cut the company's losses. Topaz made as much effort as she could to place employees elsewhere in American and see that the journalists got good settlements, but she was determined to act like a businesswoman. The decision was final.

Some things were difficult, like rehauling *US Woman* over the strenuous objections of the editorial team. But Topaz fired the editor herself and talked most of his colleagues round, with demonstrations and presentations. By the time she was through, they thought it had been their idea in the first place.

And some things were your basic nightmare. Like starting a new glossy from scratch and changing *Westside* to a national. The new title was called *Stateside* and Topaz envisaged it as a *Village Voice* for the entire country, encompassing radical views and underground culture from San Francisco to Dallas, Pittsburgh to Detroit, as well as New York. For both these projects, Topaz took over three empty offices on the thirtieth floor and converted them into a war room, where a crowd of writers and executives could be found any given hour of the day, brainstorming. The best ideas were chalked up on blackboards and left standing around the room, and the atmosphere was so inspirational that editors from existing magazines wandered in to steal ideas.

Josie Simons came up with the best one. A major feature in every issue of the new title, *Impact* – 'Not Size Eight' – which profiled women who didn't fit the supermodel straitjacket, or were older than twenty-five, or came from ethnic backgrounds; strong, beautiful women from all over the world and lots of them.

'Unadulterated sex bombs,' Jason Richman was heard to remark, and there were sighs of satisfaction from every girl in the room.

'We'll give real women something to aim at,' Josie said, underlining *How Diana Looks Better When She Puts ON Weight,* and placing a picture of Drew Barrymore next to ones of Felicia Rashad from *The Cosby Show* and Sharon Stone at her fortieth birthday party.

'That,' said Matt Gowers when he saw it, 'will sell *millions.*'

Her home life exploded too.

Joe and she seemed to fight about everything. The wedding. The reception. The honeymoon. Where to buy a house.

'I've got a lot of friends. I want them to share this with us,' Joe said.

'So do I, but I don't want a circus,' Topaz insisted.

'Let's go skiing in the Alps,' Joe suggested, bringing home a sheaf of travel brochures.

'That's about as romantic as root-canal work,' replied Topaz angrily. 'How could you think of sports on our *honeymoon*?'

'Yeah? What do you want to do? Europe and museums all day?'

'I like SoHo. We could get something really cool down there,' Topaz said. 'It's a great area.'

'You're joking, right? I want a penthouse on Fifth,' Goldstein replied. 'We can easily afford it.'

Jesus, the stubborn sonofabitch, Topaz thought furiously as Joe vetoed another idea.

She'll drive me nuts in six months. Tops, thought Joe, glaring at his betrothed's obstinate expression.

But they couldn't stay mad for long. The heady swell of love would overcome Joe or Topaz and the other would instantly sense it and get turned on, and then nobody talked for a while. They could hardly keep their hands off each other; they made slow, gentle love, they played games, they screwed each other senseless over tables and on the floor and up against the walls.

'All the therapists say this is the worst way to resolve a dispute,' Topaz managed, as Joe slipped two fingers inside her, pleasuring her most intimate places.

'Fuck the therapists,' Joe growled, aroused to boiling point by her heat, thrusting himself inside her.

'Oh, I love you, I love you so much,' she gasped.

'So I see,' he teased her.

They picked a large reception, a honeymoon in Venice and an eighteenth-century house on Beekman Place.

'I hate him,' Topaz said, slamming the phone down. Her hands were balled at her sides in tight fists. 'I *hate* him and I'm not going through with it.'

'Yes you are,' said Tiz Correy calmly, leafing through the dummy for *Impact.* The spacious director's office was a mess, the immaculate caramel carpet covered with photographs, clippings and colour charts, and Topaz's kidney-shaped desk piled high with articles, memos and financial data. For a week now she'd refused to let the cleaning staff in, because, as Jason Richman pointed out, 'Who the hell knows what you'll be throwing away?'

The launch was less than a month away and operations had moved into Topaz's office. Some of her fellow directors were more than a little bothered by this, but Gowers made it clear that she was to be given a free hand. Rossi was doing major work, however unorthodox a method she was choosing, and her reports to the board already showed improvements in operating costs.

Back in the fifties, when he'd borrowed three thousand dollars to start *Week in Review,* Gowers reflected, he'd been pretty hands-on himself. And he hadn't done badly.

'Leave Rossi be,' he commanded. 'It's only another month,' and Topaz's office descended into a maelstrom of creative chaos.

'Do you know what he just said? He said he can't believe I'm not taking his name. All this time and he never mentioned it! He just assumed I'd take his name! He can go straight to hell,' Topaz exclaimed tearfully.

Tiz tried to keep a straight face. Every week there was a new crisis, every week the wedding was off, and every week Topaz skipped back into the office like a schoolgirl, glowing from head to foot with pure happiness.

'And you assumed he'd be happy that you wouldn't,' she said reasonably. 'You know you should both have discussed this before.'

'I'm giving him back his ring,' Topaz snapped. She felt giddy and miserable. The stress must be making her ill; she'd thrown up every morning this week, almost as soon as she'd got into the office.

'Call him back, tell him you love him and you're proud to be his wife, but you want to keep your own name. Ask him how he'd feel if you wanted him to become Joe Rossi.'

Her boss gave a weak smile at the thought.

'And if he say's it's traditional, tell him he knows you're not a traditional girl.'

'Topaz, have you approved the amethyst headlines for "Not Size Eight"? Production are crawling up my ass about it,' said Tristam Drummond, *Impact*'s art director, marching into the room. 'We're two days after their final deadline already.'

'Jack Levinson in Sales wants to see you about the Revlon ads,' her secretary announced.

'Thanks, I'll be ten minutes,' Topaz promised. She passed a hand across her forehead. 'Amethyst headlines . . .'

'We thought burnt gold worked better,' Tiz reminded her.

'Henri Bendel are on line two,' her secretary said. 'About the fitting. They can't do this afternoon, would tonight suit you?'

Patrick Mahoney, *Economic Monthly*'s new editor, walked in looking harassed.

'Alan Greenspan just cancelled on me,' he told her. 'I need a replacement right away. Do you think Joe could find me someone at NBC?'

Impact and the new look *US Woman* were previewed to the trade with great fanfare. They were an instant hit. The first issue of *Impact* sold out across the country in forty-eight hours.

Joe Goldstein and Topaz Rossi were married in a private room at the Pierre, in front of a hundred guests. They held hands throughout the ceremony.

The bride wore a cream gown shot through with delicate gold thread and glittering with tiny seedpearls. Her deep red hair was caught in ropes of gold beads and hung warm and lovely down her back, under a long, romantic veil of antique English lace, secured at the top with a coronet of white rosebuds. Tiz Correy and Elise DeLuca, her maids of honour, were dressed in pink Chanel suits. Joe Goldstein and his younger brother and best man, Martin, wore traditional black tie and for once Joe looked completely comfortable in it.

The reception was a riot: their buddies from NBC, Harvard, American Magazines and Oxford downed a lot of champagne, ate a lot of smoked salmon and danced into the early evening. The speeches got bluer and bluer as the evening progressed, but most people agreed with Jason Richman, who called it 'Not so much a marriage as a merger.'

That night, when they got into the honeymoon suite at the Ritz Carlton, Joe handed Topaz a large square box.

'Your wedding gift,' he said.

Glancing up at him she opened it. Inside was a long necklace, a beautiful piece set with fifteen carat diamonds and exquisite polished beads of topaz.

'I'm sorry it's always necklaces,' Joe said awkwardly.

Topaz reached up and stroked his cheek, her eyes wet with tears. 'I love it nearly as much as I love you,' she said.

They kissed. 'You've got two wedding presents from me,' she said. 'One I couldn't bring, because it's in the garage at home. But I have the other one.'

She reached into her purse and handed him a crumpled scrap of paper with their doctor's letterhead.

Puzzled, Joe unfolded it and read it. Then he smoothed it out, looked wildly at his wife, and read it again, carefully, just to make sure.

'You don't mean –'

'I'm pregnant,' Topaz said, smiling at her husband.

For a moment they just stood there, almost drunk with happiness. Then Joe gathered Topaz into his arms, as gently as if she were made of fragile glass.

'We'll be together till we die,' he said. 'Nothing can go wrong now.'

29

As far as Rowena was concerned, it was over.

Only pressure from Barbara Lincoln staved off a lawsuit, and she was finished in the record business. All her success as a talent scout, all her achievements as a businesswoman, were swept aside in a second. She was publicly associated with drugs, and no record company would touch her.

'I tried to stop them but I was outvoted,' Josh Oberman said, calling her the day after. 'These new fucking board rules. How could you have been so *careless?*'

'Are you crying, Josh?' she asked.

'Of course I'm not fucking crying,' he sniffed. 'You fucking moron.'

'Come and work for me,' Barbara said, anxious about her friend. Rowena had lost half a stone and sunk into total lethargy. She had her groceries delivered and she rarely left the apartment.

'You must be joking. After what I said to Jake?'

'You can't blame yourself for that. As if he paid any attention to any of us,' the manager replied. 'Look, Will Macleod decided not to tell me until the lad was half-dead, but I'm not blaming him, either. What can the crew do if the band go off the rails? Jake's in rehab and we're looking for a new guitarist. The band have had it with him, Michael can't work with him . . . *you* didn't pass him a syringe, Rowena.'

'Thanks, but I can't work with you,' Rowena told her. 'I can't face any of it.'

Her friend shrugged. 'Any time you change your mind.'

'Come and work with me,' Michael said. 'You can help me choose my projects and negotiate my deals. I'll give you ten per cent of my company.'

The offer was worth millions.

'I can't ever work with you again,' she said flatly.

'Why not? We're good friends. We think the same way. I don't give a fuck what drugs you did, and I don't have shareholders.'

'It wouldn't work,' she replied. 'It's over.'

'I want you back. I miss you,' Krebs said.

For a second she closed her eyes, longing for it all to be different, longing for the blank ache in her heart to go away, for a return of the hot, passionate joy that had filled every waking second when they'd started this affair.

'We can't go back,' she said. 'Thank you for everything you did for me, Michael. Goodbye.'

She put down the receiver.

John Metcalf could only guess what she must be feeling. It happened all the time in his business, of course: scandals, resignations, corporate coups. He'd been a teenager at the time of the Begelman affair; on his first steps up the ladder when Dawn Steel was ousted whilst giving birth. Hollywood was a monster, and the only emotions worth jack were fear and greed.

The trouble was that Rowena was guilty. Undeniably so. If it had been libellous, the paper would have been sued to kingdom come by Musica's lawyers. He very much doubted whether some flippant remark by Rowena would have pushed her young guitarist down the road to addiction, but that wasn't the point. She'd condoned the use of drugs and she'd been caught doing it.

She was right, of course. Everybody *did* do it, especially in LA, and he doubted the music moguls in New York were any better. Like she said, you experimented and gave up, or you didn't give up and you screwed up your life. So she'd taken Ecstasy in the past, well, so had he. But for years they'd both been clean.

What was she supposed to say to a young rock star? 'Just say no'? And the boy would *listen* to that? 'Don't let drugs do you' was a better way of putting it, in Metcalf's opinion. If a blockbusting Metropolis star had that conversation with him he'd probably say the same thing.

It was going to be difficult, though. Metcalf knew that. As the youngest studio head in town, he'd made a lot of enemies just by having hits. What was it Shakespeare wrote? *Uneasy lies the head that wears a crown.* Right. And the shark pool circling constantly beneath him would drool at the scent of anything they could use against him. Like a girlfriend who was blackballed by her entire industry.

Fuck them all, Metcalf told himself. The closest they've come to love is Heidi Fleiss.

There was no decision to make.

'Book my table at Spago's,' Metcalf told his secretary loudly after the Metropolis production meeting, while all his VPs of Production and other development people were gathering their papers. 'I'm having dinner with Rowena Gordon. Thursday at nine.'

The VPs all studiously avoided his gaze, but John wasn't fooled for a second. Within ten minutes the word would be out round Hollywood that whatever else had happened, John Metcalf and Rowena Gordon were still an item.

He called her. 'How are you feeling?'

'I've been better,' she said. Her voice was flat and listless. 'I'm finished, John. I just don't know what to do. I can't do anything in the music business any more.'

'You can't do anything the way you did it before,' he corrected her. 'That's not the same thing.'

'I'm a non-person,' Rowena said.

'Bullshit. I won't allow you to give up like this,' he answered sharply. The resignation in her tone shocked him. She sounded as though life itself had ground to a halt. 'We've having dinner at Spago's on Thursday, and if you're not in town by Wednesday morning I'm flying up to get you.'

For the first time in a week Rowena found she actually wanted to do something. She wanted to see John.

'OK,' she said.

Was that a faint spark of animation? Metcalf wondered.

'Do yourself one other favour,' he cajoled her. 'Sort out your finances. Make sure you know where you stand.'

'I can't be bothered,' she said.

'You can and you will,' Metcalf told her. 'Do you want all those guys blanking you right now to watch you just fade to black? What would your jerk-off father say, "I always knew she wouldn't last the course"? You hold your head up, Rowena Gordon. Don't you dare let me down.'

'You're telling me I have no money,' Rowena said three days later.

She sat opposite Peter Weiss, her accountant, in the oak-panelled offices of Weiss, Fletcher and Baum, waring a short brown suit and pumps. Her hair was neatly brushed and tied back in a ponytail, and she'd put on a little foundation. She was perfectly presentable, but that was about it.

Weiss had never seen Rowena Gordon look so unattractive. Her slender frame was now gaunt, her normally healthy skin pallid, and the sparkle in her green eyes had totally vanished.

'Not exactly,' he replied cautiously. 'Under the settlement with Musica, you lost your pension funds and received no compensation, as well as having surrendered the Lotus. The financial plans we made for you' – he cleared his throat – 'didn't take account of the possibility of, uh, what happened. Which means we have to rework your numbers. Now your apartment will have to be sold because Musica Entertainment part-funded the original deal.'

'They own the apartment?'

'No, you have a share in the freehold,' he replied hastily. 'Part of the proceeds belong to you. You also have fairly substantial monies that you could realize from selling your Musica stock.'

She shook her head. 'I want to keep the stock.'

Weiss shuffled his papers nervously. 'Ms Gordon, I would have to advise you against that course of action,' he said. 'Your actual monetary savings are limited. You, uh, you've tended to live at the top of your budgeted bracket.'

'If we sold the apartment and my other stocks, and with what savings there are, how much would I have altogether?'

'I can't be exact,' Weiss replied, 'but I believe that such a sale would only realize a little over a million dollars. And with the need to find a new apartment, Ms Gordon, you couldn't live in the style to which you've become accustomed.'

'Thank you, Mr Weiss,' Rowena said. 'I'd be obliged if you could send me your final bill.'

'This firm will be happy to represent you for a reduced retainer, Ms Gordon,' Weiss said impulsively, moved by the calm dignity she was showing. 'We are sure you will make a success of whatever you next decide to pursue.'

She offered him her hand, touched. It was the first sign of confidence that anyone outside her immediate group of friends had shown in her. Record executives and promoters who had kissed her ass till it turned blue would no longer even take her calls.

'I must decline, Mr Weiss, but I shan't forget your kindness,' Rowena said.

'Why, Ms Gordon?' he asked, surprised to find he was disappointed.

'I'm leaving New York,' she replied. 'There's nothing here for me now.'

30

It was all she could do to get up in the mornings.

To begin with it was easy by comparison, because at least she had things to do. The apartment was sold. She found a relatively cheap house in the Hollywood hills above the Château Marmont; after the earthquakes in '94, prices for property on the slopes had plunged. Then there was the liquidation of her stocks and arranging for the packing up and delivery of her personal effects.

Peter Weiss had been right on the money. The value of her entire estate, without selling her Musica stock, came to $1,100,000.

For most people, a fortune. By Rowena's standards, failure.

Every single person she'd had close dealings with was worth at least ten times that amount. John, Josh, Barbara, Michael, the band. She'd been too busy flying first class, designer shopping and looking after other people's business to take care of her personal funds.

And now it was too late.

She had plenty of time to look back over things, and she knew it had been her own fault. She'd betrayed someone who trusted in her, and then refused to admit any guilt. She'd taunted Topaz again and again because she'd hated her for being her own victim, and despised her because of her own success. A flimsy enough success, as she was just finding out. As if a veil had been lifted, Rowena could suddenly see what Topaz must have seen: a haughty, arrogant bitch who cared for nobody but herself.

After Rossi's attempt to screw up the launch of *Heat Street* failed, Rowena had thought she was invincible. Never mind that it was Michael Krebs, not her, who'd turned that one around. And when she'd managed to sign Obsession and Steamer, she'd thought she was immortal.

Her comments to Jake had been just another symptom. It wasn't what she'd said, it was where she'd said it. *At Elizabeth Martin's party.* With practically every important man and woman in New York in attendance, including at least fifty of the top investigative reporters in the city.

Sticks and stones may break my bones, but words will never hurt me.
Oh yeah?
She'd been in the record business since she'd started working. She had no skills for doing anything else, and there was no way any record company would have her back.

I'll never work again, she thought blankly. Feelings of shame and catastrophe drifted through the house like black fog.

Rowena had coped with everything. Her father's rejection. Squalor in London. The struggle to find a job, and the struggle to keep it. Setting up on her own in a foreign country. Building a major new company. Deliberately walking away from the love of her life.

She had coped with everything. Except failure.

It was John Metcalf who saved her from complete collapse.

At the start he stayed away, just calling now and then to see if she was OK.

'She's hurting now. She needs a mourning period,' his therapist said.

'But she won't even go out with me any more,' Metcalf protested.

'You have to respect her space. It's a difficult time for her.'

Finally, John Metcalf handed his house keys over to a buddy, packed up a suitcase and simply drove over to her house.

'What the hell are you doing here?' Rowena demanded when he turned up at her gate. It was a cool winter's morning, the type Metcalf particularly enjoyed; a mild breeze, the flowers in Rowena's small garden faintly scenting the air. She was dressed appropriately: a dark blue pantsuit in crisp linen by Michael Kors and fawn pumps from Chanel. In the doorway behind her he could see the main room of the house, immaculately neat and tidy. *Too* neat and tidy. The place looked like a museum. And for all Rowena's careful outfit, she looked utterly lifeless. She had on no make-up, no jewellery, not even a watch.

'Can I come in?' he returned.

She unlatched the door and stood aside for him. John seemed like a refugee from another world. Someone she had known a million lifetimes ago, when she was working, when she was able to use her brain.

'It's a nice place,' Metcalf said. He glanced round at the modest reception room, the orderly kitchen and the glimpse of Rowena's bedroom and bathroom to his left. She had set up a television and stereo and there was everything you might actually need in a home – a microwave, refrigerator and coffee percolator, but that was it. She'd hung none of her paintings, unpacked none of her bonsai trees, laid out no ornaments.

'Thanks,' she replied automatically.

Metcalf hefted up his suitcase and carried it through to her bedroom. Then he picked up the remote and switched off the TV, flickering brightly in the corner. 'You shouldn't be watching that at ten in the morning,' he reproved her gently.

'Why have you brought a case?' she asked, looking at Metcalf's tanned body and luxuriant hazel hair. Almost despite herself, she was glad he was there. In fact, she was *surprised* he was there. Taken aback that someone was still interested.

'Because I'm staying for a while,' Metcalf answered impudently.

'I can look after myself.'

'I don't think so,' he replied, reaching out and loosening her ponytail. A blonde shower fell about her shoulders.

'Don't do that!' she snapped.

He grinned at her. 'At least you can still get mad.'

'Go home, John,' Rowena said. 'You can't stay. I need to be by myself.'

'You've been by yourself for too long.'

'I want to be alone.'

I can't make her accept me, Metcalf realized.

'OK, I'll go, if that's what you want,' he told her. 'But first I need your help. I've run into a problem with Picture This and we have the divisional meeting coming up – it's in San Antonio and everyone in the company's gonna be there. Including Nick Large.'

Large was his boss, a redheaded industry veteran who controlled Cage Entertainment, the company that owned Metropolis.

'So get Sam Neil to look into it,' Rowena shrugged. Sam was her successor at Musica North America and the soundtrack label was his responsibility now.

He shook his head. 'Won't work. If this was easy I'd have fixed it myself. I need you because you structured the original deal.' He gestured towards his briefcase. 'I've brought the papers with me. Please, Rowena, I know you feel lousy but I'm stuck. We have a picture opening soon with a dynamite soundtrack –'

'*My Heart Belongs to Dallas*,' Rowena agreed, with just the faintest glimmer of interest.

'Right. Anyway, word is that our numbers are gonna be just OK, but the merchandizing could turn it into a very profitable picture. The success of the record is crucial to that –'

'MTV, radio tie-ins, press,' she cut in.

'Exactly. Now we have a situation where the management for Black Ice – one of the bands featured – are insisting that the studio percentages must exclude their cut because of their original deal with Musica. They're threatening litigation and that could delay the launch of the record, which probably won't hurt the album too much but its knock-on effects for our T-shirts and sunglasses and stuff could be disastrous . . .'

As John explained the problem, Rowena began to turn the situation over in her mind, taking a pen from the sideboard and making notes. When he sat down she didn't stop him, and when he opened up his case and handed her the thick sheaf of notes Rowena took them eagerly and paced through them intently.

Half an hour later she looked up, triumphant, her face flushed with effort.

'I've got it,' she said. 'It's clause 16b. The rolling break-even states that –'

John's face stopped her in mid-sentence. He was leaning against the kitchen table, smiling gently. She realized with a start that he'd been watching her silently for the last twenty minutes.

'Welcome back,' he said.

He took her to dinner at the Ivy, where they'd first met.

'You can't understand what it's like,' Rowena said. 'When you've fought for a dream all your life, and as soon as you get it, it's taken from you.'

John kissed her hand. He wanted to let her talk, to help her admit her feelings to somebody else. He was overjoyed it was him she was confiding in.

'Everything you hated before becomes precious. Like phones ringing all the time, like the travel – God, John, I missed getting woken up at six to go to the airport every month because Atomic Mass were playing somewhere.'

She gave him a tiny smile.

'You could have done that any time you wanted,' he told her. 'Atomic Mass are on a stadium tour of Europe. It's a complete sell-out.'

'It is? How's the record doing?'

John leant towards her. 'Haven't you even been listening to the radio? Didn't you put on MTV?'

'My radio's tuned to a classical station,' she replied, the soft candlelight glinting on her gold earrings. 'And I couldn't bear to look at MTV. I knew I'd see Musica acts – *my* acts – and it was too painful. Like watching all the other kids at a party you weren't invited to.'

Metcalf shook his head in wonderment. 'I guess you're about the only person on the planet who doesn't know, then. *Zenith* is busting sales records across America. Atomic Mass have turned into U2.'

Rowena digested the news in silence. Then she said, 'Maybe I should tell you the whole story.'

Starting at the beginning, she recounted all of it. Her parents' coldness and her own independence. Oxford, and meeting Topaz Rossi. Peter Kennedy and the Union. Soho. The fruitless hunt for a band. And Topaz in America, from the launch of *Heat Street* to Velocity and finally the *Westside* story that destroyed her career.

'So don't you want to get this Rossi girl back?' he asked when she'd finished, looking at the shadows under her beautiful eyes, the tiny lines that had appeared around her mouth and forehead for the first time.

Rowena shook her head. 'Absolutely not. In Topaz's place I'd have done the same thing.' She paused, then added, 'I told myself that one day she'd give up and let it go . . . I couldn't resist taunting her. I forgot what she was like. Topaz was always passionate, always hot-blooded. What we'd consider a grudge, she'd think of as a score that needed settling.'

'Why did you make such a friend of her in the first place?'

She thought about it. 'You know what it was? We both had something to prove.'

'Because your fathers wanted boys?'

She nodded, a lovely, graceful movement. John admired her dress again, a fitted gown in moss-green velvet that picked out her eyes.

'Your fathers were morons,' he said.

'Perhaps. I've sometimes longed to be a man,' she answered. 'It would have cut down on some heartache.'

'Do you miss Topaz Rossi?' John asked.

'No,' Rowena said slowly. 'Certain things can't be undone. I miss my job. I miss Barbara and Josh and Atomic . . .'

And I miss Michael Krebs, she finished silently.

'So what are you going to do about it?' John asked.

His liquid blue eyes were intent. He was going to get her back in the game, whatever it took – pleading, bullying, threats.

He ticked the points off on his fingers. 'You used to run a record company, and that option's closed to you now. You've always worked in the record business. It's unlikely that any big corporation would be in a position to hire you right now, because you're too high-profile to be hired quietly. Those are your disadvantages.'

She looked at him as he bent over and refilled her glass with champagne; a vintage Dom Perignon, one of her favourites.

'You built up a company from scratch, so you acquired general business skills. You have intelligence and guts. You have a million dollars of your own which you could borrow against. And you will have a lot of key players in your corner – Joshua Oberman, Michael Krebs, Barbara Lincoln, Steamer, Roxana, Atomic Mass, and me. Those are your advantages. Now the question is, what are you going to do with them?'

She sipped at her drink, considering it. 'What do you think I should do?'

'I think you should set up in business. Be your own boss,' he replied. 'But I don't know *which* business. And it's not my job to find out.'

'I could, couldn't I?' Rowena asked, and with a rush of joy Metcalf saw that her eyes were sparkling again.

'Your hero David Geffen walked away from his brilliant career because they told him he had terminal cancer. A year later they say it's the wrong diagnosis and he had a load of money and nothing to do. Did he turn into a zombie? No, he went and founded Geffen Records.'

She speared a forkful of Caesar salad.

'You can do anything you want,' he said. 'Real glory isn't about a smooth ride to the top. It's about picking yourself up when you fall and building it all again.'

'John, I could fall in love with you,' Rowena said.

'That's what I'm counting on,' he replied.

31

Three weeks later Rowena Gordon was back in business.

It could hardly have been more different to her last office. No expensive carpets and designer window space. No Eames chairs. Not even a filter coffee machine.

She set up in a cheap lot on Melrose with two phones, a fax machine and an eighteen-year-old secretary. Things were different when you paid the overheads bills yourself.

John Metcalf offered her anything she wanted – start-up capital, the use of an office in the Metropolis lot. Rowena thanked him but refused. 'This is something I have to do myself,' she said. 'Taking help from anyone just wouldn't be right.'

'At least move in with me. Then you could sell your place and use the funds from that.'

She kissed him, a soft, wet kiss that stirred his groin. 'I can't. I nearly gave my independence up before. You helped me out of that, remember?'

'This isn't just for you,' he admitted, an erection growing in his pants. She saw it and pressed her hand between his legs, caressing his hardness through the cloth. He groaned. 'Please. I want you near me.'

'You're near me now,' Rowena said, reaching behind her and unzipping her slip dress. The silk slid off her like water, and with a shock of lust he saw she was naked underneath it. The long slender legs had tanned to the colour of buttermilk, and her nipples were a beautiful pink against the golden skin of her small breasts. She leant back, displaying the blonde triangle between her supple thighs. 'Want to get closer?'

Without a word he unbuttoned his jeans and kicked them off, taking her in his arms. His cock pressed against the flat of her stomach, hard and swollen with wanting.

'It's been a long time,' he said.

'Too long,' Rowena answered. She thought of the last time she'd made love to John, a week after the Martins' party, and then, unbidden, a vision of the last time she'd touched Michael like this swam into her mind.

John felt heat flood her belly. He pushed a finger into her, probing. She was already, instantly wet.

'Do you wanna fool around?' he whispered in her ear. 'Or do you wanna go right to it?'

For answer she smiled at him and spread her legs, an insolent, sensual movement.

John felt the urgency in his cock take over and he guided himself to the quick of her, pushing inside her, inch by inch, until he was sunk in right up to the hilt. She moved with him, pressing down, as though she wanted him to thrust even deeper, to fill her even more.

'You feel so good,' he said. Her eyes were shut tight and he could see her nipples harden and erect in front of his eyes. Metcalf bent to suck them, tugging at them lightly with his lips like a greedy child. Pleasure stabbed through her, and she felt herself getting hotter, needing a man's touch, loving the strong grip of his arms and the muscled torso, which she could feel through the thin cotton T-shirt he hadn't bothered to take off.

Eagerly he started to thrust, finding his rhythm, maddened by the feel of her tight, slippery clinch around his cock. As he got faster and faster her own body responded, until she blocked out everything except the sweet ripples spreading through her and his driving, relentless cock, and white-hot release came in a violent spasm which physically shook her.

John erupted inside her, held her for a second, and then pulled out of her sweating, trembling body. He put up his hands and tilted her face towards him. 'Like I told you,' he said, 'there's no going back.'

She took his right hand and pressed her lips to it, kissing him gently, gratefully. 'Only forward,' she replied. 'Which is why I can't move in.'

Nothing he could do or say would move her. She was with him almost every night, but she refused to sell her house. She was going to do all this by herself, and be beholden to nobody.

The choice of business was difficult.

She could work for a production company, or manage a band – not Michael or Atomic Mass, but others. However, that would mean working for somebody else and it would also mean she was on a percentage.

No. I never want to be in a position where I could be fired. And I want to own stock, not take a salary.

She could start a record company of her own. But any act she signed as a tiny independent would leave her for a major at the first taste of success. That was always the way. Recording costs had soared since David Geffen had founded his labels, and while it could still be done, it was much more difficult . . .

But that's not the real reason, is it? she asked herself. The fact is that Atomic Mass and Josh and Barbara and all the rest of it meant *everything* to me. When it was taken away I was devastated. Music is my life. Music is too much to risk.

No emotional capital. She would start again as a businesswoman, and keep her passions separate.

She would be in control.

Rowena settled on the best compromise she could come up with. It had to involve music, because that was her area of expertise, but it also had to be as dry as dust. Something that would let her work to live, not live to work.

She got a piece of paper and listed her main talents.

1. *A&R*. Well, that one was pretty useless now.

2. *Promotion*.

Rowena scored a line under this and sat staring into space. *Promotion ...* now there was an idea. Hadn't she pulled off the marketing rescue of the century when Atomic Mass booked the Coliseum too early in the US tour for *Heat Street*? And that was one thing Krebs hadn't done for her.

All my own work, she thought with a smile. Damn, that had felt so good.

But unforeseen disasters didn't happen every day, and the major companies had in-house marketing experts, as did the big promoters and agents.

So who needed help?

Wasn't it obvious? Everybody who couldn't afford to hire marketing specialists. Indie labels. College promoters. Small clubs around the country.

Couldn't afford them, though, that was the point. How could one of them afford her?

The answer came back instantly: *one of them couldn't. But a lot of them could.*

That evening, Rowena drove up to John's weekend beach house in Malibu to tell him her plans. After she'd taken a long, refreshing shower, washed her hair and pulled on one of his huge paisley Turnbull & Asser bathrobes, he joined her on the terrace, carrying two frosted glasses and a pitcher of margaritas.

'Do you still have that conference in San Antonio coming up?'

He nodded, a shadow crossing his face. 'Yeah. And I still have problems with the record. The plan you dreamt up stopped the lawsuit, but now the act is refusing to help promote it. And "Face Up" is the first single.'

Rowena sipped her drink. Black Ice were one of the toughest groups to deal with, she knew that. They hated big companies on principle and nothing was good enough for them: not enough posters in the stores, not enough radio play, not enough MTV. They raised objections at every stage from artwork to distribution. She remembered them and their stubborn manager, Ali Kahed, only too well.

Black Ice also sold a lot of records. They'd been the first big act on Musica North America that she hadn't signed herself, and they made the reputation of Steve Goldman, the young scout who'd risen to become her head of A&R. Their last album had debuted at number four in the *Billboard* charts.

Properly handled, 'Face Up' could sell a lot of records for Picture This, and a lot of T-shirts for *My Heart Belongs to Dallas*.

'I can tell you what to do,' she said.

'Really? Jesus, I hope so,' Metcalf said, pushing a hand through his hair. 'Because this is a total fucking mess. The new Musica guys are terrified of Kahed and they won't lift a finger to help out.'

Rowena lifted her glass to him. 'Congratulations,' she said. 'You've just become my first client.'

When Metropolis biked round the contract the next day, Rowena signed on the dotted line in front of Joanne, her secretary, and the guy who sold leather boots in the store opposite.

'They've left a space for us to include the company name,' said Joanne. Rowena shrugged. 'Any ideas?'

'Call it Cowhide,' suggested the bootseller, 'can't have rock 'n' roll without leather,' and the Cowhide Consultancy was born.

For the first two hours Joanne just sat at her desk reading *Impact*. Her boss worked in silence, spreading large sheets of paper over her desk and writing down names, phone numbers and lists of stores, radio stations and music magazines with large coloured pens, occasionally doodling lines from one to another. Eventually she came out, her hands covered with bright inkstains, and handed Joanne a small list with seventy names and numbers on it.

Joanne raised an eyebrow.

'Oh, that's just the first batch,' Rowena told her. 'Think you're ready for this?'

'I'm ready if you are,' Joanne said, smiling.

Maybe this job wouldn't be such a dead loss after all.

Once Rowena got started there was no stopping her. Carefully she'd picked out her target audience: maverick programmers, store managers who owed her favours, and writers and TV execs who'd been closely involved with her work on Atomic Mass.

'Christ, Rowena! How are you? Where the fuck have you been?' asked Jack Fleming at *Rolling Stone*.

'Black Ice? Yeah, they'll play,' said Joe Moretti at KXDA. 'They're on. My pleasure. When are you coming by?'

'I'll do what I can,' Pete Meyer at MTV promised. 'It's good to have you back.'

At lunch Joanne ordered them a pizza and a couple of Diet Cokes, and Rowena called John and listed all the stations and papers she'd delivered so far.

'I don't believe it. How the hell did you pull that off?' he asked, amazed.

'Oh, I'm not through,' she replied. 'That was the warm-up. Now, how much money would you be willing to give me for an advertising budget?'

'Advertising? Isn't that Musica's job?'

'Depends what you want. If you want to sell a few albums, we already have. If you want to help your film merchandizing . . .'

'How much do you need?' John asked, struck by the briskness of her tone. She was using his private line, but she was all business.

Jesus, we were making love on the beach this morning.

She named a figure.

'OK,' he said. '*My Heart Belongs to Dallas* is opening two weeks after this single is commercially released. Do you think you can get publicity for the movie out of this as well?'

'That's the idea,' Rowena said. 'I have something in mind, but I need an ad budget to do it.'

'All right, Rowena,' John said. 'You got it. Surprise me.'

'I will,' she said.

That afternoon Rowena gave Joanne the second list. This contained the names of programme directors and editors in the key markets whom she couldn't count on personally; men that were still friendly to her, though. The trick was to spend a little money where it would buy the most exposure; she knew better than to simply go for the magazines and stations with the biggest readership or catchment areas. Influence meant everything. That was what working with Michael Krebs had taught her.

She knew all about *My Heart Belongs to Dallas*. It was a bittersweet modern romance, the story of a woman torn between a Texan lawyer, the love of her life, and a doctor who'd fathered her child and would make the better parent for him. She chooses the doctor for her boy's sake, and then to her surprise finds herself falling in love with him after all.

Rowena didn't think it was a bad film, it just wasn't what Metropolis had expected. They'd wanted a very dramatic, highly charged Oscar winner. They'd got a wry, sexy comedy with a few tear-jerking scenes.

Personally, she thought that everyone who loved *When Harry Met Sally* would love this one too, but the Metropolis marketing guys felt differently. They'd pitched it as a classy weepy, *Kramer vs. Kramer* or *Terms of Endearment*. Rowena guessed that the reason the numbers were so low was that the *Kramer vs. Kramer* types at the previews were disappointed.

She hadn't said a word. Films were John's business, not hers. If John had offered her advice on Atomic Mass when she was at Musica, she'd have yelled at him to butt out.

But the 'Face Up' single gave her an idea.

A week before the record went to radio, huge billboards appeared in New York, LA, and Dallas, plain black backgrounds with foot-high white lettering: FACE UP TO YOUR CHOICES.

Two days later, full-page ads ran in the *New York Times*, the *LA Times* and other big papers, all with the same plain message. There was no mention of the movie, album or single.

The campaign was an instant hit. People started ringing radio talk shows to ask what the ads meant. At one intersection in Manhattan there was a logjam as drivers craned their necks up to look.

Then 'Face Up' was released.

The original work with her extensive network kicked in, and astonished Musica promo men found their brand-new single had already been plastered across the airwaves in key cities – by, get this, *Rowena Gordon*.

Then the competitions Rowena had set up started running on the other stations and in the magazines.

'What's the hardest choice you ever faced up to?'

'What would you do for love?'

It was pop psychology at the simplest level. Everyone's given something up, Rowena figured, everyone's been in love, and she was proved right as switchboards jammed coast-to-coast.

Finally there was the video. Black Ice had refused point-blank to shoot one, and the guys at Metropolis wanted to string old footage together and use that, but Rowena had a better idea. 'We won't show the act at all. We'll show the movie,' she suggested, and the result was a terrific promo, the best moments from *Dallas* segued together and laid over the funky, aggressive pop of the song.

MTV loved it.

The last calls Rowena made were to old friends of hers who worked in the industry tipsheets, both film and music – *Variety, The Hollywood Reporter, HITS* magazine and the like, and every one of them ran an article along the lines of 'Just when you thought it was safe . . .'

'Face Up' hit number one in the Hot 100 the week it was released, and a fortnight later *My Heart Belongs to Dallas* opened to packed theatres.

Ali Kahed, astonished to find his act had the biggest hit of their career, called Sam Neil and told him that they might consider doing a little soundtrack promotion.

Nick Large called John Metcalf and dryly congratulated him.

And late one evening Rowena's phone rang in her bedroom.

'Hello?' she asked, surprised. The number was unlisted, John was on a plane to San Antonio, and the only other person she'd given it to was Joanne.

'Hello, kid,' said Josh Oberman. 'What the hell took you so long?'

32

Peter Weiss stared at the young woman sitting opposite him with something approaching astonishment.

She no longer looked emaciated, listless and pale. On the contrary, she was a tanned, slender thirty-year-old woman in an elegant pink Chanel suit that fitted her to perfection. Her right wrist sported a platinum Rolex, and a sapphire engagement ring glinted on her left hand. Her blonde hair had been feather-cut to add body and movement. Her long legs were covered by the sheerest nylon stockings, and her shoes were stack heels by Azzedine Alaïa. She was lightly made-up, just enough to perfect the delicate beauty of her skin, and she wore a delightful scent – which one, Weiss had no idea, but it smelt vaguely of sandalwood. And jasmine.

It had been barely a few months since he'd seen her last, but Rowena Gordon looked like a different person.

That was partly to be expected, of course. After the Jake Williams scandal and her summary expulsion from Musica North America, Rowena had come to his offices with the weight of public humiliation and the loss of her livelihood on her young shoulders.

He recalled their meeting clearly. As the first woman to be president of a major US record label, Ms Gordon had been one of their most high-profile clients, and his partners had been insistent that, after laying out for her the sorry state of her financial affairs – relatively speaking – he let her know that Weiss, Fletcher & Baum would no longer represent her. Instead, he'd been so shocked by her emaciated body and so impressed by the quiet dignity with which she bore herself that he'd wound up offering to reduce the fee so she could keep her accountants.

It had been an impulsive offer. Completely out of character.

But now Rowena Gordon was back in his office. And this time she wasn't a private client in severe trouble, she was the chairman of her own company. Cowhide, Inc had customers all over the entertainment business – film studios, TV stations, rock bands, sports teams. They picked their events and records and shows very selectively, choosing only assignments that were both difficult and high-profile. That way, with every successive coup, Rowena's company got more famous – and more pricey.

Weiss knew that the pressure on Cowhide to expand was immense. Rowena employed sixteen people, when she could have had sixty. She took on three projects a month when thirty more were desperately trying to secure her services.

Cowhide Goes Hell for Leather, screamed *Variety.*

Rowena rules! proclaimed *HITS.*

Bullish Cowhide Wins Raiders Contract, announced *Billboard.*

They'd had offers from every conceivable source, wanting to buy them out – CAA, William Morris, ICM, Turner Entertainment, you name it. Rowena had turned them all down, as far as he knew. Certainly, she looked like a young woman who knew exactly what she was doing.

And yet he could scarcely believe what he was hearing.

'Are you sure about this, Ms Gordon?'

'I'm quite sure, Mr Weiss, I want your firm to represent Cowhide, both in general terms, for a retainer, and specifically, for – for any financial work that may arise,' she finished vaguely.

'But we handle private individuals, Ms Gordon. We're just a small firm. For a company like Cowhide, you'd be better off with a big name – Coopers and Lybrand or the like.' Weiss coughed, embarrassed. 'I would be derelict in my duty not to advise you of it.'

She smiled, a serious, courteous smile. 'And you *have* advised me of it, Mr Weiss. Nonetheless, Weiss, Fletcher and Baum is the firm I want. If you think you need more associates to handle our business, by all means hire them.'

She fished about in her purse and drew out a neat folded piece of paper. 'I hope you'll forgive the liberty,' she said charmingly, 'but I have brought a certified cheque with me for a year's retainer in advance. Assuming your partners will be willing to take on our account.'

Mesmerized, Peter Weiss unfolded the cheque. It was made out to his firm in the amount of one million dollars.

'You told me a few months ago that you had confidence in me, Mr Weiss, when circumstances were rather different,' Rowena continued, seeing he was too stunned to reply. 'Cowhide returns the compliment.'

He couldn't believe it. Jack Fletcher was going to have a heart attack.

Rowena stood up and shook his hand in a firm, dry grip.

'Nice doing business with you, Mr Weiss,' she said, and walked out of his office, leaving the old man staring after her.

In the taxi on the way to the Regent, Rowena permitted herself a small smile. The meeting at Weiss, Fletcher & Baum had been something she'd been looking forward to; it was one of the pleasures of a second wind of success to reward your friends and snub your enemies.

Well, maybe enemies was too strong a word. They existed in every business; as a new Angeleno she should be aware of that. Cowardly, greedy little types that kicked you when you were down and kissed your ass like mad if you happened to get up again. The record company execs who'd blanked her when she got fired by Musica. The promoters and agents who'd refused to take her calls. Recently, every single one of them had called up, or sent flowers, watches, other such peacemaking tokens. She had taken great delight in telling Joanne how to answer the phone to those jackals: 'Ms Gordon is not available to you, Mr X, now or at any time up to and including the Day of Judgment.'

She stirred in her seat, looking forward to her lunch meeting. First of all, it would be great to see Oberman again. For all the talking they'd done, she hadn't actually laid eyes on the old buzzard since she'd got canned. And second, meeting the chairman of Musica Entertainment at such a power-broker venue was the best way to announce that the exile was over.

Rowena Gordon was well and truly back.

As night was deepening, the electric floodlights grew more brilliant by the minute. Barbara could smell the acrid smoke from the dry ice drifting out from the venue; the sound of the people inside was a low rumbling noise, punctuated by sharp football whistles and interwoven with the pumping blast of the sound system.

On her way out of the arena, Atomic Mass's manager sighed with satisfaction. Another sell-out, and here in Barcelona the T-shirt stall was doing even brisker business than when they'd played Florence the previous night. Jim Xanthos, the new guitarist, was settling in great – there was no more sniping and secrecy among the boys, and Jim fitted in like he'd been there for ever. A happier band paid off both in better shows and more creativity; Michael Krebs had loved the demos they'd written on the road.

Jesus, that's a good sign, Barbara thought, as the limo spun out on to the main city road. Two hit albums is good, but three is better . . . we could still gain a little ground in Australasia.

She smiled faintly, catching herself plotting. God, how she'd changed in the past few years; from a cool, impersonal lawyer to a kick-ass manager with the best of them. And if you'd told her when she first saw this act that they represented the rest of her life, she'd have laughed in your face. Even when she started out with Atomic Mass, she couldn't tell Van Halen from Van Morrison.

The quiet streets slipped past her, a huge medieval cathedral at the city's centre, not much traffic in the early evening. She had time for a good two hours with Michael before they went back to watch the boys.

Imagine me *wanting to see a hard rock show! Oberman never lets up about it . . . I wonder what Rowena will say when we get her back out on the road.*

Rowena. Her most constant friend; they'd been as close as two of the busiest women in music could be, and Barbara had been appalled by what had happened to her. For the sake of that useless junkie Jake Williams, too. She hated it when Rowena went into hiding and didn't give a soul her LA number, but she understood. If somebody took this life away from her now – if Atomic Mass split up tomorrow . . .

Barbara shuddered. It didn't bear thinking about.

She knew what it was like, when you were a woman in business. You made sacrifices. If you were lucky, you had some joy out of your work. For both herself and Rowena, work and life had become inseparable.

Rowena always loved the record business, and I came to love it, Barbara thought, pulling up in the hotel forecourt. But at least I had a lover, too.

She'd met Jake Barber a week before the *Zenith* release. It was love, if not at first, then certainly at third sight. Jake worked at a cool independent record label, and they were married after five weeks at Chelsea registry office in London, with all their friends warning that it would never last. It was their eighteen-month anniversary next week.

Rowena, on the other hand . . .

Barbara got out of the car, her light Armani dress rippling in the warm breeze, and stepped into the hotel. The receptionist nodded at her and told her Mr Krebs was waiting.

On the surface it all looked wonderful. The wild success of *My Heart Belongs to Dallas* followed by the world beating a path to Rowena's door. She was her own boss now, and any corporate misgivings about ill-advised remarks had been drowned in the heavenly sound of cash tills chiming. Even *Vanity Fair* had done a profile on her – 'The Rise, Fall and Rise of the Hit Woman'. And then, on her thirtieth birthday, her engagement to John Peter Metcalf III, the brilliant young president of Metropolis Studios, had been announced. The happy couple were photographed together at the wrap party for *Steven*, the big Metropolis weepie for autumn, looking impossibly rich, powerful and glamorous. Truly two of the 'beautiful people'.

And yet, and yet.

She knocked loudly on the door of Krebs's suite and walked in.

'Barbara, you look great,' Michael said, greeting her warmly.

'So do you,' his friend replied. Krebs was wearing his usual T-shirt and jeans and still managed to look gorgeous – the muscled torso rippling under the thin cotton, the stomach trim and lean, the wiry hair at the side of his head giving him an unmistakable aura of intelligence and power.

He's not my type, but I understand what she saw in him.

'Yeah, but I have to work at it. How's Jake?'

'Wonderful. How are Debbie and the boys?'

'They're great,' Michael said.

There was always just a slight edge to this ritual exchange between the two of them. Krebs didn't know whether Rowena had ever told Barbara about their affair, and the doubt hung in the air whenever they spoke.

Since Rowena fled New York for LA, that edge had got keener. It was an unspoken bargain between the manager and the producer that her name be mentioned as little as possible, and only ever in a business sense. For after Cowhide had catapulted her back into the industry spotlight, Rowena had recontacted Barbara, the band and all her old friends – except Michael.

In interviews and on television she'd repeatedly called him a genius, her mentor, the sixth member of Atomic Mass. Rowena made it perfectly clear that she was a big fan of Michael Krebs, both as a producer and a human being.

But she didn't call.

Well, Barbara reflected, if I'm right, that's all about to change.

'Michael, when did you last speak to Joshua Oberman?' she asked him, sitting down and lighting up a St Moritz.

'About a month ago. Why?'

'Did he mention Rowena Gordon to you?'

Krebs stiffened imperceptibly. 'No, I don't think so.'

'OK,' Barbara said, taking a long, satisfying drag. 'I'm gonna tell you something, but it's totally confidential.'

'Shoot,' he said, watching her through narrowed eyes.

'Josh rang me in Florence last night. He asked Rowena to meet him for lunch at the Regent Hotel in New York this afternoon, and he's going to offer her a newly created post at Musica. They've changed the make-up of the board again, and Oberman has an absolute majority now.'

Michael leant back in his armchair. 'What new post, exactly?'

'President of the worldwide company. She'd report directly to him, but Josh is basically retiring from active involvement.'

'Holy shit,' Krebs said softly.

'We don't know if she'll take it. It would mean giving up Cowhide, and that's something of her own.'

He shook his head. 'She'll take it,' he said, and there was an expression glittering in his dark eyes that Barbara couldn't decipher.

'Maybe. Anyway, that's not all, which is why I thought we should talk,' she said. 'Oberman told me something else. One of the reasons he wants to hand over to Rowena Gordon now is that he doesn't think he'll have the opportunity in a year's time.'

'Why not?' Michael asked.

'Because he thinks Musica Entertainment is the target of a hostile takeover bid.'

'Who from?' Krebs demanded. 'Musica is a major record company. They've got the clout to hire the best investment banking in the world. Who the hell would try to swallow them?'

'Try Mansion Industries,' Barbara replied.

Rowena leant forward, trying to take in what she'd just heard. She was careful not to let her surprise show. Oberman had taken a centre table, right in the middle of the dining room, the most blatant position of all. The two of them – old corporate warrior and his young entrepreneur protégée – were on display to the business elite of Manhattan, and she knew they were being watched.

'Let me tick these points off,' she said. 'Number one, despite the fact that the company had me fired in the most ostentatious way, you now want to make me president.'

'Spoken to my lawyers,' said Oberman testily, 'and you haven't been convicted of any wrongdoing. Even if *Westside* kept the tape, it doesn't prove you did what you said you did. You might have been trying to talk Jake out of it. And if the industry thinks it's weird, so what? Everyone's read *Hit Men*. We *are* weird. I don't explain myself to them.'

'Number two, you expect me to give up Cowhide. Which is totally successful, Josh, and which I own privately.'

'So sell it. You'll be rich. And you'll be the first woman ever to make president of a major and that's your goddamn life's ambition, Gordon, so don't try and snow *me*.'

'Number three, according to you I'll only have this job for a matter of months, because Mansion Industries are going to take us over and ruin our artists' careers.'

Joshua Oberman fixed her with a watery eye. 'Listen up, princess,' he said. 'I've been working at Musica since your mom was a teenager. After my wife died, records were my whole life. I was there for the Rolling Stones and I was there for Led Zeppelin and I was there for Metallica and I was there for Atomic Mass. Now in nineteen seventy-one management, including me, took the company public, and as you may be realizing with Cowhide, that means a lot more money but the loss of your control.'

He paused, shaking his head. 'Finally, I made chairman. I'm running the whole show now. Took me long enough. Even a year ago, I couldn't stop you getting fired. But right now I have control of Musica as it stands and I'm not prepared to give it up without a fight.'

Oberman grabbed his napkin and coughed into it. 'I'm not a fool, Gordon. I know perfectly well that we may not be able to withstand Mansion Industries. But I also know that you've got the best chance of anybody around. Which is why you have to accept this job.'

'Are you asking me or telling me?'

'I'm telling you,' he said.

She nodded, blonde hair lustrous in the morning light. 'All right, Josh. I can't promise anything, though.'

The old guy smiled slightly. 'Admit it, Rowena. You missed it like hell. You want to get back to *Zenith* and all the rest of it. You want to be dealing with Barbara and the boys again and,' he added slyly, 'Michael Krebs.'

'How is Michael?' Rowena asked casually.

'Still married,' Oberman said mischievously.

'Josh' she protested. 'It wasn't like that. There was nothing going on. Anyway, I'm engaged to John Metcalf. See?' She held up her left hand, letting her new sapphire sparkle in the sun.

The old man speared a forkful of omelette and winked at her infuriatingly. 'Sure, kid,' he said.

Knowing that word would be leaking out around the record business, Rowena got in a cab to JFK the moment she left the Regent. She called John from the first-class cabin and asked him to meet her at the house at six.

This was going to be difficult. How could she tell him that she was going back to Musica Records? It would mean giving up Cowhide, which John had helped her to build. And it would also mean moving back to New York. John ran Metropolis, he could hardly come with her. Maybe one day she'd be able to engineer a transfer of the company down to LA, or set up another branch there, but at the moment taking this job involved a return to their weekend relationship.

Lots of couples live like that, Rowena reasoned. Plus, how many couples both run big companies? It'll mean that we can get on with our work in the week and enjoy each other on Saturday and Sunday . . .

'Champagne, ma'am?' the steward asked, filling her glass to the brim.

She sipped thoughtfully. *But will John see it like that? After all, we're engaged.*

And yet Oberman had been right. Amazing how well the old guy knew her. As soon as he'd offered her the job she'd known she would accept, for all her pretended outrage. She shifted a little in her roomy seat, feeling pure adrenalin pump through her veins. First woman in history to run a major record label! It *was* her dream come true. She couldn't deny it. And however mad her boyfriend got, there was no way she was walking away from it.

John was waiting for her in the garden when she got home, standing under the orange tree, a glass of iced mineral water in his hand.

Rowena fixed herself a grapefruit juice and walked out to join him. After the dirt and cold of Manhattan, the warm fragrant air of the Hollywood hills seemed especially welcoming.

I'm gonna miss this, she decided with a pang of regret.

'I had lunch with Josh Oberman today. He offered me the presidency of Musica Worldwide, with complete power to run the company. He reckons Mansion Industries is going to try a hostile takeover.'

Metcalf stared at her and Rowena felt her heart sink. His handsome face had gone tight with anger.

'Don't tell me. You accepted.'

'Yes, I did,' she replied, trying to sound confident. 'It's everything I ever wanted, John. I can't pass it up.'

'Why?' he demanded. 'So you can be the CEO who hands it over to Mansion? Don't you read the *Wall Street Journal* or *Economic Monthly*, for Christ's sake? Conrad Miles can't be stopped. If he wants Musica, he can buy Musica twenty times over. Meanwhile, you're prepared to sacrifice our relationship for the sake of an empty title and a corporation that threw you out on your ass.'

'It wouldn't be sacrificing our relationship, darling,' she pleaded, walking over to him and putting a hand gently on his arm. 'It'll just be for a few months until I can open a Los Angeles office ... I could fly down here at weekends.'

'Weekends! Jesus!' John exclaimed, pushing her away. His blue eyes were icy with fury. 'I'm not some puppy you can treat however you want.'

'That's not fair.'

'Isn't it? After the way you were when they sacked you? Is your memory so short?' he demanded, cupping her chin in his hand and tilting her face up to his. 'Rowena, you were a recluse. I had to personally go over to your house and kick your butt. And I took risks for you then. I was the president of Metropolis and you were in the middle of a drugs scandal –'

'– and I'm grateful,' she interrupted. 'But that can't change this! Please try to understand.'

'Oh, I understand,' he said savagely. 'Just like I understood when you were working day and night at Cowhide. When you couldn't make time for me then, either. Christ, I'm such an idiot. I thought that when you agreed to marry me things might be different.'

He stroked her cheek, but it was a rough, almost desperate caress. 'Your heart's a fucking fortress, Rowena, you know that?' he demanded. 'I love you. What the hell is it going to take?'

'I love you too,' she said, grabbing his hand and pressing it to her skin. 'That's why I agreed to marry you.'

'Is it?' he asked. 'Or is it just part of the masterplan?'

'John!'

'Do what you have to do,' he snarled. 'Try and remember to book some space in your fucking diary for our wedding,' and he stormed off into the house.

For a second she stared after him, and then she put down her juice and ran inside.

'Hey, hey,' she murmured, putting her arms around him. 'John. Sweetheart. Please, I'm sorry . . . I should have asked you first. I swear it'll only be for a few months. We'll open an office in LA.'

Metcalf tried to brush her away, but there was just something about the insistent press of her body, the catch in her tone, the scent of her hair. Despite himself, he weakened.

'It's OK,' he said, 'it's OK, baby,' and he scooped her up in his arms, as lightly as if she were a doll, and carried her through to their bedroom, letting her cover his chest with little breathless kisses, tiny butterfly caresses, that drove out his anger and sparked his desire.

He laid her down on the Pratesi sheets, slipping off her jacket, unbuttoning her silk chemise, his thumbs clumsy with excitement as he unhooked the lacy La Perla bra and felt his breath catch in this throat at the sight of her pink nipples, half stiffened in anticipation. His left hand slipped up her smooth thigh, a new rush of passion surging through him as it met the delicate wisp of her panties.

'I can't do without you for long,' he murmured, but then her arm snaked round his neck and her hand reached down to unzip his pants, and all protest was silenced in another hot kiss, a tangle of clothes, a liquid melting of flesh.

'Oberman? it's Rowena,' she said.

Thank Christ we bought a pied-à-terre in Manhattan, she thought, as she looked round the smart apartment John and she had picked out together last Christmas. It was a light, roomy place on Mercer Street in SoHo, with a huge window Rowena had fallen in love with and a polished wood floor. Neither John nor she had had much time to use it up until now, so her cases sat in an almost empty bedroom, with just one change of clothes for each of them hanging in the closet. A few of her files relating to the various offers she'd had for Cowhide, and her lawyers' cast-iron employment contract with Musica were strewn over the bed.

'Good, I'm glad I caught you.' Oberman's crabby voice crackled down the lines. 'I've just spoken to Barbara Lincoln and she has some ideas about the Atomic Mass contract. Like a keyman clause relating to you. Know what that means?'

'Nice to speak to you too,' she replied, laughing. 'And of course I know what it means. If I leave the company for any reason, their contract would be null and void – they could walk out of Musica and sign to PolyGram. Clive David and Whitney Houston have the same –'

'Exactly. It would be a first step in persuading Mansion not to bother,' the chairman cut in. 'So be a good girl and hop out to Spain. They're playing Barcelona.'

'But I've just got into New York this morning.'

'So take a shower,' Oberman snapped. 'You can play with your new office tomorrow.'

'Well, yes, sir,' Rowena said, smiling, and put down the phone. *Plus ça change . . .*

She opened the wardrobe. *Thank God for one sensible habit I've got into.*

She kept a small case of essentials packed and ready to go – jeans, white shirt, Nikes, two pairs of panties and bras and a nightgown, along with toiletries and her passport. Next to this case were two smaller ones with extras according to the climate: sweaters for Moscow, sunblock for the Caribbean. She picked the 'hot' case and got on the phone to Continental airlines, then booked herself in at the Meridian. Atomic Mass would be playing the Olympic Stadium tomorrow, two nights there and then up to Paris.

At least she'd get to see the lads play Europe. The last time she'd been able to get away to go to one of their concerts had been the night they stormed the Meadowlands, New Jersey, at the start of the US leg of the *Questions* tour. And that was so long ago she didn't want to think about it.

Rowena faxed John a short note, telling him she'd be back in a couple of days, and started to get undressed, deciding on a comfortable Perry Ellis suit for the flight. It was navy blue, a simple cut that flattered her figure and let her move about easily – perfect airport gear. She kicked off her beautiful, impractical Italian high heels and went for a smart pair of navy flats, taking no jewellery and snatching her purse from the dresser. She could make up on the way to the plane.

Continental Airlines flight 18635 for Spain swung slowly round on its heavy axis and prepared to head down the runway for takeoff.

Rowena Gordon, seated comfortably in first class with a blanket draped across her knees for the long night flight, was deep in thought.

Well, she told herself, you're the Chief Executive Officer of Musica Entertainment. The first woman to run a major label. Congratulations. Not quite what you expected, is it? How long do you think you'll last?

Barcelona slipped by her, neon and beautiful in the darkness. She hadn't been here for years, she'd forgotten how openly the city was laid out towards the edges, all wide roads and tree-lined spaces. Her cab driver, mercifully, did not speak English so she was able to appreciate the winding streets as they tore into the centre of town, hundreds of fly-posters lit up by their headlights. She found she was twisting and turning, looking for Atomic Mass spots. There were plenty of them, luckily for Musica Spain. The gig had sold out within hours of being announced five months ago, but that was no excuse not to promote it. If most people in Barcelona that bought records already had a copy of *Zenith*, they could get *Heat Street* too. And besides, the Knuckleheads, on as support, needed the exposure.

The Olympic Stadium was an impressive sight, floodlit towers jabbing into the sky. As Rowena stepped out of her limo, the sound of a roaring crowd drifted towards her. She felt a quick, adolescent thrill of excitement. Christ, it had been a long time since she'd seen a band.

She walked up to a security guard, flashed her laminate and was immediately ushered inside the barriers. One of the crew took her up to the production office.

Will Macleod was sitting perched on a table, yelling into a phone. When he caught sight of Rowena, he shouted, 'I'll fookin' deal with it later,' and slammed down the receiver.

'Who the hell are you?' he barked, obviously unimpressed with the all-access laminate swinging ostentatiously on her T-shirt.

'I'm Rowena Gordon, president of Musica Records,' she said hastily. Being mistaken for a groupie or a gatecrasher by this guy looked as though it could cause problems. 'To see Barbara Lincoln?' she finished, wondering why it came out as a nervous request.

'Aye. Well, you've missed her,' growled Macleod. 'She went back to the hotel. I'm sorry I cannae help, but the boys are onstage – in five minutes,' he added menacingly.

As if to confirm his words, the sound of Steppenwolf's 'Born to Be Wild,' their intro tape, flooded the air at maximum volume. A huge howl of approval tore from the crowd.

Rowena involuntarily turned towards the stage. Exhilaration ripped through her.

Jesus! she thought. I really want to see this! And why shouldn't I? Barbara won't mind, we could talk tomorrow . . . I never *did* get to see the *Zenith* set . . .

'Would you take me up onstage, Will?' she asked.

He looked at her for a second, then nodded briskly.

Rowena followed the tour manager through the labyrinthian corridor out to the back of the stage. The ramp leading up through the scaffolding to the onstage viewing area beside the wings was directly ahead of them. The sound of Atomic's bass-driven raw harmonies was bleeding into the warm night sky, mixing with the violently loud roar of the crowd. It was deafening. She loved it.

'Sixty thousand capacity here,' Macleod yelled in her ear. 'Sold out.'

The sky was misting with smoke from the stage, pierced by their trademark green lasers, caging the amphitheatre in bars of light, panning out in front of her as she followed Will up the ramp. Now she could see glimpses of the crowd, a few sweating, crushed faces in the front row picked out by the red, blue and golden spotlights that circled the packed audience as well as catching each member of the band. Giant video screens, the standard accessory for arena and stadium shows these days, were mounted at the sides of the stage so that the crowd could see the expressions on their heroes' faces, blown up to thousands of times lifesize. The fans were roaring as though Spain had just scored in a World Cup final.

She felt her exhausted body spring back into life.

'We've got a box at the side of the stage where we sit VIPs,' Will yelled. 'You can watch from there wi' the other guest.'

'Who do you have visiting tonight, then?' Rowena asked.

Will guided her along the back of the stage towards the box.

'Their producer,' he said. 'Michael Krebs.'

He pushed the little door open.

From the second she laid eyes on him, Rowena knew she was lost.

She was weakened, physically drained from the flight. And the instant she let go of all her stress, just gave up and allowed the music and the passion of the crowd to sweep into her bloodstream, she'd been shut alone in a box, onstage, in the dark, thousands of miles away from anyone either of them knew, with the man she most desired in the world.

'What are you doing here?' she said.

'I came to talk to Barbara in Modena last night,' he said, staring at her. 'Thought I'd stay for Barcelona and check out the show. It's not a crime, is it?'

She shook her head, mutely.

'What about you?'

Rowena shrugged, and gave him a simplified version. That provided a little breathing space; they talked about Josh for a few minutes.

The slow, sensual intro to 'Karla' spilled through the amps around them.

'Why didn't you tell me?' Michael said.

'Tell you what?' asked Rowena, trying not to look at him.

He grabbed her shoulders angrily and spun her round to face him.

'Don't play games with me,' he said, lifting her left hand to expose the engagement ring. 'You never told me. You never called me at all.'

'I didn't know how to,' Rowena said.

'You hurt me,' Krebs said furiously. 'I had to find out from Barbara Lincoln.'

Rowena, starved for him, raked his face with her eyes, that close-shaven grey hair, the deep black irises, his thick, beautiful eyelashes. She wanted to remember it always, to keep it clearly etched in her mind. He was challenging her, he was angry. Now that it was too late, she realized how wise she'd been to keep away from him. Love welled up in her like a flooded river.

'How do you think I felt?' she said. 'Why did you do that to me with Debbie? Do you have any idea what that was like?'

Krebs stared at her. 'Do you love him?'

'Of course.'

He shook his head. 'Don't lie to me.'

'Please, Michael, let it go,' Rowena said. She was near breaking. It was torment to be so close, and not to be able to touch him. 'This is the best way for everybody.'

'No it isn't,' Krebs said.

He moved closer, till he could hear her breathing, till there were only millimetres of space between them.

'I didn't like to see him touching you at that party,' Michael said. 'You thought I couldn't see that? He had his hand on your breasts, right in front of me.'

Rowena bit her lip. 'He can do what he likes, Michael. I'm going to marry him.'

'Look at me,' Krebs said. 'Do it, Rowena.'

She turned her head and looked at him, and felt her stomach cave in with lust. Her control evaporated. She moaned, she couldn't help it.

'I don't give a fuck what's right or not right,' Krebs said harshly. 'I won't let you go,' and he cupped her head in his hands, twisting his fingers in her long hair, and pulled her to him and kissed her.

Rowena collapsed against him, kissing him back wildly, feeling shame at the weakness and sexual heat that rushed through her. She pressed her thighs together, she was already wet, and it was getting worse. His cock was swollen and hard against her.

Krebs put his hands on her shirt, feeling her breasts through the fabric, her nipples erect, distended with desire for him. He'd never forgotten how Rowena felt to hold. Whenever he touched her, she was passionate and eager. But this time, after an absence of months, it was like the first. He felt a surge of wanting explode in his chest. She was his. He had to have her.

'We can't do it here,' Rowena gasped, pulling away.

Goddamn it, every second he had to wait now was an eternity.

'Come on,' Krebs said, and tore out of the box, grabbing her hand. She followed him, hoping her legs would still work OK. Maybe people would see them.

She didn't care. She didn't care about anything. She could only feel the blood throbbing in her legs, only hear her heart crashing against her ribcage.

They ran down the ramp and into the backstage area. Michael took a right up some deserted stairs and they found themselves in a maze of corridors on the first level, above the ground floor where the crew were working. Krebs tried some doors; they were all locked. They went round a corner, right, left, and then he suddenly stopped running and she stumbled against him.

'Now,' he said. 'Here.'

'What if somebody comes?' Rowena panted.

Krebs looked her over, pleasurably, luxuriating in her desire for him. She moved uncontrollably under his gaze, feeling it as though it were a physical caress.

'Stand against the wall,' he said, thick-voiced.

She moved back, feeling the rough brick grate against her skin through her shirt, now soaked in sweat. All her clothes were clinging to her. Her jeans felt heavy and awkward on her flesh.

'If somebody comes, they'll see us,' Krebs said, reaching for her waistband and snapping open the buttons of her jeans in one impatient movement. Rowena gasped with excitement, squirming against the wall. Michael smiled and moved closer, standing to face her, and then yanked down her jeans and panties until they were below her knees.

'They'll see you like this,' he said, and put his right hand over her pussy, lightly, feeling her heat and moisture for himself. 'They'll see you waiting for me.'

'Please, Michael,' Rowena managed. 'Please.'

He shook his head, barely controlling himself. 'I want to see you,' he said. 'Standing out here, in the light. Take your top off. Show me your breasts.'

Her fingers were clumsy, shaking as she undid her buttons and ripped at the clasp of her bra. It was sweet, protracted torture for both of them, and when she was topless, standing against the wall in the full glare of the striplights, her nipples sharp and full of blood, her flat stomach tapering down to her damp sex, displayed for him, whilst he stayed fully clothed, Michael could no longer hold back. He rammed himself against her, kissing her mouth and neck, one hand grabbing her breasts while the other loosened his pants, letting his cock spring free against her groin, and Rowena moved under his touch in ecstasy, absolutely out of control, mad for him, parting her legs as widely as she could. She'd dreamt of this, even with John she'd dreamt of it, and now he was going to fuck her and take her again, she couldn't live without it, and Michael had his fingers in between her legs, feeling his fingertips get slick with the wetness of her, feeling her move and buck under his touch, and then he found her, open and ready, and he shoved himself into her, all the way up to the hilt.

'Michael!' she gasped.

'Rowena,' he said. 'Oh, baby,' and he started to fuck her, up against the wall, and she felt him hard and thick inside her, stroking her with his cock, like he was nailing her to the wall with his cock, and she loved it, she moved with him, and Krebs felt how totally he had mastered her now, how completely she was his, and it made him harder, and he wanted to tease her some more but he couldn't speak, it was too good to speak, and he just thrust, and thrust, and thrust, deeper and harder, and she screamed a small strangled scream, gasping her ecstasy, and he burst inside her like a dam, feeling the wave of his orgasm consume him utterly, pleasuring every inch of his skin, from his toes to the crown of his skull, and he growled out her name, gripping her to him.

33

'Excuse me, gentlemen,' said Topaz, hefting herself from her chair with as much dignity as she could muster.

God, sometimes I hate being pregnant, she thought, covered with embarrassment as she waddled off to the john. What asshole invented the radiant, glowing mother-to-be? Obviously a bachelor. And a misogynist. Christ!

There were eight men and two women in that meeting, and the other woman didn't count because she was the director of Personnel. So she, Topaz, sole representative of the sisterhood – *ha!* – in the upper echelons of power at American Magazines, was soundly impressing everybody by having to rush off to pee three times an hour. Wonderful.

She glowered at her reflection in the bathroom mirror. She'd put on ten pounds apart from the weight of her lump, her face was flushed, her ankles were swollen and the pull of the child was straining her back. Her normally elegant feet were strapped into wide Dr Scholl sandals, and the only dresses she could wear were goddamn maternity tents, the ones they made in foul shades of 'feminine' pink or covered with iddy-biddy flowers. Topaz had her own made up, the best she could do: ankle-length smocks in navy, with thick white bands at the collar and cuffs, or just plain black or dark green. It was the navy today, the most businesslike outfit in her wardrobe.

Yeah, right. I look like an executive elephant, she told herself, suddenly irritated beyond belief by the sight of her red curls snaking over her shoulders. She took a velvet tie from her pocket and pulled her hair into a severe ponytail, then waddled back out to the meeting.

Harvey Smith, American's director, West Coast, was giving a short statement on the Los Angeles view of the threat they were facing. Around the table, the others listening attentively were Matt Gowers, chairman; Eli Leber, of Leber, Jason & Miller, the company's attorneys; Damian Hart, chief financial officer; Nick Edward and Gerald Quin, investment bankers from Maughan Macaskill, the firm hired to advise American Magazines; Ed Lazar, director of Sales; Neil Bradbury, director of International; Nick Thomson, director of Marketing; Louise Patton, director of Personnel; and Topaz Rossi, director, East Coast.

In other words, the board of American Magazines and their closest advisers. Matt Gowers had refused to allow anyone else to attend; even the notes were being taken by Louise, as the least senior person in the room.

This was a small meeting, but a vital one.

The company was in play.

'We've got serious concerns,' Harvey was saying as she sat down. 'The West Coast is afraid that Mansion Industries will change the entire nature of American Magazines. From what we've been told' – he waved at Gerald Quin – 'Connor Miles is only concerned with raising profits. We believe he'll close all our books that aren't making a profit yet, lower quality and ban expensive photographers and writers. The question is, how we can persuade him that magazine publishing works on different economic rules to timber-felling or food retail.'

There were nods around the table.

'What do you think, Topaz?' Gowers asked.

'I think we should fight it,' she said. 'If Nick and Gerry are right, we've got no chance of *persuading* Mansion of anything. No senior management has survived for more than a year after Mansion Industries took over their company.'

'We can't fight Mansion. We have to be realists about this,' Bradbury replied.

'American's a large corporation,' Lazar agreed, 'but Mansion Industries is a huge conglomerate.'

'Who have never lost a takeover yet,' Damian reminded them.

Topaz knew the tide of opinion was running against her, but she couldn't let it go and bow to the majority. To come so near to power, and then have it snatched away by a greedy conglomerate? Maybe she could get another job somewhere else – her record was exemplary – but she'd put a lot of work into *Impact* and *Economic Monthly* and all of them, and she was damned if she'd just walk away. Who could tell if she'd get as many chances at Condé Nast?

The boys were taking the ostrich approach. *If I stick my head in the sand, maybe the monster won't see me since I can't see him. If I'm nice to Mr Miles, maybe I can persuade him to leave me alone.*

But executive elephant or no, she knew they were wrong. When American was bought out by Mansion Industries, every board member here was history. That was obvious. But they didn't want to recognize it.

Topaz had caught that Quin boy looking at her when she spoke up to object. He sounded like he knew his stuff, and it made her even more certain she was right.

'Look, you're all way off-beam,' she burst out impatiently. 'OK, so they've never lost a takeover. Then by the law of averages, it's about time they did.'

'Really, Topaz,' muttered Louise, in a tone that clearly said *Hormones*.

'You're in Personnel. You don't know jack,' Topaz rounded on her, infuriated by the obvious glance at her swollen stomach. 'I run six magazines and that's what I intend to go on doing. If everybody else is happy to kiss up to Connor Miles and kiss their job goodbye, I'm not.'

Gowers, who had been watching her with narrowed eyes, turned to their lawyer. 'Eli, what can we do in the first instance?'

The older man spread his hands. 'Blocking petitions, ownership of magazines by a non-American citizen, the usual delaying tactics.'

'Do it. Immediately,' the chairman ordered. He gestured at the investment bankers. 'We'll hire Maughan Macaskill to represent us in a defence, as we've discussed. Topaz, Damian and myself will be your main liaisons at the company. Harvey, you, Ed and Neil are to prepare statistics and presentations that would try to persuade any predator or due diligence shark that we work best the way we are.'

'I don't get it,' Neil said. 'Which approach are we taking? Fighting or talking?'

'Both,' Gowers answered grimly. 'In this situation, we have to try everything.'

Topaz gazed out of her window at the Manhattan skyline, sparkling in the sun. She was sitting in a new orthopaedic chair she'd had installed as her pregnancy advanced – or rather, which Joe had insisted she get installed. Next to her was a small device for monitoring her blood pressure, which she was supposed to do every other day but couldn't bear to. Pregnancy was one thing, stress was another, and the combination of the two . . . well, Joe would have a fit.

He should try being pregnant in the middle of a hostile takeover. Now there's a double whammy, Topaz thought, staring out towards the Hudson.

Summer was coming to the city . . . she could see it, from this air-conditioned eyrie, the sunlight flashing on the tiny cars racing through the gridlike streets, glittering on the river. She loved summer. Even when it was too hot. And this August, of course, she'd be a mother . . .

Topaz felt her mood soar. A baby . . . my baby! she thought, with a rush of utter bliss. She placed her hands tenderly on her stomach, hoping to feel it move, and was overwhelmed by an intense surge of love and happiness. Joe's child, *our* child . . .

What would it look like? Black hair, she sincerely hoped; maybe blue eyes . . . would it be a boy or a girl? Joe had been desperate to find out, but she'd put her foot down.

'No, I want to be surprised,' she insisted, when Dr Martinez had put the question to them.

'But we could decorate the room the right colour,' Joe begged.

Topaz had shaken her head, smiling. 'Nice try.'

They'd had the ultrasound at just three months, because Topaz didn't want Joe to be able to cheat – '*Is he waving?*' '*Yes she is, Mr Goldstein.*'

When Dr Martinez had put the stethoscope down on her stomach and they'd heard the muffled, pumping little heartbeat, Topaz remembered with another rush of affection, Joe – that great hulking guy – had burst into tears. Afterwards he'd been so ashamed of this slip from macho grace that he'd watched four solid hours of football and snapped at her if she teased him about it.

Overall, though, he couldn't be more solicitous. Opening every door, refusing to let her lift so much as a coffee cup. Treating her like she was made of the finest porcelain. At first it was annoying, but as the months wore on she'd been glad of it; her stomach seemed incredibly heavy, like a dragging weight on her back and feet. She was sure a baby didn't weigh that much when you just picked it up.

The phone rang on her desk, an outside call. Topaz smiled; Joe always called her around this time of day. Every day.

'How's it going?'

'Fine,' Topaz replied, staring out at the bright blue sky. 'I can tell you more tonight.'

They had Lamaze class at eight, right after Lisa Martinez palpated Topaz's stomach at seven, and it would take some doing to make that appointment. But there was no way to cancel it. They'd had the bare minimum of checkups since the ultrasound; amniocentesis had already given the pregnancy a clean bill of health, and Topaz was a very busy woman.

'Too much for the phone?' he asked, then grunted when Topaz didn't reply. 'I hate it when they stress you out over there. Can't they see you're pregnant?'

'Joe, *everyone* can see I'm pregnant,' Topaz teased him, amused by a sudden vision of her husband calling up Connor Miles and yelling at him to lay off for another three months.

'OK, well, don't work too hard,' he said gruffly. 'I love you.'

'Love you too,' she replied cheerfully.

'Topaz,' said Matt Gowers, sticking his head round the door. 'In my office, please. Five minutes.'

She nodded at him. 'Joe, I'll see you tonight.'

If Matt Gowers noticed that his youngest director was looking extremely happy all of a sudden, he knew better than to say so. Rossi had made it quite clear that she didn't want special treatment; hormones, unruly bladders and sore feet notwithstanding, she was clinging on to her position with both hands. He knew some of their colleagues considered it perverse, but Gowers wasn't so sure. Topaz had only just completed her restructuring programme, and late nineties or no, motherhood was still a dangerous occupation for an ambitious female.

It's tough to look tough when you're expecting, the old man thought to himself as Topaz walked carefully into his office. He'd known exactly what Louise Patton had been trying to pull when she lost her temper at the board meeting, and he admired Rossi for refusing to take it . . .

She's got a good attitude, Gowers thought. Because frankly, right now we can't afford passengers.

'Have a seat,' he offered.

Topaz drew up a chair at the walnut table in the middle of Gowers' luxurious office. Sitting with their backs to the glass walls were Quin, Edward and Hart, each with several sheets of financial data spread out in front of them.

'Basic defence work, Topaz,' Damian Hart told her, passing across a sheaf of papers. 'Numbers, poison-pill safeguards, stock issues . . .'

'We've just heard that you're not alone in this,' Edward added. 'They've bid for a group of radio stations in California and a major record label.'

'Radio stations . . .' Topaz mused aloud. 'Aren't they going to run into

FCC regulations about owning radio stations and a print group? Are they after any other magazine houses?'

'Small ones,' Quin replied.

'Yeah, but how many small ones?' Gowers asked, getting his subordinate's drift. 'Can we do them for antitrust?'

'Which record label?' Topaz suddenly asked in a small voice. The banker's words had just washed over her at first.

It can't be. It can't be. Can it?

'Musica Entertainment. But they don't have any interests in print,' Quin told her. 'If we're going for antitrust, they aren't much help to you.'

Topaz took a slow sip of her coffee.

'That's where you're wrong,' she said.

The sun was setting over Fifth Avenue when Topaz and Joe arrived at Dr Martinez's clinic. They held hands in the elevator, kissing and stroking each other whenever the car was empty. Joe kept his right arm circled protectively around her, not wanting to let her go for a second.

It had been like this since the honeymoon. They still fought like cats every other day, and they still couldn't bear to be apart. Joe arrived at American Magazines the second Topaz said she'd be off work. Topaz cancelled lunch appointments, jumped in a cab and raced across town to NBC to be with him. He sent her flowers for no reason. She browsed in antique shops for hours, looking for baseball memorabilia he might like. They were so in love they were drunk on each other; Topaz had spent her first month back at the office in a haze of eroticism, walking around thinking about Joe all the time. She kept wondering if anybody guessed; somehow the sexual hunger beating between her legs seemed too powerful to be invisible, as if it could burn right through her Ann Klein suit, display her nakedness to the whole office.

The least thing could set her off. Walking past a doorway where she'd yelled at him. Walking into the *Week in Review* offices. And once, she'd arrived at a board meeting first and been so struck by the memory of making love to Joe on that table that she had to sit down, bright red and weak with desire.

Another time Goldstein called her up. 'Hi,' he said.

'Hi,' she answered, feeling herself go wet at the mere sound of his voice. The way they'd said goodbye to each other that morning ran through her mind like a dirty movie.

'How are you?' he asked inconsequentially.

'Fine,' she said, only trusting herself enough for mono-syllables.

'Topaz, you're turning to jello,' Joe observed, mock-sternly.

'Yeah,' she said, glancing round the office to see if anyone could see her. 'Should I get off the phone?'

'Yeah.'

That night when they got home, Joe had ordered takeout jello and ice cream and proceeded to eat it off the flat of her stomach.

Their fights had also been epic. Over how hard they both worked. Over whether Topaz should drive herself to the office any more. Over maternity leave, paternity leave, and hiring a nanny.

'Six weeks is not enough,' Goldstein maintained. 'You'll need at least three months to bond.'

'Don't you dare tell *me* how to bond with *my* baby!' Topaz spat, furious. 'I'm the one that's carrying it for nine months. I feel it every time it kicks. If you want to stay home and bond for three months go right ahead. Just don't expect me to turn into Marilyn Quayle.'

'Don't be ridiculous,' Joe returned angrily. 'I can't stay home. I run programming for NBC.'

'And I run the East Coast for American Magazines.'

'Really? I'd never have guessed,' he snapped.

But the next day a huge bouquet of white roses turned up at her office with a small rectangular package, and when she ripped it open Topaz found a video of *Mrs Doubtfire*.

Elise DeLuca, watching the expression on her boss's face, had shaken her head in affectionate envy. 'The rollercoaster marriage to end them all,' she said.

Work got tougher, Topaz got larger, and Joe got gentler. Paradoxically, it made her feel more vulnerable; when her love started backing off, she couldn't help sensing his desire to shield her and protect her, which meant she needed shielding. Also, at around six months, they had to stop making love, and that made her frustrated and anxious.

'Jesus, how many times!' Goldstein told her, finding her sobbing in the bathroom one morning. 'I – don't – mind. I'd wait for you until the end of time. Three months is nothing.'

'What about Jane? She's so pretty and so thin,' Topaz sobbed.

'Jane, my assistant?' Joe repeated, trying not to laugh. His secretary was a small, mousy girl with neat brown hair cut very short, a wife and mother of three. 'Are you jealous of *Jane*?'

'Yes,' sobbed Topaz, inconsolable. She remembered every touch of her husband on her skin, every thrust of him inside her, all the fevered eroticism that had consumed them both since the first time they'd made love. Joe was more man than anyone she'd ever known. How could he be satisfied without sex? How could he stay faithful to a woman who looked like a beachball?

'Remember Thanksgiving?' he whispered, gathering her into his arms.

Topaz nodded. Last November, when they'd driven to his parents' house in Connecticut, they'd had to pull over three times because Topaz kept teasing Joe, trying to go down on him while he was driving. In the end they'd parked by the side of a cornfield, spread out her coat and made love in the stubble, kissing and tumbling and screwing each other blind. It had taken another half-hour to pick the straw out of their clothes and to Jean Goldstein's fury they'd turned up very late.

'Traffic was murder, Mom,' Joe explained, kissing the old lady on the cheek and hoping she wouldn't notice the scratches on his neck.

'I remember,' Topaz choked.

Joe kissed her on the temple, a soft, sexual kiss, pressing his lips to her skin. She felt his real desire behind the gesture.

'No woman can stack up to you,' he said. 'Ever. Nobody even comes close.

Even if I didn't love you more than life, I could never settle for a substitute,' and at that moment she thought herself the happiest wife alive.

And troubles temporarily forgotten, Topaz felt pretty much like that right now.

'Come in,' Dr Martinez said pleasantly, waving them to a seat. She glanced at Topaz, briskly assessing her size and general state of health. 'How's it going? Any problems?'

'None,' Topaz lied, slipping off her dress and clambering on to the raised examining couch.

The doctor raised an eyebrow. 'No back strain? You're getting pretty large.'

'Well, maybe a little,' she admitted.

'It's a stressful time for my wife at work,' Goldstein said firmly. 'She's a key person in a reorganization which is going on at the moment, and I'm wondering if she should relax more.'

Dr Martinez suppressed a smile. Joe Goldstein and Topaz Rossi were two of her most celebrated clients, a real Manhattan 'power couple'. They were also her favourites. Topaz used to ring her up and ask her not to tell Joe if her blood pressure was too high. Joe used to ring her up and ask her to bully Topaz into taking each Monday off.

'If he knows what it's really like he'll freak,' Topaz begged.

'She thinks I'm being sexist,' Goldstein sputtered. 'You have to help me out, Lisa.'

'Let's have a look at you, Ms Rossi,' Martinez said calmly. 'You were last palpated at three months, right? That's a bit of a gap. I'd rather you increased checkups now.'

She placed a cool hand on Topaz's swollen stomach and started to press it gently. After a few seconds she stopped dead still, looked at Topaz, and repeated the process, more slowly.

Joe went white. 'What's the matter? Is something wrong with the baby? Is something wrong with Topaz?'

'Not exactly,' replied Lisa Martinez. 'But I think you should have another ultrasound.'

'Why?' Topaz asked. A wave of anxiety spread through her. 'What can you feel?'

'This reorganization, is it vital?' the doctor asked her patient.

'No,' said Joe.

'Absolutely,' said Topaz. 'There's no question of me taking time off unless it's a medical necessity.'

'No, it's not a medical necessity. But I do advise you to rest as much as you can and to avoid arguments,' she added, looking sternly at Joe. 'You'll need as much rest as you can get.'

Lisa Martinez smiled at the young couple. 'Congratulations,' she said. 'You're having twins.'

After her husband had fallen asleep, Topaz Rossi lay quietly on her black silk sheets, staring into space.

She was tired, but she couldn't stop her mind racing.

Twins. Eleanor and Maria. Joe junior and Marco. Eleanor and Joe.

Connor Miles. No one has ever stopped him before and the guys want to hand him American on a silver platter. Is having two babies gonna hurt more? Should I cut down? I can't cut down . . . Jesus, why now? Gowers won't like it, he'll reckon I'm about to walk out. Maybe he won't. He's seen what we did with Impact . . . maybe if I could get the data and work from home . . .

Antitrust. Has to be. I mean, we're not a small company, we're not Pitt Group. We can afford Maughan Macaskill . . . but we need help.

I'm not fucking Superwoman, I'm tired . . .

She's a goddamn bitch . . .

If I can save the company maybe I could succeed Matt. Harvey wants the job but he's ready to give in and Gowers hates that attitude.

Why should she help me? She hates me.

Look at the way she jumped at it when she got a second chance . . . they need us. Tradeoff. Strictly business . . . .

I want to keep my job. I love my work.

Can a woman really have it all?

Topaz swung her legs carefully over the side of the bed, grabbed her satin robe and padded across to her study, flicking on the Apple. The digits on the radio glowed 12.45 a.m.

She paged through her private addresses file, found the number she was looking for and punched it into the phone.

A voice answered, not sleepily. 'Hello?'

'Hello, Rowena,' said Topaz.

34

Rowena Gordon had never been so powerful, celebrated and rich.

She was president of Musica Worldwide, the first woman to hold such high office in the record business. She was one half of a glittering Hollywood couple. She had liquidated her own consultancy for a personal profit of $6,000,000. She was profiled in *Newsweek* and *Forbes*. Her social appearances with John Metcalf were reported by Marissa Matthews and Liz Smith.

Rowena Gordon had never been so pressured.

Day and night she found herself struggling to make sense of financial data, company histories, legal defences for her company. Rowena, Sam Neil and a bitter Hans Bauer arranged for as many big acts as possible to include 'keyman' provisions in their contracts, making Musica a less attractive target. It was a losing battle. Connor Miles bought parcels of stock wherever he could find them, hiding his interest behind webs of holding companies and fake subsidiaries.

Rowena Gordon had never been so unhappy.

'What are you thinking about?' John would ask her after they finished making love, and she would turn aside, kiss him and whisper, 'Nothing.'

Michael. Michael. Michael.

'Spain was a mistake.'

Rowena Gordon sat opposite Michael Krebs in the Oak Room at the Plaza, sipping a fine cognac and trying to sound as confident as she looked. She was wearing an Adrienne Vittadini dress in fluid peach chiffon, Stuart Weitzman mules and a sapphire bracelet, intentionally chosen to match her engagement ring.

Michael wore jeans and a black sweatshirt and beat-up sneakers, and he radiated authority and intensity. She had to use every inch of her self-assurance to prevent her response to his mere presence showing up in her face.

'No it wasn't,' he said flatly.

Oh, this was hard, Rowena thought. It truly was hard. Michael was fifty now, still with those knockout black eyes, still with that salt-and-pepper hair, still with that muscled torso that paid tribute to a lifetime of taking care of himself. Still, to her – she tried unsuccessfully to suppress the thought even as it surfaced – the most desirable man in the world. In terms of classic good looks, Michael couldn't hold a candle to John Metcalf. She knew that. She'd never, as she had with John, had her breath taken away by his pure beauty in certain positions, under certain lights.

But Michael's sexuality hung about him like perfume.

She saw he was staring at her.

'What is it?' she demanded.

'I was thinking how proud you've made me,' Krebs said.

'Thanks,' she smiled, angry with herself for being disappointed with that reply.

Come on, Rowena. He never lied to you. He was never a jerk about it. He said straight out that he didn't love you and never would, he said he was your friend and that was it. He doesn't want you.

'And I was thinking how much I want you back,' he added, not looking at her.

'Come on, Michael. You really don't mean that,' Rowena said calmly.

'Oh, I really do,' Krebs said. 'I really do.'

'Do you love me?' Rowena asked, despising herself for her weakness.

Michael battled with himself. It would be so easy just to say yes to that, and then she'd never deny him again.

'No,' he said. 'I don't love you. But I do want you. I miss you around in my life. I miss watching you have those Richter-scale orgasms.'

'I'm with somebody else now,' she said.

'But you enjoyed it. We had fun together.'

'We had a lot of fun together,' she agreed, determined to stay composed. 'But now I'm with John.'

'So what?' demanded Krebs.

'What do you mean, *so what?*' Rowena shot back. 'So I'm not gonna cheat on him.'

'You can't even meet my eyes,' Michael said, and started to look her over, slowly, a sexual, assessing look.

Rowena could feel his gaze, and blushed scarlet. He was right, she didn't dare look up.

'So tell me about John,' Krebs said conversationally. 'Is it good, with him?'

'Yes it is. It's very good, OK? Enough, Michael. I don't want to talk about this with you.'

'Does he satisfy you?'

'Yes, he does,' said Rowena defiantly. He was still looking at her like that. 'And cut it out.'

'So look at me,' Michael said. 'Come on, Rowena. I mean, your boyfriend satisfies you, so you shouldn't be afraid to look me in the face.'

She looked up and glanced at him. 'OK? Now let it go.'

She was so wet and aroused for him. *Jesus. This is killing me.*

'He must be quite a man, if he can satisfy you,' Michael said, adding mercilessly, 'so you come for him like you came for me.'

Rowena stared straight ahead of her, stony-faced.

'That is true, right?' Michael pressed her. 'You come as hard for him as you came for me.'

'Yes!' Rowena snapped. 'That's *right*. Now shut the fuck up.'

Michael put his hand under her chin, and turned her face sharply towards him. His touch on her skin was electric.

'That's the second time you've lied to me,' he said. 'I don't like it.'

'It's *over*,' she said.

'I could get us a room here, right now,' Michael said, as if she hadn't spoken. 'I could take you upstairs and push you across the desk. I could fuck you on your hands and knees on the floor.'

Rowena looked down at her untouched fruit salad, aware that she was flushing bright red with longing.

Please. You have to let me go,' she whispered.

'I will not,' he said.

'What do you want?' she demanded, raising her head and staring him in the face. 'What do you want of me? I've had success and a good relationship without you. Now you want me to come back to you and screw it all up for myself. Why? For *what*? Isn't it just sex? Isn't that what you always said?'

'You fascinate me,' he said.

Rowena closed her eyes for a split second. The force of his personality radiated across the table like heat from an open oven.

'You love me, Michael,' she said.

'No.'

'Yes, you do. You love me,' she said.

Then she stood up and walked out.

Michael. Michael. Michael.

It had become an obsession.

Even as she organized her own wedding, posed for the society photographers and worried herself sick about Musica, his name beat in the back of her mind like a drum. After the blinding, intense, wonderful ecstasy of what had happened to her in Barcelona, she was incapable of shoving him into the background of her mind.

When she'd left New York, she had left him behind her. The combination of failure in business and the sudden awareness of Michael's wife had been a double whammy that had utterly destroyed her.

Cowhide gave her back her control. Cowhide let her work day and night. It gave her something to fight for. It let her forget Michael Krebs, and gave her a little space to grow fond of John, to rediscover pleasure in sex with someone else.

But now she was back in New York, in his city, with his band, working with him every day, and resistance was futile.

She loved him so fiercely it hurt.

She wanted him so much she could scream.

One morning, on the way to work, she had found herself driving miles out of her way, to Turtle Bay where he lived. She'd parked the Mercedes a few yards down the street from the Krebses' house and just stared at it. It had been six o'clock in the morning, and the tree-lined streets were empty in the predawn darkness.

She had just stared at the front of the house for twenty minutes and then driven away.

She knew it was unhealthy. Dumb, narrow and faithless to her own partner.

Krebs had never even admitted he was *having* an affair. 'Just two friends who have great sex,' he told her.

She'd asked about everything. His brothers. His unemotional parents. High school. College. How he'd lost his virginity. Everything remotely connected with him was endlessly intriguing to her.

Now she began to dream up ridiculous ideas. Like finding where his father had his medical practice and booking an appointment, just to see what David Krebs looked like. Of finding the art gallery where Debbie worked and going to have another look at her.

Rowena did none of these things. She flew out to LA every week, avoided Michael, and worked on the defence of Josh Oberman's company. At least staying at the top was something she cared about passionately.

Because what can you do when the fairytale goes wrong? When you find the love of your life, and he belongs to someone else?

'I think we have a problem.' Hans Bauer's voice was gravelly with concern.

'No shit, Miss Marple,' snapped Joshua Oberman. He sat at the head of the Musica boardroom table, staring down at a photocopy of a letter addressed to Rowena Gordon from Waddington, Edwards & Harris, Mansion Industries' lawyers.

Central Park was bathed in the setting sun outside their windows, and the rays were reflecting off the presentation trophies hanging all over the walls, so that at certain angles Rowena was dazzled. She loved this time of day; Roxana Perdita's *Holding Out* sparkling gold across the polished mahogany floors, Black Ice's *Cry Wolf and Run* shimmering silver, and the huge Atomic Mass displays for *Heat Street* and *Zenith* glittering light back from twenty platinum discs.

'We've got a bunch of fucking problems. Like our fucking company's going up in smoke. Jesus Christ, I'm gonna have to sit here and *watch* while it slips into the hands of a bunch of fucking accountants,' Oberman cursed. He looked older and greyer than Rowena had ever seen him.

'There has to be something we can do,' she muttered.

'Actually, I don't think there is,' said Hans Bauer, sounding almost pleased about it. 'The terms of this letter are clear. If we keep on spinning keyman clauses into our artists' contracts, they're going to sue for dilution of assets. They own shares, so they have every right to do it. And our lawyers think they will win.'

'They won't win over Atomic Mass,' Rowena said, with some sharpness. 'I found them, I've been their manager's closest friend for years and I've been involved in every aspect of their career, production and touring included. If Musica wanted me back, I can legitimately say I demanded a keyman clause.'

'You might be right. But the case could take years. They could put an injunction on the release of their third album,' Maurice LeBec pointed out.

'We have clout.'

'Mansion has more.'

'Then *we* should have more! Why do they want a record company,

Maurice? Who else are they targeting? Can we get some kind of common defence?' Rowena demanded.

Jesus Christ! Like these jerks give a damn about the artists! They've all got stock and they want to be rich. Well, fuck that, I just got here, she thought furiously.

'It's a good point. We know Connor Miles is South African,' Oberman interjected. 'There are laws about foreign nationals owning media companies.'

'Communications media. Not records,' said Jakob van Rees.

'So we buy a fucking radio station. We buy three,' shrugged Rowena.

'They'll sue,' objected LeBec.

'Who are the other targets, Hans? Didn't you tell me there were others?' Josh asked.

The senior executive group president, Finance, gave a petulant shrug. 'Prime Radio in California. Four or five small print companies, a daily newspaper in Chicago and American Magazines.'

'The guy thinks the United States is his fucking supermarket,' Oberman said outraged. 'He's trying to buy Prime Radio and us and American Magazines at *the same time*? How much money does he have, anyway?'

'Enough,' said Bauer and LeBec together.

'I would like to point out that Musica Entertainment is not an American company,' van Rees added, with a sour look at Rowena. 'Madam President may have forgotten it, working in New York for all this time, but Musica is incorporated in Holland.'

'Will that make a difference?' Oberman asked her, his brown eyes ignoring the rest of the executive committee. 'Antitrust, I mean?'

'Ask a lawyer,' his president replied. 'And ask an investment banker.'

Oberman nodded, and winced.

'Are you OK?' Rowena asked.

'Sure,' the old man said, grimacing a little. 'Heartburn. I'm fine.' He turned to the men around the table and waved them away in a crabby gesture of dismissal. 'We're done for now, people.'

With a few ugly glances at their new president, Maurice LeBec, Hans Bauer and Jakob van Rees left the room.

'Rowena, can I see you for a second?' Oberman asked, putting a withered hand on her arm.

'Sure,' she said.

Josh glanced at the heavy, gleaming doors of the boardroom, waiting until LeBec had completely shut them behind him. Then he said sharply, 'Gordon, I don't want those guys within ten feet of our investment bankers.'

Rowena nodded, her shimmering hair swinging against the burgundy collar of the Hervé Leger dress she'd picked for this meeting. They called Leger 'the king of cling' in Paris, and the crossover number that hugged her handspan waist and accentuated her small breasts and the slight swell of her ass was no exception. Teamed with Versace slingbacks and a thick gold bangle, the outfit was theoretically suitable for work, but it threw off a disturbing sense of sexuality behind the neat tailoring and expensive fabric. Oberman had managed a faint smile when he saw it; he knew Rowena inside out and he knew it was a deliberate dig at the other directors, who'd made it obvious how unhappy they were at having to report to a female, especially one who was younger than they were.

The sensible female executive would have gone for ultra-conservative suits, boxy jackets and neutral colours. Rowena made a point of exaggerating her femininity – *deal with it, boys*. Oberman liked that; the kid had never been one to kiss ass.

'I was thinking the exact same thing,' she agreed. 'They *want* to get bought out. Hans Bauer hates my guts.'

'Yeah, well. He's not gonna vote me Prom King either. Who are we hiring? Maughan Macaskill?'

'They've been stalling me. I think someone else got in there first,' Rowena answered.

He noticed she seemed preoccupied, the elegant fingers tapping aimlessly on the table, the green eyes clouded.

'Spit it out, babe,' Oberman ordered, wincing again.

'It's just something Hans said about the other targets,' Rowena said. She pushed her chair back. 'I think I should make a few calls.'

'Let me know as soon as you've decided on the investment bank,' he said.

It wasn't till Oberman got back to his suite at the Pierre and found his copy of *Economic Monthly* waiting for him on his desk that he realized, with a stab of apprehension, exactly what she'd meant.

American Magazines. They're trying to buy American Magazines, Rowena thought, as she spun her Mercedes down Second Avenue.

It was late at night, and the city was melting into the bright lights of the traffic and neon billboards. She'd just come from a long dinner meeting with Barbara Lincoln, and it hadn't been encouraging.

'We want you to have that keyman clause. We don't want Josh Oberman to have to watch Musica go down the drain,' her friend had told her over grilled pheasant at Lutèce. 'But the boys are having their moment in the sun right now. I can't guarantee it'll last for ever and I have to put them first. If Mansion Industries buy you out we are *walking*. Even if I have to split them up and re-form with a different name and a keyboard player.'

Rowena had shuddered. Musica without Atomic Mass was unthinkable.

I have to stop this from happening.

With a boss who's too old to know what he's doing, a board who are probably on Connor Miles's payroll right now, and a company too small to resist this predator.

They're trying to buy out American Magazines.

She just launched Impact *there . . . she's not gonna be happy about it . . .*

She'll tell me to go to hell.

I'd deserve it.

By the time Rowena had picked up her mail from the doorman, though, her mind was made up.

John loved her, and that was good. And she was fond of him. It wasn't such a disaster.

But there had to be some passion in life. Something you love so intensely you would suffer any humiliation to hold on to it. Something that meant you were alive, not merely living.

And without Michael Krebs, Musica was all she had left.

Rowena strode through the door of her apartment, hung up her coat and leafed through her messages. John. Josh, twice. She could call him in the morning. Zach Freeman called from Berlin to say hi. That was sweet, Rowena thought, walking across the room to pick up the phone which had started trilling on her desk.

Who the hell would call me at half-midnight? Not Oberman again . . . that guy doesn't know the meaning of 'unavailable'.

'Hello?' she said.

There was a split-second pause, and in that instant Rowena suddenly knew exactly whom she was speaking to.

'Hello, Rowena,' said Topaz Rossi.

35

Nobody in the White Horse Tavern took any notice of them. Why should they? A mother-to-be and her friend sipping fruit juices in the village on a summer afternoon.

Which was exactly how they both wanted it.

'Grill Room at the Four Seasons,' Rowena had suggested.

'You have to be kidding! Entertainment industry and Wall Street – we might as well put an ad in the *Times*,' Topaz scoffed. 'How about the River Café?'

'I know too many people who lunch there,' Rowena said. 'Maybe we should go somewhere a little less obvious.'

'Fine,' her rival answered coolly. 'I know the closest thing to a pub in the United States. In the Village. White Horse Tavern on Hudson Street.'

'Tomorrow at three,' Rowena agreed, and they hung up.

It was the first private conversation the two women had had for a decade.

Rowena dressed casually: black jeans, a white Donna Karan shirt, tan cowboy boots. She wondered whether or not to take her notes on Mansion House but decided against – if they *didn't* wind up working together, Christ only knew what Rossi might do with the information.

In the cab on the way there she wondered about Topaz; it was amazing how their minds still worked the same way. She would have called American Magazines the next day if Topaz hadn't reached her first. It was surely the only way. Musica Entertainment on its own couldn't withstand a raider with such a huge capital base, and neither could American Magazines. But trying to buy both at the same time must be stretching Mansion. Maybe together they could work something out.

Maybe.

Rowena couldn't count on any more than that: a gut feeling that Topaz Rossi would fight as hard for her slice of American Magazines as she would for Musica. It wasn't an ideal set of circumstances.

Two rivals who'd been publicly scrapping for years.

Two women only recently promoted to the tops of their respective trees.

Two executives with just a heartbeat's really senior experience between them.

They might both be past thirty but in financial terms they were still kids.

Green, wet behind the ears, whatever. No knowledge of investment banking. Diehard specialists in their own industries.

Creatives, for God's sake. In a situation like this, that was a dirty word.

Topaz stepped carefully out of the cab, tipped the guy ten bucks and sat down at the first table she could see. She'd deliberately arrived early; being there when Gordon arrived was just one more way of establishing primacy.

Weird, Topaz thought. I could have sworn Rowena was expecting that call. But how could she?

Unless she was thinking the same thing. Unless she was planning to call me.

Topaz ordered a Caesar salad and fresh orange juice and considered American's position. Sales were up, profits were up, market share was up. Under her personal scheme for the East Coast, they'd closed down three poor performers, including *White Light*, totally revamped a fourth – *US Woman*, now second only to *Homes and Gardens* in its market, taken *Westside* national and, of course, launched *Impact* – the debut of the decade, the reason Matt Gowers let her get away with so much.

She shook her head, wooden bead earrings swinging in the light breeze. *No way Mansion House can outmanage us. This board knows exactly what it's doing.*

Santa Maria, she hated having to do this, *hated* it! As if twins and a takeover wasn't enough! Now she had to arrange meetings with Rowena Gordon, too. A woman whose career she, Topaz, had personally blown away.

That had made them quits. She'd hoped that was an end of it. Yeah, of course she'd read about some consultancy in California, and of course she'd seen Rowena make president of Musica last month. But it hadn't mattered to her, why should it? Rowena had got hers, and if she'd managed another resurrection more power to her. Topaz had other things to occupy her mind: marriage, the new directorship, the pregnancy, the takeover . . .

Past history. It had an annoying way of refusing to stay past.

With a slight intake of breath, she saw her old rival walking down the street towards her. Topaz waved; a short, tight movement, enough to show Rowena where she was. The other woman saw her and threaded her way through the wooden tables.

Christ! Rowena thought. Look at that!

Envy flashed through her. Topaz was hugely pregnant, beautiful in a plain black maternity smock that reached down to her ankles and bared her toned, tanned upper arms. She had her mass of red curls elegantly pinned on top of her head, sexy earrings dangling round her neck and a radiant complexion. As she shook hands briskly Rowena saw the two rings, engagement and wedding, glint on Topaz's left hand. She flashed back to that handsome NBC exec, standing with his arm round Topaz at the Martins' party, and the sense of her own loneliness was crushing.

No time for that now, Rowena told herself.

'I'm glad you came. I think American and Musica can be of use to each other,' Topaz said briskly.

'I agree,' Rowena said instantly.

For a second the two women looked at each other, and a thousand questions, remarks, accusations hung in the air.

Rowena Gordon looked away first. Obviously it would be best if their business could be conducted without personal remarks of any kind, but Topaz was so magnificently, unignorably pregnant that she just had to say something.

She nodded at Topaz's swollen stomach. 'Congratulations. When is it due?'

'Two months. Twins,' she replied coldly, acknowledging Rowena's comment with the briefest inclination of the head.

'What do you think we can do about this?' Rowena asked, beckoning a waiter over. 'The chicken salad and a glass of white wine, please. My guess is that we have roughly three weeks to put something together before our lawyers get thrown out of court.'

Topaz nodded. 'We're in the same position.' She gave Rowena a hard look, as if assessing something, and then said, 'I have a different take on Mansion to some of my colleagues.'

Rowena smiled. 'Me too. Like you believe surrender isn't the only option?'

'Exactly like that.'

'OK.' Rowena ticked off the possibilities on her fingers. 'Off the top of my head: we could merge; we could form a loose holding company for the purposes of this takeover, and buy enough communications companies to stop him buying us, because he's a foreigner –'

Like you, limey, Topaz thought but didn't say so.

'– or we could do something like pooling our capital and implementing a stock repurchase.' She speared a forkful of crunchy lettuce and croutons.

'Merger doesn't make much sense. We've got nothing in common.'

'We've got Connor Miles in common,' Rowena answered rather sharply.

'You will never sell a merger to your board, Rowena, and I know I won't. Trust me on this. But financial partnership makes more sense.'

'You've got something in mind,' said Rowena.

It wasn't a question, it was a statement. She knew that look on Rossi's face only too well – the exact same look she'd had as a student when she was about to nail some poor sonofabitch to the wall in *Cherwell.*

'Ever heard of the Pac-man defence?' Topaz asked shrewdly.

Rowena's wine glass halted in mid-air. 'You are fucking kidding,' she said slowly.

Of *course* she knew what the Pac-man defence was – the prey turns round and swallows the predator. It had happened a few times in the billion-dollar-deal explosion of '81 and more often in the takeover frenzy that had gripped Wall Street in the heady madness of the Reagan boom.

Take Mansion Industries over?

'I'm not kidding. We don't have time for jokes,' Topaz said impatiently. 'I think it could be done. They're getting greedy, they haven't thought this one through. Entertainment might be a growth sector but they're rushing into it; we're two big organizations.'

'And you think they've been neglecting their other businesses?' Rowena asked, food and drink completely forgotten.

My God. What if it is possible? What if we could pull that off?

'Totally. This will be a disaster for them. Like Sony and Columbia Pictures; they reckoned they knew how to run any industry, but films is too human, it has too many variables. Just like magazines,' Topaz replied.

'Numbers. Financing. Secrecy,' Rowena interrupted, her green eyes alight. 'How can we do this and contain it in the time?'

'Maughan Macaskill are our investment bankers —'

'Goddamn it, I've been trying to hire them.'

'I know,' said Topaz, with a slight smile. 'They have a specialist analyst who's been following Mansion for years. He thinks he can put together a proposal for breaking it down and selling it off that would make all the buyers rich. If we banded together to buy it and provided cash and equity, a number of buyout firms would come in with bonds —'

'Junk bonds?'

'It's not like it used to be, OK,' Topaz said. 'They'd be providing debt. But we'd obviously need to work out the numbers very, very carefully.'

'I'd have to sell it to Joshua Oberman, our CEO. And you'd need to sell it to your board.'

Topaz shook her head. 'Our chairman Matthew Gowers has absolute control, but I would need to sell it to him.'

The two women held each other's eyes for a long moment.

'Are you in?' Topaz demanded.

Rowena nodded. 'I'm in,' she said.

'. . . and now we have the fourth top ten smash from *Zenith*, another Atomic album that just can't be stopped! This is "Sweet Savage", right here on K —'

John Metcalf flicked off the radio and spun his Maserati up Sunset. Jesus, he thought. I can't stand to hear that fucking band.

He was as mad as hell. He couldn't believe it. His fiancée had woken him up this morning to tell him she'd be stuck in New York for the next three weeks. *Three weeks!*

'Rowena, this is getting ridiculous;' he snapped. 'We had an agreement and it involved you coming down here on Friday nights.'

'I know, I know,' she pleaded. 'But this is the last time. Either it works or it doesn't, but I'll need this time —'

'For *what? For what?* Mansion's damn takeover? Can't you see it's a lost cause? Ask a fucking banker, for Christ's sake!'

'John. You can come up here —'

'You run the company on your own, Supergirl? Uh? What about your division heads and your board and your boss? Can't they help? Musica has you Monday through Friday day and night! Since when does it need your weekends too?' he yelled, pushing his hand through his hair.

She hung up on him.

She fucking hung up on me! Metcalf thought, incensed. My own wife! Or at least about to be my own wife. I don't *need* this shit. I don't need to be fighting about work every damn day of the week!

Was it going to be like this for the rest of his life?

Unlike just about any other man in LA in his position, John Metcalf was a feminist. He always had been; it was no big deal, it seemed natural to him. He believed in the free market and that meant giving everyone a fair break ... there was no racism or sexism at Metropolis, because top management thought it was bad business.

He'd found Rowena Gordon totally attractive from the first moment he saw her and a big part of that was due to her hunger, her ambition. She was himself reflected. Metcalf saw himself in a skirt – whizz-kid, kick-ass little maverick carving out an empire in a tiny outpost of a big company. Hadn't he done the same thing? When he'd been assigned to Metropolis, it was making thirty second commercials for dog foods. He'd started with one shoestring picture and built the first movie studio to qualify as a major since Orion. No wonder Cage Entertainment had been pleased with him. No wonder he was the youngest baby mogul to hit town.

But ambition was one thing. Obsession was another. What kind of workaholic put her life on hold?

Metcalf pressed his foot on the gas. He was getting frustrated. He couldn't stop thinking about her. About that lithe, naked body leaping in his arms. About her long, feathery hair brushing his cock. About the way she moaned deep in the back of her throat when she was getting close to orgasm.

Jesus Christ!

There had been that new girl at Jack's party last week. The compliant little brunette, stacked, tanned and stupid. A *Playboy* fantasy in the flesh.

The kind of girl he'd always steered clear of.

He wondered if he still had her number.

'Really?' asked Matt Gowers.

'Yes,' said Topaz, intently.

She was sitting in the chairman's office and it was nine at night; the only time he'd had available all day. Normal defence work had started at 7 a.m. with a review of their legal position, broken at lunch for half an hour, and carried right through till half-eight. Topaz had been hunched over her computer till her eyes ached and she hated it. Maths was never her strong suit.

Still, she couldn't complain. As the hours wore on, the facts became clearer. Costs had been squeezed as tight as possible without hurting the papers; after her own revamp of the East Coast, Harvey had followed suit in LA.

'I can't get one extra dime out of these, and Mansion couldn't either,' Damian Hart asserted, and the bankers seemed to agree.

Topaz had also managed to talk a little more to Gerald Quin about their own idea. 'Are we totally leftfield with this?' she'd asked quietly.

The young man shook his head. 'Nothing's leftfield if it can be done.'

So she'd summoned up her courage and asked to speak to Gowers alone after work; if I can ring up Rowena Gordon I can go pitch my own supervisor, she told herself.

Outside his thick glass walls Manhattan was a carpet of electric light, sparkling and moving; the cars seemed to race faster, the skyscrapers to jab higher, pounding along with her heartbeat. What if he thought she was way off-base? What if he thought she was blinded by personal ambition? That she was a hysterical pregnant woman?

But Gowers hadn't thrown her out. He was listening.

'Gerald Quin has been analysing this company for years and he swears the deal finances itself,' Topaz insisted. 'Look, boss. If Connor Miles gets hold of this company we're all history.'

'We've got a duty to the stockholders,' the older man warned her.

'I realize that,' Topaz replied, trying to cool her impatience. 'But our duty is long-term, right? For all the stock might rise fifteen per cent from a takeover bid it'll have fallen thirty per cent when he publishes his first set of results.'

She leant forward, the edge of her stomach resting against Gowers' mahogany desk. 'Matt, you wanna retire?' she asked softly. 'Because there aren't that many spots open for unemployed CEOs at the other big magazine houses.'

Matthew Gowers looked down at the breakdown of Mansion Industries she'd put on his desk.

'All right, let's do it,' he said. 'And Rossi – *keep it quiet.*'

Rowena Gordon spent a couple of hours wondering how to broach the subject, then called Josh Oberman at home.

'Gordon, know what the time is?' Oberman snapped. 'This better be good. Found me an investment bank?'

'Topaz Rossi at American Magazines called me,' Rowena said. 'She wants to form a consortium with us, get some debt backing and take over Mansion Industries. They already hired Maughan Macaskill and there's a guy there, a specialist in conglomerates, who knows Mansion backwards. He reckons we'd have a good chance of doing it.'

There was a pause.

'Let me get this right,' Oberman repeated. 'Musica Records and American Magazines team up and buy out Connor Miles. In a hostile deal.'

'You got it,' said Rowena.

Oberman cackled, a great rasping laugh sputtering across the Atlantic.

'Gordon, you are one insane girl. But why the fuck not? I've got nothing better to do.'

'Are you serious?' Rowena demanded.

'If you are,' he said, his tone suddenly changing. 'And you *are* serious, Rowena, right?'

'Yes, sir. It's difficult but not impossible and it's the only chance we have.'

'Then we'll try it. I'm old, but I'm not dead,' Oberman said. 'And Rowena – I don't want the executive committee involved.'

Gerry Quin was running on high octane.

He wanted this deal so bad he could taste it. A win fee would net millions for Maughan Macaskill.

More to the point, it would make his reputation. Forget Kravis. Forget Wasserstein. He, Quin, would be Wall Street's new boy wonder – David slaying the mighty Goliath of Mansion Industries. It was the deal of the century and owing to one stupid, overconfident mistake – thinking he could have American and Musica at the same time – Connor Miles had set him up for it.

Practically an engraved invitation.

American and Musica. Big corporations, but not big enough to stand up to the conglomerate. Companies who'd only recently reshuffled their boards. Executives ready to try anything to hang on to their first taste of real power.

They were cornered.

They were desperate.

They would fight.

Nick Edward and he drew up a quick fee agreement and advised on the deal team. It had to be kept from as many people as possible; surprise was going to be key. Topaz Rossi offered the use of her house on Beekman Place, and they arranged to meet there on Friday morning at 7 a.m.

From American Magazines, Gowers took Rossi, Harvey Smith, Damian Hart and Eli Leber. From Musica, Joshua Oberman took Rowena Gordon and James Harton, the company lawyer. He also invited, at Gerry's suggestion, the producer Michael Krebs, who worked on most of Musica's star acts, and finally Barbara Lincoln, the manager of Atomic Mass.

Both these last two would be needed for public relations purposes – if he could threaten the stockholders with a talent walkout if Mansion got hold of Musica, that would be effective. Anyway, Oberman told the bankers that Barbara Lincoln was a trained entertainment lawyer and had run his Business Affairs and Legal Department for years.

'Woman's forgotten more about our contracts that I ever knew,' he said gruffly.

They'd start work tomorrow morning.

Gerry Quin could hardly wait.

It was only seven in the morning, and limos were piling up along the tree-lined street. If anybody noticed anything, though, they weren't about to say. In this part of town, most of the neighbours would die rather than admit to curiosity about a thing like that.

Topaz was ready for them.

'We have to do this, right?' Joe had asked weakly the night before, lugging in armfuls of frozen pizzas and a case of mixed Häagen-Dazs.

'Right,' Topaz answered, hardly looking up from her figures. 'You're not going to try and stop me, baby, are you? Because that would be bad for my blood pressure.' She patted her stomach gently.

'No, no, you do what you want,' said Goldstein hastily, recoiling from the threat.

Topaz smiled to herself. Who'd ever believe she'd resort to feminine wiles?

Joe had the last laugh, though. When their alarm rang at six on Friday he got up, showered as normal, and wandered off to dress.

'What are you wearing?' his wife asked, propping herself up on one elbow and sleepily pushing away a mass of crimson curls.

Her husband was pulling a Mets T-shirt over black Levi's and his favourite pair of beat-up sneakers. 'What does it look like?' he asked.

'It's *Friday*.'

'It is,' Joe agreed amiably, 'and I'm staying here with you. I've taken the day off.'

'You've done *what*! You can't do that!' Topaz protested. 'Everyone'll be here in forty minutes.'

'Try and stop me. There's no way I'm letting you run this one on your own,' he said, grinning. 'Anyway, you seem to forget that I do know a little about American Magazines.'

'No outsiders,' Topaz objected feebly.

'I'm not an outsider. I'm your husband,' Joe said, coming back to the bed and pressing her head to him in a leisurely kiss.

Matt Gowers was the first to arrive and Barbara Lincoln – resplendent in the smoothest cream cashmere by Nicole Farhi – the last, but by seven fifteen everyone had assembled. Introductions were brisk and unsociable, Joe poured out coffee, and they started right in.

'Partners,' Joshua Oberman began. 'What are the possibilities?'

Instant pandemonium. The bankers and the lawyers all started talking at once. Topaz started flicking on various computers brought over from the office, and Matthew Gowers and Josh Oberman veered off on a tangent, discussing debt ratios between themselves.

Michael glanced over at Rowena. It was Josh Oberman who'd insisted he be here, and Krebs had sensed her effort not to look at him as soon as he'd walked through the door. Her handshake and her greeting had been as dry as dust. She'd been about that cordial to Topaz Rossi.

What a weird atmosphere, Michael thought, scoping the room. All these people with nothing in common, except this deal. The lawyers – and Barbara, holy shit, I never saw that girl as a lawyer – sniping at each other. The merchant bankers doing figures with the finance guys. The CEOs obviously at the start of a beautiful friendship.

And Rowena with Ms Rossi.

'Interesting, isn't it?'

Krebs looked up to see Joe Goldstein standing in front of him with a mug of black coffee.

'Thanks,' he said. 'I'm Michael Krebs. I produce records for Josh Oberman.'

Joe nodded. 'Atomic Mass, Roxana, Black Ice. And you did *The Salute* by Three Legions. Right?'

'That's right,' said Michael, surprised. *The Salute* had been his first really big hit, out on CBS more than fifteen years ago. 'You're well informed.'

'It pays,' Joe said, shrugging.

Both men watched Rowena and Topaz. They were deep in discussion with Harvey Smith about something, but their body language ignored Smith completely. Rowena's eyes kept sliding across to Topaz while her colleague was talking. When Rowena turned to Harvey, they saw Topaz shift on her seat, watching the other woman intently.

'Yeah, it is interesting,' Krebs agreed.

'You know Rowena Gordon well?' Joe asked.

He couldn't suppress a smile. 'For years.'

'What's she like?' Goldstein asked, surprised at his own curiosity. After he'd met Rowena at Liz Martin's party he'd hated her guts. Stuck-up English bitch! No wonder she'd given his baby a rejection complex, she was as cold as liquid hydrogen. But Topaz had torpedoed her career in retaliation and when she told him she'd called Rowena about Mansion, Goldstein had been stunned that the woman even agreed to a meeting.

And now here they were, in his house, in partnership. Business is business, but still . . . there was something strange about it.

'She's intense,' Michael said, and Joe watched a strange expression come over his face.

Check it out! This guy is her lover! he realized, in a sudden flash of insight. But Rowena Gordon was in the middle of the media romance of the year! Wasn't she?

'What's Topaz Rossi like?' Krebs was asking him, equally curious.

'She's intense,' Joe replied, and they exchanged glances.

'Have you got croissants cooking through there?'

'Uh-huh. Let's go eat.'

It was impossible to remain brisk and businesslike when you were working eighteen-hour days. Something they all discovered over the first weekend, when the place was covered with empty pizza cartons and beer cans, and Matt Gowers was discovered with Josh Oberman cracking up to *Beavis and Butt-head* on the kitchen TV.

Edward had his Quotron terminal delivered to the house and hooked up. Harvey Smith started to take meetings by conference call in a spare bedroom. Rowena called Sam Neil and asked him to take over for a week. Josh and Matt worked by fax.

'There's a kind of sick pleasure in pushing yourself this hard,' Topaz remarked at eleven thirty one evening, as Goldstein's PowerMacintosh ran off yet another colour chart for Freyja Timber.

'Yeah. It's like Mods. Remember that? A huge pile of books, a huge pot of coffee and three packs of Pro-Plus,' Rowena said to her.

There was a second's complete silence.

'Let's get another pizza. I'm starving,' Eli Leber butted in hastily.

Then there was the time that Joe had been mixing Bloody Marys and Topaz said automatically, 'Rowena likes a lot of Worcester sauce, sweetheart.'

'You haven't changed at all, you know that?' Rowena told Topaz one night when she was tapping away at the IBM. 'You always used to crouch like that. Exactly like that.'

'That's right. And you always bugged the hell out of me by reading over my shoulder. The way you are right now,' Topaz replied, and they actually laughed.

'You know, I think this deal might work. Did you hear that Steel, Roven bought in?'

'For an equity stake, too. Not just debt,' Topaz agreed.

'What sex are your children going to be?' Rowena asked suddenly.

'No idea,' Topaz replied, looking round. 'Why?'

'Nothing,' Rowena said, and wondered why she was so close to tears.

Once the final break-up analysis had been completed, Gerald Quin pushed away his charts with an exhausted sigh.

'The numbers work,' he said. 'We need to find three billion dollars.'

There was an awed hush as the deal team tried to get their heads round that amount of money.

'Great,' Damian Hart said, with perfect deadpan humour. 'Now for the good part.'

36

It wasn't quite that simple.

Maughan Macaskill, the lawyers and the two chief executives finally had some numbers worked out and an idea of who might want to come in with them. They still had to hammer out a million little variables – tax problems, ownership regulations, SECC disclosures – and they also needed a creative plan that would sell Wall Street on the idea that Mansion House couldn't be trusted. Only Musica management could run Musica. Only the present board could run American Magazines.

'We have to split the team,' Gowers said wearily at half-eleven that night. 'There's just no other way to get this done in time.'

Oberman nodded. 'Rowena, you and Michael should put some kind of document together for Musica. I don't know who American want...'

'Topaz Rossi,' Gowers said instantly. 'Harvey Smith. Damian should work with us.'

'Am I needed?' Smith asked, annoyed. He wanted to be in the real action. 'LA can send up all the data through here by fax and I know some guys at RJR Nabisco we should pitch Natural Foods to.'

'Topaz?' Gowers asked.

'Fine,' she shrugged, seeing her colleagues' eyes upon her. *Why don't you just say it? No way is she professional enough to work with Rowena Gordon?* 'It's no problem,' Topaz added, her face set in a mask of perfect indifference.

Rowena, is that OK for you?' Oberman asked his president. 'We really only have a few days on this.'

'Absolutely,' Rowena confirmed.

Oh, bloody marvellous. Michael Krebs and Topaz Rossi. Just the two people I really want to be close to at the moment.

'So that's settled,' Eli Leber said, his eyes sweeping the room cautiously. Rossi and Gordon both looked as uptight as Tipper Gore at a strippers' conference, Gowers and Oberman were watching them with slightly nervous expressions, and the only person that seemed totally at his ease was Michael Krebs.

'That's settled,' Krebs agreed, smiling.

Musica Towers was electric with rumours.

Rowena Gordon could feel it in the air every day when she walked through the doors, striding through the marble lobby where she'd been served her termination notice, walking up the stairs to a marketing meeting, dropping in on a sales presentation ... as soon as she appeared, staff ceased talking, studied their shoes or picked up the nearest phone.

Not that it was easy to tell. With Roxana's *Race Game* crashing to the *Billboard* Hot 100 at number one and the next Black Ice album due in a week, the entire building was frying ice in the rush. Sam Neil had been running the place for the year of her exile and he was in total control of the organized madness; suppliers were getting served, campaigns were being run, tours were being supported – so what if the new COO wasn't in her office all the time? What was there to talk about?

Plenty, Rowena thought furiously. Evidently.

'Sam, what's going on?' she demanded. 'I can't walk in on a meeting without feeling like the elephant woman. I'm the class freak here. What's the score?'

Neil loosened his collar, sweating slightly, and looked his boss over with a wary eye. Rowena Gordon mad would give a charging rhino pause, even without those short black suits she'd taken to wearing – little Richard Tyler skirts in snug wool, DKNY fitted tops, her long blonde hair swept back in a schoolgirl's ponytail. That was Rowena's idea of dressing down. It was Sam's idea of a heart attack.

'Nothing's going on,' her division president replied, cautiously. 'Maybe some people are a little curious about you, that's all.'

Rowena fixed him with a steely glare.

'OK, OK', he added hastily, 'I guess – uh – it's just that you haven't actually been around much since you took over, and, uh, the staff are wondering why not.'

'Go on,' she said.

Sam Neil felt himself start to sweat uncomfortably. Hell, he'd taken great trouble not to show even a flicker of curiosity. If the new head of the company didn't want to show up in the office, his not to reason why. But he suddenly had the sense that he was on very thin ground indeed.

'I guess they're wondering what you and Josh and Krebs are working on,' he finished lamely.

Rowena nodded. 'I see,' she said. 'What you're trying to tell me, Sam, is that the whole building wants to know if we're off devising some kind of secret buyout defence against Mansion Industries?'

'Yeah,' said Neil, squirming slightly.

'Is the whole company talking about this, Sam?'

He shrugged. 'I don't know, Rowena, I mean, I don't have that much contact with the junior staff ... OK, all right, I suppose they are.'

Rowena pushed a wisp of blonde hair away from her forehead, feeling the tension crunch round her skull like a vice. She simply couldn't let this happen. If the staff in the New York office started to gossip about it, it was only a matter of time before her absence leaked to the trades. And if the same thing was going on over at American Magazines, it would take just one business reporter to put two and two together, and weeks of patient work would be blown sky-high.

The whole deal depended on secrecy.

She had to get back to her office, and she had to come up with the creative plan.

There was only one thing for it . . .

'Well, they can lay that one to rest,' she said firmly. 'Our legal defences are in place, you know that. I'll be back in the building from today . . . we just had some problems to do with the new Atomic Mass record, and you know Barbara and Krebs will only deal with Josh and myself on stuff like that.'

'Do you want me to tell people that?' Sam Neil asked, surprised. Atomic Mass were the Holy Grail around Musica Records. Even to *imagine* a problem with them was blasphemy.

'Sure,' his president said, expansively. 'We have no secrets at Musica Records.'

'OK,' Sam said, leaving her office with some relief.

Rowena Gordon watched him go. Then she picked up her phone and dialled Topaz Rossi's private line.

'Topaz, we have another problem,' she said.

American Magazines was just as busy and the rumours were just as wild. In fact they were worse. After all, investigation and exposure was what everybody in the building did for a living.

Topaz found that out the first day she came back to work. Sauntering into the *Impact* offices and feeling twelve pairs of eyes crawling over the nape of her neck. Dropping in on *Girlfriend* to find herself as out of place as a high-school teacher at a slumber party.

'It's what I'd expect,' Joe told her when she rang up to complain. 'At least over at Musica only the chairman and the president took off. You guys had half the board playing hookey. Of course they're talking.'

'But we can't let everybody gossip about this! It'll leak!' Topaz protested.

'Which is why you're all back in the office, honey,' Joe pointed out.

'I can't stay in the office! When am I gonna work on the creative plan? I have to present Rowena Gordon with something in the next few days!'

'I don't know,' Goldstein said as calmly as he could. *Jesus Christ, she's eight months pregnant!* 'Just try not to stress yourself out, sweetheart. If I were you I'd talk to Rowena. It would be dangerous to be away from the office now.'

'OK, OK,' his wife soothed him. *Try not to stress myself out? That's real funny.*

'Topaz, Rowena Gordon is on the line,' her assistant said.

'Joe, I have to go,' she told him. 'I'll call you later.'

Christ Almighty, Topaz thought, glancing down at the frantic rush of lunchtime traffic pouring along Seventh Avenue, sixty storeys below her. Compared with her own life, it seemed as calm as a monastic retreat. She hoped that bitch Rowena Gordon was taking at least a little of the same heat.

'This is me,' she snapped.

'Topaz, we have another problem,' Rowena said coldly, trying to hide her panic. 'I don't think I can get away from my building. The staff here are beginning to talk.'

'Me either,' her rival replied. 'And we just can't risk it getting out.'

'Nobody can do a creative plan for Musica Records but me,' Rowena said flatly. It wasn't a boast, it was a statement of fact. She knew that it was her ideas about the kind of acts they should go for, her take on marketing and distribution, and her plans for buying smaller labels that made Josh Oberman give her her job back in the first place.

'Yeah. I'm sure that's true,' Topaz said, forgetting to be icy. 'I feel the same way about American. You know? Joe thinks I should delegate this plan, but I just can't do it – it's not about the nuts and bolts of the business, it's about –'

'Vision?' Rowena suggested.

'Exactly,' the other woman said.

'So what do we do?' Rowena asked. 'We have to get this done –'

'– and we can't do it in our offices because we have to go back in to all the meetings –'

There was a pause.

'So I guess we're gonna have to work together at nights and over the weekend,' Rowena said eventually. 'We could do it separately, but then how would we check with each other over wording, the general lines of the document . . .'

'Come round at nine,' Topaz said shortly.

So it was the only way. Well, she had to do it. But she didn't have to like it.

'And Michael Krebs?' Rowena forced herself to ask.

'If your Mr Oberman thinks you need him, bring him along too,' Topaz replied.

There was another moment's awkward silence, and then both women hung up, without further pleasantries.

Michael Krebs drove his black Ferrari Testarossa up to the Musica Towers executive car park and was instantly waved in by the guard. It was an early summer evening and Krebs was enjoying everything about it. The way the golden light fell over the trees and the sidewalks. The way the Tom Petty CD sounded in his top-of-the-range in-car system. The way Rowena Gordon had sounded to him on the phone.

'Michael? It's Rowena.'

'I know who it is,' Krebs had said dryly.

'There's been a change of plan,' she went on nervously, obviously trying to get off the phone as soon as she could. 'We have to meet tonight, not this afternoon. Can you be at Beekman Place at nine?'

'I don't know. What's in it for me?'

'Michael, for Christ's sake!'

'I have some ideas I want to discuss with you,' Krebs said, oblivious. 'If we have to be there at nine, I'll pick you up at eight.'

'OK,' Rowena said, tensely.

Krebs smiled. He knew every intonation of Rowena Gordon's voice, knew it like his own. So she'd wanted to object, but she couldn't – couldn't admit that she didn't want to be alone with him.

She wants to be all business, but she's as scared as hell.

He was looking forward to this.

Rowena had just sent her assistant home when Michael arrived.

She'd spent the last two hours trying to reach John Metcalf in LA and getting the brush-off from his assistant.

'The president's in a meeting, ma'am.'

'Yes, ma'am, I know who you are.'

'Yes, ma'am, I gave him *all* your messages.'

'Uh, he went straight into a new meeting, Ms Gordon. Yes, ma'am, I know, but we're extremely busy . . .'

'Well, thanks for your help,' Rowena said as Michael walked in, replacing the receiver with a bang.

Krebs took in her lean, elegant silhouette against the windows, the last light of day catching her blonde hair so it shimmered and gleamed, her tight black outfit hugging every slender curve and her long legs seeming to stretch down for ever in sheer black pantyhose.

He felt an instant twitch of lust. 'Who were you calling?'

'Oh, nobody special,' she said defensively.

'Was that your fiancé?'

'No,' said Rowena, blushing. She grew angrier with John. Why did he have to be so childish about her staying in New York for a few weeks? Now she was embarrassed in front of Michael Krebs. The last guy in the world she wanted to know about her relationship problems.

'Well, I guess that is nobody special,' Krebs commented shrewdly, giving her an infuriatingly knowing grin.

'Do you want to work this through here, or should we go over to Mirror, Mirror?' Rowena asked, determinedly ignoring him.

'Nether. I've booked us a table at Le Cirque,' he told her, 'and don't look like that, Rowena, if we're gonna work all night I have to eat first.'

Rowena glanced at him, wanting to object but not daring to. If it was anybody else, of course they'd need dinner before working all night . . .

But it wasn't anybody else. It was Michael Krebs.

'Are you coming, or what?' he demanded, turning to go. His expression was one of complete indifference.

Pull yourself together, Rowena, she told herself severely, and grabbed her sheaf of notes and contracts.

'I'm right behind you,' she said.

They drove uptown through the twilight, talking business, watching each other. Rowena leant back against the supple leather of her seat and tried to listen to what Krebs was suggesting: buying a couple of hardcore labels, trimming the European roster, expanding the licensing division. She needed to concentrate. This stuff was important. And yet she just couldn't stop watching the way his mouth moved when he spoke, the way his large hands gripped the wheel, the sexy grey hair at the side of his head. She didn't want him to come on to her, but she was somehow resentful that he was being so goddamn professional . . . why didn't he push her like he used to? Has he given up on me? Rowena wondered, instantly ashamed to find herself dismayed at the thought.

Krebs stared at the traffic ahead of him, seeing Rowena out of the corner of his eye, talking on autopilot. This deal was Josh and Rowena's future, and he'd done a lot of work on it; besides, personally, professionally, it would be catastrophic for him to have Mansion House take Musica over. Krebs had his own proposals off by heart, which meant he could reel them off to Rowena without thinking. Leaving his mind free to consider those schoolgirl pantyhose. The clinging cut of her dress. The way her slim little body curled round in her seat. Jesus, but the way she moved drove him crazy. He remembered the tiny catlike curl she'd done on that studio chair in London, the night they'd first had sex.

I want you, I want you, Rowena thought fiercely.

She's so far under my skin, Krebs thought, heady with a sudden urge to just pull over and reach for her. He fought back the impulse and kept talking, but he was enraged. Rowena Gordon was his! She had always been his! Who was this little kid John Metcalf? Some jerk-off Angeleno who knew absolutely nothing about music, absolutely nothing about what fired Rowena's passions . . .

At the elegant restaurant on East 65th they were ushered to a secluded table, and Michael ordered champagne.

'Le Cirque is my favourite, these days,' Rowena said to him, searching for some safe ground for small talk. In the cool shadows and soft lights she felt Krebs's presence as a real threat. He'd put on a dark jacket and tie to eat here, something he never wore; it amplified his natural air of power. His charcoal eyes, fringed with those jet-black lashes, looked into hers with an easygoing interest that maddened her.

She wanted him to leave her alone.

She wanted him to forget her.

She wanted him to just be her friend.

Yeah, right.

'Its got the best diet menu in Manhattan,' she added hastily, suddenly aware that she'd been staring at him. 'I'm past thirty. I have to watch my weight.'

'Don't be ridiculous. You're perfect as you are,' Michael said, watching her drop her gaze. 'And what is this past-thirty bullshit? You're just a child, Gordon.'

Rowena laughed, and the long sweep of her hair caught the candlelight. He felt his left hand clench under the tablecloth.

'I'll always be a child to you, Michael.'

'You're a lot of things to me,' he said softly, 'but a child isn't one of them.'

He stared at her, and Rowena sensed the deep, familiar well of heat starting to pulse in her groin. Under the taut fabric of her sweater, quite noticeably her nipples tightened, swelling with blood. Lust strong enough to match his own started to trawl across her skin, digging little teasing hooks of pleasure into her groin. She felt a wave of panic, aware that her desire for him was written in bright letters across her face.

'I'm going to have you again,' Krebs said quietly, never taking his eyes from her. 'It's what you want and it's what I want.'

'No it's not,' Rowena answered sharply, reaching blindly for her wine glass. Michael lunged across the table and caught her hand in his, gripping it, his fingers pushing against the soft flesh at the base of the thumb.

His touch was like flicking on a switch. Rowena's stomach dissolved in longing and she flooded with wetness. Involuntarily she gave a little shudder of need, her whole body shaking on the chair.

'Isn't it?' Krebs insisted.

'Are you ready to order?' enquired a waiter politely.

Krebs felt the moment shatter and glared at the poor man with a look that could have melted steel.

'Thank you, yes. I'd like the monkfish with sorrel leaves,' Rowena said hastily, pressing her hot palm against the glittering coolness of her engagement ring.

She discussed contracts briskly for the entire rest of the meal.

They drew up at Beekman Place at nine exactly. Topaz Rossi let them in, elegant in an empire-waisted dress of dark blue velvet that cut off just below the knee, flowing over her round stomach and contrasting beautifully with her red curls, shiny and lustrous from her pregnancy.

'You look terrific,' Rowena told her, forgetting her reserve of that morning. 'That dress really picks out your eyes.'

'You think so? I hate it,' Topaz said. 'I hate everything in my wardrobe at the moment though. I can't find one thing that will make me look less fat.'

'Oh, you don't look fat, you look pregnant,' Rowena protested. 'Look at your arms and legs, Topaz. Look at your chin.'

'Hello, Michael,' Joe Goldstein said, appearing behind his wife. He put a protective hand on her shoulder and added somewhat coldly, 'Hi, Rowena.'

'Hey, Goldstein,' Krebs answered, feeling the renewed chill settle between the two women. Not that he would ever understand their relationship; he still remembered the unusual venom that had crept into Rowena's voice when she talked about Topaz; he could hardly forget all the barbs this cute-looking redhead had thrown at them, the sniping at Atomic Mass when they were just starting out, the way she'd blown out the Madison Square Gardens launch of *Heat Street*, the way she'd taken *Velocity* from under Rowena's nose, and the final damning *Westside* cover story that finished Rowena Gordon's meteoric career off in one fell swoop. And on their side? Joe Hunter publicly embarrassing Rossi on *Oprah*, closing *White Light* down with a few phonecalls, and the inexorable rise of Rowena and her band, right up until that final blow.

There has to be more to it than that, Krebs thought, watching Topaz Rossi's back as she led them through to the office. I know they had a history . . . it's like they know each other backwards. Half of the time they would act like sisters, fixing each other's coffee without asking how they took it, finishing off each other's sentences, complaining about the traffic. Then they would catch themselves doing it, and suddenly, instantly, snap back into the two bitter rivals who'd been forced to do business together.

But she keeps glancing over at Goldstein, keeps looking around the house, Michael thought, interested. It's like she's incredibly curious but doesn't want to show it . . . and Topaz, too, that girl's always checking me out, always striking up conversations with Oberman . . .

Of course, over the last few weeks there'd been a crowd of people around them. Now they were practically on their own.

Krebs grinned as he pulled the Atomic Mass contract out of his briefcase. This was going to be hard work, but it might be fun to watch.

Topaz shook her head, trying to clear the fumes of exhaustion and fatigue. It was ten to three in the morning, and they were still at work. Despairing of her stubbornness, Joe had long since turned in – he liked to be at NBC before seven – and Michael Krebs, who'd been up until five the night before mixing the latest Black Ice album, had passed out on the sofa.

'Do you want to call it a night?' Rowena asked, seeing her check her watch.

Topaz took another gulp of her industrial-strength coffee and shook her head. 'If we can work through this joint statement about artistic commitment we'll be finished. I'd rather do it that way, I gotta say. I don't want to have to go back to it.'

Rowena nodded. 'We did pretty well. Check this out,' and she reached down to Topaz's laser printer and pulled off thirty sheets of paper. 'Creative planning, sell-offs, the human resource factor –'

'Translation: all my writers and all your bands will be out the door in a heartbeat,' Topaz butted in, grinning.

'Exactly. Plus, detailed expansion plans, distribution details, licensing deals –'

'Translation: we know how to run these babies and Connor Miles knows jack,' added Topaz.

'Plus five-year plans for the core businesses –'

'Translation: if you sell this stock you're as dumb as Dan fucking Quayle,' said Topaz elegantly. 'Hey, Rowena, let's just be straight with this statement. Type this up – The boards of American Magazines and Musica Records –'

'Musica Records and American Magazines,' said Rowena loudly.

'– state that they have complete commitment to all their artistic principles, as long as they're making money –'

'– and if they stop making money, we'll drop them right away –'

'– and if Connor Miles buys us out we're walking –'

'– and everybody's coming with us –'

'– and your shares will be worth one-tenth of what you paid for them –'

'so don't fuck with us!' Rowena finished triumphantly.

The two women collapsed in a fit of laughter, clutching each other for support, then shushing each other as Michael Krebs turned fitfully on the sofa.

'Oh, I'm sorry,' Topaz whispered. 'I shouldn't wake Michael. He was really cool on all that licensing stuff.'

'Yeah,' Rowena agreed, turning her head to look at the producer. Topaz watched her gazing at him, her face suddenly softened and tender.

'What's the deal? You love him?' she asked.

Rowena jumped out of her skin. 'Of course not,' she said instantly. Even in the dull flickering glow of the Mac, the only light in the room, Topaz could see her old rival blushing scarlet. 'Whatever gave you that idea?'

'*Whatever gave you that idea?*' mimicked Topaz quietly. 'Oh please. How long have I known you?'

There was a pause, as the rhetorical question brought it all flooding back.

'A long time,' Rowena replied slowly.

There was another pause. Both women felt their heart-beats speed up a little. Over the course of the deal, and especially tonight, they'd been able to work together because they had to. Because there was no other way. Because they were career girls with their careers at stake.

And the unspoken, unwritten, unbreakable rule was: *Say nothing. Confront nothing. Resolve nothing.*

A temporary truce. No more than that.

And now . . .

Topaz Rossi looked at Rowena Gordon.

'Why did you do it?' she asked softly. 'We were so close.'

Rowena felt as though a fist of mixed emotions was closing around her heart.

'I was young, and dumb, and selfish,' she said eventually. 'I wanted him and he was with you. You were so . . . sexy and outrageous, and I was a virgin . . . it was just another guy rejecting me, I suppose.'

Imperceptibly, Topaz leant forward on her seat.

'And then I started to resent you, because you had him,' Rowena went on, unable to look the other woman in the face, 'and the more I was jealous of you the guiltier I felt, and I kept on wanting him but in reality, I think it was only because you had him.'

'And you were with him alone such a lot,' Topaz said, with the beginnings of understanding.

Rowena nodded. 'So I tried to justify it to myself, when there was no justification . . . I started thinking all these snobby thoughts . . . it was like all the establishment values I'd been hurt by myself I used against you. And I was ashamed of myself, so I focused all that on you. And then you blew me out for the Union Presidency, so I could kid myself that it was all your fault . . . you'd pushed me at him . . . and I hated you, because I just couldn't admit that what I'd actually done was trample all over the first person in the world who had ever cared about me for who I was. I am so, so sorry, Topaz,' Rowena finished weakly. 'I just hope you can forgive me.'

Topaz stared at her for a long moment. Then she broke into a slow smile.

'You know, if you'd said that before it would have saved us both a lot of trouble. All you English guys are such emotional cripples.'

'I'm not English. I'm Scottish,' said Rowena with dignity.

'Same difference.'

'Only a dumb-ass Yank would say something like that.'

They grinned at each other.

'Come on, Goldilocks. Let's put this thing to bed,' Topaz said, 'and you can tell me all about Daddy Bear over there while we're at it.'

37

The main conference chamber of Maughan Macaskill was packed out. Quotron screens had been installed along the length of the walnut table, and there were so many phones and fax machines positioned round the room that it looked like the Starship Enterprise. Nick Edward had also ordered up a couple of wide-screen TVs, so they could watch reactions to this deal as it broke.

The place was thronging with more millionaires than a Hamptons country club: investment bankers, debt financiers, lawyers, industrialists from eight of America and Canada's biggest conglomerates, and representatives from six banks. Twelve storeys below them, CNN reporters and *Journal* photographers were already jockeying for places on the sidewalk. There was a general sense of disbelief – *Barbarians at the Gate* Mark II and everyone had missed it! How in God's name was this bid put together without anybody finding out about it?

'Where the hell is Topaz Rossi? All hell's breaking loose up here and I can't find my fucking director!' Matthew Gowers fumed to Josh Oberman. 'Her assistant's not at her desk, Harvey hasn't seen her since lunch . . . she hasn't left any message with my secretary.'

'Rowena had a meeting with her at three,' the Musica chairman told him. 'I called her in the car on the way over. They must have left the building together for some reason, because Gordon's not answering her mobile phone. Tammy Limmon told me she cancelled Hans Bauer to go see Michael Krebs, then went straight over to American . . .'

'Yeah, but it's four thirty. They should be here! Where's Rossi's goddamn secretary?' Gowers demanded.

Oberman snorted. The bid was announced now. If Gordon was dumb enough to miss *this* party, that was her problem. 'They've probably got some excuse,' he said.

Matt Gowers looked out of the window at the crowd of business journos below him. He was annoyed; he'd been looking forward to a triumphant photoshoot of himself and Topaz as his nominated successor. Surely it wasn't asking too much for just a *little* glamour at the end of his executive career?

'Well, it better be a good one,' he said darkly.

'*Hurry*,' urged Rowena. 'For Christ's sake! Is this the best we can do?'

'I can't go any faster without breaking the law, ma'am,' the chauffeur said imperturbably.

'Then *break* the fucking law!' she snapped. 'Or do you feel like becoming an instant midwife?'

The guy blanched visibly and pressed his foot to the floor.

'It hurts,' Topaz whimpered, her right hand clutching Rowena's in a pincer-like grip. 'Ohhhh . . .'

Her face twisted with pain as another violent contraction shuddered through her. Rowena watched it in an agony of sympathy. She estimated they were about five minutes apart now.

'You're doing great,' she said, as calmly as she could. 'Hang in there. We'll be at Mt Sinai real soon.'

A quick, pained grin came over Topaz's sweating face. '"Real soon"? You're becoming an American, Rowena.'

'Am I hell,' she retorted, smiling at the woman in her lap.

'Are so.'

'Am not.'

'Are so. Jesus! *Jesus! Aaah!*'

'It's OK, Topaz. We're nearly there. They have some of the best anaesthetists in the city,' Rowena said, stroking her hair. 'Try and breathe. Don't they teach you to breathe specially, or something?'

'It's bullshit,' Topaz said through gritted teeth.

'It is?' Rowena asked, trying to take her mind off the pain. *Keep her talking, just keep it going . . .*

'Probably. I skipped most of the classes,' Topaz admitted.

'You always did,' Rowena reminded her.

Topaz managed a grimace. 'Like you were such a dutiful student.'

Rowena kept going as Topaz's grip tightened in anguish round her fist. 'Lectures weren't important. The Union was important,' she said. 'I had my priorities right.'

'Oh! *Santa Maria! Aaah, God.*'

'It's OK, sweetheart. It's OK,' Rowena said, watching her stomach convulse with yet another contraction.

God in heaven, she's gonna give birth on the back seat of this car!

'Run every fucking light! Just get us there!' she yelled at the driver.

'Rowena!' Topaz gasped. 'I'm having twins! I'm having two babies!'

'I know, honey,' Rowena said, holding her as tight as she could. 'I know.'

Michael Krebs heard the news on his car stereo.

'The Wall Street shock of the hour has to be the surprise hostile bid for the South African conglomerate Mansion Industries, owned by the notorious raider Connor Miles,' the DJ said. 'The bid, announced at four dollars thirty per ordinary share, is the work of a complex consortium of investment banks and firms operating in fields where Mansion has interests. It sets a total value of five billion dollars on the deal. So far, Mr Miles himself has refused to comment, but his board has convened an emergency meeting in Manhattan to consider the offer. In a strange twist to the sage, the two largest players in the consortium appear to be American Magazines and Musica Records, both companies recently thought to be targets of Mansion's drive into the media industry. If this is the case, we could be looking at the biggest Pac-man defence in American financial history.'

Without a word Krebs spun the wheel round, took a left, and headed downtown to Maughan Macaskill.

As with every other big moment in his career for the last nine years, he wanted to be with Rowena when this came through.

Backstage at the Globen Arena in Stockholm, Sweden, the Atomic Mass production office was hyping up for the show; Neil George, the tour accountant, was sitting down with the gate receipts, Jack Halpern, the stage manager, was yelling at a bunch of local crew guys who weren't getting the gear up quick enough, and Will Macleod was striding around looking for his boss. Eventually he found her at the main entrance to the venue, negotiating some extra Scandinavian dates with a desperate promoter.

'Four dollars and thirty cents,' Macleod said.

'I was talking,' the promoter said, pissed-off that some great hulking ape was interrupting his urgent pleas to be allowed to schedule even one more gig in the summer break.

'Oh aye?' Macleod replied, with a glare of such ferocity that the promoter physically shrank away from him. 'Well, if we *want* to play a fokkin' giant golfball in July we'll let you know.'

'Will,' reproved Barbara halfheartedly, smoothing down her Norma Kamali pantsuit in an attempt not to laugh. The spherical dome of the Globen did look kind of like a golfball ... Lord, look at Dolph Lystrom's face.

'Four dollars thirty, Barbara,' Macleod said again. 'Josh Oberman just rang the production office and said to tell you right away.'

She looked at him blankly.

'The *price*. Four dollars thirty,' he repeated. 'He said you'd know what he meant –'

'My God! They've actually done it!' the manager exclaimed. 'Didn't Rowena Gordon call?'

'Done what?' Macleod asked.

'Five-billion-dollar deal – I have to get to a phone,' Barbara said, looking about her wildly. *Had they tendered yet?* 'We have millions riding on this.'

'July eighteenth?' offered the promoter, hopefully.

'I don't care if it's Al Pacino. I'm not taking *any* calls, understand?' John Metcalf barked at his secretary. 'I'm in a meeting and I *cannot be disturbed.* The only person I want to speak to is my fiancée.'

'Yes, sir,' she said hastily, closing the door behind her.

The president of Metropolis Studios stared out of his window at the polished Century City offices gleaming in the LA sun. He was almost lightheaded with anger.

No wonder she had to have those three weeks ... Mansion Industries! Five billion dollars! An alliance with American Magazines!

The biggest deal this decade and she tells me nothing!

He recalled with perfect clarity every time he'd sworn at her that there was nothing she could do to save Musica. That resisting Connor Miles was a waste of time.

She must have been laughing her head off. Nothing she could do? They've only blown the guy off the face of the planet . . .

If this buyout came off, John realized with an unpleasant jolt, his wife would be more powerful than he was.

All along he'd encouraged her, been a cheerleader for her, and been happy to have a beautiful woman on his arm who was a success in her own right. But somehow that equation had always included the given fact that he, John Peter Metcalf III, the youngest-ever head of a major studio, would be the really important half of the couple.

What am I gonna be? Trophy husband to a female Rupert Murdoch?

He couldn't even get in contact with her. Rowena's assistant had no idea where she was. Josh Oberman could tell him nothing. And her mobile and car phones were both switched off.

Meanwhile, a hundred calls an hour were coming through to his office from West Coast players who all assumed he knew what the score was.

We're gonna have to talk, Metcalf thought grimly. We are really gonna have to talk . . .

'Any response?' Gowers asked Gerald Quin. The activity level in the dealing room seemed to have gone up several notches; traders were screaming into the phones, the fax machines were spewing paper faster than receipts from a supermarket till, and the Quotron screens were going crazy.

'Very little. Miles is on his way to JFK in his private jet,' the young analyst told him. 'He's saying that he wants time to counter.'

'Does that make a difference?'

'The longer he has to stall, the worse it is for us,' Nick Edward replied.

'We should turn the heat up,' interjected a gravelly voice. Joshua Oberman had wandered over from the end of the room, frustrated at not being able to reach Rowena Gordon. She wasn't answering in her apartment, either. '*We know* this is a generous price for Mansion. It's only worth it to *us* because everyone in the buying group has space for a piece of them.'

'True,' Eli Leber agreed. 'There's no way any bank would support Miles bidding at that price.'

'So what do you suggest?' Quin enquired, humouring the old goat.

'I suggest we call Mansion and tell their board that if we don't have signatures by close of business today, the price becomes four twenty-five dollars. And four twenty at close Monday,' Oberman snapped.

'We can't do that,' Gowers said uncertainly.

'Why not?' Josh Oberman demanded.

Gerry Quin glanced at his boss, feeling the adrenalin crackle around them.

'Why not indeed?' Edward said. 'Gentlemen, let's apply a little pressure.'

Rowena and the terrified driver supported Topaz through the front doors of Mt Sinai, where she was immediately lifted on to a stretcher and rushed off to the maternity ward.

'Don't leave me!' Topaz choked, clutching Rowena's arm as she ran alongside her.

'I'm not going anywhere. I'm staying right here,' she promised, turning to the orderly. 'This is Topaz Rossi. She was planning to have her babies here ... it's twins ... her contractions are about five minutes apart, I think.'

'Who's the husband?' somebody asked.

'Joe –' Topaz moaned.

'Joe Goldstein at NBC,' Rowena said. 'I asked her office to call him but I don't know if he's here ...'

'We'll get in touch,' the nurse said.

'I don't want Rowena to go!' Topaz gasped as they turned into the private maternity wing.

'Can you get her something for the pain?' Rowena asked.

'What the fuck are *you* crying for? *You're* not giving birth,' Topaz said gruffly.

'Try and relax,' the nurse soothed them. 'Everything's gonna be just fine.'

'Want a burger?' Josh Oberman offered Michael Krebs. 'Pizza, Bud, Chinese takeout?'

'No, thanks,' Krebs said, distracted. He looked around him at the chaotic scene in the meeting room. 'What the hell is this?'

'A consortium that's just issued an ultimatum,' Nick Edward told him. 'Welcome to wheeler-dealing.'

'And I thought the record business was full of slobs,' Michael commented. 'Did you get the number of the bus that drove through here?'

'What's the press like outside?' Matt Gowers asked.

'It's a total madhouse,' Krebs replied, grinning. 'Last time I got that much attention I was coming out of a party with Joe Hunter and Cindy Crawford.'

'Where the hell is Topaz Rossi?' seethed the American Magazines chairman.

'Where's Rowena?' Michael asked Josh.

'That's the sixty-four-dollar question,' Oberman said.

Joe Goldstein's heart had never beaten faster. Not when he was a quarterback in school. Not when he was up for his first major job interview. Not even when he'd lost his virginity.

We're having twins! I'm gonna be a father! My god, what if she's already there ...

'I'm having twins,' he said breathlessly to the receptionist. The cab had got stuck in traffic so Goldstein had jumped out and run the last six blocks.

'You are?' he replied, suppressing the laugh. 'Yes, sir. What's your partner's name?'

'Rossi. Topaz Rossi, my wife – I'm Joe Goldstein,' he said.

'Yes, Mr Goldstein, we've been expecting you,' a nurse told him, smiling. 'If you'd just like to follow me.'

'Graham Hackston is on the phone!' somebody yelled.

Instant silence in the dealing room. Hackston was the chairman of the board of Mansion Industries.

An assistant held out the phone towards Matt Gowers and Joshua Oberman, uncertainly.

'Age before beauty,' Oberman said to Matt, grabbing it.

He listened to the voice at the other end for a few seconds. 'In that case, our lawyers will be in touch,' he said calmly. 'Thank you, Graham.'

He hung up and turned to the crowd of businessmen, holding their collective breath like kids on Christmas Eve.

'We nailed the sonofabitch!' he exclaimed.

Joe burst through the door of his wife's delivery room and stopped dead in his tracks.

Topaz was sitting propped up in bed, two minute bundles cradled against each breast, her face transformed with such a look of love that he thought he'd never seen her so beautiful.

She lifted her head as he entered the room. 'We've got a son and a daughter,' she said.

'I love you, Topaz,' said Joe, looking at his family, his eyes filling with tears.

Outside in the corridor, Rowena Gordon found a payphone and rang Josh Oberman on his mobile.

'Josh? Are you at some kind of party?' she asked, hearing wild shrieks in the background.

'Gordon? Is that you?' her chairman demanded. 'Where the fuck have you been all day? Everyone's been trying to get hold of you for ever! I'm at Maughan Macaskill with the whole goddamn team!'

'What? Have we announced a bid?'

'Yes, we announced a bid! We've also given them an ultimatum, forced them to accept, exchanged signatures and *BOUGHT THE COMPANY!*' Oberman half-screamed. 'And you *missed* it!'

She glanced back down towards the delivery room, where Jacob and Rowena Goldstein were being held by their father for the first time.

'No,' she said. 'No, I didn't.'

Epilogue

Rowena and Topaz became close friends.

Matthew Gowers resigned from the chairmanship of American Magazines four months later and named Topaz Rossi his successor, making her one of the most powerful women in journalism. Topaz and Joe continued to adore their children, fight about everything and be madly in love.

The engagement between John Metcalf and Rowena Gordon was cancelled.

Barbara Lincoln divorced Jake Barber, then remarried him. The second time around they were very happy.

Atomic Mass's third album, *Questions*, sold sixteen million copies worldwide.

Joshua Oberman was rushed to hospital in New York a few days after the takeover of Mansion Industries with a heart attack, which he survived. He had been defying doctors' orders to retire for several months, refusing to leave Musica when it was under threat. This time he quit, insisting on signing all his stock over to Rowena Gordon.

'Don't be stupid, Oberman. This is worth millions,' Rowena said, protesting.

'I've got millions. Do what I tell you,' the old man snapped.

'So give it to your family.'

'I am,' Oberman said gruffly.

He came round to Rowena's apartment every Monday for dinner, and rang her every Friday to tell her how she was screwing up.

Rowena Gordon became the first woman in history to be Chief Executive of a major record label. She stopped seeing Michael Krebs.

'I want marriage and a family,' she said. 'I want us to be with each other the way Joe and Topaz are.'

'You know how I feel about that,' Krebs said. 'I care about you, but I just can't do it.'

Rowena nodded. 'I know,' she said. She reached out and stroked his cheek, softly. 'I know. And I'm grateful to you for everything. We'll always be friends.'

'What is this? Goodbye again?' Michael asked, his eyes narrowing. 'You can't be serious. What the hell's changed?'

She shrugged, her eyes bright with tears. 'I saw Joe and Topaz,' she said.

'I'm sorry, Michael. I wish I could separate everything, but I can't. I wish I didn't love you, but I do.'

'I love Debbie,' Krebs said angrily.

'So be with her,' Rowena said. 'I don't want this life anymore.'

Rowena saw Michael often, both socially and over Atomic Mass. She amazed both him and herself by sticking to it this time.

People live without love.

She loved her job, she saw a lot of her friends, and she was happy enough.

It was three years later that Michael Krebs turned up at her door.

'Notice anything different?' he asked.

Rowena looked him over. 'Since last Tuesday? I don't think so. New running shoes?'

Krebs held up both his hands.

For a second, she nearly didn't register.

'Where's your wedding ring?' Rowena asked, feeling her heart stop beating.

'I asked Debbie for a divorce,' Krebs said.

'Why?' asked Rowena, numbly.

'Because I'm in love with you,' Michael said. 'Because I haven't been able to get you out of my head. And because Josh Oberman rang me last week and told me that I'd always loved you and that I was the only person who couldn't see it. He said one day you would just leave, and I'd never see you again, and I thought about it, and it would break my heart.'

'It would?' Rowena repeated, feeling almost faint with joy.

'Yes, it would,' Krebs said dryly, producing a diamond ring. 'So what are you doing for the rest of your life?'

They called their first son Joshua.

The Movie

This book is dedicated to:
Nina Gordon and Louise Post of Veruca Salt,
because I listened to *American Thighs* constantly
whilst writing it;
George Lucas, for making *Star Wars*,
my favourite movie of all time;
and to Patrick Stewart, Henry V in a spacesuit,
for his contribution to Anglo-American relations.

Acknowledgements

I would like to thank my family for their constant support; Tilly, James, Alice, Seffi, and all my aunts, uncles and cousins, but most especially my wonderful mother and father, who have given me their unconditional love all my life, and who always told me that I could do whatever I wanted to. I owe anything I've ever achieved entirely to them.

I also want to thank my friends for alternately holding my hand or kicking my butt, as called for; Peter, Brian, Nigel, Nicky, Aidan, John, Gina, Lizzy, Ion, Fred, Joe, Simon, and the whole gang; and without Barbara Kennedy-Brown, my best friend, all my major female life-support systems would close down.

Most writers are so insecure they make Woody Allen look like Donald Trump, and since I am no exception I'm extremely fortunate to have the world's best and most level-headed agents looking after me; I would like to thank my brilliant agent, Michael Sissons, for everything he has done for me – I am truly more grateful to him than I can describe; my wonderful film and TV agent, Tim Corrie, for his magnificent work on my behalf and his permanently open ear; Fiona Batty, who is always there when I need her; Anthony Gornall at ILA, David Black in New York, and Brian Siberell at CAA for all their efforts.

Orion make publishing an art form. My gratitude is due to the entire team there for all the imagination and creativity they have put behind marketing my novels; I am especially indebted to Susan Lamb, not merely for her ironclad creative and emotional support in mass-market paperbacks, but also for having helped persuade Rosie to sign me up in the first place; Katie Pope for all her help and backup; Caroleen Conquest, for having the patience of Griselda as my copy-editor; Louise Page in publicity; Dallas Manderson in sales for his continual encouragement; and most of all to Rosie Cheetham, my editor, whose advice is always right, who seems to understand what I am trying to say before I can even articulate it myself, and who has been steadfastly supportive and inspirational from the moment I started to plan this novel to the moment the final draft landed on her desk.

1

Megan Silver woke up with an idea worth a million dollars.

Not that she realized it, of course. The excitement sweeping through her, that sweet adrenalin rush, was just a sudden panic to jot something down on paper quickly, to grab what she remembered of the dream before it faded. Groaning, Megan reached blindly for the scruffy notebook and ballpoint pen she kept by her bed, hopefully, in case something like this should ever happen. It never had before.

The pen had rolled onto the floor. Megan patted the dusty wasteland under her bed with one hand, feebly, not wanting to get up to look for it. The pain of her hangover throbbed under her temples, but she didn't care, *couldn't* care, it was such an incredible story, she had to get it down right now.

Thank God, she thought, her fingers closing round the biro.

She grabbed the notebook and began to scribble, long, flowing sentences, her spidery handwriting streaking across the page. Outside her tiny bedroom window the first red streaks of dawn had appeared over the San Francisco skyline.

'He left me,' Declan announced an hour later, marching into her bedroom without knocking. 'Do you hear me? He *left* me.' He struck a pose of exaggerated grief, looking across at his flatmate to check she was suitably shocked.

'Who left you?' Megan murmured, barely looking up from her story. Ripped-up sheets of paper littered the bed, covering the old copies of *Spin* magazine and British music papers she'd been reading last night. She'd been jotting down ideas since she woke up, not stopping to use the bathroom or make a coffee. Like she had time for Dec's crash-and-burn dramatics right now! This story was different to all the others. She was sure about that. She didn't know why, but she was sure.

'Jason,' Declan said, in tones of utter despair. 'We were at The Box last night and he left with somebody else. Some *asshole*,' he added viciously. 'The guy had a crew-cut and a signet ring. A real yuppie.'

Megan smiled despite herself. 'Dec, you've been on exactly three dates with the guy.'

'But I thought he was –'

'The One? You think every guy's The One,' Megan said, putting the notebook down. She'd just about got it now, and anyway, when Declan wanted to talk, he wanted to talk. 'Come on, you don't even care. You just want me to tell you how attractive you are and how you can have anyone you want.'

'That's not true,' Declan said, giving himself a smouldering glance in the mirror. 'Although I have put on weight lately. Does it show?'

Megan sighed, turning her full attention to the sculpture of masculine beauty that was Declan Heath. Wiry, muscular torso, thin and fit from dancing all night on Ecstasy. Eyes the colour of Irish mist with silver-grey lashes to match. Black hair curling loose round the nape of the neck in accepted Generation X style. Totally gorgeous, totally unavailable. Like just about everything she wanted in life.

'No,' she said. 'But you look great anyway.'

'Why don't you get dressed?' Dec suggested. 'We could go down to Ground Zero and get coffee ... don't look at me like that, I got paid yesterday. I'll buy. OK?'

He sauntered out of her bedroom, and seconds later she heard 'Mountain Song' by Jane's Addiction flood the tiny flat.

Megan got dressed, not wanting to face the day. She felt like shit after last night and she dreaded whatever the post was about to bring – another bill, another sheaf of rejection letters from New York agents, or worse, the printed rejection slips from publishers attached to the top of her thick manuscripts by a single paperclip, the only acknowledgment of eight solid months of work. Sometimes it was so tough to be hopeful. She'd worked so hard on that novel – nights, weekends, whatever time she could sneak out of her dismal $10 an hour job at the library – and it seemed like it was being turned down by more people than she'd even sent it to.

In a way, it was uncool to care. The slacker generation wasn't supposed to give a damn about material success. You needed some kind of job to get by, just enough money to pay for the essentials, like coffee and music and clubs and speed, but that was about it. Megan and Declan could cover a tiny rent between them, afford minimal amounts of food, and dressed at the hippest thrift stores in San Francisco – Wasteland and AAadvark's on Haight, Hunter's Moon on Valencia in the Mission district. They got into most clubs for free and went to every chic gig in the city. Declan was a failed artist and part-time comic store sales assistant, and Megan was a failed writer and part-time filing clerk at the public library. They *defined* style.

Except that Megan Silver was getting sick of style. She wanted someone besides Dec to read her book.

She dressed in seconds, snatching her oversized Levi's from the floor where she'd left them last night, belting them over a Soundgarden shirt and pulling on large, clumpy biker boots. No make-up, but she finished the effect with two armfuls of jangling copper bracelets and a heavy crystal ring. Megan didn't have that many clothes, so choosing an outfit never took long. Whatever she had that was clean lay strewn casually about the bombsite that was her room, over the bed and the tatty Indian rug, under her beloved posters of Nirvana and Veruca Salt and Dark Angel. Dark Angel was her favourite band; their huge, bleak soundscapes had been the backdrop to her college years, the hammerhead rhythms and black harmonies firing her up when she worked, lamenting with her when depression bit, slipping under her skin when she made love. A superband for the late nineties, the soundtrack of the generation.

They'd split up last week, and Megan felt ridiculously upset about it. Not that she'd been the only one – Sasha Stone, a friend of Declan's, had sat in front of them in the Horseshoe Café and sobbed her heart out, mascara running down her cheeks in grimy black rivulets.

'Come on, this is embarrassing,' Megan had said, trying to get Sasha to accept a tissue. 'They're just one band.'

'Don't be bourgeois,' Declan snapped, flinging a velvet-covered arm round her shaking shoulders. 'It's serious. All art is serious.'

'Zach!' sobbed Sasha wildly. 'Zach Mason totally betrayed everybody who believed in him!'

'He was a singer, not the Messiah,' Megan said, rather coldly. 'And you wouldn't be so upset if you didn't want to screw him so badly. He'll make some solo records, I guess.'

'Do you think so?' Sasha gulped hopefully.

'Jesus Christ, how *old* are you?'

'Megan,' said Declan. 'Sasha is hurting here! Show a little compassion.'

'Nobody died,' Megan muttered, rebelliously.

How old was Sasha? Wasn't the real question, how old was *she*? Twenty-four and not a damn thing to show for it, except an English degree from Berkeley. And here she was, sitting in a café with an adult woman who was cracking up because a rock group had disbanded.

That was the day when the restlessness had started to creep back in.

Megan twisted in front of the mirror, semi-satisfied. She looked good. Nothing special, but pretty good. She had soft chestnut hair curling gently down to the nape of the neck, clever brown eyes, a clear skin rendered somewhat pallid from too much partying all night and sleeping all day. Underneath the funky, shapeless uniform she'd pulled together her body was nicely curved in an unfashionable way: swelling breasts, feminine calves, maybe a little chunky round the thighs, weight she had never been able to shake. Megan was glad of the hip-hop culture and its outsize style. She hated her body. Most days she hated her looks; OK, so she wasn't exactly ugly, but amongst all the golden California butterflies she was a death's-head moth. Invisible.

It had been like that since the day she was born, youngest of six in a Catholic household in Sacramento, one more mouth to feed for an overworked electrician and a harassed mother who found it hard to cope. Not that she'd been abused or neglected, but they just didn't have much time or attention for her. Megan was no beauty, like her twin sisters Jane and Lucy, slim and lithe as gazelles, nor a strapping sporty guy like her three elder brothers, Martin, Peter and Eli. Not ugly enough to inspire pity, not smart enough to inspire concern, Megan grew up dating the OK guys Jane and Lucy didn't want, and making average grades, and resenting the hell out of everybody, all the time. When she did scrape into Berkeley, Megan Silver suspected that the congratulations of her family had been mingled with relief that she was leaving Sacramento.

Well, that's mutual, Megan thought angrily, tugging the Soundgarden shirt more loosely over her waist. If I never see that dump again it'll be too soon. Why should I stay and rot in Sacramento?

When you could come here and rot in San Francisco? finished the snide, carping little voice in her brain.

'Are you ready?' Declan yelled. 'We'll be late.'

She took one last look at herself, shrugged, and went to join him.

'We already are,' she murmured.

Everybody struggled out of bed at eleven, the days they didn't have to work, and sometimes on the days they did; Jesus, if you believed all the excuses and hacking coughs that went singing down the phone wires to employers every morning, you'd think a serious epidemic had afflicted San Francisco's twentysomething population. Mostly, the bosses rarely complained. What they were offering was dead-end jobs paying little more than minimum wage, hardly worth coming off welfare for; what they were getting was sullen, unproductive employees who knew their worth and thus sold themselves cheap. Everybody's just marking time, Megan thought, as they strolled up Haight towards Ground Zero. Like time will last forever.

It was quarter of twelve, and the cold mist was just beginning to clear, melting away in the thin autumn sun. Declan strutted down the street, waving and smiling at all their friends hanging out; Haight truly was the centre of his universe, Megan thought, smiling affectionately at her friend. *He never feels hemmed in. Why should he? This is more than enough for Dec ... Why can't it be enough for me?*

'Hey, Megan! Hey, Dec! What's up?'

Trey, Declan's best friend and ex-lover, waved at them from an inside table, and they threaded their way through the usual crowd to join him: beat poets, bikers, art students, potheads, and the occasional brave tourist from Europe. Megan had once seen Ground Zero listed in a student guidebook as 'the official café of the Apocalypse', a description that always made her laugh.

'Ola, what's up?' Trey said. 'Megan, Dec, this is Francine, Rick and Consuela. Consuela's a model,' he added, showing off. Trey collected cool people as if they were stamps.

Megan glanced at her as she sat down; silken olive skin, a little button nose, chic hair in a sleek bob, and no more than 105 pounds under that Nirvana jacket. Consuela didn't have the exquisite bone structure you really needed to make it in modelling – Megan could see that right off – but what did that matter? She was beautiful, confident, everything Megan had never been. When Consuela decided to get down to work, she'd have it easy. She would not wind up working at the San Francisco Public Library part-time for ten bucks an hour.

'Hi,' Consuela said.

'Megan's a writer. A *novelist*,' Trey told the others, exhibiting her for their approval.

'A novelist? Wow, that's so cool,' Francine sighed, laconically, not meaning a word of it.

'I'm not a novelist. I'm a filing clerk,' Megan said coldly, ignoring the furious gestures being semaphored across the table from Declan.

'Oh, she only says that because the big corporations haven't sent her a fat cheque yet,' he explained. 'You should be pleased they haven't let you sign your soul away.'

'Declan's an artist,' said Trey.

Declan preened. 'Of course, *life* is art,' he acknowledged modestly. 'I just express it as best I can.'

'Cool,' said Rick, not looking up from his coffee.

'I guess the only reason they haven't signed you is that they don't understand artistic integrity,' Consuela said to Megan, soothingly.

'How would you know?' asked Megan, pushing her fringe out of her eyes. 'You've never even seen my book.'

'Megan!' Declan hissed.

'Actually, they haven't signed me because my book sucks,' Megan went on relentlessly. In that moment, she knew it was true. Realization hit her like a flash of lightning; her mannered, meandering study of teenage ennui, which she had thought was poetic and evocative, was in fact stunningly boring.

'Why did you write it then?' asked Francine, stung to hostility.

Trey leaned forward, in hopeful anticipation of a scene.

'I have no idea,' Megan replied, shrugging. She felt lighthearted and free, somehow. It felt good to admit that, something she'd maybe known all along; she'd written to a blueprint her friends would approve of, eschewing such outdated concepts as plot, and the result had been just terrible.

'So what will you do now you aren't a writer?' demanded Francine, bitchily.

Megan looked at them all: so fly, so hip, so laid-back they were practically horizontal. Going nowhere fast.

Then she thought of her dream, the new story, the adventure, lying in her bedroom in twenty pages of scrawled notes.

'I *am* a writer,' she said. 'I'm just going to do it better. I'm going to write a movie.'

2

The excitement was so strong you could almost taste it.

Right now, Alessandro Eco *ruled* fashion. Where he led, the press followed panting. He was this year's brilliant new discovery, the darling of the demimonde, the first real superdesigner to shoot to fame since the meteoric rise of Donna Karan. *Vogue, Harper's, Elle, Style with Elsa Klensch* – you name it, they all swooned over his tight bodices, sculptured heels, clever little bias-cut skirts, the dramatic choice of fabrics, the way he *owned* colour, darling, it was simply too wonderful . . .

Real women loved Alessandro too. His clothes, and the cheaper knockoffs of them that reached the high street two seasons late, flattered curves, rejoiced in breasts, and forgave a multitude of sins around the thigh area. Last year every working woman had saved for that one Alessandro suit, every socialite had themed her wardrobe around him, and every teenager had bought their copy of *Vogue* and fantasized. It was fashion's version of the American Dream – that one collection by an unknown that takes the world by storm.

That was the first reason everybody was here. In *Chicago*, for God's sake. Paris, New York, Milan, even London at a pinch, but Chicago? Surely only Alessandro would dare. It was a power trip, pure and simple, for Alessandro Eco to show his summer collection – just one designer, mark you – in Chicago and expect the entire aristocracy of style to rearrange their travel itineraries around him.

Which was where the second reason kicked in.

Fashion editors and photographers milled around, mingling with famous Hollywood actors, minor European royalty, rock stars escorting their model girlfriends. The Leeward Hall was packed to the gills, bubbling with excited talk and reeking of perfume, spotlights and money. Behind the front row seats reserved for the serious players, anorexic-looking wives of Wall Street tycoons fought bitterly over the exact positions of their little gold-backed chairs. It was important to be noticed, vital to be seen. Because it wasn't merely Alessandro's new collection that was on offer here. Millions of dollars had gone into ensuring that this collection would have the eyes of the entire world trained upon it. And in the 1990s, there was only one way to do that.

Supermodels. *All* of them. It was a coup unparalleled in the history of fashion, and Lord alone knew what it had cost, but Eco's people had done the impossible, obtaining every single one for the same show. Security was tight enough for the President of the United States. If this hall was bombed tonight, the most beautiful flowers that the Western world had discovered would all be crushed together.

Cindy. Linda. Naomi. Eva. Saffron. Nadja. Shalom. It was a pantheon of goddesses, beauty in its most ideal form, from all age groups, all body types. (Jerry was returning to do this one show, that was the rumour, and there was Mick in the centre front row, sitting right next to Oprah, so it must be true!) Helena, Christy, Claudia, Isabella, Yasmin! The list went on forever! Paulina, Shiraz, Lauren, Tatijana, Kate ... if she had graced the cover of a major magazine, she would be there, a blossoming supernova, when the moment came, amongst the lesser stars that would glitter, only fractionally less beautiful, up and down the runway in a constant, seamless slipstream of perfection.

It was even being hinted that *she* might appear.

A fresh wave of suspense swept the room. The big chandelier lights faded to black, leaving the stage darkened apart from a single beige spotlight, selected from the hundreds rigged at the top of the ceiling, filtered with all the different colours of the rainbow. The only sound was the heavy, excited breathing of the spectators and the hushed whirr of TV cameras, positioned around the runway and suspended from the walls. The vast screens erected at either side of the catwalk were dull and dead.

They waited.

And then, with the perfect synchronicity of a ballet, Aretha Franklin blasted from the Siemens speakers lining every wall, the stage erupted in an explosion of coloured lights, rose petals fluttered down from the ceiling, and the first figure strutted, alone, onto the catwalk.

Naomi! It was Naomi! Opening the show in a long white dress, a formal evening gown, the last thing anybody had expected from Alessandro, but too perfect, backless and gathered, an exquisite contrast against the rich chocolate of her skin ...

Pent-up anticipation was released in an orgasmic frenzy of applause, popping flashbulbs, scribbling pens. They were in seventh heaven! And now Tatijana, in a black leather jacket and shining blue pants – what were they made of? Vinyl? Spandex? The fashion editors gave a common sigh of satisfaction. So it *had* been worth cutting Paris short. This season, at least, the king would not be dethroned.

'She won' do it, she say she won' do it!' Alessandro moaned, his words a wail of despair. He could hardly be heard in the commotion that was backstage, the supermodel sisterhood greeting each other raucously, the less famous models panicking about their hairpieces and bitching because a favoured stylist had hung a jacket wrong; the blare of the music, the din of joy and hysteria, and at least two hairdressers in tears, and Michael Winter, Alessandro's PA, had to strain to catch him. 'I cannot believe it! She is promised me, now, for two months! She will be the finale, she will make the show live forever! But now she will not come out! She will not do it! She has ruin everything, everything I work for for so long!'

'The show will live forever anyway,' Michael soothed him loudly, shouting above the noise. 'They love you, Alessandro! They're going crazy for the girls and crazy for your clothes. Like we planned. It is *perfetto*.' He kissed his fingertips in an extravagant gesture of reassurance.

The designer grabbed his lapels. '*Non es perfetto*,' he yelled. 'It is good! OK, this I understand! But it is not *perfect*! *It has to be perfect!*' He took a breath, and Michael winced; the veins on his boss's neck were standing out like whipcords.

'*Michèle*, they are vultures! They expect only the best, and if they do not get it, they will turn on me! Don't you understand? Now, yes, now they clap, now they are happy to see all the girls ... but if she does not appear, later, after the show, that is when the doubts come in. That we are *nearly* good enough, but not quite ... not good enough for *her*.'

Michael paused, unwilling to accept that possibly, just possibly, Eco was right. He had always admired Alessandro for his street-smarts and above all, for realizing that great clothes – even inspired clothes – were just half the battle. Fashion was just that. Fashion. Style. *Showbusiness*. And by promising to deliver all the world's most beautiful women, all wearing Alessandro, they'd taken a huge PR gamble. If it worked, the company name could be shot to a level where it would sit alongside not Katharine Hamnett or Ralph Lauren, but Chanel, Gucci and Christian Dior. That was the Holy Grail; to be so big no fashion ed could shoot you down.

But maybe they wouldn't get there. A show this expensive was one hell of a PR stunt, and it had better work. And if the focus was not on the girls who were there, but on the one girl who *wasn't* ...

Winter shuddered. 'Why won't she do it?'

'She is lock herself in her dressing room, she is refusing to come out,' snarled Alessandro. 'She not tell me why. I hate her. She is a grade-A bitch.'

'You got that right.'

'*Michèle*. I want you to find her agent,' snapped Alessandro, his English miraculously improving under pressure. 'Promise him anything he wants. Anything at all. We need her for the finale, and we must have her.'

'Babe, please.'

Robert Alton knelt in front of the door, models tripping over his calves as they rushed to the stage and the eyes of several amused cameramen boring into the back of his head. Sweat trickled down his pudgy neck and ran in nasty little rivulets under his collar. His career was flashing in front of his eyes.

'Sweetheart?' he tried again, yelling, his plump little chin pressed close to the keyhole.

'Get lost, Robert,' snapped the voice inside. 'I have no desire to talk to you whatsoever.'

A couple of the cameramen sniggered, and Robert felt the familiar well of hatred and humiliation boil up inside him.

'Honey, I know you like to be private, but we really have to do this show.'

'*We* don't have to do anything.'

It was a sweet voice, the tones low and dulcet, but packed with such venom that even her agent, used to it, took a step back.

'We're committed. We took a million dollars in fee.'

'You mean *you're* committed. You put the dress on, Bob. You'll probably really enjoy it.'

Bitch! Bitch! Bitch! God, how he loathed her!

'Alessandro is tearing his hair out, babe. You know that the whole deal will be nothing without you. Please, angel, everybody's counting on you.'

'We all have our problems.' A beat. 'And he has enough stars out there. He doesn't need me. There are a million girls. Tell him to use Cindy for the finale.'

Was that it? Alton felt a surge of hope at the faint chink in her armoury. A drowning man, grateful for a straw to clutch at, he thought bitterly.

'Stars? Those are *ornaments!*' he yelled contemptuously, praying to Christ that nobody heard him. Elite and Models One would put a contract out on him if they did. 'There's only *one* star here, sugar, and she won't come out of her dressing room. Cindy won't do, you know that. Christy, Claudia? Phhh!' He made what he hoped was a suitably dismissive noise.

'It won't work, Bob. I don't do cattle calls. Not even with a superior grade of cattle,' she shouted, ice dripping from every melodious syllable.

Cattle calls! Alton thought, picturing the cream of the world's superstar beauties pirouetting on the catwalk behind him. But he was encouraged. Half the battle was always finding out exactly what type of reassurance she needed that day, what precise homage she wanted to extract.

'Sweetie, think of it this way. You aren't working the main show, you're only coming on for the finale. You'll be right in the centre front of all the girls. Everybody out there is waiting, hoping, *praying* that you'll appear' – me especially, since I'm finished if you don't, he added silently – 'and they'll go just crazy when you do. Just for that one time.'

'They always go crazy,' came the bored reply, but he thought he detected an infinitesimal softening.

'Of *course* they go crazy. Who wouldn't go crazy for you, babe, if you showed up wearing a sack?' Or a body bag, preferably. 'But the point is that you'll be leading them all out. Just *once*. In *front*. For the *finale*.' Robert took a deep breath, and played his ace.

'It'll make it official, as if the world didn't already know – that you rule them *all*. It will be' – he paused dramatically – 'your *coronation*.'

Silence.

What was she thinking? Alton loosened his collar, nervous tension eating away at his stomach like corrosive acid. He could almost see his ulcer expanding under the pressure. Did she like that idea? Did she *agree* with it?

As much as he hated this woman – and oh, boy, did he ever hate her – Robert had come to understand that there was a fierce intelligence burning under that lovely cranium. You could slip nothing past her, *nothing*. If she did something he suggested, it was because she'd already decided it was a good idea. Independent. Astute. Determined. And if she wanted something badly enough, he'd learned, there was no point standing in her way. You'd be better off arguing with a ten-ton truck.

'OK, I'll do it,' she shouted.

The agent practically sobbed with relief.

'On one condition. I don't lead out the finale, I *am* the finale. Just me, by myself. None of the other girls.'

Robert wanted to throw up. 'But sugar, that's impossible! Everything's already rehearsed! You can't expect Naomi and Kate to sit still for that – '

'Kate? Why are you mentioning her name to me, Bob? I thought I told you never to discuss that anorexic washboard in front of me again.'

Mistake. Mistake. His circuits were flashing red alert.

'Honey, I'm sorry, but – '

'No, Bob. No buts. And let me tell you what's impossible. What's impossible is that I appear in this show unless it's for the *finale* and by *myself*. OK? Am I being clear enough? Now you run along to Alessandro and tell him what I said. And if he doesn't like it, call my driver, because I'm going home.'

The silken voice was threaded with absolute steel.

'Do you understand?' she demanded.

Robert Alton fumbled with his collar again, but nothing could ease this choking panic. He knew that tone. It was the end of the line.

'Sure, sweetheart,' he shouted through the keyhole. 'I understand.'

'Is this a joke?' enquired Michael Winter, glancing at his watch. The show was running on perfect time, down to the split second. They had ten minutes to the finale, and she wasn't even in make-up yet.

Robert spread his fat hands in a well-worn gesture of helplessness. 'No. She doesn't joke, as I'm sure you're aware,' he said.

'Unique took a million-dollar appearance fee on her behalf.'

'And we'll refund it if she doesn't appear,' Alton said with a sigh.

Winter glared at him. The fee wasn't an issue, and both men knew it. A million dollars was pocket change, compared with what might happen to Alessandro Eco's company if this show crashed and burned.

'Can't you guys control your clients? For the biggest show of the goddamn decade?'

Robert Alton looked him straight in the eye. 'Michael. Please,' he said. 'Nobody, and I do mean *nobody*, can control *her*.'

Nine minutes and counting.

'So you're telling me that I have to personally insult – to *demote* – eighteen of the most famous models in the world, in front of the entire fashion media, just so Her Majesty will walk down that catwalk for *thirty seconds*?'

A fresh burst of perspiration beaded Alton's neck. Winter was quite correct, of course. These backstage shenanigans would leak down to the hawks sitting out front at the speed of light. She was demanding that Alessandro snub every supermodel alive, in public, in her favour.

'That's what I'm telling you,' he said firmly.

Eight minutes and thirty seconds.

Michael Winter glanced at his watch. Either way they would only just make it. The pressure of the decision beat down on the back of his shoulders like a lead weight.

'OK,' he said. 'Tell Her Highness she's got a deal.'

Rapt, the audience, the cream of the glitterati, stared hopefully at the empty stage. Notebooks were covered in scrawls thick with underlinings and multiple exclamation marks. The T-shirt dresses, sculptured bodices and flowing coats in waterproof silk had all been sensations. The swimwear line added a whole new dimension to thigh-lines, and he'd come up with some amazing bias-cutting in the evening gowns that turned the demurest walk into a lilting dance, the tiniest movement setting off a tide of motion in the skirts. But that was hardly the point...

It was the reams of film their photographers had shot that sent moist twitches between the fashion editors' legs. That was what would sell magazines; the show as event, Alessandro as king of babe city. Kate in a strawberry satin dress that was really a T-shirt with pretensions. Goddess-like Cindy in a simple black swimsuit that would make every woman who saw it join a gym the next day. Jerry's blonde cascade tumbling around a severe tailored pantsuit. Yasmin, regal and aloof in a full evening gown with a crinoline skirt. Awesome! No other word for it.

And now the finale...

The room was thick with the sound of held breath, the photographers nervously jockeying for position. Every supermodel in the world had graced this show – with one exception. As each song shifted pace, as each new set of outfits debuted on the catwalk, they had expected to see her. But nothing.

Surely now would be the moment. With mounting excitement, the eagle eyes of the journos were trained on the black-curtained entrance to the runway, their talons scenting blood. She had triumphed yet again. God knew how, but somehow Unique had swung it. Their mega-client would appear only in the grand finale, setting herself, by definition, in a class of her own, outranking every supermodel in the world. Perhaps she would lead all the models out, or was that expecting too much? When all that female loveliness poured out together onto Alessandro Eco's catwalk, would she slip in with the others? Or would she try some new trick, some little fillip, that would 'spontaneously' catch the eye of every camera in the place?

The Leeward Hall shivered in anticipation.

There was a slight rustle of velvet at the side of the stage and Alessandro Eco, his aristocratic face reflecting nothing but the profoundest calm, stepped forward to a microphone, holding up one imperious hand in silence before the room could explode into applause.

'Ladies and gentlemen, it has been great honour for the House of Alessandro Eco to present our collection for you tonight. For your attendance and patience, I thank you.' He gave a courtly bow. 'As you may know, I have, since I was a boy, cherished the dream of one day being like the great masters – Balenciaga, Dior, Chanel – who in our modern age paid the beauty of woman the homage it deserves, a homage I attempt, all my life, to pay. The moment of greatest loveliness for woman is surely the day of her wedding, and traditionally the couturiers present last the wedding dress, a tradition I am proud to continue.'

The spotlight on the designer faded gently away, and one by one the other lights in the hall were shut down and dimmed until the stage was plunged into darkness. A haunting line of Mozart spun into the still air.

And then the curtains drew back, a web of brilliant lights lit up the platform – but instead of thirty models exploding onstage a single figure appeared from the darkness, stepping demurely into the spotlight. A simple shift of cream silk clung to her perfect body like a second skin, a bouquet of pure ivory lilies was clasped in her delicate hands and a single white rose threaded through her long, dark hair as she processed slowly, gracefully, down the front of the stage onto the catwalk.

For a second there was complete silence, as the crowd was struck dumb by her sheer beauty, by the fragile, nervous, virginal quality of her walk, the way she seemed to glance shyly out at them from under those doelike chocolate eyes, as though completely overwhelmed by the attention. Then, as the fashion world realized what they were witnessing, the hall erupted in an orgasmic frenzy of cheering and applause. The fashion editors were shooting to their feet in a standing ovation, the photographers snapping and snapping, flashbulbs exploding around her for the one picture that would make the front page of about every tabloid in the Western world the next day – the magnificent, minimalist finale of Alessandro Eco, now without the shadow of a doubt Designer of the Year, and the best PR coup for any mannequin this decade – to oust eighteen other supermodels, to appear for just these few moments, to close the show herself, as though it was she, and only she, that they had all been waiting for . . .

As she walked gracefully out towards the frenzy in front of her, Roxana Felix permitted herself a tiny smile.

'Roxana!'

'Rox! Rox!'

'Roxana, *please*! Just for one second!'

They were everywhere, clamouring for her attention, begging for the tiniest hint of a smile or a glance – reporters from the favoured shows and magazines, trade photographers, the normal fashion camp-followers. Backstage was a battleground as people scrambled for a word from Christy, a comment from Naomi, a precious shot of any supermodel in glorious *déshabillée*. But by far the largest cluster of drones hovered around Roxana Felix, undisputed Queen Bee. Disgusted, numbers of the other girls were leaving, with a curt 'no comment' and frantic agents trailing in their wake.

'Never again will she work for me,' hissed a distraught Alessandro to Michael Winter as another beauty swept past him, tiny button nose in the air. '*Michèle*, that bitch spill blood over all my collection – never another cover girl weel wear my clothes. All I hear, all I see is controversy!'

'Yeah? All *I* hear is cash tills,' replied Winter, a wide grin plastered across his tanned face. 'Controversy and coverage are synonymous in *Webster's*, amigo. Didn't you know that?'

'Roxana, did you know in advance that Alessandro would cancel the other girls for the finale?' somebody asked.

Pushing a lock of glossy raven hair out of her sparkling eyes, the young woman laughed softly. 'He did *what*? Damian, you've got it wrong. It must have been planned that way.'

'No, everybody was pulled in your favour,' another hack told her eagerly.

Roxana's sculptured cheekbones and smooth pale skin registered nothing but confusion for a few moments, while the pack bayed its assurances that she had been honoured above the rest. Then a delightful girlish blush spread across her face, and she dropped those infamous lashes, murmuring helplessly, 'Look, I don't know, you guys. Robert handles business,' and every man in the room was in love again.

'Robert Alton, was it your idea to insist on the change in choreography?'

'Absolutely,' Alton said easily. He was almost enjoying himself. In her eagerness to pass the buck, his vicious little cash-cow was turning him into a powerful Svengali of the beau monde. Surely other stars would flock to him now, he thought, and then recalled with a pang that Roxana didn't allow him to rep any other big stars.

'Why? Didn't you realize you'd be upsetting some of the most powerful women in fashion?'

Alton placed a fatherly hand on Roxana's alabaster shoulder, felt her stiffen under his touch and instantly withdrew it. 'It wasn't about egos,' he said shamelessly, 'it was about the clothes. I felt that no one but the most beautiful girl in the world should close the best show in the world.'

'Oh, Bob, really,' Roxana reproved him, in low tones of molten honey.

'Were you trying to say that Roxana is in a class of her own, like Alessandro is in a class of his own?' suggested a girl from English *Vogue* hopefully.

'No comment,' said Robert sternly, treating them all to a flamboyant wink.

'Enough, enough, please, *signoras, signori,*' Alessandro insisted, knowing a good exit line when he heard one. 'My little *bambina* is exhausted. You know how she hate publicity. Please, this way, we have much champagne...'

Roxana Felix exchanged little kisses, pressures and hugs with the favoured few as they trooped dutifully off in search of liquid and more basic refreshments, confusion and embarrassment at causing such a fuss written all over her face. As soon as the door to her dressing room closed she pulled out a small bag of white powder from her blusher box and licked a minute pile off the back of her tiny wrist, perfect bones almost translucent under the skin. Alton eyed it hungrily: the new form of ground Ecstasy that was all the rage at the shows this summer. She made no move to offer him any.

'A triumph, if I say so myself,' he announced.

'You had nothing to do with it, Bob. Play the big guy with the schmucks out there, but never try and scam *me* for credit. OK? Cause you'll be fired faster than an AK-47.'

'OK, OK,' Alton said, forcing a grin through the shame. Long ago she had cut off his balls to play marbles with. 'You're right, sweetie, of course you are. You just added another thirty thou to every single shoot.'

'Fifty.'

'Fifty, right,' Alton concurred, wondering if Madonna's manager took as much shit as he did.

'I'm not interested in that. You know what I'm interested in,' Roxana said, slowly and with menace, turning those limpid chocolate eyes at him as though they were bayonet blades. 'Have you found me a suitable vehicle yet?'

Alton twisted helplessly. 'Didn't you get *Beach Party II*? I had it messengered over.'

She gave a delicate little cough. 'Let me see. *Beach Party II*. The part was for the stupid bimbo who dates the lifeguard. Yeah, I remember that one. It came right after *Living Doll* and *Sweet Sixteen*, the ones Unique sent me last week.'

Her agent swallowed hard.

'Don't bother to send me any more scripts, Bob.'

'Honey, I knew you'd see reason. Those parts aren't worthy of you, I know that, but it's all we could come up with – lots of girls have dabbled in acting, but the studios just aren't interested . . .' Seeing her expression, his voice trailed away.

'You're fired,' Roxana Felix said calmly.

Alton almost choked in surprise and dismay. He had discovered Roxana and repped her for the last five years.

'What?'

'Lost your hearing, Bob? I said you're *fired*. As my personal agent and personal manager.'

Robert Alton's pudgy face had gone ash-grey. Over the years Roxana had demanded the removal of every other star model the Unique agency represented, for the privilege of controlling all aspects of her own career – the lucrative T-shirts, the calendars, the straight campaigns, catwalk appearances, the perfume franchise . . . it had been done so slowly and subtly that none of his colleagues had really noticed, but the Unique agency *was* Roxana, Inc. Without her they were nothing. A handful of bread-and-butter girls with no star potential in sight.

'I told you two months ago I wanted to act. And I do mean *act*, Bobby, not drape myself over some moron in a teen beach flick.'

'But the other girls – '

Roxana sighed, a deep, whistling sigh drawn in through her perfectly applied soft berry lipstick. 'How many times, Bob? I am not "the other girls". Something that SKI never failed to realize.'

SKI? She was going to Sam Kendrick? Bob felt a fresh burst of sweat erupt down his collar. He could not believe this was happening.

'I've been talking to a guy called David Tauber over there. He's young, he's lean and he's hungry. My plane leaves for LA at ten tomorrow.'

'Please,' Bob managed. 'Roxana, just give us one more chance.'

Laughing at him, Roxana Felix shook her lovely head. 'No way, Bobby boy. There are no second chances with me. You think you can treat me like a piece of pretty meat, just because I'm a woman? You have another think coming.'

'Roxana, *please*,' Bob repeated desperately. He was begging her now, and they both knew it.

'Relax. You can still book my modelling activities.'

Alton almost wept with relief.

'For the moment,' she added icily. A pleasant feeling began to contract in her upper arms, the first sign of the drug kicking in. She wanted to be alone to enjoy it. 'Get out. Bob. And tell the driver to make sure my car is ready at eight.'

'Yes, sweetheart,' Alton said meekly, the useless sack of lard. Jesus Christ, what she had to put up with. Roxana stared coldly at him until the door to her dressing room closed and she was finally alone.

Her painted nail tapped gently on the first-class ticket to Los Angeles pinned up on the mirror in front of her.

This was going to be fun.

She was Roxana Felix, and she always got what she wanted.

3

Eleanor Marshall was the most powerful woman in LA.

That was the thought that kept drumming away at the back of Sam Kendrick's mind as he turned his steel-blue Maserati into the agency parking lot, the velvet-smooth handling of the big machine slipping him into his acre-wide parking space with its usual grace. Nearly every other space in the lot was already full, but that fact scarcely registered on Sam. It was seven-thirty in the morning, and he expected his damn offices to be full. Never mind that the contracts stated nine to six. If you wanted to work for Sam Kendrick International, the third most powerful agency in Hollywood, you'd better be there by seven and you'd better not leave till ten.

Out of the corner of his eye Sam recognized David Tauber's neat Lamborghini parked in the space directly opposite his. It was the best unreserved space in the lot, which meant that David Tauber had got there first. Probably around five-thirty a.m. He smiled briefly; Tauber had wanted him to notice that, and he had. Of course. After twenty-five years as an agent, Samuel J. Kendrick II had acquired the habit of noticing pretty much everything. So Tauber – young, hungry, ambitious – was already fluent in Hollywood's secret code. *Look, boss, I was in first.* Well, OK, kid, Sam thought, dismissing it. David Tauber wasn't important right now. Eleanor Marshall was.

Don't sweat the small stuff, and remember, it's all small stuff. The nineties' stress-relief phrase of choice. Sam snorted: they were wrong on two counts. One, 'Don't sweat the small stuff' wasn't a pressure valve, it was a commandment. If you sweated the small stuff, you were dead. You'd drown. Two, it wasn't all small stuff. Some of it was very big stuff indeed, and if you planned on being a player it was highly advisable to know the difference.

Focus, focus, focus. Something else he'd learnt. In this town, where everybody had a million projects a day, focus was absolutely key. If you had a big star, satisfy that star first. If there was a bidding war for some hot property – be that a script, an actor or a director – aim your fire at that until the opposition were blown away. Maybe he didn't return a couple calls he should have for a couple days. So? That's what kids like Tauber were for. And if you had a major problem, you thought about nothing else and concentrated on nothing else until that problem was solved.

Sam Kendrick International had a major problem. But after five days of brainstorming ways to get around it, his reliable subconscious had started coming up with suggestions. And the first suggestion was Eleanor Marshall.

'Mr Kendrick, Mrs Kendrick called from the country club about catering for your party next week. Mr Ovitz's office called ten minutes ago. Fred Florescu rang at seven-fifteen,' said Karen, his assistant, briskly. She had learnt long ago not to waste Sam's time with 'Good morning' or other pleasantries of that sort. 'Plus thirty or so more which I've prioritized on your desk. Debbie has clipped the trades and the papers for you. Joanie has stacked most of the mail, there's just the Zach Mason contract and the coverage on *Hell's Daughter* that you might want to check out yourself. And everyone's ready for the meeting at eight.'

Kendrick nodded absently. 'Fred called, huh? That's good. I'll get back to him and CAA now. You can call my wife and tell her that whatever she wants is fine by me.'

He tried not to show his annoyance. How many times did he have to tell Isabelle not to bother him at the office with this dumb domestic trivia? As if he had ever given two pins for what interior designer they used, which benefit they attended or whatever idiotic food fad was being served up on smart LA tables that week. Of course, Isabelle lived for that stuff. No, the calls were a power play, pure and simple. She liked asserting her position, knowing that no matter what superstar or studio head was trying to reach him, she would always be put through first, her call would always be on top of the pile.

Kendrick strode down the soft grey carpeting of the corridor towards his offices. You had to pass through three outer rooms, each with its own secretary and personal assistant, before you gained entrance to the inner sanctum. Standard super-agent fare, but also, these days, pretty necessary. It was barely half-seven, and he'd already had thirty calls.

'Good morning, Mr Kendrick.'

'Morning, Sam. Looking good.'

'Great to see you, boss.'

Agents and assistants passed him, smiling, waving, kissing ass. Only to be expected. At SKI, Sam Kendrick was king. He'd ceased to be tickled by the routine morning contest to catch his eye.

Reaching his office, Kendrick slipped into his black leather Eames chair and reached for the phone without looking at it, a reflex movement. He left a message for Mike Ovitz – Christ knew when the two of them would ever get five minutes free at the same time – and tried Fred Florescu at home. The hottest young director in Hollywood and a new SKI client; signing Fred had been one of the few bright spots in a bleak fall.

He picked up on the third ring. 'Fred Florescu.'

'Hi, Fred, it's Sam.'

A pleased chuckle. 'That was quick.'

'You're the first call,' Sam lied easily. He was a master of the art of flattery, amongst other things. He knew how to make people feel good without sliming up to them. In the movie business, that made a nice change.

'Why? Because art comes first?'

Kendrick snorted rudely. 'You're the artist, buddy. I'm the businessman. The only art I care about is the little ink sketch they do on the hundred-dollar bill.'

Florescu laughed, delighted. 'Sam, you have no shame.'

'Did you hire me to be a blushing violet?'

More flattery. The superagent humbles himself before the talent. *I work for you. You're the boss.* Well, unless you were Julia Roberts or John Grisham, talent reports to its agent most of the time. Talent that forgets this simple rule tends to have a short-lived career.

'You're the only guy I know who watches *Wall Street* as a motivational tool, instead of a warning tale.'

Now Kendrick was laughing. 'You're calling me about . . .'

'You hinted you had a line on a certain ex-rock star. Is it true? I'd like to work with him, if it is.'

The first real satisfaction of the week flooded through Kendrick's lean torso. He had the system down so well, now his stars were starting to package themselves!

Packaging. What an '80s concept. What a beautiful concept. Everybody claimed to have invented it, CAA, ICM, William Morris, you name it. The truth was that it had just evolved, like Venus rising from the waters, like Pallas Athena springing fully formed from the head of Zeus. 'Packaging' was the name given to the process whereby an agency took one of its star actors or actresses, or preferably both, hooked them up with a director it represented and a script whose writer was being repped by their literary department, and sold the whole project to a studio as a package deal. This ensured that agency commission was maximized, all the credit went to your own firm, and maybe some client you wanted to break got their first big credit on the back of one of your major stars. Of course, it was your own big-name clients that you had to sell it to, but a package deal was worth any amount of bowing, scraping and downright begging. The studios hated it, because they had to pay through the nose – always cheaper to make a movie à la carte – and because every big package deal further increased the power of the agency shopping it. On the other hand, it minimized risk – all that talent, washed and ready to serve right on the table. Not that even incredibly large amounts of talent could guarantee filled movie theatres. Look at Steven Spielberg, Julia Roberts, Bob Hoskins and Robin Williams in *Hook.* Kendrick winced at the memory. Can you say 'over-budget'? At least that turkey hadn't been his film.

No, Sam never bothered to claim that he'd fathered the packaging idea. He hadn't, and he didn't care about being first. He only cared about being best. Fifteen years ago, he'd spotted the brilliance of the idea early on and had started tying his small, classy roster of talent together for deals. Within ten months the Sam Kendrick Agency had shifted from being a Tiffany boutique to a medium-size 'comer' with an unparalleled fee rate for its clients. In another ten, they were Sam Kendrick International, with as many cheesy superstars on their books as critically acclaimed Oscar winners, and offices in Rome and London. Sam loved it. He'd never looked back.

Packaging had made him a star; not the kind of star he bought and sold, whose box office dwindled as their looks failed, but the real kind, the type trade magazines referred to using their first names alone. The kind that pinned up the firmament, not merely glittered within it. It had made Sam his first million, and then his first ten million. But right now it was the cause of his problems.

Times were lean, margins were small, and the major film studios had become far less accommodating than most of the big players were used to. Since the recession of 1990–93 the leisure dollar had shrunk considerably; everybody who used to cackle about the entertainment industry being depression-proof had been proved horribly wrong. The record, TV, magazine and film industries had all suffered; Kendrick could still remember the wave after wave of redundancies and big-budget movies that stiffed all summer long in those two terrible years, 91 and 92. At the same time, star power, and price, had increased to ridiculous proportions as studios searched desperately for ways to ensure recouping their investment. Of course, there's no such thing, and gradually it became clear that even the biggest star and the most well-worn formula couldn't guarantee a hit. File that under *Last Action Hero*. Anyway, they became even more terrified of green-lighting anything; money committed is monkey risked, right? And when Demi Moore demanded $7 million for the third *Batman* movie, they told her to take a hike.

It had been a lean few years for SKI. Nobody was starving – they repped too many big names for that to happen – but the studios had turned aside all their package deals, permitting only named stars to sign up for fees which were high, but, despite the best efforts of Sam and his minions to the contrary, still well within the accepted ballpark. But no packages. No blockbusting movies stamped 'Property of Samuel Jacob Kendrick' on them in big gold letters. Not that the other agencies hadn't had problems, but at least they'd seen one or two fat deals come together. SKI had been coasting. And you know the old story about the LA agencies being like sharks? If they don't move forward, they die. As far as Sam Kendrick was concerned, a truer word was never spoken.

He needed to get a package deal on screen, a major movie that would grab all the headlines in *Variety* and blow away his critics. And he needed it fast. Only last week, James Falcon, the fortysomething superstar who'd been with Sam for ten years, had had his lawyers call to say he was now represented by Jeff Berg at ICM.

That was when the situation had shifted out of yellow alert. It couldn't be more than a week before *that* little snippet leaked to the papers, and then everybody else would be considering their position . . . and the shark-infested waters would be alive with movement, circling, circling, as the other firms scented blood and moved in for the kill.

Sam knew the score. He'd done it often enough himself.

Hence the full staff meeting at eight o'clock this morning.

Hence his delight that Fred Florescu wanted to work with David Tauber's new client.

Hence the reason that he'd woken up this morning with *Eleanor Marshall* branded into his brain.

'I shouldn't tell you that, man. Confidentiality,' he replied, carefully keeping the elation out of his voice.

'Bullshit, Sam. Anyway, that's a yes.'

'How do you figure that out, Fred?'

'You can't have confidentiality with someone you don't represent.'

Sam chuckled darkly. 'Wait a second.' He scribbled his name on the bottom of Zach Mason's contract, holding the receiver over the pen. 'Hear that sound? Know what that is?'

'No. What is it?'

'That's the sound of ink drying. On our deal with Zach Mason,' Sam confirmed, feeling the satisfaction return.

Fred Florescu's voice was a hiss of drawn-in breath. 'Think you can get us together?'

'Think, nothing. I know you're the only director for him, Fred.'

'I'd appreciate it. *West of the Moon* was a really vital record in my life.'

That took Kendrick aback for a second. Christ, he'd forgotten Florescu was only twenty-nine. He was a *fan* of Mason's band! He was just a kid himself! Lord, that he should live to see the day when a red-hot director was panting to work with a rock star because of the guy's *music*! Slackers my sweet ass, he thought silently. They're the pushiest little bastards since the fifties. And they gaze so hard at their own navels it's a miracle they don't all walk around cross-eyed.

'You know what I'm saying? Zach Mason is, like, a prophet of his generation. Really on the level. The shit he was singing about was important, Sam. Dark Angel are a major loss to us. I want to put him in a movie very badly, I hope I can help him share some of that vision.'

Kendrick was staggered. Not only was Florescu coming out with all this garbage, was that *humility* he heard in his tone? Fred Florescu, the director who famously told the studio head on his last picture to go fuck himself, was speaking about some two-bit singer as if he was his personal god. Sam wondered how Florescu would feel if he knew what David Tauber had told him – that Dark Angel had split up over a petty squabble about T-shirt royalties, and Zach Mason himself was a spoilt brat who threw a tantrum if the mineral water in his dressing room was the wrong brand. A real primadonna whose only concern was the megabuck career of one Zachary Mason. David was a smart kid; he could see that right off. Yolanda Henry, the band's manager from the beginning, hadn't wanted to kiss Mason's ass in the way that twelve million records had led him to expect, plus she thought it was a dumb idea for him to dabble in movies. The woman was another of these music junkies, reckoned that time spent away from the studio or the stage was time wasted. No wonder her little canary was ready to sing a new tune. David Tauber was to be commended for checking out the opportunity; he'd kissed up to Zach like he was Roxana Felix herself, and promised him the sun, moon and stars, yesterday. It had taken the 'prophet of his generation' exactly ten days to split his band, dump the woman who'd discovered him sleeping rough and busking in Miami, and ship out to LA from New York, bringing with him only the second ray of sunshine SKI had seen that lean summer. And according to Tauber, he'd picked Florescu's last smash, *Light Falling*, to watch on the private jet on the way down.

Sam leaned back against the supple leather. *He* had his mind on music, too. The sweet sound of cash tills chiming.

'I understand completely, Fred. You might not believe this, but I was young once! I think you guys can make something really magical on screen together. Forget *Reality Bites* – '

'That fakola bullshit.'

' – and just start thinking about what kind of a dream you might create with Zach. I think your generation deserves a spokesman.'

'Spokesman,' said Florescu, reverently.

Kendrick's eyes rolled in his head. 'Absolutely.' He glanced at his watch: five to eight. 'Hey, I have to split. Let me talk to Zach, set a meeting up. OK?'

'You got it,' the director said, hanging up happy.

The SKI conference room was packed and nervous. Stress hung in the air like humidity, an almost palpable feeling of tension rising from the hunched necks and taut postures of the agents seated round the table and standing lining the walls. Nobody knew what to expect; Kendrick had called this meeting personally, the word of God descending from on high, summoning the miserable sinners to account for themselves in his presence. Everybody knew that Sam was unhappy, despite the decent business SKI was doing in commissions. They were fading from the limelight, and that wasn't a good position to be in in Tinseltown. Plus, James Falcon had walked last Friday. Kendrick's Commandos, as they were popularly known, had good cause to be anxious – when Sam was unhappy, that emotion seemed to have a magical way of transferring itself to his employees.

The rookies stood against the wall; they'd been there for a couple of hours, most of them, but nobody would have dreamed of taking a chair. Those were strictly left for the head honchos, whenever they should choose to appear. No, the new kids stood up with their well-thumbed copies of *Variety* and the *Hollywood Reporter* and tried to memorize weekend grosses, commission records for the SKI stars repped by their departments, whatever significant sand-shifting had taken place in the business that week, and the current dollar exchange rate to the pound, mark, yen and Swiss franc. You never knew. It was pure torture, all the mindless cramming, but that was part of the deal. They were rookie agents. They existed to be tortured by their betters. And heaven help you if Sam Kendrick, or even your department chief, decided to call on you for a question and you couldn't answer it. They were worker ants, but they were worker ants in Hugo Boss or Donna Karan, and to a man and woman they looked forward to the time when they would be able to torment their own rookies.

The wall also gave the grunts a chance to observe those mighty merchant princes, the department chiefs and senior agents who rated the thirty or so hard chairs ranged round the long mahogany table: Lisa Køepke, the elegant head of TV, responsible for dreaming up *Beechwood Halls*, *American Hospital* and *Joe's Princess* amongst other hit shows. TV was like Lisa, a solid performer with occasional flashes of brilliance, but nothing much to write home about. Phil Robbins and Michael Campbell, the heads of the international and domestic film divisions, respectively. Phil, a slim, good-looking blond in his mid-thirties and rumoured karate expert, had less to worry about: his boys and girls had been energetic in the sale of foreign rights over the past quarter and SKI commissions in Southeast Asia had never been higher. Plus, went the whisper round the back wall, that David Puttnam/ Hugh Grant Brit flick looked as if it might be gonna happen. Now *that* would surely give Mr Kendrick something to smile about. Mike, a cropped brunette in bespoke Ray-Ban shades and a dark Savile Row suit, obviously had more problems – after all, why were they here? And finally, amongst department helmers, there was Kevin Scott, the fifty-something Boston brahmin who'd been in charge of the literary department for fifteen years. It was he who had brokered the $4 million *Sweet Fire* deal in '89, an industry record at the time, and he who'd discovered eight novelists who'd gone on to top the *New York Times* bestseller list.

But that, as they say, was then, and this is now. Kevin Scott was in over his head. The world of literary rights had changed a little from the courteous-handshake business he was used to, where a gentleman's word was his bond. Deals were now done in unseemly haste, prices seemingly bearing an inverse ratio to critical merit. The leisurely, well-lubricated publishing lunch was a thing of the past in New York. And the old school of donnish, intelligent literary agents with English degrees and a passion for the written word were being replaced everywhere Kevin looked by hyenas in designer jeans, twenty- and thirtysomething puppies with mobile phones glued to their ears and Sonic Youth blaring from their in-car CDs. He shuddered to think about it. Most of them probably read five books a year, and all of those courtroom thrillers. And yet, despite his stern protests, Sam and Mike had insisted he fill his department with these obnoxious creatures.

Somebody had turned up the volume on his world, and Kevin Scott was not happy.

Nor was his division selling any scripts.

But most rookie eyes glanced lightly over the four principals today. It wasn't the division heads they were really interested in; it was the senior agents, the comers, the two-year veterans seething for position under their bosses. Joanne Delphi and Sue Sußman in Foreign Rights. Peter Murphy in TV International, and John Carter in TV East Coast. And particularly, David Tauber, the shooting comet blazing across Domestic Movies, the most vital division they had.

Tauber lounged slightly in his chair, sitting in pride of place at Phil's right-hand side. If he was aware of all the hungry eyes crawling across his muscled torso, he gave no sign of it. At twenty-six years old, David Tauber was a gorgeous creature, and sexual charisma radiated from every inch of him. Thick hazel blond hair, cut into an almost military crop, complemented his tanned skin, deep tawny eyes and a body that paid tribute to his nutritionalist and personal trainer. Nice toys if you could afford them, and Tauber could afford them easily. He'd pulled three times the commission of the other agents of his rank last year and earned double the salary. He drove a cherry-red Lamborghini and already rated a good table at Spago's.

Hollywood prides itself on scenting out the Next Big Thing, and right now David Tauber was smelling of roses. Last week had seen the biggest coup of his young but glittering career so far: the defection of Zach Mason, ex-lead singer of Dark Angel, from the stable of Yolanda Henry to the mahogany doors of SKI.

His colleagues hated him.

'Ladies, gentlemen, good morning,' Sam Kendrick barked, striding into the meeting room and pulling up the chair at the head of the table.

Everybody stood.

'Sit down,' Kendrick said sourly.

Everybody sat.

'OK, here it is,' Sam continued briskly. Just because he was in a better mood didn't mean he was gonna cut these snivelling layabouts one inch of slack. 'This year, the agency has seen its worst billings since I founded it. We've stuck a couple of our big names in movies, but that's about it. We're trailing the fucking pack and I don't think it's the luck of the draw. I want, one, a convincing explanation of everybody's performance over the last quarter; two, a list from every person in this room of who they represent, what they're doing with them, and who they're gonna bring into this agency in the next month.'

Several faces round the room paled.

'That's the warm-up. Later we're gonna discuss the studios – and I expect everyone to have some new knowledge to share with us and how we fix this problem. I want this agency to *package a deal.* Now. If not sooner. Are we clear on that?'

Frantic nods. They were clear on that.

Out of the corner of his eye, Sam noticed that useless old lush Kevin Scott, surreptitiously pop a Valium into his mouth. Christ, he was pathetic. He should fire him, but the guy had once been so good. And they had once been friends. He also noticed the Tauber kid, slouching in an Italian suit, looking confident. He hadn't nodded with the rest of them.

Kendrick had a good feeling about Tauber.

'OK, people. Let's go,' he ordered, sitting back to watch the dogfight start.

'David, I don't think you understand.'

Kevin Scott was getting redder and redder in the face.

'With respect, I think I do, Kevin. Jason wrote a script for that TV movie – '

'*Beyond Loving,*' someone supplied.

'*Beyond Loving,* right. Sold very nicely. Seventy thousand bucks for, what? Two weeks' work? I think he'd be perfect for this project.'

Scott almost choked on his outrage. This damn junior agent from the movie division, who'd been butting into everybody's reports all meeting long, was now trying to tell him how to run his literary department? Some boy who'd just started shaving?

'Jason felt he had to take the *Beyond Loving* script on to pay his rent. He is a Serious Novelist,' he managed, hoping to shame Tauber into shutting up.

An elegant shrug. 'So explain that if he writes this movie he won't have to worry about rent. He can buy his own condo.' Tauber glanced up at Sam Kendrick. 'This is the nineties, Kevin. Starving in garrets is right out of style.'

Scott glared at him bleakly. 'Thank you for your advice, David.'

'My pleasure.'

'But the literary division need not be your concern.'

A direct rebuke! Now every agent in the room was on the edge of their seats, holding their breath, waiting for Kendrick to step in and intervene.

David Tauber sighed. 'I wish that were true, Kevin. But unfortunately, it's not . . . I represent some interesting new clients in the movie division, and we would like to be able to package them' – the magic word – 'with a script from SKI. But everything that comes down to me from you guys is an art movie.'

'We have one of the best records for Academy Awards of any screenplay department in Hollywood,' Scott wheezed. The tiny, broken red veins on his nose were glowing like Rudolph.

'We're still interested in quality here, David,' Mike Campbell said brusquely. His protégé was going too far. It was bad policy to let a two-year guy badmouth a division chief.

'Indeed we are,' added Sam Kendrick loudly.

Tauber was unfazed by the general wince that rippled through the spectators. He stared arrogantly back at Scott.

'Anyway, what do you mean, *clients?*' Kevin demanded, his gentlemanly sangfroid deserting him. 'You got one new guy. Mason.'

David Tauber stretched his legs under the table, catlike, before replying, and when he did, he looked directly at Sam. 'Well now, Kevin, that was yesterday,' he said softly. 'I had a new client sign with me this morning.'

'And who was that?' the older man enquired with acid scepticism.

Tauber studied his nails. 'A model who'd like to be an actress.'

The room groaned.

'Ten for two cents,' snapped Kevin, delighted.

David shrugged. 'Maybe. But I don't think you'd get Roxana Felix at that price.'

Instant pandemonium. Kevin Scott went purple with confused rage, Mike Campbell spun on his chair to look at his lieutenant, Lisa Køepke laughed quietly, and the rookies lost their composure, some clapping, some whistling. Tauber ducked his head minutely, acknowledging the triumph.

From his throne at the top of the table, Sam Kendrick had been watching the duel closely. He hadn't known about the supermodel, but it didn't surprise him. So, the Tauber kid was a real hustler.

Time to show him who was king of this jungle.

'That's great, David,' he began, to the immediate cessation of all other noise. 'When do we start booking her modelling?'

Tauber looked wary. 'I've only signed her to us for performance, Sam. Unique in New York are still her bookers.'

Kendrick shrugged. 'Too bad. Still, I guess she must have a hot showreel.'

'Uh, no – she hasn't acted before now.'

'Then maybe she *can't act.*' Kendrick's voice was a whiplash. 'What are you going to tell me? She looks hot, so she'll be huge box office? Did it work out like that for Isabella Rossellini? For Paulina what's her name? For *Madonna?*'

The room was stunned. Tauber shifted a little on his chair, creditably hiding most of his embarrassment, and Kevin Scott suddenly had a nasty smile fixed on his puffy face.

'We'll have to see. It's still good that you signed her, though, David,' Kendrick continued, his tone more soothing now. 'But let's not jump any guns. It's your other client I really want to build a package around. We've seen Zach Mason test, and he's hot enough to fry breakfast on.'

The room had turned from the battle between the old and new guards now. Every eye was trained on the boss. When Sam spoke like this, he sounded like the Oracle at Delphi. They waited, eager for guidance, for whatever brilliant idea Kendrick had that would add lustre to the tarnished SKI star, and therefore glitter on all their résumés.

'In fact, I think it *is* a woman who'll provide the solution to our problems,' Kendrick went on. 'But her name isn't Roxana Felix.'

He waited, letting them hang in the air, dependent on him for a few seconds.

'It's Eleanor Marshall,' he said.

4

Seven a.m. and already the morning sun was blazing down full force on the LA freeway. Driving a smooth, traffic-free path to work – there had to be *some* advantages to getting up this early – Eleanor Marshall had opened the sun roof of her dark green Lotus in order to get the full benefit of it. Her neat bob of platinum-blonde hair was still damp from the shower, and she needed it to be dry and impeccable before she reached the wrought-iron gates of Artemis Studios. Everything about her had to look immaculate, these days. Of course, elegance had always been a priority, but since last month it had become an immutable law – now she *had* to be perfect at all times.

Now she was president of the studio.

'The Boys of Summer' by Don Henley flooded the car's luxurious interior with soothing, mellow sounds, and Eleanor let the music wash over her, finding a small haven of pleasure and relaxation in the combination of speed and melody. God only knew that once she stepped inside the lot she wouldn't have a chance to breathe all day. And when she got home . . .

Eleanor shrugged, feeling guilty. She knew she ought to look forward to going home. She pictured Paul Halfin, her partner. Forty-five years old, aristocratic, thick grey hair and intelligent, cold blue eyes. Very sober, very suitable, Paul was a pin-up boy for the new, eco-conscious decade; he worked out, shunned red meat, always stood in the presence of a lady and was utterly faithful. He preferred opera and fine art to watching a baseball game, was well read and highly polished, and had been at home in the finest country clubs since birth. As a respected investment banker, his career neither overpowered, nor was overpowered by, hers. Paul had had no problem with Eleanor's promotion, the day it finally came. Why should he? Albert, Halfin, Weissman had completed another successful takeover only that week. On the contrary, Paul took Eleanor to Ma Maison for champagne and celebration, and basked in all the little tributes she received as Hollywood queued before their table to kiss the hand of the new queen in town.

He was a perfect escort. Everybody said so. And in the nineties, that was what it was all about. The days of cocaine and musical beds were long over. Now, if you weren't half of a loving, devoted couple, or at least a couple which *appeared* loving and devoted, you were nobody. And a Hollywood woman's top accessory of choice had shifted from a diamond necklace to a diapered baby.

The CD skipped to a sexy James Brown track, and the president of Artemis Studios pushed her foot almost to the floor, picking up a burst of speed, trying to drive through the sudden stab of pain, blinking rapidly to get rid of the instant film of tears that had settled across her eyes. She couldn't afford this weakness. She couldn't afford to surrender to the permanent ache, the feeling of emptiness and pressure, the terror that she'd left it too late. Not now. She couldn't think about a baby now.

By the time her gleaming car swung into the executive parking lot, past the saluting guards, Eleanor Marshall, the most powerful woman in Hollywood, looked like somebody who was always, always, *always* in control.

'Hey, good-looking.'

Tom Goldman, chairman and chief executive of Artemis for the past ten years, stuck his head round the door of Eleanor's office. 'Thought I heard you coming in.'

'I know you're a sucker for my light, tripping footsteps, boss.'

They smiled at one another, co-conspirators at the top. Eleanor felt the inevitable small shock of pleasure at seeing him for the first time that day. Goldman was her closest friend and best ally. He'd been her mentor at Artemis since the sixties, when she was a novelty woman employee, albeit just a lowly reader, and he'd been number two in the merchandising division. Their paths up the greasy pole had run pretty much together, although Eleanor had taken far longer to make that final push into the Artemis inner circle, the tiny little group of people who, despite all the fancy titles and vice-presidential perks of the common or garden management, were the only ones with any real power to get anything done. For five long years Eleanor had done time in Marketing, making buckloads of money for the head honchos in New York, all the time trying to prove that she had what it took for a creative position. Tom had always pushed for her, in the mild way senior Hollywood people push for favoured juniors. After all, no one can afford to be *too* closely linked to an untried exec. They might screw up and make you look bad. But finally, last month, Goldman had really come through for her. After Martin Webber, the last president, was fired for a hit-free year, Tom gave a slick presentation in the boardroom of the parent corporation, and Eleanor Marshall was the newest recruit to the world's most exclusive sorority. Female Players. Girls with the clout to cut it with the boys.

She was thirty-eight years old.

Goldman looked his new second-in-command over. This morning she reminded him more than ever of Grace Kelly, a soft De La Renta suit in buttery silk setting off her flawless blonde bob and impeccable complexion, and low heels from Chloe elongating her already endless, slender legs. No jewellery except a subtle Patek Philippe watch on her right wrist. No make-up except a light base, maybe a tiny dash of blusher across those high cheekbones. Elegant Eleanor. He smiled, thinking how well she dressed for the part, how perfectly she matched up to all those insulting nicknames that the male VPs threw around. The Ice Princess. The Blessed Virgin. Killer Queen.

'Always.'

It was true; nobody made him laugh like she did, nobody understood him better. Tom wondered for the millionth time if there'd been a chance for him with Eleanor once, but they had both been so wary playing the studio game, making sure the correct amount of distance was always between them . . .

Eleanor tapped a heel on the soft carpet. 'Better watch out for these footsteps, Tom. A woman's shoes can be a deadly weapon.'

'Yeah?'

'Sure. Didn't you see *Single White Female*?'

He laughed. 'You coming after me in a wig? That scene doesn't play.'

'You never know.'

They smiled at each other, but there was an edge to it. Since last month, all the rules had changed. If Eleanor screwed up, Tom would be the one who'd have to fire her. And if she did great . . . maybe he would look good to his bosses on the East Coast, or maybe they would replace him with her. They had been friends for fifteen years, but now, at the top, it was harder.

'We have a meeting with Sam Kendrick this morning,' Goldman told her, throwing himself into a leather armchair opposite her and resting his shoes on top of her desk.

'General or specific?' Her brittle professionalism always took him aback.

'General, as far as we're concerned. I wanted to brief him on what we might be interested in this season.'

Standard practice. Talk to the big agents, let them know roughly what you needed right now. It was a time-saving device; that way they weren't pitched with a billion *Pretty Woman* clones when they were looking for *Terminator XV*.

She nodded. 'OK, that's useful. But your tone would seem to imply that this isn't routine for Sam.'

Goldman shrugged. 'I got the feeling he had something in mind. I pressed him a little, but he didn't let on.'

She felt her second small thrill of the day. A deal . . . maybe. Sam Kendrick didn't usually drop false hints. She wanted to do a deal, she'd already been here a month. Not that anybody expected her to prove that she was Jeff Katzenberg in a little over four weeks, but the pressure was still there. Martin had finally got fired, but the internal whispers about him, the nasty little rumours, the lack of respect at certain key restaurants in town; that had started earlier – much earlier. Like about three months into his presidency, when no major deals had been signed. Of course, Martin's reaction had been to green-light that terrible soft-porn flick that made the grosses on *Body of Evidence* look like *Jurassic Park*, and the other dog about the handicapped cop. She wasn't about to make the same mistake, please God, but she could understand now how Martin had felt. The pressure to do a deal, to make a movie, to have a hit, mounted from the second they put your name on the stationery. And with her being a woman, not having come from the creative side of the business, and following Martin and his equally disastrous predecessor, the pressure was now up to steel-crushing levels. Artemis were desperate for a hit. Eleanor was desperate to find them one, desperate for the right deal.

Sam probably knew that. Well, she wouldn't bite unless it was good.

She hoped it was.

'We'll see in Sam's own sweet time,' she said casually.

Goldman nodded and stood up. She admired the way he moved. She had a brief flash of fantasy, of Tom inside her, stroking her with his cock, teasing her over the edge. He would be wild in bed, he would fuck like a savage. Not perfunctorily, like Paul, ticking off another goal for the day.

'Are you guys free for lunch next Saturday, by the way?' Tom asked, already on his way out. 'Jordan and I are having a small party on the yacht.'

'Surely,' said Eleanor. They would just have to cancel on the Wintertons; Paul owed her one anyway. She liked spending free time with Tom, away from the relentless pressures of work. Even if it did mean socializing with that jailbait Barbie doll he'd married; Jordan Cabot Goldman, twenty-four years old, with hair down to her ass and tits out to the horizon and baby-soft skin that always made Eleanor feel like a wizened old crone. A self-styled feminist with no career and an IQ smaller than her bust measurement, but an unerring knack for giving the right parties and supporting the charity *de jour*. Eleanor was sure her picture was in every dictionary right next to 'trophy wife'.

One look at Jordan in her skintight wedding dress, slender young arm possessively wrapped round a besotted Tom, and Eleanor had smiled gently at Paul and felt hope shrivel and die inside her.

'How sweet of Jordan to think of us. We'd be delighted,' she said brightly, smiling back at him.

The phone shrilled on her desk. 'No rest for the wicked,' Tom told her, grinning and walking out.

Eighty-nine . . . ninety . . . ninety-one . . .

David Tauber raised his torso up from the polished hardwood floor of his home gym, arms locked together over his head, bronzed legs stretched out straight in front of him, using only the well-developed muscles of his stomach. Heavy rock music thudded around him, but the melody was just so much background noise. Tauber's handsome face was set in a grim expression of pain and determination as he brought his trapped elbows down to his knees, right, left, then lowered himself back down to the floor and started again. *Ninety-three . . . ninety-four . . .* The agony was visible in the sweat that was beading all over the tanned, toned body that stared back at him from his mirrored walls, but then that was the prize. Two hundred and fifty pounds of solid muscle, with body-fat composition a mere 13 per cent. *Ninety-eight . . . ninety-nine . . .* David Tauber never gave up, no matter what torment his muscles were suffering. *One hundred.* There. Done. Tomorrow he might go for one-thirty.

Tauber stood up painfully and switched off the music, an incomprehensible rant about alienation and heartbreak by Dark Angel. Definitely not his normal thing. He preferred Gershwin and Cole Porter, but if Zach Mason was going to be his client, then David Tauber was the world's biggest Dark Angel fan, as of the second Zach's inky scrawl had dried on his deal. He was going to learn to like industrial metal. If it killed him.

'I guess I'll see you later, then.'

A tanned, stacked blonde hovered in the doorway, hesitantly. Tauber's eyes flicked over the tight T-shirt pulled across jiggling breasts, real ones, which had made a nice change for him, the equally tight jeans stretched across a butt that was fractionally too wide, the long, soft hair and the dumb hazel eyes. He was pleased to feel a twinge of desire, which was amazing really, considering that he had come in her mouth so recently.

What was she waiting for? Did she expect to be invited for breakfast?

'Sure. I'll call you, Dara.'

'OK,' said the girl, disappointed but having the good sense to pick up her purse and leave. David glanced back into the bedroom, saw that she had left a neat pile of glossy eight-by-tens on his bedside table. He smiled. Some things never change. Maybe he *would* call her . . . she had just the right looks for a small walk-on in *Baywatch* he'd heard was coming up, if she lost ten pounds. That should be no problem, it was just puppyfat she was carrying around. Only sixteen. And on the upside, you got great skin at that age. Plus, he thought he might want seconds. She'd been supple and compliant, she'd shaved herself between the legs and she knew how to suck. And she'd left in good time, too.

Tauber flashed on to a mental picture of her soft lips sliding up and down his cock, reddened with lipstick in the way he'd told her to do it, so he could get more pleasure out of watching her. He sensed himself get hard again, remembering her perfect sense of pace, the warm juices of her mouth closing round him, that tricky little thing she'd done with her tongue. Yeah, he would definitely call her.

He flicked on the percolator and went to take a cold shower. All his energies had to be directed just one way this morning. Towards the meeting at Artemis. This was exactly what he'd been waiting for and hustling for ever since he arrived at SKI two years ago, a green kid fresh from Yale with little more than a small trust fund, an OK grade-point average and limitless ambition. He'd hustled his way into a secretary's job right off – no messing around with the mailroom for David Tauber – and he'd hustled his way right back out again, making junior agent within two months. After that it had been a little tougher. No talent wants to risk association with some greenhorn kid playing agent, but no greenhorn kid gets up to agent status without a talent. Catch-22. Your problem. You figure it out.

But he had. And how.

David twisted under his power jets, letting the icy blasts instantly eradicate his moment of lust. He wanted to raise the temperature, but resisted the temptation. Two more minutes. His trainer insisted cold water did wonders for the circulation.

The first signature had been hard. Colleen McCallum, a fat, fading Irish actress with a great career as a sex bomb ten years back, now reduced to putting out decent-selling schlock-folk albums and guest spots on summer specials. ICM had basically given up on her, but that didn't mean Colleen was ready to chance it with a new face. Jesus, how he'd had to chase the bitch. A twenty to the local florist had revealed a taste for orchids, and sure, they had to be the most expensive ones, and David had sent huge bunches morning, lunchtime and night for three weeks. Cost a fortune. He called six times a day. He put clippings together of all the shows he thought she'd be right for. That was when she'd permitted him more than a few seconds on the phone when he called. He remembered now that he'd thought about taking her out and sleeping with her – that was what she'd really wanted, wearing those see-through pink chiffon robes over her chunky body when he called round. David shivered at that memory, shutting the water off. Hell, he should just think of that whenever he wanted to cool down. More effective than cold water any day. Thank God he'd realized just in time that if he faked a relationship with Colleen he'd be stuck with it. You could pack cuties like Dara off in the morning, but not so a client. Your gig was to make them big, and if they got big they could make big trouble. Tauber shuddered at the thought of Colleen complaining about him to Mike Campbell, or worse still, to Sam Kendrick. Because he *had* made her big, and now his job was to keep her both big and happy.

It had been the research that had done it. Finding out exactly where she'd come from, a little Irish village called Dunkenny, and then arranging to have the local paper flown in for a week. Other guys would have ordered a Chanel suit or bought a little sports car. But David Tauber was more imaginative than that. He'd worked on the rule he applied to everyone and everything – find out what they want, then give it to them.

It worked with Colleen McCallum. She'd signed up to SKI the day the third paper arrived, put herself in Tauber's hands, and the rest was a breeze. He'd put her on a strict vegetarian diet, sent her to a trainer and a very expert, very discreet New York plastic surgeon, and fired her old record producer. They got a stylist to eliminate the faded prettiness and pink chiffon numbers, and Tauber began the rebirth. First, they stiffed MCA for a huge budget rise and hired the best country-and-western producer in the business, and the new, mature, elegant, slender Colleen had come out with a middle-of-the road hybrid they called 'Celtic Country'. It sold across Midwest America like it was going out of style. Then, by dint of months of old-fashioned grovelling, he got Colleen onto an *Oprah* special on comebacks, where mid-show she broke down in tears, confessing a past addiction to drugs and alcohol and her rebirth in Christ Jesus. Sales in the Midwest soared, the press got involved, Tauber found her a support slot in a Fred Florescu remake of one of her old movies, playing the mother of her original character, and one season later she had an Oscar nomination and a big-rated chat show on one of the Christian networks.

Colleen McCallum had been David Tauber's shot, and one had been all he needed. Weird that it was someone like Colleen who had brought him Zach Mason. But that C&W producer knew everybody, and the music business, as Tauber had discovered, was a very small place indeed...

He dried himself briskly and slipped into his Joseph Abboud suit. Milk-chocolate cashmere, the perfect weight and cut and colour for a midmorning pitch. Set off his sandy hair and gleaming tan, too. After all, Sam had made such a big deal about Eleanor Marshall chairing the meeting, and Marshall was a woman, after all. A woman with the power to green-light his project. A woman with the power to make his career.

Then he could really tell Kevin Scott to go fuck himself. He wanted that loser out of the agency. He wanted to break Roxana and Zach *together*.

He checked himself out in the mirror. Armani shoes, leather briefcase, classic Wayfarer shades, and a movie package that Sam Kendrick had OK'd himself.

David Tauber was ready to go to work.

Sam Kendrick strode into the Artemis lobby like a pro football player or a running politician. He always moved that way when he was under stress; kind of a natural defence mechanism. Nobody would ever guess it, the way he beamed at the receptionist and headed down the right corridor to Eleanor Marshall's office without being asked. The secretaries and a few low-level female execs sighed slightly as he passed. Kendrick had that rolling confidence, that animal gait to his body that spoke of money, power and excess testosterone. Such was the force of Kendrick's personality that they almost missed the incredibly cute young guy dogging his left heel. The blond who looked like a refugee from Muscle Beach . . . kind of young to be turning up to a meeting like this. Which meant he was a new kid on the block, one of the handful that get straight on the fast track every year . . . more female sighing. Studio work didn't give a young woman a lot of time for socializing. David Tauber smiled at each one of them, right in the eyes.

'OK, guys, are we ready?' Sam asked his team as they stepped out into the back lot, standing in front of the small exclusive building where Tom, Eleanor and a few of the most senior VPs had their offices. 'Are we all clear on everything?'

They nodded: Tauber, who was repping Zach and Roxana; Mike Campbell, head of his domestic movie division, who was repping Fred Florescu; and Kevin Scott, because Sam needed a script guy to be in on this. Kendrick winced again at the sight of Kevin's crumpled tweeds. Couldn't the guy get some style lessons from his movie boys? Mike, in his regular black Armani, and the Tauber kid in that chi-chi little brown deal? Personally, Kendrick didn't like a man who so obviously took trouble over his appearance. Seemed a little faggoty. But shit, the girls in the office seemed to melt into a pool of seething hormones all over Tauber's feet. And it was his first big meeting as an equal with agency hotshots, so Sam guessed he could dress how he liked. Maybe Eleanor Marshall would go for it too, but Sam knew Eleanor and he doubted it. The Ice Queen was all business, always had been.

'We should be clear, after that briefing you just gave us,' Campbell replied.

Sam grinned. He'd had them all meet at SKI an hour earlier, just so he could hone this pitch to perfection.

'You got that right. Eleanor Marshall is our best shot. She's new, she came from Marketing, she badly wants to do a deal and we badly want to help her. And if any of you assholes screws it up for me, I'm gonna give you a new one.'

Kevin Scott frowned at his boss's language, but said nothing.

'We won't screw it up,' David Tauber said soothingly.

'Not if you want to stay working for me,' Kendrick confirmed grimly, unimpressed.

The SKI group walked inside the dark glass doors and Sam announced them to another receptionist, who rose in a graceful slither of Donna Karan and conducted them across acres of original-weave Persian carpet to Tom Goldman's office.

'That's OK, hon, we can take it from here,' Sam said.

'Welcome, gentlemen, come in,' Eleanor Marshall said, standing to greet them.

Tauber noticed that Kendrick, Campbell and Scott almost involuntarily straightened themselves. Christ, he was doing it too! How did she do that? Maybe it was the buttermilk suit, maybe it was the sleek hair, maybe just the intelligent, modulated tones. Everything about Eleanor Marshall said *lady*. It wasn't a first impression he'd had of any other woman since he'd arrived in this city.

He flashed her his deepest, sexiest smile, the one he reserved for babes already hooked up with other guys. Women had told him it made them think of his lips on theirs. And he didn't mean the pair located under the nose.

Ms Marshall returned him a steady gaze.

David snapped the smile off.

'Tom, Eleanor, you already know my guys, Mike from Domestic and Kevin from our script department.' Sam ignored Kevin Scott's imperceptible shiver of distaste. He loathed his precious literary division being called the 'script department'. As far as Kevin was concerned, Kendrick knew, scripts were a necessary evil. But they were having a meeting with Goldman and Marshall, for God's sake. Maybe little David was right about Kevin . . . 'And let me introduce you to David Tauber, a very bright young man, who represents two of our new clients.'

'Mike, Kevin, David.' Tom Goldman nodded at the three of them, polite but reserved, like a king holding court. 'Have a seat. Sam, you know we convened this meeting so Eleanor could discuss with SKI a broad framework of what we might be looking for this season . . .'

'. . . but I take it that you already have something to pitch to us,' Eleanor continued, gesturing at David. 'Since you've brought along a specific agent.'

Sam noted the way they seemed totally at ease with each other, finishing off each other's sentences, sharing that chintz couch together. Not often you saw a studio chairman and president so well attuned. He didn't like it; strong studios, weak agents.

'Let's hear it,' Goldman was saying.

'You're right, of course.' Kendrick shrugged charmingly, like a little boy caught stealing apples.

'We should know you by now, Sam,' Eleanor Marshall said, smiling at him. They had been old sparring partners from her marketing days; Sam had always wanted huge promotion guarantees for his stars, and Eleanor had always fought to keep the spend down. Eleanor had usually won.

'Well, Sam Kendrick now represents two new stars and we want to build a film around them,' Sam said.

'We have a number of very established actors who would be perfect in support roles. We think this could be huge,' Mike Campbell chimed in. 'We're looking at a motion picture that will appeal to kids *and* their parents.'

'Who?' asked Eleanor Marshall, bluntly.

'David signed them, so I think he should do the honours,' Sam said expansively. 'You guys are absolutely the first to hear about this. The deal was only finalized yesterday.'

David Tauber turned his dark gaze towards Eleanor. 'Zach Mason and Roxana Felix,' he said.

Tom Goldman breathed in, sharply.

'We have a screen test for Zach,' Sam added, patting his briefcase. 'He can really act. I'll run the tape for you.' He leant forward, looking at Eleanor, the new kid on the block. This would be the coup de grâce. 'And we have also signed a new director – Fred Florescu.'

'Does Fred want to work with Mason?' Eleanor demanded, trying not to show how excited she was.

'He *asked* Sam to hook him up with Zach,' Mike Campbell said.

Eleanor shifted on her seat. She could feel the waves coming right out of Tom's eyes and boring into the back of her neck – *Do a deal! Now! Quick! Before they show this package to anyone else!*

But although he was straining at the leash, she knew he wouldn't override her. Not in her first meeting. Tom had appointed her president, and he'd let her make her own decisions. It was one of the reasons she liked him so much . . . was that the right word?

'Sam, we'll need to see that test. But Zach Mason with Fred Florescu sounds very strong.' She didn't care about the supermodel. Not unless she could act. Most of those clotheshorses had no idea what to do once they had to open their mouths. 'And I think we can offer you a deal. But there is one condition.'

'Name it.' Kendrick was still leaning towards her.

'Zach Mason's a superstar . . . in rock 'n' roll. But there's nothing to say his appeal will hold for moviegoers. It didn't even work for Madonna. Now I know you guys have got a lot of established talent for support, but this project needs one more element. It's crucial. And we won't green-light anything without it.'

Eleanor nodded at Kevin Scott, completely certain of what she was saying.

'We need a dynamite script. Get me that, and we're in business.'

5

'Honey, over here!'

Megan paused for a second, just a second, to catch her breath. She'd managed to get the order of three plates heaped with fried chicken, coleslaw and two pitchers of beer over to table six and set down without spilling it, even when the fat slob with acne had made a grab for her ass, cackling, and she'd had to swerve away. How could they eat mounds of fried chicken in the LA summer? Sweat beaded her forehead, making her fringe cling damply to her skin. Her thighs felt heavy and sticky, gross in the too-short skirt. She'd put on twelve pounds since she started working here; at the end of the shift she was always too hungry and too exhausted to resist her free 'Mr Chicken' employee meal. Even though the mere thought of all that stale batter frying up in pools of grease made her nauseous. Jesus, she thought, when I get out of here I'm never going within ten miles of a piece of fried chicken for the rest of my life. *If* I ever get out of here.

'Honey, we need some service.'

'I'll be right there, guys,' Megan called out, threading her way past the other waitresses towards table four, nearest the bar. Oh God, it was them again. The drivers. Worked for some Hollywood chauffeuring service and turned up here once a week with their seersucker suits and attitude, boasting to the other girls about what they'd said to Demi Moore last Tuesday or Tom Hanks on Friday.

'OK, fellas, what'll it be?' she asked nervously.

'Two buckets, four 'slaws and a pitcher,' the scrawny one gabbled. Megan wrote furiously, trying to ignore the geek with the sideburns who was staring right up her skirt. She longed to slap him, but what could you do? It had taken her three weeks to find any kind of a gig. Even the waitressing slots were hotly contested in this town, and by wannabe actresses too, 115-pound babes with legs that went on forever and eyelashes so long you could braid them. Overweight and over twenty-one usually meant over and out. She had no savings. She needed this job.

'Great. Like a piece of corn with that?'

'No, but I'd sure like a piece of your sweet ass,' cracked Oscar Wilde with the facial hair. His companions roared with laughter.

Megan felt the anger bubble up inside her throat, but forced it back down. 'Not on the menu today. Sorry.'

'Mebbe tomorrow.' Oscar wasn't giving up when he was on a roll. He leant forward and jabbed a grimy finger into the cellulite on Megan's upper thigh. 'Mebbe you'd like to drop a couple pounds. I could help ya with that. Sweat it off. Get it?'

Jesus. She felt even hotter, her clammy skin prickling with rage and humiliation. Had it come to this? Being propositioned by a bunch of slobs who were telling her she was fat?

'I'll get the order,' she mumbled, and broke away from the table, her face the colour of the ketchup bottles.

'Don't mind them.' Stacey, one of the other waitresses, put a soothing hand on her arm. Stacey was a petite redhead from Indiana who'd started two weeks before Megan; and the only girl in the place who'd given her the time of day. 'They're just assholes. Standard issue.'

'Stacey, am I fat?' She was transfixed by the sight of her friend's slender legs, looking so cute in the itsy-bitsy yellow frilled uniform. And her clear skin, with no gathering pudginess under the chin. Green eyes and neat red hair. Stacey could even look good in canary, a colour Mr Chicken might have chosen on purpose to make its waitresses look sallow.

'No way.' Stacey wasn't looking at her. 'This society's all hung up on weight, anyway. It's natural for a woman to have curves.'

'I *am* fat,' Megan said, horrified.

'No you're not. You might think about losing just a touch. But only if you wanted to,' Stacey added hastily.

Both of them glanced involuntarily down at Megan's soft thighs spreading out under the ruffled hem, orange-peel dimples just beginning to form across them.

'How's the script going?' Stacey asked hastily, changing the subject. 'Got an agent yet?'

Megan laughed bitterly. 'Of course. Mike Ovitz rang yesterday. Which is why I'm still here, schlepping for standard-issue assholes.' She broke off at the sight of Stacey's hurt face. The younger girl wasn't exactly Simone de Beauvoir, and she wounded easily. 'Oh, Stace, I'm sorry,' she sighed. 'I didn't mean it like that. I guess it's just getting to me today. I got rejections through from William Morris and Sam Kendrick this morning.'

'Oh, Megan, I'm real sorry. That's too bad.'

'Yeah,' Megan said shortly. She glanced at her watch. Half-ten. Thank God. 'At least I get off in fifteen minutes.'

'You go on home. I'll cover for you,' Stacey offered, thinking how low Megan looked this evening, like a puppy with all the fight kicked out of it.

'Would you? Oh God, thanks, Stacey. I'll come in early tomorrow,' Megan promised, rushing through the dirty double doors of the kitchen to get changed. She knew she shouldn't have accepted, shouldn't have taken advantage of Stacey's soft heart. It only meant Stacey would be stuck with the jerks on table four instead of her. But God help me, she thought, tonight I just can't make it through another minute. She felt so exhausted she could lie down here and just sleep through all the racket and shouting without any problem at all. At least, she told herself grimly as she struggled out of the horrible uniform and pulled on her loose jeans, I could if the floor were cleaner.

'See you tomorrow, Megan. Quarter of nine. Sharp,' Mr Jenkins, the supervisor, said pointedly to her, nodding at the clock on the wall. 'You don't keeping mucking about with your shift times like this. OK? Shifts are set for a reason.'

Megan mumbled something placatory, hating herself.

'Want your Mr Crispy Special?' Jenkins demanded, proffering her a small tub of fried chicken wings packaged with a tub of barbecue sauce and a microscopic corn on the cob.

'Not tonight.' She was totally starving, but the humiliation had been too recent. Even her loose jeans had gotten snug around the waistband.

'Sure?' He was surprised.

She ignored the growling in her stomach. 'Yeah. Thanks.'

On the long drive back to Venice, Megan checked herself out in the rearview mirror of her beat-up Fiat. It was practically a felony to drive a car this old in the city of gleaming Mercedes and personalized Rolls-Royces, but at least it was night. And there were some advantages to having lousy wheels. Like nobody would bother carjacking someone who so obviously had nothing worth stealing, and the drive-by shooters wouldn't waste a bullet. Megan smiled to herself, with grim humour. She better find *something* to laugh about. Because her reflection wasn't funny.

The weight was the first thing; OK, so she wasn't *fat* fat, not obese. Roseanne Arnold was fat fat. Oprah before the diet. No, Megan was just – what? Plump? Fleshy? Nearly a stone heavier, and she'd been no Kate Moss before she left San Francisco. Now it showed on her face, as well as her ever-thickening thighs. An unsightly bulge under the chin. A rounding of her features, enough to give her a moon-faced expression. And a stomach that was nudging at the waistband of her loose jeans. Megan knew that when she sat down in the bathtub a small roll of flesh would crease over her midriff. She'd started to use bubblebath regularly, and now she guessed it was so she wouldn't have to look at what was happening to her. At those little dimpled cushions that were developing at the tops of her knees.

Tears started to film across her tired eyes. Oh, God. She didn't want to see this, didn't want to take a good look at herself. What would Rory say if he could see her like this? Rory, her last boyfriend up in Frisco, the one that she'd dated for nearly a year and then dumped, three months ago now. There had been nothing wrong with Rory, which is why they'd lasted so long. He'd been as comfortable to Megan as her favourite old jumper. But there had been nothing much *right* with him either – he'd never been able to get passionate about anything except sex, he was happy with their little world exactly the way it was. Though Megan had looked forward to going back to Rory at nights, she'd never managed to get worked up about it. The thought of Rory waiting for her had never given her that wet, sticky, pressing feeling in her pussy she got when she was fantasizing about Harrison Ford or Keanu Reeves in the library. And Rory on his own had only been able to give her quick little orgasms, not the more satisfying, deeper spasms she got when she shut her eyes and guiltily imagined it was Zach Mason she was fucking. So eventually she'd got round to chucking him, because she couldn't shake the feeling that as long as she was with Rory she'd be missing out on something.

Something special, something different. Passion. Infatuation. Her heart speeding up, that faint sickness . . . the stuff she saw in the movies, the stuff she read about. *Sleepless in Seattle, Romeo and Juliet,* Scarlett O'Hara melting for Rhett Butler. God, listen to me, Megan thought, pressing her foot on the gas, picking up speed. Even thinking about it, it sounds ridiculous. When does it ever happen to anyone? How many Richard Geres are out there waiting for your average streetwalker? And dumping Rory, for that. What a joke. If he'd seen her like this, he wouldn't have stayed with her for ten minutes. Even Dec would have been embarrassed by the total mess she was sliding into.

It wasn't just the pudginess. The whole thing was a disaster. Poor diet and no exercise and lack of sleep had shot her skin to hell. Her face was grey-complexioned, pallid and dull. On top of that, she had breakouts, nasty little whiteheads peppering her forehead. The lank hair was probably making that worse. She washed it every morning, but cheap shampoo was no match for the spitting oil and rank steam of the Mr Chicken kitchen. And she noticed that the real beauty, the red zit on the end of her nose, had triumphed over the six layers of cover-up she'd plastered on it this morning, and was now throbbing dully and noticeably at her in the rearview mirror.

Well, Megan thought, if the car breaks down at least I'll be able to light my way home. And then she was really crying, big, salty tears that spilled out of the corners of her eyes and tickled as they ran down her plump cheeks.

She slowed down, sniffing and reaching up with one hand to dash the water away. She didn't want a car wreck. Wouldn't that be the perfect end to the perfect day?

It had started off on the wrong foot this morning, not that there was anything new about that. Her alarm shrilling at eight, waking up with a headache, stumbling into the shower to wash it all away. That had been OK: the hot kiss of the water, the soft bubbles of her shower, her fingers slipping between her legs for a little relief, and a shockingly good orgasm five minutes later, leaning back against the thin plastic shower rack, warm rivulets of water flowing across her fingers, mingling with her own juices, letting her come, knowing that her ragged gasps would be hidden from the others by the noise of the shower. Towelling off quickly, she'd almost felt good; relaxed and unstressed, like some soothing hand had temporarily untied all the knots in her muscles. But it hadn't lasted.

'What's up?' she greeted Jeanne and Tina, her roommates, who'd already had breakfast and were sitting at their small table in the cramped kitchenette, drinking instant coffee. The apartment was grimy and too small, the showerhead needed jiggling every other day and the paint was peeling in most of the rooms, but it was also incredibly cheap. And thus in demand. She'd been really lucky to have the other two pick her out of a long list the day she answered the flatshare ad; maybe it was because she was so much plainer than all the other girls who'd applied, and they hadn't wanted any competition. Whatever, neither of them had gone out of their way to make her feel at home once she'd moved her single suitcase in. At least they weren't overtly hostile. Perhaps that was what passed for friendship in this town. And they hadn't objected when she'd tried to make the dump seem a little more like home: hanging a surrealist print over the stain in the hallway, putting her faded Afghan blanket down in the kitchen, and tacking her Dark Angel and Metallica posters up in her bedroom and the front room.

'Hi,' said Jeanne, a French girl with a chic brown bob and impeccable skin. Jeanne sold insurance over the phone, downtown, and wanted to be an actress. Central Casting sometimes called her in to do extra work, and she'd once had a speaking line in a dogfood commercial.

'Post came for you,' Tina added, not without sympathy. Tina was dyed-blonde and silicone-breasted and checked coats at a not-so-exclusive nightclub. She always had more money than her salary would explain, and Megan never asked how she got it.

Megan had walked forward to the table, her mouth suddenly cottony-dry. No mistaking it. Two fat envelopes, addressed to her in her own handwriting. Fat, about eighty pages fat. Her script. Returned to her again, rejected again. Dismayed, she looked at the franking on the top. Sam Kendrick. Oh *no*. And William Morris.

She sank into the vacant chair, feeling despair envelop her in its familiar thick fog.

'It isn't that bad,' Jeanne said, offering some uncharacteristic sympathy. 'No one gets accepted right off.'

'You have to know someone,' Tina confirmed. 'Do you want some coffee? I'm gonna get some more.'

Megan didn't want coffee or anything else unless it was laced with strychnine, but she also didn't want to offend Tina. 'Thanks.' She ripped open the envelopes, saw those death-kisses, the stapled sheets marked RETURNED UNREAD, with a form letter saying that the agency was not accepting unsolicited scripts at this time.

'That's so you can't sue them,' Jeanne told her, wisely. Jeanne considered herself a veteran, a pro. She knew all about 'the Business'.

'I don't understand,' Megan said, faintly. At least in San Francisco her novel had been rejected. Here she couldn't persuade one agency to so much as read her screenplay. 'Unread'. 'Unread'. 'Unread'. They'd all said the same thing, and they'd all sent it back by return of post. Megan couldn't afford to make huge numbers of copies, so she'd sent out two manuscripts, sending the same copies out again when they came back. Which they always did, like the world's most accurate boomerangs. Megan had started with the small agents, where she felt she had the best chance, and worked her way up. Not that it mattered; she'd struck out all the way up the pond, from the minnows to the whales. And now William Morris and SKI had told her to get lost, she was about through her entire list, with only ICM and CAA remaining. Yeah, right! Like either of them were gonna give her the time of day.

'It's so you can't sue them if they rip off your idea,' Jeanne explained. 'So if a studio makes a movie, and it's kind of like your script, you can't sue them and say they used your idea and ripped you off without paying for it.'

'Really?' Megan asked. She felt so helpless. 'But then how does anybody ever get a script read?'

'Beats me,' Tina said shortly, putting a mug of coffee down in front of her. Megan knew Tina looked down on her, compared with Jeanne. Not only did

Jeanne have looks and style; at least she was failing to be an actress. Megan was only failing to be a writer. How low could you get?

'You have to know somebody. Tina's right,' Jeanne said.

'But I don't know anybody.' Not in showbusiness, and not in this whole fucking city, Megan thought. She picked up her copies of the script, ready to slot them into new envelopes for CAA and ICM. They felt like lead in her hand, heavy with the weight of foolish ambition and frustrated dreams.

'So what are you going to do?' asked Jeanne.

Megan shrugged. 'Right now I guess I'm going to work.' And she'd gone back into her bedroom to pick up the Mr Chicken uniform, all ready for another fun-packed day in Tinseltown.

She turned down Carillo, nearly home now. Pretty quiet out there tonight; only a few bodies huddled in doorways, the normal night-time groupings you didn't look too hard at, kids selling skin or crack, more likely the latter. More money in it. The tears had stopped now; she was too tired to cry. She just wanted to get inside, get something in her stomach so she could sleep. There would be a little less time tomorrow morning, too, because she'd have to get in fifteen minutes earlier. Although there'd doubtless still be time to get back both copies of *See the Lights*, her script, from CAA and ICM. And Megan wondered for a second what she'd do then. When she had literally run out of chances.

'Hey, Megan,' Tina yelled out as she walked through the door. 'Come and have a beer.'

'What's this?' she asked, hanging up her uniform on the back of her bedroom door and wandering into the kitchen. 'Are we celebrating?'

'We are.' Jeanne had picked up two six-packs of Bud and some grass. The heady, bittersweet scent of marijuana smoke hung in the tiny room, and Megan was assaulted with a sudden rush of homesickness. 'Want some of this?' Jeanne proffered an expertly rolled joint and Megan accepted it, taking a deep drag, right into her lungs. Maybe a little dope would relax her.

'Beer?'

'Yeah. No,' Megan said, thinking of the calories. 'I'm gonna try and lose some weight.'

'Jeanne got a part,' Tina told her smugly.

'You did?' Megan asked. 'Truly?'

Jeanne nodded her sleek head proudly. 'Second lead in an art film by Ray Tyson. I'm getting twelve hundred dollars.'

Twelve hundred dollars! Megan was appalled to find herself swamped by a wave of envy and resentment. What had Jeanne ever done that was worth so much? Jeanne was stupid, a bimbo with an accent. But she was slim, she was chic. Things Megan would never be. It was so unfair.

A quotation from the Bible floated into her mind: *To him that hath, more shall be given; and to him that hath not, even the little he hath shall be taken from him.*

'Congratulations,' she said, as brightly as she could. 'Who's going to be your agent?'

'Oh, I'm not gonna bother with an agent,' Jeanne said loftily. 'Why should some jerk take twenty per cent of what I make? I got this part myself, I guess I can get other ones, too.'

Megan was too weary to argue with her. 'OK,' she said.

'Hey, Megan, maybe you should send your script back to SKI,' Jeanne said, with the generosity of the fortunate.

Megan shrugged. 'Thanks, Jeanne, but I don't see the point. If they wouldn't read it the first time, I don't see why they'd change their minds just because I repeated the process.'

'Jeanne heard some girl at the casting saying that SKI are suddenly desperate for scripts,' Tina butted in.

'It's a real hot rumour,' Jeanne confirmed. 'That Artemis are looking for a vehicle for this new star they've signed.'

Megan laughed. 'But that would only work if my script was suitable for this star.' She thought about her screenplay, the labour of love that took her less than a fortnight to finish off. God, the way the words had just tumbled out of her head, so quickly she'd been scared she might not be able to type fast enough to get them down. The movie had written itself, playing in her head as clearly as if she was sitting in some darkened theatre with a bucket of Butterkist. The bittersweet story of a young musician and how fame warps him on his way to the top, only for him to be rescued in the third act by the girl he'd previously cast aside. It had sex, drugs and rock 'n' roll and mad passionate love too. She'd been so proud of it, so filled with certainty that it was her ticket out of nowheresville.

Certain enough to draw out her entire meagre savings account from Wells Fargo and get on a Greyhound bus. Certain enough to risk everything she had. And, it seemed, to lose it.

'But it's totally suitable,' Jeanne said. 'I guess, anyway. If he doesn't mind being typecast.'

'Who is this guy they've signed?' asked Megan, only slightly interested. Like it should affect her if Tom Cruise or whoever switched agents.

'Zach Mason,' Tina informed her.

'Say that again?' Megan stammered.

'Zach Mason. You know, he used to be a rock star. Sang in that band you like,' Tina said. She added grudgingly, 'I guess he *would* be right for your script. But I'd forget about it. If Jeanne heard, every real writer in town knows about it too, and they're all connected. You'll never get them to read your script.'

Megan hardly looked at her. Suddenly she knew it was going to be OK. This movie had her name on it. All she had to do was get her script read by the right person at SKI.

'Oh yes I will,' she said.

'And how are you gonna do that?' demanded Tina nastily.

'I don't know,' Megan told her. 'But I will.'

6

His cock felt like it was going to explode. It was huge, desperately thickened, throbbing with need. When he glanced quickly down, gasping with almost unbearable lust and pleasure, Howard Thorn could see the long blue vein that ran down the side of it swollen fat as an earthworm. He could dimly register that his cock seemed to have grown to twice its usual size when he had a hard-on. That had everything to do with the slender, perfect fingers wrapped round its stem, opening and closing in a tiny butterfly movement, then pinching him very faintly around the bucking velvet tip, just enough to stop the violent orgasm he was sure would burst out of him any second. He pushed helplessly, mindlessly, guided by instinct, rubbing his dick, wet with the juices of her million-dollar mouth, against her baby-soft skin. Not that Howard was thinking about her skin. He could hardly think about anything at all. His company, his jealous wife, his power, his receding hair had all evaporated into the mist. The universe had shrunk and contracted, until the only things that Howard Thorn was aware of were his cock and her hands and his acute need to come, to end this exquisite torture she was inflicting on him. Right now, the entire cosmos was wrapped up in the nine inches of his erect, straining, pulsing dick. And the only lucid thought in his head was *Roxana Felix is the fuck of the century.*

'Now?' Roxana asked him, her gentle voice low and teasing, laced with a breathy sensuality that sent another sharp stab of pleasure right through his balls, hardened and shrunk and totally ready. Howard stared glassily at the cloud of her ultra-glossy, jet-black hair, hair he could practically see his face in. He managed to choke out the words: 'Yes. Please, yes.'

'Are you sure? I could last another ten minutes.'

She could last forever with Rudolf Valentino here. Jesus. She couldn't come for him if he was the last man on earth and masturbation was banned.

'Please. Please.' He was begging, his cock leaping at her touch, beading at the head with his liquids. He wasn't going to last ten more seconds, let alone ten minutes. 'I have to come. I'm gonna die,' Howard choked.

Maddeningly slowly she lifted herself forward over his supine body, positioning herself directly above him, sliding her pussy right down the length of his shaft with immaculate timing, so that the movement from her hands to her crotch was seamless.

Howard Thorn cried out from sheer pleasure.

'You're not going to die, baby. But you *are* going to heaven,' Roxana Felix whispered, and then, to his utter astonishment and bliss, Howard found his cock being caressed by the inner walls of her pussy, the tight, controlled muscles of her vagina milking him out like a second set of hands, and he saw her rocking above him, her small pert breasts bouncing, her flat stomach pearled with sweat, her exquisite face contorted with the violence of her orgasm, and he erupted inside her, his come ripping out of him in great spasms of ecstasy that shook his entire body, the most incredible, intense climax he had ever experienced in his entire life.

'My Christ,' he said weakly.

She was smiling at him, a languorous, sated smile, like a pedigree kitten that had just been fed, and Howard Thorn, billionaire financier and Wall Street raider, felt his heart flip over like a lovesick teenager.

'You're so good, baby. What you do to me,' Roxana Felix murmured, faintly.

Thorn felt his pride swell up nearly as much as his dick had been swollen a moment ago. He felt a wash of sheer machismo roll over him, as though he were a caveman who'd dragged the world's most famous supermodel back to his den by her long black hair, and then shown her what good loving was all about. The possibility that Roxana might have faked it never entered Howard's typically male head. The idea that one of the most breathtaking women he'd ever seen might *not* go ga-ga for his middle-aged spread, beady eyes and encroaching baldness simply did not occur to him.

'Honey, you inspire a man,' Howard said, smiling fatly at her. The little rolls of flesh on his cheeks twitched upwards in a smirk.

'If only you were free.' She gave a delicate sigh, glancing sadly at his wedding ring.

'Roxy, Roxy,' Howard said, patting her knee as though she were a favourite schoolchild. Damn, he was sorely tempted to promise to give Bunny up, the dry, frigid bitch, and take this hot tamale back to Dallas with him. But he'd married in the fifties, without a pre-nup, and Bunny had raised three kids with him and been there the entire time he'd worked to make Condor Oil a reality, including the last five years, when he'd expanded into broadcasting and real estate. Condor Industries. An American colossus, and a company that Bunny might be able to claim fifty per cent of, or so his lawyers had told him. Goddamn 'women's movement' with its goddamn communal property laws.

There was only one thing Howard Thorn loved more than sex, and that was money. He patted Roxana Felix's slim leg again. 'You know I'd love to, but I just can't do it to Bunny. We were not meant to be.'

Obviously disappointed, she turned away from him and started to dress.

'But I got you those other things you wanted,' Thorn said quickly. 'All of them. I called Tom Goldman last night about screening your tests. And my guys have talked to the trades and the press. Even the *New York Times*. It'll be pandemonium when you get there.'

Completely covered up in her opaque Mark Eisen scarlet shift, Roxana turned back to him, her chocolate eyes shining with pleasure. She took his breath away.

'Really? You called Tom Goldman?'

'Yes, ma'am,' Thorn confirmed. 'Told him he better make sure everybody watched your tests and that he'd better be positive about it.' He hoped he sounded suitably menacing. 'Jeez, I *told* him to cast you, but he said it don't work like that.'

Roxana beat down a scathing retort. Howard Thorn was not Bob Alton. He had to be played carefully. 'Why not?' she asked, disappointed, pouting, little-girl-lost.

Howard looked at her and felt his anger at that little kike come rushing back. 'Christ, honey, I know what you're thinking. He runs the damn studio. But there's a new president appointed, a woman' – and one who sat on a few charity committees with Bunny, he couldn't push Roxy to *her* – 'name of Eleanor Marshall. Seems like it's her first project, and he can't override her "creative control".' He put quotes around the phrase. The only creative control worth a damn to Howard Thorn was the kind his accounts practised on the company books.

'Oh, Howard. I want it so much. I just don't know what to do,' said Roxana, helplessly, her long lashes beading with tears.

Thorn looked at her, furious with Tom Goldman. If Roxana Felix wanted something, by God she was going to have it. Fuck Eleanor Marshall. Fuck anything that stood in his way.

'You just go to LA and do your thing, honey. I'll get you that movie.'

'Promise, Howard?'

Roxana stood in front of him, looking up at him like a little girl looking at Santa Claus. A little girl whose gorgeous raisin nipples were winking at him through the cherry satin of her dress.

For a second, Howard Thorn thought of the risks involved in messing around with the casting of a movie. A financier like him with a large stake in Artemis Studios really shouldn't be concerning himself with petty little things like that. And when Roxana Felix was the girl he was hawking, the situation more or less invited attention. *Begged* for suspicion.

But then he thought of her fingers tickling the stem of his cock, the clutching, intimate caress of her pussy, that superman-size hard-on she'd given him. Roxana Felix had shown him things no hooker he'd ever had could even dream of. But she was no hooker, she was a world-famous supermodel. The classiest piece of ass on the planet.

For fat, plain Howard Thorn, she was a wet dream come true.

'I promise,' he said.

In the relaxed comfort of the first-class cabin, Roxana Felix was doing a lot of thinking.

This wasn't behaviour she normally indulged in. Thinking was for when you were travelling by private jet, when you had time for it. When she was slumming first-class, Roxana treated it like a show. Every move worked out with precision: the dramatic entrance, just a fraction late, but never late enough to delay the plane – she'd decided the superbitch, primadonna image was passé these days – and the sexy, stylish, never overpowering outfits she picked to travel in. Her small, dark green cases, made to order on Bond Street and so much more chic than boring old Gucci or Louis Vuitton. The gentle politeness to flight attendants. The sweet but firm requests for privacy if some odious businessman wanted an autograph, and the equally sweet acquiescence if his four-year-old kid asked for one. After all, she had a duty to her public. She was more than a model. She was Roxana Felix, a lady, a role model, America's sweetheart. And you never knew who the first-class crowd actually were – heaven forbid she should lose face when a *Vanity Fair* reporter might be taking notes in the row behind her. You might even snub that reporter himself without realizing it.

Roxana frowned. Reporters took themselves so seriously. Stupid writers mistaking themselves for people other people might be interested in. Look at that Norman Mailer interview with Madonna a few years back – more about Mailer than the lady he was supposed to be talking to, and all he could ask her about was why she hadn't done beaver shots for 'Sex'. Christ. As if anyone in the whole world gave a shit about Norman Mailer, that pretentious fat fuck.

Anyway, today she just couldn't be bothered with reporters or kids or anyone else. She'd had her travel agent arrange for her to be seated at the end of an empty row, and the stewardesses were under strict instructions to keep the great unwashed away from her.

Incredibly, things were not going according to plan.

It had started with that call from David Tauber last week. Two days after her Chicago triumph, with the entire fashion business falling over itself to be the first to fling itself at her Salvatore Ferragamo heels. Bob Alton had melted into a seething pool of adoration and dollars as the phone at Unique rang off the hook. Guess Jeans. Chanel. The new Calvin Klein perfume. And best of all, Revlon's offer to feature her, alone, in a one-off lipstick campaign – 'The most beautiful *woman* in the world wears Revlon.'

When she read that she'd practically come. What was it Bob said? Her coronation. Right. Sometimes he was nearly worth tolerating. The Alessandro show *had* been her coronation, the apex, the zenith of the beauty tree. She, Roxana, had finally been crowned queen, succeeded to the throne she'd always known she was born to occupy. When she strutted into the Limelight, her favourite club in New York, the DJ had put on RuPaul's 'Supermodel of the World' in tribute, and the kids all applauded when she'd glided onto the dance foor.

How Cindy must be seething. How Linda must be livid.

As if she gave a damn!

It was all she'd ever dreamed about. As far as she was concerned, all that kissy-kissy, babe-can-I-borrow-your-blusher, Naomi-loves-Christy crap was the purest bullshit. And she was sure all the girls secretly felt the same. This wasn't about there being enough work for everyone, this was about supremacy. About who was top. Who could beat off the new girls – Brandi, Amber, Megan, Shalom *et al* – the longest.

And at Alessandro's little shebang, she, Roxana Felix, had simply walked over the pack of them in her made-to-measure sandals.

So why wasn't that enough? She couldn't figure it out, truly. She just couldn't see why the sweet sense of victory had lasted such a very short time, such a mere heartbeat of space, before all the demons had come back, all those ugly, nagging black feelings she had to work so hard to bury . . .

Roxana shook her head, hard. No. She wouldn't think about that now.

Just take it as a given that although the new contracts she'd signed since the Alessandro sensation would keep her in first-class seats for the rest of her life, that simply wasn't enough. As she'd found out when David Tauber called her from LA to tell her of the problem.

Sam Kendrick International had put her forward as a contender for female lead in the Zach Mason vehicle, to be directed by Fred Florescu. Merely the sound of his voice, hearing him say 'Zach Mason' and 'Fred Florescu' and her in the same sentence, had sent shivers down her perfect, jaded little spine. Zach Mason! She loathed that dreadful music Dark Angel spewed out, she'd had to endure it screaming from the speakers at enough of the ultra-hip shows. In fact music in general left her cold. Most things left her cold. But Zach Mason was a god to billions of kids around the globe, a sex god and soothsayer rolled into one. People she knew had reacted to Dark Angel splitting up as though it was John F. Kennedy getting shot in Dallas all over again. He defined his generation. And Fred Florescu was not only the hottest, most commercial director around after Spielberg, he was by far the most credible, the only Generation X-er to really make a mark on the American consciousness.

To play opposite Zach Mason in a Fred Florescu film . . .

She would no longer be a clotheshorse. She would be more, even, than the biggest celebrity in the world. Yeah, Roxana thought, maybe that was what she had realized – that as a model, it was her perfect face and her perfect body that were famous, not *her*. *She* was nobody. Nobody cared what her opinions were on anything, what she planned to do after she'd finished modelling. My God, she thought, I might as well be unknown.

To be a movie star would give her more than celebrity.

It would give her *fame*.

And immediately she realized this, she'd realized that she must have it. The demons had swarmed up in a black cloud like bats. Any lingering pleasure over the Alessandro triumph had become so many ashes in her mouth. And it was just at that moment when Tauber informed her that Artemis had said they weren't interested, but he'd try to get them to look at some tests.

'I guess I didn't hear you right,' she'd said, her heart hammering with blind panic. 'I thought you said you were going to *try* to get them to *look at my tests?*'

Her voice had been colder than liquid nitrogen.

Tauber sounded placatory, but he'd stood his ground. Bob Alton fainted dead away when she used a tone like that. 'Yeah, I did. And I will try my absolute hardest, Roxana, but I can't guarantee they will see your tests.'

'You're telling me that *I* have to take a screen test? Do you know how many commercials I've done? And you're telling me that even if I *accept* this insanity, Artemis may not even *look* at them? Does this Eleanor Marshall have me mixed up with somebody else?'

Tauber hadn't flinched. 'I'm – *we're* – incredibly thrilled to be representing you, Roxana. You're the most beautiful woman alive, and *I* know you're one of the most talented.' The implication was not lost on her. 'But unfortunately, the motion picture industry needs a whole new set of skills. We're gonna have to persuade them that you have what it takes.' His tone was as warm as his words were chilling.

'You're saying I can't go in at the top.' Her words were a flat monotone. Disbelieving.

Tauber had changed tack, gone for intelligent candour. 'Roxana, I told you I would never bullshit you' – she rolled her eyes – 'and I won't. This is the truth. The talent I see in you, talking to you, other people out here don't. We have to prove it to them and that's gonna take a little work,' and then he'd added the magic phrase, 'but I know you love a challenge.'

Oh yes, Roxana thought, yes, indeed I do. And this will be as nothing compared with the real challenges I've already faced. Challenges that you can't even begin to dream about, California boy, not in your worst nightmares.

'I'll do those tests, David,' she said calmly. 'You just hustle them at Artemis. They'll get seen.'

Already she had flashed onto Howard Thorn, one of the many hugely powerful, hugely stupid, hugely married names in her little black book. Men she threw a mercy fuck at now and then, who provided her with favours as needed. Howard Thorn was one of the most useful. Chained to his wife by billion-dollar handcuffs, he was guaranteed not to give her any trouble or bother her overmuch, and his massive holding conglomerate, Condor Industries, had helped her up the ladder with magazines, cosmetic contracts and many kind little whispers in smoky clubs. Naturally, Howard was besotted with her, and every time she screwed him she made sure it was better than the last. And like all her other sugar daddies, Howard thought he was the only one.

Thank God, Roxana thought contemptuously, for the fact that a girl can rely on *some* things in this life. The vanity of men was one world resource that would never run out.

Howard Thorn had bought fifteen per cent of Artemis Studios only last year.

'They'll get seen?' Tauber repeated, questioningly.

'Yes, they will.'

'OK,' Tauber answered, not pushing it.

She was glad they understood each other. Because she found herself in a position that she hadn't known for years – helplessness. She couldn't threaten David Tauber with firing him because, unlike at Unique, she wasn't Sam Kendrick International's only client. Jesus, from the sounds of it she wasn't even an important client. And anyway, Sam Kendrick had Zach Mason and Fred Florescu, and that was the *perfect* movie, the one she wanted to be in. Already she knew that much. A movie would be no problem. But it was this movie she wanted. *The* movie.

That was why she'd taken time out last week to do the test, and shown that jerk banker a little bit of nirvana this morning. She was already working for it, struggling for it. Roxana needed this film, and if laying Howard Thorn was what it took, laying Howard Thorn was what she would do. She loathed him, but this morning she'd fucked him like she was Scheherazade and her life depended on it.

The plane banked and dipped, preparing for the descent into LAX. Roxana Felix gazed out at the glittering grid of the city, laid out before her in a jewelled web of light, sparkling against the darkness.

It was a strange thing.

She was frightened.

7

Jordan Cabot Goldman was in an agony of indecision.

She twirled in front of her floor-to-ceiling mirrors, ignoring the reflection of the palatial bedroom behind her – the kingsize four-poster, an Elizabethan original imported from England, the carpet of delicate Chinese silk and the sunken jacuzzi she'd had installed at the foot of the bed. Silver vases were scattered in a careful way about the room, crammed to overflowing with white and yellow roses, flowers that were changed every morning. The huge bay windows had a polished mahogany window seat, laid out invitingly with soft downy cushions, embroidered in Scotland. The whole effect was an absolute triumph of wealth over taste, in the grand tradition of the Duchess of Windsor's jewels, and Jordan was very proud of it, just as proud as she was of their ultra-neat gardens, which she'd had equipped with the very latest in both sprinkler and security systems. Tom Goldman had taken a while to get married, but Jordan Cabot Goldman was here to see that he never regretted that decision. Not for an instant. Hence the jacuzzi in the bedroom and the cupboard full of erotic paraphernalia hidden behind a bookshelf. And hence Jordan's own slender, toned, worked-on young body that was bouncing so gratifyingly as she twisted about, pretending not to watch herself, holding up first the pink Chanel suit and then the navy Bill Blass dress. Both such *grown-up* designers. But Jordan knew it was her duty to reflect the status of her husband in the outfits she wore. She no longer owned a pair of jeans, even designer ones. It was so annoying that she couldn't get Tom to do the same thing. Hugo Boss chinos. That was what he should be wearing when he needed to go casual.

The pink was more attractive, it set off her tan and her blonde hair and her dazzlingly white teeth, but the navy had more gravitas, made her look older. She could be twenty-eight in that navy.

Isabelle wouldn't hesitate for a moment, Jordan thought, jealously. She'd know exactly what to wear. She'd know before she even got to the closet.

Isabelle Kendrick was Jordan's lunch date. Married to Sam Kendrick, she had been a social powerhouse in the city for fifteen years, and Jordan was in awe of her. She didn't like her, of course, but that didn't matter. The fact was that Isabelle sat on every important charity committee in LA, gave the definitive Oscar night party since Swifty Lazar had passed away, and somehow, invisibly, imperceptibly, marked out every new girl on the scene and ranked her desirability. It drove Jordan crazy; after all, wasn't *she* the wife of a studio head? And Isabelle only the wife of an agent, even if he was a fairly heavyweight agent. But there was no getting away from reality, and in LA the reality was that Isabelle ruled. From Cedars-Sinai to the San Francisco Opera House, she sat on every important board. Her little soirées were the most sought-after, reported-on dinner parties in the city. And at her big spectaculars once a season – there was the summer ball coming up at the end of this month – more business got done than at Cannes. If President Clinton came to town and wanted to eat with somebody besides David Geffen, Mrs Samuel Kendrick was the second name on his list. With her own ears Jordan had heard Isabelle chatting to the First Lady on the telephone as though she were an intimate friend. 'Yes, Hillary, Irish salmon.' 'No, Hillary, I promise I'll keep the cholesterol down.'

It was all fantastic, and Jordan wanted it for herself. *She* was Tom's wife and *she* should get that respect. Well, she knew how jealous they all were of her, even the ones that were nearly as young and nearly as attractive as she was. And the older women were just *green*. Too bad, Jordan thought maliciously, surveying her large, firm breasts and slimline thighs. You had your chance once, and now it's my turn.

After all, nobody had dared to actually *snub* her, much though they might have liked to. It was Los Angeles, and when all was said and done, she was the wife of a studio chairman, and thus unsnubbable. Plus, Jordan had a certain survivor's instinct that had served her very well all her life. She knew better than to try to compete with Isabelle Kendrick. No, she had to carve out a new place for herself, a complementary place, as the queen of the new generation. Jordan had started to support the more modern charities, giving nice little dances for AIDS research, sponsoring walks for the war against drugs, and throwing well-attended dinners at five thousand bucks a plate for whatever issue was in the news. Her last one had been a minor victory: An Evening to Stop the Killing, raising money for the struggle against gang warfare in South-Central LA. They'd played hardcore rap music very quietly over the speakers while entertainment industry big shots sipped Dom Pérignon and toyed with their caviar and blinis. It was too bad that she hadn't been able to get Spike Lee to attend – or, indeed, even answer her gilt-edged invitation – but then everybody knew how difficult *he* could be. Her Serene Highness Princess Caroline of Monaco had been guest of honour. Such a step up from that little tramp Stephanie. Yes, it had been quite a triumph, and Jordan had been able to seat Isabelle next to her and bask in her approval.

There was only one aspect of that evening to mar her enjoyment of it, the reason she'd pleaded with Isabelle for some time today. By deftly positioning herself alongside, and not against, Isabelle Kendrick on the LA circuit, Jordan Cabot Goldman had acquired a major advantage. Isabelle was becoming her mentor.

With a flounce of her nicely tanned ass, cheeks high and tight in the mirror as she turned round, Jordan tossed the navy dress over a Regency armchair and selected the Chanel. Just the thing for lunch. Surely you couldn't go wrong with Chanel.

'Mrs Kendrick, how good to see you. Won't you step this way,' gushed the maitre d', leading Isabelle deftly into the main restaurant and up to the second-best table. Normally, she might have protested; Isabelle had huge clout at Morton's, but her practised eye settled almost instantly on Madonna and Abel Ferrara sitting at the place she normally occupied.

Oh well, thought Isabelle. *C'est la vie.*

She smoothed down the featherweight cashmere of her Ralph Lauren jacket, supremely confident in the elegance of her look. At thirty-eight, Isabelle graced every best-dressed list in the country; her hair was a smooth, beautifully permed cap of chestnut brown, with the tiny grey streaks in it marvellously covered over every month by Dino Castoni, this year's favoured Beverly Hills stylist. Her dermatologist ensured that her skin had excellent elasticity for its age, and while Isabelle would have died at the vulgarity of a public gymnasium, Liz Xanthia, her fanatically discreet private trainer, and Margot Guise, the Kendricks' vegetarian chef, between the two of them kept her in wonderfully svelte form.

Isabelle's green eyes, so perfectly matched to her emerald earrings, latched onto Jordan Goldman immediately. Dear Jordan, she thought. Tries so hard. But pink Chanel for a blonde! So *obvious*, so lacking in imagination...

The younger woman stood up to greet her and the two women leant forward, planting loud kisses on the air next to their respective cheeks.

'Isabelle, how kind of you to come,' Jordan gushed, hoping for exactly the right mix of gratitude and graciousness. 'I know how busy you must be, with the party in a fortnight.'

'A nightmare,' Isabelle agreed. 'The flowers are giving me all kinds of headaches. You must let me have the name of that man you used at your last dinner.'

Glowing, Jordan promised to look it up for her, while Isabelle ordered a Caesar salad and mineral water.

'I'll have the same. Thank you.'

'What would we do if they ever ran out of Caesar salads?' Isabelle joked.

Jordan laughed, too brightly.

There was an awkward silence.

Isabelle looked at Jordan sharply, feeling her curiosity begin to pique. Good Lord, something was wrong! She'd assumed this lunch was just par for the course, a further sign of Jordan's respect, possibly a bid to get closer to her now that Sam was cooking up some deal with Artemis. Not for one second had she thought Jordan would actually have something to discuss. But there was no mistaking it, that hesitation, the reluctant blush, the way her irritatingly lovely blue eyes kept dropping to the table. And it wasn't as if Jordan had a job, which meant ... *trouble with Tom*. They had only been married a year.

Isabelle felt the unfamiliar sensation of excitement. What problem was the little *shiksa* about to blurt out? How did she expect Isabelle to help? And would she, should she help? Did she want Jordan Cabot to stay married to Tom?

With the lightning speed at which she made every major decision, Isabelle decided that yes, she probably did. Jordan might be annoyingly young and stupid, and disturbingly sexual, but she had paid Isabelle proper tribute. She represented no threat. Who knew what another Mrs Goldman might be like, how far Jordan's successor might try to push it?

Better the devil you know.

'My dear, I can see that you've something you want to tell me,' Isabelle said gently, ignoring Jordan's look of surprise. *Oy*, she really had no idea how obvious she was. 'Don't be embarrassed. I only hope I can help you. What are friends for, after all?'

'It's Tom,' Jordan said, carefully hiding her delight at being asked what friends were for by Isabelle Kendrick.

'Is it really? I had no idea. I thought things were wonderful between you two.'

'It's Eleanor Marshall,' Jordan said, bitterly.

There. It was out. The thing she'd been carrying around for months, wondering what to do about it, if anything, wondering if she was imagining things. She'd thought about asking Isabelle for advice ages ago, but had resisted the impulse until the last possible moment. After all, not only was there a danger in confiding worries about your relationship to *anybody*, there was the sheer embarrassment. After all, how could *she*, Jordan Cabot, twenty-four and the youngest wife in Hollywood, with her long blonde hair and *Baywatch*-approved figure, she who had introduced Tom Goldman to such excesses of sexual pleasure that he'd proposed within three months, how could she admit that she was concerned about her husband's feelings for some flat-chested bitch more than ten years older than she was?

At first she hadn't even recognized the danger, because she just couldn't conceive of it. Tom and she were so great in bed together, or at least she was great for him. She'd worked hard on that. And he'd been working with the Marshall woman all his single life and yet they'd never dated. Plus, Eleanor Marshall was *thirty-eight*. Practically forty. What man in his right mind would find that attractive? Jordan wondered, as she checked out her own supremely youthful body in the mirror every night, rubbing Donna Karan body lotion into every inch of it, the musky, sensual fragrance that drove Tom so wild. Would Eleanor Marshall know how to do that trick in the hot-tub, the one where she lifted herself slightly out of the water and pressed her wet, warm pussy against the centre of his spine, rubbing herself up and down him until he turned round with a growl and screwed her on the spot? No, she would not. The woman didn't even wear figure-hugging clothes when she came to dinner, although her figure wasn't bad. She didn't even flirt with Tom when they came round to the house. This Jordan was quite sure of; after all, she never took her eyes off the bitch for a second.

But there *was* a problem, all the same. It was there in Tom's eyes, following Eleanor round the dinner table, watching her when she got up to refill her plate from a buffet. The way he always seemed to be so damn interested in what she was saying, like business was all that mattered. He laughed at all her jokes, as if somehow they were really amusing. OK, it wasn't a crisis or anything. She knew she could still get him hard for her, even at a table Eleanor was sitting at, by lowering her hand under the tablecloth or flashing him a quick sight of her pantie-less crotch, crossing and uncrossing her legs in a way that revealed her to his eyes only. He needed her sexually. She made him feel like a man; he said so often enough.

So why was Tom so negative to Paul Halfin?

He was never rude. Quite the opposite, in fact; always pressing Paul to refill his glass, or asking him boring questions about investment banking. It was uncomfortably like watching a man who had something to prove. But she, Jordan, she noticed the way his body tensed, his eyes narrowed, and he kept glancing back at Eleanor.

So he had a little crush. She could have lived with that.

Only lately, they'd started to fight. Tom was being so crass, it was as though he didn't care about the house or their parties or *anything*. Except sex. Sex was the only way he communicated with her now. He'd even been refusing to stay on the Pritikin diet she'd put him on! And he was being such a boor. Like that night with the De Veers last week. She'd finished off her cream silk gown with her little AIDS brooch, the one all studded with rubies in the shape of a ribbon, and he'd actually got all angry with her and asked her when was the last time she'd visited an AIDS ward or volunteered at a counselling centre ...

Jordan had sobbed that she guessed he wanted her to get a job, that she wasn't as good as the women he worked with, just because she wanted to be a homemaker and raise a family.

Tom had melted, all contrite. He wanted a family too. He knew how disappointed she was not to be pregnant yet, why didn't they practise?

She shivered in her pink Chanel. Thank God Tom had never even guessed at the little white pills she hid in the kitchen cupboards.

So that quarrel had been made up.

But she couldn't help but wonder why he was getting so grouchy. And he was asking Eleanor and Paul over all the time!

Oh, Jordan Cabot Goldman was very worried indeed. And she'd never tell Isabelle or anyone else about the final straw, last Wednesday, when she'd been woken by him muttering in his slumber, and had twisted in their black silk Pratesi sheets to see his massive hard-on stiffening from the dream, ready to take him in her mouth, to wake him up in the way he most adored and make that dream a reality, when he'd jerked in his sleep, his back arching a little, and murmured: 'Eleanor.'

Jordan had been frozen to the spot. He was lying next to her, twenty-four, a world-class babe, every man's fantasy wife, and he was having a wet dream about some middle-aged career spinster with grey streaks in her hair?

She had called Isabelle Kendrick first thing the next day.

'Eleanor Marshall?' Isabelle said now, leaning forward, shocked.

'Oh, he hasn't said anything. They haven't done anything,' said Jordan, delicately.

'But you see signs. You're worried. Oh, my dear, you were so right to come to me,' Isabelle breathed, reaching across the table and patting Jordan's hand.

Eleanor! Ridiculous. Just look at Jordan ... but of course, as soon as she'd said it it made all kinds of sense, Isabelle Kendrick thought, her heart speeding up. She'd started recalling all kinds of functions where she'd seen them together. Was it possible they had been at the same studio all this time, and not? But of course it was possible . . . what an appalling thought. Eleanor Goldman. Oh, dear Lord, but that would be just too much.

'I know I must be putting you in a terrible position, Isabelle,' Jordan was breathing, 'knowing her for as long as you have . . .'

The question mark hung in the air, but Isabelle, for once, was not inclined to keep her supplicant on tenterhooks.

'Well, that's true. But it's a moral question, isn't it? After all, you are his wife.' Jordan nodded her coiffed blonde head eagerly, and Isabelle added, 'And dear Eleanor . . . she *works* so hard. I'm sure she would not wish any unpleasantness.'

Jordan breathed out as the Caesar salads were set before them, almost overwhelmed with relief. There could be no mistaking Isabelle's tone. She *hated* Eleanor Marshall, hated her even worse than maybe she did herself. Now she came to think of it, hadn't she heard stories from some of the other girls? About how Eleanor was always turning down Isabelle's invitations to sit on committees because she was 'too busy'? As if *she* was the only busy one, Jordan thought with disdain. They all had things to do. Dressing properly required an investment of your time and, of course, they were all so active in charity work, and charity work was very important . . .

Isabelle hadn't taken kindly to being blown off. And as Jordan stared at her across the table, she noticed something else — weren't Isabelle and Eleanor about the same age? That meant, she realized, that Isabelle resented Eleanor for more than just her superior attitude; the fact was that Isabelle had no hold over Eleanor because she simply did not care about the social world. Isabelle resented Eleanor for working, being a working woman, one who now wielded power, real power, in Hollywood.

Eleanor was a queen regnant, not a queen consort, and Isabelle Kendrick just hated her for it. There was no way she was going to allow her to marry Tom as well. It would be the cherry on the cake, a final triumph that Isabelle, resentful and furious, would not allow her to have.

The two women gazed at each other with perfect understanding.

'Will you forgive me if I speak frankly?' Isabelle said. 'Jordan, you must understand that men are . . . *sexual* creatures.' Her tone held up the word to the light as though it were something disgusting she'd discovered on the sole of her shoe. 'No matter what they have, they always want something else. No matter how ridiculous.'

Both women thought of Eleanor Marshall and compared her to Jordan. Unfavourably.

'The thing is, and I know this will be a difficult thing for you to accept, darling, such a newlywed as you are, but you must learn to turn a blind eye to their little peccadilloes. Men are such simple creatures, they really can't help themselves.'

Isabelle dismissed unfaithfulness and betrayal with a light laugh, aware that Jordan was hanging on her every word. Good. At least the child was going to see sense; it was never those irritating little diversions their husbands found that were a problem, it was the state of the marriage. After all, everything was founded on, centred on the marriage. A divorced queen was a dethroned queen, something she had realized ten years ago, coldly, precisely, about the same time that she'd seen the love draining out of her relationship. That was when her ascent to super-hostess had begun; recognizing that Sam no longer felt for her as a woman, Isabelle had identified a different desire in him, the beating, rampant, killer ambition that was driving him forward day by day. She had set out to help him satisfy that need, to become such a social lioness that Sam Kendrick could never divorce her, never leave her, because his business would be hurt by letting her go. Sam continued to screw around discreetly and she continued to throw exquisite parties.

Love and hope had died in Isabelle Kendrick a long time ago, but she was still rich, still stylish, and still accorded respect in this town.

She was still married.

'What shall I do?' Jordan asked her.

'In cases like this, there's only one answer, dear. Give him what every wife should. What she can't.'

'You mean – '

'Yes I do. Give him a baby.'

8

Kevin Scott was having a bad day. Another one. In fact, it was shaping up to be a very bad week. Ever since that blasted meeting at Artemis Studios on Thursday, his department had been in complete chaos.

'Ten more Elsie thinks you should take a look at,' panted Katherine, his English assistant, waddling into his office. She was waddling because she was weighed down by a pile of scripts, the paper stacking up against her bony torso, her normally pallid face bright red with physical effort.

Kevin gestured wearily to the free corner of his desk not already covered with manuscripts. That made thirty-five he had to wade through by the weekend, and there would be more in by then. Many more. The ones that had made it to his desk were typical in their variety of the hundreds that had only got as far as his subordinates – dogeared, pristine, typed on vellum, covered in clear plastic or leather-bound. Some leather-bound *and* embossed. Some with spurious gifts attached to them, like little packets of Cuban cigars or a pair of solid gold cufflinks.

Those were the ones he was always tempted to bin first, but alas, that wasn't how it worked. Suppose he were to throw away the specimen written on pink parchment, with the Mont Blanc fountain pen attached to it by orange velvet ribbon. With his luck it would turn out to be another *Ghost* or *Jurassic Park*. Just because the writer was a vulgar oaf didn't mean his script was necessarily unusable. After all, Kevin reflected, all screenwriters were vulgar oafs by definition. And in this crass and vulgar world, many of them were very highly paid.

He took a slice of that high pay, which normally consoled him for having to put up with hawking their trash for a living. Today, it didn't even come close. What had happened, Kevin wondered, to the appreciation of literature? To delicate sensitivity and fine writing? Oh, for a Proust or Joyce that he might represent, selling exquisite penmanship for large amounts of money. Or at least a Norman Mailer.

Kevin Scott was fifty-five, and a long time ago he had been educated in England. How his old beaks at Eton would cringe for him now. How his Oxford dons would wince. He considered himself a gentleman in a world overrun by ruffians, subliterate, ill-educated ruffians who wanted Judith Krantz, John Grisham and *Forrest Gump*. Even the President of the United States had had a 'popular music' group playing at his Inaugural Ball. There was simply no end to it. And now he himself was embroiled in the indignity.

For a while, at least, he had been able to carve a small oasis of sanity in the Hollywood madness – while the unpleasantness of working with scripts could not be avoided entirely, his literary division had managed to work almost wholly with quality films, producing a run of Original Screenplay and Adaptation Oscars that was the envy of all the other big agencies. Although the division hadn't turned out all that much profit in and of itself, the Oscars and Golden Globes had attracted acting and directing talent Sam's way, and once in a while one of the obnoxious kids that reported to him – all hired by Sam or Mike Campbell direct – shopped some piece of violent or pornographic trash to Columbia or Paramount, and they cleaned up. Thus Kevin had been tolerated, allowed to go about the more serious business of selling novels in New York.

Lately, that had all gone to the wind. As the packaged movies dried up, Sam had been putting more and more pressure on him to come up with commercial scripts. The pushy little Tauber brat hadn't helped that situation much, either. But after the Artemis meeting, forget about it. Word from the top was loud and clear. They wanted a script for the rock star and they wanted one yesterday.

Outside the air-conditioned, soundproofed sanctum of Kevin's office, he could see hordes of people milling about, many carrying bound manuscripts or parcels, their noiseless mouths opening and closing furiously as they argued with the harassed assistants and a couple of the junior agents. They'd been arriving all morning – the scumbags, the bottom of the pile, low-life writers with no contacts and no reputations and not so much as an article in the Nowheresville, Alabama Gazette on their résumés, and yet every one of the losers thinking that SKI would be impressed with their bravado if they crashed the doors in person.

They'd been watching too many movies, Kevin thought, pleasing himself with the ironic conceit. Turning up as singing telegrams. With huge bouquets of flowers. Holding massive bunches of balloons. One, heaven preserve him, had even sent a stripper. He recalled seeing her shaking her tassels in poor Katherine's astounded face, thrusting a script forward between two sets of blood-red talons, before the grinning SKI security arrived to throw her out on the sidewalk. There was, as he had discovered, absolutely no limits to how deeply embarrassing this business could be.

And yet the sheer volume of these wretched scripts was taking him aback somewhat. The meeting with Artemis had obviously been leaked minutes after it had finished, because by the time their limo had returned him to the SKI offices there were already ten calls on his sheet about 'the Mason/ Florescu project', and the first manuscript, about a rock star who lives a double life as a sexual serial killer, arrived an hour later. They might as well have put up a billboard on Sunset and an ad in *Daily Variety*. Forget the Information Superhighway. Showbusiness gossip was the universe's most efficient communication mechanism, because by the end of that day every two-bit hack in LA knew all about it. And by Monday six hundred of them had written instant movies over the weekend.

And yet not one of them was any good.

'Mr Scott.' Katherine was buzzing him.

'What is it?' Kevin snapped, chucking another pile of neatly typed pages onto the floor. The trash basket had given up the unequal struggle this morning, so now he was just throwing them down for the janitors to deal with. 'I thought I told you no calls.'

'But it's Mr Tauber again, sir. He insists on being put through,' said Katherine weakly, sounding distraught.

'No! Goddamnit, Katherine!'

Scott felt his blood pressure rise. Two calls per hour from Sam and one from Mike and now that – that *odious* little toad Tauber thought he had the right to bother a department head? 'Especially not Tauber! Not under any circumstances! Do I make myself clear?'

'Yes, sir,' said Katherine meekly.

He slammed down the receiver and tried to concentrate on the next script, *Hot Rockin'*.

FADE IN

INT. BACKSTAGE – A SEEDY CLUB

A SERIES OF ANGLES

A naked WOMAN is tied down with scarlet rope across two Marshall amps. ZEKE and BERTIE stand to one side, watching the DOBERMAN PINSCHER that is licking her between the legs.

Sighing heavily, Kevin Scott lifted the manuscript and threw it behind him without another glance.

'You OK, hon?'

The waitress looked Megan over with genuine concern. Most of the time she was too busy or too hardened to worry herself with the punters' problems – bleak-eyed hookers that might stumble in with bruised faces and call for coffee, or the shabbily dressed unemployment types that turned up for the cheap burgers and beer. Don't talk, don't get involved. Too much heartache that way, not to mention that you wanted them out so you could serve someone else. In cafés as cheap as this one, volume was where it was at. Pack them in and throw them out. Shit, this wasn't the Ivy. But something about this girl was touching; a little fat and plain maybe, but she'd ordered a full meal and then hardly touched it, just drunk pot after pot of coffee and sat there shaking. She looked real innocent, in a way. Soft and lost. Must be new in town.

'What? Oh, thanks. I'm fine,' Megan said, giving her a little smile to back up the lie.

The waitress hesitated, hovering, but what could she do? If they don't want to talk – 'OK. Well, if you're sure,' she said, moving off.

God, how obvious I must be, Megan thought miserably. She'd arrived there half an hour ago and ordered lunch, all keyed up, excited, nervous but a little thrilled in a way. After all, this was it. She'd taken the day off work, as little as she could afford to piss Mr Jenkins off, she'd taken the original copy of *See the Lights* out of its special hiding place in the back of her cramped closet, and she was going to come out here to storm right through the hallowed doors of Sam Kendrick International, script in hand, to make their deal come off and her dream come true.

Ha, ha, ha. Nice joke, God.

Pete's Café had been her choice for a good reason: despite being crowded, noisy, dirty and full of scumbags, it was situated just off Sunset, and through its grimy windows she could watch the immaculately clean black marble fronting of the SKI offices, check out the agents coming and going, psych herself up. Megan recalled what a good idea she thought that would be; she could get all inspired, get up the courage to just burst in there and blow them away.

It hadn't exactly worked out like that. From the moment she sat down at eleven-thirty, Megan had watched with growing horror as a stream of people – men, women, and your guess is as good as mine – all clutching scripts, or parcels that looked like scripts, or briefcases that must contain scripts, had filed steadily through the doors. Some of them wore the most outlandish rig, including some raddled hag in an overcoat and stilettos. Megan had watched with a kind of sick fascination when she landed back on the sidewalk, nude except for tassels and a gold G-string – and still clutching a script. In they poured and right back out they poured, cursing, shaking themselves down and *still clutching their scripts*. She saw some of them trying to warn off the others coming in, who merely cursed them and chanced their luck anyway.

The plan that she'd thought unique was being tried by every schmuck writer in LA, right in front of her eyes. And it was failing.

'Jerks, huh?' the waiter had asked, refilling her coffee cup. 'Some people.'

'Some people,' Megan agreed.

She wondered if she'd been this dumb growing up, or if it was a talent she'd only recently perfected. What was she going to do now? Sitting here with her script, opposite SKI, with her perfect story for their perfect deal and not a damn way she could get them to read it.

Above him, David Tauber could see the craggy side of the cliff, with a smattering of green scrub vegetation clinging gamely to the rock face, determined to survive and grow, no matter how hostile the conditions. He focused on it for a second. He empathized with it. It could have been an agent.

But there wasn't much time to start meditating on the Malibu vegetation. His dick wouldn't allow it. There wasn't much space for concentration on anything except the obvious – Gloria's heavy, sculpted silicone tits bouncing nicely in front of him, her curvy ass grinding from side to side as she danced for him, crooking her long, tapering legs as she twirled, letting him get a good look at the silky brown hair on her pussy, damp with her arousal. Jesus, this was turning him on. A little strip on the sand, a little head in his Lamborghini at the side of the road while he talked to Sam Kendrick, making his point about Kevin Scott. His cock pulsed a little harder at the thought of it, Gloria making those little sucking noises he loved to hear while he was being fellated, his hand covering the carphone so Sam wouldn't hear, while he slid the knife deeper and deeper into Kevin Scott's useless fat belly. The old guy had snubbed him one too many times and now he was going to pay.

The image warmed David's already hot blood, adding to the sensations of desire and languorous lust that were pooling in his cock. God, look at Gloria. She was totally wet for him now, her pussy flexing closer and closer towards his face, golden-brown haunches shuddering forward. That was what got him going: the way she wanted him, just for himself. Sure, David enjoyed the power-trip fucking, the little starlets, the Hollywood wannabees who'd do anything you cared to suggest, whether it involved bringing their friends round for a floor show or going down on one of your buddies in front of you. That had a thrill all its own which had nothing to do with desire. But this was different; this was a woman who desired him for himself, for the muscled body and deep tan, the hazel hair and his big, thick, beloved cock. Gloria was a corporate attorney and one of the best lays he'd ever known. Her desire, the way she choked out his name when she came, the way she'd start breathing raggedly if he talked dirty to her down the phone, all of it tickled his vanity.

Shit, they had a mutual fan club. He loved her large, berry-brown nipples and the way they jumped in his mouth, the tips of them hard as sun-dried raisins. He admired her large, toned butt and the way it tapered in to a minute waist. The original hourglass figure. Jesus, that butt was something else, the way she'd grind and swing it. David grunted, his cock aching now. Enough. He reached up to grab her, tripped her over on the sand and felt her crotch. Ohhhh, man . . . slippery wet like somebody poured a bottle of baby oil all over her.

'Want it?'

His question was a tease, asking her like that while his fingers were busy stroking her labia, making her moan and twist into him.

'Yes. Now,' she gasped. He could sense that he'd better be quick if he didn't want her to come right there. He could see her lower belly tightening up, flattening. Swiftly he took his hand away and twisted her over, placing her on her hands and knees. Gloria groaned. He put his hand under her, giving her a quick, almost patronizing caress between the legs. She knew better than to break position, just lifted her head, shuddering with arousal. His hand slipped to her midriff, lifting her up, arranging her for his entrance. David felt her respond all over her body as he touched her, the nipples on her delicious pendant breasts stiffening even more, shrinking tiny and tight like his balls. The skin of her belly was incredibly hot, warm with her blood pooling in desire. He fluttered his fingers across it and heard her gasp. That was so horny, feeling her lust literally burning at his touch. He saw a drop of moisture pearl on the end of his cock. Time to go for the main event.

David walked round behind her as she crouched in front of him like some wild beast, the smoky scent of her arousal distinct even through that designer perfume she was wearing. He put his two hands on the soft curves of her hips, allowing himself a little leverage. Then he was leaning forward, over her back, his dick finding the entrance to her like some military fucking torpedo guided by radar. He inserted just the tip, going maybe a quarter of an inch inside her, forcing himself to resist the temptation to shove it right in and nail her fabulous fucking ass until he boiled over, emptying himself inside her. Time for that later. Control, control.

'*Madre de Dios!*' Gloria sobbed. 'More! David, Jesus Christ!'

'More?' he asked softly, sinking in another inch.

She was so aroused now, she was desperate. She was sobbing openly from wanting it.

He slid in another inch, smiling despite the fury of his own lust.

'Hey, take it slowly, baby. Don't get greedy.'

'David!'

She'd come any second. So would he. David Tauber pulled out, slowly, until he was almost completely withdrawn from her, and then thrust savagely, quickly, back inside her, all the way in, right up to the hilt, hearing her ecstatic scream only dimly because of the burning blood pounding in his own ears, finding his rhythm immediately, thrusting, thrusting, feeling her spasms start up, and then there it was, that great white fucking wall. Oh JesusJesusJesus, oh, yes . . .

Gloria moved first, shifting forward and easing him out of her, and just as quickly Tauber tucked himself away and started buttoning his fly. DKNY for Men pants in the lightest cream wool, and he didn't want to be getting sand in them. The Rolex said it was five after four. Time to be heading back; a few more instances of that old faggot Scott refusing to take his calls, and he was gonna bust into his office in person. David knew Sam would back him this time. They had a window of opportunity for this deal, and he wasn't about to let that fake-ass would-be limey jerk him around because he couldn't pick one good script out of – what? – eight hundred? How many had they seen this week? And he called himself a literary agent.

Writers were scum, but even writers deserved better than Kevin Scott in their corner.

Gloria Ramirez handed him his copy of the latest Colleen McCallum contract when they got back to their respective cars, and Tauber put it carefully in his briefcase.

They shook hands briskly. He could see her mind was already somewhere else, at her next appointment, on the next deal.

'Nice doing business with you,' David said, flashing her a warm smile. She'd be back for more, he knew it. He was good, really good.

'Sure,' she said absently, adding, 'You know, David? If that Kevin guy is really so bad, maybe *you* should take a writer on. Show Sam Kendrick how bad he is by doing better.'

'But I'm a movie agent,' David said, slowly.

'So?'

He blew her a kiss as he slid into the low-slung leather seat of the Lamborghini. Not only was Gloria a great lay, she was a smart bitch, too. So, indeed. Just because it hadn't been done before didn't mean he couldn't do it.

All the way down the Santa Monica freeway the idea blossomed in his head, exciting him so much he didn't even bother to put on his meditation tape.

If he could find a writer for this movie, he could get Kevin Scott fired.

He could put a part in it so perfect for Roxana Felix they'd have to cast her.

He would represent the lead male, lead female, and the writer.

Fuck the literary division.

Jesus.

David Tauber pressed his foot on the gas.

Quarter of five, and the asshole supply had finally dried up. Maybe it was because everybody knew that Kevin's department shut its doors at five on the dot, but the singing telegrams and balloon ladies had given up the game about twenty minutes ago. The phone was still ringing off the hook, but his assistant was dealing with it. Kevin stared morosely at the huge pile of paper on his desk, waiting for somebody to take it out to his Rolls. He would have to try to look at about twenty of these tonight, but he was almost past caring. Rarely had he been so glad to get to the end of a working day.

'No. There's no way.'

Katherine's voice, louder and shriller than normal, floated towards him from the department lobby. He could see the tight silhouette of her back blocking the entrance to his office. 'You cannot come in. We only accept scripts referred to us by known sources.'

Somebody was arguing quietly, a young woman. Enraged, Kevin thrust back his chair and lumbered to his feet. This was the last straw! These people had no manners, just wouldn't take no for an answer. Well, he would give this one something to think about before she next barged into somebody's private offices.

'Katherine, what is the matter here?' he demanded portentously, flinging open the door. Yes, he'd been right. Some plump, mousy girl stood all alone in his reception, a final, forlorn figure standing on crushed flowerheads and bits of popped balloons and wrapping paper. Dear God, it looked like some child had thrown a birthday party out here. It had better, he thought ominously, be all cleaned away by the time he got in tomorrow.

'It's this young lady, Mr Scott. I was trying to explain to her that we do not accept unrecommended scripts,' Katherine said thinly.

'What in God's name do you think you're playing at, miss?' Scott roared. The girl shrank, clutching her script to her chest. 'We have a policy in this agency, you know! Didn't you understand my assistant? We do not accept unrecommended material!'

'But I'm newly arrived here,' the mouse said. She appeared to be on the verge of tears. 'How can I get something recommended when I —'

All he registered was that she had made no move to leave.

'*We do not accept* —' Kevin practically screamed.

'What's going on?'

Apoplectic with rage at being interrupted, Scott whipped round to face the intruder and promptly found his blood pressure rising even further.

It was David Tauber.

Instantly, the girl was forgotten. 'Do you have an appointment?' Scott spat, his face mottled puce with hatred.

'No, sir,' Katherine said quickly.

Tauber shrugged. 'You wouldn't take any of my calls, Kevin. So I thought I'd come to you, see how you're getting along with a script for Zach.'

Megan, watching silently from beside the desk, felt herself blush. The stranger who had so suddenly diverted all Kevin Scott's rage towards himself was the picture of nonchalant calm and composure. The nuclear blast of Scott's wrath that had threatened to break her down right there in his lobby merely washed over this guy like a gentle summer breeze. He was so masculine, so self-assured. Scott did not frighten him.

And he was so *handsome*. Movie-star handsome, male-model handsome, with thick hazel hair and an exquisitely muscled body. She could see his biceps outlined through the sleeves of his gorgeous cream wool suit, which contrasted so beautifully with his golden-brown tan. Her heart sped up, she felt a small wash of warm desire seep through her lower belly. It wasn't just his good looks and confidence, there was something else ... masculinity, sexuality. The way he moved, he just gave it off. If it hadn't been five in the afternoon, Megan would have sworn this man had just had sex.

Her mouth went dry.

Tauber turned round to the girl Scott had been yelling at, knowing she was staring at him. He could feel her eyes on the back of his neck. An unprepossessing kid, shy, needed to lose weight, but she had a pretty face – pale skin and long chestnut hair wound up in an unflattering bun. She was looking at him with a mixture of awe and admiration, maybe lust, too. No, definitely lust.

Megan dropped her gaze, flushing a deeper red with embarrassment.

'*When* I have something I think is suitable,' Kevin was sputtering, 'I'll show it to Sam.' He rounded on Megan. 'Get *out*.'

'Hey, don't be so hasty,' Tauber said. He didn't give a damn about the girl, but she was bugging Kevin. Plus, she'd looked at him in a way that he liked. 'Maybe the little lady wants to submit a script.'

'Her and a million others,' Kevin Scott hissed, hardly able to credit that Tauber would countermand him. 'This division does not accept unrecommended material.'

Megan was gazing at David Tauber, holding her breath.

He looked her over, a slow, assessing look. It felt like a caress, like feathery hands feeling up and down her body. Her nipples hardened.

'I'll bet you waited all day to come in here. I'll bet you waited until all the others had gone,' Tauber said to her, guessing shrewdly. She looked desperate, determined. He knew the type.

'I'm not looking at that script!' Scott bellowed.

Tauber held out his hand and took the script from Megan. 'Your name and number on this?' he enquired.

She nodded.

'Tauber, what the hell are you doing?' Kevin Scott shrieked.

David turned to him with an insolent smile. 'I'm accepting submission of this manuscript.' Not a hope in hell it'd be any good, but that wasn't the point. The point was a declaration of war, and this script would be as good as any for that. 'Since your department has its policy, I'm going to look at it myself. We don't demand recommendations in the movie division, and Kevin, I *do* need a script.'

'But you don't represent writers!'

Tauber shrugged. 'As of now, I do.' Ignoring the older man's incensed look, he turned to the little mousy girl and gave her a friendly smile. 'You can run along, honey. I'll take a look and be in touch if it's suitable.'

With one final glance at Kevin Scott's maroon complexion and Katherine's expression of mortal outrage, Megan turned on her heels and fled.

9

Flashbulbs exploded around her like firecrackers, microphones from local TV stations were thrust forward in a little forest under her nose, and a crowd of print reporters jostled around the airport security guards, tape recorders shoved wildly in her general direction. Behind her, Roxana could see the other passengers swamped as a pack of fans broke through the yellow security ribbons, many of them screaming her name. With a practised eye she assessed the situation: no, there were too many guards here for them to get anywhere near her.

Inwardly she smiled. Howard Thorn had done a good job.

'My God, am I safe?' she whispered loudly to her nearest bodyguard.

A hundred mikes picked up the comment. She watched the TV hacks dutifully train their cameras on the mêlée of fans behind her. That turned the story from 'Supermodel Arrives in LA' to 'Roxana Causes Riots at Airport'.

'Roxana, does it bother you to get mobbed everywhere you go?'

She bent her gorgeous head towards the electronic thicket in front of her, replying bravely, 'No, I love to see my fans. But it's a little scary when I haven't made enough security arrangements.' An elegant shrug. 'It was supposed to be a secret that I was coming to LA.'

Good-natured laughter. 'Are you here to meet with producers?' 'Are you planning on acting?'

'I'd rather not comment right now.' She smiled dazzlingly at them all, angling her head for the best pictures.

'But isn't it true that you've signed up to Sam Kendrick International for an acting career?' somebody yelled.

Score two for Howard.

Roxana turned in the voice's direction, surprise written bright across her face. 'How did you know about that?' she gasped, and then covered her mouth with her hands, as though caught out. More flashbulbs. All the other reporters babbling at once, firing off questions.

'When did you decide to start acting?'

'What's your first project? Why SKI?'

'Is this the end of your modelling career?'

'OK, people, that's enough. Let the lady through, she has no further comment at this time,' snarled the bodyguard, hustling her with admirable slowness through the journalists towards her waiting limo, giving everybody enough time to get a snap of Roxana in 'casual' clothes – cut-off denim shorts that came right up to her ass, hugging her rock-hard, slightly curved butt and displaying slender, supple thighs that tapered down to endless calves and slim ankles. This had been teamed with a Richard Tyler T-shirt in caramel silk that set off her glossy black hair and million-dollar face to perfection, clinging to her heavenly breasts that were lifted even further skywards by a satin Wonderbra. The whole effect was calculatedly casual, displaying her breathtaking body in the best possible light. The outfit cost her over three thousand dollars – the shorts were Chanel originals – but Joe Public would think she'd picked it up in J.C. Penney, and she looked stunning anyway.

Roxana smiled gently, apologetically, at the crowds of press and fans who crammed their noses and lenses against the tinted windows of her limo, maintaining her expression until the car had rolled forward onto the tarmac and the last of them had slipped away.

'The Beverly Hills Hotel,' she ordered the driver, sharply.

She'd be staying at the best bungalow in the grounds, the absolute height of luxury in a city where luxury was second nature. Not that she'd be footing the bill. Unique, her modelling agents in New York, were paying; she'd thought about asking SKI to pick up the tab, but the bald fact was that she wasn't sure they would. To Unique, she was invaluable. To SKI, she was disposable.

Roxana frowned. By this time next week, that attitude would have changed.

She flicked open her Filofax, looking for the list of numbers she'd jotted down in the plane. Around thirty calls to make before they got into the city, and her little campaign would be all set.

The first name on the list was one of the most useful; an old schoolfriend, a girl she hadn't seen since they were at the Sacred Heart, San Francisco, together. But that wouldn't matter. She wanted to be a hostess, and she, Roxana, was the biggest supermodel in the world right now.

Deliberately, she punched the number into her carphone.

Jordan Cabot Goldman.

'Hey Megan! Over here!'

So, I'm moving up in the world, Megan thought, as she dumped two trays of dirty dishes on the sideboard. They know my name now.

Bob Jenkins shoved a dishcloth at her. 'The machine's full and we need more plates. Wash these.'

Disbelievingly, Megan stared at the sink. It was piled high with greasy plates, some of which hadn't been properly scraped off, so that rank gobbets of undercooked chicken and oily skin swam around in the water. The whole sink was vibrating from the rattle of the huge antique dishwasher stacked next to it, filled to capacity and struggling to cope with the load. The movement was making the filthy water eddy about in murky rivulets.

'What are you waiting for?' Jenkins was watching her like a hawk. 'Got some problem with that? They're only plates, for Chrissake. All the other girls are busy.'

That was a blatant lie, Megan thought, looking round at Sandra, leaning against the wall with a cigarette, and Lisa who was hanging onto the payphone like it was her personal life-support system. She'd been on the damn thing all day. Maybe it *was* her life-support system. But she didn't dare object. Lisa and Sandra kissed up to Jenkins and they hadn't taken Tuesday off.

'No, it's fine,' she said, taking the dishcloth from him.

Jenkins grunted. 'Yeah, well, you better make it snappy. We got another six in five minutes ago.'

'OK.' She'd be Zen about this, take the path of least resistance, Megan told herself as she sank her arms in the washing-up, right up to the elbows. It was lukewarm and viscous, almost made her want to gag. That was the way the guys handled things in Frisco.

'Are you all right?' Stacey said. 'You look real upset.'

'I'm fine,' Megan said, but she couldn't keep it up, and the tears started to roll down her cheeks, big, splashy tears that pooled at the end of her nose and dripped into slimy water.

'Hey, don't let it get to you,' Stacey whispered, squeezing her arm. 'It's the weekend tomorrow.'

Which meant it had been three whole days since that SKI agent had taken her screenplay. Which meant he hadn't liked it. And God, that story could have been written with Zach Mason specifically in mind. If it wasn't good enough for his project at Artemis, it certainly wasn't good enough for anyone else. She was also absolutely sure that *See the Lights* was the best she could do.

Time to face reality. She wasn't good enough.

'Yeah, I know,' Megan sobbed, not wanting to discuss it. She searched for a reason Stacey would understand. 'I was thinking about my ex-boyfriend.'

'I understand,' Stacey said gravely, patting her sympathetically.

Miserably she started to wash up the dirty dishes as fast as she could, grateful to have some work to do, but she just couldn't keep her mind off it. It was so viciously heartbreaking to want something so hard, wait for it so long, and then fail so completely. And what made it even worse was that finally she had had that shred of hope. The way the young agent had taken her screenplay – the older guy, the literary guy who should have been in charge, he'd been ready to hit him, but that hadn't stopped him from taking her script. It was as though she'd eventually stumbled across an ally. And he was so hot-looking, and he'd given her that sexy once-over that made her feel so wet and squirmy, so that when she pulled up outside the apartment she'd felt more alive, more bright with hope than she'd done in years. Like she was on a threshold. And that night, a hot, sticky night, she hadn't been able to sleep, just lay on her bed with her eyes open listening to the cars and the gangbangers streaming past in the street, until finally she started to touch herself, thinking about that agent – somebody Tauber, the other guy had called him – thinking about his muscles and his eyes and his tan and his walk, what that silky hazel hair would feel like brushing between her thighs, until she'd had a gentle climax, orgasm running sweetly over her like ripples across a pool, and slept at last.

The phone had rung on and off all that week, sometimes for her. Calls from the café, even a call from Dec up in Frisco. But as Wednesday became Thursday, and Thursday became Friday, the trilling of the phone turned from hopeful music into sadistic mockery. There were a lot of calls for Megan, but not one of them from SKI. Today was Friday, Friday afternoon to be exact, and Megan Silver had learnt enough about the movie business to know that if they don't call you quickly, they don't call at all.

She shook her head, aware that Stacey was still gazing at her sympathetically.

'You must miss him like crazy, Megan. I've never seen you this upset.'

'I'll get over it.'

Stacey wasn't convinced. 'If you want to go home, you can always just go, honey. You don't have to stay here. I know you wanted to try out with your script, but . . .' Her southern twang trailed off, embarrassed. 'Well, you know how you hate the place . . .'

Megan glanced down at the greasy washing-up. 'It's not exactly Shangri-la.'

'Kids come here all the time and try out. Mostly it doesn't work, an' I seen a bunch of them slip into really bad stuff. You might be better off going home. You worked for the library, right? Maybe you could get a mortgage, get a house.' She shrugged. 'Gotta be better than this.'

Somehow Megan just didn't want to hear it from somebody else, especially not somebody as pretty and as stupid as Stacey. It sounded so true. Jesus, it *was* true. But is that all there is to life for me, truly? she wondered. A detached bungalow, a mortgage, a comfortable, passionless marriage? Was that, in real life, the highest goal, was that as high as she should set her sights? And just pray God that at least she'd feel something when the kids came along?

'It worked for Jeanne,' Megan said defiantly. 'She got a part just last week. Second lead in an art movie by a guy called Ray Tyson.'

For a second Stacey just gaped at her, and then looked swiftly down, obviously trying to stifle a laugh. 'Christ, honey, you have to be kidding. Everyone knows Ray Tyson around here. He bugged me for weeks when I first started this job. The guy shoots, you know, *dirty movies*. Sells videotapes direct to the sex stores, gets a flick screened in a porno house from time to time.'

'Everybody knows this?' Megan repeated weakly, feeling sick. 'Jeanne knew?'

'Sure. She must have done. He's a dirty old man, sixty maybe. Not even in the Guild. He pays a good rate, that's what they told me before.' Stacey wrinkled her perfect little nose. 'I'd never be *that* desperate. And I know you never would either, but this place ain't good for you. You got a college degree, you need a real job.'

'You work here,' said Megan, stubbornly.

Stacey gave her a long, cool stare, and then said, not unkindly, 'But honey, you're twenty-four. I'm still in high school.'

'What are you two gabbing about?' Mr Jenkins snarled, passing them. 'Stacey, they need two pitchers on seven. Megan, Jesus. Get a move on, willya? I told you we need this done, and that means now, not some time before you die.' He jabbed her back with a bony elbow, watching until she picked up the scourer and began to attack the plates, the slimy water splashing across her bare forearms. Mr Chicken didn't bother with mundane luxuries like washing-up gloves.

Two more hours, Megan thought, bowing her head so Jenkins wouldn't see her reddened eyes. Two more hours before I get paid for the week. And that's it. It'll be enough for a bus ticket back to Frisco, and I'm gonna be on the first one tomorrow morning.

She was ashamed at how swiftly she'd given in, turned into the quitter she swore she'd never become. She'd been so certain that she was destined for a real adventure in life, something better than Dec and Trey and Francine. So sure that there had to be something out there for her, something bigger and better than listing textbooks at the San Francisco Public Library and talking about beat poets over coffee.

Well, how wrong she'd been.

'Take a look at this.'

Sam Kendrick flung the paper across to Mike Campbell with a snort. It landed on the polished marble coffee table with a heap of other papers and magazines, all of them adorned with pictures of Roxana Felix. Smiling, pouting, winking. Standing up, sitting regally on a chair in the Polo Lounge, walking into Le Dome, lying curled on the beach like the proverbial sex kitten. In each and every shot she looked utterly stunning, endless legs stretching on forever, raven hair glistening halfway down her back, pale skin freshened with luminous blusher. The clothes were always impeccable, from the silk T-shirt she'd worn at the airport to the black cashmere blazer that had starred at her dinner at Morton's, the first evening in town. Looking at the mountain of press, you'd imagine that Roxana was on some mission to check out, and be snapped at, every star hangout in LA, from Twin Palms to the Viper Room, the Roxbury to House of Blues.

'Yeah,' Mike said, attempting to frown but unable to drag his gaze from one shot of Roxana in a copper silk dress which showed her full nipples clearly outlined under the delicate fabric. 'I gotta say I've never seen anything like it.'

'Three days! That's all she's been here, three days. She's trying to snow me.'

Sam was seriously pissed-off.

'It's not just the papers, either. She's on every radio show, every local TV station, *Entertainment Tonight*, did a guest slot on *MTV at the Movies* just yesterday,' Campbell agreed hastily. If Sam was pissed with Roxana then so was he, no matter how much of a world-class babe she was. 'I guess she's trying to force us into pushing her, going flat-out for her. If we don't get her something good after all this –' He gestured at the copy of *LA Weekly* Sam had thrown him, which had PUTTING HER FAITH IN SKI written in large black type under Roxana's picture.

'Yeah. Thanks, Sherlock,' Sam said sourly.

MTV at the Movies? Damn, the woman was better than he thought. She was running this campaign more precisely than most politicians. Of course, most politicians had a harder time getting coverage than Roxana Felix. But still! This was crazy. Surely the media would have tired of her by now, or at least kept her off the cover pages and the prime gossip slots. Her arrival in town was news, but after that? You'd think this broad was the Queen of England, the way they were fawning over her every move. They put her on the cover when she blew her little retroussé nose.

Sam Kendrick had been around the block a few times, and something about this frenzy smelt odd. To be exact, it smelt of friends in high places. Very high places. And Sam hated the idea of any shadowy puppet master trying to yank *his* strings.

Still, he had to hand it to her. She was pretty fucking determined. My God, the first night she'd arrived Sam came back home to find his wife out at an impromptu dinner with Jordan Goldman and Roxana Felix! Apparently Roxana and Jordan had been Catholic schoolgirls together in San Francisco and now just couldn't wait to celebrate their joint elevation to the Baby Millionairess Club. Obviously what Roxana wanted, and right on cue, according to Isabelle, Jordan had spilled her bimboid guts about the Zach Mason project at Artemis, including the news about the script. Jordan, meanwhile, gets a new member of the Board for her chi-chi little dinners against gang violence and AIDS and a new star at the dinner table. And Isabelle, who for some reason had lately adopted Jordan Goldman as her protégée on the social scene, just sat there and invited the bitch to their next frigging party.

Normally, both Jordan and Isabelle would have cut somebody like Roxana dead. He knew that. Roxana was far too beautiful. Too much competition. But by marking herself out as an actress, she had, in that single move, eliminated herself as a danger. She would need both Tom and Sam in her attempt to get this deal, and that meant she needed their wives.

And if Jordan was pushing Tom for Roxana the way Isabelle was pushing him, she'd succeeded.

'Did you check out her tests yet? David Tauber got the film through this morning, sent a tape to both of us.'

'He did, didn't he?'

David Tauber. His instincts had been right, yet again. That kid was a comer; the way things were going he'd have his fingerprints on three out of the four deal principals. Only Fred Florescu, the director and therefore the most important guy in the package, was repped by somebody else – namely Sam himself.

Kendrick admired Tauber, pleased with himself as he undoubtedly was. He just hoped the kid knew his place. *He better*, Sam thought, grimly.

'Not yet. I've been on the phone to Eleanor Marshall about the script all morning.'

'They're OK.'

'OK, they suck, or OK they rule?'

'Just OK. Not too bad, not too good. Like Madonna in *Desperately Seeking Susan*.'

'As opposed to *Body of Evidence*.'

'You got it. She's better than Isabella Rossellini, but not so good as Andie MacDowell. She's – '

'All right, all right.' Sam held up a gnarled hand. 'I get the picture. Why don't you shove the tape in the machine, let's see what the little *chiquita* can actually do.'

Mike reached forward and slid the video into the recorder, artfully concealed under an original Matisse. Across the other side of Sam's office, computerized dimmer switches automatically darkened the lights and a wall slid noiselessly back to reveal a huge digital television the size of a cinema screen. As the two powerful agents settled back into the Eames leather sofa, Roxana Felix's stunning face, her pores flawless and tiny even at ten times life size, swam into view.

Sam Kendrick watched with something like real curiosity. Interesting. So this was the woman who'd been turning the media heat on him like it was her personal flamethrower. Even though they hadn't bent over for her right away, and she must have been used to that as a model, it hadn't stopped her or even slowed her down. As much as he would have liked to chuck her tests in the can and send her gift-wrapped over to ICM – Sam hated clients who tried to push him around – he knew that Roxana Felix had, in three days, just about removed his power to do that. The entire LA wolf pack were now watching him with their little yellow eyes, checking out what he was going to do with his pretty new toy.

And holy shit, was she ever pretty.

Maybe it didn't all come across in still photos.

Would you look at that!

Mesmerized now, Sam Kendrick stared at the screen. The supermodel was reciting some Shakespeare with bare competence, but he wasn't listening to the dialogue. He couldn't lift his eyes from the way her skimpy little costume swung on her slender hips, the tiny flashes of brown thigh she kept turning to camera, the way she would pause every couple of minutes and run the barest tip of her tongue over her lower lip. Her bra was definitely not underwired, the way those titties were swinging. If she was *wearing* a bra. Shit, maybe if she moved a bit faster he'd be able to tell for sure. And how she walked. Demurely from the outside, a woman might say demurely, but with just that suggestion of a sway, no, more than that, of a *grind* that put you in mind of the better strip bars, up in Canada maybe. She was batting her eyes down now, playing it vulnerable, but somehow managing to suggest with her whole body that she'd be a tigress in bed, as soon scratch your eyes out as look at you.

Her dialogue was wooden, but her body language was eloquent.

> '*I am ashamed that women are so simple*
> *To offer war when they should kneel for peace;*
> *Or seek for rule, supremacy, and sway,*
> *When they are bound to serve, love and obey.*'

Unbelievable. Sam felt himself getting hard. Beautiful women were usually cold narcissists, one more LA cliché that was totally true. But Roxana Felix was obviously nothing like that.

He wondered if she'd ever been fucked the way she deserved. He doubted it. Most guys would be utterly terrified by a woman as gorgeous as Roxana, would just thrust in and out a few times before they came. Performance anxiety. Yeah, well, not him. He'd show her exactly what that flat little stomach could give her as well as him, how much he could get those perfect thighs to tremble, what happened to those plump, pointy nipples when they were sucked and stroked properly. Yeah, he'd like to have her underneath him, thrashing about in orgasm, all ready to fake it again and then suddenly realizing what was happening, tensing underneath him as her pussy started to get tight, but he wouldn't stop, he wouldn't break pace, he'd ride her like a thoroughbred filly, until she was incoherent, scratching at him and biting his shoulder, wet with her own sweat, and just at that moment he'd slip his right hand in between her legs, just above where his cock was, and rub her lightly so he'd be pressing on the clitoris above and below. He'd show her that he was a powerful man and powerful men had beautiful women all the time, that they were just a perk of his job like any other, and he wasn't afraid of her, he was going to *enjoy* her; in fact, he was going to fuck her ambitious little brains out.

And she'd love it. And she'd come for him, she'd come screaming.

As the tape ran to an end, Sam moved a copy of *Variety* onto his lap to hide his arousal. No need to get locker-room with Mike at a time like this.

On screen, Roxana's jet-black eyes, frozen in digital perfection, seemed to look right through him, as though the woman herself was up there, mocking, teasing him, calling to a part of himself that had seemed long dead, laid out cold in the headlong rush for glory.

For a second, Samuel Kendrick wondered uneasily if he had finally met his match.

David Tauber punched the redial button on his mobile phone, the other hand resting lightly on the wheel as he bombed down Sunset. Engaged again. Shit, he was making a habit of this – first Kevin Scott, and now some five-and-dime restaurant. What was the point of living in the Age of Technology, of being a surfer on the Information Superhighway, if you could never get through because people were always using the goddamn phone? Well, if you need something done, do it yourself. As he'd snidely said to Kevin Scott when Artemis finally came through with their draft screenplay approval.

He, David Ariel Tauber, the next Mike Ovitz, was *pleased* with little Megan Silver. Pleased with her for turning up in Kevin's office, pleased with her for writing such a kick-ass first draft script, not that it wouldn't need a load of work, and pleased with her for obviously not knowing the first thing about the movie business. And for being violently attracted to him. She was nothing to look at herself, but at least she had taste. And it was kind of sweet, watching her blush when he'd caught her staring at him. Sweet was not an adjective often applied to LA screenwriters; it might be fun, working with Megan, showing her a thing or two. She was close to his perfect client: talented, naive and desperate. Which was why, having failed all day to get through to the two-bit joint she was working in, David was doing her the honour of turning up to tell her the good news in person.

And shit, the girl must have been psychic. Not only was her little movie absolutely tailor-made for Zach Mason – the guy would practically be playing himself – but she'd also written in a hefty female lead for the musician's girlfriend, who was, check it out, a *supermodel.* If Roxana had looked dicey for a female lead before – and he didn't know what Sam's reactions had been to her test – surely this part would at least double her chances. The PR blitz would help as well. In fact, sometimes he got the feeling that Roxana didn't even need his help. This he didn't like. Who needed to feel like an accessory? Who needed a client who knew what they were doing and, worse still, knew what *he* should be doing? Roxana Felix kept track. She was on his case, really on his case. Six times a day. But now, finally, David Tauber reckoned he had something for her.

Yeah. Megan Silver didn't look like a sorceress, but maybe that's just what she was – waved her magic wand and made all David's problems go away. Which is why he was running red lights on the Boulevard at ten to nine, going to pick her up himself.

She *deserved* it.

Fifteen minutes. That was all she had to keep telling herself. Fifteen minutes, and then she could get out of here.

Megan kept herself busy. It wasn't difficult; what with the men all screaming for beer, and new heaps of greasy chicken and grey frozen fries being shovelled into pans a foot deep in spitting oil, and buckets of indifferent-looking 'slaw hefted round the kitchen, she hardly had time to even glance at the clock. She tried not to. If Jenkins saw her, he'd say she was slacking and dock her pay.

'Five minutes, sugar,' Stacey muttered in her ear, sweeping past with a basket of corn. She dumped it unceremoniously on the front of table twelve and came back into the kitchen, her pretty face alive with excitement. 'Look at this, Meg! The most incredible car just pulled into the parking lot.'

Megan, like most of the other waitresses, craned her neck for a quick look. 'Man or woman?'

'It's a man,' Megan said, watching a figure in an expensive-looking grey suit step out of a stunning cherry-red sports car. 'Maybe you'll get lucky, Stacey.' She dusted her hands on her canary Mr Chicken frilly skirt. Nine p.m. exactly. *Well, thank you, God.* 'I'm going to get paid.'

Utterly exhausted, she walked over to the little cash counter where Jenkins was sitting.

'So we'll see you Monday,' he said sourly.

Megan didn't have a decision to make. She'd been thinking about what Stacey had said all night and she knew she was right. It was OK to be a waitress at seventeen; twenty-four, and you had serious problems.

'No, I don't think so. I quit.' She tried to give him a smile. *That's it, Megan, kiss ass like the corporate little chicky you are.* 'Thanks for the tryout, Bob, but I just don't think it's worked out.'

His eyes had a mean glint to them. She could see it even through the clouds of steam fogging up the kitchen. 'You can't do that.'

Megan shrugged. 'I gotta go home.'

'Shoulda checked your contract.'

'My *contract?*' Megan asked, mystified.

'You signed it when you got hired.'

That little scrap of paper? That was a contract?

She tried humility. 'Look, I'm really sorry if this is any bother for you, but –'

'You need to give me a month's notice. If you ain't giving notice, you ain't getting paid for the week.'

Despite the heat, Megan went pale. 'You must be kidding, Bob. You can hire anybody, you don't want to make me stay a month. I'm a lousy waitress. You said so yourself.'

'You're not that bad.' He was eyeing her speculatively, greedily.

My God, Megan thought, suddenly realizing what this little charade was all about. He doesn't want me to stay, he wants me to get so mad I'll just storm out and he won't have to pay me for the week. Guess he doesn't realize how badly I need that cheque.

'OK.' She stared back. 'If it's what you want. Consider this a month's notice. I'll put it in writing, if you like.'

'You sure?'

She was right. Now he was mad. God, he must have been sure she'd burst into tears and run off.

'Yeah, Bob, I'm totally sure. You owe me a week's pay and I'm not leaving without it.'

'Why, you –'

'Megan.' Stacey, blushing red to her roots, had come over to interrupt them. 'Bob, I'm sorry, but we need Megan right now. There's a guy out here asking for her personally. Won't talk to anyone else.'

Dec? thought Megan wildly.

'You know the rules, Megan. No personal visitors,' Jenkins said nastily. 'I'm coming with you.'

'Jesus, Bob. I finished my shift. I can see a visitor.'

He rounded on her. 'Not on Mr Chicken premises you don't. This is where you work, not where you get to hang with your friends. Assuming you *want* to stay working here.'

'Megan?'

The three of them spun round at the strange voice to see a tall, blond man in a Yohji Yamamoto black wool suit standing at the entrance to the kitchen. He had a gold watch on his right wrist and was carrying a briefcase in soft pigskin leather. He reeked of money and confidence, absolutely aware of the sensation he was causing in a dump like this. Enjoying it, too. Stacey could hardly take her eyes off him.

Megan couldn't breathe.

'Who the fuck is this?' Jenkins demanded, recovering himself. 'Look, mister, she isn't allowed visitors here. Not if she wants to keep the job.'

'She doesn't.'

'And who says so?'

'My name is David Tauber, Sam Kendrick International,' David said, giving Megan his most brilliant, luminous smile. 'I'm Ms Silver's agent. Isn't that right, Megan?'

Megan felt faint, almost dizzy with joy. Eventually, realizing that Jenkins was staring at her with a glare that could strip paint, she found her voice.

'That's right, David,' she said. She turned round to Jenkins, suddenly unable to keep a huge grin off her face. 'Hey, Bob. You know what, you're absolutely right. You can keep that pay cheque, because I quit. Right now. And I'll tell you something else.'

She leant forward, right in his acne-pitted face. 'It's worth every cent, just to see the look on your face.'

'Ms Silver, shall we go? I've got the Lamborghini waiting outside for you.'

David Tauber stood there in the door frame, handsome as Adonis, offering her his arm. And Mr Chicken frilly uniform and all, Megan took it like a queen.

'Why not?' she said.

10

The script felt good in her hands. That was a strange thing to notice, but Eleanor couldn't help thinking about it as she walked into her office and hefted it out of her briefcase. The physical weight of the paper, the neatness of the edges, all the telltale signs that let her know it had been handled by so few people. She had a tiny thrill of electricity just picking it up.

That same electricity had been with her ever since she pulled out of the garage this morning, sending the blood tingling round her veins, giving her the feeling of wanting to get into the office, to start the day, to make this deal work. One of those mornings that reminded her why she'd longed to work in this business in the first place.

Excitement.

See the Lights was good, she could feel it, she could sense it in her bones. From the moment that slimy little jerk Tauber over at SKI had messengered it across with that pretentious note about 'the next *Close Encounters*' and '*Pretty Woman* meets *The Doors*' she'd been convinced. And God knew she hadn't picked it up with any expectations – after all, nobody had heard of Megan Silver, whoever she was, and it hadn't even come from Sam's script department. If she hadn't wanted the deal to work so badly, she might have refused to look at it, might have passed it down the food chain to one of Artemis's 'readers', the amoebae at the bottom who normally accepted screenplay submissions. She'd have liked nothing better than to snub David Tauber. He was a two-bit hustler barely out of diapers, the type who expected all women to fall at his feet with their legs open just because he had a cute smile and a tan. She was used to guys like Tauber. Probably worked out in a gym with mirrored walls.

Still, there was no way she could have refused to look at the script. Jerk though Tauber was, he was also the classic model of the Hollywood comer. Breaking onto the scene from nowhere with Colleen McCallum, and now Zach Mason as well as the model. Heavy-duty clients eventually turn the most featherweight agent into Mike Tyson. So she'd started reading it at nine a.m. that morning, intending to skim it in ten minutes.

She'd finished it at quarter of ten and called Sam Kendrick immediately.

See the Lights. An incredible love story. An action-thriller plot. A backdrop of sex and drugs and rock 'n' roll.

It was going to make her name, and she'd come into Artemis this morning with the intention – oh God, God, this was so great, and so terrifying – of green-lighting her first movie.

'You look happy.'

'Hi, Tom,' Eleanor said, looking up to see her boss standing in the doorway of her office. He was wearing some nondescript black suit that made his brown hair look darker but did nothing for the slight jowliness of middle age that had settled around his chin. He moved like a man long accustomed to power.

She felt the familiar longing twitch between her thighs.

'I brought breakfast,' Tom said, striding across the room and dumping a grease-spotted paper bag down on her desk. He took out a jelly-filled doughnut and a paper cup of coffee and offered them to her with a grin. 'Caffeine. Refined sugar. Saturated fat. Eat.'

'I can't eat that!' Eleanor protested, laughing. 'It'll head straight to my thighs. Paul wants us to go on the Pritikin diet, that one where you eat no fat at all. He says we should hire a vegetarian low-fat cook.'

Goldman shook his head. 'So? Jordan wants me to become a goddamned vegan.' He leant towards her. 'This is why people have jobs.'

'So they can secretly eat doughnuts?'

'Absolutely. Now eat it. That's an order.'

Smiling, she took a large bite. It was sweet and oily and delicious.

Tom watched her with immense satisfaction, then reached into the bag for his own doughnut, polishing it off in three bites.

'My God, it's Captain Caveman,' Eleanor said. 'And I bet you ate at home, too.'

Tom shrugged defensively, grinning. 'I work out. Sometimes.' He reached forward and wiped gently across her cheek, removing a small oozing trickle of jelly that was slowly running down her chin, licking his thumb clean. 'President of a movie studio, and she has no doughnut-eating technique at all. I find that very sad.'

'Talking of which' – Eleanor put down the rest of her doughnut and patted her script – 'I've got something you should see.'

'We can talk business later. It's only eight o'clock, you'll have all day for that,' Goldman said, impatiently. 'When do we ever get a chance to talk? Tell me how you are.'

Eleanor shifted on her seat. She was almost embarrassed. Her feelings for Tom were long recognized and admitted, filed neatly away under 'might have been'. But that didn't stop the private joy that ran through her during their early-morning moments together, when she was alone with him before any of the assistants arrived. And, she was dismayed to find, it didn't stop the wild arousal that had swum hot and squirming into her belly when his hand touched her cheek. She'd wanted to press it into his palm, to turn her lips to his wrist and cover it with hot kisses, to take that thumb into her own mouth and lick and suck it clean. From that one faintly erotic touch she was wet. There was more sensuality in Tom brushing jelly from her cheek than there was in the whole of the sexual act that she performed with Paul every morning.

The morning session with Tom was enjoyable and innocent precisely because they never did or said anything of consequence, unless it was business. But now he was looking her straight in the eyes and asking her how she was!

'Fine,' she said. 'I'm fine.'

'Are you?' Tom asked softly. 'How's life at home? How are you getting on with Paul?'

Words trembled on her lips. 'Just great.' 'Terrific, thank you.' 'Oh, he's incredible.' All the safe, stock answers she came out with every day. They were the solid couple. Rock steady, the way LA royalty should be; the studio head and the investment banker, William III and Mary II, joint sovereigns. Monogamous and neatly paired off. Very nineties.

But somehow, sitting here looking at Tom Goldman, she found it hard to say. She flashed back to the scene today. The first light of dawn creeping through the fragrant darkness of their garden, the scent of hibiscus and jasmine in the cold morning air, the way it always was when they woke at 5 a.m. to the strains of whatever soft classical music he'd programmed into the CD the night before – Bach or Mozart. And then Paul would reach for her. No preliminaries, he would just reach for her, as much a part of his early-morning routine as the jog at half-five, or the orange juice and mineral water at six.

Only this morning she'd turned away.

'Come on, what's the matter?' he'd asked sleepily, nuzzling against her shoulder. 'Don't want to?'

'I'm just tired.'

But the truth was she *didn't* want to. Not right now. Not after going to sleep on *See the Lights*, with all that raw passion and obsessive love. She'd dreamed about Tom, and just for today, just for this morning in the gentle half-light, something in her skin rebelled at the thought of Paul touching her.

'You're never tired.'

She hated that tone – it was accusatory, whining.

'You just forgot to put your diaphragm in last night.'

Eleanor started to deny it. 'No I didn't, Paul, I – '

'I don't see why I can't make love to you without it. I don't see why you always have to insist on using that damn thing.' He was angry and cold now. Thankfully, she felt his erection shrivelling against her thigh. 'You say you want kids, but you know it's getting later and later. I don't see why we can't get married.'

'We've had this discussion before,' Eleanor said, feeling her defences fly up. She hated, utterly hated, to talk about this. She didn't want to acknowledge it or see it, didn't want to confront it. 'This just isn't the right time.'

'When *will* it be the right time? When you're fifty, and we have to adopt?'

Paul threw back the covers and stood up to dress, his long, lean body blackly silhouetted against the weak dawn light from the sash windows. Eleanor could see anger in the whole way he carried himself, in the set of his muscles.

'Will you marry me?'

It was a demand, not a request.

She tensed. 'Not yet.'

'I won't wait forever, Eleanor,' he warned her as he walked towards the bathroom. 'I want kids.'

Oh, so do I, she'd thought as she lay there, Irish cotton sheets clutched protectively around her. *So do I.*

Children. A baby, maybe two or three, little infants with their wide eyes and tiny hands and all the love and fears that they couldn't even articulate. She had always wanted children, in that confident way that young beautiful women have, sure that life will send them the husband they desire and deserve, happy to trust in their wombs, unhurried and unpressured. 'Kids some day.'

She couldn't now mark out, couldn't recall, the exact moment that the first flush of youth had left her, the precise period of months when she'd started to get concerned and anxious. Maybe it combined with the period when it had dawned on her that Tom Goldman was never going to take his flirtation any further, when one girlfriend replaced another, and suddenly all the girlfriends were five, seven, ten years younger than her. Teenagers and twenty-two-year-olds.

That was when she'd accepted the best, most eligible of the bachelors who swarmed around her, fetched her drinks at charity balls and monopolized her at Isabelle Kendrick dinners. Paul Halfin had then been thirty-nine, handsome, rich, educated, charming. He was fun to talk to, if you didn't want anything too wild. Knew everything there was to know about Shakespeare and Vivaldi, and his firm was pretty hot, had been involved in a couple of high-profile entertainment deals just that year. Eleanor was thirty-two. They were two 'beautiful people'. They would be a power couple, Bill and Hillary on the way up their separate ladders.

Eleanor thought Paul was cute. She moved in with him.

The relief had been amazing, so much so that it revealed to her as though for the first time how pressured she'd felt being single. For the first time, she had nothing to prove in social situations. Executive wives thawed perceptibly to her. She always had someone to take her to Artemis premieres, and a wonderful, enviable escort for company dinners. For the first few months together they had teetered on the brink of marriage, which, inevitably, would have led to children. An ideal Beverly Hills family.

She couldn't do it.

That was what stopped her. Children, the thing she'd dreamed of since she was a child herself, tucking her doll into its cot, nursing teddies through their various exotic ailments. She'd been an only child of elderly parents, and she'd always imagined herself as a beautiful young mother with a gaggle of babies. When she got older and started to dwell on it, the precious wonder of human life, she simply couldn't understand how so many people treated their children so lightly, divorcing without the slightest effort at patching it up for the kids' sake, or starving them of affection. She couldn't believe all those deadbeat fathers that snuck away from mothers they no longer desired, frightened of responsibility or scared of another mouth to feed. God, weren't they even curious? A baby was such a miracle, it was their descendant, their link to the future, their line spanning down the generations. Did they never see it like that, those men? Eleanor wondered. Did they never look at their babies and see their own eyes staring up at them, the future small and soft in their arms when they laid it in the crib at night? To *create life*, together, was that not the ultimate bond two people could have?

And in her own mind, when she thought of her child, flesh of her flesh and blood of her blood, she could not see it with Paul's eyes, his nose, his chin.

When she saw the features of the father of her child, she imagined Tom Goldman's eyes, staring back at her.

Of course that was quite ridiculous. Tom felt nothing for her. He had this string of interchangeable nubile babes, he was her boss and her friend. So she'd had a crush on him once, so what?

It was the advent of Jordan Cabot that finally drove Eleanor to admit what she was feeling. Jordan, who'd arrived in LA from San Francisco eighteen months ago, the blonde scion of a rich, gentile family, just another stupid bimbo looking to hook a Hollywood executive. By this time, of course, Tom was chairman of Artemis and the biggest catch in town. Jordan, possibly, had simply lucked out by being the right girl at the right time, coming along when Tom was newly promoted and pleased with himself and his life. And let's face it, in a town full of pneumatic flaxen-haired cuties, Jordan Cabot was something else. A perfect hourglass figure combined with a truly pretty face of the All-American type. Great skin, white teeth, athletic muscle tone, and a mere twenty-three years old. But even that might not have been enough to get a ring on Tom's finger, as chary of tying himself down as Eleanor knew he was. What had finally swung it for Jordan was her ability in bed. Whatever skills she'd perfected, Tom was addicted to them. This Eleanor knew because he'd told her, buddy to buddy. He wasn't coarse about it; he would just come into her office and marvel at how incredible, how alive, how *young* Jordan made him feel. Said he could never get enough. Could never get tired of it. Soon, Eleanor had to knock on his office door instead of just walking in like she used to, for fear of interrupting one of his heavy phone-sex sessions.

Tom became obsessed. He said Jordan made him feel like a teenager again.

Eleanor began to have nightmares, dreaming of Jordan, young, flawless, perfect, contorting her body in wild ways which she, Eleanor, could not even begin to imagine.

Three months after he'd met her they were engaged. A month later they were married. And when Tom, two months into their marriage, confided in Eleanor that he wished Jordan would get pregnant, that children were the one remaining consuming desire of his life, she was forced into recognizing the great tragedy of her own life.

She loved Tom Goldman, loved him desperately. It was the explanation for the searing, ravaging pain that swept through her as she listened to him. And she wanted no man but Tom to be the father of her children.

It was never going to be. She knew that, accepted it as the clear truth. If she, Eleanor Marshall, wanted to be a mother, she was going to have to find a different set of genes to mix with. Moreover, she was going to have to find them pretty soon. She was thirty-eight. And if not Paul, who else? If she left Paul, would that do her any good? Whoever else she hooked up with, they wouldn't be Tom either. So shouldn't she avoid making the perfect the enemy of the good? When there was no guarantee that she was ever going to find anything better? And the feeling of desperation, of endless longing for that child waiting so impatiently to be born, was beginning to swamp her. Sometimes seeing little children with their mothers in the mall would make her cry. She'd started to dream about babies, torturingly realistic dreams, where she could smell the milky, sleepy smell of their velvety skin, see every tiny finger curl with its miniature fingernail, notice how their fragile lashes seemed too long for those minute eyelids.

And Paul was pressing her to marry him, to conceive.

So far, for three months she'd been stalling.

This morning, Eleanor had felt all the walls starting to close in. She'd have to decide. And she had no idea what to do.

Eleanor gazed up at Tom, leaning over her, staring at her with his odd intensity. 'You want the truth? Things aren't so hot.'

'Work pressure?'

He was probing her now. For a moment Eleanor sensed he didn't want her to answer yes, that he wanted to hear something more personal.

She thought about saying that Paul was swamped over at Albert, Halfin, Weissman.

'Paul wants me to marry him. I guess I'm not sure if I'm ready,' she said. 'And you? How are things with Jordan?'

'Not so hot.' Tom smiled ruefully at her, but then looked away. 'I probably didn't realize what the age difference would mean.'

'Nothing serious, though?' God, look at me, Eleanor thought, mad at herself. All I do is reach out to comfort him. Why don't I *do* something about it?

'No. I'm sure it'll all work itself out. Especially when we get pregnant.'

She nodded, trying to stifle her disappointment. Not to mention that horrible ironic stab – 'when we get pregnant'. Tom was burning to be a father, then. He longed to beget children. But not with her.

'But I gotta tell you, sometimes it's really hard. Talking to her, I mean. It's not' – she could see him struggle with his words, wanting to tell her his problem, trying to avoid criticizing his wife – 'not like it is with you. She's not interested in – '

She's not interested in anything. Except social climbing, designer dresses, and making the gossip columns, Tom thought. He'd thought that he could never get tired of sex with Jordan. And he wasn't. But he was wondering if he'd tired of everything else.

He heard his own voice trailing away. He couldn't admit it, not even to Eleanor, as well as they knew each other. In fact, especially not to Eleanor. Not as she sat there in that deep blue suit, radiating intelligence and sensuality. Flirting with her had been a constant as long as he'd known her, but lately the flirtation seemed to have taken on a new edge. He had always desired her, but his respect for their friendship, his wariness of professional misconduct, and his terror of – what? Of being tied down? Of sex that wasn't the type you could walk away from? Well, his terror of that nameless connection, all those things had kept him from making his move. Desire was joyous and clean. Desire you could control. And he had, in the end, married a girl who could satisfy his desire with the skill of a virtuoso.

Jordan. She was far more attractive than Eleanor, surely. And fourteen years younger.

So why was lust curling around his crotch? Why had he felt his sex get warmer and harder the instant his thumb touched Eleanor's cheek?

'I think I'm just too old and too square,' Goldman finished.

Eleanor looked across her desk at him, the coffee in its Styrofoam cup cooling in front of her.

'No you're not, Tom,' she said.

The silence between them hung in the air.

Then Goldman reached forward, his large right hand closing over her small left one, his grip solid, even tight, and said, 'Eleanor – '

'Hey, my two favourite people.'

Without so much as a glance at her, Tom Goldman snatched his hand away as though her skin had suddenly become corrosive acid. Past his back, Eleanor could see the dapper figure of Jake Keller, her most senior vice-president of Production. Her deputy at the department, Jake had been the man passed over for the presidency when Eleanor got the job. He'd always been totally friendly and polite to her since, but Jake was an enemy and Eleanor knew it. He was bitter. The sight of him interrupting them sent shivers down her spine. Unpleasant ones.

He hadn't seen anything.

She hoped.

'Eleanor, do you have a second? I wanted to discuss that script you sent me yesterday. *See the Lights*.'

'Sure, Jake. Of course.'

Eleanor picked up the copy lying on her desk and passed it to Tom, briskly. 'Tom, you might as well take this away too. It's the script for the Zach Mason/ Fred Florescu project, which is a go.'

'You're green-lighting this?' Keller asked. His tone was heavy with disapproval.

'I am.' She refused to be rattled, or to respond to the insult. Jake Keller was not to approve or disapprove of her decisions. She was his boss.

Tom Goldman looked swiftly from one to the other, all business now. 'Jake, maybe you should bring it up in the production meeting at ten.'

He was backing up her authority, Eleanor knew. She also knew that Tom would listen carefully to whatever criticisms Jake had. He wouldn't prevent her from green-lighting this project – after all, being president was all about making those decisions – but Jake would get to register his protest. And if this movie screwed up, Jake Keller would get credit for his warnings.

'Sure,' Keller said easily. 'See you later.'

He turned to leave, and Tom followed him. 'See you later, Eleanor.'

'Of course.' All traces of their earlier intimacy were wiped away, but she had expected that. He was probably regretting it right this minute. 'Tom, try and skim through that script before the meeting if you get a chance. It's really hot. David Tauber at SKI is representing the writer.'

'I thought Kevin Scott had all their writers.'

'All except this. Tauber found her himself.'

'He did?' Tom grinned, amused. 'That kid's in a hurry. OK, I'll check it out now.'

Eleanor watched his retreating back, realizing with a slight misgiving that already David Tauber's name carried some weight. Tom was more inclined to read it quickly because Tauber had found it. Well, that made sense: it was David Tauber who had brought in Zach Mason, and this was his movie. Fred Florescu was the most important element of the deal, and Fred was Sam's personal client, but still . . . if Hollywood was a jungle, in the nineties it belonged to jackals like David. And she noticed that Tom hadn't responded to her assurance that this screenplay was terrific. She knew him well enough by now to see when he was reserving judgement.

Eleanor glanced at the clock on her computer. Quarter of nine. The big Artemis production meeting was in just over an hour.

Damn, she hoped Tom liked it. But even if he didn't, in this meeting she was going to back her own judgement. She had found the right script for Mason and Florescu, and when they had cast the female lead – Julia Roberts, Jennifer Jason Leigh? – they were going to have a smash.

Despite her ragged emotions, Eleanor Marshall felt a small thrill. She was going to exercise her new power for the first time. This was scary. This was exhilarating. This was the *movie business*.

It was everything she had always wanted.

Well, almost everything.

11

As she threw open the last window, the scent hit her. First thing in the morning, and the air in the Hollywood Hills was fragrant with jasmine, hibiscus, she didn't know what else. Up here she was above the smog line, and the sky was humid, not exactly threatening to rain but allowing myriads of minute water droplets to hang shimmering in the air in a warm, transparent mist. Birds were singing, a sound so unfamiliar to Roxana – Ms City Girl numero uno – that for a second she hadn't known what it was. Standing there, looking out at LA, a peaceful grid laid out below her, silent from this height, she felt a strange sensation. Happiness.

Roxana shook her lovely head in a movement so graceful it was a shame she had no audience for it, her long black hair swinging behind her in a pigtail, her normally pale cheeks flushed from her morning workout. Her first morning in LA out of a hotel, and already she was getting weak and stupid.

David had found her this place and she had to admit he'd done a good job. The house was perched on a nearly secret ledge high in the hills above Sunset, protected by cleverly grown hedges from any long-range lenses or curious fans with binoculars. It had been designed by an unknown but very talented architect, probably back in the thirties, and re-equipped several times since. Now she had a Moroccan villa on the outside, all coffee-coloured plaster and Hispanic white details, with a marble fountain playing day and night in the courtyard, and a New York penthouse on the inside, with a private gym, a home office complete with several phone lines, faxes and a PowerMacintosh, the ultimate in electronic sensor security systems and plenty of natural light. Not to mention mirrors. The swimming pool was sunk in the middle of the central reception room, another detail she had approved of. Roxana didn't like outdoor pools. Any schmuck with a helicopter could gawk at you.

The rent was astronomical, but so what? She was astronomically rich. And very soon she'd be astronomically famous, too. When the call had come from Tauber last night it hadn't surprised her in the least. Everybody else, perhaps, but not her. This was what she'd come out to LA to do, and she was going to succeed, of course. She always did.

She was Roxana Felix, and she always got what she wanted.

'And what did you tell her?'

Sam Kendrick tensed, not liking Eleanor's tone. Fifteen years as one of the best agents in Hollywood had given him near-psychic powers in reading people's moods. And Eleanor was pissed-off. He scrambled to recover his ground.

'Actually, Eleanor, David called her. He told her she'd been shortlisted for the part of Morgan. Which you told us. Nothing more, nothing less.'

'Uh-huh.' The president of Artemis tapped one manicured nail on the papers in front of her. They all bore inset stories on the front page with headlines like 'Roxana Starts Acting Career', 'Silver Screen Supermodel', and the worst, the *New York Times*, ran 'Roxana Beats Out Julia, Winona, *et al*'.

Sam stifled his own fury. God, how he agreed with Eleanor. It was the most unprofessional thing he had ever seen. But he simply could not show his feelings to his old friend. The bitch was, after all, his client.

'Eleanor, I swear, we had nothing to do with this.'

'It puts me in an extremely difficult position, Sam. As you know, we're still considering casting. We haven't got back to Bridget's people, or Jennifer's people, or Julia's people *or* Winona's people. And they read this in the fucking press.'

Sam was on red-alert. Eleanor never swore, she was more decorous than a whore at a christening. 'I'll speak to her, Eleanor, I promise.'

'You do that.' She was still angry. 'I swear, I should just issue a release saying the whole thing is a fabrication by your client. But just in case we do cast her, I'll have to keep quiet about it. For now.'

'OK.' Kendrick nodded his head, accepting blame.

'You'd better go, Sam. I have to make my apologies to Mike Ovitz and Jeff Berg and every other major player Roxana Felix just spat on.' Eleanor took a deep breath, composing herself. 'And Sam, make sure you see her yourself. Don't send that little jerk Tauber in to do it. I want someone who's gonna give Ms Felix a lesson in how we do business in the movie industry, not crawl up her ass instead of kicking it.'

Despite himself, Sam grinned. 'OK, Eleanor. I'll see to it personally. It won't happen again.'

'It had better not.'

She was the Ice Queen again, cool and menacing. Kendrick almost regretted the reversion to type as he shook her hand and left. It was kind of interesting to see Eleanor Marshall steamed up, even if he was on the receiving end. He'd always imagined Paul Halfin shoved her in the deepfreeze when she got home nights, to warm her up a little bit.

Eleanor dismissed Sam from her thoughts almost before he had left, dialling CAA and ICM and everybody else to offer her apologies, smooth practised words disassociating Artemis from any involvement with these stories. They couldn't afford to offend any of the big female stars – no studio could. Female actors were still paid far less than their male counterparts, but their cents on the male dollar crawled up every year. Something she, Eleanor, welcomed, although she'd never paid a woman star a cent more than she had to. If equality happened for actresses, it would happen naturally, when market forces dictated. You couldn't bring feminism or any other agenda into it. Business was business. It was that attitude that had ensured, at long last, that she got to sit in the president's office. And it was that attitude that now forced her to look at the Roxana situation with as much detachment as she could bring to it.

God, it made her mad, the way the woman obviously thought she could just walk all over Artemis and SKI. She was incredibly beautiful and incredibly arrogant. And no Meryl Streep, either. She thought that lovely face was her passport through life, and Eleanor dearly longed to show her otherwise, to rule her out for this part and show her up in every major paper that was fawning over her today.

But she couldn't do it.

Roxana, Roxana, Roxana. That was all she'd heard for a week. As soon as the project had been green-lighted, David Tauber was calling her twenty times a day, local press and TV shows had asked for her response to the rumour, and Tom Goldman was suddenly insisting that she test with Zach for the part. Eleanor had shrugged her shoulders and agreed. After all, the original tests of Roxana Sam had sent over weren't *dreadful*, even if they also weren't good enough. With the male star making his acting debut, plus a first-time screenwriter, she'd wanted to play it safe with the female lead. After all, they had a lot of money riding on this production. As it was, Sam Kendrick International was looking at a fat package deal for the director, star and scriptwriter. And Jake Keller had raised objections at literally every stage of the process, from the first production meeting to the marketing budget. She, Eleanor, had overruled him, but effectively Jake had forced her to put her ass on the line. She'd had to sit there and watch Tom Goldman, magisterial chairman and CEO, observing the polite duels of his two most senior execs as though from the heights of Mount Olympus, not taking sides, just taking notes. Standard Hollywood-mogul practice. Tom neither blamed nor praised *See the Lights*, and that way he could take all the credit if the movie was a smash, and disassociate himself if it bombed. Every senior guy played it that way, and she had tried not to take it personally. But it still hurt. *See the Lights* was her first project, she could tell Tom loved the script as much as she did, and she longed for him to back her. Maybe because there would have been something deeply sexual in the idea of him throwing caution to the winds for her sake.

But that was dreaming.

At any rate, it had amazed her to see Tom getting involved in casting matters; he was far too busy for that, the creative side wasn't the realm of the chairman, he was the one who concentrated on making them look good to their shadowy lords and masters on Wall Street. Still, if he wanted Roxana Felix to test, so be it. He was her boss. And he had been quite insistent on the matter; why, she couldn't figure out.

'Eleanor, you must be insane. All these no-name people – '

'I wouldn't call Zach Mason a no-name,' she'd said at the casting meeting, her light tone covering a steely reproof. Who the hell did Jake Keller think he was? She hid her satisfaction at the thought that Keller was criticizing Tom's suggestion in front of him, and not her own, as he imagined. Tom had spoken to her privately, so she gave out that the decision to test Roxana had come from her.

Jake therefore attacked it, right on cue. '*Movie* no-name. OK, so he's a rock star. Like Mick Jagger and Sting and Madonna. *Great* box-office.'

'That's true. But we've seen Zach's tests as an actor, and we're all agreed he has an amazing talent.'

'OK, maybe.' Keller couldn't deny it: Mason had tested like God's gift; he acted as good as Olivier and he looked as good as Keanu Reeves. 'But it's still a risk. And we didn't like Roxana's tests.'

'That was before we had decided on *See the Lights* as the script. The male lead is a rock star, the female lead a supermodel. They'd both be playing themselves. I think that's a strong angle.'

'You can't seriously want to cast this on the basis of *publicity*,' Jake sneered.

Eleanor remembered staring at his upper-class WASPy suit, his red hair combed in a neat centre parting, and feeling a dislike of the intensity she normally reserved for Isabelle Kendrick and her coven of Beverly Hills ladies who lunch. She'd smoothed her Georges Rech pink silk skirt across her legs before answering him, a feminine, appealing gesture calculated to contrast with her next words.

'We're testing Roxana Felix tomorrow.' She paused, to let that sink in. They should all take note, all those baby vice-presidents eagerly watching the grown-ups fight. She was the president and she intended them to have no doubt about that. Jake Keller had ten years as a creative and she'd come from Marketing, and he intended to show up her creative 'weakness' wherever and whenever he could. And if she showed any weakness whatsoever, he'd exploit it like a germ-warfare expert faced with an open wound.

'Tomorrow morning. Jake, tests fall within your jurisdiction, so you can arrange it. I'll come to a screening in the afternoon; we can review everyone's tests together. Tom, will that be good for you?'

'That'll be fine. I don't have anything then I can't shift.'

Tom had looked at her with just the faintest gleam of amusement and approval in his brown eyes, nodding his head slowly, in a way that made her heart skip over, and Jake Keller had gone the colour of a beetroot.

'You OK with that, Jake?' she'd pressed him coolly.

'Sure. Fine.'

He had to agree. He knew it, she knew it, everyone in the room knew it. And, damn, maybe this was her nasty male aggressive streak, but – admit it – she'd really enjoyed rubbing his nose in it.

Walking into the darkened screening room had felt strange. All of a sudden Eleanor had a personal stake in Roxana Felix, a woman she hadn't particularly even wanted to test. It was a big deal, too: her first movie, a rock musician starring, an unknown screenwriter and a huge budget. That much she would have to give Keller, the female lead was important. And they had looked at some of the biggest females in the industry. Competition to work with Zach and Fred was intense among a whole generation of actresses, Jordan Goldman's generation, the 'X'-ers, to whom both director and star were pop-culture gods. The reaction had made Eleanor feel old and out of touch; she'd known Mason was a huge star, seen his sales figures and the rest of it, but she somehow had had no idea of the quasi-religious feeling the guy could inspire. For the twentysomethings he was a prophet, their Bob Dylan. Weird. It was why people like Fred and Julia and Winona, all Hollywood royalty and way higher up the movie-business tree than Zach, were scrambling to work with him, even before they'd seen him act.

But as the various lovely faces replaced each other on-screen, testing with

Mason, she'd had a sinking feeling in the pit of her stomach. It didn't *work*. Not with any of them. Oh, they were all great actresses and they all looked fine, even believable in the role of a supermodel. But the magic, the chemistry with Mason, that wasn't there. *See the Lights* had to crackle with sexual energy. That was why only guys normally attended these tests for female leads in blockbuster movies – a woman had to chart high, not just on her acting ability, but on what was known on the lot as the 'peter meter'. Vulgar, but effective, and for years Eleanor Marshall had not been required to attend. Well, they couldn't stop her now. Now she was president. So she got to sit in this dark baby cinema with the boys, watching unhappily as actress after actress triggered off little more than polite murmurs. Great skill, no sizzle. For *See the Lights* that wasn't gonna work.

And then, last, they'd shown Roxana's test.

Instant reaction.

As the camera panned onto Morgan, the girlfriend, making her way backstage, every man in the room shifted on his chair. Roxana was wearing jeans and a T-shirt, but as she strutted into the centre of the screen, emanating arrogance and boredom, she was as graceful and deadly as a lioness. A lioness on heat. Mason's response to her was something else, his eyes raking over her chest and crotch as they started to run the fight scene, stripping her with his eyes so blatantly that Eleanor, to her astonishment, found herself getting aroused, a silken line of sexual heat trailing down her belly. Now Roxana made to slap him round the face and Mason caught her arm, viciously, pinning her up against a crate. She twisted free, defying him, the look upon her face so feral that any minute you expected her to draw back her lips and snarl at him. The excited babble of the male executives stilled, the sound of their breathing heavy in the room. Zach and Roxana went through their lines on-screen, but Eleanor could see that nobody was listening to anything but the body language. Desire seemed to rise so strongly between the two of them that she almost felt as if she'd walked into somebody's bedroom. You expected to see them abandon their lines any second and just go to it, right there. Involuntarily, Eleanor found herself looking round for Tom Goldman, wanting to see his reaction, wanting to be near him while she felt like this. Warm, slow feelings trawled across her crotch, as though a feather-light hand were stroking her there, as though Tom were breathing softly on the nape of her neck. She was actually wet. The sexual energy on-screen was so strong she felt like holding up a match, to see if it would ignite. Was she imagining things, or had the crotch on Zach Mason's pants got tighter? And were Roxana's Felix's high, tight nipples contracting under that cotton T-shirt?

As the test faded to darkness, Eleanor Marshall listened to her male colleagues consciously control their breathing, and smiled to herself.

Fuck you, Jake Keller. This movie's gonna work.

They'd announced no decision then and there, of course. Too much of an insult to all the other candidates. Eleanor had merely remarked that it seemed an interesting performance, and Tom had agreed with her, and then everybody had gone back to work. But privately, the casting of Morgan was a given.

Which was why, even though there had been no announcement of casting and her behaviour was unforgivable, Eleanor Marshall knew that she wasn't going to slap Roxana down.

Roxana Felix was their new star.

Eleanor finished up her call to Mike Ovitz, grovelling abjectly in apology, and quickly pressed the red light on her phone. Tom Goldman buzzing her.

'Have you seen Sam?'

'Yeah. He's going to talk to her. I told him to do it himself.'

Goldman grunted. 'Good. Well, I think we better confirm it as soon as possible. If we keep them hanging on for another two days and then announce Roxana, it'll look like we're dicking them around.'

'Language,' said Eleanor automatically. 'OK, Tom. I've just got off the phone with CAA, so let me leave it an hour and I'll put out an announcement. Yes?'

He laughed, a low, warm sound. 'Sure. I'll leave it to your impeccable judgement.'

There was a moment's silence.

'Are you coming to Isabelle Kendrick's party tomorrow?' Tom asked casually.

'Only for ten minutes. We're just going to show up and leave.' Eleanor smiled into the receiver. 'If I cut the whole thing, Isabelle and' – she nearly said 'and Jordan', but stopped herself just in time – 'and the rest of them will stick all their little voodoo pins into me.'

'Oh.' He sounded disappointed, hesitant. 'I was hoping you'd stay longer. We might get a chance to talk.'

Eleanor felt herself tense up, that same sick-excitement feeling she'd had with Tom yesterday morning.

She had to test it. 'But we talk all the time.'

'Not about business.'

'We get to see each other socially, though. We all played tennis together only last weekend.'

A pause.

'I meant on our own.'

A jolt of electricity surged through her.

She tried to control it. As casually as she could manage, she said, 'Do you mean that at a big party we'd be able to slip away and talk?'

'Yeah. Exactly.' He was grunting again, obviously embarrassed.

Eleanor thought the sound of her own heart beating in her ears might deafen her. She couldn't speak.

'Whatever,' Tom said. 'I was just hoping you would stay.'

'I'll stay,' Eleanor said.

He hung up.

For a full minute, Eleanor Marshall gazed at the phone, attempting to still the wild, strange pulse racing through her blood.

David Tauber had taken over her life, and Megan didn't know which part of it had been the most wonderful – the way he'd turned up in his red charger and whisked her away from her shitty little job; the champagne and pink roses that he'd sent around the next morning; or actually signing the contract in the marbled offices of SKI, under the impassive gaze of Sam Kendrick himself and the baleful stare of Kevin Scott, a contract which, David had taken great pleasure in telling her, was for $250,000. *A quarter of a million dollars!* Tina and

Jeanne had been utterly blown away, unable to stifle their jealousy even for the sake of sucking up to her, which was what she'd expected. Maybe it was un-nineties, but Megan had enjoyed it when she saw their mouths drop open. Although it was nothing compared with the pleasure she had in driving down to Mr Chicken in her newly leased BMW to pick Stacey up on her lunch break. Bob Jenkins had tried to slime his way back into her good graces, apologizing for 'being a little short with you' and attempting to kiss her butt – 'We all knew you would make it, Megan. We could tell the second you walked in the door you were gonna be someone special.' At which she'd turned round, in the middle of the hushed diner, and said loudly and sweetly, 'Unlike you, Bob, you pimply little fuck.'

Well, it was true what they say.

Revenge is sweet.

Megan could still hardly believe it was true. She had to pinch herself every time she got up in the morning, look around her and wonder if this could actually be happening. It still took her a second or two to figure out where she was: the new apartment was so clean and spacious, compared with what she was used to, and it was as silent as the grave. Apart from the traffic rushing by, of course, but you tuned that out in a city. No, what she meant was that she didn't have to hear Jeanne and Tina bickering any more, didn't have to wake up to find all the hot water gone and some unshaven jerk that Tina had brought home with her sitting in their kitchenette drinking coffee out of her mug. This place was all hers; it had a fully equipped kitchen, soft carpets in every room and even a little home office for her to write in. David had found it for her, and when he'd shown her through the door she'd had to fight back the impulse to tears.

'It's beautiful, David! But I can't afford it.'

'Sure you can.' He'd been so certain, so confident; Megan looked at his immaculately tailored suit and platinum Rolex and felt like an idiot for even suggesting it. Of *course* she could afford it, or David wouldn't have leased it for her.

'We're paying rent and amenities directly out of your account. You don't have to worry about it. You don't have to worry about anything.'

'Out of my account?'

'We set up a facility with Norman Drew for you. They'll be your accountants now. You'll get on great with them, I always use them for my new clients.'

My accountants! She hadn't known whether to laugh or cry. What would Mom say if she could see her now? Plump, plain Megan, the perennial loser, always the last one that the family thought about, installed in a chic little apartment of her own in the heart of Century City, LA. Megan knew she should have called back to tell them the news, but somehow she'd been putting it off. Her family were normally so discouraging, deep down inside she was afraid they might snipe at her, and worse, that she might care. She didn't want any of the bloom taken off this particular rose just yet.

'*All* your new clients?' she couldn't help asking. 'Does that include Zach Mason?'

David laughed at her indulgently. Damn, what a sexy laugh, Megan thought. Sated, as if he'd just had sex. But then everything about David Tauber made her think of sex.

'It does.' He craned his head around to look inside her bedroom, noticing her Dark Angel and Metallica posters tacked up on the wall. Megan always stuck those posters up first, wherever she was – they helped keep her rooted. But for the first time she felt ashamed. He would think she was too old for posters. 'I see you're a fan.'

She nodded, blushing.

'So now you share accountants. It'll give you something else to talk about besides music when I introduce you.'

'When you introduce us?' Megan repeated, holding her breath.

'Sure. At Isabelle Kendrick's party tomorrow night. I asked Sam if I could bring you along. Everybody will be there – Zach Mason, Fred Florescu, Sam, the Artemis execs in charge of your project.'

Her project!

'And me.' David gave her that special, lazy smile, his polished white teeth dazzling against his tanned skin. In that Gucci suit that pulled taut across his impressive chest, he reminded Megan of every college football hope she'd ever seen, or of some gorgeous male model right out of an Armani campaign. She couldn't dwell on her own bad skin or her plumpness when she was with him. There was no chance to consider anything physical except David. He was so perfect, she found it tough to look away from him.

As though aware of her thoughts, Tauber winked at her. 'I'm no Zach Mason, I know. But you'll let me be your escort to this party, won't you, Megan? I can't wait to show off my latest client.'

He wants to show me off? Megan thought, wanting to hug herself.

'I'd love to go with you, David,' she said shyly.

'Great.' Another dazzling smile, and he was turning to go. 'Oh, and Megan' – he handed her an American Express gold card, made out in her name – 'you should go buy a new dress. No offence, but this is a serious party and I don't think what you have there will cut it.' He glanced neutrally at her plain black dress, her one 'good' outfit that was hanging by itself in an open wardrobe.

'No. Sure. Of course,' Megan said hastily, burning with embarrassment.

'Terrific.' He raised her hand to his mouth and kissed it, and the slight pressure of his lips burned on her skin. 'I'll see you tomorrow.'

And he'd gone, leaving Megan alone with a fifteen-thousand-dollar line of credit, one day to get ready for her *entrée* into her new life, and not a soul in the world she could talk to.

12

The Kendrick mansion was in a state of complete chaos. Only two hours to go until the party was due to begin, and a horde of immaculately groomed waiters were swarming over the grounds like black and white bees, radios crackling as though they were the Secret Service as the party director relayed his and Mrs Kendrick's orders to various parts of the ground.

Standing on the terrace, Sam Kendrick sighed inwardly. He didn't understand the subtleties of party-giving and he never would. The whole place looked fine to him: mini-orchestra set up in the ballroom, chamber quartet out by the pool, which was covered in a thousand minute sandalwood candles, floating across it like perfumed fireflies, not to mention the food and different types of champagne set up all over the house and grounds. His wife had never done things by halves. There would be caviar in ice sculptures laid out all over the place, together with real truffles, plates of oysters, dim-sum and Belgian chocolates, all the normal Hollywood titbits; but Isabelle eschewed the trend towards poolside buffets in favour of a formal sit-down dinner, with the seating arrangements worked out more carefully than most of his contracts. The pillars out front of the house were all wreathed with pink roses, solid columns of colour, and the rest of the flowers appeared to be a kind of weird mix of roses, orchids, violets and mistletoe, imported from northern Europe and flown in specially by the florist.

The effect was certainly magnificent, Sam thought wryly. Jeez, they had probably scented the air above the whole of Beverly Hills this evening. *And* provided it with a free new-age soundtrack. Talk about stress-reduction – Isabelle had wreathed their entire gardens with miles upon miles of the most delicate Japanese bells, strung on invisible silk threads, so that the slightest breeze provoked a gorgeous whispering music. He knew Isabelle would have liked to hire a few peacocks to strut around the grounds, but Elizabeth Martin had done that for one of her bashes in New York a few years back, and Isabelle would as soon call in McDonald's for her catering as imitate Elizabeth.

Sam grimaced. Maybe it was his biggest failing in their marriage, that he would never make as much as Alex Martin, the oil billionaire, and thus never enable Isabelle to throw the kind of party she would really enjoy. His budget didn't stretch to flying their guests to a tropical island for some end-of-hop beachcombing. Nonetheless, Isabelle considered Elizabeth her only rival, so peacocks were out. Instead she had, despite his misgivings, brought in sixteen tiger cubs which were tethered to different pillars and sculptures on very short leashes, their collars studded with diamonds. Insurance was costing him a fortune, and although the little bastards were semi-sedated, Sam didn't trust beasts that grew up to prey on human flesh. He had enough of those at work.

'Excuse me, sir,' gasped a waiter, staggering past him with a bowl of beluga so heavy it made Sam's wallet ache just thinking about it.

These parties were important to his position in town, vitally important. Every year he added another stack of favours in his credit ledger by granting invites to actors and directors whose wives were desperate to attend. Isabelle had worked hard at making herself a social force in the city, whatever the hell that meant. It gave him a nice feeling of male superiority not to know exactly. All these charity committees and thousand-dollars-a-plate dinners. Hospital boards and museum benefactor lists. All total bullshit, but that was the way things worked. The wives wanted to join the right committee, they had to be on the right side of Isabelle. And that gave him more pull with their husbands, it let SKI punch above its weight. You never knew when that might be important. In their recent lean patch, Sam was uncomfortably aware, it had been vital.

Well, that was all over now.

Sam fiddled with his tux in the scented air. Maybe it was a good thing that Isabelle was so obsessive about this party. Everybody would be here to congratulate him on his latest big score – Artemis Studios presenting *See the Lights*, a Fred Florescu production, starring Zach Mason and Roxana Felix. Screenplay by Megan whatsername. A great, big, fat, Sam Kendrick International *package deal*.

Kendrick smiled to himself. He was back in the game.

Megan twisted in front of her new mirror. Was this OK? She couldn't *believe* she'd spent this much money on one dress. Two hundred dollars! A month's rent back at the Venice apartment. And she still wasn't sure it looked right.

It was another long number in black. When you weren't sure, black was the only choice, you didn't have alternatives, but this was a bit more formal than her old 'good' gown that David had heaped such scorn on. It came right down to the floor for a start, hiding her still plump legs, and then gathered in gently at the waist before flaring up with an inbuilt push-up bra to give her some semblance of a decent cleavage. In San Francisco, Megan had always been faintly proud of her breasts – a good 34C cup – and Rory or whoever had always seemed impressed. Here in Los Angeles, home of Woman as Art Form, Megan felt flat-chested as well as dumpy.

Still, this dress went some way to remedying that. It wasn't silk or satin – she'd asked the price of a few designer silk numbers and nearly passed out at the reply – but it was made of a decent brushed cotton, it was bias-cut and it moved with a swing. Megan had purchased a pair of silk heels to match it, trying not to glance down at the amount she was signing for. They had made her feet look so hot, slimming her ankles and throwing a whole new gait into the way she walked.

She'd put on new L'Oréal make-up, sweeping blusher under the chin and cheekbones to give her face more definition and dabbing white eyeshadow underneath the brow as Declan had taught her. It was supposed to make you look more alive. There was no jewellery, of course, but perhaps they'd all assume she was aiming for the simple, sophisticated look, Megan thought hopefully.

Her reflection stared back at her from the mahogany frame. Not bad. No true Angeleno beauty of course, but not bad, all the same. She'd lost six pounds since leaving Mr Chicken, and though she was still overweight, most of the excess fat was hidden under the forgiving sweep of her skirt. The heels almost made her look tall, and her hair, which had been set at a beauty parlour earlier in the day, fell in loose, soft curls to her shoulders. She looked young and pretty. Feminine.

Megan tapped one silken heel to the pounding bass of 'Frozen Gold', Dark Angel's anthem from *West of the Moon*. The track was a kind of talisman for her. It had been the first rock song she'd heard and liked. But somehow the movement seemed ridiculous. Dark Angel or Pantera or whoever, you listened to them in jeans and a T-shirt, not silk heels and a black evening gown. If Dec and Trey and the others could see me now, she thought, they'd all howl with laughter and then they'd say I'd sold out. Swapped my soul for a quarter of a million. Look at me! Back home, would I ever have given a damn what a bunch of suits thought of how I looked?

The thought hovered for a while, then she dismissed it. She was going to meet Zach Mason at this party. So this couldn't be selling out, because Zach would never do that.

The door buzzer shrilled.

David!

Suddenly as nervous as a virgin, Megan went to open the door.

Roxana Felix took all of five minutes to prepare for Isabelle Kendrick's party. She had selected her look the day she arrived: strappy silver Manolo Blahnik heels, bright red lipstick, to contrast perfectly with her pale skin and raven hair, and the simple cream shift dress that Alessandro Eco had used for the wedding gown in his Chicago collection. No jewels. No make-up, either; that was a particular arrogance, to show that she had skin so flawless she didn't even need foundation. Down her back, her long jet-black hair flowed freely, shining and full of body like some ad for the world's most expensive shampoo.

She was travelling to the party in Jordan Goldman's limousine and she had no doubt that even sexy little Jordan would be sick with envy when she caught sight of her. She looked even more breathtaking than usual. If that were possible.

'You look great,' Paul said automatically, coming out of the bathroom with one hand on his bow tie.

'Do I?' Eleanor asked. 'Do I really?'

Her partner turned, surprised by the nervous tension in her voice. Her normal response was 'So do you.' Which was fine by him; why waste time on flowery compliments and checking each other out? They already lived together.

Eleanor was pirouetting in front of the mirror like a nervous teenager. Actually, she *did* look great. It was a new dress, a floating, romantic number in dusty pink chiffon, with a scoop-collar neckline dusted over with tiny rosebuds in scarlet satin. Her ice-blonde hair was swept upwards in an elegant French style, and drop diamond earrings glittered at her cheeks, a matching necklace sparkling exquisitely against her delicate collarbone. Pink satin shoes he could only just see peeped out from under the hem of her gown, and her make-up was subtle and understated.

'Yes. You look' – he searched rustily for some poetic word – 'ravishing.'

'You don't think I look too young? Mutton dressed as lamb?' Eleanor asked, anxiously.

Paul Halfin glanced at her. What was getting into her tonight? This was his wife-to-be, the queenly president of Artemis. Not to mention one of the most impeccable dressers in the city. Jumpy nerves were simply not her style.

'You're only thirty-eight, for God's sake, Eleanor. You're a young woman.'

Not as young as Jordan Goldman, Eleanor thought.

'You look lovely, dear. Really.'

'Thanks, Paul,' said Eleanor, and she wondered why his compliments made her feel so guilty.

Tom Goldman shifted on his bed to get a better look at what his wife was doing. Her tongue had ceased licking his balls for a second, but he didn't care. One pleasure was replaced by another as he watched her, eyes shut tight kneeling in front of him, slip her right hand across the downy mass of curls in between her supple thighs, rubbing her fingers backwards and forwards over herself, the knuckles suddenly glistening in their soft bedroom light, slick with her own moisture. His cock throbbed in response. Jordan always knew how to do such hidden, wicked things, it made him harder than a baseball bat. Opening one eye to check his reaction, Jordan grabbed his dick in her free left hand and started to tease him, opening and closing her fingers in a fluttering movement, then sliding up and down him with perfect rhythm, playing with herself, knowing he was watching her, mesmerized. A bead of pearly liquid dewed the tip of Tom's straining cock and he moaned, the normal signal, so she finished herself off in front of him with two deep circular thrusts, knelt forward and took him in her mouth, as deeply as she could, sucking him hard, strongly, not allowing the pace or the pressure to slip. Tom's last conscious thought was to thank God for one woman who understood that if he'd reached a certain point he wanted to come, not to be taken back down and then brought up again or whatever . . . it was never as strong if you did it like that . . . *Oh, God* . . .

His back arching as though in agony, Tom Goldman lifted himself half off the bed, thrust into his wife's throat, and came.

Jordan waited barely a second and then spat him out, turning her face aside. She reached fastidiously for a box of tissues she kept next to the bed and wiped her mouth, grimacing with distaste. Goldman watched as she went to the bathroom, reaching for the mouthwash, his hard-on shrinking almost as quickly as it had arrived. Somehow, after sex, he always felt older. More disgusting. As though she was a hooker, or he was a dirty old man, not her lawfully wedded husband.

Mentally Goldman chided himself as he reached for his shirt and pants. He should say *making love*, not *having sex*. After all, their child might be conceived on any one of these encounters.

He tried to ignore the fact that at the moment of climax it had been Eleanor Marshall's face he had imagined. And not that of his gorgeous wife.

Jordan emerged from the bathroom, dressed and ready to go in a tailored Yves Saint-Laurent pantsuit, a neat Chanel purse swinging from her left shoulder.

'Come on, honey, let's go. I promised Roxana we'd pick her up at half-eight.'

'So we'll be ten minutes late.' She looked cute in those silk pants; they hugged her ass. Tom reached for her. 'Once more, for luck.'

She swatted his hand away as though it were an irritating fly. 'Tom! We can't be late. You know Roxana, she won't wait, she'll just call a limo service. And I *want* to arrive with her. It will be *such* a coup. You know? Because she promised to get me some sponsorship from *Vogue* for the next gun-control party! Isn't that wonderful? And we did go to school together . . .'

Goldman listened to her chatter on, his mind already elsewhere, desire totally evaporated.

'Tom, are you listening to me?'

'Sure, honey, sure.' This was an important party; they had a movie at SKI now. And Isabelle's parties were always important. He didn't want to row with his wife tonight.

Besides which, if he was lucky, he'd get to talk to Eleanor alone.

Suddenly, Tom Goldman couldn't wait. 'Let's go,' he said, smoothing his jacket down.

Eight o'clock exactly and everything was in place. Not a servant, not a leaf out of place, not a ripple on any one of their four hundred Irish linen tablecloths could be seen to mark the cyclone of activity Sam had witnessed just half an hour before. My God, it's like a military operation, Sam thought. In fact scrap that. No military operation was ever that efficient these days, not with that fat asshole Clinton in charge. At any rate, their house had been transformed in just a few hours into Isabelle's personal Arabian Nights fantasy. It was perfumed, it was belled and it was wreathed in flowers and glittering with gems, like some doe-eyed houri in a pasha's harem. For a second, Kendrick imagined Roxana Felix like that, robed in see-through silk, her long black hair caught in a diaphanous veil, chained to a jewelled collar at the foot of his couch. He felt his groin grow warm and heavy with blood at the thought, desire tugging at his crotch with sharp little fingers. Yeah, on another planet that would be nice, he thought. A doubly pleasant way to take his revenge. Jesus, that bitch was running rings around him! First the little game with the PR. Then she has Isabelle nagging at him on her behalf, and Isabelle was not an easy woman to ignore. Then somehow, and he was still trying figure out exactly how, she gets Tom Goldman to push her at Artemis. Then she issues this bullshit release to the press before she's been cast, and Eleanor Marshall is eating him, Samuel Jacob Kendrick, for her low-fat lunch. Then somehow, despite all the above, she manages to get herself cast! The woman was unbelievable. And he had sworn blind to Eleanor that he was personally gonna put a rocket up her ass.

What a joke. He'd called every half-hour yesterday, and she'd simply refused to take his calls. 'Sam, I'm so sorry, I'm busy right now.' 'I'm just in the shower.' 'I'll call you right back.' Then she'd switched on the machine.

Even now, a whole day later, his blood was still boiling.

Well, he knew she was coming tonight. With his wife's latest protégée, Jordan Goldman. And that would mean she couldn't run from him forever.

Right on cue, Isabelle appeared beside him at the top of the steps in a Balenciaga original as the first headlights appeared at the end of their drive.

Banishing all thoughts of anger and lust, Sam composed his face into a rare smile.

Showtime!

Megan Silver clutched onto her agent's arm as though it were a voodoo talisman. David Tauber – she'd only known him for four days, but that was four days longer than anyone else she could see. A sense of complete unreality had descended on her. She couldn't stop looking around, her head turning constantly, as though she expected the whole place to shimmer and disappear like a desert mirage. Back in San Francisco she'd always been the clever one, intellectually self-assured, cynical, worldly. A perfect nineties twentysomething, a girl who'd been raised on grunge and political apathy. She might not have made any money, but she was cool. Megan knew every lyric Kurt Cobain had ever written, considered Jim Morrison an alcoholic loser who'd wasted his talent, and was on first-name terms with the doormen at all the hippest clubs. She wore Caterpillar trainers and Veruca Salt T-shirts and nobody fucked with her. She was in with the in-crowd.

But here! Holy Lord God, this was worse than the first time she'd dropped acid. Megan felt totally lost. Hundreds of people thronged past her, almost all of them over forty; big, powerful men who walked nowhere and strode everywhere; shorter, meaner-looking ones whom everybody else seemed to be afraid of; and women, crowds of women, practically every one of them sporting gemstones the size of small birds' eggs, floating past her, pushing past her, in clouds of taffeta and chiffon and the finest moiré silk, in designer outfits so signature that even she could not fail to recognize a few – sparkling Versace designed for a wearer thirty years younger, immaculately fitted Chanel, impossible for anyone to mistake, Gucci with its signature buttons. Every one of them had tight, clear skin that she imagined would crack if they laughed. And every one of them moved with utter self-possession, accepting a crystal flute filled with pink champagne from a waiter like she might reach for a cold Bud, or turning down caviar or truffles as though they were M&M's. Megan guessed they might add an ounce or two to all those 110-pound frames.

From the second David had helped her out of their hired limo Megan had ceased to feel successful. Looking around at her fellow guests, she knew what she was. The smallest of the smallfry. Unsophisticated. Fat. And poor.

'You're doing fine. Relax,' David whispered in her ear, steering her towards the buffet.

'Oh, David, I can't eat anything,' Megan said miserably. She was twenty-four, and she felt heavy and unattractive, as though her youth was a cruel joke. What good did it do her to be twenty-four when there were women here with thighs barely bigger than her upper arms?

'Sure you can,' David told her, a brilliant smile permanently fixed on his face, adding, 'Best go for the caviar and the fruit. No fat that way. And skip the breads. You don't need complex carbohydrates right now.'

'OK,' she said, feeling fatter than ever. But *grateful*, of course. David had been so good to her, and now he was going to help her with her diet . . . and David should know. He was a prime physical specimen, Megan thought, as she snuck a glance at her companion, waving and nodding at four different players a minute. He'd told her his tux was from Ralph Lauren's latest collection, and it certainly looked stunning on him – the wool was the darkest, deepest blue, practically black, but with just enough colour to set off his hazel eyes and sandy hair, and it was flawlessly cut, fitting his large, athletic frame to perfection.

Being with David was the only thing that gave her any reassurance, Megan thought. At least she didn't have to be ashamed of her escort. The dress she'd been so proud of earlier now looked as though it had walked right out of a Frisco thrift store, but nobody would notice the dress while she was with David. Moguls and movie stars swarmed all around her, but she knew she was with the best-looking guy in the room.

'Here.' He handed her a small plate heaped with glistening fish eggs, a slice of lemon, and a minute silver dish of sliced strawberries and gooseberries. There were two delicate silver spoons on the side. 'And take a glass of champagne, too.'

'Can I?' Megan asked doubtfully.

'This is a celebration,' David said generously. She felt his strong hand take her elbow, leading her deftly through the crowd to one of the rose-strewn tables on the terrace, the area nearby flickering and dancing with shadows thrown up from the hundred little candles drifting across the darkened surface of the pool.

He picked up the lemon and squeezed it deftly over the caviar, a thin trail of juice trickling over his palm and wrist. Megan felt need stir in her groin. She hadn't been touched since she left Rory, not that any man would want her. Still, she had a strong urge to bend her head towards him and lick him clean.

To her total embarrassment, David looked up and caught her staring at him. Megan blushed bright red.

He gave her a soft smile, and dug one of the silver spoons into the mound of caviar, scooping up a wet, shining pile of miniature black pearls, and held it out towards her.

'Try some of this.'

Dutifully Megan swallowed the caviar, taking it in her mouth as delicately as she could. Essence of salt fish and slime. Ugh.

'You like?' Tauber was asking her.

'Delicious,' Megan said.

'It's an acquired taste.' He can see right through me, Megan thought, sensing her blush deepen, but David was already on his feet. 'And you'll get used to it. All my clients do. Within six months you'll be able to tell a good champagne vintage with your eyes shut. Come on, I have to introduce you to your new colleagues.'

With a regretful glance at her untouched champagne, Megan followed him, unsteadily. Jesus Christ. She would never get used to high heels.

Jordan was burning up. She couldn't help it. They hadn't even gone into dinner yet and already she was being thoroughly upstaged! Every society wife she'd ever met was pressing Roxana to attend this dinner or that party; the news of her casting had gone round the room in twenty seconds, and all Jordan could hear was 'the next Julia Roberts'. As if the bimbo had one ounce of Julia's talent. And worse still was the way their husbands had started to jostle the Goldman party as if Roxana were some incredibly rare wild animal in danger of extinction before they'd had a chance to gawp. They stared, they ogled, they paid her inane compliments on her dress, they asked about her new career. All the attentions that *she*, Jordan Cabot, was used to receiving – for the last eighteen months she'd been the youngest woman at any high-powered party by a good ten years. And now she might as well be invisible.

Furiously, Jordan flashed Barry Diller a beaming smile and took a deep sip of her Roederer Cristal champagne. She noticed that Roxana, next to her, had not so much as glanced in the TV mogul's direction. But of *course* not, Jordan thought bitchily. Roxana waits for the Barry Dillers of this world to come to her.

She began flashing back to unpleasant memories of their shared schooldays at the Sacred Heart. Even there, Jordan had always been the prettiest girl at the convent – bar one, of course. Was she destined always to take the silver medal?

In the scented, darkened air, Jordan slipped her perfectly toned arm through her husband's. At least *Tom* wasn't fawning over Roxana, and she should know, because she'd watched him like a hawk from the moment the bitch had stepped gracefully into their limo. He had given her a once-over, of course, but in a cold, detached way. Jordan had seen him give other movie stars the same clinical look. He was checking her out for her box-office potential, nothing more. In fact, while Jordan had been explaining all about the gun-control dinner, Tom had interrupted them just once, asking Roxana if she'd spoken to Sam Kendrick recently. And Roxana had smiled coolly and replied that no, she'd been too busy to speak to Sam, and after all, David Tauber was her agent.

Jordan had no idea what all that was about. But she was glad her husband didn't seem to care for the supermodel. That would have been all she needed.

'Sweetie.' Tom was bending down to her, whispering in her ear. 'Do you need me? I have to go and talk to Jake Keller about something.'

He was amazed at the easy smoothness of the lie. Why didn't he just say Eleanor? Eleanor was his president of Production. He talked with Eleanor all the time.

'Oh.' Jordan gave him her best little-girl pout. 'You know how I hate all your silly business talk. Well, don't be long.'

'I won't.'

Why did she have to act like that? It was stupid, Tom thought, almost angrily. Since when was she six years old?

'Come back soon. Me miss 'oo.' She blew him a kiss from her full, perfectly lined lips.

Oy vey. Goldman turned away, sighing.

Sam Kendrick moved fluidly round the room, working the groups Isabelle wasn't covering. Over the years they'd got this down to a fine art: Isabelle chatted with the players and female stars, he attended to the male stars and wives. It was exactly the opposite of what everybody expected, but it worked perfectly; the men gave him *beaucoup* brownie points for being able to lay off business for one night – how many of them would be capable of the same thing?

– and their wives, normally expected to just show up, shut up and smile, were insanely flattered to have a heavy hitter, especially one as sexy as Sam Kendrick, ask their opinions as though he were actually interested. It bought him a lot of extra influence, and it was another social trick Isabelle had wised him up to. *Take care of the wives.* They won't forget it. And they'll push their husbands for you all year long.

The second trick was timing. You said as little as possible to as many people as possible; that way you could make an impression on everyone.

Sam glanced at the time on his subtly lit Cartier watch. He was making good progress.

Then, out of the corner of one eye, he saw Tom Goldman break away from the little throng of people crowding Roxana.

His blood pumped a little faster. Now was his chance. With a murmured excuse to the wife of some TV producer, Sam crossed the terrace.

'Ladies, gentlemen, would you excuse me?' he said loudly. 'I have to monopolize this beautiful lady for a few seconds.'

'Your latest client, right, Sam?' one of the suits enquired.

'She is indeed.' He smiled proudly.

'Lucky dog,' somebody else said, and there was general laughter as his guests moved away.

Roxana Felix leant back a little against the marble pillar she was standing in front of, and regarded the head of her agency with a cold stare.

Sam looked. Then he looked again. And again.

In the soft light from the Japanese lanterns, her face and hair framed by a wreath of pale pink roses, Roxana Felix reminded him of a picture by those British painters – what were they called? – the Pre-Raphaelites. Right. All pure white skin and silken black hair, her full mouth red as blood, her eyes dark as sin, and her slender, perfect figure, simultaneously hidden and revealed by the cream shift dress, the most tempting thing since Eve introduced Adam to harvesting. But no, maybe not. The way those Victorians had painted, their ladies seemed pure, ethereal and ghostly. Roxana Felix was none of those things. She was everything he had seen on screen, everything that he'd been fantasizing about. Sex projected and oozed out of every tiny pore of her flawless skin. She was no cold, narcissistic mannequin. She was a flesh-and-blood woman and she conjured up images of the hottest fuck you would ever have in your life. Even the way she was standing right now, defiant and outraged, regarding him with such hostility. Her body seemed poised to strike, as graceful and deadly as a panther.

She was the most attractive woman he had ever seen, and Sam Kendrick had seen a *lot* of attractive women.

Desire hit him like a lightning bolt. Savage. Intense. Astonishing.

'Are you done?'

She had a low, sensual voice, but the tone was absolute steel.

'Are you done, Mr Kendrick? Do you think you could pick me out of the police line-up now?'

'We have to talk,' Kendrick said, firmly. He dragged his gaze back up to meet her eyes. Jesus Christ! Just because she'd been around the block in the fashion business didn't mean that some twenty-four-year old baby was going to chew him, Sam Kendrick, out at his own party. He recognized that note in her voice. It was the same one he used to demolish his various underlings, or to pole-axe studio execs that were screwing with his clients. That was the tone of command, of a person used to authority. OK, so Roxana Felix had been boss in her world up to now. But this was a different universe and he was its resident God. This, she had to learn. This, he was going to make her learn. Sam Kendrick had not reached the summit of the game to surrender his authority to some sassy piece of ass.

'I *was* talking. To those gentlemen, whom you so rudely interrupted.'

Uh-huh. Nice grammar. Well, he got enough of the fake limey bullshit from Kevin Scott.

'Listen, princess.' He saw her eyes narrow in shock and anger, and felt adrenalin start to knot in his stomach. This was the tough bit: blasting the client without getting fired. You had to bluff, and you had to gamble on how badly they wanted the part. Poker with people. He'd always been an expert. 'You can hold court with the boys some other time.'

'Who the hell do you think you are?' Roxana demanded, scarcely able to believe her ears. Sam Kendrick was just another salt-and-pepper suit. A looker, but so what? Did he think she was going to cut him any slack because he'd retained a little masculinity? Nobody, but *nobody*, spoke to her like that. Not any more.

'I'm the head of SKI, Roxana. And if you want to stay represented by us, you'll shut the fuck up and listen to me.'

She gave a disbelieving laugh. 'My God. Do you think you're the only agency in this city?'

Kendrick looked her over, slowly. 'No. But we're the only agency with *See the Lights*.'

There was a long pause. 'I've been cast,' she said finally. Defiantly.

Sam leant towards her, a pleasant, businesslike smile on his face, so that anyone watching would think nothing of it. When he got close enough to smell the faint tang of cinnamon on her breath, he said, softly, 'And I can have you *un*cast. In ten seconds. With five words to Tom Goldman.'

'You wouldn't do that,' Roxana said, staring right back at him.

Doesn't give an inch, Sam thought admiringly. Very good.

A player less skilled than he was might even have been fooled. But Sam had been in the game too long not to notice the tiny tremor, the inability to control the breath, that gave away her horror at that idea.

Still speaking softly, he said, 'Try me.'

She didn't reply.

'The stunts you've been pulling with the press,' Sam said. 'I didn't like them, but I didn't care. When you've got to know me a little better, you'll understand that nothing you can do will pressure me into anything.' She looked sharply at him, and he gave her a knowing, indulgent smile. 'You thought I didn't realize? Come on, baby. I'm forty-five. I've been doing this stuff since before you were born. But your cute little games aren't the point here. What *is* is that you put out a bullshit release to the press about getting cast before you were. Now, that embarrasses Artemis and it embarrasses me. And if you ever, *ever* do anything like that again, this will be the last big movie you ever make. Understand?'

Roxana felt humiliation crash over her like a tidal wave. She couldn't even look at Sam Kendrick as she nodded her head.

'OK. Good.'

This was turning him on, Kendrick realized. She was too gorgeous to spar with like this and not want to fuck. Despite himself, his cock was hardening where he stood. He had to get away from her, or he'd be the chief talking point at his own goddamn party.

'I'm sure you're going to do us all proud in this picture, Roxana. See you later,' he said in more normal tones, and strode off towards the dining room.

Momentarily alone – she could see all the tame suits waiting to swarm back in on her – Roxana Felix watched Sam Kendrick go.

Jesus, how ridiculous. She sensed something stir in front of her that she hadn't felt in years. Lust. Why? Just because Kendrick hadn't crumpled in front of her like every other guy? Or because he had that strong, wild look about him, that maleness, a sense of raw power, the real kind? Sam was a lion, whereas David was just a peacock. Roxana had been around the block enough times to know the difference. And it wasn't just money. She could wrap Howard Thorn round her manicured finger, but this one was the real deal. The dominant male.

As the fawning crowd engulfed her again, Roxana seethed under her designer silk, almost paralysed with mortification. She could not and would not feel like that. Sam Kendrick had just insulted her. And Sam Kendrick would pay.

Ten minutes to go, ten minutes till dinner. Tom Goldman thrust his way through the crowd, feeling the pressure pulse against his skin with every tick of his platinum Patek Phillipe. Isabelle always held dinner bang on time, and he wanted to speak to Eleanor alone. Before they sat down. He knew that afterwards he wouldn't get a chance; Isabelle had arranged for everybody working on the Mason/Florescu project to be seated at one table, and he, Tom, a studio head, would be expected to make all the introductions and steer the fucking boring small-talk conversation.

Guests rustled past him in designer tuxes, velvet gowns, tailored suits in silk jersey. Producers, agents, actors. Blondes, redheads, blue rinses, brunettes. Long hair, short hair, balding. And just about every one of them appeared to want to talk to him. Goldman smiled and muttered incoherently, said 'Great to see you' and 'Call the office tomorrow' at least twenty times, kept himself moving, his sharp eyes scanning the crowd for Eleanor. He had to speak to her; he didn't know why, he just had to. About the way he'd been thinking of her lately. About Jordan. Or whatever. Maybe that was too indiscreet. And yet he knew he had to talk to her, even if he had no idea what the hell he was going to say . . .

'Tom.'

'Look, I can't talk right now,' Goldman snapped, turning to see who was plucking at his sleeve. He stopped walking, half jumping out of his skin. 'Eleanor!'

'Hey, it wasn't important. I'll catch up with you later.'

'No, no, wait.' He was nervous. Forty-five years old, with a woman he'd worked with for the last fifteen years, and he was nervous. Jesus. He passed a hand self-consciously across his thinning hair. 'I was looking for you.'

'You wanted to talk, right?' Eleanor said, feeling her heart speed up. 'I thought we might take a walk into the grounds.'

Away from the party. Away from all these people. OK, Goldman thought. You did deals totalling a hundred and ten million dollars last week. You can handle this.

'Sure. Let's go.'

As he followed her down the Kendricks' alabaster steps, Tom flashed for a second onto the irony of this. He, Tom Goldman, the playboy, the man of a million women, all of them as pretty and forgettable as each other. Except Jordan, who was prettier than the rest and thus his wife. He'd never had a second's trouble with girls since he'd joined Artemis at twenty-five, straight out of Yale. Making forty-seven grand a year, and that was in the seventies. If he hadn't left a trail of broken hearts, exactly, he'd certainly left a trail of disappointed starlets, students, debs. Women got nervous around him, not the other way round.

They walked together along the raked gravel path that led to the nearest sculptured grotto, silently, in the aromatic darkness, the hubbub and laughter of the gala behind them. Goldman realized that Eleanor was the only woman he knew who wouldn't have to ask where they were going. She knew the Kendricks' gardens as well as he did: she'd been a senior movie executive for more than a decade.

Just as they turned off the path into the little marble sanctuary, with its polished oak bench and statue of a rearing unicorn, he heard Jordan calling his name.

'Tom! Tom?'

Her voice carried clearly enough; she was shouting. Goldman realized with acute discomfort that Eleanor could hear her. It was unmistakable. Eleanor could hear his wife shouting for him, and they both knew that he could, too.

He should excuse himself. Go find Jordan. Bring her to join them.

'Eleanor, we need to talk.'

'So you said.' But she wasn't mocking him, Goldman realized, with a quick flash of gratitude. He looked at her, the first real chance he'd had to see her since he arrived. Jesus, she looked stunning. Elegant and classy as ever, but somehow – softer, more appealing. Those tiny rosebuds. She looked like Cinderella at the ball, her intelligent sapphire eyes glinting even in this darkness, her creamy white breasts pushed high up, spilling over the boned bodice of her gown, the minute lines around her mouth welcoming. Her hair was swept up, and even though she'd never made any attempt to cover the few grey strands weaving through the blonde he didn't care. It looked beautiful, like gold shot with silver thread. It suited her. *She* was beautiful.

Eleanor tried to look away. She knew she should break the moment. It was dangerous . . . Paul, Jordan . . .

But Tom Goldman was standing there, eating her with his eyes, looking as though he wanted to kiss her, and . . .

'Tom,' she said gently. 'You're staring at me.'

'You're so lovely,' Goldman said, without thinking.

Eleanor turned her head aside, not wanting to let him see her eyes fill with tears. At this moment, in this spot, she felt lovely. Not middle-aged, unwed, overpromoted or barren; just beautiful. For one blessed second she had seen herself in the mirror of his eyes, and she felt beautiful.

'Thank you,' she said.

'I'm lonely,' Goldman said, and felt a huge release, as though a physical weight had been lifted from his shoulders. The words had come by themselves, and the second he said them, he knew they were true. 'I'm so lonely, Eleanor. I can't talk to her.'

Eleanor Marshall felt time freeze around her, her own pulse thudding out of rhythm, out of control. She tried to breathe normally. Did he say that? Had he really said that? A million obvious responses presented themselves. 'Is this your version of "my wife doesn't understand me", Tom?' 'Shouldn't you be discussing this with a shrink?' 'Try getting in touch with your feminine side.' But she refused to trot one of them out. Tom Goldman did not play games. Not with her.

And besides, she wasn't sure if he *had* a feminine side, she thought, smiling a little in the shadows.

'It's hard, to be with someone,' she said.

The effort to keep a check on herself was overwhelming. Why do humans do this to themselves? Eleanor thought, agonized. Why have we erected these huge, sacred walls? What she longed to say was, *Tom, I love you. Get a divorce and marry me and we'll have children and we'll be happy.*

But she just couldn't. Tom was a married man and her oldest friend. For all she knew, this was a passing phase, and next month he'd be as wrapped up in his kid bride as he had been at first and then where would she be? And she, Eleanor, she was still with Paul Halfin . . . could she cold-bloodedly betray him, here, now, for the sake of a sweet look and a little perfume in the air? Expose him to knowing glances from Tom for the rest of his life? Because she was kidding herself if she thought Tom actually meant it. There was no way he was going to divorce that young, stacked, tanned sex goddess he'd married, the one who was the new social force with all the hot LA charities, for her, Eleanor Marshall, a career woman with grey streaks in her hair and the odd line on her skin. She had to get real. This was life, and not the movies.

'Are you going to marry Paul?' Tom asked her, urgently.

She shivered at the force behind his question. 'I don't know.'

'But it's not certain.'

She said as lightly as she could, 'Nothing's certain, Tom . . .'

'Eleanor,' he murmured, and then he was leaning closer to her, his body closing on hers, his head dipping towards her . . .

'Tom Goldman and Eleanor Marshall. I'm so glad I found you.'

Eleanor spun round to see Isabelle Kendrick standing in front of them, her emerald-green Balenciaga trailing in the night-time dew. Her expression was one of the purest delight at having stumbled across them, but Eleanor wasn't fooled. Not for a second. She wondered how long Isabelle had been watching them, and she didn't even have to glance at Tom to tell that he was thinking the same thing.

'Hello, Isabelle! It's a wonderful party,' Eleanor greeted her. 'You must excuse Tom and me for sneaking away. We were talking shop – about your husband's latest project, actually.'

Eleanor knew the tight-assed cow would hate that – *I'm* talking business with the boys, dear, so stuff your stupid canapés.

'But how marvellous.' Isabelle's professionally made-up face was totally inscrutable, her smiled fixed and gleaming. 'That's exactly what I came to find you for. We're starting dinner in a moment, and Sam simply insisted that all the people on this *Bright Lights* film – '

'*See the Lights,*' Goldman muttered.

' – sit together. So I've put Roxana Felix, the model, next to you and Paul, Eleanor, and the screenwriter next to you, Tom. Jordan will be sitting with the rock star.'

Her face contracted tautly with disapproval, and despite her bitter frustration Eleanor felt a flicker of amusement. So, Zach Mason had done something to piss the old witch off, had he? Maybe he hadn't pressed his tux correctly? She was pleased. When she'd been into rock and roll, musicians existed for the sole purpose of pissing off people like Isabelle Kendrick.

'That sounds great, Isabelle.' For the second time in two days, Eleanor had seen Tom Goldman snap straight back into character. Now he was all the relaxed mogul at play, being gracious to his hostess. 'Let's go.'

Megan's head was spinning. Partly from the exhaustion of following David around – he never wanted her to sit down, and he was constantly introducing her to people as his new client, the 'first-time screenwriter – she wrote the Mason/Florescu thing over at Artemis' – and partly from lack of food. She was dying to take one of the little dim-sums or handcrafted chocolates that the waiters thrust under her nose, but David kept giving her friendly little warning looks. It was humiliating, but, she reminded herself, it just showed that he cared about her. He obviously knew how to look after his own body. If she hadn't been such a pig, such a slob, beforehand, she wouldn't feel her thighs grazing each other under her skirt now. And her feet were in agony. The homegirls back on Haight didn't even own a pair of heels between them. Jesus, did women wear these things voluntarily? But she knew they did.It was a new world for her now, she was going to have to tear up her old rulebook. *We're not in Kansas any more, Toto.*

But this party . . . Tired, confused, fat and underdressed and she still couldn't get enough of it. Pure luxury everywhere you looked . . . on the walls, in the food, in the dresses of the women . . . baby tigers! In diamond collars! And no one remotely surprised! And the *stars* – she'd seen Michelle and Winona and Julia, Richard and Cindy, Arnold and Maria, Jack and Al and Robert and Harrison, and even, oh my God, it *was* him, Keanu . . .

She felt like a jerk for staring. Nobody else gave any of them a second glance. They were all too busy with their double-dutch movie conversations – 'Did you hear what the rolling break-even on that thing was?' 'Five points off the top. *And* ten per cent of the merchandising.' 'Fifteen million bucks, and that's just for above-the-line.' None of it fazed David, of course, but why would it? That was his business. So Megan Silver stood, suffered, and smiled.

But now they'd called dinner. Thank God. And David, handsome and confident as ever, was steering her through the marble lobby, past the huge crystal vases heaped with orchids, and through the vast ballroom, with its sea of opulent tables, to one particular table at the head of the room, right under two of the largest cut-glass chandeliers she'd ever seen. Most of the chairs were filled already: Sam Kendrick and his wife she'd met; the middle-aged man and elegant lady in the pink ballgown David had told her were chairman and president of the movie studio; an incredible-looking blonde girl; another middle-aged man – and oh my God, Roxana Felix! Was it? It was! And who was that in the corner, and what the hell was he wearing?

Roxana looked at Megan with contempt and indifference as David introduced her.

'Everybody, this is our screenwriter, Megan Silver. Megan, this is Roxana Felix, Paul Halfin, Jordan Cabot Goldman – Sam and Isabelle and Tom and Eleanor you've met . . .' He coughed, insistently, and Megan felt her heart lurch as the figure at the end of the table turned round. He was wearing a crumpled black jacket, thrown casually over a Metallica shirt, and his eyes narrowed, cold and hostile, as he looked at Megan, standing there with David Tauber's arm round her waist.

'Zach, say hello to Megan,' David said. 'She wrote *See the Lights*.'

Faced with her all-time hero, Megan suddenly clammed up. He was glaring at her. He seemed in a really, really bad mood.

She just nodded at him.

Utterly unperturbed, David pulled out a chair for her and the two of them sat down.

'And that makes everybody.'

Isabelle Kendrick looked round at her table with satisfaction, as though she'd personally created each one of them. 'We must have a toast. What shall we toast to?'

'Isn't that obvious, Mrs Kendrick?' David Tauber asked respectfully. He took the bottle of pink champagne nearest him and filled Megan's glass, then raised his own. 'To *See the Lights*. One thing everyone here has in common: the movie.'

'The movie,' everybody said.

Megan lifted her glass to her lips, terrified, but she managed to smile.

'The movie,' she repeated, and drank.

13

Screaming kids. Everywhere you looked. Teenagers and twentysomethings in black jeans, plaid shirts, combat boots. Longhairs and skinheads and glamorous babes in bright red lipstick and anarchy T-shirts, they formed one seething mass of rebellion, Generation X in full cry. As far as the eye could see, they crammed the stadium, heads banging, bodies flying, arms outstretched towards the stage, their expressions ranging from adulation to fury.

As the coloured spotlights swept the masses, it was obvious that this was no eighties poodle-rock crowd. Instead of standing demurely in their allotted places, the audience was cramming the aisles and standing on their seats. The crush barrier down the front was ten rows deep in human bodies. Security guards stood to one side shaking their heads, useless and helpless.

Dark Angel were onstage.

Screaming into the packed darkness, Nate Suter's guitar announced the beginning of 'Fighting Fire', the anti-government anthem that had started it all. A great howl of approval rose up to meet it, kids slamming forward as they started to chant the words, bodies drenched with sweat, a whole generation of young Americans cursing the system to eternal hell. The peace-and-love boomers were now running the banks, ruining industry, pricing them out of college. They had no jobs, no prospects, and no hope. Rage and betrayal crackled electric through the humid air. Some security men shrank back against the walls, grateful for the San Diego riot squad stationed right outside the venue. But they needn't have been concerned. All the anger, all the protest, all the energy, was being channelled into the razor-sharp riffing of this music, the raw harmonies bleeding from the giant speakers, and the furious, intense face of the singer, staring straight into the camera in front of him, so that his vast image, blown up to thousands of times life-size on two giant screens at either side of the stage, appeared to be gazing directly into the eyes of each and every fan as they chanted the lyric together.

Zach Mason. Lead singer of Dark Angel, the crown prince of the counterculture. As sensual as Jim Morrison, as angry as Malcolm X, as articulate as Kurt Cobain. Never gave interviews. Endorsed no politician. Spoke to the fans only live or through lyrics. And at moments like this, when you saw eighty thousand kids utterly mesmerized, you knew that if Mason but said the word, they would riot. They would rise up and follow him. The camera panned from left to right, across the throng of heaving, chanting kids, their aggression focused on the music with laser-like precision.

Dark Angel were the first band for years to scare parents. They appealed to fans of REM and Metallica and hardcore rap alike. They were angry. They had something to say. And looking at this wild, incensed, unified crowd, it was obvious that American youth was listening.

Zach Mason shifted uncomfortably on the soft leather sofa. 'Turn it off,' he said.

'But Zach, I thought – '

'Turn it *off.*' Mason's voice was a low growl.

David Tauber turned it off.

'I don't want to watch that,' Zach almost snarled. 'That was three years ago. I'm not interested in the past.'

His gaze swept the Artemis conference room, challenging any one of the suits to disagree. Jake Keller, the vice-president of Production, looked away, unable or unwilling to meet his glare. Sam Kendrick, the head of his agency and a man whom Mason had got to know a little, nodded sagely. Good. At least one of these fuckers understood where he was coming from. And Eleanor Marshall, the stern-looking lady in the dark green suit, was completely impassive. Only the dumpy little kid sitting next to David Tauber, the screenwriter, looked anguished. She was staring at the now blank screen with a mixture of wonder and regret. And he'd seen the way she looked across at him while the tape was playing – almost accusingly. Did he need this? He didn't need this. Not from some kid who was younger than he was. Not from some kid who looked like one of his fans, reminded him of things he preferred to forget.

Megan Silver. That was her name. He'd asked Tauber about her; she was twenty-four years old, she'd gone to college at Berkeley, and she'd written an awesome screenplay.

He hadn't said two words to her, but she still made him nervous.

'Sure. I understand,' David Tauber said smoothly. 'I just thought it might be a good idea for us all to get a *feel* for the backdrop of this movie. Fred Florescu messengered over the tapes, and I know Roxana's studying them, but since this is our first script meeting together . . .'

'I don't *need* to get a feel for what it's like to be around a band.' Mason nodded insultingly at Megan. 'Maybe she does.'

The girl started to say something, but Tauber's hand descended on her shoulder, and she relapsed into silence.

'Of course, Zach. This was more for Sam and Jake and Eleanor,' David said. 'We've all been examining the script, and I know they have some suggestions. I thought it might be beneficial if everybody knew what they were dealing with here.'

Yeah, right. Like any one of those fortysomething corporate assholes would suddenly 'get' rock 'n' roll from watching a half-hour video.

'You have script suggestions? Let's hear them,' Zach said, his green eyes narrowing. Personally, he'd thought the script was just fine as it was. But David had told him scripts could always be improved. And he wanted this movie to be the best it could be. Let's face it, for him, now, to reinvent himself, the movie had to be superb. Millions of dollars were at stake. His career. His future. His *life*.

It was the only reason he'd come to this meeting in the first place – artistic control, creative control. He'd had it with his record company and now he'd have it with his film studio. So what if the director was usually the only guy involved in the rewrite process? He was Zach Mason. Rules that applied to other actors didn't apply to him. *No* rules applied to him.

'OK, Zach.' Jake Keller was falling over himself trying to kiss his ass. 'Let's look at the opening scenes first ... I had some ideas for beefing up your entrance ...'

As the agents and executives began to rip her opening sequence into tiny pieces, Megan Silver lowered her head, scratching the odd word on the notepad in front of her. She didn't want to have to look at any of them. It was great being at Artemis, great that she was having her movie made, but ... she just wasn't prepared for *this*. The way they were all talking at once, discussing her story like she wasn't even there. Movie business terms flew around the room – 'plot point', 'the inciting incident', 'counterpointing with the Morgan strand', 'the action sequence, eight through ten', 'pushing up the CIA payoff'. And they thought she understood?

God, it was such irony. When she'd finally had the guts to call the others back in Frisco, they'd reacted with stunned silence, stammered congratulations and utter jealousy. Only Dec had the generosity of spirit to really be happy for her. He'd enthused about how glamorous her life would be now – her own office on the lot, working with bigshot studio executives, hanging out with Roxana Felix, and best of all, getting to know Zach Mason. She would actually talk to Zach Mason! On a regular basis! Dec had laughed and told her she'd be the envy of millions.

And he'd been right.

And he'd been wrong.

Megan had got her own office on the set – a windowless cubicle in the main building, with an assistant who resented her. She'd got to meet Eleanor Marshall, who seemed a nice woman but who'd explained that her script would need 'a little work'. By the time David had explained to her what 'a little work' meant, Megan was more upset than she would have believed possible. Artemis had paid $250,000 for her script, but she wondered why they'd paid anything at all – since it was patently useless and would have to be written again. More or less from scratch. Probably five or six times.

'Megan, sugar. It's all in the rewrites,' David had told her patiently. 'It never works any other way. You gave them a great first draft, but obviously, the movie will end up nothing like that at all.'

Obviously. And she'd looked at her gorgeous agent, smiling benignly at her like she was a beloved but rather slow infant, and felt like a moron for ever thinking otherwise.

Her first day at the studios, a vice-president named Jake Keller had come round and made it very clear that if she was bothered about rewriting, she could just quit and they'd hire someone else to do it. Oh, and give them back $100,000, since that was the part of her deal allocated to rewriting.

Megan had smiled sweetly at him and said she wasn't bothered.

As for hanging out with Roxana Felix – well, she'd met the lady at Isabelle Kendrick's party and been thoroughly snubbed. She'd met her a second time at Artemis and been told 'You're the writer? Morgan needs more lines. I think that's obvious. We need at *least* fifty per cent more lines for Morgan' – and here she'd been flashed a smile as cold and deadly as liquid nitrogen – 'or I'll have to find a writer who understands this movie better. Character dynamics, Megan.'

And Roxana had swept out, with a contemptuous glance at her still too-thick thighs.

For a week she'd practically starved herself. Roxana was so exquisite and so cruel she made Megan feel like the ugliest woman on earth. And she had power – she was threatening to have Megan replaced. *A writer who understands the movie better?* She'd written the damn thing!

But, as Megan was finding out, that counted for very little.

A writer is disposable.

A star is not.

In the world of *See the Lights*, her movie, Megan Silver had the least money, the least looks, the least knowledge and the least style, and no power whatsoever.

She was the low girl on the totem pole.

She didn't like it.

And as for talking to Zach Mason ... she didn't dare. He'd refused to speak to her at the Kendricks' party, and he was scowling at her every time she caught his eye. The video of Dark Angel had moved Megan almost to tears, but Zach Mason, sitting there, more physically attractive, dark and brooding than she'd ever imagined even in her fantasies, hadn't even been able to watch it. Jesus, was he saying that none of it had ever mattered to him?

Right now, for her younger self, for all her friends, even for stupid pretentious Sasha weeping her heart out in the Horseshoe Café, Megan felt deeply unhappy. Foolish and naive. Practically every kid she'd grown up with had been a fan of Dark Angel, had really believed. And was every one of them an idealistic idiot? Apparently so. How dumb of her to have thought anybody actually gave a damn.

The young man opposite her had been her idol since she was fifteen years old, and maybe she'd never even known who or what he really was. A *star* first and foremost. And music was apparently just not part of the gameplan any more.

She hadn't cried when Dark Angel split up, but she wanted to now.

'Megan, did you get all that?' David was asking her.

She looked up, startled. 'Oh yeah, sure. Thanks.' She patted her notepad. 'I'll get right onto it.'

'Well, make it snappy,' Jake Keller said coldly. 'We only have a month allocated to pre-production.'

Hating herself, Megan nodded brightly. 'Sure.'

'Thank you, Megan,' Eleanor Marshall said, more kindly. She and Jake gathered their papers together and stood up to leave. 'We have another meeting we've got to get to, but I know Zach wants to talk to you about his part.'

Oh great, Megan thought. He probably wants me to up his lines by fifty per cent as well. This should be good!

'Zach,' Sam Kendrick prompted. 'You were telling us earlier about touring, some of the script ideas that maybe couldn't really work...'

Zach Mason looked across at Megan Silver, his tongue suddenly stuck in lockjaw. It was easy enough to tell the suits where they got off – he'd been doing that all his life. It was easy enough to order SKI about, too. David Tauber was a good agent, so was Sam Kendrick, that was why he was with them, but agents were just suits that worked for you. Twenty per cent and all out for their own glory. He knew what they were like – thought all the stars were scum to be bought and sold, but still laboured under the delusion that they were stars themselves. He didn't trust any one of the bloodsucking assholes. It was just business, all the way down the line.

Megan was different.

Now he took a closer look at her, she was actually quite pretty. Soft chestnut hair that fell to her shoulders in gentle, natural curls, intelligent-looking brown eyes, and large breasts hidden away under her voluminous cotton sweater. OK, she had puppy fat, but she'd lost weight since that bullshit flesh-pressing party. Anyway, the weight kind of suited her. Made her real.

Zach Mason wasn't used to real women, and he certainly wasn't used to intelligent ones. The groupies that made it through Dark Angel's military-style security were hardened cases, bleached-blonde bitches ready to screw anything that had got within ten paces of *Rolling Stone* magazine, and to do half the crew on the way in for the privilege. Then there were the others, bored wives of record company execs, Hollywood starlets who wanted to double their chances of getting written about, models who wanted to 'date' a rock star because that was fast becoming the tradition. In fact, Zach had more respect for the groupies. At least they were honest about what they were looking for. But all of them were dumb and starstruck and greedy, all of them were trading sex for fame.

And that could make you bitter. That could make you hate. Mason had seen normal guys turn into woman-hating pigs after six months on the road, the kind who'd fuck a groupie and then kick her out into a hotel corridor stark naked. The kind who insisted they put on a show for thirty members of the crew before they earned the privilege of giving a musician head. In public. And the sick thing was, the girls almost always agreed. He'd seen guys try to outdo each other in inventing new degradations for women, and yet there was always at least one of the bitches around for whom there was nothing, absolutely nothing, too gross. It could dehumanize you.

Zach hadn't let himself slide into hatred. He didn't *care* enough to hate. He just packed a gross of condoms and fucked his way around the world – pliant groupies, fame-hungry actresses, they all wanted that fake image. Zach Mason, lead singer of the world's biggest band, the prophet, the spokesman, the *superstar*. And he wanted sex. So every encounter was a trade: cold, insulated, lonely.

Zach didn't know how to talk to someone like Megan.

She'd been to college. He knew all this, because the *See the Lights* script had just blown him away; it was more than a movie, it was beautiful and exciting and poignant and romantic. It was brilliant. It took his breath away. And then to find that the kid who wrote it was younger than he was . . .

Some of the words Zach had had to look up in a dictionary. That made him feel small, in awe of the writer's learning. He himself had started Dark Angel at sixteen, got a deal at seventeen, and when his classmates graduated high school he was out on the road. When they graduated college he was out on the road. When they graduated business, law and medical school, he was out on the road. He had never had a proper education, and it bothered him.

Most of the time that was no great problem – the record industry wasn't exactly packed with university graduates. It wasn't William Morris, where you needed a college degree even to sort the mail. No, the music business was full of talents and gangsters and street-smart hustlers who paid armies of lawyers to do their thinking for them. But sometimes, just sometimes, he'd meet a real intellectual – Cliff Burnstein, say, Def Leppard's manager, Tom Silverman of Tommy Boy Records, or Rowena Krebs from Musica, and he wouldn't know what to say. He'd grunt monosyllables, and nobody even cared. What else would you expect, from a dumb-ass musician? And so what if all the magazines called him intelligent, profound, astute? They analysed his lyrics as though he were Voltaire, and though those lyrics came right from his heart, Zach knew they would kiss his butt anyway. After all, if they didn't, Yolanda would just have denied them access to the band. And what music paper could sell copies without Dark Angel? So their opinions meant nothing. They were bought.

'Some of the stuff you have in there couldn't possibly happen,' he said.

Megan shrugged. 'OK. You tell me what's wrong and I'll change it.'

Why did I ever think somebody would actually like my work? Zach Mason doesn't like it. He thinks it's unrealistic and stupid.

Zach heard the reserve in her voice. 'The warm-up scene with the other guys in the band,' he said coldly. 'It would never happen like that. If I'm playing Jason, the audience is still going to assume the picture is about me, and if this is *roman à clef –*'

Megan giggled.

'What the fuck are you laughing at?' Zach snapped.

'*Roman à clef.* It's French. You pronounce it "clay", not "cleff" – the word means "key", not clef like a treble clef,' Megan explained, smiling.

Zach Mason went purple with rage and humiliation. Jesus Christ, the bitch was fucking *laughing* at him. 'It's French.' Like she was so fucking smart, and he was just an idiot with a guitar.

'Yeah? Well you just fix it,' he snarled.

'I'll do my best,' Megan said, shrinking back in her chair.

'You'll fucking succeed. Or you're off this movie,' Zach Mason told her, and stormed out of the room, slamming the door behind him.

14

'Come on, honey, you can do it.'

David's voice was sweet and encouraging, urging her on. Megan could imagine the cheerleading expression on his handsome face as he stood behind her, pushing her on. 'Just ten more. Let's go.'

Every nerve in her legs seemed to be screaming for mercy, but she obeyed him, her breath coming ragged and strained. Madonna was pumping from the stereo, but her tortured body had drowned out the music. All she was aware of was the floor and her elbows.

'Eight ... nine ...'

You have to. You have to.

Wearily she forced herself down and back up again.

'Ten! That's great, Megan. Just great. Now hit the showers,' David said, throwing her a towel as she staggered to her feet. 'I'll bet you feel great.'

She caught sight of her face in the wall mirror – red as a beef tomato and shining with sweat, her hair plastered wetly to her forehead, her mouth open like a fish, gulping weakly for air.

'Yeah,' she managed, trying for a smile. 'I feel terrific.'

'You *look* terrific,' her agent said, as she stumbled towards her bathroom.

Megan peeled off her Lycra leggings and T-shirt, both of which were clinging to her skin as if someone had thrown a bucket of water over them – *nice* – and chucked them in the laundry basket. Tentatively she climbed on the electronic scales David had bought for her last month. A hundred thirty-one pounds. Well, she was getting there. As she stepped gratefully into the shower and let the powerful jets of warm water hammer her aching shoulder muscles, Megan felt a small glow of achievement. She still hated seeing herself naked, hated weighing herself, but every day the mirrors were a little less insulting, the electric tally a touch less traumatic. She could see the changes in her body – the growing definition around her chin, the disappearance of the fat pockets above her knees. It *was* working. And she had David to thank for it. As he kept telling her, if he didn't show up to supervise her workouts she'd never have had the will-power to keep them up.

He was more than an agent; he was her dietitian, nutritionist, stylist, beauty adviser and personal trainer. And as the work on *See the Lights* got harder and harder, David was there, always fighting her corner. She knew Zach and Roxana both wanted her fired, as did Mr Keller, but David was in there, arguing for her, defusing everybody's anger.

She owed him her house.

She owed him her job.

She owed him everything.

'Would you like some decaff?' David called from the kitchen.

'Yes, thanks,' she yelled back.

Oh good, that meant he'd stay for a cup of coffee. Megan knew she should tell him to skip it and get back to SKI – poor David was always so overworked – but she was just too selfish to do that. Pre-production had gone into overdrive, and thanks to David's efforts she was still the sole writer. But the Artemis team changed their mind about something every single day, and it seemed that she was always working flat out to change something, then scrubbing it all the next day and starting again. Megan thought of herself as LA's Alice through the Looking-Glass, running her heart out just to stay in the same place.

So she never got out. Who had the time?

Never – unless David took her out.

Those were the nights that made it all worthwhile, when Tauber would show up in his cherry-red Lamborghini right outside her apartment and tell her he was taking her to dinner, and then she'd grab one of the outfits he'd told her to buy – oh yes, she should add personal shopper to his list of roles in her life – and drive her to Spago's or Morton's or Le Dôme, where the maitre d' would invariably greet David by name and show them to a good table, and they'd eat something low-fat, and then later he'd take her along to the Roxbury or the Viper Room, where the club doormen always ushered them past the queue and David would lead her directly into the VIP area. He was so powerful. And he knew *everyone*. 'Hello, Brad.' 'Hi, Shannon.' 'How's it going, Keanu?'

When Megan spent the evening with David Tauber, she seemed to spend most of her time blushing and trying not to stare.

He was the perfect gentleman, too, always driving her home and seeing her into her apartment building with a peck on the cheek, or kissing her hand. Megan knew it was ridiculous to hope for anything more – hadn't David done enough for her already? But she couldn't help herself. He was the proverbial knight on the white charger, rescuing her first from her mundane existence and then from herself. He had the power to open any door for her – he'd told her that often enough.

And he was so, so, so damn gorgeous. At least when he put her through this agonizing workout three times a week Megan could be sure that he practised what he preached. His lean, mean body, muscles rock-hard and gleaming with health, was a testament to that. His thick hazel hair shone with a natural vitality only gained from the ideal diet. Even his perfectly shaped teeth were whiter than her own, whether Megan was using one of the expensive cosmetic pastes or not.

Since the second he'd turned up at Mr Chicken with her contract, Megan had been daydreaming about him. But lately, those dreams had been getting more detailed. More frequent.

Shaking her head to try to clear the familiar twitch between her legs, the warm flush of desire creeping across her thighs, Megan towelled herself off and got dressed, picking a flowing Indian-print skirt and tight black T-shirt top, pulled on over a 34C-cup Ultrabra.

'Coffee's ready,' David called from the kitchen.

Her silhouette didn't look at all bad; the sweep of cotton forgave her hips a lot of their sins and in a push-up bra her breasts were impressive, even by Hollywood standards.

Megan pulled her top down tighter.

'Coming,' she said.

Roxana Felix was sobbing.

Her hands gripped the cool marble of the balustrade fence that surrounded her hilltop garden, manicured nails and tanned, slender fingers wrapped tightly around it like a drowning man clutching a raft. Her body was raised horizontally, parallel to the ground. In front of her she could see halfway to the ocean, the Hollywood Hills giving way to Los Angeles's busy grid, peaceful as ever from this height. The blazing sun sparkled off the tiny cars, logjammed on the freeway in the morning rush hour. All around her, birds were chirping and twittering, and the air was fragrant with roses and orchids and the honeysuckle wound into the tall, protecting hedges.

Her slender body bucked again as he crashed into her.

Her long black hair, normally so sleekly coiffured, fell tousled about her shoulders and back, strands of it brushing against her pendant breasts. Her skin was hot and aroused, tight with wanting. Her nipples were almost painfully erect. She was close to orgasm.

'Had enough?' he asked, teasing her, deliberately slowing his rhythm.

Roxana squirmed against him, her knuckles white against the marble, urging him on. She could feel his large, strong hands under her thighs and belly, supporting her. She knew he could feel her heat, the blood warm under the skin, her stomach slick with sweat from her desire. His hands were on her. He was holding her.

The thought sent a spasm of lust right through her. 'Please,' she said.

'Say it again.' She could feel his cock leap inside her. This was turning him on, too. His voice was rough with sex.

'Please. Please. Don't stop. Just *do* it,' she moaned, pushing the firm globes of her butt back against him, her vaginal muscles tightening around him and then relaxing again. He wasn't the only one who knew how to please, she thought, and hearing him groan Roxana had a vague awareness of triumph through the hot mist of arousal that was consuming her.

He started to thrust, and thrust, and thrust, every time going a little deeper, every time a little harder, telling her how good she felt, telling her how hot she was, asking if she liked it, if she liked what he was doing, and Roxana sobbed yes, yes, and his rhythm was perfect, and suddenly there was a new sensation in her belly and she was climbing a great wall of ecstasy, she blocked out everything except his voice and his cock, all she could feel or know was herself impaled on his cock, moving with him, and he was getting more urgent and thicker inside her all the time, and deeper, and suddenly she could feel him right down inside her, hitting that exquisite, melting spot on her vaginal wall. Jesus Christ, the g-spot, and she felt the world go black and explode in blinding pleasure, breaking and shattering around her, her pussy and her stomach contracting into spasm after spasm as Roxana Felix rode the longest, strongest orgasm she had ever known.

For a second he stayed inside her, holding her in position, letting her regain her breath. Then he gently withdrew, still holding her, and scooped her up in his arms, naked and bathed with perspiration, and carried her back inside the house.

He set her down on the polished wood floor of the bathroom, carefully, as though she were made of the most delicate bone china.

'How was that?' he asked, grinning.

Roxana brushed past him, turning the taps on her bathtub. Showering was for people in a hurry; she preferred to soak. She reached out one toned arm and selected a small crystal bottle of lavender bath oil, especially blended for her by a chic Paris *parfumerie*.

'What, do you want a rating out of ten, Sam?' she asked coolly. 'Eight and a half. You were very good. You get better all the time.'

She emptied the entire bottle into the bath and the heady floral scent rose up in clouds of steam, overpowering any lingering trace of sweat or sex.

Kendrick reached for a bathrobe, not wanting her to see him limp. 'Oh, *you were very good*, she says, so matter-of-factly.'

Roxana slipped into her bath, the perfumed oil making the water turn white. With her black hair and tanned skin she looked Egyptian. She glanced at him haughtily.

Cleopatra bathes in asses' milk, Sam thought. She was truly exquisite. And colder than ice.

'If you wanted hearts and flowers, Sam, you came to the wrong place. A great fuck is a great fuck. End of story.'

She shrugged, sending tiny rivers of scented water trickling across the tops of her perfect breasts. 'It's just friction, at the end of the day.'

'Just *friction*?' Kendrick repeated, disbelievingly. 'Is that how you would describe what happened out there?'

This was the hottest, most sexual thing he had ever dreamed of, and Roxana could dismiss it as *just friction*? Shit, one moment he was screwing her in mid-air, feeling her buck underneath him, beg him not to stop, and the next ... this? Wham, bam, thank you sir?

'Yes,' Roxana said, beginning to wash herself briskly with a sponge. 'Would you like a shower? There's a separate one in my bedroom.'

Kendrick stood up and laughed shortly. 'I don't buy it, babe.'

'Really.' There was nothing in her tone, not even a pretence at interest.

'Yes, really. No woman thinks of making love that way. Especially not when it's as intense as that.'

'I'm glad you were pleased,' Roxana said, stepping out of the bath and reaching for a towel.

The sight of her wet, naked body, the smooth flesh shining from the water, her soft pubic hair flattened against the curve of her belly, her berry nipples erect again in the cool bathroom air, crowning slick, damp breasts that tilted youthfully upwards in natural perfection, did something to Sam Kendrick.

Immediate hard-on. Despite the fact that he'd come less than five minutes ago.

Jesus, Sam thought. Is she for real?

He was forty-five years old, and Roxana Felix had him as horny as a teenager.

Roxana glanced at the bathroom clock – nine-thirty a.m. 'If you wouldn't mind showering and dressing, Sam. I have a script meeting at Artemis at ten.' She turned her back on him, heading for her walk-in wardrobe, dismissing him.

'OK,' Kendrick managed, astonished at her attitude.

'Thanks.' She gave him one quick, dazzling smile. 'Oh, and Sam, one more thing – *you* may have been making love, but *I* was having sex. That's all.'

Open-mouthed, Sam watched his new mistress walk away.

As her limo turned into the wrought-iron gates of Artemis Studios, Roxana Felix smiled to herself. She was wearing a Mark Eisen tailored suit in palest pink cashmere, her make-up a sweep of matching light rose tones; a breath of blusher on her perfect cheekbones, minimal highlights above her long black lashes, and her full mouth covered with the latest glamorous wet-look lip gloss.

She was as sexy as hell.

And that was the idea.

A month in LA, and Roxana had learned a few things. The most surprising was that, here, she was only a middling fish in a very large pond. Not everyone asked how high, ma'am, when she told them to jump. She didn't get her own way right off. And sometimes, as with Sam Kendrick at his wife's party, she even had to back down.

A lesser woman might have been disheartened. Might have shrugged it off and returned to modelling, where she ruled with a rod of hand-cured Italian leather. But not Roxana Felix. She had come to Hollywood to find true fame, to have the world fall at *her* feet, not the feet of her silent, frozen image. What had that artist done? Painted pictures of pipes and labelled them, *Ceci n'est pas une pipe*. This is not a pipe.

She had friends who'd never understood that. They'd stand there and laugh and say, 'If it's not a pipe, what is it? Sure looks like a pipe to me.'

But Roxana had understood right away.

It *looks* like a pipe, but it's not. It's a *picture* of a pipe.

Big difference.

So what if the world looked at her picture and adored? *Ceci n'est pas Roxana*. And she wanted them to adore Roxana. So *See the Lights* was more than important, it was vital. She'd had to fight harder than she had in years to get into the goddamn picture, and now, it seemed, she was going to have to fight twice as hard to stay on top of it.

It was only pre-production, and already she was running into problems. Her part was way too small, and no matter how much she turned the screws on that dumpy, terrified mouse writing the script, the little bitch stuck firm. Morgan's part was just right. To increase it would be to tilt the movie too much towards the romantic subplot.

*Sub*plot? *She* wasn't sub anything.

But the trouble was that after the first disastrous screenplay meeting, Eleanor Marshall had taken control. Nobody spoke to Megan Silver without her being present in the room. That way, it was always her fault and not Megan's – and most of the time that bearded prick Florescu, who couldn't keep his eyes off Roxana's legs, agreed with her. And after Isabelle's party, Roxana had learned that she could threaten a writer, but the director and the president of the studio? No way. It was pre-production, and she could still be replaced. So she was smiling sweetly and biding her time.

But it wasn't in Roxana's nature to do nothing. She planned ahead. Ever since . . . ever since . . .

Behind the tinted windows of the limo, a shadow of fear and pain crossed Roxana Felix's lovely face. Her lips set in a straight line. *No, no, no!* She never thought about that, *never.*

Anyway, planning ahead. In less than a month they would be on the set, filming, and at that stage she planned on throwing her weight around. She was going to make enemies. So what else was new? But she'd need allies. That much was clear. So she'd been quietly observing, surveying, calculating. Who had the power? David Tauber? No . . . it just looked that way. Megan Silver thought the sun shone out of his backside, and Zach Mason was happy with him, for now . . . but Roxana was her own woman. She had no loyalty to agents. Bob Alton could tell you that. And David was too green, too cocky. He thought he was a lion, but he didn't realize that Eleanor and Tom and Sam were just letting him tag along. Sam had Fred, and this was Sam's movie. They were all Sam's movies. He really was a lion; David Tauber was just a jackal, feeding on the carcass his master had left and calling it a fresh kill. He was a good talent scout, but that was about it. And she suspected that if he ever deluded himself that he could cross swords with his boss and win, David Tauber would find that out.

Sam Kendrick, though, was truly powerful.

Sam had proved that to her.

Sam could be useful. *She* could use him. And when she had the bastard wrapped round her finger, when she'd eked out every bit of power he had and taken it for her own advantage, she was going to *break* him. Sweet, deadly revenge.

So what if he was good in bed? So much the better, if she could enjoy herself at the same time. It made no difference. Sam Kendrick thought he could insult Roxana Felix, and he had to realize that there was a price. He was going to pay her with everything he had.

But Sam was already falling for her. He'd be back for more, she knew it. It wasn't Sam she should be concentrating on this morning.

It was the man she'd decided she needed to be *publicly* involved with – the superstar romance that would help her with this movie, help her with its launch, help her with setting up her new career.

Her next lover.

Zach Mason.

15

'I have the results of your tests,' Dr Haydn said.

Eleanor felt like yelling at her, of *course* you have the results of my tests – you called me into your office, didn't you? But she said nothing. She never did. The anticipatory fear was just too great. Her thrice-yearly check-up with the best fertility specialist in LA was something she both needed and dreaded; needed, so that she could be reassured that it wasn't too late for her, and dreaded, just in case this time it was, this time would prove to be the visit where Dr Hadyn would mutter something about conception being 'unlikely'. Not to mention the fact that actually walking into the Haydn Clinic was difficult, dragging to the surface her deepest conflicts and bitterest fears. With every day that passed, she knew she was heading closer to the line. She would have to choose. Commit to Paul, or leave him. Settle, or risk everything. Risk even her chance at a child. Because, right now, she knew no other man that she could be with, and her time was running out.

Since *See the Lights* went into pre-production, Tom Goldman had been cutting her dead. He saw her only in the company of others. Somehow, top-management issues always got discussed over the phone. And whenever Jake Keller issued a new protest about how Eleanor was directing the rewrite process, Tom went out of his way to have it formally minuted and documented. He had suddenly become the studio chairman again, the ultimate power, sitting in judgement, as impartial as King Solomon.

Eleanor was not surprised. He had come to his senses like she knew he would, and now he was retreating into his shell, embarrassed at whatever might have happened. She had thrown herself into her work, and there was more than enough work. She was solely responsible for this major, big-budget movie – a ninety-five-million-dollar gamble.

But privately, secretly, she was mourning.

Something deep inside her had died.

'I'm glad to say everything seems to be fine,' Dr Haydn went on, and Eleanor felt a sharp crunch of relief in the pit of her stomach. She glanced around the elegant consulting rooms, a fantasy of maternal pastels in pink and eggshell blue, at the posters for breast cancer research and antenatal exercising, trying to avoid revealing her feelings. Dr Haydn already thought she was weird. If she was so worried about her fertility, why wasn't she pregnant? She must be the only client on the specialist's highly expensive books who still regularly used her diaphragm. Somehow, sitting in the oak-panelled waiting room with the other patients, nervous, frightened women prepared to put themselves through drugs, calendars, artificial insemination and God alone knew what else, women who Eleanor knew would have given anything for the news she had just heard, her actions seemed incomprehensible, even to her. She wondered what Dr Hadyn thought of her. Selfish? Thoughtless? Immoral, even?

Eleanor clasped her hands firmly in her lap. Who cared what the woman thought? She could test her own fertility if she felt like it and that didn't mean she was obliged to get pregnant. My body, my choice, she reminded herself.

'However, your fecundity levels have dropped somewhat,' the consultant continued. Her voice was cold and clinical. 'A woman's fertility naturally declines with age and that process is speeding up for you now.'

Relief was replaced by a clammy fear.

'You said I could still conceive, though?' Eleanor pressed.

Dr Haydn looked at her over the tops of her wire-rimmed glasses. 'At the moment? Absolutely. But *could* conceive and *will* conceive are two different matters.' Her gaze was steady. 'Ms Marshall, you are entering the final years of your reproductive life. If you want to have a child, it is my duty to advise you that you should begin trying to get pregnant as soon as possible, and in any event, no later than six months from now.'

Eleanor sat very still.

Liz Haydn reached across the desk with her wrinkled hand and patted Eleanor's smooth one. 'It's not too late, you know.'

She made an effort and smiled. 'Thank you, Doctor.'

It's not too late, Eleanor thought dizzily, but it soon will be.

Megan said, 'I want him to drink milk. It's deliberate. Morgan is sitting backstage and we've just seen her mixing a vodka orange – light on the orange, right? She's a bad girl, she scores drugs, she drinks. But Jason, he's supposedly the wild one, but he's not really. I want to highlight that by having him reach for a carton of milk. He's clean, she's not. It's the contrast.'

The heat in the meeting room was incredible, even with all the windows open and the air-conditioning at full blast. Outside, blazing LA sun streamed onto the lot, beating down on the palm trees in the drive and the long stretch limos parked out front. Studios execs walked past with their shirtsleeves rolled up, or fanning themselves with scripts and treatments. The ice in their jugs of iced water had melted in five minutes.

Nobody wanted to work. But they had to. There were just three weeks to go before shooting started.

The studio president sat quietly to one side, dressed in a cream suit, taking notes. Roxana Felix, her long hair plaited into two thick, glossy pigtails, lay on the black leather Eames sofa, propping up her head with one hand. Her exquisite face was delicately made up in soft tones of coral and apricot, and she wore a cut-off Mark Eisen T-shirt in peach silk teamed with tight white satin shorts by Adrienne Vittadini. No longer pale, Roxana's skin had tanned all over to a honey brown, no lighter, no darker, the tone controlled exactly by her choice of sunscreen. Acres of taut, slender, golden flesh appeared whenever she shifted position, and the stomach displayed by her schoolgirl-style outfit was as flat as a board. With the pigtails she looked as though she might have been some precocious sixteen-year-old, the budding breasts and subtle make-up designed to arouse. Only her shiny wet lips with their kiss of tangerine gloss, and the two huge diamond studs that glittered in her ears, spoiled the picture. She looked breathtaking, rawly sexual. She was directly opposite Zach Mason, and every time he looked at her, she moved a little, displaying herself for him.

Why does she bother? Megan Silver thought bitterly. It's like using a sledgehammer to crack a nut.

Zach Mason would only ever consider a woman like Roxana – luminously beautiful, naturally slim, a celebrity like himself. Never mind that she was a vain, selfish bitch. Never mind that her petty objections held up the script. Never mind that all she considered was her own part, and never the movie as a whole. Roxana Felix lived and breathed in the same air of fame and riches that he enjoyed. She was designed for him – supermodel-cum-actress dates superstar-cum-actor. Models and rock stars, a classic pairing. Like salt 'n' vinegar or sugar 'n' spice.

Whenever Zach cast an admiring, stripping glance over the superbitch, Megan felt a little more dowdy, a little more plain.

She herself wore a loose shift dress in brushed cotton, sprigged with a pattern of roses, and the stacked sandals that were in fashion just now. Thanks to David Tauber's Professor Higgins routine, Megan now weighed a hundred and twenty pounds. She was slimmer than she'd ever been in her life, her skin had cleared up, and she was nicely tanned. She'd have knocked the guys dead back in Frisco. But so what? Against Roxana Felix's awesome beauty, or even compared with your normal tall, blonde, stacked California babe, she was a nothing. Invisible. The moth amongst butterflies . . .

Zach said dismissively, 'A singer wouldn't drink milk before he perform-ed.'

'Oh yeah?' she snapped. David had warned her of the need to kiss up to the stars, but David wasn't here today, and it was just too hot to take the macho bullshit. 'What's the matter? Milk lousy for your image? Does the guy *always* have to down half a bottle of Jack Daniel's before he faces his adoring public?'

Eleanor Marshall looked over at her, surprised, but said nothing.

Roxana Felix laughed. 'Well! The mouse that roared.'

You bitch, Megan thought, dropping her gaze. She bit her tongue to stop the retort that wanted to fly out of her. Mason and she were sniping at each other constantly, but so far she'd always been polite. She'd always had to be.

'That's got nothing to do with it,' Zach said.

'Give me one good reason why Jason shouldn't drink milk before he sings,' Megan insisted.

He looked at her levelly, liquid brown eyes meeting hers. God, he was gorgeous. It still got to her, sometimes, that she was fighting like mad with a guy who'd been tacked up on every wardrobe she'd ever had.

'Because milk coats the back of your throat. You'd sing like shit.'

Roxana Felix clapped her hands in delight and laughed again, cattily.

Megan blushed, embarrassed. 'OK. Sorry.'

Zach gave her a hint of a smile. 'Maybe he could drink a diet soda.'

'So, you don't know *everything*, Megan,' Roxana Felix purred, stretching on the sofa. 'Perhaps you could *listen* to Zach next time. You might learn something.'

'Roxana,' Eleanor Marshall warned her.

Roxana paid no attention. She wanted her pound of flesh. 'Right, Megan?'

Megan gritted her teeth. 'I guess.'

'I *know*,' Roxana said sweetly, and Megan saw her give Zach Mason the most dazzling smile. She lowered her head and crossed out 'milk' in the stage directions, substituting 'diet Coke'. At least the bastard was right about that. A diet soda would serve the same purpose for her characters. *Focus on your work. Focus on your work.* All she had to do was write a great script and she was out of here; she could start another one that involved absolutely no fake-messiah musicians and their bitch-goddess girlfriends.

After the session was over, Megan gathered up her notes and headed for the car, feeling a little happier. She was having lunch with David Tauber. He'd picked a new place specially, a Chinese where they had nothing but low-sodium vegetable dishes on the menu. Not normally her thing, but . . . he was teaching her how to look after herself. She should be grateful. She *was* grateful. After all, without David, she knew she'd be lost.

Megan glanced at her watch. Twenty after twelve. She was meeting Tauber at half-one, so she spun her tiny BMW towards the apartment. She could do with freshening up.

When she walked through the door Megan kicked off her shoes, revelling in the feel of the soft grey carpet against her bare feet, picked up her post and headed for the bathroom. Two bills to forward to the accountants David had found for her. A letter from Tina and Jeanne. Amazing how people got really friendly the second you picked up a little success. Well, maybe she would read it later. And a postcard from Dec. He was madly in love again.

Megan smiled. Some things never change.

She was about to hit the shower when she noticed the little red light flashing on her answer machine. That was weird. She'd only been at Artemis an hour, and she wasn't expecting any calls.

She hit play.

'Megan? This is Zach.'

Megan froze. Oh, God. Had she gone too far? Was he going to tell her he was having her replaced?

'Electric City have asked me to jam with them on Friday night. I was wondering if you'd like to come along. For research. Anyway, call me.'

Electric City. After Dark Angel, they were the second biggest band in the alternative-rock revolution; though they'd never carried the social weight that Dark Angel had, they sold millions of records. She had two Electric City albums. Dec had all of them. The gig on Friday, a stadium show at the Coliseum, had been sold out for two months.

To see Zach Mason jam with Electric City! To go as his guest!

For a second Megan stood there, thrilled. Then she remembered. Zach

Mason was a fake, a betrayer of all the things his fans had thought he stood for. He was just another egotistical jerk who wanted to be a movie star. And he'd been down on her like a ton of bricks from the second she met him.

He said research and he meant research. Zach just wanted the movie to be the most realistic it could be, the perfect vehicle to show him off in all his glory.

He'd sounded sincere, though.

Forget it! Megan thought angrily, shaking her head. She'd seen the way he looked at Roxanna Felix – his natural mate. And the bitch could have him. Those two were well suited.

She'd believed in Zach Mason once – before she'd met him.

Yeah. She would go to the show, Megan thought. Because it *was* good research. Zach could be as patronizing as he liked, but her only concern was for her script.

She turned on the shower. She couldn't keep David waiting.

Roxana favoured the gaggle of visiting executives with a slight smile as she strolled across the Artemis lot towards her waiting limousine. Tom Goldman escorting a bunch of Wall Street stiffs; young guys, analysts most likely, she guessed. It must be about time for the studio to announce its quarterly earnings – Roxana knew that some entertainment companies liked to put on a show for the bankers, take them around, show them some stars.

Well, these boys had got lucky. They'd got to see *her*. All eight balding heads had literally twisted round as she walked past, lean hips clicking and pumping under the white satin shorts. Once a model, always a model. She'd heard one of the businessmen mutter 'Jesus Christ!'

Roxana had sauntered past him, unimpressed. She always blew men away. She was used to it. If he got as rich and powerful and useful as that limp dick Howard Thorn, maybe she might have given him a second look. As it was, though . . .

Seeing her approach, the chauffeur leapt forward to open the limo door, saluting. She didn't look at him either. Zach Mason might drive himself around, but she was Roxana Felix and she wasn't into fraternizing with the help.

As the limo eased seamlessly out of Artemis's wrought-iron gates and headed towards Sunset Boulevard, Roxana bit her lip in frustration. Zach Mason. What the hell was *wrong* with the guy? Was he gay? Not unless every rumour she'd ever heard was a lie. Was he involved? All her contacts said no. And anyway, when had a man's being involved made a difference? She could make a twenty-year marriage fall apart with one flutter of her long, thick lashes. She *had* done, more than once.

Roxana was under no illusions about men's morality. Sooner or later, every last one of them thought with his dick. And ever since she'd hit puberty she had realized that her beauty was a potent weapon. If a guy was straight, she was a goddamn nuclear bomb. Nothing could withstand her. Never, not once in all her life, had she set out to seduce a man she wanted and been refused.

It just didn't happen.

It was incomprehensible.

And she was not about to permit Zach Mason to be the first to do it.

LA slipped by her, basting in the sun, palm trees waving gently in the faint breeze. The sky was a deep, cloudless blue.

Roxana noticed none of it. Her anger was consuming her. It wasn't like Zach didn't see her dressing up for him, didn't register it. On the contrary, he looked her over every time, as though rating her. Undressing her with his eyes. Sexually approving her. These were tributes she received every day of her life, of course, but from Zach Mason they meant more – for the simple reason that he'd been linked with some of the most desirable women in America. In the *world*. He was the ex-lead singer of Dark Angel, and as far as Roxana Felix was concerned, that made him a connoisseur.

So what was the fucking problem?

In script meetings, in public, no problem. He'd stare at her, flirt with her, whatever. The rock star and the supermodel. Great. And if they rehearsed a scene, there was incredible sexual heat there. Damn, she actually *wanted* him, in the way she'd wanted no other man for years, with the sole exception of Sam Kendrick – something she couldn't explain.

Desire for Mason was easier to understand. He was quite simply the best-looking, most sensual man she had ever seen. Even for a palate as jaded and cynical as hers, Zach Mason represented temptation at the deepest level. He was rangy and lean, but not in a wimpy way – more sinewy, well muscled and dangerous-looking, like a wolf. Zach had wolf eyes. Long, black, unkempt hair, a chiselled face, and menacing, glinting wolf eyes. In a still photo, she knew, he might look angelic, Greek-god beautiful, but to see him move, to watch him talk, that was something else.

Usually, Roxana was utterly uninterested in the career of anyone besides herself. And she was nobody's fan. But since she'd met Zach she had ordered Tauber to send her up some videos of Dark Angel.

The music was dreadful, of course. Meaningless white noise. She had turned down the volume and merely watched Mason, watched him move across the lip of the stage, watched him cradle his rhythm guitar, watched him speaking to crowd after crowd that rose in a body to salute him.

He was awesome. Incredible. Intense. And when those huge video screens they erected magnified his wolf eyes, staring at the crowd, staring into the camera, Roxana had shivered. It was almost as if he was gazing into her soul, burning away talk and pretence and every other civilized defence. His stare could do that to you.

For a few seconds she had been spellbound, unable to flick the television off. Just for a few seconds, of course. But nonetheless, Zach Mason was remarkable. She, Roxana Felix, had responded to him sexually. It wasn't just going to be great for her career to see him for a while, she thought; it was going to be great, period. And the next day, when she'd come on to him at the script meeting, he'd reacted perfectly; all raised eyebrows and long, slow, assessing looks.

And that was it!

He hadn't phoned. He hadn't called her over. He hadn't sent round flowers.

The next day she'd worn a shorter dress and been more obvious.

He'd noticed, but – *nada. Rien.* Nothing doing.

Roxana invited him to lunch, in front of Megan and Eleanor. Zach accepted right away. And then he'd just discussed their characters, throughout the entire meal!

She had no idea what pathetic game Mason was playing. Hard to get? Did he want her to come right out and say it, was that what this was about? When she'd tried to grab him after the session this morning he'd actually brushed her off!

Well, Roxana thought to herself, seething against the cool cream leather of her limo, if he thinks he's getting propositioned by me, he's gonna have a long wait.

But she had no idea how to break him down.

Roxana closed her immaculately made-up eyes and concentrated.

Zachary Mason is just a man like any other. There's a way round this. I just have to find it . . .

She reminded herself of her mantra.

I always get what I want.

Always . . .

16

The Manhattan skyline glittered below her, New York's concrete forest glinting in the thin autumn sun. As the plane banked and veered, preparing for the descent into JFK, Roxana took another sip of her mineral water, swirling the ice and lime wedge round in her crystal glass. She felt refreshed and ready for action. After all her problems in LA, it was a nice break to come back to New York, a city she had conquered long before, and be treated like the queen she was. Amongst the pack of reporters waiting for her at immigration there would be faces she knew. When they called the press conference at the Carlyle, the hotel management would already have prepared her favourite suite exactly as she liked it, right down to the number of kumquats in her fruit bowl. And when they set up the cover shoot for *Vogue*, Bob Alton would be there, and he wouldn't have any tiresome explanations as to why she couldn't do this or wasn't ready for that. He'd just be falling over his handmade English shoelaces to kiss her toned, tanned ass.

Exactly the way things ought to be.

The call from Unique had reached her via David Tauber on Monday morning. Robert Alton wanted to speak with her urgently. He'd rung the night before, but they hadn't wanted to wake her.

Roxana had checked her watch. Eight o'clock. Five in the morning on the East Coast. Well, it was time that fat, lazy asshole got up anyhow.

She dialled Alton at home.

'What?' answered a sleepy male voice.

Roxana tutted with impatience. 'Put Robert on the line. Right now.'

A second's silence, then Alton answered angrily, 'Do you know what fucking time it is?'

'Time you slept on the side nearest the phone, Bob,' Roxana snapped. 'I don't want to have to chat with your latest boyfriend when I need to speak to my agent. Is that clear?'

'Roxana? Oh yes, yes of course.' He was stammering in his eagerness to please. 'I'll do that. It's done. OK?'

'You called me,' Roxana said icily. 'I hope you had a good reason, Bobby. I'm trying to make a movie here.'

'Jackson Cosmetics,' Alton blurted, wisely getting straight to the point.

Jackson were the hottest new European beauty firm. Their introductory range had sold out at Saks within twenty minutes when first introduced to the States two years ago. Now they were a major house, up there with Estée

Lauder and Revlon, and they packed an extra-chic punch for being so new. Two unknown girls picked to model part of their skincare range had become instant supermodels – Adelicia Louvaine and Catherine Braganza. Jackson was *the* house for younger women: innovative, stylish and ultra-hip.

'What about them?' Roxana demanded.

'They've offered you an exclusive contract. Five years. Thirty million dollars. And the exclusivity goes two ways – you can't model make-up for anyone else, but neither can they use another model. Like Isabella Rossellini did it at Lancôme.'

'No make-up. Can I model clothes?'

'Absolutely. Of course. No problem.'

'Other activities? Acting, for example?'

'Yes. You could do anything except model make-up,' Robert wheedled persuasively.

Roxana's fist clenched by her side. Yes! Another triumph. Another laurel wreath. Another contract to end them all. And *thirty million dollars!*

'Tell them yes,' she said.

Robert was gushing with gratitude. 'You won't regret this, Roxana . . . I swear I . . .'

She cut him off in mid-flow. 'But Robert – the price is forty million. I made seven point five this year, and thirty million over five years works out at six million a year.'

She knew he wanted to argue with her, tell her that this year was exceptional, the best she'd ever had, and there were no guarantees.

'Forty million, Robert. And I want an answer half an hour after business opens. Otherwise, no deal.'

'Roxana – '

'Did you hear me, Bobby?'

'Yes. Of course.' He fell over himself to back down. 'Forty million. I'll tell them . . .'

'Get back to me,' she said, hanging up.

He had got back to her. Forty million dollars it was. And she would take two days out of rehearsal to publicize the deal and pose for covers of English, French and American *Vogue*.

'Can't you stay one more day?' Robert had pleaded, dreaming of all the juicy interviews he could arrange. *The Unique Agency Brokers Deal of Decade* . . . he'd be the talk of the town. And he'd get some snaps of the bitch to release over time, to hold her adoring public while she wasted everybody's time with this stupid movie stuff. 'I mean, honey, forty million! The picture won't make you forty million . . .'

'Money isn't the point, Robert.'

'Of course not, but . . .'

'I fly back Friday morning. I have to attend something with Zach.'

A beat.

'Are you . . . are you seeing Zach Mason?'

'Robert, whatever you think you know, you don't know,' Roxana said coldly. 'Keep it to yourself.'

As she clicked her seatbelt into place for landing, Roxana smiled in anticipation. Asking Bob Alton to keep a secret was better than an ad in the *New York Times*. She would have every reporter in the place creaming his pants, and then she'd fly back to LA and attend the Electric City show, where everybody would have heard the rumours ... Zach was going to be there, and so would she, looking the hottest she could manage, with a mega-million-dollar contract and a new rush of desirable publicity under her size-six belt.

What was it they said about self-fulfilling prophecies?

'I have to express my concerns, Eleanor,' Jake Keller said.

Tom Goldman's office was set up for the monthly senior management meeting; cut-glass jugs of iced mineral water and plates of biscuits stood untouched next to a silver coffee pot. Eleanor was the only one drinking coffee, and she needed it.

'Certainly,' she said, as calmly and coolly as she knew how.

Bill Janus, the young senior vice-president of Worldwide Marketing, glanced at his notes. 'Let's see. You list budget concerns, but I can't see anything in these figures that should worry us. For a Fred Florescu picture, this is looking pretty conservative.'

'Nobody can call ninety-five million dollars *conservative*,' Keller said, sarcastically.

'For an action movie, directed by Florescu, I think they could,' Tom Goldman said, quietly.

Eleanor turned to look at her boss, surprised. Tom hadn't backed her up on a single issue since Isabelle's party. She was beginning to wonder if he ever would again ... So what was this? A signal that normal service was being resumed?

'Possibly,' Jake said, recovering quickly, 'but his last three hits starred name actors. Big box-office – Harrison, Keanu and Tom. All three proven to open a movie. We have no such guarantees with *See the Lights* ... this project is turning into the Hollywood Unknowns Employment Centre.' He laughed loudly at his own joke. 'And I must say that the romance part of the film is being totally overlooked. The Morgan character has nothing like enough lines.'

'Jake.' After the scene with Paul this morning, Eleanor had had enough. 'First you object to my casting Roxana Felix. Then you want to triple her part. Which is it?'

'I objected to Ms Felix for the part as it was written,' Jake said smoothly. 'I think she'd be perfect if the part were expanded. That would give her a chance to show off all the emotional virtuosity I just know she's capable of – '

'Bull*shit*,' Eleanor snapped, oblivious to the stunned looks Bill and Tom were giving her. 'You want to give her a chance to show off some world-class T and A. Don't think I haven't heard from Megan Silver what you told her to include: a rape scene; a gang-rape scene; two extra sex scenes with Jason; and a kick-boxing scene where she manages to get away but half her costume is ripped off her.'

There was a momentary pause, then Keller shrugged. 'Sex sells,' he said, somewhat defensively.

'Listen up, buddy.' She was too furious to stay calm. 'Rape is not sex. Rape is violence. And I do not make movies that glamorize rape. Now, if you speak to my screenwriter again without informing me first, I'm going to inform security that you are banned from all *See the Lights* pre-production meetings.'

'You can't do that,' Keller said.

'Watch me,' Eleanor said. 'Oh, and Jake – you didn't object to Roxana being cast for the part as it was written, you objected to Roxana being cast at all.' She imitated Keller's nasal whine. ' "We didn't like Roxana's tests." I think you'd better gather up all the objections you have – casting, script, budget, marketing proposals – and put them in a memo to Tom and copy me and Bill on it. That way you can't rewrite history whenever it suits you. And that way I'll have something to frame and send back to you when *See the Lights* clears costs in its first weekend.'

'I don't think that's appropriate,' Keller said waspishly, passing a hand through his thinning red hair.

'I don't know, Jake.' Tom Goldman spoke up again. 'I think it *is* appropriate. If you want any negative comments noted, maybe you should commit them to paper. Eleanor has a point.'

Keller glanced from Goldman to Marshall, barely containing himself, but managed a nod. 'Very well, Tom. If you insist.'

'I think I do,' the studio chief said pleasantly.

'If that's everything folks, I have an eleven o'clock,' Bill Janus said, breaking the tension.

'Sure,' Eleanor said.

Jake Keller gathered his notes stiffly and left the room without a backward glance, and Bill followed him, checking his watch the entire time to avoid meeting anybody's eyes.

'Poor Bill,' Eleanor said.

Tom Goldman smiled. 'Yeah. Can't offend me, can't offend you, can't offend anybody . . .'

'. . . because Jake Keller might be running the studio next year,' Eleanor finished wearily. She sat back down in one of Goldman's cavernous leather armchairs, suddenly exhausted. Pressure. It had been crowding her from the moment she opened her eyes and saw Paul, standing in their bathroom doorway, examining her diaphragm. She'd asked him if he was planning to push a needle through it. The fight that followed had been one of their more memorable efforts. Then, arriving at her office, she'd found a bunch of anomalies in the *See the Lights* budget figures; all things she was sure she had worked out last week, but she still had to fix them again. Three of their current movies had minor problems on-set. A distribution chain was demanding a meeting. Then this happy little pow-wow, where her loyal deputy was trying to wreck her Artemis great white hope with his thousand-point objections plan.

It was too much. And her new Jimmy Choo heels in butterscotch calfskin were pinching her toes.

'Hey, Donald Duck might be running the studio next year.' Tom shrugged. He looked remarkably unstressed; his black Hugo Boss suit picked out his eyes, his smile and his tan. Eleanor thought to herself that black suits should be mandatory for all male executives. Nothing made a guy look so sexy, but nothing. Talk about power dressing. Paul didn't own a black suit.

'You can't let it worry you. The point is that you're running the studio *now*.'

'This a vote of confidence?' Eleanor asked wryly.

'You handled him great,' Tom said.

'Thanks for the back-up.'

Her boss waved his hand. 'It was nothing. You had a point. If he puts it on paper, it's fair both ways.' He grinned. 'Anyway, I asked them to make you president, not Keller.'

'Maybe you should have done us all a favour and gone the other way,' Eleanor said wearily.

'You don't mean that.' Goldman looked over at her. 'Bad day?'

'I've had better,' Eleanor admitted, getting up to leave.

'You should feel better when you read these.' He passed over a sheet of neatly typed figures. 'Results for your first quarter as president; pretty good. The sale of the merchandising division and your rationalization programme at International have made big inroads into the debt.'

'We still need some hit movies, though.'

Goldman nodded. 'Indeed. The stock won't rise unless the bankers think Artemis is going to do a real convincing impression of Lazarus. Which is why I want you to come with me to New York next week.'

Eleanor froze. 'You want me to come and present to the board?'

The quarterly results presentation to the board of directors, Artemis Studios's real bosses, was vital if the studio were to survive. Something Eleanor Marshall had learned fast was that true media power was something Hollywood rarely saw; the purse strings were clasped firmly in the hands of shadowy Wall Street financiers, media-shy moguls who gathered four times a year in some anonymous Manhattan skyscraper. The Masters of Puppets.

Tom Goldman had never let anyone but himself near the board since he'd been appointed chairman.

'You got it.' He leant forward. 'And Eleanor – be convincing. This studio is in crisis. They need to believe that *See the Lights* will be a hit and that more hits will follow.'

She nodded. 'All right, Tom. But what's the sudden crisis? You said yourself that the new quarterlies are good.'

'They are, but that's not enough. You see – and this is absolutely confidential – the board have received an offer from Michiko Corporation.'

'What?' Eleanor gasped.

'You heard me.'

'But we're one of the last two studios still in American hands, Tom!'

'Yeah,' Goldman said. 'We are. For now.'

She got in around ten o'clock, exhausted, and Paul was waiting for her. The dining-room table was set for two: their best Delft china; a silver vase crammed with scarlet roses; champagne chilling in a heaped ice bucket; and Mozart, a lilting aria from *The Magic Flute*, floating softly from their CD player.

Eleanor felt a little of the tension lift from her shoulders.

'I didn't want you to dread coming home,' Paul said, emerging from their bedroom to kiss her on the cheek. 'I know you're having a rough time at work.'

Eleanor smiled. That was the closest Paul would ever come to apologizing. 'This is lovely,' she said.

'Have a seat.' He wandered into the kitchen and brought out a steaming dish. 'Vegetable lasagne with low-fat cheese. I made it myself.'

Eleanor thought she might have preferred a rib steak or a pepperoni pizza, but still . . . at least he was making an effort. When was the last time either of them had bothered to cook a meal? They ate out or ordered in every night. *When* they managed to get home within two hours of each other.

'Sounds delicious, Paul,' she said.

'Why don't you pour the champagne?' He'd dressed up for her too, she noticed; he was wearing his loose Armani suit in navy-blue wool over a white shirt, his platinum Rolex, his gold cufflinks. Obviously this was some kind of special celebration.

She tried not to compare him with Tom Goldman in his plain black suit.

Tom would never dream of wearing blue. Or using aftershave. He wouldn't give a damn about grooming; he'd think it was effeminate to preen in front of a mirror.

Eleanor tried not to think of it as effeminate. 'What's the occasion?' she asked brightly, helping herself to lasagne. 'Are you working on a new deal?'

'No deal.' He took a champagne flute from her. 'This is just about us, Eleanor. This morning got me thinking. You're under pressure, I'm under pressure – '

She nodded.

'There's no need for us to fight all the time. We should try to spend more time together, see if we want to be with each other, see if we'd make good parents . . . figure out where this relationship is going.' He pushed a small red velvet box across the table towards her. 'Open it.'

Eleanor gently unclasped it. There was an engagement ring nestling against a bed of cream silk; a vast, dark green emerald surrounded by rubies and sapphires, mounted in white gold.

It was the most vulgar ring she had ever seen. It must have cost a fortune.

'Oh, Paul,' she said. The ring winked at her like a set of jewelled traffic lights. 'It's so . . . so . . . colourful,' she finished faintly.

Halfin inclined his head, modestly. 'Everybody goes for diamonds. And don't worry, I know you're not ready to give me an answer right now, but I want you to take your time and think about this.' His handsome face broke into a persuasive smile. 'Eleanor, I think the time has come. We're both adults. We've both achieved a certain level of success in our lives. We make a great team, and the patter of tiny feet would complete the picture.' He lifted his glass of bubbling wine. 'Eleanor, it's time for you and me to consider a merger. We'd pay great dividends.'

Eleanor smiled weakly.

'Now, I've got us tickets to the opera for next Wednesday and the ballet on Friday – '

'Paul, I can't go,' Eleanor said.

'What?' His face darkened.

'I can't go. I have to be in New York all next week for a financial presentation with Tom.'

'I see,' he said stiffly. 'Well, of course you must do what you have to. Another time, perhaps.'

'Definitely,' she said, feeling guilty. He'd gone to all this trouble to give her a perfect evening and the only thing she could do was cancel on him.

Anyway, he was right. They couldn't coast along forever. And with Dr Haydn's latest pronouncement, she knew the time had come for her to make a decision. She just couldn't put it off any longer.

'Look, I really have to do this, Paul. But I'm truly sorry I can't come to the opera with you . . . it was a sweet thought. And I promise I'll think about everything you've said, and . . . I'll give you my answer by the end of this month.'

There. It was done.

She had one month to decide.

Paul took a sip of his champagne. 'To us,' he said confidently.

'To us,' Eleanor Marshall repeated, smiling, and wondered why the only thing she could hear was the sound of gates clashing shut behind her.

17

The limo drove right up to the backstage entrance before dropping Megan off. It was the only way the driver could guarantee that she wouldn't get mobbed.

'Honey, if those kids see you walk past them with that thing,' he said, nodding at the all-access laminated pass that swung from Megan's neck, 'you are gonna get seriously jumped. Normally I'd say just tuck it inside your shirt, but right now, I wouldn't take any risks.'

She nodded her agreement. Fans were crowding every available inch of space on the route backstage; security was having a tough time keeping them back behind the ropes, and every five seconds some kid rushed up to the car and pounded on the windows before being dragged away, their faces hysterical, contorted into weeping masks of adoration or frantic pleading. Megan had thought it was merely another example of Zach Mason being ostentatious when a limousine with tinted windows, courtesy of the promoters, arrived at her apartment to take her to the gig, but now she wasn't so sure. Right now she was very glad that although she could see this seething mob, they couldn't see her.

'Is it always like this?' Megan asked.

'Not for Electric City. But didn't you hear the rumours?'

'What rumours?'

'They say Zach Mason is gonna show here tonight. They say he's gonna jam.'

Megan glanced again at the packs of yelling, screaming fans. 'Are all these kids here for Zach Mason?'

'Every last one of 'em,' the driver said.

David Tauber arrived five minutes before showtime. No point putting himself through any more of this garbage than he had to. Besides, twenty minutes before showtime he had been getting a highly skilled blow-job from a very exclusive whore, and that wasn't an experience he cared to rush. You paid enough for it. He had made her perform a slow strip, then massage him, naked, and finally wrap up a very pleasant afternoon with some expert head.

Occasionally he liked to pay for it. That way you didn't have to talk to them. Something he'd appreciated, as her warm, juicy mouth slid up and down his rearing cock, gradually increasing the pressure, her tongue swirling round the quivering head of his penis and then licking, hard, along the entire length of it. He fantasized she was Roxana Felix, on her back instead of on his, but that didn't really do it for him. Just thinking about Roxana could drop a fly into any ointment; she was the pushiest, most aggressive bitch of a woman he'd ever known. He preferred his women like Megan Silver – trusting and eager to please. She was no Roxana Felix, of course, but . . . she was pretty. Once he'd worked all that extra fat off her and put her in some decent clothes, yeah, she was quite pretty . . .

As his cock started to swell even harder and he felt his orgasm begin to build, David Tauber actually started to visualize Megan kneeling at his feet. He knew she'd love to do it. She'd love to do whatever he suggested . . .

On the short drive over to the Coliseum, Tauber thought about Megan some more. The vibe at Artemis was that she was extremely talented, but she'd made an enemy of Roxana Felix and Zach Mason. But as far as David could see, everybody made an enemy of the bitch. It was the endless sniping with Zach that bothered him. If he could get Megan to swallow her pride and kiss up to Mason a little, her future would be very rosy. As Gloria had pointed out to him, the Michael Crichtons and John Grishams of this world were making five million bucks a script.

He wouldn't mind a piece of that action.

Maybe he would give little Megan Silver a thrill.

David strolled up to the box office and collected a stick-on VIP pass Zach had left for him. Distastefully he unpeeled the plastic backing and applied it to the lapel of his Romeo Gigli suit. Ugh. It would probably leave a dreadful mess.

He noticed that none of the kids packing the foyer and entrance hall were wearing anything decent. The scene was all leather and denim and Smashing Pumpkins T-shirts. Time to head backstage; if there was one thing David Tauber detested, it was hanging around the little people.

Roxana stepped out of her limo, all-access laminate fastened conspicuously at the front of her belt. That way she could be sure it showed up in all the photos.

Zach had sent a stick-on pass, a little piece of nothing, round to her house. It was an insult, and if she hadn't been so determined to hook the bastard, she would not have shown up. As it was, she'd called Sam Kendrick.

'I need a laminate for the show tonight, Sam. Call the promoters and have one messengered over.'

'Roxana, Zach is taking care of – '

'*Now*, Sam. Or you needn't come round this afternoon. Or ever again.'

A pause. 'OK.'

She had a second to relish the sense of power. So it was starting already. By the time they started shooting the goddamn picture, Sam Kendrick would be wrapped round her little finger. When he wasn't wrapped round the other parts of her.

A small spasm of desire rippled through her at the thought. 'Thank you, baby.' She was pure sweetness. 'Why don't you bring it with you when you come by?'

'I want you,' he said, quietly, urgently.

'It's mutual.'

And it was. That was the strange thing. That was what threw her. The thought that she might enjoy fucking Sam Kendrick even if she had no other use for him at all.

'Did you really sign a deal for forty million dollars?'

'Yes, I did.'

'So you don't need to be a movie star.'

'I *want* to be a movie star,' Roxana corrected him.

'Do you always get what you want?' Kendrick asked softly.

'Always,' she told him, and hung up.

Roxana turned round and waved gracefully to the rabid crowd thronging the backstage entrance, trying not to let her momentary unease show. Dear God, what a pack of maniacs. Was this what music fans were like? Her own followers never, ever, exhibited passion like this.

As she turned and began to walk inside the stadium, a teenage girl leapt over the red crowd-control rope and lunged towards her, her face contorted with hatred. Roxana shrank back, a paralysing fear knotted in the pit of her stomach. This was what every supermodel dreaded. The one crazed nut with the knife, the gun, the phial of acid . . .

Two security men rushed the girl and overpowered her before she got two feet past the barrier. 'Bitch! Bitch!' the girl shrieked. 'It's you, isn't it? It's you! You've got him! You've got him! I love him!'

'Who?' Roxana managed, as the guards dragged her away.

'Zach! Zach Mason! You're his girlfriend! They said so on MTV!'

Stunned, Roxana managed a bright smile for the photographers waiting at the backstage door.

'Is that true, Roxana?' a reporter demanded. 'Are you here to see your boyfriend?'

'Did Zach Mason send for you?'

'Who gave you the laminate, Roxana? Did Zach fix it up for you?'

'Is the movie going to be a love story off-screen as well?'

'Were you guys a couple *before* you got cast?'

'Roxana! Roxana!'

Flinging her hair back, Roxana delicately removed her Ray-Bans.

'Zach Mason and I are working together on *See the Lights*, people,' she said, her voice honey-low, reserved and embarrassed. 'That's the only thing I can say right now. I'm here to enjoy the show.'

Immediately, cameras fired off around her, flashbulbs popping like machine guns.

'Roxana! Rox! This way, please! Just two seconds!'

She let them snap for a minute, then turned away. Always keep them wanting more . . .

'Roxana!' one of the journalists yelled after her. 'When's the wedding?'

As she headed inside the stadium, Roxana Felix smiled to herself.

The stadium headlights out front were switched on at full beam. From her viewpoint behind the stage scaffolding, Megan could see the roadies scrambling to put up last-minute adjustments to the rigging, technicians pulling at an amp here, moving a laser there. Electric City were renowned for their innovative stage set; the best thing since U2 brought the Zoo TV circus to town, they used giant holograms and computer morphing. Taped music was pumping out of the PA, loud as hell, punctuated by football whistles, screams and cheers from the crowd.

Anticipation crackled through the air like static. The headliners would be on any second.

Megan walked around, trying to look as though she knew where she was going, a mixture of seething excitement and frantic nerves at the pit of her stomach. The closest she'd ever got to being backstage anywhere was when she'd fainted in the front row of the Stone in San Francisco, during a Bad Brains set, and had been dragged behind an amp by security. On that occasion she'd got a cup of lukewarm tap water and been thrown back into the mosh-pit. Plus, the Stone was a tiny club.

All-access laminates at the Los Angeles Coliseum were outside her normal experience.

Being a guest of Zach Mason was outside her normal experience.

Where the hell is David? Megan thought, as she ducked out of the way of yet another roadie pushing a huge flight case across her path. Why isn't he here yet? I need help! I don't know where the hell I'm supposed to be!

She'd asked David to take her to the show, but he said he had to finish off some urgent work on his contracts that afternoon, and could he meet her there? Disappointed, Megan had agreed. She'd been hoping David might *want* to take her . . . but who was she kidding, right? Just because she'd lost a little weight, because he'd found her some half-decent clothes, that didn't mean she was suddenly good enough for David Tauber. David was a big agent, kicking ass on the fast-track. He was sophisticated, he was elegant, he was super-fit, and he was gorgeous. All things she would never be. No matter how many miles she ground out on the Stairmaster.

But she wished David were here now. She wished *somebody* was with her. It was terrifying, to be backstage at a stadium gig, no idea where to go or what to do, just wandering round the concrete labyrinth trying to keep out of everybody's way. And thrilling. Totally thrilling, to know she could go anywhere she wanted to, talk to the band if she felt like it, watch a concert from the side of the stage instead of two miles away at the end of a sea of seats. Instead of straining to get a glimpse of five fingers the size of match-sticks, she'd be standing behind the speaker stacks, close enough to reach out and touch the guitarist.

She would see the vast crowd stretched out before her. She would see what the band saw.

For any rock fan, this was a fantasy come true: that somebody would pluck you out of the crowd and set you down on the other side.

Megan wondered why Zach had done it for her.

'Hey.'

She jumped round. God, she was pathetic; always under everybody's feet. Now they must have sent some official to tell her to get out of the way . . .

'Megan! Over here.'

'Oh, hi, Zach,' she said, embarrassed. 'I was looking for you.'

He walked over to her, amused. 'Dark Angel shirt,' he said, reaching out to touch her T-shirt. 'Were you a fan?'

Megan looked away. Somehow, when she was getting ready to come out, this had seemed like a really good idea; black 501s, heeled ankleboots and her favourite Dark Angel T-shirt, the gold seraph logo on a black background. Dressing with a message. She would be a walking rebuke to the asshole.

As a scriptwriter, David had made clear, she was low girl on the totem pole. If she wanted to keep her job, if she wanted to write any more movies, she'd better shut up and smile; get along to go along. And a quarter of a million dollars was a lot of money. So she'd swallowed whatever insults Roxana Felix wanted to throw at her, and if she hadn't been able to control her tongue completely with Zach, she had tried her best. Minor retorts, sniping, that was about the extent of her comebacks to his constant goading. Since they'd started the rewrite process with that disastrous first meeting, Zach Mason had goaded her, teased her, called her writing unrealistic and naive. It was true that he'd got better as time went on, but still . . . and anyway, as Zach had started being a little kinder to her, Roxana had suddenly got ten times worse. And if Zach and she ever disagreed, Roxana would wade in behind her fellow star and pour acid all over Megan's point of view. Like last time. But that was to be expected; Roxana and Zach were obviously doing the wild thing, the way she posed for him in meetings and backed him up all the time. And all the press and gossip columnists said they were an item.

It would be interesting to see if the bitch showed tonight. Megan doubted she gave a damn about rock 'n' roll, but this was a high-profile event, so she'd probably turn up. Megan couldn't wait. But she hadn't worn the Dark Angel shirt because of Zach and Roxana; the Beautiful People could do what they liked with each other. No, she'd wanted to say with her clothes the things she didn't have the guts to say with her mouth.

Like, fuck you, Zach Mason.

You sold us out.

You're just another rock-star ego, a spoilt brat, a false prophet. You got rich off our dreams. You lied to us. You lied to *me*.

But then Zach had sent round a limo and this incredible laminate, told her she could do whatever she liked, go wherever she wanted. Megan felt obliged and confused. Why was he doing this? What was his motive?

He hated her! It didn't make sense.

'Yes, I was,' she muttered. 'Everybody was.'

Zach heard the criticism in her voice, but ignored it. 'Did you ever see us play?'

Megan looked him in the face. 'I saw you play sixteen times. I saw you at the Omni in Oakland when you were just starting. I saw you at the Stone. And the last gig you guys played here' – she gestured around her – 'two years ago, me and some friends from college saved up for a month so we could go.'

Zach Mason nodded slowly.

Megan looked at him again. He was wearing jeans and boots too, all black, and a black see-through chiffon shirt, the latest cool thing in alternative metal fashion. It revealed his torso; without fabric covering him, Megan could see that he was actually far more muscular than she'd imagined. He was built like Keanu Reeves in *Speed*. And his face looked even better: sculptured, masculine jaw; long dark hair that gave him a feral, menacing quality; and those incredible predator eyes, eyes that had pierced the soul of her whole generation, eyes that she'd watched from the crowd as a teenager and which had burned a fiery rebellion into her soul.

She felt a hot shock of arousal, and hated herself for it.

'Did you like us?' he asked.

Megan reddened. She didn't want to tell Mason anything. Establishing herself as a fan, and Zach as her idol, put her in a supplicant position. Now he knew she had admired him. More than that. And Megan didn't like it.

'I saw you sixteen times, Sherlock. What do you think?'

'I think you look very pretty,' Zach said. He reached out and touched her soft brown curls. 'Too pretty to be so mad all the time.'

Megan was completely thrown. He sounded like he meant it. The guy was dating the world's biggest supermodel, and he'd just called her pretty?

'Thanks,' she muttered, and then remembering her manners added, 'and thanks for the pass.'

He waved it away, still holding her gaze. '*De nada*. Which track of ours did you like best?'

'Why do you care?' snapped Megan. He was playing with her. He must be.

'I want to know. Indulge me,' Zach said, smiling wolfishly at her.

As the crowd started to chant the name of the band, Megan felt her groin contract in a violent spasm of desire. Oh God. She knew she should be stronger than this, but ... he was so beautiful. Predatory and beautiful.

' "Auburn",' she snapped. 'OK?'

'You don't sound much like a fan,' he said.

'And you don't act much like a hero!' Megan bit back, furiously.

He was silent.

Out front, the noise of the audience was deafening. Megan felt a wave of fear rush up inside her. Oh God, what had she done? Zach was the star of this picture. If he chose to, he could make one call to David Tauber and she'd be off the project for good.

'You don't know anything about my life,' Zach said softly. 'Do you want to talk about why I split my band?'

She shook her head, mutely.

I know why you split the band, jerk. Money. T-shirt royalties. A manager who didn't kiss your toned ass hard enough. David told me.

'I had my reasons.'

Yeah, about twenty million of them, Megan thought, but she said, 'It's your life, Zach. Dark Angel was your band. Not mine. You can do what you like.'

For a second he just stood there, staring at her, then looked away.

'Show's about to start,' he said. 'Come with me. I'll take you somewhere you can get a good view.'

Roxana Felix was boiling with rage. She was sitting with Megan Silver and a few other women, wives and girlfriends of the band, in a tiny concealed VIP enclosure at the side of the stage. Lasers webbed the darkness; coloured spotlights danced across the stage and illuminated hundreds of faces in the ocean of fans that stretched out in front of them. To her right, Electric City were blasting out their latest Top Ten smash. Roxana registered none of it.

She only knew that ten minutes ago she'd been sitting in here when Zach Mason personally escorted Megan Silver, that dull little puppy, into the VIP booth, and Megan – a nobody, a *writer*, for God's sake! – had been wearing a laminate which she obviously hadn't had to pull strings for. Zach had sent the little tramp a laminate!

Zach had preferred Megan to her!

And what made it worse was the look of surprise he'd shot her when he saw her pass – first surprise, and then a horrible knowing look, a sort of contemptuous stare. The mouse bimbo hadn't noticed it, of course. She was too busy gazing at the band and the crowd in some kind of pathetic wonder. Megan Silver actually cared about this stuff!

Roxana stared at the back of Megan's head. So, this was what Mason wanted, did he? A donkey instead of a unicorn. A sparrow instead of a peacock. And one who was so naive she probably didn't even realize it.

Well, the little mouse better not get in her way. Because if she did, she would pay for it!

18

Darkness had fallen over the massed ranks of the crowd. Just for a few minutes more, they would be kept waiting.

Megan twisted in her seat, her stomach knotted in excitement. It had been a great show. Watching from the side of the stage was awesome. And in between songs, when she wasn't getting carried away by the moment, she'd had time to watch what the roadies and guitar techs were doing. She had soaked up the atmosphere backstage like a sponge. It would be great research for the script; with just a few slight changes, she knew now that she could make her movie ten times more vivid and realistic. She'd get home and write new set instructions and stage directions that would change the entire way it looked on screen.

But that wasn't the point right now.

She was about to see Zach Mason perform.

Their exchange earlier had been weird . . . she'd been sure that when she came right out and condemned him, Zach would fly into a superstar tantrum, have her thrown out of the venue, have her fired. But he hadn't reacted like that, not at all. He'd been cool. Challenged her, but let her have her own opinion.

She didn't recognize the star she'd been sparring with.

She didn't recognize the primadonna David Tauber kept telling her about.

And here, in this stadium, she'd heard the Electric City fans scream his name all night long. When she ducked out of the viewing booth to use the bathroom, she'd heard near-hysterical reporters wondering aloud if it was true that Zach Mason was gonna sing. And walking through Hospitality on her way back up to the stage, the vibe was just the same – Zach, Zach, Zach. It was Electric City's show, but all the anticipation, all the rumours, were centred on the guy she'd just been fighting with.

Two months ago, Megan knew, she would have been in precisely the same state of crazed excitement. To her generation, hearing that Zach Mason was going to play a surprise jam with another band was the same as somebody telling her mother that John Lennon's death was faked and the Beatles would play at Madison Square Gardens this Christmas. Dark Angel were almost a religion, and Zach Mason was everybody's personal god.

In the heady, pumped-up atmosphere of the stadium tonight it was hard not to see it that way again. To see Zach through the adoring eyes of everyone else.

Working with him, Megan had come to think of him as a person more than a rock star. After all, he'd betrayed them . . . hadn't he?

She tried to get a grip, but she couldn't stop the butterflies squirming in her stomach. Zach would be onstage soon. Right next to her. And maybe, for a few minutes, she would see him again as the face she'd had tacked on her bedroom walls for the last five years.

Suddenly, there was a huge roar from the crowd, a howling wall of sound rising up into the warm night air. The hot rainbow of lights switched back on, bathing the crammed stadium in a pool of colours.

Electric City were back onstage for their encore. And striding out with them, one hand raised in salute, acknowledging the rabid adoration of the crowd, was Zach Mason, bathed in a single white spotlight, his hair fanning out around him like a black flame. She was close enough to see the tiny droplets of sweat beading on his chiselled face, close enough to see the intensity of his stare as he trained those wolf eyes on the crowd howling before him.

Megan's heart leapt to her throat. All her criticisms of him were blasted into nothingness. The fact that they were colleagues now was blasted into nothingness. In the heat of the moment, she had reverted to the hardcore Dark Angel fan she'd always been. Zach was her hero. And he was three feet away from her.

A raging desire gripped her, waves of lust starting in her belly and spreading out across her body, shooting little silver threads across her breasts and crotch. She felt her nipples harden under the T-shirt with his band's name blazoned across it. She felt her crotch grow warm and languid with blood, felt her pussy wetting up. Dear God, it was the most violent arousal she'd ever known in her life, and she wasn't even touching herself.

Dizzy, Megan gripped tightly onto the brass rail in front of her, leaning as closely in towards Zach as she could manage.

Electric City's guitarist, Rick de Souza, lowered his fingers to the fretboard and bled out the opening chords to 'Auburn', the title track from Dark Angel's second album. The record Megan had told Zach was her favourite.

As the crowd shrieked in ecstatic recognition, Electric City smiling and waving, the spotlight panned for a few seconds away from Zach and onto their own singer. And as he stood there, so close to Megan she could have touched him, Zach turned round in the darkness and smiled at her.

David Tauber sat on a wicker chair in Hospitality sipping a little champagne. He checked his watch. Fifteen minutes till the encores were over, and he saw no reason why he should have to stand out front, any closer to that unbelievable level of noise. From all the screaming, you'd imagine that somebody had turned a flamethrower on the audience. Which wouldn't be such a bad idea, judging from all the long hair and marijuana smoke. Thank God he had rescued Mason from this Neanderthal crap.

Colleen McCallum concerts were never like this.

He might have shown his face in the hospitality booth onstage, but had been told by a grinning security chief that his pass wasn't good enough.

'But this is the same pass Zach sent Roxana Felix,' Tauber insisted.

The guy shook his head. 'You don't get on that stage without a laminate. Roxana Felix has a laminate. Who gave it to her, I don't know.'

'And Megan Silver?' Tauber demanded, glancing up to see the back of Megan's head on the stage above him. That Roxana Felix would have pulled somebody's strings didn't surprise him in the least, but Megan . . . she hardly had the clout.

'She has a laminate too. And Zach Mason saw to that personally.'

'How do you know?' Tauber snapped, irritated.

'Because I set it up for him,' the ape replied. 'Now, you wanna keep inside your area, or you want me to throw you out?'

David had kept inside his area.

So, Zach Mason was setting up access for Megan Silver. Interesting. And Roxana was having to fight to keep up appearances . . .

As Tauber picked idly at a bunch of grapes laid out on the hospitality buffet, he started to think, fast. Right now, he controlled three out of the four principals in the *See the Lights* deal – the male lead, the female lead and the scriptwriter. Sam Kendrick represented Fred Florescu personally, and that was a pity, but even David could hardly try to poach a client from his own boss. There were limits.

At the moment.

But anyway, as it stood, his fingerprints were all over the deal. If the movie was a smash, his name would be made. His salary would quintuple. He would switch from 'up-and-coming' to 'arrived'. He would be a *player*.

There'd be a good shot at ousting Mike Campbell right away. Then he, David Ariel Tauber, would be head of Domestic Films at a major agency, one of the youngest guys ever to do it. And before too long he'd be able to walk away completely, set up shop on his own. David smiled pleasantly at the thought of it. So what if he was only twenty-six? He was kicking ass. And if Sam Kendrick wasn't exactly a clapped-out old lush like Kevin Scott, he was still getting old.

They were all old and weak and useless.

They could all learn from him. And if Sam Kendrick had to learn the hard way – so be it. That was the natural law of evolution; only the strong survive.

Well, he was surviving and thriving, but a lot of his power base was wrapped up in this movie, which was still only in pre-production. Right now, only Zach's position was absolutely secure. Megan could easily be fired, that happened all the time. Writers were plentiful, anonymous and cheap. And Roxana – well, she had more security, since her tests with Zach had practically set fire to the screen, but ultimately she was replaceable too. If Zach refused to work with her, for example, or if she tried playing the superstar with Fred Florescu. And it was important to David that neither of them be fired – he wanted as many fingerprints as possible on this picture.

That meant that all his little kids had to play nice together.

And something about this latest situation rang a lot of nasty bells.

Was it possible that Zach Mason actually wanted Megan Silver? His mousy, unassertive, bewildered little Megan? As far as the movie industry went, Megan didn't know what the hell was going on, and she took everything David told her as gospel. Somewhat understandable, he guessed.

Megan had come from the cool poverty of a slacker background in San Francisco, where she'd had a bunch of friends and been a clear part of a group, to Los Angeles where she knew nobody, got nowhere and had wound up in a nothing job – even worse than the one she'd left behind her. Then by a fortunate coincidence he'd decided to annoy Kevin Scott right at the moment when Megan was begging for a chance in his office, and her brilliant, pacy, commercial screenplay had dropped into his lap like a ripe plum.

David smiled smugly to himself. He didn't believe in luck. You made your own.

But Megan wouldn't have seen it that way. Megan would only have seen a white knight in a red Lamborghini turning up at her chicken joint to rescue her. She had pulled his whole deal together, and she still thought *he* was doing her a favour. She'd had a very tough life, and she was still functioning in survival mode. It hadn't registered with her that since she'd impressed Eleanor Marshall, there was bound to be other work for her. In Megan's mind, *See the Lights* was her only hope and David Tauber her only friend. And David liked that attitude.

He also liked the extraordinary power it gave him over her. He had taken control of her finances. He had ordered her to change her eating habits. He'd even put her through a torturous training regime; it was amusing, the way she was putty in his hands. And let's be honest, it was pretty erotic, too. Lately, he'd started fantasizing about Megan. She was attractive, in a soft, non-LA kind of way.

But what if Zach Mason had started to think so too?

Impossible. Zach fucked models and porn stars and the best that the groupie sorority had to offer. His women had thirty-eight-inch breasts and matchsticks legs and long blonde hair. And Roxana Felix, currently rated the most attractive woman in the world – top supermodel, new forty-million-dollar deal – was throwing herself at him. David had seen the headline from yesterday, the gossip running wild on MTV, the reporters outside this stadium yelling at him, asking him if he'd introduced 'the couple of the century'.

David lifted his champagne flute in the direction of the stage. He'd have to give it to the bitch, she was a smooth operator. Forget Charles and Diana or Richard and Cindy, a Zach–Roxana romance would mean banner headlines worldwide. It would guarantee huge box-office.

But if Zach decided he wanted Megan instead, and if Tauber had learned one thing in this business it was that there was no accounting for taste, the whole thing could blow up in smoke. Roxana would insist Megan be fired. Zach might intervene, have *her* fired. One way or another David would lose out.

And what if the mouse suddenly developed claws? Megan was adrift in LA. Helpless. But Tauber was sure she hadn't always been like that. Back home, she'd probably been tough and cynical.

He listened to the manic uproar rising from the crowd out front. Zach Mason's voice was coming over the PA, but the kids were so loud they were almost drowning him out. And this insanity had been Megan's world. She *knew* this. She knew Zach.

If they could just stop squabbling, Zach Mason would really represent a dream come true for Megan. She might start to get ideas above her station.

David frowned to himself. This had to be stopped. Zach and Roxana should be together, and Megan should . . .

Think, David ordered himself. *There's always a way. But you better find it. Fast.*

The last notes of 'Black Rage', Electric City's biggest hit, faded into the darkness, lost against the waves of cheering beating up to the stage. Zach had only been doing backing vocals on this one, laying raw harmonies under Karl Olafsson, the headliners' lead singer, but that didn't make any difference. No matter how far back he stood, Zach Mason was what the crowd wanted to see. And from the smiles they were flashing about onstage, Megan guessed, the band weren't too bothered. Their own street cred would soar, merely because Zach had chosen to jam with them. This was the first time he'd performed live since Dark Angel split up, and eighty thousand kids were treating it like it was the Second Coming.

Red and green Varilights swept across the stage.

'You want some more?' Karl yelled into the mike.

The affirmative roar was so loud even Megan took a step back. She was bathed in sweat from the heat of the spotlight and her own excitement. Zach had sung three songs, and each one had been a revelation . . . and to be so close to him she could watch the veins standing out on his neck when he sang, see every slight shift of expression even when the lights were on somebody else . . .

She knew one thing. When he was singing, Zach was thinking only about his song and the crowd. He took that intensity powering up from the mass and channelled it right back out through his voice. He stared into the blackness as though sheer force of will could help him see every passionate face. And his voice! Roughened with sensuality, fired up with rebellion, soaring with melody . . .

Megan was lost in it. Drowning, like the crowd in front of her. There was no fear, no embarrassment, nothing except the music and the lights and Zach. She was swept along, lost in the power of the moment.

'I guess we can do one more,' Karl agreed, turning round theatrically to his bandmates.

Rick de Souza strummed the opening chords to 'Fighting Fire', Dark Angel's signature song. The crowd screamed fit to wake the dead.

'We'd like to introduce you to the guy singing lead on this little cover – our good friend, Zach M – '

The rest of the introduction was lost in the hysterical shrieks of the crowd. Zach walked forward to the front of the stage, bathed in three spotlights, arms extended to the audience. 'I want to thank Electric City for letting me jam with them tonight. They were fucking great,' he said, nodding at Karl.

Massive cheers. The band grinned.

'This is the last number I'm gonna do; something Dark Angel used to play.'

He turned round and looked towards the concealed viewing booth. 'This is for Megan.'

Electric City crashed into the classic, dark minor-key chords exploding around them. The lights flashed everywhere, the crowd began to chant, tens of thousands of voices taking up the chant.

Megan stood frozen to the spot, paralysed with shock and delight.

'Were you pleased with that, honey?' a voice asked in her ear.

She turned round to see Roxana Felix, wearing a gold lamé mini-dress, smiling pleasantly at her. 'Yeah,' she said. At this moment, not even Roxana could upset her. Zach Mason was singing 'Fighting Fire' for *her*.

Roxana squeezed forward to the brass rail, so she was standing right next to Megan. She brushed her sweep of gorgeous, glossy black hair out of her eyes. 'I thought you would be. It was my idea, you know. I suggested it to him last week; we thought maybe we'd been a little harsh on you.'

For the first time, Megan noticed the laminate swinging from Roxana's belt. She felt herself crashing back down to earth, her stomach twisting in disappointment.

Of course Roxana had a laminate.

Roxana was Zach Mason's girlfriend.

How could she have let herself forget that? Did she really think a superstar like Zach would ever have anything more than a professional interest in her?

He'd said he was bringing her to this show for research and that was exactly what he'd meant. If he'd decided to be a little more friendly to her, that was great. It would be good for the movie. But she was an idiot to think it was anything more than that.

She was standing in this booth, right next to the world's most celebrated supermodel, and she reckoned Zach Mason was gonna pick her? Yeah, right, Megan! Nice thinking!

'Thank you,' she managed. 'It was really kind of you.'

Roxana smiled again, perfect, cherry-red lips blossoming across her face. Close-up, Megan couldn't help noticing that Roxana's skin was absolutely smooth, tight and unblemished, even without make-up. Like a searing knife, the recollection of Roxana's huge deal, announced on the news yesterday, with all the journalists bugging her about Zach, stabbed into her memory.

'And congratulations on your deal,' she added bravely.

The supermodel shrugged. 'I should congratulate *you*, dear,' she said patronizingly. 'Writing your first screenplay! I guess we're both career girls, huh?'

Both career girls . . . Yeah. I'm worth two hundred and fifty grand, less tax, less commission, less expenses, and you've just signed up to Jackson for forty million.

'Did you realize we're the same age?' Roxana asked sweetly.

'Are we?' said Megan, wondering if she'd ever felt less adequate in her life.

Onstage, Zach Mason was still holding the crowd in the palm of his hand. Megan thought he looked breathtaking; a hunter, a commander, young and beautiful but still very masculine, like the ancient sculptures of Alexander the

Great. And Roxana was slim and exquisite, a delicate, sensual Aphrodite. They were made for each other.

Zach turned round again and smiled at Megan. But this time she looked away.

As soon as the lights went down, a security guard arrived to take them into the hospitality area, where the post-gig party was in full swing.

'I think I'll skip it,' Megan said. 'I have a lot of work to do.' She glanced up at Roxana, every glossy black hair still in place. Maybe the bitch never sweated. 'Zach, uh, Zach brought me along so I could get a better flavour of backstage life. I have a bunch of new ideas to – '

'Megan, no,' Roxana insisted, threading one toned arm through hers. 'You must come along. I insist. And I know Zach will be really disappointed if you're not there.'

'Please, Roxana – '

'I *insist*,' Roxana said, steel beneath the honey-satin of her voice.

'OK,' Megan agreed miserably. Like she had a choice. But she really, really didn't want to see Zach entwined with Roxana Felix, not right now. Last week, she hadn't given a damn one way or the other. But to see Zach Mason play was to see him differently. And she was feeling like such a jerk . . .

The hospitality area was jam-packed; record company execs, loud-mouthed radio promo guys in Raiders shirts, bleached bimbos in dresses that looked like elongated T-shirts, and a few highly privileged reporters from *Rolling Stone* and other major magazines. The atmosphere crackled with excitement.

Still waiting for Zach, Megan thought, and wondered if he'd want to talk to these people. She hoped not. She wanted him to go to the backstage door and sign stuff for the fans.

'We probably won't stay long ourselves,' Roxana confided, slipping her arm free from Megan's as a small clutch of photographers caught sight of her and ran towards them. 'I want to get home.' She struck a pose for the cameras. 'Just a few, guys, please – I'm supposed to be having the night off.'

Megan stepped out of the way.

'Roxana! Great to see you, glad you could make it,' David said, swooping down on them. 'Gentlemen, that will be all for now, OK? Ms Felix is here to see Mr Mason. Can we give her some space?'

Roxana shot Tauber the faintest hint of a smile as the media guys scattered.

'Congratulations on your Jackson contract,' David added, hazel eyes sweeping across her glittering dress. 'I think you were robbed.'

She laughed. 'David, you haven't said hi to Megan.'

'No, I haven't,' Tauber said, turning towards her. Megan tried not to let her jealousy show. Wasn't Zach Mason enough? Now she had David falling down her unimpressive cleavage. 'I didn't see her there. Megan, honey, you look great.'

'Thanks, David,' Megan muttered.

She did not look great. She was wearing a T-shirt and jeans and her face was red with sweat. You couldn't jump up and down and slam against a railing for three hours and look great.

'Let me get you ladies some champagne,' Tauber offered, turning towards a passing waiter.

A sudden hum of anticipation rippled through the glitzy crowd. Zach Mason, changed into an Electric City shirt and a new pair of jeans, had emerged with the band from their dressing room. Seeing Megan and Roxana, he immediately started to head towards them.

David waved. 'Roxana,' he said, passing her a champagne flute. 'And Megan. That's for you.'

Megan took the drink, grateful to have something to do. She didn't want to have to stand there like a jerk when Zach and Roxana started pawing each other. 'Thanks, David.' She smiled at him.

'You know, when I said you looked great, I meant it,' David told her, moving closer. Megan breathed in the light scent of his aftershave. 'You've lost so much weight.'

'Thanks to you.'

'You're a really pretty girl, do you know that?' David asked. Ignoring her look of stunned surprise, he put a muscular arm around her.

At that moment, Zach Mason pushed past the last knot of people, and stopped dead. There was Megan, pressed up against David Tauber, just like the first time he'd seen her. Only now the agent had his arm possessively around Megan's waist.

'Hi, Zach,' Roxana Felix said, flashing him an incredibly sexy smile.

'You sounded terrific, Zach,' David said pleasantly. His hand moved on Megan's hip, an unmistakably sexual caress.

'Hi,' Zach said blankly.

Megan Silver looked at him, shyly. 'You were great,' she said.

Mason looked from Megan to David and back again, not wanting to accept it. But it was true, of course. Why had he thought Megan would be any different? She wasn't the Blessed Virgin. She'd fallen for his competent, slick, rich Hollywood agent. She was exactly like all the others. And he'd dedicated a song to her in front of eighty thousand fans.

He felt like a jerk.

'Glad you enjoyed it,' Zach said coldly. He turned to Roxana Felix, smiling brightly for the cameras that exploded around them, and took her exquisite head in his two hands, kissing her luxuriously on the mouth.

'Come on, sweetheart,' David whispered in Megan's ear. 'They don't need us hanging around. Let's go home.'

19

Eleanor went through her notes on the way to the airport, knowing she'd have time to practise her speech on the plane. Tom had arranged for them to fly to New York on a private jet belonging to Howard Thorn, the billionaire financier, whose conglomerate, Condor Industries, had become the single largest shareholder in Artemis Studios last year. She would have to deliver her presentation to Thorn and the other six Wall Street moguls who comprised the Artemis board.

It was odd, she reflected, how the world had suddenly become so medieval in its structures. Real power no longer resided in Presidents and Prime Ministers, but in the shadowy figures who controlled the flow of money; men with the power to devalue a currency or crash a stock market, who sent the world economy into growth or recession, and who could buy and sell the flow of ideas. George Soros. Bill Gates. Warren Buffet. Who was the most powerful man in the world? Probably Rupert Murdoch, Eleanor thought, the Australian who seemed to own half of all the papers on the planet as well as three major TV networks and a film studio.

These were the kind of men she'd be standing in front of. The modern-day equivalent of the Medici, the Italian merchant princes who had controlled Europe during the Renaissance. It was, she realized, going to be a baptism of fire. She had imagined that president of Artemis was one step away from the top of the power ladder, and she was now beginning to realize that in fact it was the very bottom rung.

She was nervous.

The carphone trilled against the cream leather of her seat.

'Eleanor Marshall.'

'So, are you ready for this?' Tom's voice crackled across the line, and she could almost see the grin on his face.

'The question is, are they ready for me?' Eleanor told him.

Goldman laughed. 'That's my girl. I'm sure we're gonna walk it. And besides, New York will be a vacation for you, the way things have been going back here.'

'That's very true,' she agreed. It would be pleasant not to have to think about Jake Keller's bitter little memos, or the *See the Lights* budget problems, and especially her one-month deadline to give Paul his answer. 'Where are we staying?'

'The Victrix,' he said. 'You're in the Presidential Suite.'

'Ha, ha, very funny,' Eleanor replied, but she was pleased. The Victrix was simply the most luxurious hotel in Manhattan, on a par with the Lanesborough in London or the Oriental in Bangkok. This trip was vital and nerve-racking, but at least Tom had made sure there would be certain fringe benefits.

'I'll see you in a while. Don't leave your briefcase on the back seat,' Goldman teased her.

Eleanor blushed. 'Tom! That was fifteen years ago.'

He was reminding her of an incident that had happened when she'd just begun work at the studio as a reader. Tom Goldman, then senior marketing manager and her mentor, had asked Eleanor to bring over his notes on a merchandising deal for a kids' feature with Toys Я Us. It had been an important presentation. Eleanor, then twenty-three, had left the wrong briefcase in her car and Goldman had had to speak extempore, pretending that the pile of rejected scripts in front of him was highly secret sales projections. He'd clinched the deal, but reamed Eleanor out. And hadn't stopped ribbing her about it for the rest of her career.

'Yeah, yeah, yeah. Once a flake, always a flake,' Tom teased. 'See you later.'

'See you later,' she agreed, hanging up.

As the Rolls-Royce glided smoothly and speedily down the freeway, deserted in the blue half-light of early morning, Eleanor Marshall felt her spirits lift a little. So, Tom was in a good mood. Whatever else happened today, at least she could be sure that the brusque, business-only awkwardness of their relationship since Isabelle's party was finished. Perhaps her performance with Jake Keller the other day had done the trick. Anyway, if Tom was joking around like this, things were back to normal.

Eleanor checked out her face in the rearview mirror. Light blusher, sugarplum lips with a neutral berry pencil, and equally subtle eyeshadow in pale pink and sand-gold. She'd gone to bed early last night with a sleeping pill, so there was no redness in her eyes or sallowness in her skin from lack of sleep. In fact, her skin looked great, under its sheer mousse foundation; the fine lines around her mouth and eyes had become far less noticeable since she'd started with that alpha-hydroxy moisturizer. Thank God, finally a beauty product that actually worked.

She could pass for thirty this morning. Sometimes life was good. Even under pressure.

When they pulled up on the runway twenty minutes later, Goldman was there and waiting for her.

'Got the briefcase? Good, let's go.'

She thanked her chauffeur, took her case and overnight bag from him and followed her boss up the steps.

'I thought you'd never get here,' Goldman grumbled as they strapped themselves in for takeoff. 'I was waiting out there in the freezing cold. Forever.'

She checked her watch. 'Tom, I'm five minutes early.'

He waved that aside as they taxied down the runway. 'Eleanor, I'm busy, Don't bother me with trivial details.'

Once the plane had reached cruising altitude, Eleanor got up from her seat to take a look around. This was a Gulfstream IV, a serious jet, not your two-bit Astra or Lear that a mere multimillionaire might use. The only other man she knew who could afford a Gulfstream IV was David Geffen.

'Impressive, huh?'

Goldman walked up to stand beside her as she gazed at the decor. Howard Thorn had rigged his little toy up in dark blue leather with gold-leaf trim, the softest wall-to-wall carpeting, leather armchairs, a bathroom, a bedroom and a kitchen.

'This baby cost twenty-five million bucks. And a hundred thousand a month to run,' Tom said. 'I know because I read it in *Vanity Fair*.'

Eleanor whistled. 'That's one hell of an expensive cab ride.'

He nodded. 'Sometimes I wonder if I got into the right game.'

'I don't even see a company logo around here,' Eleanor observed, glancing across at the young stewardesses in their smart navy uniforms. 'I must say I'm surprised. I didn't imagine Howard Thorn to be the unostentatious type.'

Goldman chuckled, clearly amused. 'Are you kidding? This is Howard's *private* jet. Condor Industries has two more of these stacked down in Dallas, near their oil company. And in those you can't move for logos.'

They sat down together on a cavernous sofa and Tom laid out his projections on a glass-topped coffee table in front of them. They worked through the figures as Thorn's flight attendants served them breakfast; Earl Grey tea from a Georgian silver service, tiny smoked salmon sandwiches, hot, flaky croissants, and racks of toast with marmalade and strawberry jelly. Eleanor declined a second course of a Brie omelette, followed by hot pancakes with syrup.

'Tom, you're going to get fat,' Eleanor warned him absently, her head buried in her speech.

'Nonsense.' Goldman grabbed her hand and laid it against the thin cotton of his Oxford shirt. 'That's all muscle. Feel it.'

He was right, Eleanor thought, her palm connecting with a rock-hard wall of flesh. It was solid muscle. Tauter even than Paul, despite his macrobiotic diets and rigorous exercising. She felt an instant stab of desire.

She snatched her hand away quickly, before things got any worse. 'Well, it won't stay that way if you keep stuffing yourself with cholesterol,' she said, hoping he wouldn't notice the slight blush.

Tom snorted, spearing a delicious-looking forkful of oozing cheese omelette. 'You sound just like Jordan when you talk that way,' he said.

Clearly, not a compliment.

'Would you prefer some fresh strawberries and champagne, madam?' one of the stewardesses asked her, clearing away Eleanor's untouched plate. 'We have Perrier-Jouet, Bollinger, Cristal . . .'

'No thanks, I'm fine,' Eleanor told her.

She took refuge in her speech for the rest of the flight.

The Artemis board had convened at the studio's New York offices, an elegant couple of floors at number 1 Madison Avenue, right in the heart of the Flatiron district in mid-town.

Tom and Eleanor said little to each other on the way in. As they drew closer to the meeting, the mood subtly changed from humour to tension. Goldman was anxious, Eleanor could see that. He kept double-checking his statistics, like some nervous housewife who can never quite satisfy herself that she's sure she's got her passport with her and needs to look in her purse every ten minutes.

What does *Tom* have to worry about? Eleanor wondered, looking out at the lunchtime traffic. He's a veteran at this, plus he knows all about the Japanese threat ... but it's my first time at a board meeting, and I have no idea what they've been offered for the stock. I'm flying blind on this. And Tom gets to present figures – nice, clean, explicable figures our accountants have been working on for months. But I've got to wade in with my pep talk about *See the Lights* and how it's gonna clean up with America's kids. Nothing provable, very touchy-feely. Very 'feminine'.

She began to wonder if there wasn't something sexist going on here. 'Who's going first?' she asked her boss.

'You are,' he told her firmly.

'Oh, terrific,' Eleanor muttered, as their limo pulled to a halt.

Tom held open the door for her. 'You're gonna be fine.'

They announced themselves at reception and Tom led her to the far elevator. 'It's right at the top, but this is one of those express cars.'

'Great,' Eleanor replied, smoothing down the skirt of her pale-pink Dior silk suit.

'You're nervous,' Goldman said, looking at her.

'You're observant.'

'Come on, Eleanor. You're the girl who was debating for Harvard when she was twenty years old.'

Eleanor shrugged. 'Between twenty and thirty-eight, I think I may have got a little rusty on the public-speaking front.'

Twenty-seven, twenty-eight, twenty-nine ... the floor numbers slipped noiselessly by. They would be there any second. Suddenly, Goldman reached past her and pressed the halt button.

'Eleanor, look at me.'

Surprised, she did. Tom was staring down at her, his black eyes picked out by his dark Savile Row suit, tender and full of kindness. 'You remember when we first met?'

'Sure,' she said, wondering where this was going. 'In the corridor by the canteen. I was running down the hall and I cannoned into you and you spilt coffee all over yourself.'

He nodded. 'You called me "sir" when you apologized. Never showed me a second's respect since.'

Eleanor recalled it vividly, just as Tom knew she would. Her first week at Artemis, when she was a lanky, nervous kid, fresh out of college and desperate to make it in the all-male business world. And Tom Goldman, with a lot more hair and a lot less style, had been thirty and already number two in the merchandising division, a senior executive as far as Eleanor was concerned. She'd been so terrified at spilling coffee down him she'd gone white with fear.

Tom had laughed and taken her to lunch, thinking she was cute. By the end of lunch, he thought he might have discovered a useful future lieutenant. Ideas, intelligence and enthusiasm bubbled out of her every sentence. He became her mentor and friend practically right away.

'We were such kids,' Eleanor said.

'We were.' He leaned towards her. 'Now, do you remember how we flew up here today? Do you remember the last time you called Mike Ovitz on his private line? Do you remember having Sam Kendrick sitting in front of you, begging you to green-light a Fred Florescu picture? We're not kids any more, Eleanor. We've done absolutely fucking great. People fell aside, but we kept on going, and now we run the whole damn studio. And don't you forget it.'

He released the halt button, and the elevator began to move again.

'You were a gangly college girl in jeans when I met you, Eleanor Marshall.' The metal doors hissed open, and Tom followed her out into the studio's corporate headquarters. Eleanor felt his hand on her shoulder, 'But today, you are the president of Artemis.'

She had to blink back tears as she glanced up at him.

'We've come too far to give it up now,' Tom Goldman said. 'You go in there, Eleanor. And you kill them.'

'Mr Goldman? Ms Marshall?'

A brisk, middle-aged English secretary in a tweed suit was walking towards them down the hushed corridor of the corporate suite. 'If you'd care to step this way, the board are ready for you now.'

They followed her past the polished mahogany tables, biscuit-coloured walls and Impressionist paintings to a large set of double doors at the end of the hallway. Opening it, the woman discreetly ushered them into the Artemis boardroom.

Eleanor took the scene in at a glance. A long, square table polished until it reflected, like a mirror, the sober faces of the seven middle-aged men seated round it. Howard Thorn was the only director Eleanor had met in the flesh, but she recognized all the others from their glossy colour pictures in the annual report: Harry Trasker, Kenneth Rich, Eli Leber, Kit Wilson, Conrad Miles, and Martin Birnbaum.

All of them serious Wall Street players.

All of them only interested in the stock.

Idly, she wondered if a woman had ever sat on the board.

'Tom, Eleanor, good to see you,' Howard Thorn said expansively.

What a breathtakingly ugly man, Eleanor thought, smiling sweetly at him.

'I know you have a report for us. So why don't we just cut to the chase and get on with it?' He motioned to the empty chair at the head of the table. 'Now, who's presenting first?'

Eleanor took one last look at the room. A porcelain coffee service. A mind-blowing view over central Manhattan, the city laid out behind and beneath them in a glittering panorama. And a bunch of financiers, completely uninterested in what she had to say – they were waiting for Tom's *real* numbers.

'I am,' she said, clearly and confidently. She strode up to the head of the table, clicked open her briefcase, and unhurriedly hung her brightly coloured demographic charts on the easel laid out behind her. Then she turned to face her multibillion-dollar audience, seven men who had the power to end her career with a stroke of the pen, and sell her studio out to the Japenese.

'Gentlemen,' she said easily. 'My name is Eleanor Marshall, and I am the President and Chief Operating Officer of Artemis Studios.'

20

They stumbled into the lobby of the Victrix together, laughing like teenagers. Goldman was still grinning at her when he checked them in, relaxed and loose in the aftermath of the victory high.

It had been a great presentation; his numbers had been scrutinized and analysed by the board and found to be impressive, but the real breakthrough had been Eleanor's speech. Goldman kept visualizing the surprised, attentive looks on the faces of the staid board members as she talked to them about the indefinable nature of the movie business, the difficulty in calculating future returns by past performance. With fluid gestures and easy words, she had demonstrated to them that just because Martin Webber had produced nothing but flops that did not mean she was going to. And finally she had begun to talk about *See the Lights*, driving home her point with such passionate enthusiasm that even bankers like Conrad Miles and Harry Trasker had begun to register what the project was all about, and how much money it could make for them. Howard Thorn had said nice things about Roxana Felix; well, Goldman expected that, after the arm-twisting Thorn had done for her earlier. He wondered briefly if Roxana was screwing the fat jerk, but decided she wasn't. She was a forty-million-dollar supermodel. Surely it wouldn't be worth it to her, to fuck Howard Thorn just for help in getting cast. Thorn had only been able to guarantee her tests got seen, not to cast her, and *See the Lights* would amount to a day's pay compared with what the woman was already earning as a supermodel. It just didn't make sense. But anyway the clincher had come when Eleanor pulled out a videotape from her briefcase, asked that a TV be brought into the boardroom, and then played the tests of Zach and Roxana together, drawing attention to the huge publicity angle in their relationship.

The suits had paid little attention to her words, though, Tom thought, smiling. They were too caught up in trying to control their erections. By the end of that five-minute tape, Eleanor Marshall had every one of the boys eating out of her manicured hand. As far as *See the Lights* was concerned, they were believers.

Goldman wasn't out of the danger zone, he knew that. The Japanese would continue to circle overhead. But at least his president had managed to convince them that selling right now would be a mistake – *See the Lights* would lift the stock price, help them to get more for the company later, if they still intended to sell. It wasn't rescue – it was reprieve. But they bought themselves a little time. And right now, that was as much as he could have hoped for.

'Here you are, sir. The Presidential Suite and the Emperor Suite,' the receptionist said, handing him their keys. 'Would you like a valet for your bags?'

Goldman hefted up his lightweight overnight case and shook his head. He picked up Eleanor's neat little Gucci case. 'No, thanks, we'll be fine.'

'Are you my porter now?' Eleanor enquired, amused.

Goldman bowed his head in her direction. 'After the performance you just gave, I'm anything you want me to be, ma'am.'

'Don't tempt me,' she teased, as they headed towards the elevator.

The car hissed up the floors as smooth as silk.

'Not going to stop it this time?' Eleanor asked Tom. She was flirting with him, light-headed with victory. The relief of getting through their presentation was so enormous that it almost made her dizzy. And reckless. A little fun wouldn't kill them, not in New York, where even Isabelle Kendrick's bat-ears couldn't pick up what she was saying.

'You can laugh – '

'Thanks,' Eleanor said, smiling.

' – but you needed that pep talk. And if it got you results like those, I reserve the right to stop your elevator car whenever I feel like it.'

'OK, coach. You got it. And how come I'm only in the Presidential Suite and you're in the Emperor Suite? Yours sounds way better.'

'Age before beauty,' Goldman said airily. 'And I *am* the Emperor around here. Bear that in mind.'

'Maybe it's about time we had an Empress,' Eleanor threatened him. 'Maybe I'll do a Jake Keller on you.'

They stepped out on the penthouse floor; their suites were right next to each other. Goldman opened up Eleanor's door for her.

'Look at that,' she murmured, impressed.

The place was a Regency fantasy in white and gold; soft cream carpet was laid throughout with a delicate pattern of gold leaves, twisting in some unseen breeze, repeated on the walls and around the edge of the ceiling. Long velvet drapes the colour of burnished bronze hung from windows twelve feet high, offering a magnificent view down the Avenue of the Americas. On a white marble coffee table with gold detailing was a crystal vase filled with pure white lilies, stamens covered in thick yellow pollen that reflected the general colour scheme. The bathroom, as large a room as the bedroom, was built round a centrepiece of a large jacuzzi, with a sunken Japanese bath right next to it. But the third room was the thing Eleanor found truly luxurious: a perfect reproduction of an English country library, complete with mounted stag's head, leather-bound tomes and a dark green leather armchair.

'Jesus,' Goldman remarked. 'Want to swap?'

Eleanor laughed. 'You haven't seen yours yet. Look, why don't you go and get changed. I need to freshen up, then maybe we can go and have tea together.'

'What, you mean cute little English sandwiches and scones with cream?'

'Exactly,' Eleanor said.

'And you're gonna have a shower?' Goldman enquired. 'Can I watch?'

She laughed lightly, but felt Tom's eyes hungry on the nape of her neck. Come on, now, Eleanor, you're imagining things, she told herself firmly.

'Nothing interesting to see,' she said.

Tom took a step back from her, staring at her, his black eyes taking everything in, from the elegant ash-blonde hair fixed neatly in place, past the slight swell of her breasts visible under her jacket, to the soft curve of her calves, tapering down into Patrick Cox pumps that emphasized her slender ankles. Eleanor was beautiful and sensual and a pleasure to look at. He took his time, and she felt his gaze like a caress on her skin, a sudden lick of sexual heat following his eyes, as though he were actually stripping her, peeling away her clothes to examine her naked body.

'Somehow I doubt that,' Tom said, eventually.

He saw her blush bright red, and the languid snake of lust curling in his belly stirred a little faster. He didn't know why he had done that, but it felt good. And it felt good that she seemed to know what he was thinking.

There was a long pause.

'I'll come and get you in twenty minutes,' Eleanor managed, with an effort.

'OK,' Tom Goldman said, and left the room.

Isabelle Kendrick didn't usually pay house calls. Either people came to her, at her convenience, or – more usually – she met with a favoured few at the most highly visible restaurants in town. After all, what was the point of being a social lioness if one didn't shine in society? But on this occasion she parked her Bentley at the front of the Goldmans' Beverly Hills mansion without even taking the time to gloat over how much more attractive her own gardens were.

Jordan had called this morning, and it was serious. *Extremely* serious. So serious, in fact, that for once Isabelle had absolutely no desire to discuss the matter in front of a crowded room. She had no wish to be seen to be discussing it with Jordan at all. And yet, as Isabelle stepped out of her car and walked quickly up to the Goldmans' pillared front porch, immaculate in her navy Bill Blass dress and Charles Jourdan heels, her heart actually began to beat faster with the unusual sensation of excitement.

A uniformed maid answered the door. 'Won't you come in, Mrs Kendrick,' she said. 'Mrs Goldman's waiting for you in the drawing room.'

Isabelle thanked her briskly and walked straight into the Goldmans' sub-Ralph-Lauren reception room.

Just as she had expected, Jordan Cabot Goldman, overdressed in a glitzy Valentino pantsuit, was leaning tragically against the fireplace, weeping into a lace handkerchief. 'Isabelle, thank God you're here,' she sobbed.

'My dear, I jumped in the car the second I hung up on you,' Isabelle said, trying to feign compassion through the thrill of it all.

Forget about the parties. Here she had the opportunity for some real social engineering. And if she succeeded, not only would it be a strike against Eleanor Marshall, but it would mean that Jordan Goldman was indebted to her forever. Indirectly Isabelle would control not only the Los Angeles establishment society, but also the flavour-of-the-week PC crowd that Jordan had started to gather around herself. And Jordan would never be a threat to her position again.

Because Jordan would owe her. Huge.

'He's taken her to New York,' Jordan sobbed, 'and he didn't even *tell* me.' Her voice rose to a little-girl wail. 'I had to find out from Joanne.'

His assistant. Isabelle's mind worked swiftly over the situation. The fact that Eleanor had accompanied Tom to New York was insignificant, just a professional feather in her cap. After all, she *was* president of the studio, Isabelle acknowledged with her usual mixture of envy and contempt. No, the significant thing was that Tom had tried to keep it from Jordan. And Jordan already knew her position was threatened, from the intelligence Isabelle had supplied her with from her party. That was why she had, on Isabelle's advice, thrown a fit of jealous rage and then wounded sorrow, demanding that Tom cease to socialize with Eleanor. He'd denied it, of course, but according to Isabelle's spies at Artemis he had been pretty clinical with Eleanor of late.

Evidently that time had come to an end, and so would Jordan's marriage, if she didn't move fast.

Tom had concealed Eleanor's presence on this trip from his wife. That was a major danger signal. Isabelle was relieved that at least the silly little tramp had had the good sense to call her about it.

'I know, dear,' she said, calmly but firmly. 'And you know what you have to do now, don't you?'

'But who knows how long that would take?' Jordan sobbed.

'Sometimes we have to anticipate problems, Jordan,' said Isabelle with authority, 'and sometimes we have to be *pro-active* in solving them. Now, I shall tell you what to do, and I want no arguments.'

'But it'll ruin my looks,' Jordan wept.

'Not if you're careful,' Isabelle told her. 'And at any rate, dear, you may be out of options at this point.' She crossed over to the mantelpiece and patted her protégée soothingly on the shoulder. 'You have to do it, Jordan, and you have to do it now. Trust me. It's the only way.'

Tom and Eleanor arrived back at the hotel around eleven. They had taken tea, gone for a walk and then gone to see a movie.

'Are you kidding?' Eleanor asked, amazed, when Tom suggested it.

'No!' he said, grinning. 'Don't you want to? I mean, when was the last time you paid to see a movie, in a theatre, with popcorn, like everyone else?'

'Uh, nineteen seventy-eight?' guessed Eleanor.

'Right! We should do this, it would be great market research.' Tom warmed to the theme. 'We can charge our tickets back to Accounts as a business expense.'

'I always liked the previews best.' Eleanor adopted a heavy mafioso tone. 'And *now*. PARAMOUNT PICTURES presents . . .'

'Exactly! Come on, let's go,' Goldman urged, and they wound up in some little cinema off Broadway, watching a rerun of *Dazed and Confused* with a jumbo bucket of popcorn and two huge Coca-Colas.

'It was a great movie,' Goldman said, as they finally walked into the

Victrix's blue marble lobby. 'Although you seemed to be enjoying it more than me.'

Eleanor shrugged. 'What can I tell you? I was sixteen in nineteen seventy-four. I lived all that stuff.'

Tom looked at her. 'You smoked dope?'

'Didn't everybody?'

Goldman shook his head, laughing. 'It doesn't compute, babe. Eleanor Marshall with a reefer?'

Eleanor shrugged defensively. 'I wasn't *born* like this, you know.'

'Do you want a nightcap?' Goldman asked, and she was surprised to hear herself say yes. But she did want a drink with him, she realized. The pleasure of spending an afternoon with Tom Goldman, talking about everything and nothing, was too great just to be suddenly switched off with a stiff good night. They hadn't talked like this for years now, maybe even five or six years. The upper reaches of the greasy pole were too slippery and dangerous to do anything but climb.

They rode up to Tom's suite in companionable silence. It was similar to Eleanor's; decorated in silver and turquoise, it had shades of an Oriental harem, and instead of a library boasted a small private gym. His reception room was also fitted with a fully stocked bar.

'What are you drinking?' Goldman asked her.

Eleanor knew Paul would want her to say 'mineral water' or 'a Virgin Mary'. 'Bourbon on the rocks,' she said. 'Wild Turkey, if you've got it.'

Tom raised an eyebrow, looking at her quizzically.

God, the guy is so handsome, Eleanor thought. 'Got a problem with that?' she asked menacingly.

He laughed. 'No, ma'am. I think I'm gonna have to bring you to New York more often. Dope, drink . . . this is a whole new side to you.'

'I haven't done dope since I was twenty,' Eleanor protested.

Goldman mixed them both a whisky and they sat down together on his soft, vast blue sofa.

'To Artemis,' Eleanor toasted him.

'To us,' Tom corrected her, 'because we got there, and today we made sure we're gonna stay there.'

They touched their crystal tumblers together and drank.

'What did you mean earlier, when you said you weren't born like this?' Tom asked her softly. 'What do you think you're like now?'

She leaned back, feeling the pleasant warmth of the alcohol spread through her. 'Oh, you know. The Ice Queen. The Statue. All those things they say.'

Tom looked her in the eyes. 'I never thought you were an Ice Queen.'

Eleanor struggled to beat back the slow, heady wash of desire seeping through her. It was too much, sitting next to him like this, after the day they'd had, up here, on their own. She knew it was dangerous. And yet she made no move to get up.

'Why did you want to make movies?' he asked her.

'Why? I'm not sure.' Eleanor considered it. 'Because it seemed like a fun thing to do at the time. Maybe because I watched so many films as a girl. Because I liked the way they always had happy endings and the heroine always wound up with the true love of her life. Every woman's dream. In the movies, everything was passionate and larger than life and nobody ever compromised, and I wanted to believe my life was gonna be that way...'

Her voice trailed off into silence.

'And now you don't believe it's possible for a woman to end up with the great love of her life?'

'I believe it's possible.' Eleanor toyed with the rim of her glass, then glanced over at Tom Goldman, sitting next to her, his black eyes staring at her so intently, his large body so close she could hear his breathing, and his left hand, gripping his tumbler so tightly that the knuckles were white, decorated with a simple platinum wedding band. 'I just don't believe it's possible for me.'

'Look at me,' Tom insisted. He put two fingers under her chin and turned her face towards him. 'You are intelligent and talented and beautiful and brave. I knew you were special from the second I met you. You can have anything you want.'

'No,' she said, feeling her skin burning where his fingers had touched her. 'Not quite anything.'

For a few seconds Goldman didn't reply. Then he began to look at her again, the way he had done in her suite, infinitely slowly, admiring her sexually, his gaze seeming to lift away her clothing, until she felt herself juicing, felt her nipples stiffen in arousal.

'Don't,' she managed.

'Why not?' Tom asked. 'Am I turning you on?'

Eleanor tried to think straight, through the warm fog of her desire. Somewhere in the back of her brain, faint and far away, warning bells were ringing frantically. But the heady, liquid pulse of her blood drowned out all her normal caution. For once she didn't want to be sensible.

She wanted Tom. She had always wanted Tom.

'Yes,' she said simply.

'I want you,' Goldman said, and Eleanor said, 'Have me.'

He leaned forward, very slowly, and brushed a lock of hair away from the side of her cheek, his rough palm cupping her soft skin, and then brought his left hand up to cradle the other side of her face, holding her head, letting her feel his strength. Then he bent down and touched his mouth to hers, a soft, dry kiss at first, then a more urgent one, and finally he ran his tongue across her lips and cheek, pushing it inside her mouth, desperate to taste her sweetness. His arm suddenly circled the small of her back and pulled her body tight against his, impatiently, insistently, creasing up her expensive silk suit.

Eleanor was overcome with desire. At the first touch of his skin on hers, fire shot through her, blossoming in her belly and breasts, everything animal and female in her in heat, her blood seeming to warm and melt. Spontaneously she moved her legs apart, the centre of them moist and ready for him. His caress was exactly as she had dreamed it would be for all these years: masculine and tender and gentle and dominant. His erection strained against her through the fabric of his pants, large and rock-hard with need.

'I always wanted you,' he was murmuring, and Eleanor said, 'Tom, my

God . . .' and then his hands were fumbling with the buttons on her jacket, clumsily, and Eleanor twisted apart from him, stripping off her clothes, kicking off her shoes and peeling down her hose, as hungry as a teenager, until she was down to her bra and panties, tiny scraps of coffee-coloured Italian lace, and then Goldman's hands closed over hers, stopping her, wanting to do that himself.

'You're so beautiful,' he whispered, and then she groaned in arousal as his hands closed on the softness of her breasts, playing with her nipples through the lace, his finger and thumb rubbing them and stroking them until she was half-mad with the pleasure, and just when she thought she couldn't stand it Tom's lips were closing over them, his tongue lapping and tugging, sucking them, the wet heat of his mouth making dark circles on the tips of her bra cups, the roughness of the lace contrasting with the smoothness of his slippery tongue until Eleanor was arching against him, thrusting her flanks against his.

'Do you like that? Huh?' Goldman was asking her, his voice hoarse with sex, and then his fingers were trailing down the front of her stomach, just the tips of his fingers brushing her skin, drawing a long, burning ribbon of fire across it. Eleanor sobbed with pleasure, unable to believe herself capable of such feelings, and then gasped out his name as Tom slid his hand into the soft, downy curls under her panties, covering her burning, damp mound with his hand, and then, infinitely gently, sliding two fingers inside her, rubbing lightly over the slick nub of her clitoris.

'Oh, Jesus! Jesus, Tom!' Eleanor gasped, feeling her womb contract into spasm, intense pleasure exploding all over her and fresh wetness flood her between the legs as she came.

'That was nothing, sweetheart. That was just the start,' Tom said, and she felt him unsnapping her bra and peeling off her panties, damp with her own juices as he rolled them down her supple thighs. When she was completely nude, he rolled her gently onto her back, stroking her lightly from her shoulders, along the curving sides of her body down to her buttocks, and before she could even twist in response Eleanor felt his warm breath on the nape of her neck, teasing her, making the tiny hairs there stand on end, and then he was kissing her, firm, circular butterfly kisses, licking and sucking at her skin, flicking it with just the tip of his tongue, taking his time, moving down her spine.

Eleanor felt conscious thought recede. She was only aware of Tom's mouth, and the heat of his body crowding hers, and his strong arms that held her relentlessly in place as she squirmed, maddened with desire, under the attentions of his tongue. Her entire body had become one huge erogenous zone; melting, pulsating streams of desire seemed to flow out of her spine, where his mouth was, and bathe her entire skin in ecstatic need. When he finally reached her coccyx, she was close to another climax.

'Tom, you're incredible,' she sobbed, and Goldman said, 'I want you so much, I've been thinking about this for months,' and his hands were on her buttocks, gripping them, stroking them.

'You've got a great ass,' he said. 'I used to fantasize about doing this every time you walked down the corridor.'

Eleanor tried to say something, but surprise and arousal strangled her voice and she could only twist under him, kissing at his forearm.

'Do you want me, Eleanor?' he was asking, and for answer she guided his hand to her pussy, open and more than ready for him, and begged, 'Please, Tom, I can't wait any more,' and he murmured, 'That's right, sugar, let it go.' He freed himself quickly, half ripping his clothes off, and Eleanor opened her arms to him, naked and hard and straining for her, his cock already dewed at the head, glistening with his arousal, and the two of them fell upon one another, kissing and biting, and he found her almost immediately and with one hard, impatient thrust sank himself deep inside her, all the way up to the hilt, and then all Eleanor knew, all she could think about, was Tom Goldman, above her, inside her, his swollen thickness drawing pleasures out of her she had never imagined existed, his intelligent, arrogant face now staring down at hers with an intense expression of desire and love, and she felt his cock, sunk deep inside her, hit some melting, blinding place, some sweet, secret trigger buried deep within her, and suddenly a new orgasm was gripping her, more powerful than the first, more powerful than any climax she had ever known, the sensations seeming to pour out of every inch of her body so she could feel the waves rock her from her forearms to her calves, her whole body convulsing in blinding ecstasy, and she cried out, 'Tom, I love you,' and somewhere very far away she felt him tense, coming inside her, and she heard him say, 'I love you, Eleanor, I always did,' and then the final, consuming, white wave of bliss broke across her body and swept everything away.

21

Eleanor woke slowly, her head swimming up towards consciousness very gradually and gently, her deep sleep pierced by soft shafts of golden morning light. She glanced at the gold carriage clock by her bedside. It was 6.40 a.m.; in another five minutes the alarm would have shrilled, waking her far less pleasantly. Sleepily she turned it off, stretching luxuriously as the memories of the night before came flooding back. Despite the lack of sleep, her whole body felt loose and relaxed, as though her very bones had melted under Tom's mouth.

She twisted a little on the navy-blue satin Pratesi sheets. Tom Goldman's large, solid back was turned towards her, moving slightly as he slept. Eleanor admired him briefly for a second or two, staring at the hard bulk of him, liking the masculinity of the tiny dark hairs on his back, the scent of his body next to hers. She debated whether or not to wake him now, so they could make love again, but decided against it: they had a flight in two hours and she wanted to dress and prepare herself, put her make-up on, be as beautiful for him as she possibly could. Her hair was a wreck, her face was a mess – well, she'd hardly had time for the cleanse-tone-moisturize thing last night – and she needed to take a shower.

Eleanor slipped noiselessly out of bed, careful not to wake him, and gathered up her crumpled clothes from the sofa and the floor. Then she tiptoed back to the bed, kissed Tom lightly at the top of his spine and crept out of his suite.

Megan tried not to give herself time to think about what she was doing. If she paused for breath, she might back out of it. This was not something reversible. This was her, Megan Silver, casting off her old way of life and plunging head first into the private swimming pool of a new one. It felt a little uncomfortable, but in Hollywood perhaps this was the only way.

The mini-library of self-help books that David had bought for her all said the same thing; you can reinvent yourself if you want to, physically, mentally and spiritually. *Awaken the Giant Within. A Course in Miracles. Stop the Insanity. The Seven Habits of Highly Effective People . . .* Megan had read them all, or at least skimmed through them. She'd had to – David Tauber quoted them all the time, and Megan didn't want to look stupid in front of David. And maybe it was about time she woke up to the message – change wasn't only possible, it was an American Duty. And if going from a caterpillar to a butterfly involved shedding a few layers of skin, well, that was simply the way it had to be.

The Electric City concert had been the last straw. She had been caught up in the magic, she had wanted so much to be wrong about Zach, to be able to believe in the idealism of her generation again, to trust in artists, to have faith in the idea that there were people who sought truth and compassion, and who rejected shallowness and glitter and surface perfection. For a few moments up there, in the humid darkness, Zach Mason had seemed to be one of those people, the true artist, the hero she'd idolized since she was a teenager.

Pulling on her Calvin Klein jeans, Megan Silver smiled grimly. Idolize was the ideal word for it. Because Zach had proved about as genuine a guru as the Great and Powerful Oz.

Was she jealous of Roxana Felix? Megan asked herself. Roxana was an out-and-out bitch, a fashion princess on the receiving end of a lucky genetic accident which she obviously thought entitled her to be queen of all she surveyed. To know her was to loathe her. She was spoilt, pampered, unreasonable and spiteful.

Was she jealous of Roxana Felix?

Absolutely.

Megan grabbed her favourite white cotton Gap shirt from her closet. A classic white shirt was the best choice for shopping – a plain background you couldn't go wrong with. She would be able to try out hundreds of different looks with this shirt. And a good white shirt, teamed with a pair of designer jeans and calf-length cowboy boots, could walk unembarrassed into the most exclusive store on Melrose or Rodeo Drive. And that was where she was headed.

Megan knew she'd never forget the image of Roxana, silken hair flowing round her tanned shoulders, gold lamé mini-dress clinging to her curveless, ultra-slim frame, leaning towards her in that viewing booth and cooing that she and Zach had discussed dedicating that song to Megan, that they felt they'd been a little hard on her . . .

Rage and disappointment had hit her with the force of a fist in the stomach. She had been so sure that Zach was finally talking to her, looking at her, communicating with her. He'd let her criticize him, he'd been kind and gracious and he'd got up on that stage and sung like God, and when he looked at her and smiled, Megan had felt, for just a few precious seconds, that Zach was everything she had always admired and that – God, how ridiculous – he was interested in her. Even though she wasn't a model, or a star, or a rich Beverly Hills babe like Jordan Goldman.

Another dumb illusion.

Well, Roxana had put paid to that. And it wasn't merely the fact that Zach was with Roxana that infuriated Megan. The fact was that every single guy backstage had been mesmerized by her, paying homage as though the bitch was the Queen of Sheba. *Including* her David. And if that was to be expected, Megan also recalled that the other women – the blonde bimbos, the groomed, polished trophy wives, the sexy female reporters in their elegant little Chanel numbers – had got their fair share of attention too, while she, the earnest, idealistic X-er in her T-shirt and jeans, with her loose brown hair and no make-up, had been completely ignored.

Zach had snubbed her. David hadn't even seen she was there, not at first. And none of the other guys in the place had so much as glanced in her direction.

David had paid her a compliment, true, but then David was her agent, as well as her friend. And he was obviously just being kind, because when he'd got her into his Lamborghini on her own, he hadn't so much as tried to kiss her – just dropped her off at the apartment with his usual pleasant goodnight peck.

Goddamnit! Megan thought, getting angry. I want more than that!

She knew what she was about to do was selling out. She knew this was the kind of status-seeking bullshit that she had despised in San Francisco . . . but that was too bad.

Megan Silver was just sick and tired of being invisible.

Jordan Cabot Goldman stepped carefully out of her limousine, trying not to scuff her Versace mauve silk pumps on the New York sidewalk. She shivered. God, she hated Manhattan. It was so bitterly cold in autumn, so unbearably hot in summer, and crammed full of people who seemed obsessed with work.

'May I carry your bags for you, madam?' a Victrix porter enquired, rushing forward from the lobby to assist her.

Jordan shook her head, girlish blonde hair flying about in the early-morning breeze. 'No, thank you,' she said. 'I'm not staying. I've come to collect my husband.' She smiled brilliantly. 'It's a surprise.'

Megan hit the town with a vengeance. She had a gold American Express card, a BMW with an empty trunk, and a ferocious hunger.

She was fed up with waiting for David to notice her. She'd lost weight, toned her muscles and learned to survive as a Hollywood screenwriter, but she still couldn't get him to do anything more than flirt with her. That, Megan told herself, was going to change. Today.

The first stop on her list was Fred Hayman. Then Frederick's of Hollywood, where she bought the most outrageous teddy in crimson lace, cut high on the thigh and plunging at the neck, a sexy, sinful scrap of scarlet nothingness that made her gasp when she saw it in the mirror. Then she headed to Melrose and the boutiques, and shopped steadily for four hours, refusing to look at the price of anything, just picking up the receipts to check later, after it was too late to back out. She got a *prêt-à-porter* Chanel suit in bold purple wool, with satin pumps to match; a minute Azzedine Alaia clinging dress in black stretch Lycra; a vermilion satin-knit skirt and flowing tunic top by Richard Tyler; an Anne Klein pantsuit in the softest butterscotch cashmere; ten different Ralph Lauren shirts; a halter-necked, bias-cut gown in bronze satin by Isaac Mizrahi, and suits in pink, dark green and turquoise wool by Dior, Saint-Laurent and Anna Sui.

'Oh, ma'am, you look *divine*!' one of the salesgirls squealed when she emerged from the changing alcove in the turquoise Anna Sui. 'That cut is so *you.* But wouldn't you rather try it in the red? Turquoise isn't the best colour for a brunette.'

Megan shook her head, a little grandly. 'Turquoise will be fine,' she said.

'Yes, ma'am,' the girl agreed, flustered, not wanting to upset a customer with so many glossy carrier bags.

After all, Megan added silently, *I'm not going to be a brunette for long.*

Once all her major outfits had been carefully packed away in the back of her car, Megan spent her lunch hour shopping for accessories. Court shoes from Kurt Geiger, two pairs of Manolo Blahnik heels, and trendy stacked sandals by Patrick Cox. A scarf from Hermès. A Gucci belt. A signature purse in cream silk from Chanel with matching kid gloves. And a bottle of Joy perfume to complete it all.

Megan tipped the girl who carried her new bags to the car twenty bucks and didn't thank her. If Beverly Hills bitch was what she had to be, Beverly Hills bitch it was. Rich, ostentatious, and don't talk to the help.

She had used David's name to get herself squeezed in at the Ivy for lunch. It was another glorious, sunny Los Angeles day. Megan admired the way the light sparkled on her water glass, and tried to calm her growling stomach with honeydew melon and a Caesar salad. For a second she longed wistfully for the char-grilled burgers she and Dec used to barbecue out in their yard on Haight, in the summer, when they had the guys round and everyone would drink cheap beer, and they'd put on a Green River CD and talk about God and sex and death and whatever else, or watch *Married, With Children* reruns. But she shoved that thought to one side. In San Francisco, she had been nothing. In Los Angeles, she was going to be a someone, and surely no self-respecting woman out here permitted so much as an ounce of spare fat on her cellulite-free thighs. Burgers and beer were out; salads and mineral water were in.

Megan made it to Le Printemps at two p.m. exactly. It had taken her a week to get an appointment with Jacques Roissy, the chief stylist, but she was certain it would be worth the wait: Le Printemps was the most exclusive, newest beauty parlour in the city, boasting a range of anti-age preparations and UV filter products that had older women panting, and a team of hairdressers, overpaid refugees from Vidal Sassoon and John Frieda in London, that had taken the town by storm. In Hollywood, where beauty vies with fame as the local religion of choice, Jacques Roissy had already acquired his own cult, with all the worshippers drawn from the richest, most privileged echelons of West Coast females.

Megan knew she didn't need the anti-wrinkle creams right now, but her hair could sure do with an overhaul, and she knew she had come to the right place. Face it – anything *this* expensive had to be good.

Le Printemps was tucked away on La Brea, behind discreet wrought-iron gates. Megan was greeted by a white-coated receptionist and her credit-card details taken while her car was driven away to be valet-parked. Moments later, when she had only just sat down with the latest Paris *Vogue* and a fat-free cappuccino, a short, plump man with slicked-back red hair and a huge diamond pinky ring burst into the lobby and swooped down on her, kissing noisily at the air on either side of her cheeks.

'*Mademoiselle Silver, n'est-ce pas? Mais qu'elle est belle! Comment ça va?*' he trilled.

'*Ça va très bien, merci,*' stammered Megan, hoping she wasn't going to have to rely on her eighth-grade French for the entire afternoon. '*Et vous?*'

'*Mon Dieu! Une française!*' the apparition squealed, delighted. '*Mais il faut parler anglais, ici, non?* We are enchanted to see you 'ere, mademoiselle. Already you are very pretty, yes? But not chic. We make you *très* chic. You will not recognize yourself.' He paused to draw breath, and Megan stood up, wondering exactly what she'd let herself in for. A second white-robed flunkey appeared with a blue cotton gown, and Megan tied it round herself as Jacques opened the door to the Printemps inner sanctum. She had a glimpse of a minimalist fantasy palace, the beauty parlour decked out in Japanese prints, chrome and dark wood. Expensive-smelling fragrances drifted towards her: jasmine, sandalwood, mimosa, attar-of-roses.

'*Ma chérie,*' Jacques enthused, linking his plump arm through her slender one, 'we are about to make you into a new woman.'

Megan thought about Roxana Felix, sashaying into the backstage hospitality area with her shimmering dress, her glossy raven hair and her million-dollar smile, and David and Zach just melting at her feet.

Firmly, she quashed her misgivings. 'That's what I'm here for,' she said.

Eleanor checked herself out in the bathroom mirror again and tried not to worry. Maybe Tom was still asleep. Or maybe he was ordering breakfast for the two of them, something romantic, like strawberries and croissants and champagne. Just because he hadn't rung through to her room yet, hadn't knocked on her door, didn't mean anything was wrong.

Her reflection stared back at her, immaculate and charming in a new suit, a smart navy Jill Sander with a white trim around the collar and cuffs. She had packed black Stephane Kelian heels to go with it, and her make-up was a fresh mixture of apricot eyes and rose lips and cheeks. Earlier, when she was feeling lighthearted, almost dizzy with happiness, Eleanor had actually put on some jewellery – two discreet sapphire drop earrings, which now sparkled attractively under her neatly brushed hair. Her small Gucci overnight case was packed and ready to go.

She had been ready to go for twenty minutes.

Tom couldn't be regretting it, could he? Eleanor wondered, the thought clenching a tight fist of panic round her heart. He'd been so tender, so passionate ... everything about last night had felt right, proper, good. She had loved Tom distantly for so long, fantasized hopelessly about him for so many years, and last night had been all she had dreamed of and more. He had taken her to a place she didn't know existed, he had changed her life forever, Eleanor knew that now. She felt more of a female, more of a woman, than she had ever done before. And she would never see the sexual act the same way again – as a mildly pleasant activity for women, something the entire world overrated in one big conspiracy, pretending it was the best thing since sliced bread, when most girls she knew would prefer a good back-rub, if they were honest. Last night with Tom had cured her of that idea for good. Eleanor could feel the echoes of that white-hot release inside her still, suddenly realized what the sexologists meant when they said that a woman reaches her sexual peak in her late thirties and early forties.

Maybe that was the difference between having sex and making love.

Last night was the first time that she had ever truly made love.

Tom *must* have felt it too, he *must* have done. It was too intense to miss. Surely there was no way he wouldn't have been touched by what had happened between them, by what he had caused to happen between them . . .

Eleanor wondered what would happen now. She had tried to put off this question, but she couldn't hide it forever. Would Tom get a divorce? He must, surely, love her . . . didn't last night prove that? And as for herself, she had been trembling on the brink of commitment to Paul, trying to talk herself into conceiving a child by Paul, but that was over now. She had to be with Tom. She couldn't settle, not any more.

The phone by her bedside purred.

Joyfully Eleanor spun away from the mirror and sprinted into the bedroom, scolding herself – this was no way for a thirty-eight-year-old woman to behave – and dived on the receiver.

'Yes?' she said.

'Eleanor?'

It was Tom. Her heart flipped over in her chest.

'Hey,' she said softly. 'I thought you'd never ask.'

There was a brief, uncomfortable pause.

'If you're ready, why don't you meet me in the lobby?' Goldman said stiffly. 'I have a car waiting to take us to the airport.'

The air seemed to freeze around her. Time pooled and stopped, and a terrible, clammy fear gripped her throat.

She knew Tom Goldman backwards, knew his every subtle nuance of tone and gesture and expression. And this was Tom at his most businesslike, his most impersonal.

He thought last night was a mistake. He wanted her to pretend it never happened.

Tears of shock and disbelief prickled in Eleanor Marshall's eyes.

'Eleanor, are you there?' Goldman asked.

She took a deep breath, composing herself, and then replied. 'Yes, Tom, of course. I'll be right down. If we're lucky, maybe we can catch the eight-thirty flight – that would give me a couple of extra hours with Megan Silver.'

'OK,' Tom said, and hung up.

Eleanor grabbed her case and her room key and walked straight out to the elevators, moving as fast as she could, trying not to give herself time to think. That was a luxury she could not afford. That would be fatal.

In the elevator car she counted each floor as it hissed smoothly downwards, recited couplets from Shakespeare, anything to stop herself from thinking about Tom and what he'd done yesterday. She realized with a sick crunch of despair that she was never going to get in an elevator again without imagining Tom, and yesterday, and last night.

Mercifully quickly they reached the ground floor, and Eleanor crossed over to reception to check out. As soon as she had signed off on the form she turned left and walked into the lobby, looking for Tom.

She found him right away.

Goldman was standing by a huge black leather sofa, dressed in a nondescript grey suit, and looking awkward and guilty ... and ... happy? And with a start of absolute disbelief Eleanor saw that Jordan was standing next to him, dressed in a fussy purple pantsuit, one hand firmly clasping her husband's.

Eleanor's mouth dropped open before she could pull herself together, but recovering at lightning speed she walked up to them.

'Jordan! This is a surprise,' she managed. 'I thought you were back in LA.'

'Oh I *was*,' Jordan squeaked, her face a mask of childish delight, 'but I caught a real late flight last night and got over here first thing in the morning. I wanted to meet Tom here and surprise him in person.' She turned coquettishly to her husband.

'Can we tell Eleanor, honey? I wanted you to be the first to hear it, but now ...'

'Yeah,' Goldman said, not meeting Eleanor's eyes. He looked away, subdued, embarrassed. 'Go ahead.'

'Eleanor, I just know you and Paul will be *sooo* happy for us,' Jordan cooed, squeezing Tom's hand ostentatiously. 'It's so fabulous! Isn't it, sweetheart? We're going to have a baby!'

22

Roxana Felix and David Tauber sat together at a corner table in the small, elegant dining room of Lutece, eating lunch. Nothing about David Tauber's manner proclaimed himself to be excited about this: he ordered comfortably, he ate slowly, and he never so much as glanced at another table. But inside, he was thrilled. The hum of discreet conversation all around him had the music of money rippling through it; this restaurant was where Wall Street mixed with Hollywood and flirted with the Social Register, and normally he would have had to wait weeks for a table. Sam Kendrick might have been able to breeze in here, but not him. Not yet. But add a forty-million-dollar supermodel to the equation, and it was a different story.

Reservations had fallen over themselves to accommodate him. The maitre d' had rushed to seat them as prominently as possible. And David Tauber had the very pleasant sensation of knowing that here, in one of New York's most exalted meeting places, the great and powerful were ogling *his* table, and not the other way round.

Word of this lunch would leak out, he knew. It would send shockwaves of fear through the fat little fucks at Unique, Roxana's model agency. And it would be another feather in his personal cap – since he'd signed her, Roxana had been dealing more through Sam Kendrick than through him. For some reason. Well, obviously that was all about to change.

'Won't you have a little more champagne, Roxana?' he asked solicitously, extending the bottle of vintage Tattinger towards her.

'Not for me.' Ms Felix shook her lovely head. 'I have to watch my figure.'

Tauber laughed, and Roxana smiled encouragingly at him.

The two of us are so alike, he thought. She'll stop at nothing to get what she wants. She's already demonstrated that beyond doubt. My God, I remember when I didn't even think I could persuade Artemis to look at the bitch's test. And she sees herself in me. She knows I can be useful to her. Face it, she didn't call me out here for the pleasure of my company.

'Your figure is beyond perfect, Roxana. Just like the rest of you,' David purred. 'And I bet your photographers out here are saying exactly the same thing.' He shrugged boyishly. 'We poor movie-business types have to hope the Jackson people will let you go in time for a few rehearsals.'

'I'll go when I feel like it,' Roxana said.

'Of course.' He was all deference.

'And I didn't ask you here to discuss my figure.'

David leaned forward. 'You know your wish is my command, Roxana.'

Roxana Felix regarded her agent through faintly narrowed lids. Hmm. He was good, no denying it. He'd dressed appropriately – Hugo Boss suit in dark charcoal wool, Turnball & Asser paisley tie, no embarrassingly loose Angeleno style. And he hadn't so much as looked away from her once.

See the Lights was about to go into rehearsals. One week of those, and they were on location in the Seychelles. That was when the fun would start.

Once she was on camera, she would be impossibly expensive to replace. She wouldn't have to take any more crap from that prissy bitch Eleanor Marshall and her mousy little screenwriter protégée.

It was going to be good. Establishing herself as a true star would be her first priority, but revenge would be number two on the list. Payback time. For every one of them that had insulted, snubbed or thwarted her.

Zach Mason. Eleanor Marshall. Sam Kendrick. They all had it coming.

But Megan Silver, the dumpy little nothing, Megan Silver who had flat-out turned down her requests to have her meagre part beefed up, Megan Silver, who had deliberately attracted Zach when she, Roxana, wanted him – Megan was going to pay the most dearly.

This was going to need delicate handling, though. And that was why she had summoned Tauber to New York. Because Roxana had some serious plans, and they went beyond just getting a few people fired.

She'd learned some valuable lessons during her time in LA. Dear God, she hadn't been screwing Howard Thorn for nothing. She was going to get more than real fame out of this movie: by the time she'd finished, she would've shifted the goddamn power balance, at Artemis, at SKI, and socially.

Those pathetic sun-dried assholes had thought they could patronize her!

Roxana's fingers tightened imperceptibly round the stem of her champagne flute. Even David Tauber thought he was using her. Did he truly believe that she could be manipulated with some decent pecs and a cosmetically whitened smile?

'Have you seen a lot of Megan lately, David?' she asked sweetly. 'Such a nice girl. I always hoped you two would get together.'

David nodded. So that was it. His orders from the Electric City concert had been confirmed: take Megan out of the picture, so I can concentrate on Zach.

'I haven't been round to Megan's since the concert,' he said, 'but I've been meaning to see a lot more of her.'

'Good.' His mistress was pleased. She shifted on her chair, displaying that magnificent body for him as it slithered luxuriously around under her amethyst silk Donna Karan slip dress.

'How *is* Zach?' David added. Let her know he was calling his marker. After all, like the old Mafia guy said – I don't do favours, I collect debts.

'Just wonderful,' Roxana purred. 'I'm sure he's as happy with you as I am, David. I'm sure he'll be boasting about being one of your discoveries in as many interviews as I shall. After all, Zach, Megan, me – *See the Lights* is really *your* movie, isn't it?'

David Tauber felt the warmth wash right through his body, with a swift jolt of adrenalin following in its wake. Great. She was going to play with him.

She would repay him. A few well-placed comments with the trades and his star would be shooting up faster than ever.

He'd have Kevin Scott fired.

He'd walk out of SKI.

With Roxana and Zach hitched to his wagon there was no limit, Tauber realized. He suppressed an urge to clench his fists. *No limit at all.* He wouldn't have to try to impress Sam Kendrick any more – he could *be* Sam Kendrick.

Forget about money. Forget about coke. Forget about sex. *Power*, power was the only drug, and power was what Roxana Felix was offering him.

'It's good of you to say so,' he replied.

'Oh, but I *do* say so.' Roxana speared a forkful of lettuce. 'And if you ask me, David darling, you should be exercising a little bit more control over it.'

'More control?' Tauber looked blank. 'How could I do that?'

The supermodel looked at her agent, a tiny half-smile playing across her blood-red lips. 'David, you don't really know Jake Keller, do you? He's the number two to Eleanor Marshall over at Artemis. He has some interesting ideas about this movie . . . I think you two would get on just fine. Perhaps I should arrange for you to play a little tennis?'

For a second Tauber sat there, frozen, his mind racing at a million miles an hour. Jesus fucking Christ. What was the bitch proposing? A conspiracy? Was she out to get Eleanor Marshall? Who did she have in her pocket? And could he risk it? Because if you weren't with Roxana Felix, you were against her.

He was only treading water at SKI anyway – and he'd always hated the idea of women running studios. They shouldn't run anything except errands.

'What a good idea,' Tauber said smoothly. 'I could do with some work on my backhand.'

Flowers. They were everywhere she looked: huge, vulgar, ostentatious bunches of them, baskets stuffed full of them, wreaths and pot plants and every variety known to man. Every designer florist in Beverly Hills must be laughing their heads off, Eleanor thought bitterly. She couldn't walk into the Artemis executive offices without being overpowered by a wash of different fragrances, assaulted by an ice-cream medley of colours; hyacinth, irises, jasmine, tiger-lilies, snowdrops – where the hell had Isabelle Kendrick found *snowdrops* in July? – and piles and piles of roses. Peonies and poppies were stacked next to orange blossom and orchids on every secretary's desk. Some of the arrangements were in cutesy shapes – a teddy bear of white chrysanthemums, a stork made entirely of cornflowers. Many of them were colour-themed in pastel pinks and blues.

Jesus, but this town was tacky when you thought about it.

Eleanor tried to ignore the living gauntlet that she had to run on the way into her own office, the one space in the building mercifully free from greenery. On the second day after word of Jordan's pregnancy had leaked out, the overflow of blossoming tributes had gotten too much for Tom's secretary, who'd innocently enquired if Eleanor would care for some pale pink tulips or light blue roses, only to be told frostily that the president suffered from hayfever. A manifest lie, Eleanor knew, but what could they do about it? She wouldn't take any of Tom's goddamn flowers. She was still president here. That was one thing she could rely on.

Eleanor sat in the spartan, businesslike fortress of her office and bent her head, examining the latest projections for *Looking Good*, the Artemis comedy that had opened the week before. The figures were creditable, but Eleanor didn't see them. They swam before her eyes, meaningless, unimportant.

Oh, dear God. All she could feel was the pain. It occupied her thoughts one hundred per cent of the time, drumming its agony deeper inside her with every pulse of her broken heart. Her skin was sallow from lack of sleep. Her eyes had dark shadows under them, and she was losing weight rapidly as her appetite slowed and died. How she got through each day was a mystery to her. How she had managed the journey down from JFK to LAX, with Jordan sitting in the seat beside her, babbling excitedly on for the whole five hours, she could not even remember.

Eleanor knew she was still well dressed, even if she no longer bothered with make-up. After all, clothes were a form of armour. And she got through meetings with no perceptible loss of control; the words flowed smoothly enough.

But behind her cool gaze Eleanor Marshall was a zombie, going through the motions. Years of businesslike behaviour had provided her with an automatic pilot, and she was just coasting along, utterly out of control.

The Panasonic on her desk buzzed.

'Yes, Mariah?'

'Mr Keller on line one,' her assistant chirped.

'Thank you,' Eleanor said, hitting the button. 'Jake.'

Her deputy's voice was brisk and calm, no hostility to it at all. 'Eleanor, I've got some more *See the Lights* budget items for you to sign off on, and a few location ideas. Is it OK if I come over and run 'em by you?'

'Thanks, Jake,' Eleanor said listlessly. 'That would be great. Why don't you bring them across now?'

A week ago she would have told him to wait until she was through with what she was working on. But who cared? Now was as good a time as any. Jake was suddenly cooperative, running off sheet after sheet of budget plans, production expenses, location arrangements. She'd thought all that stuff had been sorted out, but apparently it needed changing. Fine. Keller could change what he wanted . . . what did it matter? Minor alterations. Small adjustments. Whatever.

Two minutes later Jake Keller was in his immediate boss's office, clutching a revised set of forecasts and some new site decisions. The significant changes were buried in the middle of the third page, in a couple of clauses it had taken him all of last night to work out. They weren't hidden, though – they were clearly laid out, in language nobody could fail to understand. That was the way it had to be. If she signed these documents, the responsibility for them had to be hers – clearly, and without room for doubt.

Keller advanced towards Eleanor, holding the memos out to her. His heart was beating in a nervous samba, but he was sure it didn't show. And if it did, would Eleanor pick up on it? Would she notice *anything*?

Not in this state. He had to bet on that. She looked like shit, she looked really ill. Her cool blonde head had been someplace else all this week, and Jake Keller was not a man to let an opportunity like this pass him by. He'd had the ultra-intelligent Ms Marshall signing off on proposals an intern would have objected to. Signing off on the presidency, he hoped. But these were the big two, two simple, unrectifiable errors that he was praying would get her approval, right on the dotted line.

'Sorry to keep bothering you with this stuff, but it's best we get it right,' Keller said, watching the president's eye skim over the first page of close print. Keep her talking, keep her involved, make her trust you. 'Don't you think so?'

'Sure,' Eleanor said blankly, turning to the second page.

Keller felt the roof of his mouth dry up. She *was* reading it. Was she taking it in? 'Are you planning to go out on location yourself?'

'Maybe. I don't know.'

She turned to the third page.

'I'm glad somebody's doing some work around here,' Keller ploughed on, desperately. 'With all these delivery guys coming and going for Tom and Jordan, you'd think it was the first time anyone had ever conceived.'

He was unprepared for the effect of his remark. Eleanor's face drained of blood as though someone had slapped her. She stopped examining the document, and reached for her pen.

With a dazzling burst of comprehension, Jake Keller suddenly realized what the hell was going on. Mentally he kicked himself for not having sensed it before. Of *course*! All that jumping apart whenever he'd walked in on the two of them . . .

Oh, this was just great. His shark's nose had done more than scent blood in the water. Eleanor Marshall was badly wounded, a prey just waiting for a predator like himself to come along and restore the natural order. After all, this job should have been his in the first place, Keller thought. That Roxana Felix was a bright woman.

As he watched the Ice Queen sign her own death warrant, Jake Keller couldn't resist one final, delicious cruelty.

'Thanks,' he said pleasantly as he took the papers from her. 'That's great. You know, it's kind of sweet, about this baby stuff, don't you think?'

'Certainly,' Eleanor managed, forcing herself to meet her vice-president's eyes.

Jake Keller looked at her impassively. 'In all the time I've known him, I don't think I've ever seen Tom happier,' he said.

Then he gave her a friendly smile, turned on his heels and left.

Megan stepped smartly out of her BMW and tossed the keys to the parking lot attendant, usually a little smug and supercilious in his silver and grey Artemis uniform.

'Park it out back,' she snapped. 'And make sure it's somewhere close to the exit. I may be leaving early today.'

He gaped at her, did a double-take, then a triple-take. Megan could see the doubt forming in his eyes – could that *really* be Megan Silver? – and some of the icy block of nerves sitting in the pit of her stomach thawed a little.

Today was the first day of preliminary rehearsals. There'd be one week of them in LA, involving just Zach, Roxana and a few of the main supporting actors, and then the cast and crew would ship out to the Seychelles, to start the first part of filming on location. David had told her she had to be available, to tinker with the script as and when it needed it, and according to him, once they started shooting that would be pretty much all the time.

It would be the first day since the movie had been green-lighted that she wasn't actually supposed to work. It would also be the first time she'd meet most of the cast. Not to mention Fred Florescu, the most influential director of his generation, and her new boss. The prospect thrilled and terrified her all at once. She'd seen all Florescu's movies; they were stylish and successful, and people spoke of the guy as the 'new Spielberg'. *Light Falling*, his last picture, had made over a hundred and fifty million dollars – almost clean profit, since Florescu had shot it on a shoestring budget.

See the Lights would not have a shoestring budget – her exotic plot had made sure of that – but Megan hoped Mr Florescu would think that it had almost as good a script.

Recovering from his hesitation, the Artemis valet said 'Yes, ma'am,' to her, touching his cap as he did so, and opened her car door.

Oh yes, Megan thought dryly as she walked over to the soundstage where they were all supposed to meet up. That would be another first for the day. Everybody was going to get to see the new her.

She glanced down at herself as she walked. Well, it was certainly different. And from now on she'd be packing an attitude to match. Maybe she couldn't compete with Roxana Felix, but she'd at least give the slut something to think about.

The rehearsal group was unmistakable – even from a couple of hundred yards away Megan could hear the excited babble, see the studio production executives, low-level flunkeys, reporting to that scum Jake Keller, scurrying around like the sycophantic toadies they were. Her walk slowed as she got closer, giving her a little more time to take in the scene. There was David, looking beautifully groomed in some light brown Armani suit. He was standing next to a young guy with long black hair, jeans and a Nirvana T-shirt; it couldn't be Florescu? It was. Wow. And Zach, in a Metallica shirt and jeans, looking over at Florescu with respect on his face.

Megan snorted. Check it out. Zach Mason respects *something*! Well, once he's got the measure of you like I did, it won't go two ways, you pathetic fake.

And Roxana. No more than normally exquisite today: some kind of demure pantsuit in ice-blue silk, navy pumps and a pair of wraparound shades. Sitting next to Zach. Of course. But you're not gonna faze me, you bitch, not today.

There were the other cast members, and Megan couldn't suppress a slight blush. She'd never seen so many famous faces in one place together – Mary Holmes, Jack Richards, Robert Finn, Seth Weiss. But she pulled herself swiftly together. They were all here because *she'd* written them suitable parts

... the old Megan might have been overwhelmed, she told herself intently, but the new one wasn't going to bat a professionally made-up eyelid.

Megan strode up to them, swinging her hips as she moved, working it all the way.

'Hi, guys,' she said coolly. 'Sorry I'm a little late. The freeway was solid for miles.' Megan paused, drinking in the shock on the faces that already knew her. 'David, why don't you introduce me? I hardly know *anyone*, and that can't be right.'

'Megan?' Zach Mason asked.

'Megan?' David Tauber gasped.

'Who else?' she shrugged.

Tauber couldn't believe what he was seeing. Megan had disappeared – the old mousy, shy, invisible little Megan with her nondescript brown hair, T-shirts and long skirts. In her place was a tall, slender woman, toned, tanned flesh bared to the world. Long, lean legs stretched up indecently from outrageous stacked heels, ending only in a thigh-high Azzedine Alaïa mini-dress of clinging black Lycra, a creation that left nothing whatsoever to the imagination – and certainly not the high, rounded cheeks of her ass or the sizable proportions of her breasts, made to look even larger than normal in a balconette Ultrabra. It was as though she was flinging those curves in Roxana's face. And the surprise didn't stop there. Megan had a Gucci belt knotted loosely around her newly wasplike waist and a Piaget watch on her left wrist. The long, gentle brown curls had gone and in their place was a sleek, geometric Louise Brooks-style bob, except that Louise Brooks had never had hair so dazzlingly platinum blonde that she made Marilyn Monroe look like a brunette. And the usually naked face had been painstakingly made up, with an expensive-looking foundation, heavy bronze blusher, dark green eyeshadow melting into a dramatic plum shade swept under the brow, and full, shiny lips, lined and glossed into a wet scarlet bow.

She looked rawly sexual. Demanding attention, Megan had revealed her new, desirable body in a way that could only be called exhibitionist. And there was something more than the hair and the dowdiness that she had cast off. David had been prepared to start screwing Megan anyway – not a wholly disagreeable prospect – at Roxana Felix's orders. But now it would be a definite pleasure. The new Megan Silver was something David recognized, something he could deal with. Like Gloria Ramirez, Megan Silver was tough. Like him. Like Roxana. Like that ambitious teenager he'd fucked last week.

Megan Silver was no longer the little idealist.

She was *hard*.

'Megan, you look terrific,' David said, feeling the beginnings of an erection. 'Don't you think so, Roxana?'

'Very dramatic, dear,' Roxana Felix commented icily, in a backhanded compliment that delighted her. And as Tauber started to introduce her to Fred Florescu and the rest of the cast, Megan was aware of the unfamiliar sensation of being ogled, of men's eyes roaming across her body, of being an object of desire. Every guy in the group had to be staring at her!

Every guy but one. As she finished shaking hands with the last supporting star, Megan glanced furtively at Zach Mason.

He hadn't taken his eyes off her either, and as soon as she looked at him Zach's gaze met hers.

It was filled with shock, disgust and contempt.

Fuck you, Megan thought furiously, and turned back to David, whose eyes were roaming her with new hunger, the hunger she'd longed to see there since the day she first met him. *It was always David I wanted, not you.*

Zach Mason meant less than nothing to her. Right? Right.

Megan slipped her hand firmly into David Tauber's, and smiled, as brilliantly as she knew how.

She pulled up outside David's apartment at quarter of twelve, slipping the BMW sharply into his reserved parking space, making sure to show off acres of nut-brown thigh as she pressed down on the brake with her Manolo Blahnik shoes. Jesus, even her driving was a production now.

But, obviously, it was working.

'Thanks for the ride,' Tauber said, and Megan noticed both the hoarseness of his tone and the impressive bulge in his pants. She was triumphant. So it *had* turned him on!

'No problem,' she replied, as casually as she could.

'I was, uh, wondering if you'd care to come up for a coffee?' David asked her, and Megan turned to see the glitter of lust in his eyes. Unmistakable desire, and it was all for her.

How would Roxana play this?

'If I come upstairs, I'll be wanting more than coffee,' Megan said.

Tauber smiled at her, the smooth, practised smile she had longed for him to use on her for months now. Why isn't it more fulfilling? Megan asked herself, but then Tauber unclipped his seatbelt and leant over towards her, his hands finding her breasts, lightly rubbing across the tips of her nipples, his lips and tongue flickering across her mouth, and her body was responding to his skill; she pushed herself hard against his touch, all her doubts receding in a hot burst of physical need.

23

Eleanor Marshall rushed into the women's executive bathroom and flung herself into the nearest stall, her fingers fumbling in her haste to bolt it shut. The lock rattled into place just in time as she knelt forward, gasping, gripping the seat with both hands, and threw up. Wave after wave of nausea wracked through her, and she knelt there, shuddering and wretched, until it finally passed and she was left with a dry, raw throat and an empty stomach.

Eleanor flushed the vomit away and took a deep breath, trying futilely to calm herself. Then she reached into a concealed pocket in the lining of her smart beige jacket and took out the three essential items she'd taken to carrying around with her: a travel toothbrush and tube of paste, and a trial-size flask of antiseptic mouthwash.

Male chief executives react to extreme pressure with stomach ulcers, Eleanor thought wearily. Why can't I do that? It would be so much simpler . . .

She scrubbed and rinsed out her mouth right there in the stall, thanking God that there was obviously nobody around to hear her. So far all her attacks had come in the early morning, when none of the secretaries were around, but she dreaded the day the sudden terrible crunch in the pit of her stomach would hit in the middle of a meeting, or in the lunch hour, when this bathroom was always so full. Then it would be tough to hide, and the inevitable rumours would begin to fly around: Eleanor Marshall can't take the heat. Eleanor's cracking up. Eleanor's throwing her guts up every day at work . . .

Eleanor stood slowly, looking around her at the cool eggshell-blue walls with their pristine white accents, trying to compose herself before she walked back to her office. OK, that was better. She flushed again, unlocked the door and surveyed her reflection in the wall mirrors opposite: pallid as hell, but otherwise acceptable. A Ralph Lauren pantsuit in caramel wool, a crisp white Donna Karan shirt, Walter Steiger black suede pumps.

Elegant and understated as normal. Perfect dressing for Eleanor Marshall, president of Artemis Studios and emotionless control freak.

She smiled without humour. Some joke. Well, her universe was crumbling around her, but at least she was wearing the appropriate clothes.

Jordan Cabot Goldman was pregnant with her husband's child. *Tom's* child. The child of the man she loved, the man she had let herself hope for, with silent desperation, for some fifteen years, the man whom she had finally made love to and spent the most blissful night of her life with. The man whom she could never have.

It wasn't as though she could avoid the agony of that, run from it, ignore it, block it out the way an ordinary mistress might have. No, she had to be with Tom every day, witness an endless stream of congratulations every day. The flowers had eventually dried up, but that wasn't an end to it; every producer or agent who met them opened the meeting with good wishes, congratulations or, most often, father-to-father advice and jokes. Jordan herself had started to come by the office, and though Eleanor made an effort to be somewhere else when she arrived, she couldn't help but see her sometimes, her face so incredibly young and blooming with health, graciously accepting everybody's attentions, especially Tom's. That *really* hurt; watching Tom scramble to open doors for her, rush to get her a chair, refuse to allow her to lift anything heavier than a porcelain coffee cup. He treated his wife like she were the most precious thing in the world, and made of spun sugar, liable to break at any second.

And it wasn't merely the loss of Tom Goldman, rubbed in mercilessly every day like salt in an open wound. It was the idea of Jordan, twenty-four and pregnant with her first baby, a little Goldman son or daughter, with more to come. Eleanor had read somewhere that twenty-four was the average age for American women to marry, and twenty-five for the conception of their first child. So blonde-haired, blue-eyed, All-American Barbie was doing it exactly right, perhaps a little ahead of schedule, whilst she, Eleanor, was almost forty, still single, and childless.

A year ago she hadn't given a damn about that, couldn't have cared less. But Jordan's pregnancy had changed things, dragged all her background regrets howling viciously into the foreground of her mind. Now Eleanor *did* care, very much.

Her own longing for a child was amplified to obsessional proportions. She thought about it all the time, but then again, how could she do anything else? It was Jordan this, Jordan that, all day every day. Eleanor kept recalling the story of Elizabeth the First of England, how she had turned her face to the wall when told that Mary Queen of Scots had given birth to Prince James; on being asked what was the matter she had replied, 'The Queen of Scots is delivered of a fine son, and I am but barren stock.'

Barren stock ... that was exactly what Eleanor felt, every day. Barren. Empty. Lost.

It would be easier if she was one of those women, like Isabelle Kendrick, who only wanted to be married, to have children, to take a place in society's tight, inviolate ark of coupledom, that huge boat that only lets the animals in two by two. She knew she could have that, if she wanted it. Paul Halfin was right there, with his polished good looks and successful investment banking firm, holding out an engagement ring and a one-way ticket to permanent respectability. Eleanor smoothed down the soft lapels of her cashmere jacket, thinking how many other women would kill for that opportunity. She tried to be grateful. At least she had a ticket; do not pass go, do not collect two hundred dollars.

But she had never wanted to be married for the sake of it. She had wanted to marry for love, she'd wanted Tom Goldman. And she had wanted her child to be a bright, shining star, to meld her own genes with those of the best possible father, the brightest, funniest, most ambitious and intelligent and passionate man she'd ever known.

A month ago, perhaps she could have forgotten all that. Taken heed of Dr Haydn's six-month warning and wrapped things up with Paul. After all, what hope had Tom ever given her? He'd married his baby *shiksa* princess and there was an end of it . . .

Until those hints in the office, the stolen moments at Isabelle's party and that final, earth-shattering night in New York, when he had reached out to her and his touch had awoken her body and exalted her soul.

She *could* have lived with settling. But Tom had taken that away from her. In those few glorious hours he had opened life itself to her, revealed to her everything she was capable of feeling and being.

Son of a bitch, Eleanor thought, and struggled against the new tears forming in her eyes. *You made it ten times worse. You make it so incredibly painful.*

Shaking her head, she opened the bathroom door and walked quickly back to her own office. A plastic cup of thin coffee from the machine in the hall was cooling there, next to an untouched bagel she'd brought with her from home; she didn't have time to eat breakfast there these days, she'd been at the studio from half past six. It was necessary. Work was in crisis.

Funny, isn't it, Eleanor thought, the way you can get to be grateful for the weirdest things. She took a sip of the watery coffee and picked up her report on *Dog Days*, an Artemis comedy she had bought for half a million dollars that was now recommended for turnaround, a polite way of saying you didn't want to make it any more. The director was fighting with the screenwriter and three lead actors had pulled out at the last minute, leaving Eleanor with her fourth choice, if she wanted him, or the option to cancel. But Mary Truant, the director, had a pay-or-play clause in her contract which meant they would lose a further two million if Eleanor killed the picture. Yet a turkey of a movie could wind up costing a lot more than three million bucks.

Dog Days was only the latest crisis. There was that fiasco in Marketing in Southeast Asia, the one where their advertising for *Heavy Artillery*, a minor Artemis hit of last summer and the kind of action-adventure that normally did good in Asia, had been designed to read 'Rick Hammond Raises Hell', and had apparently wound up meaning 'Rick Hammond Desecrates Graves'. Not good, in a market where ancestor-worship was all the rage. They'd been staying away from that in droves. Plus, the Miramax distribution deal had gone sour at the last minute, with the other side claiming Eleanor's figures were false and misleading. She had a team of lawyers battling desperately to stop a lawsuit.

That was the story of her life right now, Eleanor thought, trying to take in the words and figures that swam before her eyes. Fighting fires. The last month had been a succession of disasters; ever since that triumphant presentation to the board in New York, it had just been one crisis after another. She had no time to manage the studio, to give it the kind of planned leadership that Tom Goldman had been banking on when he chose her for the job. Every spare moment was taken up with brainstorming a solution to the latest problem.

It was cool in her air-conditioned office, the silent fans cycling artificially chill breezes round the room, providing her with constant protection against the blazing LA autumn sun, already streaming over the lot outside, but the cool wasn't helping her concentrate. Eleanor had no idea how this had happened, and she felt helpless, as if her grip on her business had somehow slipped . . . but then it *had* slipped. Every new problem arose on matters she had already considered, budgets she had already approved, papers she'd already signed off on . . .

How could I have been so stupid? Eleanor asked herself, her forehead creasing in a frown. I'm usually so together. All this stuff is second nature to me.

She felt a renewed throb of anxiety. This was no time to be cracking up. If she wasn't careful, the shark pool would start to scent her weakness, and then it would only be a matter of time before she lost not only Tom, but her job too.

Eleanor began to make notes on *Dog Days*, her mouth set in a hard line. Well, if they were waiting for her to give up they'd be waiting a long goddamn time. She might not be able to prevent Tom Goldman from smashing her heart, but then love was something that was out of your control. That was why it was so dangerous. Artemis Studios was *in* her control, and she wasn't about to let it slip away from her, no matter how many fires she had to douse.

She had struggled all her life to get here. She wasn't about to give up now.

There was a knock on the door.

'Come in,' Eleanor called absently. 'Mariah, is that you? I need the Mary Truant contracts, and the production executive's notes on the script meetings. And I'd kill for some real coffee.'

'Would you go for just the coffee?' Tom Goldman asked gently.

Eleanor looked up, startled.

Tom walked towards her, carrying his normal paper bag. He was wearing the same black suit he'd worn to their meeting in New York, a gold Cartier watch and a Harvard tie. He looked great.

'No doughnuts,' Goldman said, unpacking two polystyrene cups of filter coffee and handing one to her carefully. He gestured towards the uneaten bagel. 'But then I see you're not hungry.'

Eleanor took the coffee without comment and put it down on her desk. 'What can I do for you?' she asked coldly.

'Eleanor – '

She didn't want to hear it, didn't want to hear anything. 'Tom, like I said, what can I do for you? Because if it isn't business it'll have to wait. I'm busy.'

Goldman looked at her for a long moment, his handsome black eyes soft with tenderness and compassion.

Eleanor felt sadness and weakness and longing well up inside her. Panicked, she felt a lump start to form at the back of her throat. Oh no, please, not kindness. Not pity, she thought. I can handle anything but that.

Almost of its own accord, her right hand fumbled to open the small top drawer at the side of her desk.

'We have to talk, Eleanor,' Goldman said.

'We talk every day,' Eleanor answered, 'about this studio.' Her fingers closed around the small velvet box which she kept there, flicked open the lid. 'And other than that we have nothing to discuss.'

'We can't pretend New York never happened,' Goldman insisted. 'Eleanor, you must believe that it meant a great deal to me – I know you're hurting, and I'm so sorry you –'

'Tom!' It ricocheted out of her. *How dare you pity me? How dare you offer me comfort?* 'As far as I'm concerned, *nothing* happened in New York. Certainly nothing that meant anything to me.' She turned on him, her eyes bright with fury. 'We both had too much to drink, and as far as I'm concerned it was an embarrassing indiscretion we'd both better forget.' Her tone was pure ice.

Tom shook his head. 'I don't believe you.'

'Believe me.' Her fingers were working behind the desk, out of sight. 'In fact, I hope you will be able to offer me some congratulations this time.'

He was confused. 'Congratulate you? Why?'

Eleanor Marshall brought her left hand out from behind the desk and held it up to him, defiantly. On the fourth finger Paul's ring sparkled brilliantly, rubies and emeralds glittering ostentatiously in the morning sun.

'Paul proposed to me this morning,' Eleanor said, pronouncing every word clearly and deliberately, 'and I accepted.' She looked hard at him, her whole body brittle with the pure flame of her anger.

'I'm getting married, Tom,' she said. 'And you know something? I can't wait.'

David sauntered into the bedroom, spritzing Chanel's L'Egoïste under his arms. He admired his magnificent body for a few seconds in Megan's wall mirror, then picked up a white towelling bathrobe and belted it around himself.

'Did you finish packing yet?' he asked.

'Not quite.' Megan tried to drag her eyes from Tauber's chest. She had to stop staring at him like that, and yet somehow she couldn't stop looking, couldn't stop checking to see if he was real. Naked, David was quite simply superb, even more muscular than she had pictured him in her fantasies. Standing there at the door to her bedroom, the white towelling throwing his golden-brown tan into sharp relief, he looked like some guy off a schoolgirl's pin-up calendar.

David was gorgeous. And didn't he know it, Megan thought, surprising herself with the sharp stab of disapproval that ran through her at that idea.

Come on, now, she lectured herself. Women spend hours in front of the mirror. Why shouldn't a man? You're operating the double standard.

'We leave tomorrow morning,' David reminded her. 'Nine a.m. flight.'

Megan patted her tickets, laid out neatly along with her passport on the bedside table. 'Air Seychelles number 3156 to Victoria, Mahé. I'm not planning on missing it, don't worry. I've got everything packed except for a couple of books.'

Her cases were stacked by the front door, ready to go; no T-shirts, just one pair of jeans, and all the designer outfits she'd bought last week, even the high heels. The new Megan would wear those to dinner in the hotel, she thought. Roxanna Felix wouldn't leave her heels behind just because she was heading for a tropical island, so neither would Megan. And if she looked longingly at her floppy Metallica T-shirt once or twice, she was just looking.

'Books? You're not gonna have time to *read*,' David said scornfully. 'Look, Megan, I told you, it's really unusual that you're the only writer on the project and really unusual that you've been allowed so much control – '

'I know, you've been a great agent, David,' she said hastily. 'I'm not going to let you down, I know I'll be working most of the time – '

'You'll be working *all* the time when you're on the set. Little things always need redoing. And if you're not working that minute, you have to watch what's going on, be ready to offer suggestions . . . you've got to stay around to be in control. Otherwise you turn into Sam Kendrick.' He laughed at his own joke.

Megan smiled dutifully back, but she didn't think that was so funny. David always seemed to be dissing Sam these days, except for when he dropped in on rehearsals himself, when David turned dutiful and respectful. Whenever Sam Kendrick had spoken to her, he'd always been helpful and kind, and Megan knew that Eleanor thought the world of Sam. And Sam had given David Tauber his first break. It wasn't pleasant to hear him getting at the guy the whole time.

Not to mention the way David was coming on strong to Mary Holmes and Robert Finn, the two main co-stars and both Sam Kendrick's personal clients, established stars for many years. If David were with another agency, she'd have said he was trying to poach them.

There was something about it she didn't like. That, and the way David suddenly seemed to be in conference with Jake Keller the whole time. Eleanor Marshall hadn't been attending rehearsals, so maybe Jake was the logical exec to be hanging around. Still . . .

Megan shook her head, swatting those thoughts aside. She'd longed for David, and now she had him. That was what was important.

'I brought you something,' he was saying. 'A going-away present.'

He walked over to the wall where his coat was hanging, fished in the pockets and drew out a small package wrapped in tissue paper.

'What is it?' Megan asked, delighted.

David threw it across to her. 'Open it and see.'

She unwrapped it, drawing out a tiny gold pendant on a filigree chain, a delicate gold star with a cursive letter 'D' set inside it.

'So you don't forget me,' Tauber said, giving her a bone-melting smile.

'Oh, David, it's lovely,' Megan said breathlessly. Nobody had ever given her anything romantic. And from what she recalled of the guys back on Haight, none of them were real big on gold necklaces.

'Here, let me put it on you.' Tauber was beside her, pushing her cardigan back from her shoulders. Megan bent her head, feeling his large hands skilfully undoing the clasp, hanging it round her neck. The metal was cool against her skin, and she reached up with one hand, touching the slender little star.

'It's beautiful,' she said.

'You're beautiful,' Tauber murmured, passing a hand through her newly shorn, chic platinum fringe. 'And you're wearing too many clothes.'

Megan pressed up against him as he unbuttoned her cardigan and tailored slacks, slipping the fabric slowly and smoothly away from her skin, stroking her lightly where every piece of cloth had been, then undoing her bra in a swift, practised movement, playing expertly with her breasts so that Megan was too aroused to wait for him to peel away her strawberry silk briefs and ripped them off herself, leaving her naked in his arms. David shrugged off the robe and pushed her back on the bed, bending his mouth to the newly flat surface of her belly, his dry lips and wet tongue trailing a line of fire across her skin.

Megan gasped with desire, feeling the blood in her nipples throbbing with a new intensity as his fingers started to tweak them, then caress them, rolling them around in a firm circular motion, sometimes leaving off so his hand could grab her whole breast and squeeze it.

'Yeah, that's right,' David said, his breath hot against the downy hairs of her belly. 'Tell me how much you love it, Megan. Tell me how much you want me.'

'Oh, God, you know I want you,' she groaned, feeling his mouth poised right above her, and then he was doing it, his lips on hers in the most intimate caress, his tongue swirling around, knowing exactly what he was doing, and she felt every objection, every reservation, evaporate into nothingness under the blinding heat shooting through her . . .

24

'Magic,' Fred Florescu said.

They were sitting together on the terrace of the Méridien Hotel, watching the sun set over the Indian Ocean. To the west, the sea past the Anse Polite beach was lapping gently at the shore, its heart illuminated down the centre by a red carpet of light, constantly shattering and re-forming, as the waves reflected the dying rays of the sun. On the fine powdery sand that would be picture-book white at daybreak, several bonfires were burning, throwing up sparks into the twilight, whilst around them the laughter of holidaymakers mixed with the shrieks of some Seychellois children, giggling and yelling to each other in the local Creole patois. To the east, the slopes of the mountains, covered in palm trees, wild cinnamon and thick vegetation, stretched up into the darkening sky behind them. Megan saw a flock of shadowy shapes wing up from the edge of one of the slopes and veer to the left in a ragged flurry of movement; whether they were birds or bats she had no idea.

'I think so,' she agreed.

'I hope you don't mind having a drink with me,' the director said, reaching over to refill her glass with the local speciality of crushed ice and lime, frosted with salt. The tartness was delicious after the sweetness of her evening meal: octopus curried in coconut milk, slices of baked breadfruit and a sorbet made of paw-paw and *jamalac*, a native pink-skinned fruit. David had insisted on grilled chicken and rice; as far as Megan could tell, his fitness regimen never wavered. But she had rebelled against his attempts to make her do the same; exotic travel might be commonplace to him, but Megan had never left the States before, and she refused to pretend she was still there.

'Of course not,' she said.

She was delighted to be drinking with Mr Florescu. Not that she'd have had a choice about it: his word was law on the set, and an invitation to drinks with him was like a command to tea with the Queen of England. You just didn't turn it down. But then who would want to? The guy was king of this movie now and one of the best directors in the world, and on the set everybody was clamouring for a piece of his time: Mary Holmes, Jack Richards, Robert Finn, Seth Weiss, and all the other actors; Tom Lilley, the Artemis production executive, a Jake Keller drone who slimed around the set taking notes all the time; David, whose most burning desire seemed to be to get close to him; Peter, Steven and Rick, his three assistant directors or ADs, who were glorified flunkies who slavishly worshipped their master's every utterance; and most of all, Roxana Felix, who had started acting like the primadonna from hell the second the first camera rolled.

David had told Megan to keep away from Fred. She was just the screenwriter, which put her only a few rungs above the catering staff, he said. Until and unless she was needed, she wasn't to bother Mr Florescu.

Megan resented his tone – she wasn't a child – but did as David said. After all, he was her agent, he knew what was best. And hanging around on the fringes of the set helped her to avoid Roxana Felix, who took every opportunity to insult and snub her, and Zach Mason, who basically gave her the odd contemptuous glance and apart from that ignored her.

'I wanted to get to know you better,' Florescu said. 'I never seem to see you around unless it's with David. Does he have to chaperone you everywhere you go?'

Megan blushed. She had been thinking the exact same thing, and now she felt horribly disloyal. After all, David was the reason she was here, sipping iced lime on a tropical island instead of serving greasy chicken wings to jerks. Right?

'He's been very good to me,' she said defensively.

'He's very good to all his clients,' Florescu snorted. 'You wrote a great script, plus you look great. All it would have taken was for one agent to read your script, and you would have been signed. It was his lucky break that he got to read it first, not yours. I hope you realize that.'

Covered in confusion, Megan managed, 'He's my boyfriend.'

'Sure he is,' Fred said, sounding unconvinced, and then, seeing her flustered, added more kindly, 'David's a smart guy. So long as you're happy.'

'Oh. Yes, of course,' Megan said.

The director nodded down the beach, towards the sealed-off area where they were filming. 'We might need you there tomorrow. I'm gonna want some options for the scene where Morgan confronts the drug lords, in case Roxana tries any more dumb moves and I want to shoot around her.'

'OK, no problem,' Megan agreed immediately, her mind running through the dialogue he was talking about. It would be tough to change it without unbalancing other scenes in the film, but she was glad to have something to do.

'Roxana Felix,' Florescu commented absently, 'has one major attitude problem. She's read too many magazines. She thinks that being a lead actress means being a major bitch and throwing tantrums all the time, and she really has no idea of the work an actor does.'

Megan sipped her drink and said nothing, listening to the ocean crashing on the shore. She didn't dare say what she thought of the supermodel. Roxana was David's client, and if David found she'd been badmouthing her to the director, he'd kill her.

'Your David doesn't seem to be having much effect,' Florescu went on. 'I asked him to talk to her a few days ago, and he said he did his best, but . . .' He spread his hands in a frustrated gesture. 'If it was anybody else I'd fire her. I guess I still may.'

Megan watched as his eyes glazed over, staring into space as though seeing something in his head. 'Why don't you?' she asked. 'Because she's a supermodel?'

Fred laughed, and Megan found herself warming to him, liking his easy manner and his beard and his lack of pretentiousness.

'I could get another supermodel like *that*.' He snapped his fingers. 'Or even better, a pretty actress who'd know what to do on a set already. Or Andie MacDowell – a supermodel *and* an actress. Don't get caught up in thinking Roxana Felix is as special as she thinks she is, honey.'

Megan warmed to him even more.

'It's the way she is with Zach.' Florescu sighed, and Megan suddenly felt a chill from the cooling evening breezes. She didn't enjoy thinking about Zach, didn't like remembering the offhand way he was treating her now, either with contempt or ignoring her. So he obviously hated her new look, so what? He was dating Roxana Felix. He was an asshole. And she had David, after all.

She'd always wanted David, not Zach.

Megan told herself she didn't care.

'I've never seen a sexual chemistry like it on-screen,' Florescu went on. 'The tests, and the love scenes we've shot so far – it just blew me away. I know I could get a more professional actress, but if I can just get her to work a little nobody else would be better for this movie.'

'You'd do anything for the movie,' Megan said slowly, understanding him. 'Is that what you're saying? That if Roxana Felix is the best Morgan, you want her, no matter what?'

'Exactly.' The young director leaned towards her. 'Megan, this is *my* movie now. Every director feels that way, or they should. You wrote it and Zach's acting in it and Joe Friedman lights it, but the way it looks on the screen, the whole package together, the movie itself – that's mine. And it has to be as close to what I saw in my head when I read your script as I can get it.'

'And Roxana will get you closest?'

Florescu nodded. 'She and Zach. They set the screen on fire. People will walk out of the movie theatre and go home and make love. And when you combine that with the rock 'n' roll backdrop and your CIA plot – it's going to blow everybody away. Believe me. I know what I'm talking about.'

He gazed out at the beach for a long moment. 'I don't like having to deal with Roxana, but if that's what it takes, I have to.'

'Maybe you could call Sam,' Megan suggested.

'What?'

'Sam Kendrick. When we were having script conferences, he used to come by. Roxana dealt more with Sam than with David, mostly, even though David was her agent.'

'Really? Makes a change to have it that way around,' Florescu said dryly. 'OK, OK, he's your boyfriend, I know. Don't look like that, I was just kidding. So you think Sam might have an effect? Thanks, Megan, that's exactly the kind of break I've been praying for. I'll call him, get him out here.'

'Don't tell David I suggested it,' Megan said hastily. For some reason she had a sudden premonition that her lover might be none too pleased to see his boss on the set.

'OK. Don't worry, I'll keep quiet. Maybe I just wanted to have *my* agent around for a change. But I'll owe you one.' He grinned. 'You reckon Sam might hurt the palace coup, huh? You could be right.'

'What?' asked Megan, shrinking back.

'Oh, come on, don't play it so innocent,' Florescu said sharply, picking up a sliver of sugared papaya from the dish in front of him. Megan Silver could date whoever she wanted, but he didn't like seeing her with a class-A shark like David Tauber. 'David tries to crawl up my ass every day, hands out all these little hints about how he's out on the set taking care of his clients when Sam's back in LA sunning himself – like Sam doesn't have an agency to run. I should ask him why he isn't in Texas with Colleen McCallum, but I guess McCallum's small fry when you have Zach Mason. And he's all over Seth and Mary and Jack and Robert – bends over so far backwards for them he must be double-jointed.'

'Don't talk about David like that,' Megan said.

Fred stood up, smiling at her unrepentantly. 'Hey, whatever. It's sweet that you're so loyal. None of my girls ever are – gotta stop screwing actresses, that's a director's major occupational hazard.' He winked at her. 'So I'll see you on the set tomorrow, honey.' He turned to go, then paused and added, 'Remember what I told you about the script – *anybody* would have bought it. I would have. And one other thing – do your boyfriend a favour and tell him to keep away from Zach Mason.'

'But he's Zach's agent,' Megan protested.

Florescu shrugged. 'Zach doesn't like him. That's all I know,' he told her, and then wandered back into the hotel.

Megan sat still for a few minutes, sipping her chilled lime juice and watching the beach, the fires now bright gold against the night, the last streaks of sunlight having sunk down beneath the ocean. Behind the blazes and the cries of the native children she could see the black silhouettes of the mountains, looming up into the sky. In the darkness they somehow seemed menacing; not travel-brochure playgrounds of palm trees and orchids, but a real jungle, alive, impenetrable and dangerous.

Megan arrived on the set the next morning at eight o'clock sharp, threading her way through the heavy cables of the lights, cameras and reflector shields to where Fred Florescu was sitting, aviator shades and White Sox cap firmly in place, talking to Zach Mason. Roxana Felix stood a little apart from them, in costume, but evidently not about to step into a take. She was staring at the ground, her hair blowing softly around her face in the tropical breeze, her mouth set in a mutinous line.

Megan felt her heart sink. Just another great day at the office.

'Hey, Megan! Got a copy of the script? Great,' Florescu called. 'Come over here. We need to do something with this scene.'

'Already?' Megan asked, trying not to look at Zach. The less she had to deal with him the better. She wished that David hadn't been so determined to get through his push-ups before he followed her out here; he said he'd be right there, but she wanted him with her *now*. When she had to deal with Zach and Roxana.

She tried to call on the memories of David's body moving over hers, his tongue flicking lightly across her clitoris until she'd been lost in a succession of gentle climaxes, each one bursting across her like a stream of rainbow bubbles, and then his cock ramming into her, his rhythm steady and expert, until she'd finally exploded in a hard, final spasm. Her groin was still warm from it; they'd been in bed together less than twenty minutes ago, and her quick shower hadn't completely wiped the feeling away. Sex with David was always satisfying, always ended in at least one orgasm, which was more than she could say for Rory, back in Frisco, or indeed any other guy she'd been with. Not that there'd been many. But – maybe she was just getting greedy – it still felt like there was something missing. What exactly, Megan didn't know. Perhaps it was just too smooth ... was there such a thing as being *too* good in bed? Megan wondered, and then shook her head. No way. Now she was getting seriously deranged.

Only it sometimes felt like her arousal was almost involuntary, just a physiological response to well-practised moves. Of course she knew David *would* have practised, he wasn't a virgin. But why did it feel, after the slipperiness and the heat had passed, as though she was just the latest in a long line ... Why do I snap out of it so quickly? Megan wondered guiltily. I'm thinking about something else almost the second after I've come! Isn't that what men are supposed to do, the real jerks among them anyway, just climax and then roll over and go right to sleep? I should be thinking about David, not the script ...

'I guess so.' The director's voice snapped her out of her reverie. 'Roxana doesn't want her character to appear weak.'

'Weak?' Megan asked, bewildered. 'How is she weak? This is the scene where a bunch of cocaine smugglers are threatening her with torture!'

'Oh, look. Our resident Shakespeare has finally showed up for work,' Roxana Felix remarked acidly, sauntering across to Megan with a nasty smile. 'What's the matter, honey, you missed an alarm? Or maybe college graduates need more sleep than the rest of us non-intellectuals.' She glanced across at Zach Mason, but he refused to meet her eyes.

'I was here when I was supposed to be,' Megan muttered, flushing a deep red.

'Don't talk back to me,' Roxana said with casual insolence. 'You're just the writer and don't you forget it. A film set's not about work to rule.'

'Lay off,' Zach said, very quietly.

Roxana glanced at him, but subsided.

'It would be nice if we could work at *all*,' Fred Florescu sighed. 'Now Roxana, tell me why you think Morgan is shown as weak here.'

'I don't think she would have been captured without a fight.'

'Megan?' Fred asked.

She shrugged. They had been over this scene a thousand times back in LA and Roxana had never objected to it once.

'Morgan Meyer is a supermodel. This is towards the end of the movie, and she's just been taken hostage by fifty mercenary guerrillas armed with AK-47s. How is she going to put up a fight?'

'She could kick-box,' Roxana suggested.

'Can you kick-box?' Zach Mason demanded. His tone was sharp.

'We could use a stuntwoman.'

'I don't *have* a stuntwoman who kick-boxes,' Florescu explained with exaggerated patience, 'because the script doesn't call for one.'

'So fly one in from LA.' Roxana's almond-shaped eyes were narrow with the blind fury of somebody used to having her commands accepted without question.

'How would kick-boxing help her against fifty automatic weapons?' Megan asked reasonably. 'It doesn't make sense.'

Roxana turned on her, scarlet lips drawn back in an almost feral snarl. 'Nobody asked your opinion, bitch. *I'm* the one who has to create this role, not you. And if I want Morgan to fight, she'll fight.'

'You know what?' said Fred Florescu, looking from Roxana to a mortified Megan, seething with anger and humiliation. His tone was measured, but there was a line of steel underneath it none of them could mistake. 'I don't think this is productive. We'll work something out for Morgan in that scene, but we'll do it later. The light's real good right now, too good to waste, so . . . we're gonna shoot something else. The first approach scene to the gangsters' base.'

That was an action scene. It involved only Zach, Seth and Robert.

'OK, sweetheart?' Fred asked easily. 'I'll talk to Megan about that scene. You can relax for the morning.'

Roxana stared at him for a long moment, then pirouetted on her heel and stalked off in the direction of her trailer.

'Jesus,' the director said.

David strode up to the group. 'Hey, people,' he said pleasantly.

Zach stiffened. Megan noticed it, surprised; so Fred was right about that. But why wouldn't Zach like David? He'd chosen David. Oh, they were all children, Megan thought angrily, struggling to contain the tears of frustration that rose in a lump in the back of her throat. She'd so wanted to tell Roxana to go to hell, but she couldn't, she had to sit there and swallow every insult the bitch threw at her.

Because Roxana was the star and she was just a writer. It was true. And when she'd sold this script for two hundred and fifty thousand dollars, Megan realized, she'd thrown in her self-respect as part of the deal.

She wonderd if it was worth it.

'David, good to see you. Will you do something for me?' Florescu asked him.

'Name it,' said Tauber, smiling engagingly.

'Go back to the hotel and call SKI. I've been thinking about what you said about Sam, and maybe you're right, he should be here. So call him and ask him if he'll come out.'

'You want Sam Kendrick here?' David asked, paling slightly.

'I really think I do,' Florescu said amiably.

Megan stared at the ground.

For a split second Tauber hesitated, then he said, 'Right. Great idea,' and turned back to the hotel.

Florescu motioned to his lighting director and the technicians scuffled around the sand, moving the heavy lights into place for the new scene.

Zach walked slowly over to Megan. 'Thanks for asking her to get off my back,' she muttered.

Mason ignored her. 'What if I tell you I want this scene rewritten, Megan? Would you do it? I bet you'd jump.'

'If the director agreed with you,' she replied, staring up into his breathtaking grey eyes, hating him for the derision she saw there. 'I'm the screenwriter, I'm out here to fix problems as they arise.'

'Nice speech.' He reached out and touched the delicate gold star nestling in the hollow of her neck, fingering it. '*D*. What's that for?'

'David gave it to me,' she said defiantly.

Mason raised an eyebrow, his gaze narrowing. 'He gave you a pendant and he put his *own* initial inside it? But I guess that figures. It's a badge of ownership.'

'Fuck you,' said Megan, before she could stop herself.

Zach smiled into her eyes. 'What's the matter, lost a little control there? Well, that's still more balls than David Tauber would ever display for you. Of course, I could have you fired for that. Unlike Roxana Felix, I *am* indispensable.' He leaned forward. 'And you know what would really be amusing? When David gets back here, I could tell him to give you the news. In public. And he'd do it, Megan.'

'No he wouldn't,' Megan said.

'Oh yes he would.' Mason looked down at her, intently. 'And you know it.'

She did know it, Megan realized with a sinking feeling. It was true. David would do that if Zach ordered him to. And he probably wouldn't even think twice about it.

Suddenly she felt very cold, despite the blazing sun; cold, and totally isolated.

'Am I fired?' she asked.

'No,' Mason said. He shrugged. 'I like the way you write.'

'Zach, get over here!' Florescu roared. 'Are we making a fucking movie, or what?'

'OK, I'm coming,' Zach Mason said, and he strode off towards the Klieg lights, leaving Megan Silver standing on the beach, watching them, alone.

25

'Everything's ready,' Paul said.

Yes, Eleanor thought. I guess everything is.

The house alone was decorated to the tune of eight thousand dollars; wreaths of orange blossom trailing over every balustrade, white satin ribbons looped over all the doorways, turtledoves and nightingales in silver cages piping away merrily in every room. The reception room and the dining room had been cleared of all furniture that morning in order to make room for their guests, except for the various mahogany tables which the wedding designer had draped in ivory chiffon before weighing them down with silver dishes of sweetmeats and savoury titbits and hundreds of champagne flutes in Baccarat crystal.

Of course, the main luncheon would be served outside, on the wrought-iron tables they'd had shipped in for the event, each one covered in watered silk and bearing more vintage champagnes, a Tattinger Rosé and a superlative Cristal, nestling in individual ice buckets beside the centrepieces of rare white and pink orchids. Huge oak trestle tables were lined up for the buffet, which was as sumptuous as the most expensive caterer in Beverly Hills could come up with: pheasant, grouse, wild boar, venison, pâté à la foie gras; smoked salmon, caviar, oysters, rainbow trout; fresh truffles, wild strawberries, asparagus; anything and everything a jaded palate might possibly aspire to, with special sections for vegetarians, vegans, dieters, and anyone who might wish to keep it kosher. The puddings had a table to themselves, and they deserved it: apples formed out of delicate spun sugar; freshly made ice cream and sorbets in eighteen different flavours; hot pears in a mulled wine sauce; a warm pecan pie that had made Eleanor's stomach growl just looking at it; a chilled chocolate parfait rippled with the bitter, milk and white varieties; some light concoction made of honey and burnt almonds; an exotic fruit salad; a quivering raspberry pavlova . . . There seemed to be no end to them. And next to the desserts, a bar, with everything from freshly pressed strawberry juice to a very English bowl of ready-mixed Pimms, complete with floating slices of apple and cucumber. After the meal, their guests would have their choice of ten different flavours of filter coffee, six different flavours of decaff, espresso, cappuccino or herb tea, not to mention the twelve vintage liqueurs Paul's wine merchants had recommended. At this very moment forty waiters and waitresses were hovering among the crowd, replenishing every empty glass, endlessly circulating with tray after tray of delicious hors d'oeuvres.

And that was merely a small part of it. The actual area set for the wedding was a masterpiece of floral design: each gold-backed chair for the guests had its legs and backs wreathed in lilies, roped seamlessly to the wood with invisible threads; the canopy overhead was one solid sheet of flowers, a gorgeous scented mass of pink dog roses and white orchids, irises, clematis, jasmine and freesias, strategically designed to permit just enough space for the sunlight to filter through; and the arch under which Eleanor and Paul would stand was a single, contrasting blaze of colour, a curving loop of eight hundred red roses. And as for the cake . . .

'Thanks, Paul,' she said brightly. 'Maybe you could ask everybody to take their places now? I'll be down in just a second.'

'You got it,' he agreed. In the mirror in front of her Eleanor could see him pause, look her up and down, that familiar, satisfied smile creeping across his face. It had been there a lot recently. No more fights; he couldn't agree fast enough to everything she wanted, couldn't have been more solicitous or supportive.

I have to hand it to Paul, Eleanor told herself, he's a gracious winner.

'That dress is stunning,' Paul said.

'Thank you, sweetheart. You look wonderful too,' she replied, sounding as enthusiastic as she possibly could. And he *did* look handsome: all that toned muscle and distinguished salt-and-pepper hair packed neatly into a bespoke Savile Row suit of the finest dark wool. They would look great in all the trades and society magazines and gossip columns; the hotshot banker and the studio president, Los Angeles's latest power couple.

Oh, come on, Eleanor. This is your wedding, not your funeral. Remember?

'OK, I'll see you later. Give me about ten minutes.'

'All right,' Eleanor said.

If she had her time again, she would happily have given him ten years.

'It's so beautiful,' Linda Orenstein sighed, fussing with her train. Linda was an old friend from Yale, and one of her matrons of honour. The other one was her cousin Philippa, a happily married Boston mother of two. Eleanor had seen neither of them for years, but that somehow seemed more appropriate. To any of the women producers or agents that were her real friends, her true feelings might have shown, and that was something she just couldn't risk. And anyway, she didn't have a single female friend close enough to have confided in about Tom. That was another problem; for many years now, Tom Goldman had been her closest friend. She had never bothered to maintain a tight network of girlfriends; maybe she'd let herself be put off by the social mountaineering of the Tennis Club trophy wives, all scrambling for position in the court of Queen Isabelle and her new protégée, Crown Princess Jordan.

Too late, Eleanor realized that had been a mistake.

'It's beautiful, Eleanor, really! And the bouquet is simply *divine*,' Philippa gushed, adding enviously, 'Oh, the whole thing is so *glamorous*. And Paul looks so handsome in that tux, doesn't he, Linda?'

'He does,' Linda agreed, pulling the train straight. 'There. You're perfect.'

They all looked at their reflections: Linda and Philippa in subdued, grown-up gowns of dusty pink organza shot through with gold thread, the skirts falling to their feet where matching heels in rose silk peeped from under the hem. Their bouquets were laid to one side: small bunches of the purest white roses and lilies, gathered round with a ribbon of snowy velvet.

Eleanor Marshall stood between them, gowned, veiled and crowned like a queen. She knew she looked magnificent; the mirror told her so. There was the dress, full-skirted in a crinoline style, antique lace sweeping down over rich folds of ivory satin, her white silk slippers beneath them embroidered with silver thread. The bodice was a tight whalebone corset, which she had laced into easily enough, that pushed her breasts together and lifted them up, enhancing her already impressive cleavage and encasing it in creamy silk and lace, the front of the dress studded with seed pearls and opals that glinted in the mid-morning sun. Her ice-blonde hair was swept upwards and backwards in the Edwardian style, giving height to her forehead, and her veil of the sheerest white chiffon was pinned at the crown, ready to be thrown forward as they left the room. Behind that, fixed firmly but invisibly in place by her extremely expensive hairdresser, her train of white Prussian lace cascaded down, twelve magnificent feet of it. The whole headpiece was finished off with a startling coronet; her wedding designer had worked carefully in collaboration with the florist and the contents of Eleanor's jewel box to weave strands of pearls and diamonds in with the white roses, lilies and orchids, so that she seemed to be wearing a blossoming, sparkling crown, the diamonds glittering among the petals, catching the light with her least movement.

The make-up artist had spent two hours on Eleanor's face, and now her blue eyes glistened, her lashes were long and full, her cheekbones subtly accented with a healthy, romantic-looking glow to the skin, and her lips, lined with a natural pencil and glossed over in the smoothest apricot, seemed full and soft. Of the pallor her client had shown earlier that morning, nothing remained.

Eleanor looked beautiful. No, more than that. Breathtaking.

'Shall we go?' she said.

Jake Keller, navy-blue morning suit contrasting rather unhappily with his ginger hair and sallow skin, sipped purposefully at a crystal flute of rosé champagne, his practised eyes glancing backwards and forwards over the well-dressed throng. He wasn't totally pleased at what he saw. Every player in LA seemed to have turned out for the bitch – there was Sherry Lansing, head of Paramount and the only woman in town with power equal to Eleanor's, elegant in a tailored Armani pantsuit, chatting amiably to Steven Spielberg; David Geffen was talking to Jeff Katzenberg and Barry Diller in a corner; there was Mike Ovitz and Nora Ephron; Dawn Steel with Jeff Berg . . . Jake sidestepped to avoid a curious white peacock, one of several wandering around the lawns. The place was like a goddamn Hollywood Who's Who. Well, at least there was *one* face missing, Keller comforted himself. Sam Kendrick couldn't make it – he had an appointment on the set of a 95-

million-dollar movie, only two weeks into filming and already running into problems.

Jake smirked. He'd never liked that pushy little fuck Florescu. It would be interesting watching his reaction to the events that would start to unfold in – what? A week or so from now? And once that all got going . . .

He hoped Eleanor Marshall took a long, hard look at her Hollywood A-list crowd, because it would be a long time before she saw them again.

'Jake, would you look at that?' Melinda whispered loudly. His short, dumpy blonde wife dug him in the ribs, pointing to the wedding cake, standing six feet tall under an orange-blossom canopy of its own, its myriad tiers adorned with every kind of delicacy and ornament. 'Isn't that amazing?'

'Yeah, very nice,' he said shortly. Melinda had been trying all day to work out what this wedding had cost. It was bugging him. All this conspicuous consumption . . . what, did Eleanor Marshall want her picture in the dictionary next to 'traditional' now? He could have sworn she was depressed about Tom's baby. But this display of wealth and power – not exactly hiding her light under a bushel, was she?

Keller scanned the garden, looking for Tom Goldman. With any luck, he'd get to rub it in a little more about Roxana Felix. David Tauber's information was that things were still terrible, the arrival of Sam Kendrick notwithstanding. And Eleanor Marshall had been the one who'd insisted on casting the lovely lady . . .

'Jordan! Jordan, over here!' Melinda was simpering.

Jake turned round in time to see Goldman and his gorgeous babe of a wife bearing down on them. His chairman was wearing a dark suit and looking pensive. Maybe he was worrying about *See the Lights* – he should be. Jordan Goldman, sorry, *Cabot* Goldman, Keller corrected himself sarcastically, was somewhat overdone in a skintight cream silk mini-dress with a plunging neckline, revealing acres of glorious, firm young breasts and miles of shapely calves, tapering down to the thinnest, sexiest Manolo Blahnik strappy heels in silver leather.

Not for the first time, Keller envied his boss. Jesus, it must be fun to be able to afford a cute toy like that.

'Hello, Melinda, hello, Jacob,' Jordan twittered. 'Melinda, what a lovely suit . . .'

'Tom, good to see you,' Jake said enthusiastically.

Goldman nodded at him absently.

'Did you speak to Sam Kendrick this morning?' Keller pressed him.

'Should I have? It's Saturday.'

Get with the programme, buddy, Keller thought angrily. Listen to me, and stop staring off into the middle distance like a dope fiend.

'I thought he might be sending daily reports about the Roxana situation. It's getting worse, Tom. Thursday she disrupted an entire morning's filming and so far none of the rushes Florescu's sent me have featured her.'

'Maybe we can replace her,' Goldman said vaguely.

Jake pounced. 'Nearly a month into filming? I hardly think so. She's got a pay-or-play cause in that contract, Dave Tauber insisted on it. Smart kid, Tauber. Although we may have to anyway, the way things are going. Of course, that's Eleanor's call. After all, it was Eleanor who was so insistent on casting Roxana – I tried to dissuade her, but she wouldn't listen, and now – '

Dragging his gaze down to Jake's, Tom Goldman gave him a hard stare. 'Shut it, Keller,' he said. 'This is Eleanor Marshall's *wedding day* and you're here as her *guest*. If I hear another word from you this morning, so help me, I'll fucking fire you.'

Keller flushed and threw up his hands. 'OK, OK,' he said hastily. 'Point taken. Incredible catering, huh? She's worked wonders with this garden.'

Tom gave him a contemptuous glance and walked off.

'Tom, baby, wait!' Jordan squealed, running after him.

Jake Keller seethed with anger and humiliation.

All right, you kike son of a bitch. Don't think I'm gonna forget that. I'll finish with Madam President first – but then I'm coming for you, Tommy boy.

'Eleanor, they've struck up the music!' Linda begged, her round face creased with anxiety. 'We have to go! Can't you do that later?'

Philippa shrugged and rearranged the shimmering folds of her skirts. Eleanor had always been weird, even as a child . . . if she wanted to read faxes ten minutes before her wedding ceremony, well, that wasn't totally surprising. She thanked the good Lord that her Aunt Berengaria had died before she could see the way her daughter was behaving . . .

Reluctantly, Eleanor put down the sheaf of papers Sam Kendrick had just sent through. She'd insisted on having her bedroom fax machine switched on all morning, and today, like every day, she'd been reading the reports on *See the Lights*. It was in trouble. Roxana Felix was playing the world-class primadonna, but other things were going wrong too: lights were failing, individual scene locations had proved unworkable, the crew had unwittingly violated local government rules on working practice and shoots had been forced to shut down early . . . all minor problems, so far, but they were mounting up. And as the ranking executive on the project, Eleanor was responsible. Personally.

Still, she admitted to herself as she picked up her bouquet, a heavy, gorgeous mass of the palest pink roses entwined with trailing jasmine and honeysuckle, with a pair of golden tiger lilies threaded through its heart, there was nothing she could do today anyway. It was a Saturday. And she was getting married in a few moments' time. A psychiatrist would have a field day with her.

Working, right up until the last minute, Eleanor thought. As if that's gonna help, as if that's gonna buy me any more time . . .

This could not be delayed any longer. The strains of the string quartet were floating up to them from the packed garden, crammed full of movie business royalty. They were all waiting for her, all waiting to see her finally adopt the correct LA social procedure: a husband, children. She'd be part of a couple, which was the only thing to be in the nineties, when monogamy ruled and a baby was the chicest lifestyle accessory you could have. And chic or not chic, Eleanor had longed for a child for years, but . . .

At least she was doing it in style. That, nobody could deny. This would go down as the most lavish wedding party since her friend John had married

Gina Christiansen in the medieval Greek Orthodox chapel that had been the traditional wedding site in his family for generations ... which was nice but unspectacular, until you realized that the chapel was situated right next to Dracula's castle in the Transylvanian Alps. She and two hundred Angeleno guests had all flown out for five days of intense celebrations crowned with a reception in the ex-dictator Ceaucescu's summer palace. Probably not something she could have topped, but today they'd come close. Eleanor hoped Gina and John were having a good time out there. Certainly from the windows it looked as though everybody else was. And that was the idea ... grace under pressure! She, Eleanor Marshall, was not about to lie down and die like a beaten dog. If Tom was happy fathering children on his little bimbo, her heart might be ripped asunder, but not one of the circling vultures was going to realize it. That much she had sworn. And she would have her child, even if its father was not the one her body longed for. Once it arrived, once she held it in her arms, Eleanor knew she would love it, because even if Paul and not Tom had begotten it, *she* would be its mother. And once she got married, here, now, with enough pomp and circumstance for a European princess, she would never again have to endure Isabelle Kendrick's sly whispers, Jordan Goldman's public possessiveness, Jake Keller's subtle digs about Tom. Nobody would ever pity her in that way again. On the contrary, everybody who heard about this little shebang would assume that Eleanor was the happiest woman in the world, and that was exactly the way she wanted it.

A final glance in the mirror reassured her about her looks. Superb. Sensational. Stunning. Well, God knew she had paid enough to guarantee it. She wanted to be sure that Jordan Goldman looked at her today with envy, and not pity. She wanted to be sure that Tom Goldman was blown away; she wanted him to see what he had lost; she wanted him to think that she took Paul Halfin's ring with a joyful heart; she wanted him to *hurt.*

But it was kind of sick. She had spent sixty thousand dollars on this wedding, and not one cent of that had been used to impress her bridegroom. No, this was all about business; all about pride; and all about Tom.

'OK, ladies,' Eleanor Marshall said. 'Do you want to get the train? Let's go.'

Her matrons of honour fussed happily around behind her, picked up the long, beautiful sweep of antique lace, and followed Eleanor down the stairs and out into the garden, emerging into the bright sunlight just as the musicians' melody segued into the first familiar notes of the wedding march.

The guests on their seats all turned round, as one, and Eleanor, through the faint haze of her chiffon veil, was rewarded with the sight of shocked faces and gasps at her beauty. Her gaze fastened on Tom Goldman's instantly; he was staring at her, looking directly into her eyes with an expression she couldn't read.

Immediately, coldly, Eleanor slid her eyes away and turned them to Paul Halfin, her fiancé, handsome, distinguished, powerful, waiting for her at the altar.

She'd made her choice, and now she would have to live with it.

26

Roxana Felix strolled barefoot along the shore, feeling the fine-grained sand sinking soft and dry between her toes, enjoying the cool breeze of the night air. In front of her, the inky-black sea crashed and subsided, crashed and subsided, its endless sighing providing her with the perfect soundtrack to her thoughts.

The beach was deserted, cast in the silvery light of a tropical moon, hanging low and full on the horizon, and the stars were scattered like so many icy diamonds across the jet-black backdrop of the sky. She had not seen a sky like it since she was a child; the neon boards of Manhattan and blazing night-lights of LA, Chicago, London and Paris had not left much room for real stars.

Roxana glanced up at the arc of the heavens.

They're shining and beautiful and untouchable and distant, and they wheel in their orbit miles above everybody who looks up to them, she thought. I guess it's a good metaphor for everything I'm working for.

They're also cold and dead. Just like you.

She shook her head sharply, refusing to listen to the carping voice of her demons. She never listened to them. Never let them through. They could not be permitted so much as a second of her time, a moment of her thoughts; Roxana knew that. Because if she succumbed to her memories, they would break her.

No. It was far better to look up towards the clearing in the mountainside, where they were shooting, and think about *that*. They were almost two months into filming, and everything was going according to plan – according to *her* plan, that was. For everybody else it had been a disaster – the wrong equipment arriving from the studio; location shoots set up, and then having to be dismantled at the last minute because of Seychelles government regulations; her own disruptiveness, which had been imaginatively handled. Roxana congratulated herself, smiling. After the first week, she'd alternated between superbitch and remorseful, modest actress, pretending to listen to Sam Kendrick when he arrived. That meant that she had not been fired; Roxana was a world-class expert in judging just how far she could push it. And as a result they now had two months' worth of footage featuring Roxana Felix as Morgan – footage which it would be financially impossible to reshoot. She had made herself indispensable, and now the fun had really started.

Superbitch was back, and this time she had the whip hand.

Roxana smiled as she ticked off all the other problems on her long, manicured fingers. Union. Equipment. Location. Support cast – and that was too easy, reading a line oddly to throw off Mary, feeding a poorly timed cue to Jack, or simply shifting her body before Seth or Robert so they got aroused. Subtle tricks she'd employed a million times before with fellow models on shoots across the globe, in those long-gone days when Roxana had *done* shoots with other models. Throw in David's insidious sabotage of their creature comforts – Mary's contact lens solution, unobtainable on the islands, getting delayed for three weeks, or Sam Kendrick's soothing faxes full of logic and reason never reaching Jack, for example – and compound it with the daily battle to get anything right logistically, and the co-stars' performance had taken a dramatic dive. Fred had already had to reshoot three scenes with Mary Holmes, because when he reviewed the rushes he wasn't satisfied.

They were several weeks behind schedule. Already the budget was looking hopelessly optimistic.

See the Lights was in big trouble. And that meant so was Eleanor Marshall, and so was Sam Kendrick. Eleanor's studio-saving flick was turning into a creative and commercial disaster. And Sam Kendrick's big SKI package deal was less of a big deal every day.

Of course, that was the beauty of the thing, Roxana thought to herself, the way all the blame would fall exactly where she had intended it to. Eleanor Marshall and Sam Kendrick would learn not to mess with her the hard way; they had both insulted her, and now they were both clutching a one-way ticket out of their precious industry, at which she, Roxana, had apparently been such an insignificant novice. She smiled, her lips curving coolly. As far as she was concerned, there were certain lessons in life which you could apply anywhere. As Ms Marshall and Mr Kendrick would find out. And at the end of it all, she, Roxana Felix, would be established as a great movie star, a real powerhouse, famous for herself rather than her picture – accepted, and *loved*.

See the Lights would see the end of all her enemies, but the movie itself was not dead. Just a little bit sick. And when the time was right to administer the medicine, her chosen acolytes, Jake Keller and David Tauber, would be right there to play doctor, rescue the picture and put it smoothly back on track to smash success.

Roxana breathed in deeply, drawing the fragrant tropical air into her lungs. She might head back to the hotel now, see if Sam was around to offer her a little more physical release. There was something so amusing in watching him sink deeper and deeper under her spell, and after all, he did offer her body incredible pleasures. He was good enough even to drive out the memory of her unaccountable failure with Zach. And surely there was no danger of her starting to feel anything for him, was there?

The supermodel checked her feelings as she strode back across the deserted reaches of sand, watching herself, observing her own emotions as though she were an unbiased, outside witness. That was the only way to survive, that had always been her way; to keep the core of your soul distant and unwatchable, so that nothing could crack it, nothing could violate it. She had suffered once before, and she would never do so again.

Roxanna knew that she despised men like Keller and Tauber – they were jackals, unprincipled, greedy scavengers with giant egos and a combination of cold ruthlessness and low cunning that had bought each of them every gain they had. Sam, her Sam, was not like that. He had principles. He was ambitious and tough, but not ruthless. And he was strong and bold, he played with a straight deck. You could trust him. She did not despise him. But she did dislike him, she did want revenge . . . he had insulted her in public, beaten a submission from her. Well, Roxana hoped he had enjoyed his momentary thrill of domination. Because it was going to cost Sam Kendrick very, very dear.

No, she reflected, as she walked into the orchard-scented gardens of the hotel. Her heart remained a fortress. Sam Kendrick would find no mercy there.

'There's an explanation, Tom, there has to be.'

'Not good enough!'

Goldman's fist pounded down on his desk, his angry face flushed red with fury. 'You authorized those budget projections, Eleanor. You signed off on three location choices which have proved unworkable. And you had ultimate authority over casting choices which have gone badly wrong. We developed this project from scratch, and that means *you* took on the role as producer.'

'Thank you for the recap,' Eleanor Marshall replied coldly. She stood in front of her boss's desk, poised and immaculate as ever in a navy Georges Rech pantsuit, a platinum wedding ring glinting on the fourth finger of her left hand.

'*See the Lights* was going to be our comeback movie, and now it's going to hell in a handbasket! Our pitch to New York to save this goddamn studio was based on the movie – '

'*My* pitch.'

'Oh, yeah. *Your* pitch, that's right. And your movie, your casting decisions, and your mistakes!'

'Casting Roxana Felix was not my decision, Tom, if you remember.'

'I remember that your signature is at the bottom of the memo confirming her casting.'

Eleanor took a step backwards, her expression darkening. 'You would deny responsibility for that, Tom? Is that what you're saying?'

Goldman paused, took a deep breath. 'Look, Eleanor. The board know about our problems on the set. Don't look at me like that, I know it's supposed to be top-level privileged. But Howard Thorn has heard about it and he's on my back . . .'

Eleanor felt a tendril of fear coil its way round her heart. Holy Lord Jesus, why was it Howard Thorn, out of all of them? Thorn was the one who owned stock, a fifteen per cent stake, to be precise. The director who would be most inclined to scream for blood if it all went wrong. And whose blood? Not Tom Goldman's, evidently. She had seen this kind of thing before. Greedy as he would have been to take the glory for a smash, Tom was pedalling away from a budgetary disaster just as fast as he could. And if that meant passing the buck on Roxana Felix, so be it.

The moment she had dreaded had come to pass. Tom Goldman would be responsible for firing her or sparing her, and his own job was probably on the line too.

Maybe all Hollywood friendships end this way, when you get right down to it, she thought. Torn apart in the scramble to survive. Was that what their fifteen years of companionship meant to Goldman? Kill or be killed?

'Are you saying,' she repeated slowly, 'that you would lie about the part you played in casting Roxana Felix?'

Tom Goldman stared hard at her. 'What I'm *saying*, lady, is that if you want to stay president of this studio you had better find a way to fix this mess, and you'd better do it fast.'

Eleanor turned on her heel and walked out of his office without another word.

Tom Goldman watched her go. When she had disappeared into the corridor, he slumped back in his Eames leather armchair, despair racking him. He was being hard on Eleanor, as hard as he could.

It was the only way he stood a chance of disguising his feelings for her, and disguise them he must. Because she belonged to Paul Halfin. Because he had sired a child on a woman he now realized he didn't love, maybe didn't even *like*, but who would be the mother of a baby that *he* was responsible for.

It had taken that night in New York to show him what true love was, what real passion was. It was difficult even to get aroused with Jordan now. He pretended it was her pregnancy, but he wasn't sure she was buying that . . . and meanwhile the studio and his great white hope of a movie were falling apart.

It was all turning to dust, his whole life, crumbling into ashes in front of him. Made worse because for a few shining hours he had seen it all clearly, he had had everything . . .

Too late, Tom. You're just too late.

'Fire her.' Fred Florescu's exasperated voice broke into Sam Kendrick's self-absorption. 'You've got the seniority, Sam, for God's sake. Call Eleanor Marshall and have her do it.'

'It would cost far too much money at this stage,' Kendrick said, his eyes still fixed at the projection room screen. He had seen the rushes now, all of them, and he knew this movie was salvageable – just.

If nothing else went wrong.

If he could persuade Roxana to do her job.

If the support cast pulled themselves together.

A lot of ifs, Kendrick knew. But he just could not, would not accept the alternative. She was a drug, and he was becoming addicted.

'Maybe we should consider firing Mary or Seth, or both,' the agent suggested. 'I know they're my clients, but these are lousy performances. What you've got of Roxana is actually terrific.'

'Yeah, what we've *got* of her,' Florescu ranted, passing his hand across his forehead. 'But that's not fucking enough! First I'm ready to replace the bitch, then she does a little work, and now, when we're getting too far in for changes, she starts screwing around again.'

'Mary and Seth are doing their best,' Zach Mason chimed in quietly from a corner. 'She's putting them off deliberately. Sabotaging their performances. I see it time and again on the set.'

'*Sabotaging* them? Don't you think that's maybe a little melodramatic, kid?' Sam said. 'This is a movie, not Kennedy in Dallas.'

Mason shrugged. 'That's what I see, Sam.'

'I'll ask David to talk to her again,' Kendrick said finally, standing up, 'and I'll speak to Seth and Mary and Jack. They're all my clients, so maybe I can put the fear of God into them – do something about the personnel problem.'

But even as he rolled out the soothing words, Kendrick winced inwardly at the lie. The personnel problem was sleeping with him, and he knew it.

Bewitched.

The word floated through his mind, settling on the surface level of his consciousness, above the deep levels of happiness and sensual nirvana that had practically hypnotized him. Sam Kendrick lay on top of the double bed in Roxana's hotel suite, feeling sexually sated in a way he hadn't done in years. He had started to make love to her, slowly at first, getting more and more aroused by the way she would slide that silken skin against him, trail the feathery ends of her glossy, coal-black hair over his cock, rub her erect nipples across his dry, burning lips, cup his balls in her warm hands and massage them with the lightest, most exquisitely teasing touch, until he was massively erect, his cock aching and throbbing with need, and then she had slid away from him onto those slender knees and taken him in her mouth, perfect red lips sliding up and down him in a heavenly rhythm, then breaking off to lick him seconds before the pleasure got too acute, flicking her tongue across the sensitive, straining tip of his penis, then all the way down the length of him to the base, her fingers trailing lightly over his balls until he thought he might go mad, and finally, seeing her pretty face curving into a secret smile, he had roared with amused frustration, grabbed the little minx by her underarms and hauled her onto her stomach across the bed, sliding in her inch by inch, delighted at finding her soaking wet for him, and had started to tease her, his cock pounding into her, his fingers slipping into the slick down between her legs, brushing over her clitoris, bringing her up to the brink and back several times, until she was weeping, kissing weakly at his forearm, begging him to do it to her, begging for release, and with an incredible sense of masculine power pumping through his veins Kendrick had agreed and slammed himself deeper and deeper into her velvet body, taking them both across the final barrier into an immense orgasm, one that was torn from him as though he were a boy of seventeen, one that he had felt rock his lover's slim body as her belly convulsed in spasms beneath him. Now she was curled in his arms, naked and catlike, her small, incredibly perfect body resting against his, her head nestling in the crook of his elbow, and he was almost breathless from the adoration and protectiveness that gripped him every time he glanced at her.

'I think Isabelle must be the luckiest woman alive,' Roxana murmured.

Sam laughed. 'Isabelle and I haven't slept together for years.'

'Oh, come on. You're just saying that, to please me.' She snuggled against him.

'I swear! You know she isn't interested in that kind of thing. Isabelle loves giving parties, she loves the social thing.' Kendrick shrugged. 'It works out OK; we just never confront anything. I think a lot of good marriages survive that way.'

'It doesn't sound so good, Sam. It sounds lonely.'

Her words were an icy dagger plunged right into the most vulnerable places of his heart. Until he had started to see Roxana he hadn't cared – he hadn't *known* – there was anything missing from his life. He'd been consumed with getting to the top and staying there, and there'd been exclusive whores to provide the sex which Isabelle withheld, and Isabelle to provide the social backdrop which she did not withhold. And love? Well, he loved his kids, both in their teens and away at English boarding schools. The best, apparently, and Isabelle had insisted on it. The other kind of love, the feelings he had once had for Isabelle, that had died of malnutrition, and had wasted away so silently he neither realized when it died nor missed it when it was gone.

'Are you ever lonely?'

The words came out before he could stop himself. He didn't want her to know how strongly he had started to feel for her, didn't want to scare her off. How many men would a supermodel have cast off? How many lovers would this icy beauty have broken in two? Sam didn't want to think about it. But he also didn't want to let her go.

'I'm lonely all the time. I'm lonely on this movie,' Roxana told him, her voice a whisper. 'It's hard, Sam, it's really hard. They're all blaming me.' Her words trailed away, filled with pain. 'Don't bother to deny it, I know it's true ... Seth and Mary and Jack, they're all acting so well, and I know my scenes probably aren't great on tape ...'

'Your performance is fine, sweetheart.'

She squeezed his arm gratefully. 'You're too soft with me, baby. But they make up for it. Ever since I told Zach Mason I didn't want a relationship with him, he's just made it impossible, and Fred won't cut me any slack ... but it's mostly Megan Silver.'

'Megan?'

'She keeps rewriting all the scenes and changing my part! I *try* to act it, Sam, but sometimes I just can't ... I've asked David to speak to her, as she's his client, but he's tried and I really don't know what the hell else to do – Fred just loves her.'

'Why is she rewriting scenes now?' Sam asked, bewildered and angry. The hurt in Roxana's voice tore at his heartstrings.

'Oh, she has to, I guess. Because of all that stuff that keeps going wrong, you know? It has to be changed for the new locations and stuff, but she's using it as an excuse to rip up my character, and nobody's stopping her ...'

'She's history,' Sam said bleakly.

'Oh, no, Sam. She was really sweet a couple of months ago, in LA. But she got that makeover and the bleached hair and the expensive clothes ...'

'She did change,' Sam said, recalling the last time he'd seen Megan Silver, when she'd seemed a good kid, maybe a little naive, kind of cute with her brown hair and her jeans. The stylish, sexy creature he'd encountered over here, writing furiously at all hours of the day, was someone else – a little brittle, very self-possessed. And, apparently, a new addition in the swollen ranks of backstabbing Hollywood bitches.

'She's history, Roxana. Forget about it. Just do the best you can,' he repeated, kissing the top of her head.

'I will, Sam,' Roxana promised. A small, secret smile curved across her ruby lips. 'Don't you worry. I will.'

27

'I want you to go to the doctor,' Paul repeated.

Eleanor stared at him miserably. Her husband's lips were set in a tight grey line, his face white with anger and frustration.

'It's a bad time for me at work,' she said, willing him to understand. He had to be supportive, to be there for her in her hour of need. Otherwise, what did they have together? A new respectability for the dinner parties she didn't have time to throw, a joint bank account, and rigid, monotonous sex, prescribed by Dr Haydn, designed solely for the purpose of getting her pregnant. She was due for her first check-up at the fertility clinic in a month, and every night she prayed they'd find out she had conceived. Because what with the wall charts and stupid positions and thermometers, Eleanor wasn't sure she could take much more of it.

They had the first major fight of their marriage on their wedding night. Eleanor, striving to beat back the sense of claustrophobia, the feeling of being trapped, had come to her bridgegroom's bed in the sexiest piece of lingerie she possessed – a beautifully cut black satin teddy by Janet Reger – and without her diaphragm. Trying hard for a little humour and camaraderie, she had sliced it in two with a pair of kitchen scissors, placed the remains in a small cardboard box, wrapped up like a present in red ribbons, and placed it on Paul's pillow.

He'd opened it, laughed, and then handed her a small bottle of pills. 'Sorry I didn't wrap them in ribbons,' he said.

'What's this?' Eleanor asked, smiling. 'An aphrodisiac?'

'Not exactly,' Paul told her, his handsome face suddenly serious. 'This is a new fertility drug, the latest thing. Only just cleared by the FDA. It won't work right away, but the quicker we get you on a course of treatment, the better.'

'A fertility drug?' Eleanor repeated, stunned.

'That's right.' Paul nodded proudly. 'The best available.'

Eleanor remembered that she'd had to take a second to compose herself, before managing to say, quite quietly, 'And you don't think we should allow my body to try and conceive naturally first, before you unilaterally decide I need to be pumped full of hormones and chemicals?'

It hadn't been a good evening. And lately things had been getting worse.

In perfect harmony with the rest of my life, Eleanor told herself.

'It's a bad time for everybody at work,' Paul replied, shrugging. 'You're not the only one that has troubles in the office, you know. And it isn't fair to me to use that as an excuse to shirk your spousal duties.'

'My *what*? My spousal duties?' Eleanor shot back. 'And what are those, exactly, Paul? Being ready to have sex the second I get home, in case we miss the optimum daily window for conception? Accepting that you won't make love to me at any other time in case you waste a few precious sperm? I don't have "troubles in the office", Paul, I have a huge crisis that's threatening to consume my career. I'm about to lose everything I've worked for all my life. And you expect me to come home, *every night*, and be ready for sex, *every night*, whether I feel like it or not! I'm not your goddamned brood mare!'

'We can discuss that another time,' Halfin said, his eyes cold. 'Right now I want you to get this recurrent nausea seen to. If you've got some kind of allergy or virus, it could be affecting everything we're trying to do.'

'OK, OK,' Eleanor told him wearily.

His words seemed to have knocked all the fight right out of her. She should see a doctor for her sickness – not because a virus might be causing her harm, but because it might upset her darling husband's grand conception design!

He doesn't care about *me* at all. He cares about his wife, the soon to be mother of his children, Eleanor thought. No wonder he was so furious when I insisted on keeping my own name. It took a little lustre off his carefully designed family picture. But Eleanor Halfin? Eleanor Marshall Halfin? Over my dead body . . .

She reached for her Hermès purse and slung it over the shoulder of her smart Rifat Ozbek suit in dark green cashmere, picking up her briefcase in the other hand. Suddenly she just didn't care any more, all she wanted was to get into her office and spend another hellish day trying to save her job.

I deserve this, she told herself. Maybe Paul doesn't love me, but who said he had to? I hardly accepted him in a heady rush of romantic passion.

I wanted a husband to save me from everybody's pity. He wanted a wife to complete his New Model Lifestyle. And after Charles and Diana, does anyone believe in the fairytale any more? We're alike – two cynical people in a partnership of convenience. Maybe, in the end, everything comes down to that: whether you're swapping wealth and power for youth and beauty, sexual skills for a Green Card, or social approval for an available womb in a suitable body, maybe all marriages are really just trades.

I was a fool to believe it could be any other way.

'I'm out of here. I'll have my assistant schedule me an appointment with Dr Haydn this morning,' she promised.

Her husband nodded curtly, pleased. 'Thank you.' He spread his hands. 'Who knows, maybe it's morning sickness. Maybe you're pregnant already, and we just didn't realize it.'

'Who knows?' Eleanor agreed, walking out.

She pressed a button on her remote and unlocked the Lotus, sinking thankfully into the soft leather of the driver's seat, her mind already turning to *See the Lights*, trying to figure out ways around the latest budgeting disaster.

After all, what was she going to tell her husband? That her sickness predated all their fertility contortions? As far as she was concerned, it hadn't been brought on by any allergy or virus. It had been caused by the stress of a broken heart.

Megan Silver leaned forward over the PowerBook Eleanor Marshall's office had sent out to her, typing away furiously. The scorching midday sun was beating down on the back of her neck, heat hitting her from all sides, reflected up against her face from the powdery white sand. Her skin felt sticky and uncomfortable from all the lotions and gels she was having to rub into it just to survive – factor 15 sun lotion, antiperspirant, deodorant, insect repellent, and coconut butter oil as an emergency moisturizer, and despite everything small beads of sweat kept dewing her forehead and legs. Her hands were getting cramps from overuse and her head throbbed with a crunching migraine.

Not the best way to concentrate.

Not the best way to write an inspirational script.

But that was what she had to do, or this movie was history. All the delays, equipment failure, location problems and reshooting of scenes had sent them overbudget and behind schedule. The only things that held it patchily together were Florescu, who screamed at everybody, worked like a maniac and shot and reshot until he had something he could use, and Megan herself, who found herself doing emergency rewrites all day, every day, as they were forced to change this scene or that one, bringing the mountain to Mohammed over and over again. Florescu had told her he was relying on her, and Megan, desperate to impress the one person on this goddamn movie she had any respect for, was trying hard to rise to the challenge.

The pressure was intense.

'Megan, do you think you could put something in about Peter?'

She looked up, shading her eyes with her hand, to see Seth Weiss standing in front of her. The actor was looking diffident; something she always liked about Seth, he was too secure a star, at forty-five, to have any kind of an ego. Roxana Felix could take a few lessons from Mr Weiss, Megan thought sarcastically. Although even if she won three Oscars, like he had, it probably wouldn't be enough to calm the bitch down.

'Where, in the escape sequence?'

Weiss nodded, his handsome eyes unfocused, and she could see he was going over the scene in his head. Another plus for the guy. He actually cared about *acting*.

'He was wounded when we were going to shoot in the forest, right? And he's still wounded, but now we're on a beach, and if the shot hit him in the foot, he'd get sand in there . . .'

'And sand is excruciatingly painful in an open wound,' Megan finished for him. 'Like salt. Of course, I should have thought of that before, Seth, I'm an idiot.'

'You're a bona fide heroine, Megan,' Weiss told her, grinning. 'Saving this movie single-handedly. Or at least that's what Fred keeps telling us all.'

'Get out of here,' Megan said, but she flushed with pleasure as she punched the code into her machine, looking for Seth's character, Peter Cavazzo.

'Seth, Megan, how's it going?' David Tauber asked amiably, striding over to them and giving Seth the benefit of a full-wattage smile.

'It's going,' Megan said shortly.

Why did David only ever ask her that when Zach or one of the co-stars was in her vicinity? The way he sucked up to Sam's clients was truly disgusting, she thought. Kissing ass, telling them how wonderful their performances were, contradicting any honest advice Mr Kendrick might have given them, pretending to apologize for little creature comforts SKI had failed to provide, when what he was really doing was drawing attention to the problem. And yet in private he never bothered to compliment *her* work, never gave her a shred of encouragement for the effort she was making. On the contrary, he got pissed off if she wasn't always praising him, telling him how clever he was. And if she felt too exhausted for sex, forget about it! He was furious! What had he called her last night? Totally selfish, wasn't that it?

Megan felt resentment bubble up inside her. She was starting to suspect that she'd fallen for a class A-jerk.

'We're putting in some new dialogue for Cavazzo,' Seth explained. 'More agonized than sassy. Maybe I'll be able to play agonized better.' He shook his head, a wry expression on his face. 'Sam told me straight that the forest scene didn't work well anyway. Said I looked angry, instead of witty. I told him it's hard to be witty when the leading lady keeps blowing your cue on purpose.'

Megan winked at him. Most people on the set had a strong dislike of Roxana Felix in common.

'Hey, I thought you were terrific,' David said smoothly. 'Maybe the scene needed work, but you were great.'

'Thanks, man,' the actor said, smiling as he walked away.

Megan glanced up at David. 'That's not what you said last night. You told me a cartoon would've been more convincing.'

'Jesus, you want to keep it down!' Tauber hissed, glancing over his shoulder to check that Weiss was out of earshot. 'He's talent, Megan. You only ever encourage talent.'

'I don't notice you encouraging mine much lately,' Megan said, pushing her blonde hair out of her eyes.

'You're a writer, Megan. And you've got me all the time,' David said impatiently, checking his Rolex. 'I have to get back to the set.'

'Can't miss a chance to kiss up to Mary, huh?' Megan asked, wondering where this was coming from. She'd never dared to criticize David since the day he rescued her from Mr Chicken. Maybe the heat was getting to her ... but somehow it didn't feel so terrifying, somehow it felt pretty good.

What if Fred was right? a little voice in her head was asking. What if David didn't rescue you? What if *you* rescued you?

'What?' David sputtered, glaring at her. What was this bullshit? Was *Megan* going to start up on him now? Who the hell did she think she was? Roxana?

'Mary and Seth are *Sam's* clients, David,' Megan said stubbornly. Sam Kendrick had always treated her with respect, she thought, which was more than she could say for her own agent. 'You're undermining him. I don't think it's right.'

David Tauber leant forward towards her, menacingly, his eyes narrowed. 'Listen up,' he said softly. 'It's none of your business. And if you repeat what you just said to anybody on this set – and I do mean anybody – you're going to regret it.'

Megan gazed at him coolly. 'Are you threatening me, David?' she replied.

He straightened up. Didn't want to push the stupid kid too far – who knew what she might do in this mood? Megan with an attitude? That had to be nipped in the bud, and fast. Except that right now he didn't have the time. 'We'll talk about this tonight. In private,' he said curtly.

Megan clicked off her computer and stood up, smoothing down her skirt. 'I don't think so, David,' she said. 'I'll be sleeping in another room tonight.'

'You don't mean that,' he said, unfazed, confident.

'Oh, yes, I do,' she said. 'I need a little time to myself.'

'Right. *You* need time to yourself,' Tauber sneered, and Megan found herself staring at his handsome, mocking mouth with dismay. She tried to remind herself that David Tauber was the guy she'd been longing for, but it didn't work. The polished veneer David assumed with everyone else slipped a little further every time he was alone with her, and right now he seemed less like an infallible superagent and more like a spoilt brat every second. 'It's always me, me, me with you. You're not the only one putting in time on this project, Megan. What about *my* needs? What am I supposed to do tonight? After everything I've done for you!'

Megan felt desperately tired and unhappy. She ran one sticky hand through the platinum-blonde mop she'd been regretting ever since she had it done; yet again, she'd been twisting herself into something she wasn't in the hope of pleasing a guy, only to find it was all for nothing. That short-skirted, blonde-haired designer bitch thing was a million miles from the real Megan Silver, and suddenly she felt a sharp pang of remorse. As soon as she got home it was back to brown hair, comfy jeans and Veruca Salt T-shirts. Because, as she now realized, David Tauber wasn't worth it.

She admitted to herself she didn't love him.

'David, please. I'm knocked out. I just need some sleep, a little time to breathe.'

'No. No way, lady. You'll be in our room tonight as usual.' David was bristling with anger. 'You wanted to be with me so bad? Fine. But you play by my rules.'

She admitted to herself she didn't *like* him.

'It's over, David,' Megan said wearily. And it was; yet another brilliant Megan Silver waste of energy, romantic dreams and hope. Because David Tauber, no matter how hard she'd tried to kid herself, had never been any substitute for . . . for . . .

She suppressed that idea as soon as it surfaced. Reality check, girl, he's way, way out of your league, and you know it. No amount of makeovers are gonna turn you into Roxana Felix.

'You're just hysterical, you stupid little bitch!' Tauber's smooth features were purple with fury. *Megan* thought she could dump *him*! 'You don't know what you're saying!'

Megan picked up her laptop. 'Well, David, that's where you're wrong,' she said calmly, and then she turned on her heel and walked away, leaving him standing on the beach spluttering with rage and disbelief.

Tom Goldman sat perfectly still in the air-conditioned comfort of his office, wondering if there was any way out of this situation. His normally resourceful mind would once have known exactly how to handle it; it would have presented him with several options, it would have offered him some kind of a get-out, some excuse not to do what Jake Keller was suggesting. The trouble was that right now he couldn't think of a single one.

Everything the vice-president said made perfect sense. You couldn't argue with it; he had a 95-million-dollar movie that was already a month behind schedule, nine million over budget, and by all accounts turning out to be a creative turkey.

See the Lights had been his big rescue package for Artemis Studios. If it failed, Eleanor Marshall was history. And since he had pushed for her appointment, *he* would be history.

'Eleanor Marshall took over the production on this project,' Keller was saying, his nasty weasel face looking smug. 'You heard her, Tom. She threatened to have me barred from script meetings. And she forced me to draw up all my objections to the film in a long memo, sign it and copy you on it.'

He fished about in the document wallet he was carrying and placed a copy of the memo on Tom's desk. 'At the time I was somewhat offended.' A beat, an unpleasant smile. 'But on reflection, maybe the little lady was doing me a favour. Once I finished this, I submitted a copy to Mr Thorn, too. After all, he is the chairman of the board. I felt I should have the courage of my convictions.'

Keller leaned back in his chair, enjoying the effect his words were having. At the mention of Mr Thorn his boss had gone pale.

Thanks for the tip, Roxana, he thought.

'I see,' Goldman said.

'Do you, Tom?' Keller packed sarcasm into the words. 'I wonder. Eleanor has been responsible for buying a weak script, using unnamed actors in a terrible miscasting, and for a series of location and logistical errors that are sending costs spiralling out of control. This studio doesn't even know what's going on over there. As of last week, Florescu has stopped sending me the dailies. And without rushes how are we supposed to know if there's something worth using coming out of this mess? You must admit that what we've seen so far isn't encouraging. And word is out amongst the industry, Tom.'

'Already?' Goldman asked, his expression stricken.

'Well . . . rumours are starting up. I have the publicity department working flat out to counter them, but . . .' Keller shrugged. 'You know how it is.'

Yeah, Goldman thought. I know exactly how it is. If I don't give you what you want, you're gonna put word on the street yourself, and that could be fatal for us.

On the rumours of a smash with *See the Lights*, Artemis stock had soared. They'd gone so long without a hit that it had been cruising along at the bottom of its price range, undervaluing the company when you considered its software library and real estate assets. The Mason/Florescu project had been seen as a sure-fire smash, and given Eleanor's reputation for accuracy and tight budgeting, nobody had figured it would do worse than break even. The stock price had responded accordingly. But if news of this fiasco got out . . .

My God, Goldman thought, experiencing a renewed burst of panic. How many shares have *I* got? Preferred stock options had been a big chunk of his salary package over the last twenty years.

He did a quick calculation and felt ill. Forget about losing his job. He could lose his *house*. Millions would be wiped off the value of his portfolio . . .

How would he explain that to Jordan? 'Oh gee, honey, I'm sorry, but you won't be able to throw that Save the Rainforest bash after all. And I think we should talk about selling one of the cars, to see the baby through college?' Jesus H. Christ, he could see her face now. And it wasn't exactly wearing a supportive Stand by Your Man expression!

Eleanor would stand by me, Tom thought.

No! Screw Eleanor! She got us all into this mess!

'Jake, I hear what you're saying,' Goldman told him, reluctantly. He didn't want to have to cooperate with the little prick, but Jake had been right all along and he and Eleanor conspicuously wrong. Who had a choice?

'Good,' Jake Keller smiled thinly. He had Goldman by the balls, and they both knew it. 'So it's settled, then. I'll bring my plan to save the movie and a revised budget along to the big production meeting next week. I intend to challenge Eleanor on every point in this memo.' He tapped the document arrogantly. 'That way, if she's got a defence or a better idea, she'll get a chance to counter. But if she doesn't, you put me in charge of the film, effective right away.'

Goldman sighed. Such a move would be the same as firing her. No president could accept a demotion like that from the CEO; Eleanor would have to resign, right then and there, in front of the entire management team.

'Do we have to do it so publicly?'

Keller smiled again. 'That's the only way I want to do it. Out in the open. You know how I hate sneaking around behind people's backs.'

He stood up to leave. 'Do we have a deal, Tom?'

Goldman took the limp hand thrust towards him and shook it without enthusiasm. 'I guess so,' he said.

'Jesus,' Zach Mason muttered, looking around him.

'Impressive, don't you think?' Fred Florescu asked, pleased by his star's awestruck reaction. 'I wanted you to take a look at this place tonight, get a feel for it before we start shooting tomorrow.'

The two men were standing on the side of a dusty mountain road, at the entrance to a tourists' walking path carved out of the vegetation by the Seychellois government. Photographs of the mist forest were what had made Florescu choose Mahé for his jungle, and now he was showing Zach Mason the real thing. As they climbed out of their battered four-wheel truck, the emerald slopes of Morne Blanc had looked pretty ordinary, just a dense, impenetrable tangle of trees. But two steps into the pool of green shadow and Mason's mouth hung open in astonishment.

They were standing on the edge of a mountain ridge, the path dropping away downwards and to their left. The woodland before them was a mass of open space, creepers and small green plants growing under the verdant canopy, shafts of bright sunlight piercing through here and there, illuminating the mist and the tropical palms. Gnarled *bwa rouz* trees dripping with damp red moss crowded the sides of the path, orchids curling round some of them. There was a thick scent of wild cinnamon and albazia, vast ferns were everywhere, and *coco marron* palms sprouted across the slopes. Zach saw a small electric-blue bird swoop down from some perch and flit through a sun-dappled glade. The whole jungle was alive with movement and noise; insects humming, frogs piping...

'It looks like something out of *Raiders of the Lost Ark*,' he said.

Florescu clapped him on the shoulder. 'Exactly, amigo. Got it in one. This is the most atmospheric backdrop I ever saw, I swear. Which is why I refuse to give up on this thing, despite what David Tauber is telling me.'

Zach glanced at him sharply. 'What?'

The director shrugged. 'He says that Artemis may be about to pull the plug on the project.'

'Bullshit. Why would they do that?'

'According to your agent, because of the weather.'

Zach looked up at the dazzling blue sky behind them, burning hot and clear without a single cloud. 'The weather looks OK to me.'

'It's the end of September. We should have wrapped here by now. Which would matter a lot less except that the rainy season apparently starts up round about now.' Florescu shrugged. 'Tauber says Eleanor Marshall made a huge miscalculation in picking the Seychelles; she didn't take any delay into account, and the result is that the longer we stay here the more likely we are to get caught by the rains. And I ain't talking about a little drizzle, either.'

'You mean we'll be trying to film in a monsoon?'

'You ever seen a monsoon? We'd be packed up. It would break my equipment like matches.'

Zach shook his head. 'I don't like it, man.'

'Me neither!' the director said, laughing. 'My movie is turning into a fucking disaster area.'

'No. I mean I don't like all this stuff going wrong. I don't buy it. Eleanor Marshall seemed like an intelligent woman to me. Savvy. Not the type to authorize filming in a hurricane.'

'If we were on schedule, that wouldn't have happened.'

'She'd have factored in delays. All those corporate types do stuff like that; always covering their asses.'

'Possibly.'

'And I've been watching David. He's been way too calm.'

'He's the smooth type,' Florescu said, but he was watching his star closely, intently. He knew Zach Mason now, and he sensed a picture crystallizing. Mason was uneducated, but he had a keen intelligence buried under all that ferocious sexuality. That was what made the screen come alive; that was what ignited the footage they had managed to shoot, what made it such compulsive viewing. Zach Mason was a natural. He could sink so deep into his character that when Florescu called 'Cut!' Zach would sometimes just stand there, a little dazed, taking a few seconds to snap back into the real world. Zach had been Florescu's hero, and after months of filming together the guy still overawed him; he had the soul of a poet and the aggression of a Samurai, and those deep, savage eyes that mesmerized everybody he gazed at.

God, Florescu thought, I have to show that on screen, I've got to be the one to do it. Nobody's blended beauty and masculinity like that since Marlon Brando.

'He's more than smooth, he's *calm*,' Zach said. '*See the Lights* was the big break for him, right? He has Roxana, Megan and me. He should be totally panicked to see it slipping away, but he's not – he's just hanging around Mary and Seth and Jack, always providing little solutions for them.'

'Jesus,' Florescu said slowly. 'You're right. He's acting like somebody who doesn't *need* to worry – '

'Because he knows everything is gonna be OK.'

'Jesus!' exclaimed the director. 'You think all this is deliberate?'

'Why would the studio cancel the project? They must have spent a ton of money already – '

'You got that right,' Florescu agreed grimly.

'So they *have* to finish it. Maybe somewhere else, but they have to. We're nearly done filming, we've got under a month to go. They'll need something to show to set off their losses, right? They can't *afford* to kill us off now.'

'How would Artemis know we're in trouble? I haven't sent them any rushes for months. Unless Roxana Felix is phoning in.'

'Roxana's with David,' Zach said. 'He's the only guy on the set she never gives a hard time to.'

'It has to be something to do with Jake Keller,' Fred butted in, excited. 'He hates Eleanor Marshall. He got passed over for her job.'

'I've heard David call that guy from the production office a few times.' They stared at each other.

'Speculation,' Florescu said finally. 'We're just guessing. Pretty left-field stuff.'

'But we're right,' Zach countered. He brushed a strand of long black hair out of his eyes. 'You know we are. You can feel it.'

'So what do you want to do? Confront David? Confront Roxana? I don't see what good it would do. They won't admit jack, trust me.'

'I'm gonna confront Megan,' Zach said. 'She's weaker than the other two. She'll talk.'

The director did a double-take. 'Megan Silver? Now I know you've lost it, amigo. She's been working her butt off, rewriting the script every day. She does what I tell her and she does it fast. There's no way she wants this movie to fail. The kid works harder than anybody on the set.'

Zach nodded. 'And that's something I don't understand. But she's fucking David Tauber, she's been his girlfriend for months. She thinks the sun shines out of his ass. She must know what he's doing.'

Florescu noticed that his tone was suddenly sharp with contempt.

'All right. When we climb up to the top of Morne Seychellois to shoot the hideout sequence – that's for just you, me, Jim and Keith with a high-eight camera – I'll ask Megan along. That's scheduled for tomorrow afternoon; you can talk to her then.'

'Good.' The singer stared into the tropical forest before him, his handsome face dark with anger. 'She's gonna have some serious explaining to do, and then we should know what the fuck's going on. Because she's gonna tell me *everything*, Fred. Megan is the key.'

28

'Where's Megan?' Zach Mason asked. 'I want to talk to her.'

The crew were scuttling around on the beach like tanned worker ants in a hurry, rushing to wheel cameras into position, focus Klieg lights and mike up sound recorders as quickly as possible. Eight in the morning and everybody was already in position; Florescu was standing to one side going over the next scene with the cast, huddled together for warmth against the early-morning breeze. They were behind schedule, and every minute of filmable light was precious.

'Dunno, man, haven't seen her,' the cameraman replied. 'Not like her to be late.'

'Seen Megan?' Zach asked Seth Weiss. 'She's always here on time.'

Weiss shook his head. 'You could ask David or Roxana,' he said, pointing to the two of them walking towards the set together, over the sands.

Zach shaded his eyes to see better. The two of them were walking arm in arm which confirmed one suspicion. David Tauber seemed as confident and self-possessed as ever, dressed for the heat in loose, unstructured Armani slacks and expensive-looking shades from Cutler & Gross. Roxana was in costume, a deliberately torn and dusty evening gown, slashed at the sides where her character had torn it in an escape from the gun-runners. Miles of lean, tanned legs were exposed, and there was another rip baring her left shoulder. Her long glossy hair whipped round her neck in the breeze.

What a beauty, he thought. And what a cold, selfish bitch. He'd always admired her stunning looks and never once wanted her; there had been too many beautiful girls for Zach to be impressed, and too many ice maidens melting underneath him for that trick to hold any novelty any more. True, Roxana hadn't tried to play Ice Goddess with him. On the contrary, she had thrown herself at him, but even so . . .

Zach Mason knew Roxana Felix the way these others could not. He had walked under the blazing spotlight of fame for years, longer even than she had, and he could tell what was part of the image and what was real. And while most people were comfortable believing her bitchiness was part of the package, Zach was sure it was not. Roxana was damaged. There was a fist of cold wrapped tight around her heart, and when he looked at her, he saw somebody frozen to the core. She would reach out and slash violently at anybody who approached her. Her ruthlessness, her silken savagery with underlings, was no surprise to Zach. Like most wounded animals, she was dangerous.

'Zach,' David Tauber said expansively. 'Looks like it's gonna be another hot morning.'

Yeah, you moron. Like it's gonna be twenty below in the Seychelles.

'Where's Megan, David?' he demanded.

Jesus, I can't stand this asshole, Mason thought fiercely. He's so fucking slick all the time, never gets a hair out of place. What the fuck was I on when I signed up with him? What does a girl like Megan Silver see in him? But I forgot, she's nothing special. Just another bleached LA blonde with a designer closet.

Even to himself the words rang false. Megan was working flat out for this movie. She was clever. She'd written a dynamite script. And if she wanted to be with David Tauber instead of him, so what? She could choose who she liked.

Jesus, I'm turning into Roxana, Zach thought wryly. Like I got a divine right to any partner I should happen to favour.

'Megan won't be with us,' David replied casually. 'She's packing to go home.'

'She's doing *what*?'

'I fired her,' Roxana Felix said calmly.

'Excuse me, Roxana?' Zach repeated, stunned. 'You did what? You can't fire Megan! What are you now, the director? Does Fred know about this?'

'Hey, Zach, calm down,' David Tauber said soothingly. 'In actual fact, Artemis Studios terminated her contract. They're the ones that are paying for her stay here, as well as authorizing her salary. Roxana felt she could no longer work harmoniously with Megan, and Sam Kendrick, who runs my agency – '

'I know who Sam Kendrick is.'

'Of course. Well, Sam discussed the situation with Jake Keller over at Artemis, and it was felt that for the good of the picture, Megan should start working on some other project.' David beamed at him reassuringly. 'You don't need to worry about the script. I've told Kevin Scott to fly out Gordon Walker this morning – Gordon's been familiarizing himself with *See the Lights* and he'll be able to carry out any further rewrites. You'll like him, Zach. He's very competent, he's worked on two Quentin Tarantino films.'

'I see,' Zach said, ominously quietly. 'Isn't Megan Silver your girlfriend, David?'

The agent shrugged. 'I can't let personal feelings get in the way of business. That would be unprofessional. And where *my* clients are concerned,' he added, flashing a warm smile at Zach and Roxana, 'I'm always professional. You can take that to the bank.'

'And have you told Fred about the change of plan?'

'I was just about to,' David said.

Roxana Felix gazed at him triumphantly, the light of victory shining in her eyes.

Mason took a deep breath. 'You know what, Tauber? I wouldn't bother. I'd run along back to the hotel and tell Megan you just reinstated her. Then you can call Mr Keller and tell him that *I* wouldn't be able to work harmoniously with any other screenwriter. OK?'

Paling, David Tauber took a step backwards. 'But what about Roxana?' he protested. 'Her creativity as an actress – '

'Roxana and I are going to have a little chat about that,' Zach told him, his voice cold. He stared hard at the supermodel. 'I'm sure that by the time you get back I'll have persuaded her to see things from my point of view.'

'David, stay where you are,' Roxana snapped.

'David, get your ass back to the hotel *now*,' Zach repeated. 'Or you're fired as my agent.'

'David!' Roxana insisted.

'It's a tough break, isn't it, Tauber?' Zach said menacingly. 'Whatever you do now, you're either going to annoy Roxana or me. Because if you aren't gone in ten seconds, it's going to get ugly between us.'

David Tauber hesitated, his eyes twitching from Zach to Roxana and back again.

'David, stay here,' Roxana warned him, her voice suffused with quiet fury.

'Ten,' Zach Mason said softly. 'Nine. Eight. Seven. Six – '

With a small, agonized cry, David Tauber turned on his heels and fled.

'It can't be true,' Eleanor Marshall said blankly. 'It can't be. You've made a mistake.'

'No, my dear. No mistake, I assure you,' Dr Haydn replied cheerfully. She gave Eleanor a conspiratorial smile. 'Tests these days are very accurate. Especially when you go to the best hospitals, as we do.'

Eleanor clutched onto the armrest of her pale pink leather chair, feeling dizzy. Thank God she was sitting down, she thought. If she'd heard this news standing up she might have fainted.

'Eleanor, I swear you must be the most unobservant patient I've ever had,' the older woman went on. 'Even if you thought the nausea was related to something else, didn't you realize you'd skipped a period?'

She shook her head. 'No, I – I didn't notice – it's been chaos at work, I haven't had time to think about much else. And to tell you the truth, I wouldn't have thought anything of it if I had. I skip periods occasionally, if I'm stressed.'

'You work too hard altogether,' Dr Haydn said severely. 'And you'll have to reduce as many stressful activities as you can.'

I.e. none whatsoever, Eleanor thought wryly.

'But the charts, Doctor!' she said. 'All that lovemaking in the right position and at the right time of day . . .'

'Evidently not needed,' Dr Haydn told her. 'Quite amusing when you think about it, dear. You were pregnant the whole time anyway.' She chuckled. 'At least you didn't have to start with the fertility drugs.'

'I'm *two* months pregnant?'

'You are. And quite soon we'll be able to scan for the sex of your baby, if you like. Are you hoping for a boy or a girl?'

'I don't mind,' Eleanor said blankly. Her head was spinning with all the implications of this, trying to accept it, trying to make some decisions.

Tom's baby! I'm pregnant with Tom Goldman's child!

'You must have taken my advice on your last visit, and started to make love to your fiancé without a diaphragm. And that was all it took!' the doctor said, with obvious satisfaction. She leaned across the desk towards the patient. 'Your little one will arrive eight months after the wedding, Eleanor, but that's hardly something to be concerned about in this day and age. In my young day, it was very different. I had to tell everybody that my eldest son was premature!'

Eleanor smiled at the old lady as she laughed, warming to her. She'd misjudged Dr Haydn; her joy in being able to pass on good news was infectious.

'You're going to have a baby, Eleanor!' the doctor exulted. 'Isn't it wonderful?'

And suddenly, with that simple expression of delight, Eleanor felt all her confusion crystallize into one gigantic wave of happiness. Because come hell or high water, she was going to have the baby of the only man she had ever loved.

'Oh, Liz, it *is* wonderful,' Eleanor Marshall said, her eyes suddenly full of tears. 'It truly is.'

Roxana Felix settled back against the dark blue leather sofa in Howard Thorn's private jet, making herself comfortable. She had called him that morning and told him to send it to Mahé immediately; if she was forced to leave the set for a while, she was damn well going to do it in style.

'Can I get you anything, Ms Felix?' a stewardess enquired, her eyes roaming enviously over Roxana's stunning Chanel suit in white cashmere. 'Champagne, wine, mineral water, fruit juice?'

'Bring me some fresh orange juice. Slice of lime. No ice,' Roxana snapped.

'Yes, ma'am.' The girl scurried away hastily.

Roxana took several deep breaths and tried to control her temper. This situation was going to require careful handling, and disintegrating into white rage wouldn't help her.

But it was so hard!

Who the hell did Zach Mason think he was? Taking her aside like that after he'd crushed the fight out of David Tauber, that spineless little worm, and threatening her? The conversation ran through her mind, the words searing into her memory: 'I want you to take a week off, Roxana. And back off Megan. She's the only reason Fred hasn't given up on this movie.'

'And what if I don't?' Roxana had spat back at him, her chocolate eyes narrowed in venomous fury.

'Simple, babe,' Zach replied – God, she could see it now, his gorgeous face set hard as rock against her, his grey, thundercloud eyes so alive with menace that even she had shrunk from it – 'If you don't, I'm going to walk off the film *today*. Right now. And I'm going to fly straight back to Los Angeles and call a press conference, where I'll tell the entire world what a class-A bitch you are. In fact, I'll get Florescu to sit alongside me. We'll both tell them how you disrupted this movie, and if you say anything different, I'll get statements from a hundred different people agreeing with me.' He gestured sharply towards the set. 'Little people, Roxana. The ones you tread on every fucking day – the catering staff, the make-up girls, the lighting director. That'll look good on *Oprah*, don't you think? "Working with the Beauty Queen Bitch from Hell". A nice feature in *Vogue*, too. I could give them an exclusive. And I'll tell them that you tried to have the screenwriter fired because you were jealous of her relationship with me. I'll tell them that all that coy posturing at your cosmestic deal and the Electric City show was bullshit. I'll say you flung yourself at me, but you're such a fucking snake that I'd rather fuck a leper.'

'You wouldn't,' she'd managed.

Zach Mason shook his head. 'Don't let's play games here, lady. You know I would. I don't need this movie; whatever little web you're spinning, you can't trap me in it. I'd do all that in a heartbeat. And what would that do to your fat contract with Jackson cosmetics?'

That son of a bitch! Roxana thought.

She'd been off the set, packed and waiting at the airport in Victoria within the hour. What Mason had done to David Tauber she didn't know and couldn't care less about. The little prick had zero *cojones*, not that she'd expected better.

But it didn't matter. Nothing mattered. This was just a temporary annoyance; within days Jake Keller would present his new plan to Artemis, Eleanor Marshall would be fired and the movie would be back on track. Then she could go back to the set, relocated to somewhere more suitable, and act her heart out. She'd be Meryl fucking Streep, as far as the cast was concerned. And she'd be so hard-working and so sweet to all the stupid little hired hands that Zach Mason's heart would melt.

Roxana picked up a copy of *Variety* laid out for her on the smoked-glass coffee table and idly flicked through it.

Maybe she *had* overdone the leading-lady routine a little, but so what? Everybody loves the return of the prodigal son . . . or daughter. Once Zach had been won over by the new-look, hard-working, polite and considerate Roxana Felix – that's when she could have the little mouse bitch fired. Sam Kendrick was already eating out of her hands, and Eleanor Marshall was history. She could wait for Megan. It was no big deal.

'Your juice, ma'am,' the flight attendant said, handing Roxana Felix a Baccarat crystal flute full of freshly squeezed juice and topped with a slice of lime, exactly as she'd ordered it. The girl placed a mahogany tray in front of her, laden with a plateful of lime wedges and a silver pitcher of juice. 'May I get you some lunch? The chef suggests melon and prosciutto, followed by caviar with blinis, and then strawberry sorbet with a Cointreau sauce.'

Roxana nodded. 'That will be fine.'

The familiar cocoon of respect and luxury was enveloping her again, and it felt good. She began to look forward to spending some time in LA. It would have definite fringe benefits . . . Sam Kendrick, for one. Her body pulsed at the thought of him, warm desire beginning to melt and pool in her belly. He gave her pleasures she had never dreamed of, and there was something comforting about his love, his protectiveness towards her; she was enjoying the process of enslaving this one, more so than any other man she'd yet encountered.

You're enjoying it too much, warned a little voice in her head. *You're falling for Kendrick. You think about him all the time.*

No! Roxana thought angrily. Not true! Kendrick was just a puppet like the others. If she was amused by his body, what did that signify? Nothing and less than nothing!

I know what I'll do, she thought with a sudden flash of inspiration. I'll have lunch with that stupid bimbo Jordan Cabot and tell her all about it.

Yes! That would be stage one in the progressive destruction of Samuel Jacob Kendrick – putting word out around town that he screwed his clients. Not to mention having the pleasing side effect of snubbing that old witch Isabelle. After all, what was the point of having the great Sam Kendrick dangling on the end of her strings if she couldn't boast about it a little? And Jordan would make an admirable audience – married to Tom, so it would be all over Artemis and therefore the rest of town in five minutes.

Roxana Felix laughed aloud. Great! What were old schoolfriends for?

'Can I help you, ma'am?' a steward asked, rushing over to see if she required anything.

'You know, I think you can,' she said. 'Get me a phone. I want to call Mrs Goldman.'

'Jesus Christ,' Fred Florescu swore softly. He wiped a palm across his forehead, trying to clear away some of the beads of sweat that were dewing it. 'How much longer?'

'Not far now, *mon*.' Their guide smiled at them indulgently, pushing a huge tree fern out of the path. 'We make the clearing very soon. Very beautiful view.'

'I hope so,' Zach said heavily. He plucked at the soaking cotton of his once white shirt, now plastered transparently across his chest.

Megan, panting from the exertion, looked at him and thanked God she'd chosen black. Otherwise she'd have been the top entry in a one-woman wet T-shirt contest by the time they were ten minutes into this mountain climb.

'You guys got no problems,' Keith, the Texan cameraman, butted in. He was stripped to the waist and red-faced with exertion. 'You don't have to carry equipment.'

'That's why I picked you and Jim,' Florescu said, nodding at his soundman. 'Southern boys. Real men. You're used to heat like this.'

'Fuck you, Fred,' Jim Dollar said amiably. 'In Texas you *breathe* the air, you don't swim through it.'

He had a point. The atmosphere in the jungle was not only swelteringly hot, it was humid too, the air muggy and oppressive. Megan couldn't believe that Fred would insist on climbing halfway up Morne Seychellois in weather like this, just so he could shoot Zach's hideout scene with the perfect view. Or maybe she could. Florescu was an absolute perfectionist – over the course of two hideous months on location, that much had become clear. If something wasn't perfect, they shot it again. And again. And again, until it was absolutely right. It drove the cast and crew crazy, but nobody else complained. That attitude was what had made *Light Falling* into an artistic masterpiece and a commercial smash. That attitude had won *Peter's*

Lieutenant five Oscars. And that attitude was going to make *See the Lights* one of the most shining, exciting love stories ever committed to celluloid – if the damn thing ever got finished.

But why did they need me to tag along? Megan wondered. Is he really going to want a rewrite on a scene for one character?

'*Vienz, sivouplé,*' said their guide, grinning and lapsing into Seychellois patois. 'Come, please. We continue. Not much further.'

She followed Mason up the thin path, kicking aside thorns and fungus that had crept across it here and there. This was little more than a track, a derelict trail into the heart of the mountains far from the tourist walkways, and accessible only with an experienced local guide. That was on account of the steep drops and sheer ridges that periodically curved away from the edges of the track, sheer plunging walls of granite and creepers that an unwary hiker might not have noticed.

Megan thought, Christ, I know I'd have noticed.

She kept her eyes firmly on the back of Zach Mason's legs. *One foot in front of the other, right? And don't look down.*

To take her mind off it, Megan went over that morning's events yet again, trying to make sense of them.

What the hell's going on here? she wondered. First that little asshole David comes into my new room and tells me I'm fired. No arguing, just pack up and get out, and if you make a fuss it'll go worse for you in the future. And then runs back in thirty minutes later, says he made a mistake, I should get on the set, and clears clean out of my way before I even get to call him on it! And on the set, nobody's seen David, nobody knows where he is ... Everybody's on drugs, I swear.

'*On arrive,*' said their guide triumphantly. 'We here.'

Megan looked up and gasped. The clearing Florescu had been so set on was worth every second of the climb; forty foot wide, it was an outcrop of grey granite stone on the edge of a vast precipice, backed up by the green, palm-covered slope of Morne Seychellois and overlooking the rest of the mountain range, the whole national park spread out beneath. From here you could watch the mist drifting across the jungle, look down on birds winging over the tops of the trees below, see all the chasms and peaks, the emerald valleys and lush flat plains of the undergrowth. She could hear the screech of monkeys mingling with the low calls of the bulbuls and the omnipresent hum of the insects. The sea in the distance was sapphire blue, sparkling even under the patchy clouds that had begun to drift across the sky.

The scene was utterly deserted and primeval. She could see not a single man-made structure in the whole panorama.

'Oh, man,' Jim Dollar breathed. 'This is incredible.'

'It's going to make the best long shot in history,' Florescu said, almost beside himself. 'All right, guys, set it up. I don't want to waste any of this light.'

'*Non, sivouplé.* No. You go back now,' the guide insisted, shaking his head. 'Watch, then go back. Yes?' He waved down the mountainside, pointing at the trail they had just emerged from.

'No way, buddy,' Keith said, grinning. 'We just got here. And I didn't lug that camera halfway up Mount Everest just to take a couple of holiday snaps.'

'*I* go back. You come with me.' He shifted impatiently from foot to foot, glaring at the Americans. 'Storm is coming. Very dangerous to stay.'

'A storm?' Florescu asked.

The guide nodded. 'Monsoon season. Winds, rain.' He made a sweeping gesture with his arms. 'Very dangerous. I go back. You come, or not?'

'No!' Florescu said. 'You have to be out of your mind. There's not gonna be a storm, at least not today.'

'Wait,' said Megan uneasily. 'Fred, I think we should listen to this guy. I mean, he's a native. How likely is he to be wrong?'

'Come on, Megan,' Keith protested.

'Sweetheart, take a look at the sky,' Florescu said gently. 'I know it's the start of the rainy season, but just look at it! Practically clear blue. If there's a monsoon on the horizon. I sure can't see one.'

Megan glanced up. He was right; apart from a couple of white cotton-wool clouds the sky stretched clear and blue out to the horizon.

Muttering angrily, their guide disappeared back into the undergrowth.

'That's what happens when you pay in advance,' Florescu said, shrugging. 'But we've done it once, we should be OK for the trek back down. We'll take it real slow.'

'You got that right,' said Jim, positioning the lights.

'Zach, are you ready?' the director said.

Zach nodded.

'OK, people. Let's go.'

Two hours later, while Florescu and Keith set up the equipment for a few panoramic shots before the light failed, Zach Mason walked across to Megan, who was sitting perched on a granite outcrop, scribbling ideas in the margin of her script.

'Can I join you?' he asked.

She glanced up at him, surprised. 'Sure. Pull up a boulder, be my guest.'

'I want to talk to you about David Tauber,' Zach said, propping himself against a rock. He stretched out his long legs, hard and muscular under the costume calfskin pants. Megan tried not to stare at his bare chest, muscular and covered with a smattering of wiry black hair. That was how Florescu wanted to show Zach's character while on the run: animalistic and savage, the survival instinct taking over. It was supposed to set up a mood of sensuality before he was reunited with Morgan and they made love on the beach, at night, while their pursuers could be heard all around searching for them. And looking at Mason now, Megan was pretty sure it would work.

'Don't waste your breath,' she said coldly. 'I've got nothing to say about him.'

'Yeah? Well, I do,' Mason insisted. 'You have to have been aware of –'

'Zach, we have to get out of here,' Megan interrupted him. 'Look at that!'

She pointed towards the western skyline. Zach could see it: a huge mass of dark, heavy clouds had gathered and were moving quickly towards them. The winds were picking up, and the smaller white clouds in their part of the sky were scuttling across the sun, casting swift-moving shadows across the mist forest below them.

'We'll be gone in half an hour,' Zach said impatiently. 'Don't change the subject. It's – '

'No! We have to pack up *now*,' Megan said. 'It'll take us at least ten minutes to dismantle everything. We're going to get caught in a thunderstorm halfway up a mountain if we don't.'

'You're being paranoid.'

'Am I, Zach? Look how fast those clouds are moving!'

He glanced at the sky, uncertainly. The clouds had gotten quite a lot closer in the last few seconds, even if it didn't look like they were raining.

'Fred,' he called. 'Check out those clouds. Looks like our friend's little tempest might have arrived. I think we should pack up.'

'Yeah, OK. Just give me a minute,' the director called. 'They're making for great light over the jungle. I have to get this.'

'Fred!' said Megan. 'You – '

Her words were suddenly cut off by a violent gust of wind, slicing across the clearing and pushing her back against the boulder. The mikes swayed backwards and forwards on their stands.

'Shit!' Jim Dollar said. 'Where the hell did that come from?'

'Come on, Fred. Let's go,' Zach said, getting to his feet and strolling across to the director.

'Ten minutes,' Florescu said, not taking his eye off his shot. 'That's all I ask. Then we'll have it in the can.'

Another gust of wind blasted them from the west, and this time Megan found herself spattered with raindrops. Alarmed, she spun round to see the sound equipment toppling over. Her script was wrenched out of her loose grip and went flying towards the brink of the clearing. Keith lunged for it, but too late. The white papers went soaring off the edge of the cliff, snatched up by the wind like a dead leaf, pages tearing away from it as it disintegrated over the jungle.

'Man, we're going to be in trouble if we stay much longer,' Keith told Florescu anxiously. 'I don't like the look of this.'

'All right. Let's get out of here,' the director said reluctantly. 'Shut it down, guys. Zach, can you give us a hand? We might as well leave as fast as – '

Suddenly they were plunged into gloom as a bank of black cloud swept across the sun. Almost simultaneously rain started to fall all around them, and as the technicians scurried to and fro, cursing and flicking off every switch in sight, there was a deafening thunderclap, and Megan shrieked as a dazzling flash of sheet lightning blitzed across the mountain behind them. She ran forward blindly, her feet slipping on the small pebbles and chips of stone lying loose on the outcrop of the granite. Zach Mason, his lean frame silhouetted against the light, reached out for her as the sky opened and the rain began hurling down, drenching everything in sight, the long lines of water waving through the tropical gale that was ripping through the forest, bending over young palm trees and sending sticks and bushes bowling across the ridge. As Megan reached Zach, Jim Dollar screamed in agony as his skin connected with a torn wire, and Florescu, half blinded by the rain, watched in horror as the thin blue light of an electric shock crackled around his soundman. He tried to take a step forward, pushing himself into the wind, but was flung back by a fresh blast that half lifted him from his feet, smacking him against a jutting outcrop of granite. Pain and horror surged through Florescu's body together as he watched Zach and Megan, clutching each other, lose their footing in the hurricane and bowl backwards, Megan screaming in terror, and tip over the edge of the chasm in front of them. On his hands and knees the director inched across the clearing, battling against the storm, until he reached the ledge and managed to peer over it, shouting their names, trying to see if he could see where they had fallen. There was no trace of them, just the thrashing jungle canopy, flailing in the wind and dark green from the driving downpour. It was the last thing he saw before he passed out.

29

They met at Chasen's for lunch. It was another blazing day, but Isabelle Kendrick didn't notice; she picked through her Caesar salad and sipped delicately at her chilled mineral water, exactly as usual, nodding graciously now and then at various courtiers who wandered up to their table to pay homage, but her heart wasn't in it. Under the tailored elegance of her ice-blue Bill Blass suit, the blood in Isabelle's aristocratic veins was running as cold as liquid nitrogen.

'Really? She said that, did she? Go on, dear. I'm simply fascinated to hear the rest of it,' she said, leaning forward to encourage her companion.

It was true; every word pierced Isabelle's heart like a rapier wound, setting off screaming, jangled alarms of fear and fury, but she was nonetheless fascinated. The more she knew about her enemy, the greater her ammunition against her. It was as though Isabelle herself was detached; one part of her mind remained aloof from the storm of emotions boiling within her, and merely watched the scene calmly, a dispassionate observer, curious to know just how far, just how deeply, Roxana Felix had dug her own grave.

'Oh, Isabelle, I can't,' Jordan replied hesitantly. 'The rest of it was just more of the same. You know – what Sam used to say in bed, how he used to tell her he would protect her, if anybody tried to hurt her they were dead in this town. And she discussed, uh, his, uh – *technique* –'

'Indeed?' Isabelle enquired. 'And did she say she found my husband satisfactory?'

'Oh, yeah,' Jordan replied enthusiastically, caught off-guard. 'You should have heard her. She said he was the hottest thing on two legs – said she was coming so often she lost count. Rave reviews. According to Roxie, Sam's the hottest fuck on the planet. He . . .' Jordan's voice trailed away at the sight of the frozen expression that had settled across Isabelle's face. 'He seemed to please her, anyway,' she finished lamely, trying too late to recapture a little decorum.

There was a long pause.

'How embarrassing for you, my dear,' Isabelle said eventually. She fixed Jordan with a gimlet eye. 'To have been forced to sit there and listen to such a pack of lies, and from somebody you once knew at school, too. But we must be charitable – perhaps the poor child is merely delusional, instead of being a pathological liar.'

Jordan Cabot Goldman smoothed down the immaculate rose silk of her Calvin Klein on-the-knees dress and swallowed hard. This would have to be handled delicately. At first she'd been ecstatic at the prospect of this lunch – not only would she get to do Isabelle a major favour, thus making them quits for her help with Tom, but she would have the delicious pleasure of watching the old bitch squirm as she recounted her disparagement. It wasn't often, OK, it wasn't *ever*, that you got to see Isabelle Kendrick humiliated, and Jordan had been planning to enjoy every second of it, getting to play the loyal, sympathetic friend whilst inside she was doubled over with glee, and they both knew it. But things hadn't quite turned out that way. Jordan had barely gotten five minutes into her account of lunch with Roxana when the expression on Isabelle's face gave her pause. Her mentor had sat there quite still, green eyes boring into her, her whole body tense – but not with shock, rather tensed like a cobra, coiled and ready to strike. And Isabelle's voice had confirmed Jordan's wariness: those measured, dulcet tones were somehow infinitely more menacing than any raging, teary despair.

Jordan recognized the danger signals right away and changed her approach. Out went the gory details, in came as dry a reporting of the facts as she could manage. Isabelle was watching her like a hawk, and Jordan knew instinctively that if she showed the tiniest bit of satisfaction she was a dead woman. That would mean the end of her spell as Crown Princess. That would mean social war on a massive scale. And she wasn't ready to take Isabelle on – at least not yet, Jordan thought defiantly.

Anyway, now she had received the official line, loud and clear. Roxana was lying. Isabelle was not prepared to admit, even for one second, even to her closest acolyte, that Sam had been unfaithful to her with somebody that mattered – a supermodel he was seeing regularly, as opposed to a faceless, and presumably discreet, whore. Like most of the Beverly Hills ladies who lunched, Isabelle paid no mind to *those*. On the contrary, Jordan thought, she probably relies on them to relieve her of certain 'unpleasant duties'. But Roxana was different. Roxana would mean a loss of face. And possibly, if Jordan believed everything she'd been told – which she did, implicitly – a loss of everything else, too. Jordan tossed her blonde mane, slightly annoyed. This meant Isabelle was setting herself firmly above Jordan – after all, *she* had confessed her anxieties about Eleanor Marshall to the older woman. *She* had been prepared to expose herself, to admit weakness. Apparently it was not going to go two ways. Isabelle wished her to say that Roxana was lying, when the whole manner of Jordan's report up to now had strongly implied that she believed her.

'Or don't you think so?' Isabelle asked calmly.

Jordan looked deep into her eyes and saw the steel behind them. It was a challenge. She had to make a decision – was she with La Kendrick, or against her? Evidently there was to be no middle ground.

'Oh, no, absolutely,' she said hastily. 'I expect she's horribly insecure. They say all these model types live in a fantasy world, don't they?'

Was it good enough? Jordan wondered. She'd have made a terrible mistake if she'd crossed Isabelle on this subject. You only have to take one look at the old hag to see that she was in a dangerous mood. A very dangerous mood.

'I expect that's quite right, dear,' Isabelle said, smiling softly at her.

Jordan felt herself almost sag in her chair with relief. She hurried to pin her colours even more firmly to her mentor's standard. 'That was why I came to you, Isabelle. When people like Roxana start convincing themselves of such ridiculous ideas, it's time to put a stop to things.' She took a decisive sip of her mineral water. 'I mean, she may be delusional, but we simply can't have her going around and spouting such rubbish, can we? We have to put a stop to it.'

Isabelle settled back into her chair, satisfied. 'Indeed we do, dear. Indeed we do.' She speared a few glistening green leaves with relish and popped them into her mouth, savouring the tiny croutons and Parmesan and warm hazelnut oil. Suddenly food tasted good again. Isabelle was limbering up for a fight, and she found the experience rather exciting.

It had been too easy for too long, Isabelle mused. Crushing the social pretensions of various would-be rival Queen Bees. Throwing the most glamorous and spectacular parties, year after year. Honing her guest lists to absolute perfection, until she could achieve such an incredible human potpourri at each dinner party that nobody ever turned her down – just enough glamour, nobility and sheer beauty to amuse the power players, just enough power players to attract the more glittery crowd. For years the whole town had known that more deals were done over cognac at the Kendricks' than breakfast at the Polo Lounge. Isabelle ruled LA's social set with a rod of designer wrought iron. She had no rivals. Life had become, perhaps, just a little dull.

Roxana Felix would change all that. She was a worthy rival. Isabelle acknowledged it without a qualm; she was utterly unafraid. Let the world's most famous supermodel compete with her for her husband.

Isabelle would crush her.

She would crush her so completely that she never recovered. She would *crucify* the pretty little snake. Skewer her through and through without mercy. Los Angeles would watch in amazement, because this was going to be a complete massacre. And then nobody would ever challenge her again.

'But it's so boring to discuss unpleasantness all day, don't you think?' she continued smoothly. 'Tell me about *your* life, Jordan. Your little problem is taken care of, I gather?'

Jordan nodded smugly. 'She's on her way out.'

'That was my impression.' Isabelle sighed compassionately. 'Poor Eleanor. To have worked so hard for so many years, and in the end, for what? But at least she's now married.' A pause. 'To a banker,' Isabelle concluded triumphantly.

Actually, it was rather annoying that Paul Halfin was so suitable. A successful investment banker was not the husband she would have picked for Eleanor – better a 'resting' actor, or a minor artist or something. But it would have to do. A major agent and a studio chairman far outranked any vanilla businessman.

'And what about you and Tom? Everything rosy?'

'Oh, of course,' said Jordan, uncertainly.

Isabelle shook her head. Without me, this girl's got no future, she thought despairingly. She's the worst poker player I ever saw.

'What's the matter now?' she asked patiently.

Jordan shifted uncomfortably. 'Nothing,' she lied. 'Tom just seems a little – uncommunicative. He's very solicitous, but . . . he doesn't seem to, uh, that is, he's kind of . . . we don't make love as much as we used to,' she finally blurted.

'I see. And is that because of the baby, dear?'

'He says so.' She pouted. 'But I've told him it's safe.'

Isabelle waved a bejewelled hand dismissively. 'Problems at work, dear. He's a little stressed, I expect. Now, more importantly, how *are* you progressing with the baby? Are you *enceinte?*' she enquired delicately.

'No. Not yet.'

Isabelle frowned. 'You're going to have to hurry up, dear.'

'How can I?' Jordan demanded, losing her cool. 'He doesn't hardly ever *want* it any more. I don't know what the fuck's the matter with him.' She ignored Isabelle's glacial expression at her language and ploughed on. 'And *anyway*, Isabelle, I don't know that I *want* one – once Eleanor's gone, what do I need it for?' Jordan's voice rose to a petulant wail. 'It'll *ruin* my figure – Joanna Lowell did that and she had *horrible* stretch marks and she put on *ten pounds* and her breasts! Ugh!' Jordan shuddered in horror. 'They used to be so *firm*! And now Tom is saying he doesn't want to get a nanny – it would cry all the time and – '

'Jordan, Jordan, dear.' Isabelle's voice was firm. 'It's the only way.'

'But – '

'But me no buts, dear. If you want to consolidate your position it is the only way. You can always insist on a nanny. *I* did. Now, the fact that you haven't conceived is starting to get problematic.' She paused, thinking. 'Once Eleanor has resigned, you must have a miscarriage. We can discuss that later.'

'But I'm not *pregnant* yet.'

Isabelle sighed, exasperated. Really, sometimes the girl's stupidity was just too much. 'I know that, Jordan. You pretended to be pregnant, and now you will pretend to lose the baby.'

'Oh.'

'You'll be devastated, of course. Tom will go out of his way to comfort you. At that stage you can conceive for real.' She signalled imperiously to the waiter. 'Check, please. My dear, you can call me later this week and we'll have a little chat about it.'

'Thank you, Isabelle.' Jordan bit back her protests – there would be another time. She smiled engagingly. 'You've been most helpful.'

'As have you, dear,' said Isabelle, regarding her protégée thoughtfully. 'As have you.'

Eleanor replaced the receiver on its cradle and sat bolt upright. Outside their long sash windows the sky was still pitch-dark; she glanced at the glowing red numbers on her bedside clock radio. Four-thirty a.m.

'Who the hell was that?' Paul grunted sleepily. 'Do they know what time it is?'

'It was an emergency,' Eleanor told him. 'Go back to sleep.'

'Goddamn. Can't your office call during business hours with their little crises?' he demanded. 'Your attitude to work is ridiculous. You – '

'It was a *real* emergency.' Eleanor cut him off; she didn't have time for Paul's whining now. 'And it's only half an hour before our alarm is due anyway. Now go back to sleep. I have to deal with this.'

Ignoring her husband's mumbling complaints, Eleanor stood up, reaching for her robe, and walked into the kitchen, flicking on the light switch. She blinked as her eyes adjusted to the dazzling glare, then turned on the coffee percolator. Though she would hardly need caffeine to wake her up. Despite the fear and anxiety, Eleanor Marshall had never felt more alert in her life. Adrenalin was racing through her veins. Forget business – this was a real crisis, a genuine catastrophe. Two young people might be dead, and if not, they were depending on Eleanor for their lives. And she was going to come through for them.

Four-thirty in LA. That was seven-thirty in New York. Eleanor picked up the kitchen extension and, from memory, tapped in her personal attorney's home number. If everything that Fred had just told her was true, she was going to need his help. Because if she was going to fly out to the Seychelles to coordinate a rescue mission, she intended to have her job waiting for her when she came back.

Maybe it was Zach and Megan's plight. Maybe it was the sudden knowledge of Tom's baby. Or both together, she thought: the threat of death and the promise of life. But whatever the stimulus, as she sat in her kitchen holding the phone, Eleanor felt a veil tear from her eyes.

She saw Jake Keller's betrayal clearly. Almost from the second Fred had mentioned Jake's involvement with David Tauber, Eleanor understood exactly how she had been duped. She was angry with herself, but that wasn't important. That was the past. It was her actions now which would matter.

Eleanor's eyes focused on the wall chart which Paul had insisted on tacking to the freezer door, her most fertile dates ringed in thick red marker, the days her period was due cancelled out with equally thick red lines. Well, I guess you won't have to worry about that any more, she thought wryly. She was amazed to find there was no longer any anger inside her at the sight of it, just a mild wonderment at herself for ever having let him bully her on this matter. She'd let them all bully her. Tom, who'd married a bimbo sex doll and then expected her either to sympathize or tread on eggshells around the subject, depending on how he felt about his wife that week. Paul, who demanded marriage and demanded children, not out of love, but out of some pathological desire to conform to society's latest blueprint for the successful man. And Jake Keller, who had always hated her, and whose jealousy of her career had driven him to good old-fashioned sabotage, a sabotage which she had actually assisted. Yes, Eleanor realized, that's exactly what she had done. Keller had found her in sickness and torment, and without a qualm he had taken advantage of her weakened state. And had laughed at her while he did it, like every other bully since time immemorial.

Well, they were going to be in for a suprise. Every damn one of them. Because now, as she found herself confronting a crisis situation, now, as she sensed the miracle of her child inside her, Eleanor knew she was no longer afraid. And that was going to make her strong.

The phone purred in Alex Rosen's apartment. Once, twice, and he picked up. 'Rosen.'

Five thousand miles away, Eleanor thought, and he sounds like he's in the next room.

'Alex, it's Eleanor Marshall. Did I wake you?'

'Of course not. Eleanor. I've been at my desk for an hour already, you know me. But it must be somewhat early in LA, right?'

'That's right,' Eleanor replied, smiling. Alex was more than a lawyer; they'd been to Yale together and squabbled bitterly over everything from feminism to Shakespeare for four years. And been close friends ever since. It was good to hear Alex's voice: gossipy, clever, confident, and at her disposal. And Alex Rosen was one of the most prominent corporate lawyers in the United States.

'Then I take it you have a little local trouble you'd like me to help out with. A minor problem at work, perhaps?'

'A major problem, Alex. A big, fat, hairy problem that's going to finish my career if I allow it to.'

'Oh, *good.*' Her friend's voice was a sigh of satisfaction. 'Those are the kind I like the best.'

Grant Booth leaned across the polished mahogany surface of his desk, barely containing himself. It was all he could do to keep from rubbing his hands with satisfaction, but he managed to restrain himself. Such an attitude of unholy glee would go right against the sophisticated, reliable image he was trying to project. And Booth, Warwick & Yablans were very big on sophistication and reliability. That was one reason their client was here.

Booth glanced round the air-conditioned comfort of his offices, admiring them. The dark oak panelling. The severe, masculine leather chairs in sombre shades of burgundy. The antique carriage clock placed atop the equally antique bookcase. Yes, it was quiet, expensive decor, and the firm could afford it because of clients like this one.

'Let me get this straight, Mrs Kendrick,' he began, but she held up one hand, cutting him short.

'No, Mr Booth. Allow me to repeat myself. I want you to be quite clear about my instructions.'

It was a voice used to command, and Grant Booth obeyed it. He sat back in his chair, attention focused compliantly on Isabelle Kendrick.

'I wish to find out everything about Roxana Felix, the model,' Isabelle said, calmly and clearly. 'And I do mean everything. Her parents. Her childhood. Her teenage years. Whom she is sleeping with. Whom she has slept with. Any enemies that she might have made in her modelling career, and the manner in which she made them. In short – everything. You may use whatever methods you wish, as long as you do not break the law. You will keep these instructions, the fact that I am your client, and any and all communications between your firm and myself in absolute confidence. And you will give me a legally binding written promise to that effect before I leave this office. Money is no object.'

Booth smiled unctuously. 'I am happy to hear you say so, ma'am.' He cleared his throat. 'You are aware that our retainer is fifteen thousand dollars?'

Isabelle looked at him blandly. 'No, Mr Booth,' she said. 'In my case your retainer will be fifty thousand dollars. Plus expenses. And if the investigation is concluded to my satisfaction, there will be a further hundred thousand to follow.' She gave him a wintry smile. '*Everything*, Mr Booth. I trust I am making myself clear?'

Grant Booth nodded eagerly. He had a very shrewd idea of what would constitute 'satisfaction' to this lady. She wanted blood. And for a hundred and fifty thousand dollars his firm would happily see that she got it.

'Oh, you are, madam,' he said. 'Very clear indeed.'

30

It was the heat that woke Megan up. The burning, sweltering feeling on the back of her neck was too uncomfortable to let her lie unconscious, and she groaned and blinked, opening her eyes, unsure of exactly what had happened, where she was. The pain in her neck intensified and Megan realized she was lying slumped over a fallen tree trunk, her head rammed against a branch. All around her were ferns, uprooted bushes and glistening dark green foliage, bracken and scrub, that had been drenched in the downpour. Millions of insects buzzed and chirped through the undergrowth, their low hum mingling with the constant bubbling calls of the tree frogs. Startled, Megan jerked away as a huge butterfly flew past her, brilliant scarlet wings fluttering jerkily.

She moaned in horror as it all came back to her.

The last thing she remembered was the blanket terror of her sheer fall, clutching onto Zach, then finally crashing through leaves and branches and blacking out. She glanced upwards at the emerald canopy of the mist forest; there was a patch of clear blue sky visible directly above her, in the midst of the green tangle of palms and *bwa rouz* trees. The sun had been beating down on her through that hole.

That must be where we fell, Megan thought. Zach! Where's Zach?

She tried to jump to her feet and immediately fell backwards with a piercing scream. Agony blazed through her, knives of pain lancing into her flesh. Megan glanced down and saw her left ankle, twisted and grotesquely swollen, the flesh puffed up and darkly bruised, like a purple plum.

'Megan! Megan, are you OK?'

She looked behind her to see Zach Mason, his shirt in shreds and his chest bloodied, standing in the shade of a towering palm tree. He looked shaken but otherwise all right. Megan burst into tears with relief.

'Oh, Jesus, sweetheart,' Mason said, rushing over to her and clasping her in his arms. 'You're in pain. You poor girl. Have you broken something?'

'No,' she said, and then burst into tears 'I'm all right. I'm so glad to see you, I thought you might be dead.'

He shook his head, stroking her hair with one hand. It was ridiculous, but she found the movement comforting; she wanted to nestle up against him and believe that this nightmare wasn't happening, that everything was going to be OK. She forced herself to control her tears and broke away from him.

Zach Mason is hardly my father, Megan reminded herself sternly. And anyway, my father wouldn't have wasted his time stroking my hair. So less of the weak damsel bullshit – we're in trouble here, and I have to think clearly if I'm gonna get out of this alive.

'Neither of us is dead, thank God. Let's see if we can keep it that way,' Zach said. He looked her over, and winced as he saw her ankle. 'Jesus, you poor kid. Is it broken?'

'I don't know. I think it's just sprained,' Megan told him. 'I can't stand on it.'

Infinitely gently, Zach reached out and touched the bruised violet flesh. 'Does that hurt?'

She shook her head.

'Does that?' He gave it a soft push.

'No.'

'Well, at least that's something,' Zach said. 'Probably means you haven't been infected yet.' He examined the angle of her foot. 'It looks real nasty, though. Do you think you might have dislocated it?'

'What am I, a nurse?' Megan snapped. 'How the hell should I know?'

He glanced at her. 'Hey, I didn't mean – '

'Oh, look, I'm sorry. All right? I shouldn't have bitten your head off, I know you're trying to help. It's just that I'm in pain here.' She shrugged, and Zach tried not to look at her breasts, clearly outlined under the sodden black cloth of her wet T-shirt. 'I don't think it's dislocated. I guess I'd be lying here screaming if it were. What about you, are you OK? What happened to your chest?'

He touched the dried blood on his skin, dismissing it. 'Just a few scratches from the fall. Thorns or something.'

'My God,' Megan said quietly, gazing around her. 'It's a miracle we're alive.'

Zach hooked his arms under her shoulders and lifted her up, slowly and carefully so that no weight pressed on her hurt ankle, and helped her sit upright on the trunk of the tree. Megan noticed that her hundred and twenty pounds was nothing to him; Zach's lean, hard body was evidently pure muscle. Just as well, she thought dryly. We're going to need all the muscle we can get.

Mason sat next to her, staring at their surroundings. The jungle was alive with sound and movement; they could see nameless small creatures scampering through the undergrowth ahead of them, birds flitting and swooping through the canopy. A brightly coloured pigeon, its body electric blue with a downy white chest and a crimson crest, plunged through the forest directly in front of them.

'*Pizon Olonde*,' Megan said. 'The Dutch Pigeon. They called it that because it uses the colours of the Dutch flag.'

'Yeah? Where did you learn that?' Zach asked her.

'The guidebook,' Megan said. 'I tried to get a little local colour when I wasn't on the set.'

'Did you read anything about the jungle?'

'Actually, yes,' Megan said. 'Three pages. So I can tell you some plants you better not touch. And insects to avoid.'

'Great,' Zach said, giving her a smile. 'Finally something useful from you.'

'Get lost,' Megan said, grinning.

'I got some news for you, babe.' He waved at the green shadows of the forest, pierced here and there by long, dusty columns of light where shafts of sunlight had managed to pierce through the treetops. 'We already are.'

'Apparently so,' Megan agreed, trying to keep her tone light.

'Three pages between us and certain death from poisonous berries,' Zach said, pushing his long black hair out of his eyes. 'Well, that's reassuring. You want to give me a run-through of those insects now?'

'Take your pick.' Megan looked at him, and despite their joking she felt the fear start to return. 'Tarantulas, crazy ants, yellow wasps, wolf spiders, scorpions. And the jungles are home to some of the world's crack mosquito squadrons.'

'What's the good news?' Mason asked her.

'*Good* news? Uh, the snakes aren't poisonous.'

'Terrific,' Zach said.

'Plus, I have some insect repellent,' Megan added, brightening. She fished around in the sodden pockets of her jeans and produced a large tube. 'I thought I might need it on the mountain.'

'Now you're talking,' Zach said. 'Any food?'

'No.' Megan fought to control the creeping sense of panic closing in on her. 'Zach, what are we going to do? We're miles from anywhere. You can't even see the ledge where we fell from here. They'll have no idea if we're right beneath it, or crushed on the rocks, and even if they do, how the hell are they going to find us? There's no paths into here. We're totally stranded, and I can't walk –'

Her voice began to tremble, and she bit her lip to keep herself from crying.

I won't break down in front of Zach, Megan thought fiercely. That's just what he'd expect me to do. The damsel-in-distress routine. And I'm not about to give him the satisfaction.

'Hey, I'm not going anywhere without you,' Mason said. 'Who would tell me what flowers not to touch? I wouldn't dare.'

'But you can't carry me.'

'Sure I can. I've been weight-training for years, since before the first tour. You have to keep in shape if you're gonna survive three years on the road. It's tough.'

'*This* is tough,' Megan said, staring into the dense forest.

'Agreed.' He fell silent for a few moments, thinking. Then he said, 'OK, the way I see it we have two options. One is to stay here, hope that we fell somewhere directly beneath that ridge and that they'll know where to look for us. If we do that, we have to try and figure out ways of making it obvious where we are. It would be nice to light a fire, but' – he patted the sodden log they were sitting on – 'all the wood is soaked through. Plus I don't have a lighter or a magnifying glass and I skipped boy-scout classes, the kind where they teach you that thing with the two dry sticks.'

Megan laughed. 'Me too.'

'Pity,' Mason said, giving her a warm look.

For a second Megan found herself jealous of Roxana again. Zach's thundercloud-grey eyes, his predatory wolf eyes, were suddenly softened, and she couldn't help thinking how attractive he was.

Get over it, girl.

She looked away.

'So, the other option is to get out of here. We'd have to pick one direction and keep going in a straight line, until we hit a road or something.'

'That doesn't sound too scientific.'

'Look, the whole island is only five miles across. Seventeen north to south. And the jungle's just one small part of it. We'll get out soon enough.'

'Will we? I guess that's the sixty-four-dollar question,' Megan said, looking down at her twisted ankle.

'Come on, Megan. You're not giving up on me now, are you?' Zach asked. 'Not after all that work on the script. Think of the delay this is going to cause to the shoot. We have to get back, remember? We're making a movie.'

She laughed. 'Oh, sure. Except that I'm replaceable.'

'I'm not,' Zach told her. He stood up and walked over to the nearest fallen branch, hefting it up and testing its weight.

'Don't be too sure. It's incredible what they can do with technology now,' she told him, secretly admiring his hard body as he moved, the muscles knotting in his back, the wet cloth of his calfskin pants moulded to the rocklike thickness of his thighs. 'Remember *The Crow*? Starred Brandon Lee, Bruce Lee's son. Except that he was accidentally shot dead halfway through filming.'

'No shit?' Zach asked, throwing one branch onto the ground. He took a careful look at Megan, then stepped hard on the wood halfway down it, cracking it in two.

'True story. They finished it with computer morphing. Virtual acting,' Megan told him. She laughed. 'Maybe we could use that for Roxana's part.'

'Good idea,' Zach said grimly.

'You shouldn't trash your girlfriend,' Megan teased him.

Zach shot her a sharp look. 'She's not *my* girlfriend, honey.'

'Yeah, right,' Mgan said, shrugging. She couldn't be bothered to argue with him.

'She's not. Anyway, you should talk. David Tauber's little puppy.'

'Fuck you!' Megan spat, nettled. 'I'm nobody's puppy. And certainly not David's. We split up.'

'Oh, really?' Mason asked softly. He kicked the branch to one side and walked across to her, standing over her. Megan shrank back on the log, but Zach reached forward, towards the neckline of her T-shirt, and pulled on the fine gold chain glinting against her tanned skin, yanking it free of the soaking cotton, twisting the small gold star with its cursive 'D' between his fingers. 'You're still wearing his dog-tag, I see.'

'I just forgot to take it off,' Megan snapped.

'Uh-huh.'

'God, you're so infuriating,' she said angrily, jerking the pendant out of his grasp. 'You think you're so smart. You and Roxana, you're two of a kind. Just because you're famous you think the rest of the world should be permanently on its knees in front of you. Well, fuck you. You deserve each other. And let's see how many wild animals in here are impressed because you used to sing in a rock band.'

'*I* think I'm so smart? That's good, Megan, really. Coming from the college graduate who was picking me up on my French pronunciation the first time we ever met. Do you know how that made me feel? It was like being back in grade school, I felt three feet high. And then you were always so bitchy in rehearsals, always putting me down. I never expected anybody to kiss my ass, Megan, everybody does it naturally. You get so sick of it all the time. Or they're like you, putting me down because I didn't spend years in a fucking classroom. Nobody is natural with you, except other musicians, maybe. But whatever. Any time you want to get on your knees in front of me, that's fine, sweetheart.'

'In your dreams, you son of a bitch,' she snarled. 'I wouldn't fuck you if you were the last man on earth.'

'Yeah? Because in your case, sugar, I just might be,' Zach retorted.

Their eyes locked for a second in mutual hostility, then Mason moved away from her.

'This won't help us,' he said finally, reaching for the branch he'd tossed aside. 'Like it or not, we're stuck with each other until we get out of this jungle. Right?'

'Right,' Megan agreed, although her face was still flushed red with fury.

'So let's have a truce. Temporarily. We can take up with the insults when we're back in the hotel.'

Megan looked away, biting her lip again, and just nodded. His words stirred the dread that was constantly with her. Jesus, who knew if they would ever get back to the hotel? She wondered if anybody had ever longed to walk through that lobby the way she did now.

'Check this out, another one,' Zach said, pleased, bending down to pick up a second branch with a forked tip. He flung it next to the first and cracked it at the base, smashing it cleanly with his foot.

'Zach, what are you doing?' Megan asked.

'We gotta get you mobile,' Mason said, holding up his two branches triumphantly. He smiled. 'Crutches, courtesy of Mother Nature.'

'You are out of your mind,' Megan told him, but she gave them a hard look, and added, 'Probably.'

'Try them. You can't walk on that ankle, and it's better if I carry you only when I have to – I can save my strength that way.' He came over and helped her hook her arms over the forks in the wood, then lifted her gently to her feet. 'How are they?'

'I'd prefer to get around in a cab, but not bad,' Megan said, testing her weight against the wood. It held fine. 'You got my height exactly right,' she told him, surprised.

'I should do. I've watched you often enough,' Mason said.

She glanced at him, but he'd turned aside.

'I think we should head southeast,' Megan suggested. 'I remember watching the forest from the ridge – it was thinnest to the southeast.'

'Got a compass?'

'We could use the sun. Rises in the east, sets in the west.'

'Right.' Zach smacked his forehead. 'Trust Dr Livingstone here to forget something like that.' He walked across the sunlit patch of ground, shading his eyes, and gazed up into the sky.

Megan tried not to stare too obviously at Zach Mason's sun-drenched body, the light lovingly accentuating every taut muscle, the tangled, attractive mane of black hair that fell halfway down his back, the distinct, promising bulge between his thighs... She dropped her gaze, blushing, before he spotted her lusting after him and gave her some superior put-down.

And I'm not that interested anyway, Megan told herself. Maybe it's just because he looks like a savage in those calfskin leggings, with that hair.

'Hey, Hiawatha,' she called. 'Which way?'

'Over there, I guess.' He pointed. 'Why Hiawatha?'

'You look like a Red Indian in those pants,' Megan said, grinning.

Zach glanced down and laughed. 'I see what you mean. But you kind of startled me; I'm quarter Cherokee.'

'No shit. Really?'

'My father's mother,' Zach said, nodding.

Megan shivered. *That's where he gets those strange eyes. Wolf eyes, predator's eyes.*

'I never knew,' she said.

'Never read about it, you mean. That was one of my few successes,' Mason told her, walking over. 'I tried to keep my family out of it as much as I could. Besides, with the Indian stuff they'd never let it go. I had as much "New Jim Morrison" as I could take.' He helped her over the log. 'Are you ready to go?'

'As ready as I'll ever be,' Megan said. She swung the crutches, moved her right foot, then swung her left foot after it.

'Aah,' she muttered, wincing from the renewed stabs of pain.

'I'll carry you,' Zach said immediately, leaping forward.

Megan waved him back. 'No, it's OK. It's just a twinge. Nothing I can't handle.' She tried again, took a step forward, then another. 'See? No problem. Give me ten minutes to practise, and I'll be sprinting.' She smiled at him, making light of it, trying to distract him. If Zach thinks I'm suffering, he'll insist on slinging me over his shoulder. And then it'll take us three days to get out of here, she thought. I can't let him know how much it hurts.

She wondered briefly what David Tauber would have done if she'd been stranded with him instead. And felt a chill run through her at the thought.

'You let me know if you need help, Megan,' Zach insisted, watching her carefully.

'I'm fine, really. Let's go find a nice restaurant, about four miles due southeast.'

'I mean it.' He was hesitating.

'So do I,' Megan said firmly. She gave him a bright smile and took three paces forward, walking slowly but surely in the direction he'd pointed out. 'Now, what are we going to talk about during this little stroll? How about Dark Angel? You guys meant the world to me once, if you can believe that.'

'You have to be kidding,' Zach said, but he followed her.

'No. And since I'm stuck with you, you're going to have to answer all my questions, Zach. Because I'm going to need more than the pretty scenery to distract me.'

'Will you answer all *my* questions? It has to go two ways.'

'Sure. It's a better deal for me.'

'We'll see about that,' Zach said, giving her a lazy smile. 'But OK, Megan. You get the exclusive interview.'

'It'll be the longest one you ever give.'

'You know that's the truth,' he agreed, and they set off together, slowly, walking into the green uncharted depths of the jungle.

31

Tom Goldman walked into his office with a heavy heart. Not that anybody would have noticed: he was at his desk by half-seven, as usual; he was smartly dressed, as usual, this morning in a black bespoke suit by Anderson & Sheppard of Savile Row, a Turnbull & Asser pinstripe shirt and a sober navy-blue tie; and none of the security guards or secretaries noticed anything different about his manner, because Goldman had been acting depressed and low-key for months. It was going to be another blazing hot day on the Artemis lot. Business as usual.

Except not for me, Goldman thought wearily as he logged into his computer. The password had to be changed every week and he did it without thinking. This morning he found himself tapping in *Victrix Hotel* and smiled grimly. Pretty Freudian. There was no getting away from it: he just couldn't stop thinking about Eleanor Marshall, about the miraculous night he'd spent with her, and all the nights that they could have had, and the time he'd wasted and the dumb choices he'd made. Maybe to an outsider, Tom thought, the irony of his situation would seem amusing or elegant, but to him it was simply pain; bitter, crashing waves of regret, and longing, and the hopeless sense of certainty that it was now too late, and it would be too late forever. Jordan, the sensational little sex bomb that he had so foolishly married, thinking she would add a certain *shiksa*, Bostonian class to his life – what a joke – had turned into a dead weight around his neck. It was impossible to talk to her about his work, or art, or music, or sports, or politics – in short, any of the subjects he was interested in. The sole topic of conversation that interested his wife was social mountaineering, and her babble was conducted in an arcane language that he couldn't understand and didn't want to learn – 'Co-Chairman of the Junior League', 'Secretary to the Benefit's Social Subcommittee', 'Vice-President's Assistant for Membership'.

It seemed that that was Jordan's world – throwing expensive, thousand-dollar-a-plate benefit dinners for causes she didn't give a damn about and fitting in with a bunch of overdressed, bejewelled, bored Beverly Hills housewives who all hated each other anyway.

'But sweetheart, this stuff is so petty, don't you think?' Tom had asked her last Friday, when Jordan was insisting on dragging him out to some fancy-dress ball in aid of saving the whales, or inner-city literacy, or whatever the hell it was that week. He was tired, and he really wanted to just stay home, climb in the hot tub and veg out, just stare at the stars for a while.

'I don't understand,' Jordan had replied, giving that little-girl pout he'd come to dislike intensely.

Tom tried again. 'It's not important, Jordan.'

'How can you say that?' Jordan's face was a mask of horror. 'Don't you know that Susie Metcalf is the chairman? She's *totally* important, Tom! John only married her last year and this is her first big evening! Of *course* it's important, she expects me to be there!'

'And what happens if we skip it?

'Skip it? Don't be silly, Tom!' Jordan stamped her Chanel pumps in frustration. 'If we don't show, Susie and all the other Metropolis Studios girls might not take tables out for my drug-prevention slave auction in November.'

'Heaven forbid,' Goldman said with heavy sarcasm, and went upstairs to change.

But it's my fault, Tom told himself. I married a doll, a pretty blonde toy I thought I could never get tired of. I thought I could get companionship from other friends, but it's too lonely at the top to have that many real friends, and too busy to spend much time with them. You need to be able to talk to your wife, because she's the only one who's there all the time. All Jordan and I ever had was sex, and now . . .

Something had taken the bloom off that rose, too. He had been trying not to admit it, but this morning his feelings simply could not be brushed under the carpet. It was that evening with Eleanor. No whips, no chains, no baby oil and blue movies – just two people moving together, and it had been the most incredible sexual experience of his life. Like something you read about, where the climax was more than mere physical relief, where he felt it crash around his heart and his mind, touch his very soul. It had moved him almost to tears. And when it was over, he'd had no desire to go straight to sleep, no sense of slight embarrassment at whatever scene he'd just acted out – he'd wanted to stay there, with Eleanor, holding her and caressing her and finally drifting to sleep in her arms. It was a feeling of the sweetest, purest happiness. It was total contentment.

It was love.

Goldman stood up abruptly and began to pace up and down his office, distressed.

Why do I have to dwell on it now? he thought bitterly. Why today, of all days? Today, when I have to see her, when I have to tell her she's fired?

The icy winds sliced through him, and Joey Duvall shivered as he turned into the lobby of the elegant brownstone on West 74th Street, clutching his camel-hair overcoat more tightly around him. Another freezing fall day in Manhattan, not ideal weather for trudging around the Upper West Side. But Joey wasn't complaining. So far, it had been a very profitable morning, and it was just about to get a lot better.

'Mr Duvall?' the receptionist enquired. Joey nodded curtly. 'Mrs Fransen is expecting you, sir. If you'd like to take the elevator to the fourth floor, I'll ring up and let her know you've arrived.'

Joey nodded again, picked up his burgundy leather briefcase and stepped into one of the elevators. He pressed the button and took a casual look around as the car hissed smoothly upwards. All polished brass and marble detailing; very nice. Mrs David Fransen had certainly risen in the world, Joey thought. Like most of her old colleagues. One in particular.

The elevator stopped on the fourth floor and Duvall stepped out into a long corridor, carpeted in thick, expensive-looking navy wool, its eggshell-blue walls hung with various gloomy paintings of horses and fox-hunting scenes. More English than Buckingham Palace. The Fransens' door was one of only two on that level, marked with a discreet brass nameplate for 'Mr and Mrs David Fransen'. Joey was amused. What would Babette Delors know from class? But apparently she had learned.

It was gonna be interesting to see how she handled this blast from the past, Joey thought.

He pushed the bell, listened to a few soft, musical notes chiming inside the apartment.

The door opened immediately. A young woman, the picture of a stylish New York wife, stood in front of him, dressed in a smart dark green suit, with a thin string of emeralds looped across the creamy skin of her throat. She could not have been more than twenty-seven or twenty-eight, he guessed, and she was extremely attractive, thick red hair cut in a geometric, Vidal Sassoon-type bob, bright blue eyes and long, slender legs. Everything about her screamed of money and privilege, from the soft fabric of the suit to the large dark blue sapphire of her engagement ring. But she was looking at him with hatred, and the sense of fear emanating from her was so strong he could practically smell it.

'Mademoiselle Delors?' he enquired blandly.

'My name is Barbara Fransen,' she hissed. 'What do you want?'

Duvall hefted up his briefcase. 'Information, Mrs Fransen. Nothing else. May I come in?'

Wordlessly she held open the door for him, and Duvall walked into the lower reception room of a magnificent duplex. Furnished in soft cream and butterscotch tones, it had great views over the city, antique mahogany furniture, what looked like a Ming vase on the mantelpiece, and a top-of-the-range speaker system. His eye fell upon some Baccarat crystal tumblers, one of which would have cost him a month's wage a year or so back, when he was schlepping overtime for the NYPD. Things were different in private work, but then he'd fallen on his feet. He would always be aware of the value of things, of the difference money could make in a person's life. You have to be a self-made person to really appreciate wealth, that's what he reckoned. And to truly fear having it taken away from you.

That was why he was so good at his job. And that was why Mrs David Fransen was about to open her beautifully made-up mouth and sing like a canary. Because there was no way on God's green earth, Duvall congratulated himself, that this lady was ready to swap the Baccarat for the back streets. She was standing in the centre of her Persian rug, twisting her hands nervously and not speaking.

'May I sit down, ma'am?' he asked, nodding towards the high-backed ebony chairs ranged around one of the ornate glass coffee tables.

'If you have to,' she said ungraciously, and then added, 'I don't know what you want. If it's money, I can't take too much out of David's account before he notices, and I only have a little of my own – '

'I'm sure,' Duvall interjected smoothly, cutting her off. He didn't want the bitch getting hysterical and doing anything dumb. 'Like I say, Mrs Fransen, this is not about blackmail. We aren't interested in you, ma'am. Just what you can tell us.'

He laid the briefcase flat on the shiny glass table top and clicked open the lid. Inside, neatly ranged in order of importance, were typed notes from every subject they'd interviewed around the world. A Parisian hostess. A sheik's favourite wife, safely ensconced in a luxury Cairo penthouse for over ten years – a modern take on the harem, he guessed. An impoverished policeman from Kansas City who wasn't quite so impoverished any more. A retired social worker, ditto. A court stenographer. Several ex-models, all of them current wives of wealthy, powerful men. It was a bizarre collection, but a useful one – like the oddly shaped pieces of a jigsaw puzzle, they made a very clear picture when you slotted them all together. Joey Duvall had been the operative responsible for finding three of those pieces, more than any other agent. And Mlle Delors was going to make four.

He grinned as he fished out the clear black and white photographs, chose the relevant pictures and handed them across to her. This was going to mean more than a pat on the back for him. If he read the excitement at headquarters correctly, the bonus on this baby would be the biggest payday of his career.

'Do you recognize that woman?'

She glanced at him, then nodded. 'Yes.'

'And did you have dealings with her in Paris, eight years ago?'

The answer was so low he could barely hear it.

'Yes.' The woman was biting her lip, tears forming in the corners of her eyes.

'Don't upset yourself, Mrs Fransen, my firm is *extremely* discreet,' Duvall told her softly. 'I'm just gonna ask you for a few details, and you're gonna answer me, and then I'm gonna get out of your life and you'll never see or hear from me again. Right?'

'Right,' she said, nervously, gratefully.

Duvall pulled out a silk handkerchief from his jacket pocket and handed it to her, smiling. 'Everything's gonna be just fine, Mrs Fransen. *Ne vous inquiétez pas.*'

Eight a.m. Tom Goldman spun in his chair, gripped with misery and self-doubt.

Should I go in to her? he wondered. Normally that's what I do in the mornings. But for something like this, is that wise? I should get her in here. But it's not formal – it's a warning...

Despairingly he passed a hand through his hair. I do *not* want to do this, he thought desperately. But he had to. It was now or later, and later would be worse. He just could not allow her to walk into the production meeting unprepared, to face Jake Keller's point-by-point demolition of her work on

See the Lights in front of everyone else. Eleanor had to be allowed time to write a good exit speech, something that would let her leave with dignity. Keller would hate him for doing it, but he could go screw himself.

I'm going to warn her, Goldman decided. I owe her that much.

Reluctantly, he lifted his handset and punched in Eleanor Marshall's extension.

Eleanor hit her office by six a.m., adrenalin still racing through her veins. She caught a glimpse of her reflection in the glass door of her secretary's office; despite the lack of sleep, she looked better than she had done in years, her hair newly dry and full-bodied, her make-up bold and confident – God, when was the last time I bothered with mascara? she wondered – and her eyes were bright, lively and alert.

After the conversation I just had with Alex, they should be, Eleanor told herself. She logged in to her computer, pulled up a word-processing package and started to type the list of points Rosen had dictated to her. Then she turned on the printer, accessed her private back-up files for the *See the Lights* memos and began to run off labelled, dated copies.

Her fingers were flying over the keyboard, racing to get everything done in time. Eleanor didn't bother with coffee, she was already totally wired. Next up, e-mail, she told herself, punching in another set of codes and commands. A list of memos and letters, scanned by date and subject, appeared on the screen. Silently, Eleanor blessed Bill Burton, Artemis's resident systems boffin, for forcing her to take the computing proficiency course last year. She'd wanted to refuse – who had the time? – but Bill had sternly told her that it was senior management's duty to set an example to the other staff. So she'd allowed him to lock her away for two days and show her the basics – 'There you go, princess, you'll never have to rely on your assistant again,' Bill had told her proudly. Eleanor had shaken her head – the techno kids lived in a world of their own – but he'd insisted: 'You'll be kissing my ass for this one day, Marshall, I'm telling you.'

God. I have to send that boy flowers, she thought gratefully as she punched in Jake Keller's codes and told his machine to search for, and print out, discrepancies it found against her own original memoranda.

I've got Keller's codes, but he doesn't have mine, Eleanor exulted. Privilege of office! Read this and weep, you son of a bitch. I'm still the president here. And whatever you may have thought, it's gonna stay that way.

The phone on her desk shrilled. Eleanor picked it up with her left hand, her right hand continuing to speed across the keyboard, her eyes fixed on the screen. Jesus, this was unbelievable. Except for the fact that Jake Keller was behind it . . . except for the fact that the proof was unfolding before her eyes and shooting out of her colour printer at four pages a minute. Eleanor's lips tightened. Maybe they should invent a new proverb – hell hath no fury like a male executive scorned. Especially if it's in favour of a woman.

'Marshall,' she said.

'Eleanor, this is Tom.'

'Hey, Tom. Can it wait? I'm in the middle of something here.'

'No. I have to see you now.'

There was an urgent note in his voice that Eleanor did not miss. 'OK. I'll be there in five minutes,' she told him, and hung up. Then she took her small gold powder compact out of her purse and checked her make-up, reapplying a dab of lipstick as the printer spat out the last of her files. Once it was finished, she picked everything up and shoved it in her briefcase, locking it shut. She grabbed the neatly typed list of Alex Rosen's contractual points, spritzed a little scent across her neck – Chanel No. 5, Eleanor was in a classical mood this morning – and set off briskly for Tom Goldman's office.

Isn't it ridiculous? Eleanor thought. I'm fighting for my career and in a couple of hours I'll need to be on a plane to the Seychelles. I ought to be worried sick, but I'm not. Face it! I'm feeling terrific!

As she careered into Goldman's office, Eleanor felt a minor twitch of guilt at the exhilaration surging through her. After all, she was about to hang Jake Keller out to dry. His career was over once she did this, not just at Artemis but anywhere else. And if Tom didn't like it, too bad. She had him by the balls, and she knew it. Was it unfeminine to feel such a thrill at the prospect of revenge? Eleanor wondered. But screw that. It had never stopped Queen Boadicea.

'Eleanor, come in,' Tom Goldman said, rising to meet her. He shifted uneasily from foot to foot, obviously uncomfortable. 'How's Paul?'

'Asleep,' she replied irreverently, wondering what the hell had gotten into her. And what was the personal small-talk? Tom had never wasted time on polite preliminaries before.

'You look great,' Goldman said truthfully, gesturing at her crimson Donna Karan suit and bright red lipstick. 'Married life must be agreeing with you.'

Eleanor strolled over to Goldman's desk and took the chair in front of it, confident and relaxed. 'Not so far,' she said levelly. 'But you can cut the banter, Tom. You said you had to see me. What do you want to discuss?'

He sat down heavily. 'I don't *want* to discuss this, Eleanor, believe me. But I have to. We – we've been working together for a long time, long enough for me to owe you a warning.' Goldman sighed heavily, hating what he was forced to say next. 'Jake Keller is going to bring up all the disastrous production decisions that you made about locations, casting, unions or whatever on *See the Lights*, and contrast them with the objections he lodged in that memo you made him write. We're facing a bath on this movie, Eleanor, and if word gets out it could affect the stock. That would be the end of the studio.' He glanced at her, then looked away again. 'Keller says he has a detailed plan for completing this film at a minimal further cost, but the price he's demanded for giving it to me is that he replace you as the executive in charge of the project, and that I announce it publicly. He wants me to do it at the meeting this afternoon.'

Goldman paused, took a breath. Why had he put it like that? He'd meant to say, *I'm going to do it at the meeting this afternoon. I'm sorry . . . I have no choice.* He'd meant to sit here and break it to Eleanor Marshall as gently as he could; he was sacking her.

It was his duty as CEO.

There was no other way.

It would be nothing personal. Right?

She gazed back at him, those sparkling eyes calm and unfazed. Tom felt his heart contract with respect and love. Eleanor was as brave now as she'd been when he first met her fifteen years ago. He flashed back to those same eyes, warm and brilliant, looking up at him in bed in New York, filled with sweet love and hot desire.

Now he had to look into those same eyes, look at this woman who'd been his friend and partner for fifteen years, and tell her she was fired.

'And are you going to, Tom?' Eleanor asked quietly.

For a second she held her breath. So this was it. He was about to break faith with her, for the sake of business, for the sake of his job. And even though she knew that Alex Rosen could save her position, there would be no saving her love for Tom Goldman. Not after this.

Once he said the words, it was all over.

Tom Goldman looked at Eleanor Marshall, and suddenly, irrationally, felt a great weight lifting off his chest. He couldn't do it. It was that simple.

'No,' he said. 'No, I'm not. I can't do it to you, kiddo. Not that it'll help you any; the Artemis board will have you out in a heartbeat. But I'm not gonna point you at the exit sign. I'll resign first.' He shrugged. 'What the hell? We came in together, we'll go out together.'

Eleanor stared at him, a thrill of exultant love rushing through her. My God, she thought. If I'd waited one more day to do this, it would have been too late.

Goldman misinterpreted her silence, and felt a surge of pain and compassion. 'Look, I do know how hard this must be for you. If there's anything I can do, anything at all, just name it.'

Eleanor shook her head, smiling. 'Tom, I'm sorry. I was thinking of something else.' She cleared her throat, held up Alex Rosen's list in front of her and said coolly, 'Now, let me tell you what's actually going to happen. My lawyer is taking the first plane out of New York, and he should be here by lunchtime, so he can go over it with you then. But I thought I'd give you a little rundown first. Number one, my contract as president of Artemis states that nobody can be hired above me or below me without my approval, unless the company is sold. I would regard Artemis placing Jake Keller in charge of production on my movie as placing him above me. And so would a court. They'd be in breach of contract, Tom, and I'll file a suit against the studio this afternoon. And I'll announce it at a press conference.'

'Eleanor – '

She held up a hand. 'I'm not done. Furthermore, I cannot be dismissed without three written warnings, none of which I have received, and a review with the board in New York. Again, if Artemis violates these conditions, I will sue. And I have the guaranteed right to see my first green-lighted project through to completion and release.' She smiled gently. 'If you recall, Tom, you advised me to have that clause inserted in the deal, so they couldn't do to me what they tried to do to Martin Webber. And Alex Rosen, my lawyer, is very hot on this issue. He says if Artemis tries to get out of it we'll sue for millions. Moreover, this binds any future owners of the studio. So Howard and his buddies can't just ship me off to the Japs and let them fire me, either.'

Eleanor tapped her long, elegant fingernails on top of Rosen's list. 'We've got three major breaches, right there, Tom. And it will be a splashy trial. I'll turn it into a feminist *cause célèbre*, and the nation can turn a spotlight on how Hollywood treats women – *all* women, not just the handful of us who make it to senior executive level. Remember when Dawn Steel was president of Production at Paramount, and they ousted her while she was in labour with her little girl? Nice, huh? Well, they can *forget* about trying that with me. Or I'm going to make every Artemis stockholder rue the day they were born.'

Tom Goldman sat back, gazing at her in total shock. He opened his mouth to say something, but no words came out.

'What about Jake's plan for *See the Lights*?' he managed eventually. 'We have to rescue that picture, Eleanor. We're looking at a hundred-fifteen-million-dollar loss! We can't survive it!'

'We couldn't survive a loss that size, true. But we aren't going to take a loss. I spoke to Fred Florescu this morning, and he tells me that they'll be all done in a month, and what they finally have down is awesome. Now, let's talk about Mr Keller.' She reached for her briefcase, unlocking it, drew out the sheaves of memos and e-mail messages and passed them across the desk to her boss.

'What are these?' Goldman asked, mystified.

'These are copies of my original memos, laying out all the location sites and production details we had decided on, after I took reports from my location scouts.' Tom nodded. 'And these are copies from Jake Keller's computer, showing where he altered them. The discrepancies are highlighted in bold type. You'll see that most of the changes are minor – one beach versus another, that kind of thing – although the changes resulted in lost hours and costly reshoots. Keller was switching locations to nature reserves, protected or dangerous areas, or beaches where the tide would come in too fast and cause a shoot to be abandoned.'

'But how could this have happened without you noticing?'

She nodded. 'You're right. And that was my fault; it won't happen again. I was too trusting, it never occurred to me that a senior executive at this studio would actually stoop to sabotage. But Jake asked me to sign off on some "minor changes", as he put it. The big one I missed was the warning about the weather in the Seychelles. I advised the crew to switch to Hawaii if filming hadn't wrapped by a certain date, to avoid the rainy season. And Jake deleted that from my instructions.'

'I don't believe it,' Tom said, dumbfounded.

'Nor did I, but there's your proof. If you access his computer now, before he arrives, you'll see the same thing yourself. And there is one other matter – casting. Jake's condemnation of me for picking Roxana, and then his desire to enlarge her part.'

'We did have major trouble with Roxana, Eleanor. We still do,' Goldman said, feeling he should make some kind of a rally on the studio's behalf. The documents he was holding seemed to smoke in his hands. Jesus Christ? How come *I* never thought to investigate, either? he asked himself, utterly dismayed.

'Yes. And perhaps these will explain some of that,' Eleanor told him, passing across one final pile of papers. 'I pulled them out of Jake Keller's private e-mail file. They're faxes sent to David Tauber at the Méridien Hotel, Anse Polite, Seychelles, discussing Roxana Felix's deliberate disruption of the shoot, and when it would be best for her to start working properly – after I had been fired.'

Tom Goldman took them and glanced through them, his face darkening.

'Cancel the production meeting, Tom. You can reschedule it a week from now. That'll give you time to discuss Keller with our lawyers.'

'Very well,' he said quietly. 'What excuse should I give?'

'Unfortunately, you don't have to give them an excuse,' Eleanor told him. 'The main reason Florescu rang me this morning is that Zach Mason and Megan Silver are missing.' She gave him a brief description of her phone call. 'You can tell them that I had to fly out to Mahé this morning to supervise a rescue effort. In my absence, you'll be taking over my responsibilities. Right?'

'Right.' Goldman paused, leant towards her. 'Eleanor, I – '

'Save it.' She gave him a quick smile. 'We can talk when I get back.'

32

'I hope you can appreciate, Mrs Kendrick, that we have only been conducting the investigation for a matter of days,' Grant Booth said nervously, as he watched Isabelle sort through the foolscap document wallet, occasionally holding up a photograph to the light, her face expressionless. 'I realize that there is a certain lack of witnesses to the findings we have come up with so far. We normally obtain at least ten witnesses per incident or fact that we allege took place.'

'Can you get me more witnesses to this?' Isabelle enquired.

Booth nodded hastily, flicking a finger across the navy-blue sleeve of his suit, a masterpiece of immaculate tailoring by Turnball & Asser in London, as if removing an imaginary piece of lint. It was so important to impress Mrs Kendrick. Not only was she paying them more than handsomely, she was a social power in the city. Her recommendation to the wives and ex-wives of Hollywood moguls could double the firm's revenue in a year. He would bend over backwards to please her. Indeed, he would contort himself into any position the lady required.

'Certainly, madam, certainly. And we have various employees doing just that as we speak. But since the story that was emerging was so, uh, so *surprising*, we felt you would want to have the basic skeleton of the matter right away. An interim report, if you like.'

Isabelle closed the lid of the document wallet. 'Can I keep these?' she asked.

'Please, be my guest.' Booth nodded reassuringly. 'We have several copies of everything.'

Isabelle nodded, pushed back her chair and stood up to leave.

'Is – is everything satisfactory so far, Mrs Kendrick?' he asked her anxiously.

For the first time that morning, Isabelle Kendrick favoured him with a slight smile. 'I look forward to receiving your full report, Mr Booth, but I must say your work so far has been excellent.' She glanced coolly down at the document wallet, placed neatly inside her soft leather Gucci tote bag. 'Absolutely excellent.'

Grant Booth's pudgy face beamed with relief as he sprang forward to hold open his office door for her.

Isabelle parked her Bentley in front of the house, trying to contain herself. It wouldn't do to let Sam see her in this state. She was bubbling over with happiness, her manicured fingers tapping out old Sinatra tunes on the steering wheel. A long time ago, when she'd been interested in things like music, Sinatra and Tony Bennett had been her favourites. Kind of appropriate, really, Isabelle thought, restraining an unseemly grin. She was about to do it Her Way. But Sam mustn't know until it was too late; according to these reports, Sam had actually developed *feelings* for the little slut. A blast of cold anger sliced through her elation, but she suppressed it. Never mind what her husband chose to do with his empty little heart. She had lost that years ago. And it was hardly important. It was Sam who was important – the man himself, and the status that his thick platinum band on her left hand represented. Isabelle had not come all this way to lose it to some twenty-four-year-old mannequin now.

But peace, peace, Isabelle soothed herself as she stepped out of the car, smoothing her peach Bill Blass suit as she did so. That was all taken care of – Mr Booth and his cohorts had seen to that. Now the only thing that remained was for her to pick a reporter to give this story to. She would choose carefully, for it was the showbusiness scoop of the decade, and whoever she handed that foolscap binder to would owe Isabelle huge forever. She had to select somebody with appropriate clout, somebody worth having in her designer pocket. There was no point in rushing things, Isabelle thought. She had to keep one eye on her future. Unlike Ms Felix, who after today didn't *have* a future.

Isabelle practically bounded up the steps of the terrace, nodded curtly at the maid who admitted her, and walked through to her study right away. First things first. Because she wanted so desperately to believe what Booth, Warwick & Yablans were telling her, that didn't mean it was true. For her own peace of mind she wanted to check up on a couple of details. She dialled Jordan Goldman's number and waited, one foot tapping impatiently on her antique Chinese rug.

'Goldman residence.'

'Isabelle Kendrick for Mrs Goldman,' Isabelle said impatiently. She wished dear Jordan wouldn't insist on having the servants always answer the phone. Really, so affected.

'Isabelle! I'm so glad you *called*.' Jordan was gushing. 'I've been wanting to speak to you about my slave auction next month. Do you think I should make togas mandatory?'

'Oh, definitely not, dear,' Isabelle said, shuddering at the thought of all that wrinkled male flesh exposed. 'But we can talk about that in a second. I want to ask you a few questions about Roxana Felix.'

'Anything, Isabelle,' Jordan said obediently.

'You always said Roxana had been a schoolfriend of yours, dear, but how long was she actually at the Sacred Heart?'

'Only one year. She was enrolled in senior year,' Jordan said, surprised at the question. 'She was eighteen when she arrived.'

Isabelle gave a sharp intake of breath. So it was all true.

'Are you OK, Isabelle?'

'I'm fine. Tell me, did you ever see her mother or her father at the school? Did they ever come to pick her up, or attend graduation?'

'No. As a matter of fact, they didn't come to graduation,' Jordan mused thoughtfully, remembering it. 'We all thought that was weird, but Roxie said they were in Europe on business and couldn't be there. But they never came to pick her up, either; at the end of term, she always left for the airport in a cab.'

'Thank you, dear. That's very useful,' Isabelle said, one hand balling into a fist of triumph at her side. 'I have to go now. I've got a few calls to make.'

'But what about my togas?' Jordan whined.

'I'll call you back,' Isabelle said firmly, hanging up.

She stood there for a few seconds, racing through the possibilities, and finally settled on the ideal person. Marissa Matthews, the most widely read gossip columnist in New York, an old acquaintance, and syndicated all over Los Angeles. Isabelle congratulated herself: Marissa would kill for a story like this. And she would be the perfect ally for an entrée into New York society. After all, she had already conquered Los Angeles, and one had to expand one's horizons.

Smiling, she lifted the phone and punched in the number.

'Marissa? Darling, it's Isabelle Kendrick. I have a scoop for you. Rather a big one, in fact. Do you have a decent fax up there? . . . Oh, it can take photographs too, can it? Splendid . . .'

Eleanor leaned back in the air-conditioned comfort of the hotel's sedan, sent to collect her from Seychelles airport, and gazed out of the windows. Physical fatigue was beginning to hit her, but she forced herself to stay awake. This was going to have been a big day for her, but it wasn't over yet. Not by a long shot. First, she'd managed to save her job, and that had been fun; Tom, looking gorgeous in that sombre black suit, and sitting there with his mouth hanging open in astonishment, was a sight she would never forget. Blown away by the new, tough, improved Eleanor Marshall. But that was the easy part; she just prayed she could be tough enough for Megan and Zach. If there was any Megan and Zach left to rescue. But somehow Eleanor was sure they had survived. She could feel it in her bones. They were alive, and stranded somewhere in that emerald-green jungle she'd stared at from the windows of her plane.

Fred Florescu, looking pale and anxious, was waiting for her in the lobby when she arrived. 'Thanks for getting here so quickly,' he said. 'It's the second day they've been missing. I've notified all the authorities, and they've got a search under way . . .' The young director shook his head. 'I don't know what else we can do. There's been no news.'

'OK. Here's what I've been thinking,' Eleanor said. 'First up, I'm going to hire every private helicopter available on this island to fly over the national park, with spotlights backwards and forwards all night.'

'That'll cost you,' Florescu said.

'That's my problem, Fred. I'm authorized to draw on Artemis funds for this search. Next, I'm hiring locals to go into the jungle and look for them.'

'The mist forest they're lost in is eleven miles square,' Florescu told her, despairingly. 'You'd need hundreds of people to make any impact.'

'And I'm prepared to hire hundreds. Thousands, if necessary. We'll pay them five hundred dollars each to look for Zach and Megan, and give the guy that finds them a five-thousand-dollar reward.'

Florescu looked at her with a new respect. 'Jesus, Eleanor. Studio execs are supposed to be tight-wadded assholes. Where did you come from?'

She laughed. 'Hey, we *are* tight-wadded assholes. This is just an investment, as far as I'm concerned. A dead Zach Mason means a big loss for Artemis Studios, and Megan Silver will make a lot of money for us, down the line. I've got a lot of personal capital in *See the Lights*, Fred. I want to see this movie released.'

'And you know what? You're going to be sitting on one hell of a goddamned smash when it is,' Florescu told her.

'Good. Now, you get the rest of the cast together and start shooting.'

'Do *what*?'

'Start shooting,' Eleanor repeated. 'Film some scenes without Zach or Roxana in them. There have to be a few left, right?'

'There are, but – '

'Forget *but*, Fred. You're no use to Zach and Megan sitting here moping. None of you know the forest, and I'm not risking any more of my people in there.' She gave him a soft smile. 'I intend to get those kids out alive and well. I want them to have a picture to go back to. Now, are we making a movie here or not?'

'Yes, ma'am!' Fred Florescu replied, smiling broadly.

'It's getting dark,' Megan said.

She tried to keep the fear out of her voice. They had already spent one night in the undergrowth, but then she'd been unconscious, knocked cold by the fall. This evening it would be different. Megan doubted if she'd sleep at all, despite her exhaustion, every muscle seemed to shriek in protest as she took another step forward with her right foot, balanced her weight on the makeshift crutches and swung her useless left foot forward to join it. She had gone as fast as she could all day, refusing to stop for a rest despite Zach's urging; Megan knew that if she sat down she'd never have been able to get back up. Twice she'd stumbled and fallen, screaming with pain as her swollen ankle jarred against some hidden rock or branch, and Mason had insisted on carrying her until her kicks and scratches finally persuaded him to put her down. Megan refused to wear Zach out: deep inside, although she was too scared to face the possibility right now, was the feeling that maybe Zach was their only hope; maybe he'd have to leave her in the jungle and run on ahead, gambling that he could get out of the forest and that help would arrive quick enough to save her. Although somehow she doubted that they'd find her again; one patch of jungle looked much like another.

Well, Megan thought, gripped with gallows humour, at least this is a pretty spot for a grave.

Beautiful but deadly; that summed up the mist forest. Gnarled northea and screwpine palms covered with damp moss and creepers, bright sunlight penetrating into the green gloom of the woodlands, primeval giant ferns rearing up everywhere under the jade canopy overhead. Brightly coloured birds swooped and plunged through the trees. The scent of wild cinnamon, vanilla orchids and passionflowers hung in the air, underlying everything along with the buzz of insects and the calls of the tree frogs and the geckos. Never in her wildest dreams had Megan imagined any place so strange and lovely. But it was terrifying, too: twice Mason had scooped her into his arms, trembling and frozen with fear, and carried her several yards away from a scorpion; they had passed three huge hanging nests of yellow wasps, a savage genus of the species that could paralyse if they attacked in numbers; a thick Seychelles wolf snake had slithered out of some leaves and writhed right through Megan's crutches, and although she knew they were harmless Megan had trouble suppressing her natural dread of the giant palm spiders, each one the size of a human hand, that hung from every other tree in thick white cobwebs. She was frightened of nightfall, she couldn't help it. She kept thinking about tarantulas, and the jungle would be swarming with bats. What she could cope with in the green and gold of daylight would become horrible, unbearable in the dark, the blackness crawling and slithering with nameless terrors.

Thank God she wasn't alone. Zach had been with her when she woke up and he had been by her side every step of the way, carrying her, comforting her, protecting her. Megan felt suffused with gratitude for the way the guy had behaved: picking her up when she needed help, joking around to distract her, forcing her to talk about herself incessantly, so that she could get through the day. He'd never once complained over the way she was slowing them down; he would wait for her, with total patience, for as long as it took. And Megan knew she'd slowed them down. Despite all the agonies she'd put herself through, they couldn't have travelled more than two miles in the whole day.

Mason looked up at the patches of sky visible through the treetops. Sunset was definitely falling, streaks of red and gold blazing across the darkening blue heavens like so many banners.

'Looks like it. We'd better stop,' he said, leading her across to an overgrown mossy stump. 'You sit there while I build a shelter. I'll do it right away, before the light fails.' He gave her a warm smile. 'Relax, you get to rest now. You did great.'

'Can I help?' Megan asked, watching him cracking branches and stacking them against the bark of the nearest large tree.

'No. This won't take me five minutes,' Zach told her, jumping up to rip off a few large leaves for thatching. He moved confidently, quickly, the muscles in his back sliding around under his tanned skin, his back covered in a thin sheen of sweat, the tattered shirt long since discarded in the heat and tied around his waist. Megan couldn't help noticing how firm his thighs looked under the calfskin leggings, moulded round his body like a second skin. And his biceps were pretty impressive too, large and rock-hard, as though sculptured by a master craftsman.

David would kill to look like that, Megan thought, and was suddenly overwhelmed with embarrassment at her own stupidity. How could I ever have looked up to that guy? she wondered, blushing a deep red. He's such a weasel, such a peacock, such an ass-kisser! And I acted like putty in his hands! I thought *he* was the talented one, even when somebody like Fred Florescu told me different. I let David dictate to me what I ate, what I wore – I let him stand over me while I worked out! How pathetic can you get? And just because I lost a little weight I convinced myself that I should put my life in his hands. But I was unhappy with how I looked anyway – I would have slimmed down of my own accord, with him or without him . . .

'There you go,' Zach said, standing back. He had finished a small wigwam-style hut of branches, palm fronds and leaves, backed up against the tree for security. 'Not exactly the Ritz-Carlton, but it'll have to do.'

'It's wonderful,' Megan told him.

Zach glanced at her. 'You're blushing.'

'I was thinking about David,' Megan said truthfully.

He turned away and started threading a few more leaves into the thatch.

She took a deep breath. 'I was thinking what an idiot I was ever to see anything in that guy. You were right, you know. He's a complete jerk. We were fighting before we finally split up – I told him I was moving out of the hotel suite – and the next morning he came up to my room and told me to pack, because I was fired. Then he came running back twenty minutes later to tell me I wasn't fired. But I did realize he was an asshole before. Now, I just don't understand why I ever thought any different.'

'Now?' Zach asked, his grey eyes watching her steadily.

'Now I'm here with you,' Megan said, unthinkingly.

Mason gave her a slow smile.

Megan felt the blush deepen to a rich crimson. 'I didn't mean it how it sounded. It's just that you – I meant, you've been so good to me today, you've been really manly about it. David would have left me – ' Her voice trailed off in confusion.

'Me Tarzan, you Jane,' Zach said, but his gaze was travelling slowly up and down her body, and Megan wasn't completely sure he was joking.

'Why did you go with David? I knew you were hanging out together but I never saw you with him until the Electric City show.'

Megan shrugged. 'He decided to make a move on me then, though nothing much happened that night. Actually, I was grateful – I was kind of embarrassed, standing there while you and Roxana were getting close.'

Zach glanced at her. 'I only did that because I saw you with Tauber. After we'd been talking. I was jealous, I guess.'

'You were jealous? I don't understand,' Megan said, feeling a warm wash of desire flood through her groin. Could he be saying what it sounded like he was saying? 'You were with Roxana Felix. She told me so, in that little booth on the stage, remember that? She was wearing the laminate you got her.' She tried to take the accusing note out of her voice and failed. 'When you dedicated that song to me – this is going to sound really stupid, I know – I was so pleased. It meant a lot to me – because you were my hero, once. I grew up on Dark Angel.' Now she was really abashed, blushing harder than ever. She looked down. Was there any way to say something like that and not come off as another dumb groupie? Megan wondered. Because if there was, she surely hadn't found it.

'Why would you think that sounds stupid?'

'Because I sound like a fan.'

'Do you think I despise my fans?' Zach asked. 'I'm glad it meant something to you. That was the point. We didn't write those songs so we could play them to ourselves in Nate's garage. Even if we never expected what happened, we wanted to be heard.'

'She told me that she and you had discussed it together. That you thought the two of you had been a little harsh on me, so you'd do that onstage to make me feel better. And then I felt like a moron, because it wasn't your idea. It was Roxana's.'

Zach Mason stared at her for a long moment, and finally shook his head, laughing.

'What?'

'Megan. It *was* my idea, of course it was. Roxana had nothing to do with it. The pass she was wearing, Sam Kendrick got for her. Roxana Felix was never, ever, my girlfriend! She was sleeping with Sam. She still is. God, you must be the only person on the set who never realized that. She wanted to get together with me, but only for the publicity, or so she could use me. I told her I was interested in somebody else.'

'Oh,' Megan said blankly.

Somebody else? Did I miss something here? Who? I haven't seen anyone else around – he can't mean Mary, surely, she's way too old . . .

'I told her I was interested in you,' Zach said.

Megan sat very still on the tree stump, trying not to breathe.

'But you hate my hair. You were always so rude to me. You don't like me,' she stammered.

'I preferred you the way you were before, that's true. But I figured you were doing that for David.'

'I was doing it to get some attention,' Megan muttered.

Zach smiled at her, his eyes now full of desire. She felt her nipples stiffening in response.

I don't care if this is happening because we're standing together. I don't care if this is all lies, Megan thought fiercely. I want him. I must have him.

Long-submerged waves of longing were beating up in her, making the blood warm under her skin, need pulling at her crotch.

'You always had my attention.'

'I was frightened of you, because of who you were,' Megan admitted.

He nodded, dark hair cascading round his shoulders. 'And I was kind of frightened of you. Because you were so smart, so well educated, and I never even finished high school.'

She stood up and walked carefully over to the hut.

'Let me take those for you.' Zach supported her as she let go her crutches, one arm carefully encircling her waist, then lowered her down onto the ground.

'You are one of the most intelligent men I've ever met,' Megan told him, her brown eyes fixed on his. She could feel the warmth of his body, the tight, naked skin next to her face, and fought back the urge to press her lips against it. This had to be taken slow. 'You must be crazy. Don't you understand that you were the voice, you were the focus, for our whole generation? What did you think made them respond like that?'

'It was just lyrics,' he said, sitting next to her.

'Yeah? And who wrote them, Zach? Who wrote all those songs? You did! And you said what we all believed. You spoke for us. That's something you should be proud of, Zach. You have a genius with music and lyricism that thousands of kids would do anything for, *and* you've proved to be an incredible actor. You don't need a little paper certificate to tell you you're smart. And deep down inside, you know that.' She paused. 'Why did you split the band?'

'You really want to know?'

She nodded, and he settled next to her, pressing his body up against hers. The touch of his skin was electrifying.

Zach closed his eyes briefly. 'I had always written everything. And last Christmas, Nate came to me with two songs he'd laid down, on his own, when there was a break from touring. I told him I couldn't use them. He said he wanted to talk to the other guys. And I freaked. I said I was always going to write all the songs.' He tapped one rough hand on his knee. 'Dark Angel was my baby, Megan. It was my vision, it had been from the beginning, from before our first guitarist left and Nate joined. Maybe I was feeling threatened. I don't know.'

'So what happened?' she asked gently.

'We had a fight.' He shrugged. 'A lot of shit got said that couldn't be taken back. And then Yolanda Henry, our manager, came in on Nate's side. She said they were good songs, and we should use them. I was bitter, I was really incensed. I fired Yolanda and split the band. And within days there was David, pouring oil all over my wounded ego, pushing the right buttons. He asked me if I'd like to try acting, and it sounded good – a chance to show the other guys that I had talent, I could make it without Dark Angel. And that's it. Not very noble.'

'But you believed his songs would hurt your vision of the band,' Megan said.

'You know what? I wish I could tell you that was true. I wish I could say that I acted with integrity. But it's not, and I didn't.' Mason glanced at Megan. 'They were great songs. Really beautiful. And I got jealous, I got protective . . . I thought I was so cool, but when it came right down to it I was just another bigshot with an ego. Yolanda wouldn't bullshit me when I wanted her to. *She* had integrity. So, I fired her.'

He fell silent.

'Go easy on yourself, Zach.'

'I can't. I split my band, for nothing.'

Megan grinned. 'So what? When we get out of here, you fire David, call Nate Suter up, apologize, put the band back together, reinstate Yolanda Henry and apologize to her too. I think it's great. I get to be responsible for Dark Angel getting back together. I'll be the biggest underground heroine since Courtney Love.'

'Just like that, huh?'

'Yeah. Just like that. What's stopping you?'

'Are you serious?' Zach asked, turning to her. His thundercloud eyes stared right into hers, and Megan felt her crotch tighten.

'I'm totally serious. Why not? I'm sure they're feeling just as bad about it as you are.' Feeling hot, flustered at his gaze, she reached into her pocket and drew out the tube of insect repellent. 'Let me put some of this stuff on you. At dusk we're going to need it.'

Zach said, 'Take off your top.'

'What?'

'Take off your top.' He patted the damp ground beneath them and reached to his waist, untying his shirt. 'We have to get some kind of solid covering underneath us, so nothing crawls out of the leaves while we're asleep. The gel should keep the bugs away from our upper bodies.'

Megan did as he said, spreading her shirt next to his on the ground, trying to act naturally. This is a survival situation, she told herself firmly. Right? Just like going to the doctor. He won't think anything of it.

'My God, you're beautiful,' Zach exclaimed softly. He reached out and stroked the soft, creamy flesh of her left breast with one finger, and Megan felt a liquid rush of renewed wanting surge through her like molten lava, his touch burning against her skin. Her nipples stiffened with pleasure, and they both saw it, the swollen buds pressing through the thin chocolate lace of her bra. Half hypnotized, Megan glanced down at Zach's crotch. He was already erect, the hard outline of his cock, large and thick, clearly visible as it strained inside the calfskin. Instantly, a burst of wetness exploded inside Megan's pussy in response, making her rub her thighs against each other with impatient need. She moaned.

'I want to make love to you,' Zach said urgently, his voice rough with desire, and Megan reached out to caress his chest, saying, 'Oh, yes, Zach, please, *now*,' and then his hands were on her breasts, not softly this time, grabbing them, cupping them, his thumbs brushing her taut nipples, sending little shocks of sex through them, and Megan leaned forward, her fingers shaking, and unknotted the laces at the top of his crotch, pulling them halfway down his thighs so that he sprang free, and she took his thickness in her hands and began to play with him, her fingertips lightly brushing against the warm skin of his balls, her fingers wrapping themselves round the stem of his cock, until Zach groaned with pleasure and broke away from her, ripping off his clothes as if he couldn't undress fast enough. Megan, her heart hammering against her chest, snapped open the buttons on her 501s and started to yank them down, then stopped, dismayed.

'What's the matter?' Zach asked her, seeing her sudden distress.

Megan pointed to her injured ankle, bloated and discoloured above the leather of her shoe. 'I can't take my jeans off. I'll never get them over that,' she said, almost choking on her disappointment.

Mason took her head in his hands and kissed her, a long, luxurious kiss, his tongue meeting hers, teasing the inside of her mouth, flicking under her top lip, then taking her bottom lip in between his teeth and sucking it. Lust bathed her entire body and she pressed against him, her breasts swelling with need, her nipples now sharp as a razor blade against his chest.

'You don't need to take them all the way down. They go far enough,' Zach said, giving her a slow smile. Megan gasped as his left hand snaked round behind her, cupping the back of her neck, supporting her weight, and his right hand plunged between her thighs, covering her mound, his palm first barely touching the damp, silken down, then pressing harder, sending a blaze of pleasure through her crotch. Automatically she bucked underneath him, trying to move her thighs, to twist away from the caress, but she couldn't. Her jeans held her locked securely in place, her crotch exposed to him. Zach looked into her eyes and laughed, a low, throaty laugh, full of delight and desire. 'No way, baby. You're not going anywhere,' he said, and then his fingers were inside her, two of them, stroking her gently, probing her heat and her wetness, and he began to caress her, intimately, fingertips sliding over the smooth nub of her clitoris. Megan cried out, her back arching involuntarily under him, and waves of pleasure began to beat up in her, the ecstasy overtaking her, and she came in a blind rush, spasms of bliss rippling across her belly.

'We're just warming up,' Zach Mason said, and he laid her down on their flattened clothes with infinite gentleness, taking care not to jar her ankle, and then Megan's fingers tightened in his dark mane as he lowered his head to her skin, his tongue flicking the erect buds of her nipples, so that she moaned again, feeling a new warmth between her thighs, and then shuddered with longing as he sucked her breasts, licked down past her navel, holding her body firmly in place with his hands as she moved under him, and then finally, wonderfully, he reached her pussy and his mouth was on her, licking her, sucking her, playing with her, and Megan was transported into a new place, a new kind of passion, her universe contracting and shrinking until she was aware of nothing except her own crotch, and Zach's head, and her breath, coming in ragged gasps, and the pleasure was so intense, it was so hot and unbearable and incredible that she thought she might pass out, and then, just as she was sure she was going to explode, Zach took his mouth away and moved across her and she felt him enter her, his cock thick and hard as stone, throbbing, pulsing with need for her, and he was inside her, making love to her, fucking her, deep and slow and rhythmic, the strokes coming harder, faster, pushing into her, driving her further up, so she couldn't breathe, couldn't think, had never imagined sex could be like this, and then, deep within her, his cock was thrusting against her g-spot, that tender, sensitive little kiss of flesh, hidden so far inside her that no man had ever reached it before, and she heard herself cry out, as though far away, and suddenly the pleasure exploded around her, dizzying her so that she couldn't see, her whole world dissolving around her, her bones liquefying, her body melting into a sea of bliss, absolute, complete nirvana, the spasms seeming to contract her every muscle, groin, calves, forearms, back, and she sensed his climax rushing up to meet her, and finally the waves of rapture slowly receded, and Megan was left, sweating and shaking, gazing into Zach's wolflike eyes, and locked tight in her lover's embraces.

33

Roxana Felix was under siege. Literally. The reporters were everywhere: massing the road outside the front of the house, sneaking through the neighbouring grounds, even flying past in helicopters to get a few aerial snaps of her gardens. The discreet seclusion of her coffee and white Moroccan-style villa was no match for the tabloid's rat-pack, every one of them desperate for a photo or a comment or, better still, a snippet of footage. Her tall private hedges rustled with unauthorized movements every few minutes, and all the available viewpoints on nearby tall trees or mountain outcrops were being bitterly fought over. She no longer dared even to sneak into a bedroom to take a look outside, because the slightest twitch of the curtains would set off a flurry of flashbulbs. Roxana Felix had graduated into the hottest type of celebrity around – the fallen angel, the Madonna exposed as a whore. It was a perfect piece of white-trash culture – the story of the supermodel everybody adored. America's sweetheart, the bashful, modest heroine of a million magazine puff-pieces uncovered as a teenage prostitute and brothel-keeper. America and the world licked sleaze-hungry lips. Who didn't relish something like this? It was the best story since the Michael Jackson thing broke. Marissa Matthews had been first with her scoop, announcing the grisly details to New York society over breakfast – a special edition of *Friday's People* released on a Wednesday – and the rest of the pack had followed enviously in her wake an hour later. Orders were dispatched and shuttles jumped on in London, Paris, Madrid, Sydney. Bribes were offered wholesale to anybody who would talk – old clients, old hookers, old schoolfriends, anybody – and suddenly acquaintances were pouring out of the woodwork faster than the TV shows could line them up. Her hairdresser. Her New York chauffeur. A secretary to her booker at Unique. And with every passing minute another news crew or freelance hack arrived at the 'secluded' villa tucked away in the Hollywood Hills, now about as secluded as Times Square on New Year's Eve.

Roxana sat on a chair she'd dragged into the bathroom with her head in her hands, listening to the phone ring. She'd chosen the bathroom because it was the only room in the house without windows, the only room where she could be sure that she wasn't seen. She wouldn't disconnect the phones or the fax machines; that was what they would expect, but she would not do it. She was no coward.

So it had finally happened, Roxana thought. After all these years, they had found her. They knew almost everything. And the fame, the conquest, the safety, the adoration – her iron castle, the fortress she had built up, over eleven long years, inch by painstaking inch – in a matter of hours it had melted away, vanished like dew in the morning sun.

The demons had come for her. She had always known that some day they would.

Roxana sat on the chair and rocked herself backwards and forwards, singing gently, as though lulling a little child.

'Mr Goldman, I think you should see this.'

'Not now, Marcia. I have to call New York.'

Tom Goldman did not conceal his impatience. It was one thing after another: first, Zach and Megan's disappearance; next, deciding on the best way to handle Keller; and now, the second he got into his office, he found piles of pink-slip telephone messages from various members of the board. Jesus, Tom thought as he sank into his black leather Eames chair, those sons of bitches better not be selling the company. Not now. Because when what's happened to Zach Mason gets out, the press'll be all over *See the Lights* – and then it's all over for the stock. Right now, if those pencil-pushers decide to sell, they'll find Artemis Studios trading for thirty cents and a can of Coke.

'Yes sir, I know,' his secretary said apologetically. 'But you should really see this before you make any calls.'

Tom glanced at his assistant, cradling the morning papers to her chest. Oh, God. 'Is this something to do with Zach Mason, Marcia? I'd better have a look.'

'Not exactly, Mr Goldman,' she said cautiously, handing them across to him.

Goldman felt his jaw slacken in blank astonishment.

The *New York Post* had two pictures of Roxana Felix: smiling, poised and confident as the forty-million-dollar face of Jackson Cosmetics, and wafer-thin, over-made-up and dressed in a miniskirt, spike heels and sequined top, leaning against a wall in Paris, a teenage hooker in an unmistakable pose. In bold black type the headline screamed – MODEL MADAM! and underneath. *The sensational story of Roxana Felix – from streetwalker to supermodel! How teenage tart turned from brothel-keeper to America's Sweetheart!*

Aghast, Goldman pulled out the *New York Times*. WHY THE LADY IS A TRAMP. The *Washington Post*. FASHION PRINCESS WAS FRENCH PIMP. The *Los Angeles Times*. REAL ROXANA REVEALED. They were all the same.

'Those are the late editions, sir,' Marcia said, adding weakly, 'they couldn't fit it in the earlier ones.'

'Is this all over the radio and TV, too?' he asked, although it was a form question.

'Yes, sir. I thought you might have heard it on your car radio.'

Dazed, Goldman shook his head. He'd driven in silence this morning, radio off, carphone switched off, so he could have a little time with his thoughts.

Just as well, Tom thought grimly. Because that's the last peace and quiet I'll be getting for a while.

'No calls for ten minutes, Marcia, OK? I have to read this story through. Tell them I'm on my way into the office.' She nodded, but Goldman was suddenly struck with a dreadful, clammy fear. *The directors had been calling. The board was worried . . .*

'Wait! Marcia, get me Joel Steinbrenner on the phone, right away.'

'OK.'

Goldman spun his chair round, his fingers drumming nervously on his mahogany desk. Steinbrenner was on the phone in seconds.

'Joel, it's Tom.'

His broker's voice was a screech of agony. 'Goldman, where the fuck have you been? I don't have power-of-attorney! You've been unreachable for the last hour, and I can't sell jack for you without an instruction! You know that!'

Tom nodded, pain crunching through his temples. The carphone. It had been the first time he'd switched it off for months. Christ, why today? Why had this happened today?

'Yeah, I know that. What's the damage?'

'The stock's going *south*, Tom. Nobody can dump it fast enough. I'm telling you, it's in fucking free-fall!'

'What did we lose?'

Steinbrenner snorted with disgust. 'On paper? Your holdings have lost about eighty per cent of their value. But it might be more by the time I get to lose whatever I can. Even the bottom-fishers don't want to touch it.'

Eighty per cent. The words echoed in Goldman's brain, sending new shockwaves through his system. Eighty per cent, possibly more, wiped off the value of his Artemis holdings. Holy Lord God, Tom thought, I'm ruined.

'So? Talk to me, Tom, goddamn it!' Steinbrenner howled. 'Give me a sell order, for God's sake! Let's salvage *something* from this mess!'

'No,' Goldman said.

'*No?* What the fuck do you mean, *no*? We have to move *now*!'

'No, Joel. Don't sell anything,' Tom said. 'This studio is in trouble. I'm the chief executive, and I'm not going to dump my stock in the company during a crisis.'

'Are you out of your *fucking mind*?' Steinbrenner screamed.

'When you think the stock has hit bottom, buy ten thousand units.'

'Do *what*?'

'You heard me. You're my broker, right?'

'Yeah, but – '

'No buts, Joel. Carry out my order,' Tom said, and hung up.

He stared at the pink slips on his desk. Every one of them had rung in: Conrad Miles, Howard Thorn, all of them.

Marcia buzzed him. 'Mr Goldman, should I get Mr Thorn for you now?'

'In a minute, Marcia,' Tom said calmly. It was strange; he knew his world had just blown up in his face, the studio, his personal fortune, all of it, and yet he suddenly felt as clear-headed as he'd ever done in his life. Joel Steinbrenner and everybody else would probably think he was insane, but Tom Goldman had a responsibility to this studio and he was going to carry it out. 'I'll call everybody back in a minute. But first I want you to call the Méridien Hotel on Mahé in the Seychelles. I need to speak to Ms Marshall.'

Isabelle Kendrick sat in a soft oyster-white armchair in her drawing room, composed and relaxed, and faced her husband. On a small Regency table, by her side, the late editions of the day's papers were neatly stacked. Next to them rested Isabelle's half-drunk cup of cinnamon coffee in a blue Sèvres cup, her normal morning refreshment. She had not eaten breakfast for the last ten years, and as far as she was concerned, this morning was just the same as any other. Possibly a little more enjoyable. Isabelle seemed just as collected and unruffled as ever; she was wearing an elegant caramel Georges Rech pantsuit, her hair was neatly coiffed, and a subtle seed-pearl necklace gleamed against the slack skin of her throat. Totally unperturbed, Isabelle glanced up at her husband as he paced back and forth, passing his hand through his hair repeatedly, his black eyes burning with rage and pain.

'You never said anything. You never asked me,' he said, glaring at her. 'How could you do it, Isabelle? *Why* would you do it? You're a monster, do you know that?'

'Don't be melodramatic, Samuel.' His wife's voice was ice-cold, absolutely emotionless. 'I only told you it was me as a courtesy. And so that you wouldn't indulge in any similar foolishness in the future.'

Kendrick stopped moving and looked Isabelle directly in the face. 'What are you saying to me? That you were jealous?'

She shook her head, as if finding the suggestion distasteful. 'Of course not. We don't have that kind of marriage.'

'The real kind, you mean,' Kendrick said bitterly.

'Our marriage works very well, Sam.' Isabelle felt the adrenalin start to flow again as she spoke, saying aloud the things that had been taboo between them for so long. This was her moment of victory; she was going to flex her muscles, lay it out for him. He was not the only power in this house, Isabelle thought viciously. He owed her. Let him see what she was capable of if he forgot that fact. She would fry Roxana and any other little toy that he got too public with. Nobody threatened *her* position, not Roxana, not Sam, not anybody. 'You know I've never objected to your various liaisons, but this was different. This was public. And you may do as you please, as long as it does not reflect on me.'

'You don't care if I screw prostitutes?'

Isabelle waved a bejewelled hand. 'Not at all, dear.'

'You don't care if I see other women? If I love another woman?'

'Not as long as you're discreet.' Isabelle took a delicate sip of her coffee. 'Good gracious, Sam, did you think I didn't *know* about your other girls? How many have there been, eight or nine, is it? Aside from the hookers. I simply hoped that you had the good sense to take precautions. All these nasty diseases going around, and of course there's always pregnancy to consider. That can get messy. But beforehand, none of the girls came from our world.'

'You knew, and you said nothing,' Kendrick whispered.

The woman sitting in front of him was a stranger, a machine. He couldn't believe that the change in Isabelle ran so deep. She looked the same, but the blonde elegance covered stone, pure rock. It was true they hadn't been close for years, but somehow he hadn't realized, not completely, that the women he lived with was such an automaton. It terrified him.

'Why should I care, dear? We're a highly successful couple.'

He stared at her. She meant it.

'What about love, Isabelle?' Sam said quietly. 'We loved each other once.'

She gazed levelly at him. 'That was a long time ago.'

He made one last effort. 'You can't mean that, Isabelle. You can't. There has to be more to your life than giving parties and ruling all the wives. You can't be that shallow. Tell me you hate me, or you were jealous of her, or you want all the affairs to stop. Tell me you feel *something*.'

Deliberately, Isabelle reached into her bag and drew out her silver Chanel compact. She snapped it open, regarded herself in the mirror and dabbed a little powder onto the end of her nose. When she had quite finished, she snapped it shut, and finally turned to her husband.

'Why should I say that, Sam? It would be a lie.' She nodded at the pile of papers next to her. 'Roxana boasted about you to Jordan Goldman. I can't have that, I won't be humiliated. So if you keep your indiscretions quiet, I shan't have to do this again.'

Kendrick shook his head. Then he turned on his heel and walked towards the door.

'Where do you think you're going?' Isabelle demanded angrily.

'I'm going to see Roxana Felix,' Sam told her.

'You can't do that!' she hissed, enraged.

He turned towards his wife, a certain sadness clouding his eyes.

'Yes, I can, Isabelle. I love her. I didn't realize how much until this moment, but now I do. And when I find her, I'm going to ask her to marry me.'

Isabelle Kendrick paled in shock.

'I can't live this charade any more,' Sam said quietly. 'Whether Roxana accepts my proposal or not, I want a divorce.'

And he walked out.

'Wake up.'

Megan stirred fitfully, restlessly, dragged out of an exhuasted sleep by Zach Mason's warm, large hands gently shaking her shoulders. As her senses struggled towards consciousness, she felt overwhelmed by the sudden rush of feeling, her mind and her body mingling pain and pleasure in an extraordinary way. The wretched ache in her muscles, the sharp pain of her left foot, the hunger now raging in her empty stomach, were all balanced by the recollection of last night. Just remembering it brought a new softness to her groin, a joyful lightheadedness that had nothing to do with being half-starved. Megan's first conscious thought, embarrassingly enough, was that she hoped she looked OK for Zach.

How's *that* for shallow, she chided herself as she opened her eyes to look up at him.

'Hey, sweetheart,' Mason said gently. 'Sorry to do this to you, but we really have to get going now.'

She groaned. 'I can't have had more than an hour's sleep.'

Barely ten minutes after they'd finished making love, the noisy roar of a helicopter, spotlight blazing through the towering trees, had swept past their area of the forest and continued to make passes throughout the night. Zach had left the makeshift hut to try to attract attention, waving clothing, whatever, but he just couldn't get seen. The thick jade canopy of branches and leaves above them prevented any real chance of the searchlights finding them. About three Zach gave up and came back to take Megan in his arms, holding her and kissing her until she blacked into unconsciousness just before dawn.

Mason hadn't slept. One good thing about being a rock star, he'd had plenty of practice at that. Once he was sure Megan was finally out, he'd slipped away from her, checking out their immediate surroundings and looking for food and water. He reckoned they were gonna need some fuel if they were ever going to make it out of here; that broken ankle was looking bad. He wouldn't let her continue to drag it around. Zach thought Megan was in more pain than she was making out.

He'd looked at her tenderly when he got back, curled up where he'd left her, blonde fringe curling incongruously over that cute forehead with its thick dark brows, her soft lips half-open in sleep, her muscled arm flung awkwardly over the heavy, beautiful breasts that had responded so superbly to him last night. Zach felt such a surge of protectiveness he was short of breath. He marvelled at himself. He, Zach Mason, the rock icon who'd fucked a million groupies and turned down ten million more, who'd had his pick of starlets and models for the last five years, he'd finally fallen. Pole-axed by this embarrassed, clever, gauche, determined, idealistic little bunch of contradictions. Pretty, but no more than that. Feisty. Naive. Brave. His Megan.

Great time to pick out your true love, Mason, he told himself. Starving and stranded in the middle of the fucking jungle.

'You had at least an hour and a quarter,' he teased her. 'Stop whingeing and get your ass in gear. I reckon we'll be out of here by sundown.'

Megan lifted a cynical eyebrow. 'Right!'

'At least we know they're looking for us.'

'That's true.' She levered herself up, reaching for her shirt where they'd left it on the floor of the hut. 'What do you have there?'

'Room service,' Mason said cheerfully, tipping his findings onto a palm leaf in front of her. He'd managed to find one wild pineapple, growing in a crack in the granite glacis boulders that thrust through the forest floor all around them, a couple of leaves that his nose told him were cinnamon, and an armful of small pinkish-white fruits, the size of apples, that covered a grove of bushes to their left.

They looked at this harvest doubtfully.

'Call yourself a hunter-gatherer? Pathetic,' Megan grinned.

'I blame women's rights. I've been robbed of my natural instincts,' Zach said, carefully peeling the pineapple. He tossed Megan a white sphere. 'So is this poisonous?'

'Only one way to find out,' she said, and before Zach could stop her, took a large bite. The flesh tasted like damp cotton wool. She devoured it.

'Coco plum,' Megan told him. 'Tasteless but harmless.'

They ate in silence for a few minutes, Megan trying to slip most of her share towards Zach and Zach refusing to allow it. The fruit sugars weren't much, but on their empty stomachs they provided a surge of energy, and as soon as Mason had swallowed the last fragment of coco plum core he lifted Megan to her feet and ducked under her legs.

'What the hell are you doing?' Megan shrieked, clutching his shoulders. 'I've got my crutches, Zach! Put me down!'

'No,' he told her firmly, getting a restraining grip on her calves. 'I'm not letting you walk. Shut up, this is non-negotiable, OK?'

'But I'll slow you down,' Megan protested. She tried to be nonchalant, but her eyes were brimming up with tears. She dashed a hand quickly across her face. 'I'm serious. Only one of us has to . . . I mean, it'd be better if you went for help and left me, came back for me . . .'

'Get this straight,' Zach said, taking a deep breath and squaring his shoulders under her weight. 'I'm not leaving you. Not ever. We're in this together, live or die, for better, for worse. All that stuff. Anyway, you're as light as a feather. Consider it an extended piggyback ride. You can navigate.'

'I love you,' Megan whispered.

His hands tightened on her legs. 'Let's get out of here, OK? You can go all mushy on me later,' Zach said firmly, but as he strode carefully forward, his heart was singing.

It took Sam over an hour to make it to Roxana's front door, ploughing the Maserati first through the rabid pack of journalists, camera crews, photographers and gawking sightseers that crowded the road leading up to her villa, and then past the LAPD roadblocks that by this time lay seven layers thick. Eventually he managed to convince the sergeant in charge that he *was* Sam Kendrick of SKI by calling up Troy Savage, the guy's favourite soap star and a SKI client, on his carphone, and having him verify it. Thank God for starstruck cops, Sam thought, as he swung the silver car into Roxana's drive, got out and locked it. He glanced up at the villa. Every shutter was lowered, every curtain closed. Yeah, well. That didn't surprise him.

Kendrick felt compassion overwhelm him as he walked past the uniformed men on the door and pressed the buzzer on her entryphone. His poor baby. What she must be feeling today he could only begin to guess at. He'd seen clients go through scandals, but never anything as bad as this. Only Jackson and Madonna had it as bad as this. And neither of them had been exposed as a teenage madam, running the most exclusive call-girl service in Paris at the age of sixteen. He still couldn't believe it. There were so many pieces of the puzzle that didn't make sense: an American girl, hooking in France at fourteen years old, graduates to brothel-keeper at sixteen and makes enough money by eighteen to buy herself a whole new identity and a new life – then enrols at a Catholic convent school in San Francisco. Hits the model agencies the day she graduates and the rest is history. But why France? How had she done this? And why? His Roxana, his shy and fragile girl? Was it possible? But it had happened. He'd seen the pictures, watched the news. He knew it was true.

I didn't know Isabelle and I didn't know Roxana, either, Sam thought, bewildered, as he stood there. All the time I was such a mogul, such a player, and I thought I read everybody like a book. But the people closest to me were the ones I couldn't see. And Florescu tells me David Tauber was working behind my back all the time . . . Tauber, who I thought was so smart, such a killer. I guess I was right. He'd have killed me, if he could.

The anger rose in him, thick and blood-red, and it was almost a relief. At least one emotion was clear. Once the little prick got back to LA Sam was going to smash him.

It was my own fault for not noticing, Sam berated himself. But I'd have seen it eventually. On the set I was distracted, couldn't think about anything except Roxana . . .

'Who is it?'

Her voice on the speaker was cautious and muted.

'Roxana, baby. Let me in. It's Sam,' he said.

There was a long pause. He could hear the crackle of static through the metal grille.

'It's Sam Kendrick, sweetheart. Let me in,' he repeated.

Finally he heard a click as she released the lock. Sam pushed the door open and walked into the house, shutting it carefully behind him.

'Roxana?' he called.

She was nowhere to be seen. He could hear the constant sound of phones ringing and the babble of different voices, angry voices, as four separate answering machines took messages. Through the door to the home office Kendrick saw the lights of her fax machines glowing red as sheets of paper inched slowly out of the tops of the machines and crashed onto the floor.

'I'm in the bathroom,' Roxana called. Her voice was flat and strained, hoarse, as if she'd been crying. Sam raced upstairs to the bathroom, that sanctuary of polished wood and brass and cool marble, a place where he'd made love to her so many times he'd lost count. She was sitting on the floor, wrapped in a voluminous white towelling robe, her legs crossed, her eyes glazed, seemingly staring into space.

'Roxana,' he murmured, and then she looked up at him, her liquid brown eyes narrowed with such vicious hatred that he took a step backwards.

'You took everything,' she said bleakly. 'Everything. Bob Alton was so pleased to be able to tell me I was fired. Unique won't represent me. Elite and Ford and Models One wouldn't take my call. Jackson Cosmetics cancelled the contract – forty million dollars, Sam. And no other house will use me. I can't work. My *Vogue* cover for next month is going to Christy now.' She took a breath, and continued. 'Jordan won't talk to me. She wouldn't accept a call. Neither would Susie Metcalf or any of those society bitches. I'm dead, Sam. You took everything.'

'It wasn't me, sweetheart,' he said, inwardly recoiling at the poison in her gaze. 'It was Isabelle. And I told her I wanted a divorce, I wanted to marry you.'

'It was *your wife*. It was because of *you*,' Roxana hissed, her gaze still filled with venom. '*She* did this, she led them to me. But you don't know what it was like, none of you! *None of you!*'

Her voice rose to a banshee wail, and she started to weep, hot blinding tears coursing down her cheeks. Sam took a step towards her but Roxana lashed out at him, wildly, like a madwoman, her long fingernails slicing through the cloth of his pants.

'Get the fuck away from me! Don't touch me!' she screamed, and then, as he watched in horror, she started to tear at her hair, ripping strands of it from her head, rocking backwards and forwards in a violent fit of grief. Kendrick lunged forward and caught her wrists, trapping them, forcing her to be still.

'Roxana! Roxana!' he said, and was shocked to hear the tears choking his own voice, so distressed was he at the sight of her anguish. 'Whatever it is, you can tell me. You can trust me. I love you, whatever you did. I don't *care* what you did. I love you, don't you understand that?'

She froze, staring at him, her eyes suddenly calmer, flatter. It was as if the hatred had vanished, to be replaced by . . . what? What is she feeling? Sam wondered uneasily. He didn't understand the strange look on her face. She seemed to be . . .

. . . *laughing at me* . . .

'You are so fucking dumb, you know that?' Roxana said, her voice suddenly subdued, filled with scorn, mocking him. 'I was using you, Sam. For the picture, so that you wouldn't stop me wrecking the shoot. So that you would help me fire Megan Silver. For whatever you could do for me. And because of the way you spoke to me at Isabelle's party, I was going to break your heart as soon as it was over. Why do you think I told Jordan? I *wanted* her to tell everybody else. I wanted to show the world the great Sam Kendrick was just another puppet dancing on my strings.'

Dazed, Sam released her wrists, stumbling backwards, numb from the malice of her tone.

'Your wife did this. You mean nothing to me. *Nothing.*' Roxana's brown eyes held only contempt. 'I despise you, Sam. Get the fuck out of my house.'

Sam turned blindly round and walked down the stairs, his heart so full of pain it felt like a thick stone in his chest. He said nothing to the policemen standing around his car who looked at him curiously as he came out. He couldn't speak. For the first time since he was a boy, Sam Kendrick was fighting back tears.

34

Eleanor Marshall walked quickly up the sunlit steps of Victoria Hospital, followed by Fred Florescu, her agitation betraying her nerves. Zach Mason and Megan Silver had been found alive, shortly after sunrise, by a guide trekking through the Anse Jasmin estate in the northernmost part of the jungle. He had fetched help and had the two Americans taken to the nearest village, where somebody called an ambulance. Beyond that she knew very little.

'Ms Marshall and Mr Florescu,' Eleanor said to the thickset woman staffing the reception desk. 'We've come to see the two people that were found in the mist forest this morning. Are they OK?'

The receptionist checked the names on a printed sheet in front of her and nodded, giving them a warm smile. 'You want rooms twelve an' thirteen, jus' down the corridor there.' She pointed straight ahead of her. 'The gentleman told us to call Mr Florescu here. You with him?'

'Yes. Thanks,' Eleanor replied, striding down the corridor the woman had showed them.

'Jesus, do you think they're all right?' Florescu asked, his face clouded.

'We know they're alive,' Eleanor said, checking the door numbers.

'Yeah. But it was a long way to fall,' the director said.

They looked at each other, neither wanting to say it. What if either of the kids had cracked their heads open, or broken their necks? What if they were paralysed? Or if they'd cut themselves open and the wound had become gangrenous?

'Twelve,' Eleanor said, coming to a stop outside a closed blue door. There was no sound from inside the room. She hesitated.

'We have to see them,' Fred Florescu told her softly.

Eleanor nodded, her heart crashing against her chest.

What if they *are* paralysed? she thought miserably. It was my fault that they were filming in a monsoon. I didn't double-check my own location reports because I was so wrapped up in Jordan Goldman's baby. If I'd have been doing my job, Jake Keller would never have gotten away with it. And this would never have happened.

Florescu glanced at Eleanor Marshall, standing there twisting her hands, her face as white as chalk. He was frightened too; Zach and Megan were such talented kids, both of them, and so young, and who knew what the hell had happened to them out there?

He slowly twisted the handle and opened the door.

Zach Mason was sitting up in bed, an empty cereal bowl stacked on the table behind him, sipping from a long, tall glass of milk, fresh dressings wrapped round his bare chest. Megan Silver, in a pair of green hospital pyjamas and a dressing gown, was lounging in a spartan easy chair beside him, eating a delicious-smelling croissant and looking at a copy of the *Herald Tribune*, her right foot in a tartan slipper and her left foot bandaged up in a splint. Both of them looked up, smiling, as Fred and Eleanor walked into the room.

'Hey, guys, it's good to see you,' Zach Mason said.

'Are you OK?' Florescu asked, hardly daring to believe his eyes.

'We were a little hungry, but we're fine now,' Zach told him, adding, 'I sure as hell hope those scenery shots were worth it.'

Eleanor felt weak-kneed with relief.

'Eleanor! What are you doing here?' Megan asked her.

'Looking for you,' the older woman said.

'Oh yeah? We wondered if all those helicopters last night were something to do with us,' Megan said. She held up the paper she was reading. 'So what's the story with Roxana Felix?'

By the time the cab drew up to her house Eleanor was feeling jet-lagged and exhausted. She tipped the guy a twenty and carried her small Louis Vuitton case into the porch, reaching into her purse for the keys. Her fingers fumbled around for a minute before she found them and managed to let herself in; she was so tired she tried to unlock the front entrance with the back door key.

I'll take a nap for a couple of hours before I head back to the studio, Eleanor told herself. I'm no use to Tom or anyone else in this state.

It had been a sleepless night, all coffee and doughnuts in a suite at the Méridien, supervising the air searches and taking phone call after phone call of reports – somebody had found a strip of cloth from Mason's shirt, another man said he'd seen footprints – but there'd been nothing of substance, and despite her best efforts Eleanor had slumped into unconsciousness towards dawn. When the phone shrilled by her bedside to say they'd been found, she'd been asleep for barely three hours. The relief at knowing Zach and Megan were alive and almost completely unharmed had carried her through the rest of the morning as she paid off the Seychellois involved in the search, packed her handful of clothes and booked herself on the first flight off the islands. But that euphoria couldn't last forever, and when the jet had taxied off the runway and soared into the clear blue skies above the Indian Ocean, Eleanor Marshall had had to face the rest of her problems.

Tom Goldman's call had come through at eight p.m. the night before – eight a.m. in Los Angeles. Roxana Felix was the newest front-runner in the worldwide bad-girl stakes – a prostitution scandal that had completely buried her career in a matter of hours. And he wasn't exaggerating: a flick of the remote control and CNN confirmed everything to her, right there and then in her hotel room.

'The markets think this will kill the movie,' Goldman had told her, his voice terse and pressured. 'They know it was a costly flick. They know we're in desperate need of a hit.'

'What's happening to the stock?'

Goldman laughed caustically. 'Are you kidding? What stock? It's going downhill faster than an avalanche! At this rate the SEC's gonna suspend trading, before it hits zero.'

'Christ,' Eleanor muttered. 'I've got about two million dollars' worth of stock!'

'Well, now you have about forty thousand dollars' worth. If it's any consolation, I've got a lot more than that. Do you want me to call your broker and give him your number there? Perhaps you could still off-load some of it.'

'No. No, thanks,' she replied. *Two million dollars, up in smoke!* 'I'm the president, I don't want to be seen to be dumping stock in my own company.'

On the other side of the world, Tom Goldman smiled, feeling a strong rush of affection for her. 'You know, I said exactly the same thing.'

'Great minds think alike,' Eleanor told him.

'And fools seldom differ.'

She chuckled. 'You've got me. Look, just hold on, OK? The second I know what's happened to Zach and Megan I'll be on my way home. We'll figure something out.'

'Will we?' Tom sounded sceptical. 'I called so you'd know what was happening, Eleanor. I don't think I'll be here when you get back. I have sixteen messages in front of me from assorted board members, and I don't think they want to chat to me about the weather.'

'No way, Tom. You're not going anywhere. They can't fire you for something Roxana Felix did, and if they try, you just pull the same number on them I pulled on you before. Call your personal lawyer and check your contract. Tell them you'll sue. I'm sure they won't want any more scandal right now.'

A pause, then, 'You could be right.'

'You *know* I'm right. And you'd have thought of that yourself given time,' Eleanor said. 'Tell them all to hold onto their stock. If it's plunged that low, there's no point in selling now anyway, right?'

'That's true. Maybe we should look on the bright side – we've got nowhere to go at this point except up.'

'That's my boy,' Eleanor said. She glanced down and noticed that she had her hands on her stomach, covering her womb. Somehow, without having even consciously considered it, she knew she was going to tell Tom the truth about this child when she got home. What would he say? And should she tell Paul? What would be best for her baby? All the anxieties pressed around her, crowding her, crushing her. Eleanor felt as if she were being swept along in the most fearsome current, swimming with all her might against the flow, fighting not to give in, not to be felled by each fresh disaster. It was her baby that gave her the strength, the deep, new knowledge of what was really important. They could take away her reputation, her wealth and her job, but they couldn't take that. And she was going to fight like hell before they took *anything.*

'And there's another silver lining you haven't thought of,' she added. 'Now the stock's dropped through the floor, Jake Keller has nothing left to threaten you with. So you might as well sack him this morning.'

'Don't you want to wait until you get home?'

'No,' Eleanor told him. 'Sam Kendrick's already recalled David Tauber. I think you should just sack him now – no reference, no compensation. Make it as public as you can. Humiliate the son of a bitch.'

'You got it,' Goldman told her, hanging up.

So now she was back, Eleanor thought wearily. Back to a company in crisis, a media frenzy, an exposed leading lady, and . . .

'Where the hell have you been?'

Paul stood in the doorway of their bedroom, his arms folded, glaring at her. He was wearing a dark blue suit and smelt of too much aftershave. He had a brightly patterned tie on, and his hair was meticulously parted. She hated this side of him: the peacock, the dandy. It seemed too vain, almost effeminate. Tom Goldman wouldn't be seen dead in that outfit, Eleanor told herself.

'You know where I've been, Paul. I called and left messages here and at your office.'

'You went halfway around the world to supervise some pathetic little rescue attempt,' he said angrily. 'Who do you think you are? Rambo?'

'Don't be stupid, Paul. Two of our people were missing and in danger.'

'So you had to go out there, I suppose.'

She was too tired for this. 'That's right, I did. Because it wasn't the kind of job I like to delegate. Now if you'll excuse me, I'm worn out and I need to get some sleep.'

Paul didn't move. 'Do you realize you missed days thirteen, fourteen and fifteen of your menstrual cycle, Eleanor?' he demanded furiously. 'You *owed* it to me to be here.'

She bit her lip to stop herself from screaming out the truth. If he had to know, it wasn't going to be like this, not blurted out in the middle of a quarrel.

'Well, I owed it to Zach and Megan to try and save their lives,' she said, as calmly as she could. 'Let's talk later, OK? This isn't a good time. I'm really tired.'

'*I'm* tired!' Paul snapped petulantly. 'Tired of how lightly you take this marriage! Have you *heard* about Roxana Felix?'

'Yes, I – '

He wasn't listening. 'Do you realize how much crap I had to take in the office? All the analysts sniggering behind their desks. People going quiet when I walked past them. Don't you do *checks* on people before you hire them?'

'She wasn't an employee. She was an actress,' Eleanor said, trying to keep her temper in check. 'And Artemis is a motion picture studio, not the Federal Government. We don't tend to call in the FBI.'

'Artemis *was* a motion picture studio, I think you mean.' There was a curious note of satisfaction in her husband's voice. 'The stock's plunged. It almost hit the one-day floor for losses, Eleanor. You've lost millions.'

Eleanor took note of the 'you'.

'Well, at least I still have you to put bread on the table,' she said sarcastically.

'This is no time for jokes!' Paul Halfin almost screamed. He was puce with indignation. 'While you were playing around in some goddamn tropical island, your studio was crumbling! And your stock became worthless! I'll bet you didn't even manage to lose it in time! Don't you understand what this does to our reputation?'

'You mean, now I'm no longer the respectable studio president you married?' Eleanor asked him very quietly.

'Yes!' Paul said. It was a screech.

'Do you love me, Paul?'

He took a breath, backed down. 'Of course I love you. But this behaviour can't continue.'

Eleanor nodded. 'You're right. I want a divorce.'

'You can't be serious.' He looked at her with disbelief. '*You* want to divorce *me*? Don't you understand that you're history in this town? You've lost your job and you've lost your money! What else do you have?'

'My pride,' Eleanor told him simply.

Then, as Paul stared after her in blank astonishment, she picked up her case, walked into the guest bedroom and bolted the door behind her.

Tom Goldman had looked better. His skin was sallow from lack of sleep, his eyes had dark circles under them and he hadn't had time to shave. He'd been under pressure before in his life, but never had it been anything like this. The phone was ringing off the hook: distributors angrily demanding to know if the studio was bankrupt; directors, producers and actors all frantic about their Artemis projects; media hacks clever enough to fool his assistants and get through; agents hysterically claiming that their clients had 'senior debt' if the company went under; and distraught stockholders who screamed abuse. His neck was aching from the number of calls he had taken, and they never seemed to stop, six, seven callers holding at a time. Marcia had brought him in a pizza at lunchtime but he hadn't been able to stop talking long enough to eat it, and by four p.m. it was still cooling on his desk.

Eleanor stood in the doorway to Goldman's office, watching her boss pronounce soothing reassurances into his handset, his neck lolling at an exhausted angle against the headrest of his chair, his eyes closed as if in pain.

'I couldn't buzz him to tell him you were here, Ms Marshall,' Marcia Hearn said tearfully. 'I couldn't get through. All his lines have calls holding on them.'

'That's fine, Marcia. Forget it,' Eleanor said gently. The secretary looked completely stressed-out and shaken up; she was twisting her hands compulsively and she looked as though she might be about to burst out crying any second. On her desk, behind them, four different phone lines were ringing insistently and the fax machine was pouring out letters, old faxes spilling slowly over the edge of the containment tray and cascading onto the floor, mingling with a white and grey pool of paper. Marcia was a fanatically neat woman, and Eleanor realized with a start that she hadn't even had time to pick up the faxes.

'OK. Here's what we're going to do,' she told her. 'You switch all incoming calls to Mr Goldman's answering machine. As of now, he's in a meeting and can't be disturbed.'

Marcia looked doubtfully towards Tom, sitting at his desk with his eyes closed. 'But –'

'He's in a meeting with *me*,' Eleanor said firmly. 'Senior management only. And you take the rest of the day off, Marcia. That's an order.'

'Yes, Ms Marshall,' she said gratefully, and scurried back to her desk.

Eleanor closed Tom's door quietly, then tiptoed up to his desk, grabbed the receiver out of his hands said, 'He'll call you back,' and hung up.

'Eleanor!' Goldman said, not believing his eyes. 'What are you doing here? I didn't expect you until tomorrow!'

'Gee, everybody seems so pleased to see me,' Eleanor said dryly.

'I am pleased to see you. You have no idea how much,' Goldman said, giving her a weak smile.

'Has it been bad?'

He raised an eyebrow. 'I'm not even going to bother replying to that.'

'I told Marcia to take the phones off the hook,' Eleanor told him. 'We need to talk.'

'Want some cold, greasy pizza?' Tom asked her, ripping off an unappetizing slice and stuffing it in his mouth.

'You tempt me, but no. Did you speak to the board?'

Goldman nodded. 'Yeah. Told them what you said. They hated it, but they played ball. Present management stays in place for the time being, and they'll do what they can with the banks to shore up the stock. I guess they didn't have a choice; it was that or lose their whole investment.'

Eleanor paced round the room, thinking fast. 'Good. Have you spoken to Roxana Felix?'

'Left a message. No reply. No surprises there,' Goldman said, thinking how good Eleanor looked. Even in the midst of complete and total disaster, she managed to appear poised, calm and elegant. She was wearing the scarlet Donna Karan suit she'd had on for her confrontation with him a few days ago; bold, confident colour and meticulous tailoring, it accentuated her slim figure and it looked terrific.

She's got such style. Such grace under pressure, Goldman thought, and tried not to dwell on the image of his wife last night – weeping uncontrollably, shrieking with fury that he wouldn't sell his stock, mascara running down her heavily made-up face, throwing a tantrum like a spoilt brat. *How could you do this to me!* As if he had ruined himself and destroyed his career purposely to spite her. And all she could think about was her stupid slave auction, screaming at him that now nobody would come.

'What about Sam?'

'Sam called to say SKI didn't represent her any more.'

'That's not like Sam, to run out on a client.'

'He wouldn't discuss it with me. He sounded pretty upset, actually,' Tom said. 'But maybe that's because he's getting a divorce.'

'Sam too?'

'What?'

She shook her head. 'I'll tell you later. First, I want to tell you what I want to do.'

Goldman leaned back, smiling. 'Go ahead. You're the only person around here with any fight left in you, Eleanor, I swear. I don't know what happened to you last week, but I sure as hell wish it would happen to me.'

'I want to speak to Roxana Felix and persuade her to come back and finish the movie.'

'You are certifiably insane,' Goldman said amiably.

'Hear me out, Tom. Zach and Megan are in good health and the doctors told me he could be back on the set in a day or so. I had Fred continually shooting while we were looking for them. I've seen some of the rough cuts, Tom. *See the Lights* is an incredible movie and production is almost complete. They'd only need Roxana for a week or so to finish up, and you know Florescu edits fast.' She held up a hand. 'No, let me finish, please. I know what you're going to say: Roxana won't do it, and even if she does, nobody will want to distribute.'

'Right.'

'Wrong. I'm sure I can persuade Roxana to come back to the set. She has nothing to lose, and precisely because she *was* such a class-A bitch she won't want the world to see her running away with her tail between her legs. I want to drive over there and speak with her tonight. And as for the distributors – once everybody's calmed down, people will go *crazy* to book this film. We're getting a billion dollars' worth of free publicity right now.'

'Even if you're right about Roxana, I'm telling you, Eleanor, the chains don't want to do business with a bankrupt company. And if the stock crashes – '

She made an impatient movement with her hands. 'The stock won't crash. In a day or two people will realize that we have a certain bottom-line value for our library and our real estate.'

'True.'

'And the only way they can write us off is if *we* write off *See the Lights*. But I won't do that.' Eleanor walked towards her old friend, her eyes bright with passion, and put her hands on the front of his desk, leaning towards him. 'Tom, look. *We have nothing to lose.* Everything has already gone up in smoke – our careers, our bank balances, everything. But I want *something* to come out of the time I was president of a studio. I want to be able to point to this film and say, I helped to do that. I got into this business fifteen years ago to make pictures, Tom. And *See the Lights* is a truly wonderful picture. I believed in it when I first got the script, and I still do. If it's a success, we win. If it isn't – we have nothing left to lose. But I have to finish it. This is my movie.'

Tom Goldman looked at Eleanor. There were tears in her eyes. 'Go talk to Roxana,' he said softly. 'I'll call my lawyers again. We'll make your movie before we quit.'

'Thank you.' It was all she could say. 'Thank you, Tom.'

Goldman reached forward, closing his hand over hers. 'We started together, and I guess we're gonna end together. I'm just sorry it had to be this way.'

'Me too,' Eleanor whispered, briefly closing her eyes.

She had to say it now, she knew that. Tom had a right to know, and she had to tell him. If she waited for the right moment, she'd wait forever. There was no good time. She pulled her hands away. 'I have to tell you something else, Tom. I'm getting a divorce. And I'm pregnant.'

He gazed at her, puzzled. 'You are? I don't understand. What does Paul say about it?'

'I don't know how to tell you this,' she said. 'But I always used a diaphragm with Paul. We didn't make love without protection until after the wedding. And I'm two and a half months pregnant.'

'What are you saying?' Goldman whispered.

Eleanor gazed at him steadily.

'It's your baby, Tom,' she said.

35

Roxana Felix opened the door to Eleanor Marshall and stared at her defiantly. It was four a.m., early enough for Eleanor's forest-green Lotus to crawl through the police roadblocks without attracting too much attention, and the elder woman had begged her for a meeting, leaving thirty-two messages in succession on the answer machine in Roxana's bedroom, until she'd finally picked up. There were no recriminations in Eleanor's voice, but Roxana wasn't fooled: the bitch had come to rave and shout and threaten. As if she cared. She had hit bottom, and there was no further to fall.

'Roxana. Thank you for seeing me,' Eleanor said gently. 'May I come in?'

She stood aside. 'Be my guest. Come in, say what you want to, and leave. I just want to get this over with.'

'Didn't you disconnect any of the phones?' Eleanor asked, listening to the constant jangling echoing through the house. Roxana was dressed in a tailored Ralph Lauren pantsuit in royal-blue cotton, her long hair was swept into a chignon, and she was fully made-up, a soft berry gloss on her beautiful lips and a sweep of damson blusher accentuating her razor-sharp cheekbones. She had even clipped on a small pair of gold earrings. She was wearing a subtle, sensuous perfume. She looked every inch as stunning as the last time Eleanor had seen her, as if she had just stepped blithely off another catwalk.

I was right about her, Eleanor thought. Roxana won't show me any weakness, she'd die first. She wants me to tell the world that she couldn't care less. She has her pride.

Yesterday's scene with Paul flashed back into her mind. Maybe, in the end, pride was all any woman had to cling to.

'What for? I'm taking messages,' Roxana said. 'People can say whatever they like. I'm not running from them.'

'That's what I hoped you would say.' Eleanor walked into the kitchen. 'Can I make us some coffee? I have a proposal for you.'

'If you must,' Roxana said ungraciously. 'I hope this isn't going to take long, Eleanor. If it's about your stock – too bad. There's nothing I can do. I didn't plan this. And if you want me to sign some statement saying that you had no knowledge of my past when you cast me, have it messengered over. I have no problem with that. I just want you to leave me alone. And if you came here for more information' – her lips tightened – 'you should ask

Isabelle Kendrick. She was the one who did this. You can blame your company collapse on her.'

'None of the above,' Eleanor said, spooning French Vanilla ground into the percolator. *Isabelle Kendrick!* Because Roxana had been sleeping ... with *Sam*? 'Did you know Sam Kendrick is getting divorced?' she asked casually.

Roxana shook her head. 'I think you'll find he decided to stay with his wife.'

'No. I spoke to Sam earlier this morning,' Eleanor said. 'He's moved into the Bel-Air. He seems really upset.'

'Yeah? There's a lot of that going around,' Roxana replied, but Eleanor thought she detected a touch of confusion beneath the flippancy.

'Roxana. Listen to me,' Eleanor Marshall began. Her heart was thumping against her chest; she *had* to convince this girl, she just had to. It would require a huge act of courage on Roxana's part, even a little selflessness, not qualities most people would associate with her right now. But Eleanor had to back her instincts, she knew that. She had given everything she had fighting for this movie. She wasn't about to give up now. 'I didn't come over here today to shout at you, or demand information, or to get you to sign something. What happened to our stock was not your fault. Nobody said you had to confess your sins to us before you got to act in our movie. But I am here to ask for your help.'

Roxana leaned back against the door, watching her with narrowed eyes.

She's learned to trust nobody, Eleanor thought. Why? What happened to her, all those years ago?

'What do you want?' Roxana asked warily.

'I want you to go back to Mahé and shoot the end of *See the Lights*.'

She held her breath. There, it was out. This was the moment of truth; if Roxana wanted to shriek, or yell, or order her out of the house, it was all over.

There was a moment's silence.

'Why?' Roxana asked, looking at her steadily.

'Because if we get this thing finished, it's going to be an incredible movie. Fred Florescu showed me some of the footage. When you were actually acting, Roxana, and not trying to screw up everybody else's performance, you were brilliant. Really talented. And in the love scenes with Zach, you just set the screen on fire. I think if we ever get this film out to the theatres, and people can see it, the world will agree with me.'

'And why should I do this?'

'Do it for yourself,' Eleanor said. 'I could tell you to do it for me, or Zach, or Fred, but I won't. You should understand that I know about your cooperation with David Tauber and Jake Keller, and I really don't care. That's all in the past. The only thing that matters to me is this movie, getting it completed and released, and for that I know I need you. But what you get out of this is some self-respect. You told me when I arrived that you weren't gonna run from anybody. So don't! Make this movie! You wanted the world to see you as an actress, you came to LA, you forced us to cast you – God knows what you did, but you ended up cast – '

Roxana gave her the briefest flicker of a smile.

' – and you made most of a great movie. They all expect you to crawl away and die, Roxana. Now, I'm not going to stand here and tell you that what you did was OK. It wasn't. And if that's what you have to hear, I'll get out of your house right now, because I won't say it. But I *will* tell you that I know we don't know the whole story. You were a fourteen-year-old American girl, so why were you in Paris? And how does a teenage hooker get to run an upmarket brothel in two years? It doesn't make sense. But what I do get from your story is a fierce need for independence – you came back to the States, you took your final year of high school privately, you got a new identity and a new career and then you climbed higher in that field than anybody had done before. I'm not asking you to tell me anything, Roxana. I don't judge you, because I don't know you. But what I am asking you is to show them a little of that independence now. You couldn't be broken before; don't let this break you now.'

Roxana Felix burst into tears.

'Hey.' Eleanor moved forward and took the sobbing girl in her arms, stroking her hair, cradling her as she wept. 'It's all right now, honey. It's going to be all right.'

It was night over Mahé by the time they arrived, the stars glittering above the Anse Polite beach, dancing round a huge harvest moon hanging low and orange in the clear sky. The taxi drove straight past the hotel and pulled up two miles further along the shore, at an anonymous-looking ocean-side diner which seemed to be closed. Eleanor paid the driver and helped Roxana out of the cab, checking the café for a single light in the downstairs window. It was on; that meant Florescu was waiting inside with Zach, Megan, Seth, Mary, Robert, Jack and the rest of the cast.

'Are you sure you want to do this?' she asked. 'You know you don't have to tell them anything. I can go up there and simply announce that you have returned to complete the film. Nobody will harass you. I can talk to Fred and make sure of that.'

Roxana shook her head, her long black hair shining in the moonlight. 'No. I don't want to hide this any more. If I can speak to those guys, maybe they'll understand the way you did, and they'll forgive me for the way I was before.'

'You're a very brave woman,' Eleanor told her.

'So are you,' Roxana said simply.

Eleanor offered her her arm, and the two of them walked into the tiny shack together. The wooden door opened into a warm, sweet-smelling room, lit by three oil lamps. Fred and the others were sitting round a long trestle table, eating something that smelt like spiced lobster, and drinking long glasses of the local *bacca* sugar-cane liquor. The conversation was loud and raucous, but as soon as they walked into the room it went totally quiet. Eleanor felt Roxana stiffen a little beside her; thirty pair of eyes were staring at her in complete shock.

'Ladies and gentlemen,' Eleanor said. 'I asked Fred to book this place for your meal tonight because I wanted someplace private for Roxana to speak to you. I realize this may come as a surprise, but Roxana has decided that she wants to come back out here and finish off this movie. You will have read the recent stories about her in the press. They are true, but Roxana has something to add to them. It took great strength for her to decide to tell you the things she is about to say. I want you to listen to her quietly.'

She squeezed the younger girl's hand, and then walked across to the table and sat down next to Fred Florescu.

Roxana took a deep breath as she stood there in the soft light of the lamps, looking at the actors she'd been screwing over as they sat in front of her, watching her curiously. There was no sympathy in their faces, just a neutral interest.

But I'm not asking them for sympathy, she told herself. Just understanding.

'My name *is* Roxana Felix,' she said. 'Legally. I had it changed by deed poll when I was nineteen years old. But I was born Heather Piper in Kansas City, twenty-four years ago. My father worked in construction and my mother had a part-time job working in the local supermarket check-out. We were poor, but I don't remember much about it. I was four when they were killed in a car crash. They didn't leave much, so I wound up in an orphanage, because my momma had no relatives, and my father's brother didn't want me.' Her voice was dry, emotionless. 'I stayed in that home until I was eleven. Then I was adopted, by a retired judge named Eli Woods and his wife. It's unusual for kids to get adopted that late, you understand. Most couples want babies. But I was real pretty by the time I was eleven, and I soon realized why the judge had chosen me. Two days before my twelfth birthday, Eli came into the bathroom when I was drying myself. That night he came into my bedroom and raped me.'

She paused, swallowed hard, and then continued. 'He raped me for two years, and he told me all the things they all say – nobody will believe you, you led me on, it's your fault. I told his wife, and she slapped me around the face and called me a good-for-nothing welfare slut and a dirty little liar. A year later, when I was thirteen, I walked into town and spoke to a police officer. He said he would file a complaint. But that evening Eli came to my room and he beat me until he drew blood. Then he broke my little finger.'

The tears were coming now, she couldn't stop them; they rolled out of her eyes and trickled down her cheeks, so she couldn't even see the faces of her small audience, staring at her, horrified. She ploughed on. 'As soon as it was healed, I stole his credit cards and his wallet and his wife's jewels, pawned the money and skipped town. I took my passport and booked a one-way ticket to Paris; told them Judge Woods was sending me on an educational trip. I don't know why I picked Paris. It just seemed so far away, and I was very good at French. He didn't speak French. Maybe I thought he'd have trouble tracking me down. So I got there, and I started hooking. I hated myself, but I was good at sex and it seemed like the fastest way to make a lot of money. Eli had power in that town because of his money. And I didn't trust anybody, I wanted enough cash of my own. I guess I was better-looking, more promiscuous than the other girls, because I made a lot of money very fast. I was off the streets in two months, graduated to a call girl serving rich businessmen, discreetly, at fancy hotels. That's where I met a couple of other girls doing the same thing. One of them wanted to leave her pimp, because he'd been hitting her. I told her she should come and work for me, because I'd never hit her. I was only fifteen, but I looked older. I was already cold, hard, ruthless – the person you're used to. By the time I was sixteen I'd rented my own small house for my girls on the Champs-Elysées. We were successful; a lot of the call girls working for me became models, got new names, married out of the life. I thought I could do that; I was eighteen years old, and I had nearly a million dollars in savings and deposit bonds. A real entrepreneur.'

She stifled a sob. 'So, I got a new passport, moved to California, picked the most conservative private school I could find – a Catholic convent – and contacted the model agencies. A scout had already tried to sign me in France, but I wanted to start fresh, back home, where nobody knew me. I wanted to be the biggest, richest, most famous woman in the whole world. I was determined I'd never love anyone and never trust anyone, because nobody had ever loved me. And you know the rest. So, I've been a bitch to you, and I realize it. I'm not asking you guys for anything, I just want you to understand why, so we can finish this film. Because Eleanor persuaded me to do something with my life, so at least when all this is over I can walk away with my head held up.'

Roxana sank onto the nearest chair and dashed her hand across her eyes, trying to brush a few of the tears away.

For a moment or two there was a stunned silence, the only noise in the dim room Roxana's soft weeping and the breaking waves on the beach outside. Finally Fred Florescu cleared his throat.

'Roxana, I can't pretend that we know what you went through. I don't think anybody who hasn't undergone the kind of horrors you endured could ever begin to imagine what that must have been like. But I know I speak for everybody in this room when I say that I totally admire your courage in being able to tell us what happened to you. However you behaved doesn't matter in the least. So you were a little cold, so what? I think you had every right to be mistrustful. But I hope you'll trust me now when I tell you that you are a truly fine actress, and you're somebody I'm proud to be making this movie with,' he said gently, and the whole cast began to applaud.

The sun was sinking over Beverly Hills when Tom Goldman arrived home. He parked his car in the garage and sat slumped in the front seat, his eyes staring into space, wondering how in God's name he was going to explain this to Jordan. The loss of most of his fortune would be the first blow: he realized his wife had expensive tastes, and he was about to tell her that they had to cut back drastically. Sell this house, for example, her favourite toy. But Lisa Weintraub, his accountant, had been totally clear: he could no longer afford to service the four-million-dollar mortgage on his five-million-dollar house. So, goodbye Beverly Hills, hello Laurel Canyon. He could live with that, but the question was, could Jordan? And there would be no more of those goddamned stupid parties she seemed to live for, either. With his new net worth of a million and a half, which had to cover a new house and a new baby, there was no way he could go for the caviar dinners and the Chanel suits any more. It was only after sitting down with Lisa and going through the household accounts that Tom realized just how much money Jordan had been spending on clothes. An original Chanel couture suit cost $20,000 dollars a pop. *Twenty thousand dollars!* And Jordan owned *five*!

Now he was going to have to go in there and tell her it had to stop. Not only were the big spending days over forever, she was going to have to sell most of her jewellery. He'd spent over three-quarters of a million on rocks for her since their marriage, and they needed the money. She was going to hate that. She was going to hate everything about this conversation.

Oh well, Goldman thought wearily. She has her baby on the way. Once it arrives, maybe she won't be interested in the social scene any more – because we sure as hell aren't gonna be hiring a nanny now.

The baby. Body-blow number two. He had to confess to his wife that he'd cheated on her, and that he was having another child by another woman.

Tom rubbed his fingers across his temple, feeling every second of his forty-five years. How in God's name had he screwed up his life this badly? he wondered helplessly. As long as he lived, he would never forget the torrent of emotions that had raged through him when Eleanor dropped her bombshell. Astonishment. Exhilaration, for a fraction of a second. And finally, the searing, overwhelming, hopeless waves of regret.

Seeing Eleanor so decisive, so calm, so controlled under pressure had underscored a truth he now realized he had always known – he was in love with Eleanor Marshall, and he probably always had been, from the day that bright, gawky graduate crashed into him outside the studio cafeteria fifteen years ago right up to that moment when she told him she was carrying his child. If he was honest, the appalling jealousy that had racked him at her wedding was the first real signal he was in trouble – Christ, had she ever looked so radiantly lovely as she did that day? Or was it before that? In New York, when he had found such total release in her arms, when he had sired the child that she had carried ever since? Too late, Goldman understood everything: the flame that Eleanor had borne for him in silence for so long, and the pain she must have gone through when Jordan turned up in the lobby of the Victrix; even at the time, he had been embarrassed that Eleanor had to hear it like that, but only now did he understand the full depths of what she had gone through. It explained her weakness, her loss of control at work when she returned to LA – weakness that Jake Keller had exploited.

The same weakness that Goldman was feeling right now.

What a tragedy that he had never seen what was right under his eyes, all the time. She had been his best friend, his protégée, his most trusted lieutenant. She had been the first person he would run to with a new idea, his sounding board, his best critic. He had tried to spend as much time as he could with her in and out of the office. He'd never confronted the root feelings behind his strong dislike of Paul Halfin, not until yesterday, not until it was too late.

Three months ago, and he could simply have asked Jordan for a divorce. But not now. His wife was an adult – of sorts – and though he might have hurt her, it would have been better that way than trying to inch through a sham of a marriage. But all that had changed in the lobby of the Victrix. Because the child Jordan was bearing had to come first, whatever he wanted to do. He had conceived that baby in wedlock, and Tom Goldman knew he had a duty to his kid. He had to stay with its mother until such time as it was old enough to understand – at fifteen or sixteen, say. He'd support the other baby if Eleanor required it, but he could have only one family. And he had married Jordan first.

Goldman got slowly out of his car and walked towards the house, thinking about his mother. Hannah Goldman had been dead now for seven years, but he knew she would tell him that this was the only choice. He had to stay until he had seen this child's bar or bat mitzvah.

But dear God, it was a terrible price to pay for his mistake.

He let himself in through the back door, punching their security code into the entry system. A flashing red light above the panel told him that Jordan was already home.

So what were you hoping for? Tom asked himself wryly. That she was out shopping on Rodeo? You're gonna have to do this eventually, so it might as well be now.

'Jordan!' Goldman called. 'I'm home!'

'Oh, *really*.' His wife's Bostonian tones were dripping with acid. 'Well, I'm in the drawing room. I hope you don't expect me to come to *you*, Thomas.'

Here we go, Tom thought, walking through to their lavish reception room. It was an ornate fantasy of William Morris wallpaper and English Regency antiques; the decorator had charged him a small fortune for them, Goldman recalled. Well, possibly he'd get another quarter-million from an auction of every goddamn antique in the place. Nothing but functional twentieth-century American for the Goldmans now.

Jordan was sitting bolt upright on one of their chintz armchairs, her long blonde hair clipped behind her head in a severe ponytail, wearing her pink Chanel suit and her long diamond drop earrings. He noticed she had also put on her pearl and sapphire choker and the diamond and ruby eternity ring he'd bought her to celebrate her pregnancy. She was obviously making a point. And from the way she was scowling at him, she was pretty mad already, before he'd even started.

'I hope you're about to tell me that that you've changed your mind about that *horrid* stock,' Jordan snapped petulantly. 'It was *hell* at the health club this morning, you know. Everybody whispering and pointing.' She pulled a small lace handkerchief out of her sleeve and dabbed at some nonexistent tears. 'I can't take much more of this, Tom. How could you do this to me?'

'I met with Lisa Weintraub today,' Goldman began. The quicker he came out with it, the better. 'She told me that we've lost a lot of our money. Almost eight million dollars.'

'*What?*' Jordan shrieked.

'We're going to have to sell the house, most of your jewellery, and auction off a lot of our effects. Lisa knows a good real estate broker who'll get us a discount on a new place; we can get something compact in Laurel Canyon or Pasadena for about half a million. That'll leave us a million in disposable capital, so we should be able to get by until I find another job.'

'It's not true,' Jordan whispered, shaking her head. 'You're making this up to scare me.'

'Jesus, Jordan. Don't be so childish. This is tough, but we'll pull through it. We're a family; we've got each other.'

The words rang hollow in his ears.

'I'm going to stay at my job until our current movie is released, then I'll resign. And I won't easily be able to get another job in the industry, certainly not at the level I was at before, so I'm afraid all the socializing is going to have to go. We don't have the money for expensive parties, anyway – we're going to have to economize, honey. I'll need to cancel most of your credit cards and arrange a small allowance for you. And you realize that we certainly won't be able to hire a nanny now, so it'll just be you, me and the baby,' Tom concluded, trying to give her a smile.

'No! I won't do it!' Jordan shrieked. 'You can't do this to me, Tom! I won't live like that!'

'We don't have a choice,' Goldman answered, suppressing his anger. She was reacting like a spoiled teenager, even now, in the midst of this catastrophe, at the one time a husband might look to his wife for support.

But I don't have the right to be angry with her, Tom reminded himself, considering what I have to tell her next.

'Jordan, listen to me. There's something worse.'

'Something *worse*?' Her angelic young face was pink with fury. '*Something worse?* You son of a bitch, what the hell could be worse than that? Don't you understand that you've *ruined my life*?'

'You remember when you flew up to the Victrix, in New York, to tell me about the baby? Jordan, I have something to confess to you.' He swallowed. 'I slept with Eleanor Marshall the night before – it was the first and only time – and yesterday she told me that she conceived that night. She has decided to have the baby.'

Silently he waited for the storm. Over this, she had every right.

'Is that it?' Jordan asked.

'Isn't that *enough*?'

'I thought you were going to tell me we were being investigated by the IRS,' Jordan sniffed. 'You slept with *Eleanor Marshall*? Tom, how could you? She's so old!'

Tom Goldman stared at his wife, but the words wouldn't come. He wondered if he was hearing things. Jordan went into utter hysterics at the thought of lowering her lifestyle, but to his admission that another woman was also bearing his child she acted as if it was a minor lapse of taste. Could she really be that petty? Could anybody?

Maybe she'd misunderstood him.

'Jordan, I just told you that Eleanor is also pregnant. By me. Don't you have anything to say?'

'Yes! Yes I do!' she screamed. Suddenly all the fury was back, and it was almost a relief. But then she continued, 'How dare you humiliate *me* like that! Don't you realize how everybody will laugh at me? They'll say you preferred that *wrinkled old woman* to me!'

'Eleanor's thirty-eight – '

'And I'm *twenty-four*! And *don't* think *everyone* won't point that out! She doesn't even *work out*. She's just a bluestocking! How could you?'

He couldn't hide his disgust. 'Jordan, that's the most – '

'*I want a divorce!*' She was yelling at him, the veins on her slender neck standing out like a whipcords. '*I want a divorce right now!*'

'But our baby,' Tom managed.

'What baby? I'm not pregnant, you stupid fool! There never was any baby! Isabelle told me to say there was, so you'd leave that old bitch alone!' She laughed hysterically. 'Do you think I'd get pregnant with the baby of a stupid *asshole* like you? You just *wanted* me to *ruin* my figure! To stay home all day with some *screaming brat* when I'm young! You're just jealous of me because *I* know how to have *fun!*'

Goldman's head was reeling. 'There's no baby?'

'No! Don't you understand English? I was going to tell you I'd had a miscarriage. If I *was* pregnant you'd have *made* me have a miscarriage!' Jordan was sobbing with rage. '*You* can live in Pasadena! *I won't do it!* I want a divorce! And I came to this marriage with two million dollars of my own in savings, and you're not having *any* of it!'

'You never told me that,' Tom said quietly.

'You're not having any of it! It's *mine!*'

'I wouldn't touch a cent of your money,' Tom told her with contempt. 'You're welcome to walk away with everything you brought to this marriage. I'll have my lawyers get in touch tomorrow.'

'I'm keeping the diamonds!' Jordan screamed after his retreating back.

Tom Goldman walked out of his house and out of his marriage. And by the time he hit the back door he was smiling.

36

'All right. OK,' Goldman said resignedly, looking across at Eleanor and shaking his head. 'Two weeks. If that's the best you can do . . . yeah, I know. Thanks, Janice.'

He hung up.

'What did we get in Seattle? Two weeks?' Eleanor asked, disappointed. 'I was hoping for a little more time than that. It's supposed to be the Generation X capital of the universe. You'd think that Zach and Florescu alone would be enough to guarantee some box-office down there.'

Tom shrugged. 'What can I tell you? Everybody's fighting shy of the Roxana thing, I guess.'

'No, it's not that. A scandal like that is just free publicity. My guess is that it's Jake Keller and David Tauber.'

Tom Goldman and Eleanor Marshall were sitting together in Tom's office at Artemis Studios, surrounded by phones, piles of notes and the remains of a tray of coffee and bagels. It was seven p.m., and the sun was just starting to sink in the rosy sky outside Goldman's huge windows, the pollution in the atmosphere hanging over LA distorting the light into wild streaks of scarlet and copper. That was one thing you could say for the smog: it made for great sunsets. But today neither of them had had much time to notice the beauty of nature. They had spent the entire day trying to persuade distributors to book *See the Lights*; this morning it had looked as though the picture would get shown in two art-house theatres in Minnesota and one multiplex in Tucson and then die an ignominious, straight-to-video death. Nobody wanted to touch it with a disinfected ten-foot pole. Word was out that *See the Lights* was going to be Fred Florescu's *Last Action Hero*; even Steven Spielberg had bombed with *1941*, and now it was about to be Florescu's turn. The Artemis marketing team had gotten the same message over and over: this movie is a total failure, absolutely unreleasable, how can you even ask us to book a flick which is practically forcing your studio into bankruptcy? It had taken Tom and Eleanor all day to salvage a minimal opening distribution for the movie. They'd exhausted a lot of stored goodwill and personal credit in the process, cashing in fifteen years of favours owed, and even then the two of them had only been able to get a skeleton release. But that was the most they could squeeze out of the market. People just did not want to know.

'Tauber and Keller? I guess it's possible,' Tom mused.

'You know I'm right. After Sam Kendrick finished trashing David Tauber round this city no other agencies would pick him up, and he wound up working for some fly-by-night schmuck with one phone line and a PO box number down in West Hollywood, casting pet food commercials.' Tom grinned. 'And as for Keller, when you put the word out, he was all washed up too, so he's – '

'Fulfilling his boyhood dream of becoming an indie producer,' Goldman finished off, laughing.

'Exactly. So I think we can take it as read that neither one is wishing this movie the best of luck. David Tauber was out there on the set, and Jake Keller has a lot of memos detailing stuff that went wrong. All they had to do was plant a few whispers – you know, Florescu wouldn't let anybody see the rushes, Artemis was in despair over a creative and commercial disaster, Roxana Felix couldn't act her way out of a paper bag . . . It's very simple to do, and those two assholes want revenge.'

Tom nodded slowly. 'You have a point. Plus, we have to remember that the industry knows we only get to stay in our jobs for the release of *See the Lights* because we have good lawyers. As soon as this movie is out, we're out. Howard and Co are making that pretty clear. So nobody cares if they offend us by blanking this picture. Why should they? We're as good as gone.'

Eleanor gave Tom a soft smile, nodding at his T-shirt and jeans. 'At least you don't have to dress up for work any more.'

'If it's good enough for David Geffen, it's good enough for me,' Goldman said unrepentantly. 'I should have done this years ago.' He reached across the desk and took Eleanor's hand, stroking it softly. 'I should have done a lot of things years ago.'

Eleanor looked at him, his dark eyes fixed so intently upon her, and felt the familiar warmth of desire blossom across her skin. But it was too soon. She had to be sure he wasn't on the rebound from Jordan, that he meant what he was telling her, that he wouldn't wait another couple of months and then trade her in for the latest trophy wife *de jour*. The pain of losing him was too recent; she just couldn't risk her heart again. Because if he smashed it this time, Eleanor Marshall knew in her deepest soul that it would be broken forever.

She pulled her hand free, gently but firmly. 'Maybe it'll be a huge hit. Maybe we'll rescue the studio with this picture. Fox was in trouble when they put out *Star Wars*, and nobody was expecting that movie to do anything either.'

Tom Goldman swallowed his disappointment. Eleanor needed time to trust him, he realized that. But it was so hard, to be near her, to know she was carrying their child, and not to be able to hold her and caress her.

'Eleanor, you have to understand something here. We've done what you said; we beat all the odds in forcing the board to let us stay and finish the movie, persuading Roxana to go back to the set, and getting some kind of basic release going. But this was a hundred-and-twenty-million-dollar movie! Do you realize the kind of distribution, marketing, or whatever that we'd need to earn our money back? *Star Wars* cost *seven* million dollars. You've done the right thing, creatively, for your project, but you have to face facts. We're going to bomb, and we're going to bomb *huge.*'

'It's possible that we could have a word-of-mouth hit.'

'A hundred-and-thirty-five-million-dollar word-of-mouth hit? You're asking for a miracle.'

Eleanor Marshall thought of Tom's baby, growing inside her womb. 'I believe in miracles,' she said.

Tom shook his head. 'You just don't know when to quit, Eleanor, do you?'

'Absolutely not,' she agreed. 'So are you coming out to the wrap party on Saturday? I'm going to book my ticket tonight.'

'Are you kidding?' Goldman replied. 'After everything we've been through to see this goddamn movie finished, I wouldn't miss it for twenty monsoons.'

See the Lights held its wrap party on the beach, under the stars. Tom and Eleanor arrived to a hotel already in chaos as hundreds of crew technicians lugged packed suitcases down the main stairs or hogged the elevator, stacking all their stuff in the hotel lobby in great colourful piles of leather and plastic, ready to be ferried out to Seychelles airport the next morning. The party atmosphere was in evidence even before they got out to the beach, the lighting director staggering past Tom with his hair covered in sticky coconut milk and the chief grip passing out thick pre-rolled joints to everybody in sight. Relief was hanging so thick in the air you could almost smell it. And once the two of them stepped outside onto the soft, powdery sand, it was insane.

'Is this a wrap party or Mardi Gras?' Tom asked Eleanor, gazing at the scene on the shore. Four huge bonfires were stacked along the beach, throwing up towers of flame against the inky black sky, silhouetting the dancing figures jumping crazily around them to the strains of some extra-loud rap music that was pumping from a beat-box somewhere. Florescu had organized a trestle table piled with food they could smell two hundred yards away: Creole lobster, octopus curry, sharkmeat with ginger sauce, parrotfish soup. As soon as they walked over, somebody from the catering crew shoved a tall glass of something tall and colourful into their hands.

'What's this?' Goldman asked warily, putting an arm round Eleanor's waist.

'*La purée,*' the girl said, laughing. 'Local speciality. Try it!'

Tom took a gulp and gasped for air, the crushed fruit brew searing the back of his throat. 'Jesus Christ! What *is* this?'

'Fermented fruit alcohol. It's pretty strong,' she said.

'No kidding,' Tom said, putting it down on the table.

'You have anything non-alcoholic?' Eleanor asked. 'I'm pregnant.'

'Sure.' She handed her a plastic beaker of *citronelle*, the light Seychellois brew of mineral water, honey and crushed lemon.

'I'll take one of those,' Tom said.

'Hey, you guys! You're late,' Fred Florescu said, walking up to Tom and slapping him on the shoulder.

'It's good to see you too, Fred,' Tom said, smiling.

'Plane was delayed in Singapore,' Eleanor explained. 'How are you?'

'Pretty fucking pleased with this movie,' the director told her. 'I gotta thank you guys for fighting so hard to let us finish it. We've made an incredible film. It's gonna win the Palme d'Or at Cannes next year, and it's gonna break box-office records.'

'Really?' said Eleanor.

'Sure,' said Tom.

Florescu glared at him with mock severity. 'Oh ye of little faith. You care to place a bet on that? A hundred dollars says you make at least thirty million dollars' profit on this thing.'

'Sold,' Goldman said, clasping the younger man's hand. 'God knows I could use the money.'

'We're out of a job after *See the Lights* is released,' Eleanor told him.

'No you're not. You can come and work for me,' Sam Kendrick said, emerging from behind a crackling bonfire. 'Artemis may be history, but we're not. Since the divorce I've thrown myself into work. We wrapped a fat deal from Troy Savage at Universal just this morning. I'm snowed under, I could do with some help. You gamekeepers should turn poachers. It'd make you more well-rounded human beings.'

'By becoming an *agent*? You're on drugs, Sam,' Florescu teased him. 'Kendrick's just a money-making machine with a greedy, ruthless, one-track mind. Which is precisely why I signed to him.'

'All directors are just kids whose bullying instinct never found enough expression beating up small children in grade school,' Sam rejoined amiably.

'What are you doing here, Sam? I thought you didn't represent Roxana Felix any more,' Eleanor said, curiously.

Kendrick's face darkened, and he looked away.

'I don't,' he said. 'But Fred, Zach and Megan are still my clients, and so are all the co-stars. I was never about to miss this.'

'Where is Roxana?' Eleanor asked. 'I'd like to see her.'

'You will. Real soon,' Florescu said. 'Zach and Roxana are both about to make speeches. Have a seat.'

He waved them to a place at the trestle table, and they sat down, aware of figures beginning to gather around and sit cross-legged on the sand, crowding the benches. Suddenly they exploded into cheers and wolf whistles as Roxana Felix, looking stunning in a sheer white silk dress, her long hair braided in a sophisticated French pleat, climbed nimbly on top of a pile of crates which somebody had erected specially for the occasion.

'Wow, they really love her,' Tom Goldman muttered.

'Yeah, well. She turned from bitch queen of the universe into Mother Theresa,' Florescu whispered back loudly. 'Turned up early every morning, made coffee for the wardrobe girls, asked if she could help packing up the equipment – you name it, Roxana was in there giving a hand. Everybody on the crew was shellshocked. Now they worship the ground she walks on.'

Eleanor cast a sideways glance at Sam Kendrick, but he had lowered his eyes, refusing to look at Roxana as she started her speech.

'On behalf of the cast, I want to thank everybody in the crew who worked so hard to make this movie,' Roxana said, to loud applause from the supporting actors, who banged the tables and whooped. 'It was you guys versus spoilt models, Murphy's Law, studio politics and the forces of nature – so naturally there was no contest.' There was a lot of raucous laughter. 'I should also give special thanks to Megan Silver, for writing us out of more dead ends than anybody can count' – huge applause and whistles – 'and Zach Mason, for kindly getting his ass back here alive, so I didn't have to do love scenes with a cadaver. Although on second thoughts, maybe that might have been preferable ... and lastly, let me say that I have always dreamed of working with the most talented young director in America.' A beat. 'So when I get home, I'm going to call Quentin Tarantino right away and ask him to give me a test.'

The party exploded into laughter and cheering, and Roxana bowed and sat down, blowing a kiss towards Florescu.

'Bitch,' he yelled, grinning.

Roxana's place was taken by the tall, musclebound figure of Zach Mason, his long black hair blowing against his bare shoulders, his broad chest silhouetted in the firelight.

'Jesus, he looks terrific,' Eleanor said.

'The guy's been pumping iron like a madman ever since he got out of hospital,' Fred explained. 'He says he's going to get back on the road and he needs to be in shape. It's either that or it's love. He's been inseparable from Megan Silver since the moment they were found in the jungle.'

'Ahhh, how romantic,' Eleanor murmured, and Tom tightened his grip around her waist, squeezing her softly. She hesitated a moment, then settled back in against him. It felt good to be out here with Tom, in the darkness, Eleanor thought. If this was their final bow, it was right that they were doing it together.

I won't pull back from him, Eleanor told herself. At least, not this evening.

'They say a thing of beauty is a joy forever,' Zach Mason began, 'although in Roxana's case I think I speak for everybody when I say that for most of the time a thing of beauty was a pain in the ass.'

'Amen,' Florescu yelled, to more cheers.

'Seriously,' Mason went on, holding up a hand for silence, 'I have to thank Roxie, Seth, Mary, Jack, Robert, Fred and the whole cast and crew for letting me see what it's like to make a movie. And when I next want to do something a little less stressful, I'm going skydiving over the Grand Canyon without a parachute.' He waited for the laughter to die down, and then held out his hand. 'Megan, get up here.'

Eleanor watched quietly as Megan Silver, chic and slender in a short Donna Karan dress and loose sandals, climbed up next to Zach and nestled against him, her small hand clasped in his. She looked gorgeous, confident and radiant with happiness.

'Is that Megan?' Tom whispered to Eleanor, staring at her disbelievingly. 'What happened to that dumpy little mouse I met six months ago?'

'She made this movie,' Eleanor replied, finding that she had tears in her eyes. 'It changed all of us.'

'I've got a couple of announcements to make,' Zach said. 'The first is that I'm really glad to have had the opportunity of seeing what it was like to act, particularly in such a great film as this turned out to be, because I won't be doing it again. I've talked to the guys in Dark Angel, and we're getting back together. Movies are fun, but music is my life.'

There was deafening applause.

'Thanks,' Zach said. 'And talking of my life, the second thing I've got to tell you guys – saving the best for last' – he looked tenderly down at Megan, smiling into her eyes – 'is that this morning I asked Megan Silver if she'd agree to marry me, and she said yes.'

Anything else he might have wanted to add was lost in pandemonium, as the cast and crew burst into congratulations, everybody yelling and whistling and stamping their feet, and Megan and Zach were pulled down off the crates by people crowding around to shake their hands. Eleanor saw Roxana hugging Megan, and then Zach.

'Are you going to say something?' Tom asked Florescu.

'After that? Are you kidding? It would be the anticlimax of the century,' Florescu said dryly. 'No. I spoke to the crew when we did the final take of the final scene. That'll have to do.' He swung his legs over the bench and stood up. 'Excuse me for a second, OK? I have to go congratulate them.'

'Me too,' Sam Kendrick added, following his client. 'I'll see you two later.'

'Come on, Tom,' Eleanor said. 'Let's go.'

'In a second.' He moved closer to her on the bench and grabbed her two hands, holding them tightly in the shadows, looking at her in the flickering light of the bonfires as people rushed past them towards Zach and Megan, the party raging around them, ignoring them, leaving the two of them alone at the end of the table.

'Not now,' Eleanor whispered. There was something about the way Goldman was looking at her that made her nervous. His liquid black eyes were fixed on her, scanning her face as though he wanted to memorize it, as though he would never take his gaze off her.

'Yes, now,' Tom insisted. 'Now. I have to say it, Eleanor. I can't wait any longer.'

She was silent.

Tom reached out one hand and cupped her cheek, softly, gently, rubbing his rough palm across the softness of her skin.

'I love you,' he said. 'I've loved you since the day I met you. Maybe you felt the same way, maybe it happened to you a little later, but I *know* you feel something for me. New York proved that to both of us.' He took a breath, struggling to find the right words. 'I guess we were both too timid, or too comfortable, or too shy, but neither one of us said anything until it proved to be too late. I hadn't been with Jordan long when I realized what an idiot I'd been. I thought about you every second of the day. I thought about you when I was with her. I tried not to, but I couldn't help it. And the night we had together was the most perfect communion I ever had with another human being in my life.'

Eleanor Marshall sat listening to him, tears forming in her eyes and rolling softly down her cheeks.

'The next day, when I thought Jordan was pregnant ... I was trapped. It was too late. And I realized the full depths of what that meant when I saw you marrying Paul. So help me, Eleanor, I wanted to kill him. I wanted to rush up there and carry you away by force. And I couldn't do a thing about it.' He touched his finger to one of the tears rolling down her face and brushed it away. 'Eleanor, I know I hurt you. I know you're frightened now. But I swear, I love you with all my heart.' His voice was hoarse with the intensity of what he was saying. 'Look at me. You know I mean what I say. I love you and I love our child with all of my heart. God gave us both a second chance, Eleanor. Don't let's waste this half of our lives.'

'Oh, Tom,' she whispered.

He slipped from the bench and sank to his knees in front of her, on the sand, holding her hands to his.

'I love you more than life,' he said. 'So help me, I don't want to live without you. Eleanor, will you marry me?'

She gazed at him for a long moment. Then she bent her head and kissed him softly, passionately.

'I thought you'd never ask,' she said.

In the darkness, Roxana Felix hung back from the crowd, watching them all swarm around Megan and Zach, shouting congratulations and cracking jokes. She was truly pleased for both of them. Since the night she had spoken to the cast, neither of them could have been more compassionate or friendly towards her. Zach in particular had gone out of his way to be kind; Roxana knew that he realized, more than any of the others ever could, what it was like living in the centre of the spotlight, where nobody could be themselves with you and everybody already had an opinion the first time they met you. He'd told her last night that she'd gone from the most lonely kid in the world to the most sought-after-woman alive, and added, 'Maybe now you'll get a chance to be normal, Roxie. I really hope so.'

God, I hope so too, Roxana thought fearfully, her eyes fixed on one figure breaking away from the crowd.

Sam Kendrick.

He had arrived yesterday, and refused to see her, refused to speak to her, and hung up on her when she'd called his hotel room. She'd sent a note, asking for five minutes of his time, and received no reply. Sam didn't want to know, and he was making it painfully obvious.

Roxana felt her heart crashing against her ribcage. She was so nervous she half expected to look down and see herself bathed in a cold sweat. But she had to do this; she had to speak to him.

Sam Kendrick was the only man who had ever been able to reach her, whose caresses had actually aroused her, the only man whose touch she had ever truly desired. Oh, she might have kidded herself that she wanted Zach, but Zach Mason, to her, had only ever been another link in the masterplan. She had set out wanting to use Sam Kendrick, to be revenged on him for some minor insult, and then . . .

. . . and then she had fallen in love with him.

Sure, she'd tried to deny it to herself. The more she thought about him, the more she told herself that she loathed the guy, the more ferociously she tried to break him. As though she were proving something to herself.

And when that terrible phone call had woken her up, Isabelle's mocking voice bringing her ice fortress crashing down all around her, Sam had been the only one to come and see her, the only one not to condemn her, the only one who would stand by her side and tell her he loved her. And then, terrified by the feelings he was evoking in her, seeing them as pure weakness, in her desperation she had turned on him like a wounded beast, snarling, and hurt him as desperately and as deeply as she knew how.

Only when Eleanor had arrived, later, offering her a second chance, had Roxana managed to let everything go. Weeping in the older woman's arms, too tired to fight the world any longer, she had discovered that at least one other person gave a damn about her. Then the cast had accepted her back amongst themselves, with complete forgiveness and acceptance, and working her butt off to finish *See the Lights* had provided her with her own small redemption; a chance to work with other people, and to be considered, for once, just as an actress, just as herself. After Florescu had yelled 'Cut! – and *print!*' to the cheers of the crew, he'd come across to Roxana and told her he'd like to work with her again. Not such a big deal to most people, maybe, but at that moment it seemed better than the most flowery compliment she'd ever been paid.

And finishing the movie had given her a little space to confront her feelings about Sam Kendrick; to acknowledge that she'd fallen in love, to look at Megan Silver as she walked around the set hand in hand with Zach, and know that she wanted that for herself, that simple, profound affection, that bond, the love that Sam had offered her. He was angry, and he had every right to be. She knew that. But she also knew, as she stood there and watched Kendrick walking back towards the hotel, alone on the beach, that she had to try to reach him. At least *try*. Or he'd be out of her life forever.

This was her only chance.

Roxana moved out of the shadows, running across the beach, down to the water's edge, and touched Sam Kendrick on the shoulder.

He spun round, smiling, but the smile died and froze on his face when he saw who it was.

'What the hell do you want?' he demanded, his tone sharp. 'Can't you just leave it alone, Roxana? What more do you want from me?'

'Sam, please,' she said. 'Give me a chance. I just want to tell you I'm sorry. I truly am.'

His eyes were cold.

Roxana tried again. 'I've changed, Sam. I truly have. Can't we make a fresh start?'

Kendrick stood there, watching her for a second, and slowly shook his head. 'I don't think so, Roxana. I'll accept your apology, OK? Let's leave it at that.'

She took a step backwards in the damp sand. The finality in his voice was terrible.

'I know it's too late,' Roxana whispered. 'But for what it's worth – I love you.'

For a moment she thought she saw a light flare in his eyes, but then Kendrick looked away, and the moment passed.

'You're right,' he said. 'It is too late.'

And as Roxana Felix stood there, watching him, Sam Kendrick turned his back on her and walked away.

The crew flew back home the next morning, together with Sam Kendrick and most of the supporting cast. Tom had arranged for Zach, Megan, Fred and Roxana to take Howard Thorn's private jet in the afternoon, along with himself and Eleanor.

'Privilege of office,' he explained as they soared into the dizzy blue skies above the Indian Ocean. 'And since this is the last time we're ever gonna get to enjoy them, we might as well make the most of it.'

'So do you think you guys will take up Sam's offer?' Florescu asked Eleanor, as she sat on the comfortable leather sofa, curled up against Tom.

'And become an agent? No way,' Goldman said.

'Speak for yourself. I might give it a try,' Eleanor replied, digging Tom in the ribs.

He caught her hand and kissed it. 'Eleanor Marshall Goldman. What do you think?'

'Sounds terrific. Apart from the "Goldman" part,' Eleanor told him, laughing.

'You guys too?' Florescu asked in mock horror, glancing at Zach and Megan. 'Jesus. I hope it isn't catching.'

Zach laughed. 'Fred, you're too macho to be infected.'

'You got that right,' the director told him, winking at Roxana. 'So where are you going to be when the movie opens?'

'At the Bel-Air. We're renting a suite while we look for a new house,' Eleanor told him. 'In fact, everybody should give me a contact number, so I can let you all know how we're doing.'

'Roxana, Paramount want me to do a remake of *Breakfast at Tiffany's*,' Florescu told her. 'You interested?'

She nodded, delighted. 'Are you serious?'

'Absolutely. You're a great actress,' Florescu said, adding mischievously, 'not to mention a world-class babe, which never hurts.'

She threw a cushion at him.

Obsequious stewardesses bustled round them, handing out crystal glasses of champagne.

'I think we should toast the movie,' Florescu said, raising his glass. 'Because after this, nothing is ever gonna seem difficult again.'

The plane was filled with laughter as they raised their glasses.

On Saturday afternoon, Zach Mason and Megan Silver were lying in bed together, wrapped in each other's arms.

'Stop looking at the phone,' Zach teased her.

'I am not looking at the phone.'

'Yes you are. You've been waiting for the phone to ring all day. When Yolanda called this morning, you jumped three feet in the air.'

'I did not,' Megan said indignantly, then gave him a sheepish smile. 'It was only two feet.'

Mason laughed, cupping her breasts in his hands and kissing the tips of her nipples.

'You have a one-track mind. Will you cut it out? We've done nothing but make love all day.'

'You have a better idea?'

'Maybe not,' she said, reaching down between his legs.

They kissed softly.

'Declan was totally blown away when you called,' Megan said. 'He thinks I'm Cinderella, running off to fairyland and winding up with the handsome Prince.'

'Well, you are,' Zach told her, stroking the back of her neck.

'Are you kidding? I wound up with the frog,' she giggled, squirming away from him. 'I can't believe I'm going to spend the rest of my life in a tour bus.'

'Writing novels. Your choice, babe,' Zach reminded her.

'Stop changing the subject,' Megan teased.

The phone rang. They both jumped out of their skin.

'You get it,' Megan said breathlessly. 'It's probably for you.'

He shook his head. 'No way, sugar. *You* wrote the fucking movie. You get it.'

'Get the phone.'

'You get it.'

'Get the goddamn phone, Zach!' Megan squealed.

He snatched the receiver off its cradle.

'Zach Mason. Oh, hi, Tom. Yeah, she's here too . . .'

Roxana Felix sat alone in her chic Century City apartment, curled up on her favourite easy chair, reading Florescu's latest script and trying not to think about the movie. Since she'd given her press conference on her return to the States, life had gotten a whole lot easier. She had forgotten nothing, but she'd also discovered one fundamental truth: that demons turn to stone when exposed to the light. The cosmetics people had all come crawling back to her, even pathetic little Bob Alton had tried to reingratiate himself, but she just didn't want to know. There was more to being a woman than physical beauty, a lucky combination of genes and something that had a sell-by date imprinted in every atom of her DNA. Eleanor Marshall and Fred Florescu had shown her that she had something worth nurturing; real talent that would grow with her, that would blossom with her age and experience, instead of fading away. That was something she could truly be proud of. And she was trying to concentrate on that, and not keep obsessing over *See the Lights* and a phone that obstinately sat there, not ringing. She was more mature than that.

The phone rang.

Roxana leapt out of her armchair and pounced on it before it had a chance to ring twice. 'Eleanor?' she asked.

'I'm afraid not,' came a low voice at the other end.

Her heart stopped.

'This is Sam Kendrick.'

'Hi,' Roxana managed.

'I'm sorry, I forgot. You'll be getting the opening figures for the movie today. I should have thought.'

'Fuck the movie,' Roxana said elegantly. She could hardly breathe.

Sam laughed. 'I was going to ask if you had a date for the European premiere.'

'Oh, Sam,' Roxana said.

'I saw your press conference,' he said, and paused. 'I nearly didn't call, because I figured you'd hang up on me. I'm sorry I was so blind, Roxana.'

'That's OK,' she said, feeling her heart starting to pound against her ribcage. Oh God, was there another chance for her? Could there be?

She struggled to sound calm. 'I know I gave you every reason to hate me.'

'You know that Isabelle and I, we're still getting divorced.'

'Yes. I heard. I'm sorry,' she lied politely.

'I'm not,' Kendrick said grimly.

There was a long pause. Roxana found she was literally holding her breath.

'Uh, look. I was wondering if we could have coffee, get to know each other . . .'

'Start again?' Roxana whispered.

'Something like that,' Sam admitted. She imagined his smile as he cradled the receiver. 'We'll take it slow, just see what happens.'

'Good idea,' she agreed coolly, then lost it and added in a rush, 'Are you free now? I have a great coffee cake in the oven.'

'I'm on my way,' Sam said, and hung up.

Roxana kissed the phone before she put it down on its cradle, and danced around the room, skipping like a ten-year-old.

The phone rang again, and she snatched it up.

'I love you, I love you, I love you!' Roxana sang.

'Roxana? Are you OK?' Eleanor Marshall asked her.

Tom Goldman had been sitting in his hotel suite reading a novel when the call came in from Artemis; Eleanor lay on the couch eating a bowl of strawberries. She sat bolt upright, watching him as he nodded expressionlessly, scratching some figures on a piece of paper, saying 'Yeah, OK,' and then 'I see.'

He put the phone back on its hook.

'Well? Jesus, Tom, don't play poker-face games with me now,' Eleanor said, twisting her fingers around. 'Say something, for Christ's sake! Or I'm going to have a major coronary!'

Goldman let her hang for a second longer, then gave her a slow smile. 'Well,' he said. 'It looks like I owe that Florescu kid a hundred dollars.'

She sank back onto the couch, holding her breath.

'There are queues around the block in every theatre that's booked it,' Tom said. 'Box-office is totally sold out. There were riots in New York when the tickets sold out. They had to call the police.'

Eleanor Marshall stared at him, tears forming in her eyes.

'The studio's been inundated with requests to show this movie,' Goldman went on, coming across to her. 'They're telling me some theatre owners are going to court to get another chance at it. CBS are going to run a news segment tonight on the kids in Seattle who've taken sleeping bags to camp out on the pavement so they get a chance to see it tomorrow... Howard Thorn is desperate to get hold of us, apparently. It would appear that they want to offer us our jobs back ... the stock is going through the roof...'

'It's our miracle,' Eleanor whispered.

Tom Goldman shook his head. 'What miracle? I knew this would happen the second I read the script. I always had complete and total faith,' he said.

'Faith in me?' Eleanor asked, kissing him.

'In the movie,' Tom replied, and they melted into each other's arms, laughing.

Tall Poppies

This book is dedicated to
Rosie Cheetham, Susan Lamb, Barbara Kennedy-Brown,
and Tall Poppies everywhere.

1

'No! Stop it, we can't do this!'

Nina squirmed away. She kept her eyes down, hoping he wouldn't see that telltale glitter, her dilated pupils. Her face was flushed from wanting, but it was too soon.

'Come on, sugar, gimme a break,' Jeff said. His voice was rough, and she could see the outline of his hard-on through his grey flannel pants. Nina tried to be cool about it, like Judy or Melissa or any of those popular girls, and not think how much it would hurt if he put it inside her. Perhaps he wouldn't get it in, Nina thought wildly. She'd checked herself out in the bathroom mirror last night – pretty small. He'd split her in two.

'You drive me crazy,' Jeff breathed, running his hands inside the burgundy school blazer, finding her voluptuous breasts under the thin cotton of her outsize shirt. She was wearing some kind of coarse, heavy sports bra to hold them back, just like she wore her kilt a size too large, to cover up her tiny waist and full, round butt – but not even Nina Roth could hide for ever. Jeff grinned with triumph as her nipples stiffened against his palm. He'd been after her ever since he'd come off the basketball court, thought he'd like a swim, and found Nina doing twenty laps. After hours, guess she thought she'd be by herself. Jeff had hidden in a corner to watch. Christ! Who knew? Nina Roth, scholarship girl, major nerd, charity case – had a figure like Playmate of the Month! Va-va-voom, instant hard-on! When she had climbed out of the pool Jeff couldn't believe it – water streaming from her hair, trailing down across a cheap black swimsuit, outlining big firm breasts, a tiny waist, a flaring ass and long, curving legs. He'd felt his cock throbbing so urgently in his pants he had to slip into the guys' bathroom and jerk himself off. That was three weeks ago.

'Not here,' she said, looking up and down the corridor, trying to back away. 'Someone might see . . .'

'So what?' Jeff demanded sullenly. Nina was hard work for a chick that never had a guy look at her before. Sometimes he wondered if she was worth it. He had a hundred skinny blonde cheerleaders who'd jump through hoops for the chance to lay him. 'Don't you care about me?'

'You know I do—' The bell rang for third period and she jumped aside, shaky with relief, as kids came streaming out of their classrooms. 'I have to go, I got physics. I'll see you later . . .'

Melissa Patton came sidling up to Jeff's locker, her arms laden with cute pink files covered in butterflies. Melissa was blonde, thin, bouncy, scraped by in most of her classes. She always talked about being an actress or a model. Real popular with the girls.

'Hey, Jeffie ... some of us were going to see *Rage*, that movie? D'you wanna come along?' Melissa smiled invitingly, tossing one shiny blonde ringlet out of her eyes.

Glazer shook his head, liking the way her eyes moved appreciatively across his chest muscles. Missy and her crowd never missed a football practice.

'I'm going to hang in the park.'

'With Nina Roth?' Melissa's manicured nails curled around her gold eternity ring. He could smell Chanel No. 5 mingling with the newly washed scent of her hair; his mom would love Melissa. Jeff shrugged.

'I don't know why you bother. She's only into math,' Melissa snapped, and flounced away, blonde curls flying.

Right! But Nina made Melissa look like a stick of spaghetti ...

Jeff Glazer slammed the door of his locker.

Inside the quiet, gleaming classroom Nina Roth took deep breaths, taking in the smell of chalk and polish and disinfectant, trying to concentrate on what Sister Bernadette was saying. Normally this was one of her favourite classes; Sister Bernadette had been a research fellow at MIT before taking the veil, and it was cool to learn from somebody like that. But not today.

The class sat hunkered down at their desks, bored and restless, drawing in their margins with one eye on the clock. Rows of smart burgundy blazers and crisp cotton shirts, tailored linen pants or neat, swinging kilts were turned towards the teacher, eyes staring glassily at the blackboard where Sister was outlining equations in chalk. They did things the old-fashioned way here: the College of St Michael the Archangel was big, impersonal and expensive, one of the most prestigious schools in Park Slope. Brooklyn's richest parents had been sending their kids here for decades, paying through the nose for the nuns, the uniform, the Catholic education. Most of the trust-fund babies ignoring Sister Bernadette were atheist or Episcopalian, but so what? St Michael's was all about *cachet*, not the Church.

The kids shifted in their seats. One or two glanced over at Nina, the nerd, the scholarship girl. Her uniform was stretched and shapeless, but everyone knew she had to buy stuff secondhand. Anyway, she never cared how she looked; she was always lost in her stupid books ...

'So, the sum of the angles is ... ?'

Silence.

'Nina?'

Nina jumped in her seat, dragging her mind away from the feel of Jeff's hands on her breasts. She flushed a dark red.

'Excuse me, Sister?'

The teacher pursed her thin lips. 'Nina, what did I just ask?'

'I – I don't know, Sister.'

'I'm not surprised. You're miles away. How do you expect to get anywhere in life, Miss Roth, if you don't pay attention in school?'

Mean giggles from the class. Nina felt the familiar haze of humiliation creep over her again. They all knew she was the only one here who'd have to work her way up: their folks were lawyers, doctors and bankers; hers were a retired cop, a slob who lived for beer and *Jeopardy*, and a wasted alcoholic who ran their rundown deli between blackouts.

'Miss Whitney?'

'Ninety degrees, Sister,' Josie Whitney said smugly, shooting a look of triumph at Nina.

But Nina didn't care, not today. Because *she* was dating Jeff Glazer, the hottest guy in the school. Maybe things would be different now, Nina thought as she scribbled furiously. Maybe her luck was finally about to change.

Nina Roth was an only child, which was just as well, since her parents couldn't have afforded a second. According to her father, wheezing and complaining whenever he signed a cheque, they barely managed the first. Mark and Ellen Roth shared a dingy walk-up on South Slope and an air of bitter disappointment. They also shared a daughter, but for as long as she could remember, Nina had only got attention during their endless fights. A pawn to be squabbled over. Pop was in his fifties, fat, squalid, a major armchair jock. He mouthed off about the government and the Yankees and the weather in front of the TV, never shifting his blubbery body to do a thing about it. Pop said he was retired from the force, but Nina heard on the street he'd been canned for theft, siphoning off confiscated money and goods for himself. She never asked him about it. She knew it was true.

Then there was Mom. Nina thought she remembered a time when her mom loved her, took her walking in Prospect Park, bought her Italian ice cream on Court Street, or best of all, took her out to magical Coney Island in the summer, to ride the funfair and eat cotton candy.

But that was when she was very little. Before Dad had come home. Before Ellen started to drink.

Then things got bad very quickly.

These days Mom only hugged her in a drunken stupor, with her breath rank and tears of self-pity streaking her thin cheeks. Nina hated it, hated her, preferred to be left alone. Ellen didn't really love her daughter, Nina knew that. She took comfort solely in a bottle. Her mom was a sour woman, cocooning herself in an alcoholic fog from the misery of her life, often blacking out for entire days. She kept just enough control to staff the family store, a scuzzy 7–11 with peeling Coke ads on the door and a loaded pistol under the counter. Ellen sold cigarettes, booze and candy bars and counted the money. Matthew took deliveries, stacked shelves once a week. The important stuff, like accounts and reordering, Nina took care of. She'd asked to do it when she turned thirteen. Somebody had to put bread on the table.

Nina was sixteen years old. She knew her rich classmates despised her. She hadn't been popular at Beth Israel Elementary, either, when she was ten years old and studying desperately for the St Michael's scholarship, but she didn't give a damn, because school was the way out. Her whole life had one blind obsession: to get out of the South Slope, away from the drugs and the garbage, the graffiti, the gangs, the stray dogs.

Away from all the dirt and despair. Away from home.

Even so, it hurt, the way the other kids shunned her, never inviting her to hang out, snickering at her patched-up uniform and secondhand blazers. Nobody ever asked her to sit at their table at lunch. Nobody picked her for their team at games. She'd gotten the reputation for being a loner, and nobody ever bothered to disprove it – at least, not until three weeks back.

That miraculous day, Jeff Glazer had actually strolled up to her locker after French, and casually asked if she'd like to go out with him.

At first Nina just stood there blinking, convinced this had to be some particularly cruel joke. Glazer was seventeen, school quarterback, the only son of very wealthy parents, and a major hunk; muscular, tall, with Viking-fair hair and ice-blue eyes, Jeff had every babe in school flirting with him constantly. He'd dated and dropped half the best-looking ones already; ex-girlfriends swore he was a stud but a user, but that never stopped the next crop of giggling cuties trying out as replacements. Nina Roth would as likely fly to the moon as be asked out by Jeff Glazer.

But he was there. And he was asking.

'Like a date?' she stammered.

Jeff gave that indifferent shrug of his. 'Sure. You want to?'

OK, so it wasn't exactly *Romeo and Juliet*, but when he'd sat next to her at lunch, Nina wouldn't have traded the envious stares of Judy Carling and her crowd for all the roses in the world.

She pinned her compass to the paper in front of her and mechanically traced out a couple of angles. It couldn't last like this, she knew that. Jeff wanted to make love to her, and if she didn't let him, he was going to dump her. Even when she said she was too young, Jeff told her that everybody did it, she was way too uptight, and if she loved him she would *make* love to him.

Nina thought of the sniggering when Sister Bernadette said she'd have to get on in the world. They were all snobs and she hated them. But it didn't matter when she had Jeff – he'd picked *her*, not them. And some of the guys on the football team, even some of the girls, had started including her in stuff since she'd been dating him. Was she going to give it up? Just 'cause I'm chicken? Nina thought. He does love me, why would he touch me like that if he didn't love me? And I know I love him . . .

Nina breathed in deeply, trying to stop her heart thumping so hard against her chest. She could be as good a girlfriend as Melissa or Judy or Josie . . . as any of those rich babes. Jeff was gonna expect an answer in Prospect Park tonight. And the answer was going to be yes . . .

2

The turrets of Caerhaven Castle towered black as coal against the twilight sky, darkened from the rain and wind. The bitter storm had raged all day, churning the sea to fury against the cliffs below and uprooting two pear trees in the castle orchards. But tonight nobody noticed the weather. Light streamed from every window in the medieval walls, from the sturdy marquee set up on the croquet lawn and from the stream of Bentleys and Rolls-Royces crunching past the stone dragons on the front gates and up two miles of gravel drive.

The Countess of Caerhaven was giving a ball.

'Goddamn it, Monica. Where is that wretched child?'

Tony Savage, Thirtieth Earl of Caerhaven, tugged at the waistcoat of his immaculate white-tie suit. He hated being defied. Not only was he holder of one of the oldest titles in Wales, lord of Caerhaven Castle and seven hundred acres of rich farmland, Tony was Chief Executive of Dragon plc., the family company. Founded on blood money from the slave trade, Dragon was a pharmaceutical giant, with divisions worldwide. It was publicly held; Tony Savage had eleven per cent.

At his side Monica shrugged, offering her hand to a new batch of arrivals. 'Joanna, delighted you could come. Richard, how good to see you …' Tall and elegant, the second Lady Caerhaven swished around in a sea-green Balençiaga, pearls looped round her neck, sapphire clips pinching delicate earlobes. She smiled dazzlingly at every unfamiliar face: Cabinet ministers, industrialists and investment bankers, along with the society set. She was charming to them all. So important for Tony's business.

The earl nodded softly to himself. Monica looked wonderful, behaved perfectly. Never gave him a second's concern. She knew her place was at his side. None of that feminist claptrap had ever sullied her brain; she just liked spending his money, hosting his parties and dazzling the *Tatler* set every season. Women envied Monica and men wanted her. She was the perfect wife.

Monica Savage had done her duty in every way. There was Charles, Lord Holwyn, and Lord Richard; the heir and the spare. And if she no longer welcomed him into her bed, that was fine too: Tony Savage had women whenever he wanted them. Monica pretended not to notice and got her little baubles from Tiffany or Garrard's as a reward.

Tony grinned. If he'd chosen the Hon. Monica Fletcher first, he'd have had no problems whatsoever. As it was, there was only Elizabeth.

Tony glanced at his sons. Charles, Lord Holwyn, thirteen. Dark and intense, he was destined to look like his father. Charles was handsome and callous, calculating like his mother and ruthless like Tony. Just into his teens and already cocky and self-possessed. It was easy to be confident: Charles was heir to a title, a castle, London property and a vast fortune. Eleven-year-old Richard would get a slice of that too, though nothing like as much. Another boy might resent it, but Richard was lazy and easygoing. Charles had dominated Richard since they were tiny boys, and Richard never complained. Richard was popular with the girls because he was so pretty; he made average grades in school; he'd be a gentleman of leisure and do very well. The kid was only eleven but Tony could tell. Richard was the image of his mother.

If only they had not had Elizabeth.

The earl checked his watch and felt rage stealing over him. Elizabeth was late for her own ball.

Elizabeth. Daughter of Louise, Countess of Caerhaven, his first wife and the only woman ever to make him look a fool. To this day Tony hated the bitch. Louise worked when he asked her not to, refused to play hostess, and cuckolded him with Jay DeFries. His former best friend. Careless whether they were seen in public, Louise made Tony Savage a laughing stock and then divorced him before he'd had a chance to divorce her. He'd hated everything about her, even his infant daughter. Louise perversely delighted in the fact her baby was a girl. And little Elizabeth was just like her mother: the same downy, dark blonde hair, green eyes and long, lean body, not a sign of her father on her. Tony was sure she wasn't even his, but admitting his wife might have borne another man's child would have been too shameful.

When Louise died, aged twenty-seven, of breast cancer, the infant Lady Elizabeth moved back to her papa. She grew up a green-eyed, rebellious minx, her mother blossoming back up in her like a flower, an almost uncanny replica, laughing at Tony even in death.

Tony ruined Jay DeFries. Dragon was powerful: it wasn't difficult. He took over DeFries's business, muddied the books, got the Fraud Squad in. His former best friend had gone down for eight years, bankrupt. Hanged himself in jail.

As Dragon grew bigger, the whispers grew smaller. Soon nobody dared mention Louise or Jay; Tony Savage, Wall Street's Robber Baron, heard nothing but flattery. But young Elizabeth, running wild, flirting with the local boys, dressing indecently, blossoming into exquisite, dangerous beauty, was in his face every bloody day. She didn't mix with her brothers or stepmother. She was her mother's kid. The cuckoo in his golden nest.

'I have no idea,' said Monica, beckoning Charles over. 'Darling, do go and find your sister. Tell her to come down here *at once*. It's *her* sixteenth, and David Fairfax has been waiting for her all evening.'

Tony Savage looked across the grey stone of the Great Hall, lit by torches flickering in iron sconces and the roaring fire burning in the grate, past the rich swirl of silk, lace and velvet, to where the plump figure of a young man stood, surrounded by toadies and cradling a glass of vintage champagne. His

Grace the Duke of Fairfax, one of the most eligible men in England. Suitor for the hand of his only daughter.

'Can't think what he sees in her,' Tony said.

In her bedroom in the West Wing, Lady Elizabeth Savage leaned against the chill stone of the turret window and stared out into the night. Her eyes were used to bleak darkness and she could make out most of the landscape: the stable roofs, the black stretch of forest outside the castle walls, the low hills in the distance. She ignored the sounds of the glittering party below her and listened for the endless sigh of the sea. The cold air tasted of salt.

Granny was dead. Only two days ago she had been sitting with her in the East Wing, chattering about business, politics, and the roaring twenties. Granny never minded her talking on, her curiosity and ambitions. Two days without her already seemed like an eternity.

Despite what she said – 'Don't be ridiculous, child, everybody loves you' – Elizabeth knew Dad and Monica didn't care for her. She thought it was because she wasn't a boy.

Elizabeth grew up eager and vivacious. Scandalously careless of her station, she made friends with the servants' kids, climbed apple trees in her vest and knickers, and got suspended four times from Cheltenham – twice for smoking, twice for swearing at her teachers. A cold letter to the countess had threatened expulsion. She wasn't bookish, but Elizabeth was fascinated by business, the only thing about her dad she admired. There was an almighty row the day Tony discovered she'd been sending away for Dragon company reports.

'What is this nonsense, young lady?' he spluttered.

Elizabeth hurried to explain. 'I'm just taking an interest, Daddy. I thought I could study how Dragon does its marketing – you know I'm interested in how people sell things—'

'How people *sell* things? What are you, a *salesman*?'

'I want to work at Dragon,' Elizabeth said stubbornly.

'You have no idea what you want to do.'

'I do. I'm fifteen years old. I want to work in advertising, in Dragon . . .'

'Over my dead body.' Tony actually laughed. 'The *company* is going to your brother! Behave like a lady for once in your life.'

White faced, Elizabeth had turned and raced away up the stone staircase, looking for her grandmother. Flushed with anger, her father drew a deep breath and walked slowly back to his offices. With every year that passed, he was more certain Elizabeth would disgrace the family just like Louise.

But no. He would never let it happen again.

Elspeth, the dowager countess, had occupied the East Wing for twenty years since her husband died. She loved Elizabeth, although she too was convinced the girl was Jay DeFries's bastard. Elspeth's heart sank each year Elizabeth grew older, looking like a younger, prettier version of Louise. She knew Tony would never give the child a chance.

When Elizabeth sobbed out what her father had said about Dragon, the old lady coughed drily and gave her a hug.

'Never mind, Lizzie. He'll come round.'

'He won't.' Elizabeth buried her face in the stiff cotton petticoats. 'He doesn't want me to do *anything*! He said it wasn't ladylike … and he said if I'm expelled he'll have Dolphin put down!' Dolphin was her Labrador puppy. He slept on her bed and she loved him fiercely.

'Did he?' Granny said, frowning. 'I was expelled once, dear.'

'You? When? Why?'

Elizabeth's face was blotched red and puffy from crying. Her son was going to crush this one, unless somebody stopped him. Liz was a merry little thing. She wouldn't let Tony snuff the child out.

'The year before I married your grandfather. From finishing school in Switzerland.' A wicked chuckle. 'For painting my nails red.'

'Just for that?'

'Very wanton in those days.' Elspeth smiled, slipping her wrinkled hand over Elizabeth's smooth one. 'So, you want to work? If that's what you want, dear, you shall.'

Elizabeth shook her head. 'Daddy said the company belongs to Charlie. He won't let me anywhere near it.'

'But it isn't up to him. *I* own fifteen per cent of the stock … it was a wedding gift. It would get you a seat on the board. If you like, I'll call a lawyer and change my will. You can have it on your eighteenth birthday.' Granny's wrinkled face creased into a smile. 'I don't need to play at tycoon any more.'

Elizabeth stared at her grandmother. 'Truly? But what will Daddy say?'

'He can like it or lump it,' the old lady said crisply. 'Oh, don't worry, child. I'll speak to your father tomorrow. He can bluster away, but that never frightened me.'

She knew Daddy had called on his mother the same day.

When he went up to her again the following morning, however, the earl found Granny stiff in her chair. Dead, from what the family doctor called a 'routine coronary'.

Elizabeth resented every smiling idiot at the ball downstairs. All she wanted was to be alone, to have a little time to mourn. The wonderful news about Dragon was dust and ashes without Granny. How can I bear being stuck with the rest of them? Elizabeth thought, blinking back tears.

There was a heavy creak as the ancient oak door to her bedroom swung open.

'I should have known you'd be hiding up here,' Charles said. His low voice was full of disapproval. 'Everybody's waiting for you. It *is* supposed to be your party, Lizzie.'

'Nobody asked me if I wanted a party!'

'You're spoiling things again, as usual. Mamma can't believe how selfish you're being. Don't you know David Fairfax wants to see you?'

'I couldn't care less about David.'

'What's that dress you're wearing? That's not the gown Mamma bought you!'

He was annoyed. Elizabeth glanced back at the plain green Laura Ashley dress with the huge bow on the bottom, lying rejected over a Regency chair.

She'd known there was no way out of this horrible ball, so she'd snuck upstairs to Granny's rooms last night. Undisturbed by the cleaners, she'd unpacked the gown she wanted from Elspeth's chest of drawers; under folds of crisp white tissue, hidden away for nearly sixty years, was this vision of a dress. It was a cloud of the palest gold silk trimmed with cream lace, a whalebone corset tapering down to a billowing skirt over stiff petticoats of ivory lace, a discreet pattern in gold thread and seed pearls dusted over the bodice. It fit Elizabeth's long, lean body snugly, pushing her small breasts together and lifting them up, the skirts sweeping gracefully with every movement of her legs. She'd pulled her tawny hair up into a formal French pleat, added topaz drop earrings and slipped her feet into apricot satin heels.

Dad could try and ignore her *now*.

'It was one of Granny's,' Elizabeth told him. 'Just go away, Charles, please.'

'All right, I'm going, but you'd better get down there. Otherwise, Father's going to come up here and drag you down, in front of everybody . . .'

He would, too. Elizabeth knew that. She had to face her parents and all their vacuous friends . . .

Taking a deep breath, Lady Elizabeth Savage composed herself, opened her bedroom door, and walked slowly down the winding stairs to her sixteenth birthday party.

3

'I told you before. I can't come back early tonight, I have economics,' Nina said.

'Yeah? And what are we supposed to do? The stock needs checkin'.'

Nina shrugged. They were arguing in the tiny, cramped kitchen, standing shoulder to shoulder while Nina washed the dishes. Ellen gave them a perfunctory wipe with the towel and stashed them in the rack. She was only interested in haranguing her daughter.

'You're never around,' Ellen whined. 'You're always studyin' or out with your friends. Don't even have time for your mom.'

'Mom, I have to go to school, and I took that job at Duane Reed,' Nina told her shortly. She was too tired for this. SATs were two months away, she worked weekends and two nights a week at the local drugstore, and three evenings she had to be as fresh as she could for Jeff. The deli was just too much extra grind. They'd have to work it out by themselves.

Mr David had been right. Nina's math teacher had called her in last semester and laid out the facts.

'Nina, I have to tell you, I'm concerned about your grades trailing off.' He'd looked at the solemn little face bunched with worry under its mop of raven hair. 'Your concentration seems to be wandering, you're constantly tired, and Sister Agnes tells me you fell asleep during chemistry practical last week.'

'I'm sorry, sir. I'll try harder.'

'I don't think that's the problem.' He paused. 'Are things difficult at home?'

Nina stiffened. 'No, sir.'

Peter David gently motioned his star pupil to a chair, wondering how to handle this. He took a personal interest in the welfare of Nina Roth. She had an instinctive grasp of economics, the like of which he had not encountered since leaving Harvard. What most of the other teachers took for shyness and quietness, he knew was something very different – a blind concentration, a steely determination to master her subject. Nina might be a gangly, awkward teenager, but there was a core of iron in her soul that almost scared him. Nina Roth was destined for great things.

And now she was letting it crumble to dust. Her grades had plunged. Her essays lost their sparkle. The Ivy League scholarships he'd assumed were sure things were slipping away.

Mr David felt close to this girl. He'd asked around when Nina first came to St Michael's, knew all about the lazy father and the lush mother, heard on the grapevine that the kid practically ran the family store herself – no wonder she was so clear about basic business economics. You didn't have to be a shrink to see that Nina was compensating hard for her parents' failure, and he approved of that. But now something had changed; she was getting exhausted at school.

He knew Nina was too proud to discuss it, but everything would go up in smoke if he didn't do something.

'You work for your parents, don't you?' Mr David asked gently. 'Have you taken on any extra duties besides that? School clubs, for instance? Drama, volleyball, something like that?'

Nina smiled slightly. Drama or volleyball, indeed. He must think she was like Missy or Josie or the rest of them.

Since she'd been dating Jeff, she needed more money. He liked her to look pretty, to have good Levi's, cool boots, whatever the other kids took for granted. And though he always picked up the cinema tickets or the beer or whatever, she wanted to spring for it sometimes, and there was no way her parents would come up with an allowance.

Before Jeff Glazer she hadn't had a social life, but that had changed, and she needed money.

St Michael's, Jeff and her parents all taught Nina the same lesson: money *was* everything. It was new uniforms and fancy cars. It was American Express cards and respect. It was a house on the North Slope and your own business, versus a walk-up on the South Slope and a rundown deli. Jeff's folks versus her parents. Hope versus despair.

People who said 'Money isn't everything' had one thing in common.

None of them was poor.

Nina Roth had known since she was a baby that the worst thing in life would be to turn out like Mom or Dad, sitting around, waiting for rescue, waiting for something to happen. She was filled with contempt when she thought about it. There was no White Knight. You made things happen yourself. When Duane Reed advertised for a junior clerk, Nina marched off to the interview, lied about her age, and was hired on the spot. First week, she'd taken her paycheque and opened an account at Wells Fargo. Each month, she checked her balance, watching the tiny green glowing numbers with intense satisfaction. She spent only what she had to, and those numbers were creeping up. They were small, but they were growing.

Money was independence, power, freedom.

Nina's eyes narrowed as she looked at her teacher. No way was she giving up her job.

'I work at a drugstore part-time,' Nina said. She sat up in the chair, determined. 'I need the money, Mr David.'

'Well, we all need money,' the older man replied, surprising her, 'but you'll be giving up a lot more money if you go on this way.'

'I don't understand,' Nina said, but she was listening. She respected Mr David; he took an interest in her when other staff hadn't bothered, just dished out good grades and no feedback. Early on, Peter David graded one of her projects a 'C' when any other student would have gotten an 'A'. When Nina complained, he told her she was smarter than the rest of the class, and therefore he wanted better results. She'd get graded by her own standards, and she'd only get an 'A' for outstanding work. If she didn't like it, she could drop his class.

Nina never got a 'C' since.

'You have your SATs coming up, assessments, reports. You'll need all that for college. Now, we both know that you're good for an academic scholarship to NYU, Mount Holyoke, Brandeis, maybe Vassar, but you can do better than that, Nina.'

'Better than Vassar?' Her eyes widened.

'Sure. Sure.' Peter David nodded impatiently. 'I'm talking Harvard or Yale. Maybe MIT if you planned to specialise.'

She shook her head, glossy raven hair gleaming in the light from the office window. 'I'd need a full scholarship for that, and they only give out a handful each year.'

'That's right. You could easily take one of them, Nina, but not the way you're performing now.' Her teacher brushed aside her protests with an impatient wave. 'No, stop giving me excuses. You are a student gifted with outstanding mathematical ability. Your economics are fluid and perceptive. You're strong in physics, chemistry and business studies, but you're letting yourself down.'

He leaned forward.

'It amazes me that someone like you would sacrifice longterm profit for pocket money. Look, Nina, the graduate market is a *market*. Maybe it doesn't matter to some of your fellow pupils, but when you come out of college, do you want a résumé from somewhere OK, or do you want to be the best?'

Nina sat there, taken aback.

'Something's got to give,' Peter David said.

She pushed back her chair, stood up straight, and offered him her hand. She's so dignified, David thought, his dry academic's heart touched by this tall, awkward teenager, standing there so seriously.

He shook it warmly.

'I hear you, sir,' Nina told him. 'I'll work something out.'

From now on, she thought grimly, Mom and Dad are on their own.

Starting that day, Nina cut back on her hours in the deli. She told Dad he'd have to check the books himself; she told Mom she'd need to spend more time behind the counters. But they didn't like it, and every day they let her know.

'You're workin' for them when we need you here,' her dad grunted. Nina looked behind her to see him slumped in his easy chair, eyes fixed on *Wheel of Fortune*.

'You don't need me, Daddy, you could do the books,' Nina said. 'You're just as smart as me.'

'*I* know that, miss. Don't you sass me,' her father said. He fancied himself a great brain, always quoting from Shakespeare and Whitman. Nina despised him all the more because he was intelligent: an intellectual, real proud of his education and never doing anything with it. 'I'm busy enough with deliveries . . .'

'They only deliver once a week,' Nina tried.

'*And* I gotta stack the shelves. That's real work.'

Nina waited for Mom to wade in shrieking, but there was only silence. They were united for once. Against her.

'You spend way too much time with that fancy jock you're seein',' her mother snapped.

'He's not a jock, he's just athletic,' Nina said, her buttermilk complexion lighting up. She couldn't help it. Just the mention of Jeff was like the sun bursting through the thick clouds all round her. She'd be going round to the park to meet up with him tonight . . .

Her stomach felt squirmy with excitement, hungry for his touch. Sometimes she was ashamed to find how hot he could get her. Lying in her cramped bedroom at night, Nina would stare at the damp cracks in the ceiling and think about Jeff, about his smooth strong chest and the flat of his stomach with its smattering of wiry hair, trailing down to his cock, and she'd feel weird, hot and edgy, and her hand would slip between her legs, rubbing herself frantically for some release. Somehow it was better when she was imagining it than when it happened. In her dreams, Jeff's tongue was gentle over her aching nipples, his hands would stroke her butt and her back and tease her the way she teased herself . . . Nina's hands would start to move of their own accord under the languorous heat of her body, her mouth slightly open, panting softly as she thought about Jeff inside her, kissing her and saying soft things but somehow fucking her harder and harder all the time, until she'd lose control and her stomach would contract and expand in an exquisite, savage flash of white fire . . .

Actual lovemaking with Jeff wasn't quite that way and sometimes Nina thought about it guiltily when she began to pleasure herself. But it was thinking about Jeff that got her that way, after all, and she loved him so much, it just couldn't be wrong.

'He's not interested in you, girl. He's playin' with you,' her dad grumbled.

'Jeff's in love with me,' Nina said fiercely.

'Oh yeah?' Her father's pudgy face creased in scorn. 'He take you back to meet his folks yet? White trash, that's what we are. You reckon he thinks any different? Don't kid yourself.'

'You're wrong!' Nina shouted. She grabbed her coat from the back of the door.

'Where d'you think you're going, Nina Roth? You got work to do *here*!' her mother yelled.

'Sharper than a serpent's tooth it is, to have a thankless child,' Matthew pronounced.

'I'm going to meet Jeff,' Nina told them. She nodded back at the ragged pile of papers stacked on the couch. 'You should deal with those, Mom. I don't have time.'

The door slammed on its hinges behind her.

Ellen Roth stared at it. 'Little bitch thinks she's too good for us,' she said bitterly.

'You got that right,' grunted her husband.

A fresh fall wind whipped around Prospect Park, sending golden leaves dancing across the paths as Nina hurried towards the Long Meadow. She drew deep breaths, elated to be out of the claustrophobic apartment. Tantalised by the thought of seeing Jeff. A pair of joggers huffed past her and Nina flashed them a beaming smile. No matter what, when she was with Jeff, life was good.

'Hey!'

She spun round, the wind lifting her coal-black hair, and saw her boyfriend lounging under an elm tree. She felt her heart jump. God, he was so gorgeous, all those muscles huge and hard under his navy sweatsuit, picking out his cornflower-blue eyes. He was wearing the latest black Nike runners and a steel Rolex. Nina pulled her threadbare duffel tight against the chill and told herself clothes didn't matter.

'Hey,' Jeff repeated, when she caught up to him. He smiled, his eyes trawling lazily over her wrapped-up body. 'Where you been?'

'Sorry I'm late. I had some trouble back home,' Nina apologised. She knew he hated to be kept waiting. 'I got out as soon as I could.'

'No problem,' Jeff said graciously. He turned and started walking west out of the park, heading for the cheap hotel on Eighth Street they always used. Nina used to think that was so cool of him, the way he'd casually spring for a whole night although they only took a couple of hours – 'So we don't need to sneak around at my place,' he'd explain, kissing the nape of her neck. Often he'd order up room service, too, and that made her feel spoiled and exotic; waited on hand and foot, even if it was only cheeseburgers and beer. The sex was usually just OK; she always felt hot and weird when he started, but after Jeff collapsed across her with that strangled groan, bathed in sweat and looking drained, she felt ... unsure. Left out. Maybe the flashes of excitement and tenseness she felt sometimes were an orgasm. Maybe that was what they felt like when you weren't doing it to yourself ... She wasn't sure, and something told her there was no way she could ask Jeff. It was being alone with him, being kissed, stroked, told how beautiful she was – *that* was what Nina loved. In bed with Jeff she was accepted. Desired. That made up for everything else.

But today Nina could still hear her mother's carping voice. Suddenly the hotel didn't seem so magical ... it seemed a little cheap, a little seedy.

'Hey, Jeff?' She caught up with him, putting a hand on his arm. 'Could we maybe do something else tonight?'

He stopped short, frowning.

'You don't like the Payne? Where d'you want to go?'

'I was thinking maybe we wouldn't go *anywhere*.' Nina paused nervously at the shadow that crossed over his face. 'I'd like to go to your house and meet your mom and dad.'

'Oh yeah? What for?' Jeff demanded, irritated. Nina Roth looked pretty sharp, despite the cheap clothes and lack of grooming: her creamy skin, perfect without make-up, was flushed and glowing from the fresh air; her heavy-lidded eyes glittered like polished slate and her ebony hair cut down across her cheekbones in a gleaming cap. But he could imagine the reaction if he took her home! His mother would go ballistic! She was always nagging at him to find a 'nice girl', but to the Glazers, that meant someone like Melissa or Josie ... someone like themselves. Not a Jewish checkout girl from South Slope, a scholarship kid with a lush for a mother.

'It's a dumb idea. We can't just drop in on them like that.'

'Why not?' Nina asked stubbornly. 'Are you ashamed of me? That's what my mom said.'

'She's nuts,' Glazer said warily. He didn't like that mutinous look she was giving him, though. Nina's body had nearly given him a heart attack once he finally coaxed her into bed, and there was no way he was letting her go now. 'Look, we can't go tonight, because, uh, we're having some people over for dinner. Let me talk to Mom and you can maybe come for tea, or something. OK?'

'Sure.' Nina smiled up at him, bursting with happiness.

He does love me, she thought triumphantly. He does, he does, he does!

4

Murmurs rose from the crowd as Elizabeth descended the stairs, floating on a glorious cloud of pale gold silk. The apricot satin shoes, topaz earrings and coral necklace were perfect with her glowing skin and tawny mane.

Monica's first frown of disapproval at Elizabeth's rejecting the Laura Ashley melted into a warm smile. Her one aim in life was to get rid of Elizabeth as quickly as possible. Her husband's discreet nudge pointed out the young Duke of Fairfax, at the door to the Great Hall, gasping like a dying trout. The countess heard wedding bells.

'Happy birthday, darling. I must say you look splendid,' Tony boomed, moving to grip her elbow firmly as Elizabeth started shaking hands. He felt taken aback. His tomboy daughter looked enchantingly feminine. David Fairfax was interested, and if Love was that blind – well, Elizabeth might bring something besides trouble to the family. He thrust her forward briskly through the glittering crowd.

'Evening, David. Glad you could make it,' the earl said genially.

Elizabeth blushed scarlet. How could he be so obvious! She wanted to pick up her cascading skirts and scamper away. Anything rather than listen to Father suck up to David Fairfax while he showed her off like a prize heifer.

'Good of you to ask me, Lord Caerhaven,' Fairfax replied. His gaze swept approvingly across Elizabeth's figure-hugging bodice and lingered on the freckled swell of her breasts. 'Hullo, 'Lizbeth. Happy birthday. Smashing dress,' he added with more spirit.

Elizabeth looked at him wearily. David had had a crush on her for years. He was ordinary looking, with sandy hair and a strong jaw, graduated from poly with a spurious degree in estate management. In real life, if you were David Fairfax, that consisted of hiring a manager to run your estates. They'd met often at parties and later hunt balls and Tory fundraisers Dad wouldn't let her duck. He was OK, but pretty boring, and he was twenty-four, while she was sixteen today. She secretly thought he was a bit of a perv, chasing after a girl eight years younger.

Dad had made himself crystal clear. To him, no duke could ever be boring, but David was a young fogey: he actually wore tweeds and he listened to Cole Porter instead of Bowie or T-Rex.

Granny's spirit bubbled up mischievously inside her.

'Hiya, Dave. How's it hanging?' Elizabeth asked, grinning.

Her father stiffened, but when Fairfax laughed he just glared at her and moved off.

Elizabeth chatted briefly to David and then tried to get away. Her heart sank as she saw Monica swooping down on her.

'What do you think you're doing? Can't you see the way David's looking at you?' Monica hissed.

Elizabeth sighed and glanced back to the fireplace. Mother was right, His Grace was gazing after her with a particularly annoying sort of moony-calf expression. Like a spaniel after you refused to give it a bit of your cheese: all helpless misery and silent pleading.

'I want to dance with Richard Villiers,' she snapped.

Richard was the bluff son of Dragon's finance director, a massive Blackburn Rovers fan. She'd rather talk about football than David Fairfax's gardeners any day of the week.

'For God's sake, Elizabeth!' Monica spat.

Elizabeth pouted. There was no way out of it, if she wanted to avoid a scene. She walked back across the room and watched the moony eyes light up with the enthusiasm of a border terrier spotting a rabbit.

'Smashing dress, smashing,' David repeated. 'D'you like a dance?'

She surrendered sullenly to the inevitable, much to the fury of the gaggle of hopeful debs who'd been hovering in the duke's vicinity all night.

'Sure, Dave, that'd be cool.'

David hauled her bodily round the draughty hall, stepping anxiously all over her apricot slippers. Elizabeth was selfishly furious. Why couldn't the great hulking lout take dancing lessons? He spent his life attending these wretched things!

'I say, Bessie – can I call you Bessie?'

'No,' replied Elizabeth coldly.

'You're wasted at school. Really, you know. You're very pretty. Ever thought about gettin' hitched?'

Elizabeth withdrew as far as the waltz allowed her, but was caught by David's plump arm squeezing her waist.

'Definitely not. I'm only sixteen, I haven't even been to college yet.'

The duke looked nervous but tried again. 'What does a pretty girlie like you want to bother with college for? Bet your ma and pa wouldn't mind.'

'I wouldn't dream of it,' said Elizabeth sharply. 'Anyway, I've got a boyfriend. Joe Sharp in the village.'

'Sharp? Never heard of him.'

'You wouldn't.' Elizabeth grinned again, picturing Joe, stained overalls, swearing, muscular, the forbidden taste of cigarettes in his mouth when she kissed him. 'He's an attendant at the garage, he goes to St Joseph's school.'

'Ha ha,' Fairfax chuckled, annoyingly, 'don't be ridiculous.'

Suddenly he caught her to him as they whirled in time with the Strauss, thrusting his face into her neck and kissing it. Revolted, Elizabeth braced herself and shoved him away.

'What the hell do you think you're doing? Get off me!'

She was a strong girl. Fairfax tripped and fell sprawling, and there was an agonising crack as his head hit the flagstone floor.

Around them couples stopped dancing to stare. The string quartet faltered in its playing for a second because of the commotion at the centre of the ballroom. It struck up again as the countess made frantic motions to continue, but David Fairfax lay crashed out on the polished marble, groaning in agony. Blood was seeping out of one cheek.

There was a stunned silence amongst the assembled guests.

Leaning back against the tree trunk, Elizabeth winced at the memory. Her father's face had set like granite and the ball had started breaking up as of that moment. Suddenly all the tycoons remembered important breakfast meetings and the socialites developed headaches, as the guests made polite excuses to their hosts and scurried away. David, helped to his feet by the onlookers, gave Elizabeth an embarrassed nod and hobbled towards the door. It had taken barely half an hour for the piles of fur coats and cashmere shawls to disappear from the cloakroom, and once the last guest had hastened outside the earl sent his daughter to her room, the quiet menace in his voice worse than any shouting fit.

Neither last night nor this morning had Tony wanted to hear her explanation. As far as her parents were concerned she was simply a disgrace.

Elizabeth sat under the mossy trunk of an apple tree, biting into the crisp, smoky flesh of a windfall. She loved it out in the orchard: the dry-stone walls covered with bindweed and ivy, the warm scent of mown grass, the tiny white moths that fluttered around her like scraps of lace. They kept pear, apple and plum trees, and if you didn't mind the wasps that gathered greedily around all the ripe fruit, the orchards were a glorious place to get lost in. Elizabeth discovered them as a child, to her parents' dismay. She liked nothing better than shinning up the ancient, gnarly trunks, finding a nook to sit in, and hiding there all afternoon, while the stable-hands combed the grounds calling for her.

Maybe that was the start of my rebel streak, she thought ruefully. It had been so exciting, clambering up a tangle of branches and leaves like a squirrel. If she got high enough, she could see over the orchard walls, to the red-roofed stables and the manicured green of the croquet lawn, and even past the bounds of the estate, to the clifftops and the silver glitter of the sea. She would trek back up to the castle around teatime, with grazed knees and torn stockings, leaving mud and leaves all over the kitchen flagstones, and be marched off to bed without supper.

Elizabeth smiled. Sixteen years old, and she was still in trouble.

Even the servants had been giving her stern looks at breakfast. Mother had been reduced to taking a tray of coffee and dry toast in her bedroom, while Daddy and that little prig Richard had glowered their way through the kippers and marmalade without so much as a 'Good morning'.

My God, if he wasn't already leaving everything to the boys, he'd disinherit me, Elizabeth thought, then hugged herself. Granny had put a stop to that. She needn't be afraid of Dad any more.

Even so, she had saddled up one of the bay mares as soon as breakfast was over and taken her out for a gallop across the cliff tops. It was good to be out of his way; the turrets and battlements rearing behind her seemed gloomy and menacing in the chill morning light. She'd never known Tony so furious. It was dawning on her that he had been *serious* about her marrying David. He was outraged that she'd blown her chances of becoming a duchess . . .

'Lizzie!' called a reedy voice.

'Right here, Richard,' Elizabeth said, throwing her apple core into some bracken. Her brother came clumping through the trees, looking annoyed.

'Where on earth have you been? You'd better get yourself inside, sharpish. Father wants to see you in the library, right away.'

She got up, ignoring the gloating tone to Richard's voice. What an unpleasant little brat he was, he loved to see her in trouble.

She tried to ignore the nagging voice inside her that told her she'd behaved like a spoilt brat herself last night. Poor clumsy David, he hadn't meant any harm.

But no! Elizabeth thought sulkily. Why should *I* have to put up with him on *my* birthday!

When they reached the dark-panelled hall Richard turned pointedly away towards her stepmother's morning room, leaving Elizabeth standing in front of the library door by herself. She looked at the brass studs in the old oak door and drew herself up bravely. Father's bullying needs standing up to, Elizabeth told herself. She smoothed down her long mane of hair and knocked sharply.

'Come in,' the earl snapped.

Elizabeth pushed the thick door hard and it swung open, creaking on its hinges. The library was a large room, tapestries and antique swords mounted between rows of dusty, leatherbound books. A mahogany grand piano stood to one side. Behind it, his back to her, her father was sitting in front of his writing desk, a sheaf of papers laid out neatly on the green baize.

'Elizabeth,' he said icily without turning round, 'your behaviour last night was unforgivable. You disgraced yourself in front of all our friends. You made a public exhibition of yourself. Your stepmother was so ashamed she has made herself ill.'

'David Fairfax kissed me. What was I supposed to do? He was slobbering down the front of my dress—'

'Elizabeth!' Her father spun round on his seat, glaring at her. 'Not another word, do you hear me? Stop lying!'

'But I'm not lying!' Elizabeth protested, feeling the tears well up despite herself.

The earl raised a warning hand, his expression dark. 'For the sake of sheer impudence and disobedience to us you chose to assault one of your own guests.'

'That's not true!'

'Why in the name of God a decent young man like that should have been interested in you, Elizabeth, is quite beyond me, but you could not even accept a small romantic gesture—'

'There's nothing romantic about being pawed by that baboon!' Elizabeth cried angrily. 'You and Monica just want to marry me to a duke! You're nothing but a pair of snobs!'

Father gazed at her impassively. Then he reached down to his desk and picked up a piece of paper.

'This is a letter of registration, enrolling you at the Ecole Henri Dufor.'

'The Ecole Henri Dufor?' Elizabeth repeated blankly.

'In Saas-Fée.'

'You're sending me to *Switzerland*?'

Her father nodded coldly. 'Since you cannot seem to behave yourself here, I am sending you to your stepmother's finishing school to learn some manners.'

Elizabeth stared at him in disbelief. 'To learn flower-arranging and deportment? This is the seventies, Daddy. Nobody does that any more. What about my A-levels?'

'You can take the Baccalaureate, for all I care.' He laid the letter purposefully in front of him. 'You have gone too far, young lady. I tell you that I will not permit you to make a mockery of this family.'

She thrust her hands deep inside her jodhpurs. 'I won't go.'

'You'll go. Or I will cut you off without a penny.'

'I'll borrow money from the bank.'

'Indeed. Do you imagine that banks take charity cases? Against what would you borrow money? Your pony, perhaps?'

Her father's expression frightened her, but Elizabeth stubbornly shook her head. 'You know perfectly well. Granny told you about her will the day she died. She left me fifteen per cent of the company.'

There was a silence, broken only by the crackle of the pine logs blazing in the fireplace.

'Your grandmother left me her entire estate,' Tony Savage said.

'No.' Elizabeth paled. 'Granny wouldn't lie to me.'

Her father picked up a tiny brass key from the green baize, reached under the desk and unlocked a small side drawer. Elizabeth felt her heart thumping as he drew out a thin sheaf of vellum, yellowed somewhat with age.

'This is Mamma's will, Elizabeth. If you doubt my word, you are at liberty to read it yourself.'

'She was making a new one,' Elizabeth said.

'She did *not* make a new one. She did *not* leave you any stock.' The earl glanced down at the parchment. 'I seem to remember there is a small jewellery bequest to you in here, but you won't inherit that until your twenty-first birthday. A bank wouldn't think much of it.'

Elizabeth stood there trembling with shock. The bequest had been her protection; she had counted on it.

'Phone her solicitors, if you like,' her father told her coolly, indicating the telephone that stood next to her on a card-table. 'They will confirm it.'

Fighting to stay calm, Elizabeth shook her head. Father wouldn't make that offer if he was bluffing, but Granny had given her a solemn promise just a few days ago.

'She can't have got round to changing it, then,' Elizabeth managed, 'but you know she intended to, Daddy. That was what she told you when you went upstairs to see her. She wanted me to have her stake in Dragon. You have to respect her last wishes!'

'Mother told me no such thing.' The earl's tone was flat. 'I confess I am sorry that you choose such a subject for more lies.'

'I'm not lying,' Elizabeth gasped. 'You know how much I loved Granny!'

'Did you? It sounds to me as though you were trying to influence a frail old woman for your own benefit. You have been a thoroughly selfish girl for far too long.' Her father leaned forward, his sallow face set hard. 'For your information, Mamma and I were discussing your brother's trust fund. The world does not revolve around you, whatever you may believe. And I notice you never mentioned this so-called bequest until this moment.' He snorted with contempt. 'You fool only yourself, Elizabeth.'

Panic and doubt washed over her in a wave as she looked at her father's cold, certain face. Did he really think she would lie about Granny? Was it possible that Granny had planned on telling her father later? And never had the chance?

The earl was holding the vellum will firmly. Elizabeth realised, with a terrible sense of desertion, that she had lost. She wasn't a major stockholder in Dragon. She had no chance of a marketing job, no right to a seat on the board. She was just a rebellious teenager whose parents were determined to crush her.

For one wild moment Elizabeth thought about running away, but where would she go? Cardiff? London? With what money, and to do what? She was only a schoolgirl, and she'd lived in luxury all her life. She knew she'd last about ten seconds on the streets.

'You *will* go to Switzerland, one way or the other,' the earl snapped, as though reading her mind. 'If you behave sensibly, we will continue your allowance at the Ecole. If, on the other hand, you decide to cause your stepmother or me any more distress, you will receive not one centime. Which is it to be?'

At least she would get away from him.

'I'll go to Switzerland,' said Elizabeth.

5

'Would you like some ham, Nina?' Mrs Glazer asked.

Nina shifted uncomfortably on her seat, unsure if she was being deliberately insulted. Jeff had mentioned that she was Jewish at the start of tea, and an extra chill had settled over the already icy table.

'No, thank you,' she replied quietly, taking a sip of her tea. The cup was made of bone china and rimmed with gold leaf. The cutlery was silver plate, the table made from some dark wood that looked very expensive, and the Glazers' carpets were so thick her shoes sank into them as she walked. They lived in a redbrick townhouse on Willow Street in the Heights; the neighbourhood was rich, the streets leafy and clean. Mrs Glazer answered the door in a smart red woollen suit, with gold earrings and Italian leather shoes.

Nina smoothed down her own cheap black dress. Nothing could quiet the bolting nerves in her stomach. She'd known Jeff was rich, but it was still a shock. They might both reside in Brooklyn, but he lived in another world.

Clearly his mom thought so too. Her thin, polite smile never reached her eyes.

'It's a beautiful neighbourhood,' Nina said, trying hard to make conversation. Jeff was no help; he'd spent the meal with his head lowered, pushing blueberry pancakes round his plate.

'Isn't it?' Mrs Glazer answered coolly. 'Henry Ward Beecher used to live right opposite us.'

'Is that so?'

'Nina, tell me again about your parents,' Ken Glazer said. Ken was looking uncomfortable in weekend clothes. She'd asked around and found that Mr Glazer had a job with IBM, supplying mainframe computers. The computer industry was in its infancy, but growing every year. Most people thought of the huge machines as a science-fiction fad, but Nina was certain they had a big future. Maybe every company would need a computer of its own one day . . .

At any rate, computers had been good to the Glazers. She'd have liked to discuss it with Jeff's father, but every time she looked over at him his eyes were glued to the large swell of her breasts. Maybe that explained Mrs G.'s obvious dislike. Nina didn't know which was worse.

'Jeff tells me they have their own business.'

'Well, uh, not exactly.' Nina coloured. 'My mom runs a store.'

'Oh?' Mrs Glazer took a tiny bite at a chocolate wafer. 'What kind of goods does it sell? Clothes, cosmetics . . . ?'

'It's just a deli,' Nina admitted.

Jeff's mother gave a tinkling laugh. 'How refreshing. And whereabouts is it? I must pop in some time.'

Nina wanted to die. 'I think it would be out of your way. We're on the south side of Park Slope.'

Mr Glazer frowned disapprovingly at his son.

His wife pursed her lips. 'Yes,' she said after a moment. 'I'm not down that way very often.'

I'll bet you're not, Nina thought miserably. She gave Jeff a pleading look but he reached for another scone, refusing to meet her eyes.

It was another dreadful hour before Jeff lumbered to his feet, muttering something about football practice, and they were able to escape. Nina thanked her hostess for the tea in as dignified a manner as she could, and took her time about putting on her coat, as though it were a silver fox instead of her threadbare duffel. She felt Mr Glazer's eyes roaming hungrily over her body the whole time, but she tried not to show it. As Jeff's girlfriend, she knew she had to win his parents over. That awful woman would be her mother-in-law eventually.

As she descended the Glazers' scrubbed stone steps, Nina turned round and gave the townhouse a long, cool look. Some day, I'll be richer than you are, she thought. I'll own a bigger house, wear better clothes and have the kind of success you've never even dreamed of. I swear it.

Her small fist clenched under her cheap coat. *I swear it.*

'God, aren't families the worst?' Jeff said lazily. Outside the house, his confident swagger reappeared. 'That was lame. Come on, baby, let's go and make love.'

He admired the way Nina's glossy hair caught the light as they walked off down the street. Damn, she was a hot babe. He got turned on just thinking about peeling those heavy clothes off that dynamite body. It was worth all the shit he was going to get tonight.

Beside him, Nina dropped her eyes so Jeff wouldn't catch the contempt glinting in them. Ordinarily, she'd have laid into him for letting her down like that, but not tonight. They had more important things to talk about.

She had a sneaking suspicion she was pregnant.

'What do you mean?' Jeff asked her half an hour later. They were sitting on the bed of the same room they always used, but for once the coverlet remained straight, the sheets unrumpled. Nina could see their reflection in the dresser mirror and shrank inwardly at the sight of Jeff, his athlete's body hunched up in tension and disbelief. 'You think you're pregnant? You can't be.' He passed a hand through his gleaming fair hair. 'We've been careful.'

It was true that they'd followed all the current teen wisdom on sex – antiseptic douches and avoiding the middle of the cycle – but Nina had no money for a doctor and no access to a birth-control clinic. South Slope was big on coat-hanger abortions and welfare mothers instead. Jeff had tried condoms before he met her, and refused to do so again. Douches worked, he promised her: 'I've been around, baby, even if you haven't.'

'I'm late,' Nina said dully. She hadn't expected him to jump for joy – at least not right away – but this blind panic was making her nervous.

'How late?' Jeff demanded.

'Two and a half weeks.'

He shot up from the bed and started pacing the room. 'But it could be stress, right? Girls sometimes skip one for stress. You had all those college exams last week. It must have been pressure.'

Nina shook her head. As if! 'I've been under a lot of stress before, and I've never missed a period.'

Jeff rounded on her, his handsome young face suddenly aggressive. 'You don't know for sure. And anyway, who says it's mine?'

'What?' Nina gasped.

'Don't give me that weepy look. Come on, Nina, I'll bet you've been seeing other guys as well as me. It's been three months. Nobody's that saintly.'

'You know there's only you!' Nina cried, battling tears. How could he say that to her? Didn't he love her? And what did that mean, was he saying he'd been cheating on her? 'Have you got somebody else?'

Jeff leaned heavily against the window and thrust his hands into his jeans. He shrugged defensively. 'Sure. I've seen Melissa Patton a few times.'

Nina's beautiful face went grey with shock. She felt ill.

'See? I knew you'd start gettin' heavy,' Jeff sneered. 'Why the hell shouldn't I? We weren't married. I never said I wanted to go steady. That was your deal.'

Despite herself, Nina felt two huge tears well up and trickle down her cheeks. She felt like such a fool. 'I thought you loved me. I thought we'd get married,' she said bleakly.

Jeff gave a harsh laugh. 'You're kidding. You thought I'd *marry* you?' His stare was cruelly indifferent. 'OK, now I got it. You reckoned I'd fall for this baby crap and get you a one-way ticket to the good life. Huh?' He pulled out a cigarette from his jacket pocket and lit up with shaking fingers. 'Don't pull that with me, sugar. I'm not getting married at nineteen. And when I do, it won't be to some white trash.'

Nina couldn't speak. She couldn't take it in. Was this the same Jeff who had held her close all those nights, whispered sweet things in her ears, covered the back of her neck with downy kisses? Was this the boy she'd spent hours daydreaming about, the lover she'd killed herself to get time with?

Just a few hours ago she'd been eating with his parents, thanking God that Jeff was nothing like them. And he wasn't. He was worse. At least his mother hadn't been a hypocrite as well as a snob.

She'd thought Jeff Glazer was her Prince Charming: the most popular guy in school, the football hero, big and brave and daring. Now Nina saw him for what he was, as he stood scowling by the window: an immature boy, a coward, a bully, a cheat.

And she had his child growing inside her.

'I shouldn't have said that. We'll work something out.' Relieved that Nina wasn't arguing, Jeff looked away. All that white-faced melodrama, he couldn't stand it. It was kind of a shame, but there was no way he was up for this. Marry Nina Roth! She must have been out of her mind. It had been tough enough getting her invited to the house.

Sooner or later, he thought sourly, they all start whining.

'I know this guy works out of Sixth Avenue,' Glazer said, calmer now. 'Dr Fenton. He's sorted out some of the girls from St Mike's before – he's a real doctor, qualified, he'll give you anaesthetic and he's clean and stuff. It's expensive, like five hundred dollars.'

Nina was gazing at him, her face expressionless.

'Hey, I'll spring for it,' Jeff said magnanimously. 'I know my responsibilities. I'll get the money to you in school next week.' He paused. 'No hard feelings, Nina, right?'

Nina stood up slowly and reached for her coat. She let herself out of the hotel bedroom without looking round and quietly closed the door behind her.

The journey home through the park had never taken so long. The bluster of the early afternoon had given way to a glorious sunset of rose and gold, but Nina was blind to the beauty of the day. Nobody watching the tall young girl striding home, her black hair tousled and ivory complexion flushed pink from the fresh air, could have been aware of the dark thoughts racing through her. As she walked slowly home, grief gave way to furious anger, and by the time she reached Third Avenue she had started to form a plan.

'Can I see you for a moment, sir?'

Peter David turned round in the corridor to see young Nina Roth standing patiently behind him, a heavy sports bag slung over one shoulder. Not for the first time, he thought what an attractive kid she was. Her hair was swinging around her face in a shining bob, and she smelt of some delicate perfume. School uniform looked disturbing on that voluptuous body. He could feel the gaze of the boys linger on her as they streamed past. Only some heavy, dark circles under her eyes marred her beauty. He supposed a girl like Nina would be out late with some lucky boyfriend. And why not? It was the last few days of the semester. If any kid deserved a little partying, it was Nina Roth.

'Of course, Nina.' Mr David opened his office door. 'Come in.'

'How long will it be before my college results are back?' Nina asked him directly.

'About a month, but you don't need to worry, Nina. I'm sure you'll be offered a scholarship – probably several. Since we last talked, your work has improved one hundred per cent.' His smile was reassuring.

'What if I wanted to put off college for a year?'

'Delay a year?' Her tutor was shocked. 'You can't do that. We've made the applications. You enrol in the fall.'

'And what if I couldn't?'

Mr David leaned forward, his kindly face concerned. 'Is there some problem, Nina? Is it something I can help with?'

She gave him a small smile. 'Not really, sir. I just need to know.'

'Ah, let me see ... I don't think that's a good idea. Competition for assisted places is so fierce. I think you'd lose your chance. Better to reapply the following year,' he said, pushing his wire glasses back up the bridge of his nose, 'but even that might be a problem. Take your place up this year, young lady.' He attempted to look stern. 'Time enough for a year's fun *after* you've taken that degree.'

Nina nodded and rose. 'Thank you, Mr David.' She clasped his hand and shook it briskly. 'Thank you for everything.'

The teacher watched her go and wondered why he felt so uneasy.

Nina went to her locker and opened it. The space behind the grille was empty; twice Jeff Glazer had stuffed an envelope full of bank-notes in there, and twice she had returned it. Perhaps he'd finally gotten the message. She pulled out her running shoes and one file of math notes, unzipped her sports bag and packed them inside. The rest of the space was full of the clothes she had taken from her bedroom this morning – two pairs of jeans, her boots, underwear, a few shirts and sweaters and her one good skirt. Her toothbrush, soap and flannel were packed in a side pocket from which she now removed a sealed envelope, addressed to Sister Ignatius, the principal. A similar note was tucked under her pillow at home, for her parents to find when they bothered to make the bed. She didn't expect them to show any concern for at least a day or so, which would give her ample time to do everything she needed to. Without rushing, Nina stacked her textbooks neatly inside her locker. Then she carried her tote bag into the girls' restroom, shut herself in a cubicle and changed into her skirt, a neat blouse, dark hose and a pair of flats. She emerged with her uniform folded in a neat pile, laid it on top of the textbooks and closed her locker door.

The bell rang for second period. Nina ignored the strange looks her classmates gave her as they hurried off to geography. She turned left at the end of the corridor and walked straight through the double doors, down the marble steps and out of the gates.

The bag was heavy but Nina marched down the street like she hardly noticed it. Yesterday afternoon she had gone to see Jo Kepler, her supervisor at Duane Reed, and explained that Mom had been taken ill. She was going to have to quit her job right away. She was terribly sorry for the inconvenience, but could Ms Kepler give her a reference she could use in the future?

'Sure, of course. I hate to lose you, Nina, but of course I understand,' Ms Kepler said, shaking her head. She was really sorry to see Nina go; the girl had been one of the brightest assistants in the store, suggesting products to customers and helping them out instead of merely ringing up the purchases. She had awarded her two pay rises in two months and had been planning to offer her a place on the trainee management course next year. 'I'll give you an excellent reference, and maybe we'll see you back here when your mother gets better.'

'Thank you, ma'am. Would it be a lot of trouble if I asked you to write it out now? I don't know when I'll be able to look in again.'

'No trouble at all.' Ms Kepler stepped into the back office, slotted a headed sheet of paper in her typewriter and dashed off a reference, couched in the most glowing terms. She signed it, slotted it in an envelope and handed it to Nina. 'There you go, honey. Now you take good care of yourself.'

'Don't worry, I will,' Nina promised her gravely.

The letter was tucked safely inside the outer pocket of her purse, and now there was only one task left. Nina turned right down a side street and headed for the nearest branch of Wells Fargo. There was an empty teller window and she went straight up to the smiling clerk.

'Good morning, miss. May I help you?'

'Yes,' Nina said. 'I'd like to close my account.'

The smile was replaced by a frown, but five minutes later Nina was back out on the sidewalk with a brown envelope in her hand. It contained $627; all she had in the world.

6

'Six thirty! Six thirty, *mesdemoiselles.*'

Elizabeth could hear the maid coming along the dormitory corridor, tapping on doors to wake up the young ladies. There was nothing so vulgar as an electric bell at the Henri Dufor, but if you were more than ten minutes late to the dining room, you'd miss breakfast.

'Six thirty, my lady,' the maid announced, opening Elizabeth's door a fraction.

'*Merci*, Claudette,' Elizabeth said, quickly swinging her bare feet out from under the eiderdown duvet before its cosy warmth could tempt her back to sleep. The beds were heavy, old-fashioned things carved from solid oak, with pretty Alpine flowers painted on the headboards, made up freshly each morning with crisp linen sheets. Elizabeth loved her bed and collapsed into it at night without a second thought. Yet it wasn't difficult to get up in the mornings, she had so much to look forward to.

'There's been a new snowfall.'

Penny Foster, her room-mate and the only daughter of a property tycoon, was standing at the window looking up at the Alps. Saas-Fée was ringed with a massive horseshoe of mountains, great stretches of shadows and brilliant white velvet bisecting each other. Green pastures full of tiny flowers lay at their feet in the summer, and the chalet school was perched low down on one of these, east of the main village. Elizabeth padded across the polished wooden floor and craned her neck past the apple-green shutters. Penny was right: even in the dark of early morning she could see a fresh blanket of white covering the upper meadows.

'Terrific!' she grinned. 'More skiing. I can do a run straight back to the village.'

'Is that all you ever think about?' Penny sniffed, pushing a lock of red-gold hair out of her eyes. Where Elizabeth had a strong, athletic body, Penny was slim and constantly worrying about her weight. She had a pair of the latest electric scales by her bed and weighed herself morning and night. She'd been taught to ski by the school instructors but preferred the ballroom dancing classes, as exercise made her even hungrier. Elizabeth thought Penny was neurotic. Penny resented Elizabeth's energy and the way she ate mountains of food without ever getting plump, but she was also in awe of her room-mate's daring. Elizabeth Savage had a wild reputation, in school and the village as well; a natural on the slopes, within months she was taking on the local hotshots, Swiss boys who had started skiing when they started walking. Elizabeth skied with ferocious passion, ignoring all the school rules about forbidden areas. Saas-Fée had practically year-round snow, and even after the tourists departed, admiring locals noticed Elizabeth's graceful young body in its snug lilac suit twist sharply down a mogul field or bomb down a black run, crouching into the trajectory like a brightly coloured bullet. Penny heard the other girls gossiping about Elizabeth's nickname in the village, 'Coup de Foudre', the thunderbolt. She was sure it was no accident that the phrase also meant 'love at first sight'.

Six months of Switzerland had changed Elizabeth dramatically. Her curves had become high and tight, her legs powerful. Her glossy hair had grown longer and thicker and the mountain sun had highlighted it with rich streaks of gold, the colour of warm honey. Away from Tony's constant disapproval, the sullen rebellion had disappeared. There was a fresh flush to her complexion and a dancing light in her green eyes. Elizabeth would never be model-thin like Penny, but she didn't seem to care. She practically glowed with health, and looking at her standing there in her white cotton nightgown, breathing in the cold morning air, Penny felt another stab of envy.

'Come on, we've only got twenty minutes,' Penny said, and the two of them scrambled into the school uniform: ivory shirt, fitted navy blazer and skirt and knee-high black socks and shoes. Elizabeth caught her hair back in a ponytail, Penny spritzed herself with Miss Dior, and they rushed out into the corridor to join the other girls.

The dining room was laid out with long tables and hand-carved, high-backed chairs, its windows looking out towards the pastureland and the dark, scented pine forests beneath. Herds of belled cattle were already grazing, and below them the girls could see the lights of Saas Grund. After the first week, though, nobody paid attention to the view, as all the young ladies were constantly gossiping about boyfriends or rock stars. Penny's wardrobe door was covered with pictures of T-Rex and The Who; it was another weird thing about Elizabeth that she seemed totally unmoved by pin-ups, and had *her* wardrobe tacked up with ads – a pregnant man encouraging men to think about condoms, 'Go to Work on an Egg', 'Guinness Is Good for You'.

Elizabeth rushed towards the buffet and loaded her plate: newly baked bread, warm croissants, a bowl of steaming hot chocolate and some fresh apricots. Penny took a small helping of cornflakes and a cup of black coffee and they sat down.

'Hey, Elizabeth, something to interest you,' Vanessa Chadwick announced. Vanessa was a shipping heiress, a willowy blonde and a prefect, who obeyed school rules and found the Savage girl rather shocking.

Elizabeth grunted. 'I doubt that.'

Mornings at the Ecole Henri Dufor were spent practising music, dancing or deportment and then attending 'lectures'. These were supposed to broaden the mind but normally sent Elizabeth to sleep; Mademoiselle Charmain, the French mistress, would blather on about Marie Antoinette, or Herr Flagen, the history tutor, would drone on about the Confederation in his dense *Schweizerdeutsch* accent. Occasionally they were treated to outside guests with links to the school. These ranged from the Mayor of Zermatt to some pupil's filmstar mother. The girls still talked about the visit Yves Saint Laurent had once made.

Vanessa sighed at this sad lack of school spirit. 'His name is Herr Hans Wolf. He helped organise the Winter Olympics here last year.'

'Not Hans Wolf the skier?'

Vanessa flicked back her shiny blonde hair and consulted her lecture notes. 'He coached the Swiss ski team, if that's what you mean.'

'Yes, but he was a skier long before that.' Elizabeth tore off a piece of croissant and dipped it in her chocolate, eyes sparkling. 'Back in the twenties, when people used wooden skis they tied on to their boots.'

'That don't sound too safe,' remarked Chantal Miller, an American banker's daughter.

'It wasn't. It was incredibly dangerous. Hans Wolf set five downhill records that way during his career.'

'I'll never hear the end of this,' Penny sighed.

'How long is he staying?'

'Just to give the lecture.'

The others started chatting about the Robert Redford film showing down in the village, but Elizabeth ate her breakfast silently. Her head was miles away in a world without safety nets, padding or crevasse warnings, imagining a young Hans Wolf tearing down a mountainside on a pair of shaped planks, lashed to his feet with hempen rope. She found she was almost blushing with excitement. Perhaps she could talk to him after the lecture, ask him what it had been like. Maybe he would let her watch the Swiss team train . . .

After breakfast the girls cleared away their plates and trooped into the music room for piano practice. Elizabeth was dreadful as usual but smiled engagingly at Madame Lyon; she wanted some new ski-boots and that meant Dad had to receive good reports. She plunked awkwardly at the keys, one eye on her watch, longing for nine o'clock. As soon as they were dismissed – all the girls bobbing a curtsy to the old lady – Elizabeth rushed down the corridor to the lecture hall to bag herself the best seat.

The room filled slowly with laconic, overprivileged teenagers, and Herr Geller, the headmaster, peered in to check that his flock was settled. He noticed Penny Foster and Elizabeth Savage sitting centre front and raised an eyebrow; most unlike Lady Elizabeth to take an active interest in anything.

Still, he was pleased to see it. It had been a great coup for the Ecole to land the daughter of Lord Caerhaven – titles always looked good in the pupil register – and in many ways, her ladyship had proved ideal. The earl had written him a frank letter before Elizabeth was admitted, explaining that she was a wilful girl and likely to cause trouble; on no account was she to be given business education, maths lessons or allowed to have marketing journals delivered. He wanted a young lady and not a tomboy to return from the Alps. Geller had called Elizabeth to him when she arrived and explained her father's prohibitions, expecting a storm; instead, all he got was a nod and a shrug of the shoulders.

Elizabeth had resigned herself to the inevitable. She knew the dream would have to be postponed. She wasn't going to work in Dragon, and if she was ever going to escape her parents' clutches, that meant money. Tony had it and she didn't. For the moment, it was better to play along, let the family think she'd given in. She should be studying for her A-levels, but instead she was stuck in this relic from the past, learning *cordon bleu* cookery, flower-arranging and ballroom dancing. Whenever she heard Penny talk about her brother at Oxford, or Chantal's at Wharton, or Thérèse Lecoute's cousins at the Sorbonne, she felt a tight knot of anger in her stomach; no university for her – Dad only wanted her qualified for the Mrs degree. Enthusiasm was asking too much, but Elizabeth dutifully stuck roses in jars and waltzed to the 'Blue Danube'. At the end of her first term her report said, 'Modest and well behaved,' and gave her average marks for everything.

Tony doubled her allowance.

Besides, Elizabeth was enjoying herself. She thought she would loathe Switzerland, but within a week she was in love – the soaring, white-capped mountains, green Alpine slopes covered with Eidelweiss and grazing cattle, the belled goats and clear mountain air. She adored Swiss food, thick black bread and *Kaise*, cuttlefish soups, fondues and *Kirschtorte*, or cherry tart. There was spicy *Glühwein* and perfect chocolate, and the village of Saas-Fée was enchanting, with its narrow, winding cobbled streets and gabled shops.

Elizabeth made friends easily despite her reckless streak; some girls disapproved violently, but others secretly admired her. Elizabeth tried hard to sort out the real friends from the crowd of *nouveaux riches* who sucked up in the hope of an introduction to her brothers. She never trusted Vanessa since the morning she caught her doodling 'Lady Holwyn' all over her art history file.

Good behaviour and a large allowance meant she was allowed to join the termly school trip to Zurich. Penny and Chantal dived into the expensive hotel shops packed with Hermès scarves and Louis Vuitton luggage, but Elizabeth liked to stare at the towering banks, with their mirrored walls and discreet brass plaques. Businessmen in dark suits and Cutler & Gross sunglasses strode past and the news stands were full of financial journals in every conceivable language. Zurich had none of the commercial buzz of London or New York, but its sober atmosphere was impressive. Elizabeth felt she was breathing money. Finance, secrecy and power practically bled from the paving-stones. She would sit in a roadside café, sipping a glass of schnapps, and think slowly about what she was going to do about Dragon. That company was her birthright, and she wouldn't let it go.

She turned the problem over and over in her mind – in class, in her bedroom, in the village. *One day*, Elizabeth promised herself. *One day.*

Meanwhile, she toed the line. It was easy enough to turn up for classes, and it was necessary. Then she had her first skiing lesson, and her life was transformed.

Alone on the black runs from Felskinn and Langflüh, slicing down the glittering, pearl-white tracks, her blood racing, she felt more alive than she had ever believed possible. Elizabeth had two years of finishing school and from now on she looked forward to every second.

She heard the other girls rise to their feet in a rustle of lambswool and cotton as Herr Geller and his guest entered the room. Hans Wolf marched rapidly up to the lectern amidst the polite applause, with the air of a man who wants to get something over quickly. His long stride and erect back were in strange contrast to his wiry white hair and the deep wrinkles scoring his face. Elizabeth knew he was seventy-six, but he looked fifty. That's what a lifetime on the slopes will do for you, she thought, thrilled.

Sighing, Hans Wolf regarded his bored, beautiful audience for a second. Then he reached into his jacket pocket, fished out some crumpled notes and a pair of wire-rimmed spectacles, slid them up his nose and started to read. What a waste of a morning. He resented having to do this; the young prodigy, Franz Klammer, was racing down the Lauberhorn right now and Wolf had hoped to be there, checking him out. But a banker from Geneva with a daughter at the school had asked him for this favour, and since the banker made a breathtakingly large contribution to Swiss athletics last year, Wolf reluctantly agreed. Money, after all, was sacred.

He rattled on in a dry monotone about the Olympic ideal and the healing powers of sport, occasionally glancing up at the bored faces in front of him. Most of them were examining their manicures, or staring at him with glazed eyes, except for one girl in the centre front. She was a pretty, healthy-looking child with bright green eyes and a dusting of freckles around the nose. Wolf galloped through his clichés at a rate of knots. He paused for breath and noticed the same girl looking at him as if spellbound, leaning forward on the edge of her seat. Disconcerted, the old man gave her a brief smile, lost his place, found it again and ploughed on to the end. Then he sat down, mopping his brow, and wondered how soon he could get out of here without being rude.

Herr Geller was on his feet. 'I'm sure we're all most grateful to Herr Wolf for that fascinating talk.' Dutiful applause. 'Now, *mesdemoiselles*, do you have any questions for our distinguished guest?'

The prefects duly raised their hands with prepared questions about sporting behaviour and it being the taking part that counted. Wolf answered them in an equally pat manner and waited for the attractive blonde to speak. He was slightly disappointed that she did not. After a few minutes Geller thanked him to a fresh round of applause and dismissed the school.

'Many thanks, Herr Wolf. I'm sure that was very instructive for our young ladies,' Geller was saying.

Wolf picked up his notes and thrust them back into his jacket. 'My pleasure, Herr Geller.'

'I hope I can persuade you to stay for lunch. The school maintains an excellent cook ...' Geller began obsequiously.

Wolf suppressed a shiver of dislike and was starting to decline when he felt a small tug on his sleeve.

'And what do you want, young lady?' Herr Geller snapped, annoyed at being interrupted.

'I'd like to ask Herr Wolf a question,' Elizabeth said nervously.

Wolf turned to see the girl from the front row. Close up, she was even prettier and she had a lean, fit figure.

'You had a chance during the talk, Lady Elizabeth.' Herr Geller was never too sharp with an earl's daughter.

'Well yes, sir, I know, but this isn't about the talk.'

'Don't worry, Herr Geller, I'm happy to answer the young lady's questions.' Wolf was interested despite himself. 'Go ahead.'

'Well, Herr Wolf,' Elizabeth said nervously, ignoring the annoyance on the headmaster's face, 'I was just wondering what it was like to break the record on the Hahnenkamm?'

'What?' Wolf stuttered, taken aback.

'In nineteen twenty-five,' the young girl added helpfully.

'*Ja*, I remember when it was,' Hans Wolf replied. He took a closer look at the pretty eyes and saw the pale ring of goggle-marks. 'It was terrifying. Wonderful. You are interested in skiing?' How many of his own countrymen knew he'd broken that record? It was half a century ago now.

Elizabeth nodded eagerly and Herr Geller, wanting to impress a member of the Olympic committee, added, 'Lady Elizabeth is a very good skier, I believe, Herr Wolf. Our own instructors taught her. The Ecole has an excellent record in—'

Wolf caught the scornful glint in Elizabeth's eye and was suddenly vastly amused. Maybe he could take the young *Fräulein* out for lunch at a mountain café. Good sausage, black bread, soup. A glass of *Pflaumen*. No doubt she would enjoy the chance to get out of this ridiculous establishment for a while, and it would be fun to tell war stories from his youth. The Hahnenkamm in 1925! A lifetime ago.

'So I hear, Herr Geller. I would very much like to see for myself, though.' He turned to Elizabeth. 'Young lady, will you show me what you have learned? We could take the gondola up to Plattjen.'

'I'd love to, sir.' Elizabeth glanced at Herr Geller.

'*Natürlich*, go ahead,' he said expansively. 'We have many skis, suits and boots in the games room, Herr Wolf, if you would like to join her yourself.'

'I hung up my skis a few years back.' Wolf eyed the young woman speculatively. 'Are you good?'

'Very good,' Elizabeth said boldly.

Wolf grinned. 'There are some nasty mogul fields up there. We'll see.'

Hans Wolf leaned over the rail on the restaurant balcony, wondering if he could believe his eyes. Down the steep, unforgiving slope opposite him, Elizabeth's strong young body was flying around the moguls. The stick was planted firmly and removed cleanly, she jumped high and twisted sharply from the waist. Slice, leap, slice. No mogul seemed too large, no jump too high. The teenager moved with instinctive grace and skill. The technique was unpolished, but *Gott in Himmel*! she was superb.

Ten minutes ago he'd been looking forward to an encouraging chat and a pleasant lunch. The *Engländerin* aristocrat was very down to earth and warm, openly admiring of him, obviously passionate about skiing and funny about her school. He had settled on the restaurant balcony and told her to have a go at the short, steep mogul run while he ordered lunch. The first time he watched her descent Wolf thought he must be imagining things. He waved at her to do it again, to check it was not a fluke. And then again.

She was so good, it set his adrenalin flowing just to watch her. For a second the old man imagined Heidi Laufen and Louise Levier, their own

World Cup hopes on the Swiss women's team. They wouldn't thank him for what he was about to do, but he didn't hesitate for a second.

He beckoned to a waiter. 'Do you have a payphone in the back?' he asked. 'I need to make a telephone call.'

'Of course, sir. Let me show you,' the waiter said, and led him into the bar. Wolf dropped some coins into the slot and dialled the number from memory.

'British Ski Federation,' replied a female voice.

'This is Hans Wolf calling from Switzerland,' he said. 'Is the director around?'

7

Six hundred and twenty-seven dollars didn't get you very far, even in Brooklyn.

'Fifty a week,' the landlord said.

Nina shrugged and looked scornful. She was staring into a tiny, cramped little room with damp stains on the walls, a tiny chipped basin and one closet. The communal bathroom was down the hall.

'Thirty-five,' she said.

He laughed sourly. 'C'mon, sugar, we charge fifteen bucks a night.'

The Ocean Motel was in the scuzzy Red Hook area and it blended right in, catering mostly to sailors working on the docks.

'Yeah, but you won't fill this every night. I'll stay at least three weeks.'

'Forty, baby, and you're robbing me,' the landlord said. His eyes flickered hungrily across her large breasts and small waist. The kid was weird, kind of like a co-ed but with street-smarts. She was so serious she freaked him out. Not a hooker, he could tell that much. Pity, 'cause she could have made the rent in kind, any time. He'd have offered her a drink, but she had this stand-off vibe around her.

'Thirty-five.' Nina locked into his eyes and killed the fire there with an icy stare. 'It's all I got. It's not enough, I'll need to go somewhere else.'

The guy frowned. He smelled of sweat and cigarettes and Nina wanted him out of her room.

'OK. But two weeks in advance.'

She fished in her pocket, peeled off the bills from her small roll. He left. She sat down on her small bunk and put her head in her hands.

Nina wondered what her parents were doing now. Calling the police? Did they miss her? They had to miss what she could do. But even so, Red Hook was a no-go area, nobody knew her here. The cops wouldn't find her.

She felt surprisingly calm. She'd been self-reliant for a long time; the only thing different now was the circumstances. Looking back on it, Jeff Glazer had been such a stupid mistake for a clever girl. What was he? Just a good-looking jock who'd used her and then run for cover. She'd trusted him, and look where it got her. Yeah, whatever. She wouldn't make the same mistake again.

Nina got up from the bed and went to the grimy window. Outside was an alley; beyond that, the bustle and noise of dirty, dodgy Brooklyn. She had $557 and the clothes she stood up in.

Tomorrow she would go get a job. It was time to get out of here.

Nina didn't find a job the next day, nor the day after. She spent two anxious weeks trudging down Flatbush Avenue and around the Civic Centre, terrified her money would run out before she found work. Even her reference was no help.

Brooklyn was sunk in the late seventies recession. Nobody was hiring: the drugstores were full, the banks had enough tellers, even the delis didn't need a clerk. She was desperate when she had her first stroke of luck. A boy named Leon was standing in front of her in a checkout queue, bitching about the health food store that had just fired him.

Green Earth was a small Mom-and-Pop joint, a hippy-looking place. Fading paint peeled from its storefront and dusty windows, displaying an assortment of candles, vitamins and joss sticks. Not promising, but her heart beat a bit faster. Surely this place would need someone new.

A bell jangled as she pushed the door open.

'Hi, can I help you?'

The storekeeper was grey haired, maybe sixty. He was sitting behind the counter, hunched over a stack of loose receipts.

'I hope so,' Nina said politely. 'I heard you fired Leon. I'd like to apply for the job.'

The proprietor shook his head. 'I'm not replacing him. Third kid I tried in a month. All they do is sit around chewing gum and talking back to the customers.'

'I'm not like that, really. I've got experience and a reference,' Nina persisted.

'Sorry, honey. Try somewhere else.' Nina swallowed her bitter disappointment and was about to leave when he added, 'What I need is an accountant. Or a magician.' He patted the forms in front of him with a good-natured sigh.

'What are they, your records?' Nina asked.

'Uh-huh.' The old guy shook his head again. 'Never keep a store, kid. You'll go blind before your time.'

'I can organise those for you,' she said, walking towards the counter and ignoring his disbelieving expression. 'Really. My folks kept a seven–eleven. I used to –' she nearly said 'do the', but changed it to '– help with reordering and stock-taking.'

'Yeah? You good at math?' he asked, a slight interest creeping into his tone.

'Top of the class. Look, why don't you let me sit with you and sort those receipts? If you think you can use me, give me a month's trial. If not, I'll stop bothering you.' She fought to keep the anxiety out of her voice.

He paused for a second, then nodded. 'I guess it couldn't hurt.'

'I'm Nina Roth,' Nina said, weak with relief.

'Frank Malone,' the old man said, shaking her hand. 'So you understand these order forms?'

Nina started at Green Earth at six bucks an hour. She reordered stock, washed the windows, and hand-painted the storefront a cotton-candy pink. The small price list Frank kept at the counter was replaced by bold cardboard signs for special offers and discounts. Compared to the chaos of her mother's deli, Green Earth's simple product line was a breeze to keep track of, and soon Nina could tell her boss what was selling and what wasn't. Word got around fast, and more customers started coming in. Nina gave them all polite, efficient service, and made sure she learned the names of the regulars. Frank was impressed.

'How come you work so hard?' he asked her one night, as she combed through a pharmaceutical catalogue. 'You don't have to stay this late. You should be out having fun.'

'I like to work,' Nina said truthfully.

It was true, she did like to work. She had a million ideas for improvements, and Frank Malone was eager to try them all. A widower of seven years, the store was all he had left, and Nina Roth made it an exciting, friendly, bustling place to be. As they started making a little money, he gave Nina a raise; not much, but better than nothing. Nina slaved all hours, she worked like a demon. For one thing, the bright, airy store was better than her dingy motel room. For another, she wasn't the fun-seeking type. And finally, she knew she had to make herself indispensable to Frank Malone before the inevitable happened.

It took four months.

'How's my favourite girl?' Frank asked one morning, as Nina unlocked the front door.

'Good. You know, Frank, we should think about advertising. Posters round town. The local paper.'

'Too expensive.'

'It'll pay for itself in a month.' She took off her coat and hung it in the back.

'Well, I'm glad to see that.'

'What?' Nina asked, turning round.

He gestured at her stomach. 'You're putting on a little weight at last. It suits you, you should eat more.'

Nina braced herself. He'd have to know some time.

'It's not that, Frank. I'm pregnant.'

Blank astonishment. 'You're pregnant?'

She nodded.

The old man's face darkened. 'Boyfriend's not around?'

'No.' Nina's grey eyes were expressionless, and for a moment Frank Malone felt uneasy. Nina was such a serious, determined kid. Seventeen going on forty-eight. It was clear she was in no mood for arguments.

'You need any help?'

'No.' She wondered if she was being too snappy. 'But thanks all the same.'

When she'd picked up her meagre savings, Nina had just one thought in her head. She'd get a place, find a job to cover the rent, and spend her money on an abortion. It was terrible to lose her scholarships, but she couldn't stand it a second longer; she had to get out of Park Slope. Nina wanted a place of her own, away from her selfish parents, away from St Michael's and the kids who laughed at her, a million miles away from Jeff Glazer. The pain of what he'd done to her was unbelievable. Jeff said she was nothing. Her parents treated her like nothing. Nina felt so lonely and so hurt she'd thought she would die.

There was no way she'd take a cent from Jeff. In his world, money bought everything, but Nina swore she was not for sale. Once she had a job, she'd pay whatever it took to rip his bastard out of her. By next year, she'd be in control of her own life – she could reapply to college then.

It was difficult to pinpoint the moment she'd changed her mind. After she started at Green Earth, Nina meant to make a doctor's appointment, but she kept putting it off. She told herself she was settling in, but two weeks passed, then three, and she still hadn't done it. Walking down Atlantic Avenue in the summer evenings, past the Arab bakeries and falafel stands, she'd watch the black-robed mothers cuddling their downy-haired babies, and feel an unexpected tenderness. Or she'd notice a little girl trotting behind her mom in a shopping mall and wonder what her own baby might look like. Somehow she shoved the issue to the back of her mind. It was easy to ignore it, at least at first. Nina had no morning sickness, no cravings for sardine and jelly sandwiches, nothing. Her already voluptuous body didn't seem any different, except for a little tenderness around the breasts.

Two months into her job, the third month of pregnancy, Nina found herself stacking jars of baby apple-sauce. She froze as she stared at the label, showing a chubby baby with a gap-toothed smile. And she knew she'd changed her mind.

Nina *wanted* her child. No matter who the father was. She wanted someone to love. She wanted to take her to the park and buy her dolls and building bricks. She wanted to play with her. She wanted to give her all the joys, all the caring, that her own parents never bothered with. She knew it sounded selfish, but that was the way she felt.

Come on, Nina, you have to be kidding, she lectured herself. What about college? You think you can work your way through college with a baby?

But what *about* college? That was unreal, that was another world. St Mike's and Jeff's world. This was life, earning a wage and making the rent. She could survive without a college degree. She looked again at the apple-sauce.

A baby would be family, and that would be worth anything.

It's going to be tough, the nagging voice of reason warned her. But Nina had made up her mind. *Tough I'm used to.*

Nina always remembered the day she told Frank. It was bitterly cold, freezing grey slush on the streets, gaudy Christmas decorations everywhere, Chanukah lights in a few windows, another New York winter. She found herself looking in toy stores, full of holly and kings and neon Santas, and wondering how she'd handle Christmas with her kid. The only thing she didn't like about being Jewish was Christmas. There was no getting around it, Chanukah gifts couldn't compete with the orgy of Christmas celebrations, food and trees and lights and cards and presents, bombarding you everywhere you went. You felt guilty as a kid for feeling so left out, because even if it was all about money, lots of Jewish parents scrupulously ignored the twenty-fifth. Hers had, for sure, although Nina was sure it was more to avoid spending any dough than for God.

She decided she'd just make a bigger deal of Chanukah. Her baby would have no cause to complain.

That was when she knew for sure.

'Frank, I got something to tell you.'

'You're leaving,' Frank said anxiously. Nina had only been around a few months but it felt like for ever. He didn't know how he'd get along without her.

'No, but I hope you won't be mad ... I've decided to keep the baby.'

'That's wonderful,' the old guy said. His face blossomed into a vast crinkly grin. 'You'll be a great mom. I guess I'm gonna have to give you a raise.'

He trundled over and hugged her. Nina almost wanted to cry. Nobody had given her such simple friendship for as long as she could remember.

Frank added, 'I been thinking about giving you a share in the profits, anyway. Five per cent on top of your wages. Since we're making some, these days.'

'Oh, Frank,' Nina said. She knew it wasn't true, and maybe she ought to turn him down, but money was so tight, she couldn't afford to. Frank Malone was a lonely man who felt paternal towards her, and she *had* made a big difference in the store. 'I shouldn't,' she said weakly.

'Take it.' Frank brushed aside her objections. 'I got a cousin in Queens, a lawyer. Did my will. I'll get him to draw up the paperwork.'

Nina hugged herself. Five per cent of one tiny store, hardly an empire. But it was something, it was her first step on the ladder. And Frank was a friend, and she was going to have a baby. The future wasn't rosy, but perhaps it wasn't so black either.

Three days later Frank Malone had a stroke. He was rushed to hospital, but there was nothing the doctors could do. He died an hour later.

'Nina Roth?'

Nina looked up from sweeping the floor as the door jangled. A tall, stocky man in a homburg and a black overcoat stepped into the store, ignoring the 'Closed' sign. She frowned wearily; there was so much to do before the funeral, and nobody else to do it.

'That's right,' she said, holding on to the broom in the hope he'd take the hint, but the stranger didn't budge.

'I'm Connor Malone.'

'Oh.' Nina blushed, wiped her dusty hands on her apron and came forwards to shake his hand. Connor would be Frank's son from Albany, the one he was always moaning never came to see him. Connor had a sister, Mary, in Texas and Nina hadn't been expecting either of them so soon. She wished she'd been wearing something more appropriate than her tatty blue jeans and red checker shirt to meet her new boss. 'Hi there. I'm so sorry about Frank, Mr Malone. He was always very good to me.'

She decided not even to mention the five per cent. Connor Malone wouldn't believe her, she could tell that right away.

'Yeah, he was a generous guy,' Connor said vaguely, glancing around the shop. 'He really pulled it together since the last time I was here.'

Nina couldn't exactly say that it was mostly her doing, so she just nodded and smiled. 'Green Earth is doing really well.'

'That's good, we'll get a better price for it.'

Connor Malone was an insurance salesman, used to sizing up assets, and he liked what he saw: great retail space, attractively laid out, nicely kept. He missed his pop but they hadn't been close for years, whereas fifty per cent of this store would be a great windfall for Cheryl and the kids. He was so pleased he missed the look of panic on the face of the small, dark-haired clerk in front of him.

'You're not going to sell, Mr Malone?'

Connor glanced at her. 'Sure, who'd run this place now?'

'Why not me?'

'I don't think so.' The salesman smiled politely. 'OK, well, thanks for looking after the place till I got here, Miss Roth. I know you didn't have a contract, but I'll see you get a full month's severance. That's only fair.'

'Mr Malone, don't you think you should keep Green Earth open? It's making a nice profit—'

'But my father's dead,' Connor explained patiently.

'Yes, sir, but I did all the book-keeping, I ran the promotions and ordered the stock. I could go right on doing that, and you could hire a junior to help me out.'

Malone looked at the earnest little face and almost laughed.

'How old are you, honey, twenty-two?'

'I'm eighteen,' Nina admitted.

'Yeah? You look older . . . but still, I didn't get where I am today by hiring teenage girls to take care of business, even pretty ones,' he added with a laboured attempt at gallantry.

'But I have been taking care of business,' she protested.

Connor Malone's face lost some of its genial air.

'Nice try, Nina, but no dice. Sorry. I'll get you that cheque tomorrow.'

Nina didn't attend the funeral. Instead she stayed back and organised what passed for an Irish wake, a restrained affair with a few glasses of Scotch and some tired sandwiches, which was what Connor thought appropriate. She worked methodically in the store before the guests came back, tidying the last few boxes of pills and bottles behind the counter. Connor would be pleased to see the place straight and somehow it seemed a better farewell to Frank than a bunch of flowers anyway. Nina buffed the mahogany counter until she could see her own face and tried to figure out what Frank would have advised her. First up, don't panic.

She leaned back against the empty shelves and took a deep breath. On her own again. Well, she'd been there before.

It was scary, but she did have some options this time. The local storekeepers knew her and a couple of them had been over making probing noises. Fatimah Resaid in the large grocery across the street had even offered her a job, so she wasn't going to starve. But Nina had the baby to think of now. Even if it was frightening, she had to hold out for something better. A career with potential.

Mrs Minsky in the hairdresser's opposite, who was fond of the grave, quiet kid who'd turned Frank Malone's sorry little store around, had tried to do her a good turn just that morning. Abraham & Straus, the huge department store on Hoyt Street, ran a management trainee programme.

'My niece's husband works over there, he could put in a good word for ya,' Mrs Minsky announced. 'You got your pay, your benefits . . . that's a real business, Nina, ya could go places with an outfit like that.'

'Thank you, Mrs Minsky, I appreciate it,' Nina said uncertainly.

'What, ya don't like Abraham and Straus? Ain't it big enough for ya after the empire here?' Mrs Minsky snorted, waving her hands round the empty room.

'It's not that,' Nina said.

'Ya worked in retail, in a drugstore,' Mrs Minsky pointed out. 'Now the question is, where can that take ya? In the store business, in Brooklyn? A and S is the best there is, honey, think about it.'

When the mourners returned and pounced on the whisky and salmon, Nina was still thinking about it. By the time pompous young Connor took her aside and magnanimously announced he was adding one extra week to her severance pay, Nina had pretty much made up her mind.

She was more interested in 'drug' than 'store'. Abraham & Straus *was* glamorous, for Brooklyn; a retail career could lead to Saks and Bloomingdale's, to pretty cosmetic counters and staff discounts on perfume. It would be fun and fashionable.

However, the real money was elsewhere. A year's book-keeping had taught her the kind of cash that the prescription-drug companies made, despite lazy salesmen and lousy service. New York was hooked on its vitamins and minerals, its pills and potions, and it would stay that way. There were vast improvements needed in the pharmaceutical business. She'd been a customer and she knew it. Thinking about that gave her a little frisson of excitement.

The drug business would be less diverting than a big retail store and much harder work, but it would provide better for her kid. As far as Nina was concerned, that was all that mattered.

8

Elizabeth arched her back under the caress of his tongue. Gerard's grip was firm, one hand expertly brushing across her breasts, the other stroking between her legs as he moved down her spine. Her skin was hot and slippery, making her long, burnished hair damp around the forehead and dewing the chiselled outlines of her muscles. Gerard was so lost in lust for her incredible body he never noticed her eyes were closed. His own were fixed on the gilt-edged mirror opposite the bed, its ornate frame belying the wild scene it was reflecting. Silk sheets and pillows crumpled on the floor. A primrose satin Dior gown and evening suit flung casually over a chair. And Elizabeth's firm body curving back against him, his cock pushing in and out of her ... too hot to wait, Gerard felt himself speeding up, his breath coming shorter, starting to thrust. He gasped.

'Chérie, chérie, je t'aime...'

She said nothing but he felt her press against his hand. In time to his thrusts, he brushed his fingertips lightly back and forwards, the way she liked it. She moaned, and his touch got faster. He felt his orgasm gathering, struggled to control it until he could make her come. Two strokes, two more, and then he pressed hard against her clitoris and heard her cry out, the flat of her stomach pulsing. Groaning with pleasure, Gerard exploded inside her and collapsed. They slumped back together on to the sheets.

Elizabeth panted as her climax subsided, coming out of her fantasy. For a few seconds she was dizzy, disorientated. Then she felt Gerard slip out of her and remove the condom, snapping her back to reality. The James Bond sex scene dissolved into her hotel suite, Sean Connery reverted to her boyfriend, and Moscow turned back to St Moritz.

'You're so beautiful, Elizabeth. *Je t'adore,*' Gerard murmured.

'You were great, Gerard,' Elizabeth said coolly. She could never reach a climax with Gerard without fantasising. Once the pleasure had ebbed, she found she always wanted to be alone. She wondered how to get him out of her suite without actually being rude.

'You've worn me out, baby.' Elizabeth stretched out as though exhausted. 'Better get back to your own room. I need some sleep before tomorrow, and if you stick around, I'll be up all night.'

'OK, sure. I understand. The races come first.'

He was too eager to please, pulling on his clothes right away. Elizabeth couldn't stand that puppy-dog look. Gerard had seemed like he'd be different from Karl and Richard, but in the end they were all the same: knocked out by dating the famous Lady Elizabeth, society darling and starlet of the slopes.

'Well, it *is* the World Cup.'

'And you'll go home with the title, *chérie, j'en suis sûr.*'

His enthusiasm annoyed her. Who did Gerard de Mesnil want to be with? Elizabeth, or the World Champion? She knew he'd be right at the bottom of the black run that plunged down from Diavolezza tomorrow, waiting to hug her for the cameras after the ladies' downhill. It was boring. He was boring.

Elizabeth stirred restlessly. 'See you tomorrow.'

'*A demain.*'

After Gerard left, Elizabeth got up from the bed and wandered into her bathroom, a fantasy of ivory and gold. She ran a bath, pouring a stream of expensive scented oil under the foaming taps. The fragrance of lavender and thyme filled the room and she willed herself to relax. The bathroom had a large window overlooking the lake, and as Elizabeth sank into the water she could see the spires and turrets of the luxurious Palace Hotel, where her parents would be checking in tonight. For all she knew they might already have landed. Monica could be strolling through St Moritz right now, picking up some new toys at Cartier or an extra scarf at Hermès. Dad would have gone straight to the Corviglia, the most exclusive ski club in the world. Despite a total lack of interest in skiing, her parents had bought some equipment and joined last year, skipping the long waiting list. Lord Caerhaven was old money and head of Dragon plc.; cash *and* class. The Corviglia was just another open door.

Relations with her family had changed completely. When Elizabeth was offered a place on the British ski team, Tony agreed at once. Skiing was a frightfully pukka sport, almost as good as showjumping. They could talk about Elizabeth at dinner parties again.

Soon it was clear they could do more than that. Elizabeth came second in her first slalom, actually won a downhill at Méribel. To the amazement of the Europeans, the British teenager came from nowhere to finish fourth overall in her first World Cup.

Elizabeth was an overnight sensation. The story had it all – a beautiful, sexy-looking young girl, with a strong body and cascading honey hair; a British amateur beating the Alpine nations at their own game; and best of all, she had a title. Photos of Elizabeth smiling on the rostrum in her sapphire Ellesse skisuit were splashed all over the papers. The BBC put her on the news. Reporters were hastily dispatched to Cortina to grab a quote. She was the pin-up of the moment – recession-bound Britain, with strikes paralysing the Labour government and rubbish piling up on the streets, was in need of a bit of glamour. In the 'Winter of Discontent', sexy Lady Elizabeth Savage gave people something to smile about. The press called her 'plucky' and 'gorgeous' and praised the earl and countess for letting her have a go. To their amazement, Tony and Monica found Elizabeth was an asset, her black fleece washed white by the Alpine snow.

That Christmas, Elizabeth cautiously asked her father for a favour. She wanted to spend the summer working at Dragon plc.

Instead of the curt refusal she'd been dreading, the earl calmly agreed.

'If it would amuse you, Elizabeth. I believe there's some space at head office.'

Elizabeth gaped with disbelief and stammered a thankyou.

'Switzerland has obviously been good for you, you've been a credit to the family. Is that going to continue?'

Shock was replaced by understanding. Swallowing a sarcastic retort, Elizabeth nodded.

'Good. I expect you'll enjoy it. As long as you realise the arrangement is temporary. You're bound to meet a decent chap on the winter circuit, and you'll be far too busy with wedding plans . . .'

Tony couldn't have been plainer. As long as she played ball and behaved herself, she could do what she wanted, but they were still planning on marrying her off. They just liked the added extras she could bring them right now: a whole new set of parties, terrific social clout, a new sparkle on the family crest.

To underline the point, Monica gave her a diamond bracelet for Christmas, and on New Year's Day Tony quadrupled her allowance.

Elizabeth sold the bracelet. She opened a secret bank account in Geneva, and fed her allowance into it every month. The new star of the British team didn't need money. She raced as an amateur and wasn't allowed pay, but after the World Cup success companies fought to sponsor the team. Suddenly the Federation was swamped with funds. The team got aerodynamic, body-fitting suits especially made by Ellesse, and customised Rossignol skis with an extra edge. They booked suites at the best hotels and flew first-class instead of club. For Elizabeth, nothing was too much. She demanded an iridescent suit that caught the light when she hit the slopes, so she looked like a flashing rainbow against the snow. She never shared a room; she ignored the British coach; and she stayed up all hours on the circuit, partying, glittering, flirting, a butterfly playgirl in the skiing jet set.

It drove her team-mates mad. When they were getting up at six to sweat in the hotel gyms, Elizabeth was lounging in bed with hot chocolate and a croissant. When they were slamming down the practice runs, being screamed at by the coach, Elizabeth would turn up late and do her own thing. When they were ordered to bed at nine p.m. before a race, Elizabeth would be downstairs in the cocktail bar, living it up with the Austrians, swapping notes with Franz Klammer, or draping herself over the arms of the latest beau.

Janet Marlin, Karen Carter and Kate Cox, the other British girls, thought Elizabeth was a bitch. A spoilt teenage brat, she loved the limelight and rewrote the rules. It drove them nuts the way the men swarmed around her, begging for a date, drooling over the tight young body with its firm curves, the suntanned face with its big green eyes. Bad enough that Elizabeth was so gorgeous, without her showing up in sparkling diamond earrings and Perry Ellis cocktail gowns. And on top of that, she had a title. It was 'Yes, my lady', 'No, your ladyship', wherever they went. Even the press hounds called her 'Lady Elizabeth' when they were baying for a quote. Elizabeth never did what the officials told her, but nobody dared complain.

The bottom line was, on the day of the race, Lady Elizabeth Savage was a crouching she-wolf, one of the top ten females in the world. She was the best skier from Britain in fifty years. And she knew it.

Elizabeth clung to her new freedom fiercely. For the first time in her life, she had nobody bossing her; not her father, not her finishing school. Unsure of what to do, she tried to act as sophisticated as possible. The skiing circuit was full of ultra-glamorous types: billionaire Americans, old English money, European princes, *comtes* and margraves. Everybody admired her skiing and it was easy to fit in; she was rich, titled, talented. The team didn't bother her while she kept winning races. She was the *coup de foudre*, the thunderbolt, famous across the Alps. She felt edgy and rebellious, she didn't listen to her trainers. International skiing didn't have much to do with sport: the events took up one per cent of her time; ninety-nine per cent was press, publicity, planes, and parties.

In the eye of the glittering storm, Elizabeth Savage felt lonely and empty.

She got a reputation as a playgirl. Soon she accepted one of the persistent suitors: Karl von Hocheit, a male model and son of a German car tycoon. Karl introduced her to sex, and she felt defiant and wild, but they had nothing in common. Karl was handsome, but he was blond and bland. She dumped him for the Hon. Richard Godfrey, an Old Etonian, heir to a hotel empire; her parents were thrilled. Then Richard said she should win the title and settle down to child-rearing.

'Who cares?' he asked when she talked about Dragon. 'Lizzie, don't you realise you don't *need* to work? I'll take care of the cash.'

They broke up the same night.

Now there was Gerard, Comte de Mesnil. Gerard was a good lover and made no demands. She had been with him ever since.

In her second year of competition, Elizabeth took the individual silver for the slalom, gold for the downhill and overall bronze medal. The country went nuts, but she was bitterly disappointed. She stood beside Heidi Laufen, triumphant on the winner's rostrum, and heard them play the Swiss national anthem.

Next year, Elizabeth swore. Next year it'll be 'God Save the Queen'.

That autumn, Elizabeth flew out to Davos to begin training again. She met up with Gerard and started to party. Once again, though, she began to feel a gaping emptiness inside her.

It was true that she loved to ski, but she didn't want to *be* a skier. Yet she wasn't equipped to do anything else.

All the flashbulbs, laughter and chiming champagne glasses in the world couldn't drown out the question pounding in her head.

My God. What am I going to do?

9

'Elizabeth, you have a visitor.'

Ronnie Davis, the British coach, studied his star athlete with an exasperated expression. Elizabeth had come third in the downhill at Val d'Isère, trailing Louise Levier by a good six seconds. Shrugging, she had promised to do better at Méribel, but she'd still cut training yesterday. How could he ream her out for coming third when the media were all over her, celebrating another bronze? The kid had professional talent but an amateur attitude. It drove him crazy.

'Is it Gerard again? Tell him I'm busy,' Elizabeth said, pushing her dark glasses further up her nose. 'I want to unpack and take a shower.'

They were standing in the lobby of the Antares, Méribel's smartest hotel. Janet was already strapping up for the slopes; Kate had gone to work out in the fitness room. Ronnie knew that Elizabeth would head for a café and a paper, despite the slalom tomorrow. It was her third World Cup. You could lead the mare to water . . .

'No, it's not Gerard. Regretfully.'

'Hans!'

Elizabeth spun round to see a tall, white-haired figure standing behind her. She rushed to give him a hug. 'What are you doing here? I thought you retired last year.'

'It's true I don't coach, but they can't get rid of me that fast,' Wolf told her gravely. He nodded at Ronnie. 'An honour, Herr Davis. You have your country wining races again.'

'That's all down to Elizabeth,' Davis said flatly. 'I'm sure you two will want to catch up. I think I'll find Janet and run through the slalom.' He shook hands with Hans and headed for his room. Great, just great. Another hanger-on to tell Elizabeth how wonderful she was.

Hans took Elizabeth out to lunch. They rode the La Saulire gondola, suspended high over the Trois Vallées, the biggest skiing area in the world. Mountains stretched below them, vast craggy peaks covered with smooth blankets of snow, pine forests bisected with open trails. People swooped down the runs like colourful ants, but at this height the frantic activity seemed calm, minute, dwarfed by the immensity of the Alps.

Wolf had chosen the Pierres Plates, a chalet restaurant at the gondola station with breathtaking views down the valley. They sat on the sun-drenched terrace, the light burnishing copper highlights on Elizabeth's tawny hair, and watched the skiers swoop away down the black runs. Pulling on his own shades because of the glare of the mountaintops, Hans ordered for them both: soup with thick, black bread, sausage and sauerkraut, and a beer and Orangina.

'It's a beautiful view, *nicht wahr*? The top of the world.'

'Stunning,' Elizabeth agreed.

Hans waved a wrinkled hand at the scene in front of them. '*Ja*? What do you see?'

'See? Skiers, I suppose.'

'Skiers. I am surprised you recognise them.'

Elizabeth glanced sharply up at the old man, and found the pale blue eyes were narrow with disapproval. 'What are you talking about?' she protested. 'I took the bronze in the Cup last year.'

'If I was Herr Davis, I would send you home. I would not let you ski. You are a disgrace to your country.'

Hans Wolf was leaning towards her, his weatherbeaten face angry and passionate. 'Everyone talks about you, how you do not train, you will not learn, you refuse all instruction. With these boys, always you are running around. You are not a skier, you are a tourist.'

Elizabeth dropped her hunk of black bread and pushed back her chair. 'I don't have to listen to this. Don't you read the papers, Hans?'

'*Ach*, the papers. Of course, you are a big star. *Coup de foudre*, the thunderclap, yes? A woman Prime Minister, and now a girl ski champion.' He snorted with disgust. 'You don't notice the others saying that.'

'Which others?'

'Other *skiers*. The pros. The men and women up here who are not impressed by your pretty face, your noble family. They know you are not trying. You have talent. So? Talent, you were born with. That is nothing to respect. What matters is what you do with it.' Ignoring her look of outrage, Hans Wolf dipped his spoon in the spicy soup. 'You, *Fräulein*, turn up to race like you were punching a clock.'

'Hey, I took fourth, then the bronze. I'll make gold this year.' Elizabeth tried to pretend she didn't know what Hans meant. 'Maybe I need a little polish—'

'Polish! You think taking gold is as easy as that? Yes, you took bronze last year, but only because Heidi fell in the Lauberhorn. Otherwise, it would have been fourth again. You are four, five seconds behind Heidi and Louise, each race.'

'That's nothing,' Elizabeth muttered.

'It is eternity. The Swiss girls train every day, while you go shopping. They rest every night, when you giggle with your young men. But then they are not here to catch a husband; they are here to race. And win.'

'Hans . . .'

'The young Comte de Mesnil? Very rich, a good estate. A fine catch.' He shook his head contemptuously. 'Aah, Elizabeth. When I first met you, you had the passion. You could have been one of the best. I saw a great skier, not some gilded *Hausfrau*.'

'I don't intend to marry Gerard. In fact, I'm going to break up with him,'

Elizabeth said, knowing it was true. 'Hans, I'm not out here to get a husband.'

'Why do you resent the sport, then? *Liebchen*, I can't help if you won't tell me.'

Behind her sunglasses, Elizabeth's eyes filled with tears. Nobody had dared speak this way to her since she'd started racing, but it was all true. She was coasting; she was pathetic. Hans was deadly accurate: along the way, her love of the silent, plunging world of the skier had turned into a brooding resentment.

'Because I like to ski, but they're making me a *skier*. Just a skier. I want to be in business, Hans.'

Her mentor's face was a mask of astonishment. 'Is this all? You do that later, no? When you finish on the slopes.'

'No! I can't! You don't get it. My parents wouldn't let me qualify for college; they don't want me to work. I've got no degree, no experience, nothing. This is all I can do.' She gestured to the crowds behind her, and then, to her embarrassment, burst out crying.

Hans Wolf handed her a handkerchief and coaxed out the whole story. Her miserable childhood, Granny, her disastrous sixteenth-birthday ball. The showdown with Tony over the will, Switzerland, and now this.

'So. You have no way to fend for yourself.'

Elizabeth shook her head. Now wasn't the time to bring up her Zurich bank account; she'd been salting money away since the start of last year, but it still totalled only £15,000. Not enough to live on.

'Well, maybe there are other things you can do. Other firms you work for, not only Dragon. Perhaps the FIS, *hein*?' The Fédération Internationale de Ski was the sport's governing body. 'You are clever, Elizabeth. Nobody needs pieces of paper to see it. You are glamorous, well known. You might help promote the sport, but not if you continue this way – they know you are faking, they won't touch you.'

'OK, OK. I hear you.' Elizabeth felt a tiny ray of hope pierce the shadows. Sell skiing for the FIS? God knew she had first-hand, customer experience. All it would take was one post, one job where she could shine.

'What do you suggest I do?'

Wolf speared a forkful of sauerkraut. 'You stop wasting time this season and you start to train. For the first time, you work with the other athletes. You will need to sweat blood to get that five seconds back.'

'All right. I suppose I could try.'

'You will *succeed*. I will arrange for you to train with some of the men's teams – don't think of beating Heidi Laufen, think of beating Franz Klammer.'

'Klammer!'

The legendary Swiss racer had won twenty-five titles.

'You must try to be *best*. Not just as a woman – best overall. Then, you might take the gold. Anyway, this World Cup is a warm-up.'

'To next year's Cup?'

'No, idiot child. To the Olympics.'

Darkness. Panic. Elizabeth woke with a start, the shrilling of the telephone shocking her out of sleep. Semi-conscious, she grabbed at it blindly.

'Good morning, my lady,' a French voice said calmly. 'It's five a.m. Your wake-up call.'

The slalom was at twelve, and she'd agreed to be ready for practice at six. Hans had arranged for her to meet up with the US men's team; there was a long mogul run down from Mont de la Challe, an unrelenting bastard of a run that would have her turning and slicing like her life depended on it.

It would be hard, hard work.

Sighing, Elizabeth hit the shower.

'Where's our princess?' Kate Cox asked at nine, when the team assembled in the lobby for training. 'Still in bed?'

'Some rich French Romeo's still keeping her up,' Janet guessed.

Karen Carter shook her head. 'We won't wait for the thunderbolt. Let's just hope she turns up for the race.'

Ron Davis joined his team, a scrap of paper in his hand.

'It's a note from Hans Wolf. Apparently Elizabeth's already on the moguls. Training. She got there three hours ago.'

'You're joking. Who with?' Janet demanded.

Davis scratched his head. 'With the Yanks.'

'Kim and Holly are training with *her*? They're letting Elizabeth see their technique?'

'She's training,' Davis said slowly, 'with the men.'

When Hans Wolf arrived at five forty, Elizabeth Savage was already waiting. He had a flash of admiration for her curvy figure, the stylish way she carried herself on those skis; he might be fifty years too late, but some guy was going to get very lucky. It annoyed him to think of a girl like that with Gerard de Mesnil. That milksop was just a snow groupie with money.

Of course, people said that about Elizabeth, but they were wrong. There was some spark about the girl he'd never forgotten; enough to make his blood boil when he saw her wasting her talents. At Saas-Fée she'd looked one with the slopes, a snow-leopard, but a year into international competition, she was a robot. Bored and cynical, lost in the glitterati.

Wolf didn't know himself why he cared. He was retired, and Elizabeth wasn't even Swiss. But it was the chill twilight of early morning, and here they were.

'How you feel? Muscles all warm and relaxed?' he asked as they jumped on the draglift.

Elizabeth nodded, adjusting her goggles.

'After four hours with Brad they will be screaming for mercy,' Wolf told her smugly.

He could see her body in front of him tensing with anticipation. Every muscle in her thighs was lovingly outlined in that shimmering Lycra; her tight, round butt sat high on her long legs.

For a second he worried that Brad would get mad at him. Brad Hinds, the US men's coach, was training for the Super-G tomorrow. The demands he made of his boys would be a shock to Elizabeth's system, but if they took time out to look at their guest, she'd have them all crashing into the mountain.

'I can't believe you're making us do this, Brad. It's a waste of fucking time.'

Jack Taylor leaned against his ski-pole, his two hundred pounds perfectly balanced, barely denting the snow. It always amazed the team, how such a big guy could be so fluid, so smooth, once he strapped his boots into the skis. Taylor was six-three, bench-pressed three hundred, refused to check into a hotel without a weights room. But get him on the snow and he moved like a ballerina.

Sam Florence, Rick Kowalski and Pete Myers had all been on the team longer than Jack, but they didn't resent him. Taylor was the great white hope for the Olympics next year. He'd taken the silver in his first World Cup, overall gold last year and was running a comfortable lead over his Austrian rival this year. Despite the overnight success, though, Taylor had worked for it. His dedication took even champion athletes aback. Taylor would be up before dawn working out, ran five miles each evening before supper, skied all year long to train, following the snow round the world as the seasons shifted across the globe. Jack studied videos of the competition, tested out countless pairs of skis to find a millimetre advantage for his edge. It wore you out just watching him.

Jack Taylor had his sights on next year. An Olympic gold medal for his country, nothing less. The World Cup was a practice run.

The team admired him more because he didn't have to do it. Now twenty-four, Taylor had been tapped for the US three years back, when he was skiing for Harvard at Aspen. That year he'd graduated magna cum laude in English and put off a business degree for the sport. He could only dedicate one more year to amateur competition – his one shot at the Olympics. But Taylor was never going to need the glory for a résumé. His father was a multimillionaire, one of the few Texans to make a fortune outside oil and cattle. John Taylor, Sr, had a Thoroughbred horse ranch outside of Dallas and traded Grade-A bloodstock across the world. The Aga Khan and other Arab princes made the trip across the Atlantic to buy from him.

Jack Taylor was an only child. One day he would own four hundred acres of prime Southern land, two Dallas hotels, a large stock portfolio, a colonial mansion and an exclusive stable of racehorses.

In addition to this, there was the slight matter of his looks. His mom used to say that when God was making Jack, he forgot to press the 'stop' button. Sometimes it didn't seem fair. Not only was he smart, rich and athletic, Jack Taylor's tall, muscled body was crowned with a face that stopped girls in their tracks. Women passed him on the street, paused, and turned round for another look.

Taylor had jet-black hair, so smooth and glossy it looked like the flank of one of his mares. He cropped it close to the head in a severely masculine cut, which complemented the frank brown eyes with their dark, long lashes, the square jaw and the sensual, slightly cruel mouth. Jack couldn't help his mouth, but it was the finishing touch that broke so many girls' resistance. Set against his all-American, open good looks, the faint sullenness of the mouth, the ruthless set of his lips, spoke of a hidden darkness, a pitiless male sexuality.

Girls fluttered around him like butterflies.

Jack was selective about the ones who made it to his bed. He'd been hit on since junior high, the envy of all his friends who found it Mission: Impossible just getting to second base. Jack was thirteen years old when he lost his virginity, and thirteen and a half when his pop caught him on a haystack with his riding mistress. The riding mistress was fired, and Jack was given a lecture. Horrified by his father's lurid descriptions of what venereal disease could do to his cock, Jack was supposed to abstain. Instead, he learned everything there was to know about condoms.

His pop did nothing because he was secretly delighted. Every good ol' boy would be proud of a son who got laid at thirteen.

By the time he was fifteen, Jack Taylor was a connoisseur.

By the time he hit college, he was sexually mature. Dynamite in bed, he was dominant and skilful. Non-orgasmic women often climaxed for the first time with Jack. He learned to savour going slow, to enjoy relationships, not just two-week flings without strings. His pop boasted that if a stallion of his could sire like Jack, he'd retire ten years early, but slowly the string of cute faces were replaced by steady girlfriends who lasted four, five months at a time.

Still, Jack had never fallen *too* hard. Six girlfriends at Harvard; six broken hearts by the time he left.

Clarisse Devlin was the last candidate. Blonde, slim and pretty, Clarisse had hung on for a year post-graduation, but eventually the constant travel broke them up. Against the dream of Olympic gold, Clarisse never stood a chance, and Jack was secretly glad. He didn't need a girl hanging round right now. There were enough Identikit Euro-babes on the circuit to keep any guy happy, and being single gave him more time to train.

Taylor took practice deadly seriously. He was none too happy right now.

'It's not a waste of time. It's a favour to Hans Wolf.'

'Yeah? Why can't she train with the British guys? Or have Hans ask favours from the Canadians, not us?'

Brad Hinds shrugged. 'He wants her to train with the best. She's the women's bronze medallist. This year she wants gold.'

'Elizabeth Savage is no gold medallist.'

'I didn't know you followed the women's competition, Jack.'

'Enough to know that Savage is lazy, disruptive.' Jack's voice was ice. 'We don't need that attitude around.'

'So, not everyone's a fanatic,' Brad Hinds said doubtfully. He'd heard the same things. 'But it's only once, and we owe Hans. Come on, Taylor. He helped *you* out enough last year.'

Sighing, Jack Taylor nodded. Last year he'd pulled a ligament and might have dropped out if Hans Wolf hadn't found him the best doctor in Switzerland.

'OK, OK. But don't expect me to slow down so she can study my technique.'

His team-mates laughed.

'You wouldn't slow down for the President,' Rick Kowalski pointed out.

At that moment the draglift pulled two figures into view and started carrying them up the mountain to the top of the mogul run.

Sam, Rick and Pete stared at Elizabeth's curvy frame with open admiration.

Jack shook his head. Sex kittens were great, but not while he was working.

'Here already,' Hans said cheerily as he slid off the draglift. 'Brad, it's good to see you. Hello, guys. Brad, can I present Lady Elizabeth Savage.'

Brad Hinds leaned forward and took Elizabeth's gloved hand. He tried hard not to show how surprised he was. Christ, the kid was gorgeous! High cheekbones, brilliant green eyes, full lips, kick-ass athletic little body. She had a tight butt, long legs, sculptured shoulders. Goggles and rainbow Lycra that clung like a second skin did a lousy job of wrapping her up. He couldn't stop his eyes flickering over her breasts. They had to be the only part of her that wasn't firm and toned. To his dismay, he felt the beginnings of a hard-on. Thank God he'd picked bulky nylon pants today.

'Uh, how do you do, my lady,' Hinds said uncertainly.

'Please call me Elizabeth, Mr Hinds. It's such an honour to meet you. I really appreciate your making time for me today.' Her small hand shook his huge paw enthusiastically.

'Hey, no problem. I'm Brad, and these are Sam, Pete, Rick and Jack.'

'Elizabeth.' Sam Florence's grin was fit to split his face. Kowalski and Myers nodded hi and undressed her with their eyes. Nothing she wasn't used to.

However Taylor's reaction was a surprise. He gave her a cold stare, shifted impatiently on his skis, and turned away. 'Brad, can we get going? We've hung around long enough.'

'Sure.' Hinds pulled out a stopwatch. 'You take the first run.' He turned to Elizabeth as Taylor settled into a crouch. 'Don't mind Jack. He's World Champion, it makes him a little excessive about training.'

'Oh, I understand,' Elizabeth said warmly. 'Jack, you were superb at Garmisch—'

She never got to finish her sentence. Ignoring her completely, Taylor pushed off with a mighty lunge and tore down the mogul run, planting his stick cleanly and with perfect rhythm, his heavy body leaping, twisting and landing cleanly and sharply.

'Jack Taylor is a real skier. He does not want to know you,' Hans whispered in her ear. 'You have not earned his respect.'

Elizabeth stood at the top of the run, her eyes narrowing.

That smug bastard. She was going to teach him a lesson.

Two hours later, Elizabeth was ready to drop. Hans had been right: training with the men pushed her to the limit. Her muscles were burning with effort, her body bathed in sweat under the suit, her head throbbing from the gritted focus it took keeping up with them. After Pete Myers sliced his way down the mogul run barely a second behind Jack, Elizabeth took a go. Swooping, turning and jumping with ferocious concentration, she made the run three seconds ahead of her personal best.

She was miles behind the men. Taylor's stare was scornful.

Elizabeth listened to Brad's comments with unusual humility, but she was biting her lower lip with rage. The second descent, she shaved off two extra seconds, but still trailed Taylor. The third time she pushed herself too hard and fell, bruising her outer hip painfully and jolting a ski out of its bindings.

'Are you OK? Maybe you'd better take a breather,' the coach suggested anxiously. Ronnie Davis would skin him alive if the Brit's star girl was injured before her slalom.

'You made a great time for a woman, anyway,' Sam told her.

Jack Taylor caught her looking at him. She was stunningly beautiful. The type of chick who thought the world owed her a living. Or a gold medal, in this case.

'The idea is to stay upright, Cinderella,' he remarked coldly. 'Don't bite off more than you can chew. Women's training is effective for women – if they bother turning up for it.'

'I'll go again,' Elizabeth told Brad furiously.

On the fifth attempt, she managed to beat Pete Myers by half a second.

'Jesus!' Pete swore, disgusted with himself.

'Come on, Pete. You're way off today. Just concentrate,' Jack Taylor said loudly, belittling her achievement.

The girl flashed him a look of pure disdain, which Taylor pretended to ignore. He thought she was an arrogant bitch, and he wanted her to know it.

Privately, he had concluded something else.

Elizabeth was the best female skier he'd ever met.

And she was the sexiest, best-looking babe he'd ever seen.

10

Nina was writing a job application when it happened, sitting in Green Earth in the gloom. Connor had boarded the place up, ready for sale, but Nina had kept a spare set of keys. She snuck in the back most nights and hammered out résumés and letters, a torch propped up behind her, bombarding the big drug giants until somebody said yes. At first she felt like a thief, but Nina was getting used to being ingenious. You could only ever rely on yourself. Until she landed a new job, she couldn't afford a typewriter of her own. Most of her severance cheque had been eaten by her new, tiny walk-up studio; you couldn't afford to head letters with a motel address.

She was trying ICI when the first pain came. A sharp twinge in the gut that she ignored – she was always getting pains from her pregnancy. Then it was worse. Nina pressed a hand to her taut midriff. God, it hurt, it really hurt; like the worst period she ever had. Gasping, she doubled forwards, clutching herself. There was a pause, then another wrenching, flaming stab. Nina staggered out of the door and on to the sidewalk. There was a payphone there and she dialled 911.

When the ambulance got there five minutes later, they found Nina clinging to the phone, tears streaming down her face. Her slacks were drenched. She knew what was happening. She was going to lose her baby, like she'd lost everything else.

St Jude's Blue Cross Hospital was staffed with brisk, fatigued junior doctors. A black gynaecologist saw Nina.

'I'm sorry you lost the child, but you're OK. No reason why you couldn't have another.'

'Thank you, Doctor,' the girl said quietly.

'Got a husband?'

'No.'

'Got a job?'

'No.'

Dr Kenmore shook her head. The kid was still the light side of twenty. Most girls in that position would be pleased to miscarry. 'You're nineteen? You look older.'

Nina pushed herself up on her pillows. 'When do you think I'll be fit to leave?'

She was taken aback. 'You're fit now, physically, but you can stay and rest, that's fine. We do Medicare.'

'I have to go,' Nina said, and pushed back the covers.

'Don't you want any counselling?' Dr Kenmore asked. 'We have a rabbi here, he could talk to you.'

'No. Thank you.' Nina Roth looked up at the doctor, her face beautiful despite its pallor, heavy, silky hair ringing her face. 'No counselling's gonna change what happened. I'm alive, I have to get on with it.'

What a cold young woman, Dr Kenmore thought as she left.

Nina felt weak enough to take a cab home. She let herself into her apartment, collapsed on the bed and cried like she would never stop.

When she woke up, it was six p.m. It was bitterly cold, her rickety radiator barely blunting the edge of the chill. Her stomach hurt, but the emptiness and the loss hurt more.

Nina forced herself out of bed and went to the window. It was sparkling clean, like the rest of her tiny place. Food stacked neatly in the cupboards, rejection letters piled on the kitchen table. Total contrast to the grime and dirt outside: hookers and dealers hanging out on the street corner, sirens screaming, traffic noises and drunks. All those people, millions of people, and not one of them who cared about her. She'd lost Frank. Jeff. And now, her baby.

Idly she picked up the bottle of painkillers Dr Kenmore had prescribed. A junkie was yelling on the sidewalk below her. She could probably get about a hundred bucks for these; powerful shit, Valium mixed with opiates. Easy to get high on, easy to check out with. She would float away on a hazy, warm cloud and just never wake up.

There was a cheap hand-mirror propped against the Cheerios packet. Nina looked at the reflection inside the ugly pink piping; she was red eyed but beautiful, pale, exhausted. She saw too much experience and cynicism in her own dark eyes. She was still just eighteen years old.

Nina unscrewed the bottle and counted out two tablets. Recommended dose. She'd never seriously consider taking the coward's way out. She'd made herself a promise on Jeff Glazer's front steps, and she was absolutely going to keep it.

Two days later, she got her first positive reply.

Dolan MacDonald was the tenth drug firm she'd applied to. The position was for an assistant sales manager at $21,000 a year; a pittance by industry standards, but a fortune to Nina. She wanted the job so much she ached. Anything, anything to get her out of here.

In her first interview, she answered questions on her work experience and Dolan. Today she was meeting her prospective boss.

Nina left the subway at the Jay Street exit and headed for Dolan's offices, a functional block of grey stone behind the Borough Hall. It looked dull, but she was excited. Dolan MacDonald, with its boring pill bottles and plain white packaging, was the place to be.

Her second interview took place in a drab room somewhere on the second floor, with a bored-looking flunky who chewed a pencil the whole time, and Ivan Kinzslade, head of the vitamins division.

'You don't have a degree, but you made good grades. Why you drop outta school?' he asked without preamble.

'I wanted to get on in the world, make something of myself.'

'So why you join a tiny joint like Green Earth?'

'It was tiny, but it made a good profit,' Nina said defensively.

Her interviewer's eyes narrowed. 'Not when you joined.'

Nina sat up a little straighter, realising Kinzslade had been asking around.

'I couldn't get a job anywhere else. It wasn't such a great idea, dropping out of school.'

The Russian laughed. 'You got any family?'

'Only my parents, and I don't talk to them.'

Kinzslade called her at home that afternoon to tell her she was hired.

Nina insisted on her first paycheque in advance; she needed it for a deposit on the rent. She was surprised that demanding the money didn't hurt her image, in fact it impressed her bosses. Nina found that if she acted seriously people respected her. For the second time in a month she moved, to a small one-bedroom off Flatbush. It wasn't much, but to Nina it was a triumph. Her own apartment! For the first time in her life she had a respectable place of her own, she was doing good at work, she could pay all her bills.

It was hard, though. Nina's creamy complexion was dull with fatigue by the end of each day, even though she was eating well. She couldn't afford unhealthy convenience meals; it was all cheap pulses, potatoes and veggies from the local markets, fish and chicken if it was on offer. Nina could cook, just about. Still, she was pathetically grateful when Mrs Minsky, her neighbour, dropped round with the odd apple pie.

'Lord, child,' Mrs Minsky said, sniffing, 'they work ya too hard, you're white as ivory. Didn't your momma tell ya you're too cute for this? Ya need a man to take care of ya. I gotta grandson, Carl—'

'Thanks, Mrs Minsky, but I like things this way,' Nina said politely, but in a tone of such finality the old lady actually gave up.

'If those guys at your work don't ask ya out, they should be takin' their own medicines,' was her parting shot at the door.

Nina could have laughed. Ask her out! Like they ever did anything else! Almost every man on her floor, from the geeky researchers to the cash 'n' flash commission salesman, had tried his luck already. Slowly but surely Nina got the word out that she wasn't interested. That might have caused resentment, but who could resent the quiet Ms Roth, that mousy, dedicated little toiler with her reports and calculations, always either glued to the phone or hammering at her computer screen? Nina got a skewed reputation. She was a major babe, but uninterested in men. She was ambitious, but bored by office politics. Nina stayed well away from the water-cooler crowd, just doing her job, finding her feet. And soon enough, the boys ignored her.

All except Ivan Kinzslade, who had an instinct about Nina. The job he'd hired her for was simple, form-filling and number-crunching. At first she seemed happy just to do that, but after the first month, Ivan noticed her calls to the field offices were taking longer, she was asking for more data.

First thing one Monday morning she showed up in his office.

'Morning, Nina, you gotta problem?' the Russian asked, offering her a bite of his jelly donut.

'An idea,' Nina said, coming right to the point.

Ivan liked it. Roth was more upfront than any other young girl he'd hired. She seemed much older than her years. Ivan was an immigrant who'd escaped from Russia and taught himself English before winding up in Brooklyn. Sometimes he thought he saw a similar hardness in Nina, the look of a person who'd been through a furnace and come out tougher the other side.

'Go on, then.'

'We're wasting a lot of money in the way we sell our stuff. Look at this,' Nina said, spreading out research in front of her boss. 'We tailor journeys to our salesmen. If we paid more attention to retailers, we could focus our efforts.'

'You think so?'

'I know it. Look, Ivan, I've been the customer. I know what they want.'

Kinzslade glanced up at the grave young woman standing over him. 'I guess you can try it,' was all he said.

Over the next year, Nina crammed as much work as possible into an eight-hour day. She tried to alter Dolan's sales, organising training programmes and policy around the needs of the customers, not the company. Dolan's sales force got a reputation for friendliness and efficiency. Orders picked up, and Ivan gave her a pay rise.

Nina opened a new account at Wells Fargo, with a first deposit of five hundred dollars. Every extra cent she earned, she salted away. Waiting till she had enough money to do something.

In her second year, Nina talked her boss into thirty new computers. The expense was a black hole in the quarterly budget, but quickly paid for itself. Productivity went up two per cent; clerical expenses fell.

It was hard, grunt work, trying to change a system that had been in place for decades, but her colleagues listened when Nina talked, even the flyboys who thought any women in offices should be taking dictation.

'Nice idea you had for Ohio,' Grant McCoist, a flash Midwestern rep, told her after one strategy session. 'It'll help get our profile off the floor.'

'Thanks,' Nina said coldly.

The handsome young comer didn't take the hint. 'You know, that dress is real pretty. You should let me buy you dinner, we could discuss it some more.'

'If you want to discuss it, send me a memo,' Nina told him.

'Good morning, Ms Roth,' Ally Hendry announced confidently, turning up in her office at nine a.m. with a huge bunch of roses. 'Wanna have lunch? We could swap computer strategies.'

'I mostly eat at my desk. And they're sweet, but I get hay fever,' Nina said bluntly.

'You know, you're quite the rising star,' Jock MacCallister, a finance manager, told her as he leaned over her computer and stared soulfully into her eyes. 'You got some free time? You could tell me your secret.'

'I can tell you that now, Jock,' suggested Nina sweetly.

He leaned forwards.

'Hard work and imagination,' she said, trying not to laugh at the offended look in his bloodshot eyes.

'What, you're frigid? Or you gotta boy in your life already?' Jock demanded, acting like a spoilt brat. Nina regarded him coldly. That's all they were, these boys, spoilt brats whining when they couldn't get the toys they wanted. She made twenty-six grand a year now, she paid her own way. Independence that was very precious to her. Mrs Minsky might see it as natural to seek out male protection but Nina was determined never to have to. She had no respect for men and no time for romance. Jeff Glazer had bruised her heart so badly Nina never wanted to risk pain like that again.

'Yeah, I do. I have a boy in my life,' she lied.

Jock puffed up like a mating pigeon. Of course, or how could she have ignored his advances?

'OK, I guess we shoulda known,' he said magnanimously.

After that the guys left her alone. Nina was a beauty, but she was off the market.

Nina climbed quietly, seriously, relentlessly, hand over fist, without stopping for friendship or looking back for love. She didn't care. She thought that stuff was for weaklings.

The phone trilled on her desk right after one. It was Edwin Jensen, a prestigious firm of head-hunters who specialised in pharmaceuticals. She was getting herself a reputation, they said. Dragon was looking for a business development exec. Would Ms Roth be interested?

Nina lowered the soggy tuna sandwich that was her idea of a lunch break and took a deep breath. Dragon Inc. The big time. The bluest of blue chips, Dragon had pharmacies, drugstores and health food places across Europe and the States. Their executives were highly paid, with hefty bonus schemes and expensive company cars. The head offices on Park Avenue were a fantasy of marble and gold, burgundy leather and oak, exuding old-world elegance and Fortune 400 wealth.

Nina hadn't even considered the British giant. Dragon was not known for its political correctness. Just for its profits.

Dragon acted like a gentleman's club. The dress code was strict, recruitment conservative. Dragon wanted clean-cut young men, the cream of the Ivy League. Out of Harvard via Brooks Brothers. It wasn't big on ethnic minorities, City College grads, or women.

Why me? Nina thought.

'So, would you consider interviewing, Ms Roth?'

'Absolutely,' she said. It was certainly worth a shot. At worst she'd get a little flavour of life inside a market leader.

The interview took place a week later. Uncharacteristically nervous, Nina arrived at the Dragon building on Park Avenue ten minutes early, wearing her best suit and imitation leather shoes. Dragon's HQ was a palace. The reception area was a study in burgundy leather, mahogany and marble, bustling with middle-aged men in expensive suits. The receptionist looked at Nina like she was gunge sticking in the sink drainer.

'Yes, miss, can I help you?'

'I'm here for a job interview.' Nina's voice sounded very small in her own ears and she cleared her throat. 'My name's Nina Roth.'

The woman tapped her hi-tech keyboard and unbent slightly. 'Yes. You take the elevator to the thirteenth floor. You'll be seen by Mr Gary Bellman from our Personnel division, and Lord Caerhaven.'

The back of Nina's throat dried up. 'Lord Caerhaven, *personally*?'

'That's right. He's visiting New York,' the receptionist said blandly.

Nina could feel the hostility rising off the older woman like steam. There you go, cutie, it said, how do you like them apples?

Tony Savage. The Robber Baron. She'd clipped countless articles about him at Dolan, everything from *Vanity Fair* puff pieces to *Fortune* assessments. Savage had ripped the heart out of countless small firms and research teams, invested brilliantly, fired thousands of workers, and turned his moribund family business into a global giant. He was respected but loathed. The drugs business feared him. And adored him. What the hell was he here for? Why was he attending this interview? Nina buzzed for the elevator and tried to calm herself. Thank God, she thought, I don't have too much time to think about it.

Upstairs a secretary ushered her into Gary Bellman's spacious office. The two men were sitting casually on chairs behind a long table; one, smaller chair was set in front just for her. It felt like a long walk before she could sit down.

'You're Nina Roth?'

'Yes, Mr Bellman, how do you do.' Nina shook hands, hoping she sounded confident.

The sandy-haired guy raised an eyebrow. 'How do you know I'm Bellman?'

'Because I recognise Lord Caerhaven.'

Tony grinned. He liked to sit in on odd meetings around the world; lightning visits to keep his people on their toes. Today he was inspecting Human Resources. Bellman, his new guy, liked to pick people from different backgrounds to the norm: scholarship kids, entrepreneurs, comers cherry-picked from Glaxo or ICI. This girl, Roth, had brought in some reforms at Dolan. Her file said she had a reputation already. She was clearly terrified, but putting on a good act. It impressed him; her lovely face and sexy figure impressed him a lot more.

He didn't mind the odd woman around. They cost less, they worked harder. The Dragon boys' club was no place for a lady, but then this kid wasn't a lady, she was a working-class hustler from the wrong side of Brooklyn.

And she knew who he was.

'Tony Savage,' he said.

His strong, fleshy hand gripped hers like a vice, dark eyes sweeping across her body like they could X-ray her.

Nina blushed. Savage was physically overbearing, large and muscular. He had an air of ruthlessness that matched his reputation. She had to fight not to flinch under his stare. Next to his charcoal wool Turnbull & Asser suit, his gold Blancpain watch and his immaculate manicure, Nina felt cheap and underdressed.

'Thank you for seeing me,' she replied coolly.

'Lord Caerhaven has some questions for you, Ms Roth,' Bellman said.

Tony Savage looked Nina over for a long, luxurious moment, careful to keep his eyes expressionless. The scout reports on her work suggested some ugly bluestocking.

Nina Roth was anything but. An awesome body under that shapeless suit. A flaring bosom tapering down to a handspan waist, a tight, round ass, creamy white skin, nicely turned calves. Her body language was repressed, though. Knees pressed together. Back rigid. Clothes designed to play down that sexy shape.

Savage fired a question. Nina answered it sharply. He fired another.

Nothing seemed to faze her. As Nina talked, Savage's thoughts drifted. He wanted to see if his hands would really fit round that waist. What colour the nipples were on top of those creamy breasts. She looked uptight: great. Not the kind to sleep around.

A challenge.

Tony nodded coldly and made a small note on his pad. Nina Roth had a great future with Dragon.

11

Nina gave herself a last check. It was her first day at Dragon and she wanted to look perfect. She'd chosen her new suit at Saks on Saturday, something she could barely afford, but it was an investment. The eighties were here.

It was a brave new world, and women executives had a new rulebook to go with it – John Molloy's *Dress for Success*. Nina had a well-thumbed copy of this bible next to her bed, and she obeyed it to the letter. Adopt a business uniform. Blouse lighter than the suit. No bright red, bright orange or bright anything. Avoid emphasising the bust.

Easier said than done, Nina thought uneasily. Her suit comprised a white cotton blouse, a boxy jacket with the latest 'power dressing' essential – padded shoulders – a skirt that hovered precisely on the knee and low pumps with natural hose. In her one concession to individuality, Nina rejected navy in favour of rich burgundy. Hopefully the jacket was boxy enough to disguise her breasts.

Nina fiddled with the floppy bow tie at her neck, and picked up her new leather briefcase.

'Let's go to work,' she said.

As her yellow cab crawled up Park towards the Dragon building, Nina read over her product marketing file. She didn't think about the oddity of her situation. A young woman with no formal training, from the wrong side of the tracks, storming one of corporate Manhattan's most exclusive male bastions ... it was unheard of. But it had happened, and Nina didn't waste time wondering why. That was the past. Her eyes were fiercely trained on the future. She'd make her mark fast and keep moving up.

She soon realised how tough that would be.

'Good morning, Ms Roth,' an elegant blonde receptionist greeted her as she stepped inside the Italian marble lobby. Nina had thought she would be early, but the lobby was full of Identikit young men striding purposefully towards banks of elevators. It was eight-twenty a.m. She made a mental note to arrive at eight tomorrow.

'I'm the new Business Development manager,' Nina explained, trying to sound like a businesswoman. 'I'm due to report to Mr Jax at nine.'

The receptionist's gaze swept across the glossy black bob, the grey eyes and ivory skin. Then she stared almost rudely at the hourglass figure only half-hidden under the burgundy suit, and the long, curvy calves that tapered down to the neat pumps. Nina had to restrain herself from checking to see if she had coffee stains on her lapels.

'Yes, ma'am,' the girl said thinly. 'Business Development is on the twelfth floor and you have offices next to Mr Robbins and Mr Daly. They've already arrived.'

'Thank you,' Nina said, but the girl had already returned to her magazine. Clearly that was it. Uncertainly, Nina picked up her briefcase and headed for the nearest elevator bank. Three young men were standing inside one car, but as Nina hurried towards it, the doors hissed shut. They didn't try to hold them open for her. She took a deep breath and pressed the button for the next one. Maybe this was just how people behaved in a big corporation, Nina told herself as she waited. After all, they didn't know her yet, and time was money. Right?

In the slow ride up to her department Nina fiddled anxiously with her buttons. The reflection in the mirrored doors showed a pretty girl, maybe a little flushed, but neatly, conservatively dressed. She examined it carefully but still couldn't see anything wrong. Shrugging, Nina shook it off. Two minutes inside the corporate jungle and already she was getting paranoid ...

At the twelfth floor the elevator stopped gently and the smoothly hissing doors opened on to a luxurious corridor. The floor was carpeted with a soft grey weave and elegantly framed prints of Dragon products. Men and women were walking in and out of various offices, but only the men were executives. The women wore short skirts, heels and pretty dresses in pastel colours, and they all hovered and smiled deferentially. Nina glanced around but could not see one other woman in a business suit.

'Excuse me.' She stopped a young redhead carrying a freshly made mug of coffee. 'I'm new. Could you tell me where to go?'

'Sure,' the girl said neutrally, giving Nina a once-over. 'The typing pool's at the end of the next corridor. You should report to Mrs Finn.'

'No, I mean – I'm the new Business Development manager. Apparently I'm going to be working with Mr Robbins and Mr Daly,' Nina explained. 'Could you direct me to my office?'

The girl did a double-take. '*You're* N. Roth?'

'Yes. Nina Roth,' Nina confirmed.

There was a second's stunned silence, and then the girl said, 'If you'll follow me, Ms Roth,' with barely concealed hostility. Making no effort to put her coffee aside, she led Nina down the length of the corridor and to the right. A small group of tiny, windowless offices nestled in a corner, with names stencilled in thin black lettering on the doors. 'N. Roth' was in between 'S. Daly' and 'T. Robbins'. You had to peer closely to read the titles and Nina was shocked to see that all three of them had the same status: Manager, Business Development. She had assumed she'd be the only one doing the job.

'This is your office,' the secretary said, showing Nina into the cubbyhole of a room. Between the desk, the filing cabinet and the trashcan, there wasn't enough room to swing a kitten.

'Tracy Jones is the assistant assigned to you. You'll be sharing her with Mr Robbins and Mr Daly,' the girl continued, her tone making it clear she felt for Tracy. 'You can buzz her if there's anything you require. All the new managers have an appointment with Mr Jax at nine and his office is on the thirteenth floor.'

'Thank you,' Nina said faintly, opening her briefcase and starting to lay out her documents.

'Uh-huh,' the girl said, and closed the door.

Gee, Nina thought wryly. What tells me they don't have many women in management roles?

Five minutes later, as she was busily setting up her computer passwords, there was a smart rap on her office door.

'Come in,' Nina called.

It swung open to reveal two expensively dressed men, both of them wearing big smiles and sombre pinstripe suits. One had a gold watch and one a steel Rolex, and Nina could see at a glance that the shoes were handmade European leather.

'Hi, I'm Simon Daly and this is Tom Robbins,' the taller one said, indicating his colleague. 'You must be Ms Roth.'

'Nina.' She stood up and shook their hands. 'I'm looking forward to working with you.'

'Ditto,' Robbins said. He had sandy hair and freckles and she didn't care for the twinkle in his eye as he took in her figure.

'Are you guys new here too?'

'Yes, ma'am.' Simon, the blond, seemed more open and relaxed. He had a slight Chicago accent and a straightforward manner. 'First day of my working life. Dragon yanked me out of my student haven and now I'm supposed to sing for my supper.'

'Goes for me too,' Tom added, eyes still roving over her jacket. 'I majored in economics at Cornell and Simon did math at Yale.'

Nina straightened up. 'I went straight into business from high school. I worked at Dolan most recently.'

'And now the big time. Well, you're a liberated lady,' Tom teased her, with an obnoxious smile.

'I like to think so,' Nina replied calmly.

'That's the reason, then. You don't have a degree and we don't have any experience. That's why we get forty-five thousand and all the others get fifty-two,' Simon grouched. He checked his Rolex. 'Ten of. Come on, let's get upstairs. We don't want to be late for our first pep-talk.'

Nina nodded and followed them into the elevator, trying not to let her feelings show on her face. Obviously, working at Dragon would be like running up the down escalator.

She'd thought thirty-five thousand was a fortune, but they'd hired two younger guys with zero experience to do the same job as her. For ten thousand bucks more.

The thirteenth floor was already pretty crowded. Around thirty people were standing in the sumptuous waiting area Nina recognised from her interview, admiring the oil paintings of hunting scenes, sitting on chintz couches, or gazing out of the stunning floor-to-ceiling windows. Nina was relieved to see four other women, but as she introduced herself, the relief lessened. Two of the girls were in Human Resources, one was a creative in Packaging, and one was assigned to PR. As they shook hands, Nina sensed her isolation creep back. The girls had jobs that *sounded* impressive but kept them well away from the bottom line.

The door swung open and they filed in. Small, gold-backed chairs had been lined up in rows in front of the elegant mahogany desk. Nina noticed the other women automatically seating themselves in the back, anxious not to appear pushy. Squaring her shoulders, she headed for the centre front row.

Dragon hadn't hired her to be a shrinking violet.

All conversation ceased as Gerald Jax strode into the room. He was wearing a dark suit and a platinum Gucci watch. His grey hair was severely cropped and his dark eyes hard and uncompromising. The head of Dragon US, Jax was Tony Savage's right-hand man in the States. He radiated ruthless power.

'Dragon Chemical is the largest drug company in the United States. We have revenues of half a billion dollars on turnover of three billion.'

There was absolute silence as they gazed at their new boss.

'That's not enough,' Jax continued coldly. 'Lord Caerhaven wants to be the biggest in the world. We aim for radical improvements in US market share. We pay the highest salaries and we expect the best. Dragon is looking to you to implement its expansion.'

Jax surveyed the spellbound new recruits.

'We're not easy to work for. We want results fast. Those who do not deliver will be fired. Those who do – will become extremely rich. I expect to see tangible progress in the first month of your employment. Then we'll know who's intended for which fate.'

He leaned forward slightly, as hypnotic and menacing as a swaying cobra.

'We remain the best because we *never* let up. Remember this: if you rest on your laurels, they become funeral wreaths.'

Dismissed, they rose from their chairs and began to leave. As Nina stood up, Jax motioned to her to stay.

'Good morning, Nina. Welcome to Dragon,' he said.

'Thank you, sir,' Nina answered carefully.

Jax nodded at the crowd of young men. 'By now you may have realised that you're quite an exception. We haven't had many women applicants with your ability.' His tone was unapologetic. 'I hope that's not going to be a problem for you.'

Nina looked the vice-president straight in the eyes.

'No, sir. No problem at all.'

'Glad to hear it,' Jax said coolly, turning aside.

His gaze followed Nina with vivid interest as she left the room. Tony had asked for a report on this one. She didn't know it, but Nina Roth was going to be very closely watched.

The speech might have been macho melodrama, as Nina told herself once she was safely back in her office, but a part of her thrilled to the challenge.

She had one month to come up with something hot. Brainstorming all afternoon, her first day, Nina fished out a dramatic idea from her fertile subconscious. Dragon was richer than Dolan MacDonald, but it followed a lot of the same practices – shipping the same drugs at the same prices right across the States. There was huge wastage, but that was 'the price of doing business'.

What if I could change that? Nina thought. What if I could get Dragon to invest in another mainframe, a computer that could track what drugs sold where? If we had a clearer picture of the market . . .

Nina titled the project 'Customised Response'. Her phones buzzed incessantly and the mailcart stopped by her door five times a day as data she requested came flooding back. It was a mammoth task, and even harder than it had to be.

Simon and Tom kept pretty much to themselves. Nina's trouble was the support staff. There was no sisterly feeling at Dragon Chemical. The receptionists and secretaries, far from being pleased to see a woman executive, all resented her bitterly and let it show. They called her 'Ms Roth' and made it sound like an insult. They took for ever to do her filing and often did it so sloppily Nina found herself staying late to correct things.

But the major problem was her assistant.

Tracy Jones had been assigned to the three of them. A sexy-looking redhead with wild hair, short skirts and long nails, she hated having to work for a woman. Tom's letters and Simon's charts always came before the work Nina needed typing.

Nina didn't complain at first. She was new. But eventually she had to say something and told Tracy she wanted her reports assigned equal priority.

'They are,' Tracy insisted insolently, with a flick of her rosy curls. Nina flushed, hating the confrontation, but saw all the other girls in the pool slow down their typewriters so they could eavesdrop.

She knew she had to assert her authority.

'I'm sorry, Tracy, but I don't think so. I want these letters on my desk first thing tomorrow.'

'Yes, ma'am,' Tracy said icily.

The letters were delivered to her by mailcart at nine a.m. the next day. They had two spelling mistakes and a word Tipp-Exed out in each of them.

Gritting her teeth, Nina did it herself.

Three weeks into the deadline she was seriously behind. Her proposal needed detailed statistics, and she'd have to check it before it went off to Jax. If she gave it to Tracy on schedule, Nina realised, it would be handed in late or so messy she couldn't use it at all. Gerald Jax wasn't interested in excuses.

Besides, there *were* no excuses. Nina wanted to get to management, but right now she couldn't manage her own secretary! Tracy and all the others assumed a woman had no place being an executive. They preferred flirting with the boys and Nina was basically letting them get away with it.

The bright, polite schoolgirl in Nina shrank from appearing a bitch. She remembered how hard it had been when she started at Green Earth, and she had no desire to be anyone's boss from hell. But as the deadline got closer, she had no other choice.

On Friday Nina went down to the typing pool at eleven a.m., to find Tracy sitting at an empty typewriter, painting her nails. As Nina approached, she brazenly continued.

'Hello, Tracy. I need this report typed up today. It's got quite a few statistics,' Nina told her, laying the sheaf of neatly written notes on her desk. 'Do you think you could get it done for me?'

The girl barely glanced at her. 'Sorry, I'm too busy.'

Aware of the others watching her, Nina drew breath. 'How can you be too busy? Coffee break is over and you're painting your nails. *Whenever* I need something done, you're always too busy. I think the problem is that you just don't want to work for me.'

At that moment, all the girls in the pool stopped typing.

Tracy shrugged, without looking up. Then she turned to Maria, a hard-working Spanish girl who sat next to her. 'Maria, can you do this?'

Nina tapped the paperwork sharply. She was red faced, but her voice was firm. 'No, Tracy. You are my assistant and I want you to do it. I am leaving it on your desk and I'll be back for it at three. If it isn't done by then, I am going to fire you.'

'Oh, really,' Tracy said with a sneer.

'Try me,' said Nina.

There was complete silence as Nina walked back down the corridor. Her heart was hammering in her chest and her palms were sweating, but she held up her head. She could feel the eyes of all the typists boring into her back.

Nina tried to get on with her research. It was impossible to concentrate. She didn't eat at lunch and wondered what on earth she was going to do. Nina was a new hire, very junior, and already she was making waves, but it was a matter of principle and she knew nobody else could get her through it.

At five of three Nina marched down to the typing pool to find Tracy languidly tapping at her keyboard. One look at the paper told her this was a letter of Tom's. Nina's own project was resting on Tracy's desk, exactly where she'd left it.

The typing pool fell completely silent as Nina stood in front of her secretary.

Tracy shot Nina a defiant look.

'You haven't typed up my report,' Nina stated flatly. 'I gave express orders that it was to be ready by three. Is there a reason why you haven't done it?'

'I told you. I'm too busy,' Tracy said rudely.

'And I told you. You're fired,' Nina said. 'Collect your papers from Gary Bellman in Personnel.'

The room was so quiet she could hear the other girls breathing as they watched the confrontation.

'You can't do that. You don't have the right,' Tracy challenged her.

'I've just done it. If your desk isn't cleared in ten minutes security will throw you out,' Nina replied.

Then she turned on her heel and marched back to her office.

Breathing deeply to calm herself, Nina lifted the phone and dialled an extension in Human Resources. Her palm was clammy with sweat where she gripped the receiver.

'Gary? This is Nina Roth in Business Development,' she said when he answered the phone. 'I've just fired Tracy Jones.'

'Nina, you can't dismiss anybody. You don't have the authority,' Gary Bellman said, sounding worried.

'Gary, I have fired her,' Nina told him firmly. 'And I have fired her in front of thirty-five other secretarial staff.'

There was a long pause.

'In that case, she's fired,' said the personnel director.

That night, Nina could hardly sleep. She lay on her bed and stared into space. What if Tracy had needed the money? What if she herself had been responsible for not fixing the problem sooner?

But she knew that under the same circumstances, she'd do the same thing again. Tomorrow, if necessary.

12

Hans Wolf was right. The amount of work it took to claw back just a few seconds on each race was staggering. That first day at Val d'Isère, even with the ferocious training she'd done that morning, Elizabeth still came third in the slalom. It didn't help that Jack Taylor watched at the finish line, and left without comment.

'I can't believe it,' Elizabeth said, heartsick with disappointment.

'*Ja*. You have a long way to go. Heidi does not give up the crown just because now you want it,' Wolf replied, but then he softened. 'You were only three seconds behind.'

'For ever!'

The old man smiled grimly. 'Listen to my little snow-leopard, who yesterday is calling five seconds nothing.'

Elizabeth nodded briskly, preparing to face the barrage of cameras for her post-race interview. 'Yeah, well. Today, things are different.'

Things certainly were different. As the World Cup continued across the Alps, the British team watched her transformation open mouthed. Ronnie Davis couldn't believe it was the same girl: Elizabeth rose early in the morning to jog, practised with Karen, and turned up to formal practice religiously. She apologised to him for being so bloody minded before.

'I was a jerk, Ron. I'm sorry. I'm paying for it now.'

'No problem,' said her coach, waving it aside. Ronnie was a bus-driver's son from the East End of London. He'd never voted Tory and despised the upper classes, but Lady Elizabeth was sweating it so hard she'd almost changed his mind. 'You're Welsh. You're stubborn. Goes with the territory.'

'*Diolch* for nothing, *cariad bach*,' Elizabeth retorted, pulling her mane of shiny honey-blonde hair back from her face.

Ronnie whistled under his breath as she plunged off down another downhill. Prolonged exercise, sun and crisp mountain air made that girl more attractive every season. They were having to lay on extra security at the hotels to keep the reporters away. Back home, Britain was slumping further and further into recession, and his dazzling champion offered a total contrast. The Ski Club of Great Britain had reported a four hundred per cent increase in membership, especially from girls. Skiing holidays were selling out. He knew several travel agents had tacked posters of her young ladyship up in their offices.

This time she wasn't letting it swell her head, but they still had problems.

If Elizabeth was ever going to get that gold medal, she needed to go an extra mile. Reluctantly, Ronnie concluded that it couldn't be with him.

It was all very well, Elizabeth turning up for practice. Trouble was, there wasn't much he could teach her. Now she was making an effort, her real talent was coming through.

She was leagues ahead of his other girls. She was leagues ahead of *him*.

Ronnie called the office back home and secured some extra funding. Then he called Hans Wolf.

'We want you to come in as coach for Liz Savage.'

A dry chuckle. '*Ach*, Ronnie. You know I am retired.'

Davis swallowed his pride. 'She needs more than I can give her, Hans. What's the point of you discovering her, if you don't see it through?'

'She's the world bronze medallist.'

'So fucking what? Come on, Hans. Don't muck me about. Are you up for it?'

Hans Wolf took over as Elizabeth's coach. It was the first time in her life she'd known what real work was. To her runs, he added heavy backpacks. In gym training he upped her weights. When she studied videos of Heidi and Louise, he made her write notes. The second an event was finished, Elizabeth barely had time to shower before she was being hustled on to a plane. If they got to the next stop ahead of time, Hans explained, there'd be an extra evening for practice runs.

'Don't I ever get a break?' Elizabeth gasped, as Hans rushed her away from the press after a downhill victory in Grindelwald.

'*Nein*. Plenty of time to sleep when you're dead,' Wolf told her briskly.

Travel, train, race. Travel, train, race. Elizabeth spent day after day lost in the brutal cycle of competition. The chic bars and glittering hotels she'd hung out at last year faded from view, replaced by an endless, interchangeable set of cable-cars, black runs and slalom poles. At night she dreamed about run layouts. On planes she fantasised about sleeping till noon. But in spite of the punishing pace, she never considered cutting back.

Motivation was easy to come by. It was right there in the stocky, skilful form of Heidi Laufen, twice World Champion, and the aerodynamic crouch of Louise Levier, her heir apparent. The commentators called them unbeatable.

Elizabeth knew better. She sweated, strained, pushed her way forward, eroding the lead. Bronze turned to silver, then to gold. In one punishing month she wiped out Louise's lead. Now there was only Heidi to chase. The two girls struggled for supremacy across Europe. Sometimes Heidi topped the table, then Elizabeth, then Heidi again.

Elizabeth found she suddenly wanted victory desperately. She was twenty years old, with nothing to show for her life. She didn't even have a degree, thanks to Tony's attitude. In the World Cup, her breeding and her bank account meant nothing. Talent was the only thing that counted. And she wanted to show she was worth something. She wanted to be the best.

Basically, Elizabeth admitted to herself, she wanted to be like Jack Taylor. She couldn't stand him, but she had to admire him. Hans forced her to watch tape after tape of Taylor's victories, pointing out the speed, the technique, the mastery.

Jack Taylor wasn't just poetry in motion. He was a symphony, an epic. He had blasted through the sport like an F-14 jet fighter. Jack might have come from nowhere, Elizabeth thought, but my God, the guy is ruthless on a pair of skis.

The Swiss, the Austrians, the Scandinavians, the French – none of them knew what had hit them. Over and over, the Stars and Stripes flew on the winner's podium.

'I cannot understand it,' the Swedish coach had shrugged. 'He is a freak. After all, there is no skiing in Texas.'

He's the best, but doesn't he know it, Elizabeth thought, annoyed. Jack bloody Taylor, with his magna cum laude from Harvard and his blatant sexuality. She'd heard the stories from some of the other girls, and tried to dismiss Taylor as a womaniser. What else could he be, with that Southern drawl like slow-pouring treacle, and that cruel, sexy mouth?

She thought about Jack Taylor a lot. It bugged her that she thought about him so much. Though she pretended not to care, his derision at Val d'Isère cut her to the quick. Elizabeth knew the American was a one-off, a once-in-a-generation kind of talent. She wanted his respect. She wanted his approval. The bastard could snub her all he liked, but she wanted him to rate her. As an equal.

When the women's and the men's events coincided, Jack Taylor turned up to the female event to cheer on Kim Ferrell and Holly Gideon, the US team. At those races, Elizabeth tried to squeeze a little more excellence from her performance. She could see Taylor watching her as she crouched forward, schussing over the finish lines. His handsome face was assessing, taking notes. But though she took three wins and a second in front of him, he never offered her a word of encouragement.

It became ever clearer that Elizabeth stood a chance, and the British media went nuts. The 'battle of the slopes' was the second favourite tabloid story, right behind the rumours that Prince Charles had a thing for Lady Diana Spencer.

Hans kept her away from the media, but that only made them chase her more.

'These people are fools,' he snorted, when he caught Elizabeth reading *The Times* at the airport. The headline 'Lightning Strikes' showed a glowing Elizabeth after a four-second slalom win at Val Gardena. 'They think you are good *last* year.'

He couldn't afford her to relax one millimetre. It was the final stage of the Cup, and things were too close to call.

'Ronnie Davis called the hotel. CBS wants the team to go on *Good Morning, America*,' Elizabeth told him, hopefully.

She wouldn't mind becoming well known in the States. Maybe it would help convince the FIS to let her do their marketing. Or be leverage to change Dad's mind about Dragon.

'The team, indeed! They want your ladyship, *nicht wahr*? Certainly not.'

Wolf snorted with disgust. 'We have only two more races, and you are just one point ahead of Fräulein Laufen. The only Americans you mix with will be Taylor and Kowalski.'

Elizabeth felt her heart skip a beat under her Jean Muir suit. 'What did you say?'

Boarding for first-class passengers was announced, and they stood up, picking up their hand-luggage. Wolf glanced at his protégée, a smartly dressed young woman, beautiful, vibrant, her hair flowing loosely about her shoulders, her elegant hand resting on a Gucci purse. Her forest-green eyes sparkled like snow in the sun.

'They are already at Kitzbühel for the slalom. Thursday they ski the Hahnenkamm.'

'We've got slalom Tuesday, downhill Wednesday.'

'*Ja*, and I have asked Kowalski if you can train with him Wednesday morning. He agreed.'

'And Jack Taylor?'

'Taylor always trains with Kowalski. Rick is the American number two,' Wolf reminded her. 'He will not alter his plans for you.'

Elizabeth handed her boarding card to the attendant, smiling.

'You are excited, *Liebchen*,' the old man teased. 'Just make sure you keep your eyes on the snow. Taylor is very good looking, no?'

'No.' Elizabeth sounded dismissive. 'Jack's the best in the world. *I'm* the best in the world. Who else would I ski with?'

'*Natürlich*,' Hans said, grinning.

The final slalom of the women's World Cup was a nail-biter. Girl after girl swooped off from the summit, planting their ski-poles, turning, planting again, control and speed in brilliant balance. Kitzbühel cheered the Austrians and Louise Levier, the Swiss now certain to take bronze. But it was Heidi and Elizabeth everybody was waiting for.

Elizabeth said a prayer at the starting gate and thrust forward. Three hours of practice, days of layout study, a week of videos, all down to these few minutes. Plant, turn. Stick, slice. The cheering crowd lining the run, deafening her with whistles and cowbells and ululating shrieks, urged her forwards. Out of the corners of her eyes she saw Union Jacks, even the Red Dragon flag of Wales. She ignored it all. There was nothing registering except the flagpoles and the snow. Concentrating furiously, her technique was perfect but she lost a little speed. Elizabeth shot through the finishing line one point five seconds behind her best time on this course. She led the field comfortably.

Hans slapped her on the shoulder and Elizabeth turned to the cameras to give her reaction. She kept it short. Nothing to do but wait for Heidi.

Kim Ferrell took fourth place for the US and Kate Cox came in eighth for Britain, a terrific result for her. Elizabeth congratulated her warmly.

Finally, to roars of approval from the Swiss in the crowd, Heidi Laufen was called to the start. Time seemed to stop for Elizabeth as she reached the first gate and twisted through it cleanly. Slicing, sticking and lunging, Heidi tore through the flagpoles. White plumes of snow sprayed up behind the edges of her skis. She wasn't as exact as Elizabeth, but she was quicker. With each gate Elizabeth felt her heart sink. She didn't need to look at the clock to know Heidi's pace; she could see it in her rhythm. Laufen was letting go and she was fast.

Heidi came bombing through the finish line over a second ahead.

Elizabeth could feel the eyes of her coach, her team and the press burning into her back as she walked over to shake the World Champion's hand. Now they were level. It would all depend on the downhill tomorrow – the legendary Hahnenkamm, the fastest, toughest, most dangerous run on earth.

At the side of the ropes, Jack Taylor, looking stunning in black jeans and a sweater, was standing with the US team. Elizabeth walked across and pumped Kim's hand. 'Nice racing.'

'You too,' the redhead said. 'Bad luck. Heidi was on top of her form, right then. Didn't you think so, Jack?'

Jack Taylor shrugged, looking straight at Elizabeth. His eyes flickered over her body, but their expression was unfathomable.

'You could have done better,' he said.

Elizabeth stiffened. She pulled up to her full height.

'And I will. Tomorrow.'

Wednesday morning, Elizabeth was up before her wake-up call. She'd tried to rest but she hadn't slept much. The thought that everything was riding on this afternoon had been too exciting for sleep. She only hoped that Heidi Laufen had been similarly affected.

Quickly, Elizabeth selected a training suit in scarlet Lycra and began to get dressed. Outside the windows of her hotel suite the massive mountain peaks were jagged silhouettes against the early-morning light. A telltale brightness in the sky let her know there'd been a fresh snowfall during the night. Adrenalin pumped through her. Today would be sudden death; she was challenging the world's best skier on the world's most dangerous course. It had a hospital purpose-built at the bottom, to cater to the dead and wounded the mountain regularly claimed; victims of the Mausfalle, the sheer drop you hit just after the starting gate, or the 180° Panorama turn, or the plummeting dive of the Steilhang . . .

Enough. Enough, Elizabeth told herself, selecting her training skis. Practise first.

It would be a great warm-up to the downhill, to show that son-of-a-bitch Jack Taylor just what she was made of.

Before she headed out the door, Elizabeth spritzed herself with Chanel No. 5 and slicked a dash of Elizabeth Arden over the sunblock on her lips.

Not only was she going to ski the pants off him, she was going to do it in style.

Rick Kowalski had arranged to meet her at the top of the Resterhöhe. Seven thousand feet above sea level, it was the highest ski area in Kitzbühel, guaranteeing no problems with the snow. This morning he needn't have worried, Elizabeth thought as she leaned back in the cable-car. The fresh fall in the night had blanketed the whole resort, and the peaks and valleys lay covered with a thick, unmarked blanket of soft white velvet. The forecast had been for clear skies, but she was sure there was more to come. Clouds were gathering darkly behind the mountains. She prayed no blizzard would delay the race.

The car clanked to a halt and Elizabeth stepped out, hefting her skis on to the flattened snow. She was ready for some serious training. They would be heading off-piste; apart from the Hahnenkamm there were no black runs at Kitzbühel hard enough for a world-class skier.

She looked around for Kowalski, but couldn't see him. Maybe he was out there wearing an ivory suit, or something. Elizabeth cupped her hands over her mouth and yelled.

'Rick?'

Suddenly, from behind her, a black-suited figure shot out of nowhere and sliced to a halt.

Elizabeth jumped out of her skin.

He raised dark goggles and regarded her steadily.

'Jesus Christ, Jack. You scared me,' Elizabeth said angrily. 'Where the hell did you come from? Where's Rick?'

'Good morning to you, too, ma'am,' Taylor replied. The Texan drawl was cold. 'Kowalski couldn't make it. He's in bed.'

'Really.' Elizabeth's nerves made her snappy. 'Too much *Glühwein* last night? I'd have thought even you Americans might give the partying a rest two days before your last downhill.'

Jack's eyes narrowed with anger. He paused, then said calmly, 'Actually, he has flu. He's in bed on doctor's orders, so he stands a chance of competing tomorrow.'

Elizabeth blushed. 'Oh, OK. I'm sorry.'

'He asked me to come train with you. Rick never breaks a commitment.'

'I said I was sorry.'

'And there's nothing Rick could teach you about partying, my lady. Not from what I hear.'

She bent down and locked her boots into their bindings, forcing back the reply. She was here to train, not to fight Jack Taylor.

'My name is Elizabeth, Jack. Are we going to ski, or do you prefer talking?'

Taylor studied her a moment, then lifted his stick and pointed off down the mountainside towards a dark pine forest.

'Brad found a route for me yesterday. It's got a sixty-five-degree sheer drop, a tough mogul run, some tree skiing, lots of powder on the straight.' He shrugged. 'Reasonably challenging.'

That meant white-knuckle terror, Elizabeth thought. A shiver of spine-chilling pleasure rushed through her.

'I'll want you to stick with me. There are crevasses and the new snow will have covered some of them. We'll be going close to a lot of mountain edges; concealed boulders, outcrops, stuff like that. Think you can handle it?'

'Hey. I do have a little snowcraft, Taylor.'

'You want to train with me? You *follow* me.' He was uncompromising. 'I'm not explaining to some English lord how I watched his daughter ski off the edge of a precipice.'

'I'm the best female in the world.'

'You're not as good as me,' Jack Taylor said flatly.

Enraged, Elizabeth glared at him, but Taylor held her gaze calmly, refusing to back down. He was resting his huge body on his ski-pole, dark brown eyes studying her impassively.

He was right and she knew it.

'You win.' Elizabeth swallowed her pride. 'I'll be right behind you. But this better give me a workout.'

'Hey, Princess,' Jack said, and now his look was sexual, flickering over the tight red Lycra, stripping, assessing, lingering on her breasts. 'You haven't been trained at all. After this, the Hahnenkamm's gonna look like a nursery slope.'

He pulled down his goggles and pushed off to the right, schussing swiftly down towards the forest. Elizabeth followed, gathering her body into a crouch. The snow glittered like crystal dust in the rosy dawn light, arching up behind her skis in a feathery spray. The air had the crisp, clean sparkle of high altitude. She gathered her body into an aerodynamic crouch, skis close together, picking up speed. Jack's tracks were deep tramlines on the virgin slope, their smooth, sharp angles displaying his skill like a signature. Thrusting harder, she caught up with him. His black-clad figure was aiming straight for the forest; he said nothing to her, was acting like she wasn't there. Angrily, Elizabeth skied closer, crowding him, until there were just a few inches between them. Taylor swung sharply left. Elizabeth followed. He immediately took a hard right. She matched him, inch for inch. Fighting. Challenging. Competing.

Without so much as a glance at her, Jack leaned forward into his crouch and disappeared. Gasping, Elizabeth found herself plunging down a sheer icy curve that had looked like an ordinary ridge a second ago. Instinctively she righted herself and hugged the gradient, while her stomach somersaulted.

You son-of-a-bitch! She was barrelling into the schuss now, beside him again, but Jack tilted away left, bringing his skis together. Why was he doing that? And then she saw it – two patches of dark shadow, bridging white ground barely two feet across. Shade like that could be covering a ravine, a crevasse. You would plunge down a hundred feet of solid ice to your death. Elizabeth broke into a cold sweat as she swung her body violently, making sure she was behind him, not beside. The broad muscles of Taylor's back, skiing without even a hint of tension, seemed to taunt her as he schussed coyly across the strip of solid ground. Elizabeth followed, dry mouthed with fear. Now she was across!

Her heart was hammering against her ribcage. Her palms were clammy under her gloves.

He wants me to beg him to ease off! she thought. Jack Taylor thinks I'll go crawling up to him, admitting I can't keep up with him! I'll die of a heart attack first, you bastard!

She settled into a racing position, chasing Taylor's handsome silhouette in front of her.

'So, how are you doing, honey?' Jack asked as she drew level. 'All warmed up?'

Warmed up? 'You said you've skied this before.'

'Yes, ma'am.' The Texan drawl was relaxed.

'So when does it start getting hard?' Elizabeth asked casually. Two could play that game.

Taylor looked across at Elizabeth, imagining that strong, sexy body curled up naked on the rug beside his chalet hearth. She was stunning. It was turning him on, watching her move. If only she wasn't such an arrogant bitch.

Jack didn't want to admit he was changing his mind about Lady Elizabeth Savage. He'd been determined to despise her – just a haughty British piece of ass who was squandering her talent, dissing her team-mates and turning on the charm for the cameras – but it was hard to dispute that her attitude had changed. And despite the fact that he'd rated her as competent but boring – a robot in rainbow Lycra – this year she'd been something else. Heidi Laufen had perfect technique, but Elizabeth Savage was inspirational. Fluid and fast. One of the best he'd ever seen.

This run would have beaten most guys he knew by now.

'Right about now,' Jack said, and shot over a mogul, executing a perfect helicopter spin. He plunged full-throttle towards the pine forest which now loomed up over the second ridge, shooting past a triangular sign with an exclamation mark on it. Elizabeth could only make out the word '*VERBOTEN*' as she raced forwards. Then she brought her knees together with a crash. Taylor had headed down the steepest, largest mogul field she'd ever seen. Her breath coming short, Elizabeth twisted, jumped, landed, twisted. Every muscle was shrieking for mercy. Jack Taylor was a big, strong man, and jumps he took easily Elizabeth strained to clear.

Panting for breath, she righted herself at the foot of the run. Taylor cut an S-bend between a boulder and a shadow patch, heading down the mountain. Elizabeth followed grimly as he made for a boulder, shot over it, and soared into a twenty-foot jump due south, landing cleanly and hurtling forwards.

I don't get it, Elizabeth thought as she flew into the air. Where's the break in the trees?

Jesus! Oh, Jesus! There isn't one! That maniac is heading straight into the forest!

She was going too fast to think. Jack shot into the trees and Elizabeth, terrified, shot after him, hugging his trail as close as she could. Suddenly the bright glitter of the mountainside disappeared, and she was swallowed up by green, scented gloom. Elizabeth was dimly aware of the fresh snow piled on the branches, the twigs and cones snapping under her skis. Instinct took over as she lunged, skied, and thrust around the trunks, ducking under branches, making the fastest, sharpest turns she'd ever done in her life. No slalom ever invented could match up to this, and you took the slalom slow, not at Warp Factor Nine! Elizabeth tried to beat back the rising panic. Follow Jack. He's got the trail. She kept her eyes on those wide shoulders, dodging rocks, bushes, branches. A crash at this speed would snap her legs like matchsticks, wrench a shoulder from its socket! Not only would she lose the World Cup, she might never ski again!

Then, blessedly, there was light. The trees thinned. She swerved right, left, right again and schussed out on to the clear snow.

Jack Taylor had pulled up a hundred yards in front of her, resting on his poles and nodding in admiration.

'Congratulations. That was some sharp skiing.'

Elizabeth sliced to a stop and ripped off her goggles. Scalding hot tears burst out of her eyes, cooling instantly against her flushed cheeks. She was sobbing, hyperventilating.

'You bastard, you absolute bastard! I hate you!' she spat at him.

'Hey, come on. You did fine—'

'Is that your idea of a joke, Jack Taylor? Your stupid macho games could have fucking killed me!'

'Honey, I wouldn't have taken you any place you couldn't handle. I've seen how you ski.' He smiled at her. 'That's why I insisted you follow me. I was going first, so if you stuck behind me you'd be fine.'

'Is that right.' She wiped the back of her hand across her eyes, furious with him, furious with herself for breaking down in front of him. Jack stretched out a hand towards her, but she was still seeing red. Angrily she shoved his arm away and pulled up her goggles.

'Elizabeth, I'm sorry. I—'

'Jack, do me a favour and get lost,' Elizabeth snarled, and thrust off violently, skiing away from him down the mountainside as fast as she could.

'Wait! Elizabeth, stop!'

Taylor's voice floated down towards her, but, still sobbing, Elizabeth ignored it. She had no idea where she was, but the lights of Kitzbühel in the valley below gave her some sense of direction. She would schuss to the next ski area and ride a lift back home. Get to the hotel, calm herself down before the Hahnenkamm.

Jack had stopped shouting, but she could hear the faint hiss of his skis some way behind. Glancing round, she saw him settle into a crouch, as though desperate to reach her. As he saw her look at him, Taylor shook one pole frantically. She ignored him. Now he could try catching up with *her*.

She was hugging the mountainside, following the steepest gradient down. Powder snow plumed around her. The world was returning to what she knew and loved – whiteness and silence – except for—

A faint rumbling sound like a growling stomach. Nervously, Elizabeth looked up. Not thunder! A blizzard was all she needed.

The sky was still cloudy, but calm. And yet there it was again. Louder this time. Out of the corner of one eye, Elizabeth saw a rocky outcrop quiver. A pile of snow loosened and dropped heavily on to the slope.

Elizabeth slowed in an S-bend, suddenly petrified. Her face drained of blood.

There was only one explanation for that sound.

Jack Taylor was bombing after her at a speed which suggested he'd already figured it out.

Oh, Christ! She didn't know where she was! Where this slope led! If it was a precipice, she was dead! Elizabeth turned to the right, back the way she'd come, and pushed off with all her strength. She could see Taylor do the same—

And then it came! A deep cracking sound, a slow boom of breaking rock, with the ground under her feet quivering like jelly, and small pebbles and twigs falling from the cliff-face behind her!

Avalanche!

Elizabeth's body flooded with adrenalin. She pointed her skis straight ahead, crouching as low as she could safely go. Skiing for her life. Racing the snow.

Jack was heading hard right, motioning for her to follow. He knew the danger, and he came after me anyway, she thought miserably. Jack had risked his life to try and save her, and now she'd probably got him killed.

Oh, God, I'm sorry, Jack, I'm so sorry . . .

Her eyes were blurry with tears of terror. Sobbing, gasping, she blinked them away. She had to be brave! If she lost control, she was history.

Abruptly Taylor's black-clad figure stopped and swung round, skiing towards her. Elizabeth schussed frantically forwards. My God, don't come any further this way! she thought desperately. But he was barrelling her way, the heavy body plunging forwards.

As he reached her, another huge rumble shook the mountainside. Elizabeth's head whipped round to see a vast, menacing wall of white, piled eighteen feet high, sliding steadily down the rock face above them, gathering speed and size with every foot. Mesmerised, she gazed at the tidal wave of snow, freezing like a rabbit caught in a car's headlights.

Jack Taylor's big hand jerked her back to reality.

'You shouldn't have come for me! Jack, I'm sorry,' Elizabeth gasped.

'Tell me later, OK, sugar? Let's go. This way,' Jack said shortly, and jetted off to the right. Elizabeth followed blindly.

'This slope leads to a cliff edge!' Taylor yelled, as they bombed down the mountain together. 'We need to get to the right! You have to outrun it! Point your skis straight down and just wing it, OK?'

'OK!' Elizabeth managed. She copied him, pointing her ski-tips straight downhill, leaning into the gradient, sticks tucked under the arms. Downhill racing was instinct and gravity. If you were thinking about it, you weren't going fast enough.

'Get to the forest!' Taylor shouted.

Elizabeth headed after him, rocketing towards another grove of trees. Her body was soaking in sweat, but it wasn't enough. Behind her the avalanche had hit the slope and was cruising forwards, its mammoth weight hissing as the air rushed past the towering snow-wall. She didn't need to look round to see how fast it was gaining – a black shadow loomed over the ground in front of her, silent as death.

Jack was nearly at the trees now. She had two hundred yards to go. To her left, the slope finished abruptly, dropping down into a rocky chasm a mile deep. The avalanche was closer, closer, gently nudging her towards the precipice. She wasn't going to make it. Desperately, Elizabeth pushed to the right, towards the trees at the edge of the cliff. Jack was standing three yards into the forest, his arms wrapped round a tree trunk. The forest could resist twenty foot of snow, but she couldn't! The breath sobbed in Elizabeth's throat as she saw snow spattering across her skis, was engulfed in the shadow of the avalanche. She'd failed by a few feet, she was going to die. Air shot out of her lungs as the snow hit her, freezing, heavy, and she waited to be swept into the void—

But something held her back. A hand, *Jack's* hand, his vast palm clamping her left wrist, strong fingers like a vice around it.

Elizabeth's body was flung forwards, her skis knocked off balance, right pole ripped from her grasp, but she didn't fall. Jack Taylor was holding on to her wrist with a mighty grip. Her arm burned agonisingly as it took the full weight of her body. She couldn't scream, because her mouth was muffled with snow. For a few horrible seconds, the avalanche trundled over her back, pressing her down into the slope. She thought she might pass out from the pain and terror, but bit her lip to keep herself conscious.

And then suddenly there was light, the weight bearing down on her slid away, and as she sucked air into her lungs the wave of snow teetered slightly and crashed slowly, unhurriedly, into the ravine.

Jack pulled her up, away from the cliff edge. Her shoulder socket screamed and she scrambled forwards with her legs. Taylor was holding on to a tree trunk with his left hand, his right hand clutching her. She could see every muscle in his arms rigid with the effort. He had been a human bridge, clutching her against the force of the snow.

Elizabeth flung herself into his arms.

'You didn't let go, you didn't let go!' She was crying, her whole body trembling against him. 'Jack, you saved my life!'

'We all make mistakes,' Jack Taylor said.

Then he tilted her face up to his, and kissed her, hard.

13

Jack bore down on her, kissing her frozen mouth open, the tip of his tongue tracing a fiery line across her bottom lip. One arm was circling her back, pulling her to him, and one was cupping her ass and sliding up and down her thigh. Elizabeth felt burning warmth rush through her icy flesh as his body warmed hers. His chest was rock hard, his strength incredible. Jack was sucking snow crystals from her mouth as he kissed her and Elizabeth found herself flooded with a different kind of heat, a wet rush of lust that curled like smoke in the pit of her stomach.

She'd never been with a man like this. All the suave, Eurotrash men she'd ever dated with their flowery compliments and sexual proficiency had never affected her like this man who was crushing her to him. Jack was handsome, brilliant and fearless. He was also a stubborn, ruthless bastard.

Elizabeth told herself to go slow, but her muscles were melting with longing. She felt weak against such raw male strength. Pleasure fluttered across her groin. Despite herself, she moaned softly at the back of her throat, pressing herself against him.

Taylor's hand immediately slid up over the tight, cold red Lycra of her skisuit, his huge paw brushing her breasts softly, teasing the tips of her nipples. Elizabeth gasped as a burst of heat exploded between her thighs. Glancing down, she saw the outline of his erection and her eyes widened. He was massive, not just long but thick, too. It frightened her a little.

What did you expect, with a man this size? Elizabeth asked herself, but then Jack moved forward to cover her, pressing her back against the tree roots. The rough bark prickled against her back, breaking the tension just long enough for Elizabeth to gather her thoughts.

You nearly died. You're not thinking straight. You can't sleep with Jack Taylor! You only just met him!

Firmly she pushed against his chest, shaking her head.

'Jack, no.'

He leaned back a fraction. 'What's wrong, sugar?'

'We can't do this.'

'We can do anything we want,' Taylor said. His brown eyes were full of hunger for her, glittering with desire. Elizabeth dropped her eyes. She couldn't look at him.

'You just saved my life, Jack. I – I'm not clear-headed. I don't even know

691

you!' She was stammering out explanations. 'And we have to get back to Kitzbühel! I've lost a ski-pole and I'm racing in three hours!'

Jack stared at her for a second, then sighed and stood up. He stood with his back to her and took a deep breath, trying to stamp out the fire blazing in his groin. Liz Savage wanted him. He could feel it in the hot flush of her skin, the tantalisingly erect nipples. His cock was so hard it ached. Jesus, how he wanted her. He wanted to nail her right there on the snow, peel that teasing Lycra off her and just fuck her brains out. Kiss her mouth off. Stroke her and lick her until she begged him to take her . . .

'Jack?' Elizabeth asked, scrambling to her feet.

'All right, Elizabeth. I'm not pushing you.'

'Thank you,' she said, hoping she didn't sound disappointed.

Taylor gestured to her boots. 'Fix your bindings and we'll get back.' He unhooked the ski-pole from her left wrist and handed her his own pair.

'I don't need these—'

'Take them,' Jack said.

She didn't argue.

When they reached the Pass Thurn skiing area, Ronnie Davis and the other British girls were standing by the gondola station, waiting for them.

Elizabeth glided to a halt and offered Taylor back his ski-poles. He hadn't said a single word to her all the way down.

'Right on time,' Ronnie said. 'We're going to head back to the hotel. So, Jack, how was she?'

'She was the best female skier I've even seen,' Jack said, without looking at her.

'Thanks for helping me practise,' Elizabeth said, blushing.

'My pleasure, ma'am,' Taylor replied softly. He nodded to the British team, turned, and schussed away down the mountainside.

'God, he's so gorgeous,' Janet sighed.

'That guy was made in heaven,' Kate added wistfully.

'I see you lost a pole, Liz. How was the training?' Ronnie asked.

Elizabeth's eyes were following Jack's tiny black figure as it plunged away to the south.

'Oh, pretty quiet,' she said.

When they got back to the hotel there was a telegram for Elizabeth. Tony wished her luck. The dry, restrained language was a message from another world. The Cup was so intense, so focused, that Elizabeth had almost forgotten about the real world below the mountain peaks. She was certain that her success this year would be enough for the FIS, but still . . . Dragon was the family company. Dragon was what she wanted. It was 1980 now; maybe she could change Tony's mind . . .

Just one more reason not to fail today. More pressure to perform.

Hans Wolf found her clutching the crumpled scrap of paper when he arrived in her room. He pulled it out of her grasp and tossed it on to the bed.

'Tony and Monica wrote.'

'So I see.' Wolf scowled. 'Today you do not need distractions.'

'My father will be so pleased if I win this,' Elizabeth told him.

'Child. You cannot control your father. Business is business, but skiing is life,' the old man told her, so seriously Elizabeth had to smile. 'Think about your company tomorrow, *Liebchen*. Today is for the mountain. Today is for *me*.'

'Oh, Hans, you've been so good to me,' Elizabeth said tearfully. 'What if I let you down? I screwed up yesterday.'

'The only way you let me down is if you do not try. Do your best. Not for me, for your father, even the gold. Just because you are a skier, and this is the greatest race in the world.'

The foot of the course was a zoo. Press, radio and TV crews from all over Europe were jostling for position, shouting out reports in ten different languages. Elizabeth waited with the others to hear her draw – it might be anywhere in the top fifteen numbers, the earlier the better. Heidi Laufen was drawn number three to thunderous applause from the Swiss in the crowd. Elizabeth was drawn number fourteen.

She shrugged elegantly to the BBC cameras, but she was very disappointed. Fourteenth versus third. A bad, bad position. A bad omen?

Looking graceful, polished and stunning in her signature rainbow suit, Elizabeth tried not to show her nerves. It was always bad before a race, but this time she had eels writhing in her stomach. A few hours ago she'd been close to death. She'd lost an easy slalom yesterday. Heidi Laufen was hitting perfect form.

Her parents were watching, Hans was watching, the world was watching . . .

'How's it going?'

Elizabeth jumped out of her skin.

'Jack, don't sneak up on me like that!'

'I wasn't sneaking, baby. You were miles away.'

Jack Taylor was wearing dark jeans, cowboy boots and a black windcheater with the Stars and Stripes embossed on the pocket. Goggles had been replaced by black Wayfarers. He looked just as impressive off skis as on.

The memory of his hands on her breasts sent a stab of wanting right through her. Under the sheer Lycra, her nipples tightened.

She saw Taylor watching them.

'It's cold, isn't it?' Elizabeth said quickly.

'No,' Jack said, giving her a lazy smile. The sun was blazing down on the slopes.

Elizabeth blushed and tried to cover herself. 'I got number fourteen,' she said quickly.

'I heard. But it don't matter.'

'What do you mean, it doesn't matter? I—'

'Forests, ravines, avalanches,' Jack said, cutting her off. 'Remember? This is a walk in the park.'

'For you.'

'For both of us,' Jack replied. His easy air was infuriating.

'Oh yeah?' Elizabeth snapped. 'That's just great, Jack. Anything else?'

'Yes, there is.' He touched the side of her waist, pressing her skin. 'You were lying up there, sugar. You do know me.'

An official marched up and tapped her on the elbow. 'You should go to the start gate now, my lady.'

'Elizabeth,' Jack said.

'What?'

He looked her right in the face. 'Just ski. Everything else is talk.'

Heidi Laufen made the run of her life. Jumping, schussing, hugging the treeline on the Stemmle stretch. It must have been perfect snow for her, Elizabeth thought jealously, as she heard the shrieks of joy, the football whistles, the ringing cowbells drifting up from below. The TV screen outside the start gate told its own story. Heidi made a textbook run. Dismayed, Elizabeth watched the spinning numbers freeze as she shot through the finish line. A new record. Position: first.

Waiting was eternity. Elizabeth took deep breaths, tried to stay calm. She studied the TV, watching the other top seeds, trying to get a feel for the course. Kim Ferrell came in second for the US. Then Louise Levier pushed her back to third. The Austrian and French champions were quick, too, but Heidi held firm at the head of the table, four seconds clear of Levier.

Then finally her number was called. Instructions, technique, layouts raced through her mind as she settled into her starting crouch, waiting for the bell. Trying to remember everything . . .

The countdown finished. Three, two, one . . .

And then, as Elizabeth thrust off down the mountain, Jack Taylor's voice drowned out the theory. *Just ski.*

The run fell away under her, a steep drop before the first two gates. Sharp swings, right, left – and now she was hitting the Mausfalle, sheer ice plummeting down, her stomach flipping over as she hit the hundred-and-fifty-foot jump. If she turned right she'd jet into the trees. Flying by pure instinct, Elizabeth skied straight ahead. She was going too fast for thought. She hit the Panorama turn like a bullet – 180° left – throwing herself into it with her whole body, dragging herself round. The run soared over a hill and she twisted rightwards, ready for the Steilhang – hard left, then down through the forest, reaching the Woodcutter's Path. Her head rattled inside her helmet, the sounds of the shrieking crowds deafening her. Now the Stemmle stretch – if you played safe here you'd slow right down. Elizabeth swung hard towards the net, hugging the line, going 140 km per hour. A crash at this speed could maim or kill, but she felt no fear. She was soaring. Off at the Alte Schneise – nearly over, but here you could drop precious seconds if you lost position. Elizabeth held her crouch rock solid, every muscle screaming as she rode the bumps – Larcheschuss, swerve right – a huge jump by the Hausberg! Elizabeth took it high and hard. Landing swiftly, poles tucked under her arms, she could see the finish – a racing crouch down the Zielschluss, she was almost prostrate now . . .

She fired past the finish line, heart ricocheting under her chest, and sliced to a clean halt.

Panting, Elizabeth tore off her helmet and spun round, as the press did, as

Louise did, as Heidi did, waiting for the announcement. She'd been fast. But how fast?

There was a second's silence as the dry Austrian tones announced the time.

Then pandemonium. Cameras flashing, reporters thrusting forwards, Hans fighting to get to her, and Elizabeth burst into tears.

She was twenty years old. She had just won the World Cup.

As she was swallowed up by TV cameras, Elizabeth caught sight of Jack Taylor, hanging back by the netting.

He nodded once, calmly. And then they both smiled.

14

Tony Savage stirred restlessly in his bed. The girl in front of him looked as pretty this morning as she had last night – slim, silky legs, large breasts, glossy hair the colour of candied chestnuts – but he felt no desire. He was done, and it was six a.m.

He slipped carefully out of bed. Camilla didn't stir; he didn't want her to spoil things by waking up and starting to talk. She was a great lay, but that braying voice annoyed him. Not to mention the whining she was likely to do with it.

Tony dressed quickly. He kept one eye speculatively on the fuzz between Camilla's legs, but his mind was already elsewhere. His research team were presenting today on slimming drugs. It was the holy grail of pharmaceuticals. The first firm to develop a safe slimming drug would own the biggest moneyspinner since aspirin. Conventional wisdom was that it couldn't be done, but Tony didn't believe that. And then there was Elizabeth. Her demands to work at Dragon were getting more insistent, and this time, she had some leverage. She was World Champion; famous. If she made a fuss, the press would notice it. Run stories. Embarrass him. Dredge up the past . . .

A quick burst of anger sizzled through him. Blackmail, it was blackmail. Liz wouldn't let it go. Standing there in Kitzbühel, a gold medal round her neck, defying him. Like Louise . . .

With an effort Tony pulled his mind away and fastened his cufflinks. Nothing for it, he'd have to fob her off. Maybe a taste of work would actually calm Elizabeth down. Switzerland had settled her, hadn't it? And there was Jack Taylor, a Texan, lots of money, Harvard. Apparently interested. He could do worse; Taylor was no duke, but then again, America was thousands of miles away. If he could pack DeFries's bastard off to the South, maybe he could forget about her. Those Southern men kept their women in line. Yes, maybe it would be expedient to keep Elizabeth sweet, for once.

Tony's elbow knocked a crystal champagne flute on to the ground. There was a dull thud on the thick carpet, but it was enough to wake Camilla. He sighed as she propped herself up sleepily, magnificent tits swaying slightly as she turned to accuse him.

'Darling, you're not leaving already! It's only, my God, it's only six.' The horsy Berkshire tones turned plaintive. 'You were going to leave without saying goodbye . . .'

'I didn't want to wake you,' Tony said coldly.

'When will I see you again?'

'I'm not sure. I'll call you today.'

'When?'

'When I can,' Tony said, and let himself out of the suite. He could shower and shave at the office; there was always a freshly pressed outfit ready for him there.

Downstairs in the lobby Tony settled the bill. 'Have breakfast delivered to my guest at half-seven.' He wanted her out of there, but there was no point in being too harsh. Breakfast was a neat way to say it.

'Very good, my lord.' The receptionist's face was as blank as a discreet British hotelier's could be.

'Send up some champagne and some flowers. Not roses.'

'Yes, m'lord. Any message?'

'No,' Tony said, passing over his gold Amex.

As he strode out to a waiting taxi, the clerk shook his head in admiration. No false names, separate suites or embarrassment for Caerhaven. You had to give it to his lordship, he was a cool bastard. Flowers and champagne; he wondered lasciviously just how the latest bit of fluff had earned them.

'Where to, guv?'

Tony relaxed slightly as the cab drew away from the Ritz and headed down Piccadilly. At this time in the morning traffic was sparse; they should be on the South Bank in less than ten minutes. He made a mental note to ring Camilla before lunch and finish with her. A pair of diamond earrings, a line about feeling guilt towards Monica, that should do it. He was bored of her; she was clingy and tiresome when she wasn't performing. And good as she was, he'd had better. She wouldn't cut up rough if she knew what was good for her. Her father worked for one of his subsidiaries, her brother for another. Anyway, Camilla was pliant and nervy, another reason he'd picked her.

Tony had other business this morning. First, a quick call to Los Angeles, to check in with Jax, out on the West Coast. Get the vibe on New York; the stock was jittery on the Street and he wanted to know why. Also, to see if their latest crop of bright boys had come up with anything in the initial brainstorming period.

The Dragon building loomed massive in the pre-dawn twilight. Tony paid the cab and stepped into the deserted place, nodding at the security guard's obsequious greeting. He ordered coffee, toast, marmalade and crisp bacon sent up from the kitchen and then took the executive elevator to his private office. It was good to get in early; it added to his intoxicating sense of control. Today the *frisson* of power was particularly enjoyable. He felt lustful. Wondered about Camilla's replacement. Whoever she might be.

Nina walked in to work feeling nervous. She knew she wasn't alone there: every man of the new Dragon intake had submitted their reports on Friday. Jax would have leafed through them this weekend and today they got their results. Everyone was on a two-monther, so unless you got it renewed today, it was a case of clear your desk and sayonara.

She was wearing a short dress with a cropped jacket, cream cotton with navy piping, and navy pumps. She'd taken extra care this morning with her make-up, her dark hair and eyes set off with subtle shades, charcoal around the eyes, matt plum lipstick and tinted moisturiser to smooth out the skin. Her thick, dark hair had been cut and curled under at the edges in a sleek pageboy. If she was going to get fired, it would help her out to look good. She'd be stronger about it.

Nina walked into her tiny office. Her desk was almost totally clear; she'd done that Friday night. There couldn't be anything worse than standing there, maybe crying, ladling your personal effects into a black plastic bag while the secretaries watched. This way, if Jax handed her her pink slip, she could just ride the elevator down to the lobby and walk smartly out the door.

Simon and Tom were laughing together in Tom's office. She could hear the thuds as the boys lobbed paper at Tom's basketball hoop; obviously they had a bit more confidence than she did.

It's not the project, Nina reminded herself. 'Customised Response' was good, computerisation was her bag, she knew it would be effective. It was the fact that she'd exceeded her authority. Fired Tracy Jones last Friday, in public, forcing Gary Bellman to back her up. Gary Bellman, a division chief! Gary had been furious and she knew Jax would have seen what she'd done. Women in Dragon were expected to keep their heads down. Already, they'd see her as a troublemaker.

Eventually, there came the rattle of the mailcart from the corridor. Stopping at Tom's office. She heard muffled speech, then whoops of glee. New contracts for those two, then.

There was the knock on her own door. Heart hammering, Nina pulled it open to be faced with Abdul. He was handing her a small, thin envelope; didn't look like a contract.

'Is this all? You're sure?' Maybe she'd been expecting it but her heart plunged.

'Yes, ma'am. Sorry.'

Great, now the mailboy's feeling sorry for me, Nina thought dully. It was a memo envelope and she ripped it open. From Jax himself. 'Nina, please come to this office at ten a.m. sharp.'

Would Dolan take her back? God, why couldn't she have just put up with it? Now she was not only getting the can, she was going to get carpeted first. Wonderful. Simon and Tom must have realised by her silence what the score was, but they weren't exactly hurrying in to comfort her. That was business here: failure was regarded as an infectious disease.

Sighing, she looked at her watch. Best get it over with. Nina picked up her bag and closed the office door behind her, heading for the elevator bank.

Jax's secretary looked at Nina gleefully. She must have heard about the Tracy thing too.

She recognised Jack Fletcher, new at Accounts, as he stormed out of the office, his face white. Clearly, another candidate for the black plastic binliner and the cab home.

The secretary buzzed her boss. 'I have Nina Roth for you.' She listened a second, then, 'You can go in, Ms Roth,' like butter wouldn't melt.

Actually Nina was grateful for the hostility. No danger of dissolving into tears when that was their attitude; pity would have been a lot worse. She squared her shoulders under the cream cotton and marched into Jax's office.

The boss was sitting behind a heavy oak desk, his room decorated in clubby burgundy leather and dark woods. It was so traditional and masculine Nina almost expected to smell cigars.

Jax waved her to a seat. He had a file open in front of him; her project. 'This is good work,' he said.

Nina was so shocked she didn't say a word.

'Precise and focused,' Jax went on, and she carefully wiped the astonishment off her face. 'You didn't try anything too flashy, but this could save us a good lot of overhead. It's similar to what you did at Dolan, but that's OK. This isn't the movies, you don't get Oscars for creativity. We can use it.'

'Thank you, sir,' Nina said.

Jax looked the girl over appreciatively. A cool customer, this kid. She must have figured she was getting fired, but look at her. All poise and calm. A real beauty, too, in that understated way, dark hair, sharp cheekbones, huge black eyes. You couldn't tell what she was thinking, with that alabaster mask up all the time. And no matter how she dressed, she couldn't hide those curves. He felt desire ripple through him, mixed with annoyance. It would have been great to have her stay here. Under his authority.

'You fired your secretary Friday.'

'Yes, sir.' Nina's hopes sank again.

'You had no authority to dismiss another member of staff. Tracy Jones reported to Mrs Harris in Support Staff, even if she was assigned to you. Discipline is undertaken by the relevant department head and Personnel. Mr Bellman's office was furious.'

'But she defied me openly.'

'So you fired her, just like that?'

Nina squirmed. 'No, of course not. It was the end of a long line of incidents.'

'I see.' Jax's voice was mercilessly cold. 'So you had previously discussed this problem with – which one of Ms Jones's supervisors?'

'I didn't.' Now, it sounded impulsive and childish. Nina couldn't help herself, she blushed a rich red. 'I guess I thought I could handle it myself. I thought I had to, as a—'

'As a what?' Jax demanded.

Nina couldn't bring herself to come right out and say, 'as a woman'. She knew Jax knew exactly what she meant.

'Well. Your action was certainly decisive, Nina, but it was way out of line. Next time, contact somebody appropriate.'

Next time? It sank in: she wasn't getting fired. She felt almost light-headed with relief.

'Oh, yes, sir. I'll contact Mr Bellman's office right away—'

'It won't be Mr Bellman,' Jax said.

'I'm sorry, I don't understand.'

'It'll be Mr Keith Sweeney. In London.'

'London?' Nina gasped, startled out of her composure. 'I'm being posted to London?'

'That's right. The earl saw your report and requested you personally.' Jax leaned forward. 'That's not a problem, Nina, is it? You don't have any family here, or property? Nothing you can't leave behind?'

'No.' Nina bit her lips to stop a stupid grin from spreading right across her face. 'Nothing at all.'

'Good. The firm will pay rent on your apartment while you're away. You'd better take the rest of the day off to pack.'

'When am I leaving?'

'Tomorrow morning. Nine thirty out of JFK.' Jax allowed himself a small smile at the girl's shocked face. 'This is Dragon Chemical, Nina, we move fast here.'

Elizabeth smiled and bowed for the millionth time that evening. If her calves and quads were supple and limber, the muscles in her cheeks were definitely starting to ache. At least they'd cleared out the photographers, finally, and now the athletes present were helping themselves to champagne, starting to loosen up, to celebrate.

It was the US team's victory ball. Schloss Lebenberg, the modernised castle that was their team's hotel, had been taken over. Everywhere from the casino to the pool was draped with vast Stars and Stripes and blow-up photos of the team. Jack Taylor had insisted on it; the most he would do solo was pose with the medal for the networks. The States were trumpeting their triumph from the rooftops, as usual, Elizabeth thought, amused. One individual gold, and already the TV stations, sports people, even food chains were begging to throw sponsorship at them. The British camp had its feet on the ground. After all, the Alpine nations were still skiing them off the snow in the team events.

Still, it was fun, to come out and party. She'd almost forgotten how to do it. Elizabeth's dark blonde hair hung loosely down her back; her dress was a gorgeous, slim column of white silk and gold thread, spiralling into a loose fishtail. She danced the first stately waltz with Hans Wolf, to huge cheers, then whirled gracefully round with Ronnie Davis, Brad Hinds, Pete, Sam and Rick. Everywhere she went people murmured appreciatively, pumped her hand, asked for her autograph. Elizabeth told herself she was having a good time. She wasn't going to be put out just because a certain person hadn't come to find her. After the joint photocall, Jack Taylor had disappeared. Probably with some groupie.

I'm not disappointed, I'm the World Champion, Elizabeth thought fiercely. Who does he think he is, anyway? Arrogant bastard!

She reached for another flute of champagne and then stiffened. Someone was resting their hand on the tight curve of her back. Angrily Elizabeth whipped around to be confronted by Jack, his tall frame bang up against her. His white shirt was unbuttoned at the top, displaying a tanned chest and just a smattering of hair. He looked relaxed.

'Congratulations,' Jack said softly.

'And to you.' She was stiff with him.

'You been looking for me?' Jack asked. He reached down and made to brush some hair away from her cheek but Elizabeth pulled back sharply. God! He thinks he's God's gift, the infuriating jerk! But Jack did look wonderful, the formal dark cloth picking out his eyes, the confidence, the aggression. Stuff had already passed between them that couldn't be taken back. Even if she had skied away down that mountain, Elizabeth knew, she'd lain under him, responded to him. Her nipples had stiffened under his hands, her body had flooded with heat for him. He knew it. She knew it.

'And why would I be doing that?' Elizabeth snapped.

Jack laughed. 'Thought you might like to dance.'

'I've done nothing but dance.'

'With me,' Taylor insisted.

'Well, I've had to make do with the lesser gentlemen that were on offer,' Elizabeth answered icily.

They were standing close to the dance floor. Skiers, their coaches and families were whirling around merrily and clumsily to 'She Wore a Yellow Ribbon'.

'Come on.' Taylor held out one large hand for Elizabeth's tiny one. He was looking her right in the face with insistent, come-to-bed eyes. She felt a new flood of lust, no doubt about it. Strong arms, he had. Elizabeth badly wanted to be held by them. Pinned down again, made love to. The certainty that Jack would be great in bed mingled with the certainty that he'd done this to loads of women before, and that they'd all been eager to comply.

Her bodice was reinforced satin. Her hardening nipples would not betray her this time. He owed her an apology. Right now he's acting like he's got some *right* to me, Elizabeth thought crossly.

'I'm sorry. I'm feeling a little tired.'

Jack let his hand drop, annoyed. 'Please, girl. Stop playing games.'

'*Excuse* me?' Elizabeth said, coldly.

Jack bristled. This wasn't going the way he'd planned it at all. So he'd had a few drinks before coming to find her, so what? He'd noticed her casing the crowd. Certainly she was looking for him. They could dance, sip a little champagne together, go upstairs. Women, he hated it when they got coy.

'I booked a private suite here especially,' he said. 'There's no point, Elizabeth, I know how you feel.'

A private suite? He was planning on hauling me into bed? Elizabeth's brows knitted together.

'Clearly you've got no idea how I feel, Mr Taylor.' She drew herself up, took a step back from him. 'I wouldn't place too much emphasis on what happened earlier. It was a near-death experience, I wasn't thinking.'

'Yeah. I liked that,' Jack said.

They were interrupted by a waiter heading towards them with a salver. On it was a thin yellow envelope: a telegram.

'Excuse me, my lady, but it's a message from your father.'

'Thank you.'

Jack stood back, seething with irritation, as Elizabeth ripped it open. She read the message quickly, then looked up at him.

'I'm afraid I have to say goodbye. I've got to get back to the hotel. Dad wants me to come home tomorrow morning: he's going to give me a job at Dragon,' Elizabeth said triumphantly.

Jack read the exhilaration in her tone. Was there something else there? Regret? Hey, clutching at straws now, champ, he chided himself. He wanted to kick something. He was angry. Frustrated.

With an effort he made her a little bow. 'Then allow me to escort you home.'

'Thank you, I can manage.'

'I insist.' Jack took Elizabeth's elbow and steered her towards the cloakroom. Normally, when a girl got an attitude he lost interest, but right now he was dreaming up excuses to be in London.

Jack Taylor looked down at Lady Elizabeth Savage, walking stiffly at his side, refusing to look at him. Maybe she'd blown him off tonight, but only tonight. He had her down as unfinished business. He'd never lost a battle of wills with a woman, and he wasn't gonna start now.

15

Nina looked round her new apartment and smiled. Two bedrooms, a tiled bathroom and neat, fitted kitchen, in a tree-lined Camden street. She had selected it from a list of company-approved flats, as the English called them, and eighty per cent of the rent would be coming out of her overseas living allowance. Then there was the displacement bonus, the relocation expenses scheme and her rise for signing the new contract. Dragon had locked her up for five years, but they were paying handsomely for the privilege. She'd never seen anything like this in her life. Tom and Simon and her old colleagues back in New York were probably used to it, but after years of walk-ups, living over stores and in rank motels, Delancey Street was a palace.

On the plane she had done the sums in her head. She was going to be very comfortable; the allowances, the rise, and the strength of the dollar would see to that. Britain had just emerged from years of socialist government, the country was in a mess, and the austerity measures employed by the new Prime Minister had plunged it into deep recession. Inflation was still high, but she was being paid abroad. Her dollars would go even further. She'd winced when she paid the bill on her new wardrobe – dark blue suits, smart heels, severe dresses and jackets in pinstripes, burgundy, black and chocolate brown – but then realised that it would barely dent her new monthly cheque.

The weather outside was gloomy – grey skies and threatening rain. Nina could not have cared less. Camden was funky, full of musicians, long-haired students, stylish mod artists blasting the Jam. And Britain was full of opportunity. Nothing like the Queen-and-cucumber-sandwiches image back home – a woman could even be Prime Minister here. A woman President seemed about as likely as a man giving birth. Clive Sinclair had launched the ZX-81, a tiny home computer that played games and ran programmes off tape recorders. It was a big craze. They were wired here, they were going places. London was the city both of punk and princesses – Lady Di souvenirs from the summer's big royal wedding adorned every market stall – and the City was the financial centre of Europe.

She'd had three days to settle in. Today was the first at work. Nina felt a rush of nerves, but they were swamped in her bolting excitement. Dragon HQ, after all, was not in Park Avenue, it was right here, south of the River Thames. She was going to work in the heart of the company, directly for the earl. Tony Savage, the Robber Baron, had ordered this posting personally.

Nina picked up her briefcase and set off for the Tube. Even London's subway system beat New York: tickets and automated gates, no fumbling about with rolls of quarters and filthy tokens. A fast train would take her practically to her office door. She was over an hour early, and she couldn't wait. New decade, new city, new job. Maybe she was finally getting somewhere.

'Good morning, my lady.'

Elizabeth beamed at the receptionist as she handed over her security pass and a sheaf of company recruitment forms. They looked so official. Everything was great, even the wet, crowded streets full of businessmen barging past her, even the grey ugliness of the Dragon tower. She was used to being stopped and asked for an autograph, but in the City, nobody gave her a second glance. That was great too. They were all serious people, seriously busy. Doing real work. She had been trying to gain admittance to this world for ever.

'Mr Sweeney is the head of Personnel, and he asked if you could fill these in today.'

'Of course, thanks,' Elizabeth said.

'New Products Division is on the ninth floor, just take the lift to your left.'

Elizabeth nodded and joined a crowd of men in dark suits. They immediately parted and let her stand at the front. When the lift arrived, everybody waited until she had stepped in.

'What floor, Lady Elizabeth?' a grey-haired executive asked politely.

Elizabeth brushed back her glossy hair and told him, returning everybody's beaming smiles. Of course they all knew who she was, she was famous. Everyone was going out of their way to be nice and welcoming. She felt super-confident. Dad was wrong, she was going to fit in here just fine.

'Initial tests look promising.' Tony grinned, seeing the flash of greed lighting up Frank Staunton's eyes. 'Appetite suppressant, amphetamine base.'

'Could be big,' Staunton agreed.

Fifty-five, Frank Staunton was thin and wiry, nicknamed the Terrier by his subordinates when his back was turned. He went after results like a dog after a rat, and he displayed utter loyalty to Savage, his master. Frank Staunton had run New Products for ten years, ever since Tony poached him from Glaxo. Most of his pay was stock options, so that Dragon's success was his success. Frank loved money. Self-interest made him reliable.

Tony knew Frank would never leave. The carrot had been perfectly effective, and he was also keeping the stick in reserve. Photos of Frank in drag at clubs like Heaven; arms round a fourteen-year-old cherub on Hampstead Heath; getting his cock sucked in a notorious gents' lavatory outside Waterloo Station. Not a portfolio he'd want flashed around the Travellers' Club, or the Carlton. Or mailed to his wife. Tony had never had occasion to refer to them, but the thought made him relaxed. Frank, like all the big Dragon players, had a weakness. Whereas Tony had nothing but strengths.

Frank was discussing the prospects for the new slimming drug they were developing. If toxicity and addictive problems could be ironed out, they were looking at a whole new level of power and wealth. One tiny tablet for doctors to prescribe, and the stock would be on automatic pilot to the moon.

'Your drones need to concentrate on this.'

Frank nodded. 'Including her young ladyship?'

Tony did not return the grin. He hadn't forgotten that Elizabeth was coming in today. He had to find her something to do, something to keep her quiet. The necessity ached in him like a rotten tooth; even though it was temporary, it felt too much like a victory for her. Louise's bastard, forcing her way into the heart of his kingdom. He grunted.

'And we have some others new in this morning.' The Terrier sensed his master's blackening mood and changed the subject fast. 'Joe Walsh, an analyst. Hotshot from Morgan Grenfell. Lionel White, a systems kid. The New Yorker.'

'Nina Roth.' Tony leaned forward, animated. 'I forgot, she starts today.'

'She's working in the same area as Lady Elizabeth.'

Tony didn't listen. His pulse quickened as he flashed on the girl from Brooklyn, with her strong accent and dark, grave beauty. Intelligence and drive combined with great tits, a great ass and a handspan waist. Very different from his usual blonde bimbos, she was sexy, but a scrapper. Dimly he recalled some story about her firing her secretary when she was still a brand-new rookie. And she'd known who he was. Nina was different, very different.

Beneath his sober bespoke trousers Tony felt his cock stir. Since Camilla Browning had got her marching orders he had only had Monica and one high-class hooker. He hated having to pay for it; mistresses were the better bet. His memories of the Roth girl sharpened into focus. She'd come up from the street, fast, still only twenty-one years old.

It occurred to him that was Elizabeth's age. Fucking Nina would be like fucking one of her schoolfriends. That thought sharpened the twitch between his legs into a real hard-on.

'Uh-huh.' He was casual. 'I'll take the first meeting with you. I'm going to be working with some of them myself.'

'Then you'd better come with me.'

Nina was shown into Frank Staunton's office, where ten other people were waiting: nine men and a girl. Two of the men were in their early twenties, looking expectant. New hires like herself. The girl was probably a secretary. She was wearing a pretty little dress in a Liberty print, and fashionable high heels, together with bracelets and earrings. Nina smiled at them all and began to introduce herself, but she kept one eye on the girl. There was something familiar about her, but she couldn't place her. Was she a secretary? She must be. And yet she had a soft, rich look about her, a polish. The hands were manicured, the eyebrows beautifully plucked, and now she was a little closer, the bracelets were real, gold studded with diamonds. Plus, she was sitting on a chair like the executives. Nina felt confused, more so when she caught a breath of expensive scent. Long, shiny hair worn loose, not even tied back for the office. Very beautiful, slim and delicate. Who's the bim? she thought. Sleeping with somebody?

The men were all smiling at the girl. There was a nervous deference in their body language. Nina frowned. She *was* sleeping with somebody important. Like Honor Feathers at Dolan, a talentless twenty-five-year-old piece of ass who was the managing director's regular date. Honor had gotten promotions and raises so regularly you could set your watch by them, and all the boys had been terrified of her, because she told tales out of school and got her enemies fired. Nina had disliked Honor intensely. Women like that made it harder for all other women. She had more respect for whores – at least they were open about what they were doing. This beautiful rich chick set her teeth on edge.

Elizabeth glanced up as Nina entered the room. A dark-haired, voluptuous woman, very young, wearing a tailored black suit, flat shoes and a steel watch. Immediately she blushed. The men's quick glances of approval told her that this was the right look, this girl was wearing the right clothes. She felt embarrassed. Now the woman was shaking hands, briskly and impersonally. The others greeted her as one of them. No joking or banter, they were talking business right off the bat.

The girl came closer. Elizabeth heard an American accent. And then, she glanced right at Elizabeth and gave her an unmistakable look of icy derision.

Elizabeth bridled. So she'd got the wardrobe wrong, so what? This girl looked her own age but *she'd* clearly been working for years. She hadn't had to blackmail her way into an office. Dad's company had hired her and given her a real chance. She's got no business looking at me that way!

There was only one empty chair, right at the front, by Elizabeth. Nina slid into it and sighed inwardly. There was no getting away with it. She offered her neighbour her hand.

'Nina Roth. Just over from Manhattan. I cut my teeth with Dolan for a couple of years.'

The blonde showed no sign of recognising the name. Nina was shocked. Dolan was a big player, hadn't the cutie here even heard of them?

'I'm Elizabeth. I – well, this is my first job.'

The accent was plummy and patrician, accompanied by a little flick of the hair. The girlish gesture was out of place. What the fuck was she doing in New Products? It was a vital division!

'Oh. And what are you gonna be doing?' Nina asked politely.

'I'm not sure.' Breathy upper-class voice was accompanied with rounded green eyes. 'I expect they're finding something for me to do.'

Nina was dumbstruck. She looked down at her lap in case anybody saw how pissed off she was. Finding something for her to do!

'Elizabeth who?'

Elizabeth heard the hostility and bridled. It had been a long time since anyone had shown her contempt.

'Lady Elizabeth Savage,' she said coolly.

Nina looked at her sharply. Of course. Lady Elizabeth, the Brit skier, she'd seen her on CNN getting her medal with Jack Taylor. So, she wasn't a girlfriend, she was a *daughter*. Christ, she was just playing around on Daddy's patch. She hadn't even heard of Dolan, and here she was. No messing around with experience or education for the boss's kid.

Nina knew she should be sucking up, like all the men, but she couldn't do it. The thought of her own struggles boiled up in her like acid.

'And I'm *Ms* Nina Roth.' The sarcasm was unmistakable. 'You can call me Nina.'

One of the younger men behind Elizabeth sniggered, then clamped a hand across his mouth. Elizabeth blushed a rich red. Bitch! Who did the Yank think she was? She spun round to fire something back but at that moment the door swung open and Frank Staunton walked in. Followed by her father.

'London. Y'all have to be kidding.'

Jack reached down and patted Queen of Arabia on her sleek white neck. It was still cool enough in the early morning, but the gallop around his Texas farm had left him sweating and sore. Pop looked comfortable enough, but he lived in the saddle. Plus, he'd set Jack up on this fine, half-tamed mare, a huge beast, gorgeous but hard to control. Like Elizabeth.

'No. I'm used to Europe from the circuit.'

That was plausible. He might buy that.

John Taylor, Sr, waved a hand at the vista before them, the green lawns kept lush by sprinklers, the palm trees, gaudy flowers and rows of neat stables. Jack had loved the stud farm since he was knee high.

'But we keep the horses here. Main office, here. Major hotels. London's just an outpost, boy.' The sharp blue eyes twinkled. 'You're hidin' something.'

Jack shook his head and squeezed his knees round the mare's flank, to still her. 'I think we're wasting opportunities over there. Too many Brit and Irish stables need good studs, we're ignoring that market. Waiting for them to come to us. Plus, there are horses we never see. Meets we don't go to.'

'Y'all only have a few months off,' John said shrewdly.

'Exactly.' Jack pounced. 'Not enough time to do anything major here, but I can see if we're missing anything in London.'

'OK, if that's how you wanna spend Christmas.' His father snorted. 'This ain't about a girl, son? You got em' linin' up in Dallas! You didn't used to chase any pussy halfway round the world.'

Jack almost blushed. 'C'mon, you know me. No girl's worth making a fuss over.'

'I know you.' John spurred his stallion round to face the woods, preparing for another run. 'That's the problem, son.'

Tony listened with one ear as Frank ran through the new protocols. Most of the men in this room knew exactly what they had to do. The new kids were thrown in at the deep end.

He was watching the men take notes. Joe Walsh knew the market – he would be ferreting out info on their competitors, finding out what Glaxo, ICI and SmithKline had in the pipeline. Lionel White was already sketching computer codes for a modelling system, seeing how the numbers would affect them.

Elizabeth was writing it all down, laboriously, occasionally looking up at him and catching his frown. She seemed uncomfortable, out of her depth.

He bit back a smile; her defiant streak would mean trouble unless he found her some pretence of a role.

Nina Roth sat next to her. He liked what he saw. She wasn't writing, she was drinking it all in. Leaning forwards, straining at the leash like a bloodhound, her thick, raven hair fell heavily round her high cheekbones, the young, pale skin dusted with excited pink. Under that sombre suit her body was magnificent. The breasts looked heavy, but still firm with youth. Her ankles and calves turned beautifully, her ass flared out from a tiny waist. Unlike his boyish, muscular daughter, Nina was womanly, all curves. A go-getter. Nothing ladylike about her. His imagination stripped her slowly, so she was sitting there naked. He knew she was aware of him, nervous in his presence. Her eyes kept sliding towards him, and if he caught her looking, she blushed and glanced back at Frank.

The earl was good at body language. Elizabeth sat stiffly next to Nina. For her part, Nina's eyes never even flickered towards Elizabeth's busy pad; the gesture was contemptuous, like, *I'll never need notes.*

Nina didn't know how he felt about Elizabeth. If she pissed off the chairman's daughter, she was taking a big risk. He wasn't used to females who did that.

Tony smiled. He'd made it a rule not to mess his own doorstep, but none of the pretty, blonde and bland girls stuffing Personnel or PR had ever really excited him. Not like the curvy, prickly little Brooklyn smartass.

His hard-on was refusing to go away. Rules were made to be broken.

16

Elizabeth leaned over and pressed the button on her treadmill, pushing it up to maximum. It was already tilting at an angle, simulating uphill running. The responsive growl from the machinery blasted her ears; her space was by far the loudest in the Chelsea gym.

Several flabby ladies-who-lunch looked over, annoyed. Elizabeth was drowning out their new Sony Walkmans as they pedalled sedately on stationary bikes or trod slowly up a Stairmaster. Elizabeth was aware of them dimly, like she was clocking the admiring stares from the men's weights room next door, although she couldn't care less. Nothing mattered but the workout.

Her strong body was clothed in the bare minimum. Hi-tech sneakers, Lycra cycling shorts and a leotard in icing-sugar pastels. Blonde hair swept back and up in a raised ponytail, to keep it out of her eyes. The heart-rate monitor was flashing, but she didn't have time to look down. Sweat dewed her body, her fringe was plastered to her forehead. Arms raised for maximum motion. Balls of the feet pushing off the rubber with every pulse. Her heart beating like a roadside drill, Elizabeth Savage lost herself in vicious, punishing speed. She'd already done the weights and the crunches, training every major muscle group in the upper body. Now the endurance work.

In under an hour she'd be reporting to that utter bitch, Nina Roth. This was a pleasure in comparison.

The thought of Nina drove Elizabeth into a fury, feet flying up the mechanical hill. They called her the Brooklyn Bomber in the office, the men, almost admiringly. She still hadn't worked out what Nina did but she sure was good at it. Phone glued to her fucking ear, barking orders and tapping out computer programs and talking science gobbledygook Elizabeth couldn't work out. Never losing an opportunity to put Elizabeth down.

Dad had given her the job she begged for. Advertising on New Products. But whatever she suggested to Nina, the cow lost no time in vetoing. It was so unfair: Jake and Richard and Dino, the other advertising guys, all loved her ideas, but Nina stopped her work from getting anywhere.

Anger burned in her face as bright as exertion. Bitch! Nina had a chance to learn; Elizabeth never would. And Nina was Daddy's bright-eyed little girl. She worked directly for him, she was his right-hand girl on the slimming drug thing. Elizabeth hated the way she smarmed up to Tony. Those two deserved each other.

She leaned forwards to increase resistance, throwing herself into the final burst. Elizabeth needed her fitness. While she was struggling at Dragon, Heidi Laufen was practising in the Alps.

Tony Savage stepped out of his car and paused while his chauffeur handed over his briefcase. Breakfast at the Connaught had been light: coffee, bacon and toast for him, enough to stave off hunger without dulling his senses. Not that there had been much danger of that. Sir Leo York, his companion, gorged himself on eggs, kippers and pastries, with a bottle of Krug. Leo called it a champagne breakfast to celebrate the deal. Tony called it a surefire sign of a lush.

He had been the one doing the celebrating. Disposing of Idun Cosmetics had completed his firesale of Loki Medicine. Leo overpaid. Now Tony was only left with the key labs division. The disposal of the rest covered his original payment. It was like getting a company for free, plus twelve million cash as a bonus.

Tony's blood sang as he walked into the building. He checked his Tag Heuer sports watch. Ten to eight.

In the express elevator Tony went over his plans for the day. Talk to New York and Sydney. Interview with the *FT* at lunch. Strategic planning in the afternoon. Tory donors do at the Opera House tonight.

He was pumped up, he wanted to celebrate.

Almost without thinking Lord Caerhaven unlocked his office, went straight to his phone and dialled the extension for Nina Roth.

Nina glanced at the scrolling text on her computer screen. The glass reflected the view behind her, the wide Thames glittering in the chill winter sun, commuter traffic streaming across Westminster Bridge, the Houses of Parliament grey and forbidding in the background. But it had been weeks since she'd noticed the view.

The earl had assigned her to his own task force. She supervised Lionel's computer modelling and found out which companies Joe should be investigating. That meant research, and lots of it. She had to find out who their most likely competitors were, and how far their slimming projects had come; what the distribution impact would be; and how it might affect their antitrust status. Nina gathered facts all day.

Because she was Tony's direct inferior, the boys at Dragon fell over themselves to help her. It was the total opposite of New York. She felt she was finally making inroads. The world drug market was coming into sharper focus, like a city emerging from a blanket fog.

If only she didn't have to waste her time with that stuck-up Sloane, Lady Elizabeth. Nina couldn't stand her: the prissy, entitled air, the super-confidence of a star and an aristo at the same time. Elizabeth kept offering stupid ideas, but all the boys here couldn't wait to tell her how great they were. Elizabeth was rude to her own father, she was bolshy with Nina, she took every opportunity of rubbing her nose in it. 'No better than you ought to be.' That was the Brit expression. Lady Elizabeth's slap in the face: you're just a piece of Yankee white trash from the wrong side of the tracks, whatever suits you wear or job you do.

The phone trilled.

'Nina?' She started as she recognised the cut-glass tones. Lord C. 'You're in early.'

'I've been at my desk for an hour,' Nina shot back without thinking, then bit her lip. Oh, God. You didn't cheek Tony Savage.

'Glad to hear it. You should be up to speed on the FDA scan, then.'

'Yes, sir,' Nina said quickly. She glanced down at her dress, a dark red cropped affair with a long, slimming jacket, by Jil Sander. Wolford tights, low Cartier heels, and fortunately, she was already made up. The earl expected all Dragon employees to look polished and pulled together.

'Then come upstairs to my office,' Lord Caerhaven said.

'Yes, sir. Right away.'

Nina carefully replaced the receiver on the hook and took a deep breath. One on one with the Robber Baron. It was the kind of chance she used to daydream about.

As she stood up she saw her hands were trembling.

Tony's office was fairly modest. It had a private bathroom off to one side which was shut, and a secretary's annexe as yet deserted. Neat windows looked north over the Thames to Soho. The décor was light and modern. It was far more impressive than Jax's clubby cavern on Park Avenue, or Frank Staunton's expensive art; Tony Savage, Nina realised, didn't need the English gentleman look, because everyone knew he was one.

The earl was sitting behind his desk, waiting for her, wearing a dark, nondescript suit, immaculately cut. His hair was close-cropped chestnut, only lightly speckled with silver. His eyes were hazel and he had a broad, strong chest. He looked powerful physically as well as financially. There was something cold about the alert speculation in his eyes. Nina sensed a fresh, spicy scent; Floris maybe, the lightest tang, pleasant but perfectly masculine.

Anthony Savage was the best-groomed man she'd ever seen. He looked almost predatory. He wore no jewellery except a gold signet ring, stamped with his family crest.

Nina had heard all the rumours. Now she wondered if they were true. He wasn't pretty, but his sexuality was magnetic.

She blushed. She couldn't believe it, she felt a ripple of desire. Something she hadn't felt since Jeff Glazer.

Tony Savage was more man than a million Brooklyn high-school jocks. *Watch it, girl,* she told herself, *you are out of your league.*

'Take a seat.'

Tony looked at the new kid. Short, but exquisite. Alabaster skin and a long, refined nose. A stylish suit that played up the coal-black eyes and hair. And close up, those curves were even more impressive.

He settled back languidly.

'I sold Idun this morning. For eighty.'

'Eighty?' Nina asked. Tony watched the wheels in her brain whirr; the very tip of her tongue touched the dark berry gloss on her full lips. 'That's twelve million more than it's worth.'

'That's what I thought,' Tony said. He was impressed: she'd pegged the market value off the top of her head. 'Tell me about the FDA.'

Nina swallowed drily. She had news she was sure this man did not want to hear.

'They don't like drugs based on amphetamines, and even with those they sanction, you have class action suits. A single bad reaction, a good lawyer, and you have a dented quarterly or worse. The appetite suppressant has an addictive effect and suppresses various auto-immune responses. I found well over thirty landmark rulings over eight separate states, then you have Federal liability . . .'

Tony watched Nina as she blasted through her findings. It was good work, well presented. She wasn't flinching; no soft soap or small talk. He enjoyed the rhythmic swell of her breasts and the sharp little hand gestures she used, long, elegant fingers tapering down to blood-red nails. Her calves slithered against each other. Despite the grown-up dressing and clever talk, she was very, very young.

'Hmm,' he said when she had finished. 'So the drug won't work?'

'Not in its present form.'

He leaned forwards.

'I want a slimming drug. One that they *will* ratify.'

'Yes, sir.' Nina didn't know what else she could say.

Tony looked at her; his gaze was hypnotic. 'And how are you settling in? Do you like London?'

'Very much, I—'

'How are you getting on with my daughter?'

Nina coloured. She felt fearful again. 'I, that is, she—'

Tony cut her off. 'You think she's a waste of space?'

Nina thought fast. Somehow, she knew that if she lied, this man would know. 'Well, Elizabeth's learning,' she replied.

Elizabeth. Tony noticed the deliberate lack of a title. She had balls, this girl, something he usually hated. In Nina it was erotic. Maybe it was the contrast, the rounded softness of her body and the hard coldness of her manner.

'I agree with you. I don't think work is any place for a young lady.'

Nina flinched. It was like a punch to the gut. He didn't think she was a lady, then? Too common, wasn't that what the English called it?

On the other hand, he was looking at her like an equal. Giving her an amazing job for a new kid. Power and position she hadn't thought she'd get for years.

'No, no place for a lady – or a gentleman.'

Tony glanced up sharply. The girl was staring at him boldly, her pale cheeks flushed from her challenge.

'I could have you fired.'

Nina lowered her eyes. She had the thickest lashes he'd ever seen. 'Yes,' she said, 'my lord.'

He almost laughed. She was fencing with him. No female had tried that on with him since Louise. But Nina was no Louise; she was earthy, she was street, she was Jewish. Tony could handle her, easily.

'We still need to find a plan B for the drug. Do some thinking. We'll have dinner tonight at the Groucho, eight p.m.'

Nina stood up. 'Right. Thanks for the invitation.'

'It wasn't an invitation,' Tony Savage said.

'This won't work. It's flashy, consumer orientated.' Nina didn't bother to hide her exasperation. 'You keep coming to me with ad campaigns.'

'It's a good idea.'

Elizabeth burned with resentment. Her ads for their Soothex throat pastels were arresting, original. Dino loved them.

'It's not what I asked you to do, Elizabeth.'

'Lady Elizabeth,' Elizabeth snapped. She couldn't help it; something about Nina's dismissive attitude made her lash out.

The two girls glared at each other. The men in the room stood stock-still; you could almost see their ears pricking up. Nina felt adrenalin surge through her.

'I don't think so. Social titles are not appropriate in the office. Not for a junior.'

Elizabeth flushed darkly.

Nina spoke up, so the rest of the room could hear her. 'If you have a problem with that, you could take it up with your father. I'll be happy to call you Lady Elizabeth, if he tells me to. Otherwise we'll keep it informal.'

There was a pause, then Elizabeth muttered, 'That's fine.'

Nina brushed a lock of black hair out of her eyes. Now she wanted to smooth things over.

'I love your bracelet, by the way. It's gorgeous.' She gestured to a thick silver cuff around Elizabeth's left wrist, covered in delicate engravings of ferns and ivy. 'Where did you buy it? I'd adore one.'

The other girl looked up at her. The green eyes were chips of ice, the aristocratic brows lifted in supercilious disdain.

'I don't buy my jewellery, I inherit it.'

Now it was Nina's turn to stiffen. 'I'm sorry, I didn't realise you were so grand.'

'Don't worry, Nina. You couldn't possibly know about things like that. Considering your background.'

Nina paled as the insult went home. For a moment, the two young women just glared at each other. Then Elizabeth gathered up her rejected work and walked back to her own department.

Nina stepped out of the taxi and tipped the driver almost absentmindedly. It had been a rush, racing home at quarter of seven, tearing off her suit, fixing her face at the speed of light. She knew the earl would not expect her to change for dinner, but she wanted to be impressive in every way.

A three-quarter black Prada jacket covered her dress, a loose, flowing sheath of Thai silk in metallic blue. The bright reds and charcoals of the day had been replaced with subtler shades: clover on her full lips, plum across her cheekbones, nails painted silver to match her necklace. The lids over her dark eyes were slate-grey, blue and black; all the colours of a dark English sky. Nina's black hair fell thickly over a grey cashmere wrap. The mirror had been kind; she was stunning, and she knew it.

Despite the long day and the rush at the end of it, Nina felt composed. Somehow, Lady Elizabeth's challenge had made up her mind. The confusion she'd felt in Tony's office had vanished long since. Nina knew what she was here to do.

The outfit she was wearing had cost over a thousand pounds. All the new money she'd thought she had was vanishing in things like this: good suits for the office, decent shoes, coats, accessories. As a Dragon executive, you couldn't shop at Marks & Sparks. You had to have an abundance of the right clothes, the stuff Elizabeth merely 'inherited'. Nina thought about that when she was dressing. How the few square feet of fabric clinging to her curves would, less than a year ago, have paid for months of food and lodging.

Elizabeth and the well-heeled young men at Dragon looked on her as nothing. An upstart, almost a child. They don't realise, Nina thought sourly, that I've *never* been a child. I've never had that luck.

Her past was a prison. Growing up in that slovenly apartment, carrying the can for Mom and Pop. Her mother a lush. The teasing she'd gotten at St Michael's for being white trash, well, some things never changed. The dizzy hope of Jeff and then the crunch of betrayal. Rooming with drunk sailors. Passing up college. Frank dying, Connor throwing her over. Miscarrying in a dark room.

But she'd done it. She'd gotten away. Two years at Dolan, now Dragon, Nina thought, and no one to help me but me. She'd turned twenty-one a few days ago and hadn't even noticed until the evening. Birthdays just didn't seem important. Elizabeth Savage might be the same age as her, but she was younger, lifetimes younger. Even though she was untrained and inexperienced, Lady E. was drawing a salary like Nina's and getting respect and position. Because she'd been lucky enough to be born on the right side of the tracks.

Nina pulled her cashmere scarf tighter and picked up her skirts, carefully stepping across the Dean Street slush. Her coat was smart, but not practical against the biting December air. She hurried across to the nondescript entrance to the club and ducked inside. When she told the receptionist she was meeting Lord Caerhaven, the woman melted.

The Groucho was a hot place to be. Full of media executives and stars, Nina recognised a couple of famous actors, a newscaster and a pop star. There was also a division chief from Hanson and the Treasury Secretary. Every one of them eyed her up as she walked over to the restaurant.

The attention thrilled her. It was perfect, she thought cynically. Men were all the same, no matter who or what they were. Some curves and a pretty face, and they were baying for it.

So why shouldn't she take advantage? Nina felt tired of being bruised. Of being the last person on the field playing by the rules.

Tony Savage was an attractive man. She knew the gossip round Dragon was that she was his pet. Elizabeth never lost a chance to sneer about her by the water cooler. Nina respected the earl, although she didn't like him, or trust him. However, he was her boss, the ultimate power. Lord Caerhaven was known for making his favourites rich and destroying his enemies. She was sure he wanted her. Well, maybe she wanted him. Maybe it was time to do something for herself.

Tony was seated at a discreet table in a corner of the room, still wearing his work suit. He stood up when Nina appeared and waited as she shrugged off the scarf and coat, appearing in a slither of cobalt and silver.

She saw desire blaze into his eyes.

'You look wonderful, Nina.'

'Thank you, Tony,' Nina said softly.

17

'So what do you think?'

Jack looked at Rupert Beeching and shrugged. He thought it was too cold, too windy, and too damn close to Christmas to be conducting serious business, but he'd asked Pop for the assignment, and now he had to live with it.

He was standing with a Gloucester farmer in a rundown stables, inspecting one of the finest colts he'd ever seen. Beeching was a part-timer with a useless trainer, but this one had come third in a minor race he'd attended down in Sussex. Beautifully proportioned, bursting with potential. Trouble was, his interest would spark off other buyers. Rupert wasn't so dumb he wouldn't have figured that one.

Jack thrust his hands into the pockets of his thick overcoat. The farm behind him looked out over sweeping hills; elm copses and dry-stone walls glittered under midwinter frost. In London, his secretary was drowning in messages from Paris and Galway; his book of photos and stud pedigrees was attracting a lot of interest. Jack was a good salesman, and the warm Texan accent was a help. Breeders were looking into Taylor Stud who had never considered it before. It had been a successful couple of months.

Jack named a figure, ignoring Beeching's theatrical scowl. 'Look, bud, I ain't haggling. He's pretty, but he's got no blood.'

'He *is* the blood.'

Jack laughed. 'Unplaced in three meets, third in one minor race? It ain't the Derby winner we're talking about.'

'Kerry Stud left me a message.'

'Ireland's in deeper trouble than Britain, right now. They can't match my price, and you know it.' Jack looked at his Rolex Oyster. 'Come on, Rupe. I want to take him home. I'm too tired for hassle. You think you can get a better price, be my guest, but I'm leaving now and so's my chequebook.'

The farmer winced at the familiarity, but he also looked wary. I've got you, you stupid, greedy jerk, Jack thought.

'You've got me,' Beeching said. He smiled foolishly as Jack sat down on a bale of hay and pulled out his chequebook. Coutts & Co. A lousy bank with high charges, but in England, appearance was everything.

First-class on a rickety BR train back to London, Jack sipped a watery Earl Grey and grinned to himself. Piece of cake. What should he call the animal?

A funky racehorse name. Maybe Easy Money. His fledgeling operation here had been as successful as everything else in his life. It was a nice surprise to find that the business school principles he'd picked up at Harvard actually worked. Plus, it was a buyer's market. Britain was tightening its money supply, and the medicine was hurting. Jack had toasted Margaret Thatcher, strident at her party conference in a frumpy suit and floppy bow tie. 'You turn if you want to. The lady's not for turning.' Stirring stuff, sure, but monetarism was hard. Inflation fell, but recession was biting deep. Luxury, high-end businesses – like racehorse stables – were feeling it. Closing down, selling up, desperate for cash influxes. And here was the young Texan champ, riding to the rescue like Zorro. A bit of schmooze, a bit of bluff, a macho chat about skiing and sport. Amazing how all the round, red-cheeked country gents with their gin and tonics and massive girths loved that stuff.

Jack bought himself a malt whisky and soda from the drinks trolley and smiled at the ogling waitress. He sipped the drink and watched rural England slide past him, the beautiful riverside meadows and thick forests belying the turmoil the country was going through.

Old money – landowners like Beeching – was on the slide, and a new breed was on the rise. Young, smart entrepreneurs, working for themselves, clawing up the ladder hand over fist. Men just like him.

To the victor the spoils. Jack had nearly everything he wanted. And finally, he had a chance at the one prize he hadn't been able to reach. Though she'd been turning down his calls all winter and refusing all his invitations, this one she couldn't duck. An order from Ronnie Davis, the British coach, to start her training again in preparation for the Olympics. The whole British women's team to meet in Kent at the weekend. And Ronnie, bless his cockney heart, had heard Jack was in town.

'Don't tell her I'm turning up.' Jack grinned as he remembered his own words. 'It'll be good to see all the girls again, but let's keep it a surprise.'

Elizabeth tried to get her brain in gear. Skiing. The Olympics. It was important, she had to focus on it. A weekend at base camp doing fitness routines and studying videos would be a good warm-up to the new training season, but it was hard to fight the sense of failure that swamped her.

Life at Dragon had proved to be one big disappointment. She was sure her ideas for ad campaigns were good ones, but Nina Roth was having none of them. And nobody was going to listen to her over Nina, that robotic cow. Nina, with her years of experience and her in-at-seven ferocious energy. Whatever Nina was up to, in that search for a new drug, she was given total backing from everyone who mattered. With her severe suits and her humour bypass, everyone took the New Yorker seriously. Especially darling Daddy.

Constant failure had worn Elizabeth down. She stopped presenting new ideas to Nina, and contented herself with reading company reports and typing market research. At least there was enough of that to keep her looking busy, and she'd learned more than she ever wanted to know about the pharmaceutical marketplace in the UK. Which hospitals bought what, which new pills were in development. Maybe it would be valuable knowledge – if they let her do anything with it.

Elizabeth's blonde hair whipped back under her Scotch House scarf as she emerged out of the Leicester Square Tube. The cinemas flashed ads for the big Christmas movies – *Raiders of the Lost Ark, On Golden Pond.* Tinned carols bled out of tourist-shop windows and mixed with pop music from a breakdancer's transistor. It was freezing. She bought some chestnuts from a brazier stall to try and jolly herself out of it. What was Hans Wolf doing at this moment? Sipping *Glühwein* by the lake in Lausanne? Waiting for her to come back, in January, ready to forget playing shop and get on with her real job?

That was how everybody else saw it. Certainly Nina. And certainly her noble papa. Elizabeth never even thought about complaining to him. Hand Tony that satisfaction? She'd rather die. He thought the sun shone out of Nina Roth's backside. He was happy to give her all the chances of real work, real satisfaction, he'd always denied his own daughter.

Elizabeth strode briskly through the crowds down to Charing Cross. Tunbridge Wells, great. Home of rich dowagers and the biggest drugs problem outside of Glasgow. Plus dry-skiing slopes. As if! It was like asking Picasso to practise on a painting-by-numbers book. Oh well, maybe they *were* all right. Maybe she should just try and ski.

Jack Taylor had called this morning. Again. And she'd blanked him, again. It didn't help to see that arrogant bastard doing so well, his every triumph reported lovingly in Dempster's diary, his social exploits pictured in *Tatler* for the last couple of months. When she really didn't need to feel any lower, there Jack was, staring out at her, his muscled arm slipped round some bland blonde: Violet Tomlins at the Royal Ballet do, Ursula Fane-Harvey at the Waldegraves' party, even Vanessa Chadwick, her old schoolmate from Switzerland. God, to think she'd nearly fallen for him!

Elizabeth scurried into the station, her Louis Vuitton overnight bag slung across her shoulder, and ducked into W. H. Smith's to pick up some reading for the journey. Nothing about fucking business. A Jilly Cooper and a *Standard,* that should do it. Her train was already at the platform and she secreted herself in first-class, ready to try and relax with a KitKat and the paper.

She opened it at the sports pages.

There was a picture of Jack, his warm smile beaming brightly at her through the muddy newsprint. He had his hand on the neck of a young horse, a magnificent-looking colt. The caption called it 'Another score for Taylor Stud.' Jack had named the beast Easy Money. Elizabeth flung the paper into the luggage rack.

The Alpine Hotel was primed for their arrival. A twee, purpose-built affair on the outskirts of town, it overlooked the distinctly non-Alpine dry-ski slope and was decorated with Holiday Inn-style mountains, pigtailed Heidis and cuckoo clocks. A giant Christmas tree in the lobby fought for attention over the huge display of banners and balloons welcoming 'Our Lovely Olympic Hopefuls'. Elizabeth signed in, furiously embarrassed, under a huge poster of herself, as the hotel manager fussed over her.

'Mr Davis has left a message in your ladyship's suite. Let me get a porter for your bags.'

'There's just the one. I can manage,' Elizabeth muttered, lifting her small bag.

'No, really, my lady—'

'Honestly, it's good for me. The exercise,' Elizabeth pleaded, scribbling an autograph and escaping to the lifts.

Her 'suite' was two rooms done up in tasteless pink and grey, with noisy air-conditioning that she knew would dry out her skin. Her spirits perked up for a moment as she noticed a bottle of champagne in an ice bucket and moved to pick it up, but the cork had been popped and it was empty. A small note was tucked under the neck: 'You won't be needing this. Or the chocolates, which I threw away. Meet us in the gym at six thirty.' It was signed Ronnie Davis.

Elizabeth flopped down on the bed. She wouldn't even have time to clean up. The mirror opposite showed a cross, red-eyed young woman with hair that needed a wash and skin that needed some sleep. In her futile efforts to make a dent at Dragon she'd let the gym work slide, and now she was unfit, out of condition and muscularly weak. She was tired and she looked dreadful.

'Welcome back,' she said aloud.

The gym was reserved for the team. Elizabeth could hear Ronnie's trademark growl as she arrived, in a sports bra and Lycra leggings over Adidas cross-trainers. No point trying to hide in baggy jog-pants, Ron would see right through that.

'Fucking 'ell, Karen, is that the best you can do? Pick it up, girl, gawd almighty …'

Elizabeth stuck her head through the door. Poor Karen, Janet and Kate were racing around a circular track, sweating bullets. Tinny music, Adam and the Ants, was drifting out of a portable radio. It was no competition for the strident voice of her coach, yelling scornfully as his athletes completed their endurance tests. A group of men in BSF tracksuits lounged at the side of the track but Elizabeth didn't look at them. She was staring horrified at her team-mates. Ron didn't think any of them were up to it, and all three of them looked way, way fitter than she was.

'Hold it.' Ron switched off Radio One and and waved Elizabeth over. 'It's the nobs' answer to Anita Roddick! Good evening, milady, you've finally turned up.'

'Nice to see you too, boss,' Elizabeth said, waving at the girls who all collapsed on the linoleum.

Ronnie came forwards and cast a critical eye over her body. Clearly he didn't like what he saw.

'Flex. Biceps, triceps, delts –' Expert stubby fingers probed her cotton-wool arms. 'Quads, glutes –' Now he was pushing against her bottom, checking her out like one of Jack's horses. Elizabeth blushed scarlet. She was as soft as a marshmallow.

Ronnie frowned thunderously. He grabbed her wrist and took her pulse.

'You're jokin', aren't ya? Seventy-five beats per minute? I'm sorry, miss, you'll have to leave the gym. I'm expecting a World Champion athlete to show up any second.'

Elizabeth paled. Seventy-five? Just three months ago she'd been a steady fifty-eight. That was an athlete's rate. Joe Blow's average was eighty. Could she really have lost it that fast?

'You can't be serious.'

'*I* can be serious, darlin'. The question is, can you be?' Ronnie threw a towel at her. 'Warm up. You got five minutes. Then we're gonna see just how bad the damage really is.'

Barely forty minutes later, Elizabeth was gasping for air. Her feet hurt, her calves were screaming. The clock on the wall told its own sorry tale: forty minutes, Christ, just a warm-up session normally, and here she was, totally worn out. Her sprint speed was still OK but her endurance was shot to pieces. Fifteen minutes of vicious squat thrusts had her in tears, Ronnie screaming at her, the officials shaking their heads, Ronnie screaming at the officials. At least he'd sent them out of the room. Then Elizabeth had to endure the humiliation of a crunch routine and push-up routine in which Janet, Kate and Karen, three girls not usually in her league, outperformed her easily.

'Go and 'ave your dinner,' Ronnie barked at them eventually. 'Not you, milady. You ain't going anywhere. Drop and give me fifty.'

'Fifty!' Elizabeth gasped, wiping the trickles of sweat and dust out of her eyes. 'I can't manage fifteen.'

The coach settled himself on a gymnast's mattress. 'Fifty, Elizabeth. Hans had you on sixty for routine—'

'But that was—'

'Back when you were a skier?'

Elizabeth responded to this with such fury that she didn't hear the gym door creak open again. She tried to ignore everything; the pain in her upper arms, the ache lancing over her back, Toyah Wilcox lisping on the radio, Ronnie's cheerful hello to someone or other. *Come on!* She wasn't so bad that she had to take this shit. Surely. The floor and her upper body. Fifteen, sixteen . . . now the lactic acid was burning, blazing fire around the weakness of her biceps . . . Another pair of boots had joined Ronnie's an inch from her nose. She was sweating, gasping, grunting like a stuck pig, willing herself through the red mist of exhaustion. Feeling like a tomato with the blood flooding her face. Twenty-two, twenty-three . . . but there was only so much that will power could do. Elizabeth felt failure hovering over her like a vulture. She groaned. Her body simply could not cash this cheque. With an agonised moan she swayed and collapsed, her cheek hitting the dusty linoleum, gasping for air.

'We've got a lot of work to do,' Ronnie said into the silence, 'if you're gonna go to the 1982 Olympics. Let alone win 'em.'

Elizabeth nodded. She didn't have the breath to say anything.

'Oh well.' Her coach's voice shifted back into a friendly, non-business mode. 'Time for supper. You can catch up with the girls, Liz, you'll enjoy that. And your mate here.'

A sudden sickening revelation hit Elizabeth as she stared at the second pair of boots. Cowboy. Chestnut leather. She'd seen those somewhere before.

She raised her reddened, sweating face from the dust and looked up into a pair of twinkling brown eyes. The neat suit and Gieves & Hawkes shirt could not conceal the perfect strength and proportion of his iron, obviously super-fit muscles.

'Hi there,' said Jack Taylor.

Elizabeth scrubbed angrily at her hair in the pouring shower. The fragrance of lavender and thyme drifting up from her Floris conditioner, and the burning heat attacking her soreness, could not wipe away the sense of outrage. If she wasn't so mad she'd be crying. Seventy-five bpm, looking like shit, flabby, weak – couldn't even do *thirty* reps on the floor, and Jack, bloody Jack Taylor, actually standing over her, watching her collapse!

How could Ronnie do it to her? She was going to complain in the strongest language. Get the insufferable bastard thrown out. What was a Yank doing in the British training camp? What, oh God, if word of her condition leaked out? Heidi Laufen would have a very happy Christmas!

She switched off the water and started to dry her hair. Miserably she wished she'd packed a few more cosmetics. There was nothing in her bag but basic foundation, blusher and lipstick. Not much to counter the first impression Jack must have got. He was probably still laughing about it now. Vanessa and Ursula and co. had all looked like they'd spent the morning at Molton Brown. But God, she'd only packed for the girls!

Elizabeth dressed in her travelling outfit, a long, simple knitted jersey sheath from Sonia Rykiel. It was OK, but she had no jewels to dress it up with. The pale pink shade matched her lipstick and blusher and that was about all you could say. It was off the shoulder, and Elizabeth wished it had sleeves. Dinner with four athletes and a coach, it was like advertising her wimpy delts.

She didn't know which was the more humiliating – looking so ugly or looking so weak! Jack had been as polished and gorgeous as ever, and he was clearly still at his peak performance. He could race a downhill tomorrow and cruise it. Most likely he was laughing about it in the hotel bar, right now. With whatever bimbo he was here with.

That thought stopped her hairbrush in mid-stroke. She pounced on her telephone and stabbed out the number for Ronnie's room.

'Hi, it's Elizabeth.'

'Want to talk about it already? Look, Liz, it's early days. No need to panic just yet—'

'No, no.' She cut him off. 'Jack Taylor, Ronnie! What the hell's he doing here? I want him gone by tomorrow morning!'

'He's here because I invited him. He's going to be doing a little pre-season training with us. It's just fitness.'

'Fitness, hell! He could report back to Kim or Holly.'

'Jack's hardly a spy. You didn't exactly complain about training with him before.' Ronnie's voice was sharp. 'In fact, it did you a lot of good, I seem to recall.'

'He *goes*! I'm not having it!' Elizabeth heard her own voice rise. She felt like stamping her feet. 'I'm the World Champion, it's my team—'

'Hey! It's the British team, Liz Savage.'

'Bullshit!' Some part of her mind told her to give in, but the shame and the anger wouldn't let her stop. Karen, Janet, who the fuck were they? She was the only hope they'd got! '*I'm* the medallist here! I refuse to train with a foreigner! You get him out of here, Ronnie, or I'm filing an official complaint to the Olympic Council.'

'All right, that's enough.' Davis's surprise was as obvious as his anger. 'I'm the gaffer, Elizabeth, simple as that. You say one more word about it and I'll call in the OC myself. There's a minimum fitness standard for all Olympic athletes, do you hear me? If I have you tested officially tomorrow, you're scratched.'

Elizabeth took a deep breath, frozen to the spot.

'You do exactly what you're told, girl, or you wind up a "Where Are They Now" clue on *Question of Sport*. Jack stays. You come down to dinner in ten minutes, and we never had this conversation.' Davis paused; his fury crackled down the line. 'Your attitude needs as much work as your body. You got two weeks to get both in shape or believe me, milady, you are *out*.'

18

Nina pulled her Golf GTi sharply to the right and parked neatly. It was the black darkness of early morning in December, but the Dragon car park was flooded with light. It gave her a little thrill to see her name stencilled in white against the wall. 'Reserved, Miss Nina Roth, New Products.' Last week she had passed her driving test first time; no trouble learning the English system, because she'd never had a car in the States.

The Golf had been the first tangible benefit. The day after that long, teasing dinner with Tony, Keith Sweeney from Personnel had summoned her and shown her a range of cars. Pick one. Any colour. Red is the most popular.

Nina thanked him and took a dark blue.

She smiled softly as she left Sweeney's office. Dinner the night before had rewritten the rulebook around here. As she casually ran through chat about drugs, approvals, regulations, Nina made sure her body did all the real talking. Leaning into Tony, letting those hard eyes flicker over her bodice, her inviting smile and long legs. Tony Savage had started bringing up figures of his own. Money. Market share. Personal profits. Letting her see just how powerful and rich he really was. He was brash and obvious, but it had worked. Savage was magnetically sexual. Nina knew it was throwing her principles to the winds to flirt with Tony like that, but he was the boss, and it was what he wanted.

She tried not to think about the fact that it was what she'd wanted too.

Tony's kiss on her hand at the end of the night was slow, toying with her skin, his lips touching her hand just that fraction too long.

He wants me, Nina thought triumphantly.

She got out of the car and pressed a button on her keys. Central locking, a new invention. They were all over the place. Atari games consoles were cramming the West End toy stores, and yesterday someone at Phillips had shown them a flat, rounded metal disc, loudly proclaiming it to be the future of music. In television, video recorders were the new craze; now you could tape pictures as well as sound. Betacam and VHS were fighting it out as operating systems.

'Buy VHS. And buy stock in VHS,' Nina had told Tony last night.

He had smiled at her, a little patronisingly. 'Betacam is clearly superior.'

She had ducked her head, letting her newly waved, softly curled hair skim her shoulders. 'Yes, but VHS have more software available. Superior pictures don't matter if you can't watch any movies.'

Once more she had felt his eyes lock on hers as the finance director launched into his report. For two weeks they had been circling each other; Tony, with his diary crammed full of year-end speeches and Christmas dinners, hadn't had any evenings free since he took her to dinner. Nina, pressing her advantage, put together a file on freelance drug researchers that she hoped would blow Frank Staunton away. It was clear to her that the current slimming drug was a bust. Effective, but not safe. If Dragon put a pill out there before it was ready, the company could be ruined. Like Betacam would be.

And there was more work to do. Nina knew Tony was chasing his holy grail, but what if that was a mirage? Right here and now there was a lot more work to do. Inefficient customer response. Poorly advertised standard drugs that were losing market share. Dull stuff, maybe, but their bread and butter. Nina made sure she had that stuff covered too. It wouldn't look good on her résumé if she spent all her time on a project that ended up a failure.

So Tony was busy and she was busy. But that was about to change.

The building was half-empty. In the last week before the Christmas holiday, many staff had taken up holiday time and gone home. Balloons sprouted from computer monitors and gaudy paper-chains looped across ceilings. There was a definite sense of unreality. In the States, Nina thought wryly, you'd get a couple of cards stood on a desk, that was it. The Brits did it differently; 1981 seemed already over for most of the drones sitting here making half-hearted calls. Partly that was because of Europe. The Swiss had packed up and gone home, retailers had placed Christmas orders long ago, research labs stocked with international teams were dispersing across the globe. Who would you call? Even the Stock Exchange was sluggish. The Brits were like a bunch of schoolchildren, watching the clock and waiting for the bell.

Nina threaded her way through Marketing. Lady Elizabeth's desk was unoccupied except for a huge pile of cards and presents. The staff sucking up. Sports fans' tributes, forwarded by the BBC. But Elizabeth wasn't here to pick them up, she was off at training camp in Kent.

Nina paused. 'This looks ridiculous.'

Dino Vincenza, senior marketing manager, looked up from his terminal. 'Lady Elizabeth is very popular,' he said silkily. 'Many people like her skiing. And her ideas.'

Nina heard the rebuke just as he meant her to. Popular, unlike you. And you're stamping on her. Technically Dino outranked her, but she was a comer in a more important department, and a favourite of the Robber Baron.

She reached forwards and picked up an envelope at random. It was very stiff, thick card inside creamy paper. An invitation. Nina flipped it over and found a gold coronet franked on the back. What was it? A New Year's ball, Boxing Day sherry, a hunt meet somewhere? She didn't look to see whose the crest was. It didn't matter. It was another sign of Elizabeth's world, of her class, her privilege. All the things that Nina could never get.

'I'll call Maria in the postal office. Get this cleared, and future mail routed to the castle. It may be Christmas, but that's no excuse for the place looking a dump.'

'Of course,' Dino said sweetly.

Nina stormed off to her area with her cheeks flaming. She hated being mocked. Her own desk was fastidiously neat; since she was Jewish, nobody had sent her cards. Yesterday she had been pleased by this sign of respect. Now she found herself riddled with doubts. Was it respect? Or were they all snubbing her?

Come on, girl. Since when did you care what a bunch of limey assholes thought of you?

Angrily she switched on her computer and started to cross-reference. To Nina the end of the year represented opportunity. It was a chance to get her act together and her findings in order. While the rest of the company sipped sherry and stuffed mince pies, and that blonde dilettante went jogging in the countryside.

I'm efficient, Nina told herself, pulling up a new spreadsheet. I *work* during the working day—

The phone buzzed on her desk, making her jump. She snatched it up.

'Roth, New Products.'

'Tony Savage, Chairman's Office.' The dry voice sent a shiver through Nina's stomach, an electric crackle like radio static. She wasn't expecting his call until late this afternoon. 'Do you have that report on the research teams?'

'I was just tidying it up.'

'I need it now. You'd better come upstairs and present.'

'But I haven't even typed it up—'

'Now, Nina.' The earl hung up.

For a moment she sat frozen. Bastard! It wasn't ready! He'd said tomorrow, hadn't he? But repeating that to Tony Savage wouldn't help her any. He didn't like excuses; he was merciless to underlings that proffered them. Quickly she dumped her early notes out to the printer and rushed over, ripping the still-warm sheet out of the machine after it inched through. Present? To whom? The virtuous smug feeling of a few moments before evaporated.

The elevator arrived. Piped carols rang out annoyingly as Nina stood there fidgeting. 'God rest ye, merry gentlemen, let nothing you dismay ...' Which was great for the merry gentlemen, but bugged the hell out of the harassed lady.

Tony met her as she stepped out. He looked crisp as ever. No novelty Rudolph ties for his lordship.

'I have the basic gist, but it was due tomorrow,' Nina said.

Her boss frowned. 'Unlike the rest of the bloody country, we don't deal in work to rule.'

'No, sir, but I had to do the sales projections and—'

'I told you what your priority was to be.' Lord Caerhaven's angry voice had nothing of flirtation about it. 'The slimming drug. It's not for you suddenly to decide what you concentrate on. Now go in there and present it.'

Nina looked up into the dark eyes and found them unyielding. Reluctantly she walked into his office. A long table had been set up in the middle of the room and was surrounded by middle-aged men. She recognised Gerald Jax and Don Hadley, head of Finance US. Plus there was a banker from Credit Suisse whose name she couldn't place, but his jowly face was familiar – a heavy hitter.

Tony sat at the head of the table and introduced her briefly while Nina's heart flipped slowly in her chest. She didn't need lapel badges to realise who this lot were. Investment bankers, Dragon Europe heads, American management. The big boys. The guys who ran things.

Men you seriously didn't want to screw up in front of.

'Thank you, Lord Caerhaven,' Nina said faintly. 'The first thing we have to face is that Steele Ripley, our current research team, is not up to the job. Their drugs are effective but consistently unsafe. We must look for other R and D sources . . .'

Her throat was dry. The room seemed dreadfully bright. Not so much as a sprig of plastic holly lightened the tone up here. The eyes of her superiors were fixed on her and Nina had to fight back panic. Not a natural public speaker, without orderly notes she was flustered. She forgot company names, track records. She kept looking at her paper. She fumbled questions from around the room. Sometimes she didn't even know the answers.

Nina couldn't look at Tony. She had the awful feeling that she might be going to cry. She didn't want to cry, it was a reflex action against the embarrassment. She didn't look super-smooth now; these men were seeing just what she was, a young girl, floundering miserably, out of her depth.

'But you're arguing the allocation of massive resources. Steele Ripley are a known quantity,' Gerald Jax was objecting.

'Yes, sir. But known to be greedy and lax on safety.'

'The B-28 damage isn't as bad as you're making out.' Heinrich Günther, Dragon Deutschland. The West German was bony and florid, anger making him more ruddy than usual. He'd discovered Dr Steele and Professor Ripley. 'Nobody has died.'

'Not yet, Herr Günther, but they would, long term.' You fucking Nazi, Nina thought, what were your parents doing in the war? 'Look, we might as well package up cocaine! You'd enjoy it, you'd get thin, at first you'd be fine. But in the end you'd be a useless junkie.'

There was a heavy silence. Jax lowered his eyes.

'Get out!' Günther shouted. 'You incompetent, you are wasting our time!'

Nina froze.

'Didn't you hear me? Get out!'

Shellshocked, Nina grabbed her sheet of notes and bolted for the door. Once she was safely in the corridor, her eyes filled with tears. She ducked into a restroom to get herself together. Christ! What had she said? Was she really that bad? Was she going to get fired?

Tony watched Nina scarper like a startled doe. Her pretty turned calves flashed out of the room, black tights with seams at the back rising up to a smart turquoise wool skirt. She'd been scrappy and scared, but she'd got the information across. He was pleased with the result. His lieutenants had something to think about. And Ms Roth had been scalded out of her complacency.

She'd been doing well, but he never liked any junior to think they were doing too well. Especially not a woman.

She was bruised now, he thought; that would soften her. That débâcle with Heinrich was wonderful. Poor little Nina, how was she to know about his longstanding fondness for a snort of Charlie? His head of Dragon GmbH thought he was being deliberately insulted.

Tony reached into his breast pocket and pulled out a folded red spotted handkerchief. He threw it at Günther.

'Here, Heinrich. Terrible sniff you've got, old man. I should see a doctor about that cold. And now, gentlemen, let's consider the points Miss Roth made.'

Back at her desk Nina typed furiously. She worked through lunch without taking a break. She couldn't afford to be caught napping twice. When the travel office sent someone upstairs with her air ticket for tonight, Nina almost told them to check if she was still meant to be travelling. But if Tony wanted her out, she'd be out soon enough. Christmas was no protection. Tony would fire someone at the office party if he felt like it.

By the end of the day her stomach was growling and her fingers were cramped. She filed everything into a briefcase and set off for Heathrow. She guessed she was still going, since nobody said otherwise.

London and its suburbs slipped by her in a cold drizzle. The sky was already black, but there were too many clouds for stars. Nina drove as fast as she could without breaking the law. She didn't want a ticket or a delay; no more black marks, please, Lord.

The Human League, Madness and Diana Ross blared out of her car radio. When Haircut 100 came on Nina switched off. Shitty music, shitty weather, stuck-up old-money pricks! she thought. I hate this fucking country!

But did she want to go home? After today, maybe she'd have to. All the money, the allowances, the car and nice clothes, vanished. The thought made her sweat. Back to Brooklyn? No job, no references ... when you were in with Dragon, great; when you were out you were usually dead. People who pissed them off didn't work again. At least, not in the drugs business.

At the airport she checked in for Dublin with British Midland and was directed to the VIP lounge.

The earl was standing to one side in the middle of a knot of men. With a start Nina recognised Harry Cohen from Planning, Joe Bould from Strategic Accounts, even mousy, capable Maggie Stevens from Customer Relations. For the second time today she was taken aback. She'd thought she was the only one Tony was taking to Dublin, to attend a Europe-wide conference on distribution routes. But there were at least seven others!

Trying to hide her discomfiture, she walked over.

'Miss Roth. Good. I thought you were going to delay us,' Tony said coolly.

Nina smiled lamely. She didn't dare say a word. Tony wasn't smiling at her or glancing over; he seemed deep in a discussion with the Cohen boy. Clearly she'd got it very wrong. She was just one more junior exec; nothing special.

From Dublin airport they were ferried in limos to the Shelbourne Hotel. The hotel was old fashioned, with art deco nymphs at the gate looking out on a small green park; it was bustling with delegates in evening dress, packing the Horseshoe Bar and talking shop. The Dragon contingent filed into a packed conference room to listen to speeches; they would be changing for dinner later.

Exhausted and upset, Nina tried to force herself to listen. She saw Maggie taking notes but this was kids' stuff for her. Stuffed shirts from ICI, SmithKline Beecham and Glaxo droned on about healthcare providers. The room was warm from the packed audience, and Nina was fighting to stay awake, to fake some enthusiasm, and to avoid the besuited assholes all round her trying so obviously to catch her eye.

And then it was his turn.

Tony Savage stood up at the podium and noted the immediate response. The packed room jerked to life. Heads lifted. Whispers ceased.

He was the Robber Baron.

As he talked – with enough gravitas for a Lord Chancellor, rather than a takeover pirate – Tony felt the pleasure of it all flood through him like adrenalin. His quarterlies looked great. Recession? What recession? Look at these pricks, he thought: drab, plump, soft-bellied losers, the lot of them. He knew they'd all heard the rumours: the debauchery, the vengeful streak. They loved it. They wished they were him. Like Machiavelli, Tony thought, I'd rather be feared than loved. And nobody said a word. He took his pleasures like a City barrow-boy, but last July, he'd been there with Monica in Westminster Abbey, a sombre and dignified peer, watching Diana Spencer waltz off with the Prince of Wales.

Louise and Jay DeFries were the last people ever to make him look a fool; and look what happened to them.

As his speech raced to its conclusion, Tony let his gaze find his own people. The boys and Miss Stevens were watching with appropriate awe, but it wasn't them he was looking for. And then he saw her: a flash of light blue in the drab browns and greys; pale face framed with that thick cloud of black hair; a dragonfly amongst the midges. Nina. She was watching him, and Tony was amused again. Because even though she quickly dropped her eyes, it wasn't fast enough to hide the blazing anger, the rage in them, burning in her dark pupils like fire on coal.

19

After Tony's closing address, the room broke up to prepare for dinner. Nina rushed upstairs, feeling stressed out. She knew she'd glared at him, knew he'd seen it. The misery and rage would not be held back. He had lectured her and humiliated her. God knew how she was going to get through tonight.

Her bedroom was decorated with genteel, faded charm: Victorian prints and a radiator whose age could not be disguised by its new coat of paint. But it was luxurious, after a fashion; the bed made with heavy Irish linens, fresh lavender and roses scenting the air, the wall mirror mounted in an antique brass frame. Nina unpacked her overnight bag quickly. She wished she'd been smart and brought some Pro-Plus. If the rumours were true, Joe Bould across the hall would be refreshing himself with a quick line or two of fine Peruvian marching powder right now. But Nina didn't do drugs. Loss of control equalled weakness.

In the pretty mirror she repaired the damage to her exhausted face. Concealer under the eyes, white pencil along the bottom lid for that alert look. Light turquoise shadow with sea- and dark greens at the edges, a bronze slash of blusher painting the colour back into her cheeks, berry lipstick with a neat matching liner, her dark hair curled gently into her face. It took less than five minutes; Nina planned everything in advance now, it was a habit. Even her make-up. She pulled on a pair of dark-green velvet mules by Ferragamo and grabbed her dress from the hanger. Full-length, bias-cut jade crêpe, layered thickly enough to be opaque, it was a creation by a hot new Manhattan designer, Donna Karan. Looked nothing on the peg, but when Nina slipped it on, adjusting the thick gilt clasp on the left shoulder, it clung to her curves then fell from the waist, making her look like a Greek goddess. And it moved like a sea wave.

Nina smiled softly. She looked beautiful. On nights like this one, you could put on your beauty like armour.

Downstairs the Dragon party had assembled already. Maggie Stevens's jealous scowl – she'd picked a boring black velvet number, probably from Next – reassured her.

Harry Cohen coughed. 'Shall we go in? They've set our placings.'

Nina followed her colleagues. The conference had set out tables back to back, dispersing delegates from different firms around the room. That was the point: you swapped business cards, made contacts. Nina was cynical. She didn't believe real work got done at these places. Conference jaunts were an institution, an excuse for a booze-up and salary-swapping, comparing your status. Whatever.

The menu plan had Nina on Table 1. She checked it again just to be sure. Table 1 was surely for the MDs and directors, wasn't it? But there she was, so she mounted the wooden steps at the end of the room.

'Nina Roth,' she told the hovering waiter.

He glanced at a list. 'Yes, madam. Just over here.'

Nina followed the man right to the head of the table. She was two places down from the Chairman of ICI. To her left was the Finance Minister of the Republic. The chair to her right was empty. Trying to hide her surprise, she smiled and shook hands in complete confusion as she sat down. And then a shadow passed over the table and the waiter was seating her other neighbour.

Tony Savage.

He looked great. Tony had been born to black tie. The other bigshots here were grey and bespectacled, nerdy, or plump. The earl was lean; spare and muscular, his hair dark, his eyes glittering as he sat. Nina couldn't help but notice the table's reaction, how these gentlemen smiled at her boss with their eyes full of envy, curiosity, and loathing. The alleycat was among the tame pigeons.

She had to say something.

'I'm – I – good evening, Lord Caerhaven.' She didn't dare call him Tony, not after today. 'Aren't the delegates supposed to be sat separately?'

'Umm.' The arrogant tilt of his head looked down on her. 'They are, but I ordered that you be sat next to me.'

Nina swallowed.

'Is that a problem?' Tony asked. His eyes were dancing, observing her discomfiture. 'Would you rather be down there, with the others?'

'No, sir.' She was blushing. Although everybody at Dragon called Tony sir, in a work situation, there was something disturbing about it right now. The formalised submission. The sense of his power. And his closeness. Nina took refuge in a gulp of champagne. 'I'm sorry about this morning, sir. I should have been ready.'

'Yes, you should have,' Tony said. 'I set the priorities. You follow them. Is that clear?'

The rest of the table were talking amongst themselves while the starter was laid out. Nina knew they were being rude, but Tony clearly didn't give a fuck. She swallowed the rest of her glass. She was a mess of fear and desire.

'Yes, sir.' She couldn't help it, she blurted out, 'Am I fired?'

He grinned. His eyes flickered down the bodice of her dress. The look burned a wash of fire across her skin, like the alcohol was burning down her throat. Under the silk, her groin tightened.

'You're good. I can use you. You're just not as good as you thought you were. Don't act on your own initiative, act on *my* initiative. Dragon is not a democracy. You're not at your five-and-dime store in Brooklyn now.'

The reference to her past jerked Nina's eyes back up to his. The earl was looking at her in that superior, maddening way Elizabeth had. Don't forget who you are, it said. I took you out of there and I can send you back.

With an effort Nina nodded. Bastard, she thought, he's got the whip hand and he loves it. She turned to the Minister for Finance and made some desultory conversation, pushing her oysters round her plate. She couldn't eat. Tony Savage, on her other side, was lording it over the rest of the table; sometimes their eyes slid over her dress, but then it was always back to Tony. That was his magnetism, and anyway, for guys like these, sex always came second to power.

Nina drank champagne for courage, enjoying the icy, bubbling sting in her mouth. I might be white trash, she thought angrily, but I'm *smart* white trash. The best. I got here myself, asshole, and you were born in a goddamn castle!

She forced herself to take a little of the *entrée*. Grouse and roast parsnip. The earl was still watching her. She felt his gaze on her shoulders, the curve of her waist. The champagne was buzzing round her bloodstream. Despite herself, Nina felt herself tense again, moisten between the legs.

The Minister turned to Tony. 'Lord Caerhaven, Miss Roth does you credit. She's got a better grasp of EU regulations than some of my officials.'

Tony smiled. 'Nina's got a top-drawer brain, Minister. That was my first reason for hiring her.' When the old buffer reached for more cranberry jelly, he grinned down at Nina.

The alcohol made her brave. 'And what was the second?'

'The packaging,' Tony said lightly. Then he turned to his neighbour, and didn't speak to her again for the rest of the meal.

Once the plates were cleared the room broke up.

'I'll go and mingle.'

The earl was shaking hands, but he broke off to put one on her shoulder. 'No. Wait in the lobby. I'll be right out.'

Nina picked her way through the crowd, weaving and smiling. She was dizzy and carefree. Maybe she should have gone easy on the wine, with an empty stomach, but what the hell. She wandered out and stood by a dusty palm in a large brass pot, refusing to meet the hungry male eyes that followed her.

Tony was out less than a minute later, striding through a crowd that seemed to part around him. Nina noticed how tall he was; even with her heels, he towered over her. He beckoned to her curtly and they walked into the Horseshoe Bar together. Nina found she was backed into a corner.

'I like your dress,' Savage said.

'I'm glad you like something.'

He laughed softly. 'Prickly. Let's see how good you really are.'

Nina caught her breath. The dark eyes and predator smile were fixed on her, and the desire in them was naked. So blatant she felt herself tighten some more, the downy hairs of her belly lifting in response. Jeff had never looked at her that way, with such expertise, such pure confidence.

'Are you asking me on a date?'

'No. I'm asking you to bed. Don't tell me you're surprised.'

'I guess not,' Nina murmured. She kept her voice down, afraid people would hear them. Caerhaven didn't seem to care about that; or anything, she thought. She stared back at him. 'And what if I say no? You sack me?'

He moved a step closer. Crowding her. Bending slightly, so his face was close to hers, so that when he spoke, she was looking at his mouth.

'You're a clever girl, you know what I do for my friends. And you want me. So let's not play games.' Savage held out his hand to her. 'Come with me.'

'We're going up there together?' Nina whispered. Tony smiled; he liked the way the kid kept blushing, eyes darting about, like a hare looking to bolt. 'But what will people think?'

'Who gives a damn?' Tony Savage said.

They rode up together in a stately, creaking elevator, joining some suits and a couple of dowagers. When the last of them left at the fourth floor, Tony turned to her, casually, and reached for her breasts through the silky crêpe, feeling their heaviness, palming them deftly, feeling the sharpness of her nipples. Nina gasped. Her knees weakened. He didn't say anything but he smiled, letting her know he could feel her response. Nina felt ashamed but also flooded with heat. Experimentally Tony moved one hand down to the flat of her stomach, resting it there, feeling the warmth of her burning through her gown. The other came up to cup her chin, and he slowly pushed his thumb into her mouth.

Nina started to suck it. She didn't know what he was doing to her. She was light with lust, almost collapsing, pressing herself against his hand.

'Steady,' he said. Like he was laughing at her.

The elevator juddered to a halt. Nina tried to pull herself together. Tony waited politely for her to walk out first.

The penthouse suite was to the left. Nobody passed them. Tony reached for his key calmly, without hurrying, but Nina could see his hard-on outlined through his pants. His desire was as strong as hers, he was just more used to it. How many women has he had? she thought. A hundred? More than that? Every touch, every look of his was assured. Business and society whispered about him. His girls, his Teflon romances. Not one of them had ever breathed a word. For a second that made her uneasy; how could that be? Was it a Brit thing, a code of silence? Or did Caerhaven use the carrot and the stick?

Come on, girl, you're not afraid . . .

The key connected with the lock.

Tony held the door open for her as he flicked on the light. Nina looked round a gorgeous suite, crammed with flowers, baskets of fruit and nuts and chocolates on a silver tray. The furniture was mahogany, Georgian antique, including a full bookcase. There was a white damask chaise-longue and armchairs in navy-blue leather. A huge mirror dominated one wall; oil paintings the others. The bed was a double, pillows heaped on a snowy coverlet; lambswool blankets and broderie anglaise.

Tony shut the door.

'Are you nervous?'

'No,' Nina said boldly.

He came over to her and steered her into the centre of the room, at the foot of the bed. Facing the mirror. Then he tipped her face up to his with both hands.

'Liar,' he said.

Then he bent down and kissed her. Nina breathed in cigar smoke, light, sexy masculine sweat, that expensive aftershave he used. His lips were brushing hers softly, not gentle so much as exploratory. Tasting her. Pushing on her. Getting a feel for her mouth. Then he was rougher, kissing and breaking off, using his tongue, biting her, his hands slipping round her face, yanking her to him, and then his hands moulding the roundness of her butt, stroking her breasts, her belly, pushing down between her legs. Tony was strong: he wouldn't let her force the pace, holding her back when she squirmed under his touch, closing her mouth with his when she wanted to speak.

When he broke off, Nina's breath was ragged.

'Have you ever had an orgasm?'

She blushed. 'Of course.'

'With a man? No, I thought not.' Tony broke away from her and reached for the clasp on her shoulder, unpinning it. 'Let's have a look at you, baby.'

Nina just stood there as her gown slithered to the floor. The dizzy, squirmy mixture of embarrassment and excitement was almost too much to bear. To want a man like this and have him know it. A man you didn't even really like. But the antagonism made it better . . . carefully she stepped out of the dress and kicked it aside.

She stood naked in front of the mirror except for a tiny scrap of lace at the groin; full, firm breasts, a sleek waist, and a high, rounded ass. Soft upper arms, sweetly turned calves, small feet. She saw the light in Tony's eyes burst into flame. He groaned and pulled her to him. Nina felt his hands everywhere, tugging her panties down her thighs, his fingers sliding into her, feeling her arousal. The rough cloth of his suit brushed against her everywhere. His erection was larger and harder now. She wanted to undo his belt but her fingers wouldn't work, they were shaking.

Tony reached for his shirt buttons. He broke two ripping them open, he couldn't get naked fast enough. His cock was throbbing in his pants, he was a teenager again, fighting to control himself. The girl was light headed from the champagne, but even so, magnificently responsive, and naïve at the same time. Passionate but clumsy, clearly not used to it. If not her first, he'd be one of the first. The thought was exquisitely exciting. She'd been worth waiting for. Check out that body, those incredible breasts with the gorgeous, dark-fleshed nipples, tight as raisins, waiting for him. He could get his hands round her waist and her ass was out of this world, he could fuck her all night long. He'd been with no really clever woman since Louise but Nina didn't turn him off. Her brain would make her inventive. She thought she could get round him, but as he'd shown her today, he had her future, everything, right in the palm of his hand. He had her where he wanted her, and that was just how it'd stay.

'God, you're beautiful.' He pulled her on to the bed. 'I could fall in love with you.'

'Bullshit,' Nina said sweetly.

Tony reached for her.

20

The phone buzzed. Elizabeth's left hand reached out to grab it while her right hand flung back the blankets and her feet swung down to the carpet.

'This is your wake-up call,' the recorded voice intoned. 'The time now is . . .'

Five forty-five a.m. She dropped the receiver back on the hook and bounded towards the bathroom, flicking on all the switches. Light stops the production of melatonin, the body's natural sleep hormone. After frustrating months of reading, Elizabeth knew her biochemistry back to front. Anyway, the morning routine was conditioned now. Quickly she washed her face and showered briefly, dried herself on an ugly peach towel that looked like a reject from BHS, and pulled on her running gear. Four days in Tunbridge Wells had tightened her butt and strengthened her legs. Ronnie's threat hit home; whatever else happened, she had to be fit. The team had followed a set training routine, but that wasn't enough for Elizabeth. When Karen, Janet and Kate had finished, Elizabeth would change suits and head back out the door. Five extra miles every night, then team dinner, then free weights. Seeing the other girls with better physiques than her fired Elizabeth's competitive edge.

And it was a good way of avoiding Jack Taylor.

Elizabeth pulled on her sports bra, ignoring the little thrill of excitement and anger Jack always provoked. Sitting there at dinner, pretending to discuss business with her. Ronnie refused to get rid of him, and Elizabeth just had to take it: Jack lying next to her in the weights room, bench-pressing three hundred, his chiselled muscles contracting, sliding back and forth, his jaw clamped tight in ferocious concentration. She hated him. His perfect body. His peak conditioning, his fucking business success.

Elizabeth flung herself into a warm-up routine, lifting her heels up to her butt to get the blood flowing round the hamstrings.

'He's got the best body I've ever seen,' Karen had gasped last night. Ron had put them all through a second fitness test. Jack joined in, and Elizabeth was forced to watch Jack's powerful quads tensing as he ate up the squat-thrust routines. His back muscles knotting and sliding in the press-ups. And his bicep curls, God, the weights he could lift. Elizabeth felt her team-mates' eyes just eating him up.

'He's nothing special,' she muttered.

They'd gaped at her in disbelief.

When Elizabeth hit the machines, Jack was watching her. She was clamped in place like a prisoner. And flexing, clamping her legs open and shut for the inner thighs, Jack had hung back and just blatantly stared between them.

'Open.' Ronnie yelling at her like a sergeant major. 'Close and open. Come on, Elizabeth! Open. *Open*. Great . . .'

Elizabeth pushed up from the soles of her runners, swinging her arms, blushing furiously. Remembering the betraying, ridiculous rush of sexual heat as she sweated and struggled, forcing her thighs apart, trying not to let that arrogant fuck see what effects his little games had on her. It was killing her, that was a plain fact. If Ronnie didn't get him out of here, there was a terrible danger Elizabeth was going to crack. She'd lain awake for an hour last night, dizzy with longing, not daring to touch herself in case that made it worse.

She took a swig of water from an Evian bottle, stretched out her calves and hamstrings, and opened the door. The hotel was just stirring, waiters setting out places in the awful buffet dining room, papers being shoved under doors. Outside, the roads were still quiet in the morning darkness. Elizabeth's blood was flowing now and she was looking forward to her run. For forty minutes she was alone with her body, nobody hassling her. She was hungry to get back out there to the snow. Louise and Heidi would be practising on World Cup courses, while she had to muck about on nylon fibres in distinctly non-World Cup Kent.

She jogged out of the lobby and stopped dead.

Jack Taylor was standing there, wearing pro Adidas runners and a US Olympic tracksuit.

'What the hell do you want?' Elizabeth demanded.

Jack gave her a lazy smile. 'To go running, Sherlock.'

'Who told you? Ronnie?' She stopped herself. 'Actually, I don't care. I run by myself.'

'Well.' He shifted on his feet, a movement that reminded her of his skiing. 'I know you're scared of me, sugar, but—'

'Scared? Don't be ridiculous.'

'Sure scared. You've been avoiding me ever since I got here. Which I think is kind of unfriendly, for a guy that saved your life.'

Elizabeth flushed. 'You provoked me into skiing off.'

'Provoked you?' Jack shrugged, his handsome, cruel mouth twisting a little scornfully. 'Because I took you on a hard run? I thought you could handle it, girl, but maybe I was wrong. I guess you've always been afraid of real competition.'

Elizabeth gave him an icy stare. 'You're heavy, Taylor. You're not built for speed. Your muscles are all wrong.'

'Try me,' Jack said.

'OK.' Already she was turning the local roads round in her mind, rewriting the course. 'We'll start by the station, then up the High Street.' That was two miles of solid uphill work.

'Fine by me, Princess.' Jack didn't flinch.

She turned away from him and loped off to the right, heading for the pool of neon orange under a far streetlamp. Her feet were lifting off the asphalt, rising to the challenge, flying away from him. Behind her Elizabeth heard Jack's grunt of surprise and the heavy thud of him on the ground as he raced to catch her. It took him four or five seconds. As Jack pulled up beside her, Elizabeth effortlessly increased the pace.

'Come on, Taylor,' she said coldly. 'Let's see what you got.'

Thirty minutes later she was covered in sweat. Straight hill running, then hill running on a curve, with small flat stretches to keep it aerobic. Elizabeth was working at the top of her range but she could feel Jack really suffering. He *was* too strong for sprinting.

'It's called muscle memory,' Jack gasped when they finally hit the Pantiles. Royal Tunbridge Wells was a ghost town at this hour, its prosperous red-brick houses and pretty Georgian streets deserted. He watched Elizabeth fly past countless gift shops and antique dealers, her long neck lifted, her haunches in front of him tight and fluid.

'What is?'

'Your fitness. How fast it's coming back. Even if you lose it, you're not starting from scratch. You should be ready for snow work in a couple more days.'

'Well, thanks, Coach,' Elizabeth snapped. She was annoyed that Jack hadn't cried off yet, the stubborn bastard. 'Let's see if *you're* ready for this. Toad Rocks. Half a mile up this curve.'

Four minutes later she turned into a dirt track off the main road. The prehistoric rock formation thrust out of thick woodland, surrounded by sand; a giant beachhead hidden in the middle of Kent. Elizabeth usually ran there in the mornings, via a much softer route. Overhead the sky was lightening, the pink and gold streaks of dawn creeping in from the east. She forced herself to bounce on her feet and breathe regularly.

Behind her Jack Taylor caught up, hit a rock, and collapsed, gasping, tearing the air into his lungs. Unbelievable. That exhaustion was all the reward she was going to get. He'd taken everything she could throw at him.

Petulantly Elizabeth ignored him and started some deep stretches. Jack said nothing, so when she was done she turned to face him. He was still lying prostrate, clutching his ankle.

'What's wrong?'

'It hurts. Christ, I think it's fractured,' Jack muttered.

Guilt surged through her. Who'd been playing macho games now? If Jack's ankle was fractured, it was highly unlikely it would heal in time for the Olympics. He was the favourite for gold. She'd have robbed him of that just to make a point.

Elizabeth gasped in dismay and sunk to her knees by Jack.

'Oh! It's all my fault, I'm so sorry.' She reached out and touched his lower leg but Taylor flinched away from her. Elizabeth's eyes prickled with tears. 'Can I test it, Jack? I'll be very careful . . .'

He nodded, biting his lip, and spread his legs a little to make room for her. Gingerly Elizabeth draped herself across him, her breasts brushing his thighs, and reached forwards with both hands. His ankle was lying in a pool of shadow from the rock. She couldn't see if it was discoloured.

'Gentle,' Jack murmured.

Elizabeth took his foot in her hands like it was made of eggshells and massaged it lightly, expertly, her long fingers working the muscle and bone, probing for any swelling.

'You seem OK to me—'

Suddenly Jack pounced, slipping one arm over the small of her back and tipping her into the sand. His legs kicked underneath her and his mouth fastened against hers in a deep, rough kiss.

'Bastard,' Elizabeth snarled.

'You play rough, sugar. You nearly killed me.'

He tasted of sand and sweat. He kissed her like he knew what he was doing. His arms were thicker than her upper thighs. She was back on that mountain, lifting her body into his, remembering herself dangling into space, hanging on to life by the strength of that arm. There were no men like Jack in her father's office.

'I came to England to find you,' he said, looking right down into her eyes.

'What, you can't live without me?' Elizabeth asked, trying for sarcasm and failing.

He grinned. 'Sure I can live without you. It just wouldn't be nearly so much fun.'

Then he kissed her again, and again, covering her face and her neck and ears with downy, butterfly kisses, till Elizabeth gasped and pressed her body into his.

'Come on.' Jack hauled her easily to her feet. 'We'd better get back, or I'm gonna take you to bed right here.'

She trained that day in a fever of anticipation and happiness. Partly to prove something to Ronnie, partly to show off to Jack.

'I can't believe it.' Ron was fulsome in his praise as they lined up in the Alpine View buffet restaurant for lunch, Elizabeth heaping her plate with pasta salad, baked potatoes and tuna. 'You're almost at race fitness.'

'Cow.' Karen's jokey insult had a slight edge to it. She could sense that the antipathy between Jack and Elizabeth had gone. As had the other girl's fantasies of displacing Lady Liz as number one.

'Umm, I must admit, I didn't think you'd be ready.' Janet had a dig too. It wasn't fair. Ronnie's threat had leaked out and she'd hoped Elizabeth might just be dropped. Now she was going to waltz off with a medal and maybe Jack Taylor. None of them could miss the way his eyes had fastened on her all day.

'It's called muscle memory,' Elizabeth smiled sweetly. 'My body just needed reminding.'

'You've worked hard.' Ronnie grinned as they all slotted into a table. He liked the resentment crackling round the room, it would make them more competitive. 'I think you're ready for snow training too. Hans Wolf called from Lausanne today. He wants to get you back on the snow, mid-Jan.'

That would mean giving up on Dragon. But then, thanks to Nina Roth, I'm going nowhere fast anyway, Elizabeth thought. Maybe it was time to cut her losses.

'Great,' she said.

Jack called for her after dinner.

'Let's go out for a drive.'

Elizabeth looked up at him in surprise, but Jack gestured to her tacky room. 'We can do better than this, don't you think?'

They passed Janet in the lobby. 'Training starts at six tomorrow,' she said, staring jealously at Jack's arm threaded through Elizabeth's duffel coat.

'And she'll probably be there,' Jack replied. Elizabeth bit back her smile, but Janet's eyes glittered with dislike anyway.

A hire car was parked in the forecourt, a sleek Mercedes. Elizabeth slid into the passenger seat while Jack jumped in beside her. A set of keys were resting on the dashboard.

'Where are we going?' Elizabeth asked.

He smiled. 'You'll see.'

They drove out of town towards East Sussex, dipping up and down country hills. Jack drove smoothly, unfazed by the narrow woodland roads and sharp corners. The night was crisp and cold, the stars brilliant in the clear sky. Rabbits scurried away from the headlights, and once she saw a white owl's wing ghosting up out of the trees in front of them.

He parked outside a cottage on the edge of Frant village. 'My country retreat. I stay here when I'm going to meets.'

Jack jumped out to open the door for her. His Texas gallantry made her nervous.

What's wrong with me? Elizabeth thought. Suddenly she cared desperately about the kind of impression she was giving him. It had never been that way with Gerard de Mesnil, or Karl, or any of the others.

'Come in.' Jack flicked on lights and ushered her into the cottage. It was beautiful, with timbered ceilings and wooden stairs curving upwards. Elizabeth hung up her duffel on an old-fashioned coat-stand and followed him into a tiny drawing room. A careful pile of kindling, coal and logs was all ready in the grate. Jack took a box of Ship matches down from the mantelpiece and lit a firelighter. It crackled into flame at once.

'Cheat,' Elizabeth teased.

Jack turned his head and gave her a wicked smile. 'I'm not that rustic. Want a drink? Port, sour mash, champagne?'

Elizabeth shifted on her heels as he drew the curtains. She wanted to drink herself brave. 'Maybe a little champagne.'

While he rummaged in the kitchen Elizabeth snuck upstairs. The bathroom was painted a child's blue with yellow ducks in the basin, and the single bedroom was papered with a Laura Ashley burgundy sprig. A pair of dumbbells lay at the foot of a large bed covered in a pretty eiderdown. Something about the place made her happiness tighten around her heart.

She went downstairs. 'It's lovely, but it doesn't seem very you.'

'How do you know what's very me? You don't even know me,' Jack said.

Elizabeth felt shy. 'I'd like to,' she said.

Jack leaned over and kissed her very softly on the lips. Then he handed her a chipped stone mug, half-full of champagne.

'No glasses. At least it proves I didn't take you for granted.'

They drank the champagne by the fire, Elizabeth nestling her head in the crook of Jack's arm. He didn't make any move on her, and slowly the nerves started to fade. When he finally started to stroke her, Elizabeth wanted it, she was light with desire for him. They started to kiss, gently, then more urgently.

'Are you ready?' Jack whispered.

Elizabeth nodded, even though she was still scared.

He took her head in his two hands and kissed her again. 'Sugar, I was dying for you the first moment I saw you. It's not an audition. I won't do anything you don't want.'

She smiled and held out her hand to him.

'I got a better idea,' Jack suggested. Then he scooped her up in his arms like she was made of cotton wool, and carried her slowly up the stairs.

21

Snow lay thick on the ground in her tiny scrap of garden. Outside on the street it was already turning to slush. Nina let herself out and set the burglar alarm. It was still a thrill to do that; the two-bedroom, three-storey house in Tufnell Park, ninety grand, her first piece of property. Tony had recommended her to the Hong Kong & Shanghai for a wonderfully low mortgage, and the smart Camden flat went to somebody more junior. Her Christmas present had been a diamond necklace and earrings from Asprey's, which Nina was planning to sell after a decent interval.

'I don't celebrate Christmas,' she said when he handed over the box.

Tony was unabashed. 'You do now.'

Despite the glorious chill fire of the jewels, Nina thought how easy it would have been just to say, 'Happy Chanukah.' But that was Tony, he didn't move an inch. For anybody.

Nina climbed into her Golf and swung out into the traffic. January was a buzz; maybe it was Britain's long, booze-soaked holiday, but once New Year's was over, the capital seemed full of fresh vigour, as though desperate to make up lost time. Nina spent the holidays in Companies House and the library of the British Medical Association. She knew Frank, Carl and her other colleagues thought she was a crazy workaholic. They also despised her once the rapid promotion came through. Senior manager, that young? Nobody said anything to Caerhaven's new piece of ass, but the frostiness was there.

She flicked on the radio as she turned past King's Cross Station. The news was dolorously announcing flooding round the city of York and a passenger train marooned in a Welsh blizzard. The Americans were stalling over the Falklands. Unemployment was up again.

Anger doesn't bother me, Nina thought, it's the other thing. Junior pricks of the type that always sucked up to Liz Savage had started to suck up to her. That was branding as bad as any scarlet letter. The irony was that she *deserved* the new slot. Busting her ass all vacation, she'd found an answer, to both of Tony's problems.

The last time she'd seen him was Christmas Eve, in a suite at the St James's Club. He was taking a lunchtime Intercity to Cardiff to be ferried back to his castle, and he wanted to see her before he left. Nina was flattered by his hunger for her, but unsettled by the Christmas present. She took it and then him, straddling him on the bed, riding him almost violently. Tony provoked her. He was good in bed, very expert in his moves, and his power was a turn-on, but it wasn't like it had been that first time. It hadn't been that good again.

Dublin was the climax of a lot of things, she saw that now. Fear, and greed, and anger against a world from which she was permanently barred. Anger at Elizabeth, making her feel once again that she was just white trash. Nina lifted her chin and flicked the dial to Radio One. They could all go to hell. She deserved this promotion, even if that was not why she'd gotten it. The Police were yelling, 'We are spirits in the material world!' Nina tapped the steering wheel in time. Yeah, brother, Amen to that.

Tony had his problems too.

'They involve you,' he'd said, reaching across her breasts for the Cristal, his green eyes bland.

'How?'

'My darling daughter isn't happy. She thinks we are stifling her creativity. Or more to the point, that you are. Ever since she came back from her bloody training camp she's been making merry hell.' The aquiline face was tight. 'She's aggressive. Insistent. She wants me to fire you.'

Nina sat bolt upright, the silk sheet slithering to her waist. 'What?'

'That's right.' He was amused at her outrage. 'She says you never consider her work—'

'That's because she never does any. I ask for market research on hospitals, she turns up with cut-and-paste adverts for aspirin.'

'Do you look at her stuff?'

Nina seethed with resentment. 'Fuck no. I'm New Products. I want market research. Facts. She reports to me, she should do what she's asked. I'm not looking for the next Charles Saatchi.'

'But you may have to humour her, I'm afraid. She's making good skiing times and she's in the Olympics this year. She's talking about making a fuss in the press. Giving interviews.'

'And you don't want that to happen?'

'And that isn't going to happen,' Tony said, his voice light as silk round a blade. The darkness in his eyes made Nina shiver. 'Make her happy, darling, would you? Smooth things over. She is my daughter, after all.'

Nina slipped out of bed as Tony pulled a cigarette from his silver monogrammed case, heading for a shower. She'd been furious. She relied on him to block Elizabeth's moves in the office, and now the snobbish little cow was going to win? She didn't understand Savage. He talked about Elizabeth with passionate dislike, but now he was ordering Nina to roll over! Maybe blue blood was thicker than water, after all.

Nina spun her car into its new slot, closer to the building's entrance. The paint was still gleaming. She knew she was making a lot of enemies here, and Lady Elizabeth was just at the head of the queue. They would tear her apart like a pack of rabid dogs if Tony ever took his protective hand off her shoulder.

She took out her slim dossier from the back seat. To hell with them all. If she couldn't be liked, at least she could be good. And that would have to do.

'Catch!' Jack spun the box across the room and Elizabeth's hand shot upwards to grab it. He thumped the table. 'Reflex like that, you should be in baseball.'

'Cricket, please.' Elizabeth smiled as she ripped off the wrapping. 'Garrard's! What's this, another present? Christmas is over, don't tell me you haven't noticed.'

She flicked open the small box to find a pendant, a platinum ski on a long chain. 'Jack, it's so cool . . .'

'It's not cool, it's romantic. Look.' He fished the matching ski out of his pocket. 'I'm keeping this half. Thought it was better than a split heart or a sixpence or something corny like that. It's a goodbye present.'

Elizabeth jumped on the eiderdown to kiss him. 'I love it.' She wanted to say, 'I love you,' but didn't dare. When you said, 'I love you,' men heard, 'I've got meningitis,' they ran away so fast. 'But what do you mean you're going away? It's nearly a month to snow training.'

Jack took the chain from her hands and looped it around her neck. He was quick with the clasp; it still amazed her, the guy was so big and yet so graceful. 'I got to go back to Texas. Check on my studs, check on the new orders.'

'Oh.' Elizabeth frowned. 'Can't that wait? Don't you want to be with me? We're going to be so busy once training starts, they'll have the national officials all over us . . .'

'It's business. I have to go.'

'You don't have to, you want to. Whatever.' She was really pissed off. They'd waited so long, and now all she got was a few days snatched before and after Christmas. His business success was waved like a flag in her face, and Elizabeth felt miserably conscious that her own grand scheme had come to nothing.

'Hey, you'll want time at Dragon, right? You made your old man take you on, you might as well make it count for something.' Jack dropped to the ground and began a fast set of stomach crunches.

'You're right,' Elizabeth said. It was true. She had made Dad take her on, and the power she'd had then she still had now. If that bitch Nina Roth was going to block her, she could have her fired. What was the point of leverage, if you didn't use it?

Nina went up to see Tony as soon as she arrived. Mrs Perkins, his secretary, tried to brush her off.

'Are you down in the book, Miss Roth?' She made a great play of consulting her diary. 'Oh dear, I'm afraid there's been a mix-up, you're not here.'

'I didn't make an appointment.'

'You didn't *schedule* an appointment? Then it won't be possible to see him now.'

'He said I should drop by any time,' Nina said, trying to smile. Mrs Perkins was giving her a superior gate-keeper's look that said, I know what you're all about, you hussy. She probably had a huge crush on Tony herself. Casually Nina fiddled with her cuff to flash her gold Cartier tank watch, set with diamonds, another Tony bauble she could never have afforded on her salary.

Mrs Perkins went white. Bingo, thought Nina maliciously, and he probably sent you out to buy it for me, you uptight old bag.

'Lord Caerhaven is very busy. He doesn't see anyone without an appointment.'

'Mrs Perkins,' Nina said sweetly, 'I don't have much time. I'm afraid I must insist you buzz him for me.'

She faced the older woman down. Nina knew she was an insolent Yank brat to her, but still, she was a senior manager and Mrs Perkins was a secretary. Nina had earned her status and she was never going to be put down or blocked off again.

Mrs Perkins's whiteness blossomed with rage, two red spots blooming on her cheeks like berries in cream, but she icily depressed her intercom.

'I'm sorry, my lord, but Miss Roth *insists* on my disturbing you.'

'Nina? Terrific. Send her in, Mrs P.'

'He'll see you now, Miss Roth,' Mrs Perkins said unnecessarily, her voice thin with annoyance. Nina gave her an insolent wink as she opened the door.

Tony was standing facing his windows, gazing out over the river that glittered in the weak January sun. He turned to face her, his eyes assessing her pale blue suit and green silk shirt, her expensive Patrick Cox mules and sheer Wolford stockings. Looking her over with sensual possessiveness. Nina found it arousing but disturbing, the way his eyes stripped her, like a boy appreciating a favoured toy.

'You like your new parking slot? And you're wearing your watch.' He smiled. 'What about the earrings?'

'Too much jewellery's not appropriate for the office.'

'But I like to see you in them. Wear them tomorrow.' Tony gestured to the notes she was carrying. 'What's this?'

'I think I've found you some answers. To the slimming drug problem. And to Lady Elizabeth, too,' Nina said.

'Good girl,' Tony said warmly.

Elizabeth got into the office to find her friends genially welcoming her back. She smiled and asked them all about their Christmases, but she felt empty inside. Jack had actually flown off and left her, and she wouldn't see him for weeks. Then there would be a hard haul to reach Olympic Champion skiing level, then the Games themselves. Elizabeth felt sick with nerves. It was '82 now, the Olympic year, and the bloody rings were appearing everywhere, on Mars bars and Coke cans and in the papers and on the telly, with endless profiles of herself. Along with Jayne Torville and Christopher Dean, the ice skaters, Elizabeth was apparently Britain's other dead cert for gold. She thought Heidi and Louise might have a few words to say about that. Heidi was three times World Champion and only beaten by a nanosecond last year. Plus, she was Swiss, she'd have been skiing all winter. Cabbies, socialites, and now the rest of the office, everyone was wishing her luck, cheering her on, treating her with a kind of awed respect that felt like a vice crunching her skull, the pressure was so huge. It was incredibly difficult to focus on anything else, but she knew she had to. If she couldn't wring something out of her bastard father now, she never would later. Win or lose, by Easter the Olympics would be over, and she wanted some kind of role to go back to.

She picked up her internal phone directory and skimmed the pages, looking for Nina Roth's extension. It had been changed. Now it began with a five. Elizabeth frowned; five was for people with their own offices.

'Hey, Tom, has Nina Roth moved departments?'

Tom pointed at the ceiling. 'Only upwards. She got a promotion while you were away. She's got her own room now, her own assistant. It's some kind of record.'

No way, Elizabeth thought angrily. 'You're kidding, she only just got here.'

Tom nodded. 'Umm, and the boys in New Products aren't too happy about it either.'

'But why? What on earth did she do that was so great?'

Elizabeth saw poor Tom suddenly blush and look down. Then it hit her.

Of course. She was always close to Daddy. So now she's a bit closer; another tart for the harem. Sleeping her way effortlessly up the ladder. Well, that was the only thing Daddy ever rewarded women for, or in the case of Monica, for not making a fuss. Was he bored of the girls in pearls now, Elizabeth wondered acidly, and moving on to career women? What did a hard-nosed robot with breasts do for him?

At any rate, she wasn't going to let either of them stand in her way.

The phone on her desk buzzed loudly. Elizabeth picked it up.

'Elizabeth, is that you, darling?' She tensed at the sound of Daddy's voice; the nice words flecked with sarcasm, the way he always spoke to her. She'd spent the whole Christmas break riding out over the freezing Caerhaven fields, or going for long hikes along the clifftops, just to get away from that utterly bloody tone. 'Could you come up to my office? Nina Roth and I have a little suggestion for you.'

Elizabeth checked her reflection in the mirrored door of the lift. Her hair fell loose and glossy over a Jaeger jacket in butterscotch cashmere and matching tweed skirt. She wore low brown heels and eight-denier tights, the thinnest wisps of nothing she could find for her legs. The pre-training session had got her back into shape; she fit the same size twelve now but she was half a stone heavier, her weak legs and buttocks firmed into muscle, her taut upper back making her look taller. A gold cuff bracelet fell over her left wrist and Jack's long platinum ski glinted against a cream silk shirt. She had no make-up but she didn't need it. The healthy athlete's glow was back in her skin.

The lift doors hissed open and she stepped out to face Mrs Perkins, who gave her an obsequious smile. 'Lady Elizabeth, how nice to see you, you look beautiful ... did you have a nice Christmas? Lots of exercise, I expect?'

Elizabeth smiled graciously and chatted but her heart was thumping loudly in her chest. She could feel the adrenalin surging through her bloodstream, like it did before a race. Nina and Tony. Together. Was she going to need it? Was there going to be a fight?

'No, no, go in, Lady Elizabeth, of course he's expecting you,' Mrs Perkins was twittering. Elizabeth stepped through her father's lobby, unconsciously rubbing the signet ring he'd handed over at Christmas. All Savage children got theirs at twenty-one, the heavy gold circle cut to fit, stamped with the family crest. I've got a bloody right to this, Elizabeth thought, summoning up her anger. He can't shut me out any more.

She walked into Tony's office.

Nina stood by the desk, listening to Elizabeth and Mrs Perkins murmuring outside. Mrs Perkins sounded remarkably friendly and deferential; but then Elizabeth was quality, after all, and I'm just the help, she thought cynically. Tony got up when his daughter entered the room and walked across to kiss her on the cheek. Nina pasted a smile on her face as she watched them. Christ. Look at the stuck-up little cow. This was the girl who wanted to take her job away! A castle. Swiss finishing school. Hunt balls and tweed skirts!

The earl and Elizabeth said hello and kissed the air by each other's cheeks. The words were friendly, but the ceremony was stiff. Nina forced the grin off her face. They're as screwed up as me and my loser folks, in their way.

Tony waved both girls to a seat.

'Elizabeth, darling, Nina's had an idea.'

22

'Lady Elizabeth.' Nina nearly choked on it. 'Do you recall that New Products was working on a drug, B-28?'

'The slimming pill,' Elizabeth said.

'Yeah. That drug was a bust, but the research on it turned up some interesting side effects.'

'Part of the pill components were vitamins,' Tony said, 'intended to replace lost nutrients if the appetite suppressant stopped the punters eating. B-28 failed toxicity tests, meaning it poisoned the system—'

'I know what toxicity means, Daddy.'

Daddy! Speaking quickly to cover her annoyance, Nina ploughed on. 'Vitamins may be the next big thing in retail. Along with bottled mineral water and keep-fit, we think they're going to be the craze of the eighties. We were hoping you could help.'

'So was I, but every time I came up with an idea – for anything – you refused to look at it.'

Elizabeth held the American's gaze and saw the dark pupils flash, Nina's lush beauty spiced with anger.

There was a pause. Elizabeth saw Nina glance at Tony, but her father looked blank.

'Yes, Lady Elizabeth. I realise I may have been too hasty,' the dark-haired girl said slowly. She dropped her eyes. Clearly furious.

'You can be a special help to us with a new pill we're launching,' Tony said smoothly. 'People want one pill for everything. It's been difficult in the past.'

'And we've got one?'

'Well, we've found a way to combine iron and calcium,' Nina Roth said. 'Usually, calcium blocks the absorption of iron. So our new pill will be the most complete thing out there. And you are the perfect person to sell it. You could combine the campaign with your skiing career. You see, we're thinking of calling it Dragon Gold. As an Olympic hopeful, a World Champion already, you would be the perfect face for the brand.'

'You want me to be in adverts?'

'Only print ones, Elizabeth. I'd find television ads a little vulgar,' her father said. 'But you would also be in charge of the campaign. Designing it. Selling it. You can create copy, oversee the agency account, everything.'

Elizabeth found her fist had curled into a tight ball. Amazing what a little blackmail could do. It sounded like a good product, and she would have total control. She was careful not to betray her elation.

'Is the pill gold?'

'Yellow, from the beta-carotine,' Nina explained. Elizabeth hated her patronising air. She might not be a lab rat like Nina Roth, but she wasn't stupid. Nina thought she had a monopoly on anything needing a double-figure IQ.

'What do you think, darling?' the earl asked lightly. 'Right up your alley, isn't it?'

'Right up my alley,' Elizabeth agreed. 'If you mean it, about my having total control.' She leaned forwards, looking at Tony challengingly.

She's ignoring me, Nina thought.

'Of course,' Tony said.

'If I'm to control this line, I shouldn't have to report in to Nina.'

Nina sat perfectly still, anger blazing through her like fire through petrol. She had no doubt at all that Tony would cave in. All he wanted was the quiet life. And if that meant humiliating Nina then that's what he would do. She looked over at her young ladyship, the girl so poised and polished in her upper-class clothes, and her eyes were flint.

'No. Nina will be out there, supervising the actual launch, but your work will be overseen by Dino Vincenza. He's in charge of marketing, after all.'

'Suits me, Daddy. Although maybe it would be better if I reported in to Dino on everything. In the future.'

Nina bit her bottom lip. Caerhaven had tensed, and she sensed he was very angry, but he was the consummate pragmatist.

'If you like,' Tony said.

'Then that's fixed.' Elizabeth stood up, pushing herself up on the soles of her feet, perfectly balanced. It was a strong movement. She gave Nina a barely perceptible nod, then shook her father's hand.

'Well, that's all,' Tony said, dismissing the meeting.

Nina got up, unable to look at father or daughter. She followed Elizabeth's stiff back out into the corridor and waited by the elevator bank with her. She wondered if Mrs Perkins had been listening in to that exchange, thought about the look of triumph that would greet her next time she entered Tony's office.

Elizabeth stepped into the lift. Nina followed her.

'You know, this works great for me,' Nina said. 'I really have so much work to do already, one less job will be a relief.'

Lady Elizabeth's green eyes fixed on hers. 'Nobody asked you if it would be great for you or not,' she said.

'That's right.' Nina couldn't help herself. 'I didn't go running to Papa to ask him to fix things for me. But then I'm not a part-timer. I really work for a living.'

'Yeah, you don't bother having a life. I heard that,' Elizabeth Savage mocked. 'Except when you go running to your boyfriend's bed. *That's* why he lets you do real work, sweetie. Daddy's not big on women, except the ones he wants in his bed. That's the only reason you made the grade.'

'You silly, spoilt little cow,' Nina snarled. 'You've got no idea how I made the grade. I'm the smartest person in this goddamn company.'

'Certainly the best at Daddy's *special* assignments.' Elizabeth reached out and slammed the pause button. 'But don't get any illusions, Nina. You'll never replace my stepmother. You're nothing special. Girls like you come and go, you're just a toy to him.'

'He doesn't give a damn about you. He's only doing this to shut your stupid little Sloane mouth up.'

Elizabeth smiled. 'You think I need you to tell me that? And you think I care? I've got a right to this company. I'll get my chance any way I bloody well can. Although I expect you'll be blabbing all this to him next time he takes you to bed.'

'No chance, bitch,' Nina snapped. 'I can look after myself.'

'Ditto.' Elizabeth let the lift slide downwards. 'And I can handle you. In fact I just did, didn't I? I'll be trotting off to Dino now, since he's my new boss.'

'Watch your back, kiddo,' Nina said.

Elizabeth laughed. 'I don't think so. I'm more than a match for you. And give it a rest with the melodrama, would you? You're in England now, you know, not a bit player on *Starsky and Hutch*.'

The lift slid smoothly to a halt and the doors hissed open.

'After you, milady,' Nina said softly.

Elizabeth turned and gave her a brilliant smile. 'Oh, you can call me Elizabeth, Nina. I like to encourage familiarity from the staff.'

She walked off towards Marketing in a soft swish of cashmere and tweed, her long, honey-blonde hair gleaming neatly down her back, her elegant walk giving Nina visions of deportment lessons and private dances. Fury balled like a fist in Nina's stomach.

I might be in England, she thought, but I'm still playing by Brooklyn rules. And girl, you just had your first and last warning.

Nina sat down at her desk and tapped into her computer absently. Her mind was already in Switzerland. And on what it would take to bring Lady Elizabeth down.

'So. Tell me more about these *Wünderkinder* you've discovered,' Frank Staunton said.

Nina crossed her legs and leaned back in her chair. Lady Elizabeth had flown off to Switzerland, and no one else around Dragon dared to give her a hard time. She was wearing a navy suit with white piping, a *prêt à porter* from Chanel. Gucci heels gave her an extra inch of height and Tony's diamonds glittered on her lobes. The Swiss team she'd found were a slam-dunk. Right now she could face Heinrich Günther, Don Hadley and the rest without a qualm.

For a moment Nina remembered the frightened, desperate teenager she'd been barely three years back. Well, that girl was dead. She'd killed her. The power she felt right now was worth any amount of catty looks from Tom, Elizabeth and the rest of them.

'I've found a primary research source I think should replace Steele and

Ripley.' Nina passed folders around the table. 'Dr Henry Namath, Dr Lilly Hall and four technicians under their employ are currently operating in Zurich. They're freelancers and have supplied specialist work to pharmaceutical giants and bio-tech companies. They work on complex computer modelling systems. Dr Hall's the biochemist, Dr Namath the computer expert. Their ratio of success to failure is very good.'

'But slimming drugs, Miss Roth,' Heinrich Günther objected. 'Your folder refers to cardio, respiratory, anti-inflammatories . . .'

'If they already *had* a slimming drug, we wouldn't be taking this meeting.' Nina risked insolence; she saw the amused gleam in Tony's eye. 'The reason I propose we annex them is that they have recently done some interesting veterinary work. A drug called Leptate has helped to slim pigs.'

There was silence. Pigs weren't humans, but they were mammals; they were close.

'And why has not ICI jumped on them already?'

'Only because they aren't scanning the breakthroughs in animal medicine, I guess. It occurred to me to cross-check over the vacation.'

There, Nina thought. Under the table her manicured fist curled softly in on itself. Now they'll stop despising me, she thought. They'll have to. That kind of lateral thinking is what's lacking over here. And with one brainwave I just got them closer than they've ever been before.

'We should move fast, though. Somebody else is bound to notice soon.'

'I agree.' Frank Staunton was looking at Tony, nodding.

'And I.' Seeing which way the wind was blowing, Herr Günther had decided to jump in there too.

'My daughter will be out there supervising a new product launch. As she's skiing in the Olympics, it will be perfect cover. Meanwhile Nina will be in Switzerland, essentially to cover sales and shipping, but actually talking to Doctors Hall and Namath.'

'Terrific, sir,' Gerald Jax said admiringly.

'*Ja*,' Günther agreed. 'Nobody will think twice about it.'

'Then that's settled.' Caerhaven smiled softly.

The meeting broke up. Nina noticed that the soft murmurs of congratulation were all headed Tony's way. Heinrich Günther gave her a sharp look of dislike, which was the best compliment she was likely to get. She glanced angrily at Tony. Why did he want to steal her idea?

The earl looked over from his crop of courtiers and caught her staring. He frowned slightly and Nina dropped her eyes. He didn't appreciate the protest. *I'm still the boss*, his dark eyes warned. *Don't fuck with me.*

Nina walked through to Marketing at five p.m., carrying a folder on Dragon Gold. Ad executives and their secretaries gave her nasty glances and stopped talking when she passed by their desks.

She stopped in front of Elizabeth's little cubicle, expecting to see it plastered with pictures of Elizabeth holding medals or grinning out of the pages of *Tatler*. Maybe some shots of Jack Taylor; she'd heard the rumours they were seeing each other. One rich-kid jock screwing another, just perfect. She knew Tony thought so. And she was with him there: Elizabeth married and in Texas meant Elizabeth out of her hair, giving dinner parties and throwing charity balls like little ladies were intended to. But the walls were covered with ads. Saatchi's pregnant man, the Honey Monster, some apes throwing a tea party. Nina recognised each one of them. Maybe looking up at other people's triumphs was the closest her little ladyship would ever come to work.

Elizabeth looked up. Her long hair was caught back now in a velvet clip. It looked ludicrously fresh faced and boarding-school-ish.

'I've come to bring you the notes on the new product, Elizabeth.'

'The notes? Oh, thank you, but I have them already. Mrs Perkins is making sure I'm up to speed.'

Nina shrugged.

'I'll get everything I need direct from my father,' Elizabeth said, 'so you needn't concern yourself.'

'OK,' Nina said, through gritted teeth.

'And I've just heard that you'll be out in Switzerland too. Do you like skiing? Maybe you could come out and watch the Olympics.'

'Thanks, but I find *work* keeps me busy. I prefer to concentrate on the job in hand.' Nina dredged up some murky names from her memory. 'I guess I'll just keep my fingers crossed for Kim Gideon and Holly Ferrell, those are our girls, right? Or if not, Louise Levier and Heidi Laufen. The Swiss. If you're neutral, it's nice to support the host nation.'

Lady Elizabeth's green eyes regarded her with maddening coolness.

'How silly of me. You're the total professional. Just work, work, work, but then of course that's how you've been getting all your wonderful promotions. Pretty earrings, by the way. They look rather expensive.'

'I earned them,' Nina said.

'So I hear,' Elizabeth replied.

Nina turned on her heel and walked away. She didn't want the rich bitch to see her riled. She wanted to slap that silly, smug little face until the ears bled. Goddamn, I've been working since I was seven years old, I don't need to come to England and have some no-nothing blueblood call me a whore to my face.

Nina's office was a haven of silence. She looked round: soft, dove-grey carpets, an orthopaedic chair, a kidney-shaped desk and top-of-the-range computer. She was a senior manager now, with her own secretary and two fax machines.

I earned this, she thought fiercely, I did, I did.

The wall opposite her desk was decorated with a large square photograph. Nina had chosen a Patrick Demarchelier shot, a black and white showing a grimy Brooklyn street scene. It was nowhere near her old neighbourhood but so what, poor was poor. As Nina stared at it her heart hardened up again, shaking off the insults and misgivings.

Jeff Glazer. The laughing kids at St Michael's. Her fat fuck of a father slumped on the couch in front of *Jeopardy*.

Never, never again. She was sitting here wearing Chanel. It was gonna take more than a few dirty looks to faze her now.

23

Tony Savage lay back in bed and watched Nina. He felt marvellously relaxed. The ultra-modern, Japanese décor of the Halkin Hotel matched his mood perfectly; soothing, with no fuss or bother. He congratulated himself as Nina dressed. The girl had been quite a find; an off-the-wall thinker, with relentless ambition. And the best piece of ass he'd ever had.

He thought of Camilla Browning, with her horsy voice and clingy manner. Looking back on it she seemed as exciting as a lowing cow. Nina was in another league. She turned him on like a light switch. Nina Roth would die before she'd cling on to anything. Tony casually studied the soft creamy flesh at the top of Nina's thighs as she pulled on her panties, plain white cotton from Marks & Spencer. Nina had the best pair of breasts he'd ever seen, she was all soft curves and hard-assed Yank attitude. Tony knew it was one more source of jealousy around Dragon that he was laying her. Heinrich, for example, looked at her when her back was turned like a slavering dog. He'd even caught the bellboy tonight with his eyes on her butt like he could see through her dress. Tony liked that. He loved lesser men drooling over what he had.

'My flight leaves at noon,' Nina said. 'I'm going home now. To pack.'

'Are you taking your bracelet with you?'

Nina picked up the trinket he'd bought for her tonight. It was a light twist of silver set with opals and sapphires.

'I don't think so. I don't plan on going to many parties.'

'I want you to take it,' Tony said.

Nina stiffened. She hated it when he used that tone. The jewels she'd loved at first were now beginning to annoy her; she couldn't say why.

'I went to a lot of trouble to get it for you. Why won't you take it?'

'I guess,' Nina agreed after a pause.

Tony smiled. Nina was too prickly for hearts and flowers, fine. But he was still in charge. That was the best thing about this little one: she was smart and driven, but still too young to really see things straight. When she got a good idea, she came right to him. Women did that a lot, he noticed. They picked up silly romantic ideas about work, they invented spurious loyalties and clung to the idea that hard work would be rewarded. People worked hard in quarries, but rarely got rewarded. Results. It was all about results. Nina would give him her best work, she would be comfortable, she would wind up a middle manager and be grateful for it too. The jewellery made a nice point: he didn't want her getting too independent.

Recently she'd been hanging back a little in bed. Initially she'd been passionate; lately it was like the bloom had gone for her. But Tony was skilled, he knew how to ride over that first reluctance. His desire for her was still at full throttle. He had no intention whatsoever of letting her go.

'Good girl, that's the ticket. You'll want something to wear to the Olympic parties and launches that Liz dreams up.'

'Yeah.' Nina's dark mood blackened further. She reached for her bra and dress and pulled them on quickly.

'You must send me reports on her. See that she's keeping out of trouble. And what the story is between her and the Taylor boy,' Tony said.

'Of course. I'll keep you updated.'

'I knew I could count on you, darling. We'll rush forward with wedding plans as soon as he pops the question. Throw her a spectacular bash, and then it'll be off to darkest Texas.'

'But never mind.' Nina walked forwards and perched on the end of the bed. Tony's wallet was laid open on the side-table; there was a prominent photo of the countess, Monica, with two teenage boys. Elizabeth was noticeably absent. She watched her lover as she added, 'You won't be so much gaining a son as losing a daughter.'

Lord Caerhaven gave a short bark of laughter.

God, you really do hate her, Nina thought drily. How interesting.

She took a taxi back from the lobby of the hotel. The receptionist kept shooting her sidelong glances, until Nina turned dark eyes towards him and stared him coldly in the face, at which the man dropped his eyes at once.

The cab took her up to Tufnell Park. It was only two a.m., but the roads in the city centre were already deserted. Nina stared out of the windows; a thin drizzle was lashing little beads on the windowpane that sparkled in the lamplight. Her new bracelet sparkled too, twisting between her fingers. It was a wonderful piece; expensive but not overpowering, impeccably tasteful. Just what you would expect from the Robber Baron.

The house was deserted and still. Nina had shoved most of her furniture into storage and switched her bills to Dragon. The answerphone was blinking furiously: six messages from New York and Europe that had missed her in the office; one from Anita Kerr, her secretary, inviting her out for a goodbye drink. Nina was sorry she'd missed that one. Anita, who knew how hard she worked, was the closest thing she had to a friend in the office. Anita and Brian Kane, her neighbour, who she sometimes jogged with on a Sunday, represented her non-Dragon social life. But I don't need one, Nina told herself. I don't need to be a butterfly like Elizabeth. I have things to do with my life.

She went into the kitchen and pulled out the last Tesco pizza from the freezer. Then she started to fix a pot of coffee. She drank so much caffeine these days, she could drink coffee right before bed without any problem. Coffee and pizza was a small pleasure, a solitary moment in a day filled with people she didn't really like. Take the function last evening, a stuffy

Caerhaven party at the House of Lords. Senior Dragon people went. Why had she been asked? Because Tony wanted to impress her? Or his cronies? It was the eighteenth birthday of Charles, Lord Holwyn, Tony's eldest son. Charles was a miniature version of his papa, striding through the crowd, being heartily congratulated by obnoxious schoolfriends and bluff business associates of Tony's. Lord Richard, his little brother, seemed blond and bland, like his mother. Nina watched Tony's wife curiously. She seemed sexless, almost faceless, despite her inoffensive prettiness. Yet she moved through that crowd with a poise Nina would never have, looking bored but charming at the same time. There were more titles and money together in that room than Nina could get her head round, and she hated every last second of it. An attractive but stupid girl named Camilla Browning kept bumping into her all night long, showering her with clumsy insults and cutting remarks about Americans. Eventually Nina escaped with a glass of bourbon to the terrace, to watch the Thames roll sluggishly by. When Tony wandered out and casually suggested the Halkin as a rendezvous, Nina was relieved. But by the time she met him in the lobby, her attitude had hardened. She disliked Tony almost as much as the rest of them.

The microwave pinged.

Even if it meant more run-ins with Elizabeth, she was looking forward to Switzerland. That country was all about money. And Nina knew money. Maybe in Zurich she could make the deal that would gain her respect once and for all.

Before she ate, Nina picked up her new bracelet and dropped it in an envelope, addressed to Anita Kerr. Her note asked Anita not to wear it around the office. It might be a foolish gesture, Nina thought, but it felt good. If rather dangerous.

The plane dipped towards Kloten airport, overlooking Lake Zurich and the snow-capped mountains around the city. Nina watched the scenery with idle curiosity. It was her first time in Continental Europe but she couldn't spare much interest in picture-postcard views. Her mind was racing through the biographies of Dr Lilly Hall and Dr Henry Namath.

They were a strange pair. Dr Hall had been a full professor of biochemistry at the University of Western Australia. She was a holder of the Order of Australia for her breakthrough work in disease-resistant crop genetics. Lilly was a practical woman, she didn't take time to publish her work. Her college demanded more name recognition, there was a spat over tenure, and Dr Hall left for the private sector. Her work since then was ambitious, and often failed, but the scores she did make were serious. Lean pigs! Nina could shiver just thinking about it. Her photograph in the file was ten years out of date; it showed a jowly woman in her forties, short, squat, with leathery skin from too much exposure to the sun. If there was a romance, nobody knew about it.

Dr Henry Namath. Pictured four years ago, nothing to write home about in the looks department – Buddy Holly glasses and facial hair that would do credit to Chewbacca the Wookie, but a razor-sharp mind. Between the lines of his file Nina read him as your classic nerd. As a teenage boy from a cold northwestern suburb outside Minneapolis, Harry Namath had been twice expelled from school for crashing a mainframe computer. Later he had done two months in juvenile detention for doing the same to a state mainframe, causing all the lights in Pennsville, MA, to stick on green for a full day. Namath had been writing code and programming machines for ever, since that meant feeding strips of paper with holes punched in them to metal behemoths working the binary system. He'd maxed out his SATs, but with the criminal record, only scraped in to University of St Thomas, a Catholic college, where he'd barely cruised through. Nina grinned when she recalled that. Maybe UST didn't have any computers.

Now he was writing programs as a freelance. Picked up an easy doctorate at the London School of Economics, hired by IBM, fired in six months. Clearly a maverick. Bumped into Lilly Hall at a hospital fundraiser in London, when she was completing a project for the Ministry of Agriculture. They'd been together ever since. Lilly did the pharmacology; Harry wrote programs for companies, showing how her drugs and genes could be used.

Both of them were arrogant, rebellious and probably as greedy as she was for the big score.

Just the kind of hustlers I can do business with, Nina thought.

After Customs she picked up her baggage and jumped in a cab. Tony had personally selected her apartment off the Storchengasse.

'Very nice,' the cabbie said pleasantly when she gave him the address. 'Very good area, you will like.'

They drove through the jazzy Niederdorf area, past outside cafés, tobacconists and bookstores with slanted roofs. After London everything seemed very clean. Nina watched an ancient *Kirche* slip by, then banks with brass nameplates. It was very cold and the sky was a dazzling blue. She could see mountains in the distance. It felt like an alien world.

The Storchengasse turned out to be a major shopping thoroughfare for the seriously rich. Hermès, Chanel, Cartier; it was thronged with women in silky-looking furs. When the cab drew up outside a smart, flat-fronted building with a uniformed doorman, Nina stepped out with a sigh of pure satisfaction. She gave the driver a generous tip.

Her apartment was fully automated. Nina punched a combination into a wall panel and the front door slid open. Doubtless Dr Namath would approve. It was decorated in white and cream with touches of gold, very Swiss and baroque. The refrigerator was fully stocked; a basket of fruit was laid out on a small ebony table by her bed. The card was a sterile, printed welcome message from Luc Viera, MD of Dragon Switzerland. Tony kept a skeleton office in Geneva. Mostly Viera and his gnomes kept abreast of the gossip floating out of the banks. Nina imagined the Robber Baron's orders coming through, how annoyed the career suit Viera would be to be told he was point man for a kid. That idea pleased her almost as much as the apartment.

Money and power, that's what Tony Savage was dangling in front of her face. Nina selected a bitter Swiss chocolate from the open box in the kitchen and bit into it carefully. It was sublime. Maybe she should wear his jewellery, next time he told her to. After all, wasn't this everything she'd always wanted?

'So.' Elizabeth dumped her skis down in the boot room for waxing and pushed her goggles up over her face. Her skin was stung red from the cold; white wax was smeared clown-like over her lips but right now she wished she'd done her cheeks too. She clump-clumped her way into the hotel foyer. It was so ironic: good boots anchored your turns like rocket boosters on the slopes, bombing you forwards with perfect weight precision, and yet the second you unclipped the skis you were crippled, tripping and lurching like astronauts on the moon. She sat down carefully on a step and unstrapped them, ignoring the stares from the tourists and sports groupies. 'At least I haven't forgotten how to ski.'

'You could have fooled me,' Karen Carter sniped. 'Still four seconds off your best. And five off Louise's – she did that course in two-twenty over Christmas.'

Elizabeth shrugged. 'I'm improving every session.'

What the hell was your time, loser? she wanted to snap, but bit it back. She was coming in for unexpected stick from the press. Slagging a fellow Brit would only make things worse. Karen or Janet Marlin would be bound to leak it. Jealousy over Jack Taylor had soured the team spirit, and the Olympic setting made things a lot worse. Everywhere the team trained they were greeted with huge five-ring banners, cheering Swiss and multinational officials, sports journos and television crews. The World Cup felt like a local gymkhana in comparison. Big stars were wandering round every venue: Torville and Dean, Robin Cousins, and the rest. Since it was Switzerland, the bobsledders would be tackling the Cresta Run. Glamour and glory were in the air; deadly rivalry and the weight of history. You couldn't escape the atmosphere. Adrenalin crackled around like electricity up the cable-cars. The élite were here for Olympic gold medals. Nothing less.

Karen Carter, Janet Marlin and Kate Cox were not here for Olympic gold medals. Or for Olympic medals of any description. They had no chance. Martin Bell in the men's team had no chance. Lady Elizabeth Savage was the UK's only real contender. All the other girls got asked was, what was it like to ski with her, didn't they feel privileged watching such a great talent emerge? Des Lynam contented himself with Karen, because Elizabeth was too busy to speak to him. And the stuck-up cow had somehow waltzed off with Jack bloody Taylor, after pretending for months and months that she hated him. Janet told Karen Elizabeth was a proper little madam, and Karen had totally agreed. Ronnie Davis kept his distance, because Ronnie would soon be training only the main team. Elizabeth would zoom off again with Hans Wolf, the genius coach they'd all have given their eye teeth to work with. Elizabeth was just too good for the rest of them.

'Did you take a look at the *Sun* this morning?' Janet asked.

'Yeah, but it doesn't bother me.' The tabloids were all running nasty pieces about Elizabeth's lack of commitment, commenting on her Alpine rivals' current times. 'I'm heading out to Klosters with Hans tomorrow to start the real work,' she said lightly.

'Well, hold the back page,' Karen sniped.

Elizabeth smiled softly at her. What was the point? Did Jack get this crap from his team-mates?

'Will you be packing all your pictures with you?'

'Yes, I will.' She grinned as she thought about her piles of ad mock-ups. Elizabeth had been spending every moment she wasn't skiing working on Dragon Gold. Nina Roth was due in Zurich soon and Elizabeth wanted to have something to show her.

'I don't think you should be doing anything but skiing, Elizabeth,' Karen lectured. 'It's not proper.'

Elizabeth squeezed her feet into trainers and eased into some deep stretches.

'England rugby players work in banks. Sally Gunnell's got a fulltime job. So have Jayne and Chris. It's supposed to be an *amateur* event.'

'Amateur is right,' Karen muttered.

Elizabeth rounded on her. 'Yeah? Think you can do better? I don't *need* to train as hard as you, Karen, because I'm twice as good. You can stick to opening supermarkets and writing columns for *Cosmo*. I'm out here to do something for Britain. You don't have a prayer, not if you spend every day of the year on the snow. So get out of my face.'

Karen's mouth dropped open as Elizabeth stomped off to the elevator bank.

'Snobby cow,' she said.

Kate Cox moved closer. 'Don't worry, she'll get hers. I heard Louise Levier's been training with Franz Klammer. She'll be lucky if she scrapes a bronze.'

Janet glanced down at a ski brochure franked with the Olympic rings. Jack Taylor's bronzed, square-jawed face.

'Can't think what he sees in her.'

'Not that much,' Karen said gleefully. 'He hasn't called her once, not at this hotel. I checked with the operator, pretending to be her.'

'You never.'

'I did. And you know his reputation: find 'em, feel 'em, fuck 'em, forget 'em. He fancied her, she dropped her pants, end of story.'

'You reckon?'

'She's had it far too easy for far too long,' Karen muttered. 'She's got it coming, that girl.'

24

Nina shivered and looked at her watch. Quarter of nine in the cold morning light, no sign of life. The bell on the fading pistachio paint buzzed insistently; the grubby steel plaque read Hall/Namath Consulting. She was in the right place at the right time, representing Dragon's global power and wealth. And nobody seemed to care.

This was the sleazy part of town, facing away from the lakeside. The main rail station was a few blocks away, the *Straßen* packed with dull, shabby apartment blocks full of unskilled workers. Maybe this was the only low-rent street in Switzerland. The shuttered stores used Chinese letters; the wrappings dropped in front of the delis were Turkish and Polish. It was almost like being back on Flatbush, except the air was clean.

Nina shifted from foot to foot. The neighbourhood wasn't stirring yet from whatever trouble it had seen last night. Otherwise she'd have been scared to be stood here, wearing an expensive, tailored suit of dove-grey cashmere, a silver cuff bracelet and prim little studs. Her make-up was pulled together, a pale foundation, clover lips and cheeks. She'd made sure she dressed as formal and old as possible. In her experience, mavericks liked to keep all the craziness for themselves. If executives showed up in jeans and T-shirts they panicked. No, Nina wanted to look dull and trustworthy. And rich. As much like a nice Swiss banker as she could manage.

She picked up her briefcase and depressed the buzzer again, a long, hard push. Namath's deep, warm voice had said eight thirty. Real insistent.

'Are you sure?' Nina had asked, surprised.

'Eight thirty's good for me, Ms Roth. Best time of day. Clear head, you can think straight.'

Now she'd been stood here for fifteen minutes. It was freezing, but little midges were already buzzing around. This quarter had been built on former swamps. Fuck, she was going to have to leave and get to a phone, rearrange.

Angrily Nina took her finger off the buzzer and kicked hard at the door.

It swung open, yanked back by a tall man with a broad chest, a square, clean-shaven jaw and handsome brown eyes. He was wearing a robe and not much else. He was very tanned. He looked furious.

'*Gott in Himmel, was ist geschah? Was ist los?*'

Nina swallowed hard. 'Dr Namath?'

He straightened up. 'Yeah. Who the fuck wants to know? Are you from the embassy? I sent the visa papers over last week. Don't you people have phones?'

Nina flushed scarlet. She didn't dare look at him, he was almost naked.

'I'm Nina Roth from Dragon. I – don't we have an appointment?'

'You're who? Oh, sure, the drugs people.' He was still pissed off. 'What the hell do you want now?'

Nina was miserably confused. 'Sir. It's quarter of. I've been here since eight thirty. That's when you told me to turn up.'

Dr Namath paused, then shrugged his shoulders and grinned. 'You're kidding. You thought I meant eight thirty as in a.m.?'

Nina had absolutely no idea what to say. If it hadn't been for the voice she'd never even have recognised him. She was expecting a bearded geek with bottle glasses she could sign up on the spot, a poor researcher who'd be grateful for her attentions. Not this big hulk standing here in his robe, laughing at her.

'I meant at night. When we're done. Lilly doesn't even open her eyes till ten, kiddo. Go have some breakfast and come back then.' He gestured to the thin Paisley robe covering his bronzed chest with its wiry black hair and cutting off above stocky legs. 'I'd ask you in for coffee but I'm not exactly dressed for it.'

'Yes. Sure. Uh, I'm sorry I got the time wrong. In Dragon we tend to—'

'Eleven,' Namath said firmly, and shut the door in her face.

Nina went to the chrome and glass temple of the Container design centre for breakfast; something ludicrously expensive to charge to her platinum company Amex. Spending money would help her feel back in control. She was still blushing with embarrassment and annoyance when the coffee came, a large espresso so thick and bitter she could almost rest her spoon on it. The restaurant was full of businessmen. Nina ordered a *Wall Street Journal* and *Financial Times* sent over and breakfasted on croissants and a bowl of wild strawberries. She buried her face in the *Journal.* Kiddo! He'd wrongfooted her, dressed her down whilst nearly naked, then called her kiddo! How frustrating was that, to be all revved up for the big poaching operation, and then . . .

Namath had made her blush. Not just because she'd gotten the times mixed up, either. Whenever he'd lost the shrubbery and got himself the lenses he'd unwrapped something pretty special. That was no nerd. He looked like Sean Connery with an American accent, when she'd confidently been expecting Pee-Wee Herman. And her Swiss banker look hadn't taken him in for a millisecond. It was just like being back at Dolan in her first week, when she'd got everything wrong and stumbled round with her face permanently set to strawberry.

Nina began combing through the financial reports. Boring stuff about interest rates and EC budget quotas. But Dragon stock was up significantly. That must be Tony's latest raft of disposals; he was getting sharper and deadlier every day.

A small heading in the Marketing section of the *FT* caught her eye. A nice photo of Dragon Gold, the new vitamin pill, in new packaging. The revamped label was bold even in black and white, and showed a Dragon sitting on a hoard of vitamin pills. A raft of slogans jumped out of the text: Dragon Gold – Go for It; Ill-Getting Gold; Gold not Cold; Golden Wonders. Despite her mood, Nina started grinning. Then she stopped.

The next picture was very familiar. Too familiar. Lady Elizabeth Savage, posing her lean, hard body in a new skisuit, black with gold detailing. Skis resting against her shoulders, holding up a bottle of pills and smiling that arrogant smile.

'British Olympic hope Elizabeth Savage launching Dragon Gold in Kitzbühel yesterday. Breaking her training to supervise the launch, Savage has commissioned a bold ad campaign that seems to have been an instant hit. UK retailers' advance orders are high, and with Savage also personally involved, Dragon Gold looks set to become an important retail line for the UK giant.'

Nina felt a thin coat of ice settle on her heart. Elizabeth's launch plans had been faxed to her last week and ignored. Who cares what the princess does with her stupid pill? But this looked good. Amazingly so. She reread the piece and stopped dead at the order figures. Goddamn, that was terrific. There was no denying it. It's got to be a massage by the sales department, Nina thought, then shook her head. No. There was no way Tony would hand Elizabeth any extra credit.

She made herself look carefully at some of the follow-up slogans, due to be wheeled out next month. After novelty, Elizabeth had decided to use the pill's medical advantage, calcium and iron together. Again, the line was short and sweet – 'Blood. Bones. Brilliant.'

Nina called for the check and pushed the papers away. She didn't know anything about advertising, but she trusted her instincts. They were screaming. Underestimating your enemies was a dumb mistake, and clearly, Elizabeth had hit paydirt.

It doesn't bother me, Nina thought. So she's got some talent? Great. It takes more than talent to survive out there. Assuming she doesn't scamper off to Texas with the playboy.

If Elizabeth was more of a danger than she'd thought, Elizabeth would be more fun to bury. Simple as that.

Nina glanced back at the grinning picture before she threw the text away. She longed to wipe the grin off that rich-girl face.

'Come in,' Namath said grinning, opening the door for her. He was wearing a grubby white lab coat and tinted goggles, but she could still see the faint trace of mockery behind the eyes. 'Lilly's just in the kitchen, waiting for you.'

Nina followed him inside, taking a deep breath. They'd probably been laughing at her all morning long, but she had to be in control here. As far as these people knew, she was an angel from heaven bearing gifts: secure funding, top equipment, fat salaries. Namath and Hall were fly-by-night researchers, hawking their projects round hospitals and drug firms; they had to be up for this. She wasn't going to be shaken just because Namath had opened the door semi-naked.

The kitchen was clean and functional. They'd converted this building themselves; the table looked through a reinforced glass window over the lab, where pigs and rabbits were crouched in wire cages and computers perched on tables strewn with messy notes. Dr Lilly Hall *did* resemble her picture, short and squat. She was wearing blue slacks and a red shirt, sitting at the table sipping an Orangina.

'Dr Hall, I'm Nina Roth,' Nina said confidently, leaning over and shaking her hand. 'I'm with Dragon. We'd like to talk to you about a joint venture.'

'So take a seat. We're listening,' Harry Namath said.

Nina sat.

'You look pretty young to be a pharmaceutical exec,' Lilly Hall commented. She was unimpressed by Nina's expensive suit. Nina also guessed she might be irritated by her looks. 'How old are you?'

'Twenty-eight,' Nina lied.

Harry Namath snorted. Quickly she moved on. 'Doctor, we're aware of your recent biochemical work on pigs. We're very impressed and we'd like you to come and work for us, exclusively. We have a heavy package on offer including your own lab and guaranteed non-interference in your research. We understand how Hall/Namath do things.'

'Done your homework, yeah?'

'What do you want us to work on?' Harry asked.

'Same area.' I don't want *you* at all, flyboy, Nina thought, but I gotta kiss your butt to get Lilly here. 'We don't like to get too specific before you're actually on board.'

'Well, I wanna know,' Dr Hall insisted. The Aussie accent was as thick as sourdough.

'Slimming pills, Lil.' Harry regarded Nina. 'That's what they all want. Especially Dragon: they hired Steele and Ripley—'

'Strewth!' Lilly laughed rudely. 'Is that right? That what you're after?'

Nina's fingers balled into a fist under the table. 'Yes, ma'am,' she said calmly. 'You've seen the benefits we're offering. Plus autonomy. You'll get full funding and remuneration but be free to do things your way. All the other big firms have tried to stuff you into suits and ties.'

Lilly Hall looked up at her partner. Harry shrugged. 'I want to go back to London,' she said eventually. 'You cover relocation as well?'

'Yes, ma'am.'

'Then if we can work it out, legally, I'm game.'

Nina froze. Just like that? She had them? Could it really be that easy?

'But we'll want more money. And a legal guarantee, we're in charge, you just own the results,' Harry Namath said.

'There's no more money,' Nina said authoritatively. 'You already have our absolute best offer.'

Dr Namath stood up slowly and looked her up and down. Then he opened the kitchen door out of the hallway.

'OK, well, thanks for dropping by,' he said.

'What?' Nina said.

'Come on, kid. We've both been around the block a few times more than you. You'll go, best guess, fifty per cent higher than your "absolute best", and believe me, you'll need to. Or I just get right on to Glaxo.' Namath picked up an imaginary phone. 'Yeah, hi, is that legal?' Cause Dragon are lying in front of us with their skirts up and their legs open, but they're only offering a quarter mil . . .'

'OK. OK.' Nina knew she was scarlet. 'It's negotiable.'

'And I want to deal with a lawyer on the cash,' Lilly added, 'no offence, kid.'

This is about the deal, it's not personal, Nina told herself, biting her lip. 'Sure.'

'That's better.' Harry Namath's face was straight but Nina heard the laugh in his voice. 'If we're gonna work together we've got to be able to trust what you tell us. Like, for example, how old are you?'

Nina couldn't believe it. She swallowed hard. 'I'm twenty-two.'

'Really,' Lilly Hall said, rather coldly.

'But I went into work straight from school. I've worked in retail, at Dolan MacDonald and now Dragon. I have years of experience.' Nina knew she was justifying herself but she couldn't stop. 'My computerisation programmes at both Dolan and Dragon were instituted across the whole of the US. I'm a senior New Products manager, and,' she added with an acid stare at Namath, 'it was my research that discovered the breakthrough pharmacologies you've been working on.'

Dr Hall nodded. Nina got to her feet, leaving a couple of business cards on the table. She'd done it, she'd got them. That was what she should focus on, not the fact that the good-looking cowboy in the goggles and white coat had just utterly humiliated her.

'I'll see you out,' said Harry Namath.

He walked her to the door. Nina offered him her hand.

Namath shook it. He had a dry, firm grip. 'Brooklyn, right?'

'Right,' Nina said flatly.

He shook his head. 'Twenty-two. Pretty funny, but then it was a good save.'

She smiled slightly. 'Maybe it was.'

'I'm an American too, kiddo. You can't put it past me.'

'My name is Nina, Dr Namath.'

He fielded the rebuke easily. 'Only if mine's Harry. So, your lawyer will be in touch, we'll talk again.'

'Right.' She glanced up the street, looking for a cab.

'Hey Nina,' Harry said, 'great suit.'

'Thanks,' Nina muttered.

He closed the door.

Tony Savage picked up his phone with a shiver of pleasure. Sex rippled through him now whenever he heard any mention of Nina's name. She'd been away for a week. He wanted her to get through her deals quickly and get back. He was missing her softness and prickly ambition; lays like Nina didn't grow on trees.

'Go ahead, m'lord.'

'Nina? I read your fax. Good work.'

'Thank you, sir.'

Tony grinned. She wouldn't use his first name on a company phone. Whether it was paranoia or her stupid pretence that she separated business and pleasure, he didn't care. He liked Nina to call him sir; for her he was great God from whom all blessings flowed.

'How long is it going to take for you to wrap things up? You're missed around here.'

'A while yet. Legal is on it, but I want to get to know them. Dr Hall is thorny, but she knows exactly what she's doing.'

'And Henry Namath?'

There was a pause. 'Harry's real interesting, sir. No bullshit. When we talk about computers, he's . . . intense. He'll go with us if he thinks it's right for Lilly.'

'You like him.' Tony was surprised. 'Good. It'll be helpful in getting them to commit. Just don't like him *too* much, there's a girl.' Nina said nothing, so he ploughed on. 'Maybe I should come out there, Nina, get a sit-rep,' Tony added, silkily.

'I can fax you detailed reports. You don't need to come out.'

Tony glanced down at the receiver. 'No. You don't understand. Maybe I *want* to come out. And how's Elizabeth?'

'I don't know, sir. I'm seeing Lady Elizabeth next week. Where she's training.'

Tony grunted. 'What about her and Jack?'

'As I said, I don't know. I've been busy with Harry.'

'It's important to me to know the state of that relationship, Nina. It's a priority for me. Remember? Namath can get on just fine without you. My priorities are the ones that count. Don't forget it. Do you understand me?'

'I understand you perfectly, Lord Caerhaven.'

Tony flipped through the thick, gold-leaved pages of his desk diary. 'First Saturday of the month. I think I'll come over. To your apartment. We can have a chinwag before I fly out to Elizabeth. You'll enjoy that.'

There was a small silence. 'I might not be free on that Saturday.'

'No, you're not free. You're tied up with me,' Tony said.

He hung up. The pleasurable *frisson* had vanished completely. Tony glanced at the phone, then across his desk to the latest bunch of reports from sales. After the success of Dragon Gold, his wretched daughter had started taking matters into her own hands. They were small things, both of them, but not to be tolerated. Tony had learned early on that rebellion was there to be stamped on. In London, Switzerland, or anywhere else.

And the natives were getting restless.

25

'Yeah, the response is fantastic.' Jake Ansom's voice crackled down the hotel telephone. 'Boots just put in another major order. Central buying says they're thinking of stocking it as standard.'

'Brilliant.' Elizabeth grinned. 'What about the independents?'

Village chemists were important too. She wanted her pill to be flying off shelves everywhere, right now, while it was still hot. They wouldn't allocate advertising money for ever. Elizabeth had spent months going over boring sales projections and histories for lots of their past brands. Now it was paying off. Once Dragon Gold was a household name, half the battle was won.

'You've got a real instinct for this stuff,' Jake said. 'Everybody's talking about it.'

Elizabeth laughed. 'Look, I want to launch in France. And put a major push into hospitals.'

'Hospitals? But—'

'Trust me, OK? Then we need to talk to water companies. Vittel, Evian . . .'

Jake snorted. 'Bottled water? That's never going to catch on. Why should anybody pay for *water*? You get it free out of the tap.'

'Just set it up, Jake.' Elizabeth didn't mind his teasing, she was brimming with confidence. The years of reading trade magazines and pinning up Clio award-winning ads on her walls were all bearing fruit. Ideas were tumbling out of her like water bursting through a dam. And Elizabeth knew what the stakes were. She had something to prove. By the time she was through, not even Daddy would ignore her any more.

Jake was still fretting. 'If you *insist*, but Liz – you can't launch in France, just like that.'

'Why not?'

The line to England gave a crackle as though amazed. 'Because it costs money to set it up! Lots of money! You don't have the authority—'

'I do. I've got total authority for Dragon Gold. But you're right, it's a waste to set up distribution in just one foreign country.'

Jake sighed with relief.

'We need to go across the whole continent. No, it's OK. I spoke to Father this morning, he wants me to go ahead.' That was a lie, of course, but Jake wouldn't know it. Everybody at Dragon assumed Tony adored his only daughter. 'You can check with him, if you need to.'

'No, that's fine,' Jake said hastily. 'I'll get our people in the local companies—'

'To call *me* direct. Father's very busy, he doesn't want to be bothered. That's why he gave me sole responsibility.'

When Ansom rang off she smiled. Maybe she was taking a risk, lying about Tony, spending millions, but someone else would soon discover how to link calcium and iron. Right now they had a USP, as Procter & Gamble would say, a unique selling point.

I know how this company works, Elizabeth thought, her heart quickening with excitement. As her father's daughter, nobody would question her. And with the power and wealth of Dragon right behind her, she could launch her product and make a success of it Europe-wide before anybody had time to stop her.

Elizabeth launched herself into her warm-up routine, flexing, stretching. Outside a new blanket of snow had covered the mountains and she was late for meeting Hans and Jack. Oh well, they could talk theory for a bit. It was going to take some doing, supervising Gold and training hard, but she was sure she could handle it. Like they said round the office, if you want something done, ask a busy person.

Surely this boldness would win Tony over. That was the way he worked: jump first, ask questions later. Tony was always saying that the person swearing it couldn't be done was run over by the person who just did it. It was daring, ruthless daring, that had made the Robber Baron – why shouldn't it make his daughter?

She grabbed her lilac skisuit with the iridescent stripes. Success made her feel romantic. The skintight Lycra was what she'd been wearing during her first battles with Jack. It hugged her tight butt and chiselled quads, and it shimmered thousands of rainbows as she plunged down the slopes, flashing bright as a starling's wing.

Elizabeth was annoyed with Jack for not calling, but she shoved that feeling aside. Today they'd be skiing again, skiing together, for the first time since she got to Switzerland. She twisted her glossy hair into a neat ponytail and picked up her goggles. No forests, no avalanches, God, this was going to be fun.

Elizabeth smiled softly at the bowing concierge as she left the Hotel Möller. It was one of the most exclusive in Klosters, unmarked from the outside, at first glance just another gingerbread-gabled townhouse in the heart of the old town. Places like the Möller did not advertise for guests. Hans knew the proprietress, so Elizabeth got the best of both worlds: as much privacy as you could get in the Olympic capital, stately courteousness and old-fashioned elegance, but also a first-class suite wired with faxes, three phone lines and even a small Quotron terminal, linked to the markets via Zurich. That was for the gnomes, rich Swiss financiers who used the Möller regularly. And despite the apparent rustic nature of the receptionists, they were ruthless on the phone. No journalist had scammed his way through to Elizabeth yet. The first night she arrived they camped outside the door; but when one tabloid hack tried sneaking into the lobby two gigantic bouncers had appeared silently from nowhere. The press let her alone.

It all came at a price, of course, but Elizabeth didn't worry about that. She charged it as a business expense and used her Dragon corporate Amex. Well, she couldn't ask Ronnie Davis to fork out for it, and the other girls were still sulking in St Moritz.

She caught the cable-car up to Gotschnagrat. Klosters dropped away beneath them, and Elizabeth's heart lifted along with her stomach; the sun was brilliant in crisp blue sky, new snow on the mountains glittering like powdered glass. Skiers were out in force, neon specks blazing over the runs, hundreds-and-thousands spattered on ice cream. This was skiing, this was coming home. Rocky crops and plunging walls of ice vanished below them as they moved on. Everything was so vast in the roof of the world; the sky so close you could touch it, crevasses that would drop you straight into hell.

Elizabeth moved among the tourists. She kept her dark goggles on so she wouldn't be bothered. Now Klosters was some brown speckles on the snow, they were passing Davos, with its dreary purpose-built blocks and endless lift queues. Traffic was toytown cute from the cable-car windows, bright sun flashes sparking from tiny windscreens. She felt an edgy knot in her gut as she looked down. Funny, you really felt how high up you were in one of these, whereas a plane seemed clinical and safe. Sometimes a car would stop for a few moments, and hang creaking over the void. That always scared her. Maybe it was too many Bond flicks: they made you expect a wheel failure, a lurch southwards, sickening drops into a fireball death. Chairlifts were worse. Years out on the circuit, and Elizabeth still thought that was a dodgy idea, park benches that flew. She never told Hans about her little phobias, he'd have teased her unmercifully. And as for Jack . . .

Elizabeth grinned at that thought as she stepped out at the Gotschna station, selected a flat patch of snow and buckled on her skis. Rossignol had custom-made these for her; they slid and turned, almost weightlessly, slicing and twisting in motion like part of herself. The snow was good, well packed but not icy, and the air at altitude had a perfect champagne sparkle. Just a few brave souls were pushing off towards the start of the Gotschnawang, and she recognised Hans straight off; you couldn't mistake that ramrod stance, nor the incongruous shock of white hair above the ancient goggles.

She glided over with one effortless push. '*Güten Morgen, mein Herr, wie geht's Ihnen?*'

'Elizabeth!' Hans smiled, clapping one mitt on her shoulder. 'You are well? Good!' He glanced her over critically. '*Ach*, not bad. It almost seems that you are fit. But fitness in the gymnasium does not equal speed on the slopes. All winter Heidi Laufen has been practising, and you are dabbling in business. What have you to show for it?'

Elizabeth grinned. Same old Hans. 'Maybe something big, in a couple of months.'

The old man's face creased. 'In a couple of months, *you* will see something big. Heidi Laufen with an Olympic Gold.'

'I don't think so. You don't get them for second place.'

'So,' Herr Wolf was sarcastic, 'you think Louise Levier will beat her to it?'

'I'm not that bad, boss, I'll show you,' Elizabeth said cheerfully. She waved down the plunging drops of the Gotschnawang run with a ski-pole. Ski-instructors scared tourists with tales of this one; the Wang route to the south was unmarked, full of stomach-lurching dives and vicious mogul fields. If you were trying to crunch your way back into contention, there was no time for easing into it. Elizabeth's nipples tightened pleasantly from more than the cold. She'd been looking forward to taking this on with Jack, the adrenalin, bobsled-speed, his hard quads and glutes straining and pushing beside her . . .

'OK. We go.' Hans pushed off.

'Wait! Where's Jack?'

'Jack?' Wolf blinked; his mind was already locked into the run. 'You were late.'

'You mean he's *left*?' Elizabeth asked. 'He can't have done, Hans, I'm only fifteen minutes—'

'*Ja, ja.*' Hans was impatient. 'He is by now halfway down. He said, this is too important to waste time, he does not like waiting. Maybe at the bottom he stays for you, maybe he takes the gondola to Parsenn.'

'I see,' Elizabeth said coldly. She couldn't believe it. Son-of-a-bitch, selfish, arrogant bastard! Fifteen bloody minutes! First he didn't ring her, now he wouldn't wait for her . . . As she followed Hans over to the lip of the first schuss, Elizabeth ran over all the moments they'd had since he presented her with her little platinum ski. There weren't that many of them, really. Phone calls in the office, mostly brief news updates on their lives.

Jack's platinum trinket pressed against her collarbone as she thrust off from the top. Instantly her reflexes took over as her body hugged the ice, her stomach floating fifty yards behind her as she flew behind her coach. Elizabeth flicked into ski mode like she'd turned on a light, keeping her eyes a hundred yards in front, turning to the left cleanly. The slicing edges of her skis threw up a small arc of ice. She barrelled left again, then right, hugging Hans's tracks so perfectly you could hardly tell there were two people on the track. But Jack was still in the back of her mind, even while she concentrated on her technique. Resentment lay clammy over her heart. Maybe she'd been right the first time. Jack Taylor just lived for the chase, and now he'd had her, he was going to—

Elizabeth swung right a fraction too late in an ugly turn, the angle was huge. Hans glanced behind him and frowned as Elizabeth ducked her head, abashed. Bloody Jack had put her off. A howler like that could lose you a third of a second, maybe more, if it happened on race day. Her annoyance intensified. Maybe Vanessa, or Clarisse or all Jack's other groupies put up with it, but she wasn't going to.

You'd better buck your ideas up, mate, or else—

'Elizabeth, *lieber Gott!*' Hans grumbled, as she smoothly fell in beside him. 'Horrible, you ski like a farmer's wife, and slow as a cow.'

'Sorry,' Elizabeth mumbled.

'Sorry won't save you.' On a small flat patch Hans carved to a full stop, Elizabeth just fast enough to match him. Her coach was shaking his head. 'Come, show me something, *Fräulein*, the World Champion I ski with!

Where is your head? Not on the schuss.' The bright old eyes watched her clearly. 'Heidi pines for her *Jungen* only *after* she skis. Forget him for now.'

'I wasn't thinking about Jack!' Elizabeth protested hotly.

'No?' Hans said shrewdly.

Elizabeth flung herself into the next barrelling drop before Herr Wolf saw the blush on her face. Was she really that obvious? It was embarrassing. And he was bloody well right, Taylor wasn't worth it.

With a wrench she turned her gaze to the plummeting white track before her, settling her body lower towards the ground, feeling the gradient in her belly. She hurtled forwards so fast it seemed her skis barely grazed the snow, flying over the ice crystals until the horizons were bleeding into each other. Hans dropped behind her, and all the world was whiteness and freefall, angles and sticks, her strong muscles twisting and leaping. The Wang run fired her downwards to its finish like a bolt from a crossbow.

No posts announced the end of the piste. The kind of skier that tackled the Gotschnawang runs didn't need them. Elizabeth simply ground to a halt, a vertical wave of powder pluming up behind her like the tail of a giant white peacock. She ripped her goggles from her head and stood there panting, still recovering when Hans zoomed the last schuss a full nine seconds behind her.

'*Ja*,' Wolf gasped, breathing hard himself. His eyes twinkled. 'That is the girl I remember. You are now fast. But reckless.'

'Overcautious, undercautious,' Elizabeth grumbled.

'Speed *and* skill. That is what we need. But with much work we shall have it.' Hans brightened and waved at the café. 'A schnapps? We will celebrate, but it will be the last before the Games.'

'What?'

'No alcohol. Also early bed, strict diet, no caffeine,' Hans said happily as Elizabeth unlocked her boots.

Great, Elizabeth thought glumly, trudging up the wooden steps behind him. Skiers sipping their *citrons pressés* or *Glühweins* gawked at them, whether it was recognition or just the speed of their arrival she didn't know. As Hans led her inside, the familiar waft of frankfurters, soup and cheese with black bread hit her. A pine-log fire crackled in one corner and her heart rate dropped steadily. That was good; real fitness meant quick recovery, and—

'Hello, milady,' Jack Taylor said. He was perched on a barstool, drinking mineral water, wearing the red, white and blue suit of the US team. Obviously the recognition thing is not too much of a problem for *you*, Elizabeth thought, swiftly clocking at least five Swiss girlies with their eyes constantly flickering Jack's way. Hell, why not? He looked great, as usual: bronzed, huge, the dark hair cropped a little tighter than when she last saw him, the cruel mouth set in that maddeningly confident way. Maybe it was the snow. Or the suit. In a Savile Row three-piece Jack looked a real babe; but in a skisuit, out here, he looked like a champion. A world beater with the gold already reserved. How great it would be, Elizabeth thought a little sourly, if *I* had no competition.

'Jack,' she said. What was he expecting, a fucking ticker-tape welcome?

'Are you coming up to the Weissflujoch? We're just going to have a quick schnapps.'

'You're drinking alcohol?' Jack asked.

'Yeah.' She heard herself get curt. 'I'm not a Muslim.'

Jack put some money on the bar and waved at Hans. 'No, I want to do some Strela blacks. You were late, Elizabeth.'

'It was only a quarter of an hour,' Elizabeth said angrily. 'You were rude, Jack, you should have waited for me.'

Jack shrugged. 'Sugar, I wouldn't ask *you* to wait. You want to drink schnapps, relax your schedules, ski tramlines like the Weissflu? It's the Olympics. I never screwed up a schedule in my life for anything, especially not for manners.'

'Nice to see you too.'

'Hey. I'm thrilled to see you. Look, if it was anyone else, I'd be on the gondola right now, but I gave you guys an extra five minutes to get here.'

Elizabeth was furious. 'Look, Jack, don't do me any favours, all right?'

'What's your problem?' the Texan demanded, brown eyes narrowing.

'I don't have one.'

'I'm letting you train with me, Elizabeth,' Jack said softly. 'Wouldn't do it for any other female. This is—'

'The Olympics, yeah, so I gathered. And I know what you think of females. But you needn't bother yourself,' Elizabeth snapped. 'I'm skiing a tramline run right now.'

Jack looked at her for a few seconds. Then he said, 'OK,' casually, waved at Hans and stood up. 'I'll call you tonight.'

Elizabeth turned away to pick up her schnapps. 'Like I said, don't do me any favours.'

She picked up her glass and sipped it slowly, listening to Jack's heavy footfalls as he clumped out to the terrace.

'Problems?' Hans asked, but Elizabeth shook her head. She started to talk techniques with the coach, while glaring at one of the adoring Swiss girlies, who was irritatingly staring at her as if she were mad.

26

'Great, so we'll complete next week.' Nina was filing more notes as she talked to Luc Viera. She rubbed her aching temples; it was the end of another long, busy day. She'd been setting up contracts and offices and new administrative structures; she dreamed of figures, she woke up with crunching migraines and rows of accountant's print swimming before her eyes.

A shadow fell over her desk. Nina looked up.

Dr Henry Namath, Dragon Inc.'s latest contractual supplier, was looming over her. He wore a pair of jeans and a Yankees sweatshirt. Behind him Frau Bierhof, Nina's new assistant, was looking outraged. Obviously Harry had barged past her. As usual.

Nina sighed. 'Hold on, Luc.' She looked at him, exasperated. 'Harry, what's wrong with the phone?'

'Nothing. If you answered it.' Namath pointed to the pile of message slips on her desk.

Nina shrugged; if it was Tony, legal or a vital call, Steffi Bierhof let her know, otherwise, sure, she ignored them. Who had time? 'Can't it wait? Guess not. OK. Look, Luc, Dr Namath's here, I have to go. You know the fax in my apartment, right? I'll check the details tonight.'

She hung up. 'OK, Dr Namath, I'm all yours.'

'Great,' he said, pulling her coat from the rack. 'Let's go find a restaurant.'

'We'll discuss it here. I have too much work to do, and—'

'Nina.' Namath bent over her, his black hair and blue eyes seriously distracting. 'Let me tell you something. Biochemical principle. The human body needs food.'

'Really, I—'

'And mental agility suffers without it. Come on, it's an investment, it'll stop you screwing up from low blood sugar.'

Nina couldn't stop a tiny smile as she accepted her coat.

'That's better.' Namath looked her over with a forty-watt grin. 'Come on, I got a table. Best place in town.'

Well, she *was* hungry, Nina rationalised as she followed him out.

The cab pulled up off the Dörfli and Nina stepped out, looking at the narrow Gothic houses, antique shops, cafés and bookstores mingling with underground nightclubs. That was Zurich, if you had time to enjoy it. Grimm's fairy tales by day, Soho by night. She felt too exhausted to be appreciative, wondered what Namath had in mind: another fancy Swiss eatery, full of bankers and ladies in furs, unpronounceable dishes and alcohol strong enough to fuel rockets. If she ate one more lamb and dandelion salad she was going to explode.

'So, we're going somewhere ethnic?'

'Very ethnic.' Namath pushed her to the right and pointed. 'The Hard Rock Café.'

Nina laughed.

'Well, American is ethnic,' Namath said, grinning, 'and I felt like Bud and a cheeseburger, I hope you don't mind.'

They were shown to a small table in the back. It was cramped and in sight of the kitchen but Nina couldn't have cared less; it was dark, busy, full of American babble and waiters carrying trays piled with fries and ice cream. A girl materialised right away and Harry asked for a cheeseburger, beer and fudge melt chocolate cake. Nina went for grilled chicken and Diet Coke, with a fruit salad.

'That's really going to do your cholesterol a lot of good.'

'So now you're worried about my cholesterol?' Dr Namath asked.

Nina blushed. Harry had been a hellish pain in the butt; he ran their lawyers ragged, he insisted on supervising all the lab details, wouldn't buckle on a goddamned thing. Once the ink was dry, Lilly Hall had gotten the best terms any Dragon contractor had ever had. She had to admire Namath, he knew what he was doing. Impressive for such a young guy, but like Harrison Ford once said, it's not the age, honey, it's the mileage. Young kids were coming up everywhere. The eighties was the decade of the entrepreneur. Even if Namath didn't fit the red-braces-with-dollar-signs stereotype. For a man who'd be a millionaire in less than two years, Harry dressed like a workman.

But face to face he was real attractive. The logician's brain came gift-wrapped: short hair, raven black, and sharp azure eyes. He had none of Tony's powerful elegance. Namath was brutish to look at, stubborn, annoyingly light hearted; getting his own way while refusing to take life seriously. Nina thought about him often, caught herself, and tried to stop. She told herself it was her scientific side, how could she not admire a man who thought in code, a mathematician who could read numbers like a language?

'Well . . .'

'I can handle it. Or maybe you think I'm too fat.'

Nina was forced to glance at his body under the loose shirt. Nice, very nice. He was big but lean, well balanced, one of those naturally strong guys who didn't need the gym.

'What did you want to discuss? Lilly's bonus? It's being credited to her tomorrow. The lab? That's ready to inspect Monday. Or was there another contract problem? I hope not because we've moved on from that . . .'

'None of the above.' Namath dipped a handful of fries in barbecue sauce. 'I wanted to talk about us.'

'Us? I thought we'd straightened those problems out, Harry. I know you think I've been harsh but—'

'Harsh? You're a nightmare. I buckled in to you more times than I want to think about.'

'Like hell,' Nina said.

Harry smiled. 'I mean *us*. Now it's a done deal. You and me. Dates.'

'Dates?'

'Dates. You remember them,' Harry said maddeningly, 'not the dried fruit or the calendar kind, you must have had some. Girls like you don't get away without them.'

'Girls like me?' Nina repeated stupidly. It was dumb, but with those clear eyes looking right at her she felt silly, like an idiot teenager. Somehow she'd never expected this. Namath was mildly flirtatious with every female, and they'd fought so much, and she was the corporate enemy . . .

'Girls who are so radiantly lovely,' Harry said.

Nina blushed deeper. She had no idea how to react. Nobody had ever said anything like that to her in her life – it was always catcalls, or 'babe', or Tony's explicit praise. She was used to Tony making her feel like an erotic sculpture. Did he really call me radiant? she thought, and felt strange, different. Vulnerable and shy.

'I don't have boyfriends,' she said flatly.

'Good. I don't want you to have boyfriends, I want you to have me,' Harry said, taking a bite of his cheeseburger. He looked like he was loving it. Nina flashed on Tony, eating and drinking with perfect restraint. In public the earl was always totally dignified, the Robber Baron, impeccable and ice cold.

'No. It's nothing personal, but I tried it once and it didn't work.'

'Some guy treated you bad?'

'You don't want to know.'

'You're wrong there, toots, I want to know everything.'

'It's private,' Nina said coldly. 'Happened a long time ago.' Yeah, when I was a different person on another planet. Nina brushed the beautifully cut cotton of her moss-green Martine Sitbon jacket, matched with a white silk shirt. Her strength, her hardness, had taken her from that girl to this one. Tony Savage she could handle. She wasn't scared of him. But right now she was very, very scared of Harry Namath.

'OK.' He accepted that, but wasn't put off. 'So that means what? You're going to punish every other man you meet for the rest of your life?'

'I'm not going to punish anybody, I just don't want to deal with it.' Nina stabbed defiantly at her chicken. 'I have enough on my plate. I'm trying to build a career.'

'Surprisingly enough, I had noticed that. But that's no way to live, you can't take a computer to bed with you at night. Do you read Kipling? The *Just So* stories?'

'No,' Nina said, smiling faintly at the thought of her ever having time to read fiction.

'You should do.' Harry looked across at the young woman in front of him, groomed, self-possessed, lifetimes older than her age. There was something in that beautiful face he couldn't read, some veil those dark eyes were pulling down. God, but Nina was so lovely, dark hair round her face like a thundercloud, cheekbones like knife-slashes in her pale face. He had ached for her since the second he first saw her, then his lust had mixed with something else; he'd never known a girl like her, breathlessly efficient, such a worker, so organised and pushy and quick. It was easy to tell she'd never been educated, but she was vividly smart. Nina was *it*. Weird and obsessive, but she was it, she was the one for him. And vice versa. Harry wanted to rip all that armour off and make her see it too.

'There's one about you. The animal who doesn't need anybody, just sways around all day, going, "I am the cat who walks by himself." '

' "I am the cat who walks by himself"?' Nina smiled despite herself. 'I like that.'

'Even cats need company. It'll be wild, we can discuss Turing machines and Church's lambda calculus under the stars.'

'Don't tempt me.'

'See? You're laughing,' Namath said triumphantly. 'Come on, try being happy for a while, what could it hurt? If you don't like it you can always go back to being miserable.'

He winked at her and Nina felt a warm flush of desire lap around her belly and tighten between her legs. Oh God. She should never have agreed to dinner. She wanted him now, wanted him pretty badly. But of course, that was impossible.

'I can't go out with you.'

'You're in love with somebody else?'

'No!' That idea was so off-base she really did laugh. 'Definitely not. I just need my independence.'

'Independence, hell. You're terrified of me,' Harry said shrewdly.

Nina tilted her head. It was such an arrogant, lovely movement he wanted to reach over and kiss her.

'I'm terrified of nothing. But I don't want a man, Harry, it's not compulsory.'

'Then a friend. I could do with some company.'

'You've got Lilly.'

'Lilly? No, we're just professional partners. She likes classical opera and shit that bores the hell out of me. And she's nuts about her work, whereas I like to switch off.'

Nina weakened. What could that hurt? Could it hurt? She'd never had a real friend since Frank Malone. Now he was making her think about it, she *was* lonely, she did feel . . . 'But you don't mean *friends*. You'll just try and take advantage.'

'Nina.' Harry reached over and grabbed her hand. His fingers felt rough and calloused, covered in tiny scars and burns from acids or Bunsen burners. 'I swear to you, I won't do a single thing to you you don't ask for. In so many words.'

Tony rang Nina a week later. 'Getting on OK, darling?'

'Fine,' she said. She launched into a summary of the new division she was setting up, a restructuring of all their research projects. It was Nina's idea to have their various teams – human, medicinal, animal and supply – all report to the same people. That way knowledge would be pooled. It was already starting to pay off: a useless side-effect in a Dutch team's experiment was the clue their coronary people had been looking for. And Lilly was a landed fish now. Nina was confident.

'I know all that.' Tony was brisk. 'Stock's up two and an eighth. I'd like you to knock something out for the quarterly newsletter.'

'Sure.' Nina was pleased. Their newsletter for analysts was important to Dragon; it led to big orders from the pension funds and institutionals. Now she'd really get noticed. 'I'll get a promotion for this, and a rise?'

'You just had one.'

'Come on, Tony, Dragon's about results, not tenure!'

There was silence on the end of the line. 'Where were you last night? I got the machine. Same thing on Wednesday.'

Nina looked down at the phone she was holding and felt a soft chill dance across her spine. 'I was out.'

'Really?' Caerhaven's voice was measured. 'With whom?'

Never complain, never explain, Nina thought. 'With Harry Namath.'

'Of course, the charming Dr Namath. You went to the ballet, or the theatre? How delightful.'

Nina's heart thudded against her ribcage. 'Uh, we went to the movies. *An Officer and a Gentleman.*'

'Maybe we should get you home, darling. He sounds like a bad influence. Just as we were getting you civilised, you start watching drivel like that.'

Nina said nothing. She'd loved the movie. Maybe she was meant to identify with Debra Winger, although she felt like Gere instead; she knew what it was like to have a worthless lush of a father and grow up feeling like dirt. Something in Savage's voice warned her not to say that, however.

'I spoke to Lady Elizabeth's coach yesterday. She's moved up to Klosters, away from the team hotel, so she can train with Jack Taylor.'

That was a lie. She'd been too stretched to give the Sloaney bitch a second thought, but Tony would explode if he thought she'd ignored his orders.

'That sounds promising, but you should go yourself. I'll call her and tell her you're coming.'

'OK.'

'You don't sound too enthusiastic, darling, but I think I can cheer you up. Tell you what, knock that newsletter into shape for me and we'll talk about it.'

'Why can't we do that now?'

'No. I mean face to face,' Tony said warmly. 'I actually found some space. I'll be in Zurich next Friday.'

Harry picked her up on Wednesday night, late enough so Frau Bierhof was gone and she didn't have any excuse to hand. Night was falling outside the office window, the phones had stopped trilling and even the fax machine was silent. He found her crouched over her IBM, tapping away obliviously, her face lit up in a ghostly pallor by the light of the screen. Namath recognised that Nina sunk-in-my-work look. It was easy enough to sneak up behind her, lean over the keyboard, punch a few buttons and shut it off.

'What the hell—' Nina shouted.

'Calm down, kid, I haven't lost your work, it's saved.'

'Are you sure? You better be.'

'Hey, this is Dr Henry Namath, remember, fluent in processor, computers are my friends.' He yanked her up from her chair and started waltzing her round the darkened office, humming the *Doctor Dolittle* theme. 'Oh I can *walk* with the monitors, *talk* to the monitors …'

'OK, OK,' Nina said, smiling. What the hell, it was nine p.m., and she was taking a morning train to Klosters. She let Harry throw her her coat and pull her down the stairs. 'Where are we going?'

'To my apartment.'

She pulled back. 'Hey, Harry …'

'Where is the trust?' Harry asked rhetorically. 'I told you, you needn't expect anything from me until you ask for it. Maybe not even then.'

Nina gave him a suspicious look but climbed into the cab. She could always brush him off if he decided to try it on. She tried to ignore the half of her that was longing for him to do just that. So far he'd been as good as his word: fun to be with, great company, but nothing more. A peck on the cheek was all she got when he dropped her home. Did he really think she was going to ask for more? Was she going to?

Stop that! Come on, girl, you know he's out of bounds. He's a prize asset, he's business, you can't risk it, you don't want to get involved …

She was wildly curious to see Harry's place. A neat penthouse on the Niederdorf, a one bedroom with *Sports Illustrated* on the couch, a mess in the drawing room, functional black and white. Thick books on pure mathematics and piles of computer paper everywhere, not much luxury apart from a huge TV. But he'd set it up for her: two chairs in front of the widescreen, home-popped corn, chilled Millers, nachos, a large bowl of M&Ms …

Nina burst out laughing as Harry reached for the remote and pressed play. The screen flickered into life, the CBS commentators started yelling, goddamn, it was the Superbowl, last year's final she'd complained to him she missed.

'Have a beer,' Harry said, 'I got chilli dogs waiting to be heated up.'

'Oh, this is great,' Nina said, smiling, 'this is so great—'

Harry walked up to her and kissed her full on the mouth.

Nina melted. Instantly. It was thermonuclear meltdown, weak at the knees, her lips parting, his pressing, her back arching into his arms, his tongue—

'No!' She pushed him away, breathing hard, fought for control. For time. 'You said you'd wait till I—'

'I lied,' Namath said.

Nina forced herself to sit down and crack open a beer. 'Don't spoil it, Harry. Let's just watch the game, all right?'

She refused to look back as he went into the kitchen. She was so turned on, just from that. Oh God, help me, Nina thought. She wasn't in control any more, she was out of control. He was so gorgeous. And so smart, and so sweet. Regret stabbed at her like a dagger. Harry liked her, because he didn't know her. He just had no idea what he'd be getting himself into.

She wanted him so badly. She wanted to cry.

27

Nina checked in to the Fluela at noon. She hated Davos. Huge cinder-block hotels, roads clogged with traffic, gawking Eurotrash tourists lumping skis and boots on their way to the endless lift queues. This was town as theme park: skiing, skiing and more skiing. Snow, fondues and ugly nylon suits. Elizabeth's world.

She got her room key and went right upstairs. Last night with Harry had unsettled her, she felt nervous and edgy. She wasn't *like* this, her confidence gone and her armour dented. Tony was turning up tomorrow, and she didn't even know how she felt about that. Soon it would be time to transfer back to London, with a promotion. More money, more status ... I'm writing a section of the *analysts'* report, Nina reminded herself, staring out of her window at the icy massifs in front of her. I'll see less of Harry, I'll get back on track, it'll be great.

She thought about Tony as she dialled Elizabeth's hotel in the valley below. He seemed to miss her. That had to be a plus.

So why was she wishing so hard that he wouldn't show up?

'Hotel Möller, *güten Tag.*'

'Can I speak to Lady Elizabeth Savage? This is Nina Roth.'

A few seconds before Elizabeth picked up. 'Nina! Daddy told me I might have the pleasure.'

Nina's confusion vanished in a hot surge of anger. She said politely, 'I wonder if I could have a few minutes of your time? Tony would like a progress report.'

'But of course.' Silky limey tones, sounds just like her papa. 'Would three o'clock suit?'

'Not really. If we meet then I can't get on a train until—'

'That's the only time I've got today.'

Nina bit her lip so hard it hurt. 'Then three o'clock it is. I'll come to you.'

'Wonderful. I'll look forward to it.'

She got to Elizabeth's hotel at ten of, after twenty fruitless minutes tramping Klosters' fairy-tale streets trying to find it. She was cold and exasperated, her Jimmy Choo boots probably ruined, her ass freezing off under her primrose Galliano skirt. Nina wanted to show up for the bitch wearing Levi's and a sloppy Joe, Harry-style, but Elizabeth might have reported her to Tony. Nina knew they hated each other really, but she didn't understand them any more.

And she didn't trust either of them. As well as the cold, Klosters oppressed her with its huge Olympic rings everywhere, TV crews on every corner, the Games paraphernalia limbering up. A picture of Elizabeth herself, green eyes limpid, gazed out from an import cover of a British sports magazine.

Jealousy flashed through Nina. Elizabeth had all this, but it wasn't enough, she wanted her playtime in Daddy's back yard as well, all the trappings of the businesswoman without doing one thing to earn them. In Klosters Nina was forced to think about the loathsome prospect that Elizabeth actually won an Olympic gold. Then she really would be famous, she'd be a heroine to the Brits. World Champion was good, but those things came and went. The Olympics had that magic. What would Elizabeth do with leverage like that?

It made her sick just thinking about it. Today she was here, wasting her time, freezing her butt off, playing a stupid game – Elizabeth thought Nina was taking a report on the vitamin pill but all Tony was interested in was Jack Taylor. Nina smiled grimly as her new boots scuffed on icy cobbles. Jack, another rich kid, another snow jock. What was there to admire in skiers, anyway? Only rich kids *could* ski. You wouldn't get many competitors from the Bronx or the East End, not like running or soccer or something. That must cut the competition pretty good. Probably ninety per cent of potential champions would never even see a goddamn mountain.

Lady Elizabeth's hotel was right next to the Walserhof, where Charles and Di had stayed last year. It looked rich but utterly discreet and secure. Nina picked out the guards right away: burly 'guests' who didn't quite fit in by the elevator, reception area and front door. One of them caught her assessing look and turned away, not used to being identified. But I'm not like the press, *paisan*, Nina thought. We can spot muscle in Brooklyn.

The receptionist showed her to an anteroom and Nina settled down to wait. And wait. Her anger grew as the minutes ticked by, her mind on the trains, rearranging her travel plans. This selfishness was gonna get her home at nearly midnight.

The door opened and Elizabeth strode in. She was dressed in some kind of sexy, clingy rainbow-suit with black sneakers. Goggle-lines marked her tanned face. She was glowing from exercise, tawny hair pulled back in a girlish pigtail and her gold signet ring glinting on her left hand. Elizabeth looked like a convent girl on a school outing, and this, *this*, was the kid who fancied herself as Charles Saatchi, that tried to have Nina fired?

Elizabeth smiled defiantly and dumped a pile of fax papers on the table.

'Sorry I'm late. Got caught up in a crash on the Strela. Really vile, one of the Spanish girls twisted her ankle. She's out, most likely.'

'Oh.' Do I care? Be polite, Nina, be polite. 'Was she a contender? They can't have much skiing in Spain.'

Elizabeth smiled. 'I suppose you didn't do much European geography. Spain's got a lot of decent spots – Sierra Nevada, Formigal, Baqueria-Beret ... and anyway, most people would say I couldn't have much skiing in England.'

'Unless you'd been to Swiss finishing school,' Nina said, unable to resist.

Elizabeth inclined her head. '*Touché*. How's Zurich?'

'Busy. We have a lot of ground to cover, it's like setting up a new business.'

'Just like me, then. Why don't you have a look at my stuff, tell me what you think?' Elizabeth asked.

Nina reached over and took the pile of faxes she was proffered, pretended to look through them. The ad slogans seemed snappy enough, there was lots of butt-kissing from France and Germany. She'd check this rubbish on her way back tonight, just in case, by some fucking fluke, there was anything interesting in it.

'It's doing very well back home, the sales are still holding.'

'Yes.' Elizabeth nodded proudly. 'Did you realise that's almost three weeks since our last TV slot ran, and they're *still* selling?'

'I'll admit, you seem to have a flair for advertising.'

'I do indeed. A talent you could have used.'

'I needed you to work on other things. Market research matters, Lady Elizabeth.'

'Yes, I realise that now,' Elizabeth said coolly. 'As you can see from my work, I've managed to use what you made me learn. Now I know more than most account executives about what our market *wants*. And when we tailor the work to that – bingo.'

Nina pressed her manicured fingers deep into the table mat. *Oy*, I can't take much more of this, with madam sitting there condescending about geography and telling me about the market!

'Well, that's about it. How's the skiing coming along?'

'Why do you care?'

Nina flushed. 'It could be good for the product.'

'I suppose that's true. Pretty well, so far, but we'll have to see,' Elizabeth said vaguely.

'Are you training with your boyfriend?'

Elizabeth seemed to freeze for a second. 'I don't have a boyfriend.'

What? 'Isn't Jack Taylor your boyfriend?'

'No, Jack's just a friend,' Elizabeth told her. 'We do ski together. Sometimes. But if I get any free time I spend it on work, not socialising.'

She flashed Nina a brilliant smile from perfect white teeth and stood up, extending one hand. 'I must dash, meeting the coach on the Weissflujoch and the queues are horrible! Will I see you at the Games? Or maybe in London. Give Dino my best. And say hello to Father for me.'

Nina picked up Elizabeth's notes with a sinking heart. *Just a friend.* Was that a cover, or did she really mean it? Had they busted up? There were a lot of papers here, it looked like she was taking it seriously. Maybe in that bimbo's head she was involved in Dragon for real.

Tony wasn't going to like it. And neither did she.

Elizabeth watched Nina leave from her bedroom window, the dark hair immaculately styled against the designer clothes. Roth looked as professional as always. She could scarcely believe they were the same age. Were all career women like that, or just the Americans? Nina Roth had that low-class tough-guy attitude, a real don't-fuck-with-me type. Dad had surrounded himself with those men; Elizabeth recalled hundreds of them over the years, guests at the castle, tennis-tournament partners, padding the crowd at Monica's receptions. Faceless stormtroopers with that jungle vibe underneath the sombre suits, she'd called them 'the piranhas' when she was a kid. The big difference being that all those lackeys were male.

While she snapped on her boots and reached for her racing helmet Elizabeth thought about Nina for a while. She was sleeping with Tony, but there was something else there. I have to face up to it, Elizabeth thought, she hates me, and she's *good*. She's really good. It made her edgy when Nina asked about Jack. There was something behind that – Nina Roth wasn't interested in her love life . . . or lack of it – but she'd have to worry about it later.

Elizabeth arrived at Drostobel feeling tense. The sky was slate blue, thick, pregnant clouds lumbering over the sun, dappling the slopes with shade, and creating small pools of vertical beams where the light broke through, like medieval paintings of divine grace. The air was thick and close as well as chilly. Hans had been pleased with her progress so far, she could tell because she spoke fluent Hans, although to anyone else his endless lectures on angles and crouches and now we try once more, *Fräulein*, would seem unbearable. Hans only cheered you once the medal was won. Or lost.

Her fitness hell in Kent had worked. Cross-training had given her extra strength and flexibility. Her records showed that she'd shaved almost a second off her World Cup time for the Davos meet. Trouble was you couldn't count on that – the rumours were that the Swiss team had also come up with new routines.

Heidi and Louise were skiing the course in Verbier. The Austrians were in Grindelwald and the French in Flims, the main contenders spreading themselves out amongst the courses by mutual consent. Hans and she would rotate as well. Heidi and Louise had real good fortune; every meet was home base for them. And there was more that upset her. The Strela crash she'd nearly skied into, Grace Cortez lying there, her foot twisted, back arched in agony, every skier's nightmare. Poor Grace, she'd nearly made the top ten last year. Now the dream had skidded away along with her skis, for these Games and maybe for ever. Elizabeth's mouth dried up thinking about that. They were all just one fall away from oblivion.

Focus, focus, Elizabeth warned herself. Hans was taking her down the Drostobel, less scary than the Wang but about as steep. Difference was, he'd had it fenced off and poled up. She sighed. Slalom and Super-G, her weak points, but they needed work.

At the top of the lift she slid on to the snow and tightened her helmet strap, looking round carefully. Where is he? I should be able to pick Hans out of the crowd by now . . .

Somebody rapped on the Union Jack emblazoned over her visor. Elizabeth looked up crossly. 'Hey, cut it out! Oh, Jack, hi, I was looking for Hans.'

'He couldn't be here.'

'But we've got a session. He never misses training.'

'I'm sure he's got his reasons,' Jack said lightly. 'Wouldn't share them with me, which is something I purely hate.'

Suddenly she was glad she was wearing the helmet. Didn't want Jack to see the silly, puppy-like longing probably written all over her face. It was the warm Texas sun in his voice on this gloomy day. Or maybe the matt-black suit, no goggles, that made him look like a thug from a spy movie. It was awesome on that body, moulded to his chest and quads, with just a discreet Stars and Stripes over the heart, US training colours.

'Thanks for the message. See ya,' she said, but Taylor clamped a massive paw on her gloves before she could push off.

'He asked me to help out.'

'Hans asked you to train me?' Elizabeth repeated.

'I guess,' Jack said, shrugging, his dark eyes fixed on her. 'I'm polishing Super-G this afternoon. I don't mind showing you what you're doing wrong.'

Hans, you bastard! Elizabeth thought. This would be good for her and Hans knew it – he didn't give a damn about anything except her skiing. It was murder to have to take it from Jack Taylor. 'Show you what you're doing wrong!' And she *would* have to take it, because Jack's Super-G was outstanding. Possibly his best discipline – and with Taylor, that meant a hell of a lot. She had no choice here at all.

'Thank you. That'd be great,' Elizabeth muttered. She'd been avoiding him since the day she arrived. It occurred to her that this would be the first time she'd seen him ski since the World Cup.

'OK,' Jack said evenly. He cursed Hans Wolf silently under his breath. He owed Wolf too many favours to turn him down, but the old guy just didn't know what he was asking. Elizabeth, he must have been out of his brain, thinking he could make a future with the spoilt, stuck-up little brat. First she got on his case about leaving England to train, like the Olympics didn't matter, like her dumb-ass job at the drug company really meant something. Her pa was never giving her a shake, and she should have seen that.

She should have been *here*, like I was, he thought. Then when she does turn up she's foolin' about in the hotel, she ruins my schedule, snaps at me . . .

Jack took his skiing seriously. It took the last World Cup for Elizabeth to get his respect. Now the rumours from the British camp were she was back to her old ways, her prima donna mode. This time her distractions were 'business', quote unquote, and not boys, but it was all the same thing. Toys. Games.

All that time I pined for her, Jack thought, but I wasn't with her. Wasn't seeing how she acted. She turned up to team camp looking like cotton-candy, she was so weak. It killed him to see her, weeks before the Games, being late, temperamental . . . it wouldn't matter but Savage was a world-class talent, she had the potential to be one of the true greats. Jack just knew it, he smelt it in her like a fox scents a vixen. For her to throw it away like this was disgraceful. If a kid of his acted that way he'd tan her hide. She made him mad.

But then there was the other little problem, the one he'd brought on himself. It was real, real easy to get pissed at Elizabeth. Not so easy to ignore her. Or forget her. Why should I care if some limey chick doesn't take my calls? Jack thought angrily. It bothered him that she was blanking him again. He couldn't forget that kiss on that freezing winter morning in England, the waiting for her sharpening the pleasure, feeling her resistance melt, and then the cottage, and everything he'd imagined – but better. Elizabeth's long honey hair drifting over his chest, her flat stomach fluttering under his hands, her endless legs and sinewy body writhing over him, those little bud nipples taut on her pale breasts . . .

Elizabeth was looking at him from under that biker's helmet. Impatiently. That tilt of her head bugged the shit out of him.

Come on, Jack, that was it, she's a great piece of ass, but there are lots of those. Now you gotta train with her so let's get on with it.

Well. He *would* train her. He'd show her exactly what standard was required to be an Olympic champion, what she'd forfeited with all her stupid games and scrappy practice. What sweat bought you.

I'll show you, sugar, Jack thought.

'I'll watch from the top the first time. We'll do the three slalom courses, then the Super-G, then you follow my instructions. Just holler if you want to drop out.'

'I won't want to drop out,' Elizabeth said, glaring at him.

Jack smiled coldly. 'We'll see. On my mark, left gate . . .'

28

The doorbell buzzed. Nina jumped, startled. She was still tugging her brush through the ends of her hair, she'd only gotten to the tinted moisturiser stage of her make-up. Her watch said eight a.m. It couldn't be him, it had to be a mistake. She ignored it and rubbed pale concealer under her eyes; God, she was so tired. Up at five to wash her hair, but she'd gotten in at midnight and been forced to stay up till two, trying to think of some way round the Lady Elizabeth problem. Her body had broken through some kind of barrier. Being tired like this gave you a jittery false energy, like the kind you get on too much caffeine.

The buzzer again. Shit. Nina slipped her feet into the Stèphane Kelian stacked mules and stumbled to her entryphone.

'Tony! Sorry, you're so early – come right up.'

She rushed back to the bathroom, frantically scooping up last night's underwear from the tiles and shoving it into the laundry basket. No time for make-up now, she might smear it. Tony, oh God. Her heart started hammering, she felt a nervous sweat break out across her back. Flung open the window to the freezing morning air to lose the steam from her shower. The mirror cleared and she caught a glimpse of herself as the doorbell trilled: dark hair damp and sleek, her body-hugging Chanel number in navy and white over a crisp Prada shirt. The most expensive suit she owned. There could be none of the casual pants and jumpers she wore out with Harry; for Tony, nothing but the best was acceptable. You had to be it and look it, for the greater glory of the Robber Baron. Her face was bare, but there was no time to put that right.

'Coming, Tony, just one second!'

She spritzed herself with Joy, his favourite, and sprinted to open the door.

Harry Namath stood there, holding a video and a packet of Butterkist.

'Oh.' Nina gasped with surprise, then recovered herself. 'Er . . . Harry! Come in, sorry, I was expecting someone else.'

'So I gathered.' Harry stepped into the apartment, looking her over. He was wearing jeans, runners and a sweatshirt, with a battered khaki rucksack slung over one shoulder. '*Tony?* I thought it was always "the earl" or "Lord Caerhaven", some feudal bullshit like that.'

Nina wanted to die. 'Well, I usually refer to him that way to outsiders – I mean, other people. He's the boss, I have to be respectful.'

'But privately you're friends?'

'I wouldn't say *friends*,' Nina said evasively. 'Not strictly friends ...'

'That's good.' Namath's handsome, open face curled a little with dislike. 'He's sharp, but I hear bad things about that guy.'

'Successful people always have enemies.'

'OK, OK, if you like him ...' Harry handed over the cassette and the popcorn. 'Brought you the game and some supplies. In case all this culture gets too much for you. It's a goodbye present.'

'It's a what?' Nina said. She clutched the video to her chest. She couldn't believe the dismay she felt. 'Where are you going?'

'To England, honey, remember? To London.'

'But I thought—'

'So did I, but Lilly's found a place she wants to be. Says she's seeing some interesting results on the latest batch of mice.'

'But why does she need you with her?' Nina pushed her hair back from her eyes. 'You run the computers ...'

'She's real insistent. I don't like to let her down,' Harry said. He moved a little closer. 'You look upset, don't tell me you're gonna *miss* it. All those fights and screaming matches ...'

Nina dropped her head so he wouldn't see the look on her face. He was grinning, teasing her, but she didn't feel like laughing. A big wave of loneliness and loss rolled right over her. It dawned on her like a flash of lightning, what a lifeline Harry had been out here, how she was already relying on him, how fucking miserable it was going to be without him. Yesterday she'd wanted him gone, and now he was going, so why wasn't she thrilled?

Namath walked up to her and cupped her chin in his hands, gently tipping her face up to his. She looked so beautiful, trying to be polished but rushed instead. Her hair was damp. He breathed in the faint scent of her perfume. Desire and frustration clamoured inside him, he felt himself stiffen just from getting close to her. He wanted Nina so much. When she'd pushed him away the other night he'd found it hard to sleep. Yesterday evening he'd picked up a tourist in a bar, gone back to her hotel and banged her mercilessly, but it hadn't helped. A one-night stand wouldn't do it any more.

'Like I'll miss a migraine,' Nina smiled weakly. She knew she should prise his hands off her face, but she didn't move.

'I guess I'll see you in a month.' Harry was still looking right into her eyes. 'Do I get a goodbye kiss?'

'Do you want one?' Nina whispered.

Harry looked at her for a second. Then he bent his head, very slowly, touched his lips on hers, just brushing them, lightly, drily, an echo of a kiss.

'Is that it?' Nina whispered. Harry was hovering there, his mouth close to hers, she could feel the heat of him, hear his breathing. Lust crashed over her like a wave, and she couldn't stand it, she lifted herself up to him, pressing her lips against his. Harry pulled her to him, kissing her over and over, biting, licking the inside of her lip, kissing her neck wildly, his hands moving up to her hair, tousling it, not giving her time to think.

'God, you're so lovely,' he murmured.

Nina felt her knees give. She was arching against him, totally, helplessly responsive. His fingers flickered at her waist and then his hand was on her, pulling her shirt out, his palm moving upwards to the wire and lace of her bra, brushing over her nipples.

'God ...' Nina gasped. She felt a sharper tug of lust shoot right down her body.

'Baby.' He was cupping her breasts now, groaning softly with pleasure, his thumbs stroking, just the right pressure. Nina forgot about telling him to stop. She couldn't say a word. A spasm of pleasure exploded across her groin, she felt herself moisten, he was almost too slow, she wanted this, *needed* it now, and there was none of that squirmy, ugly undertone she felt with Tony, it was real straightforward.

Harry's other hand slipped down from her waist, past the tweed and gilt buttons and up her skirt. He was tugging the silken waistband of her hose, twitching off her panties. Tony's due at ten, what if he's early? flashed through Nina's mind but then right out again. She felt herself part her legs slightly, involuntarily, and then his hand was on her, covering her, two fingers tracing the slickness, unbearably softly, Harry's breathing rough and unsteady, and then he pressed his whole hand on her and she shook, a light, sweet orgasm rippling through her. Nina's cry was muffled by his kiss, her legs gave, she was dizzy from the pleasure of it but still hungry, still tight with desire. They collapsed backwards on to something, the sofa, Harry pulling her up almost harshly, climbing on top of her, lying against her still dressed, kissing her, his fingers darting over gilt and silk.

'Your flight ...'

'Screw my flight. I'll get the next one.'

'We can't,' Nina managed.

Harry bent his dark head to her ear and shoved himself against her. He was hard, really hard and thick. Nina felt herself move against him, beneath him, she couldn't think straight, she felt an animal longing to have that in her, filling her, plugging her.

'How wrong you are,' Harry said, and then his hands tightened round her again, circling her waist, lifting her up as easily as a rag doll, flipping her on to her stomach. Nina turned her head around, sooty hair tumbling in a thick curtain over her face, to see him unstrapping his belt, dragging the shirt over his head, tearing at his jeans. His chest was paler than his face, smattered with wiry curls, the muscles wonderful, tight but not huge, natural and perfect. His powerful thighs pinned her legs down, she felt denim brush the back of her thighs as he threw off his jeans. Nina's stomach clenched with longing. Harry grabbed the hem of her thousand-dollar skirt and shoved it unceremoniously up round her waist, exposing her butt, the lean, tapering line at the back of her thighs, Nina's rounded softness. She inhaled sharply and pushed up on her elbows. Harry wanted to shout out loud from the glory of it, how perfect she was, he could almost see the blood rushing to his cock, he was so hard for her now it hurt. His fingers trembled a little as he unsnapped her bra. In the gilt mirror opposite he saw her, totally disarrayed, her face flushed with heat, her incredible breasts lifting out from the unbuttoned shirt, the nipples dark and tight like black cherries in cream, tiny waist and round ass lifted towards him. So many girls these days didn't eat.

Harry had taken a few home, gotten them undressed and found an ironing-board backside, sexless and boring. But Nina, his Nina, she was all girl, the way her ass flared out from that tiny waist, goddamn . . .

He had to get inside her or he was gonna come. As gently as he could he made to open her thighs, but Nina thrust back, impatient, she wanted it too, and Harry pushed in and took her, first time, right there, feeling her tight and hot around him, moving with him, urgently . . .

'You like that?' Harry whispered. Nina's breath came in sobs, she could feel every thrust, she could see herself in the mirror, Harry moving behind her, taking her, his hands gentle on her tits but still teasing, moving over them so that the intensity of the thrill spread right across her body, a neon web, lighting up wherever he touched her now, even her legs where his thighs were pinning them down, her back when his chest rubbed against it, wiry hair brushing her spine and making that wall of pleasure bigger and closer.

'Yeah . . .'

'You know, this is how we used to make love. Humans.' Harry was talking low and fast because he found it hard to breathe. His arousal poured over Nina's skin like a caress, like downy kisses. Every atom of her felt suffused. 'It's the best way.'

'Why?' Nina choked.

Harry thrust again, picking up the pace, going harder and faster. Perfect rhythm. Slamming into her.

'Because it goes in deeper.' His breath was hot on her ear, he felt hot blood surging into her belly, she was pressing back into him, writhing under his touch, abandoned, God, she was passionate, she was so beautiful. He pushed again. 'Like that.'

'Harry!' Nina said, and there was a note under the heat, something strange, almost sad, but she wanted it because she was moving with him, Harry felt sex overwhelming him, Nina grabbed his hand and grabbed it to her mouth, kissing it, he felt her tighten and stiffen, saw her eyes close and her lips part . . .

Nina couldn't think or move, the pleasure, the wanting was so huge now and she felt the sweet pressure filling her and blocking her, like a tidal wave rearing up, building, and then Harry's arms were hooking under her armpits and pulling her closer and he was taking her stronger and harder and the wall exploded, white light behind her eyes, and she came, sobbing out his name.

Harry's orgasm burst from him like Nina had ripped it out of his heart. Which maybe she had. He collapsed against her, relaxed and perfectly happy. He wanted to stay there for ever.

'You've got to leave,' Nina panted.

Harry reached over and kissed the side of her neck. She was warm, soaked with sweat.

'Really,' Nina insisted. She pulled her clothes away from him, got unsteadily to her feet. Namath stared at her; black hair was falling over her pretty face.

'Is that all I get?'

'It was great,' Nina said softly. She padded over to him with her shoes in her arms and kissed the top of his head, but reticently. She's holding something back, Harry thought uneasily. 'But really, I have a meeting, and I can't wear this.'

'We'll do this again. When you get to London.'

'Sure.' Nina dashed round, picking up her stuff, as Harry pulled his clothes back on. 'Look, you can still make your flight ... call me when you find a place.'

She pecked him on the cheek as he left. Taken aback, Harry found he was standing in her hallway, his sneakers unlaced.

'Gee, thanks for stopping by,' he muttered.

Nina waited until she heard Harry's footsteps on the stairs. Then she sat down weakly on the floor and started to cry.

29

Tony stepped into Nina's apartment with a smile. He enjoyed travel. Flights in first-class were never too dreadful; Mrs Perkins organised his drivers, hotels and suites with military efficiency, he was always checked in automatically, and grovelling staff greeted him wherever he went. That hardly registered; the earl barely thought of them as people at all, they were part of the wallpaper. What he enjoyed was the barometer his travels gave him. How he was doing. What the rumours were this week. Each flight involved some waiting in a VIP area, some mingling with other first-class travellers when one boarded, usually last, and the common or garden businessmen filed past. Tony pretended supreme indifference to the whispers, the recurrent glances and nudges, the occasional obvious stare. But he loved it. They reacted to him like schoolboys to a football striker, drama-group actors in front of Robert de Niro. He'd noticed it gradually, years ago, as his empire started to build and his strings quietly started to jerk. It got more pronounced as Dragon took off, building to a crescendo as he became England's foremost takeover shark. When Jay DeFries was ruined and dragged off to jail, perversely, the whispering stopped for a short while. They were too scared to say anything at all. He sometimes thought he'd enjoyed that period most of all.

Today, of course, he was famous. The Helmers buyout had been concluded last week, a perfect hostile raid that left the stock in Tony's hands and the chairman in tears, or so the City whispers had it. On this morning's low-key flight they had chattered like starlings. Lowered voices, naturally, and pretend-casual looks in his direction, but it was wonderful, the sense of jealousy and curiosity all those losers were giving off. Satisfaction had lined his stomach as pleasantly as the warm croissants and coffee he'd breakfasted on. If they thought he had it good now, Tony wondered, what on earth would they say once the latest newsletter went to the number-crunchers?

Nina's find was looking exceptionally promising. He'd called Lilly Hall in for a meeting; frightful harridan, but she knew what she was about. The photographs of slim mice and svelte monkeys were exquisitely dramatic. Human trials would take a long time. It was hard to get permission to experiment on human beings in the West, which was nonsense, of course, how could science ever improve that way? Tony reflected calmly on his methods of avoiding that problem. Quiet little research centres in Africa and South America, where indigent adults would fight each other for the chance to earn twenty US bucks a day. And to think, they'd all get slim as well. Whilst the real beauty of the thing was that Nina's reorganisation of his research divisions would prop up the share price all by itself. Delicious rumours of his new bombshell would leak out, and then, by God, it was open season. Dragon Inc. would be on automatic pilot to the stars, and he, Tony Savage, would be lifted along with it into orbit.

Tony was tired of being a big fish in a small pond. He was an hereditary peer, and since the Queen had legendarily proclaimed there were to be no more dukedoms created – apparently she was very relieved when Churchill turned down the chance to be Duke of London – he wasn't likely to get bumped up, a gong could have no meaning. He had a perfect social life, the respect, or better, the fear of his fellows. Charles and Richard were shaping up nicely, Monica was an asset. There was no further to go in the UK, he needed to set his sights a little higher. In the States he'd still be a minor figure, not like those slick bastards Hanson and White, or the half-Frog Sir James Goldsmith. And that was what Tony desperately wanted. Success on a global scale. He wanted to hear that muttering at other airports besides Heathrow. Hanson, White and Goldsmith were up there with the oil owners and the finance boys like George Soros. There were only a couple of hundred men like that, it was the world's most powerful and exclusive club. Tony hungered for admittance. And he felt he was just about on the brink of it.

Nina's grace-and-favour company flat. White and gold, modern and automated. He'd been here before years ago but forgotten all about it. She was probably overwhelmed by the luxury of it, Tony thought. She has no idea what she's doing for Dragon. Not the first clue what she really deserves.

'My dear girl, you look wonderful,' he said warmly. She did. His dick was stirring pleasantly right off the bat; Nina Roth wearing a fluid suit in creamy pink, the colour picking out the lush blackness of her hair and the purity of her pale skin. Tony's experienced eye identified the cut, that was a Ralph Lauren, one of her more demure numbers. It hovered just below the knee and buttoned up past her magnificent cleavage. He grinned. So unlike Nina to be prudish. Her make-up was minimal, a little blusher on the sharp cheekbones and a clover lip-gloss. Tony breathed in but scented no perfume. How amusing, she was being so businesslike. It was almost as if he hadn't fucked her.

'Thank you. I hope you had a good flight?'

'Quite acceptable, darling, thank you.'

'Great …' Nina pushed a stray lock of hair out of her dark eyes. 'Shall we get right to it?'

'Fine with me,' Tony said, making to slip off his cashmere overcoat.

'No.' Nina put her hand on him to stop him. Tony looked down and saw that she was bright red. 'I didn't mean that …'

He looked at her sharply. 'What's the problem?'

'No problem, we just have a lot to discuss first, about work, and your daughter, and I think we should do it right away.'

'Right you are.' Savage shrugged himself back into his coat. 'We'll go and have some lunch; business before pleasure, I suppose.'

Tony took her to the Merci Hotel. Nina felt the fear gripping her heart squeeze a little tighter as the staff recognised him at once. There was an orgy of bowing and scraping as they were ushered to a discreet table overshadowed by an ornamental tree. She wondered if they were expecting him to take her upstairs and bang her after the meal.

While Tony confidently ordered for both of them Nina opened her file. Her mouth was dry and she felt her heart palpitating. Maybe she'd always known, in her head, what manner of man the Robber Baron was. But when he was sitting in front of you it was different; the aquiline face, the hawk's eyes scouring the room, like he was permanently scoping for targets. She knew he had always watched her in the same way, the powerful rajah stripping her with his eyes, assessing her like a farmer at a cattle market. In London she'd enjoyed it, but that was before she'd met Harry. The jewels, the callous sensuality, started to rankle. Sitting here while the waiter wheeled over their champagne Nina saw clearly why she'd sent Anita that opal and sapphire bracelet. What looked like generosity was something very different. Tony knew it and she'd known it, but she'd been too cowardly to admit it. He forced her to wear those jewels because she didn't like to; because they marked her out as his property. His plaything.

She could put a label on that uncomfortable feeling now. It was the way Tony made her feel like a high-class hooker.

Tony leaned over her as he poured the Cristal into cut-glass flutes. Nina breathed in his aftershave. She had to fight the impulse to shrink back. Oh, God, she thought, nervously. She was going to have to tell him it was over. She wondered how he was going to take it. She felt petrified.

'To Dragon. May she spread her wings and fly,' Tony smiled, touching his champagne flute to hers.

Waiters set a starter before them, braised veal and truffles in a white wine sauce. It was delicious but Nina could hardly taste it. Nervously she handed her boss the notes for the quarterly report, the piece she'd been sweating over all week.

Tony scanned it quickly, glanced up at Nina, nodded. Then he leaned back and read it more slowly.

'Very good.' The patrician tones were smoothly pleased. 'Very nice, exactly what the institutional boys are looking for.'

'And will I get a promotion?' Nina screwed up her courage. She'd delivered for Dragon: once in finding Lilly and twice with the reorganisation.

'Nina.' Tony looked faintly amused. 'You've just had a promotion. What will your colleagues think?'

'Only to senior manager. That's nothing. And since when did you give a damn about what your employees think?'

He nodded faintly to that. 'You're doing very nicely.'

'I've set up a whole new division, sir, it's going in the newsletter—'

'Sir? We are being formal today.' Tony speared some veal and truffles and made a cutting motion with his left hand, his gold Rolex flashing in the sunlight, ending the discussion. 'It was a very simple idea.'

Nina didn't push it, but she was annoyed. Simple idea it might have been, but none of his gilded flunkies had ever thought of it. And it was on simple ideas that business empires were built.

Oh well. Once her report was published, and credited, to her, Nina knew she'd be in a much stronger position. She had no doubt this was going to send Dragon stock to the ceiling. At that point, headhunters would start calling with tempting offers from other firms. Tony'd have to give her her due, pay her for her results.

Patience is a virtue.

'We'd better talk about Elizabeth.'

The tiniest cloud settled on Caerhaven's forehead, a minute frown as her name was mentioned.

'Yes. She's getting rather ubiquitous at home. There are too few British athletes in with a chance at these Games.' Tony shrugged. 'So give me good news, tell me when the Taylor boy's going to pop the question.'

Nina breathed in. 'I'm afraid I can't. I don't think they're together any more.' She watched Tony's expression darken. 'It's impossible to check on that relationship right now, with the Games so close. Elizabeth isn't training with her team, she doesn't socialise, she just skis and works out.'

'I don't believe it,' Tony said angrily.

Nina shivered. Oh God! 'There's something else. It's about Dragon Gold.'

'What? Oh yes, her little pill. Managed to make a go of it, a few orders from Boots.' Tony took a belt of champagne, then another, refilled his glass. His flirtatiousness had vanished. It was amazing, the way you could almost see the little cogs whirring as his mind worked, analysing, planning, hovering round the problem like a vulture round a corpse. 'Maybe I can give her a few UK products to play with until we *can* get her married off. At least she'd be content.' He almost spat out the word. 'And unnoticeable.'

'I'm afraid not. Not if I read the figures she's been giving me correctly. She's tried to bury what she's doing, but reading between the lines . . . Lady Elizabeth's trying to launch Gold in Europe. She's dealing direct with the national offices, she's talking to German and French ad agencies, and she appears to have got herself a budget from central funding.'

There was a crashing silence. Tony Savage lowered his knife and fork and stared at Nina.

'I could have it wrong,' Nina muttered.

'I see.' The earl's voice was ice. 'And with what authority is she doing this? How could she unlock our monies like that?'

'I believe she's doing it with your authority. She refers to you a lot in the correspondence I've seen. She's just giving orders, and they're assuming she has the right to do it.'

'You're serious.'

'Yes, sir. Dragon is a family company . . . Lady Elizabeth is your daughter, and she has sold a lot of pills. Maybe they thought it was natural to expand – nobody would dare challenge a Savage. It is fairly . . . unorthodox. And bold.' Nina had to admit it, she loathed the princess, but you had to give it to her, it was gutsy as hell. And with someone less sussed than me, she might even have got away with it; presented Daddy with a Europe-wide success as a *fait accompli*. She tried to smile at Tony. 'Like father, like daughter, I guess.'

The earl's head jerked up. His eyes stared right through Nina, the fury in them blazing like coal, so fierce she shrank back in her chair.

'I don't have a daughter,' Tony Savage said.

'No.' Jack's voice was impatient, almost disdainful. Elizabeth smarted under it as under a whip. Bastard! She'd been dropping and twisting for hours, trying to follow Jack's bawled instructions, till her waist was sore and her butt ached and the whole world was a blur of flying snow and flapping flagpoles. '*Left* a little, then right, lean into the curve for extra room!' He was shouting as she screeched to a halt, skis digging into the ice. Elizabeth was panting, red faced under the helmet. Fucking bloody Jack, if only he had been a little less good at the Super-G and she'd got something to throw back at him. But whenever the arrogant jerk sliced down in front of her his sodding technique was perfect. Elizabeth had watched in dismay. Next to Jack's grace and precision she felt like a fat builder trying to dance *Swan Lake*. Taylor was so big, such a burly git, where the hell did it all go? He took those turns like he was computer controlled. Jack Taylor, the skiing Texan android.

'I'm doing the best I can,' Elizabeth shouted back.

Jack shook his head and pointed to her helmet. 'Say what, milady? You're gonna have to do better than that.'

Elizabeth's Lycra gloves fumbled with her straps, ripped off the helmet. Her scrunchie came with it and a great cloud of tawny hair tumbled down round her shoulders. Her green eyes were sparkling; Jack fought back the surge of desire lapping round his groin. Goddamn, he wanted to trip her up, right here, right now, and just—

'Christ! I *know* that, I'm trying my best! Can't you be a little encouraging?'

'I could. But I won't.' Jack shrugged; his handsome face was glowing gently from exercise, like he'd just completed a few pleasant strolls. Elizabeth knew she was a wreck and that made her crosser than ever. 'I'm not British, sugar. I'm not here to fly the flag and get your autograph.'

'What the hell's that supposed to mean?' shouted Elizabeth.

'It's supposed to mean that you need a lot more work.' Jack lightly lifted his ski-pole and touched her on the chest. 'You need to quit being late, quit skipping practice, quit playing shop.'

'I'm doing something real—'

'Oh, like hell.' Jack was too annoyed to take this bullshit any more. 'You got no future there and you know it. You've got some ego thing going on with your Dad, you're letting it waste the best chance Britain's got for a gold.'

'Jack, I don't know where to start.'

'Then don't.' Jack's dark eyes were uncompromising. 'The world doesn't owe you a living, Princess. You got no degree, no experience, but somehow you think you can barge in and take over from day one.'

Elizabeth said nothing.

'You got the talent, you should stop fucking around, or you're not going to win, sister, and that's the bottom line,' Jack said harshly.

'You know, you sound just like my father,' Elizabeth said.

Jack was angry. 'Fuck you, babe.'

'I don't think so, Jack. Once was enough.' Elizabeth strapped her helmet back on and lifted the visor. 'Thanks for the workout.'

She lowered her poles to the ground and pushed off southwards, disappearing in a flash of iridescence down the Strela black that led down to Davos.

Jack Taylor watched her go. He'd made her sweat it, he'd made his point, and he'd also spoken his mind. Those things needed saying.

Damn it! he thought.

30

Tony stepped out of the limo at the airport concourse and motioned for Nina to get out.

'Sorry I can't stay, darling. I must go back and sort this out.'

So I gathered, Nina thought. Tony had called for the check right away and bundled her into his waiting car. On the drive to Kloten he'd made her go through the figures over and over. 'Why don't you just call everybody and tell them it's all off? If you want to do that. I mean, it's not such a bad idea . . .' Nina stopped herself mid-sentence. What was she saying? That was her practical streak speaking, she wanted Elizabeth Savage to get busted, and brutally.

Tony looked at her blankly. 'You don't understand. I'll deal with it, and not a word to anybody, or you can kiss Dragon goodbye.'

'I won't mention it.' Nina drew back from his intensity as their car pulled smoothly over to the kerb.

Tony's expression softened. He lifted one hand and tucked the wind-blown hair back behind Nina's ears, looking her over pleasurably. 'Really, darling, so sorry we've been interrupted. But you'll be home very soon, we can take up where we left off.'

Tony bent to kiss her, but Nina turned her head, so it landed on her cheek instead of her lips.

He pulled up sharply. 'What's the matter with you?'

'Tony,' Nina said, and her voice suddenly sounded like it belonged to someone else, someone a lot calmer than she actually felt, 'I'm sorry, but that side of our relationship has to finish.'

Caerhaven looked down blankly at her. 'Don't be ludicrous. We're perfect for each other, we enjoy each other.'

'It doesn't feel right any more. I'm sorry, Tony. I'll return all your jewellery,' Nina said.

Tony almost laughed. The luminous dark eyes locking on to his were so serious. As though she had any idea, as though there was any way he was actually going to permit this.

'Nina, Nina.' The fingers stroking her hair suddenly moved on to her cheekbones, tracing their line. 'You don't understand. *I* enjoy *you*. We stop when I get tired of it.'

'What?' Nina whispered.

'You heard me.' Tony checked his watch. 'Now, I don't have time for this,

I'm on the two thirty. Don't send me back the jewellery. Wear it the next time we go out.'

'I'm not going to see you socially any more,' Nina said.

Tony's hand cupped her face and tightened. He spoke softly and smiled deep into her eyes.

'I gave you everything and I can take everything. You'll be reasonable, darling, or it will be the worse for you.'

Elizabeth's feelings were mixed as she stepped out of the courtesy bus, its new gold paint emblazoned with the Olympic rings hoping to compensate for the ramshackle suspension. Monica would have had kittens, negotiating the winding Alpine roads in that, but she was used to it. You had to be, if you were skiing for Britain. Apparently not even the thought of a glorious women's gold could persuade the BSF to part with hard cash, so the team arrived at Flims in a nicely painted old banger, courtesy of the Swiss Confederation.

'Did you see the French coach?' Janet Marlin asked as she grabbed her bags and dumped them on to the snow. 'It passed us driving up to Davos. Madeline de Lisle showed me around. It had Ataris and bunk beds and everything. Just like rock stars use.'

'How would you know what rock stars use? Been in the back of the bus with Duran Duran?' Kate teased her friend.

Elizabeth leaned forwards and grabbed her purple hold-all.

'Careful, milady, don't strain yourself,' Karen said nastily. 'Carrying your own bags? Is the butler off sick, then?'

'Sod off, Karen,' Elizabeth snapped.

'Forget about the French coach, did you see the American one?' Kate added, with a sly glance at Elizabeth. 'It's a bloody palace. Ford are sponsoring them and they've got a lounge area, a video …'

'What, don't they have their own mountain?' Elizabeth replied sarcastically.

'You should know, love, didn't Jack show you around?'

Elizabeth stiffened. She'd walked right into that.

'Why should he? I hardly see him any more.'

'Yeah, I heard something about that,' Karen said. 'Or maybe he just didn't want you to bump into Holly Ferrell. The US team travel together, they just sleep on separate floors. Bad news if the ex bumps into the current, ain't it?'

'Holly?'

'Yes, Holly. Didn't you know? He's been skiing with her day in, day out since they went to Grindelwald. Doing the Lauberhorn and the White Hare …'

Elizabeth couldn't help it, she paled. Hans and she had just done that area, the best in the Bernese Oberland, skiing the legendary runs around Wengen and the Eiger. Gradients that were so steep, runs that turned so well they were pure motion, a champion's dream, like the mountain's own gift to the skier. Her heart did a slow flip in her chest at the thought of it. Jack skiing the Lauberhorn with someone else! Charming Holly Ferrell, a blonde society babe who had never greatly troubled the timekeepers nor the sports writers.

A meat-and-potatoes athlete, a richer, prettier Karen. Holly would not fight with Jack. All she would do was watch him in dewy-eyed wonder, Elizabeth thought viciously, and they could hum 'The Star-spangled Banner' as they schussed back to their hotel at night. Holly, yes, Holly would be Ms Perfect, a nice wholesome Miss America with white teeth and no personality . . .

The other girls were watching her.

'Why should I care? I've seen Jack ski, I don't think I can learn anything more from him.'

'Sure. It's all about skiing,' Karen said.

Ronnie Davis arrived from the back of the coach and the girls fell silent. He glanced from one flushed face to another.

'Catfights again? Just cut it out! We've got a couple of weeks until the start of the bloody Games. None of you has trained on Crap Sogn Gion yet, yes, Janet, ha ha, very amusing . . . wait till you're halfway down to Murtscheg. And Elizabeth – don't even think about skiing off-piste from Cassons.'

Elizabeth's head lifted, startled. She had been planning exactly that tomorrow, once Hans Wolf settled into his chalet on the slope above them.

'But Ronnie, it'll be perfect practice . . .'

'Perfect for you to schuss off the edge of the cliff. No way, girl, you're back under my orders for the duration.'

Elizabeth nodded sulkily. He was taking away her drug. Nothing but the hardest, harshest white slopes, peppered with moguls and virgin powder, could distract her from all the stress. And Jack. She wanted to forget him but that was easier said than done, with all the US media out here on a feeding frenzy. Taylor this, Taylor that, it was the gossip that leaked out from the Olympic Village, it was the profiles in *Newsweek* and *Time* and the *Herald Tribune*.

'I've already spoken to Herr Wolf.' Ronnie's rough voice spoke the name deferentially, you couldn't deal with a legend any other way. 'He agrees with me. From now on, it's Olympic courses only. You ski them till you can see them with your eyes shut.'

'Ronnie.' Kate spoke up winningly. 'If Hans is coming up here tomorrow, why don't you have a word with him, see if he'll take us for some training too?'

'Get lost, Kate!' Elizabeth exploded. 'Hans is *my* coach, he doesn't waste time with fifth-raters—'

'That's *enough*!' Ronnie rounded on Elizabeth. 'Christ almighty, this is supposed to be a team.'

'So the papers are right about you,' Janet said to Elizabeth, pink faced from being called fifth-rate. 'The things they're saying.'

'What things?' Elizabeth demanded.

'I said that's enough.' Ronnie's bark was sharp enough to scare them all into silence. Elizabeth saw him give Janet a death-stare. 'You're sharing a chalet, Janet and Kate, and Karen, you're in with Elizabeth. One more word from anybody and I'll report in to the Sports Council and FIS. Nobody talks in bars, and nobody,' he added with a sweeping look, 'speaks to the press. There are all the home comforts you'll need in these chalets, including a weights room.'

'Are there the papers? I'd like to see how we're getting on in the Falklands,' Karen said smoothly. Elizabeth looked at her; she wanted news from home as well, but there was something in Karen's tone that made her edgy.

'I can tell you that, love. We're winning. There'll be *no* papers, no radio, no distractions. From now on we're just here to ski.'

Elizabeth unpacked her hold-all in her room. It was soulless and functional, maybe the best way for an athlete's quarters to be; a hotel-style uniformity could be Zen-like in calming the brain. There was nothing here to make her nervous, except the view from her pale blue blinds. When you opened them up you saw Mount Startgels looming over you, the vast rocky outcrop blanketed with snow, spearing the deep clear blue of the sky. When Elizabeth slept under mountains she felt them as a presence, frozen giants who could almost breathe if you had the spell to unlock them. Startgels was the site of an Olympic slalom. She would be out on it soon, in the red, white and blue. The downy snow that looked so virginal covered so many things: abysses, crevasses, cliffs, soul-searing pleasure, death and glory.

'Horrible, isn't it?'

Elizabeth jumped; Karen noticed the long, glossy hair shimmer as she moved, the expensive burgundy cashmere dress, the Italian shoes. As well as the sports hold-all, Elizabeth's clothes cases were at the end of her bed; moss-green leather, embossed with some heraldry thing in gold. They looked antique. Fucking hell, she was so posh you could wonder if she ever used the toilet, Karen thought. Dislike seethed in her stomach. Pictures of milady were all over Flims, usually grouped with Louise and Heidi of Switzerland. You didn't have to speak the language to get the idea – they all thought Lizzie was the only threat. Karen had felt it keenly when Elizabeth jetted off to Klosters with Hans; the press that stayed with the official team had only asked about Elizabeth. The rest of them were a Mickey Mouse outfit, and nobody bothered pretending otherwise.

Karen was the best, though. She'd held the UK record before bloody Hans Wolf called up from Saas Grund and suggested they give the stuck-up cow a trial. Karen wouldn't have creamed off any World Cups but without Liz she'd be the UK champion and she'd have respect.

'What do you mean?'

'That.' Karen pointed at the Alp. 'Oppressive, makes you want to see pubs and cherry trees.'

'We get enough pubs at home, don't we?' Elizabeth asked mildly. She thought about Jack with a sharp ache. He felt like she did about mountains. He loved them and lived them, but they were still strange enough to enchant him; to Franz Klammer and Louise Levier they were everyday.

'Can't think your sort ever sees much of a pub.'

'You'd be surprised.' Elizabeth looked away, partly because she didn't want to fight, partly because she'd just flashed on Jack again; drinking with him in the White Swan at Frant, watching the firelight crackle shadows across his face and hearing how strange he sounded under all the horse-brasses and dried hops hanging from the timbers. 'How was Verbier? I heard you did the mogul field at Mont-Fort in record time. That must feel great.'

Karen flushed. Condescending bitch, she sounded like the Queen asking what you did for a living. Karen had squeezed everything she had to shave one second twenty off that run, a tough mogul field, relentless and very steep. And she knew she was still three or four seconds off Elizabeth's average.

'Hardly a record. Heidi Laufen has that and you have the British.'

'English, then, you'll have the English record.'

Yeah right. Karen shrugged and left the room.

Elizabeth flopped down on her bed and stared out at the pistes. What the hell, it was good to have the hostility. Something other than Jack to occupy her mind.

At six p.m. sharp Elizabeth appeared in the drawing room for supper, a tasteless fish and pasta thing cooked up by the team nutritionist.

'Protein, carbs, bit of fat, the boffins know what they're doing,' Ronnie Davis said cheerily, thanking God he could go down to the Little China in the village later. 'Here are your schedules, girls. Elizabeth, here's yours. Hans has called and he'll be meeting you tomorrow.'

Elizabeth dutifully wolfed her food while the other girls chattered. Teams and times and who was going to get busted in the drugs samples, the Spanish team's new skis and who was screwing who. Janet had been asked on to *A Question of Sport* and Karen thought a sponsorship deal with Nike was in the works. God, as if any of it mattered! Elizabeth thought. She said nothing after Ronnie went to go and check the weights room, eating her tasteless food and trying to rehearse the courses in her mind. She was trying to become a race machine. Maria Peraña's new skis and Freyja Gundstrom's drug test, so what? If it was Louise Levier, now ...

Elizabeth took her plate to the kitchen and washed it up. None of the others said a word, but she didn't give a monkey's. They could try and send her to Coventry like a pack of bitchy schoolgirls; she was going to work out and then head straight for bed.

On her way through to the chalet gym Elizabeth paused in the TV room. There was a bunch of papers strewn prominently over the sofas. She grinned as she saw they were English, great! Ronnie's censorship hadn't worked that well.

Elizabeth flopped down and leafed through them. *Sun*-speak doggerel about Our Boys in the South Atlantic, but it was good to get news from the outside world. If only to remember that there *were* other things in this world besides the Olympics. Shooting in El Salvador, John de Lorean had gone bust and some English cricketers were banned for busting sanctions to tour South Africa. There were no ads for Dragon Gold, maybe they'd all run yesterday. Elizabeth flipped to the back pages. Nice snaps of Christopher Dean doing a faultless double-axel. She hoped the rumours about those two were true, that they could skate both Yanks and Russians right off the ice ... her green eyes flicked determinedly over the story topped by an unsmiling Jack Taylor, his cruel mouth set hard as a gladiator. Then there she was: big picture, her ski-poles in one hand, goggles round her neck, hair pulled back from a chiselled face. Elizabeth recognised the shot, her triumph after a personal best Super-G in practice, back at Davos. At that moment she recalled the mix of triumph and annoyance, because it sunk in how much Jack's training had helped her. She looked gorgeous. She couldn't suppress a thrill of pride.

She soon stopped grinning.

'SNOW HELP TO BRITAIN,' sniped the *Sun*. 'TEAM SPIRIT SAVAGED,' screeched the *Mirror*. 'SELFISH, SECRETIVE, SAVAGE,' screamed the *Star*.

The articles were pure acid. Elizabeth was a playgirl who insisted on luxury hotels and refused to train with the team. Not a word about the fact that her training was agreed by Ronnie, that the hotels were to keep her away from the press . . . if you read this you'd think Elizabeth was betraying her country, taking a skiing holiday at the nation's expense.

'We hope Lady Elizabeth knows what she's doing,' said the *Sun*. 'If she gets the gold – terrific. If not, we'll need some answers, Lady E – England expects, you know.'

'What the hell's this?'

Ronnie Davis reached down and tore the papers out of her hands. 'Don't pay any attention to that crap, love.' He stuck his head into the kitchen. 'Ladies, get in here *now*.'

'What's the problem, Ronnie?' Kate asked innocently.

Ronnie shook the crumpled sheets of newsprint. 'This. English papers I told you we weren't having. Somebody must have ordered them up here. They've been printing crap about Elizabeth I didn't want her to see.'

All three denied it, Karen shaking her head like butter wouldn't melt.

Elizabeth made a real effort and shoved the lump back down her throat. Somebody had not only wanted her to see that, they'd been feeding the media those lies in the first place.

'It's OK.' She looked at the girls with measured calm. 'After all, I *am* World Champion. I don't let fish-and-chip wrapping put me off my stroke.' She paused and looked directly at Karen. 'I can promise you, it'll take a lot more than that.'

31

Nina's heart lifted as she stepped out of Swissair Flight 223. There were no soaring mountains as you came in to land at Heathrow. The sky was overcast and the plane was full of grumpy passengers carrying their Lindt selections and cuckoo clocks, all wishing they were still out on the slopes. But not Nina.

A Dragon driver, mercifully untalkative, had been sent to pick her up. You had to give it to Tony. When you were with Dragon, life was smooth.

'Home or office, madam?'

'Home, please.' Nina was still young enough to get a kick out of being called 'madam'. She settled back into the soft leather seat and watched the motorway slip past. She thought pleasantly that soon this would be normal for her, once she was promoted. A Golf GTi wouldn't cut it then. And hell, why not? It happened to the young Turks in the City and Wall Street all the time. Nobody could say she didn't deserve it.

There was a minibar, a TV and a copy of the *Financial Times* on the back seat. Nina flicked to the share listings. Sure enough, Dragon was up, a real big jump – two and an eighth – and if she was right, this was just the beginning.

She poured a glass of mineral water with a slice of lime. It was good for the skin. She didn't want to be all dehydrated when she saw Harry again. Once she'd talked some sense into Tony, they could start dating. Nina shifted a little. Harry still left an echo, that sweet crunch she thought she'd never get without shame. Wow, kid, what a discovery, Nina teased herself, there's more to life than work.

Namath had made her less hard but more alive, like somebody unthawing after an age in an ice-box. It was better than triumph or satisfaction. It was simple happiness and hope, because maybe, at last, things were going to be different.

Her place was perfect: furniture replaced, radiators on, warming the house against the March chill. Anita had even gone to M&S to stock the fridge.

Nina rushed upstairs and took a long, blissful shower, then phoned the office.

'Coming in today? Surely there's no need,' Anita protested.

'There's lots of need.'

'You could take the afternoon off. Nobody expects you in. Maybe you could go shopping.'

Nina chuckled; she hadn't changed that much. 'No, I'll be there in an hour. Could you possibly call Frank Staunton and let him know?'

'OK, I'm sure the boss'll want to see you.'

True, Frank Staunton was her boss. Well, not for much longer.

'And somebody else will want to say hello, I expect. Friends of yours from Switzerland: Dr Hall and Dr Namath, they've popped in to see Frank.'

Even though there was nobody around Nina blushed. 'Er, great, sure. See you soon.'

The Dragon tower on the South Bank loomed forbiddingly into the grey sky as Nina stepped in out of the drizzling rain. She'd changed into a Donna Karan tweed, with Manolo Blahnik heels and a thick silver cuff bracelet, one she'd bought herself from Mappin & Webb. Tonight she was going to send Tony a thick parcel of jewels. If he refused to take them she'd send them to charity. She was never going to wear them again.

'Good morning, Miss Roth,' the receptionist said. Nina clocked the quick flash of hostility from one beautiful girl meeting another. She was pleased, that meant she looked good. Men she recognised smiled and waved. A good sign. They thought it was worth kissing up to her. The quarterly report must have made quite an impact.

The elevator hissed smoothly to a stop and Nina stepped out, smiling and glad-handing her way to her office. Anita greeted her with a mug of coffee and a mountain of notes.

'Just to get you up to speed on recent developments. The Helmers acquisition went through, Clophramine has been approved for beta-testing. Frank Staunton wants to see you in twenty minutes. I'll buzz you, OK?'

'Fine.' Nina sat down and leafed through the headlines. Only one page got her attention: a curt memo from George Gage, in Production, copied to New Products.

'Owing to quality control concerns, company product no. 87569 is being temporarily discontinued. Sales are to be withdrawn until further notice.'

Memos like this were the kiss of death. Advertising was immediately stopped and further orders not accepted. The last time Mr Gage's clammy spectre had fallen on her division was with Protaxin, their hotly tipped anticoagulant, when one final batch of tests had shown delayed side-effects – two chimps became impotent. Nobody in pharmacology liked the word 'lawsuit'.

Nina lowered her coffee and tapped her computer keyboard. Interesting – normally products didn't get out there unless they were super-safe. The cost of recall was huge.

Her IBM flashed up the name: 87569, product, Dragon Gold, executive in charge, Lady Elizabeth Savage.

She gave a low whistle. Goddamn, he really knew how to bear a grudge. Elizabeth's strategy had been groundbreakingly successful. Nina knew it could have opened the door to the vitamin market. Three billion dollars a year's worth of trade, parcelled up between three of their rivals – Hoffman LaRoche, Eastman Kodak and Pfizer. Caerhaven had wanted a way in for years, but he'd rather throw it away than take it from Elizabeth.

For a second she almost felt sorry for Elizabeth. Tony was a hell of an enemy.

Not my problem, Nina thought.

'Come in, come in.' The Terrier gave Nina a thin little smile, his eyes sliding over her suit without seeing it. 'The traveller returns. Good work, by the way.'

'Thank you, sir,' Nina said, as Staunton ushered her in. Harry and Lilly were sitting on his burgundy leather couch.

'A great achievement, the liaison with two of our prized assets.'

Liaison? I *found* them! Nina smiled as neutrally as she could at Harry and his partner. Lilly looked at Nina coldly, said, 'G'day, kid.' Harry sprang to his feet. He walked over to her.

'You look gorgeous,' he murmured. Nina flushed and shook hands. Harry traced a small line on her palm, one fingertip stroking the soft flesh between her thumb and forefinger. It was too sensuous. Nina yanked her hand away.

'Hello, Harry, I hope you're settling in OK.'

'No complaints,' Namath replied. His tone was grave but his eyes were dancing.

'Dr Hall was just going through her latest results with me,' Frank Staunton said.

'Then I won't bother you,' Nina said with relief.

'I'll drop by your office when we're done,' Namath said.

'That would be fine.' She smiled briskly.

Frank Staunton turned back to the dumpy woman on his couch. How delicious, her attempts to hide it were pathetic. Nina had something going on with Namath. He was sure that would interest Tony. It was just the kind of thing the Terrier loved to ferret out. For the daughter *and* the girlfriend, things were going to get a little hot around here . . .

In her office Nina pressed a cooling hand to her brow. Oh God, Harry, you shouldn't have let anything show . . .

Anita poked her head round the door. 'I've got the priority mail for you, and your copy of the quarterly report.'

'Great! Let me see it,' Nina said. Anita handed the newsletter over; the Dragon logo stamped in gold on thick vellum, charts and projections at the front, new business at the back. She found her piece right away: 'A New Approach to Drug Research'. Nina felt victory flood through her. She settled down to read.

Two minutes later, her heart stopped.

For a few seconds she felt dizzy, so stunned and betrayed she didn't know what to do. Then Nina lifted her phone and tapped out Mrs Perkins's extension.

'Chairman's office, can I help you?'

'Yes you can, Mrs Perkins. This is Nina Roth. I'd like to speak to Lord Caerhaven.'

'I'm afraid that won't be possible.'

'Mrs Perkins, I must speak to him. It's urgent.'

'I'm afraid it's still not possible,' Mrs Perkins told her smugly. 'Lord Caerhaven isn't in the country. He can't be reached. I can take a message—'

Which he'll never get. 'I see. Where is he?'

'He's out in Switzerland, Miss Roth. Cheering on Lady Elizabeth.'

'It's going to look bad,' Ronnie Davis warned Hans. 'The papers are eating her alive.'

'*Ja*, and now she knows this!'

Ronnie quailed a little before Hans's fury. Amazing how the old man could screw with your head.

'That wasn't my fault.'

'I know, Ronnie. But look at her.' Hans pointed to Elizabeth, sweating bullets as she peeled off her goggles. 'What says your stopwatch?'

'Five-forty on the Cassons. Two-ten on Nagens-Startgels,' Ronnie agreed. 'And her Super-G's picked up almost a second and a half. She's making amazing times.'

'She can do better. We have but two days. No more distractions and envy.' Hans glared at the silhouette of Karen Carter. '*Bitte*, Elizabeth leaves the team chalet and moves in with me.'

'OK, guv.' Ronnie threw up his hands. 'If it's right for the team . . .'

'For the team? *Ach!* I do not know, I do not care. For Elizabeth, it is right.'

Both men glanced back at Elizabeth. On the wooden slats of the cool-down room, her long, lean body was twisting itself backwards and forwards as she bent into her deep stretches. Elizabeth wore the geometric slashes of the red, white and blue, a mobile Union Jack. Hans had deliberately delayed the time she would put this on; when she wore the national colours it had to be significant, like donning armour for battle. Suddenly it was about more than times, rankings and rivals. Fräulein Laufen was not just Heidi, she was Switzerland; Marie Le Blanc was France; and for these few weeks, Elizabeth would be Britain, taking her country's flag into battle. That was the magic of the Olympics. For yourself, you could get tired and weak and jaded. For your country, you would fight till you dropped.

'So what's the story?' Ronnie Davis asked. 'She will get a medal?'

'Of course.'

'And what colour?'

The old man gave him an incredulous stare. 'She will get the gold. I am surprised you even ask. I have never been more certain of anything in my life.'

'Lovely,' Monica said. She reached over and gingerly unwrapped a whisky silk scarf from its layers of tissue. Their suite at the Park Hotel was the best Flims had to offer. Every place in town had been sold out for weeks. TV crews swarmed over the resort like ants, besieging the skiers' chalets and the Olympic Village. Spectators arrived every day, a polyglot crowd packing everything from the Park to the lowliest rented chalet. Even if you were the parents of a medal hopeful, there was no room at the inn.

Unless of course you were Tony Savage.

'We'll stay for Elizabeth's races, then we'll go straight back,' Tony said. His face was expressionless as he stared up at the mountains. The competitors' chalets were fenced off; some common little man named Davis had curtly told him he couldn't speak to the little bitch. But words were being had in London right now, and that would change.

'Oh, really, darling?' Monica murmured, admiring herself in the wall mirror. The Nicole Farhi in orchid lambswool clung to her concave stomach and slender shoulders, swaying below the hem when she moved. And Tony's latest offering, a necklace of diamonds and lapis lazuli, just this side of vulgar, would set it off beautifully. She knew she'd photograph wonderfully tonight. And tomorrow night. And every day that the cameras asked for comments from the proud parents. 'I think we could stay, don't you?'

'If you like,' Tony agreed absently. The fax machine in the drawing-room was spewing out confirmations of everything he wanted to hear. Elizabeth's pill, all her sales routes and advertising, had been withdrawn from every region like it was toxic. His word had gone down, and her work was snuffed out like a candle.

The phone rang. Monica picked it up.

'Monica Caerhaven . . . oh darling, it's you, how thrilling. Yes, he's here.' She languidly handed the phone across to her husband. 'It's Elizabeth, dear, for you.'

'Thank you.' Tony cupped one hand over the receiver. 'Darling, why don't you find Charlie and Richard and go out shopping for a while?'

It was a clear dismissal, and Monica didn't hesitate. Smiling blandly, she nodded and left the suite.

'Hello Elizabeth,' Tony said. 'I've got some rather bad news for you.'

32

Outside the chalet windows it was still dark, the deep blue shadows of the Alpine massifs blocking the rising sun. There had been a snowfall last night. Elizabeth could tell from a faint scent in the freezing air, and from the way the sky was brightening, the streaks of dawn lighter than usual. She'd slept fitfully, tossing and turning in the hard orthopaedic bed. She'd tried to sleep but it was no good. The conversation with Tony had filled her with a white-hot rage that just refused to simmer down.

He'd torn apart her work, her baby. No consultation, nothing. Sure, she'd expected him to be a bit annoyed, but nothing like this. To stop her having any success, Tony was prepared to wipe out all their market gains and take thousands in losses. She felt the bitterness as strongly now as she had last night. Once the Games were over, she was going to have to decide what to do. Father had buckled in in the first place, why? Because he was scared she'd make a scene. Not such a strong reason, Elizabeth thought, but it was to him. So what would Tony do once she was gold medallist? She'd be famous back home. Like they said, you were World Champion for a year, but Olympic Champion for life.

The desire for revenge. It was incredibly strong. It was blazing up in her. She started to march on the spot, swinging her arms and heels through the warm-up she could do in her sleep. Hot blood started singing round her body. She hadn't needed more incentive, but there it was – the gold would give her the means to get back at Tony. And Nina Roth. How could she figure it out from the notes I gave her? Elizabeth wondered, but clearly she had, and she'd shopped her straight to Daddy. Oh, the delight Nina must have felt, bringing her down—

She stopped herself as she lifted one leg on to the windowsill, bowing into the stretch. Come on, girl, not now. You've got exactly one day to the start of the ninety-fifth Olympiad.

There was a sharp rapping on the door. Hans poked his head round.

'Hey, I didn't mean to wake you.'

The old man waved that aside. 'Only in the morning you ski, you must rest all afternoon.'

'OK, boss.'

'Where are you going?'

'Sogn Gion this morning.' The men's World Cup run was a women's

Olympic downhill for the first time. Tomorrow afternoon Elizabeth would be out there for real.

'Some others are also there.'

'No kidding, it must be a regular traffic jam,' Elizabeth said wryly. Everybody would want to get last-minute dry runs in.

'Do not be distracted, *Liebchen*,' Wolf lectured her sternly.

'Don't worry.' Elizabeth turned her head to him. It was amazing, Wolf thought, how she could be covered with streaks of sunblock and goggle-lines and still look so beautiful, so dignified. The blonde hair had lightened two shades in the mountain sun and her green eyes sparkled with fierce determination. 'Nothing is going to distract me now.'

Elizabeth skied down to the first lift areas. Hans was right, it was busy. Practice suits were out, national flags were in; unless your suit was stamped with an official number, you didn't see snow in Flims today. She waved cheerfully at Robin Cousins, walking past her to the ice-rink; Martin Bell was queuing for the cable-car up to Cassons; the Swiss hero Pirmin Zubriggen was chatting to Alte Skaardal from Norway. The women were busier around the Murtscheg gondola. Most were clutching their skis to them like shields. French flags, Swedish, Norwegian, Austrian, Swiss. Elizabeth's heart gave a sick little flip when Louise Levier passed her; there were six girls in the blood-red suits with the white crosses, but she knew Louise by the tight waist and lean, mean quads. The Swiss turned her head and nodded politely. Neither of them felt like small talk.

Somebody tapped her on the shoulder as she shuffled into the line. Karen Carter.

'Shall we ride up together?'

'Sure,' Elizabeth said blandly. She breathed in, the chilly morning air stinging her nose. Steam was rising from their breath like cows standing in the farm back home.

'You might as well. The press heard Hans moved you out of the team chalet.'

'I wonder how that could have happened,' Elizabeth said mildly. She wasn't rising to it. She gestured over at the queue for Cassons. 'Look at Martin and Graham. Martin was top ten in practice yesterday. Wonder what they're talking about?'

'Most likely Jack Taylor,' Karen said, glancing at her with nasty pleasure.

Elizabeth shrugged. Maybe it was. The rumours of Jack's total dominance in practice surprised nobody. If he won his gold as easily as they were expecting him to, he'd be a legend, the new Franz Klammer. To Karen she only said, 'Look lively, dear, or we'll miss our spot.'

The gondolas swung round, scooping up the athletes. Elizabeth and Karen climbed in with some French officials and half the Spanish team, two hefty girls ranked twentieth and thirty-first in the world. They stared at Elizabeth most of the way up, whispering in awe. Karen was really pissed off.

Elizabeth smiled at her serenely and turned her attention to the crisp new snowfall on the Olympic runs beneath them. The gondola swung upwards and onwards, into space, flying them to the cold, white roof of the world. It was the last session before the Games, and skiing, thought Elizabeth, would be the *only* thing on her mind.

At Sogn Gion Karen got out, strapped up and skied off without another word. There was no way she was going to follow Elizabeth and be shown up. Elizabeth smiled at the Spaniards and some others pressing round the top of the run. She felt warmly about the lower-level girls; kids for whom it was the thrill of a lifetime just to be in the Games, to march out tomorrow in their national blazers. When she saw the threats – the Austrians, Louise, Heidi or any others – Elizabeth looked away. It was like an electric shock. Those super-fit, super-skilled she-wolfs stood between her and the dream. There was no point in false friendship when the piste was the arena, and the skis on your feet were swords.

Elizabeth pulled her dark blue helmet on and clicked her Rossignols into place. This run was straightforward. Long, almost 3,500 feet vertical, with spectacular views. Not that she had any time to look at scenery.

She took a deep breath and pushed off. Straight away she was picking up speed, leaning into the first left. Elizabeth was skiing by reflex, her body adjusting, leaning, pushing, her weight shifting on the skis, mingling with the mountain's slope. Fresh morning snow plumed up around her, downy as feathers, flying back from the slicing cut of her edges. She was threading her way through other girls, diving and leaning through them with precision that left them gasping. Over a stomach-flipping ridge, Elizabeth's strong back flattening almost to horizontal, perfect lift as she landed. Exhilaration flooded her like oil round an engine, she was hot, she had it! There was Karen, Jesus, look at her, boring textbook skiing. Elizabeth flew past her. Now the run was clear for a little while, she could see the red and green of the Italians towards the finish. She turned to hug the treeline, she felt weightless, the speed and gravity had dissolved her mass. First past the ridge and then through this glade . . .

There was another figure on the course. Skiing in the blind spot under the forest, so she hadn't expected anyone there. Far too big and fast to be a female. Wearing the starry costume of the USA.

Jack Taylor.

Elizabeth reacted fiercely. Her heart was pulsing, it happened in a millisecond of real time, but this was ski time, parcelled in half seconds and point two-fives. She barrelled slightly to the right, her skis shooting across the diagonal, arcing powder up behind her and all over Jack as she jumped the ridge in front of him. She had faster momentum, it bombed her right in front of him, flying over the jump and landing. Point, plant, lift, slice to the right and fly down the home straight. He was coming after her. She didn't look behind her, but his shadow was on the snow, dark on the crystals glittering sunrise pink. Furiously Elizabeth skied from the gut, her waist crunching as she whipped in to the final turn, close by the orange nets. It was silent out here, their blades just skimming the snow, but the fury of her competition was totally real. Jack was gaining on her inexorably, he had too much muscle, he was going to win . . .

No! Elizabeth's body screamed. No! No! She thrust violently with her poles and willed herself forwards as Jack arrived beside her, every tendon in her legs blazing, and shot across the finish line, first by less than a head.

Elizabeth unhooked her helmet. Jack Taylor ripped off his goggles, glaring at her. She turned and pushed off without a word, skiing on to the start of an easy red.

Jack schussed down behind her, both poles tucked under one arm, his balance perfect, fluid and controlled. He grabbed her by her arm.

'What the hell was that all about?'

'You were in my way,' she snapped.

'No, ma'am, but you sure got in mine,' Jack said. The dark eyes flicked over her body-tight suit. Elizabeth felt herself respond, an involuntary twitch between her legs, her nipples hardening under the thermal fabric.

'If you can't take the competition, Jack ... I hear Zubriggen's looking good this year. It must be nasty, to get beat out by a girl.'

'You moved pretty fast.'

'Fast enough to ski you off the snow, Taylor,' Elizabeth snapped, 'and you must have made a damn slow time from the top for me to catch you like that.'

'Well now. Wrong again, sugar. I stopped to tighten up a clip. I'd just started up again when you came tearing down with a bug up your ass.'

'Yeah? But you took me on, and you lost.'

Jack snorted. 'Because you had a fifty mph start, girl. You couldn't beat me if I was skiing on one leg.'

Elizabeth glanced up to see a small crowd of girls pretending not to watch them fight. Angrily she flattened her edges and slipped down into the trees. Jack tilted his skis in perfect harmony, so they moved with each other like synchronised swimmers.

'Bullshit. It's all macho bullshit, Jack,' she taunted. 'That what Holly Ferrell tells you when you hold her hand down the Lauberhorn? Oh, Jack, you're so good, nobody in the world can touch you ...'

'Cut it out. Holly's a good skier.'

'Holly's a moose,' Elizabeth said, recalling a school insult, 'she brays in the forest.'

'You want to put up or shut up, baby,' Jack said angrily.

Elizabeth fought down the desire. Inside her catsuit she was slippery with perspiration, and not just from the run. She rounded on him.

'I beat you a minute ago, I can do it again.'

For a second she thought he was going to laugh in her face. Then the brown eyes narrowed. 'Princess, you're on. Right after the Games. You get ten seconds' start on the Lauberhorn.'

'Five will be fine.'

'Sure, if you really want to embarrass yourself. We'll ski for a wager. If I lose—'

'You endorse my next Dragon product. Free of charge and for as long as I want.'

Jack's face clouded. 'I'm not a goddamn used-car salesman.'

'Afraid you're going to lose?'

'Then if I win, you fly out to Texas, you spend the night with me.'

Elizabeth flushed. 'What, you'd have sex with me?'

'Till you could hardly walk,' Jack said slowly.

She said nothing.

'Scared?'

'Drop dead, I'm not frightened of a bet I won't be paying. You're on.' Elizabeth thrust out one gloved hand. Jack took it in his bare one and shook it, squeezing hard enough to let her feel his strength.

'See ya, honey,' Jack said, then reached down and patted her on the butt. Elizabeth whipped round but he was already a hundred yards in front of her, skiing back down to the village.

She pushed forwards and laboriously started to step up the slope. Boring, but good work for the thighs. The morning sky was bright from the snow, sunny and rosy with promise. Above her, she looked up and saw Christy Lansch, the Austrian number one, turn in tightly at the end of the piste. She looked good, but Elizabeth knew she could do better.

She took a deep breath of crystal-cold air and joined the chairlift queue, rank-and-file skiers staring as she passed. She was going to do the Sogn Gion until she could ski it blindfold.

The Arena Olympique was packed out. Waiting in their tunnel, the British teams fidgeted, listening to the hubbub of the crowd, watching the flash of television lights. The president of the IOC droned on about the Olympic ideal. The nations would march out in alphabetical order.

Ronnie Davis, wearing the white trousers and navy blazer of a UK official – 'Makes me look like a soddin' bellboy' – smiled encouragingly at his girls. Opposite them stood the giant Olympic torch, dull now, waiting to blaze up the sky like a bonfire.

Elizabeth was trembling. She didn't want to cry but she was fidgeting, easing her nerves away. Right now she was just one of the crowd, until the BBC cameras closed on her face. Lucy Mansfield, a bobsledder, was carrying the Union Jack, how must she be feeling?

Out there were her family. Tony, that selfish bastard, flighty Monica and two half-brothers she hardly knew. They'd have Frank Staunton and a bunch of corporate types in their box, but she wasn't going to worry about them. More to the point, there was Hans, somewhere in the stands, unofficial. He had declined to march as a British official; he was Swiss, he said firmly. Elizabeth wondered if Hans would cry, then dismissed that idea. Hans Wolf never cried. Not even when was he born, most likely.

Karen, Kate and Janet stood around her but didn't bother making conversation. She almost smiled. Family and team, it was just the same; surrounded by people but on my own, Elizabeth thought.

She wondered how Jack was feeling right now.

Over her blazer her tawny hair lay long and glossy. Under the TV lights it would show up almost platinum. Maybe it would—

'*Royaume-Uni!*' bellowed the announcer. '*Great Britain!*'

Elizabeth straightened up as the column began to walk forwards, Lucy tilting the flag just right so it fluttered free. She thrust back the butterflies squirming in her stomach, smiled, and waved like the Queen.

After all, the world was watching.

33

Nina sat in her office and considered her future.

Her options were very limited now. She had to believe that Tony had some explanation. Without the newsletter giving her credit, it looked like this was just another success for Dragon's team. She wasn't even mentioned by name.

After a lot of pushing, Mrs Perkins had admitted that Tony was due back in England tomorrow. He couldn't spend a whole week in Switzerland glad-handing his cronies when Dragon's stock was rising so fast. She knew the Robber Baron. Buy something fast, before all that extra cash sloshing around becomes a homing beacon for a takeover shark even bigger than him.

'Could you try and reach him in Flims, Mrs Perkins? I need an urgent meeting.'

'About what?'

'I'm afraid that's really between me and Lord Caerhaven,' Nina said smoothly. Stick it up your ass, she thought sourly. Whatever Tony was playing at, she was still *persona grata* at this firm. The airport limo, the obsequious doormen, the very fact that Mildred Perkins was taking her calls; these things only happened to Friends of Tony. In fact Mrs P. would probably assume Nina wanted to arrange a rendezvous, and it would be more than her job was worth to stand in the way of any pleasure of Tony's.

'Certainly, Miss Roth,' said Mrs Perkins thinly, then hung up.

When Nina came back from lunch there was a message on her voice mail. Tony telling her to meet him at the Halkin at nine p.m. He sounded pleased, like she had finally seen sense. And he had nothing on the agenda but sex.

Elizabeth stood at the start of the Lauberhorn, quietly flexing her quads and calves, waiting to be called. First in Super-G and the two Flims downhills, second in the slalom to Levier. Best of all, Louise had crashed in the Cassons race and Marie Le Blanc came second in Super-G, so right now, her competitors were spread out. The British tabloids were reserving judgment, but they'd stopped slagging her off.

Hans was icy cool. He let her give one-line statements to ITV and *Olympic Grandstand*, that was it. After Flims all he said was that she needed to work on the slalom. Good old Hans; Elizabeth knew he'd be down at the bottom right now eating his heart out.

This was the Blue Riband race. Women had never been permitted to ski the Lauberhorn before in any World Cup. People died on this run, their skis tangling in orange netting, shooting into trees in the fog, taking too much speed after the endless right-hand bend; men broken like dolls under the shadow of the Eiger, looking out at the Schilthorn valley. The safety officers were screaming in protest, but the girls wanted to ski it, and TV wanted the ratings. There was no women's record for the Lauberhorn, so Janet Fraser of Great Britain had set the first; three minutes fifteen, the first and last record she'd hold in her life.

Louise Levier made three-eight. Heidi Laufen three-seven. Marie three-ten. All blazing performances. Ingmar Lystrom, the Swede, crouched in the starting hut in her blue and yellow suit, heard the gun and slipped noiselessly out into the descent. The crowd went nuts, yelling and ululating, shaking their cowbells and football rattles. She was next.

'Number eight, representing Great Britain, Lady Elizabeth Savage!'

Elizabeth stepped up into the starter's hut. She was the favourite, the noise was deafening; a few boos were mixed in with the bells and whistles, the home crowd were for Heidi and Louise. The countdown began, she felt strangely calm. Nerves that seethed minutes before you skied sort of evaporated once you were actually up there. Out of the corner of her eye she saw the crowd packed behind the nets, Union Jacks waving brightly against the snow. Behind them and the Olympic media towers the Schilthorn loomed up, white snow and craggy black rock. It was settling; the Alps were uncaring, unchanging; the Olympics would blink in and out of this valley and leave no trace behind it.

She pushed off.

The schuss, leaning as low as possible, feeling the speed pick her up like a bullet and fire her down the track. Plant, slice, she had it covered, she saw the jump, soared clear and landed smoothly. The crowd shrieked but she was hundreds of yards on already. Now hug the trees, careful, careful, lower with the body – Elizabeth's tight quads steering her. Through the tunnel, bombing over the snow, the other girls had already packed it a little lower, squeezing out some air, the surface was faster that way. Long, long right, Jack's instructions flashing up and she shifted left milliseconds before the turn. For a moment she thought she wasn't coming back up, her gravity was too low, but then she tilted, righted herself, she was upright again, too fast to see flags or register cheering. There was the gate! Low, if you were thinking you were too slow . . .

Elizabeth thrust through the gates, couldn't slow down fast enough and tumbled over under her own tidal wave of powder. She felt like an idiot, scrambled to her feet.

For a moment they all just waited. Elizabeth hated this: your racing heart stopped, you couldn't breathe until the time flashed up. Hans walked over, put his bony hands on her strong shoulders.

Three-six point five-five. A roar went up from the crowd, Ronnie Davis jumped three feet in the air. 0.45 of a second faster than Heidi Laufen. The Swiss team turned away in disgust, the camera crews rushed forwards and Hans gave her a dry little nod. Her lead was extended yet again. Less time than a heartbeat, but it said, Britain one, Switzerland two and three.

'Lady Elizabeth – CNN—'

'Lady Elizabeth, can ITV have a few words—'

Camera lights shone brightly into Elizabeth's rosy face; microphones like fluffy marrows hung suspended over her head and hand-held ones were thrust under her nose.

'How does it feel to win the first women's Lauberhorn?'

'I wouldn't know, I haven't won. Christy and other great skiers have to go yet. It was a thrilling course to race, and I'm just going to concentrate on the next slalom.'

'That's it, ladies an' gents,' Ronnie said, beckoning to officials to get the rat pack off his girl. 'Liz, that was brilliant, you were flying down the fucking thing, I thought you were going to take off!'

Hans Wolf gave him a reproving look. 'You lost control at the end.'

'Yeah, but only after I was through the gate.'

'It's not good, it shows you lose control. If it happens on the run, *glaub' mir*, you can die.'

Elizabeth lowered her head, annoyed. She was burning with triumph, she thought Hans might have been a bit more upbeat.

'Elizabeth, your dad's flying home today,' Ronnie said. 'He wanted you to give him a call before he leaves.'

Elizabeth smiled. 'I don't want to talk to him. If he asks again, tell him I can't be bothered, simple as that.'

'Right,' Ronnie said uncertainly.

Elizabeth reached over and took a yellow flask of isotonic squash from an official. Tony could go screw himself. Once she had the gold in her pocket, she could make his life a misery.

'Still we have more work to do,' Hans said, like he could read her thoughts.

Elizabeth nodded and smiled. Behind them Stars and Stripes were waving, the crowd cheering Kim Gideon's competent three-eleven.

'I know. It's not over yet.'

The words sounded blissfully unconvincing. Bring them on, Elizabeth thought, Heidi, Louise, Tony . . . she was going to blow everyone away. This was her moment.

She was invincible.

Nina arrived at the Halkin at nine precisely. Tony had avoided her calls all day, but he was going to have to deal with her now.

She checked herself out in the elevator mirror as she rode up to his suite. Her raven hair was twisted up in a formal French pleat; her suit was Comme des Garçons, chocolate brown piped with cream. Low mahogany heels from Pied-à-Terre, opaque silky tights, no jewellery. Her make-up was shades of brandy, berries and gold. She looked five years older in this rig. Beautiful, but serious too.

The elevator slid noiselessly to a halt and discharged her. Nina stared to feel a little scared. God, she wished she'd been able to get hold of Harry. They'd had just one Chinese together, the first night she got back, then he'd jetted off to France with Lilly. The dinner had not been the slam-dunk Nina wanted. She was tired and edgy from the flight and the shock of the report, and mad at Harry for coming on to her in front of Frank Staunton. Harry was loose and she was wound up like a string ball. They hadn't fought, exactly, but Nina left early. Nina's fortune cookie told her to beware the dark forces lining against her. Harry's said he would be successful in all he did.

She wished she'd been a bit softer with Harry. She could have done with a friend right now.

Nina pressed the doorbell outside the earl's suite.

Tony opened it and ushered her in, smiling softly. Inside the expensive Japanese minimalism of his suite someone had laid a table laden with extravagant dishes, vintage Krug chilling in a silver ice-bucket and warm bottles of saki next to plates of sushi and vases of purple orchids. Nina's glance swept to the single bed. There was a large, royal-blue box laid out on it, stamped with the gold crest of some jeweller or other.

She wanted to laugh. That was his answer to everything.

'I don't buy it any more, Tony,' Nina said harshly.

He lifted an eyebrow. 'What don't you buy?'

'This bullshit.' She pointed to the table and the box. 'Whatever it is, I hope you got a receipt.'

'Nina.' Tony Savage sat down calmly on a cherrywood-backed chair and looked her over. 'What are you talking about? Come on, darling, I hope you're not going to be difficult. You're a clever girl, you know how stupid that would be.'

'Are you threatening me?'

'Threatening you? Don't be idiotic. Think about who I am and who you are. Sounds like you have delusions of grandeur, Nina. You're really not that important.'

'I'm the reason Dragon went up five points in two weeks,' Nina said fiercely. 'That work was mine. My words in the report. But you didn't credit me, you didn't even mention me.'

'Why should I?' Tony said, and there was an edge to his voice. He reached for the champagne, popped the cork and poured out two glasses. 'It wasn't *your* work, it was Dragon's work. Done with our funds, achieved with our name. We did struggle along quite nicely before you arrived.'

'You have to give me credit for the work I've done. Nobody else in this company managed it. You owe me promotion and—'

'I don't owe you a bloody thing,' Tony said, standing up and walking towards her. He didn't shout, but there was a quiet menace in his voice that made Nina shrink inside. 'I rescued you from Nowheresville, Brooklyn, I made you a wealthy young girl—'

'Out of the kindness of your heart.'

'Nina, this is silly,' Tony said silkily. 'I think I've been generous to you. Come on, darling, I can't remember a woman I've enjoyed more.' He leaned down and stroked the black satin coverlet on the bed. 'You want a promotion, more money – that can be arranged, I'll dream something up. Providing you stop all this nonsense about credit.'

Nina stared at him. 'You think I'd sell myself to you? My God, is that the kind of woman you think I am?'

'It's the kind of woman I *know* you are.' Now his eyes were black pinpricks of cold rage. 'You proved that in Dublin.'

'I wouldn't touch you again if you were the last man alive!' Nina snarled.

'Of course. You prefer something a little more basic. Like Harry Namath?' He laughed to see her pale in front of him. 'You know me, Nina, I like to have my finger on the pulse. But I wouldn't put too much store in that one, darling, he's not interested any more.'

Tony's aquiline mouth was twisted in amused contempt, watching her reaction eagerly. She felt sick.

'You told him,' she said dully.

'Of course I told him. In some detail,' Tony said lightly. 'We had a long chat over the phone while I was in Switzerland. I like to keep on good terms with the staff.'

Nina said nothing. She could almost hear him doing it.

'It was a pity. He seemed rather put off, didn't have much to say. You Americans can be so prudish . . . a shame, I'd have liked to swap notes.'

'Go to hell, you bastard,' Nina spat, her eyes flooding with tears.

Tony reached up and traced his finger round her jaw. 'But angel, you still have me. As long as we understand each other, I can make life very sweet for you.'

Roughly Nina pushed him away. 'Yeah, we understand each other. I got your number. I would rather fuck a leper with syphilis.'

'I don't think you understand. I'm not asking you for this, I'm telling you. Otherwise,' Caerhaven said blandly, 'it's over for you. You'll be fired. You won't find work at any other drug company, once I put the word out. You're an alien in Britain, you have no friends here, as you so correctly put it, no credit outside. And I don't think you've got many friends *inside* the company, Nina, in fact I gather you're rather unpopular. People will assume that you're just another tramp, this time one who worked for me and whom I've now tired of.'

'I do understand,' Nina said, quieter now.

'Good.' Tony ticked the points off on his fingers with a maddening smile. 'You're fired. You're kicked out of the country. You have nothing to show for your time with us. Word will go out loud and clear that you're a bimbo with an attitude problem. And you won't have your boring little boffin to run to either. He had you all wrong, sweetheart; he doesn't want used goods.'

He picked up a flute of champagne and held it out to her.

'Or we can forget this unpleasantness, and you can look forward to a very pleasant life and a bright little future.'

Nina hesitated for a second, then took the glass.

'You were wrong about Dublin. I didn't sell myself; I used you for what you could do for me.'

'See? We're so alike, Nina, we're two sides of the same coin.'

Nina smiled back. She moved closer to him.

'Wrong again, my lord,' she said. Then she flung her chilled champagne right in his eyes, and walked out of the suite.

34

The alarm went at six as usual. Nina was halfway to the shower when she realised there was no need. She wouldn't have to be in the office today.

She got up anyway, washed and dressed. She put on a butterscotch suit, Wolford hose and flat heels. There was no way she could feel comfortable in jeans on a Friday morning.

Her head ached but she was dry eyed. She'd done all her crying last night. Tony was gone, all her work had vanished like a puff of smoke. Harry was gone too, and maybe that was the worst thing. She wondered why it should matter so much; it was stupid, a few meals, a movie and one good lay. She wanted to batten down the hatches on her weak, leaky heart. Wasn't this why she'd sworn never again? Namath had snuck his way in there and now she was hurting, really hurting, a fresh burst of that soul-searing pain she thought had gone for ever.

Nina put on a little make-up. She didn't feel like it, but it was about dignity. Tony would love to picture her sat here crying, red nosed, with suitcases under her eyes. She felt hollow with grief and loss, but she wasn't going to put it on a billboard.

Outside her window the sun rose into a balmy spring sky. Nina fixed herself coffee and listened to the *Today* show on Radio Four. She was never home this late. Outside her kitchen window Nina saw scrappy little flowers bobbing under the fence, crocuses next to wilting snowdrops and a couple of waxy yellow daffodils bobbing cheerfully. She stared at the flowers and wondered how they'd got there. She'd never had any time for gardening.

At nine a.m. Nina rang Dragon.

'Can I speak to Anita Kerr in Nina Roth's office, please?'

'One moment.' A brief pause, then, 'There is no such office registered here, madam. Anita Kerr has been transferred to another department.'

God, that bastard works fast. 'Which one?'

'Label Production.'

Nina felt a chill run over her forearms. Labels – that was worse than getting fired. Anita would have to spend her days double-checking tiny E-numbers and drugs and RDAs. And it was based in Slough.

'But she's on vacation for a week.'

'Then Personnel. I need to discuss collection of my personal effects.'

'You've been terminated? Whom am I speaking to?'

'This is Nina Roth,' Nina said, as calmly as she could. The scorn in the girl's voice was something else. She knew exactly who it was, but she was loving making Nina jump through all these hoops.

'I'll see if Mr Sweeney can talk to you. Hold please.'

She put her on hold for a full five minutes.

'I'm sorry, but he's not available.'

'Then his deputy.'

'Nobody in Personnel is available. Would you like to leave a message?'

Nina left her number and hung up. She had personal notes and research papers, phone numbers for the scientists she'd talked to, project studies on all the rival companies. Invaluable when she was looking for a new job. She decided to wait until lunchtime for Keith Sweeney to call her back. The blazing humiliation was bitter as raw sloes; she paced around her drawing-room, restless, her mind racing as she tried to seize on something, anything, she could do. She came up with zero. Nina Roth, mid-twenties *putz* from Brooklyn, versus the Earl of Caerhaven? Dino, Tom, Luc Viera, they'd be lining up to deny anything she said.

At nine forty the doorbell buzzed. Nina opened it to find a spotty kid in a grubby T-shirt clutching a cardboard box.

'Nina Roff? Delivery for yer,' he said, thrusting the box into her arms. 'Sign 'ere. If that's your car out front, someone'll be round to collect it in a minute. And the furniture.'

'The furniture?' Nina said blankly.

'Yeah, it's all in the papers,' he said indifferently. 'See ya.'

She slammed the door behind him and sat down on the couch. The small box contained her pens and pencils, a pad of W. H. Smith writing paper, and three postcards from Zurich. Her notes and notebooks were nowhere to be seen. There was also a thick envelope franked Berman, Graves & Bowler. BGB were Tony's front-rank legal firm; they were the ones he used for serious shit, the real heavy-hitters. She ripped it open. A pink P-45 form from the UK government, a 'you're history' form, fluttered to the ground. She ignored that and went straight to the letter.

Dear Miss Roth,

You are hereby advised that your employment has been terminated for cause, as verbally advised. You are prohibited from entering the premises of Dragon Chemical. Your work and contact notes are proprietary intelligence and will be retained. Your car remains the property of Dragon and you are required to return it immediately or face legal action. Other personal items, purchased for you on the 'Settlement' company allowance, are also to be returned (see itemised list attached). You will not be receiving a reference from the company. The Home Office has been notified of the change in your residency status . . .

There was another sharp rap on the door. Nina jumped to her feet and opened it, to be confronted with five burly men in red and black Dragon Security outfits. A white van was parked outside her fence.

'Owright?' said the team chief, pointing to the letter in her hand. 'We've come for the stuff. You got the car keys?'

Nina stood aside to let them in. Silently she fished in her pocket for the keys to the Golf and handed them over as the other men filed past her and started to carry off her furniture.

'That's it,' the foreman said approvingly. He handed her a small receipt. 'Best to get it over with quickly, like. I knew you wouldn't make no trouble.'

'No.' Nina was quick to reassure him, if it would get these baboons reeking of curry out of her place. 'I won't make any trouble.'

At least, she thought in silent fury, not yet.

Friday morning dawned crystal clear over Verbier. The sun shone brilliantly over the rocky mountains. Snow had been patchy, and the piste at Veysonnaz had been thickly blanketed overnight with artificial snow.

'Suits me fine,' Elizabeth remarked to Hans over her creamed porridge and lean ham. 'Artificial packs down those little air pockets, it'll be faster.'

'*Ja*, and that is not so good. Veysonnaz, only a red, but very fast. Maybe now too fast.'

'Too fast? That's like too happy, there's no such thing.' Elizabeth smiled, her teeth white against her golden skin. She had the tight, healthy glow of the peak-performance athlete, and confidence dripped from her like jewels from Monica's neck. Three days of events and she had built up unstoppable momentum. Hans had never seen her ski like this. It was like she had reached down right into her guts and pulled up her last reserve of speed and skill. He had to struggle to keep her away from the media, in case the things they were saying went to her head. Her nearest rival was Louise, with Christy second and Heidi third, but they were way behind Elizabeth. Hans had never seen a female like her. And he knew she knew it. She was so confident she reminded him of Jack Taylor.

'You have two more days of races. You *can* be caught, *Liebchen*.'

'Yes, Chicken Licken, and the sky might fall down.'

'I don't understand . . .'

'Oh, don't worry, Hans. I promise I won't be complacent, not till I'm wearing the gold. Louise's really hot on this one.' She shook her head for a second. 'What do I do if she skis a perfect run?'

'You want to beat someone, there is only one way,' Herr Wolf said drily. 'Ski it faster.'

Elizabeth took a final slug of her freshly squeezed orange juice, jumped up from the table and poked her head out of the kitchen window. 'I'm going to go out for a quick run down the Savoleyres.'

The speed-skiing course. Hans knew better than to forbid it, she was just crackling with energy.

'Elizabeth, only once, *verstehst Du*? Or it can take the edge off your run this afternoon.'

Magic words. The green eyes were instantly grave.

'You got it, Coach, just one trip.'

Stepping off the draglift at the top of the run Elizabeth wondered if this was what it was like to get high. She felt beautiful, invincible. The electric lifts were running for the benefit of the Olympians alone on several runs, but spectators on neighbouring pistes stopped to cheer her and wave at the Union Jack suit. The icy *couloirs* of the speed-skiing run were fenced off and almost deserted, apart from two or three athletes with some adrenalin to burn. Savoleyres was a real speed kick – leave your stomach at the start and rocket to the bottom, the skiers' version of bungee-jumping. A plunge on this baby would fire her up. Elizabeth knew her brain was mainlining serotonin, the happiness hormone you got from perfect exercise. And victory. And the high, desert whiteness of this mountain.

She unhooked the metal circle between her legs and schussed forwards.

'Lucky seat. I sure wish that was me.'

Elizabeth jumped out of her skin. Jack Taylor was standing there, wearing a USA practice suit in subtle navy. The men were skiing the Tortin downhill today, a tough customer full of moguls. Elizabeth scowled a muttered hi.

'We must stop meeting like this,' Jack said easily. 'How's Holly bearing up? She's making real good times, you be sure and tell her how proud I am.'

'Give your messages to your girlfriend yourself, Jack, I'm not AT&T,' Elizabeth snapped. 'I have other things on my mind.'

'So I see. You're skiing pretty hot as well.'

'God!' Elizabeth exploded. 'You are the most arrogant man I have ever met, Jack Taylor! Don't you dare patronise me! I have this gold in my pocket, and *you're* getting caught up by Zubriggen.'

'I tripped on the last race.'

'Always some excuse.'

'No excuse, Lizzie, I'm going to win this with a ten-point margin,' Jack said angrily.

'I'm skiing as well as you are, Jack, and I've had to with your putdowns. You're only faster than me because you're a man.'

'You noticed, how sweet,' Taylor said icily.

'Don't flatter yourself, Jack, you were five minutes' fun,' Elizabeth said, hissing like a bobcat.

'Well, baby, you sure gave me a real *quid pro quo*,' Jack said slowly, his Southern drawl crawling over her like his eyes. 'And I'm lookin' forward to my next piece, when you lose our bet. Though be warned, it'll last a lot longer than five minutes. I'm going to collect in full.'

'Ooh, what would Holly say?' Elizabeth taunted. 'Except she doesn't need to worry, because you won't be collecting anything. Now excuse me. I came here to ski.'

She snapped up her visor and pushed forwards, disappearing in a flash of primary colours.

Jack glared after her. He'd chased halfway round the world for that?

'Jesus fucking Christ!' he said.

At the top of Veysonnaz the athletes stood around, shifting on the snow and not talking to each other. Most were silently following the monitors rigged inside and outside the hut. There was nothing to say.

At the starting gate Elizabeth was ready to go. Her heart was racing as though she were halfway down already. Two minutes to triumph or defeat.

The news wasn't good. Her championship lead just narrowed. Heidi had led until Louise skied, two girls before Elizabeth. A bravura race; less than two-hundredths of a second slower than the world record. The race of Louise's career. And the only thing between the Swiss girl and the podium was Lady Elizabeth Savage. The crowd thought it was sewn up. Obviously so did Louise, thrusting both fists skywards in a victory salute and hurling a pole into the air like a cheerleader's baton.

There was no more time to think. The klaxon sounded and Elizabeth settled forward, as low as she could go. Within the fifteen-second start time she could choose when to push off and she composed herself, keeping Hans's words drumming through her head, settling low, low as she could to the ground . . .

Elizabeth shoved herself forwards, violently, launching due south like a rocket, the packed snow hurtling beneath her long skis, the edges turning nicely as she soared over a hill, a mini-jump taking her twenty yards ahead. How do you top a perfect run? You go *faster, faster!* Her muscles burned as she forced herself down for the vertical plunge, hugging the netting line for greater velocity. Wind howled past her helmet, the crowds near by shouting and clanging bells behind the rope. From the blurred red, white and blue of the Union Jacks Elizabeth knew she was ahead. Yes! Yes! She'd beat Louise, she just needed to keep it up, to get that speed – run a sharper angle by the netting . . .

As she headed into the final furlong Elizabeth saw the Brits jumping up and down, hysterical with joy, waving flags and yelling. *She must be ahead!* But she couldn't take chances, had to clinch it. Elizabeth thrust herself forward, taking the last turn at a dangerous tilt, her chest inches from the ground, right by the netting as she—

Suddenly she was out of control! A small, sick lurch she tried to steady but was going too low and too fast to stop, and Elizabeth slammed into the side netting, screaming in pain as the tips of her skis thrust through the woven nylon, halting instantly as her body travelled forwards at over a hundred and twenty miles per hour. Her legs were spreadeagled, flung against the solid grip of her boots, the world was a white and blue tumble of sky and snow, then cracking bone, her own distant screaming, and a warm red stream of blood on the icy ground before pain washed everything away in a terrible darkness.

35

All she wanted to do was crawl away and die, Nina thought. The young, beautiful woman who gazed back at her from the mirror seemed a mirage. Surely she was a raddled old hag of seventy; she had to be, feeling so weak and so exhausted. All the years she'd been working, at Green Earth, Dolan and Dragon, Nina had kept up the pressure, climbing hand over fist up the ladder with blinkered determination. Now the sweep of events had hurtled past and left her behind, and she felt drained. Dragon was rewriting her history as ruthlessly as the KGB; she had been a nothing, a non-person. Every day she saw the upward march of the stock. Little articles about Dr Hall's research appeared in the bio-tech sections of the papers. And big, commanding photos of Anthony Savage, Earl of Caerhaven, the Robber Baron, dapper and collected as he ramraided yet another three companies while bravely coping with the tragedy in Switzerland.

That was the thing that saved her.

No matter how lifeless she felt, there was still a core of strength buried deep inside. Too much pride to look at those charming pictures and just take it. Nina clipped the photos of Tony and pinned them everywhere – above her kettle, on her mirrors, by her bed.

It worked like a voodoo charm. Soon grief was only her second emotion. The first was rage.

The first thing to do was sell the house. Knight Frank & Rutley gave her ninety-five thousand, a profit of five grand on the purchase price. Then there were the jewels. Since Tony had refused to take them back, Nina wasn't going to offer twice. She needed the money. Every penny of it. You had to have funds to go to war. A place in New Bond Street, the leathery old tortoise behind the counter fairly drooling over the quality of the carats and the filigree workmanship, offered six thousand. Nina laughed and started to walk out. She left with fifteen.

Then she checked into a cheap hotel for a week to try and figure out what to do. Flights home were cheap, money went further in the States. Plus she had right of residence there.

But I'm used to Britain, Nina thought. I know the European market. And this is where Tony Savage operates.

It might be ridiculous, she knew, but she wanted revenge.

If the authorities didn't know where she lived, they couldn't serve her with any nasty letters. Nina knew about English bureaucracy – she figured she would have some breathing space. She rented a cheap flat in Highgate for cash, using a false name – a nasty shock, when she'd got used to luxury. The clothes hanging in her tatty wardrobe were thousand-dollar suits, she had silk shirts and Italian leather shoes and a Patek Phillipe watch, but a tiny table, a creaking bath and paint peeling off the door frames. The TV was secondhand and she didn't have a kitchen, just a fenced-off little enclosure that was part of the drawing-room, but Nina had been in worse dives than that.

She bought a used computer and fax machine from *Exchange & Mart.* That ate up a thousand pounds but she needed those things for survival. Once they were set up in her cramped little bedroom Nina's spirits lifted just a touch.

Now she was ready to go to work.

She couldn't find a job.

Glaxo, Wellcome and ICI turned her down flat. At Hoffman LaRoche, Eastman Kodak and Pfizer she talked her way to a first interview but that was all. She was trying to explain her 'upset' at Dragon, and as she sat there fumbling the shutters came down in the interviewers' faces. Nobody was listening.

Tony Savage had been as good as his word.

He was clever, very clever, Nina thought bitterly as she left SmithKline Beecham. He let her have a few interviews. Even a couple of job offers. She could never prove any blacklisting, but she knew just what was going on.

The jobs she was offered were suitable for an entry-level executive without a degree. Procter & Gamble's science trainee programme, Johnson & Johnson's marketing course. She got five or six offers like that. She turned them all down. They would mean years of working her way back up; the same frustrating struggle for promotion and recognition. It would be like starting over.

Nina couldn't live with that. She was going to have to find another way.

Elizabeth blinked dizzily, her mind struggling to the surface through pain and fatigue. She was desperately thirsty and there was a wrenching ache in her left ankle. Her body felt wrong. Unbalanced.

'She's coming round.' A clipped English voice, a grey-haired doctor leaning over her bed. 'Lady Elizabeth. Do you know where you are?'

Elizabeth whispered, 'Pain. Water.'

The surgeon lifted a beaker of water to her mouth and motioned to a nurse. 'Give her ladyship some pethedine.' He gave her a brisk, impersonal smile. 'I'm Dr Jopling, one of your father's regular consultants. He had me flown out here to attend to you after your accident. You're in the Clinique Reine Catherine, outside Geneva. We'll be flying you home as soon as you're fit to travel.'

The nurse silently injected something cold into her side.

Elizabeth stared at him, groping for meaning. Images flooded back into her mind: the race, her fall, agony and blood.

'I fell.'

'I'm afraid so. We removed your spleen. You had a serious accident and underwent several operations, but you're all right now.'

'No.' Elizabeth shook her head. The pethedine was working, making her dizzy as the comforting warmth flowed through her body, washing away the pain, but something was very wrong.

Dr Jopling's face was professionally reassuring. 'We can discuss everything later, once you've had a chance to adjust. I'll call your family; they've been waiting for you to recover consciousness, and I'm sure you'll want to see them—'

'Doctor.' Elizabeth's voice was a weakened croak. 'I want to know what happened. Please tell me now.'

'Very well.' Jopling came closer to the bed and looked like he might be going to take her hand, but then thought better of such familiarity. 'You suffered a severe fall – at intense velocity – sustaining serious internal and external injuries, including haemorrhaging, broken bones and fractures.' A beat. 'The worst damage was done to your left foot, which was broken by your fall and then sliced to the bone by your right ski. This injury was further compounded by your ski boot. It crushed the severed portion of the foot.'

He paused. There was no way to soften the blow.

'Every effort was made to reattach, but the nerve endings were beyond repair. I'm sorry to have to tell you that we amputated your foot at the ankle.'

Blood drained from Elizabeth's face as she glanced down to the end of the bed. Two feet seemed to point upwards under the blankets, but she only had sensation in the right one.

'A prosthesis,' the surgeon explained. 'It's plastic; attached to your leg with a metal frame, jointed on the ball of the foot to simulate as normal a walk as possible. The best on the market; your father insisted.'

Elizabeth quietly said, 'Thank you, Doctor.'

'You won't be crippled, Lady Elizabeth. Recovery will take a while, but you should be able to manage a medium-paced walk eventually.'

There was a deathly silence.

'I'll never ski again?'

'I'm afraid not.' Jopling's words were measured, but his tone was final. 'No running, no skiing. Apart from possible gentle swimming, no athletic activity of any kind.'

He pretended not to notice as tears filled Elizabeth's eyes and trickled silently down her cheeks.

When she felt she had control of herself she buzzed for the doctor.

'I'd like to see Herr Hans Wolf,' Elizabeth said.

The name seemed to shock Jopling. His face creased just a fraction. 'Herr Wolf was refused permission to see you.'

'Refused permission? Don't you know he's my coach?'

'Of course, Lady Elizabeth. It was precisely because he was your coach that it was felt he would upset you – considering how you received your injury.'

'Hans had nothing to do with this. Accidents are risks we take every time we strap up.' She pushed herself up on her elbows and glared at Jopling with fiery eyes. 'Who refused him permission? You?'

'Not at all, my lady,' Jopling said hastily. 'It was Lord Caerhaven. He has control over all the arrangements here.'

I'll bet he does, Elizabeth thought. 'OK, Dr Jopling, please call Hans and ask him to come and see me.'

Jopling nodded. 'I believe Herr Wolf is staying in the city. Despite your father's ban he refused to leave. He has called to check on your condition every day.'

Elizabeth started to cry, she couldn't help it. She brushed back the tears. 'Has anyone else called?'

The doctor spread his hands. 'Hundreds. The officials, the British team coaches, your team-mates, many other competitors, and the media . . . I have a roomful of flowers waiting for you, now you are recovered.'

Am I? 'Did . . . did Mr Jack Taylor ask to see me?'

'He rang to ask after your condition, and he sent flowers, but he didn't request an appointment, no.'

'I see,' Elizabeth said dully.

'Do you want your flowers?'

She shook her head. 'I don't think I'm in the mood. Give them to other wards.'

'Certainly, Lady Elizabeth, and I will call Herr Wolf.'

'Thank you. Doctor, who won the medals?'

Jopling looked at her with a certain amount of pity. 'Louise Levier took the gold, Christy Lansch the silver and Heidi Laufen the bronze.'

'And Jack Taylor took the men's gold?'

'Of course,' Jopling said absently as he checked the charts at the foot of her bed. 'There was never any doubt about that.'

The door opened at three p.m. Elizabeth sat up, hoping to see Hans, but it was her father.

Tony thanked the nurse and waited until she had vanished before closing the door. He walked over to Elizabeth with a vast bunch of blossoms in his arms, and laid them on her bedside table. White roses, the roses for mourning.

Elizabeth flopped back on her pillows. She knew disappointment was all over her face but she didn't have the strength to care.

'Darling, you look terrible. Are you feeling OK?'

'I've lost my foot, I'm never going to ski again,' Elizabeth said flatly, 'and I've lost an Olympic crown I had sewn up.'

'We don't know if you had it sewn up. There were lots more races to come.'

'I tell you, it was sewn up,' Elizabeth repeated angrily.

'Well.' The earl perched himself on the edge of her bed. 'Never mind about that now. I've come to discuss your future. Clearly you're not going to be skiing, and I gather Mr Taylor is out of the picture.'

'Who do you *gather* that from? Your girlfriend?'

'I don't have one of those, Elizabeth, but if you're referring to Nina Roth, she's been dismissed. For insubordination.'

'You're breaking my heart,' Elizabeth said bitterly. 'You get good information, though. Jack was never *in* the picture. So I'll have to come and work at Dragon.'

'Yes.' Tony leaned forward and spoke softly. 'I've thought about that. I have some terrific openings for you.'

He reached into his jacket and handed Elizabeth a sheet of paper. Her eyes flickered quickly across it, then rose disbelievingly back up to his.

'You have to be joking. Corporate Hospitality, Events Organisation, Promotional Literature – why don't you just assign me to the typing pool?'

'Why, can you type?' Tony asked urbanely.

'It's not a joke, Dad!' Elizabeth shouted. She jerked her leg under the covers. 'My foot's made of *plastic*! I know you were angry I did Dragon Gold without your permission—'

'Angry? Yes, I was angry. What you fail to understand is that Dragon is *my* company. Nobody does anything without my approval. Nobody is going to make me look a fool, Elizabeth, you least of all.'

'I won't do those two-bit dressmaker jobs.'

'Then I'll give you a small allowance, as long as you behave yourself and keep out of the spotlight. Don't think there's a third option. There never was.' Tony's smile was full of malice. 'Do you know, I thought of you just yesterday. I was talking to Dean Bradman in the Sydney office, and he told me the most marvellous Australian proverb: you've got to cut down the tall poppies. You were a tall poppy, Elizabeth, you and Nina both.'

Elizabeth looked right into his eyes. She couldn't believe it. She was lying here with her foot shorn away, and this was what he was saying.

'I—'

Tony held up one hand. 'Don't spoil things, Elizabeth. You don't have the same power to embarrass me now. You're not quite the national heroine you were. It seems the press are blaming you for reckless skiing, and apparently you were rather disliked by your team-mates . . . nothing official, of course, but that's what's leaking, and that's what they're printing. One can't trust the press. And none of them will be too eager to print any muckraking stories about me, considering the source.'

'You *owe* me,' Elizabeth said fiercely. 'I'm your *daughter*. Don't you owe it to my mother?'

The earl sat up as though he'd been stung. He looked at her again, more carefully, a musing expression on his face.

'You look so like her,' he said absently, then, 'Those are my offers, Elizabeth. Take them or leave them. To be honest, I don't give a damn either way.'

He tapped the paper again.

'In fact, Elizabeth, I'm doing all of this *because* I owe your mother.'

Elizabeth had nothing to say. She watched him as he left the room.

He hates me, she thought. My God, he actually hates me.

36

Hans came by to see her. Despite his stiff manner, he was brokenhearted and it showed. A light had gone out in those clear blue eyes. Elizabeth had sworn she wouldn't cry but it was no use; Hans Wolf's grief, contrasting with Tony's casual cruelty, opened the floodgates.

'*Ach, est ist unmöglich . . .*' He rattled off a torrent of bitter *Schweizerdeutsch*, cursing the mountain, the course, the weather, everything. 'It should have been me. I am an old man, but—'

'But you can still ski? No, that's how it should be. You lived for the snow long before I was born and you'll live for it till you die. I was careless.'

Hans's bony hand gripped hers fiercely. 'Never again do you say that, Elizabeth. Never have I seen you ski that way. You had wings, you were an eagle. You had the gold in your pocket.' He snapped his fingers. 'Mademoiselle Levier was a dairymaid next to you.'

'You didn't say that at the time.'

'*Liebchen*, you know your old Hans. I was only being cautious . . .'

'Wish I had been,' Elizabeth said. She struggled for a brave face in front of him, but despair was squatting over her heart like a toad. Every day she forgot it when she was medicated to sleep, then when she woke up there were a few cruel seconds of not realising before it clicked back in. Her prosthesis was cleverly made and fitted to her ankle, no expense spared, a thick metal cuff covering the join between flesh and plastic. But the basic fact was still there. She was a cripple. Right now, her strength was flowing away. Her muscles were softening as she lost her appetite and couldn't exercise. Her reserves of energy were draining, her heart rate speeding up. But what does it matter, when you'll never need to be fit ever again?

Memories were torture. The crash, the Veysonnaz run, she hardly thought about. It was her supreme, immortal confidence. Elizabeth died when she remembered what she'd said to Hans, and worse, to Karen and Kate, and Jack Taylor. All the people she'd fought with. She'd thought that gold was in her pocket like a Swiss franc. Well, her enemies could surely laugh now.

'Cautious skiers? There is a place for them,' Hans said stiffly. 'Teaching the snowplough to *Kinder* on the nursery slopes. There has never been a woman skier like you.'

Elizabeth looked away before the tears started again. The dreadful thing was, she thought that too. Deep inside, she thought she was the greatest, could have been the female Franz Klammer. But everybody would forget her now, not right away, but soon. One single World Cup does not a legend make. Louise Levier was the gold medallist, and soon history would be rewritten. Savage took her world title by a hair's breadth. She lucked out once. She wasn't *that* good.

'Easy, when you have the best coach ever.' She tried to be British, brisk and impersonal. 'Anyway, I came to it so late. I've only been skiing for a few years. There are other things that I can do.'

Hans Wolf made a clear effort and agreed with her. Elizabeth smiled wryly; for the old man, life off the slopes was life hardly worth living.

'What will you do? Work for your father?'

'I don't think that's going to work out. He and I have fallen out. He won't let me do the kind of work I want.'

'I see,' Hans said. He looked at her with a fierce protectiveness. He knows where I'm at, Elizabeth thought, he knows I don't have a degree or any experience outside of Dragon.

'There are many options for you. I can speak to the Swiss Sports Council. Or the FIS, they will be thrilled to have you market the sport. Not all of Europe reads the British tabloids,' Hans added, his wrinkled face creasing in disgust. 'Or Britain – Ronnie knows how bitchy are the lesser girls, and how hard you work. The British authorities can find you a place—'

'I don't think so. Thanks, Hans, really, but no.' She shook her head and Hans watched the hollow shadows under her eyes, the new gauntness in her face. 'Spend my life publicising slopes I'll never ski again, writing puff pieces about Karen's amazing reign as UK champion, or Jack Taylor's next World Cup?'

'You have not heard, then? Herr Taylor has retired from the sport. After this gold. In one year we lose both our brightest hopes.' Hans bent over and smoothed her coverlet. 'But what about him, child? I am not so old that I see nothing. You love him, he loves you. He is a rich, powerful young man, he can look after you.'

'Oh, Hans,' Elizabeth said, stroking his hand. 'It's all over between Jack and me, it has been for ages. He's got another girlfriend, Holly Ferrell.'

'The *Mädchen* who skis like a drill sergeant?' asked Hans, outraged.

'And anyway, I've had enough of being looked after. I'm going to take care of myself.'

Wolf looked down at his pupil. Under the misery there was something he had not seen in her before. A quiet fury, a cold chip of ice at the heart of her pupils. A certain foreboding mingled with his pity.

'You have a plan?'

'Something to start with,' Elizabeth said softly. 'Get on my feet. And get some answers.'

There were a lot of empty hours in the hospital bed, waiting for reflex tests and anodyne clinic food. Enough time to watch a lot of CNN or read months' worth of *Paris Match*. Or to brood.

Monica, Charles and Richard all paid dutiful visits. They weren't malicious like Tony, they just didn't care. Which made them and her about even. Ronnie and others asked for appointments but Elizabeth told Jopling to make medical excuses. She wasn't interested in other people. She was interested in Tony.

Elizabeth started to eat. She did intensive physiotherapy four times a day, against the doctor's advice. It was hateful, having to stand in between two poles, resting her weight on a foot that wasn't there. After years of instinctive balancing, her body was all out of kilter, every step felt like she was lurching drunkenly. And her foot. It was solid, plastic. She hated it. She thanked God she couldn't see her stump under the metal casings but she had nightmares about it, a hideous mass of red, nubby tissue at the end of her leg. Even though she was the same from the calves upwards, Elizabeth felt ugly, like her beauty had fled along with her hopes. But the cruellest dreams of all were pretty: soaring down the Hahnenkamm, slicing through the mogul fields in Saas Grund, running barefoot over the clifftops at Caerhaven Castle. All the things she would never do again. Her body was changing too: from lean strength to slim, softer and weaker. It was the fashion model look and she hated it, she felt like a coathanger. But through all the pain and frustration, and the nightmares, Elizabeth never wavered. She ordered a new wardrobe and stuck it on Tony's account; clothes in smaller sizes and specially made boots and shoes.

She wanted answers. And she wasn't going to find them behind the walls of the clinic.

Jopling peered over the top of his wire-rimmed spectacles at the young woman sitting in front of his desk. Elizabeth's hair was washed and styled, newly dyed to a radiant blonde. She was made up in attractive shades of peach and gold, wearing a long Prada dress in moss green, a fitted jacket and chocolate leather boots. From the patient he knew in white hospital wraps to this sophisticated young lady was some transformation.

He didn't want to discharge her – the rehab period had been chopped in two by her exhausting schedule, but her ladyship resisted any attempts to slow down. Now she wanted out, and Jopling knew he was going to concur. Elizabeth Savage had arrived here a broken young girl and she was leaving a hardened woman. She had clearly done some fast growing up.

'Lady Elizabeth, you should really stay.'

'No, Dr Jopling, I should really leave. There are things I have to do.'

'Very well,' Jopling said thinly, scribbling her discharge papers. 'We'll send the account to Lord Caerhaven, if you could just sign here.'

Elizabeth initialled the bill and shook his hand.

'You do that, Doctor. Thank you. Goodbye.'

Well, she doesn't waste any time, Jopling thought as he watched the valet load her cases into the car. There was something about Elizabeth's attitude that made him very nervous.

Oh well; like father, like daughter.

Elizabeth had Mrs Perkins book her on a flight under a false name. Enduring the gushing sympathy of Tony's lapdog was worth it, if it meant she could get away in peace. The last thing she needed was paparazzi at Heathrow.

First-class was comfortably empty. Elizabeth took a glass of champagne, her first drink since that schnapps on the Gotschnawang. She took notice of the pleasant food served on real china, the luxurious seats and individual videos. It might be the last time she travelled this way. Since she was being compliant, Tony would send a limo to drive her up to the castle.

'I've thought about what you said, and I've decided to quit the company.'

'I'm glad, darling, I think that's probably best,' the clipped voice replied without warmth.

'Since the accident, I don't feel the same about things any more. If you'll give me an allowance, I can talk to Monica about finding something to do.'

'Fine. We can discuss it further when you get back.' Tony rang off.

Elizabeth felt her dull anger sharpen into a kind of strength. It was a vicious motivation, revenge. But very effective.

She made it through Heathrow in shades and a Burberry raincoat, so nobody recognised her except a respectful customs officer. He said he was sorry, and welcome to England. Elizabeth smiled bleakly. She got more goodwill from a total stranger than her own family.

It was raining lightly as the limo purred up the M4, water spattering over the glass so the traffic slipped by in a soundless blur. Elizabeth switched on the radio for privacy so she wouldn't have to chat to the driver. She had a stiff pad and a pen and immediately started making notes, letting the formless suspicions in her mind swirl into some kind of definite shape.

The Radio One news was all fresh to her. British troops had landed at San Carlos in the Falklands, preparations were stepping up for the Pope's visit, and the pound note was going to be replaced by a coin. It was another world, she had to adjust to it. Her reflection stared back at her from the glass, thin, blonde, fashionably lanky. She looked like a different person, and she felt like one too.

By the time they pulled in to the narrow country road twisting through gnarled hillside woods that led to Caerhaven, Elizabeth had an idea.

'Darling!' Monica kissed her. 'You look wonderful, so glad you're better after such a shock. And the hair, well, it's *very* dramatic . . .'

You hate it, you think it looks too good, you cow, Elizabeth thought. She smiled back. 'It's nice to be home.'

'Jenkins will unpack your bags, and there's a wonderful salmon mousse crying out to be polished off.'

'I don't feel that hungry, really,' Elizabeth murmured, petting Dolphin who was bounding all over her. 'I think I'll just have a bath, change, make a few phone calls.'

'Of course,' Monica said with perfect disinterest. 'Do whatever you want.'

In her room Elizabeth stripped and grabbed a warm sweater, her cowboy boots and some Levi 501s. They were hanging off her, but she fixed that with a thick buckled belt. Then she brushed her hair loose and picked up the phone. Joe Sharp, her old village boyfriend, had a brother who worked on the *Bangor Courier*. She hoped he hadn't moved.

'Hello?'

She felt a silly relief. 'Joe, it's Liz Savage.'

There was a stunned pause, then he laughed. His voice was a lot deeper, but it was definitely the same old Joe, redder than Stalin and a staunch Plaid Cymru man. She'd swear blind that Joe would still help her out.

'Christ! I haven't heard from you in years. *Shwd mae pethau?*'

'It's going OK, *iechyd da*, but could we stick to English? My Welsh is sort of rusty.'

'*Peidiwch troi i'r Saesneg*... OK, OK, if you must. Not that your sort were ever really Welsh anyway.' The teasing changed to concern. She could just see his beat-up face on the other end as he gingerly approached the subject. 'Liz, I'm really sorry, I heard—'

'Thanks, but I'll be fine. Things happen for a reason.' That sounded unconvincing even to her. 'The stuff in the papers was all bollocks, but never mind about that now, I need a favour from Aled, as soon as possible.'

'Anything for you, *cariad*.'

'I want to check some old press cuttings. They've got that database up in the *Courier*, I need it to check something out. Family history.'

'That'll be no problem,' Joe said. 'I was going into town to meet a few mates. I could give you a lift if you like.'

'Now?' Elizabeth said, a bit startled. She checked her watch; it was still only three p.m. 'Sure, why not? Thanks, Joe, I really appreciate it.'

'Then I'll pick you up outside the front porch in ten minutes. Tell her noble ladyship not to set the dogs on the peasant boy.'

Elizabeth slipped out to find a black Mini Metro and a grown-up Joe Sharp. He was twenty-nine now, bigger and thicker, and the caterpillar fluff on his chin had turned into thick stubble. He was ugly as hell but very coarse and masculine. She could see why she'd been attracted to him as a teenage convent girl.

Joe whistled as she climbed in the front seat. 'You've dyed your hair, you look great.'

'How do you know that?' Elizabeth belted herself and turned round anxiously to see if Monica was watching them, but there was no sign of her.

'Come on, girl, you're all over the papers. I won fifty quid when you took the World Cup,' Joe said amiably, shifting fluidly into gear and speeding off down the gravel drive. 'First use a Caerhaven's ever been to anyone. God, will you look at this place.' They were passing the croquet lawn now and turning right past the orchards. A few horses were grazing in rolling meadows punctuated with landscaped oaks. 'Come the revolution—'

'I'll be first against the wall, yes, I know.' Elizabeth found she was grinning openly for the first time since the accident. 'Bloody Sharp the Mouth, I see nothing's changed.'

Bangor was relentlessly gloomy as ever, though by some oversight it wasn't raining. Elizabeth twisted around in the car. She always felt excited when they drove here. It was a relic from the time when Bangor was 'town', with real pubs and the Cannon cinema and Boots and W. H. Smith's.

'The *Courier*'s just down there. Aled knows you're coming in. I'm having a few jars with the lads, so come to the Royal Oak when you're ready.'

Elizabeth thanked him and climbed carefully out. A few people stared at her, then looked away again. The hair's confusing them, Elizabeth thought, and anyway, I won't be famous for long. She made it into the functional slab of grey concrete that was the local rag's office, home of the front-page lead on planning permission scandals, NUM fundraisers and village fêtes, and Aled Sharp came and met her at the front desk.

'My station's over here if you want to have a go,' he said, leading her to a beat-up IBM behind a plywood screen. He was blond and thinner than Joe, and he also seemed nervous. 'Just tap in the reference you want, press this, and then this to print it, er, Lady Elizabeth—'

'Elizabeth. Please. You're a lifesaver, Aled.'

'Well.' He smiled shyly. 'It's not strictly allowed, but seeing as how it's you . . .'

'I just need half an hour,' Elizabeth said, then she had an idea. 'Look, tell your boss you did me a trade. Time on the clippings service, in exchange for an exclusive. I'll give you a great interview, really gory, I haven't talked to any national press. He can license it to the *Sun*.'

'Would you do that?' Aled's face pinkened with excitement. 'Oh, brilliant, terrific. I'll go and tell the editor.'

Elizabeth watched him go. Poor kid, it was probably the closest to a scoop he'd ever come. Quickly she entered into the database.

SEARCH PARAMETERS:

She tapped in EARL OF CAERHAVEN, and LOUISE, COUNTESS OF CAERHAVEN, 1956–60

CROSS REFERENCE:

LADY ELIZABETH SAVAGE

She thought a moment, then added one more name.

JAY DEFRIES

It took a little while for the computer to scroll and select. Elizabeth read it over. Double-checked to be sure. Then with a calm she didn't feel, she sent it all to the printer.

'He wants me to come over and interview you tomorrow,' Aled Sharp told her eagerly when he came back. He pointed to the wad of paper she was holding. 'Find anything interesting?'

'Yes, I did.' Elizabeth stood up to leave. 'I found the answer.'

'Oh yeah?' Aled ushered her out, smiling like he'd just won the pools. 'The answer to what?'

'The answer to everything,' Elizabeth said.

37

Nina sat alone in her office.

London in April was a beautiful place to be. The scabby cherry trees that lined the street had burst into glorious froths of white and pink. It was sunny enough to set the cabbies whistling and bring out the ice-cream vans. Advances in the Falklands had united everyone here in a sort of friendly patriotism; dirty windows in the houses round about were covered with bright Union Jacks. Nothing like war to help you forget the recession.

It was not something Nina could forget.

She was only just realising how cocooned she'd been at Dragon. In a huge drugs company, the recession was just an idea. Boom or bust, people always got sick. Hospitals bought their drugs, institutions bought their shares, and the Robber Baron was cash rich. No wonder he'd been on such a shopping spree. Retail chemists and others were closing down everywhere. For bottom-fishers like Tony Savage, trawling for cheap market share, 1982 was paradise.

For everybody else, it was a nightmare.

Nina's premises were located on Wardour Street. Rent was high in Soho, but that was how it had to be. She had a tiny space in a good location. The office was two rooms, and it had come with peeling walls and filthy windows. Nina had rolled up her sleeves and repainted herself in a soothing apple green, then scrubbed the windows until everything gleamed. The front door was stencilled: 'ROTH CONSULTING'.

Roth Consulting. It sounded so grand. Six weeks ago when Nina registered at Companies House her head had been full of dreams of glory. She was going to start a bio-tech consultancy. Management consulting was the hot new business sector, and who knew more about European markets than her? Just a few contracts would let her hire staff . . .

Nina realised certain doors were shut to her. The big companies wouldn't need her help, and word had gone round from Tony. It was the little fish she'd set her sights on: outfits with one product, or a single office in another country. Firms that Tony would never consider. Minnows.

Great theory. But lousy reality. The little firms she approached were too strapped for cash even to think about consultants. To them, it was a luxury. Meanwhile, the rent on the office, its equipment and her flat were eating up Nina's savings at a rate of knots. As she sat here looking out at the cherry blossom, tapping a pencil on her empty in-tray, Nina knew she was in big trouble. She needed a contract. And fast.

'Son?'

Jack tugged on the reins and turned round, his Arab stallion half-rearing in annoyance.

'You ain't been listening to a single word,' John Taylor said wearily. He pricked his mount forwards, breathing hard. Jack had ridden him right off the course today, flying over the ranch fields like he was riding for his life. Whatever Europe had done, it hadn't softened him.

Back to the States with a gold medal. Him and LouAnne had been right out there to see it. Watching their little boy stand up on that podium, taller and stronger than a Greek god, with the Stars and Stripes behind him, his hand on his heart as they played 'The Star-spangled Banner' – it was the proudest moment of their lives. The TV people and the papers made such a fuss, you'd fairly think the whole country loved Jack as much as they did. Even the movie people had come buzzing round like flies on horseshit, wanting to turn Jack into a picture. Like Robert Redford in *Downhill Racer*, but this time for real.

Jack should have been prouder than a white peacock.

He wasn't. The one time he looked happy was when they looped that burnished disc around his neck. Saving that, he was moody and restless. Had the family lawyers serve injunctions on the Hollywood boys. Gave no interviews. Nothing like their Jack, the arrogant glory junkie. And he was moody back home; no interest in anything, even the ladies. The Dallas babes were queuing up for it. John had grinned a quiet male smile when he saw the bunch of females pressin' round his boy everywhere he went like they were in heat. When he was here a couple years back, Jack woulda bought a few rubbers and taken 'em on one at a time in a line-up, but he was real strange about it now. LouAnne had insisted he date Clarisse again – now that little lady was a perfect ten, a walking Barbie doll with sweet Southern ways. Jack had taken her out a couple of times. Probably got laid, too. But he did it by rote, and for Jack, that was acting like a goddamned monk.

Today their ride around the ranch had ended ten minutes ago, that was how long it took John to catch up with their son.

'Sorry, Pop.'

Taylor patted the horse's sweating flank. 'Boy, I don't need no shrink to tell me something ain't right. You'd better spit it out. I don't need no zombie round here.'

Jack looked down. 'It's Elizabeth.'

'Elizabeth? Her again? I thought that was all over. You're upset because she got into that accident? Hell, she'll be OK, her folks have money. You can't help her none by vexin' yourself, kid.'

'It's over, but I can't stop thinking about it. To come that close and then . . . she'll never ski again.'

'There's worse things than that.'

'She wouldn't see me, you know? Her doctor said no visitors. I sent flowers, I called, but she never answered.'

'Dealing with it her own way. Now, Jack.' John dismounted and started to tether his beast to a post. 'I am mighty sorry for a girl who has something like that happen, don't get me wrong, but last time you spoke you were sayin' how you were through with her, what a stubborn, ornery bitch she was, how you couldn't even speak but you were gettin' into a fight. It's crazy how you're gettin' riled up. There's lots of pretty girls right here, and y'all know you got work to do.' He waved a leathery, suntanned hand around the rolling acres. 'The stud farm, the hotels and the land, it ain't going to nobody but you. You gotta start taking an interest.'

'Pa.' Jack looked down at him distractedly. 'I have to go and find her, tell her how sorry I am. In person. It's a skiing thing.'

'Back to Europe?' He snorted. 'Like hell, it's a skiing thing. Look, son, go if you have to, bang her again if that's what you gotta do—'

Jack frowned thunderously. 'Don't talk about her that way, Pa.'

'Hey.' Now John was mad. 'Y'all have had enough time for foolin' around. You want to waste thousands of bucks jettin' over to dry some chick's tears, be my guest. But then you get your butt back here.' He jabbed a finger at the stables behind him. 'This is your future, Jack. Texas. Not London. You'd better have that real clear in your mind.'

The car came crunching down the gravel drive to park in front of the house. Elizabeth sat at her turret window and watched it come, Tony's sleek Silver Phantom Rolls-Royce gleaming whitely in the warm spring sun. She was surprised he hadn't fixed a Dragon company flag to the front. Tony's monster ego suggested that was just a matter of time.

Now he was actually here, Elizabeth's calm deserted her. She felt the adrenalin surging through her as she watched Monica glide out and offer her husband that reserved, passionless kiss. There was none of the good, enhancing stress she got before a race, though. This was different, a sour mixture of anger and fear. But she knew she was ready; it couldn't be postponed.

Elizabeth picked up her folded set of clippings and looked at her reflection. She'd chosen an outfit Tony would hate: black CK jeans and a tight green T-shirt by Donna Karan. With her ankle boots and steel sports Oyster, it was aggressive and sexy. That had always bothered him; now she knew why.

She limped downstairs and walked stiffly across to Tony where he stood ignoring the ecstatic welcome of the dogs.

'Elizabeth, darling,' he said, his brow creasing at her new look. 'It's a bit too dramatic, wouldn't you say?'

'Not really. Look, why don't you step into the library, and we can have a little talk.'

Tony nodded his head towards Monica, busying herself in the kitchen. 'I was going to have a spot of tea first. You can wait?'

'If you like,' Elizabeth nodded with equal reserve, 'but I think you'd prefer to hear this now.'

He looked her up and down with that cold assessment that had been so hurtful before, but now just slid off her.

'As you wish.' Tony walked across the uneven flagstones to the old library door, pushed the studded wooden door and held it open. Elizabeth walked into his green baize den with a flash of *déjà vu*. This was where they'd had their last confrontation, when she was sixteen years old, over Granny's will.

His victory then had been complete, but that was not going to happen this time.

Tony sat at his desk again, comfortably, and glanced at her. He looked utterly self-possessed. Elizabeth shut the door firmly behind her and sat down herself. He thought she was crushed; her spirit as broken as her leg. At least she would have the element of surprise.

'You've always hated me, Tony. And now I know why.'

His Christian name. His eyebrows arched.

'Don't look so surprised.' Elizabeth smoothed out her list of cuttings and passed them over, seeing Tony's shock at the old articles. 'I never knew Mother, but I wish I had. She had you over six ways till Sunday.'

'Nobody had me over.'

'I look so like her, don't I? Nothing of you at all, Lord Caerhaven. Or of Jay DeFries, for that matter. But my, how awkward it would have been, for the Robber Baron we know and love.' Her voice was thick with sarcasm. 'Whispers at the Athenaeum. Jokes in *Private Eye* and the House. Tabloid fun at your expense. Of course, it simply wouldn't do, I see that. You had to take in the little cuckoo.'

'Well.' He did a creditable job of hiding the rage. 'You've become a PI, how inventive. You always were an unladylike little tramp, just like Louise—'

'A tramp? Because she wouldn't play dumb in the gilded cage like Monica? I can see just why she'd prefer Jay, even without money, or a title. I know I would have.'

'You cheap little bastard,' Tony said, with real viciousness.

'Well, that's the difference between us. I *know* you're a bastard. You don't know if I am.'

'You're no child of mine, Elizabeth. I have sons.'

'Lucky you, since we all know just what you think of females. Having been trampled by one of them.'

'She was a ball-breaking whore,' Tony snarled.

'I've always thought,' Elizabeth said slowly, 'that a man who could have his balls broken by a woman wasn't much of a man in the first place.'

'A pity your Mr Taylor didn't agree with you,' Tony said.

It was a direct hit. Elizabeth flushed, and the earl made an effort to settle himself. He pushed back into his armchair and looked at her coolly.

'What do you want? I think I should remind you, you don't have quite the same *cachet* you once did. The press think you're a spoilt, petty little brat. That you threw away a British medal.'

'I still have the capacity to embarrass you, my dear papa,' Elizabeth spat. 'We both know it. So if you still value your reputation—'

'To an extent. Don't think you have a blank cheque. I'd rather take my chances than have you back at Dragon.'

'I'm sure we can come to an arrangement.'

Tony steepled his fingers. He looked at her like she was something unpleasant he wanted to scrape off the soles of his handmade brogues. 'Then I repeat, what do you want?'

Elizabeth smiled. 'You'll like this one, Tony. I want out. Away from you, away from this freezing old relic, away from that vacuous bimbo in the kitchen, all your hypocrisy and high-class whores. I want enough money to look after myself. In exchange, I will always be Lady Elizabeth. A million pounds, that should do it. You won't even notice it.'

He shook his head. 'No guarantee.'

'You have my word.'

'Worthless. I might agree to a trust fund. A million, paid at intervals over the next five years, conditional on your silence. You sign a contract; if you ever breathe a word, the money is repayable with punitive interest.'

'Fine with me, old man, but I want something now. My cases are all packed; I don't want to spend another night under this roof.'

Tony stood up and drummed his fingers on top of the grand piano.

'Fifty K and Walgrave Road.' That was a Dragon house, kept furnished for visiting executives, a beautiful mews in a villagey, tree-lined street tucked away in Earls Court. Elizabeth had stayed there once; it was a little jewel of a house, with a small walled garden out back full of roses and wisteria. The neighbours were an opera singer and a Saudi princeling. 'There's a housekeeper who will let you in, the lawyers will bring papers round tomorrow. That's the first year. It's worth two hundred grand easy.'

'Fine,' Elizabeth said. 'Go out and tell your chauffeur he has a passenger for town.'

Tony nodded. 'So, darling, I suppose this is goodbye.'

'I suppose it is, Father,' Elizabeth replied.

'You'll keep that promise or lose everything. You'd better realise that. I don't know what you think you're going to do with yourself, but I would strongly advise you to keep away from me.' He smiled thinly. 'You'll find out, Elizabeth – once you're outside, you stay there. I have a lot of enemies, and they all know the score. They hate me, but they don't mess with me. I don't think there's a soul in London who's prepared to risk that.'

Elizabeth left the room without replying. At that moment, she wanted revenge worse than anything else in the world. She would endure any humiliation to get it. And Tony's last bit of pomposity had put a name glowing into her mind.

The woman she'd disliked but respected. A blinkered workaholic with a razor-sharp brain, a vicious bitch, maybe, but that was what she needed. Someone who had been close to Tony. Someone who might know a way to bring him down.

Nina Roth.

38

Harry Namath slowly pulled off his white coat and looked over at Lilly. 'What?'

'I said she's left the company.' The older woman tried to sound casual, but it didn't come off.

Harry frowned as she sat there on their lab sofa, fag in one hand, sprawled out against the leather cushions. It was dark outside, three in the morning. They'd just come off a gruelling session of proto-lipid tests. Lilly was injecting her baboons while Harry ran complex computer models. He'd been seeing endless DNA strands revolve against his eyelids, double-helixes in purple and green spinning into his brain. But the tiredness melted away when she dropped this little bombshell. It was as bracing as a cold British shower. Harry sat up again and stared at Lilly. She looked worse than usual tonight: her skin was pallid and grey from fatigue, and she was ill tempered too.

'You're over-reacting. She got us the deal, she's gone, so what? Those corporate bods will get another suit to replace her.'

'She's a friend of mine, Lil. Why didn't you tell me?'

'I didn't think she was such a mate of yours.' This was so obviously a lie that Harry didn't bother replying. Lilly threw up nicotine-stained hands. 'OK, fine, but you hadn't been speaking, you hadn't seen her ...'

'We were in France working.' Harry's voice was cold.

'You were bummed out about her after that talk you had with Tony. So I reckoned it was all over.'

Harry pressed a hand to his aching forehead. He could feel the pincer-like claws of a migraine wrapping themselves round his skull. 'What would you know about that?'

Lilly sat up and glared at him. 'Tony talked to me too, all right? He told me the score. Little tramp. What would you want to hang out with her for?'

'Hey, bud, my friendships are my business.'

'She was bad for you.'

Harry paused. He couldn't believe what he was hearing. Lilly sounded really sour. '*Bad* for me?'

'That's right. I told Tony that too. He said he was going to can her, and I said good on him.'

'Lilly, you have no right to interfere in my private life.'

'Oh don't I?' the dumpy woman said bitterly. 'When I'm the one who's

836

been your partner for years! When I'm the one who's doing the work they want! I'm the biochemist, Harry, they don't want computers. I could just have taken this whole thing for myself. But I carried you along with me and what happens, you run off with some floozy brunette, some career prostitute who slept her way—'

'That's enough!' Harry shouted, then calmed himself. 'Lilly, we hardly even socialise.'

'We're together enough,' she muttered.

Harry shook his head again. Lilly. She had a brilliant mind but she was squat, ugly and way too old. Yet somehow she had managed to delude herself that their working together was a relationship. She'd never said a word. Maybe she'd known inside that it wasn't gonna happen, she didn't want to spoil the dream. He remembered her disapproving looks at Nina. Harry thought it was the youth; now he thought it was the beauty. He had shattered her illusion like ice over a dirty puddle, and now she was sitting here screaming about betrayal.

It was worse because it struck a chord. Lord Caerhaven had reached into his heart and squeezed a burning fist around it. The words in that laconic English tone were almost more than he could bear: ugly pictures of Nina, screwing Tony, on her back for a promotion. Harry was already halfway in love with her. Making love to her had been incredible, he couldn't wait to hook up with her again. That memory had been tainted, corrupted with acid. Now he knew why she'd been so jumpy back at Dragon's office. She didn't want anybody to tell the boss that his mistress had her own bit on the side.

Harry had tried to shove Nina from his mind.

But he couldn't forget her. He thought about it every day. How could she? Was she really that cheap?

Harry decided to get an answer. That didn't mean anything – just curiosity. He wanted to confront Nina. To say all the things that were burning up his chest.

And now it looked like he wouldn't have the chance.

'When was she fired?' he demanded.

'How would I know?' Lilly asked sullenly. 'A few weeks back? Who cares?'

Harry turned away from her and started to pace up and down. He felt almost regretful; he would have been a millionaire in a few years.

'Sorry, Lil,' he said, 'I quit.'

'Don't be a jerk.'

'Whatever you think we have, we don't. I'm sorry. And nobody telling me about Nina Roth – I don't like being played for a schmuck. Or manipulated.'

'If you go,' Lilly said meanly, propping her fat torso up on her elbows, 'you're breaking contract with me. Your work on our research becomes my copyright, and you'll lose all your royalties and points from Dragon. Do you get that? You'll lose everything.'

'I'll lose this project.' Harry shrugged and reached for his overcoat.

'You're bluffing! What the hell will you do?'

He turned at the door and gave her a quick, dazzling smile. 'What I always do, Professor. Land on my feet.'

Elizabeth took the keys from the housekeeper on Tuesday night and signed the papers Wednesday morning. Tony's lawyers came by at nine a.m., on the dot. That was no surprise. She knew he was as eager to be shot of her as she was to go.

She had got Walgrave Road lock, stock and barrel, so she spent a morning checking it out. Dragon's corporate hospitality people were very efficient. There was everything a fat cat could wish for, from a power-shower to a study that came complete with IBM, home printer, copier and fax machine. There was a Quotron terminal in one corner of the room. Elizabeth checked the share price: up three points. Tony must be confident he could never be beaten. The garden was as pretty as she remembered, the refrigerator, freezer and wine cellar were fully stocked, and there was a small home gym in the basement. Elizabeth looked at it dispassionately. She could only use arm weights and a stationary bike now. If there was any point.

She arranged to have all the bills transferred to her name and called Coutts & Co., where a smug functionary confirmed the deposit of fifty thousand pounds. Then she went to the Lloyd's round the corner and picked up an account transfer form. Stuffy pomp and circumstance were behind her now.

'We'll handle that for you, miss,' said the teller. 'Name?'

'Lady Elizabeth Savage,' Elizabeth said, and smiled briefly as he gave her a quick, embarrassed stare.

'Yes, milady, right away.'

She wondered idly if that was really her name. Tony didn't think so. But Tony was wrong about a lot of things. In the end it didn't matter: Savage or not, she was out on her own.

Nina flicked through the pages of *American Scientist* and tried to pay attention. She knew she should use dead time to keep learning and improving, but it was no good. She dropped the glossy on to her desk and looked at her reflection in the switched-off computer screen.

Yesterday she'd gotten her first break. Peter Meyer, president of a small bottling plant, had returned her call. She'd had dealings with him at Dragon. Meyer had been impressed then and invited her in to head office. His firm was in trouble: one of their biggest clients was about to cancel a longstanding order, switching bottling function to their own firm. He knew Nina was a lateral thinker; maybe, he said without enthusiasm, she could come up with something. He'd tried every option he could think of – discounts, increased productivity – but their finance guys weren't going for it.

Nina hadn't needed asking twice. She had extensive notes on both Meyer and the client company when she'd showed up this morning, wearing her most businesslike charcoal suit and carrying a mobile phone and a briefcase. In a meeting with Peter and Linda, his secretary, Nina went over the options.

'In the short term, I can fix this,' she said confidently. 'In the long term, you'll need to diversify.'

'What do you mean?' Peter asked her.

'You can't die of hypothermia every time Tropex sneezes. They may want to cut costs again. You need other options.'

'And your firm can supply them?' Peter Meyer asked sceptically.

'We can indeed,' Nina said, ignoring the secretary's sniff. 'If you're not satisfied, you pay nothing more than expenses.'

'Thank you. I'll think about it,' Meyer said.

She had gone back to the office on a cloud of hope. It had lasted all of two hours. That was when Linda called her back and said the board were minded to turn down the proposal.

'We'll give you a final answer by the end of the day, but I can't see them changing their minds.'

'I see.' Nina struggled to control her disappointment. 'Thanks for letting me know.'

Now she sat here facing the facts. The Meyer call was the first bite she'd gotten in weeks, and now the fish had almost wriggled off the hook. She'd offered him a no-win, no-fee deal and he still wasn't interested. If Peter Meyer didn't think it was worth the effort, even at zero cost, Nina stood no chance. She was going to have to give up. Pack in the office and take some menial job, entry-level like the ones she'd been offered before. If, indeed, they were still open. Or maybe she should go back to America ...

No! Nina thought. No! I can't let him win! She couldn't, couldn't quit! She jumped up from her chair and kicked the desk in a rage. There were no options, but she couldn't accept that. Her mind was dashing against the brick wall like a bee trapped by a windowpane—

There was a knock on the door.

Nina stopped dead. Somebody must have got the wrong address. Or really be looking for the psychic next door.

The knock came again, louder, impatient.

'Hold on,' Nina called. She walked over to the door and opened it.

Elizabeth Savage was standing there. She had lost the golden tan and about a stone, and she looked thinner and tireder than when Nina last saw her. She was still beautiful, skinny and tall, however, the kind of figure Melissa Patton and her cheerleader buddies had always idolised back at St Michael's. The startling blondeness of her hair framed the sharp cheekbones like a glossy halo. She was wearing tailored slacks, a close-fitting military jacket and a pair of heeled boots. Nina couldn't help but notice the boots, glancing down involuntarily.

'No, you heard right,' Elizabeth said wryly. 'I did lose a foot.' She banged her left leg on the cracked linoleum. 'Hear that? It's a prosthesis. Plastic.'

Nina opened her mouth to say something but nothing came out. Attack Savage? She could do that, but not to a cripple. It was like speaking ill of the dead or something, although Elizabeth, slim and blonde and designer top to toe, didn't look like your average zombie. Offer her sympathies? No way, that would sound as false as it would feel.

'Come in,' she said neutrally. 'I guess you had a reason for coming here, Elizabeth, unless you were in the neighbourhood and felt like dropping by.'

'You guess right.' Elizabeth walked into Nina's office and looked round.

'It's not the Stock Exchange,' Nina said defensively.

'It must rent cheap.'

'Well, that was the plan. Did you come here to gloat, milady? If so, you can just leave the way you came in. Or is it a message from Tony?' Nina's brown eyes glittered with distaste. 'Because the answer is no, no, and no. Whatever it is.'

'Neither one. Can I sit down?' Elizabeth asked, gesturing to a secondhand black leather chair.

Nina's eyebrows arched. She looked hard at the other girl. 'I'm busy, but you can have ten minutes.'

'Sure, you look busy,' Elizabeth wanted to say, but bit it back. 'Nina.' She sat down and brushed the hair out of her eyes. 'I don't like you, you don't like me. Fine, that's a given. But you've got something I really need, and vice versa. I was thinking we could help each other out. On a purely business basis. A pact of convenience.'

'Go on,' Nina said.

'I have fallen out with my father. It's been brewing for a while but now it's final. I've left Dragon – I was kicked out, or as good as. I've moved out of the family home. He expects me to live off the pocket money I've got in exchange for that, but I have other ideas. I want to make money myself and I want revenge.'

Nina laughed. 'You expect me to buy that? Why would he do that to you? You're family!'

'He hates me,' Elizabeth said intently. 'Look, I can prove it to you. He took all the Dragon Gold stock off the market. He incurred millions in losses just to spite me. I swear it's true.'

'I know it's true. I saw the memo,' Nina said slowly. Something about Elizabeth's face was convincing. The look in her eyes was one Nina recognised. She saw it every time she looked in the mirror.

'When I came out of recovery, he told me I could only work in Corporate Hospitality, Events Organisation, or Promotional Literature.'

Nina snorted. 'Might as well type the letters.'

'I said exactly the same thing. Come on, Nina, you knew him, you slept with him. He disliked me intensely. You must have been aware of it.'

'Yes, I was.'

'Then you should believe me. He destroyed my life.'

'He let you ski.'

'Because it suited him. Skiing was the one thing I did he could approve of – it fitted the great Robber Baron image. You used to hate me because I went to finishing school, I had no real education. I wanted to – you have no idea how much – and I wanted to work, but he wouldn't let me do either. That way he could control my destiny, can you understand that? No degree, no experience, I was qualified for nothing. Except winning races. The marketing skills I always knew I had, I studied in my spare time, I read *Campaign*, even those fucking boring stats you made me learn.'

Nina smiled suddenly, caught off-guard. It was so funny to hear that cut-glass limey voice say 'fucking'.

'Dragon Gold was *mine*. I made something of it.'

'You did. It was pretty gutsy, faking Tony's authority like that. He was so mad when he found out he dropped everything to fly home.'

'I'll bet,' Elizabeth said softly. 'You can imagine what that was like. He did the same thing to you, and you were his girlfriend.'

'Correction. I slept with him. When I no longer wanted that to continue . . .' Nina shrugged.

'Then help me.'

Nina stood up. 'Look, Elizabeth. I don't know what you think I can do. If I could have hurt him, I wouldn't have waited for your permission.'

'So. You've got the same problems I have. No credibility,' Elizabeth said shrewdly. 'Once you're out of Dragon, you're a non-person. And to start anything up, you need money, you need staff.'

'You got that right.'

'OK.' Elizabeth's green eyes narrowed. 'I'm not the president of your fan club, but I have money and I can sell this firm. You *know* I can, because you've seen me work. We could make something together.'

Nina stared at her. 'You mean that?'

'Every word.'

'Look, Elizabeth.' Nina sighed. 'It sounds good, on paper, but I can't take your money. There *is* no business. I got the first break I've ever had yesterday.' She explained about Peter Meyer. 'That phone's going to ring any second to turn me down, and it'll be the first and last bit of business I ever do. I can't afford to pour rent money down the drain any more.'

Elizabeth leaned forward urgently. 'Let me call them,' she said. 'I've got an idea. If you're going to fold anyway, what could it hurt?'

Nina shrugged. For a polished Sloaney princess, she was certainly persistent.

'OK.' She pushed the phone across the desk. 'I guess you can give it a try.'

39

'Come in,' Peter Meyer said expansively, ushering them both into his office. He smiled briskly at Nina and shook hands with Elizabeth. 'Nina, you never said Lady Elizabeth was on board with you.'

Nina nodded quietly. Meyer was grinning and bowing like a nervous butler. He had agreed to another meeting right away, because he was terrified of Tony Savage.

That little deception got Elizabeth through the door, but she'd need something more to get them any further.

'This won't take long, Mr Meyer,' Elizabeth said. Her voice was rather cold. 'I called as soon as Nina told me you were in negotiations. It's just a good-faith visit, really.'

'Good faith?' Meyer repeated. Under other circumstances, he knew he'd have been admiring the view across the desk – one young woman dark and lush, the other slim and blonde, both gorgeous – but he couldn't manage it. They were so well dressed, serious and relentlessly formal. Looks of twenty-five with an attitude of forty-five. It was unsettling.

'Yes. Lolland Jars have also replied to our pitch.'

Nina stiffened. Meyer sat upright and frowned. Lolland Jars were his biggest rival; they had narrowly lost out on the Tropex contract. Now he feared they were going to have their shot at it.

'They want to get their firm in shape for the future.' Elizabeth's smile was apologetic. 'Knowing how tough it is for independents out there. So, we'd be obliged if you could sign the formal "no" from your board and give it to us, so we'll be legally clear to start dealings with Rob Lolland.'

'Wait a second!' Meyer said anxiously. He hated Rob, the guy ate into his customer base a little further every month. What had he missed here that Rob had seen? 'You can't work for Lolland if you're in negotiations with me!'

'I'm sorry.' Elizabeth leaned back, an expression of confusion on her patrician face. 'I thought you were turning us down.'

'No, that's not correct. We were just trying to rejig the budget,' Meyer said hastily.

'I'm afraid we do need a fast decision. Mr Lolland needs an answer, one way or the other.'

Meyer glanced at Nina's briefcase. 'Do you still have that contract you brought round before?'

'Of course.' Nina unclipped her case and handed it across to him.

Elizabeth added, 'If you do want to hire us, we need expenses payments in advance. Two thousand for the first month.'

Meyer nodded and scrawled his signature at the bottom of the page. 'If that's your company account, I'll transfer the funds across at once. I'm afraid you'll have to disappoint Mr Lolland. Meyer Bottling got there first.'

Nina and Elizabeth exchanged a quick glance. Nina took the signed contract, and they shook hands.

'Good to have you with us. I'm sure with such a capable deputy you'll make very rapid progress,' Meyer told Nina with relief.

'Thank you.' Nina smiled back. 'But I should set you straight. Elizabeth is my partner.'

In the cab on the way back to Soho, Nina looked at Elizabeth with amazement. 'Lolland replied to our pitch? They turned me down flat!'

So?' Elizabeth grinned. 'That's a reply!'

Nina streamlined Meyer's operations and cut costs, while Elizabeth provided them with a marketing prospectus for fresh clients. Tropex retained their account, and Meyer entered discussions with three more companies. Nina sent Peter Meyer pitching segments of the market he'd never even considered.

'How can you possibly know so much? You're so young!' he said, the night they toasted the Tropex renewal.

'Dragon teaches you fast,' Elizabeth muttered.

'I've been in this game for over seven years,' Nina said.

Meyer needed no convincing. He paid Roth Consulting, with a bonus. And he spread the word.

A month later, they had more work than they could handle.

Elizabeth and Nina found it hard going. They hired a secretary, a mature woman returning to work. She was cheap, but ten times more efficient than the gum-chewing teenagers with uninterrupted experience. Helen Potts kept them civil to each other: they couldn't snipe in front of her, although they were respectful of each other's talents. Elizabeth's effortless confidence and polished manners worked beautifully with clients, but they still got under Nina's skin, and Elizabeth hated the draconian way Nina ran the place: in at eight a.m., out at eight p.m. Plus, there was mountains of work, with little reward. All the money they saw went as fast as it came: hiring new equipment, moving offices to Hammersmith, paying lawyers and accountants as they set themselves up. Nor were their fees large. They were undercutting the big boys, and all their clients were baby firms.

However, they were too busy to snipe much. It was like scraping your way out of prison with a grapefruit spoon. At night they fell asleep when their heads hit the pillows.

It was a makeshift alliance, but bills got paid. Jobs got done.

They were in business.

'Mrs Potts, could you hold the fort for half an hour?'

It was a cold June morning, rain pouring down on Hammersmith Broadway. Nina could see it splashing on the red roofs of the buses that crawled past their windows. Elizabeth was silhouetted against the dull grey sky, her blonde head bowed over transparencies for a new brochure. Wellkin Pharmacies was their biggest client yet, but that wasn't saying much. They had six shops in the West End, a lot of clutter and no way to keep up with Boots. Nina was trying to persuade the chairman to specialise and Elizabeth was dreaming up a new look. The fee on this job was ten thousand – it would cover overheads for months.

'Certainly, Miss Roth.'

Elizabeth glanced up. 'Something up?'

'Let's go into your office a second,' Nina said. Elizabeth followed her into the orderly room she'd had decorated with framed ads, and settled into a chair. Nina seemed edgy and tense, and Elizabeth's guard flew up.

'I've got a proposition, but I need your consent for it.'

'I'm listening.'

'I think we're in the wrong business.'

'Oh! Is that all? Well, that's reassuring,' Elizabeth said irritably. 'Is this New York angst? You should leave Woody Allen on Manhattan, Nina. We have six jobs in hand and three more waiting.'

'Yes, but what are we getting out of them?'

'Money. OK? Are we done with the therapy session now? Because I'm really busy.'

'Jesus Christ, will you hear me out?' Nina snapped. 'We're not making *enough* money. We're keeping ourselves afloat, that's all, and since we can only handle so much consulting work, that's not going to change. We're just going to trundle along making a minor profit. We've been so busy we haven't looked at the big picture.'

'Can't see the wood for the trees? You're right, but I think we're working as hard as we can.'

'It's not about working harder. It's about working smarter. We need to advise bigger firms, and to do that we need something more concrete to offer them. Sterling Health don't need us to teach them how to suck eggs, but there's still a lot of wastage in their systems. If we can fix that, we can command *real* fees. Hire staff, expand—'

'But we can't fix that. You just said so.'

'Not on our own, no, but what they need is computer help. I can pinpoint market improvements – did it for Dragon *and* Dolan.'

'Yeah, but you never even graduated high school, you can't write a major computer program. It would take a genius like Clive Sinclair—'

'I know somebody. I think he'd go for it, but I'd have to offer him a partnership. Do you agree?'

'Providing our decisions have to be made unanimously,' Elizabeth said coolly. 'I'm sorry, but I'm not going to be outvoted by you and a friend.'

'Understood. Though I'm sorry to say he and I aren't exactly friends,' Nina admitted.

Elizabeth gave her a small smile. 'Hasn't hurt *us* so far.'

Nina used Elizabeth to track Harry down. She knew the numbers for Lilly's French lab like the back of her hand: she'd fought so hard with Harry over the location.

'I'm sorry, Lady Elizabeth, I can't help you.' Dr Hall's Australian accent was thick and rather sour. 'Henry Namath walked out of this firm months ago. Don't tell me Dragon has more business with him.'

'Absolutely not.' Elizabeth played a hunch. 'You sound as angry with him as I am.'

'You've got a beef with Harry?' Lilly snorted. 'He means nothing to me.'

'Actually, he owes me money. Quite a lot. I loaned him twenty grand when he moved to England.'

'Well, that's different. Twenty grand?' Lilly laughed meanly. 'I have an address here somewhere. Unless he's fled the country. Thirty-four Fount Street, South London. Phone number . . .'

Nina caught the Tube to Charing Cross and picked up a cab at the station rank. She wanted to turn up looking successful. That would convince Harry to listen to her. She told herself she had to be strong, very dry and businesslike. It would do no good pleading with him to give her a second chance. Tony told him the truth and he was disgusted; that's why he didn't call or write when she was fired. She hadn't seen him since that Chinese dinner.

I was right the first time, Nina thought. I should never have let another man into my heart.

She was getting stronger all the time. She never let Elizabeth see she was unhappy, and she'd die before Harry got a chance to realise it.

For this meeting she had dressed with incredible care. Her raven-black hair was spritzed into neat submission with a burst of Elnett, she wore a dark green Jil Sander pantsuit, crisp and attractive, with Stéphane Kelian pumps and camel leather gloves. Simple gold studs in the ears, soft make-up, Mac colours and Shu Umera brushes. Nina wasn't going to hide away from him. She refused to apologise for being attractive. Dr Namath could take her or leave her.

The taxi pulled up outside his house. It was a quiet street near the Oval, a pretty mews house with a cherry tree in the front yard. She could see a light burning in the upstairs window. He was there.

She felt almost light headed with nerves as she paid the driver and walked up the steps.

Nina rang the bell. She was afraid she might run away, so she rang it three times, pressing really hard. The faint sounds of the Rolling Stones clicked off from upstairs and she heard him racing down the stairs. The door wrenched open.

'All right, all right, Jesus fucking Christ, what's the—'

Harry jumped out of his skin. He did a double take, then a triple take.

Nina tried to keep her impassive look but her control was deserting her like water sloughing off Vaseline. Harry was so surprised he hadn't said a word. It suddenly occurred to her he might just slam the door in her face.

'I do have a telephone,' he said slowly.

'I thought you might just hang up on me. I've got a proposal for you, Harry,' Nina said.

'Well.' Namath scratched his head and gave her a strange look. He was so attractive, he took her breath away. He was wearing a T-shirt, and it was plastered to him, sticking to his lean torso. His legs were covered in a black pair of workout shorts, black socks and beat-up sneakers. His chin was peppered with two days' stubble. His face was glowing; he'd clearly just been working out. Erotic images flashed uninvited into her mind: Harry doing push-ups, Harry laying into a punchbag. She felt the sudden pulse of lust all through her body. Like a hunger you didn't know you had until you smelt food.

'You're making quite a habit of it.' He lifted his T-shirt. 'I'm as unprepared as the first time. You can come in, but you'll have to wait while I have a shower.'

Nina went dry mouthed. She said, 'Fine, thanks.'

Namath stood back to let her in. His London house was an extension of the Swiss place, furnished minimally, with hardwood floors and exercise equipment stacked in a corner – a bench, heavy-looking dumbbells. Only a set of shelves on one wall, stacked with computer texts, spoilt the seamless line. It was a small slice of TriBeCa in South London.

'Kitchen's right through there. Coffee's freshly made,' Namath said. He bounded back up the stairs two at a time.

Nina went into the kitchen and fixed herself a coffee. It was so American, so recognisable it hit her in the gut. Coffee beans from Gloria Jeans, wafting cinnamon amaretto all round the kitchen. An empty Häagen-Dazs pot by the bin. Where did he get this stuff? She tried to take her time with the coffee, noisily opening cupboards and choosing a mug and switching off the machine. Trying to take her mind off the faint hiss of water coming from upstairs, trying not to think of him, standing there, with the water sluicing him down, pushing the soap across his armpits and his back . . .

She set the coffee down and leaned against the side, light with longing. It was bittersweet: he was so sexy and so close, and she had lost him. Did he have a girlfriend? He must have, by now. The thought made her wretchedly jealous, more pictures drifting through her mind like toxic gas. She felt physically nauseated. And sick with desire.

Thank God I'm not a man, Nina thought. It would be so obvious.

'So.' Harry's voice jerked her out of it. He was wrapped in a voluminous navy bathrobe and rubbing his hair with a towel. 'What's the story?'

'You broke the partnership with Lilly. Why did you do that?'

Harry reached over to the coffee pot and poured himself a mug, took a sip and gave her a cold glance. 'That's really none of your business. I guess you must have got this address out of Lilly. Don't ask her any more questions about me, Nina.'

She flushed. 'You're right. I apologise, I just needed to see you.'

'Why?'

'I want to suggest something to you.'

'Oh?' Harry dropped the towel on the floor and leaned back against the oven. He watched her neutrally, like he was trying to read her. 'Business or pleasure?'

If I said pleasure, would he kick me out of the house? Nina wondered miserably. Then she shoved that thought aside. She was offering Harry something she knew he'd be into, but she had to pitch it right. She squared her shoulders and looked him right in the face.

'Business. Strictly business. And believe me, Harry, this is perfect for you.'

40

'There is a train strike. Please make alternative transport arrangements. Contact your local tourist information office.'

Jack grinned at the announcements crackling out of the Underground tannoy at Heathrow. Welcome back to Britain. Life sure was a lot easier in this country when you had money. He bought a paper, jumped in a cab and gave the guy directions to the Regency Hotel in Marylebone. *The Times* was the usual mix of optimism and outrage: victory in the Falklands, birth of Prince William, an IRA attack in Hyde Park. The photos showed Household Cavalry horses with their necks ripped from their torsoes. Sickening. Italy had just won the World Cup. They took soccer real seriously here: the sports pages were full of dissections. The US had come last in its qualifying group. What the hell, soccer was a limey game anyway. Jack flicked to the business pages.

He wondered how Elizabeth was doing. *What* Elizabeth was doing. When he'd called Dragon it was like butting into a wall. No, sir, they had no information, Lady Elizabeth had left; no, sir, Lord Caerhaven wasn't available; no, sir, under no circumstances could they release her address. Perplexed, Jack rang the castle. Monica Caerhaven had been vague but jumpy; she muttered something about Earls Court, excused herself, and put the phone down. Something was definitely up.

The British Ski Federation gave him her address with no trouble. Ronnie Davis, reduced to coaching third-raters like Karen and Kate, almost fell over himself in his eagerness to help.

'She's running some computer firm. Consultants . . . they just changed the name. I got a number here, if you can ever get through. I keep trying to get her to come and coach, maybe do something with the youth programme, but she's way too busy.' Ronnie sighed. 'Gawd, I wish she would, great to have her teaching the kids.'

'You can't teach what Elizabeth had, Ronnie.'

'Bloody hell, mate, you got that right.'

In his room Jack unpacked, dropped to the floor and did fifty stomach crunches to shake off the lazy feeling he'd gotten from the flight. Then he dialled the number that Ronnie had given him. The company was out in Hammersmith, West London.

It was called Tall Poppies.

'Just one second, Mr Taylor,' Mrs Potts said brightly. She waved at Elizabeth, crossing to her office with an armful of ad layouts. 'Personal call for you on line two. It's a Mr Jack Taylor.'

Elizabeth froze. Then she said, 'Yeah, right, put it through.'

She put the layouts down on a nearby desk and shut her door behind her. The red light on line two was blinking silently at her. She felt herself break out in a sweat, a light dew of fear. Jack. He could still hurt her, and badly. What was he going to say? An invitation to a wedding? His wedding? The picture she saw in *Vanity Fair* last month had pierced her like an arrow. Jack, impossibly gorgeous in a tux, with Clarisse Devlin on his arm. Clarisse, his longtime girlfriend, revealed in the flesh to be just the daintiest, creamiest little piece of Texas honey you could possibly imagine, and Daddy probably owned two oil-wells with it. 'Olympic and World Champion Jack Taylor with Miss Clarisse Devlin at the opening of the San Francisco Opera House.' She was sure Clarisse would never argue with Jack or talk back to him. She would be gracious and submissive and all the things Elizabeth could never be. And would never be. No matter what.

I've got no choice, I've got to talk to him, Elizabeth thought. She steeled herself and picked up the phone.

'Jack! This is a surprise.'

'God, girl, are you ever hard to track down.'

'You could have tracked me down in the clinic,' Elizabeth said angrily, then kicked herself. Great, where did that come from? She could control her end of a booming business operation but she still hadn't got a handle on her runaway mouth.

There was a pause. Then he said, 'I've got to see you.'

'I'm really busy, Jack,' Elizabeth said negatively. Talking to him was one thing; she didn't know if she could handle a visit.

'Elizabeth Savage, I flew in from Dallas just to see you. I fought like a bobcat with Pa to let me go.'

'Well, I'm sorry about that, Jack, but I never asked—'

'Elizabeth.' His exasperation as he cut her off was just like old times. 'I am here and I am *going* to see you, if it means campin' outside your door on the sidewalk. Now do I come over there and punch out your security guards or are you going to be a lady about this?'

'Be a lady about it?' Elizabeth chuckled despite herself. 'Jack, you don't know how to take no for an answer, do you?'

'No, ma'am, guilty as charged.'

'Come to my house. Twenty-four Walgrave Road in Earls Court. I'll be there in forty minutes, but I warn you, I can only give you a little time.'

Jack smiled to himself as he hung up.

'We'll see about that, sugar,' he said.

He found the place without any trouble. It was a cute little house, tucked away in a tiny corner of village hidden in the heart of the city. Reminded him of their townhouse in Greenwich Village, New York, that Mom used for her shopping base. It struck him that he'd never been to any place of Elizabeth's before. They'd always met up on the circuit, in hotels or gyms. Apart from that one time in Sussex. That suddenly seemed so wrong and wasteful. Jack shook his head, smiling confidently. No more. Now he was going to rewrite the book.

He bounded up the small stone steps and hit the bell.

'Hey,' Elizabeth said. 'Did it insult your mother, or something?'

'And good morning to you too, sweetheart,' Jack replied.

She looked different. Real different. The athletic frame was gone, slimmed off her. No problem, she was beautiful either way. The competitive fire had also disappeared, but Elizabeth still looked tough and focused. He wondered what the new place was, Tall Poppies, that had given her a look like that. For Elizabeth, he'd have said you couldn't get it outside of a race piste. She was wearing a tailored pantsuit in dusty pink, cream leather boots, an ivory shirt and a gold bangle. Her hair was coloured a dazzling blonde, layered all round her face in a feathery cut. She blew Clarisse Devlin and all the simpering Dallas debs right out of the water.

'Come in,' Elizabeth said.

Jack stepped inside the house. It was sparsely but elegantly furnished, a few old oil paintings on the walls, rows of leatherbound books, the normal rich-limey clutter.

'Very nice. Your pop give you some spares?'

'I bought everything you see,' Elizabeth said flatly. 'Tony and I have split for good. The house was part of the settlement.'

Jack walked over to a far wall and examined a small pastoral. 'Looks Pre-Raphaelite. What is it, Burne-Jones?'

'Very good. I've started collecting.'

'Without the earl's help? Come on, Elizabeth, where would you get that kind of money?'

Jack settled himself in a deceptively plain leather armchair and found he was sinking into perfect posture. It must be orthopaedic. Eames, most likely. He took another look around the room, paying greater attention. Sure the décor was sparse, but everything here was top quality, costly stuff.

'I can't believe you, Jack.' Elizabeth sat opposite him and allowed herself to sound annoyed. That was simple, so much easier than actually confronting what she was feeling right now, a sort of dizzy joy combined with sick apprehension, the way she was desperate for him not to leave, how she was telling herself to get a grip and failing so miserably. 'You come over here, you drag me out of work, and all you can ask is how I pay for my decorating?'

'So you think I should ask you about your leg?'

'Shouldn't you?' Elizabeth demanded. He was totally wrongfooting her. She'd expected belated tears and hand wringing, and here he was, joking and squabbling with her like nothing had happened.

'Honey, there's nothing to say. You know how sorry I am. I know how it would feel.'

'Oh, you do?'

'Yes,' Jack said gently. 'Of all the people in the world, I do know what it would mean not to ski again. What it must mean to you.'

Elizabeth looked away before she started to cry. That was perfectly true.

Only Jack, and maybe Hans, could have any idea. She swallowed hard to push down the dry lump in her throat.

'Think what it means to *me*, babe. You can't ski, so I can't collect on my bet. That would have been real intriguing. We'd both have got the golds—'

'You think I'd have won?' Elizabeth blurted out, then kicked herself. That was not the next thing she was planning on saying.

'There was never any doubt,' Jack replied. 'I wouldn't have let you bet me otherwise. When you had to come to my room and pay up, it had to have been at least a little interesting.'

Elizabeth pushed herself to her feet and rounded on him. 'For God's sake, Jack! I'm a fucking cripple and all you can do is fly over here to make sex jokes! Where were you when I needed a friend? Out partying with Holly Ferrell and all your stupid American groupies—'

'Hey. Hey.' He jumped up and grabbed her hands. 'You know I tried to visit. I begged to. Your father told me to get lost. And I never partied from first to last. Got the medal, flew home and tried to forget all about you.'

'And you couldn't?'

'I'm here, ain't I? And you're no cripple, girl, you're standing up like Lady Liberty.'

'But I've lost my foot,' Elizabeth muttered. 'I've got a plastic foot.'

'So what? It was never your foot I was interested in.'

'But what about Holly Ferrell? And Clarisse Devlin?'

Jack's hands had left hers and were cupping her face now, one finger delicately tracing the line of her jaw and her cheekbones. His touch on her skin was like an electric charge. Her stomach was melting into a liquid, shifting pool, she wanted him so badly.

'Y'all want the truth, or the PG version? PG, I never touched them, I sat in my room and pined like a dog. Truth is, I saw them both for a little while and I slept with them. I was mad at you, and you weren't there. It was OK. And then,' Jack added with a disarming grin, 'I sat in my room and pined like a dog.'

'Jack ... it won't work, it never does.'

'It won't work? Baby, you know we ain't ever tried it.'

'What about Sussex?'

'Not bad for a warm-up,' Jack said, reaching up to the ivory silk at her neck and undoing one of the buttons. Elizabeth knew this was her cue to push him off but she didn't. It was weird, like one of those running-in-treacle nightmares when you couldn't move. Except it didn't feel too much like a nightmare.

'But that's not a relationship, Jack ...'

'Yeah?' He breathed it, bending down to kiss her, just brushing her lips. 'That's just fine with me, sugar. I don't want a *relationship*.' Jack's tanned face was tight with scorn as he pulled her to him, one arm cradling the small of her back, supporting her whole weight like she was made of straw. 'I got a *relationship* with my cousin Sarah in Fort Worth. I want you. In case you're too blind mulish to notice. This makes twice I've flown round the world for you, and I'm not doing it again.'

'Jack—'

'Jack, Jack.' He kissed her again, briefly and impatiently. 'Is that all you want to say? Objections? Reasons we both should be somewhere else, right now? If you don't want me, Elizabeth, you just say so. Look me right in the eyes and say go.'

He tipped her face up to his. His eyes locked on hers were probing, intense. Elizabeth didn't say a word.

Jack pulled her closer still. Close enough to feel him hard up against her groin.

'That's what I thought,' he said.

It was wonderful. Elizabeth's fears and nerves couldn't withstand the hot longing for him that was racing through her. She let Jack undress her, because he wanted to and because she was trembling so much her fingers were all fumbling. When he peeled off her shirt and the filmy scrap of nothing over her breasts she was anxious, because she'd always been small and now she was flat, but Jack breathed in sharply at the sight of her, brushing his fingers over the pale-pink buds, then bending to suck them, until she was almost crying from pleasure. The feelings in her breasts distracted her from the way he was unzipping her boots and trousers, and then she was naked, and Jack took her left ankle in his hands, curiously, muttered, 'Poor baby,' kissed the flesh where her calf met the metal band, and moved right back up her leg, slowly, deliberately, kissing and biting the skin at the back of the knee, trailing his tongue up a little way and then stopping, his strong hands locking her in place; Elizabeth gasped at how he made her feel, she was squirming around under him, losing her control, it was all she could do not to moan out loud. Jack kicked off his shoes, tore off his shirt. Elizabeth heard the buttons thud on the carpet as he unzipped his fly.

'Your shirt—'

'Fuck my shirt.' He was naked now, leaning over her, his hands all over her, his fingers palming the slickness between her legs. It was broad daylight, pale sun streaming through her window, letting her see every inch of him: just like her fantasies, huge chiselled muscles, his arms were thicker than her thighs; not narcissistic like a bodybuilder, but about as big as you could be and still look like a normal man. Elizabeth knew girls that hated that look, said it was too big and too macho, and it was true, under him she felt as fragile as a reed; but it was painfully erotic, and she felt heat blaze through her like a forest fire. Something female and primal responded to that physical strength, that total masculinity.

'You're so beautiful,' Jack said. She saw him register the hunger in her eyes. He smiled, but there was nothing of humour about it. It was pure sex, that smile; pure triumphant sex. 'You like?'

'You're huge,' Elizabeth said.

'And you like that.' Jack straddled her. He was like a Greek sculpture of Hercules. He lifted one knee and firmly, slowly, pushed her thighs apart. Elizabeth heard the breath wrenching out of her in a sob of desire. Jack pushed his knee up just a little, pressing into her, pushing against the wetness there, looking her right in the eyes so she could see he felt it. 'You like me to be a man. Admit it.'

'Yes,' Elizabeth managed. 'You know that.'

'You're right, sugar,' Jack said thickly, 'I do know that—' and suddenly he slid down the bed, cupped his two hands under the globes of her butt and pulled her up to his mouth, like she weighed nothing, burying himself in her. His tongue flicked over her in a light, sweet rhythm, sexy, relentless, ignoring her when she cried out. Her fingers twisted in his hair, and her fingernails dug into his back. Jack drove her forwards, until he felt her involuntary surrender. Her body melted against him, her back arched, and right at that second he grabbed her hands, pinning them back over her head, up against the bed-rails. She was open and waiting. Jack thrust right into her, all in a single motion, not gently, giving her exactly what she wanted, thrusting, as deep and as hard as he could go, automatically now because he couldn't wait either. Elizabeth rose to meet him and he was still pinning her there, it made the orgasm stronger. Their eyes were wild, locked on each other, as the white-hot scalding spasms broke over Elizabeth and her fierce clenching and releasing set Jack off, and then they were in each other's arms, drenched with sweat, fighting for breath, and kissing.

41

'I can't believe it,' Jack said.

'Believe it,' Elizabeth answered. She showed him round the crowded offices packed with people, sixteen different programmers hunched over their workstations. Tall Poppies had taken over two floors of the Hammersmith offices. Downstairs was Elizabeth's own marketing division; a fancy name for a team of four people, but they were all rising stars poached from the big agencies, and the way things were going she might need to hire some more. 'Yesterday was the first day off I've had in four months. We're growing so fast I'm getting altitude sickness.'

Jack stared at her. Elizabeth did look frazzled, but she was happy too. 'We're stretched to the limit, but we're making a lot of money.'

'And it wasn't working before?'

'Oh, it was working, but in a small way. We fixed that when Harry came on board. He's a genius programmer. He creates the software, Nina applies it to the market, I spread the word.' She tugged at Jack's hand. 'Come over here, see the boardroom.'

Jack laughed. 'The boardroom? Oh babe, you're kidding.'

'Good morning, Lady Elizabeth,' said a middle-aged woman in a smart navy suit.

'Good morning, Mrs Potts. Jack, this is Mrs Potts, our executive assistant.'

'Good morning to you, ma'am,' Jack said politely, trying to hide his disbelief. Elizabeth showed him into a small, well-equipped conference room, with a mahogany table and four chairs. Then she shut the door behind her and kissed him triumphantly on the lips.

'I'm not kidding,' she said. 'I'm deadly serious, Jack. This time it's working. And we're in charge. If it keeps up this way, I'm going to be a multimillionaire before I'm thirty years old.'

'Is Elizabeth still busy?' Harry asked, slightly annoyed.

'Is this about your new project?'

'Yeah. I'm done with the conceptual stuff. I need to know if we can sell it. I only have forty minutes before the Unilever meeting.'

'You're starting to sound like me,' Nina said, glancing across the hall. The boardroom door was still closed and she smiled. 'Elizabeth's got a lot of history with Jack Taylor. I think you should just let her alone.'

'It's going to mean working late tonight.'

'So what else is new? Success is tough,' Nina replied.

It was true. The addition of Harry had given them everything Tall Poppies needed. Nina's cold efficiency was offset by Elizabeth's warm English-rose persuasiveness, and the addition of the older American scientist banished any remaining doubts. The small companies they'd worked with before recommended them highly, but now they had something fresh to offer. Computerisation. What sci-fi writers saw as a sinister force, and Establishment fuddy-duddies regarded as a passing craze, was taking over. Namath's maverick code-jockeying now had a legitimate target. Tall Poppies became IT consultants to the UK drugs business. They were in demand right away. Nina made her first really big score, an efficiency programme for a division of Procter & Gamble. After that it was open season.

Nina was straining to go like a Dobermann on a leash. She'd waited for this all her life. When Harry complained he was being pushed too hard, they hired more programmers, all the brilliant, unorthodox talents the hi-tech giants wouldn't touch. At Tall Poppies, staff wore Hawaiian shorts, Beatles T-shirts, anything they liked. And they kept their own hours, as long as the work got done. Soon Elizabeth needed marketing help too. They physically outgrew their surroundings, rented another floor.

Nina was now speaking to the landlord about a lease on the whole building, and they hired accountants and lawyers. Elizabeth arranged interviews in the business press.

'What do you feel about this overnight success?' the *FT* asked Nina.

'Overnight?' she'd laughed. 'It's taken me years.'

'Never mind my partner,' Elizabeth butted in. 'You have to speak fluent obsessive to understand her.'

The uptight, besuited journalist tried another tack. 'Female entrepreneurs seem to be the wave of the future – Anita Roddick at the Body Shop, Debbie Moore at Pineapple. Why do you think this is?'

'Well,' Elizabeth said, looking over at Nina, 'we women have to give ourselves a chance, because nobody else is going to.'

'And have you girls always been friends?'

Nina shrugged. 'We *girls* have always hated each other.'

The hack put his pad down. 'I don't understand.'

'Why not? I'm speaking English,' Nina told him curtly.

'And is that still the case?' asked the stuffy jerk, with a look that clearly said they were mad, hysterical females, and how the hell were they making all this money?

'No.' Elizabeth grinned over at her partner. 'We tried to keep it up, but the truth is, we were just too busy.'

'We understand each other better now,' Nina added.

'And the third partner? Dr Namath?'

'I like Harry,' Elizabeth said carefully, 'and our working relationship is terrific.'

He'd been satisfied with that because he had to be, Nina reflected. Elizabeth was too smooth to let anything slip out: how they worked together fine, but Harry and Nina fought all the time. Pushing. Yelling. Stand-up fights, blazing arguments the staff could hear through Harry's office wall, the two Americans jabbering at each other in a barrage of slang. Elizabeth acted as a bridge between them, and there was too much work and new business to have it get in the way. Nina knew it was mostly her fault, but she couldn't stop.

It was torture, having him there all the time. Watching him as he crouched over a computer station, his eyes locked on the scrolling numbers, his face lit up by a monitor. Sometimes they worked together late at night. Nina took care to keep out of his way. Otherwise, the urge to reach over and ruffle his hair might be too strong. She couldn't bear the way he looked at her sometimes, a guarded glance, like he was trying to figure out how he'd gotten her so wrong.

Every day she hoped he'd turn up and announce a new girlfriend. Every day she was terrified of it. When she had to be physically close to him, it was almost too much to bear.

But Nina couldn't do without Harry. His reputation grew every week. He was the engine for her revenge on Tony Savage, and for her and Elizabeth both, that was the absolute priority.

Elizabeth had told her what Tony said: 'You have to cut down the tall poppies.' Every job they landed, every new bill that got paid, was a slap in that bastard's face. Tony refused to comment on all the good-natured questions about his daughter's success. When Nina imagined the journalists bugging him, it gave her exquisite pleasure.

And even better, they were hurting him.

Nina pitched Dragon sometimes, just to be spiteful, and when they turned her down, she went to their competitors. Dragon had its own IT people, but they were hidebound, way behind Tall Poppies. In the UK, on the Continent, rivals were chipping away at Tony's market share.

The first day Dragon's stock dipped, Nina opened a bottle of Cristal. Tall Poppies was still a small business, but it wouldn't stay that way for long.

'Yeah, success is tough,' Harry said. 'Just like you.'

'Me?' Nina tried to smile. 'I'm just a marshmallow. Look, is it really urgent?'

'Damn straight, it's urgent.' Harry ran his hands distractedly through his hair.

'Then how about I go over it with you?'

'Tonight?'

'Not if you don't want to,' Nina said, blushing.

'No, it's OK. Your place or mine? Or does that sound too much like a date?'

'Your place is fine. And no, it doesn't sound like a date,' Nina said with a touch of bitterness. 'Don't worry, I know better than that.'

'Let's go back to the hotel,' Jack said, kissing her forehead and eyebrows. 'You're turning me on, sugar, I swear.' He bent her back, both his arms resting on the boardroom table. 'There's a desk in the bedroom, I want to get you butt naked and push you down across it and—'

'Jack!' Elizabeth pushed him off her. 'Jesus! Is that all you ever think about?'

He grinned. 'Nope. Sometimes I think about having you go down on me. Or getting you in the tub and washing you with a little bubblebath...'

Elizabeth's creamy skin blushed a deep rose. 'Cut it *out*! This isn't some kind of sex-trip, Jack. This is serious, this is seriously my business!'

'I know that.' Jack stood upright, letting her wriggle out of his arms. 'And I'm totally impressed.'

'And surprised.'

He shrugged. 'That too. OK? I admit it. But come on, baby. You know things are changed now. You don't need to be worrying, y'all are going to get a whole lot of money for your share in this thing, and when we're in Texas you and me can—'

'Wait a second.' Elizabeth held up one hand. 'Back up. What did you just say?'

Jack shook his head. 'You're right, I'm all messed up. Going too fast. But I've had years of practice at that.' He dropped to one knee and took her hand in his. 'Elizabeth, you know I love you. And you love me, unless you're one hell of an actress. Will you marry me?'

'Jack ...'

His handsome face clouded slightly. 'Yes or no, sugar.'

'Maybe,' Elizabeth said.

Jack looked at her disbelievingly. Then he scrambled to his feet, frowning like thunder. '*Maybe*? You know, I had this scene all figured out.' He fished in his pocket and drew out a blue velvet box, flicked it open. Inside was a huge solitaire diamond, emerald-cut on a ring of white gold. 'Real romantic and all. I have to tell you, girl, *maybe* wasn't a part of it. Are we still playing games? Aren't we done with that?'

'Oh, yes.' Elizabeth nodded and blinked back tears. 'We're done with that. Which is why I say maybe. I do love you, Jack, I always have, and I want to marry you.'

'Then I don't see the problem.'

She waved at the busy offices behind them. 'That's the problem, Jack. Tall Poppies. It's my thing and I'm not selling up. Not now. We're on the threshold of something extraordinary ... I've been waiting for this all my life, to be somebody in my own right. I can't give it up to go back to ... to *Southfork* and play at being Sue Ellen.'

Jack sat down heavily in one of the carved oak chairs. 'Sweetheart, I don't have a choice here. I'm an only child. I got hundreds of acres of prime Texas land, two hotels and a stable full of the best studs west of Arabia. I can't sell it.'

'You can do whatever you want.'

'You can come and help out with the business back home. I know how you feel—'

'No,' Elizabeth said. 'No, clearly you don't. Or you wouldn't ask.'

Jack scowled at her. 'Honey, get real! You're saying you want me to *live* over here, like a goddamn househusband? My business has been in my family for six generations.'

'And mine has been in mine for one generation.' Elizabeth blinked back a film of tears. 'Look, thank you for the offer, truly—'

'No!' Jack shouted. He caught her hand and pressed it on to his heart. 'You can't say no to me! We were meant to be together!'

Elizabeth looked at him. He was so beautiful, so perfect, and she loved him so much. She also knew if she gave up Tall Poppies to be with him, she would wind up resenting him so bitterly that love would turn to hate.

Sorrow clogged her heart so thickly she felt like she could hardly breathe.

'God,' she said, and one big tear trickled out on to her cheek before she could get a grip on herself. 'I thought so too.'

Nina left Elizabeth alone for the rest of the day. It was strange, seeing Jack Taylor in the flesh; so tanned and Texan, he was Marlboro Man in the flesh. She couldn't imagine him on a pair of skis. Or ever dating a cool customer like Lady Elizabeth. He was real courteous when Elizabeth introduced them, said something about them being fierce enemies and fiercer friends, but Jack seemed distracted. That way they were matched: Nina was distracted too.

'Nice to meet you,' she said. 'Elizabeth, can you come round to Harry's house this evening, any time you can make it? We need to check out his new product.'

'Sure. Sure.' Elizabeth turned to go. 'I'm not going to be in this afternoon, is that OK? I'm going to drive Jack to the airport.'

'Whatever you need,' Nina said.

It was still light when she got to Harry's, the gold and pink streaks of the summer evening silhouetted behind the pretty Georgian houses in his street. London was a beautiful city, when you thought about it. Nina watched a pair of pigeons flurry on to Harry's roof, strutting around cooing to each other. The tree outside his front door was in full green leaf. She stepped up and rang the doorbell wearily. How nice it would be, just once, to have an evening off. She hoped whatever Namath had dragged her out for was worth it.

'Hey, come in, come in.' Harry led her into the kitchen where he liked to work at night. He had a terminal set up in the far corner, so he could programme and never be too far from the cookie jar. Tonight he was wearing grey sweats and sneakers; he looked relaxed and confident. Nina was wearing the same John Galliano she'd been in all day. She was frazzled from clients, and her neck hurt where the phone had been glued to it.

'You look tired.'

'You got it.' Nina rubbed the back of her neck. 'Can we get to it? I'd like to go over what you're proposing.'

'Something I've been working on,' Harry said. 'Proprietary software. I'm calling it Home Office.'

'Home Office?' Nina repeated. 'But we do consultancy—'

'And we still will, but this is going to take us to a whole new level. You won't just sell to big drugs firms, you'll sell to every small businessman in the country,' Harry said.

'OK.' Nina knew better than to laugh at Harry when he got that look on his face. 'Layman's terms, try and tell me what you've written.'

Over the next couple of hours he explained it to her. Nina tried to follow;

she lost him in the jargon, but the concept was simple. Home Office was a software program you could sell in the high street. Disc-drive computers could access the full thing, smaller Spectrums and Amigas could run a mini-version on their tape recorders. It would centralise word processing, spreadsheet and inventory functions in one programme.

'What are we doing?' Namath asked enthusiastically, watching his partner with her head bowed and her neck aching, trying to read his graphics designs. 'We're reorganising all these giant firms to make them more efficient. Well, that's something *everyone* needs. The florist. The guy with the corner store. Didn't you tell me once you'd run a deli?'

Nina glanced up at him. That was the first time he'd ever referred to their time together before. But Harry didn't look sarcastic; he was just asking a question.

'Sure, South Slope, Brooklyn.'

Harry winced. 'Nasty neighbourhood. You ever have inventory problems?'

'Every week,' Nina agreed.

'Well, if you'd had Home Office, it would have done your inventory in ten minutes max.'

Nina looked at her watch. Quarter of eleven. 'Elizabeth's not coming, but I know what she's going to say.'

'She's going to turn it down?'

'She's going to love it.' Nina shook her head. 'It's brilliant, Harry, it's going to lift us to the next level.'

'But we'd need money.' Namath looked at her hopefully. 'To manufacture it, I mean. Unless you think I should license it?'

'Like hell, we'll do it ourselves,' Nina said firmly. 'That means a factory, sales force, packaging, the works. That means capital. And that means bank loans, or going public.'

'Which do you prefer?'

'A bank loan,' Nina answered. 'If we go public we'll get taken over, and we're not ready for that yet.'

'But if we go for a bank loan and it goes wrong, we've lost this company. My credibility. Everything.'

'That's right. So will it go wrong?'

'Not the code, sister,' Harry said with a grin.

'Then we'll do it,' Nina said.

Namath let out a whoop of joy. Then he came over and started to massage the back of her aching neck. He was strong, his fingers were pleasurable, she wanted to melt into it, just melt against him and let him take all her pains away.

Roughly Nina pushed him off. 'Cut it out, Harry,' she snapped.

'Right.' He lifted his hands and spun away from her. 'Business, I forgot. That's all life ever is with you, kid. Business. Is that it? Don't you want anything else?'

Nina got up to leave. 'It's a great idea, Harry.'

'Don't dodge the goddamn question.'

She turned at the door. 'You know what? You're right, they're all right.

There's nothing but business in my life. I really don't see the point, because every time I've tried something else, I've always got burned.'

'By who?' Harry sounded furious. 'Tony Savage, the great heartbreaker? Are you going to pine after him for the rest of your life? Because he burned you?'

'Get this straight,' Nina snarled. 'If there's any burning between me and Tony, *he's* the one that's getting fried. And you can take that to the bank.'

She slammed the door behind her.

42

When Nina woke up, it was a bright, cold morning, the early light crisp with the promise of great heat later on. For the first time in years, it reminded her of Brooklyn: summer on the Slope, when she'd woken up early in order to get a few moments on her own before Pop dragged himself out of bed to switch on the cable. But now her sheets were Irish linen, and her window had William Morris curtains instead of grimy slats. This morning felt significant somehow. And then she remembered. They were going to gamble.

A million things could go wrong. Her instincts, for a start. Maybe shopkeepers would be technophobes, maybe the village trader would as soon fly to the moon as buy a computer program. Tall Poppies was still small. If they blew several million pounds of financing, they were history. Like Elizabeth's skiing career.

This was the biggest stake she'd ever risked. For the first time in her life, she had something precious of her own to lose.

What the hell. Nina jumped out of bed and into the shower. She had never second-guessed herself. Make a decision, then go with it. Win or lose. Move to London, or sleep with Tony Savage. Start her own firm, or fall in love with Harry Namath—

Angrily she grabbed a towel from the rail. Bullshit, Nina thought, I'm *not* in love with Harry. I just find him attractive.

She went into the hall and phoned Elizabeth.

'Hey, kiddo, you awake?'

'I am now.'

'Come on, it's quarter of seven. No rest for captains of industry.' Nina teased her partner a little, but she could hear pain in her voice. Was she missing Jack already? You had to really know Elizabeth to hear anything under that well-bred Brit politeness. Elizabeth would have to be tortured before she complained about anything in public, still less something so private as an emotion. 'Get up but don't get in the car. I'm coming round. We need to have a meeting, I've got some great news.'

'Marvellous,' Elizabeth said, with a total lack of enthusiasm.

Nina reached Elizabeth's thirty minutes later. Her house near Green Park was direct on the Piccadilly Line, and that meant pushy, grouchy crowds of early-morning bankers facing another boring day with their caffeine and migraines, but she didn't care. Turning into Elizabeth's little tucked-away street she almost ran.

'You look happy,' Elizabeth said.

'You look terrible,' Nina replied. It was true. Her partner wore a defiantly pretty amethyst DKNY, and her blonde hair was gleaming, but she'd obviously been crying all night.

'I feel terrible,' Elizabeth admitted, then sank on to her chintz sofa and burst into tears.

Nina put aside her notes and finance projections and gave Elizabeth a hug.

'Jack and I are through.' Elizabeth explained what she could, in between sobs.

'But that's terrible. Did he fly back to Texas?'

'Just to Dublin.' Elizabeth was distraught, almost choking on her tears. 'He said he's got stud business there and in England … God, if he comes back to London I don't think I'll be able to bear it.'

'London's a big city, babe, and he likely won't be here for long.'

'I don't know if that makes it better or worse,' Elizabeth said, wiping her hand across her eyes.

'Look, we'll buy you out if that's what you want,' Nina said bravely, wondering where the hell she was ever going to get the money. 'You should be happy.'

'But that's just the problem. I can't be happy in a gold cage. I should know,' Elizabeth said. She picked up the notes Nina had put down. 'Come on, tell me what's going on.'

'Are you sure? It's … a pretty big deal. Do you want to look at it now?'

Elizabeth nodded. 'Don't worry, my head's still intact. It's just my heart that's broken.'

Outside Tony Savage's windows, all was calm. The sun glittered on the sluggish Thames, lambswool clouds bobbed across a periwinkle-blue sky, traffic flowed serenely across the bridge below them. Inside the office, things were not so calm.

'They're doing *what*?' Tony barked.

Frank Staunton recoiled from Tony's anger, the Terrier shrinking from its master's boot. 'Bank financing,' Staunton repeated. 'Maybe they suspect that going public would see them taken over.'

The earl got to his feet and started to pace around his office. The anger in his stomach was going to give him an ulcer. In the early days he'd kept tabs on Nina Roth's little adventure through a discreet but expensive private investigator; looking for the moment it got off the ground, so he could crush it. Then Elizabeth had hooked up with her. He had to hear that news twice before he believed it; didn't the silly little bitches hate each other? Evidently, not so much as they hated him. Tall Poppies! Elizabeth's long-distance insult, her arrogant slap in the face. And when they'd gone out and picked up Namath, that unshaven, unbusinesslike slob, Tony had fired three of his personnel directors in a blind fury. His company had discarded the programmer as so much excess baggage. At Lilly Hall's request, all Namath's royalties were sequestered; the bonus was eliminated; he'd got nothing. But

Lilly's work was an expensive bust, while Harry Namath was already paying off. For a company that was turning into the London School of Dragon Rejects.

Yesterday at lunch Bob Cohen had teased him unmercifully. 'And you let them go, Tony! Talent like that?' The financier clearly enjoyed the joke as he speared his rocket salad. It had been a long time since the Robber Baron had looked this dumb.

'They're riding a craze,' Tony replied tightly.

'You think?' Bob shook his head. 'Home computing's not just Pac-Man any more. If this new venture is as hot as the money is saying, all bets are off.' Cohen lifted his Château-Lafite. 'Your daughter's company could be as big as yours in a year, Tony, it must run in the family. Good Lord, you must be busting with pride.'

Tony pleaded sickness and called for the bill. He couldn't deal with this, just couldn't bear it. All round the Square Mile they were whispering at him and laughing. He hadn't felt such powerful rage since Louise ran off with that prick DeFries.

'It *would* see them taken over. By me.'

I expect they know that, Savage, Staunton thought but didn't say. 'Of course, if the product fails—'

'They fail. So we must make sure it does.'

'I don't see how we can do that, sir. Dr Namath is a genius programmer, the Roth girl seems to know what she's doing and the banks are queuing up to lend them money. Lady Elizabeth has them mad with curiosity already. I must admit,' Staunton said admiringly, 'they move pretty fast.'

'There's a simple way to stop them,' Tony said. His manicured fists clenched on top of the table. 'There's always a simple way. Get out, could you, Frank, I need to think.'

Without saying a word, Staunton glided out of the room and shut the door behind him. Tony stared angrily into his Quotron screen. The Dragon share price was blinking down another eighth. In the dull glass screen he saw himself reflected: handsome, urbane, beautifully dressed. It didn't satisfy him. Nothing did that any more, not the limpid debs he was screwing, not his sons' bland obedience, nor the crawling of his corporate vassals like Frank Staunton. The explosion he had thought would catapult him into the really big time had fizzled out with a whimper. He wasn't ruined, but this felt almost as bad. Small stock dips. Loss of respect. *Treading water.*

And two young women laughing in his face.

They were laying themselves open now, though. All he had to do was see that this product failed miserably. Sabotage? No, too clumsy, and he didn't have the time. He recalled the smug face of Bob Cohen.

'Home Office. A tailored software package, a Filofax for the PC. Wave of the future, old boy, and Tall Poppies will be the first ones out there. Nobody can catch Namath, and he's immune to poaching.'

The earl caught his breath. It was so damn obvious, he was amazed he hadn't thought of it before. He lifted his Sèvres coffee cup in a toast.

'Bob, you're a bloody genius,' he said.

They divided up the tasks between them. Elizabeth toured the finance sources with the company lawyers, raising the money. Nina went round the country, interviewing software manufacturers for the subcontracting, and talking to sales reps. By the time Elizabeth had moved on to packaging and promotion, everything was in place. They were all waiting on Harry.

'Look, when I said it was ready I meant the basic code,' Namath said.

'You needn't talk to us like we're retards,' Nina snapped.

'Time out,' Elizabeth protested, holding up one hand. 'Isn't that what you Yanks usually say? Harry, just how far along are we?'

'Two weeks away from beta-testing.'

'Speak English,' Nina said.

Harry shrugged angrily. 'Hey, make your mind up, toots. Either you understand or you don't. Two weeks away from customer try-outs, a month away from production.'

'Who's in charge?'

'I'm doing the user interface – graphics, sound, cartoons, all the stuff that'll make it attractive to the buyers. Tim Paris is finishing up the platforms. John Cobb is checking the code, and Lee Reddy's troubleshooting.'

'We should be ready earlier,' Nina fretted.

'OK, Nina. You want to write the program yourself, be my guest. Otherwise it's one month. You must have business stuff you can do.'

'No.' Nina shook her head. 'The "business stuff", as you put it, is all done.'

'Then the only thing you can do is wait,' Harry said.

'Take a holiday,' Elizabeth said. 'Oh, don't look at me that way, Nina, just a week. Recharge your batteries. Like an investment in your energy.'

'I can't, you need me.'

'No way.' Harry grinned at Elizabeth. 'She's right. She's going ahead with the marketing and I'm writing. What I need is for you to get out of my hair.'

Reluctantly, Nina agreed to a holiday.

It was a mistake. She found she was scouring the business press every day, devouring Elizabeth's banner adverts and PR pieces. She couldn't relax with a book, knowing that her whole future was riding on this. She tried turning up to work on the Wednesday, but Elizabeth pushed her back out the doors again.

'But I'm going stir crazy,' Nina pleaded. 'I want to do something to help the company.'

'You really want to do something? Then you should go see Harry,' Elizabeth told her. 'Seriously. I mean it. When Home Office is launched, Tall Poppies will take off like a rocket, but the rocket will explode unless you guys sort yourselves out. Whatever the problem is, you need to talk it through. We're partners.'

'You don't understand.'

'On the contrary. I *do* understand. Look, Nina, if you and me can wind up friends, so can you and Harry. You're both adults.'

'OK.' Nina nodded. 'OK, I'll go round right now. We won't be friends, but . . . we can work something out.' She pressed Elizabeth's hand. 'How are you?'

'Me? Terrific, this is an easy sell.'

'I meant personally. With Jack. Is he still around?'

Elizabeth's beautiful face took on a tight look. Her smile no longer reached her eyes. 'Yes, but he's going home next week, so I'll be able to forget all about him.'

Nina smiled back and turned to hail a taxi. She knew neither of them believed that, but there was no point in saying so. Elizabeth was trying to get on with her life, and, as Nina knew herself, there was really nothing else for a woman to do. It was why she'd agreed to see Harry. To put the past in the past, and move on, like a grown woman.

'Hey, what a pleasant surprise,' Harry said wearily as he opened the door. He was wearing jeans and a faded blue shirt and he looked great, despite the red eyes and stubble. That's what you get, Nina thought, if you're shackled to a computer screen for days on end. 'What have I done now?'

'Nothing. Absolutely nothing,' Nina said, squeezing past him. 'Except work like a slave. It's OK, Harry, I've come to apologise.'

He looked at her suspiciously. 'Either this is a plot of Elizabeth's or I'm having caffeine hallucinations.'

'Right first time.' Nina went into the kitchen and reached for his coffee jars. 'See? I'll make decaf.'

She glanced around the pretty kitchen, taking in all Harry's chaos: drying clothes strewn everywhere, food left out on the side, running shoes kicked casually under the table. It was so homely and domestic. She fought the urge to mother him, to tidy up the mess. She had no right to do that. She had no true place in Harry's life. Elizabeth was right, this was a conversation she had to have. You couldn't fight with your partner all the time; it was bad for business.

But Nina was scared. She was about to face things she'd long since swept under the carpet.

'No way.' Harry followed her into the kitchen and Nina tried not to flinch at how close he was standing. 'You have some agenda, Roth, you're permanently on my case.'

'I came over to talk about that. To ... apologise,' Nina repeated. Her mouth was drying up, this was a bad idea. She was feeling nervous. God, he shouldn't be able to do this to her. Not still. 'We're partners, we shouldn't be at each other's throats like hyenas. I think you're doing a great job.'

'You think I'm doing a great job.' Harry looked at her searchingly. 'Jesus. Do you have any idea how clinical that sounds?'

Nina shrugged. 'What do you want me to say?'

'I want you to tell me the truth.'

'Harry—'

'No. I want you to tell me the truth. You came over to clear the air, right?' Harry said mercilessly. 'So clear it.'

This was it. He's going to make me say it, Nina thought miserably. She couldn't stave off the confrontation a moment longer. It was so hard, though, with Harry standing there, looking so handsome, his gorgeous eyes with the thick black lashes staring at her so challengingly. He would never understand why she'd done what she'd done . . .

'OK.' Nina took a deep breath. 'I thought it was easier to be aggressive than let you look down on me.'

'I didn't do that.'

She flushed. 'Come on, Harry. I know what Tony Savage said to you, and – it was all true.'

Harry nodded. 'I know that.'

'Then you must despise me,' Nina said, and to her horror she heard her voice break and felt her eyes film over.

'No. It's true, I wanted an explanation, but you made it very clear I had no right to one. You broke up with him, and I couldn't compete with some ghost. I hoped I might win you over, once we were colleagues again, but that hasn't exactly worked out.' He gave her a small grin.

'You couldn't compete? I *hate* Tony Savage.'

'So you must have loved him once, right?'

'Wrong! Are you insane?' Nina said. 'I hate him because he told you, he took you away from me!'

There was a moment's dumbstruck silence. Harry just stared at her. Then he reached forwards and grabbed her two hands in his.

'But you were having a relationship . . .'

Nina tugged her hands away. 'No. I slept with him because I was young and tough, or I thought I was tough. I didn't love anybody. I was new and hungry, and everyone assumed I was sleeping with him anyway, so I thought, what the hell? He can be of some use to me.'

'So why did you break up with him?'

'Because it didn't feel cut and dried like I thought it would. It made me feel . . . bad. I realised I was talented, I had promotions due me anyway.'

'And he didn't like it when you walked.'

'First he threatened me. Then he told you. Then he offered me rewards. And then he fired me.'

Harry Namath looked like a man processing a lot of information, Nina thought bitterly.

'But you did find him attractive.'

'Yes, at first I did, but I never loved him.'

'And I made you feel there could be something more to it.'

'Yeah, well. That was obviously another mistake. I should learn to trust my instincts. Look, Harry. I won't snipe at you any more, but I'll tell you right now,' Nina said, 'that's the way it was. I'm not apologising for it. You can judge me when you've walked in my shoes, and not before—'

'Jesus!' Namath said. He moved closer to her, lifted one hand and clamped it over her mouth. 'You know your trouble, honey, you never listen. I don't judge you. You don't love him?'

He lifted his hand. Nina muttered, 'No.'

'You never did?'

'No.'

'Then that's all I give a damn about,' Harry said, and he pushed her back against the cooker and kissed her.

43

Nina didn't go into work the next day. Or the next. She moved her stuff into Harry's, and every moment he wasn't working on Home Office, they went upstairs and made love. She got that same thawing feeling she'd had in Switzerland, only this time there was no fear, no ghosts lurking in the darkness of her past. Harry filled in something missing from her life she didn't know was gone. In his arms she felt safe and relaxed. Except for the times when safe was the last thing she was feeling. Sometimes it was tender, but mostly it was harshly sexual, animal coupling, his hands twisting in her hair as she went down on him, their naked bodies writhing in front of the mirror, Harry talking dirty in her ear until she was half-maddened, and then thrusting savagely into her until she came. But there was no shame to that, no nasty, guilty tang in the mouth afterwards. It was the difference between having sex and making love. Nina climaxed effortlessly every time.

On the Saturday Elizabeth came round for a council of war and found them curled on the couch in their dressing gowns.

'Hey, don't mind me.' She held up a hand to block Nina's protests. 'It was always going to be when, not if. When's the wedding?'

'Whenever we have time,' Harry said, grinning.

Elizabeth looked horrified. 'You're going to wait that long?'

'So what's the news?' Nina asked.

'Thunderbirds are go, kids. The good news is the loans went through this morning. Our asses are in hock to the banks to the tune of four million quid.'

'I'm on schedule, despite the distractions,' Harry said calmly, 'if John Cobb and Tim Paris are ready.'

'Well, if not, they haven't said anything to me.' Elizabeth got up to leave. 'I hate to spoil the mood, guys, but maybe Nina should come into the office again. We need to be totally ready, and we can't afford to have Harry delayed.'

Elizabeth tried to analyse her feelings as she turned into Earls Court Road. She hadn't felt so upset in a long time. She was happy for Nina and Harry, wasn't she? They were two of her dearest friends now, and the atmosphere at work would be smooth as silk. But she didn't feel happy, she felt wretchedly miserable. It was too saintly to try and rejoice for other people when your own heart felt shattered.

She was glad the Tall Poppies situation was so urgent. It took her mind off Jack, off the dust and ashes in her mouth every morning when she woke up.

She parked the car and stepped out on to the sunny pavement. And stopped dead.

Jack Taylor was sitting on her steps.

Elizabeth's eyes lit up like floodlights. 'Jack!' She rushed over and hugged him. 'What are you doing here? I'm so glad to see you!'

He's changed his mind! He wants me, he can't stand it, he wants us to get married—

'You won't be, when you know why I've come,' Jack said.

Elizabeth pulled back and looked at him. He was grave. 'What's wrong? Is somebody dead?'

'No. Nobody's dead, but it's not good, sugar,' Jack replied. 'You're in big trouble. I'm real sorry.'

Elizabeth unlocked her door and took him inside. Jack told her everything he'd heard, and Elizabeth sat down, shakily.

'Are you OK?' He looked anxious. 'Let me get you a drink, or something.'

'No. Thank you,' Elizabeth said, distractedly. 'I need to call Nina, and my lawyers. Look – thanks for letting me know.'

'Hey.' Jack pushed the phone towards her. 'You call who you want, but I'm not leaving. Right now, you need a friend.'

Tony Savage walked into the lobby of the Dragon tower and smiled with perfect triumph.

Though it was a Saturday, the place was buzzing. Production designers had been recalled from their weekends, sales staff were busy placing calls and faxes, and Dragon factories were unlocking their gates for a little extra overtime.

'Your guest is waiting in your office, my lord.' The receptionist smiled deferentially. 'Good morning.'

Tony nodded. 'It is indeed.'

'They're going to do *what*?' Nina gasped.

'Put out a program of their own. "Executive Package." TV advertising starts tomorrow, a huge spend, commercials during the news and *Coronation Street*. Billboards in the City and the West End.'

'But that would cost millions!' Elizabeth said. 'It would swallow up initial profits—'

'He's got millions, and it don't look like he cares about profits,' Jack said. 'He just wants to be first. He's got all the machinery in place already. Factories. Sales forces hundreds of guys strong. Instant packaging expertise. And with the reputation of a big, cash-rich company behind it the analysts love it. They've seen the response to your proposals, you see? They know people are waiting for this.'

'You mean to tell me we've just prepared the ground for Dragon?' Nina spat.

'Looks that way. I'm truly sorry.'

Elizabeth pushed her hands through her hair. 'If he takes the first wave of customers—'

'It could become industry standard,' Nina said dully. 'Nobody will buy a competing product from a baby firm.'

'But I don't *get* it,' Elizabeth said, jumping up and pacing around the room. 'Harry knows he was way in advance of the pack on this. How could anybody have overtaken Harry's team?'

The two women looked at each other.

'Oh my God,' Nina said. 'I can't believe it. That slimy prick. He's poached one of our team. He's creamed off Harry's work. It's the only answer.'

'If that's true, you got resources,' Jack pointed out. 'You can sue.'

'By then the horse would have bolted. And anyway, lawyers cost money,' Elizabeth said. 'It wouldn't do any good.'

'We need to call Harry. He's in the office, working on some last-minute stuff.' Nina punched in the number and Harry picked up right away. They talked quietly for a few minutes.

Jack looked at Elizabeth. 'If you want to hire lawyers, you can use my money, but I guess you wouldn't take it.'

'You guess right,' Elizabeth replied, 'but thanks, Jack. You've been a good friend.'

He nodded. 'I wanted to be a lot more than that.'

'Maybe you still will.' Elizabeth was on the brink of tears now. 'If my company isn't – if I turn into the most famous bankrupt in Britain, I wouldn't stick around out of pride.'

Jack lifted her hand to his mouth and kissed it softly. 'I hope you can believe I didn't want you that way.'

'But truly.' She smiled bravely at him. 'You must be pretty glad this has happened.'

He thought about that for a little while. 'No. I'm not,' Jack said finally. 'I can't stand to see you in pain.'

Nina hung up and turned round, shattering the moment. Her eyes as she looked at Elizabeth were bright. 'Harry and I have had a little chat. He doesn't think we should do anything. Just carry on as before. No statements to the press. No panic.'

'Pretend it's not happening?'

'John Cobb's gone,' Nina said. 'Left a message on Harry's answerphone. Tony hired him for over a million a year.'

'What?' Elizabeth's mouth dropped open. 'A million quid? We were paying him twenty-three grand! That's a hell of a pay rise! What does he have that's worth a million?'

'Experience.' Nina looked grim. 'He was in charge of checking Harry's code. He had total access to Home Office.'

'And Harry thinks we should just keep our heads down, carry on regardless?'

'If that's Harry's advice, we have to trust him.'

'You're right there,' Elizabeth said furiously. 'There's bugger all else we *can* do.'

It was agony to watch. The mighty Dragon sales machine swung into action with devastating effect. TV screens were bombarded with ads. The computer press ran profiles of both systems and concluded there was nothing to pick between them. Except for one key point. Dragon's was out first.

The press Elizabeth had courted were now hounding her wherever she went. If Tall Poppies had had a share price, trading would have been suspended. The hacks who'd loved them last week were now full of scorn. Trust two stupid bimbos to put all their eggs in one basket! Their bankers were on the phone every day, demanding clarification. When Tall Poppies' own campaigns, modest and well targeted, started to run, people poured scorn upon them. Scenting blood, the tabloids even got in on the act. The idea of a deadly rivalry between Tony Savage and his estranged daughter was just too delicious to resist. How stupid we were to criticise the Robber Baron, the papers crawled. Letting those three losers go was a great idea.

Lord Caerhaven gave a few triumphant interviews. Dignified pieces in serious organs: the *FT*, *The Times*, *The Economist*. Everybody feared him again. Dragon's stock took a massive ten-point jump.

Executive Package launched on the first of August in a blaze of publicity. Elizabeth and Nina stayed quietly in their offices, putting the final touches to Home Office. They took no calls from the press.

Sales for Dragon's package, as predicted, went through the roof. A super-efficient sales force was on hand to see huge piles of the beautiful box stacked everywhere from toy stores to stationers. Initial stocks soon sold out and Tony switched two more factories to EP. More copies were rush-produced. Linguists produced interfaces in French, Spanish and German. For two weeks, Executive Package was the computer craze of the moment.

Tall Poppies bowed Home Office on schedule, but they were way behind. Lukewarm reviews said there was nothing wrong with the product, but so what? With its no-nonsense packaging, no sales discounts and lack of publicity, Home Office was a moth to Tony Savage's glittering butterfly. Their loans were due in two months. It looked like the game was up.

'He's won,' Nina said dully.

'Wait and see.' Elizabeth was defiant. 'I don't hear any fat lady singing.'

Exactly twenty-one days after the launch, Dragon took a call. A sweet shop in Birmingham complained of a bug. Instead of printing out its normal spreadsheets, Executive Package was typing a nursery rhyme. Over and over. Nothing they could do would stop it.

Tony called the customer personally. He thought it was a masterly piece of PR.

'Must be a faulty copy. What's the message exactly?'

The man sounded embarrassed. 'It goes, "I'm the king of the castle, and you're the dirty rascal," uh, milord.'

'What?' Tony coloured. 'Never mind. Just a glitch. We'll replace it right away.'

That same day, the Customer Service Department received ten more calls. The next day, twenty. By the end of the week, they were flooded.

'Jesus Christ!' Tony said, raging at John Cobb. '*Fix* this! Don't you understand, we have half a warehouse full of returned copies?'

Cobb looked helplessly at Frank Staunton. 'I can't fix it. It's programmed into the code. It, uh, appears to be a time-activated thing.'

'It prints the message three weeks after EP is turned on, sir,' Frank Staunton said smoothly.

Tony looked at his underling with loathing. The little jerk was enjoying this!

'If it's in the *code*, write new code! Change it!'

Cobb ran his hands through greasy hair. He looked like a man who hadn't slept. 'But I can't do that, milord. It was Henry Namath's code.'

'Get out,' Tony snarled.

Cobb scuttled out. Tony sat down heavily in his carved chair and stared at Staunton. 'I can't believe it.' The clipped tones were tight with humiliation and fury. 'It's a trap. The little bitches have trapped me.'

'We'll have to recall the entire line,' Staunton said blandly. 'I'm afraid the television stations are starting to pick up on it.' He tossed Tony a copy of that night's *Evening Standard*. Twin shots on the front page showed Tony and a computer screen, blurting out the EP message. The headline was, 'DIRTY RASCAL TO LOSE HIS CASTLE'.

'To do what?' Tony snorted. 'What are they talking about, Staunton?'

'I think it's this comment from Marcus Fitzallen, sir,' the Terrier said with undisguised pleasure, 'speaking as Chairman of the Board of Dragon. He says they want a word.'

Epilogue

'But he survived,' Nina said.

Elizabeth shrugged. 'Of course he survived. Men like that always do. My father knows too many people, he's spent a lifetime covering his back.'

They were in the office, sipping champagne and leafing through the papers at a celebratory Tall Poppies brunch. All around them was the chaos of last night's wild staff party. Friday morning, when Tall Poppies went public, the issue was an immediate success. After the bank loans had been repaid, they were all three millionaires, a few times over. Today they were looking at pictures of themselves in the financial pages, smiling broadly. Many of them were placed next to a grim-faced Tony Savage exiting his board meeting. The 'Rascal' fiasco had cost him a profits warning and a public reprimand.

'What made you suspect John Cobb?' Jack asked Harry.

He grinned. 'I didn't. I just didn't trust anybody. I booby-trap every programme I write against hackers.'

'Come on, sweetheart.' Nina stood up and beckoned Harry. 'Let's go home.'

'OK.' He reached over and briefly touched her cheek. 'I'll wait for you in the car.'

'Goodbye, Jack,' Nina said, waving to him.

'Nina.' He winked.

Elizabeth said, 'I'll walk down with you,' ran over and threaded her arm through Nina's.

'We did it,' Elizabeth said.

'We did the first part of it,' Nina replied, smiling softly. 'We've got a long way to go to get where I want to be.'

'Tony'll be back, you know? We hurt him badly, and we made him look like a fool.'

'Yeah, ain't life grand,' Nina said, her eyes sparkling. 'We can handle him, no problem.'

'It's true: he couldn't stamp us out when we had nothing . . .' Elizabeth grinned. 'Living well is the best revenge, but misery and humiliation's pretty good too.'

They hugged, and Nina slipped out to the back, to where Harry was waiting for her.

Elizabeth walked slowly back up the stairs. The place looked like it had been hijacked by a gang of marauding kids. Squishy cake on the steps and balloons drifting everywhere.

Jack was perching on the edge of her office couch, wearing jeans, cowboy boots and a thick blue jumper. He looked so gorgeous. Bittersweet pleasure, because now, Elizabeth thought, he's got nothing to stick around for.

She walked over to him and sat down. Don't cry, Elizabeth warned herself, as her exhilaration burst like one of the balloons. Don't ruin the happy mood by getting all emotional.

You know the score.

'So, I guess you'll be leaving soon.'

'Hmm. Maybe.' Taylor nodded. 'But first, I got a business proposition for you.'

Business. Right. Elizabeth tried to look enthusiastic. 'Sure, go ahead.'

'Well now,' Jack said slowly. His Southern accent dripped over her like honey, she hated how his voice turned her on. 'I spoke to Pop last night. Thought if y'all could make so much money with lateral thinking, we should give it a try. I was talking to him about property over here. The Viceroy Hotel.'

'The place on the river?'

'Yes, ma'am. We reckon it would look real good in the portfolio, but it'll need upgrading. We thought maybe Tall Poppies could do it.'

Elizabeth sat stunned. 'But that would take you—'

'At least six months. By which time, you'll probably need to open an office in the States.'

'Jack!'

He caught her left hand and pressed it to his mouth. 'Baby, I'll say it again. Will you marry me? We can be together, we'll work something out. Hell, you take all these dollar-and-cent gambles every day. Why don't you risk a little on something important?'

Elizabeth leaned up and kissed him. He tasted of sun and champagne and Texas, Jack, her Jack, absolutely the only man she had ever loved.

'Aggressive as ever.'

'Is that a yes?'

'Oh, yeah,' Elizabeth said, 'that's a yes, sugar.'